Marge Doss

Russka

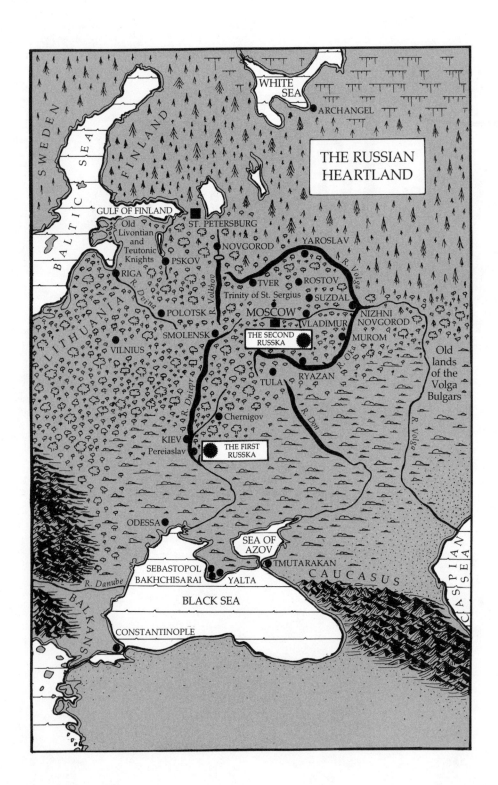

RUSSKA

THE NOVEL OF RUSSIA

Edward Rutherfurd

CROWN PUBLISHERS, INC.

New York

This book is respectfully dedicated
to those now rebuilding the monastic
community of Optina Pustyn.

Published by Crown Publishers, Inc.,
201 East 50th Street, New York, New York 10022.
Member of the Crown Publishing Group.

CROWN is a trademark of Crown Publishers, Inc.

Manufactured in the United States of America

Library of Congress Cataloging-in-Publication Data
Rutherfurd, Edward.
Russka / by Edward Rutherfurd.—1st ed.
1. Soviet Union—History—Fiction.   I. Title.
PR6068.U88R8 1991
823'.914—dc20 90-34457 CIP

ISBN 0-517-58048-9

10 9 8 7 6 5 4 3 2 1

First Edition

Acknowledgments

I am deeply indebted to Dr. Lindsey Hughes of the School of Slavonic and East European Studies, University of London, and to Miss Cathy Potter of Yale University and the University of Wisconsin, who between them read the entire manuscript of this book and corrected errors. Any that remain, however, are mine and mine alone.

Thanks are also due to Prof. Paul Bushkovitch of Yale University, who set me upon my path.

I am most grateful to Mr. E. Kasinec and the staff of the Slavonic Division of the New York Public Library, to the staff of the Butler Library at Columbia University, and to the staff of the London Library, for their unfailing help and courtesy. Special thanks are also due to the staff at the Synod of Bishops Russian Orthodox Church outside of Russia, New York, and the staff at Saint Vladimir's Seminary, Crestwood, who helped me obtain many books.

Thanks are also due to Mr. John Roberts, who kindly provided me with helpful contacts, and to Mr. Vladimir Stabnikov of the Writers Union in Moscow, who greatly facilitated my travels in Russia and gave much useful advice and encouragement. I am grateful also to the staff of the Hermitage Museum in Leningrad, who so kindly arranged private tours for me.

There are also many other people, too numerous to mention here, both in the West and in the USSR who, in a private capacity, gave me great help and hospitality for which I shall always be very grateful.

I am most fortunate in having an agent, Gill Coleridge, and two editors, Betty A. Prashker of Crown Publishers and Rosie Cheetham of Century, whose patience, encouragement, and unstinting help made this book possible.

I am deeply grateful to my wife, Susan, for her kindness and patience during the long process of this book's gestation.

And once again, special thanks are due to Alison Borthwick for her expert map.

Finally, I should like to express a special debt to the Archimandrite and monks of the monastic community of Optina Pustyn for affording me an unforgettable glimpse of Russia.

FAMILY TREE

CHAPTERS

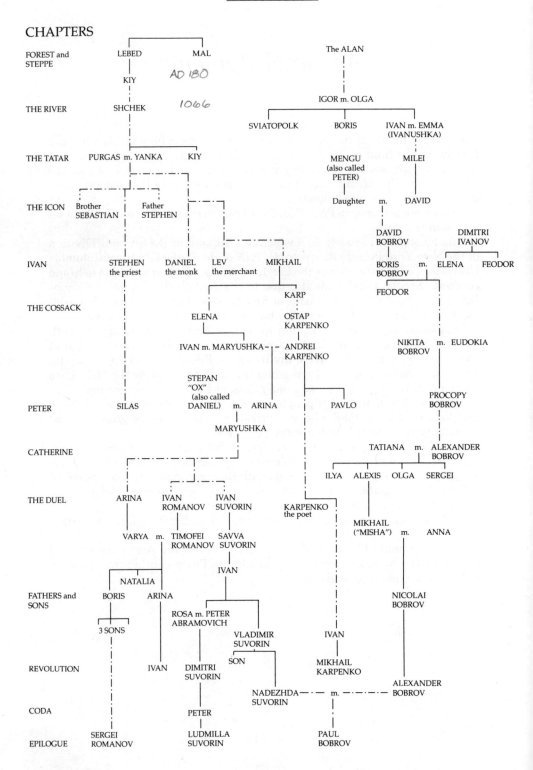

FOREST and STEPPE   LEBED   MAL   The ALAN

KIY   AD 180

THE RIVER   SHCHEK   1066   IGOR m. OLGA

SVIATOPOLK   BORIS   IVAN m. EMMA (IVANUSHKA)

THE TATAR   PURGAS m. YANKA   KIY   MENGU (also called PETER)   MILEI

THE ICON   Brother SEBASTIAN   Father STEPHEN   Daughter   m.   DAVID

DAVID BOBROV   DIMITRI IVANOV

IVAN   STEPHEN the priest   DANIEL the monk   LEV the merchant   MIKHAIL   BORIS BOBROV   m.   ELENA   FEODOR

KARP   FEODOR

THE COSSACK   ELENA   OSTAP KARPENKO

IVAN m. MARYUSHKA — ANDREI KARPENKO   NIKITA BOBROV   m.   EUDOKIA

STEPAN "OX" (also called DANIEL) m. ARINA   PAVLO   PROCOPY BOBROV

PETER   SILAS

MARYUSHKA

CATHERINE   TATIANA   m.   ALEXANDER BOBROV

ILYA   ALEXIS   OLGA   SERGEI

THE DUEL   ARINA   IVAN ROMANOV   IVAN SUVORIN   KARPENKO the poet   MIKHAIL ("MISHA")   m.   ANNA

VARYA   m.   TIMOFEI ROMANOV   SAVVA SUVORIN

IVAN

FATHERS and SONS   NATALIA   BORIS   ARINA   ROSA m. PETER ABRAMOVICH   IVAN   NICOLAI BOBROV

3 SONS   VLADIMIR SUVORIN

REVOLUTION   IVAN   DIMITRI SUVORIN   SON   MIKHAIL KARPENKO   ALEXANDER BOBROV

NADEZHDA SUVORIN — m. — ALEXANDER BOBROV

CODA   PETER

EPILOGUE   SERGEI ROMANOV   LUDMILLA SUVORIN   PAUL BOBROV

Preface

Russka the Place

THE TWO SETTLEMENTS named Russka in this story—the first in the south and its successor in the north—are both imaginary, although a small town bearing this name did once exist elsewhere in former times. Each of these imaginary Russkas is an amalgam of features drawn from its respective region. In the northern Russka, where the principal action is set, the old town and monastery somewhat resemble, on a smaller scale, the ancient city of Suzdal, where part of the book was written. The magic springs I saw by the old fortress of Izborsk, in the northwest. The Bobrov country house is not unlike the country estate of the Pushkin family.

Russka the Novel

RUSSKA IS A historical novel. All the families of Bobrov, Suvorin, Romanov, Ivanov, Karpenko, Popov, and the character Pinegin are fictitious. But in following their stories down the centuries, I have set them among people and events that did exist, or could have.

For many reasons, despite the ever-growing fascination with Russia in the West, the history and geography of this huge and sweeping land are only slightly familiar to most readers. Insofar as possible, therefore, I have tried to provide a historical framework for the reader that I hope will be informative without being burdensome. Here and there I have allowed myself some very small telescoping of events to simplify the narrative, but none, I believe, that does violence to history.

In an attempt to convey something of the astonishing richness and the special character of Russian culture, I have felt free to draw extensively from the wealth of Russian folklore and literature. The result, for better or worse, is certainly my own; but it is my hope that those familiar with these subjects may find that they recognize some old friends in these pages.

Names and Pronunciation

THERE IS no agreed system for writing Russian words in English. In each case I have, therefore, chosen what I believe to be the most familiar, or that which is most currently used.

In cases where place names change, I have again used my own judgment. For nineteenth-century Vilna, in Lithuania, I have used today's more familiar Vilnius. Present-day Istanbul remains Constantinople throughout the narrative.

There is one other peculiarity of Russian transliteration. Sometimes the letter written *e* is pronounced *o* as in *of,* or *yo* as in *your.* Certain important words and names that appear in the book are therefore pronounced as follows:

chernozem: chernozyóm   Potemkin: Potyómkin

Pugachev: Pugachóv   Rublev: Rublyóv

Summary

THIS BOOK was written in the period 1987 to 1991, in the course of which I visited Russia upon numerous occasions totaling many months. Traveling individually, I was able, besides my stays in Moscow and Leningrad, to visit the northwest as far as Kizhi, the Baltic, the ring of medieval cities around Moscow, Kiev, Chernigov, and the Ukraine. My southern travels also took in Odessa, the Crimea, the Cossack country of the Don, the Caucasus Mountains, and the desert cities of Khiva and Samarkand. Thanks to friends I was able to visit the town of Gus Chrustalnyi, in the region where the fictional northern Russka is set. The Writers Union also kindly took me to the ancient city of Riazan (Ryazan) and the still older site of the former city, destroyed by the Mongols—a haunting experience.

But most important of all was the day when, thanks again to the Writers Union, I visited the recently reconstituted monastery of Optina Pustyn. We arrived, as it happened, just after the monks had discovered the remains of the famous nineteenth-century elder, Father Ambrose, an event that was being celebrated the morning we arrived. It was an event of great simplicity, but one which, I like to think, vouchsafed an outsider a precious glimpse of the real Russia—and which convinced me, once and for all, that if we hope to understand anything of this extraordinary country's present and possible future, it is of great importance to delve, as far as we may, into her past.

ONE

Forest and Steppe

A.D. 180

THE STEPPE was quiet that night. So was the forest.

Softly the wind moved over the land.

In the hut—one of six that nestled together in the little hamlet by the river—the sleeping mother lay with her child.

She had no sense of danger.

High in the starlit summer sky, pale clouds passed from time to time, drifting in a leisurely procession, glowing softly in the reflection of a crescent moon that rode to the south.

Like horsemen they came from the east with their billowing white canopies, from who knew what endless steppes—sweeping majestically over the little collection of huts by the river's edge and continuing their journey behind the hamlet over the dark forest that very likely was also without end.

The hamlet lay on the southeastern bank of the stream. There, the woods of oak and lime, pine and birch grew thinner, gradually giving way to glades and the broad stretches of open grassland that were the outermost edges of the mighty steppe. Across the small river, on the northwest bank, the forest was thick, dark, and unbroken.

The three families who inhabited the place had arrived five summers before and, finding there an ancient, deserted earthwork enclosure overgrown with scrub, had cleared it, put up a wooden palisade on the low earth wall, and built half a dozen huts inside. Nearby two large fields cut untidy swaths into the trees. Farther into the woods, a messy patchwork of smaller clearings appeared.

A few hundred yards downstream, the land on both sides became marshy and remained so for a couple of miles.

Softly the wind moved over the land. It caressed the tops of the trees, so that the light undersides of the leaves shimmered pale in the starlight. The waters of the winding river and the marsh glimmered in the woods.

There were few sounds except for the gentle stirring of the leaves. Here and there might be heard the sounds of small animals, or of the deer quietly walking. At a certain point near the marsh, against the monotonous background of the frogs' croaking, an attentive ear might have picked up the crackle of a bear making its way along the wood's edge. But by the hamlet the only sound was that of the leaves, and the intermittent rustle as the breeze stroked the long field of barley, sending a

1

ripple like a momentary shiver down its length.

The wind moved, yet did not move. For sometimes the field stood still, or swayed in another direction, as though the wind from the east had paused, lazily, before brushing the ripened barley once again.

It was the year A.D. 180—and yet it was not. That is to say, although future times would give to this year such a number, as yet the Christian calendar was not in use. Far south, in the Roman province of Judea where Jesus of Nazareth had lived, learned Jewish rabbis had calculated that it was the year A.M. 3940. It was also the one hundred tenth year since the destruction of Jerusalem. Elsewhere in the mighty Roman Empire, it was the twentieth and last year of the reign of Marcus Aurelius, also the first year of the single rule of Commodus. In Persia it was the year 491 of the Seleucid era.

What year was it here then, in the tiny hamlet at the forest's edge? So far as history is aware, it was not any year. It was five years since the last village elder died. The huge systems of numbering familiar to the civilized world, and kept in written texts, were unknown here.

For this was the land that would one day be known as Russia.

Softly the wind moved over the land.

She lay with her little boy. The worrying thoughts of the day before had passed from her mind in sleep like the pale clouds receding over the forest behind the river. She slept at peace.

There were twelve people sleeping in the hut. Five of them, including Lebed and her child, lay on the broad shelf that ran across the room over the big stove. On this warm summer night the stove was unlit. The air was thick with the sweet, earthy smell—not unpleasant—of folk who have worked all day in the field harvesting. To this was added the fresh scent of grasses carried in by the breeze through the square, open frame of the window.

She lay at one end of the wooden shelf—a lowly position—because she was the most junior of her husband's wives. She was twenty-seven, no longer young. Her face was broad and her body had already developed a stocky roundness at the hips. Her thick fair hair had slid over the edge of the shelf.

Beside her, in the curve of her plump arm, lay a little boy of five. She had had other children before him, but they had died, and so he was all she possessed.

She had been fifteen when she married and she had always known that her husband had only taken her because she was strong: she was there to work. But she had few complaints. He was not unkind. Still a tall, good-looking man at forty, his weather-beaten face had something soft, even wistful about it, and usually when he saw her his light blue eyes would gleam with a gentle, mocking amusement as he called, "Here comes my Mordvinian."

With him, it was a term of affection. With the others, however, it was not.

For Lebed was not a full member of the tribe. To her husband's clan she was a half-breed: after all, what was her mother—one of the forest folk? A Mordvinian?

Since time began, the forests and marshes that stretched northward for hundreds of miles had contained the scattered tribes of Finno-Ugrian peoples to which her mother's tribe belonged. Broad-faced Mongoloid folk with yellowish skins, they hunted and fished in those huge, deserted regions, living a primitive existence in their little huts and pit dwellings. At the solstice they would stand in a circle and sing, in a high, harsh, nasal chant, to the pale sun who, as one traveled farther north, would scarcely show his face in winter and in summer would deny the earth her nightly rest as he bathed the land in a long, white twilight and made the horizon tremble with pale flashes.

In recent times her husband's people—fair-skinned folk speaking a Slavic tongue—had been sending out little colonies east and north into this forest. Some of these, like her husband's clan, cultivated fields and kept cattle. When these Slavs and the primitive Finns encountered each other in those vast regions, there was seldom any conflict. There was land and hunting enough for ten thousand times their numbers. Marriages like her mother's took place. But the settlers of the hamlet looked down upon the forest folk all the same.

It was her husband's joke to call her by the name not of her mother's little tribe, but of the great tribe of Mordvinians that lay far to the north. It made her sound more foreign, even though she was half pure Slav. And, she reflected sadly, it reminded the rest of the clan to look down on her.

Especially her mother-in-law. For nearly thirteen years her large, powerful figure had loomed over Lebed's life like a threatening cloudbank in the sky. Sometimes, for days at a time, the other woman's leonine face with its big, heavy cheeks would seem to be serene, even friendly. But then some small mistake on her part—a spindle dropped, sour cream spilled—would call forth a thundering rage. The other women of the house would be silent, either looking down at the floor or watching her furtively. And she knew that they were glad—both that they had escaped and that the anger was falling on her, the outsider. After the burst of rage, her mother-in-law would abruptly tell her to get back to work and then turn to the rest of them with a shrug.

"What can you expect from a poor Mordvinian?"

It was easy to bear. But her own family made it harder. Both her parents had died the previous year, leaving only her and a younger brother. And it was he who had made her weep the day before.

He meant no harm. But he was always in trouble with the village elder. His broad, slightly foolish face was always smiling, even when he was drunk: and he seemed to have only two desires in life—to hunt and to please his little nephew.

"Kiy doesn't need you," she would tell him, "and nor do I if you won't obey the elder." But it was useless. He hated the work in the fields, would disappear for days into the forest without permission—while the villagers muttered about him angrily—and then she would suddenly see his strong, square form come striding back, with a dozen pelts hanging from his belt and his habitual, foolish smile on his face. The elder would curse him and her mother-in-law would look at her with renewed disgust, as if it were her fault.

And now, that day, with complete foolishness he had promised the little boy: "Next time I go hunting, Little Kiy, I'm going to bring you a baby bear. You can keep him tied up outside."

"But, Mal," she reminded him, "the elder said you'll have to leave the village if you disobey him again." As a punishment because of his absences, the elder had already forbidden him to go hunting anymore that year.

But her brother only bowed his big, fair head, still smiling foolishly, and said nothing.

"Why don't you take a wife and stop this nonsense?" she shouted at him wretchedly. "As you command, Sister Lebed." He bowed his head, grinning.

He said it to exasperate her: for almost no one in the village was addressed by his full name. The little boy, whose name was Kiy, was usually called by a diminutive, Little Kiy. Her own full name, Lebed, was seldom used. Since childhood she had always been known by an affectionate nickname—Little Swan. Mal had a nickname, too, which people used when they were angry with him—they called him Lazybones.

"Lazybones!" she countered angrily. "Settle down and work."

But Mal would never do that. He preferred to live alone in a small hut with two old men who were no use for anything, nowadays, but a little hunting. The three of them would drink mead together, hunt and fish, while the women treated them with a mocking tolerance.

She had gone to him twice more that day in the fields, the second time in tears, trying to make him forget his stupid plan. Though he brought her nothing but trouble, she loved him. It would be lonely if he were sent away.

And each time, though there were tears in her eyes, he had only grinned at her, the sweat trickling down his big, broad face, as he carted the bales of hay to the stack.

Which was why, at the end of the day, it had taken her a long time to get to sleep; and when at last she had slipped into unconsciousness, her mind had still been full of foreboding.

But now, night had washed her mind to a state of blankness. Under her coarse, plain shirt, her breasts rose and fell regularly. Softly the breeze from the window stirred her thick hair and the fair hair of the child.

Nor did anyone awake when the dog by the doorway sat up expectantly as two shadows glided past. No one, that is, except the little boy, whose eyes briefly opened. A sleepy smile appeared on his face, and had his mother been awake she would have felt the suppressed tremble of excitement go through his body. He closed his eyes again, still smiling.

Soon, he knew.

* * *

Softly the wind moved over the land.

But where were the hamlet, the river, and the forest?

In order to explain the significance of the magical place, a few words are needed.

Geography, by convention, has long divided the huge landmass of Eurasia into two parts: Europe in the west, Asia in the east. But this convention is misleading. There is, in fact, a more natural division, which is between north and south.

For stretching across this vast landmass, from northern Europe, across Russia and the frozen wastes of Siberia, all the way to the high grounds above China, that reach north almost to touch Alaska, is the world's greatest plain.

The mighty north Eurasian plain is over seven thousand miles from west to east. From the Atlantic to the Pacific it stretches, a series of huge, interlocking plates, covering a sixth of Earth's land surface—the size of the USA and Canada combined. To the north, most of the plain is bounded by the icy Arctic Ocean. From there it descends, sometimes two thousand miles, across huge belts of tundra, forest, steppe, and desert to its southern border. And it is this border that may truly be said to divide Eurasia into two.

For if northern Eurasia is a vast plain, southern Eurasia consists of the huge regions, from west to east, of the Middle East, ancient Persia, Afghanistan, India, Mongolia, and China. And dividing north from south, like a wall, is the mighty crescent of mountain ranges containing some of the highest summits in the world—from the Alps in western Europe to the mighty Asian Himalayas and beyond.

It is hard to see, therefore, why Eurasia was ever divided by geographers into west and east.

About a third of the way across the great plain, roughly above today's Afghanistan, there is a long, low, north-south line of ancient hills that reach from the tundra to the desert's edge. These are the Urals. Modern convention has called them mountains and designated them the border between Europe and Asia.

Yet in truth, with the exception of a few quite modest peaks, these gently rounded hills often rise only hundreds of feet above the plain. By no stretch of the imagination do they form a continental divide: they form scarcely a ripple on that ocean of land. There is no border between Europe and Asia—the plain is one.

As it sweeps across northern Europe, the plain is quite narrow—only some four hundred miles wide. As it goes farther, across eastern Europe, it begins to widen, like a wedge. Its northern border becomes the large, cold gulf of the Baltic Sea, which lies under the curving overhang of Scandinavia. Its southern, mountain border becomes the magnificent Balkan and Carpathian Mountains that guard the north of Greece. And then it opens out.

Russia: where the plain is endless.

Russia: where east and west meet.

Russia: the borderland.

Here, at the beginning of Russia, the northern border of the mighty plain starts to sweep up, to the Arctic Sea. In this northern land begins the world's greatest forest—the cold, dark empire of firs called the taiga, that stretches for thousands of miles to the Pacific shores. In the middle section of the plain is a huge, mixed forest. And in the south begins the endless, grassy steppe land, that leads down, at this point, not to desert or mountain, but to pleasant, sunny seashores, like those of the Mediterranean.

For the southern border of the Russian heartland is the warm Black Sea.

The Black Sea, lying as it does above the eastern end of the Mediterranean, is rather like a reservoir. The great southern crescent of mountains hold it in like a vast dam: to the southwest, the Balkans of Greece; to the south, the mountains of modern Turkey; to the southeast, the soaring Caucasus Mountains. Between the Balkans and the mountains of Turkey, a narrow channel allows the Black Sea to connect with its greater sister sea. This connecting link is known, at the Black Sea end, as the Bosphorus, and at the southern end as the Dardanelles.

The sea is large—some six hundred miles from west to east and four hundred north to south. It is fed by innumerable rivers including, on its western side above Greece, the stately Danube. Its waters contain traces of sulfur, which may at some point have caused it to be called "Black."

In the center of the northern, Russian shore, jutting far out into the sea's warm waters and shaped like a flat fish, is a broad peninsula. This is the Crimea. On each side of it, nearly four hundred miles apart, two enormous river systems descend across the steppe from the distant forests. On the western side, the broad river Dnieper; on the eastern, the mighty Don.

Between these two river systems therefore, the Dnieper and the Don, and from the steppe above the Black Sea shore all the way up into the northern forests, lies the huge, ancient Russian heartland.

Russia the borderland.

For still the great plain continues, even eastward. At its southern border, east of the Black Sea, the huge range of Caucasus Mountains stretches for another six hundred miles. Famous for their wines and fighting men—Georgians, Armenians, and many others—their shining peaks reach several thousand feet higher than any in the Alps or Rocky Mountains.

They end at a remarkable phenomenon, the second of the two seas inside the mountain crescent of the south. It is huge, running north to south—roughly the same shape as the Florida peninsula but twice as long—and the great crescent of mountain ranges makes a downward loop to accommodate it. This is the Caspian Sea.

Technically it is the world's largest lake: for it has no outlet. It is surrounded by steppe, mountain, and desert, and it loses its water by evaporation into the desert air. And it is fed, on its northern shore, by Russia's best-known river.

Mother Volga.

The Volga starts her great journey far away in the central forests of the

Russian heartland. From there she makes a huge loop, up through the distant forests of the north, before turning southward; then, having embraced the northern heartland, she turns away and flows across the Eurasian plain eastward and then southward until at last she makes her way slowly down, out of the forest, across the windblown steppe to the distant desert shores of the Caspian Sea.

And still, beyond the Volga, the mighty plain sweeps on, becoming less and less hospitable. In the south there are terrible deserts. In the north, dark taiga and permafrost spread down and finally conquer all the plain. To this day these vast regions are scarcely inhabited. Past the Volga, across the Urals, across the frozen wastes of Siberia to the distant Pacific Ocean: still there are three and a half thousand miles to go.

And where was the village, with its river and forest?

It is easy for us to say. It lay at the edge of the south Russian steppe: a few dozen miles east of the great river Dnieper, and roughly three hundred miles above that huge stream's estuary in the northwest corner of the warm Black Sea.

Yet, strange though it may seem, had a traveler from some other land asked, at that date, how to reach the place, there was scarcely a person living who could have told him.

For the state of Russia did not yet exist. The ancient civilizations of the East—China, India, Persia—all lay far away, below the huge crescent of mountains that was the southern border of the plain. To them, the empty plain was wasteland.

In the west the mighty empire of Rome spread all around the Mediterranean's shores and even as far north as Britain. But Rome had never penetrated beyond the outer fringes of the forests of the great Eurasian plain.

For what did Rome know of the forest? Only that east of the river Rhine were warlike German tribes, and that north by the Baltic lay primitive peoples—Balts, Latvians, Estonians, Lithuanians—they had vaguely heard of. But that was all. Of the Slav lands beyond the Germans they knew little; of the Finno-Ugrians in the forests that stretched beyond the Volga, nothing at all. Of the Turkish and Mongol tribes that lay in the huge Siberian hinterland, there was, as yet, not a sound over the forest, scarcely a whisper across the steppe.

And what did Rome know of the steppe? True, at the eastern end of the Mediterranean, Rome had expanded as far as Armenia, below the Caucasus Mountains; and she had for centuries known the little ports on the Black Sea's northern shore, where mariners came to buy furs or slaves from the interior, or to meet the caravans that had journeyed across the desert from the mysterious Orient. But the huge plain beyond these places was terra incognita—an unknown land of barbarous tribes, dangerous steppe, and impassable rivers. Long before the little hamlet was reached, the lines and names on the maps of the classical world—of Herodotus, Ptolemy, Pliny—dissolved into rumor or simply petered out.

Nor could the villagers themselves have explained where they were.

Even today, to the confusion of strangers, the people of Russia have difficulty in giving directions. Ask if a road runs east or west, north or south, or how many miles, and a Russian will not know. Why should he, in that endless landscape, where horizon succeeds horizon, always the same?

But he can tell you how the rivers run.

The villagers, therefore, knew that their little stream ran down into another small river; and that after a little time that river joined the mighty Dnieper. They knew that somewhere, far across the southern steppe, the Dnieper ran into the sea.

But that was all they knew. Only five of them had even seen the Dnieper.

To convey the truth, as it then was, we cannot speak of Russia, which did not exist, nor can we build an exact framework by which position may be defined. We can only say that the hamlet lay in the lands above the Black Sea, somewhere to the east of the river Dnieper and to the west of the river Don; a little to the east of the forest, a little to the west of the steppe; by one of a thousand uncharted rivers. For to be more precise, in this imprecise land, would be meaningless.

Softly the wind moved over the land, and a summer's night stretched over the vast plain. At the great plain's western edge, dusk was falling. Here, in the southern hamlet, it was starry midnight although, far to the north at the Arctic's beginning, a pale polar twilight persisted. East, by the Urals, it was the early hours, the depth of night. In Central Siberia it was dawn; by the Pacific Shores it was now well into morning; and farther yet, at the northeastern end of the huge landmass opposite Alaska, it was already high noon. Huge weather systems could be lost in the night upon the plain. Two thousand miles northeast of the hamlet, a shattering electric storm was raging over the forest: yet here all was still. And who knew what storm clouds crossed the forests, what tents were pitched upon the steppe, or what fires burned upon that endless land in the many chambers of the night?

The little boy smiled as soon as he woke.

The breeze was coming through the window; the sunlight from the square window frame made a large pale rectangle across the earth floor.

"Awake, my little berry?"

His mother's broad face, close to his. Past her, people were moving about the room. In one corner a cradle hung from a long, curved stick attached to the rafters.

It was a large room. The walls, made of clay plastered onto a wooden frame, were a grimy color. This was because, like the other huts in the hamlet, the little house with its long turf roof had no chimney: instead, the smoke from the big stove was left to fill the room before being allowed to escape through a small shutter that could be opened in the ceiling. It was an efficient way of warming the place quickly and, to the occupants, the darkened walls seemed familiar and friendly. Today however, the stove was not lit. The air within was clear and the room pleasantly cool.

The hut had two other compartments: behind the stove was a passageway where one entered the hut, and on the other side of this passage, another space, a little bigger than the main room, which served as a general workplace and store. In this stood a loom, various barrellike containers, hoes, sickles, and, hanging on the wall in a place of honor, one axe belonging to the master of the house. The whole building, framed by oak pillars, was dug about eighteen inches into the ground so that one stepped up from the passage to pass through the outer door.

His mother was washing his face with water from a brown earthenware pot. He gazed past her at the strip of gleaming sunlight on the floor.

But his mind was elsewhere.

She smiled, seeing his eyes on the sunlit floor. "What do we say about the sunlight?" she asked softly.

> Sweet milk poured
> on her floor;
> Neither knife nor your teeth
> Will ever get it off.

He chanted obediently. He looked out of the window. The breeze from it stirred his fair hair.

"And what about the wind?"

> Father has a stallion fine
> Not all the world can him restrain.

Already he knew a dozen such sayings. The women knew hundreds of them—homely riddles, word games, proverbs, likening light to spilled milk, the wind to a stallion. In these countless sayings the simple folk delighted in the gentle wordplay of their Slavic tongue.

In a moment she would let him go. He longed to run to the door. Would the cub be there?

She quickly examined his teeth. He had lost two milk teeth but grown two new ones. One more felt loose, but at present none was missing.

"Two little perches, full of white hens," she murmured happily. Then she let him go.

He ran to the doorway, into the passage and to the outer door.

Opposite the hut there was a vegetable patch from which, the day before, he had helped his mother pull a large turnip. To the right a man was loading farm implements onto an old wooden wagon with sturdy wheels each carved from a single block of wood. To the left, a little farther off beside the river, was a small bathhouse. It had been built only three years before and was not for the present members of the village, who had a bigger one of their own, but for the ancestors. After all, Kiy knew, the dead liked to take their steam bath, just like the living, even if you did not actually see them. And as everyone in his young life had told him, the ancestors became very angry if one left them out of anything.

"You wouldn't want people to forget about you, after you've gone, would you?" one of his father's other wives had asked him; and he had thought, no, he would not like to be forgotten, cut off from the warm company of the village.

He knew that the dead were there, watching him, just as he knew that in the ground under a corner of the barn in front of the elder's house, lived the tiny wrinkled figure of the village *domovoi*—his own father's grandfather—whose spirit presided over all that passed in the community.

He stepped outside. Nothing. He looked right and left. The bath-houses, the huts, all looked the same: there was no sign of the bear cub. The little fellow's face fell; he could not believe it—hadn't he seen Mal and the old man slip by in the night?

The man by the cart, who was a brother of one of his stepmothers, turned and looked at him. "What are you looking for, little boy?"

"Nothing, Uncle." He knew he must not say anything.

The pit of his stomach became cold and the bright morning sky seemed suddenly gray. He wanted warm tears to bring relief but, knowing Mal had sworn him to secrecy, he bit his lip instead and sadly turned back into the hut.

Inside, his grandmother was scolding the women about something, but he was used to that. He noticed his mother's tambourine hanging in one corner: it was colored red. He loved the color red; to him it was warm and friendly. Indeed, it was natural that he should think so, for in the Slav tongue the words *red* and *beautiful* were one and the same. He gazed at his grandmother's heavy face: how large her cheeks were—they reminded him of two lumps of lard. She noticed his gaze and stared at him balefully, pausing to indicate to his mother that he constituted an interruption.

"Go outside, Little Kiy," his mother said tactfully.

As he came out, he saw Mal.

It had not been a good night for Mal. Together with one of the older hunters he had set a trap for the bear cub in the woods; and they had nearly been successful. He'd have had the cub now if he hadn't lost his head at the last moment, made a false move, and been chased away by an infuriated mother bear. It made him blush just to think of it.

He had been planning to help the men get the hay in that day—attract the attention of the elder with his hard work and avoid embarrassing conversations with Kiy.

It did not occur to the little boy that his uncle was hurrying by the hut in order to avoid him. He ran over to him and stood looking up at him expectantly.

Mal glanced guiltily right and left. Fortunately the cart was unattended now and they were alone.

"Did you bring him? Where is he?" Kiy cried. The sight of his uncle had raised all his hopes again.

Mal hesitated. "He's in the forest," he prevaricated.

"When are you bringing him here? Today?" The little fellow's eyes were sparkling with excitement now.

"Soon. When winter comes."

The boy's face clouded with puzzlement and disappointment. Winter? Winter seemed half a lifetime away.

"Why?"

Mal thought for a moment. "I had him. He was walking beside me with a rope around his neck, Little Kiy; but then the wind took him away. There was nothing I could do."

"The wind?" His face fell. He knew that the wind was the oldest of all the gods. His uncle had often told him: "The sun god is great, Kiy, but the wind is older and greater." The wind blew by day, and also by night, when the sun had departed. The wind blew whenever it wished, over the endless plain.

"Where is he now?"

"Far away, in the forest."

The child looked heartbroken.

"But the snow maidens will bring him back," his uncle went on. "You'll see."

Why did he have to lie? He gazed down at his trusting little nephew and knew very well. It was for the same reason that he lived with the two old men and defied the village elder. It was because they all despised him and because, worse, he was ashamed of himself. That was why he could not admit the truth to the eager child. I am foolish and useless, he thought. Yes, and he was lazy, too. He had planned to work hard in the field that day, but now he felt like fleeing into the forest again to escape the ugly truth about his character. He could feel his resolution slipping away from him.

Yet perhaps there was still hope.

"I know where the wind is hiding him, though," he said.

"You do? You do?" Kiy's face lit up. "Tell me."

"Deep in the forest, in the land of Three-times-Nine."

"Can you get there?"

"Only if you know the way."

"And you know the way?" Surely a fine hunter like his uncle would know the way even to magic lands. "Which way is it?" he demanded.

Mal grinned. "To the east. Far to the east. But I can be there in a day," he boasted. And for a moment, he almost believed it himself.

"Will you fetch him then?" the little boy pleaded.

"Perhaps I will. One day." Mal looked serious. "But that's our secret. Not a word to anyone."

The boy nodded.

Mal walked on, glad to have escaped from his embarrassment. Maybe in a few days he would think of another trap for the bear cub. He did not want to disappoint the little boy, who trusted him. He would find a way.

He felt better. He would work in the field that day.

Kiy watched him go sadly. He was thoughtful. He had heard the women laugh at his uncle Mal, and the men curse him. He knew they called him Lazybones. Was it true after all that he could not be trusted? He looked up at the huge, vacant morning sky and wondered what to do.

*   *   *

The line of women spread out across the golden field in a broad V, like a flight of swallows in the summer sky.

In the center, with the line of women sweeping behind her to right and left, moved the large form of Lebed's mother-in-law. The wife of the elder had died that past winter, and she was the senior woman of the village now.

It was a hot day. They had already been working for several hours and now it was nearing noon. For this work the women wore only simple dresses of linenlike shifts, and shapeless bast shoes of woven birchbark. Each carried a sickle.

As they inched their way up the long field of barley, they sang. First the senior woman led with a single line, then the rest would chime in behind her, singing in a high, nasal tone that sounded sometimes harsh, sometimes mournful.

Lebed was covered in sweat; but she felt comfortable, working in that steady rhythm under the sun. Although they sometimes treated her scornfully, each of these women was in some way her kin—another wife, the other wife's sister, her husband's sisters and their daughters, these daughters' aunts, and cousins. For each there was a precise form of address that noted their complex relationship, the appropriate degree of respect, and to which was usually added the diminutive so beloved of all Slavs, and which turned every form of address into an expression of affection. "Little mother"; "little cousin": how else would one speak to another speck of poor humanity here in the immensity of the endless plain?

These were her people. They might call her a Mordvinian, but she was part of them. This was the community: the *rod* as the folk in the south called it, or the *mir* farther north. They held their land and village in common—only a man's household possessions were his own; and the voice of the elder was law.

Now her mother-in-law was calling to the women, encouraging them with the soft, caressing names. "Come, my daughters, my swans," she called, "let us reap." Even to Lebed she cried softly: "Come, my little swan."

In a way, Lebed loved even her. "Eat what is cooked, listen to what is said," the older woman would tell her sternly. Yet apart from her outbursts of rage, she could sometimes be kindly.

Lebed glanced across the field. Beyond, a few hundred yards away, her husband and the men were loading hay onto carts in the meadow. Her brother was there, too. By the side of the field, three of the oldest women were quietly resting. She looked for Kiy. He had been sitting with the old women a little earlier, but perhaps he had gone to watch the men.

> The golden sun is in the sky,
> Moist Mother Earth will never be dry.

The women sang and swung their sickles, stooping once more, as though in prayer to the greatest goddess who fed them all: moist Mother Earth.

The great goddess of the Slavs took her finest form in that region. For the hamlet lay on the edge of the best of all the bands of soil on the great plain: the black earth.

There was nothing else like it on the Eurasian plain.

Up in the north, under the tundra, the soil was a peaty gley, poor for cultivation; next, under the forests, lay the sandy podzol soils—gray under the northern deciduous forests, brown as one came to the broad-leaved forests farther south. In these soils, too, the yields were relatively poor. But as one came towards the steppe belt, a very different soil appeared. This was the black earth, the chernozem—glistening, soft, thick, rich as honey. And it stretched, for hundreds upon hundreds of miles, from the western coasts of the Black Sea, eastward across the plain, past the great river Volga, and far into Siberia. The Slavs who lived at the forest's edge had only to clear a field and then crop it continually: on that rich black soil they might raise crops for many years before the soil was exhausted, and then they would leave the field to grass over and clear another. It was a primitive and wasteful form of agriculture, but on the chernozem a village could survive in this way for a long time without having to move to fresh soil. Besides, what need was there to worry— were not the forest and the plains both endless?

It was as the women paused between songs that she saw Mal strolling towards them. His face was red and covered with sweat.

"Here comes Lazybones, looking for more work," one of the women cried mischievously. Even her mother-in-law laughed, and Lebed couldn't help smiling. It was obvious from the slightly guilty look on his face that he had sneaked away on some pretext for a rest. She was only surprised that Little Kiy had not come with him.

"Where's Little Kiy?" she asked.

"Don't know. Haven't seen him all morning."

She frowned. Where could the boy be? She turned and called to her mother-in-law, "May I go and find Little Kiy? He's gone off somewhere."

The large woman scarcely paused as she looked impassively at Lebed and her good-for-nothing brother. Then she shook her head. There was work to be done.

"Go and ask the old women where he went," she said to Mal quietly.

"All right." And he ambled amiably towards the edge of the field.

It always amused Mal to compare the lives of the people in the village. Those of the men were more vivid, perhaps, but shorter. A man grew strong, either fat or thin; and when at last his strength deserted him, like as not he would suddenly die. But the lot of women was quite different. First they would blossom—pale-skinned, slim, graceful as a deer; then, all and without exception, they would thicken—first at the hips as his sister had done, then about the midriff and the legs. And they would infallibly continue to get stouter and rounder, burned by the sun, like a pear or an apple, year after year, until the taller of them might reach the stately massiveness of Lebed's mother-in-law. Then gradually, still keeping their comfortable, rounded shape, they would begin to get smaller, shrinking gradually until at last in old age they shriveled up, like the little brown kernel inside a nutshell. And thus the old woman—the babushka—with her wrinkled brown face and shining blue eyes, would live out her long last years until finally, as naturally as a nut that has fallen, she sank at last into the ground. It was the pattern for all women. His sister Lebed would go that way, too, in the end. When he looked at an old babushka, he always felt a wave of affection.

There were three babushki sitting together at the edge of the field. Smiling kindly, he spoke to them each in turn.

Lebed watched him as he spoke to them and wondered why he was taking so long. Finally he returned grinning.

"They're old," he explained, "and a bit confused. One says she thought he went back to the village with the other children; the second thought he went to the river; and the third thinks he went off into the forest."

She sighed. She couldn't think why Kiy should have gone into the forest; and she doubted that he had strayed to the river. The other children were back in the hut in the charge of one of the girls. Probably he was there.

"Go and see if he's in the village," she asked. And since it was better than working, Mal wandered contentedly.

As the women worked, they continued to sing. She loved the song—for though it was a slow and mournful one, its tune was so beautiful it seemed to take her mind off her troubles:

> *Peasant, you will die;*
> *Plow your bit of earth.*
> *Neither water nor the fire*
> *Comfort you at your last hour;*
> *Neither the wind*
> *Can be your friend.*
>
> *In the earth*
> *Is your end:*
> *Let the earth*
> *Be your friend.*

The long line of women moved slowly forward, stooping as they cut the heavy-eared barley. The field was full of the soft swish and rustle of their sickles cutting through the browning stalks. The thin dust from the toppled barley hung low over the ground, smelling sweet. And Lebed, as she often did, experienced that half-pleasant, half-mournful sense—as though a part of her were lost, unable to escape from this slow, hard life in the great silence of the endless plain—half mournful, because one was forever trapped; half pleasant, because these were her people, and was not this life, after all, as things should be?

Some time had passed before Mal returned. His face still wore its usual vacant smile, but she thought she noticed a hint of uneasiness in it.

"Wasn't he there?"

"No. They hadn't seen him."

It was strange. She had assumed he would be with the others. Now she felt a trace of anxiety. Again she called to her mother-in-law. "Little Kiy isn't at home. Let me go and find him."

But the older woman only looked at her with mild contempt. "Children always disappear. He'll come back soon enough." And then with more malice, "Let your brother look for him. He's got nothing to do."

Lebed bowed her head sadly. "Go to the river, Mal. See if he's there," she said. And this time she saw that Mal walked more quickly.

The work went on steadily. Soon, she knew, it would be time to stop and rest. She suspected that her mother-in-law was keeping them at it for longer so as to have an excuse to stop her from leaving. She looked up from her work to the long horizon. Now it seemed almost to mock her, to remind her as brutally as her mother-in-law: "There is nothing you can do—the gods have already ordered all things as they are destined to be." She bent down again.

This time Mal came back in only a few minutes. He looked worried. "He didn't go to the river."

"How do you know?"

He had met the old man he went hunting with, he told her, who had been at the riverbank all morning. The old man would surely have seen the little boy if he had come by.

She felt a stab of fear.

"I think he's gone into the forest," Mal said.

The forest. He had never wandered there before, except with her. She gazed at her brother. "Why?"

He looked embarrassed. "I don't know."

Obviously he was lying, but she knew better than to cross-question him about his reasons. "Which way would he have gone?"

Mal considered. He remembered his foolish words to the little boy that morning: "To the east. Far to the east. I can be there in a day."

"He's probably gone east." He blushed. "I don't know where."

She looked at him scornfully. "Here, take this." She thrust the sickle into his hand. "Cut!" she ordered.

"But this is women's work," he protested.

"Work, fool," she shouted at him, and strode towards her mother-in-law, while the other women, watching the scene, burst into laughter. "Let me go and find Little Kiy," she begged once more, "my brother has sent him into the woods."

Her mother-in-law did not at first look at her, but glanced across at the meadow. The men had stopped work there and several, including Lebed's husband and the village elder, were walking towards them.

"Time to rest," she called to the women, and then, curtly to Lebed: "You can go."

As her husband and the elder arrived, Lebed told them briefly what had happened. The elder was a large, gray-bearded man with small impatient eyes. He showed little interest. But her husband's softer face creased into a look of gentle concern. He glanced at the elder.

"Should I go, too?"

"The boy will turn up. He won't have gone far. Let her find him." His tone was bored.

She saw the flicker of relief pass across her husband's face. She understood. He had other wives and other children to worry about.

"I will go now," she said quietly.

"If you're not back when we start work again, I'll come after you," her husband promised with a smile.

She nodded, and she went upon her way.

How pleasant the woods seemed, how friendly. Above, in the brilliant blue sky, billowing white clouds passed from time to time, gleaming in the reflection of the late-morning sun. They came from the east, over the green forest, from who knew what parched and endless steppes. By the forest's edge where the little boy walked, the wind passed softly over the tall grass, making it whisper. Half a dozen cows grazed there in the dappled shade.

It was already some time since Kiy had slipped away from the old women. Now he made his way happily along the familiar path that led into the woods. He had no sense of danger.

All morning he had brooded about the bear cub. His uncle Mal knew where it was—in the magical kingdom far to the east. And had he not said he could reach it in a day? But somehow, young as he was, Kiy knew: his uncle would not go. And the more he thought about it, the more it had seemed to the little boy that he knew what to do.

As the long morning grew warmer, the field where the women worked had begun to shimmer in the heat. He had wandered to and fro, apparently listless, until at last, as though in a daze and moved by an invisible hand, he had found himself drifting towards the woods.

He knew the way. East meant away from the river, along the track where his mother and the women came to pick mushrooms. At summer's end they would come this way again, to pick berries. East was where the white clouds were coming from.

He did not know how far it was; but if his uncle could get there in a day then so could he.

Or two days anyway, he thought bravely.

And so, dressed in a white smock with a cloth belt, little bast shoes, and still clutching a wisp of barley he had picked up from the field, the chubby little fellow made his way along the path into the pine trees with the dreamlike determination of the small child.

It was about a quarter of a mile to the series of small glades where the women went to pick mushrooms. More than a dozen varieties could be found there, clustered in the deep shadows, and he smiled with pleasure as he reached the place. He had never been beyond the spot before, but he pressed on with confidence.

The narrow path led down a slope, sometimes over pine needles, sometimes over gnarled roots, then up again into a coppice. He noticed that there were fewer pines now among the oaks and beeches, but he saw more ash trees. Squirrels watched him cautiously from the trees. One, by the path, seemed about to bound away, but changed its mind and instead sat alertly, crackling a rusk between its teeth, as he went by. After a little the coppice thinned. Everything seemed very quiet. The path was grassy here. A few hundred yards more and it led to the right, then turned to the left. Another clump of pines appeared.

Little Kiy felt happy. He was still excited by this adventure into an unknown land.

He had wandered over half a mile when the path led into a thick screen of trees and became narrower. He pressed on: the trees closed in upon him. There was a faint, peaty smell.

And suddenly, right beside him, was a dark pool.

It was not large—about ten yards across and thirty long. Its surface was still, protected by the trees that concealed it. While he looked though, a little gust of wind stirred a faint ripple on the surface. The ripple came towards him and lapped, with scarcely a sound, against the dark earth and clumps of fern by the water's edge.

He knew what it meant. He looked at the pond and all about him cautiously.

In the still pool, the devils dwell.

That was the saying the people of the hamlet used. There were sure to be water maidens—*rusalki*—in there, and if you were not careful they would come out and tickle you to death. "So don't ever let the *rusalki* get you, Little Kiy," his mother had warned him laughingly. "You're so ticklish they'd finish you off in no time!"

Keeping an eye carefully on the surface of the water, the little boy moved around the edge of the dangerous pool, and he was glad when the path led him away from it. Soon the trees opened out into an oak grove. The path wound through them until it came to a large empty clearing. Tall grasses moved gently in the clearing. On the right was a stand of silver birch. Kiy paused.

How quiet it was. Above, the blue sky was empty, silent. Which way should he go?

He waited a few minutes until a cloud drifted soundlessly above the clearing. He watched carefully, to make sure of its path.

East lay straight ahead. He began to walk again.

For the first time, now, he wished he were not alone. Several times he glanced around the clearing. Perhaps, he hoped, his mother might appear. It seemed to him natural that she should suddenly be there, where he was. But there was no sign of her.

He entered the woods again and walked another ten minutes. There was no path at all: the short grass under the beeches did not seem to have been trampled into tracks of any kind by man or beast. It was strangely empty. He paused, disconcerted. Should he go back? The familiar field and river seemed very far behind. He suddenly wanted to be near them again. But then he remembered the silent, hidden pool with its *rusalki* that lay beside the way, waiting.

The trees grew close together, tall, frightening, and aloof, soaring up and blocking out the light so that one could only see little fragments of sky through the screen of leaves—as though the vast blue bowl of the sky had been rudely shattered into a thousand pieces. He looked up at them and again hesitated. But what about the bear? He would not give up. The little boy bit his lip and started to go forward.

And then he thought he heard her voice.

"Little Kiy." His mother's cry seemed to have echoed softly through the trees. "Kiy. Little berry." She had called him. His face lit up with a smile of expectation. He turned.

But she was not there. He listened, called out himself, listened again.

Only silence. It was as though his mother's voice had never been. A gentle gust of wind made the leaves rustle and the upper branches sway stiffly. Had the voice been no more than a moan from the wind? Or was it the *rusalki* from the pool behind, teasing him?

Sadly he walked on.

Sometimes a thin ray of sunlight from high above would catch the fair hair of the little figure as he made his way across the forest floor under the tall trees. And occasionally he felt as if other eyes were watching him: as if silent forms, brown and gray, were lurking in the distant shadows; but though he looked about him, he never saw anything.

It was five minutes later that he nearly ended his journey.

For just as he had paused once again to look for signs of movement, there was a sudden, loud screech above him; and as he turned in fright, a dark form burst through the high foliage.

"It's Baba Yaga," he shrieked in terror.

It was a natural reaction. Every child feared Baba Yaga the witch. You never knew when she might find you as she flew through the air in her mortar, her long feet and clawlike hands outstretched, ready to seize little boys and girls, carry them off, and cook them. You never knew. He stared in horror.

It was only a bird, however, flapping noisily as it plunged through the leaves and swooped through the high branches.

But the shock was too much for him. He was shaking uncontrollably. He burst into tears, sat on the ground, and shouted for his mother again and again. Yet as the long, silent minutes passed, and nothing stirred, he ceased to cry and gradually became calm.

It had only been a bird. What was it his uncle had often told him? "The hunter has nothing to fear in the forest, Little Kiy, if he is careful. Only women and children are afraid of the forest." Slowly he got up. Hesitantly he moved forward, a little farther, through the dark woods.

And it was only a short while later that he noticed that, to the left, a different region was starting to appear, where the woods were thinner and the light permeated more easily. Soon this other wood seemed to be glowing with a golden light and, drawn by the light, he made his way across.

It was warmer there. The trees were not so tall. Lush green grass grew beneath, and bushes, too. There were clumps of moss on the ground. He felt the hot sun full on his face, heard the buzz of flies, and soon felt the tiny bite of a mosquito. His spirits lightened. At his feet a little green lizard darted away through the grass.

He was so glad to enter the place that for several minutes he scarcely noticed in which direction he was wandering.

In fact, though he did not know it, Kiy had been walking for almost an hour and it was now high noon. He still did not notice that he was hungry and thirsty; nor, in his relief at escaping from the dark woods, did he realize he was tired. Glancing back now, he could no longer see the dark wood; indeed, as he turned full circle, the sunlit place seemed strangely unfamiliar. Nearby, silver birches were gleaming in the sun. A small bird on a branch stared at him as though too hot to move; and suddenly he, too, affected by the powerful sun, felt as if the whole day had taken on a dreamlike quality. Ahead the undergrowth grew thicker and there was a low screen of reeds.

And then he saw the shining light.

It came from the ground, from under a tangled mass of roots. It flashed suddenly in his eyes and made him blink. He took a pace forward. Still the light glittered. A light in the ground. He moved closer, and as he did so a thought formed in his mind.

That light, he wondered, could it be the way into the other world?

Surely it might be. For the Slavic word by which the people of the hamlet referred to the other world sounded identical to *light*. And Kiy knew that the place where the *domovoi* and the other ancestors lived was underground. Here, then, was a shining light, in a mysterious place, in the ground. Perhaps this might be it—the way in!

Moving closer, he discovered that the light came from the smooth surface of a tiny, half-concealed stream, where it was struck by the noonday sun. It wound its way in and out of the undergrowth, sometimes entirely disappearing into a trough, and then reappearing in the long grass a few yards farther on. But the fact that the light came from a stream did not make it any less magical to the little boy. Indeed, as he looked around at the stream, the shining birch trees, and the lush grass, another and still more exciting idea was forming in his mind. I've reached it, he thought. This is it. He must have arrived at the start of the secret kingdom—the kingdom of Three-times-Nine. For what place could be more magical than this?

Wonderingly he followed the tiny rivulet: it led him for fifty yards through the greenery until he reached a pair of low rocks with a hazel bush growing in the crevice between them. There he paused. He touched the rocks: they were warm, almost hot. He felt suddenly thirsty, hesitated for a moment to drink from the magical stream, and then, his thirst overcoming him, knelt on the grass and scooped up the crystal water with his hands. How sweet it tasted, how fresh.

Then, to get a better view of where he was, he began to scramble onto one of the rocks. There was a ledge just above him. He raised his hand over the ledge, cast about for something to grasp.

And felt his hand close upon a snake.

He himself could not have said how, a second later, he came to be ten feet away from the rock, trembling from head to foot. His head made tiny, convulsive movements, jerking this way and that, as he looked at the trees, the stream, the rocks, for signs of the snakes that might be about to strike him. A stalk of grass brushed his foot, and he jumped into the air.

But the snake on the rock had not moved. He could see the end of its tail lying along the edge. For two long minutes he waited, still trembling. Nothing on the ground stirred, though high above a buzzard, wings stiff and still, swept noiselessly over the scene.

Slowly, his curiosity overcoming even his terror, the little boy crept forward again.

The snake was dead. It lay in a twisted mass on the broad ledge. Fully stretched, it would have been two, perhaps three times as long as he was. Its head had been split open and gouged: he wondered how—by an eagle perhaps? He could see that it was a viper—there were several varieties in the region: and although it was dead, he could not help shuddering as he looked at it.

Yet even as he looked, he realized something else: something that, despite his fear, made him tremble less and even smile. Yes, indeed, this was the magic kingdom. The snake lay under the shadow of a bush that grew in the crevice between the two rocks. And it was a hazel bush.

"So now I'll be able to find my bear," he said aloud.

For the dead snake could give him one of the greatest secrets in the world—the secret of the magic language.

The magic language: it was silent. All trees and plants spoke it, so even did stones and streams; animals too, sometimes. And you could obtain the secret in several ways—no less an authority than his grandmother herself had told him. "There are four ways to discover the secret language, Little Kiy. If you save a snake from the fire, or a fish from being caught, they may give it to you. Or second, if you find fern seed in the forest at midnight on midsummer's eve; or third, if you find a frog when you're plowing and put it in your mouth. Or lastly, if you find a dead snake under a hazel bush, you must bake it and eat its heart."

If I could speak to the trees and the animals, they'd soon tell me where my bear cub is, he thought. And he gazed at the fearsome snake with satisfaction. Only one big problem remained, though: how to bake it? For there was no fire. Perhaps, he considered, I could take it back to the village.

He did not take his eyes off the snake. It lay only a few feet away and it had not been dead for long. Except for its torn head, it looked as if it might come back to life at any moment, and as he felt the heat of the rock through his little bast shoes and thought of the heat warming the snake, he still could not help trembling a little.

No, he could not drag it home alone.

But then a simple and comforting thought came into his head, and in his mind's eye it seemed a broad path had just opened up before him through the lonely woods. I'll go back and fetch Uncle Mal. He'll come and bake the snake for me.

How easy it seemed. For a second he felt as if his journey were over and he was safely back already. With relief he scrambled down off the rock to the little brook below, and he began to retrace his steps along it.

The whole scene seemed less magical, more familiar now, as he began the return from his successful journey.

It was five minutes before he realized that he was lost.

Having turned back into the woods from the shining pool, he had taken his direction from the passing clouds. How was it, then, that the place looked so unfamiliar. The trees were starting to grow taller and closer together. There were some scattered boulders and bushes, quite different from the woods where he had been before. He would have been glad, now, to see even the dangerous pond with its *rusalki*. Again he looked up to see the clouds. He did not know that, since before noon, the wind had been gradually changing direction.

And only then, at last, did the little boy slowly give way to panic. As the minutes passed, and he knew with greater and greater certainty that he was lost, a coldness seemed to envelop him. He stopped, looked right and left, saw only the endless ranks of tall tree trunks stretching in every direction, and realized that it was hopeless.

There was no way out. He called out, shouted his mother's name four, five times. But his cries were only lost in the forest. It was as though the day itself had decided to trap him, imprison him in the forest under the endless blue sky, and was now watching him from far above, mocking. Perhaps he would never get home. There was a fallen tree nearby and he sat beside it. Waves of misery passed over him as he sat on the ground with his back to the tree, too discouraged to walk anymore. He began to cry.

Twice more he called out, but there was no answer. A large mushroom was growing beside him. He stretched out his hand and stroked its soft form for comfort, then cried a little more. And so several more minutes passed as his crying brought him warmth and his wet eyes grew heavy. Then, for a little time, his head fell forward and his chin rested on his chest.

At first he wondered if he was dreaming when he saw the little bear.

It had obviously wandered away from its mother and it was loping along, almost tumbling over its own large paws, hurrying to catch up with her. The bear cub passed only fifty feet from where Kiy was sitting half asleep.

Rubbing his eyes, Kiy struggled up, pinched himself to make sure he was awake, and stared after the cub. Could it really be, after all, that he had found the cub? He could hardly believe his luck. The cub was still visible, scurrying towards a brown form about a hundred yards away that must be its mother. The brown form vanished behind a tree.

Forgetting everything, the little boy started after them. He had only one thought: I must see which way they go. Excitedly, hurrying as quickly as he could, he followed.

They led him through the wood, across a glade, into another wood. He did not care how far it was. Sometimes he caught a glimpse of them and froze, in case they saw him. But mostly he was following the sounds they made as they plunged and scuttled through the forest. He did not know how far from home he was now; nor how he would find his way back. He was too near the object of his quest to think of that. Eagerly he pressed on.

Several times he almost lost them. In the middle of a seemingly endless grove of oak or beech, he would suddenly encounter silence. All around would be trees, with no special feature. And he would pause, wander, pause again before at last hearing their rustling sound coming from some direction.

He had no sense of danger. For after so many magic signs—the hidden pool, the light in the stream from the other world, the snake under the hazel, it was clear to him that this must be a magical day and that the spirits of the forest were leading him to his goal.

It was in one of these silences that he saw that, over to his right, there was a patch of sunlight behind a screen of birch trees that suggested a glade. Perhaps the bear cub had gone there. He moved towards it.

And then ahead of him at the edge of the glade he saw a flash of light in the trees. It was not very high up. Something in the lower branches was glittering. He could not see what it was for the screen of birches, but the sun's rays were dancing on it, darting this way and that among the trees, flashing bright colors of red, silver, and gold. What could it be?

And then he realized, with a rush of joy—of course, what it must be. What else lived in a tree and shone like this? What else guarded the valuable things that people searched for—and must surely be guarding his bear cub at this very moment? What else, but the rarest and finest of all the forest's wonders?

It could only be the firebird itself.

The firebird had plumage of many colors. It glistened and sparkled, even in the dark. If you could creep up and seize one of its long tail feathers, you could have anything you wanted. The firebird meant warmth and happiness. To be sure, the bear cub would be waiting there with the firebird, now. The glinting light seemed to beckon, inviting him.

He went forward, until he was only a dozen yards away. Though he could not see it clearly, the firebird did not move but still sent out flashes of light: it was waiting for him. With a little cry of joy he ran through the screen of birch trees into the clearing.

The face of the horseman that looked down at him from under a metal helmet was motionless. The helmet had several colored gems set around the rim that flashed in the sunlight—like a firebird. The face was dark, with a large aquiline nose. A mane of black hair cascaded from under the helmet to his shoulders. And his black, almond-shaped eyes were cold. Behind his shoulder hung a long, curved bow.

The little boy stood before him, transfixed. The horse this awesome figure rode was black. Its leather trappings were richly decorated. The horse had been cropping the grass in the shade beside the trees: now it raised its head lazily to look at Kiy.

The face of the horseman did not move.

Then he swooped.

*   *   *

High above, in the vast blue sky, the heavy sun beat down upon the land at silent noon; through a faint, sultry breath of wind made a whisper in the dry barley that brushed against Lebed's waist as she left the golden field. The dusty smell of the barley permeated the edge of the wood, too. As she made her way along the open ground by the wood's edge, a field mouse scurried out of the barley and hid under a tree root.

Perhaps the child had only strayed to the shadows by the trees. As she walked, she called out gently: "Kiy, my little berry. Little Kiy, my dove."

The grazing cows looked up but did not trouble to move. Across the field, skirting the woods, a buzzard glided over her in search of prey. Kiy was not there.

She took the path that led to the place where they picked mushrooms. The woods at noon were as silent as the field, and the sun broke through the cover with a harsh light. She called again: "Little Kiy. Kiy, my duck."

Hanging on a length of twine around her neck was a little talisman—a tiny goose carved out of pine wood—that her mother had given her. She pulled it out and kissed it.

Then she searched the glades where the mushrooms were. But Kiy was not there.

She went on to the pool. Might he have tumbled in, she wondered? Could he be there, under the still, dark water? She gazed at it. There was no sign of any body floating, and surely there was no reason why he should have fallen in, she reassured herself.

Loudly her voice rang through the wood.

She followed the path to the clearing. There she called out several times more, half expecting to hear his reply. Surely he could not have wandered much farther?

She went over to the stand of silver birch at the far side of the clearing and, standing still for long moments, she bowed her head before the shining screen they made. The birch was sacred, and friendly: it could help you if you prayed to it. After this she moved on. But now she went the way she knew was eastward, not guessing that her child, unaware that the wind had changed, had taken the path of the clouds, in another direction. Once she saw a pair of wolves, standing like pale gray shadows by a tree, watching her. For a moment her heart missed a beat. What if Kiy had met them earlier? She could only remind herself that wolves seldom attacked humans in the warm, plentiful summer.

As she went, images came slowly into her mind, lodging themselves, refusing to be cast out: uncertain figures from her people's folklore— birds of joy and sorrow, birds of prey. For ten minutes her mind was full of the image of fire—fire in the stove at home, bringing comfort; fire in the forest, bringing fear. The two images seemed to impose themselves, one upon the other, so that she could not tell which was which.

Sometimes the trees seemed friendly, about to deliver her son to her from their silent protection; at other times they were dark and threatening. At one moment, in an oak grove, she thought she heard his voice echoing plaintively somewhere to the left and listened, and called, and listened again before moving forward.

She thought of life without him. She imagined the space beside her over the stove, empty. How could she fill that desolate emptiness? Would her kindly husband fill it? No. Another child? She had seen other women in the village who had lost their children. They had wept, pined for a time, then settled down again. They had had other children, lost more. The life of the *rod* would always go on. But what use was that knowledge to her now? Lebed had known a mother's anxiousness many times, but never a fear like this. It gnawed at her, caused her a pain that she could hardly bear.

If only she could fly, like Baba Yaga the witch, to the top of the great dome of the sky and look down upon all that moved in the forest and upon the steppe below. If she could only see, and cast a spell upon the boy to bring him back.

As she went farther east that early afternoon, two thoughts occurred to her. The first was that the child could not have wandered much farther: so, as long as he was still alive, he must be lost somewhere in the forest to the right or to the left, if only she could guess which way.

The second thought was more frightening.

For very soon, to the east, came the end of this part of the forest; and there began a new danger: the steppe.

She imagined Kiy walking out from the line of trees into the tall grasses. Nothing would protect him from the burning sun. The grasses would close behind him: he would never find his way out and she would be unable to see him. And what of the animals there? Though the chances of a bear or a wolf attacking the child in high summer in the woods were not high, she had no such hopes if he met a viper, wild dogs, or a polecat in the steppe.

She decided to go on through the wood and then walk along the edge of the steppe, calling into the fringes of the forest as she went. Perhaps after all, if he had come so far, he would be tired and might rest in the shadows at the edge of the wood. Anxiously she quickened her pace.

Five minutes later she emerged from the trees.

The steppe lay before her, a vast open sweep. The silence of the summer noon extended to the horizon and beyond. The light fell like a weight upon the land, which shimmered. For a hundred yards, patches of short grass and sedge, blistered but still green in places, provided an introduction to the steppe. Beyond that the tall feather grass—so called because of the long, trailing wisps of plumage it exhibited in spring—stretched in a boundless expanse. Its bleached feathers blended in the middle distance so that the yellow haze of parched grasses seemed to be covered with a white down. Farther on the plain looked brownish, and beyond that, glimmering under the line of the horizon, it was the color of lilac. At first glance, emerging into the heat, there was a sense that the heavy sun had reduced, quelled all living creatures into sleep.

But it was not so. A grasshopper sounded near Lebed's feet. To her right a woodlark rose and hovered, bravely singing in the blazing heat. She noticed some hyacinths and irises at the wood's edge, shriveled by the summer. Some way in front of her, a dark green patch in the yellow grass told her that a marmot colony inhabited the place.

Several times she called, but she neither heard nor saw any sign of the child. She turned left and began to walk northeast, along the forest edge. Ahead of her and to the right, perhaps two miles out into the steppe, was a small but clearly visible mound. It was a kurgan—a tomb—but she did not know who had put it there or when. Her own people seldom built such things.

Some time passed, yet strangely, through the heat haze, the kurgan never seemed to get any closer. The steppe played many such tricks with light, she knew; but today it seemed sinister, ominous. In the far distance she saw an elegant demoiselle crane with its blue-black neck and white back make its way swiftly towards a hidden nest. Frequently, several times as she went along, she turned back into the trees, making a circle to search for Little Kiy before emerging into the glare of the steppe again.

At last the kurgan seemed to be getting nearer, and at the same time she came to a thin promontory of woodland extending from the left out into the steppe. She started to walk through the line of the trees.

The camp of the horsemen lay just on the other side of the trees. She saw it as she came through, not a hundred paces away.

And she saw that they had her child.

The five wagons had canopies made of bark. They were arranged in a circle, making a modest ring of hot and dusty shadows in the huge brightness of the steppe. Several of the horsemen had dismounted and lay under the wagons.

Outside the little circle, two men remained mounted. One of them was fair haired, the other dark. The dark warrior addressed the other, the leader of the expedition. "Brother of mine, let us find the village."

The fair-haired horseman gazed at the child his blood brother held before him on the neck of his powerful black horse. The child was pale and stared about him with large frightened eyes. A good-looking little boy.

His blood brother's long raven hair glistened in the sun, almost as sleek as the flanks of his black mount.

The village could not be far from where the boy had been wandering. They would take a few of the young men and male children away with them while the villagers protested powerlessly. And these would be trained as warriors—not as slaves, but as adopted members of the clan. Two of the horsemen resting under the wagons had been taken from Slav villages in this way when they were young. A strange people, he thought: they had no god of war, yet once trained they made brave and excellent fighters. No doubt the little boy in front of him would be a credit to the clan one day.

That hot afternoon, however, he did not want to raid a village. "I came for another purpose," he said softly.

The dark horseman inclined his head. "Your grandfather did not live to be old," he replied gravely. "Not for nothing was he called the Deer."

These were the highest compliments among the horsemen of the steppe. Among them, an old man was without honor—brave men died in battle before they grew old.

It had been a little while before, as the sun reached its zenith that day,

that the fair-haired warrior had stood on the top of the solitary kurgan that lay in the steppe nearby and plunged a long sword into it. For
this was the tomb of his grandfather, killed in a skirmish in this half-
forgotten place; forgotten, that is, except by his family, who would
return every few years to honor him in this remote corner of the steppe.
The sword stood there now, its crossed handle just visible from the
wagons, a gleaming iron reminder of a noble warrior clan.

Kiy stared at the horsemen. He had never seen such men before, but
he had heard of them. The man on the black horse, he guessed, was a
Scythian.

"If a Scythian catches you," his father had once told him, "he'll skin
you alive and use your skin for horse-trappings." Kiy looked at the reins
anxiously. His first sight of the dark warrior's cold eyes had made him
expect the worst and now he supposed they were discussing how to cut
him up. He was trembling. And yet, as he stared up at the fair-haired
horseman, he wondered if there might be hope. For, despite his terror,
he was also thinking that this was the most splendid figure he had ever
encountered in his life.

Unlike his Scythian blood brother, the tall fair horseman had his hair
cut short. The features of his handsome, oval face were regular, refined,
almost delicate; his expression was open and pleasant. But when his pale
blue eyes flashed in anger, he was truly terrible—more frightening even
than the dark Scythian in front of him. So fearsome was the gaze of the
men of his tribe that it was remarked upon by several authors in antiquity.

For he was an Alan—the greatest of all the Sarmatian tribes—and the
mighty clan to which he belonged was one of the proudest of all, who
called themselves the "pale" or "radiant" ones.

Since time out of mind, horsemen had come from the east, from Asian
lands that lay beyond that huge crescent of mountain chains that bor-
dered the mighty Eurasian plain to the south. Through the passes above
India and Persia they had ridden, through the shimmering haze of the
foothills, streaming down onto the vast plain. From the desert they had
come, round the Caspian Sea, over the River Volga, and thence to the rich
steppe north of the Black Sea, to the lands of the Dnieper River and the
Don. They had even penetrated to the eastern Mediterranean and the
Balkan mountains above Greece.

First, in distant antiquity, came the Cimmerians, Iron Age horsemen.
Next, about 600 B.C., the Scythians—an Indo-European people with a
mixture of Mongol race, who spoke an Iranian tongue. Then, around 200
B.C., and mightier yet, another Iranian-speaking people—the Sarmatians—had swept over the land, reducing the Scythians to a small area
and dominating them.

They came from the east, these warrior clans with their noble princes.
They gave an Iranian name—Don, meaning water—to the rivers Don,
Dnieper, and even the more westerly Danube. They were nomadic war-
rior lords of all the steppe.

From the Black Sea to the forest's edge, the Slavs feared and admired
the radiant Alans. Some Slav tribes worked for them; others paid tribute.

Widely indeed did they roam: as they proclaimed in their heroic folk-tales, they rode the wide prairies from the land of the warm sun to the land of the sunset.

The Alan glanced up at the sky. The afternoon was still hot, but in a little while the men under the wagons would finish their sleep and it would be time to move.

"We return today," he said quietly. "You have the boy."

Kiy could not take his eyes off the tall warrior. Unlike his Scythian blood brother, the Alan used stirrups. He wore soft leather shoes and billowing silk trousers. By his side hung a long sword and a lasso—a favorite weapon of his people; and a dagger with a ring on top was fastened to his leg. His coat of mail and pointed helmet were strapped to a pack on the ground near the wagons, together with two of the long spears that the Alans used to mount their devastating charges. The cloth doublet he wore was sewn with little open triangles of gold; around his neck was a torc of golden wires with ends fashioned as golden dragons. Over his shoulders was a long cloak made of wool and held with a huge pin richly studded with Oriental gems. And that was all his personal ornament.

The Scythian was differently dressed. Kiy felt his back scratched by the gold and silver ornaments sewn onto the Scythian's leather jerkin. On the dark arm that held him was a bracelet carved with fantastic gods and animals. Kiy did not know that this wonderful work was Greek; all he knew was that it hurt his eyes as it flashed in the sun. At the Scythian's side hung a scimitar, its handle carved with Greek designs.

But even more splendid and more enthralling to the trembling child were their horses. Though he could only partly see the jet-black horse beneath him, he could sense the huge power of the animal as he sat astride its neck. And as for the horse upon which the Alan sat—it might have been, for all he knew, a god.

It was silver gray, with a black mane, a black stripe down its back, and a black tail. The Alans called his noble coloring "hoarfrost." As he watched this graceful animal move, it seemed to Kiy that the horse stalked over the ground as though it barely deigned to touch it. Such a creature, he thought, would not gallop: it would fly.

And indeed he was right: for there was no fleeter mount in all the Alan's tribe. He called this noble animal Trajan, after the Roman emperor whose heroic reputation had spread around the shores of the Black Sea and who had been adopted as a minor god even by the far-flung Sarmatians. Three times, in battle, Trajan had saved the Alan's life by his extraordinary sureness of foot. Once, when he had been wounded, it was the horse who had got away from his captors and come to search for him. It was as a compliment to the Alan and his horse that men said of him: "He loves Trajan more than his wife."

Trajan was still now; but the faint breeze on the steppe caught the small golden disks that hung from his bridle and made them twinkle. On each disk was incised the *tamga*—the emblem of the clan of which the horse, like his master, was considered a member. The *tamga* of the clan was a three-pronged trident—a sacred sign that hung over the hearth in the clan's ancestral tower, hundreds of miles away to the east.

The Scythian, too, looked at Trajan. And he almost sighed. Among his native people, such a godlike steed would be buried with his master in the kurgan when at last he had fallen in battle. The Alans, great horsemen though they were, usually were content to go to their rest with only their horse's bridle and equipage.

His father and the Alan's had fought together as mercenaries for Rome, and he and the Alan had become blood brothers when they were boys. No bond was more sacred: it could not be broken. For years they had traveled together, fought side by side. Never, in anything, had the Scythian ever failed the Alan. If need be, he knew without a doubt, he would die for his friend.

Yet as his hard eyes rested for the thousandth time on Trajan, they took on a strange, dreamy quality. If he were not my brother, he thought to himself, I would kill him, even a hundred like him, for such a horse. The horse stared back at him proudly. Aloud the Scythian said: "Brother of mine, will you not let me take two of our men, raid the village, and follow you? I will come up with you by sunset tomorrow."

The Alan gently stroked his horse's neck. "Do not ask this of me now, brother," he replied.

The Scythian was silent and thoughtful. Both men knew that the Alan could not refuse his blood brother anything—no gift, no favor, no sacrifice could ever be too great. This was their custom, and their honor. Had the Scythian asked formally for the horse, his brother would have given him Trajan. But a blood brother did not abuse his right: he must know when not to ask. And so now, the dark man bowed his head and it was as if the suggestion of the village raid had never been.

Then Little Kiy looked across the grass and cried out.

She came walking towards them in the heat of the day. The long yellowing grass brushed harshly against her bare legs.

Lebed did not know whether they would kill her or not, but she had nothing to lose. As she approached, something told her that the handsome Alan was their leader, but she was not sure. The two men were watching her impassively. Even their horses did not move.

Kiy instinctively struggled to get free, but he found that the Scythian's dark arm, which seemed to hold him so carelessly, was as hard as iron. Yet even now it did not cross the child's mind that, once his mother arrived, these strange and terrible horsemen would not deliver him up to her.

She called to him: "Little Kiy."

And he replied. How was it, he wondered, that the horsemen were ignoring her?

Lebed looked up at their eyes; the dark eyes of one, the pale blue eyes of the other: both seemed equally hard. The Scythian slowly began to reach across towards his scimitar; but then his hand hovered in front of the child and came to rest on his horse's mane.

She was only ten paces from them now. She could see Kiy's expression and understood it—his face first lit up with joy and hope at the sight of her; then his face puckered up in frustration and misery at his powerlessness to reach out to her. She noticed that some of the men and the horses by the wagons gazed at her curiously, but without stirring. Then Lebed stopped, folded her arms, and stood there with her feet apart, facing the two horsemen.

A breath of wind sent a faint ripple across the tall feather grasses that smelled sweet. The sun shone heavily upon their heads. The helmet of the Scythian glittered. No one spoke.

The Alan knew some words of Slavic. Finally, from his great height looking down from Trajan, he addressed her curtly. "What do you want?"

Lebed did not look at him. She looked at her son on the Scythian's black horse and said nothing.

"Go back to your village. The boy is ours."

She looked at Kiy's round cheeks, not at his eyes. She looked at his small, plump hands that held on to the black mane of the powerful horse. But still she said nothing.

For silence is more powerful than words.

The Alan watched her. What could she know, he thought, of the destiny that awaited the boy, over the horizon? What could she know of the busy Greek and Roman Black Sea ports; of the tall gray cliffs that shone like molten ash upon that southern sea; of the smooth, humpbacked promontories that looked like great bears come to drink the waters? What could she know, this poor Slav woman from the forest's edge, of the rich grain trade by the Crimea, of the caravans that traveled to the east, of the snow-topped Caucasus Mountains, the forges where men tempered iron in the passes or of the green vineyards on the lower slopes? She had never seen the great herds of magnificent horses, like gods, that dwelt by the mountains, or the proud stone towers of his people.

Soon, in a few years, this boy would be a warrior—ride a horse like Trajan, perhaps. He would be one of them, the radiant Alans, whose charges and feigned retreats the Romans themselves had copied. Had not the emperor Marcus Aurelius himself recently given up his attempts to conquer them? Had not the Romans seemed glad of their help against the fiery Parthians?

There was so much to see and know: he might visit the kingdoms of the Cimmerians, or the Scythians in the Crimea; he could converse with Greeks, Romans, Persians, Jewish settlers in the ports; meet Iranian and Asiatic people from who knew what distant eastern lands. He might win glory fighting the Persians in the east or the troublesome Goths from the north. Above all, he would experience the huge freedom of the mighty steppe—the thrill of the gallop, the comradeship of their brotherhood.

As a Slav, what could he do—live in the forest and pay tribute, or move south and till the land for the masters of the steppe? But as a member of their clan, he would be a lord of men.

With these thoughts he stared down at the woman who wanted her child.

"The boy is ours." Little Kiy heard the words and looked first at the

Alan, then at his mother. He tried to see if the Alan meant to kill him. Surely if they meant to, they would have done so by now. Yet what was to become of him? Was he never to see her again? The sharp smell of the big horse and the hot tears that welled up in his eyes seemed to fill the whole afternoon.

The men by the wagon were stirring, harnessing up. The Alan allowed his gaze to wander over the steppe. Lebed stood where she was.

The dark Scythian watched her as impassively as a snake. His horse shook its head. The village must be close indeed, he thought. How he longed to raid it. But he had twice suggested it and his blood brother had been unwilling. His arm flexed around the boy. "Let us go, my brother," he said quietly.

The Alan paused. Why should he pause? There was no reason to do so. But since it would be a long journey, and since the boy his blood brother had captured was about to begin a new life, and since he wished to show some small act of kindness towards the little boy to reassure his watching mother, he moved close and, drawing it out from his chest, hung a small amulet around the boy's neck. It was a talisman of the magical bird Simrug, whose eyes point in different directions—one to the present, one to the future. Pleased with this gift, he nodded to the Scythian, and the two men wheeled their horses.

As they did so, Kiy's face filled with fright. He wrenched himself around, stared back, across the Scythian's unyielding arm.

"Mama!"

Her body quivered. Every muscle she possessed wanted to move, to rush at the horseman. But she knew that if she did, he would strike her down. For some reason she herself did not understand, she knew that stillness and silence were her only hope.

"Mama!" A second time. They were thirty paces away now.

She did not move. Slowly the two men walked their horses into the long grasses, towards the east. Seventy paces. A hundred. She watched the small round face, its eyes very large, looking strangely pale above the dark horse that carried it away.

"Mama!"

Still she gazed at the face intently. The tall feather grass was starting to obscure him.

The carts were moving now, lumbering after them, accompanied by the other horsemen. They did not even bother to glance towards her as she stood, watching them go.

She had been praying in her mind since the moment she had first seen them; and although her prayers had been to no avail, she continued to pray, nonetheless. She prayed to the god of the wind, whom she felt against her face. She prayed to the god of thunder and lightning, and to the sun god who even now beat down upon them both. She prayed to the god of cattle. She prayed to moist Mother Earth, who lay everywhere, under their feet. She prayed to all the gods she knew. But the empty blue sky looked down upon her—and gave her nothing. It seemed metallic, hard as the horsemen's eyes.

The wagon went away through the swaying grasses. After a time she could no longer see even a faint cloud of dust. And now it seemed to her that the blue sky itself was slowly receding from her. And though she continued to pray, after the manner of her people, she bowed her head in tacit acknowledgment—it was fate.

It was mounting a small hillock, and looking back that the Alan saw her: a tiny figure in the distance, still standing there, watching after them.

And then he took pity on her. For by chance, that year, he, too, had lost his only son.

When the Scythian heard what his blood brother asked of him, his eyes shone.

"Twice today, my brother," he replied, "you have said to me—Do not ask—when I desired to raid the village. But that you may know my love for you, ask anything of me, and it shall be yours. For did we not put our sword points in the cup of blood together? Did I not swear by wind and scimitar to be yours in life and death?" With an easy movement, he passed the little boy across to the Alan. "He is yours."

Then he waited.

Had it not been against his honor, the Alan would have sighed. Instead, with a light smile, he answered, "My faithful brother, you have journeyed far with me to honor my grandfather, and you have done all that I have asked, not only today, but many times. Nor have you ever asked anything in return. Now, therefore, I beg you, ask a gift of me that I may show my love for you."

He knew a gift was due; and he knew what it would be.

"Brother of mine," replied the Scythian gravely, "I ask for Trajan."

"Then he is yours."

It hurt, physically, when he said it. Yet even in his pain he felt a surge of pride: to give such a horse away—this, truly, was the mark of a noble man.

"One last ride on him," the Alan said gaily. And without waiting, he wheeled Trajan about and, with no more than a touch, and holding the little boy easily in his arms, he put the horse at a gallop across the steppe.

And as Little Kiy looked about him in bewilderment, clinging instinctively to the splendid beast's mane, the Alan said to him in the Slavic tongue: "See, little boy, you are returning to your village: but all your life you will be able to say—'I rode on Trajan, the noblest of all the horses of the radiant Alans.' "

The little boy had no idea that there were tears in the Alan's eyes. All he knew was a thrill of joy, and of excitement greater than he had ever known before.

So it was that Lebed, staring hopelessly at the empty steppe, suddenly saw, as though it were the wind god himself, the flying form of Trajan racing over the ground towards her. Almost carelessly, and without a word, the Alan dropped the child at her feet, then turned and rode away into the shimmering steppe.

She hugged the child to her, in disbelief, while he clung to her.

And she scarcely took in the fact that, after a moment, he abruptly turned in her arms, pointed to the disappearing figure on the pulsating steppe, and cried out, "Let me go with them!"

Carrying the child in her arms, lest he be taken from her again, she hurried back to the woods.

Lebed did not return to the village at once. Instead she went to a quiet place beside the river. Close by there was a sacred oak tree, to which she gave thanks, and then, wishing only to be alone with her child, she sat in the shade and watched the little boy while he played by the water and then slept a while.

It was evening when they emerged together from the wood's edge. The big field had been cleared and was empty. Like two little clouds, they drifted slowly across the big open space.

The harvest was done. In one corner of the field, as was the custom, a sheaf of barley had been left standing—a gift to Volos, the god of wealth. At the top of the field, a group of little girls were standing in a circle, playing a clapping game and laughing; and as they entered the village, the geese by the huts greeted them with their usual din.

The first person Lebed saw was her husband. His face lit up with joy as he lifted the little boy high into the air above his head, while her mother-in-law came out of the hut and gave her a curt nod.

"I looked for you," he said. No doubt he had. Indeed, she knew, his warm heart might have driven him to search for them for days—except that there were so many other things he had to do.

"I found him," she said simply. Then she told them about the horsemen, and they went to the village elder and made her tell it all again.

"If they come another time," the elder said slowly, "we shall move north again." For the little community had come north to that place only five years before to avoid paying tribute to the horsemen of the steppe.

But that day there was nothing to be done except celebrate the ending of the harvest.

Already the young men and girls had gone out beside the field and were rolling and turning somersaults on the grass. In front of the elder's hut, the women were putting the finishing touches to a small figure in the shape of an old man, made of barley. It had a long, curling beard which, just then, they were anointing with honey. This was the god of the field, whom they were about to take to the boundary where the field met the edge of the woods.

And it was only now, as the villagers were gathering, that Mal emerged from the doorway of his hut. He hesitated when he saw Lebed and the child, but the little boy ran up to him. "I saw the bear," he cried. "I saw him."

And Mal blushed deep red, as Lebed pulled Kiy away.

As the villagers started to move out into the field, Lebed felt her husband at her side. She did not glance up into his face, as she knew he hoped she would, but she already knew the soft expression it wore. His eyes were glowing with eagerness like a boy's—she knew this, too, without looking. His long arms hung beside her and now one of them moved as his hand took her by the arm and gently squeezed. That was the signal—she knew it was coming.

She kept walking. Other women, she guessed, had noticed the little signal too. It was a strong arm, she thought, though rather bony, and by walking on, by not looking up, she could best conceal her lack of enthusiasm. He would come to her that night: that was all. She pushed the little boy in front of them so that their eyes could rest upon him, and so, as they entered the field, this was their communion.

While the sun began its slow descent onto the trees, and the long shadows streamed across the cut field, the villagers began the songs and dances. In a circle now, led by her mother-in-law, the women who had been reaping sang:

> *Stubble of the summer grain*
> *Give me back my strength again.*
> *I reaped you and now I am weak,*
> *But winter is long, winter is bleak:*
> *Harvest field and summer grain*
> *Give me back my strength again.*

The warm rays of the sinking sun caught the soft honey that trickled off the beard of the barley man, so that it shone.

By the side of the field, three old women, each a babushka too old now to dance or sing, watched them placidly. As she glanced at them, Lebed smiled to herself. She knew that she, too, would pass that way. They say that the god of the field shrinks to a tiny old man when the field is cut, she thought. Humans, too, shrink into the earth, dwelling underground like the ancestral *domovoi*. That was fate. Nature could not be mastered; man or woman could only accept seed time and harvest. And her individual destiny—this, too, she knew, was not important. No, not even the loss of her child would be greatly noticed, whatever her pain. So many children were lost. Nobody counted them. But some survived; and the life of the village, of the *rod*, only this would continue, always, through the harsh, remorseless cycle of the seasons in the endless land.

When the song was done, she went over to Little Kiy. He was sitting on the ground, fingering the talisman the horseman had given him; his mind was not on her, but moving upon the open steppe. He scarcely looked up at her.

And now her husband was in front of her, hovering over the child, his face smiling, eager.

He, too, was necessary: at certain times, at certain seasons, she had need of him. Yet although she was his to command, although it was the men who ruled in the village, it was the women, she knew, who were strong and who endured. It was the women, like moist Mother Earth herself, who protected the seed in the ground and who brought forth the harvest for the sun god and for man with his plow.

He smiled.

"Tonight."

It was after dusk, when the splinters of resin wood that served as candles were lit, that the feasting began in the elder's hut. The loving cup and its ladle, brimming with sparkling mead, was passed from hand to hand. And with each course of fish, millet bread, and meat, a dish was offered to the *domovoi* who it was assumed had emerged from his lair under the barn to join them.

When the food was eaten, the whole village continued to drink, and to dance. Kiy saw his mother take her red tambourine and dance before his father; and he watched, fascinated, until in the heat his head finally fell forward on his chest and he slept.

Twice her husband touched her and murmured: "Come." Twice she shook her head and continued to dance. She, too, had drunk, though less heavily than the others, and now her body was suffused with warmth. Excited by her own dancing, she began to crave him; but still she danced and drank, to bring herself to the moment when she would truly want him.

Gradually, as men and women alike reeled drunkenly out into the night, Lebed, too, allowed her husband to put his arm around her waist and lead her out. All around, by the huts, towards the field, indiscriminate couplings were taking place: who knew, who would remember, who had lain with whom? Who would know whose child was whose, in any results of that general sexual encounter? It did not matter. By such careless means the life of the *rod* would go on.

They went down to the river, past long grasses where the fireflies were shining in the darkness. Together they gazed at the river that gleamed in the moonlight. To this little river the villagers had given a name, taken from the horsemen of the steppe they feared. For as the Slavs knew well, some of the greatest of the Alans had described themselves, in their Iranian tongue, as *Rus*—meaning "light," or "shining." And so, since to a Slav ear this word had a pleasing feminine sound, well suited to a river, the villagers had called the little gleaming waterway *Rus—the shining one.*

It was a good name. And no doubt it would have pleased them still more had they known that this same Iranian name—*Rus* or *Rhos*—was also to be applied in these early ages to that mighty river far to the east that later times would call the Volga.

Rus they called the river; and the hamlet beside it they called, similarly, Russka.

The night was quiet. The stream shone, moved, yet did not move. They lay down on the grass. High above in the starlit summer sky, pale clouds came from time to time, like horsemen in an unhurried procession, glowing softly in the reflection of a crescent moon that rode to the south—and who knew, out in the forest, what bear or fox, wolf or firebird might be moving through the shadows, or what horsemen camped by their fires upon the endless steppe?

But the only sound that Lebed heard was a whisper in the leaves, as the wind moved softly over the land.

TWO

The River

In the year of the Lord 1066, in the month of January, a terrible sign appeared in the heavens. It was seen all over Europe.

In the Anglo-Saxon kingdom of England, threatened with William of Normandy's invasion, it was recorded in the chronicles with gloomy expectation. In France, Germany, and all around the shores of the Mediterranean it was seen. In eastern Europe, in the newly formed states of Poland and Hungary, the dreadful object dominated the nights. And beyond them, on the eastern borderland where forest meets steppe and the broad river Dnieper runs down to the temperate Black Sea, the great red comet hung, night after night, over the white and silent landscape; and men wondered what new evil was to befall the world.

And now that world had changed. In the nine turbulent centuries since the days of Trajan and Marcus Aurelius, Western civilization had passed from classical to medieval times in a series of huge events. Rome had become Christian; but soon after, its sprawling empire, now divided between its western and eastern capitals of Rome and Constantinople, had collapsed under the weight of huge barbarian invasions.

From the Mongolian lands above the Great Wall of China they had come, wave after wave from the East, crossing the great southern crescent of mountain ranges and sweeping down onto the desert and steppe of the vast Eurasian plain. Some white, some Mongoloid, mostly speaking forms of Turkish, these terrible invaders swept all before them. Thus came Attila and his Huns; after them the Avars; then the Turks. But it was not their sudden invasions, nor their huge, short-lived empires in the steppe that broke the Roman Empire: it was the enormous chain reaction of migrations that they set off as they crashed into the tribes of eastern Europe. These were the migrations that brought the Franks to France, the Bulgars, descendants of the Huns, to Bulgaria, the Saxons and Angles to Britain, and gave the names of tribes to regions like Burgundy and Lombardy.

By the end of this process, the old world had been shattered. Rome had fallen. Western Europe, though the barbarians were slowly converted to Christianity, remained a disorderly patchwork of tribal and dynastic regions. Only in the eastern Mediterranean and the Black Sea did a semblance of the old order remain. For here, just above Greece and beside

the narrow channel that links the Black Sea to the waters of the Mediterranean, stood the stately city of Constantinople, also known as Byzan-
tium. Unconquered, guardian of classical culture and of eastern Christianity, its character Greek rather than Latin, Constantinople remained
inviolate: the city where, right through the Middle Ages, there would still
preside—even if only in name—a Christian Roman emperor.

But this was not the end of the West's troubles. For in the year 622,
the prophet Mohamet made the first *hijrah* from Mecca and the mighty
power of Islam began its explosive expansion. "To the Garden, Muslims,
not the Fire," their leaders would cry as they went into battle: for those
who fell were assured a place in heaven. From Arabia the Muslim armies
swept through the Middle East, then eastward to Persia and India, and
westward across North Africa and even into Spain. In another drive, they
even reached the gates of Constantinople. And for centuries yet to come,
Christian Europe was to tremble at the prophet's name.

Lastly, to trouble the world yet further, came the Vikings.

Pirates, merchants, colonists, adventurers, from around the year 800
these Scandinavian voyagers burst upon the stage of history. They took
over much of central England; they set up colonies in Iceland and Greenland and even visited the North American coast. They founded the state
of Normandy and swept around into the Mediterranean.

And it was one group of Swedish Vikings who, having founded trading
colonies around the Baltic Sea, made their way down to the river system
of that great eastern hinterland, the land of the Slavs.

Varangians, these Norsemen were sometimes called. They set up a
huge, north-south trading network—collecting goods at the Slav city of
Novgorod in the north, and sailing down the rivers Dnieper, Don, and
Volga. On the Black Sea coast, near the mouth of the Don, they set up
a trading post known as Tmutarakan. And whether it was because they
were fair, or because they traded or fought side by side with fair Alannic
peoples in those southern lands, or for some other reason we do not
know, these piratical Norse merchants soon came to be known to the
civilized southern world they entered by that ancient Iranian name still
borne by some of the Alans—a name meaning "light" or "shining"—*Rus.*

And thus the new state of Russia was born.

High on the palisades the boy gazed out at the huge red star. His mind
was in a fever of excitement.

Far below in the darkness lay the broad river Dnieper; the ice at its
edges dimly reflected the star's blood-red light. Behind the boy, the city
of Kiev was silent.

It was nearly two centuries since this ancient Slav city by the Dnieper
had become the capital of the state of Rus. Lying in rolling woodlands
a day's journey from the beginning of the southern steppe, it was the
collecting point for all the trade from the northern forests that was to
pass downriver to the faraway Black Sea and points beyond.

What could the star portend for the city? the boy wondered. Certainly
it must be a sign from God.

For the land of Rus was Christian now. In the blessed year of the Lord

988, Vladimir, Prince of Kiev, had been baptized, with the Roman emperor of Constantinople himself acting as his godfather. Did not many already, for this conversion, call Vladimir a saint? And was it not said that two of his sons, young Boris and Gleb, had also joined the blessed?

The story of their death, just half a century before, had immediately entered popular folklore. For in the springtime of their lives, these two royal princes, facing assassins sent by their wicked elder brother, had meekly submitted, spoken only of their love for each other, and commended their young souls to God. The sadness, the gentleness of their deaths had touched the Slavs, and Boris and Gleb became the best-loved heroes of the land of Rus. The Passion-Sufferers, they were called.

Kiev was a city of churches now. In her streets one heard not only the sounds from the merchant boats upon the river, but also the chanting of monks and priests in a hundred churches; and the squat, Byzantine cupolas of the greatest of these, covered with gold, gleamed warmly in the sun. "One day," the nobles claimed, "we shall be like Tsargrad itself." For this was the name they often gave to the Roman emperor's city of Constantinople. And if, as the chroniclers in the monasteries had to confess, there were many peasants in the countryside who still preferred the old pagan ways, it would only be a question of time before they, too, joined the great commonwealth of the Christian world.

And what did the star mean for him? Did it mean danger? Would he be tested in some way?

For the coming year was to be the most important in his life. He was twelve years old. He knew his father was looking for a place for him in the entourage of one of the princes; there had been words about betrothing him, too. And even more thrilling was the fact that this very summer his father was sending a caravan across the steppe to the east. For weeks he had been begging his father to let him go with it. And then, he thought, I shall ride all the way to the great river Don. His mother was against this dangerous ambition; but just the week before his father had said he would consider it, and the boy had been thinking of little else since. And when I return, I can train to be a warrior, he promised himself. Like his noble father.

So intent was he upon these thoughts that he hardly noticed the approach of two figures, until they were standing beside him.

"Wake up, Ivanushka: you'll turn into a tree."

His name was Ivan; but he was called by the diminutive: Ivanushka. He smiled, faintly, but did not take his eyes off the star. He knew his brothers had come to tease him. The younger of these two, Boris, was a fair-haired, friendly-looking fellow of sixteen, already sprouting a beard. The elder, Sviatopolk, had a long, serious face and dark hair. He was eighteen and already married. After Boris had tried to coax the boy home for a minute, Sviatopolk gave him a sharp kick. "Stop freezing. Think you're an ice maiden?"

Boris stamped his felt boots to keep warm. Sviatopolk muttered a curse. Then they left.

Still the red star hung, silently, in the heavens. This was the fourth night Ivanushka had watched it, standing alone, and refusing all calls to

return home. He was a dreamy boy. Often one of his family would find
him staring at some spot outside, go away, and return to find him still
there, with a half smile on his broad face, his pale blue eyes still fixed
on the same place. Nor could they stop him from doing it. For these little
acts of contemplation were necessary to him. He was one of those beings
who, for better or worse, have a sense that all nature is speaking to them
directly. The minutes passed, therefore, and still he continued to gaze,
without moving.

"Ivanushka." It was his mother now. "Foolish boy. Your hand is like
ice." He was aware of her putting a fur coat on him. And though he did
not take his eyes off the star, he felt her gently squeeze his hand. And
now at last, Ivanushka turned and smiled.

They shared a special bond. How many hours he could happily spend
sitting with her by the fire in their big, wooden house, listening to her
recite the courtly tales of the heroic warriors—the *bogatyrs*—or a fairy
story of Baba Yaga the witch, or the firebird in the forest.

Olga was a tall, slim woman, with a broad forehead but rather small,
delicate features and dark brown hair. Her family had been great chiefs,
once, of the ancient Slav tribe of Severiani. As she sang these tales in a
soft, faraway voice, Ivanushka would gaze up at her, spellbound. The
image of her beautiful yet tender face was often in his mind; it was a
presence, like an icon that he carried with him through his life.

When she sang for his father, she could sing very differently. Her voice
would descend to a harsh contralto, her manner assume a laughing,
teasing scorn. Did he guess that her long, pale body had hidden strengths,
that she could make it behave in a way that drove his father wild with
desire? Perhaps, like all children, he had always had a natural sense of
these things.

Sometimes they would read the holy books together, both leaning
forward eagerly, with difficulty but always triumphantly making out the
Slavic words, written in bold uncial script, of the New Testament and
Apochryphal stories. He would study the sermons of the great preachers
of the Eastern Church—John Chrysostom or St. Basil; or better still, a
Slav preacher like Hilarion. He had also learned several of the lays of the
great singer Bayan, whom his own grandfather had known; and these he
could recite faultlessly, to please his father.

Ivanushka shared something else with his mother. It was a little gesture that she used to make. One would often see it when she was
standing and talking to someone—a slow raising of her arm from her side
towards them, as if ushering her listener through a door. It was such a
gentle movement, though—almost sad, yet tender and caressing. Of the
three brothers, only Ivanushka had taken this gesture from her, though
whether by inheritance or unconscious imitation he did not know.

He was always conscious of one other important fact about his mother:
unlike his father she was a Slav. So I am half a Slav, he thought.

What did it mean, to be a Slav? It was, he knew, a huge community.
Over the centuries Slavic people had spread to many lands. The Poles in
the west were Slavs; the Hungarians and Bulgarians partly so; farther
south, in the Balkan Mountains of Greece, the people were Slavs, too;

and though their languages had drifted apart from that spoken by the East Slavs who lived in the land of Rus, one could still easily hear the similarities.

Were they really a race? It was hard to say. Even in the land of Rus, there were many tribes. Those in the south had long ago mixed with the invading peoples of the steppe; those in the north were part Balt and Lithuanian; those in the east had gradually mixed with the Finno-Ugrian peoples of the forest.

Yet when Ivanushka looked at his mother, and compared her with his father and the other foreign retainers of the heroic Scandinavian ruling dynasty, he could say at once that she was Slav. What was it? Was it that she was musical? That she could be suddenly sad, then suddenly gay? No, it was another quality, he realized, that he especially associated with the Slavs. You see it in the peasants too, he considered. For even if they get angry and violent, they change back again in a moment. It was that they were gentle.

His mother was moving away now. Once more Ivanushka stared at the star. What was it telling him? Some of the priests were saying it meant the end of the world. Of course, he knew that the end of the world was coming—but surely not just yet.

He remembered the preacher he had heard, only a month before, who had profoundly impressed him. "The Slavs, dear brother in Christ, have come late, it is true, to work in the vineyard of our Lord," the priest had said. "But does not the parable tell us that those who come last shall be rewarded no less than those who were there before? God has prepared a great destiny for His people the Slavs, who rightly praise Him."

The words had thrilled him. Destiny. Perhaps because he was approaching puberty, the subject of destiny was much on his mind. Destiny: surely he would be part of it. And surely, too, Ivanushka prayed, the Day of Judgment would not come before he had had a chance to perform the great deeds for which he felt he was intended.

He did not know that, at this very moment, his destiny was being decided.

It had been a bad day for Igor. A promise of betrothal that he thought he had secured for Ivanushka had fallen through that very afternoon, and he did not know why. The family—a noble one—had suddenly backed off. It was an irritation, though one that he would normally have shrugged off.

But now this. Silently he gazed at the man before him.

Igor was a tall, impressive figure. He had a long, straight nose, deep-set eyes, and a sensual mouth; and his striking and exotic appearance was accentuated by the fact that the hair on his head was jet black, while that of his pointed beard was gray. From his neck on a chain hung a small metal disk on which was incised the ancient *tamga* of his clan: the three-pronged trident.

Like many of the noblemen in Kiev, it would have been hard to guess with certainty his ancestry. Indeed, even the many princes of Rus, whose origins were Scandinavian, by now were as likely to be dark and olive skinned as fair. But Igor's descent was from the radiant Alans.

They had come from the east. With others from ancient Alan and Circassian clans, the father of Igor had joined a great warrior Prince of the Rus in his campaigns beyond the river Don; and having fought well—there had never been a finer horseman—he was even admitted to the prince's council, the *druzhina*. When the prince returned, he had accompanied him; and so he had come across the steppe, to the rivers and forests of the land of Rus. There he had married a noble Scandinavian girl; and now their son Igor, in turn, served in the *druzhina* of the Prince of Kiev.

Besides his role as a warrior, Igor had many business interests. And in the city of Kiev, there was much in which a man could trade. There was the grain from the rich black earth of these southern lands, which was sent to the cities in the great forests of the north; there were the furs and slaves sent down the river to Constantinople. From the west came silver from Bohemia, and Frankish swords from the distant countries beyond. From Poland and the far western provinces of Rus came the all important salt. And from the east, downriver or in caravans across the steppe, came all manner of wonderful goods—silks, damasks, jewels, and spices—from the fabulous Orient.

The trading empire of the Rus was formidable indeed. All the way down the great north-south network of waterways that led from the cold northern forests by the Baltic, to the steppe above the warm Black Sea, there were trading posts and even substantial cities. In the north was Novgorod. Halfway down, by the headwaters of the Dnieper, lay Smolensk, and west of that, Polotsk. Above Kiev lay Chernigov; and below, as a last outpost on the borders of the steppe, Pereiaslav. Each of these cities, and others besides, could boast populations in the thousands. An estimated thirteen percent of the population were engaged in trading and artisan activities—far more than feudal Western Europe. Upon the vast landscape where ancient hunting and primitive agriculture ruled, therefore, were dotted these lively centers of commerce, cartels, and a money economy. And their lords were merchant princes.

After the disappointment about the betrothal, Igor had been hoping that this evening's meeting at his partner's house would improve his temper. For a long time he had been planning a caravan across the steppe to the southeast. There, beyond the great river Don, where the Caucasus Mountains descended from the skies to meet the Black Sea, lay the old peninsula settlement of the Rus: Tmutarakan. And opposite that, on the broad Crimean peninsula that jutted out into the sea from the center of its northern shore, were huge salt flats. In recent years a powerful tribe of steppe raiders, the Cumans, had weakened this trade with Tmutarakan; but as Igor had said: "If we can bring back a large shipment of salt, we can make a fortune."

The details had come together well. In early summer, several shipments would be brought to a little trading post and fort called Russka, at the edge of the steppe, where his partner had a storehouse. From there, with an armed escort, the caravan would set out. "And I only wish I could go myself," he remarked truthfully.

And then he had made the request that so embarrassed him.

The man who sat opposite him was a few years younger than he. He was not as tall as Igor, but he was massive. He had a heavy chin, a large curved Turkish nose, and drooping lids over his black eyes. He had thick black hair and a black beard cut in the shape of a broad wedge. Balanced, it seemed precariously, on the back of his head was a skullcap. This was Zhydovyn the Khazar.

His were a strange people. They were Turkish warriors who, for some centuries, had controlled an empire in the steppe that stretched from the desert by the Caspian Sea all the way to Kiev. When Islam had swept through the Middle East and tried to cross the Caucasus Mountains onto the great Eurasian plain, it was the mighty Khazars of the steppe, together with the Georgians, Armenians, and Alans in the mountain passes, who had barred its way. "So it's thanks to us Kiev isn't Muslim now," he liked to remind his friend Igor.

The Khazar empire had faded now, but Khazar merchants and warriors still often crossed the steppe from their distant desert base, and there was a large Khazar trading community in Kiev, beside the entrance known as the Khazar gate. Of all the men he knew to organize the caravan and lead it across the steppe, Igor could think of none he trusted more than Zhydovyn the Khazar. And indeed, he had only one regret about his partner.

Zhydovyn the Khazar was Jewish.

All the Khazars were Jewish. They had become so when, at the height of their empire, their ruler had decided that his people's primitive paganism was not worthy of their imperial status. And since the caliph in Baghdad was Muslim and the emperor in Constantinople was Christian, this ruler of the steppe—who did not want to seem the junior partner of either of them—sensibly chose the only other religion with a single God that he could find: and the state of the Khazar warlords converted to Judaism. Thus it was that Zhydovyn spoke Slav and Turkish—and preferred to write both using a Hebrew alphabet!

"Will you take my young son, Ivanushka, with the caravan?" That was all his friend Igor had asked him. Why then should the Khazar hesitate? He knew the boy quite well. His father was his partner. The answer, however, was simple: Zhydovyn was afraid.

I can see it all, he thought. If we get caught by the Cumans and he's killed—that will be understood. But I know this little fellow. It won't be like that. He'll go and fall in a river and drown, or something stupid like that. And then I shall get the blame. And so he prevaricated.

"Ivanushka's rather young. What about one of his brothers?"

Igor's eyes had narrowed. "Are you refusing me?"

"Of course not." The Khazar looked awkward. "If you are sure it's what you wish . . ."

And now, suddenly, it was Igor who felt awkward. Under normal circumstances he would simply have told Zhydovyn that this was his wish: and that would have been that. But now, fresh from the humiliation over the betrothal that day, he found himself overtaken by a wave of embarrassment. The Khazar was an excellent judge of people. He didn't want Ivanushka either. For an instant he had felt a surge of anger towards his youngest son. He disliked failure.

"No matter." He got up. "You are right. He's too young." The incident was closed.

Or almost. For just as he was leaving the Khazar's house, he could not resist turning to ask his friend: "Tell me, what do you think of Ivanushka—his character."

Zhydovyn had thought for a moment. He liked the boy. One of his own sons was a little that way.

"He's a dreamer," he said pleasantly.

As Igor rode home, he scarcely glanced at the red star. He was a sternly religious man and he had no doubt that God was sending a message. But it was his duty to suffer whatever would come, he supposed. Instead he thought of Ivanushka. "A dreamer," the Khazar had said. He knew what his own brothers called the boy. Sviatopolk calls him a fool, he thought sadly.

And what could one do with a fool? He had no idea.

It was three days later that the red comet passed out of sight, and there were no more signs in the heavens that winter.

Spring. In the beginning of each year in this fertile country, water covered the land, and the water was the river. Kiev: city by water. They would see it in a moment. The long boat moved steadily down the broad, placid stream of the Dnieper. Four men pulled gently on the oars, guiding it towards the city. Ivanushka and his father stood in the stern, the tall man's arm around the boy's shoulders.

The boat, though it was twenty feet long, was hollowed out of a single massive tree trunk. "No trees," Igor told his son, "are as big as those in the land of Rus. A man with an axe can carve himself a small ship out of one of our mighty oaks." And it seemed to the boy, feeling his father close beside him, that in all his life, no morning could ever be more still and more perfect than this.

Ivanushka wore a simple linen shirt and trousers, over which he had pulled a brown woolen kaftan, since the morning was still cold. On his feet were small green leather boots of which he was very proud. His light brown hair was cut short in the pageboy style.

They had been upstream at dawn to inspect the traps where the men were fishing. Now, still early in the morning, they were returning to the city for breakfast. And after that . . . Ivanushka felt a tremor of excitement in his stomach. For this was to be the day.

He looked up at his father. How often he had seen him, on some vantage point high on the wooden walls above the river, gazing down like a silent eagle on the watery landscape far below. Standing in the stern of the boat now, wrapped in a long black cloak, tall and spare, one might indeed have supposed that Igor had only to unfurl his cloak in order to rise up into the sky and hover, high over the river and woods, before swooping upon some luckless prey.

How powerful his father's arm was as it rested against his neck: not only with the strength of mere muscle, though. For when he was close to Igor, he sensed another strength that came from the past: haunting like an echoing memory, yet flowing into his being like a warm river. "You have the blood of mighty warriors in your veins," Igor had often told him. "Giants in battle, splendid horsemen like my father and his before him; our ancestors were strong before the Khazars came, in times when even the mountains were young. Remember, you are one with them; they are always with you." And then his heart would thrill when his father added: "And one day you, too, will pass all this on, to your sons and those who come after." This was what it meant to have a father and to be a son.

And today, he was sure, he would begin his career, following his elder brothers and his father, as a warrior, a *bogatyr*.

The monk would settle it all.

Softly the boat moved with the current. In the morning silence the great river spread towards the south. The air was sharp but still. Traces of mist remained upon the surface of the river whose huge, ceaseless movement was barely perceptible, thus creating a watery landscape that was always receding, yet motionless. As one looked south, gray-blue water and pale blue sky seemed to melt together at the horizon in a single, liquid softness, becoming indistinguishable one from another in the distance, while, to the east, the golden sunlight diffused in the haze.

They were coming in sight of the city now, and Ivanushka let out a little sigh. How beautiful Kiev was.

It sat on the right side of the river. On banks that rose steeply over a hundred feet above the water, and topped with high wooden palisades, it stretched for a couple of miles, staring—strong but secure—over the gentle, placid landscape.

The city consisted on three principal sections. First, at the northern edge, on a modest tumulus, stood the stout old citadel. This contained the prince's palace and the large church founded eighty years before by the Blessed Vladimir himself, the Church of the Tithes. Next, to the southwest and only separated from it by a small ravine, was the new citadel—a considerably larger area, built by Saint Vladimir's great son, compiler of the Russian Law, Yaroslav the Wise. Outside this, and running down to the river, lay another, still larger area, also protected by wooden walls. This was the suburb—the *podol*—where the lesser merchants and artisans lived. And down by the river were the jetties where the cumbersome, masted boats were moored.

In the two citadels many of the larger buildings were made of brick. In the *podol* all but a few churches were constructed of timber. All around, pleasant broad-leafed woods covered all, including the high, steep slopes that fell to the river below.

Everywhere in the city, golden crosses bearing the extra diagonal bar that represented Christ's footrest in the Eastern churches, caught the morning sun; and the golden, shallow domes of the churches glowed. Indeed, the great city itself looked like some vast and gleaming ship floating upon the waters.

For at Kiev, although the right bank of the river was high and topped with palisades, the left bank was low; and here, as at countless other places in the Dnieper's vast system, the river had flooded its banks. It lay glistening over the fields, which received its water and its rich silt. Each spring, through this wonderful immersion, all things were made anew.

As the city came closer, the boy fidgeted. Recently he had been having growing pains in his knees. But above all, he could hardly contain his excitement.

For just the week before Igor had told him: "It's time to decide what we shall do with you. I shall take you to see Father Luke."

It was a tremendous honor. Father Luke was his father's spiritual counselor and Igor never made a major decision without going to see him. When he spoke of the old monk, he would lower his voice in respect, for the old monk knew all things, he would declare. And he always went to see him alone. Even Ivanushka's two elder brothers had never been taken to see him. No wonder then that Ivanushka had blushed and then gone pale when his father had told him.

Again and again he had already pictured the scene. The kindly old man—tall, with a richly flowing white beard, a broad, seraphic face, eyes like suns—would see at once he had before him a young hero, would rest his hands in a blessing upon his head and declare: "It is God's will, Ivan, that you shall be a noble warrior." This was how it would be. He gazed first at his father, then towards the rampart, with happy trust.

And Igor looked at his son. Was he doing right? It seemed to him that he was. For he was going to betray him.

How handsome his family was. It gave him a thrill of happiness just to look at them. They were in the main room of the big wooden house. Light was streaming in through the windows, which were made not of glass, but of mica, the translucent silicate found in local rocks. The light also caught the yellow clay tiles on the floor, so that the room seemed flooded with light.

On the table lay the remains of breakfast. By one wall was a large stove; in the corner opposite hung a little icon of Saint Nicholas with a small clay lamp hanging from three silver chains in front of it. On a chest on the right side of the room stood two large copper candlesticks, gleaming dully. The wax candles in them were, for the present, unlit. In the center of the room, in the heavy carved oak chair that had been waxed and polished until it shone like ebony, sat his mother.

"Well, Ivanushka, are you ready?" He was ready. He gazed at her joyfully.

A rich, deep pink brocade gown fell to her ankles. Her girdle was sewn with gold. The sleeves of her gown were wide, and the slender arms that emerged from them were encased in white silk. On one wrist she wore a bracelet of silver, set with stones—green amethysts from Asia, warm amber from the Baltic north. Her pendant earrings were set with pearls. From her slim neck hung a golden crescent on a chain. Thus did the noblewomen of Rus dress themselves, like the Grecian ladies of imperial Constantinople.

How pale her broad brow was; how elegantly her hand rested on the carved lion on the arm of the chair, her long fingers, with their golden rings, gracefully pointing downwards. How sweet her face was, how kind. Yet, as she gazed at him, her face seemed somehow sad. Why was she sad?

His two brothers were there as well. They were both dressed in gowns, with rich belts and handsome sable collars: Sviatopolk, with his pale and lovely Polish bride; and Boris. He tried to love them equally; but though he admired them both, he could not help being a little afraid of Sviatopolk. People said Sviatopolk was the image of his father: yet was he? For while Igor often had a distant and reserved look in his eyes, there was something in Sviatopolk's face that was secretly angry, bitter. Why should that be? And though both brothers would occasionally cuff him, when Sviatopolk hit him, it always hurt just a fraction more than he had expected.

On his father's instructions, Ivanushka wore only a simple linen shirt and trousers—the long shirt hanging outside and held in with a belt. Somewhat against his mother's will, he had been allowed to keep on his favorite green boots. But his face and hands had been thoroughly scrubbed, in the big copper basin that stood on the washstand.

Igor, too, was similarly dressed, his shirt only distinguishable from that of a peasant by the fineness of the embroidery at the edges. "For rich ornament is not fitting, up there," he would say severely. Ivanushka's eyes were shining. He had been too excited to eat more than a little bread and oatmeal porridge called *kasha.* Now, kissing his mother and his brother, he ran out, and moments later, mounted on his pony, he felt the cool, damp morning air on his cheeks as he clattered into the street.

It was muddy. The houses of the nobles were mostly large wooden structures on one or two floors, with tall wooden roofs like tents and outbuildings behind. Each was in the middle of a small plot of ground enclosed by a stake fence; and these plots were, at present, so sodden from the melted snow and spring rain that planks had been laid on the path from the outer gate to the stables. The street outside was boarded in some places too, but where it was not, the horses' hooves almost disappeared into the mud.

Ivanushka, on his gray pony, rode respectfully behind his father. The nobleman was a splendid figure: a simple black cloak hung from his shoulders over his white shirt, and Ivanushka stared at his proud, straight back with boundless admiration. The jet-black horse that Igor rode was his finest. The ancient imperial name it bore had undergone a slight modification in its passage across the generations into Slavic: it was called Troyan.

The simple folk that father and son passed put their right hand on their heart and bowed from the waist; even the robed priests inclined their heads respectfully. For Igor was a *muzh*—a nobleman. The blood-money to be paid if he was killed was forty silver grivnas, whereas killing a free peasant, a *smerd,* cost a fine of only five.

Even the names of the ruling class were often different. The princes, and a few of their greatest retainers frequently bore the "royal" names that ended in *slav,* meaning "praise" or *mir,* "world." Such, for instance, were the great Vladimir and his son Yaroslav. For the nobility, Scandinavian names like Riurik or Oleg still quite often appeared. Even Igor's wife, though of noble Slav family, bore the name Olga, the Russian version of the Nordic Helga. A peasant, on the other hand, would probably bear some simple old Slavic name like Ilya, or Shchek, or Mal.

But it was a special form of address that marked out the noble beyond doubt. For while a peasant might be plain Ilya, a noble also added his father's name, his patronymic. Thus young Ivan was called Ivan, son of Igor: Ivan Igorevich. And the three brothers might be referred to as "sons of Igor"—the Igorevichi. For Igor was not only a noble: he was a valued member of the *druzhina* of the Prince of Kiev himself.

There were many princes in the land of Rus. Each of the trading cities on the great river routes had a prince as its protector, and all of them were descendants of the Norseman named Oleg who had taken Kiev from the Khazars two centuries before. At the moment the greatest cities in the vast river-trading empire were in the hands of the sons of the last prince of Kiev, the mighty Yaroslav the Wise. The sons of Yaroslav had organized the succession by rote—the eldest brother taking the greatest city, Kiev, and the rest taking the lesser cities by order of seniority, and owing obedience to the eldest. Thus while Igor's master was now the senior, or grand prince of Kiev, the city of Chernigov, to the north, was in the hands of his younger brother Svyatoslav; careful Vsevolod, younger still, held smaller Pereiaslav in the south. If one of the brothers died, he was succeeded not by his son, but by his next brother, so that all the younger brothers in the pecking order would move up to a greater city.

Igor served the Prince of Kiev himself. Indeed, he was almost in the inner council. Ivanushka's brothers, too, were already in the outer *druzhina,* although Boris was still only a page; and it thrilled Ivanushka to think that soon he, too, would follow them.

"Dismount!" His father's curt voice cut into the boy's reverie and he started. They had only gone a few hundred yards, but Igor had already swung out of his saddle and was striding away; and as Ivanushka looked up, he saw why. They had reached the cathedral. He sighed. He dreaded the cathedral.

The walled citadel of Yaroslav the Wise contained many fine buildings. Besides the handsome wooden houses of the nobles, there were monasteries, churches, schools, and a splendid gateway—the Golden Gate—built in stone. This gateway was especially fine because on top of it, soaring up into the sky, stood the little golden-domed Church of the Annunciation. But nowhere in all the lands of Rus was there anything as magnificent as the great cathedral that rose before him now. For just as his father, the Blessed Vladimir, had built his great Church of the Tithes in the old citadel, so Yaroslav had begun his own huge cathedral in the new one.

He called it Saint Sophia: what other name would do, when everyone knew that the greatest church in the Eastern Roman Empire, the seat of the Patriarch in Constantinople, bore that sacred name? Saint Sophia, Holy Wisdom.

For though this new northern nation might proudly declare "We are the Rus," it was the civilization of the Greeks that they copied. The senior priests were mostly Greek. Even the one Slav, the mighty preacher who had headed the Russian Church a decade ago, had taken the Greek name of Hilarion. When noble children were baptized, they took a second, Christian name to complement the Slav or Scandinavian names they mostly bore. Thus a Yaroslav or a Boris would also carry a Christian name like Andrei, Dimitri, Alexander, or Constantine. And all these names were Greek.

How huge the cathedral was. It was built of red granite, laid in long thin strips and fixed with almost equal layers of pink cement. It rose up a massive, rather square, red-and-pink block, a holy fortress designed to impress upon all the people the might of the newly adopted Christian God. Upon its center sat a great burnished dome, in the shape of a flattened helmet—like that of the church in Constantinople—and around it were grouped twelve smaller domes. "They stand for our Lord and the twelve disciples," Igor had told him. The cathedral was almost finished. Only a small scaffolding on one side showed where work was still being done on the outside staircases. With a shiver Ivanushka stepped inside.

If the outside was like a fortress, the high, broad, gloomy spaces within seemed as vast as the universe. In the manner of the great churches of the Roman Empire, it proceeded from west to east in a broad line of five naves—a wide central nave, with two more on each side. At the eastern end were five semicircular apses. At the western end, high above the floor, were galleries where the princes and their courtiers gathered to pray, looking down upon the people. And at the center of the church, under the huge dome, was the great airy space where the priests in their shining vestments stood before the congregation and heaven met the earth.

But it was not the high dome, nor the five naves, nor the massive columns that dominated the cavernous interior. It was the mosaics.

They made Ivanushka tremble. From floor to distant ceiling they covered the walls. The Blessed Virgin with hands outstretched in the eastern attitude of prayer; the Fathers of the Church; the Annunciation, the Eucharist: in blues and browns, in reds and greens, against the background of shining gold, these awesome, august figures stared down upon the world. Enormous, pale, oval faces with dark hair and huge, black eyes gazed mournfully yet impersonally from their golden setting upon the little people in the passing world. And highest of all, the Pantokrator, creator of the world, gazed from the central dome, his large Greek eyes, seeing all, seeing nothing—knowing all men yet unknowable, beyond all earthly wisdom.

Earth met heaven in the church; hundreds of candles flickered in the gloom; and upon the walls the golden mosaics glowed, their great and terrible light shining in the darkness of the world.

Some priests was chanting.

"Gospodi pomily." Lord have mercy. They sang in Church Slavonic—a nasal version of the spoken tongue that was both understandable and mysterious, hieratic.

Igor lit a candle and stood, in silent prayer, before an icon by one of the heavy pillars, while Ivanushka looked about him.

Everyone knew the story of the Blessed Vladimir's conversion: how he had sent out to the three great religions: Islam, Judaism, and Christianity, and how his ambassadors, having visited Constantinople, reported to him that in the Christian church of the Greek, "We did not know whether we were on earth or in heaven."

In such cathedrals as this, the emperors of Constantinople—and now the princes of Kiev who copied them—brought the visible heavens to earth and reminded their people that they, the rulers who prayed in the galleries above, were regents for the eternal Godhead whose golden universe was present, though unknowable, among them.

Igor, part Oriental, found peace in the contemplation of this absolute, unknowable authority. Ivanushka, half Slav, instinctively shrank from such a God; he yearned for a warmer, softer deity. And this was why, in the great church, he shivered as though from cold.

A few minutes later he was glad to be out of the church and riding towards the gate, beyond which lay the track through the woods to the monastery, and his destiny.

At last they were at the monastery gates.

Their ride along the path from the citadel had been so delightful it had filled Ivanushka with joy. After passing through the scattered huts of the lesser folk outside the city walls, the track had led southward, up to the little promontory of Berestovo, now a suburb, where Saint Vladimir himself had kept an extra residence. Over the treetops on the left, one could see the river shining far below, and past that, on the other side of the broad expanse of floodwater, the woods stretched across the flat plain into the distance. The oak and beech coming into leaf spread over the landscape like a soft, light green mist under the washed blue sky. Nothing disturbed the gentle sounds of the birds in the stillness of the spring morning, as Ivanushka rode happily behind his father towards the wide southwestern promontory, two miles from the citadel, where the monks lived.

And still Ivanushka had no idea why he was really there.

Igor was silent, deep in thought. Was he doing the right thing? Even for a boyar as devout and austere as he, this morning's expedition was an extraordinary step. For Igor's idea was that Ivanushka might enter the religious life.

It had cost him dear. No boyar normally wanted his son to be a monk or even a priest. The life of poverty seemed like a reproach; and those of noble blood who chose the religious life did so, almost always, against their family's wishes. True, a boyar like Igor might spend many hours in prayer each day; a prince, on his deathbed, might take the tonsure of a

monk; but for a young man to bury himself and take vows of poverty—
that was another matter.

It was just after the appearance of the red star that the idea had taken
shape in his mind. "I do not say Ivanushka's a fool," he had said to his
wife, "but he is a dreamer. That night I found him gazing at the star—if
I hadn't fetched him in he'd have frozen to death. The boy should be a
monk." Igor had worked so hard to make himself a man of affairs, a
warrior and member of the *druzhina:* he knew what was required. "And
I cannot see Ivanushka succeeding," he admitted sadly.

"You are too impatient with him," Olga had replied.

Was he impatient? Perhaps. But what father can tolerate the weaknesses of the one who was—though Igor would never admit it—his
favorite son? And did a tiny voice, deep inside him, say: The boy is like
you, as you might have been.

So it was that, as the weeks passed and no opportunities seemed to
present themselves for the boy, he wondered: Perhaps, though it is not
my desire, God means to claim this son for His own service. And then,
since it was his nature, he began to make plans for this undesirable
outcome.

These included a long talk with Father Luke, to whom he confided all
these thoughts. Indeed, he might slightly have exaggerated Ivanushka's
interest in the religious life. He had begged the old monk to take a look
at the dreamy boy and to encourage him if he showed any signs of
vocation. For if Father Luke himself suggests it, he reasoned, that will
greatly influence the boy.

He had only told his wife the day before, and when he did, Olga's face
had gone white. "No! I beg you. Don't push the boy away," she had
begged.

"Of course not," he had answered. "He will only go to a monastery
if he wishes."

"But you mean to encourage him."

"I shall show him the monastery, that is all."

Olga's face had remained distraught. She, too, knew her little son.
Who knew what might seize the boy's imagination? "He might easily
take it into his head to become a monk," she said. "And then I'll lose him
forever."

"He can be here in Kiev," Igor had replied. Secretly, because he was
ambitious, he had hoped that the boy might go for a time to one of the
great Greek monasteries at faraway Mount Athos—for that was the way
to reach the higher church offices. The boy might even be another Hilarion! But he did not tell her this.

"I shall never see him."

"All sons must leave their mothers," he went on. "Besides, if it is God's
will, then we must submit. And who knows, he may truly find happiness
in the religious life. He may be happier than I." And this, though he
scarcely knew it himself, was as near to the truth as it was tactless. "I
shall only take him to visit the cathedral and the monastery," he promised her. "Father Luke shall talk to him. That is all."

And what of the boy?

Let's hope he sees the monastery and takes an interest, he thought. Then he would have to tell Ivanushka the truth, that he would never succeed in being a boyar. That will break his heart, he acknowledged to himself. But by then there would be an alternative. And then we shall see, he concluded.

And so it was, that morning, that Ivanushka came to the monastery.

He had never been there before.

They reached the top of the promontory, then continued until, by a clearing in the trees, they came to a stout wooden gateway. A monk in a black habit bowed to them as they passed through, while Ivanushka, pale with excitement, looked about him.

It was not much of a place. There was a small wooden chapel and a cluster of dwelling houses, together with two low, barnlike structures, one of which was the refectory where the monks ate, the other a hospice for the sick. It was nothing like the grand cathedral, and Ivanushka was rather disappointed. It seemed to him that there was something sad about the place.

The morning dew still clung to the dark wooden huts although the sun was well up in the sky, as if the buildings had been permeated by the cold, wet ground. Rocks appeared among the trees. Here and there in the clearing were patches of light brown mud. Yet somehow, in the midst of rising spring, there was a feeling of autumn, as though leaves were still falling.

It was hardly twenty years since Anthony the Hermit, traveling from Holy Mount Athos in distant Greece, had come upon this deserted spot and found the caves. Soon others had joined the holy man in his cave above the Dnieper, and this little community of a dozen or so hermits had burrowed out a network of tiny cells and passages deep underground. These cells were under their feet now; and it gave Ivanushka a strange feeling to know that the holy men were down there, like rabbits in a warren, aware no doubt of his presence above.

Anthony himself, he knew, dwelt apart from the community in a cave on his own, occasionally appearing for some important purpose, such as to demand that the prince of Kiev give the monks the hill, and then disappearing again. But his saintly spirit was said to hover over the place like a wreath of mist over the ground. Meanwhile the faithful monks, led by kindly Theodosius, had built up the monastery above the ground as well as beneath. And of this number of saintly men was Father Luke.

Ivanushka and his father dismounted. One monk had led their horses away; another, after a whispered conversation, had walked to a small hut and disappeared.

"That is the way down into the caves," his father explained.

They waited. Several minutes passed. Two elderly monks accompanied by a young monk in his twenties walked slowly past and into the wooden chapel. One of the old monks, Ivanushka saw, wore a big, heavy chain around his neck and seemed to walk with difficulty. "Why does he wear a chain?" he whispered. His father looked at him as though he had asked a foolish question. "To mortify the flesh," he answered abruptly. "He is close to God," he added with obvious respect.

Ivanushka said nothing. A faint, cold breath of wind made itself felt against his cheek.

Then the door of the hut opposite slowly opened and the monk emerged, holding the door open for an unseen figure. Ivanushka heard his father whisper: "Here he comes." He held his breath. He saw the skirt of a robe in the doorway. This was the moment—the splendid figure who was to tell him his destiny was approaching.

And then from the doorway emerged a small, scrawny old man.

His hair was gray and, though he had combed it, not very clean; nor was his black habit, tied with a leather belt that was mottled with mildew. His beard was straggly and untidy. He shuffled slowly towards them, the younger monk walking just behind him as though to catch him should he stumble.

Father Luke's face was wrinkled and ghostly white, and his brows hung over it heavily, partly because he stooped so much. As he came slowly forward he opened his mouth once, as though flexing stiff muscles in preparation for a smile he knew he must make. Ivanushka saw that several of his yellowed teeth were missing. The eyes were not, as he had imagined, like suns. They were old, a little rheumy and, it appeared, slightly cross. The old man seemed mostly concerned with staring at his feet, which were encased in leather shoes that were full of holes, so that his grimy feet could be seen within. But there was something worse than his appearance, something Ivanushka was completely unprepared for.

It was the smell.

For those who live long underground acquire not only pale skins like corpses, but also a terrible aroma; and it was this smell, preceding Father Luke, that came towards the boy. He had never encountered anything like it: in his mind rose a vague image of wet clay, dead flesh, and rotting leaves.

And now the monk stood beside them.

"This is Ivanushka," he heard his father say.

Ivanushka bowed his head.

So, this was Father Luke. He could not believe it. He wanted to run away. How could his father have cruelly deceived him in this way? If only, he prayed, he does not touch me.

When he looked up, he was aware of his father and the old man talking quietly. The monk's eyes, which looked up from time to time, were blue, sharper and more inquisitive than he had first supposed. They glanced at him from time to time, before staring down at the ground again.

His father and the monk were discussing quite mundane affairs in a matter-of-fact way—the trade and politics of Tmutarakan, the price of salt, the building of the new monastery of Saint Dimitri inside the citadel. He found this surprising and rather dull. So he was taken off-guard when Father Luke suddenly nodded towards him and remarked, "So this is the young man you told me about."

"It is."

"Ivan," Father Luke went on, half to himself, though smiling slightly at the boy. "A very Christian name for a young man."

It was true that as yet few Russians had taken the name Ivan—the Slavic form of John—as their first name. But while Igor had given his first two sons the usual Slav names and reserved the Christian ones for their baptismal names, he had for some reason given his third son only a single, Christian name.

Ivanushka saw that his father was giving him an encouraging smile that was meant to reassure him, but in fact told him only that Igor was anxious he should make a good impression: and, as always upon such occasions, he immediately felt something tighten within him, while his mind became a sea of confusion. The monk's next question completed his confusion.

"Do you like it here?"

What could he say? He was so upset, so disappointed, and the direct question seemed suddenly to bring all his misery to the surface. With tears coming into his eyes, half in fury at his father, half in numb disappointment, unable to look up at them, he blurted out: "No."

He could feel his father stiffen with rage. "Ivan!"

He looked up and saw Igor's furious look. The monk, however, did not seem put out. "What do you see here?" he asked quietly.

Again, the question took him by surprise. It was so simple that, too agitated now to collect his thoughts, he answered it without thinking at all: "Rotting leaves."

He heard his father's gasp of exasperation, then saw to his surprise the monk reach out his pale, bony hand and take Igor gently by the arm. "Do not be angry," Father Luke admonished softly. "The boy has only spoken the truth." He sighed. "But he is young for such a place."

"Some boys have come here," he heard his father say crossly.

The monk nodded, but apparently without much interest. "Some." He turned back to Ivanushka.

What was coming next? Ivanushka could not imagine. Certainly not what did. "So, Ivan, should you like to be a priest?"

A priest? What could the old man be thinking of? He was going to be a hero, a boyar. He stared, openmouthed, at the monk in horror.

With a wry smile Father Luke turned to Igor. "Are you sure about this, my friend?"

"I thought it would be best." Igor's brows were knitted, both in anger and embarrassment.

Ivanushka looked up at his father. It was hard for him, at first, to understand even what was being said; but through the fog of his confusion he began to realize: if his father thought he should be a priest, then he must be judged unworthy to be a boyar. And so now, fresh from the disappointment of finding the awesome Father Luke to be nothing more than a shabby old man, two thoughts formed themselves in his mind. His father had betrayed him, never even told him about his plans; and he had rejected him.

Father Luke now drew out a book from the folds of his habit and opened it. "This is the liturgy of Saint John Chrysostom," he said. "Can you read this?" And he showed him a prayer.

The boy stumbled through it and Father Luke nodded quietly. Then he drew another little book out and showed it to Ivanushka; but in this one the writing seemed different and Ivanushka shook his head. "This is in the old alphabet that the blessed Saint Cyril invented for the Slavs," the monk explained. "In fact, some monks still prefer this old writing, which uses some Hebrew characters; but today we use the alphabet designed by Cyril's successors, which is mainly Greek and which people call, incorrectly, Cyrillic. If you were a priest, it would be useful to know both."

Ivanushka hung his head and said nothing.

"We in this monastery," Father Luke went on quietly, "live by the rule that our abbot Theodosius has chosen. It is a wise rule. Our monks spend much of the time singing and praying in the chapel, but they also occupy themselves with useful tasks like caring for the sick. Some, it is true, follow a harsher discipline and remain in seclusion in their cells or in the caves for long periods. But this is their own choice."

"It is a holy choice," Igor said respectfully.

Father Luke did not look impressed. "But not for all." He sighed, though it sounded more like a short hiss. It seemed to Ivanushka that the monk used less breath than other men. "The life of a monk is a constant drawing closer to God," he went on quietly. Whether he was addressing Igor or his son now was hard to say. "In this process, the flesh dries up, but the spirit is fed, and grows, through communion with God." To Ivanushka, the monk's quiet voice sounded like the falling of leaves.

Then Father Luke coughed, with a dry, rasping sound. And Ivanushka thought: He is like a husk, buried in the earth.

"And so the body dies, that the soul may live."

Ivanushka knew that some monks kept their coffins in their cells, in this long preparation for death.

He realized that Father Luke was watching him dispassionately, observing how he received these words. But he could not conceal his disappointment, his desire to escape from this image, as it seemed to him, of death.

"Yet it is not death," Father Luke went on, as though following his thoughts. "For Christ overcame death. The grass withereth, but the word of the Lord does not. So it is that, even in our mortal condition, our souls live in the world of the spirit, humble before God." But if this was meant to bring him comfort, it brought him none.

It was an old idea, this ascetic ideal of the withering of the body. For centuries it had been practiced by single-minded hermits in Christian Syria. This was not the wild infliction of pain that was often practiced by the flagellants in the West, but rather the slow process of sapping the vital juices from the body, reducing it to a useless husk that would not interfere with the life of the spirit and the service of God.

Still watching him carefully, the monk continued: "These extremes are only for a few. Most of the monks here live a simpler life, devoted to the service of God and their fellow men. Indeed, this is the rule favored by our abbot Theodosius."

Ivanushka was too discouraged, however, to find comfort even in this.

"Do you wish to serve God?" the old man asked abruptly.

"Oh yes." He was almost in tears, though. The idea of serving God had always been such an exciting thought before. With a single heart, a single mind, he had seen himself riding in God's service over the waving grasses of the steppe, fighting the heathen horsemen.

The old man gave a grunt.

"The boy is young. He loves his body." It was said calmly, without anger, but it was obviously the monk's final judgment. He turned his back on Ivanushka.

"You do not think he would make a priest?" Igor asked anxiously.

"God touches each man at the proper time. We do not know what we shall be."

"He should not be trained for the priesthood then?" Igor sought clarification.

Instead of answering, Father Luke turned back to Ivanushka, and laid his hand on his head, in a gesture that might, or might not have been a blessing. "I see that you are going on a journey," he said, "from which you will return." Then he turned away again.

A journey? Ivanushka's mind was racing. Could he mean his plan to go to the great river Don? Surely he must. And he had said nothing about his becoming a priest. At last there was hope.

Meanwhile, the old monk was gazing at Igor rather severely.

"You fast too much," he said abruptly.

"Surely fasting is permitted?" Igor said in surprise.

"A fast is a tithe we pay to God. And a tithe is a tenth, not more. You should limit your fasts. You are too severe with yourself."

"And my prayers?"

Ivanushka knew that his father prayed for a long time at dawn, and then again, three or four times before the day was over.

"Pray as much as you wish, as long as you don't neglect your business," the monk replied sharply. He paused for a moment, then went on: "This fasting, you know, came into our church from the Latin west, through Moravia. I am not one of those who condemn the West, but too much fasting among the laity is foolish. If you want to do that, you must join the Romans and say their creed," he added with a faint smile.

For more than a decade now, there had been, technically, a breach between the eastern and western Christian churches—between Constantinople and Rome. The disagreement concerned mainly the form of addressing God and the Trinity in the creed, though certain differences in style and theological emphasis underlay the division. The Pope claimed the highest authority. The eastern Church did not agree. But it was not as yet a deep rift.

The monk's gentle taunt, therefore, was merely a way of reminding Igor that, as his spiritual son, he owed him obedience.

"I will do as you say," the noble replied. "As for the boy, if he's not to be a priest, what's to become of him?"

Father Luke did not even look at Ivanushka. "God knows," he replied.

1067

KIEV the golden. But there was one problem in the land of Rus. Its rulers had devised a political system that did not, and could not possibly work. The problem lay in the system of succession.

For when the royal clan had chosen that cities should pass not from father to son, but from brother to brother, they had not foreseen the consequences, which were disastrous.

First, when a prince ruled a city, he might set his sons to rule over the lesser towns in that territory. But when he died, they usually had to give these up to the next prince in line, perhaps without compensation. Worse still, if one of the princely brothers died before being granted a city, his children were completely left out of the long chain of succession. There were many such landless princes without prospects, and these political orphans were known by the same name that was applied to other dispossessed or dependent folk in Russian society: *izgoi.*

And even when the succession of brothers did not create *izgoi,* it still produced ludicrous situations.

For the princes of Rus were often long-lived, and they had many sons. What if the eldest son produced children who were fully grown warriors and statesmen by the time his youngest brother, their uncle, was still a boy? They would still have to give up power for their boy-uncle. No wonder if they were angry.

Indeed, as the generations passed, it became harder and harder even to work out who was entitled to what, let alone to get the parties to agree to it. Thus the ruling clan of Kievan Rus spent generations devising makeshift arrangements within a system that was inherently unworkable. They never solved their problem.

Kiev the golden. Of late it seemed to Ivanushka that a harsh, angry light menaced the golden city. Treachery was in the air. And now, a year after it had appeared, in the dead of winter, the meaning of the terrible portent in the heavens was becoming clear in the land of Rus.

At first, Ivanushka had even been afraid for his father.

Of all the princes in the land of Rus, none was stranger than the Prince of Polotsk. Men said he was a werewolf. He was certainly terrible to look upon. "He was born with a caul wrapped over his eye," Ivanushka's mother had told him, "and it's there to this day."

"And is he really so evil?" Ivanushka had asked.

"As wicked as Baba Yaga the witch," she had replied.

The revolt of the Prince of Polotsk was a typical dynastic quarrel. Though not a landless *izgoi,* this grandson of the Blessed Vladimir had been cut out of the main chain of succession: so while he kept the city of Polotsk, which lay towards Poland in the west, he could never inherit Kiev, Novgorod, Chernigov, or any of the greatest cities of the land of Rus.

For a time, while other, less important *izgoi* princes had been creating trouble in the outlying territories, the Prince of Polotsk had remained quiet. Then suddenly, at the dead of winter, he had struck in the north, at the great city of Novgorod; and as the snow lay thick upon the ground, Igor and his two eldest boys had ridden north with the Prince of Kiev and his brothers.

If only he could have ridden with them. Since the interview at the monastery, Ivanushka had spent a miserable year. Because of human raids in the steppe, the caravan with Zhydovyn the Khazar had been postponed. Igor had made several attempts to place him in one of the princely households, but with no luck. More than once his father had asked him if he would not like to visit the monastery again; but each time he had hung his head, and Igor had shrugged and turned away. And now his father and brothers were hunting the werewolf.

"Father will kill him," Ivanushka had cried as they left. But in his heart he had not been so sure. Three weeks had passed. They heard that the western rebel city of Minsk had fallen, and that the armies had passed on towards the north. After that, silence.

Then, one afternoon in early March, while the snow still lay on the ground, Ivanushka heard the stamp and jingle of a horse coming into the courtyard and ran out to see a tall, stern figure dismounting.

It was his brother Sviatopolk. How handsome and brave, how like their father he looked. He glanced at Ivanushka. "We won," he announced drily. "Father's on his way back with Boris. He sent me ahead to tell mother."

"And the werewolf?"

"He lost and ran away. He's finished."

"What happened at Minsk?"

Sviatopolk smiled. Why did his mouth look bitter when he smiled, and why did he only do so when he was talking about people being hurt? "We butchered all the men; sold the women and children as slaves." He gave a short laugh. "There were so many slaves it drove the price down to half a grivna a head."

Ivanushka followed him into the house. At the entrance Sviatopolk paused and half turned to him. "By the way, there's good news for you." He spoke the words casually.

"For me?" Ivanushka's mind began to race. What could it be?

"God knows why," Sviatopolk remarked. "You've done nothing to deserve it." The words were spoken lightheartedly, but Ivanushka knew Sviatopolk meant them really.

"What is it? Tell me what?"

"Father will tell you." It seemed that Sviatopolk was not particularly pleased with the good news, whatever it was. He smiled thinly, then turned away. "You'll have to suffer until he comes, won't you?" he said, and stepped into the house.

Ivanushka heard his mother's cry of joy. She loved Sviatopolk, he knew, because he was so like his father.

The news his father brought, the next day, was so wonderful that he could hardly believe it.

The younger brother of the Prince of Kiev, Prince Vsevolod, held the splendid southern border city of Pereiaslav, which lay some sixty miles downriver from the capital. Vsevolod had made a marriage that impressed the nobles of Rus, for his bride had been a princess of the royal house of Constantinople itself, the family of Monomakh. And their son Vladimir was only a year older than Ivanushka.

"We've still to arrange a meeting of the two boys," Igor proudly explained to his wife, "but Vsevolod and I became friends on the campaign and he's agreed in principle—in principle," he emphasized severely, looking at Ivanushka, "that Ivan should be attached to young Vladimir as a page."

"This is a great chance, you know," his mother said to Ivanushka. "They say this Vladimir is gifted and has a great future ahead of him. To be his close companion when you are still both so young . . ." She spread her hands in a way that suggested the treasure house of Kiev and the imperial city of Constantinople all rolled into one.

Ivanushka was beside himself. "When? When?" was all he could ask.

"I shall take you to Pereiaslav at Christmas," Igor told him. "By which time, you had better have prepared yourself." And with that he dismissed him.

"I'm sad to see Ivanushka go, though," his mother confided to her husband afterwards. "I shall miss him."

"That is a woman's lot," Igor remarked coolly, unwilling to admit that he felt the same.

It was shortly afterwards that a small incident took place in the stables that would have shocked Igor and his wife had they known about it.

The three brothers were together. Boris, grinning broadly, had clapped his little brother on the back in a friendly way that sent him sprawling; then he had given him a whole silver grivna for luck and ridden down to the *podol.* That left Ivanushka and Sviatopolk alone.

"Well, brother, I told you the news was good," Sviatopolk remarked quietly, as he gazed admiringly at his horse.

"Yes." Ivanushka had an uncomfortable feeling, however, that his brother was saving something unpleasant for him.

"In fact, I'd say that you had probably done better than Boris or me," Sviatopolk added thoughtfully.

"Oh. Do you think so?" He realized it was a fine opportunity, but he had not thought of it that way.

"Oh," Sviatopolk mimicked him, without turning around, "do you really think so?"

Ivanushka stared at him blankly, wondering what was coming next. Suddenly Sviatopolk turned. His dark eyes seemed full of hate, yet also contemptuous.

"You've done nothing to deserve this. You were supposed to go into the church."

"But it was Father . . ."

"Yes, it was Father. But don't think you can deceive me. Because now I see you for what you really are, little boy. You're ambitious. You want to do better than us. You think only of yourself behind that dreamy mask."

Ivanushka was so taken aback by this unexpected attack that he had no idea what to say. Was he ambitious? It had never occurred to him. He stared at Sviatopolk, confused.

"Yes," his brother went on acidly. "The truth hurts, doesn't it? So why don't you just admit it like the rest of us? Except that you're worse than us. You're a schemer, little Ivan, a little viper." He hissed the last word so that it hit Ivanushka like a physical blow. Sviatopolk was getting into his stride now. "And no doubt you're waiting for Father to die, too," he added.

Whatever did he mean? Ivanushka had no idea.

"What do you think it costs Father if you become a monk?" Sviatopolk enlightened him. "Some donations to the monastery. But your new position means that one day you'll be left the same inheritance as us. So you'll be taking from me, too."

Ivanushka was scarlet. The tears were welling up.

"I don't want Father to die. You can have my share. Have it all."

"Oh, very good," his brother sneered. "And how easy to say. Of course, you would say that, now you've escaped from the monastery. But we shall see."

Ivanushka burst into tears. Sviatopolk watched him.

And this was only the beginning of Ivanushka's troubles.

1068

IVANUSHKA was disobeying his father.

But such astonishing things were going on in the city that day.

For two years, it seemed to the boy, the influence of the evil star had been constantly at work. Even so, there were things that were hard to understand.

They had never taken him to meet the young Prince Vladimir. The reason, they said, was that the boy's mother, the Greek princess, had died. "Vladimir and his father are mourning her," Igor told him. "It's a bad time. Next year, though, things will be better." Why, then, before the year was out, had Vladimir's father taken another wife—a Cuman princess?

"It's politics," Igor explained. "Her father's a powerful Cuman chief, and the prince wants to protect Pereiaslav from attack from the steppe." Yet only months later the Cuman horsemen had come, and now they were burning the land of Rus in greater strength than ever before.

And still no word had come from Vladimir's father about a visit. The prince had promised; now it seemed he had forgotten, leaving Ivanushka still drifting, uselessly, at Kiev.

Perhaps his brother Sviatopolk was telling the truth when he had hissed in his ear, one cold morning that spring, "You'll never be Vladimir's page, you know. They've heard how useless you are." For when he had wondered aloud who would have told them such a thing, Sviatopolk had smiled and whispered, "Maybe I did."

Then there was the matter of the Prince of Polotsk. After defeating him, the Prince of Kiev and his brother had offered the werewolf a safe-conduct to a family meeting. Then they had shamefully trapped him and thrown him into jail in Kiev, where he still remained. Yet when Ivanushka had asked his father whether such treachery was not a sin, Igor had only told him, grimly, that it was sometimes necessary to lie. Ivanushka was still puzzled about this.

Finally, threatening to destroy them all, came the Cumans. Less than a week ago, at dead of night, the men of Rus had gone out to deal the steppe raiders a decisive blow near Pereiaslav. And they had lost. To their shame, his father and the princes had fled back to Kiev and retired to the fortified safety of the stone-walled palace in the citadel. Worse yet, a strange lethargy had set in among the *druzhina*. Day after day, Ivanushka had expected that his father and the boyars would go forth again. Yet nothing happened. Surely they could not be afraid? Surely they would not leave the people to the mercy of the invaders while they stayed safe behind their high walls? They must, the boy thought, have fallen under the spell of the evil star.

And now, this bright September morning, the whole city was in an uproar. Terrified messengers came at the gallop to say that the Cumans were advancing. In the *podol* outside the citadel, the city assembly—the famous *veche*—was meeting. All the people had gone there.

And the talk was of revolution.

That was why, this morning, instead of staying with his family in the high brick hall of the prince's palace, he had sneaked out, crossed the bridge over the ravine that led from the old citadel to the new, and made his way past Saint Sophia's cathedral towards the gates into the *podol*.

The new citadel was eerily quiet. The nobles' houses were deserted: not even the horses and grooms had been left at his father's. There were a few women and children, and the occasional priest in the streets, but it seemed that the whole male population had gone down to the *veche* in the suburb.

Ivanushka knew about the *veche*. Even the Prince of Kiev himself was afraid of it. Usually, of course, it was tame enough and run by the leading merchants. But in times of crisis, every free man of the city had the right to attend and to vote. "And when the *veche* revolts, it is terrible," Igor had told him. "Even the prince and the *druzhina* can't control them."

"Are the people angry now?" he had asked.

"They are beside themselves. You're not to go out."

As he made his way through the citadel, Ivanushka was so excited he almost forgot that he was disobeying his father. He hurried through the gate to the market square.

It was full. He had never seen so many people in his life. They had even come in from the outlying towns—merchants, artisans, the free traders and workers of the Russian city-states—several thousand of them. On each side of the square was a church: one a stout, brick, Byzantine affair with a flat central dome, the other a smaller wooden structure with a high gabled roof and a little octagonal tower in the middle. They seemed to be overseeing the proceedings, giving them a religious sanction. In the

center was a wooden platform, upon which all eyes were fixed. A huge
brown-bearded merchant in a red kaftan was standing there. In his hands
was a staff, and, like some terrible Old Testament prophet, he was de-
nouncing the authorities. "Why is this prince here, in Kiev?" he shouted.
"Why does his family rule in other cities?" He paused until he had drawn
an expectant silence from the crowd. "They are here because we invited
their ancestors to come to us." He hammered his staff. "The Varangians
came from the north to us Slavs because we brought them in!"

This rewriting of history that had grown up over the generations had
suited both sides—the Norsemen because it gave legitimacy to their
original piratical rule, and their Slav subjects because it salvaged their
pride.

"Why did we bring them in?" He glowered from side to side, as though
challenging the churches themselves to interrupt him. "To fight for us.
To defend our cities. *That* is why they are here!"

There was truth in this. Even now, the relationship between the
princes and the cities they governed was ambiguous; the prince protected
the city but he did not own it, any more than he owned the land, much
of which still belonged to free peasants or communes. In the great northern city of Novgorod, the *veche* of the people had been known to reject
princes, and never allowed their chosen protector or his *druzhina* to own
land in their domains. So Ivanushka did not find the merchant's words
strange. Indeed, he flushed with pride to hear his father and men like him
called protectors of the land of Rus.

"But they have not defended us!" the merchant roared. "They have
failed! The Cumans lay waste to our countryside, and the prince and his
generals do nothing!"

"What shall we do then?" shouted several voices.

"Find a new general," cried another.

"Find a new prince," bellowed a third.

Ivanushka gasped. They were speaking of the Prince of Kiev! But the
idea seemed to please the crowd.

"Who then?" a chorus demanded.

And now the big merchant on the platform hammered his staff again.
"These troubles were begun by treachery," he roared. "By treachery,
when the sons of Yaroslav broke their word and put the Prince of Polotsk
in jail." He gestured towards the citadel. "An innocent prince lies in
prison up there."

He did not need to go on. It was clear even to Ivanushka that many
in the square had been carefully prepared for this moment. "Polotsk!" the
crowd roared. "Give us the Prince of Polotsk."

Ivanushka could never say, afterwards, exactly what followed. All he
knew was that a minute later the crowd, as though it had a disciplined
will of its own, was surging into the citadel; and he was being carried
with it. In front of Saint Sophia's cathedral, the river of people split into
two streams. One half turned off to the left towards a stout brick building
near the cathedral where the strange prince with the caul over his eye was
being held. The rest flowed across the narrow bridge towards the palace.

It was time to get back to his family. He must warn them of the danger. He tried to get ahead of the crowd as it surged across the narrow bridge into the old citadel, but he soon realized that he was too late.

What had not occurred to him, however, was that he would be unable to get back in. But minutes later, as he found himself in the square before the tall, thick-walled block of the prince's palace, he realized his predicament. On the left side there was a high wall; on the right a broad flight of stone steps led to a large oak doorway that was barred. The line of windows here was twenty feet high, well out of reach. Before him, the brick palace consisted of a series of towers and slit windows, set irregularly and high above the crowd. The two doors at the base were locked and bolted. Even if he could work his way through the crowd, he was closed out.

The crowd was hurling abuse.

"Traitors! Cowards! We'll feed you to the Cumans!"

But the high red wall of the palace seemed to stare back at them with blank indifference.

Minutes passed. Nearby, a bell began to ring, summoning monks to prayer. Ivanushka glanced across to his left where the golden domes of the old Church of the Tithes were gleaming. But the crowd paused in its shouting only for a moment.

It was then that Ivanushka saw, high above, in a small window of the palace, a large red face staring down at the crowd—a face he recognized at once as belonging to Izyaslav, the Prince of Kiev himself. The crowd caught sight of him, too. There was a roar of rage, a surge forward. Then the face disappeared.

It suddenly occurred to Ivanushka that if the crowd realized who he was—the son of one of Izyaslav's boyars—he might be in danger himself. I must get inside, he thought. There was only one other way into the palace: through a courtyard that lay behind it. This would mean working his way around the complex of buildings, along a side street, and thence to the gate. He turned and began to push his way towards the back. But it was difficult. The thick crowd seemed to sway from side to side, almost knocking him off his feet each time he tried to press through, and after several minutes he had only moved a few yards.

And he was still far from the exits to the square when a murmur began somewhere in the crowd that gathered into a general hubbub, and which finally turned into a roar. "They've gone! They've run away!"

He looked on in astonishment as a man, climbing on the backs of others, managed to reach one of the windows and then vanished from sight. Three minutes later one of the doors of the palace in front opened and the crowd, meeting no resistance, began to burst in.

The prince and the *druzhina* had left the palace. They must have escaped through the very courtyard where he had hoped to enter. He stared, momentarily numbed. In that case, his family must have gone, too. And he had been left behind!

The crowd was surging forward now, into the empty building. Figures began to appear at the windows, high above. Suddenly he saw a golden flash. Someone had thrown a goblet down to a friend in the crowd; a moment later a sable coat followed; and with a shock he realized they were looting the prince's palace!

Ivanushka turned. He had no idea what to do, but he knew he must get out of the square. Perhaps he could find his people somewhere in the woods below. As the crowd pushed forward towards the palace, he managed to reach a small gateway to one side and find a way out. Moments later he was in a half-deserted street.

"Ivan. Ivan Igorevich!" He turned. It was one of his father's grooms, running towards him. "Your father sent me to find you. Come."

Ivanushka had never been more glad to see anyone. "Can we ride to join him?" he cried hopefully.

"Impossible. They've gone, all of them. And the roads are being sealed off."

As if in confirmation, at that moment a party of men came running up the street: "The Prince of Polotsk is free!" they cried. "He is coming!" And indeed, as Ivanushka gazed down the street, he saw a dozen mounted men cantering in their direction: and in the middle of them, and quite unmistakable, the terrible figure himself—the werewolf.

He was of above middle size and he was riding a black horse. It was hard to tell what he was wearing for he was wrapped in a large brown cloak that looked none too clean. His face was large, rather broad at the cheek-bones, and his whole bearing exuded a sense of tense power. But it was his eyes that riveted Ivanushka's attention.

One was indeed hooded with a caul of skin; yet the effect of this was not monstrousness, as Ivanushka had expected. The face did not look as if it had been twisted, or burned; instead, one side had a strange stillness, a sort of blank detachment from the world such as one sometimes sees with the blind. But the other side of the face was alive, intelligent, ambitious, with a piercing blue eye that took in everything.

It was a fascinating face, half handsome, half tragic. And the good eye, he suddenly realized, was resting upon him.

"Quickly, this way," the groom pulled him insistently to one side. "They mustn't know who you are."

Ivanushka let himself be dragged away. The half-blind prince and his escort clattered by. And as the werewolf passed, Ivanushka had a strange sense that the prince, like some creature with magic powers, had both noticed and identified him.

"Where are we going?" he asked.

"You'll see." And the groom led him hurriedly towards the *podol*.

The house of Zhydovyn the Khazar, though not as large as Igor's, was a stout wooden affair of two stories, with a steep wooden roof, two large rooms at the front, and a courtyard behind. It stood just outside the Khazar gate near the wall of Yaroslav's citadel. "They will look after you here for a few days," the groom explained to him, "until it's safe to smuggle you out of the city."

Already bands of men were searching for the families of the *druzhina* who had fled.

"What will they do if they find me?" Ivanushka asked.

"Lock you up."

"Nothing worse?"

The groom gave him a strange look. "Don't ever go to prison," he said slowly. "Once you're in prison . . ." He made a gesture as if dropping a key. "But don't worry now," he added more cheerfully. Zhydovyn will take care of you." A moment later he was gone.

Ivanushka enjoyed being with the Khazar and his family. Zhydovyn's wife was a dark, stout woman who seemed almost as massive as her husband. There were four children, younger than he, and Ivanushka spent much of his day playing with them indoors. "For it's not safe for you to be seen outside yet," the Khazar warned him.

Sometimes Ivanushka would tell them a fairy story. And once, to the Khazar's amusement, his children helped Ivanushka to read a story from the Old Testament in Hebrew: which he then pretended to translate, since he knew it by heart in Slavic.

It was on the third day that the crisis broke. It began early in the morning, when Zhydovyn came hurrying into the house and announced to the family: "The Prince of Kiev has gone to Poland. He's asking the king for help."

Ivanushka looked up in surprise. "Does that mean my father has gone to Poland too?"

"I assume he has."

Ivanushka was silent. Poland lay far to the west. Was his family really to pass away into those distant lands? Suddenly he felt very deserted.

"Do you think the Poles will invade?" Zhydovyn's wife asked anxiously.

"Probably." The Khazar grimaced. "The Polish king and Izyaslav are cousins, you know." Then his eyes traveled back to Ivanushka. "There's another problem, as well." He paused. "There's a rumor that someone in the Khazar quarter is hiding a child of one of the *druzhina*. And in case things get rough with Izyaslav and the Poles," he hesitated momentarily, "they're looking for hostages. They're searching the citadel now."

The room seemed to have become very quiet. Ivanushka felt their eyes upon him. Clearly his presence there was becoming increasingly inconvenient to them. He started to grow pale, with an awkward embarrassment, and glancing up at the big, sensuous face of Zhydovyn's wife, he saw at once that if he were a threat to her comfortable family, she would as soon be rid of him.

Yet it was Zhydovyn's wife who, after a pause, remarked slowly, "He doesn't look like a Khazar. But perhaps we can do something." Then she gazed at Ivanushka and laughed softly.

So it was that, later that day, a new figure appeared in the household of the Khazar.

His hair, carefully died, was black. Juices had somewhat darkened his skin. He wore a black kaftan and a little Turkish skullcap. He even, with more coaching from Zhydovyn and his wife, mumbled a few words of Turkish.

"He is your cousin David from Tmutarakan," their mother told the other children.

And the next day, it was this quiet, studious figure who the werewolf prince's guards saw sitting with the children when they entered the house and confronted the Khazar's wife.

"They say one of the Igorevichi remains in Kiev," they announced, "and your husband has dealings with Igor."

"My husband has dealings with many people."

"We shall search the house," the decurion leading the little troop said abruptly.

"Please do."

While they did so, the decurion remained in the room with her. "Who is that?" he suddenly demanded, pointing at Ivanushka.

"A young cousin from Tmutarakan," she replied coolly.

He stared at the Khazar boy.

"David, come here," she ordered in Turkish.

But as Ivanushka rose, the decurion turned away impatiently. "Never mind," he snapped. A few moments later they were gone.

And so, in the year 1068, Ivanushka waited to face an uncertain world.

1071

It was spring, and in the little village of Russka all was quiet.

The little river Rus had overflowed its banks so that below the settlement it was impossible to say which was marsh and which was field.

On the eastern bank, the village consisted of two short, muddy streets with a third, longer one running at right angles across them. The huts were made of various combinations of wood, clay, and wattle. Some of them had roofs of turf, some of thatch. Around this cluster of huts was a wooden palisade, but one that seemed more designed to keep in animals than repel any serious invader. On the north side of the village stood a small orchard of cherry and apple trees.

Just below the village, on a piece of land where the floodwater was shallow, small stakes stuck out of the water. This was the area where vegetables were grown, richly flooded each spring. Cabbages, peas, onion, and turnips would all appear here in due course. Garlic, too, was grown; and later in the year, pumpkins.

On the western, forest side of the river, however, where the banks were higher, a new feature had recently appeared. Here, where the bank rose to its highest point of some thirty feet above the river, it had been further heightened by a rampart of earth with a stout wall of oak on top. This fortification, enclosing nearly two acres, had been constructed some fifty years before. It contained, besides some long, low quarters for troops, and stables, two large storehouses for the use of merchants, and a small wooden church. This was the fort. It belonged, as did most of that land, to the Prince of Pereiaslav.

There was one other notable feature of the village. About fifty yards from the entrance, on a pleasant spot overlooking the river, was the graveyard, where the ashes of the dead were laid in the ground. Beside this spot stood two stone pillars, each about seven feet high and carved so that each appeared to be wearing a tall, rounded hat with a big fur brim. These were the chief gods of the village: Volos, god of wealth, and Perun, the thunder god. For despite the attempts of the prince's priests, out in the countryside many a village like Russka still quietly continued the old pagan ways. Even the village elder had two wives.

And it was by the cemetery, this clear spring afternoon, that a single figure was moodily walking.

Someone who had not seen him in the last three years would not have recognized Ivanushka. He had become as tall as his brother Sviatopolk, but in the process he had also become thin and pale. There were dark rings around his eyes and he seemed gaunt and haggard.

But there was something else, even more striking than these physical changes. About his whole person now, there was an aura. The way his head hung, his downcast eyes, the careless walk he affected, all seemed to say: I do not care what you think; I defy you all. And yet at the same time, this silent voice added: But even my defiance will fail.

In the last three years, nothing had gone right.

At first one important event seemed to give him hope. After waiting nearly a month in Kiev before being spirited away by Zhydovyn to join his family in Poland, he had discovered that his father, disgusted by the cowardice and treachery of the Prince of Kiev, had exercised his right to change masters and transferred to the *druzhina* of his younger brother Vsevolod, who ruled the southern frontier city of Pereiaslav.

This did indeed seem a stroke of fortune. Not only was Vsevolod known as the best and wisest of the ruling brothers, but by his Greek wife he was the father of the brilliant young Vladimir, to whom Ivanushka had been promised. Surely now that Igor served his father, Vladimir would send for him.

Yet no word had come. Even Igor was surprised. "But I've joined Vsevolod's service too recently to demand it," he admitted to Ivanushka sadly. Sviatopolk served with his father. Boris went to the court at Smolensk. Yet though his father tried to find him a place at Chernigov, Smolensk, and even distant Novgorod, nobody seemed to want Ivanushka.

He thought he knew the reason. "It is Sviatopolk," he sighed.

Wherever he went, people treated him with a distant kindness that told him they thought he was a simpleton. He could almost hear them thinking: Ivanushka's a fool. Once he had even confronted Sviatopolk and demanded: "Why have you ruined my reputation?"

But Sviatopolk had only looked at him in mock amazement.

"What reputation, Ivanushka? Surely nothing from my poor tongue, for or against you, would make any difference to the impression you produce yourself."

As time went on, this expectation of stupidity began to surround Ivanushka like a wall. He even began to say and do foolish things, as though hypnotized by people's opinion. He felt trapped, and the city of Pereiaslav with its stout earth ramparts became like a prison to him.

Indeed, he was only happy when he was out in the countryside.

It was a year after the move that Igor was put in charge of the defenses along part of the southeastern border. And it was at the center of this area, now one of the prince's estates, that the little fort of Russka lay.

It was an insignificant little place—one of dozens of little frontier forts along the borderlands—of no interest to anyone. Indeed, Igor would hardly have troubled to pay it more than a cursory visit if his friend Zhydovyn the Khazar had not reminded him that the warehouses there could serve as a useful depot for the caravans they still hoped to send to the East.

Ivanushka liked to visit this place. He would help the men repairing the fortress wall, or wander along through the woods, enjoying their peaceful quiet. And since Igor did not know what else to do with his youngest son, he would send him down there from time to time to help Zhydovyn receive shipments at the warehouse.

Which was the cause of his misery today. He had been in charge of receiving a consignment for furs that morning while the Khazar was away. He had heard the villagers and the men who brought the furs downriver laughing together; he had seen them look at him with amusement. And somehow, though he could never make out how it happened, two valuable barrels of beaver furs were missing. Now the Khazar was due back shortly, and he had no idea what to say.

It was just as he was gloomily pondering this matter that he saw the peasant.

Shchek was of medium height with a broad, stocky, square body upon which rested a round face with broad cheeks, soft brown eyes, and a wavy aureole of black hair that stood up like a soft brush; he wore a linen shirt and trousers, with a leather belt outside the shirt, and bast shoes. There was something about his whole body, thick-set and square though it was, that seemed to suggest a gentle, if possibly obstinate character. He was standing at the corner of the graveyard, and he was watching young Ivanushka carefully.

In Shchek's mind was a very simple thought. They say this young man's a fool. But I wonder if he has any money. For Shchek was about to be ruined.

Shchek the peasant was, like most of his kind, a free man. True, his status was humble. The very name of the class to which he belonged— the *smerdy*—meant "the dirty ones." But he was free, in theory, to live where he wished and sell his labor to whom he chose. He was also free to incur debts.

He ran over them in his mind. The horse, first. That had not been his fault: the animal had gone lame and died. And since he was obliged to supply a horse to the prince for his soldiers in time of war, he had to buy another. But that had only been the start. He had gone drinking in Pereiaslav. Playing dice, too. Then bought his wife a silver bracelet out of guilt; and obstinately borrowed again, and gambled again, to retrieve his money.

Now, as a member of the village commune, he owed the prince's steward a tax on his plow, and he knew he could not pay it.

Thoughtfully he moved towards the youth.

When Zhydovyn returned that evening and discovered the loss of the furs, he could only shake his head. He liked Ivanushka; but it seemed to him that his prospects were poor. And though nothing was said, Ivanushka sensed that he was unlikely to be sent to Russka again.

Only one thing puzzled the Khazar. He could understand the theft of the furs, but how was it that the money Ivanushka had been left was short by two silver grivnas? The young man said he had lost them. But how the devil could he have done that? It was a mystery.

Ivanushka did not mind. He had known after the furs had gone that his own cause was lost. He had felt sorry for the peasant. At least the fellow could pay his taxes now.

And he scarcely thought about the incident again.

1072

TODAY, it was said, there would be a miracle. The people confidently expected it. And with good reason. For today they were honoring the remains of the two royal martyrs, the sons of the mighty Saint Vladimir, Boris and Gleb, whom the Slavs already called saints.

It was half a century since they had died; now their remains were being taken to their final resting place, a newly constructed wooden church at the little town of Vyshgozod, just north of Kiev.

Would there be a miracle? Surely there would. But what form would it take?

In the upper circles of the nobility and the church it was known that the Greek metropolitan, George, had grave doubts about the martyrs' sanctity. But what could one expect from a Greek? And besides, whether he believed it or not, he had had to perform the ceremony.

They were all there: the three sons of Yaroslav, grandsons of Saint Vladimir himself—Prince Izyaslav of Kiev and his brothers, the princes of Chernigov and Pereiaslav; Metropolitan George; Bishop Peter and Bishop Michael; Theodosius of the Caves monastery, and many more—all the greatest dignitaries in the land of Rus.

The procession wound its way up the hill. A light drizzle was falling, nestling softly on the heads of those who made their way slowly up the slippery path. Despite this fine rain, it was warm. It was the twentieth of May.

First came monks, shielding their candles. Immediately after them, dressed in plain brown cloaks, came the three sons of Yaroslav. Upon their shoulders, like humble men, they carried the wooden casket containing the remains of their uncle Boris. After them came deacons, swinging censers, then priests, and behind them Metropolitan George himself and the bishops. Behind them, at a certain distance, followed a company of noble families.

"They died rather than resist their brother. Now they shine like beacons over the land of Rus." "Boris, look down upon me, a sinner." "Lord have mercy." These and other pious remarks from the crowd reached the ears of the tall, gloomy-looking boy who walked up the slope beside the handsome family in the company of nobles behind the coffins. "Perhaps today we shall see a miracle." "God be praised."

A miracle. Perhaps God would send a miracle; but not, Ivanushka felt sure, if he was there.

Nothing good happens when I'm around, he thought despondently; and his shoulders drooped as he trudged upwards.

In the last year, things had gotten worse. A few weeks after the embarrassing incident at Russka, he had overheard a brief conversation between his parents.

"There's so much good in Ivanushka," his mother was pleading. "One day he'll do something and you'll be proud of him."

"No, he won't," Igor's voice had replied. "I'm certain now. I've given up." He heard his father sigh. "I can't get anyone to take him. And I know why. I can't trust him myself."

He heard his mother murmur something; then his father replied: "Yes, I love all my children. But it's hard to love a child who always lets you down." Indeed, Ivanushka thought miserably, why should anyone love him?

He began asking for things—money from his mother, a horse from his father—to test their reaction and see if they loved him. But soon this, too, became a habit. He grew lazy, and he did as little as possible for fear of failing yet again.

He often loitered in the market at Pereiaslav. It was a busy place; on any day one might see a shipment of oil or wine arrive from Constantinople; or a cargo of iron taken from the swamps near the river and bound for Kiev. There were workshops where they made glass, as fine as any in the land of Rus; there were stalls where merchants sold bronze clasps and jewelry; and there were the food stalls.

But as he watched, Ivanushka gradually became aware of a secondary activity going on all around him. One stall holder always shortchanged his customers; another sold short measure. A gang of boys roamed by the stalls and stole fish from the sellers or coins from their customers with absolute impartiality. He came to watch all these arts, to admire the neatness with which they were done. And the thought arose in his mind: These people depend upon no one for their living; by taking, they are free—free as the horsemen on the steppe.

Once he even stole some apples himself, to prove how easy it was. No one detected him.

Yet the emptiness of his life was still a misery to him. He still felt that same vague longing he had had as a child: the desire to find his destiny.

And so it was that at last, three weeks before the ceremony for Boris and Gleb, and having seen all other opportunities evaporate, he had finally told his parents: "I want to be a monk."

After all, it was the only thing that anyone seemed to think that he could be.

And the effect had been remarkable.

"Are you sure?" his father had asked him in a tone that suggested Igor was only anxious that he should not change his mind. Even his mother, whatever her private misgivings, did not object.

Indeed, it was as if he had been born again. By that very evening his father had formed a plan. "He can go to Mount Athos in Greece. I have friends both here and in Constantinople who can help him. From there"—Igor smiled with satisfaction—"he might yet make a great career." And the next day his father took him to one side to assure him: "You need have no fear about your journey, Ivan. I shall see you are well provided for. And there will be a gift for the monastery too."

Even Sviatopolk, no doubt glad to see the last of him, came up and said, in what appeared to be a friendly voice, "Well, brother, you've probably chosen the right course after all. One day we'll all be proud of you."

They were proud of him. And now, in two more days, he was due to leave. Why then, as he walked up the hill behind the two saints, did he look as miserable as ever?

Only once, passing a guelder rose, did he seem for a moment to smile.

Would there be a miracle?

Ivanushka had never seen one. If God sent a miracle, then perhaps his faith would be restored.

I am going to bury myself in a monastery, he thought gloomily. Perhaps, in a few years, they will make me live underground in a cave. I shall certainly die young—all the monks do.

Would it be worth it? If only God would speak to him, reassure him, lighten his spirits. If only He would send a sign.

The procession had stopped. The coffin containing Boris was being carried into the little wooden church. When it had been placed there and prayed over, they would bring up the second coffin, containing Gleb. The drizzle fell. One could hear a muffled chanting within.

And then something happened.

It was as though the gasp within the little church could be heard all through the waiting crowds outside. The singing, which had been proceeding quietly, suddenly broke off, and then began again with an altogether new force. A murmur went through the crowd. And Ivanushka, glancing at the sky, saw to his surprise that the drizzle had abruptly stopped and the sun was shining through.

What had happened? Long moments passed. The crowd waited tensely.

And then the tall figure of the Metropolitan appeared at the church door. He looked up at the clear sky, then sank to his knees. From where Ivanushka stood, he could see that the Greek was weeping. "A miracle has been granted." The Metropolitan's voice rang out. "Give praise unto the Lord!" And while the crowd buzzed and people crossed themselves, those near the church door could hear him add: "God forgive my unbelief."

For when they had opened the casket, it had given out the sweet aroma that God grants only to His saints.

A few minutes later they brought up the remains of Gleb. These were in a stone sarcophagus; and since it was too heavy to carry, they followed the ancient custom of the land of Rus and pulled it on a sled.

And yet again, before Ivanushka's eyes, God sent a sign. For when the men pulling the sled reached the church door, the sled stuck fast. They pulled, people from the crowd even came to push. But the sarcophagus would not budge.

Then the Metropolitan gave instructions: "Let the people cry the Kyrie Eleison." And Ivanushka with all the crowd cried out: "Lord have mercy." And again: "Lord have mercy." And then the sled was easily moved.

Ivanushka felt the hairs on the back of his neck stand up. As the sled moved, he found he was trembling. He glanced across and saw that even Sviatopolk was trembling, too.

For by these signs, recorded in the Russian chronicles, the people of the land of Rus ever since knew that Boris and Gleb were truly saints.

It was just at this moment that Ivanushka saw Father Luke.

The old monk had been inside the church but had emerged for a moment into the open air. Ivanushka recognized him at once, yet could scarcely believe it was he.

For in the four years since he had visited him at the Monastery of the caves, his father's spiritual guide had passed into utter decrepitude. He seemed to have shrunk. One leg now dragged uselessly behind him as he pulled himself slowly forward with the aid of a stick. And his eyes, which before had been rheumy, now stared helplessly before him, sightless. He was like a small brown insect, crawling out blindly into the light where someone, no doubt, would step on him.

He glanced towards the family, and Igor respectfully bowed. But Father Luke saw nothing. Ivanushka stared at him. And the euphoria of the miracle suddenly evaporated.

This, he remembered with terror, is what it means to be a monk.

It seemed to Ivanushka, though he could not be sure, that he was in the woods near the village of Russka.

At least, when he remembered the dream afterward, this was where it had seemed to be.

It was late afternoon. The shadows were lengthening, but there was still a brightness in the sky which told him it was summer. He was riding along a path—he thought it led to the east, though he could not be certain. The trees, mostly oak and birch, seemed to be speaking to each other as he rode past them in the dappled light. His horse was black.

He was searching for something. But he did not know what.

It was not long before he passed a pool on his right. Turning to look at it, he noticed the pale glint on its smooth surface; and at the same time thought he heard a faint cry from the water—was it a moan or a laugh?

Realizing that it was the *rusalka* of the place, he put spurs to his horse and hurried on. The woods grew darker.

It was morning next, and he was still in the wood. His horse, for some reason, had now changed its color to gray. The path led to a glade, where there was a stand of silver birches; and at the far end of the glade was a crossroads. Standing by the crossroads was a small, brown figure that somehow looked familiar. He approached slowly.

It was Father Luke. His eyes were quite bright now. It was evident that he could see. Ivanushka bowed to him respectfully. "Which way should I travel, Father?" he asked.

"There are three ways to choose from," the old man said quietly. "If you go to the left, you will preserve your body but lose your soul."

"And to the right?"

"You will keep your soul, but lose your body."

Ivanushka thought. Neither sounded attractive to him.

"And straight ahead?"

"Only fools go that way," the monk replied.

It was hardly more encouraging, but as he considered, it seemed to him the only choice. "They call me Ivanushka the fool," he said. "So I may as well go there."

"As you wish," Father Luke answered, and then vanished.

And so Ivanushka rode forward, he knew not whither. It seemed to him that he heard a raucous bell clanging in the sky; and his horse, for no reason, had turned from a gray into a roan.

This was Ivanushka's dream, the night before his journey.

It was still morning as the two boats, one laden with goods, the other carrying only a few travelers, glided silently down the huge, pale, moving surface of the river. Above, a washed blue sky; on the right, high, sandy banks above which, here and there, cattle grazed. In the yellow banks nearest to them, Ivanushka could see a mass of little holes around which small birds were darting. Far away, on the left bank, stretched a light green plain dotted with trees.

He was well provided for. The bag of silver grivnas his father had given him was safely attached to his belt. "By turning monk, you've got your inheritance long before me," Sviatopolk had remarked drily as he set off.

And now the great river Dnieper was carrying him southward towards his destiny.

They had traveled all morning, and Ivanushka was just about to close his eyes for the midday nap when he was startled from his drowsiness by a loud cry from the boat in front. "Cumans!"

The passengers strained forward in astonishment; but there was no doubt: the dark Turkish faces in the longboat pushing out from the shore on their right were certainly Cumans.

The travelers had reason to be surprised. It had been thought that the Cumans were resting in their camps at this time, far away on the steppe. And besides, it was almost unheard of for them to attack by water. They usually preferred to wait far to the south, where there were rapids, and attack the caravans as they were carried around them overland.

"They've forced some Slavs to row them out," someone muttered, and Ivanushka saw that the oarsmen were indeed some unhappy Slav peasants. As he watched, one of the Cumans took a long, curved bow; an arrow flashed over the water; and one of the men in the cargo boat slumped over the side. "Behind you!" came a shout across the water. And he turned and saw another boat cutting them off upstream.

"There's nothing for it. We'll have to make for the left bank," the skipper of the little vessel cried.

Yet it was far away. To Ivanushka at that moment, staring across the soft blue waters, it seemed to be almost on the horizon. Grunting with the effort, the oarsmen pulled, and the boat slipped quickly across the flow.

Turning around, Ivanushka saw that the boat with the cargo was already lost. He wondered if the Cumans would be satisfied with that. Moments later, however, he saw that the other Cuman boat was pulling after them.

"There's a little stream that joins the river over there," the skipper called out. "There's a fort a few miles up it. We'll make for that." And Ivanushka found himself mumbling a prayer. For he knew the fort in question very well.

It was strange to be back at Russka. Zhydovyn was not there, but half a dozen soldiers made them welcome. The Cumans had given up soon after they had left the Dnieper; but the travelers had decided to wait two days in the fort before tempting fate again.

He had trailed about the fort, visited the village, and wandered along the quiet paths in the woods, feeling strangely contented. He had even walked out to the edge of the steppe, and gazed out across the feather grasses to where an ancient kurgan could still be seen.

On the third day the travelers set off again.

And Ivanushka did not go with them.

He hardly knew why. He told himself that providence had granted him a respite. I can pause here, take stock of life, and prepare myself for my journey, he reasoned. The fact that all his decisions had been made and that he was already on his journey, he somehow put at the back of his mind. All that third day he walked about by the river.

On the fourth day he was overcome with a feeling of lassitude, and he slept.

It was on the next day that he met the peasant Shchek. The fellow was thinner than before, but he greeted Ivanushka warmly. When Ivanushka asked him if he had paid his debts now, he grinned sheepishly. "Yes and no," he replied. "I'm a *zakup.*"

This was a harsh institution. A man who could not pay his creditors had to work for them, virtually as a slave, until the debt was paid off. Since the debt continued to accrue interest during this period, however, these unfortunates seldom managed to get free again. "I got the prince's steward to take over all my debts," he explained, "so now I work for the prince."

"And when will you get free again?" Ivanushka asked.

Shchek smiled ruefully. "In thirty years," he said. "And what are you doing, young lord?" he inquired.

Ivanushka explained that he was going on a great journey to Constantinople and to Greece, to become a monk.

Shchek listened carefully, then nodded in understanding. "So you'll never be free either," he remarked. "Just like me."

Ivanushka gazed at the peasant. The similarity between them had not occurred to him. But I suppose he's right, he thought. I'm a prisoner of fate, too. And, reaching into his pouch, he gave Shchek a silver grivna. Then he passed on. He wondered if he should have given him more. But I need my money, he considered, for my journey.

The day afterwards he left Russka on foot, going towards the river Dnieper.

It was after parting from Ivanushka that Shchek the peasant had wandered out from the village towards the steppe.

Though the little fort had somewhat enlarged the significance of the hamlet of Russka since ancient times, it was still a tiny and deserted place. To the south, two miles away, lay one of the prince's estates; to the east, the steppe; and to the north, nothing at all for fifteen miles, where there was another similar hamlet and a fort.

As he walked, Shchek was rather cheerful. Since he had become a *zakup*, his life had not been easy. The prince's steward worked him hard. His wife, ashamed of his status, had become sullen. But this unexpected gift from the young noble was a great windfall. A silver grivna was worth about three months' wages to a peasant like Shchek.

He took the path through the woods and continued along it to the glades where the women picked mushrooms. He pressed on, past the pool where, the villagers said, *rusalki* dwelt. It was a little way past the pool that he came to a crossroads. The right-hand track, he knew, led south to the prince's estate. The left-hand track led northward; but since it passed through a place where one of the villagers had been killed by a boar, few people took that route, thinking it unlucky.

On impulse, however, the peasant decided to do so. That Ivanushka brought me luck, he considered. I've nothing to fear today.

Some way to the north of Russka, the river made a large curve around a low and densely wooded hill. It was here that the villager had been killed. Thick undergrowth had formed around the base of the hill, much of it bramble and thorn. It was not an inviting spot, and he would not have paused had he not suddenly seen, a hundred yards ahead of him, a large fox slipping silently into the undergrowth.

I wonder if he has a lair in there, Shchek thought. Fox fur was valuable. As quietly as he could, and suffering a number of scratches, he made his way through the undergrowth and began to climb the hill. And a few minutes later, having almost forgotten the fox, he was grinning with delight and astonishment.

For the hill, so densely covered with oak and pine, and which no one ever visited, was a treasure house. It was crowded with beehives. He could smell the rich, thick smell of honey up in the trees everywhere. As he wandered around, he counted no less than twenty hives up in the branches; until finally he laughed aloud. "That Ivanushka has brought me more luck than he knew," he cried.

He did not plan to tell anyone about it. For already he could see how to make use of it. I might even be able to get free one day, he mused.

1075

IN THE YEAR 1075, few men in the land of Rus were considered as lucky as Igor the boyar.

His master, Prince Vsevolod of Pereiaslav, showered gifts upon him. No one was held in more honor in that prince's *druzhina*.

The greatest nobles, now, had a new status: instead of the old blood money of forty grivnas, their lives had been set at eighty. Even to insult them carried a fine of four times the value of a *smerd*.

Igor had been granted this high status. More than that, so impressed was the Prince of Pereiaslav with his loyal servant that the previous year he had given Igor the lordship of extensive lands on the southeast border of the principality, including the little hamlet of Russka.

These outright gifts of land were a new method of rewarding faithful retainers. Cheaper than gifts of money, in a state where land was plentiful, these land grants began the process whereby the term *boyar,* which originally meant a retainer or nobleman of the *druzhina,* came to signify "landowner."

Igor the boyar had reason to be happy. Yet behind his aloof and busy manner there was a sadness. Seeing Igor and his graying wife together, a stranger might have thought that they shared a love of quietness. Yet in fact they were quiet because each was afraid that almost anything one of them said might bring to the surface the sadness concealed in the other.

Boris was dead. He had been killed in a skirmish at the edge of the steppe one winter day. As was the custom, they had brought his body back on a sled.

Igor would never forget that day. It was snowing, and as they pulled the sled up the slope to the city gates, the snow flurries had slapped, softly, across his face so that at times he could scarcely see the sled. He had prayed in front of the icon for long hours at that period and sought the comfort of Father Luke.

But the loss of Boris was a wound that could heal.

Not so the loss of Ivanushka.

Where was he? A month after he had left for Constantinople, they had heard from Zhydovyn the Khazar that he had been seen at Russka. But where had he gone after that? Word came from the Russian merchants in Constantinople: he had never arrived there. A year of silence followed; then a rumor that he had been seen in Kiev; vague reports came also from Smolensk, Chernigov, even distant Novgorod. He had been seen gambling; he had been seen drinking; he had been seen begging. There were few reports, however, and none of them very reliable.

And from Ivanushka, for three years, came not a word to his parents to let them know if he was alive or dead.

"He is searching for something," his mother said, after the sighting in Kiev had been reported.

"He is ashamed," Igor concluded sadly.

"Yet even so," Sviatopolk remarked, "he cannot love any of us, to behave like this."

And as the third year passed, and no word came, even his mother began to believe Ivanushka did not love her.

The jetty was crowded. Above, a long path of dry earth made an untidy diagonal gash across the tall ramparts of Pereiaslav. In the faint sun, the ramparts, where they were not dirty brown, had a pale green covering of tired autumnal grass. The summer had passed. There was an air of lassitude about the place. The broad river, too, looked brown and dreary, stretching away like a monotonous echo under an iron sky. At the end of the jetty, a stout boat was about to cast off—an event that would have attracted no special attention but for a little incident concerning a young man.

He was a strange figure. His whole person appeared to be filthy. The brown cloak wrapped around him and the peasant's bast shoes he wore had almost disintegrated.

He was sitting with an air of sullen helplessness on a small barrel by the end of the jetty, while the master of a stout boat was yelling at him, "Well, are you coming or not?"

It seemed he nodded.

"Devil take it! Then get in, man!"

Again the young fellow assented. But he did not move.

"I'm casting off, you fool," the master shouted in an excess of fury. "Do you want to see Tsargrad or rot in Pereiaslav?"

When there was still no movement: "You promised me the fare. I could have had another passenger. Give me my money!"

For a second it really seemed the passenger would rise, but he did not. With a curse the older man gave the order, and the stout boat with its single mast and bank of oarsmen pulled out into the broad, sluggish river and headed south.

And still Ivanushka did not move.

How long he had wandered. In the first year, several times, he had started to go south. At least he had found merchants who were prepared to take him, and he got as far as inspecting their boats. But each time some invisible force had pulled him back. Just as surface tension holds a light object one pulls from the water, so a subterranean force seemed to make it impossible for Ivanushka to break free from his native soil and set out upon the great river that would carry him towards the religious life. It was almost, sometimes, like a physical force, a huge inertia dragging at his back.

As his money had been eaten into, he had started to gamble.

If I win, he reasoned, it means that God wants me to go to the monastery. But if I lose all my journey money, then obviously He doesn't. It seemed a good argument, and he did not have to gamble long before he lost.

It was not that Ivanushka consciously turned away from God, but rather that he hoped, by these devious means, to slide towards Him comfortably. As time went on, however, he had sunk into lethargy, punctuated by increasingly frequent bouts of drinking. He wandered from city to city, unable to go south or to return home. In the second year he began to steal.

They were only small amounts; and strangely enough, he even persuaded himself that he was not really stealing. After all, he told himself, if I take from the rich man, what does it matter? And besides, did not Our Lord Himself let His disciples pick the ears of corn in the fields? Often, before stealing, he would work himself up into a kind of angry scorn. He would tell himself that he was a man close to God while those from whom he stole were contemptible, lovers of money who should be punished. And after stealing, and buying food and drink, he would wander through the countryside for days with that slight elation from a half-empty stomach that he took to be a state of grace.

The winters were very hard. Even stealing had not helped him: one could not live in the open. He had traveled from church to monastery as an *izgoi*, picking up what charity he could. Several times he had nearly frozen.

Once he had seen his father. He had been wandering through the woods near Chernigov one spring day, when suddenly he heard the sound of approaching hooves, and a cavalcade had swept into sight.

He had hidden behind an oak tree as they had come by, a big party of noblemen with their retainers. He had seen young Prince Vladimir among them, and almost beside him his father and brother Sviatopolk. Igor was carrying a hawk on his wrist. He wore a hat made of sable, and he was listening with a cool sardonic face while the young prince, laughing, told him some story.

And to his astonishment, Ivanushka had been afraid: as terrified as any peasant might have been; yet more than that: ashamed. "Dear God," he prayed, "do not let them see me." For was not he the failure, now the outcast, from this glittering world, with his gnawing hunger and his filthy rags to prove it? The thought of their embarrassment, of their disgust were they to recognize him, was more than he could face. How tall, how hard, and how terrifyingly magnificent they looked. That world is closed to me now, he thought.

Yet he could not take his eyes from them.

It was as they had almost passed that he saw something else that made him gasp aloud. For riding together at the rear of this hunting party were two young women: one a young lady, the other little more than a girl.

They were sumptuously dressed. They rode well, with gracious ease. And both were fair haired and blue eyed—fairer than any women he had ever seen before. And it suddenly seemed to him, as he crouched behind his tree, that he had seen a vision not of the royal court, but of heaven itself. "They are like two angels," he murmured, and he wondered where they could possibly have come from.

Moments later the vision faded and the sounds died away. But the memory of the two girls remained with him, hauntingly, to remind him as the months passed: You are just an animal, now, in the forest.

It was that spring, when by chance he found himself near Russka, that Ivanushka had finally made one last attempt to recover himself. I can't go on like this, he had decided. I can either end it all, or go to the monastery. The thought of death frightened him. And no monastic rule, he considered, could be worse than this life I lead.

Only one problem remained. He no longer had any money.

It has been a warm spring morning when Zhydovyn had glanced out from the warehouse in Russka to see, loitering opposite, the shabby figure of the wanderer. Russka was very quiet that day. The little fort, unguarded at present, was nearly empty.

The Khazar had recognized him almost at once, but being a cautious man, he gave no sign; and it was midday before the wanderer ambled, a little stiffly, towards him.

"You know who I am?"

The voice was quiet, yet there seemed to be a hint of abruptness, even scorn in it.

"Yes, Ivan Igorevich." The Khazar did not move or make any gesture at all.

Ivanushka nodded slowly, as if considering something far away. "You were good to me once."

Zhydovyn did not reply.

"Could I have some food?"

"Of course." Zhydovyn smiled. "Come inside." He wondered how he could keep the young man there. If he tried to seize Ivanushka himself, he wasn't sure of holding him; but by midafternoon, two of his men were due back at the warehouse. With their help he could secure the youth, then ship him back to his parents in Pereiaslav. Leaving Ivanushka in the warehouse, he went into the yard behind where his quarters were, and a few minutes later returned with a bowl of kvass and a wooden plate of millet cakes.

But Ivanushka had disappeared.

It was foolish of the Khazar not to remember that Ivanushka knew where he hid his money. There had not been a great amount, but enough to get him downriver and even to Constantinople. At least I shall see the place, Ivanushka thought.

He was sorry to steal from the Khazar, even in a good cause. Yet it isn't really stealing, he told himself, because he can just recover the money from my father. I daresay Father would even be glad to know that I've

finally gone. For as he made his way through the woods, Ivanushka had
no doubt that it was to the monasteries of the Greeks that he was at last
going.

As for Zhydovyn, he had cursed himself for his stupidity, then wondered what to tell Ivanushka's parents. After thinking it over for a long
time, he had decided to tell them nothing. For what could he have said
that would not give them pain.

And now, sitting alone on the jetty, Ivanushka stared blankly at the
water. He knew the boat had been his last chance of reaching the imperial
city before winter set in.

He had wanted to go. At least he thought he had. But during the
summer something new and terrible had occurred within him: he had lost
his will.

Often, recently, he had found that he could do nothing except sit,
helplessly, staring in front of him for hours on end. And when he did
move from place to place, he was like a man in a dream.

The money he had stolen was more than half spent. Indeed, that very
morning he had found he had only eight silver grivnas left—just enough
for his journey. And he had dragged himself to the jetty today, fully
intending with the last of this money to get on the ship. But, to his own
despair, he had found he could not move.

And now it is over, he thought. There was, it seemed to him, no course
left open to him, in his abject failure. I shall walk along the river, and
end it all, he decided.

It was just then that he became aware of a noise behind him, from a
row of slaves sitting on the ground, waiting to be led to the marketplace
for sale. He looked up without interest. One of them seemed to be excited
about something. He shrugged and stared at the water again.

"Ivan. Ivan Igorevich!"

He turned.

Shchek had been staring at him for some time. Now he was sure. He
was so excited he even forgot that his hands were tied. It was the boyar's
son. The one they called the fool.

"Ivan Igorevich," he cried again. And now, it seemed, the strange
young man had vaguely recognized him.

Shchek's position was grim. He was about to be sold. Worse yet, one
of the other prisoners had just whispered the awful news: "The merchants are looking for men to row the boats." They all knew what that
meant: backbreaking work on the river; carrying the boats past the rapids; perhaps even a dangerous sea journey. And like as not they might
be sold again as slaves in the markets of the Greeks. Anything could
happen to a slave.

One thing was sure: he would never see Russka again.

Under Russian law, Shchek should not have been there. A *zakup*
working off his debt could not be sold like an ordinary slave. But the
rules were often broken, and the authorities had long since turned a
blind eye.

In his own case, he should have seen it coming. For two months now, it had been clear that the elder at the prince's nearby village had taken a liking to Shchek's wife, and she to him. Yet the treachery had been done so suddenly that it had caught him off-guard.

Just a week ago, early in the morning, the elder had appeared with some merchants and literally dragged him from his bed. "Here's a *zakup*," the elder had told them roughly. "You can have him." Before he could do anything about it, Shchek had found himself skimming down the river towards Pereiaslav. There was nothing he could do about it: five of the other slaves on the jetty were debtors like himself.

And yet—here was the irony—given time he could have paid off the debt and be free again. Even in a mere ten years.

It was the honey from the beehives in the forest that were his secret. Ever since his discovery of this hidden treasure, he had been discreetly making use of it—selling a honeycomb or two to any passing merchant, or even taking some into Pereiaslav. He had to be very careful, for he had no right to those trees. But by selling a little at a time he had already been able to put by the sum of two silver grivnas.

He had even made more hollows for the bees. The hidden wood had become a treasure house; and although he could not profit from this extra labor, his secret seemed to give him a purpose in life. It almost became an obsession. He felt himself to be the guardian of the place. And he had kept his secret well. From time to time he had fostered rumors: that he had seen a witch along the path that led there, or snakes. The reputation of the wood remained evil and no one went there.

So it was with irony that he had been brooding: I lived beside great riches. Yet they lie useless and I am poor. He supposed it must be fate.

And now, here was that curious young nobleman, walking slowly towards him. "I am Shchek," he cried. "Remember me?"

How poor Ivanushka looked; and how sickly. Despite his own miserable condition, the peasant felt sorry for him. And for want of anything better to do, while the strange young man stood vacantly in front of him, Shchek told him his story.

When he had finished, Ivanushka stared at the ground for a moment. "How strange," he murmured. "I, too, have nothing."

"Well, good luck to you anyway," Shchek said with a grin. For some reason he felt affectionate towards this nobleman in tatters. "Remember Shchek in your prayers."

"Ah, my prayers." The young fellow seemed lost in thought.

"Tell me again, he said at last, "how much you owe."

"Today, I owe the prince seven silver grivnas."

"And that would make you free?"

"Of course."

Slowly Ivanushka removed the leather bag that hung from his belt, and attached it to Shchek's.

"Take it," he said. "It's eight grivnas. And I have no use for it."

And before the astonished peasant could say a word, he moved away. "After all," Ivanushka thought, "this peasant may as well have it, since I am about to depart this world."

* * *

The decurion in charge of the slaves was not a bad fellow, and when he returned a few moments later from the booth where he was drinking, he was genuinely delighted by Shchek's good fortune. He knew Shchek was a *zakup* and had felt sorry for the man's bad luck. "The Mother of God herself must be watching over you," he cried, as he cut Shchek's bonds and embraced him warmly. "What devil's luck you have, my boy," he added. "I've never heard of such a thing. We'll have to tell the prince's steward in the market." He glanced up. "And here he comes."

Shchek had never seen the tall, dark young nobleman who now stalked down onto the jetty; but he noticed that he looked irritable. When the decurion told this nobleman the story, he only glowered at the peasant, then turned coldly to the decurion. "Obviously he stole this money," he snapped.

"The other slaves saw it," the decurion suggested.

The noble looked at the slaves with disgust. "Their word is worthless."

"How could I steal, lord, with my hands tied?" Shchek asked. The noble glared at him. It was all one to him whether this indebted peasant lived or died, but he had just informed a merchant that there were twenty slaves to sell, and this would leave him one short. He did not like to be inconvenienced.

"The fellow who you say gave you this money. Where is he?"

Shchek looked around. Ivanushka had vanished.

"Take his purse," the noble ordered the decurion. But before he could do so, there was a cry.

"Look!" It was one of the slaves. He was pointing excitedly to the riverbank below the city. About a quarter of a mile away, a single figure had just emerged from a clump of trees.

"That's him."

"Fetch him," the noble ordered.

And so a few minutes later, to his utter astonishment, Sviatopolk found himself staring at his brother Ivanushka; while Ivanushka, his eyes glazed and his mind apparently far away, looked back at him dully and said not a word.

"Let the peasant go, he has paid his debt," Sviatopolk said calmly. "As for this vagrant"—he gestured to Ivanushka—"throw him in prison."

His mind was working quickly.

The candles were lit. The icon in the corner glowed softly as the Mother of God gazed out from Her golden world into the dark spaces of the large room. The remains of the meal on the table were being cleared away by the slaves.

Igor was sitting in a heavy oak chair. His long head, all gray now, was inclined forward, his chin resting upon his chest. His eyes were open, watchful, his face still but grim. His wife sat on a chair beside him. One might have guessed that, an hour or two before, she had been weeping; but now her face was pale, drawn, and upon her husband's orders, impassive.

Sviatopolk was scowling with barely contained fury.

What unlucky curse, he wondered, had caused his father to walk out to the city wall just as they were leading the silent Ivanushka to the little jail where he would have been out of the way. He would have been drowned by now, Sviatopolk thought. For his intention—not knowing that Ivanushka was going to drown himself anyway—had been to take him down to the river that night and hold him under himself. Better for him. Better even for my parents, he had told himself. They'll find the body, suppose he took his life, and end all this agony over a useless son. Besides, the fool would only ask for money.

But fate had intervened. True, his father had been grim-faced about it from the moment he had encountered him. He had marched his youngest son back to their house almost like a prisoner. And now, over the evening meal, the young man had been forced to explain himself.

It had scarcely been necessary for Sviatopolk to accuse him. He had, in his stumbling way, accused himself. Indeed, Sviatopolk had thought it wisest to say nothing against him but to suggest: "My brother has lost his way. I think he has almost lost his soul. Perhaps he may regain it as a monk." Monks usually died young.

Igor had put the questions, while his wife watched in silence.

Once, Sviatopolk had murmured: "Can such a son love his family?" But the rest of the interrogation had gone on without his aid. And now at last, the stern nobleman summed up.

"You have lied to me, and to us all. You have thrown away the money, your inheritance, which I gave you. You have even stolen. By no word did you tell us whether you were alive or dead, breaking your mother's heart. And now, having stolen yet again, you give the money to a stranger and try to depart from the very place where your parents are living."

It seemed to Sviatopolk that no indictment could be more complete. He watched, contented, while no one spoke.

Then Igor forgave his son.

The great Russian winter, terrible in its mighty cold, is also a time of joy. For Ivanushka, it was a time of healing.

At first, during the autumn months after his homecoming, his body and spirits seemed to collapse. The end of his long ordeal, as so often happens, caused a surrender in his system. He fell prey to a cold that soon turned into an illness that made his throat swell up, his limbs ache, and his head throb so violently that he blinked with the pain. "It feels like an anvil," he muttered, "upon which two demons are hammering."

It was his mother who saved him. Perhaps because only she understood. For when his father had wanted to send for one of the Armenian or Syrian doctors of the prince's court, men skilled in the medicine of the classical world, Olga had refused. "We have folk remedies, better than the medicine of the Greeks and Romans," she said firmly. "But send to the monastery if you wish, and ask the monks for their prayers." Then she had locked the door of the room where he lay, and let no one in but herself.

While he tossed and turned, she would remain in the room, a gentle, quiet presence, bathing his brow from time to time, saying little. Sitting by the window, she seemed quite contented to stare out at the sky, or read her book of Psalms, or half doze while he lay. She would speak if he wanted to talk, but she never addressed him, or even looked at him. She was there, yet not there, calm and unmoving.

Outside the rains of autumn fell, the countryside became a morass of rich, black mud, and all nature seemed like a wet and wilted bird. The skies were gray and heavy, the horizon blank. Somewhere, behind the long gray-black skyline, a huge, white cold was preparing to advance from the east.

Then came the snow. The first day it came over the steppe, in an endless orange glow, and fell upon the damp streets in soft gray flurries. As Ivanushka stared past his mother's quiet, pale face, he had the impression that nature was closing a door outside, shutting out the light from the sky. But alone in his room with her, he did not mind. The second day came a blizzard. Now the snowstorm howled, as though the endless steppe had conjured up and sent an infinite army of tiny, gray demons who intended to hurl themselves furiously upon the citadel and overpower it. But the third day a change occurred. The snow fell softly. For a time, in the middle of the day, the sky even cleared enough for a few shafts of sunlight to shine through the clouds. The snowflakes that fell, morning and evening, were large, soft as feathers. And it was after this that he began to recover.

The Russian winter is not, in truth, so terrible. Even the smallest hut, with its huge stove, is piping hot inside.

A week after the snows fell, on a bright sunlit day, Ivanushka, wrapped in furs, was carried to the high walls of Pereiaslav.

How the land sparkled. The golden domes of the churches in the city flashed in the sun under the crystal-blue sky. Below, the river was flowing past a gleaming white bank, and in the distance the woods on the other side were like a dark, glistening line. To the east, and south, over patches of wood, laden with fresh snow, the beginning of the mighty steppe could be seen: a huge, white carpet, stretching endlessly, shining softly.

Thus, through the Russian winter, the thick blanket of snow protects the earth.

And through that winter, as the land by the snow, Ivanushka was protected by his mother.

At times it was as though he were a child again. They would sit by the fire, or by the window, and read the fairy stories or recite the *byliny* that he had known as a boy.

The firebird, the tales of snow maidens, of bears in the forest, the stories of princes in search of wealth or love: why was it that these childish tales, now that he was older, seemed so full of wisdom? Their very language, with its subtle sense of movement, wry humor, and gentle irony seemed to him now to be trembling with life and color, like the endless forest itself.

Death came once to the family that winter, when Sviatopolk's wife suddenly sickened and died. Though he had hardly known her, Ivanushka would gladly have gone to comfort his brother; but Sviatopolk did not seem to wish it, and so Ivanushka had said no more.

Slowly the long winter with its covering of snow passed; and Ivanushka, in this little womb prepared for him, recovered his life and
emerged, in early spring, while the snow was still upon the ground, ready
to join the world again.

His brow was clear; his eyes bright; and although he was a little
subdued and often thoughtful, he felt cheerful, whole, and strong.
"Thanks to you," he told his mother, "I have been reborn."

The world of Pereiaslav into which he emerged was a busy one.

While the princes had fought over golden Kiev, cautious Prince Vsevolod had kept his grip on Pereiaslav, the hub of the southern frontier forts,
and raised the city to new importance. Compared to Kiev, of course, it
had only a few fine churches, and most of its buildings were of wood.
But the stout, square fortress town represented a force to be reckoned
with. Above all, the Church there was so powerful and so loyal to the
Patriarch in Constantinople that the metropolitan of Pereiaslav was
sometimes more favored in the imperial city than that of Kiev.

As he walked through the broad main square and gazed at the stout
little Church of the Virgin by the prince's palace, or the chapel they were
building over the gate, Ivanushka felt a sense of well-being. He would
visit the glassmakers and lovingly handle the brightly colored pieces
bound for a church or nobleman's house. He even found a workshop
which made bronze clasps for books, and he bought one for his mother.
They were pleasant days.

And yet, strangely enough, he was no sooner recovered than he began
to experience a vague sense of unease. He could not put his finger on it:
the sense was only a vague intuition. But as the days passed he began
to get the distinct feeling that there had been some intrigue concerning
him—as though, while the snow covered the earth, someone had been
burrowing dangerous channels underground. What the devil could it be?

At first, however, he had put the suspicion out of his mind. For the
news his father shortly brought him was wonderful indeed.

"I've done it," the boyar proudly told his wife. "Prince Vsevolod is so
much my friend I can even beg a place for Ivanushka!" And to his son
he had joyfully declared: "You are to join young Prince Vladimir after
all. Sviatopolk is in his *druzhina* and has done well. Now's your chance
to prove yourself, too." And Ivanushka had beamed with delight.

It had been just two days later that his father had casually remarked:
"By the way, while you were ill, your brother and I paid off all your
creditors, you know. You name's quite clear now."

Supposing this to be a reference to Zhydovyn and one or two others,
Ivanushka had thanked his father and thought little more about it. It was
only when, the next day, his mother made a reluctant reference to his
debts that he had thought of asking to see the list.

And now he saw what had been going on. For the list was staggering.

At the top, of course, came the debt to Zhydovyn. But after that came
a list that took his breath away. People that he had never seen, in places
he had scarcely visited, had claimed either that he had robbed them or
that they had lent him money. In all but two cases, he knew that their
claims were false. "Who found these creditors?" he demanded.

"Sviatopolk," his father told him.

So this was the dark labyrinth that had been burrowed in the ground all winter.

His brother had been thorough. It seemed he had been to every town in the land of Rus. The amounts were not large. Sviatopolk had been clever. But their number was astonishing. "You owe your brother a debt of thanks," Igor told him sternly. "He insisted on paying half of these himself."

"He feels responsible for you, too," his mother added.

Ivanushka understood. His experiences had made him a little wiser. "I fear a great many of these folk have cheated my brother," he remarked sadly. But seeing they did not believe him, he said no more. The incident was closed.

The next day, at last, his father took him to meet the young prince whom, on account of his royal Greek mother, men called Vladimir Monomakh.

The meeting took place in the long, high hall of the prince's palace. With its small windows set high in the thick walls, the palace had the feeling of a church.

The young prince was standing at the far end as Ivanushka entered with his father. There were half a dozen nobles standing respectfully on each side of him. Vladimir was wearing a long cloak, trimmed with sable. It reached almost to his feet and was encrusted with gems so that, even in the dimness, it shone softly. Upon his head was a cap trimmed with ermine. His hands were at his sides.

From his Greek mother, no doubt, came the handsome face with its long, straight nose and large dark eyes, which stared before him calmly. He awaited their approach like a priest before an altar, motionless, as if his dignity came not from himself but from an authority securely lodged in the other world.

Father and son bowed low before him, advanced a few paces, bowed again. He is like a painting in a church, thought Ivanushka, as he stole a glance up at the motionless black eyes. When he reached him, Ivanushka went down upon his knees and kissed the jeweled shoes.

"Welcome, Ivan Igorevich," the young prince said solemnly.

The courts in the land of Rus were not like those of Western Europe. The Russian princes did not seek, like the rulers of Bohemia and Poland, to join the elaborate feudal network of Europe; nor were they interested in its manners or the new ideas of knightly chivalry. Their models, rather, came from the Orient. For had not all the rulers of these vast lands come from the East?

From the ancient Scythians and Alans who could still be found in their *druzhina,* from the once vanished Avars and Huns, from the mighty Khazars, the rulers of the borderlands had always been godlike despots from far away. And what power in that quarter of the world was more ancient and civilized than the Christian empire of the Greeks in Constantinople?

So it was that Russian princes were learning oriental luxury, and to

copy the jeweled, hieratic formality of the Eastern imperial court. Monomakh knew how to do so from birth.

But now, to Ivanushka's surprise, the prince smiled pleasantly. "I hear
that you have traveled widely." At this there was a laugh from the
courtiers and Igor blushed. They had all heard of this foolish Ivanushka's
wanderings.

"Do not laugh," Vladimir corrected them. "If he has observed well in
his travels, our friend may know more about the land of Rus than I do."
By this simple sentence, the prince secured the eternal loyalty of his man;
and Ivanushka witnessed the grace that made Monomakh loved as well
as feared.

With that, Monomakh waved Igor and the other nobles away and
drew Ivanushka to one side. Sensing Ivanushka's nervousness, he began
to talk to him quietly and easily until the young man was ready to speak
for himself. Vladimir asked him about his travels, and Ivanushka answered very honestly so that, though Vladimir once or twice looked at
him in astonishment, he seemed well pleased.

And strangely, the young prince reminded Ivanushka of his own father. There was a stern self-discipline about him that was impressive. It
soon became clear that he spent long hours in prayer, four or five times
a day, and this he spoke of with a calm grimness very like Igor. But when
he mentioned one subject, his whole face changed and he became quite
boyish.

"Do you like to hunt?"

Ivanushka told him he did.

"That is good." He grinned. "Before I die I mean to hunt every wood
in the whole land of Rus. Tomorrow," he added happily, "you shall come
and see my hawks."

Before their conversation ended, however, the prince became serious
once again. "You are new here," he said quietly, "and there are others
who have been here before you." He paused. "Including your brother."
It was a warning. But though Ivanushka looked at him carefully, Monomakh's expression was quite impassive, giving nothing away. "Go about
your business quietly therefore," he instructed. "I shall judge you by
your deeds alone."

The interview was over. Ivanushka bowed gratefully. Vladimir turned
back to his courtiers.

It was at this moment that Ivanushka saw her.

She came in directly behind her mistress. She was no longer a girl, but
a young woman; both she and her mistress were so fair they seemed
almost unearthly: and he remembered at once how he had seen them
before, two years ago, riding through the forest with his father and the
court, while he hid behind a tree.

"Who are they?" he asked the nobleman beside him.

"Don't you know? The elder is Monomakh's wife. The other is her
maidservant."

"Where do they come from?"

"Why, from England. Gytha is the daughter of the Saxon king, Harold, who the Normans killed at Hastings ten years ago. The girl's called Emma. She's an orphaned nobleman's daughter that the princess brought with her."

Ivanushka knew that there had been many exiles from England after it was conquered by William of Normandy in the terrible year of the red star. Some Saxon warriors had traveled all the way to Constantinople and joined the elite guard of Norsemen who served the emperor. Others had wandered Eastern Europe. And this princess and her companion, with their ethereal looks, had somehow arrived in Kiev and thereby joined the blood of the Saxon king of England to that of the ruling house of Rus.

Ivanushka stared.

The noble smiled. "Of Gytha we say: 'She came from a crystal pool and her father was the sunlight!' "

Ivanushka nodded slowly.

"And of the girl?"

"The same. She is not yet betrothed," the man added casually.

It was on a bright morning five days later that, having finished his prayers, Igor summoned his sons to him at breakfast.

They found him alone. He looked cheerful, yet Ivanushka could see, from a certain faintly troubled look in his eyes, that he had been deep in thought.

"I have decided," he announced, "that it is time you each received the income fitting to a nobleman." Some of the greatest boyars of Kiev even kept small courts of their own. The honor of the family dictated that the sons of Igor should live at least with comfortable means.

"As you know," Igor went on, "the Prince of Pereiaslav has rewarded my services well. I am by no means poor." He paused. "But when I left the service of the Prince of Kiev, I suffered several financial reverses. As a result, we are not as rich as I might have hoped, and the cost of maintaining one's state seems to increase with every year. "Sviatopolk: you already have your household. Ivanushka: so you will no doubt marry and require a household too." He paused gravely. "With this in mind, I am making the following disposition."

The two brothers listened attentively.

"Of the income from the estates the prince has given me, I retain half for myself. The income from the other half is for my sons." He sighed. "Normally, of course, the greater portion should go to Sviatopolk and a lesser portion to Ivanushka. But since Sviatopolk already has a good income from Prince Vladimir, whereas Ivanushka as yet has almost nothing—and since the income I have to give you is limited—I am allotting the two of you equal shares." He stopped, as if tired after making a hard decision.

Ivanushka stared before him, hardly able to believe his good fortune. Sviatopolk was silent.

When at last Sviatopolk spoke, it was with icy coldness. "My father, I thank you, and I bow to your will," he said quietly. "I have served my prince; and I have served this family. But is it right, I ask, that Ivanushka, who has done nothing except bring dishonor upon us, and whose debts we have just paid, should receive exactly the same?"

Igor did not answer, but Ivanushka guessed that the same thought had been troubling him.

He hung his head. What Sviatopolk said was true. He did not deserve it. And he could understand his elder brother's anger. Until he had appeared—from the dead as it were—all Igor's limited fortune would have passed to Sviatopolk. Now he was to be denied half his expectations—and all for a stupid wastrel.

"I have decided," Igor said abruptly, and the interview was over.

As they left, Sviatopolk gave Ivanushka a single look. There could be no mistaking its meaning. It said: Death.

It was not until the following day, when he was sitting in the corner of the marketplace, that Ivanushka reached his decision.

The meeting the day before and the look on Sviatopolk's face had shocked him. Can he really hate me so much, for money? he wondered. And it reminded him, with force, of a conclusion he had reached during his slow convalescence. For when I was wandering in the world, stealing from others and enduring those terrible winters, he had considered, I had nothing. In the end, I was ready to take my own life. Only when I returned and found the love of my family did I once again desire to live. It is true, therefore, what the preachers say: the world is good for nothing without love. And gradually in his mind a new formula had taken shape: Life itself is love; death is lack of love. That is all there is to it.

That day, therefore, as he considered the situation with Sviatopolk, he finally concluded: What use is my good fortune to me if it only creates hatred in my family? I'd sooner be without. So I think, he had decided, that I should give up my inheritance. Let Sviatopolk have it. God will provide. And satisfied that this was the only sensible thing to do, he was about to move across the market.

It was just then that he felt a tug at his sleeve, and to his surprise saw a sturdy peasant grinning beside him.

"Why, you're the fellow I gave the money to." He smiled.

"That's right," Shchek replied cheerfully. "And, if I may ask, what are you so down in the mouth about, my lord?"

Shchek had reason to be content. Not only had he regained his freedom but, thanks to his secret treasure house, he expected to put some money in his pocket, too. He was glad to see the strange young man again, if only to thank him. And since there was already a bond between them, and he had no one else to talk to, Ivanushka told him the whole story.

What a good fellow this noble is, Shchek thought as he listened. He has a warm heart. And besides, he reminded himself, as he heard the final details, I owe him my liberty after all.

So when Ivanushka had finished, the sturdy peasant saw what he should do.

"Don't give up everything, lord," he advised. "Your father, however, possesses the Russka estate, which is poor. "But I think I know a way to make it rich. If you want to give up your share, then ask your father for only the village of Russka—together with the wood to the north of it," he added.

Ivanushka nodded. He liked Russka. It didn't seem a bad idea.

When, that very evening, Sviatopolk heard what Ivanushka had to say to himself and his father, he could hardly believe his ears.

"Russka?" Igor said. "You want only the income from that miserable little village? How will you live?"

"I'll manage," Ivanushka said cheerfully.

"As you wish," Igor sighed. "God knows what is to be done with you."

Praise the Lord, Sviatopolk thought. My brother is a fool.

And with a tender smile, he went forward and kissed Ivanushka on the cheek.

It was two days after this that Ivanushka astonished his father with a bold request.

"Go to Prince Vladimir, Father, and ask on my behalf for the hand of the Saxon girl, his wife's handmaiden. He is her guardian." Igor stared at him. What could he say? The boy had renounced most of his income and he knew very well that young Monomakh, who took a fatherly interest in this Saxon girl, would hardly give her to a poor man. But even if it were not for that . . . "My poor boy," he replied sadly, "don't you know that Sviatopolk asked for her himself yesterday?"

Ivanushka's face fell. Then he looked thoughtful.

"Ask all the same," he said finally.

"Very well," Igor replied. But after Ivanushka had gone he sighed to himself, "I'm afraid there's no denying it: the boy's a fool."

The reply from Monomakh was given within two days. As usual, it was both kind and sensible.

"The girl will be betrothed at Christmas. She may choose herself, at that time, from among any suitors I approve. I hereby approve both the sons of my father's loyal boyar, Igor. However," the prince had very properly added, "any suitor who cannot come forward with proof that he is free of debts, and has an income of thirty silver grivnas a year, will be disqualified."

Sviatopolk smiled when he heard it. His income was over fifty grivnas: Ivanushka's could not possibly be more than twenty.

Ivanushka said nothing.

It was two days later that Ivanushka, its new lord, rode into the village of Russka.

Spring was everywhere in the air. There was a warm glow coming from the ground. The cherry blossom was already making a first, shy appearance, and, as he rode towards the river crossing, he heard his first bee.

As it happened, Shchek had gone downriver that day. So Ivanushka ordered the elder to give him a thorough inspection of the village. The main income he could expect came from the taxes paid by each household. A third went to the prince; he could keep two-thirds; but there were expenses at the fort that he had to meet. True, if he could afford to hire laborers or buy slaves, he could develop unused land in the area; but that would take time as well as money, and he had neither. Even with luck, he could not see how his income would reach more than twenty grivnas that year.

That damned peasant's probably made a fool of me, he thought, as he returned that afternoon to the fort. And when Shchek appeared a few hours later, he was ready to be angry with him. But the peasant promised him: "We go out at dawn tomorrow." And so he waited one more night.

Then, while the sun was still low in the sky the next morning, Ivanushka discovered the secret treasure of Russka.

All that spring and summer, Ivanushka was busy.

He served Vladimir, as required; but because there was always a slight friction in the air whenever Ivanushka and Sviatopolk were at court together, the prince often let Ivanushka know that he was free to go to Russka to inspect his estates where, it was said at the court, the eccentric young man had even been seen working with the peasants in the field.

In the early summer, Prince Vladimir went west to help the Poles in a campaign against the Czechs, staying some four months in Bohemia, and taking Sviatopolk with him. Reports of his elder brother's valor came back to Ivanushka at Pereiaslav, and although he was proud of Sviatopolk, he could not help being a little sad. "I fear, in the girl's eyes, I must cut a sorry figure beside him," he admitted to his mother.

He saw little of the girl during these months. She spent most of her time with her mistress, who was now pregnant.

But the work at Russka continued apace.

All through the summer, lord and peasant tended the precious honey forest. It consisted now of a thousand trees: one hundred oak and nine hundred pine. There were well over a hundred swarms, and Shchek kept the hives occupied at a rate of roughly one in seven.

He had also built a stout storehouse in Russka for the beeswax.

Shchek now had two men to help him guard the place, for word of it had reached as far as Pereiaslav and, as Shchek assured Ivanushka: "If we don't protect it, people will come and rob it."

Already Ivanushka was sure the forest would easily give him the required income. But what of the girl herself? Would he win her?

For the truth was, he had no idea.

He had managed on various occasions at court to snatch a few words with her; and he thought—no, he was sure from her look—that she liked him. But he had to confess there were many suitors, including Sviatopolk, who were far better matches than he was.

"And you're sure you want her?" Shchek asked curiously. The ways of these nobles often seemed strange to him.

"Oh yes." He was sure.

Why was he sure? He did not know. Was it just her magical appearance? No, it was far more than that. There was a kindness in the sparkling blue eyes; there was something in the way she walked behind the princess, something indefinable, that told him she had suffered. And this was very attractive to him. He thought he could imagine her life: an orphan, left to wander with a dispossessed princess; a proud girl who had nevertheless had to learn the humility that is forced on those who are dependent. In their brief talks he had sensed in her an understanding of life and its difficulties that he had seldom seen in the proud but protected daughters of the boyars.

"Yes, she's the one." He nodded.

The harvest was good that year. The production of honey an outstanding success. Ivanushka's income was assured. In the autumn he managed to speak to the Saxon girl several more times. But as the Christmas season approached, he had no idea where he stood with her.

When the great day came therefore, before Vladimir Monomakh, four suitors appeared for the hand of the Saxon girl. Two were the sons of Igor.

The whole court had been astonished at the good fortune of Ivanushka.

"While his brother fights, the sly young fellow gathers honey," some cruel wit observed.

But the fact was, he had fulfilled the prince's conditions.

Yet more astonishing was the fact that Emma, having politely thanked all four men for the honor they did her, whispered to the prince that she chose Ivanushka.

"As you wish," he replied, but he felt obliged, out of loyalty to Sviatopolk, to add: "His elder brother is one of my best men, you know, whereas they say Ivanushka's a fool."

"I know," she answered. "But," she smiled, "it seems to me he has a warm heart."

So it was that the very next day Ivanushka, the son of Igor, and the daughter of a Saxon English noble, were married.

There was a splendid feast given by Vladimir where they were served roast cockerel; and a merry company then showered them with hops as they retired. And if Sviatopolk had any further designs against his brother, he hid them behind a mask of dignity.

While these small events, of such importance to Ivanushka, were taking place, the attention of everyone else at court was directed towards the political arena.

On December 27, the Prince of Kiev died, and Vsevolod of Pereiaslav himself took over Kiev.

"It's a great move for your father," everyone told Ivanushka. "Igor is a great boyar of the Grand Prince of Kiev now."

For Vladimir Monomakh these events meant that he became master of Pereiaslav in place of his father, so that Sviatopolk and Ivanushka now had a richer master, too. And the joy of the court was completed by the birth to the Saxon princess of a baby son.

Yet for Ivanushka these important events seemed of small significance.

He was married. He had discovered, in the depth of winter, a joy far greater than he had ever known—so much so that at times, as he looked across at the wonderful, pale form at his side, he could scarcely believe that such continuous joy was not stolen. Yet the weeks passed and, far from being taken away from him, this joy was only increased. So it was that at last Ivanushka found not merely happiness, but the sense of wholeness that, sometimes hardly aware of what he was doing, he had so long sought.

"When I was a boy," he told Emma, "I wanted to ride to the great river Don. But now I'd rather be here with you. You are all I want."

She smiled, yet asked him: "Are you sure, Ivanushka? Am I alone, really enough?"

He had stared at her, surprised. Of course she was.

In March she had told him she was pregnant.

"Now, what more could I want?" he asked her playfully.

A few days later he went to Russka.

It was early in the morning, three days after he arrived there, that Ivanushka came out of the fort soon after the sun had risen above the trees, and sat on a bare stone gazing across the landscape to the south.

How silent it was. The sky above was pale blue, so crystalline that one might, it seemed to Ivanushka, have soared unimpeded into the clear air and touched the edge of heaven. The snowy landscape extended as far as the eye could see, the darker lines of the trees stretching until they seemed to become one with the snow of the endless steppe beyond.

The edges of the river had recently begun to melt. Everything was melting. Only a little at a time, softly, so that you could scarcely hear it; yet inexorably. The more one listened, the more one became aware of the faint popping, the whispering of the whole countryside melting.

And as the sun acted upon the snow and ice, so, Ivanushka could almost feel, were underground forces similarly at work. The whole gigantic continent—the world itself as far as he knew—was softly melting, snow, earth and air, an eternal process caught, for a moment, in this shining stasis.

And everything, it suddenly appeared to Ivanushka, everything was necessary. The rich black earth—so rich that the peasants scarcely needed to plow it; the fortress with its stout wooden walls; the subterranean world where the monks like Father Luke had chosen to live, and certainly to die: why it should be so was beyond him, but it was all necessary. And so, I see, was the winding path of my own confused life, he thought. That, too, was necessary. Father Luke had perhaps seen it all, years ago, when he had said that each mortal finds his own way to God.

How soft the world was, how shining. How he loved, not only his wife, but all things. Even myself, unworthy that I am—I can even love myself—because I, too, am part of this Creation, he pondered; this being, he perceived, his Epiphany.

1111

DARK CLOUDS passed silently over the empty land. Slowly the mighty army made its way past the forest's edge, past the lonely wooden walls that joined the line of little forts, staring at the emptiness beyond, and emerged onto the open steppe, where it fanned out. As the spring sun struck through the clouds, in powerful stanchions, it caught sections of the horde so that, here and there, patches of the line dully glittered.

The army spread for about three miles across the steppe. Seen from above, as the clouds temporarily passed away and the afternoon sun fell bleakly upon it, the army looked like the shadow of a vast bird with outstretched wings, moving quietly across the grasses.

On the ground, the huge movement of chain mail and weaponry filled the air with the clinking sound, as though the whole steppe were echoing with a million metallic cicadas.

Sviatopolk's face was dark. Now and then the light fell upon his face and one could see his eyes, hard and clear, upon the horizon. But his mind still dwelt in the shadows.

Though he was in the Prince of Kiev's *druzhina,* he rode alone. Now and then, though no one noticed it, his black eyes turned to glance at his brother, riding some distance away. But each time they did so they flicked quickly away again, as though pursued by fear, or guilt. Guilt makes a proud man dangerous.

It was the year 1111, and one of the greatest expeditions ever mounted was setting off from the land of Rus towards the east. It was led by the Prince of Kiev, with his cousins the Prince of Chernigov and the great Vladimir Monomakh, Prince of Pereiaslav; and its object was to destroy the Cumans.

The huge force had waited only for the start of the warm weather, when the ground was firm. With long swords and scimitars, curved bows and long spears, fur caps and chain mail, they rode and marched. Preceded by gongs and trumpets, wooden pipes and kettledrums, singers, dancers, and priests carrying icons, this huge Eurasian horde made its awesome way from golden Kiev, eastward towards the endless steppe.

Sviatopolk surveyed the men around him. It was a typical Russian army, containing all kinds of men. On his right two young men, both of the *druzhina* and pure Norse—though one had married a Cuman. On his left a German mercenary and a Polish knight. Sviatopolk respected the Poles: they obeyed the Pope in Rome—that was a fault, he supposed—but they were independent and proud. And what fine brocade the fellow wore.

Just behind him marched a large party of Slav foot soldiers. He glanced at them with contempt. Brave fellows, lively, wonderfully obstinate; he did not even know why he despised them, except that it was his habit.

Ahead of him rode seven Alan horsemen. Beside them, a company of Volga Bulgars—strange fellows, distant descendants of the terrible Huns, with oriental faces and black, lanky hair. They were Muslims nowadays, and they had gladly come from their trading stronghold on the Volga to help crush the troublesome pagan raiders of the steppe.

"If I were a Cuman, though, I know whom I should fear the most," he remarked to his page. "The Black Caps."

For a long time the princes of Rus had encouraged settlements of steppe warriors along their southern borders, to act as a buffer against the

Cumans. But this group was special. These Turks had formed their own military cadre; they even had a garrison in Kiev now; they hated the Cumans and they had an iron discipline. They rode with their bows and lances, on black horses, wearing black caps, their faces hard and cruel. Sviatopolk admired their bitterness and their determination. They were strong.

Again he glanced at his brother Ivan, riding with Monomakh.

Ivan was in his fifties now, a little stout and ruddy-faced, but still fit. Why was it, Sviatopolk wondered, that where other men's eyes gave away their lives—looking shifty, cunning, proud, or simply weary— Ivanushka's blue eyes were still as clear and open as they had been when he was young? It wasn't stupidity. For the man they had once called Ivanushka the Fool was now known as Ivan the Wise. And he's rich, too, damn him, Sviatopolk thought. He has all the luck.

They seldom saw each other now. Twenty years before, when the old Prince of Kiev had died and another of the periodic relocations of the princes had taken place, Sviatopolk had left Monomakh and joined the Prince of Kiev. He had thought the pickings would be better. Ivanushka had remained with Monomakh at Pereiaslav.

Now they were together again, in the same army.

And only one of us, he secretly swore, will return alive.

"So at last," Ivanushka had told his sons, "I am to ride to the great river Don." It was strange that only now, in the fifty-seventh year of his life, God had granted this childhood desire. Yet God had given him so much.

The estate at Russka had made him rich. For although Cuman raids had several times destroyed the village, the bee-forest lay undisturbed. And he had other estates, too.

For the land of Rus was still expanding. While the princes traded and fought in the south, they had continued to colonize the huge unchartered regions of the northeast, pushing into the hinterland where the primitive Finnish tribes had always dwelt—into the deep forests by the headwaters of the mighty Volga. The Rus had many settlements there, from substantial cities like Tver, Suzdal, Riazan, and Murom, all the way down to little fortified hamlets, like the village of Moscow.

The Prince of Pereiaslav controlled the part of this region around Rostov and Suzdal, and it was in this hinterland that he had given Ivan a second big estate.

Though the soil was poor compared to the black earth of the south, the forest of the northeast was rich in furs, wax, and honey. Above all, it was far away from the raiders of the southern steppe. "Remember," Ivanushka would say to his three sons, "your ancestors were the radiant Alans who rode the steppe, but our wealth now lies in the forest, which protects us."

God had been good to him; He had also given him a perfect master: Vladimir Monomakh.

How could one fail to love Monomakh? For, by any standards, the half-Greek prince was remarkable. It was not only that he was brave in battle, and daring in the chase; he was also a truly humble Christian. For decades all Monomakh's energies had gone into trying to preserve the unity of the royal house. Time and again he had called together conferences of the feuding princes and begged them, "Let us forgive each other. Let us hold the land together and unite against the Cumans, who would rather see us divided."

"One day," Ivanushka prayed, "his turn will come to rule in Kiev."

Meanwhile, Monomakh's city of Pereiaslav was a fine place now. Twenty years before, its bishop had built a huge stone all around it. The place boasted several more brick churches and even a bathhouse of stone, so that Ivan could say proudly: "There's nothing else like that bathhouse unless you go to Tsargrad."

Two of Ivanushka's three sons served Monomakh; the third served the prince's half-English son, who now ruled over northern Novgorod.

Ivanushka had brought a strong contingent with him. From the village of Russka came a party of Slavs, under old Shchek, who, despite his advancing years, had insisted on coming with his lord. From his estates in the north came a group of bowmen, some mounted, some on foot, from the Finnish tribe of Mordvinians. Quiet, surly fellows with high, Mongoloid cheekbones and yellowish skins, they kept to themselves and in the evenings crowded around their soothsayer, whom they refused to travel without.

Apart from two of his sons, there was one other addition to his party—a handsome young Khazar from Kiev. Ivanushka had not wanted to take him although the boy's father, a longtime trading associate of his, had pleaded for the boy. "He's not trained to arms," he had said sternly. "And besides," he had finally confessed, "I'm terrified of something happening to him."

Only when his grandfather Zhydovyn had gone to see Ivanushka, had he at last agreed to take the boy on.

"Keep the Khazar boy near you," he gruffly ordered his two sons. "And now," he addressed all his men, "we'll smash the Cumans so that they will never recover."

The strife with the Cumans had continued all through his life.

To the south, along the edge of the steppe, the little frontier forts had been strengthened and huge ramparts of earth and wood had been built, so that there was now an almost continuous wall to keep the raiders out. But they still either broke through or made huge sweeps across the steppe, far over the horizon, to circumvent the defenses and come down unexpectedly from the north.

Ten years ago the Rus had launched a massive attack across the steppe that had left twenty Cuman princes dead. Four years later, led by Boniak the Mangy, the Cuman warlords had struck back and even burned churches in Kiev itself. And now the Russians were going down to break them. It was God's work: Ivanushka had no doubt of that.

"We know their usual grazing grounds and their winter camp," he said to his sons. "We're going to hunt them down." Though the business was grim, as he looked about him, at his strong sons and the mighty army of the three princes, he was confident.

But even so, having at last achieved his life's ambition to ride to the

Don, he felt melancholy. He could not help it. The main reason was his father. That at least he understood. The other reason was less clear to him: it was something vague, uneasy. And it was made worse when, on the day they entered the steppe, Monomakh turned to him and quietly remarked: "They say, my Ivanushka, that something is troubling your brother Sviatopolk."

Day after day, southwards and eastwards across the steppe they rode. The grass was green, the ground draining. Across the vast, rolling plateau, for hundreds, thousands of miles, the land was drying out, from the rich steppe to the mountains and the deserts where, even now, the delicate spring flowers were being burned by the sun only to vanish without trace into the sand.

Within days the pale feather grass began breaking out—a white sheen spreading in front of them like an endless mist over the rich black earth hidden below. Horses and men hissed through the grass like myriad snakes; where the grass was short, their feet drummed upon the ground. Birds skimmed anxiously across the feather grass before this huge advancing host. Sometimes an eagle, a blue-gray speck, hung high above the moving mass.

Ivanushka rode quietly on his finest gray: Troyan. At midday the sun overhead grew so bright that, to Ivanushka, it seemed as if the whole army, his horse, the day itself, had grown dark because of it. Steadily they went on.

Monomakh was cheerful. Often he would canter ahead, a favorite falcon on his wrist, and hunt across the steppe. And in the evenings he would sit by his tent with his boyars while a minstrel strummed his lyre and sang to them:

> *Let me die, noble men of Rus,*
> *If I do not dip my sleeve*
> *Of beaver fur,*
> *Or drink from my helmet filled*
> *In the blue river Don.*

> *Let us fly, noble men of Rus—*
> *Faster than the gray wolf,*
> *More swiftly than falcons—*
> *Let the eagles feast on the Cumans' bones*
> *By the great river Don.*

It was after these evenings, when the fires were low, and all but the men on watch were sleeping, that Ivanushka found himself most melancholy. For he was sure he would not see his father again.

He had gone to Kiev to take leave of him and had found him almost helpless. A sudden crisis the year before had left him partly paralyzed: he could smile, faintly, with one side of his mouth, but his speech was very slurred.

"You should not be grieved," his mother told him. "He is to depart soon, and so am I. But see what years God has granted us, and be grateful."

The old man was still handsome. His gray hair was still thick. Like others in that period of better nutrition in Russia, he had kept most of his teeth. Gazing down at his long, noble face, Ivanushka had wondered whether he should go on campaign, but Igor, seeing his thought, had done his best to smile and whispered: "Go, my son."

He had kissed his father, long and warmly, before striding out.

Often now, as he rode across the steppe, with a feeling of tender sadness, his memory returned him to that morning when he was a boy of twelve, as he floated down the great river Dnieper with his father, his mind full of high hopes. Like a physical presence he could feel his father's hand on his shoulder, feel his powerful heart beating behind him, and he wondered: Is he still with me, my father? Is he still alive in Kiev, perhaps remembering that very day, sharing my dream with me, his hand around my shoulders? Or has he gone, into the great cold?

And around the campfire, he remembered his father's forgiveness, and his mother's healing presence.

And then there was Sviatopolk. Though he rode some distance away, with the Prince of Kiev, it was easy to pick him out by the banner carried before him that bore the three-pronged trident. It was not that his face was hard and bitter—it had always been that—but there was a new look in his eyes, a faraway gaze that Ivanushka, having known desperation himself in his youth, recognized at once. And his attitude towards Ivanushka, though always cool, had taken on a new tension which, to those who knew him well, was a sign of danger.

On two occasions Ivanushka had gone up to him: once to ask, "Have I offended you?" The second time, with some misgivings, he had asked, "Is something wrong with you?" But each time Sviatopolk had bowed to him coldly and inquired, with sarcastic politeness, after his health.

Sviatopolk lived well in Kiev. His sons were successful. What, Ivanushka wondered, could it be?

It was when Sviatopolk was asleep that the monsters troubled him.

During his waking hours it was only a question of calculation: even if that always brought the same conclusion. But in his sleep the monsters came.

How had he got into debt? Even now he could hardly believe it had happened.

If they'd let me into the inner circle, he told himself, by now I'd be rich. That was the trouble—he told himself several times a day.

Everyone in Kiev was speculating. Most of the merchants and boyars were. Even the small merchants and artisans did if they could. But the greatest speculator of all was the prince himself.

Salt. That was the key. In the good old days, when his father Igor was in his prime, they brought salt across the steppe in caravans from the Black Sea. But now, with Cumans breaking up the southern trade route, the only places to get salt safely were in the west: from the southwestern province of Galicia, or from the kingdoms of Poland and Hungary. And the plan of the Prince of Kiev was to form a cartel that would get control of all the salt sold in the land of Rus.

This campaign was dearer to the prince's heart than even the crusade against the Cumans. He had prepared the ground for years, marrying one of his daughters to the King of Hungary and another to the King of Poland.

"Nothing will stop him," Sviatopolk often declared. "Then they're going to force up the price and make a fortune." Even now, the beauty of the scheme filled him with a kind of cold joy.

But he was not in the cartel. Though he had served the Prince of Kiev well—and no one ever accused him of failing in his duty—he had never been invited into the inner circle; and as time went on, he knew that his influence was slowly waning. "He's not the man his father was," people said. "Or his brother," they sometimes added. It was his awareness of this last comment that ate into his soul and made him all the more determined to impress the world.

If the prince would not make him rich, he would find other ways.

So had begun the series of bad investments. There was the futile attempt to bring salt from the Black Sea. Who knew what had become of those Khazar merchants and their camels in the southern steppe? He had tried to extract iron from some marshlands he owned. He discovered, after two years of obstinately pushing his men, that the little iron he found cost more to extract than he could sell it for. All his schemes had failed; yet the poorer he became, the greater the state he maintained in Kiev. "I must impress them," he vowed.

He had succeeded in masking his losses. Using his reputation and his father's good name, he had got credit from merchants as far afield as Constantinople. And now that debt had become a mountain, the size of which no one guessed—neither his father, his brother, nor his own children.

And so the monsters came. They came to him in his sleep.

Sometimes his debt came as an eagle—a huge, brownish bird sweeping over the Caucasus Mountains, flying swiftly over the bones of his camels in the steppe, soaring over the forest in search of him until at last, with talons outstretched, its huge wings filling the sky, the furious bird swooped and he awoke with a cry.

Another night, searching in the forest, he came upon a girl, lying naked upon the ground. Coming up to her, he saw to his excitement that she was the most beautiful creature in the world—even lovelier than the Saxon girl his brother had taken from him. But as he reached down to touch her, she had turned to solid gold.

With even more joy, he lifted her and carried her on his horse until, coming to a small hut in the forest, he decided to rest.

It was empty. He carried her in and laid her on the table by the stove. "I'll carry you to Kiev and melt you down," he muttered, and turned round to look for water. But when he turned back the golden girl was gone.

And in her place, sitting on the table, with a leering grin on her wrinkled face, was Baba Yaga the witch.

He felt himself go pale and cold. Her hands reached out to him.

"Let me go!" he shrieked.

But Baba Yaga only laughed, with a cackle drier than the sound of cracking nuts. The room had filled with the acrid, stale smell of rotting mushrooms, and she replied: "Pay me your debt."

Then, turning to the stove and opening the oven door, her long, bony hand had grabbed him and drawn him, slowly, towards the flames, while he wailed, like a frightened child, in his sleep.

But the worst dream was the third. This was the one that haunted him. It began, always, inside a building, though whether it was a church, a barn, or a prince's hall he could never be sure, since it was dark. He would be trying to find a way out, searching for some sign of a window or door in the cavernous gloom. But as far as he looked, it always seemed that the high, empty spaces stretched away without end.

And then, before long, he would hear it coming.

Its heavy footsteps crashed upon the iron floor with a terrible reverberation that echoed in the distant roof above. If he turned and fled, he would find that the awful footsteps were suddenly coming from the direction in which he was running.

And he knew that this fearful creature was his debt. It would come closer. There was no escape.

Then he would see it. The creature was as high as a house, and as broad. It was dressed in a long dark habit, like a monk, so that its feet, which were surely made of iron, could not be seen. But far more frightening than this was its face: for the creature had none. It had only a huge, gray beard where the face should have been: no eyes, no mouth. It was deaf and sightless. Yet it always knew, infallibly, exactly where he was, and as it slowly, blindly crashed forward, he would fall helplessly onto the iron floor, unable to move his legs, and awake in a cold sweat and with a scream of terror.

There is only one way out, he told himself.

The will of his father Igor was a simple one. In line with the princely practice of inheritance, the boyar's did not concern itself with grandchildren, but only with sons.

The wealth remaining to Igor, which was now substantial, was to be divided equally between his surviving sons, who were to take care of their mother as long as she lived. That was all. If one of the two remaining sons died before the will was executed, then the other son would inherit both shares. It was a typical will for those times.

Sviatopolk knew roughly what Igor's estate was worth. Half of it would not pay his debts. All of it would leave him a modest income over.

Shchek was uneasy. He could not say exactly why.

That afternoon the scouts had returned with good news. They had found the Cumans' winter quarters. The main Cuman horde had already gone out to its summer pastures, where it would dwell in tents. The permanent winter quarters—a walled town—lay before them. "The place is half empty," the scouts reported. "There's only a small garrison."

"We shall attack tomorrow," the princes announced.

All through the camp there were happy faces. It seemed an eternity since the empty steppe had closed behind them; and now, at last, they would take a Cuman town. With luck, the looting would be excellent. In the warm night under the stars, the sound of quiet singing could be heard around every fire.

Yet Shchek was uneasy. Perhaps it was just the battle ahead; but he had had evil dreams; and as night fell on the happy camp he drew the Khazar boy aside. "Stick close to the lord Ivan," he said. "Guard him well."

"Tonight, you mean?"

Shchek frowned. What did he mean? There were a few trees nearby and some clumps of tall grasses; he watched them waving in the slight breeze. Were there Cumans lurking in there? "Yes. Tonight, tomorrow, every night."

Was this half-empty town perhaps a trap, a lure? He did not trust the Cumans: he hated them. Four years before, they had killed his little wife and one of his four children. They had been killed for sport. It was another reason he had begged his lord Ivan to take him along.

What is it you fear? he asked himself again. He did not know. But he was certain he felt it, a pervading sense of danger, something treacherous in the air.

The battle did not last long. The town was a large, rectangular enclosure with low walls of baked earth and clay. The army drawn up before it must have been a fearsome sight. The Cumans appeared on the walls and fought well; but they were horribly mauled by the volley after volley of arrows that poured from the men of Rus. By midafternoon, though they had scarcely lost any men, the Russians saw the gates open and a parley party coming out, bearing gifts of wine and fish.

The city had been partly emptied; but even so, in the low rows of clay and wooden houses, they found quantities of fine silks from the Orient, gold and gems, and wine from the Black Sea coast and the Caucasus Mountains. They feasted that evening, both inside the city and in their camp, which they pitched before its walls.

It was just as the sun was sinking that Ivanushka, together with Shchek and the Khazar boy rode away from their camp, by a little stream and made their way slowly around the city. The boyar was riding Troyan; the Khazar also had a fine, black horse; Shchek a more modest beast.

It was by the cemetery of the Cumans, on the far side of the city, that Ivanushka paused.

The graves of the Cuman warriors were marked with strange stones: they were four, even six feet high, and carved in the shape of men—with round faces, high cheekbones, short necks, broad mouths, flowing moustaches, and thin, basin-shaped helmets on their heads. Their almond eyes mostly seemed to be closed. Their bodies were distorted, with wide hips and shortened legs; and their arms, unnaturally long, were bent at the elbows so that their hands were clasped either at their midriff or between their legs.

Though unnatural in shape, these thick, stone figures had an extraordinary life to them, as if they had been temporarily frozen, dreaming while they rode upon some endless journey across the steppe.

Ivanushka turned to the young Khazar. "They are dead. Do you fear death?"

The young man visibly braced himself. "No, lord."

Ivanushka smiled. "And you, Shchek?"

"Not much. Not these days," the widower said glumly.

Ivanushka sighed but said nothing. Yet silently, to himself, he admitted: I fear death.

Then they rode on.

It was the dead of night. There was a quarter moon in the sky, but it had not risen very high and it was frequently obscured by the long, ragged clouds that passed from time to time. A light breeze stirred the reeds that fringed the little stream. Apart from that there was silence over the steppe. The whole camp appeared asleep.

The three Cuman figures made almost no sound at all, as they waded carefully through the shallow stream. Now and then a light splash or the noise of drops falling from an arm onto the water's surface might have been heard. But the bank of reeds muffled these sounds. They carried swords and daggers. Their faces were blackened.

When they reached the place where they meant to climb the little bank, they paused for some time. Then, very slowly, parting the reeds less than the breeze might have done, they slipped through them and out onto the bank. And they might have given no sign of their coming had not one of them, whose expertise was widely acknowledged, foolishly made an answering call to a frog.

Shchek froze. He had been only half asleep. Immediately his heart began to race. There was no animal in forest or steppe whose call he did not know. Even the most perfect animal call from a human was immediately recognizable to him. He sat up and stared towards the reeds, straining his eyes in the darkness.

They watched him. One of the three, the leader, was already on his belly some twenty feet across the grass, and only a dozen paces from where Shchek sat.

Shchek got up. He touched the Khazar boy lightly, to wake him, then, taking a spear in one hand and a long knife in the other, he started to creep cautiously towards the reeds. The Khazar boy wanted to go, too, but Shchek impatiently waved him back. "Stay with Lord Ivan," he whispered.

It was this sound that woke the boyar.

Ivanushka saw the peasant creeping towards the reeds. He started up. And his mind, too, worked quickly.

"Shchek, come back," he hissed. He reached for his sword. But Shchek was already a dozen paces away, intent upon his task.

He never saw the Cuman at his feet. He was aware, only, of a blinding, searing pain in his stomach, as though a huge serpent had suddenly reared up and buried its fangs just under his heart.

He gave a loud cry, and he observed to his surprise that his arms had suddenly become quite useless, while the stars were unaccountably falling from the sky, taking him with them to the earth. Then redness. Then, strangely, a great cold whiteness, shining, like the morning mists.

The other two Cumans had rushed forward while the first, having struck Shchek, had leapt like a gray wolf towards Ivan and the Khazar boy.

The boy struck at him, but the Cuman easily sidestepped him and swung at Ivanushka with a curved sword. Ivanushka parried. The Cuman moved swiftly in a circle around him, cutting cleverly at his legs.

The Khazar boy shouted. His voice echoed round the camp. One of the Cumans swung his sword and, by good fortune, the boy managed to parry. He shouted again.

And to his surprise, the Cuman hesitated.

He struck at him wildly, felt his blade just graze his shoulder, struck again. But the fellow was gone. At the sound of other voices around, he and his companion were running lightly back to the reeds.

He turned. By the moonlight, he could see Ivanushka and the first Cuman locked in combat. It was impossible to see who had the upper hand.

At last, he thought, I can prove myself. And, gripping his sword tightly, he rushed at the assailant.

And then, to his amazement, this one, too, turned and started to run.

He hurled himself at him, caught his sleeve, and as the man staggered, reached for his legs.

Only to find himself in a viselike bear hug, from behind, as the Cuman made his escape.

How strange. The arms holding him were the lord Ivan's.

"I had him, lord," he protested. "I had him. Let's go after them," he pleaded.

"In the dark, like this?" Ivan still held him. "You'd get your throat cut. Let them run. You can kill Cumans tomorrow."

The boy was silent. He supposed Lord Ivan was right. The arms slowly released him. "What cowards these Cumans are," he muttered.

"Perhaps," Ivanushka said drily. He turned. "They've killed my poor Shchek, though," he added mournfully.

It was true. The boy looked at the sturdy old peasant, who now lay still, his blood making a black patch on the moonlit grass.

But neither then, nor later, could he understand why Ivan had let the last Cuman go. Nor did Ivan ever tell him who his attacker was.

They found the main Cuman force a few days later. They were drawn up beside a river. Ivanushka and Vladimir ran their eyes along the huge, dark, menacing line. They had drawn themselves up well, on a slight slope that favored them. To the right their carts and light chariots were set in two enormous circles into which they could, if necessary, retreat.

It was the biggest force that Ivanushka had ever seen—line after line of mounted men in leather or light armor with lances and bows, who could charge, wheel, or fly across the steppe like so many falcons.

"I can count more than twenty princes there," Vladimir remarked. He knew the Cumans well.

"And Boniak?" Boniak the Mangy, the most terrible, the most ruthless of them all.

"Oh yes," said Monomakh cheerfully, "he's there."

The two armies faced each other in silence.

It was then that Ivanushka noticed something. It happened gradually, softly, so that even the sharp-eyed Monomakh did not at first perceive it.

The wind was changing direction.

He reached out, touched the great prince on the arm, and nodded at the swaying grasses. "Look."

Monomakh looked. "Praise God." The wind would carry their arrows towards the enemy. God meant them to punish the pagans.

The battle that took place that day lived in the memories of the men of Rus.

"Our arrows floated on the wind," Ivanushka told Emma afterwards. "They sailed like swallows." The slaughter was terrible: for Monomakh, though generous in peace, was terrible in war. His contempt for Cumans, whom he often accused of breaking their oaths, was complete. No Cuman who came within his reach could hope for the slightest mercy. "They tried all their tricks," Ivanushka said of that day. "They even pretended to run away. But we stayed put, until we could trap them against the river." The victory was total.

But there was one event that Ivanushka never spoke of. It took place a little before the end of the battle and was seen by nobody.

He had scarcely thought of his brother during the battle; there was no time. But suddenly, glancing to his left, he saw a single Russian boyar surrounded by three Cumans, who were hacking at him with their curved swords, and he instantly knew it was Sviatopolk.

He did not trouble to think; he spurred away from his sons towards him. They had backed him against the river so that his horse's hind legs were already digging feverishly in the crumbling earth of the bank. As they closed, he valiantly lunged forward, knocking one of the Cumans from his horse. Then, as one of the attackers slashed at its nose, Sviatopolk's horse reared and he fell, over the steep bank into the swirling river some ten feet below.

Ivanushka caught one of the Cumans from behind, killing him with a single blow; the other fled. But by the time he looked down into the river, Sviatopolk was already several yards out into the stream. The water was moving fast. Half stunned for a moment, Sviatopolk was struggling now to reach the bank, but his chain mail was dragging him down. He looked up, hopelessly, at the bank above, then, seeing his brother, turned away his head. Then he sank.

For a moment, Ivanushka hesitated. The water was deep. Sviatopolk had vanished. If he went in, his chain mail would probably drag him under, too. The words of the Old Testament story suddenly flashed through his mind. "Am I," he murmured, "my brother's keeper?" And for the first time in many years, as he gazed at the water, he knew fear.

Am I to give up my life for the brother who tried to kill me? he asked himself. He looked around. The battle had moved away towards the wagons. It was strangely quiet there. Then he took off his helmet and dived in.

No one else ever knew how close he came to death that day.

As the cold waters closed over his head, he felt himself being dragged down by two forces—the strong river current and the weight of his mail. It took all his strength to fight his way to the surface, to gasp for air and dive again.

But he found Sviatopolk. His face was already gray; he was tangled in some river reeds that seemed to wrap themselves around him like insistent, importunate *rusalki*. How Ivanushka got him free, he hardly knew; but somehow he did, and drifted with him down the stream until he could pull him to the riverbank. There, turning him over, he forced the water from his lungs.

Together the two brothers lay, exhausted, on the riverbank. For several minutes neither spoke. The sun was high in the sky. Birds were flitting, curiously, over the long grass around them. The sound of the battle had entirely died away.

"Why did you save me?"

"You are my brother."

There was a pause. Ivanushka could feel Sviatopolk preparing himself for the next question. "But . . . last night. You knew?"

"I knew."

Sviatopolk groaned. "And now I must bear the burden of your forgiveness, too." It was said without rancor. Sviatopolk sounded infinitely weary.

"You forget," Ivanushka calmly reminded him, "that I, too, sinned. Perhaps more than you, when I was wandering and I stole. I returned with nothing, yet our father forgave me and took me in. Tell me now, my brother, what it is that drove you to such a thing?"

It seemed to Sviatopolk that he could hate no longer. For hatred, feeding upon him year after year, driving him forward like a cruel rider pushing his horse, hatred and misery had finally worn him out. Slowly, a few words at a time, staring straight up at the blue sky, he told his brother the whole story.

"You had only to ask me for help," Ivanushka reminded him gently.

"But what man can ask?"

"You are too proud," Ivanushka said with a smile.

"It has brought me despair, and death," his brother sighed.

"The preachers tell us it does," Ivanushka replied drily.

And that summer, having at last visited the great river Don, he paid his brother's debts.

They had returned in triumph. Yet in the long warm days of autumn, that very year, the sage counselor of great Monomakh, for the first time in many years, gave all Rus the chance to say: "Ivan's a fool."

He decided to build a church.

That would have been normal enough, for a rich boyar. But he decided to build it in stone. Even that, if extravagant, might have been thought handsome had he decided to build it in Pereiaslav, or even perhaps in the fort of Russka.

But he did not. He decided to build it outside the fortress walls, on a little rise looking over the river towards the village on the eastern side.

"And since I see now that, without help, all men are lost," he declared, "I shall dedicate it to the Mother of God when She begs God to forgive the sins of the world."

So began the construction of his little church, which was dedicated to the Virgin of the Intercession.

It was a modest building.

It had four walls made of brick, stone, and rubble that formed, near enough, a cube. Over the center of the cube was a small, squat octagonal drum, and this was topped with a shallow dome—only a little deeper in shape than an upturned saucer—with a little rim of roof around it. That was all: it was just a cube with a hole in the top.

Had one looked down from the sky at this little building before the roof was on, one could have seen that it contained four pillars, making a smaller square in the middle, and thus dividing the interior into nine equal squares. The drum and dome rested on the four pillars in the middle.

Within the church, however, this simple arrangement of nine squares could be seen another way. It appeared as three sections, dividing the church laterally. First, as one came in from the western end, came the introduction—a sort of vestibule. Then one passed into the second, central section, under the dome. This was the heart of the church, where the congregation stood and worshiped. Lastly, at the east end, came the sanctuary, with the altar in the middle. Upon the altar stood the cross and seven-branched candelabra, rather like a Jewish menorah; and to the left stood the oblation table on which the bread and wine were prepared for the liturgy.

To relieve the harshness of this design and add a sense of direction to his building, there were three little semicircular apses on the eastern end.

The roof was made with sets of simple barrel vaults, resting on the walls and central pillars, and open in the center where the cylinder and dome rose. There were long, narrow windows in the walls and small windows in the octagonal drum under the dome.

This was the standard Byzantine church. All the great churches and cathedrals of the Orthodox Church, like Saint Sophia in Kiev, with their many arcades of pillars and their multiple domes, were only elaborations of this simple arrangement.

There was one technical problem to solve. This was how to support the octagonal drum over the square formed by the four central pillars.

Though much brick building could be easily enough accomplished by the skilled wood-builders of Rus, this particular problem was of a different nature. There were two chief solutions, both from the East: the

Persian squinch, a kind of fan vaulting; or the one the Russians usually preferred, the pendentive, which had originated eight centuries before in Syria.

This was simply a spandrel—as though one had cut a V shape, or triangle on the inside of a sphere. Curving out from the supporting pillar, the top of this V could support a circle or octagon above.

As simple as it was elegant, this arrangement allowed the dome above to seem to float, weightless as the sky, over the congregation.

On the outside of the church, Ivanushka copied the great churches in Kiev, alternating brick and stone, joined by thick layers of mortar mixed with brick dust so that the whole building had a soft, pinkish glow.

At the outer edges of the three curved roofs, with their barrel vaults, he added a little jutting overlap so that the roofline's triple wave, like a triple eyebrow, was pleasantly accentuated.

Such was the little Russian–Byzantine church the eccentric boyar built. It was very small. There was only room for a small congregation. Indeed, had the inhabitants of the village been Christian, the place would have been full to overflowing. Work was begun in the autumn of 1111 and, pushed ahead vigorously by Ivanushka, it proceeded through the following year.

1113

THE FIRST Russian revolution—that is to say, the first organized uprising, by the people, against an exploiting mercantile class—took place in the year 1113. And it was successful.

The grievances of the people were entirely justified and were caused by an unpleasant mixture of what amounted to laissez-faire capitalism, widespread corruption, and cartels—in all of which the ruling princes were involved.

The general speculation that had drawn Sviatopolk into debt had continued and got worse. It was led by the Prince of Kiev himself who, with increasing age, had grown not wiser but lazier and more rapacious.

There was corruption everywhere. Debt, often at crippling interest rates, was positively encouraged. Small artisans and *smerdy,* in considerable numbers, had been thus forced into becoming *zakupy.* It was, after all, a very cheap form of labor for the creditor. And if, on distant estates, the friends of the prince ignored the laws concerning the *zakup* and actually sold him as a slave, the prince turned a blind eye. Because of these widespread abuses, the people were furious.

But worst of all were the cartels: They were organized by the great merchants. Their object was simple—to obtain monopolies on basic commodities and raise their basic prices. And the greatest of all was the salt cartel.

The Prince of Kiev had been successful. His plan for controlling the Polish supply had been effective and prices had soared.

"Are we to welcome visitors with bread alone?" his people demanded ironically. For every Slav, since time began, welcomed a stranger at his door with bread and salt.

But the Prince of Kiev was corrupt and cynical. The abuses continued. And then, on April 16, 1113, he died.

The next day an almost unheard-of event occurred.

Years before, after the troubles of 1068, the Prince of Kiev had moved the meeting place of the *veche* from the *podol* to the square by the palace, where he could keep an eye on it. Nor did the *veche* meet unless summoned by the Metropolitan of the Church or by the boyars. But these safeguards did nothing for the ruling powers now. Without consulting anyone, the *veche* of the people met of its own accord. And their meeting was both stormy and determined.

"They make slaves of free men!" they rightly protested. "They conspire to ruin the people," they said of the cartels.

"Let us return," many demanded, "to the laws of Yaroslav." Although in fact the *Russkaya Pravda*—the Russian Law—which had been collated by Yaroslav the Wise and his sons, was chiefly concerned with the payments due for harming the prince's servants and boyars, it did contain a provision protecting the *zakup* from being made into a slave.

"Let us return," they cried, "to another just prince who will maintain the law."

There was only one such man in the land of Rus; and so it was that the *veche* of Kiev, in the year 1113, offered the throne of Kiev to Vladimir Monomakh.

"Praise the Lord!"

It seemed to Ivanushka that at last there would be order in the land of Rus. He had been in Pereiaslav when the news of the Prince of Kiev's death had come, and without even waiting to summon his sons from the estates, he had ridden hard to the capital.

He had long been disgusted by the old prince's rule. At Russka, and on his estates in the northeast, things were well run and the laws were obeyed. But he knew this was an exception. For the reigning prince's brothers he had no great regard; and it was good judgment as well as personal loyalty, he believed, that made him declare: "Only Monomakh can put things right."

With admirable good sense, he discovered on his arrival in Kiev, the people's *veche* had decided the same thing.

Before even going to his brother's house, he sent one of his grooms with all speed to Monomakh with the message: "Ivan Igorevich awaits you in Kiev. Come, take what the *veche* rightly offers you."

So he was saddened, as he strode into their childhood home, to find his older brother in a gloomy mood, shaking his head.

"It can't work," Sviatopolk told him.

Since the campaign against the Cumans they had developed a quiet relationship that suited them both. They were not friends, but Sviatopolk's hatred, having smoldered all his life, had burned itself out. He felt old and tired. Thanks to Ivanushka, he was well provided for. He lived entirely alone. His sons were serving in other cities, but he preferred to remain in Kiev, enjoying the respect due to him as a boyar and a reputation—alas undeserved—as a successful man of affairs. In general, on most subjects, he was pessimistic. "And I tell you," he reiterated, "Monomakh cannot become Grand Prince."

Two days later, it appeared, he was right. For word arrived in Kiev that Monomakh had refused.

In a way, he had no option. By the rules of succession he was not the next in line—there were senior branches of the family who should precede him. And had he not, all his life, strove so that the orderly succession should be preserved and peace kept? Why should he throw away his principles now, especially at the bidding of the lower classes whom, as a prince, he knew must be kept in their place? He did not come.

And then the revolution started.

Ivanushka had gone riding in the woods that fateful morning, across to the Monastery of the Caves and back. He had no idea that anything was amiss until, coming in sight of the *podol,* he suddenly saw a dozen columns of smoke starting to rise over the city. He spurred forward. A few moments later he met a merchant in a cart. The fellow was sweating profusely and whipping his horses along for all he was worth.

"What are they doing?" he cried.

"Killing us, lord," the man shouted. "Merchants and nobles alike. Turn back, sir," he added. "Only a fool would go in there."

Ivanushka smiled grimly to himself and rode forward. He passed into the *podol.* The streets were full of people, running to and fro. The uprising looked spontaneous and seemed to be universal. Some of the small traders were boarding up their houses, while others were forming into armed groups in the street. Several times he had difficulty getting through.

In one small street, he came face to face with a group of twenty or so.

"Look," one of them shouted, "a *muzh*—a nobleman." And they rushed at him with such fury that he only just managed to get away.

The crowds were surging towards the center. Already he could see flames coming from the citadel of Yaroslav. And a single thought formed in his mind: I must go and save Sviatopolk.

It was as he came towards the Khazar gate that he saw something that made him go cold and for a moment drove even thoughts of his brother from his mind.

The crowd numbered at least two hundred. They had entirely surrounded the house. And whereas the people he had seen so far looked either angry or excited, the faces of these rioters had taken on a cruel aspect. A number of them were grinning with obvious pleasure at the punishment they were about to inflict.

The house belonged to old Zhydovyn the Khazar.

An expectant murmur rose from the crowd.

"Roast them a little," he heard a voice cry.

There was a chorus of approval.

"Roast pig belongs on a spit," a large man shouted jovially.

Some of them, Ivanushka noticed, carried flaming torches. They were already preparing to set light to one side of the house; but it was obvious from their faces that their desire was not so much to burn it down as to smoke the inmates out.

"Villains," a man cried.

"Jews!" shouted an old woman.

And at once, several more in the crowd took up the cry. "Come out, Jews, and be killed."

Ivanushka understood very well. The fact that many of the Jewish Khazar merchants were poor; the more significant fact still, that nearly all the leaders of the exploiting cartels had been Slavic or Scandinavian Christians; both these truths had been temporarily forgotten. In the heat of the moment, the angry crowd, looking for objects to attack, had remembered that some of the capitalists were foreign. They were Jewish. There was now a grand excuse for acts of cruelty.

It was just then, scanning the house, that Ivanushka saw a single face at a window.

It was Zhydovyn. He was looking out gloomily, unable to guess what he should do.

One of the men had pushed his way to the front. He was carrying a long, thin pike. "Show us your men," he shouted.

"There are no Jewish men," someone replied. And there was a general laugh.

In fact, as far as Ivanushka could tell, old Zhydovyn was probably alone in there except for some servants.

"Show us your women, then!" the man bellowed, to a general guffaw.

Ivanushka braced himself and started to push his horse forward, through the crowd. People began to turn. There were cries of anger.

"What's this?"

"A damned noble!"

"Another exploiter."

"Pull him down!"

He felt hands grabbing at his feet; a spear was thrust up at him, only just missing his face. He wanted to strike at them with his whip but knew that if he made the slightest angry movement he was lost. Slowly, imperturbably, he coaxed his horse forward, gently nudging his way through the parting crowd to the front. Then he turned.

Ivanushka looked at the crowd; and they stared at him.

And to his surprise, he experienced a new kind of fear.

He had never faced an angry crowd before. He had faced the Cuman horde; he had several times looked at death. But he had never faced a wall of hatred. It was terrifying. Worse than that, he suddenly felt numb. The crowd's hate came at him like a single, unstoppable force. He felt naked, fearful, and, strangely, ashamed. Yet why should he feel ashamed? There was no cause for it. True, he was a noble; but he knew very well that he had done these people no harm. Why should their rage make him feel guilty? The force of their united hate was like a blow to the stomach.

Then the crowd fell silent.

Ivanushka gripped the reins and gently patted his horse's neck, lest he, too, take fright. How strange, he thought, to have survived the Cumans only to be killed by a mob.

The man with the pike was pointing at him. Like most of the others, he wore a dirty linen smock with a leather belt; his face was almost wholly covered with a black beard and his hair fell to his shoulders.

"Well, noble, tell us what you want before you die," he called out.

Ivanushka tried to meet his angry eyes calmly.

"I am Ivan Igorevich," he replied in a loud, firm voice, "I serve Vladimir Monomakh, whom you seek. And I have sent him a messenger, in my name and in yours, begging him to make haste and come to the *veche* in Kiev."

There was a faint hum in the crowd. They were clearly uncertain whether to believe him. The man with the pike narrowed his eyes. It seemed to Ivanushka he was about to thrust the pike at him. Then, from somewhere, a voice came: "It's true. I've seen him. He's Monomakh's man."

The man with the pike turned around to the speaker, then back to him. It seemed to Ivanushka that there was a trace of disappointment on his face.

But now, like a tide receding, he felt the wave of hatred from the crowd drawing back. "Welcome, Monomakh's man," the fellow with the pike said grimly. "What are these Jews to you?"

"They are under my protection. And Monomakh's," Ivanushka added. "These ones have done no harm."

The fellow shrugged.

"Perhaps." Then, suddenly, seeing that this was the moment to strengthen his temporary street-leadership, he turned around upon the crowd and bellowed: "For Monomakh! Let's find some more Jews to kill."

And within moments, he had led them away.

Ivanushka went in. He found the old Khazar alone except for two women servants. He stayed with him until late afternoon, when the city was quieter. Only then did he proceed to his brother's house.

It was as he had feared. They had reached the tall wooden house in midafternoon. As far as he could judge, Sviatopolk had made no attempt to run. Supposing the boyar to be far more successful than he was, the furious crowd had killed him, ransacked the house, and burned it down.

Ivanushka found the charred remains of his brother's body, said a prayer, and then, in the failing light, returned to seek shelter as he had so many years before at the Khazar's house.

How strange it was, after so many years, to find himself in that house again, sitting alone in the candlelight with old Zhydovyn.

Zhydovyn had recovered from the attack now. And Ivanushka, though saddened by Sviatopolk's death, found that he did not feel unduly melancholy.

They ate together quietly, saying little; but he could see that the old man, still brooding about what had happened that day, was longing to say something. And so it did not surprise him when, at the end of the meal, the old man suddenly remarked sharply, "Of course, none of this would have happened if the country was properly governed."

"What do you mean?" he asked respectfully.

"Your princes of Rus," the Khazar replied scornfully, "those fools. None of them knows how to organize an empire. They have no proper laws, no system."

"We have laws."

Zhydovyn shrugged.

"Rudimentary laws of the Slavs and Norsemen. Your church laws are better, I admit. But they are Greek and Roman, from Constantinople. Yet who runs your administration, such as it is? Khazars and Greeks half the time. Why are your people revolting now? Because your princes either break the law or don't enforce it—or just have no laws to prevent them from oppressing the people."

"It is true we have been badly ruled."

"Because you have no system within which to work. Your princes fight among each other all the time, weakening the state, because they can't devise a workable system of succession."

"But, Zhydovyn," he protested, "is it not true that the succession of brother by brother is derived not from the Varangian norsemen, but from the Turks? Did we not take this, too, from you Khazars?"

"Perhaps. But your rulers of Rus are incapable of order. You can't deny it. The royal house is in chaos."

He looked at him fondly. What the old man said was true. Yet he was not convinced.

For despite his disgust at the people that day, with their foolish, anti-Jewish rallying cries, he could not help thinking, How wrong they are, these Jews. How far behind us, with their endless trust in laws and systems. He sighed, then said aloud, "The law is not everything, you know."

Zhydovyn gazed at him. "It's all we have," he replied bluntly.

He shook his head. How could he explain? That was not the way to think.

No. There was a better way. A Christian way.

He could not, perhaps, find the words himself; but that did not matter.

For were they not already said, better than he could hope to express them, in the most famous sermon ever given in the Russian Church?

It had been preached just before his birth, yet so well recorded that he had learned sections of it as a child. The sermon had been given by the great Slav churchman, Hilarion, in memory of Saint Vladimir. He had called it "On Law and Grace." And its message was very simple. The Jews had given mankind God's law. But then had come the Son of God, with a greater truth—the rule of Grace, of God's direct love, which is greater than rules and regulations. This was the wonderful message which the new Church of the Slavs would demonstrate to the vast world of forest and steppe.

How could he tell old Zhydovyn this? He could not. The Jews would never accept it.

Yet had not his own journey through life been a pilgrimage in search of Grace? Had he not—Ivanushka the Fool—discovered God's love without a textbook of laws?

Ivanushka had no wish for the Jew's world of systems. It was not in his nature. The solution, with God's grace, must surely be something simpler.

"All we need," he told him, "is a wise and godly man, a true prince, a strong ruler."

It was a medieval phantom that was to be the curse of most of Russian history.

"Thank God," he went on, "that we have Monomakh."

It was a few days later that, by the grace of God, the princes bowed to the *veche,* and that, thanks to a revolution, there began the rule of one of the greatest monarchs Russia ever had: Vladimir Monomakh.

Ivanushka's joy was even further increased when, that very autumn, the little church at Russka, with what seemed like miraculous speed, was completed.

He would often make the journey down to the village, staying days at a time, pretending to inspect the estate but in fact just enjoying the astonishing peace of the place.

Above all, at the end of the day, he liked to look at this little master-piece. How gently it glowed in the evening light, its pink surface warmed by the departing rays of the sun.

He would sit, contentedly, gazing at the brave little building on its platform of grass above the river, with the dark woods behind, as the sun slowly went down.

Was there a threat of menace, a sense of melancholy over the golden Byzantine dome as it caught the last flashes of light at sunset? No. He had faith. Nothing, it seemed to him, would now disturb the tranquillity of the little house of God, before the forest and above the river.

All nature seemed at peace in the vast Russian silence.

And how strange it was, he sometimes thought, that when he stood on the bank by the church and gazed out at the vast sky over the endless steppe, the sky itself, no matter which way the clouds were passing, seemed, like a great river, to be motionless yet retreating, always retreating.

And often, even on summer days, a slight wind from the east came softly over the land.

THREE

The Tatar

1237   December

THE HORSEMAN's broad Mongolian face was weather-beaten to an ocher brown.

His beard and mustache were thin, rather stringy, and black.

Since it was winter he was covered with thick furs, although hidden underneath were underclothes of the finest Chinese silk. He wore felt socks and, over them, heavy leather boots. On his head was a fur cap.

He was, in fact, twenty-five; but wind and weather, war and the hard living on the open steppe had made his age seem indeterminate.

Tied to his belt was a leather drinking pouch containing the fermented mare's milk—kumiss—that his people loved. Attached to his saddle was another pouch, containing dried meat. For, as a Mongol warrior, he always traveled with all the essentials that he needed.

These also included his wife: together with a baby child, she rode with the huge camel train that carried the baggage behind.

There was only one physical characteristic that distinguished this warrior from other men. Four years before, a spear had just missed his left eye but made a gash from his high cheekbone, across the side of his head, and taken off his ear, leaving only a jagged stump. "I was lucky," he had remarked, and thought little more about it.

His name was Mengu.

Slowly the vast army rode across the frozen steppe. As usual, it was drawn up in five large contingents of roughly equal size: two—a vanguard and a rearguard—on each wing; and a single division in the center.

Mengu was on the right wing. Behind him rode the hundred men he led. They were light horsemen, each carrying two quivers and two bows, with which they could shoot at the gallop. The bows were fearsome—very large, composite, with a pull of over one hundred and sixty pounds—more powerful, that is, than the famous English longbow. They had a destructive range of up to three hundred yards. Like all his men, Mengu had first learned to draw a bow when he was three.

To his left moved a party of heavy cavalry, who carried sabers and lances, a battle-axe or mace, according to preference, and a lasso.

Mengu himself rode a coal-black horse, which at once marked him out as belonging to the black brigade of the elite imperial guard. With the great herd of spare horses behind went his four remounts, all black.

He was glad his wife and his firstborn son were with him. He wanted them to see his triumph. For this was his first command.

The Mongol army, and the empire that grew from it, was modeled on the decimal system. The lowest command was ten men. Then a hundred. The senior men commanded a thousand and the generals led the myriads, the ten thousands. Mengu commanded a hundred. "But by the end of the campaign," he promised his wife, "I'll have a thousand." And by the time the rest of the western lands were conquered, the lands that merchants had told him stretched to the end of the plain, he might even lead a myriad, a ten thousand.

Promotion: how he desired it. But one had to be careful.

For although all men were equal in the service of the Great Khan, and promotion was on merit, the most important things were judgment and tact. The old proverb of the Asian steppe said it all: "If you know too much they'll hang you, and if you're too modest, they'll walk all over you."

It also helped to belong to a successful clan. And I am, he mused, using the Mongol phrase, of the same bone as two generals already. That had helped him get into the imperial guard.

There was another factor, however, that he thought might advance him even more.

In the beauty contests regularly held by the Great Khan, to which all the prominent Mongols sent their daughters, his sister had been singled out. "A moonlike girl," the Great Khan himself had remarked: this was a term of high praise. She had been allotted, as a senior concubine, to Batu Khan himself. Several times he had seen her by the khan's tent.

She will find a way to bring me to his notice, he thought confidently. And his hard, impassive face looked towards the horizon with satisfaction.

Soon, Mengu knew, they would reach the edge of the forest.

In the twelve-year animal calendar of the Mongols, there were two years to go until the year of the rat. By the end of that year the land of Rus would be conquered. This he knew as certainly as that the sun would rise and the stars shine.

For the Mongols were going to conquer the world.

It was Genghis Khan who had told them so. Genghis Khan, by birth the leader of a noble clan, who in 1206—only thirty years before—had united all the Mongol clans under him and taken, from the ancient Turkish empires of the Asian plain, the title of kagan, or khan.

Others before had born this title; but none had ever built an empire as the Mongols were to do.

Genghis: also called the dalai—the all-powerful.

From their homeland in the pasturelands above the Gobi Desert, these warriors born to the saddle and the bow struck southward across the Great Wall into China, and westward against the Turkish, and now Muslim states of Central Asia and Persia. These were not defenseless states, but powerful. The fighting was tremendous. But Genghis crushed them. In a few years the northern city of Peking had fallen; by 1220, most of Persia was his; and then, like all the conquerors from the East, the

Mongols came to cross the crescent of mountains and ride down into the great open north Eurasian plain.

It was the aim of every Asian empire to control the rich caravan routes to the West. To do so was very profitable. But it was the aim of Genghis Khan not only to do this, but to set up a state to rule the entire world. It was not only his mission but his duty.

"Tengri, the god of the Great Blue Sky, has granted me to rule all who live in felt tents," he declared. But if this meant the nomad dwellers on the plains, he took it to mean the world. And like the Chinese emperors he conquered, he claimed a mandate from heaven.

His object—which popular history, with some reason, often forgets—was universal peace. The rules of this new world order were all set forth by Genghis in his code—the great Yasa—a copy of which was kept, like the Covenant, sacred and hidden from the eyes of the people at each of the Mongol capitals.

"All men are equal," declared the Yasa, "and all, on their merits, shall serve the Great Khan." It was a formula that other empires, like the Chinese, had used. "The old and the poor shall also be protected," the Yasa ordered. And indeed, in the empire of Genghis Khan, there was a kind of welfare state.

Wiser than many despots, he also allowed freedom of religion. "You may worship as you please," the conquered were told, "but in your prayers, you must also pray for the Great Khan." And all this was bound together with the simple formula: "There is one God in heaven, and one lord upon the earth—the Great Khan."

In 1227 Genghis died. Like the falcon that was the *tamga* of the clan, he had flown up into the heavens, many believed. But his empire did not falter. For centuries the khans would elect from the large number of his direct descendants, the state clan.

The empire Genghis left his sons and grandsons in his will was divided into four parts. In the Oriental world, each of the four points of the compass had a color: the north was black, the south red; the east was blue, and the west was white. And the center, the royal center, was gold.

Thus it was that the descendants of Genghis were called the Golden Kin.

To his sons, Genghis gave the order: expand. And to each, in his will, he left not silver and gold, but armies with which to get it.

The great army that descended upon the Western World in 1237 was led by Batu Khan, a junior ruler and grandson of Genghis. At his right hand was the great Mongol general Subudey. The clan council of the Great Khan had decided that his army, though it belonged to the western of the empire's four divisions, should be supplemented by large detachments from the other divisions as well. It consisted, it is estimated, of about one hundred and fifty thousand men: the core Mongol, the rest mainly Turks from the conquered lands of Central Asia.

History, since that time, has usually referred to this army, and the vast western empire it was to rule, as the Golden Horde. In fact, this name comes from a misreading of a text written centuries later. The huge western Mongol lands were not called golden: being western, they were white. And the horde within this vast white division, that had come to subdue Russia, was called the Great Horde.

The Mongols' information was excellent. Back in the time of Genghis, they had sent an expedition across the southern steppe, past the river Don; but the Russians had not understood who these soldiers were. Since then spies had come, and merchant caravans had told their story: there were always many whispers across the steppe. While the Russians hardly knew of their existence, the rulers of the mighty empire had prepared their plan.

"It will not be a long campaign," Mengu had told his wife.

Indeed, while the Mongol council believed that to subdue the entire empire of the Chinese, north and south, might take sixty years, they had estimated that the conquest of the Rus would take three.

In order to understand the shape and nature of the Russian state, it is necessary only to consider her greatest rivers. And the pattern they make is very simple: for they form, roughly speaking, the capital letter R.

First, from the beginning, there was the great north-south network of waterways that led from the cold northern lands by the Baltic Sea down to the broad river Dnieper, and thence through pleasant forest, across the dangerous southern steppe, and at last to the warm Black Sea. This was the upright of the R, on which lay Novgorod in the north, Smolensk in the middle, and Kiev just above the southern steppe.

The tail of the R, stretching southeast from the center, out across the steppe, and down to the eastern corner of the Black Sea shore and the settlement of Tmutarakan, was the great river Don.

The loop of the R was made by two rivers: the upper part by the mighty Volga as it started its journey with an enormous curve up through the dark northeastern forest before turning south again; and the lower part by another river, the sluggish Oka, that came out from the center and curved northward to meet it. From their meeting point, about halfway up the loop, the Volga flowed away to the east again, to continue its journey across the endless Eurasian plain.

Within this huge loop—a land of forests and marshes, where primitive Finnish folk had dwelt since time immemorial—had gradually been established towns: Suzdal in the central section, sometimes called Suzdalia; Rostov farther north; and, on the outside of the loop, on the river Oka, the towns of Riazan and, above it, Murom.

Four chief rivers: Dnieper, Volga, Oka, and Don. From the frozen north to the warm Black Sea: about a thousand miles. From west to east across the loop: nearly five hundred. This was the R of Russian rivers, the shape of the state of Rus.

In the century that followed the reign of Vladimir Monomakh in Kiev, however, one great change had taken place in the state of Rus. Its leaders had taken an increasing interest in the lands within the loop of the Russian R. New towns like Yaroslavl and Tver grew up. Monomakh himself had set up an important city in Suzdalia and given it his own name: Vladimir. Meanwhile, in the south, not only did the Cumans continue to raid from the steppe but—thanks to the near wrecking of

Constantinople during the West's confused Crusades—the Black Sea trade had weakened and the great city of Kiev entered a slow decline.

As a result of these developments, the center of gravity in the state of Rus had shifted to the northeast, into the loop. The proud descendants of Monomakh preferred the forest lands where the Cuman raiders did not penetrate. The senior member of the royal clan called himself Grand Duke of Vladimir now; and golden Kiev, like a famous woman growing older, but still glamorous, became only a possession that rich and powerful princes liked to display at their side.

The Grand Dukes of Vladimir were mighty indeed. They usually controlled Novgorod, and its huge trade with the Hanseatic German towns and far beyond. They received the great caravans that came across the steppe and forest from the lands of the Volga Bulgars and the Orient.

And, to add religious importance to their new northern capital, they brought from Greece a sacred icon of the Mother of God and installed it in the new cathedral of Vladimir. No object was more reverenced in all Russia than the icon of Our Lady of Vladimir.

There was, however, one central weakness in the state of Rus: it was disunited. Though the rules of brotherly succession still applied for the position of Grand Duke, individual cities had gradually become power bases for different branches of the numerous royal houses. Their disputes were endless. No ruler in Vladimir ever imposed unity upon them from the center.

The state of Rus was disunited. The Mongols knew it very well.

1239

YANKA was awake at dawn. The sky was growing pale.

Quietly she slipped off the warm shelf over the stove and made her way to the door. She could hear her parents and her brother breathing. No one stirred.

Pulling on her furs and her thick felt boots, she unlatched the door and stepped out onto the crisp snow.

In the half light the village seemed gray. A few feet away on the right was a small dark dot on the ground. She inspected it. It was just a dog's mess that had frozen to stone in the cold clear night. There was no wind, and only the pleasant smell of woodsmoke that emanated from the chimneyless huts. No one was about as she began to walk.

There was no particular reason why Yanka should have walked through the woods that dawn; except that, after a restless night before, she was glad to go out into the cold open spaces away from the village for a while. She began to walk along the path through the trees.

She was seven years old: a quiet, rather self-possessed little girl, with blue-and-hazel eyes and straw-colored hair. Of the children in the village of Russka, she was one of the most fortunate. For her mother's family were descended from the peasant Shchek, the keeper of the honey forest in the days of the boyar Ivan and the Grand Prince Monomakh.

By the time of his death Shchek had acquired numerous beehives of his own and even now, generations later, in addition to the traditional distaff, salt box, and butter press that came with every bride, Yanka's mother had brought a handsome dowry, including several beehives. She was a gay, quick-witted woman, resembling her ancestor mainly in their thick dark hair and square build; and she loved to sing. Sometimes, it was true, Yanka had noticed some tension between her parents. She had even heard her mother speak words of scorn. But for the most part their household seemed happy.

The sun was about to rise. Its rays caught a single, small white cloud overhead, causing it to gleam. Yanka wandered on. She smelled the faint earthy scent of a fox that must have crossed the track. Turning, she saw it, watching her through the trees thirty paces away on the right. "Good morning, fox," she said quietly.

The fox slipped away across the snow, like a shadow dropping footprints as it passes.

It was time to turn back. Yet she did not. Something seemed to beckon her to the edge of the steppe. I will look at the sun rising over the steppe, she thought, before I go back to the village.

The settlement of Russka had become rather isolated in recent times. The fort was still there, but poorly manned, for recently there had not ever been a prince in Pereiaslav. The boyar's family had long ago become strangers to the village. Ivanushka's grandson, another Ivan, had married a Cuman girl, and their son, a strange, fair-haired fellow called Milei whose blue eyes were set in a rather high-boned, Turkish face, had taken no interest in Russka. The Turk, the villagers called him; although by the standards of the Russian princes, some of whom were now seven-eighths Cuman, he was not particularly Turkish. Apart from this, the boyar's family owned large estates in the northeast, beyond the river Oka. The boyar lived in the city of Murom. His steward came to inspect the village from time to time, and to take the profits from the honey. The family also kept up the little church, although it was sometimes left with only an ancient, half-blind priest to look after it.

During Yanka's brief life, the village of Russka therefore was a place of benign torpor, its inhabitants gathering harvest and honey, cheating the absent boyar, sitting outside in the long summer months, and, often, singing in the summer evenings at the border of the southern steppe.

Except for the threat over the horizon.

Yanka did not know what to make of that. A huge raid from the steppe had taken place in the north the previous year. The Cumans, or whoever they were, had done enormous damage. And that autumn the boyar's steward had not shown up. Who knew what it meant? "But don't worry," her father had told her. "You'll be safe with me."

When she came to the edge of the trees the sun had just cleared the horizon. Ahead, to the east, the white snows seemed to stretch forever, as though the sun had come from some hidden declivity in their distant wastes. Now, the great golden sun was rising like an emperor in the blue sky of the east as she stared, transfixed at its splendor.

The air was completely clear and silent. About a mile away, a little to the left, a small bump marked the place where there was an ancient kurgan. Far to the south, long layers of grayish clouds stretched along the horizon from steppe to forest, their edges gleaming gold.

Yanka stepped out from the trees and walked out onto the plain. Almost at once, its huge, empty silence seemed to envelop her. She took a deep breath of icy air and smiled. Now she was ready to go home.

Just as she was about to turn, however, her sharp eyes noticed a minute dot, far away on the horizon. She stared at it, shielding her eyes from the sun, not even sure if there was something there or not. It did not seem to be moving. Was it growing? She finally decided it was not. How strange, she thought, as she gazed. It must be a tree, casting a long shadow in the sunrise.

And then she turned to go home, while the sun, lord of the blue sky, took possession of the morning.

Mengu watched her.

He had ridden out from the camp at first light and before long had come to a low rise that gave him a good view. Across the open steppe, ten miles away, he could clearly see the line of trees and he had seen the little figure even as she emerged from the wood.

For while Yanka's eyes were sharp, the eyes of the man of the steppe were far keener.

In the clearness of early morning, before dust or haze have risen, the men of the desert and prairie can make out a man at fifteen miles and more. Even at four miles, such warriors can spot the arm of a man hiding behind a rock.

So Mengu, like a falcon, watched the little girl as she ventured out onto the steppe and then went back.

Then he smiled. How easy it had been. The cities of the north—Riazan, Murom, Vladimir, had fallen helplessly before them. The Grand Duke and his army had been destroyed. It was only a pity that the wet spring weather had forced them to turn back before reaching Novgorod; but that great trading city could be dealt with later. These poor Russian cities, despite their high walls, never had a chance. To the siege engineers, used to dealing with the stupendous fortified cities of China, these western places seemed puny.

Now they had come again, in winter, to smash the south. And in this, too, they had shown their wisdom.

For the general view, that Russia is protected by her winter, is incorrect. The winter is a very good time to attack Russia. In spring and autumn, mud makes the land impassable. In summer, there are large rivers to cross. But in winter, the rivers are frozen solid and it is easy to travel if one is prepared for the cold and knows how to move over the snow. The Mongols were no strangers to harsh winters. They liked them.

Mengu continued to gaze thoughtfully at the distant treeline where the girl had vanished. The campaign had been satisfactory so far; his men had performed well; he had nothing to complain of. There was only one trouble; he had not yet been able to attract the general's attention.

His sister had done her best for him with Khan Batu. But the message she gave him was as bleak as it was simple. When the great man had heard about her brother and his hopes he had merely remarked: "Good. Let him distinguish himself."

All he needed was a chance—even a skirmish would do, as long as it took place under the general's eye. He nodded thoughtfully. An opportunity was about to come. But let it come soon.

Again he scanned the woods. If the girl had been wandering at the treeline, there must be a village nearby.

They would be there by noon.

Moments after Yanka awoke, her face was white with terror.

They were everywhere. And she had been deserted.

She stood, shaking convulsively, by the window. She could smell the sweating flanks of the horses, almost touch them, as the horsemen in thick furs, with huge bows slung on their backs, went by, brushing against the eaves of the huts. Some of them carried burning torches.

Where was everyone?

Still not fully awake, she looked behind her. The hut was empty. For a second she had to collect her thoughts.

At midmorning, she remembered, her father had harnessed the old mare and taken the sled down the frozen river to the next village. The clear sky of the dawn had disappeared. The cloudbank from the south had moved slowly up and by the time her father left, the light in the village had seemed almost brown. Nothing had been happening. It was dull, rather oppressive. Her mother had decided to go over to the fort; but Yanka had stayed behind and fallen asleep.

She had not heard the shouting.

And now she had awoken to this. Coming out of sleep, it seemed like a nightmare. The sounds of the horses' hooves on the frozen snow echoed eerily in the room.

Though Yanka did not know it, it was only a minute since the villagers had fled. For everything had happened so fast. Suddenly at the far end of the big field, a horseman had appeared. Then three. Then, as people began to shout, a hundred. It was as if all the trees had suddenly turned into horsemen, advancing with bow and spear.

Silently the Mongol army had melted through the woods in five enormous groups along a front about three miles across. The village of Russka lay near the center. Now they were flowing through like a dark flood upon the snow.

The villagers had been so surprised that they had not had time to do anything but run. Three people had banged upon Yanka's door before tearing away, supposing the hut must be empty. They had run across the frozen river, driven like game, looking for shelter. Some rushed up into the fort; a few ran to the sanctuary of the church; others preferred to try the woods beyond.

It was at the first shout from the village that Yanka's mother looked out from the gateway of the little fort. First her breath caught in her throat. Then her heart began to race wildly.

She saw the villagers streaming out—small, pathetic, dark bundles running raggedly across the gray-white ice towards her. But where was Yanka?

A moment later she saw what none of the fleeing villagers could see—the full extent of the Mongol line, stretching up and down the river.

She scanned the fleeing villagers again—where was Yanka? There was no sign of her.

She started to run down the slope, towards the river and the Mongol horseman, who had already reached the opposite bank, and she did not know that, seconds later, the villagers had stupidly closed the fortress gates behind her.

Mengu could hardly believe his luck, when, as the gates shut, the general rode over to him. He was a stout, surly man, given to few words. He raised his arm and pointed his whip across the river. "Take that fort."

It was a chance to show himself. For a second, the image of his sister flashed across his mind. He knew very well that in the universe of the Great Khan, nothing, not even the smallest seeming diversion, happens by chance, and now his brain was working rapidly, calculating.

Scarcely pausing to acknowledge the order, he wheeled his horse and, with two curt commands, like a couple of harsh grunts, directed the nearby squadrons into two lines who immediately forked right and left, riding across the ice to encircle the fort and the church.

Beckoning a decurion, he commanded: "One siege engine. A catapult." And the fellow clattered away up the frozen river.

They were bringing the engines across at a place where the woods were thinner, a few hundred yards to the north.

The Mongol siege was very like the hunts of the Great Khan. One circled the fortress entirely, excluding any possibility of escape. Sometimes, if a major town looked obstinate, the Mongols would build a wooden wall right around it as though to say: "You think your walls protect you. Now look: you are trapped inside ours." Then, at leisure, they would knock down the fortress defenses, or fill in the moat and build bridges over the walls. There was no possibility that they would ever give up. The surrounded fort was doomed.

Mengu looked at the pitiful little wooden fort. What fools they were to shut the gates. The army would never have even bothered to burn the place down if they had just left them open.

But how convenient. What an easy way to show his mettle.

The thing must be done quickly: that was the key. The general would not want to see his forces delayed. "Hurry," he shouted after the decurion, who was already too far away to hear him.

He frowned, impatiently.

Yanka hesitated.

The horsemen had passed out of the village. They had set two of the huts on fire but they had not paused to do more. A shouted order from somewhere in front had caused them to move swiftly towards the river. Suddenly it was very quiet.

Perhaps her family were out there somewhere. Perhaps they were lying dead. Or they might be fleeing without her, and she would be left alone. What should she do? She was terrified of the horsemen, but even that was not as terrible as the fear of being alone.

She stepped outside.

The horsemen had already been drawn down to the river. As she came out of the hamlet she saw the back of the two files of cavalry trotting across the ice to surround the fort. Away to her left, past the old grave-yard, was a body of about three hundred infantry. The men wore heavy leather coats, like armor, and their lines bristled with long, dark spears. In front of her and to the right, half a dozen horsemen waited impassively upon the bank, and directly ahead, on the edge of the ice, a single horseman seemed to be giving directions. No one even noticed her existence.

Then she saw two sights that made her want to cry out for joy.

It was her brother Kiy who saw her first.

The nine-year-old boy and his father had been almost back from their trip, and they were approaching the last bend in the frozen river before the village when Kiy suddenly heard his father exclaim: "Devil take it. Look at that. It's a Cuman raid."

He looked to the right. Three horsemen were calmly riding through the trees by the bank. Then he saw ten. Then fifty. His father jerked the rein. The sled swerved. "What's behind us?"

Kiy looked back. "More. They're crossing." And his father cursed. "What about Mother and Yanka?" the boy cried out.

His father said nothing but cracked the rein savagely along the old mare's back. She flinched, tossed her head angrily, and they raced to-wards the bend. "Please, God, they aren't in front as well," the peasant muttered.

The little sled whisked over the ice. Father and son held their breath. It must be a big raid. Kiy started silently to pray. Thank God, the bank seemed for a moment to be clear as they raced round the curve . . . and ran into the Mongol army.

The line of horsemen was trotting across the ice to surround the fort directly in front of them. Kiy did not see his mother. But just as his father wheeled the sled around to race towards the woods on their right, he shouted: "Look! It's Yanka. On the bank. She's seen us."

He was surprised when his father only muttered: "Devil take it. You'll get us all killed."

Then he saw Yanka start to run down towards the Mongols.

For Yanka had not only seen them. She had seen her mother, coming across the ice, between the two streams of horsemen. She opened her mouth to shout. But as though she were in a dream, no sound came, except a tiny whisper that nobody heard. She tried to step forward. Nothing happened. And then her mother saw her.

Suddenly the little girl felt a flood of relief. She was safe. Without pausing even to think, she ran down the bank onto the frozen river, straight towards her mother, oblivious even of the Mongol on his horse who stood in the path between them.

Mengu stared. What was this peasant woman doing?

He had been looking for the siege engine anxiously. Another few moments and it would be in position. He glanced at his troops. The ring around the fort was almost complete. This would be his day. Studiously he avoided looking towards the general. "I'll have the whole place under control in an hour," he murmured.

Though his face showed nothing, he felt a surge of excitement. It was like the great ring in the royal hunt. And today the ring was his. For a brief hour he was to be general, like a prince. I'll show them, he thought elatedly.

But who was this peasant woman coming towards him?

It was just then that he suddenly remembered a story he had heard some months ago. A peasant woman, no doubt very like this, had made a sudden rush at a young captain when they were burning the city of Riazan. She had pulled out a knife and killed him, too. "So watch out for their women," the fellow who told him had warned. He frowned, irritated. Who was she, to disturb the imperial hunt? He was not going to have a Russian peasant woman threaten his career.

Now she was breaking into a run, making straight for him.

At the lightest pressure from his knees, his horse clattered forward. He took out his saber and with a single, curving slash, cut straight down to her breast, and she crumpled and slid across the ice. He turned back to look for the siege engine.

"Mama!"

A scream. He wheeled again, sword in hand, to face this new threat. Even before he knew it his curved saber was raised high, his face tense, his mouth a snarl.

A little girl, white faced, in terror on the ice, kneeling beside the woman. Blood was pumping from the huge gash. The woman's eyes were open; she was gazing at the child, trying to say something.

For a second he, too, forgot everything. He saw only the faces of the mother and her child.

"Yanka!"

A shout, this time from a boy and a peasant on a sled two hundred yards away. He had not noticed it before because his horsemen, now across the river, had been in the way.

"Yanka!"

The peasants stood there by their sled with no idea of what to do, in front of several hundred bowmen who could have killed them in a second.

The woman's eyes were glassy. It was over.

There was a clatter upon the frozen river as the Mongol reached down and scooped the little girl up in one arm. The flakes of ice flew as his horse raced across the ice towards the sled, where he threw her carelessly to the ground. Looking down contemptuously at the boy and his father, he waved them away.

A second later, their sled was racing through the trees.

It was not the policy of the Mongols to kill the peasants in the lands they conquered. The peasants tilled the soil, paid the taxes, and supplied recruits. The Mongols only killed those who were foolish enough to resist them, like those who had closed themselves in the fort.

Mengu turned back. The entire incident had taken rather less than a minute, during which time he supposed everyone had been too busy to take much notice.

The troops were all in place. The catapult was coming up, and an engineer was awaiting his order. He put the foolish incident out of his mind. Secretly he felt ashamed of killing the woman. As for the little girl . . . His face showed nothing.

With a curt nod, he signaled the catapult to proceed.

The inhabitants of Russka had never seen a catapult like this. Its technology was simple enough—a massive counterweight at one end of a lever caused the arm to hurl a stone from the other. But its power was truly extraordinary. For the engineers of China had constructed a machine that could be loaded with a stone it took four strong men to lift, and then hurl it with devastating accuracy almost a quarter of a mile.

The first stone completely broke down the parapet over the gate. The second smashed the gate itself.

At Mengu's order the Mongols streamed through into the fort. They moved rapidly but methodically. Every door was kicked open: every room, every crevice searched. They used spears and swords. Any living creature, man, woman, or child was quickly and efficiently butchered. They were so quick and thorough that, apart from a few moments of sheer terror, few of their victims even suffered very much.

Inside the fort they found some modest quantities of food, but ten tons of stored grain, which they removed in carts taken from the village. Then, leaving the bodies where they were, they set fire to every building and to the wooden walls.

The huge bonfire on the little hill grew rapidly. Soon the whole fort was alive with fire, and above its walls, new walls of roaring flames appeared, hurling smoke and sparking cinders high into the air above the forest. As the broad-faced Mongols watched below, the whole place seemed to shudder with the roar, crack, and whine of the little town's destruction.

Mengu turned to a decurion. "Twenty bowmen, with fire arrows," he ordered. "Surround the church."

A few moments later there were broad-chested Mongols, in leather jerkins and with huge, curved bows at the ready, before each of the church's walls. At a nod from Mengu, they took out long, heavy arrows with huge cloth heads that had been dipped in pitch, and lit them.

"Fire." The arrows began to fly and to crash through the church's narrow windows. Soon smoke emerged; then flame.

Mengu wondered whether the people inside would come out of the door, and he stationed more bowmen opposite. But though the force of the fire within seemed to be causing the door to tremble, it remained closed.

After a time the little dome collapsed and fell with a crash into the building. No one could possibly be alive in there by now, he thought. The place must be a roaring furnace. Even the bricks were starting to glow. A wall fell, then another. It was good. In case the general thought him soft about the child, he meant to show he knew how to be harsh.

That evening, as a few villagers crept out of the woods, they saw in place of the fort and the brave little church only blackened ruins, beside which the birds were swooping curiously.

The report the general made to the mighty Khan Batu that evening was sensible and clear-headed.

"He lost concentration because a woman ran towards him. He should have seen her before and ordered his men to cut her down or remove her. He didn't. He waited until she reached him, then he killed her. He took his eyes off the job."

"Then?"

"There was a little girl. He picked her up and threw her out."

"Waste of time. What then?"

"He took the fort. Burned it down."

"Very well. Anything else?"

"He burned down a church."

"Inside the fort?"

"No. Outside."

"Was it defended?"

"No."

"That is bad. The Great Khan respects all religions."

"I do not think he has a cool head," the general concluded.

That night, the mighty Khan Batu changed his mind and did not sleep with Mengu's sister.

That same night, as she rocked herself to sleep in a shelter her father and brother had improvised in the bee-forest, Yanka remembered only two things about the Mongol who had killed her mother: he had a scar across one side of his face and was missing one ear.

She would never forget: never.

1246

Softly the raft drifted through the early morning mists. Until the previous month, to escape detection, they had traveled only at night, inching their way upstream, reconnoitering every village in case of patrols. Once, on a moonlit night, they had almost run into a party of soldiers camped on the riverbank.

It was August. Making their way northward by the curving rivers, they had already covered a distance of some five hundred miles. It had taken them three months.

Last month they had left one river system and made their way across land to another. The boat by which they had come so far—a huge single tree trunk, hollowed out—was too heavy to carry. They had left it therefore and, having reached the other stream, they had built themselves a raft, which suited their purposes well enough since, from now on, instead of working their way upstream, they would be drifting with the current. Their mood had also begun to lighten. It had been possible, now, to travel by day. But they were still cautious.

For Yanka, her father and their companions were doing a very dangerous thing. They were trying to escape from the Tatars.

The Tatars. Even now, most Russians did not really understand the nature of the empire of which they had just become a part. Failing to perceive the absolute importance of the Mongol elite from their distant eastern homeland, the Russians confused them with the subject Turks who fought under them, and therefore gave the Horde a Turkish name that was to remain in use throughout history: the Tatars.

The estimate of the Mongol war council had been exactly right. Russia had fallen in three years. The great army that had passed through the village of Russka had swept on to destroy Pereiaslav utterly; within a twelvemonth Chernigov had fallen and golden Kiev was a ghost town.

The ancient state of Rus was finished.

For convenience, the Mongols divided it in two. The southern half—the territories around Kiev and the southern steppe—were placed under direct Mongol rule. The north—the lands in the great loop of the Russian R, and in the deep forests beyond—were left under the nominal control of the Russian royal house. But with a single, simple proviso: the Russian princes ruled, henceforth, only as the representative of the Great Khan. They were there to keep the people quiet and collect the khan's tribute. That was all.

Some chronicles of the time—and many Russians, too—liked to pretend that the Tatars were just another, if impressive, group of steppe raiders whom, for the moment, the Grand Duke had to buy off.

The reality was very different. The Grand Duke was summoned eastward, even as far as Mongolia, to receive his badge of office—the *yarlyk*. He ruled only at the khan's pleasure. "Remember, you belong to us now," all princes were told. No disobedience was tolerated. When a bold prince from the southwest refused to bow to an idol of the Great Khan, he was executed on the spot. This imposition of rule was immediate and total. Indeed, the only reason the Russian princes were allowed to exist at all was that the Mongols, unimpressed with the wealth of the northern forests—puny indeed, compared to the rich caravans and cities of Asia— had reckoned that the Grand Duke's territories were not worth the cost of direct administration.

It is likely, had the Mongols not paused for the elections in the Orient of a new Great Khan, that all Europe might have fallen at this point, too. But the new khan decided instead to consolidate his western empire: a new capital, Saria, was built on the southern Volga and his army commanders were told: "Wait."

And in this matter, too, the Mongols displayed their excellent understanding. For there was one other relevant fact that they had quickly understood.

Russia was Orthodox; the West Catholic.

Back in the days of Monomakh, the split between Rome and the Eastern church had been one of liturgical niceties. But since then the gulf had widened. Questions of authority were involved. Was the Patriarch of Constantinople—or his fellow patriarchs in the east—prepared to submit to the Pope's authority? Had the Eastern—Orthodox—Church showed a proper interest in the Pope's crusades? Feelings ran high. When the Russians sent frantic appeals to their fellow Christians in the West for help against the heathen Mongols, they were met with silence. Indeed, the West watched with satisfaction while the Orthodox were being punished for their mistake. Worse yet, not only did the Catholic Swedes start to attack them in the north, but a pair of crusading orders—the Livonian and Teutonic Knights—whose headquarters were up by the Baltic Sea, started with the Pope's approval to raid the lands of Novgorod. "Let the heathens smash them," said the Catholic West, "and we'll gobble up the pieces." So it was that the Russians concluded, more firmly than ever: "Never trust the West." And the Mongol leadership cleverly calculated: "Take Russia first. The West can wait. Russia belongs to Asia now."

Yanka's father was not a bad-looking man.

He was just above average height and fair, though his beard was thin and the crown of his head was covered by only a few strands of hair. His features were small and regular, though the upper part of his face seemed rather bony. His pale blue eyes were generally kindly, though they sometimes looked at people as though he were counting something. He was, in a nondescript way, quite pleasant looking. Occasionally he drank too much.

Sometimes he would punish her with a beating if she had misbehaved; this was always in the evening—and at such times he could be stern and frightening. But he was less severe, she knew, than the other fathers in the village.

He himself supposed that in earlier years he had taken less notice of her than he had of Kiy, his son. But the terrible events since the Tatar invasion had changed all that; and now, as they continued on their journey, he realized that he had undertaken it chiefly for her sake.

For if they did not leave, he had thought that she would die.

At first, after the terrible destruction, a strange silence had fallen upon the village. News of the fall of the cities of Pereiaslav and Kiev came; then nothing. From the boyar in the north, not a word. Perhaps he was dead. Meanwhile, in the shattered village, seed time and harvest came; Yanka's father took up with a stout, dark-haired woman, though he did not marry her, and she taught Yanka to embroider; Kiy became a dexterous woodcarver. And then, the previous year, the blow had fallen.

On an autumn day a small Tatar troop led by an official from the newly created governor of the region, the baskak, marched briskly into the village. All the people were lined up and counted—a thing that had never been known before. "This is the census," the official said. "The baskak numbers every head." Then the men were divided into groups of ten. "Each ten is a tax unit and is fully responsible for maintaining its full complement," they were told. "Nobody may leave." A peasant who foolishly tried to argue was immediately whipped. They also discovered that the village was to have a new significance.

The imperial post service, the *yam,* connected every part of the Great Khan's empire. His messengers and selected merchants could use it. There was a station every twenty-five miles, where mares and sheep were kept to supply kumiss and meat. Also a quantity of spare horses. For when the khan sent a messenger, the man wore bells to warn the station of his approach so that a fresh horse would be ready, onto which he could leap, never pausing in his journey. The baskak had decided that the ruined fort would do very well for a *yam.* An official stationed there would oversee the village, too. "Which means," a villager whispered, "that we shall all be slaves."

But it was the final action of the official that had destroyed Yanka. For suddenly, turning to the village elder, he had demanded: "Who are the best woodcarvers here?" And being given five names he had called them out. The youngest was Kiy, age fifteen. "We'll take the boy," the Mongol snapped. For the Great Khan had asked for artisans to be sent to him. And for a long time that evening, as the party went away across the steppe, Yanka had gazed after the distant figures who began to look like tiny shadows that might sink, at any time, into the reddening sea.

Life for both father and daughter had been miserable after that. His woman had left him. Several times, to drown his own bitterness, he had got drunk and foolishly frightened the girl. Meanwhile Yanka had gone into strange decline. During the winter she had grown progressively thinner, eating little, speaking less. And by the spring, when she showed no signs of improving, her father had confessed: "I don't know what to do."

It was a family from the next village who had announced their intention to leave. "We're going north," they told him. "There are endless lands up in the northern taiga," they explained, "going right across the Volga, where men are free, without a master. We'll escape up there."

These were the so-called Black Lands. In fact, they were in the prince's land, for which the settler paid him a small rent; but the farther north and east one went, the more settlers became frontiersmen, recognizing no authority. Such freedoms were exciting, even though the life could be hard. "Come with us," they suggested. The father of the family had once been north as a young man. "I know the way," he claimed.

"And if we get caught?"

The fellow had shrugged. "I'll take the risk," he said.

The great river journey they had undertaken was very simple. They were slowly ascending the great Russian R. First up the Dnieper; then cutting across eastward until, after their brief overland journey, they had joined a small river that took them to the underside of the huge northern loop—the sluggish river Oka. Once in the Oka they were in the Grand

Duke's lands, where the Tatar patrols did not bother to come.

How pleasant it was, at last, to drift along the river Oka. Fish were plentiful. Forgetting her grief in this great adventure, Yanka had started to eat again. One day they even caught a noble sturgeon. As they went north and east, they saw signs of a gradual change in vegetation. There were fewer broad-leaved trees, more firs and larches. Their guide also pointed out another important feature. "We're getting into the country of the old Finnish tribes now," he explained, "like the Mordvinians. And the names of places are Finnish too." The Oka River itself was an example. The cities of Riazan and Murom likewise. And one day, passing a modest river that joined them from the left, their friend remarked, "That river's got a primitive Finnish name too: it's the Moskva."

"Anything up there?" Yanka's father asked.

"A small town called Moscow. Nothing much."

Yanka's father had considered carefully what they should do. He was attracted by the idea of these distant free lands of which the others spoke. But he was cautious, too. Life could be very hard for a settler. He had with him a quantity of money, which he kept carefully hidden. He could start up anywhere. But I might be able to get more out of a landlord who needs a tenant, he thought.

So he had formed a simple plan. When we get to Murom, he decided, I'll look for the boyar Milei. Perhaps he'll help us. But if he won't or he's dead, maybe we'll try the north.

And so, that August, Yanka and her father went along the Oka.

The boyar Milei was a large man with a family of five. He was very proud of his physical strength. He was also cunning.

When the news had come upriver, eight years before, of the Mongol attack on Riazan, he had not waited to be summoned to battle. "The Grand Duke of Vladimir will order us to join him if he gives battle," he remarked shrewdly, "but he'll do nothing for us if these raiders come to Murom." In this assessment of the relationship between the Grand Duke and the princes of the minor city of Murom he was entirely correct.

The little principality of Murom lay at the eastern edge of the loop of the Russian R. West of it lay the rest of the great loop—the wide lands of Suzdalia, ruled by the Grand Duke of Vladimir. Once Murom had been a senior city, greater than Riazan. But in the last century Riazan had become richer, and Suzdalia had become mighty; and now the princes of Murom did the bidding of the Grand Duke without question. So, therefore, should Milei the boyar. Unless it did not suit him. Faced with this new threat, therefore, Milei the boyar had discreetly withdrawn, with his entire family, for a visit to the most remote and obscure of all his estates, where he had wisely remained until the following year.

The estate in question was isolated indeed.

Across the great loop of the Russian R, and dividing it horizontally in half, there runs eastward a pleasant minor river called the Kliasma. It was upon this river, a little to the east of the loop's center, that Monomakh had set up the present capital of Vladimir. Other fine cities like Suzdal, Rostov, or Tver, all lay in the northern half of the loop. The southern half of the loop, however, until one came to the cities on the Oka—Riazan and Murom—contained very little except hamlet, forest, and marsh. It was here, in the southern half of the loop between the Kliasma and Oka rivers, that the boyar Milei owned an estate. From this place a stream obligingly ran northward up to the Kliasma, not far from Vladimir. It was also possible, some miles away, to pick up other streams that led south to the sluggish Oka.

The boyar Milei's grandfather, who had been given the place, had decided he did not like its barbarous Finnish name. So he had renamed both the little stream that ran northward and the settlement beside it. He named them after an estate he was fond of, in the south: the stream he called the Rus, and the village, Russka.

There were many such names that were carried like this from the south into the north.

It was not a bad place. And the winter that the boyar Milei spent there had convinced him that it had more possibilities than he had first supposed. "Indeed," he told his wife, "from what I've discovered at Russka, we could make it highly profitable. All we need is more people." But then finding enough peasants was the perennial problem of the Russian landlord.

The next spring he returned to Murom to find that his house outside the city walls burned down, but that the large cache of coins he had hidden deep under the floor was quite safe. For the time being there had been plenty to do, for the Mongol invasion left much to repair. But the little village of Russka was often in his mind.

"We must attend to it when we have time," he often remarked.

And so, late in the summer of 1246, he was surprised and delighted to find before him two peasants from his estate in the south.

Since the Mongol invasion, he had found it harder than ever to get enough peasants to work his land. So far, he had only managed to add three families of Mordvinians to the settlement at Russka. "And two of those are drunk most of the time," his steward told him mournfully.

Now, as Yanka looked up at this tall, powerful man with his fair beard, only half gray, and his broad, Turkish face, she saw nothing but friendliness. His hard blue eyes beamed. "I have the very place for you," he announced. "The Russka of the north."

"I've no money," her father lied.

The boyar gazed at him, not deceived for a second. "It's more profit to me to give you land and have you work it than get no return at all," he replied. "You can build yourself a house—the villagers will help you. And my steward will take you there and set you up with everything else you need. You'll repay over time."

He questioned them about their journey, and when he heard they had come with another family, with two strong sons, he at once made an offer to them, too.

But they refused. "The offer's good," he told Yanka's father, "but I don't want a landlord. Come with us," he urged instead.

"No," her father was shaking his head. "We prefer to remain. Good luck to you, though."

The next day their companions were on their way. "God knows what they'll do up by the Volga," her father growled. "We're safer in the village." Then he turned away.

Russka.

This northern Russka was a very different place from the village in the south that she had left.

Its only similarity was that, like most Russian villages, it lay beside a river: that was all.

At the site chosen for the settlement, the river made a large, S-shaped curve. The western bank here was about fifty feet higher than the eastern, so that the curve formed a promontory on the west side, and left a large, sheltered space on the eastern bank just below it. This sheltered area had been made into a meadow.

There had once been a settlement in this meadow; but over time it had been moved for greater safety to the promontory, where there now stood a dozen wooden huts with a strengthened fence around them. On the western side the land stretched away, almost flat. A few vegetable plots had been scraped bare near the fence, and two poor fields could be seen through a thin screen of trees.

There was no church.

The northern Russka.

The nearest village lay three miles away, to the southeast. This, too, was on the little river Rus. Just behind this village lay a low wooded ridge. But below the ridge, down by the river, the land was marshy, and so when the Slav settlers had first come upon it they had called it Dirty Place—which remained its name thereafter. Past Dirty Place it was another seven miles to any village.

At first sight, it seemed to Yanka that the forest was all fir. But a walk around showed her that there were, in fact, a huge variety of trees: larch and birch, lime, oak, pine, and many others. Back along the Oka, around Riazan, she had even seen orchards of apple and even cherry trees. But she did not notice any here. The vegetable patches were not very impressive either. They grew peas and cucumbers mainly, as far as she could discover. And she observed something else: their horses were all tiny.

The houses were made of wood—huge, solid logs from base to roof: there were none of the clay walls and thatched roofs she had known in the south.

But above all, the people were different. "They are so quiet," she whispered to her father, the first morning as they walked around the place. "You'd think they were frozen."

There was a mix of people in the village. Before the boyar's family acquired it, the inhabitants had been mostly Slavs of the Viatichi tribe. "Pagan animals," she had always heard these Viatichi called, for they were among the most backward of the Slav tribes. There were six Viatichi families now. As well as these, there were three families who had moved up from the south a generation ago; and finally the three families of Mordvinians brought in by the boyar, with their high Finnish cheekbones and almond eyes.

Different as these all were, to Yanka they seemed all the same in this one, crucial respect. For whereas the Slav villagers she knew in the south were expansive, argumentative, and full of droll humor, these people of the north were quiet, undemonstrative, and seemed to be slow. In the south one sat in the sun and talked. Here people went quietly into the warmth of their huts.

They were not unfriendly, though. On the steward's orders, half a dozen of the men appeared with axes by midday. "We'll build you a hut," they announced, and showed them a site at the southern end of the hamlet.

Then they set to work.

And Yanka's opinion of them changed.

She had never seen anything like it. Huge logs appeared, seemingly from nowhere. The sturdy little horses she had seen were dragging in tree trunks you could almost have hollowed into boats. Great timbers of oak were used for the foundation, then softer, easily worked pine.

The plan of the hut was much the same as in the south: a central entrance corridor with a large space for keeping one's equipment and stores on one side of it, and a room on the other. A good part of the wall between corridor and room was taken up with the stove, which they built of clay.

They worked entirely with their axes—stout, broad-bladed implements with rather short, straight handles, the blade extended towards the butt. And whether Finn or Slav, they seemed equally skilled. Each log was neatly jointed and slotted into its neighbor so that, although the lines between the logs were filled with moss, they were so tight it was scarcely necessary.

And there was not a single nail in the whole house.

It was not only the neatness of their work that amazed Yanka, but the speed. She was used to the busy people of the south, but there was something in these northerners' quiet, ferocious pace that was heroic. They worked into the dusk. The women brought torches and lit fires so they could see better. By the time they stopped that night, the whole house except for the stove and the roof was completed.

The steward and his wife gave them shelter that night. By noon the next day, their hut was complete.

"There," the men said. "This is your place. It will keep you warm and it will last for thirty-three years."

This was the northern hut—the Russian *izba*. Its huge stove and tightly sealed walls would keep its occupants baking hot through the coldest winter as its very name implied: for *izba* meant "hot room."

After they had thanked their new neighbors, the steward led them out to show them the plot of land he had chosen for them.

As they walked they chatted, and she told the steward how impressed she had been by the men's work. "With men like this"—she gazed about her, envisioning cities in the forest—"there is nothing we Russians cannot do."

The steward was a small man with a shrewd face. He laughed. "This is the north," he told her. "Up here we can do anything—for a short space of time." Seeing her puzzled look, he smiled. Then he gestured to the forest all around. "You're in the north now," he explained. "And up here it's like this: we do our best, of course. But whatever we do, the forest reminds us that the land, the winter, and God Himself will always be stronger than we can be. Too much effort is in vain. So then we don't work so hard, except when there's something definite to do in a hurry." She laughed, thinking this a joke, but he only replied, "You'll see."

The estate, he explained to them, was of medium size—about four hundred desiatin, or a thousand acres. Only part of it was worked at present. It lay on both sides of the river.

Many landlords preferred to give these remote estates over entirely to peasants and collect a modest rent, usually paid in kind. It was not like the old days in the south, he told them, where landlords ran their own estates and shipped the surplus to markets. "You'll find things simpler up here," he continued.

But the boyar Milei had the resources to buy slaves and hire laborers. "He's planning to bring more people in and build this place up," the steward said, "and work some of the estate himself. So although it's small as yet, you'll see changes here soon."

One thing troubled Yanka. "We are Christians," she told him. "Are all the people here pagan?"

She had noticed some strange, hump-backed graves outside the fence that did not look Christian to her.

"The Slavs from the south are Christian," he replied. "The Mordvinians." He laughed. "They're Mordvinians. As for the Viatichi, they're Slavs, but pagan too. Those were their grave mounds you saw by the fence."

"Will there ever be a church?"

"The boyar plans to build one."

"Soon?"

"Maybe."

After this she returned to the hut, while her father and the steward went to see the land he was to be given.

The land that he was allotted was the standard peasant plot of thirty chets—about thirty-six acres. But it was poor woodland, west of the village, that would need to be cleared. For this, however, he would only have to pay a small rent, with none payable in the first year. The steward would advance him a small sum, in return for which he was to do some light work for the boyar. And so began his career in his new home.

For Yanka this was a time of discovery. The summer drifted on far into autumn that year, into the time of Indian summer that the Russians call "Granny Summer."

She walked all around the area, sometimes alone and sometimes with the steward's wife. The steward's wife was a small, rather cold woman, but she wanted to make sure this new girl was useful to the estate, and so she showed her around thoroughly.

The woods were richer than Yanka had imagined. The older woman showed her where to find herbs—Saint John's wort, betony, ribwort—

and where there were medicinal ferns. They walked through a little pine wood to the south, above the river, and there on the mossy ground grew bushes of bilberry and cranberry. Here and there, as they walked, she would point to a particular tree and say: "There's a squirrel's nest up there. Look." And she would point to the little tracks made by the squirrel's claws on the trunk as it went up, again and again, to fill the deep hollow in the trunk with nuts for the winter.

"We have special wooden spikes you can put on your feet," she explained. "You can climb up any tree in them and steal the squirrel's nuts—or honey from the bees as well. Just like Misha the bear." She laughed drily.

One spot that Yanka particularly liked lay about half a mile south of the village. Here, the high bank was set about ten yards back from the river, providing a little glade of trees, reached by a steep path down the bank, at the water's edge. And from the bank, about twenty feet up, burst a little spring of bright, clear water, wonderfully cold even in midsummer. The spring water divided into three little falls, dancing down the mossy bank, over gray rocks, and running away in tiny pools among the ferns.

"One waterfall is for love, one for health, one for riches," the steward's wife told her.

"Which is which?"

"No one knows," came the wonderfully Russian reply, and they turned back to the village.

As they parted, the older woman gave her one piece of advice, which reminded her of the house building she had witnessed. "This year's unusual, a very long summer. Don't expect it again, though. The summers are short here; so you work very hard while they last—harder than they do in the south."

"And after that?"

The other woman shrugged. "Nothing."

The other change in Yanka's life was that she was becoming a woman.

She had known it, physically, for some time; but the journey upriver and the offer from Mal's family had made her conscious of new stirrings and vague desires, which on some days filled her with a new confidence and on others made her unaccountably blush, uncertain about herself. She had a wonderful, pale complexion with a delicate pale rose color in her cheeks, and long, yellow-brown hair of which she was rather proud.

Yet some days her skin became oily and pimples appeared; or her cheeks felt blotchy; or her hair seemed sticky and hideous to her. Then her downward-turning mouth would contract into a tight line; she would frown and stay indoors as much as she could.

She was more pleased with her body. It had filled out that summer, and though she was slim, there was a warm, gentle curve around her hips that she supposed some man, some day, would find delicious.

For the time being, as winter approached, she took pride in making a home for her father.

While he was out working with the village men, or building a cart for their needs, she busily wove cloth, built up their food stocks, smoked fish, and put all her skills to good use so that he would come in in the evening and say with a smile: "What a fine nest you are building, my little bird."

He seemed in better spirits. The hard work and the new life had challenged him. There was a new hardness and strength about him that filled her with pleasure. And as he came in, his face glowing darkly in the dying sunlight before dusk, she would turn and think to herself: There is my father, the man I can be proud of.

Nor did she take an interest in any other man in the village.

There were reasons for this; they dated from the first day when the steward had shown them around the village.

For it had been only halfway through that afternoon when her father had burst in through the door, leaned against the warm stove, and cried: "Have you seen their fields?" And before she could answer, "Slash and burn. It's all slash and burn. Mordvinians! Pagans! They haven't even got a decent plow!"

"No plow?"

He gave a disgusted snort for reply. "You hardly need one for this land. Come, I'll show you."

The problem that her father had discovered was one of the major disadvantages that were to plague the state of Russia for the rest of its history.

For the land in the north is very poor.

There are, on the great plain of Russia, two kinds of soil: leached and unleached. In leached ground, the water in the soil does not evaporate fast enough and washes the rich salts down, leaving a poor, acidic topsoil of little agricultural value. This leached earth is called in Russian *podzol*— literally "ash-soil."

Unleached soils occur where evaporation is good. The rich salts remain in the soil, which is usually neutral to alkaline. Here agriculture is good. The richest of all the unleached soils is the deep black earth, the chernozem of the south.

Between these two soil types, however, lies a third—a sort of compromise. This is the gray earth—technically a leached podzol—which is moderately good for agriculture.

Roughly speaking, the good black soil lies in the south, on the steppe; the gray in the center of Russia, in the lands from Kiev up to the river Oka. But in the great loop of the Russian R, and thence northward until one reaches the peaty, waterlogged soil of the tundra, the ground is poor podzol, and yields upon it are low. This soil, together with the cold weather, is the reason why the agriculture of north Russia is very poor.

And upon this earth one did not need the heavy iron plows that had already been used for centuries in the thick, rich black earth in the south. The peasants in the north used the *soka*—a light, wooden plow with a modest steel tip that only scratched the surface of the thin, infertile land.

It was this feeble little plow, and this half-barren soil, that had disgusted Yanka's father. But even more to be despised was the method they were using to organize their holdings.

For instead of having two or sometimes three big fields upon which crops would be rotated, the villagers were using the ancient slash-and-burn technique: cutting down a piece of woodland, burning the debris, and then working the resulting carbonized field for a few years before moving on to another and leaving the previous one to become wilderness again. It was an ancient form of subsistence agriculture.

"Pagans," her father repeated in disgust. But there was little, as a single newcomer, that he could do about it.

And it was this primitive aspect of the place that confirmed Yanka's opinion of the villagers and her lack of interest in them.

The steward, servant of the boyar, was technically a slave. The Viatichi families, besides being uncouth, were the poorest kind of peasants—sharecroppers—who instead of a fixed rent paid the boyar a third of their crop. The Mordvinians were hired laborers, who worked a part of the estate some way from the village that the boyar had decided to retain in his own hands; and the other Slav families from the south had already adopted the primitive ways of the northeast, it seemed to her, and were contentedly using the primitive slash-and-burn techniques on their modest holdings.

There were, as it happened, no unmarried young men among these Slavs in any case. The nearest to her in age was an eleven-year-old boy. As for the three Mordvinian and two Viatichi youths, although they all seemed kindly, she did not care for them.

This place is primitive, she decided. Whoever I find to marry, he certainly won't come from here.

It was three days later that her father had made a discovery that infuriated him even more. "There is good land here after all," he told her in frustration that evening. "Yes: chernozem. But they won't let me work it."

"Where?"

"Over towards the village they call Dirty Place. Can you believe it? I went over there today with those damned Mordvinians."

For nature—the retreating glaciers from the last ice age, to be exact—had here and there deposited in the region of the sandy podzols small stretches of good gray soil. There was a large area of this so-called chernozem above Vladimir, stretching towards Suzdal. And another, much smaller deposit had been made to the east of Russka.

"The boyar's keeping back that land. He's leaving us only the poor soil."

As it happened, this stretch of chernozem was divided into three parts. One part, somewhat to the north, was a private estate that belonged to the Grand Duke himself. The village there had been destroyed by a plague some years ago, but in time, no doubt, the Grand Duke would use it again. The part to the east was Black Land—nominally the Prince of Murom's—but let to the free peasants.

And the nearest, smaller part, belonged to Milei the boyar.

When the boyar had encountered Yanka and her father he had said
nothing of this. A single man and a girl were hardly such desirable
tenants for the best land. Let's keep them in reserve and see what turns
up, he reasonably judged.

Meanwhile he had decided to work a part of the good land for himself
with some slaves he had been able to find.

"Perhaps we could work some chernozem," Yanka suggested.

"No. I already asked the steward. He only wants hired laborers like the
Mordvinians. I'll not sink to that."

She put her arms around her father and kissed him, aware of the faint
smell of sweat from his shirt and the deep lines around his neck. She
hated to see him frustrated like this. "We can leave," she suggested. "We
have money."

The money they had brought was safely hidden under the floor.

"Maybe. Not this year, though."

"No," she agreed, "not this year." Winter was too close.

Yet despite the unsatisfactory life of the village, she felt a certain sense
of peace in these new surroundings. "At least," she remarked to her
father, "we are a long way from the Tatars."

The warm weather, surprisingly, continued through until mid-
October. Yanka became used to the quiet rhythm of the village. She went
out with the villagers to collect nuts in the forest; and when the men
killed an elk one day she helped the women prepare a splendid feast.

He moved along the track, letting the water pouring down from the trees
settle on his fur collar or run freely down the creased back of his neck.
Below him, at the bottom of the little cliff, the lucky spring burst from
the bank and seeped through the ferns into the river. He did not pause,
except to glance across the river below. Twice he cursed out loud.

Damn the girl.

Her fresh young body—what did it smell of? Roses? The wild carna-
tions in the woods? Nuts. Roasted nuts. Could it really smell of roasted
nuts?

Damn her, doesn't she see me? he almost said aloud. Perhaps she
doesn't know, he considered, but at once dismissed the thought. Oh yes.
She knows. They know everything, women.

So what did it mean? What did she mean by it? What did she suppose
he felt in that room, alone with her, with the rain pouring off the eaves
all around like a waterfall? What did she mean, arching those young
breasts when she knew he was watching, and turning towards him—her
whole, young body, and telling him in that soft voice that she was bored?

Is she teasing me? Does she despise me?

Pretending not to understand. That was her defense. And her weapon.
She was good—oh yes, she had been good to him. And she loved him.
At least, she had once. But since that boy on the river, he wasn't sure
what tricks she might be up to. It was as if she were his, yet not his; as
if she understood everything, was ready to open herself to him, yet
turned away whenever she sensed he might approach.

She was his daughter, of course.

Was that it? Of course that was reason enough, in theory. Forbidden. They both knew that.

But surely after all they had been through . . . They had a special bond, didn't they? Was there not in her calm eyes that seemed to stare at the world with a kind of sad understanding—was there not a perfect understanding of how they were, he and she?

The way her mouth turned down, he thought—a little sad, a little cynical, and also, yes, sensuous: very sensuous when awakened. Those lips, those sad, obstinate lips with their hint of a pout—the pout that never developed because her strong mouth kept everything under control—were they going to refuse to part and open for him? Were they going to smile and then open for another? The thought had become a torture to him.

He was her father. He stamped furiously down the path. He had heard of other fathers . . .

Besides, there was no one for either of them. No one else in this God-forsaken place.

"I'll be a father to her. I'll discipline her if she wants to play games with me," he muttered.

He had been so immersed in his thoughts that he had not noticed where he was going, nor realized how far from the village he had gone, until suddenly he looked up and saw a strange sight.

It was a bear. He stopped in his tracks. It was quite large. It was also very old. It was moving with great difficulty across the path ten yards in front of him. The bear saw him but seemed uninterested. It was moving very stiffly.

And then he realized: the bear was going to die. It was only searching for a final resting place.

Cautiously he went forward.

"Well, my Misha," he murmured, "what use can you be to me?"

The bear gave him a baleful look but was too weary to threaten him. How old, sad, and bedraggled the animal looked. The rain had soaked it; the bear's coat was caked with mud and smelled dank. Moving closer, Yanka's father drew his long hunting knife. A good idea had just occurred to him.

He would give Yanka a fur coat for the winter. That would please her. Not every man could say: "I have killed a bear for you."

It required great skill to kill a bear. Even though it had almost collapsed, an instant's revival, one swipe from those mighty arms, and he would be done for. But he thought he could do it.

He edged behind, paused, then suddenly leapt onto the creature's huge back.

The bear started, began to stand up; and he ripped his long, sharp blade right across the animal's throat.

The bear rose fully with the man on its back and tried to get at him. Again Yanka's father plunged his knife into the throat, attacking the windpipe and searching for the huge veins. After a moment he was sure he had succeeded, and he leapt down into the mud before running behind a tree.

He heard the bear gurgle. Then it came down heavily on its front legs again. Blood was pouring from its throat. The bear seemed to see him, but it did not move. It stood there miserably, knowing this was the end, and, for some strange reason, blinking uselessly. Then it crashed into the bushes and he heard it coughing.

An hour later he had skinned it.

Yanka found the muddy season depressing. It was made worse by her decision, on a day when the rains had stopped, to go down to the nearby village of Dirty Place.

What a dreary spot it was. Half a dozen huts clustered by the riverbank. The land there was Black Land, like the northern territory where Ilya and his family had gone, so that the peasants there were, in practice, free. Better than that, the village's land lay directly on the chernozem that the boyar Milei coveted.

Yet still it was dismal. The riverbank was very low. The ground immediately to the south was waterlogged and smelled of marsh.

And when Yanka spoke to some of the village women, she found that four out of the six she met suffered from some strange affliction that made the skin on their head spongy to the touch and their hair perpetually oily and matted.

Instinctively she drew away from them.

She was glad to get back, to put wood in the stove and feel her own hair, soft and light, as she ran her hand through it for reassurance.

It was that very evening that her father came in with a wonderful coat, made by one of the Mordvinian women from a bear he had killed for her himself. He had kept the incident a secret from her. Now he handed the coat to her with a smile.

"You killed a bear? For me?" She was half delighted, yet half terrified. "You might have been killed."

He laughed. "It will keep you warm up here in the north."

She kissed him. He smiled but said nothing more.

Three days later the snows came. It was cold, very cold; though one was perfectly warm inside. Yet once winter had sealed the little village she could not escape the sad fact: it was boring.

She had no friends. The village, it seemed to her, was quiet as a tomb. They did not mix much with their neighbors and, though they were only yards apart, days might pass without her speaking to another soul. There was not even a church to draw them together.

To pass the time, she began to make a large embroidered cloth. It had a white background, and onto this she sewed, in bright red, the striking, geometric birds that the village women had taught her when she was a child.

So, in this remote northern hamlet, appeared a design drawn directly from ancient, oriental patterns familiar to the Iranian horsemen from the steppe a thousand years ago.

November passed. The cloth progressed, and the girl and her father lived alone.

The change in her life came in the first half of December. It took place rather suddenly.

Her father had been very kind to her of late. He knew that she was sometimes afraid of him if he drank too much, and so he had hardly touched any mead since autumn. In the last two days he had been especially warm with her, often giving her friendly hugs and a gentle kiss.

One evening, however, he did drink mead. She saw the faint flush around his neck; she looked at him a little nervously, but decided that he had not drunk enough to make him depressed. Indeed, she felt a little surge of happiness to see the smile of well-being on his face. She noticed his hands, resting on the table. For some reason she noticed the thick fair hairs on the back of them and this, too, filled her with a feeling of affection.

And then she did something very foolish.

She had been heating some red dye for the thread: it was almost boiling; and she decided to carry it across the room.

Her father had been sitting very quietly at the table now, for several minutes, without speaking. She did not particularly look at him, though she was aware of his strong back, and the bald top of his head as she brushed past him with the pot of dye.

Perhaps it was glancing at the top of his head that made her lose concentration. But suddenly her foot caught against the leg of the little bench he was sitting on. She started to fall, desperately righted herself and, by a miracle, only slopped a quarter of the boiling contents of the pot onto the table.

"The devil take me!"

He had leapt back, upsetting the bench on the floor.

She stared at him horrified, then at the dye on the table.

"Your hands?"

"You want to scald me alive?" He clasped one hand in the other with a grimace of pain.

She dropped the pot onto the stove.

"Let me see. Let me bandage it."

"You careless idiot," he roared. But he did not let her come near.

She was terrified, yet also anguished.

"Let me help you. I'm sorry."

He took a deep breath, gritted his teeth. And then it happened.

"You will be," he suddenly said, very quietly.

She felt the inside of her stomach go cold. She knew that tone. It came from her childhood; and it meant: "Wait until this evening."

She trembled. In an instant, it seemed to her, the relationship of the last few months had vanished. She was a little girl again. And as a little girl, she knew what was to follow. Her knees began to shake. "You should look where you are going with scalding water," he said coldly. She was so upset she had hurt him that, in a way, she almost preferred it if he would punish her. It was two years since he had last done so, before Kiy had been taken away. Yet it was strangely humiliating to be addressed like a child again.

"Go to the bench."

She lay on the bench. She heard him undoing his belt. Then she felt him pull up her linen shift. She braced herself.

But nothing happened.

She closed her eyes, waiting. And then, to her surprise, she felt his hands upon her. Then she felt his breath by her ear.

"I won't punish you this time, my little wife," he said softly. "But there is something else you can do for me." Now she felt his hands moving over the back of her legs. She frowned, what was he doing? "Hush now," he breathed. "I won't hurt you."

She began to blush furiously. She did not know what to do. Even now, she could not quite understand what was happening.

She felt his hands advance. Suddenly she felt naked as she had never felt before. She wanted to cry out, to run; yet a hot sense of shame held her strangely helpless. Where was she to run to? What could she say to their strange neighbors?

At this terrible moment, this man, her father, in this stifling hot room, was trying to do something strange to her. And now she realized exactly what it was.

His touch terrified her. Her body suddenly arched, rigid, and she heard him gasp.

"Ah, that's it, my little wife."

Moments later, after a sudden spasm of pain, she heard him moan: "Ah, my little bird, you knew. You always knew."

Did she know? Did a little voice within her tell her that she had known this was to be, that she shared some complicity with him?

She wanted to cry, yet strangely, at this instant, she could not.

She could not even hate him. She had to love him.

He was all she had.

The next morning she went out early in the snow.

It was going to be a bright day. The sky was pale blue. Pulling snowshoes on over her thick felt boots, she trudged towards the high riverbank. The sun was gleaming on the edge of the bank. Below, the forest was bathed in golden light as the sun rose.

A ragged figure was coming towards her. It was one of the Viatichi men. He was leaning far forward, dragging a pile of logs on a little sled behind him. His dark eyes stared at her, piercing, from under his heavy gray eyebrows. He knows, she thought. It seemed impossible to her that everyone in the hamlet did not know what she had done the night before.

The bearded figure went silently past her, without a word, like a sullen, elderly monk.

There was the lightest breath of wind, but it was very cold. Her heavy coat kept her warm; yet she was unusually conscious of her own body inside it, a body that felt naked and bruised.

She turned.

A few yards in front of her there was a silver birch tree. Its branches were bare, wintry; but the eastern morning sun was making its silvery bark shine. The black ribs on its bark reminded her of the rich black earth in the south. You look as if you were made of snow and ice, she thought, yet inside you are still warm.

The birch was a hardy tree. It would grow anywhere, in any conditions, supplanting trees that had been burned or cut down. I will be like that, too, she vowed. I shall survive.

Slowly she trudged back to the *izba*. An old woman peered at her from a doorway.

"Perhaps she knows; perhaps not." Though she did not realize it, Yanka had said these words out loud.

She decided that she did not care if her secret were guessed.

She went inside.

Her father was there. He was sitting on a bench eating kasha. He glanced up at her, but neither of them spoke.

It happened again, a few days later; then again the next day.

She was puzzled herself by her own attitude.

On the first of these two occasions she had tried to resist him. It was the first time in her life that she had realized, actually physically felt, how much stronger he was than she. He had not hurt her; there had been no need. He had simply taken her arms and she had found that she was completely unable to move them. Unless she chose to kick, or try to bite him, she was easily in his power. And even if she had: what then? A physical fight she would lose? The breakup of the only home she had?

In silence she had braced herself against him, trying to ward him off, then given up the futile struggle.

And as he had possessed her she had thought, grimly, of the birch tree in the winter snow, surviving, always surviving.

Her confusion, in the weeks that followed, was natural. For he was never brutal. Despite herself, she could not help the fact that her body responded to his lovemaking.

He no longer called her "little wife." That would have seemed, now, a too blatant reference to their secret. Nor did he put his arm around her in public, as he had used to do.

Yet she came to see him, now, as a woman sees her husband.

She still loved him. She became aware in a different way of the rhythm of his body. When he sat at the table and the back of his neck seemed taut, or his hands slightly clenched, she felt sorry for him, as she had when she was a child; but now, instead of thinking he needed comfort, she knew that these were simply physical symptoms for which there were simple remedies.

Sometimes—even if with a secret inner sigh, because she knew what must follow—she would walk over to him when he sat like this and, instead of throwing her arms around him as she would once have done, she would knead the back of his neck and his shoulders.

It was a strange relationship: she was never lighthearted; she never ruffled his hair or teased him as she might have done with a friend or husband; there was always a slight constriction in her manner towards him; she was timid, yet practical.

As the winter months went by, a new and curious bond grew between them. Once the door of the *izba* was open, they were a perfect father and daughter. If the other villagers knew or suspected, no one said anything. And the very fact that they shared this secret meant that there was a complicity between them.

Complicity. They both knew.

It was only a short step from there to the development that, in secret, she realized she had been dreading.

In the month of January, several times, she gave herself to him with pleasure.

Why should it matter so much to her that, for a few brief minutes, her young body had taken pleasure and found release in the function for which it had been created? Why were they so much worse, these particular intimacies, than those which had already taken place?

She knew very well. It was a long time since she had seen a priest, but she knew what this meant. The Devil had her. She had not only sinned: she had rejoiced in her sin.

It was after these that she entered the abyss of self-disgust.

"I am like the women at Dirty Place," she moaned.

She felt as if her hair were matted like theirs, and as if her whole being was defiled.

And when she was alone, in her misery, she turned to the distant, sad-faced little icon in the corner and prayed: "Save me, Mother of God, from my sins. Show me a way out of this darkness."

The boyar Milei was cautious and shrewd.

He had three daughters and two sons and he meant to leave them rich.

He trusted nobody.

And though he served the princely family of the little eastern territory of Murom, he did so cynically.

His attitude was perfectly reasonable. For a long time now, the greater boyars had seldom actually served day to day in the princely retinues, leaving that to their sons or to poor cousins. And though they were theoretically at the prince's service in any emergency, they had minds of their own. In the larger territory of Riazan, immediately to the south, the boyars were well known for their independence, and the Riazan princes had some difficulty controlling them. In other principalities—in the distant lands of Galicia in the southwest, let alone over the border in Poland, the nobles and gentry were strong, and a prince needed their agreement to any major decision.

There was another factor, too.

While the princely families were royal—for they still all descended from the family of Saint Vladimir—they had become large. Unlike the great days of Kiev, when each prince ruled over a huge territory, some of the notable princes now ruled over minor towns, and their children and grandchildren might have less in land than the greater boyars. These small appanages, as the princely inheritances were called, meant that a boyar like Milei might have a more aggressive view of his own status: and as he looked out upon the changing fortune of the many little princely towns, he saw a more relative political world than his ancestors had.

As for his own princes, those of the ancient city of Murom, they were puppets of the Grand Duke, who, in Milei's opinion, was not to be trusted.

"In any case," he shrewdly remarked, "even the Grand Duke, whatever he may like to pretend, is only a servant of the Tatar khans from now on."

So where did his advantage lie? How was he to get richer?

The most telling development to Milei was not the fact that the Grand Duke had had to travel across the steppe to submit, humiliatingly, to the khan. It was not that the Tatar army had destroyed cities—they could be rebuilt. It was not that the Prince of Chernigov had been executed.

What Milei wisely observed was that, unlike the Russian princes since great Monomakh, the Tatar khan minted his own coins.

"It's the Tatars who will hold the moneybags now," he told his two sons. "They won't destroy all the trade—why should they?—but they'll reap the profits."

The province had been very depressed since the invasion. Though Milei owned slaves who produced some handicrafts he could sell, and though his villages brought him some brightly woven cloth and quantities of furs, there didn't seem much room for expansion at present.

We must look to our own land, he decided.

He knew several boyars who had even been spending months at a time on their estates recently. Where before they always lived in the town, traded, and received their rents in money, they had been forced to live off the land.

"And you know," one had said to him, "it may not be silver coin, but when a peasant of mine turns up with two sacks of grain, a cheese you can hardly carry, fifty eggs, and a wagonload of firewood for his rent, I find I'm quite pleased to see him. When I go into the country, I may look like a peasant"—he had laughed—"but I live well."

Which had made Milei think carefully about Russka.

How big was the place anyway?

Here Milei had to guess.

For like most such documents in this huge and imprecise land, the title deeds to the estate stated no exact boundaries.

> On the west; north and south
> side, the boundary shall be
> as far as the axe, the plow
> and the scythe have gone.

It was the usual formula. Only the local people, long familiar with the place, could say with any certainty where these traditional limits to cultivation lay.

But these three sides, lying as they did upon poor podzol, were of less interest to Milei than the east side across the river, where the chernozem was rich and fertile. And here the boundary, where it joined the prince's Black Land, was well established.

Since there was no present reason why the Prince of Murom should grant it to him, Milei had several times offered to buy the village of Dirty Place from him. So far he had got nowhere. But as his steward had pointed out, he had only partly cultivated the chernozem he already had.

"Send me more slaves," the steward said, "and I can yield you good returns."

It was with these matters on his mind that, late in the August of that year, Milei the boyar came to visit Russka.

The hay was already cut and the cone-shaped stacks were casting shadows on the meadow across the river when he rode into the settlement.

He had given the steward fair warning, and a stout new hut, with a tall, steep roof and a fenced plot of land around it, awaited his arrival. He came alone with a single servant and immediately called for fodder for his two splendid horses.

When the steward started to bring hay, he immediately cursed him. "Oats, you fool. These aren't your pitiful village horses."

Indeed, the splendid beasts were half as big again as the sturdy little northern horses the villagers used.

Milei himself ate quickly, made a few testy comments about the turnips they offered him, and then at once retired for the night.

But when the steward's wife complained to her husband about the lord's bad temper that night, the steward grinned. "It's a good sign. I know him," he told her. And when she looked surprised. "See, he wouldn't bother to get cross if he hadn't decided to take an interest in the place."

The old fellow was right.

Milei was up at dawn the next morning, riding out to inspect the estate, with a few curt nods to the inhabitants as they went out to the fields.

The largest crop, the spring-sown rye, had already been reaped in July. They were reaping barley that day.

Milei rode around every inch of the place, with the steward running along beside him. He paid special attention to the chernozem.

"We don't grow any wheat?"

"Not at present, lord."

"We should try." He gave a short, hard laugh. "Then you can make communion bread."

Communion bread? So the boyar meant them to have a church. The steward smiled to himself. He must really mean business.

He made other suggestions, too. They had started to grow buckwheat in the south when he was a boy. He wanted to try that at Russka. In particular he seemed to have taken offense at those turnips they had offered him the previous night.

"Damned peasants' food," he said in disgust. "You hardly grow any peas here."

"No, lord."

"I want peas, and lentils, too. Hemp as well. Grow it with the peas. Hemp seeds are full of oil. They keep you warm in winter."

"Yes, lord." What on earth could the boyar want with all this? Could it be that he not only wanted to build the place up but actually live here himself? "Will this be for yourself, lord?" he rashly inquired.

"Mind your own business and do as you're told," the boyar replied sharply, and the steward immediately bowed.

So that's what he's up to, if I know him, he thought happily.

Milei was pleased with the flax.

"But I want more," he announced.

This was the basic fiber product of northern Russian agriculture and it was one commodity that could be profitably transported to market. The northwestern city of Pskov was even exporting flax abroad.

When he inspected the livestock, the boyar did not complain. The sheep were not bad: they were small, hornless animals with rather long bodies that he had introduced himself. The pigs did well. But the cattle made him shake his head sadly. They stood less than three and a half feet high at the shoulder; at winter's end a single man could carry them out of their stalls to pasture.

Milei said nothing and passed on.

It was afternoon before the boyar finally returned.

He ate, then slept. And then, in the early evening, he made a tour of the village huts and inspected the peasants.

He was not pleased.

"A dirty, miserable collection of people," he remarked with irritation to the steward. "And don't bother to remind me I sent most of them here," he added with a grim smile.

But his temper visibly improved when, last of all, he came to the house of the father and daughter he had sent the previous year.

"At last," he said with satisfaction, "a clean *izba.*"

It was better than that. There were fresh herbs hanging from a little straw rope over the stove. The place smelled sweet. Everything was beautifully cared for: the loving cup on the table, in the shape of a duck, was a little work of art. In the red corner, a candle burned before the icon; in the corner opposite, three beautiful embroidered cloths hung.

This was what Yanka, in eight months of the blackest inner torment, had achieved.

And in front of him, it appeared to the boyar, stood a model father and his child. Though Savva had been working in the field all day, his thin brown beard was neatly combed. He had put on a fresh blouse in the boyar's honor, and he smiled respectfully but manfully, like a fellow with a clear conscience.

The girl was a pearl. Neat, clean, and, he was bound to say, good looking. For once, even the cynical Milei's heart was touched.

"A good man deserves such a daughter to look after him," he said with a pleasant smile to them both.

How the girl had improved since he saw her. She was still slim, but her body and face had filled out a little in this first season of her womanhood. Her skin was wonderfully clear, yet a little pale.

He looked at her carefully. Was there a trace of worry in her eye?

Then, thinking of his own daughters, he reminded himself that all girls worry about something at that age.

"A pretty virgin to pluck," he could not help murmuring to himself once they were outside again.

He went to Dirty Place the next day, then announced that he was departing, and that he would return shortly.

"So be ready for me every day," he shouted to the steward as he left.

He did not come back for a month.

When he returned, in late September, he was followed by four boats which his men were pulling up the stream with ropes.

In the first was a family of slaves.

"Mordvinians, I'm afraid," he said to the steward, "but you'll make them work."

In the others there was livestock: Milei had bought young calves from the Riazan region.

"They grow them bigger on those Oka meadows," he said. "Give two of them to that new man with the daughter to look after for the winter. He'll take good care of them."

He settled into his house and announced that he would remain there a week, at the end of which we would receive the rents.

"Then," he told the steward, "I'm going to Novgorod on business. I shall return from there in the spring."

He made no inspections this time, but contented himself with walking around and watching the villagers at work.

One of the activities he liked to watch was the threshing.

This took place on a space cleared beside the little kilns where the grain was dried by smoking.

The sheaves were threshed in two ways. Some were hit with sticks and flails: this was the men's work. But the more delicate method, performed by the women, used a horizontal log, on two upright supports. By tapping the sheaf on the log, the grain was knocked out but the long straw was preserved for weaving and plaiting. The rye straw was especially long and soft, yet strong enough for rope making.

Milei often walked past and paused to watch. Though the women were at first a little frightened by the presence of this big, Turkish-looking lord with his hard eyes and yellow hair, they soon got used to him. He did not seem to be looking at anything in particular.

But Yanka soon sensed that he was. She could feel it.

She was always neatly dressed; but the second day he came by, he noticed that the smock she was wearing had one of her bird designs embroidered on the front, and that she had tied her belt just a fraction tighter than usual, so that as she bent and then raised her arm, he could clearly see the outline of her body.

Indeed, to Milei, worldly though he was, there was something magical in this little village scene, miles from anywhere, with this pretty, clean young creature working with the other women before him.

He had been away from home for a long time. He felt strong, but he knew he was getting older; and this girl was different.

He felt strangely refreshed, as though in this magical late summer season, in this place apart, it had been granted him for a few days to step outside the passing of the years.

He did not speak to her, nor she to him. But they were both aware of each other and of this thought which, as inevitable as the coming of the shadows, seemed to join them in the bright silence of the afternoon.

On the fourth day, in the early evening, as he was standing alone gazing out over the reddening field across the river, she came towards him, smiled, and passed on.

The day before he was due to leave, Milei the boyar received his rents.

They brought him sacks of grain and young pigs. Half the pigs were usually slaughtered before winter. They brought him lambs and baby goats. One family, who had elected to pay in money instead of kind, brought him a pile of the rabbit skins bearing an official stamp that were the small currency of that time and place.

They brought him beaver skins that he could trade.

It was a haunting little scene, with peasants dragging forward pigs and cattle. The cattle still wore the wooden bells that were hung around their necks when they were put out to feed in the woods after harvest. A melancholy clinking filled the autumn air as they came before the lord and were marked for killing.

Milei, though he was pleased with the rents, felt a sadness at the thought that he was about to leave this place. At the end of the proceedings, when it was almost dusk, he rose and, signaling to the steward that he wished to be alone, left the hamlet for a last walk along the river's edge.

The shadows were long; the trees seemed very tall in the silence.

He was surprised a little later, though not displeased, to find the girl in front of him on the path. Below them lay the still, glassy river. He saw that she wished to speak, and stopped.

This time, she looked straight at him, with those strange, half-sad eyes. "Take me with you, lord."

He gazed at her. "Where to?"

"To Novgorod. Isn't that where you are going?"

He nodded. "You don't like it here?" he asked quietly.

"I must leave."

He looked at her curiously. What was troubling her? "Is your father unkind?"

"Maybe. Maybe not. What's that to you?" She took a deep breath. "Take me with you."

"You want to see Novgorod: is that it?"

"I want to go with you."

There was something desperate about her. He had not observed it before, and if he had been a young man he might have found it a little frightening. She was like a *rusalka,* haunting him from a river. Yet all the same, she seemed quite self-possessed.

He thought of her body.

"What would your father say?"

She shrugged.

So that was it. He thought he guessed. He looked at her calmly, with a new frankness. "And what would you do for me, if I took you with me?"

She stared back at him, with equal calmness. "Whatever you want."

It was her only chance. He did not know that, if he refused, she had decided to kill herself.

"Very well," he said.

He turned to go back. The river below was a pale ribbon of light; the woods were already dark.

It was a long journey—nearly four hundred miles northwest to the lands by the Baltic Sea. Yet as soon as she left Russka with the boyar and his retinue of half a dozen men, she felt a sense of excitement.

It was also, for a time, uncomfortable. For the boyar had sent the boats downriver again and told her they were to ride to Novgorod.

"You can ride, can't you?"

She could ride the farm horses, of course; but it would not occur to a peasant to undertake a long journey except by boat. By the end of the first day in the saddle she was sore. By the third, she was in agony. Milei thought this was amusing.

"Anyone would think I'd beaten and raped you," he remarked jocularly.

He was a large and powerful figure; and when he rode his tall and splendid horses, he looked larger and more impressive still. He wore a fur-trimmed coat and hat, which had a diamond in it. His big, high-cheeked face; his hard eyes, set wide apart; his rich fair beard, all seemed to proclaim: "I am power itself, untouchable by mere peasants, for whom I care nothing."

And with a trace of pride she watched him as they rode and murmured to herself: "This is my boyar."

He had wasted no time. He had made love to her the first night after they had left the village.

But though, for a moment, she had been a little alarmed by the size of this powerful man whose tent she was sharing, he was surprisingly gentle with her.

He made love skillfully. She hoped she pleased him.

He was kindly as well. A few questions had before long drawn from her the whole story of her recent months with her father, and the boyar was comforting.

"Of course you want to get away," he told her gently. "But don't think too badly of him, or of yourself. In these small villages, miles from anywhere, I can promise you these things are not uncommon."

Her father, to her surprise, had not raised great objections to her leaving. Strictly, since they were free peasants, Milei could not order her father to give her up. But when the powerful boyar had summoned the peasant to him and informed him of his decision, he gave him such a piercing look that her father went scarlet.

He did not altogether lose his presence of mind, though. "The girl is of great help to me, lord," he said carefully. "I shall be a poorer man without her."

Milei had understood. "How much poorer?"

"My land is very bad. And you see I am a good workman. Let me have some of the chernozem."

Milei considered. He supposed the fellow would work it well. "Very well. Five chets. You'll pay a fair rent. Talk to the steward."

And he had waved him away.

When Yanka had parted from him, there had been tears in his eyes. She saw him for what he was and felt sorry for him.

They rode up to the Kliasma River.

Yanka would have liked to enter the capital city of Vladimir, which was not far away, and see the famous icon of Our Lady. She had heard that it had been painted by the Evangelist Saint Luke himself. But Milei shook his head, and the little party turned westward. They rode along the Kliasma for ten days until they were just north of the small town of Moscow. Then they struck northwest.

The rains caught them just as they reached another minor city, Tver, that lay below the gentle Valdai Hills, on the banks of the upper reaches of the Volga. It was a small town, rather like its neighbor Moscow. They found an inn there and waited for ten days. Then the snows came.

A week later, sitting in a large and comfortable sled now, Yanka began the last, and magical, part of her journey.

Some days there were icy winds and blizzards. But on others the sun shone over a sparkling northern scene.

How softly and easily the sled had raced down the slope by Tver and across the frozen Volga. They traveled swiftly across the snow, sometimes following rivers, sometimes plunging into dark woods and following endless tracks between the trees.

West of Moscow, she had noticed, the woods had become mainly broad-leaved again, like those of the south. As they went farther west and north, the tall firs and pines of the taiga reappeared together with these trees.

Then, late in November, the countryside began to change. It opened out into huge flat spaces with mixed woods broken up into coppices and small stands. Often she realized that they were gliding over ice rather than earth, and that there was frozen marsh underneath. The ridges were very low. It felt as if they were approaching the sea.

Milei was in high good humor. He began to sing the song of Sadko, the merchant of Novgorod, smiling to himself as they sped over the flat, open land. Then, one afternoon, he pointed. "Lord Novgorod the Great."

From a distance it was not so impressive, because the citadel only rose a score of feet above the river. But as they approached, she began to realize the remarkable size of the place.

"It's huge," she said.

He laughed. "Just wait till we get there."

The mighty city of Novgorod lay on the slow-moving river Volkhov, just north of the great lake Ilmen. It consisted of two halves, one on each side of the river, surrounded by tremendous wooden palisades and joined by an enormous wooden bridge. In the middle of the western half, and raised above it, stood a stout citadel with thick, blank stone walls.

They came in from the east, clattered through the eastern quarter and across the bridge.

Yanka cried out in wonder.

The bridge was massive. Sailing boats could go under it.

"There's not another like it in all the lands of Rus," Milei remarked.

The bridge led them straight under a huge gateway. Immediately before them towered a stern-looking cathedral. They turned right and passed through the northern quarters of the city until they finally came to rest at a large wooden structure that was an inn.

And already Yanka was gasping.

For all the streets were paved with wood.

The early part of her stay in Novgorod was happy.

Milei was busy, but although she was there, ostensibly, as his servant, he often let her walk along behind him and, from time to time, curtly pointed out the sights.

The western side, containing the citadel, was called the Saint Sophia side, because of the stern-looking cathedral she had seen. It contained three quarters, called ends: the most northerly, on the edge of which they were staying, was the Leatherworkers' End; then came the Zagorod End, where the rich boyars had their houses. Then came the Potters' End.

There were fine wooden houses everywhere, wooden churches, it seemed, by the hundred, and even stone churches by the dozen.

How solid and strong everything seemed. The streets were not very wide—mostly about ten feet. They were made of big logs, split end to end and laid, the flat side up, across the framework of poles, like rails, that ran along under the street. At one place, where they were repairing the street, she saw that underneath lay layers—she could not see how many—of older wooden pavings.

"So the streets of Novgorod are slowly rising," she said to Milei.

"That's right," he replied. "You'll notice that you have to take a step down, now, into some of the older stone buildings."

Every street was enclosed by fences—not like the modest fences she knew at Russka, but thick, solid wooden walls, almost like small palisades, that seemed to say: "Bump into a fence in Novgorod if you like, but you'll get hurt."

When she was a girl, in the south, the people from Kiev or Pereiaslav were always a little contemptuous of the distant people of Novgorod.

"Carpenters," they still called them.

But she found nothing to laugh at in their carpentry now. She found it a little frightening.

The great cathedral in the center of the citadel had been built to rival its namesake at Kiev: Saint Sophia.

Like the Kievan church, it had five aisles. But its walls, instead of soft glowing pink brick in tidy lines, were made of large irregular stones. Its whole aspect was harsh and austere. Instead of Kiev's thirteen shining cupolas, it had five large domes, plated with lead, that gave off a dull, dark gleam. Inside, instead of glittering mosaics with their mysterious, otherworldly Byzantine light, huge frescoes stared coolly down from the flat, soaring walls. The building expressed not transcendental mystery, but high, hard, unyielding northern power. For this place, it reminded the beholder, was Lord Novgorod the Great.

"The painting here was done mostly by Novgorod artists, not Greeks," Milei explained to her. And when she admired the huge bronze gates of the west door, carved with rich biblical scenes, he told her: "We took them from the Swedes, but they were made in Germany, in Magdeburg."

When they came out, she pointed to a huge wooden palace standing nearby. "Is that where the prince lives?" she asked.

"No," Milei told her. "The people of Novgorod won't let the prince live in the city. He has to live in his own little fort, just to the north. That's the archbishop's palace you're looking at. It's the archbishop and the people's *veche* who rule in Novgorod. The prince defends the place and they won't accept a prince they don't like."

She had always heard that the city of Novgorod was free, but she had not realized that such expressions of power, as she saw all around her, could belong to the people.

"They are truly free then," she remarked with admiration.

"They are truly obstinate," he replied curtly, and glancing down at her puzzled face he remarked: "You'll see."

But if Saint Sophia's side was impressive, it was nothing compared to the astonishment she felt when they crossed, on their second day, over the river.

From the citadel they passed under the huge Virgin gate with its stone church over the arch and across the great wooden bridge. Below them lay the frozen river Volkhov that led north-southward on the ancient trading route down to the Dnieper and Kiev, and flowed northward to a huge lake called Ladoga, that was joined by the river Neva to the Gulf of Finland and the Baltic Sea.

And before them lay the Market side.

"There are two ends," Milei announced, as the sled went over the bridge: "the Slovensk and the Carpenters' ends. And in the middle is the market. That's where we're going."

She had never seen anything like it. Beside another impressive church spread a huge open area stretching to the river's edge and the wharfs.

It was covered with frozen snow, yet on the snow were long lines of brightly colored stalls, more than she could count.

"There must be a thousand," she said.

"Probably."

Milei had business to conduct, so he left her to wander alone all morning. She was astonished by what she discovered.

For this was the ancient trading emporium of the north. There were all kinds of people there, even in winter: not only Slavs, but Germans, Swedes, and traders from the Baltic states of Lithuania and the lands of the Latvians. One stout man selling salted fish even told her that in his youth he had been with the herring fleets all the way to the Western island of England.

One could buy anything.

There were all manner of foods: huge pots of honey, barrels of salt and blubber oil. Fish there was in abundance, even in winter. There were barrels of eels, of herring and of cod. Bream and turbot, she soon learned, were popular. There were great piles of furs everywhere: bear, beaver, fox, and even sable. There was bright pottery and acres, it seemed, of beautifully worked leather.

"At the end of summer," a woman told her, "they bring in the cart-loads of hops. Ah," she smiled, "the smell of them!"

There were neatly carved ornaments of bone and reindeer horn from the northern forests. They sold walrus tusks, which they called "fish teeth."

And there were icons.

As she looked at these, she noticed a difference between these and the icons she had always seen as a child.

These seemed brighter, their outlines clearer and harder. Strong reds burst gaily out upon the icy scene, as though in these bracing northern climes a more boisterous deity was emerging over the coasts and forests. She had just observed the newly developing and soon-to-be-famous Novgorod school of icon painting. She was not sure that she liked them.

But the goods she coveted came from the East. They had come from the caravans of the steppe, from the vast lands the Tatars now controlled. They had come through the cities of Suzdalia to the great emporium of the north.

There were spices, on their way to the West. There were combs made of boxwood and beads of all kinds. And there were dazzling silks from old Constantinople. She ran her hand over them sensuously.

"Can you imagine feeling that soft silk on your skin?" the stall-holder asked her.

She could.

It was while she was watching a large man counting a pile of the stamped squirrel skins that the Novgorodians, too, used as small cur-rency, that she noticed something else. He was making small notes for himself with a stylus on a little wax tablet. She had seen Milei the boyar do this, but here was an ordinary small merchant doing so, too. She wandered around the other stalls. Other merchants, even artisans, had wax tablets or, very often, little pieces of birchbark on which they had made notes and drawings.

"Can you read and write?" she asked a woman minding a fish stall.

"Yes, my dove. Most people can," she answered.

It made a deep impression on Yanka. No one at Russka could. And it opened up new possibilities in her eyes.

These people, she realized, are Slavs, yet they are not the same as us.

And as she looked around the huge square, which was also where the *veche* met, she began to have an idea of the thrusting, adventurous power of the Baltic north.

That night, in the inn, Milei summoned her to eat with him alone. He was in excellent humor. Whatever his business was, it had gone well.

She had never eaten like this. Fishes she had never had before, rich venison, huge bowls, carefully arranged, of delicacies and sweetmeats. At one point they brought a bowl of shiny roe that she had never seen before and placed it before her.

"What's this?" she asked.

"Caviar." He smiled. "From a perch. Try it."

She had heard of caviar; she knew it came from perch, sturgeon, and other fishes; but she had never eaten it. This was boyar's food.

He plied her with mead and watched with amusement as her face grew flushed.

Towards the end of the meal, the door of the room opened and a thin old man looked in inquiringly. The boyar gave him a quick nod, and he entered. He was a minstrel, a *skazitel.* In his hand he carried a *gusli*—the small harp of his trade.

"What will you sing, *skazitel?"* the boyar asked.

"Two songs, lord," he replied. "One of the south, one of the north."

He spoke with an accent that made Yanka think he had originally come from the south himself.

"The first," he explained, "is a composition of my own. I call it 'Prince Igor.'"

Yanka smiled. There had been several popular tales in her childhood of the noble Igor—a southern prince who had led a great raid against the Cumans of the steppe. It had been a valiant expedition, but it had failed and Prince Igor had been killed. Every Russian knew the story.

The old man had composed a haunting song. As his thin voice filled the room with a melancholy, oriental sound, she could see, almost smell, the endless grasses of the steppe, the great empty spaces of her childhood.

The message of the song was simple: if the Russian princes were only united, the men of the steppe would never defeat them; and it seemed to apply even more poignantly now that the Tatars had come.

She looked up and saw that Milei, too, was misty eyed. Were not his own ancestors these very men, Rus and Cuman, who had fought upon the steppe?

It was now that he reached behind him and pulled from a leather bag a small bale which he put in front of her.

It was a roll of the finest oriental silk.

"A present for you," he said, and, seeing her look of utter astonishment, the big boyar leaned back his head and let out a huge laugh.

"Milei is generous to those who please him," he cried. "Sing your other song," he commanded the *skazitel.*

This was the Novgorod song of Sadko the rich merchant. It was, in part, the Russian version of the Orpheus story, with the merchant minstrel charming the Finnish sea god in his palace at the bottom of the sea, and thus winning his return to life. It was also a reminder of an actual merchant of the city.

The minstrel had set it to a lilting, sensuous tune.

Yanka lay down at Milei's feet and slowly drew the soft, shining silk through her fingers; as the song described the sea god churning the ocean waves while Sadko played his harp, she stretched out luxuriously, hugging the bale of silk to her and looking up at the boyar. The top of his kaftan was open. She stared at the curling fair hairs on his chest and at the little metal disk that hung from his neck, that bore the three-pronged *tamga* of his ancient clan. She looked up at him and smiled until, at last, he, too, gave a soft laugh and waved the minstrel away.

She abandoned herself to Milei the boyar that night. Everything was right. And afterward, it seemed to her, that something more than usual had opened within her and that she, too, had been with Sadko the merchant minstrel in the palaces in the deeps of that northern sea.

Yet although Yanka was learning more every day about the world, it was two weeks later that she made her greatest discovery, and it came as a terrible shock.

For if there was one thing she had looked forward to in Novgorod, it was the chance of seeing that city's famous prince: Alexander.

He was an extraordinary man. At the very moment Russia was cowering before the Mongols in the east, this young prince, descended from Monomakh, had won stunning victories over Russia's foes from the west, smashing the Teutonic Knights in a battle on the ice, and halting the mighty Swedes, in an action by the river Neva that was to earn him his title—Alexander Nevsky. Yanka had already heard of this hero, even in faraway Russka; yet here, if she mentioned his name, people only shrugged. She could not understand it.

Since leaving the south, she had never heard anyone discuss the political situation and when, once or twice on the journey, she had asked Milei some naïve question, he had only laughed.

But all that changed the night that the boyar gave a feast.

It was for the men with whom he had been doing business, and she was allowed to remain in the room to serve. There were about a dozen of them—mostly large, bearded men in rich silk kaftans. Several wore huge sparkling stones; one was so fat it seemed astonishing to her that he could walk at all. Some were boyars, others wealthy merchants, and two, including a younger man with a thin, dark face, of the middling merchant class.

Only as she heard them talk did she realize the richness and size of Novgorod.

For they spoke of estates scores, even hundreds of miles away in the forests and marshes of the northeast. They spoke of iron from the marshes, of great salt beds, of huge herds of reindeer that roamed by the tundra's edge. She learned that for a month in summer, in these northern climes, there was no darkness but only a pale twilight, and that in midwinter trappers roamed the wastes which scarcely grew light. A boyar of Novgorod might own whole tracts of land that he never even saw, and receive rents of furs from trappers who had traveled a hundred miles to their rendezvous and had never in their lives set eyes on a town of any kind.

Truly, this was the land of the mighty, the endless taiga.

But when she heard them speak of politics, she was astonished.

"The question is, what are you going to do about the Tatars?" Milei began. "Will you submit or will you fight them?"

There was a murmur round the room.

"The situation is delicate," an elderly boyar remarked. "The present Grand Duke will not last."

Yanka knew the last Grand Duke of Vladimir, the father of the great Prince Alexander of Novgorod, had died on his way back from a submissive visit to Mongolia. Some said the Tatars had poisoned him. That year his brother had succeeded him and confirmed his nephew Alexander as ruler of Novgorod. But this new Grand Duke was said to be weak.

"The real struggle for power," another said, "will be between Alexander and his younger brother Andrei."

She had heard of his brother but knew nothing about him.

"That's where we shall have to take sides." The old boyar nodded.

And then she heard the first astounding words.

"To some of us," the thin-faced young merchant remarked, "they are both of them traitors."

Traitors? Prince Alexander, the valiant conqueror of the Swedes and Germans a traitor? To her amazement, no one protested.

"It's true," the fat boyar said with a sigh, "that Alexander is not loved. People think he likes the Tatars too much."

"Is it true," Milei asked, "that at his battle with the German knights he used Tatar bowmen?"

"It's been said, but I believe it's untrue," the fat boyar said. "But you must remember that not only do people dislike his friendship with the Tatars, but there are those in this city, and still more in our neighbor Pskov, who would be happy to see the Germans ruling here."

As he said these words, there was an awkward silence.

Since being in Novgorod, Yanka had heard that, at the very time when Prince Alexander had been defeating the Swedes and Germans, the leaders of the city of Pskov had actually taken the German side.

"When Alexander came back to Novgorod, he hanged the German sympathizers here, you know," the fat boyar explained to Milei, "so even if someone felt that way now, he might not say so."

For a moment the silence in the room grew very deep.

"The rumor is," the young merchant went on quietly, "that young Prince Andrei secretly prefers the Catholic Germans and Swedes. So to us small merchants, it seems there isn't an honest Russian prince to be found."

Could this really be? Though Yanka in her simplicity understood that some princes might be stronger and braver than others, it had never occurred to her that they might be playing cynical games with the lands of Rus.

The discussion went on in this way for some time, the various members of the group giving their views on the likely and most profitable outcomes. Finally the fat boyar turned to Milei. "Well now, you've heard that none of us can agree: so what does the boyar from Murom say?"

They looked at him with interest as he paused, taking his time. Yanka, too, waited expectantly. What would her powerful protector say?

"First," he said at last, "I understand the Catholic camp. You're close to Sweden, Poland, and the Hansa trading towns of Germany. They're all Catholic, and fairly strong. In the same way, the Prince of Galicia down in the southwest thinks he can hold off the Tatars with help from the Pope. But the Catholic party is wrong. Why?" He gazed around the room. "Because the Tatars are much stronger, and the Pope and the Catholic powers are unreliable. Every time the Prince of Galicia tries to assert himself, the Tatars crush him."

There were some murmurs of agreement. What he said about Galicia was true.

"Novgorod is mighty," he went on. "But beside the Tatars, Novgorod is puny. They'd crush your fortifications in days if they wanted to, as they did Vladimir, Riazan, Kiev itself. You were lucky that they happened to turn back before reaching you."

"The Tatars will vanish like the Avars, the Huns, the Pechenegs, and the Cumans," someone objected.

"No, they won't," Milei replied. "That is exactly the mistake half our Russian princes are making. They don't like the truth so they won't admit it. These Tatars are not like the Cumans. They're an empire like no other the world has seen. And"—he paused for a moment to make his point—"if you oppose them, they'll crush you like a fly upon a gong."

"So," said the young merchant sadly, "you think Prince Alexander is right and we have to submit to these pagans?"

Milei looked at the thin young man with calm disgust. And now there came into his eyes a look of ancient, cynical cunning that Yanka had seen before but never known enough to understand.

"I think," he said very quietly, "that the Tatars are the best friends that we have."

"Exactly," the fat boyar broke out. "I saw at once, my friend, that you were an intelligent man."

Yanka was aghast. What could he mean?

"Of course Alexander is right," Milei continued. "We have no choice. Mark my words, in a few more years they will rule us all. But that is not the point. Who runs the caravans from the East with whom you trade? The Tatars. Who mints coins and who keeps the steppes free of Cumans? The Tatars. Where shall our sons find profitable service and plunder? With the Tatars, just as my Alan ancestors served the Khazars before the state of Rus existed.

"And what is the alternative? The princes of Rus? The Grand Dukes who never lifted a finger to help Riazan or Murom when the Tatars came?

"The Tatars are strong and they love the profits of trade. Therefore I will cooperate with them."

Yanka was white.

Before her, at that moment, rose up the vision of her mother, falling before her eyes. Then the Tatar with the missing ear. Then her brother, disappearing across the darkening steppe.

So he was for the Tatars.

She had not known. How could she, a poor Slav peasant from a little village? She had not understood that, for more than a thousand years, Sarmatian, Khazar, Viking, and Turk, the men of steppes, of rivers and of seas, the powerful wanderers on the earth, had seen the land and the people of Russia only as objects for use to be ruled for profit.

Several of the older men were nodding wisely.

It was fortunate that, standing quietly in a corner, virtually forgotten, she was too shocked even to speak.

But at that moment she felt more utterly defiled by the nights she had spent with him than she ever had, even in the depths of her despair, by those spent with her father.

It was a week later that she first suspected she might be pregnant.

She did not tell him. She said nothing to anyone. In any case, there was no one to talk to. But what should she do? At first she did not know. She walked around Novgorod each day, trying to make up her mind.

Looking for quiet places, away from the noisy bustle of the narrow streets, she visited the outlying monasteries, and the prince's hunting grounds to the north of the city. She came to know the place quite well.

Yet the better she came to know Great Novgorod, the less she liked it. Even in the nearby Yuriev monastery, where she had expected to discover a peaceful haven, she found a huge, square cathedral that was so high and harsh that it seemed almost cruel.

Similarly, when she entered the church of those gentlest of saints, Boris and Gleb, what she saw was a big, rich building, housing pompous oak coffins of the nobility at one end. An old woman told her: "This place was built by Sadko—the merchant in the song." And as she gazed around at the impressive interior the old woman added approvingly, "Yes, he was rich."

Day by day Yanka was discovering that this was all that mattered in Novgorod—how much money one had.

Not only when she went to the market, but at the inn, or in the streets, whoever she talked to seemed to speak of their neighbors and to value them only by their wealth. To them, she realized, I am not a person. I am only a sum of money. And as the time passed, this harsh, unyielding world began to repel her. I don't belong here, she decided. I have no wish to remain.

It was not easy, being obliged to make love to the boyar at nights and going out into this harsh, mercantile world by day. The image of herself that she had once conceived—as a silver birch tree, withstanding wind and snow—no longer helped her. If she closed her eyes and thought of it at nights, it seemed puny and far away. By day she became depressed and listless; at night, full of self-loathing. There was no sanctuary.

Sometimes she would visit the lesser churches. There were many of these, in wood and stone. The smaller stone churches were especially beautiful to look at. The Novgorod architects not only favored the placing of Greek crosses over the domes, as was often done in Russia now, but they liked to alter the shape of the old Byzantine dome. Instead of the broad old cupola, like an upturned saucer, they sometimes squeezed the top up into a point, so that it resembled a helmet. And more elaborate still, they might even give the sides of this helmet dome a slight bulge so that it looked like a large shining onion.

They were miniature versions of the cathedrals, with a main chamber above and a smaller cellar below where services could be held when it was cold. Yet though they were of stone, many of these churches had been built by boyars and merchants just like those who had visited Milei that terrible evening. Instead of the high galleries where princes could look down upon the people, they contained on their upper floors little corner chapels where the family of the founding merchant could worship and where, often as not, the merchant's dark bearded image stared out severely yet smugly from a fresco on the wall.

Perhaps it was her mood, but these places, too, soon filled her with repulsion.

And still she was pregnant with the boyar's child. What was she to do?

She had no doubt he would provide for the child. But what would become of her? Where would she live? And would she ever get a husband? Though the married women in Slav villages might take part in the careless sex that sometimes followed the end of a drunken feast night, it was a shame to any man to find his young wife not a virgin. If his neighbors knew, they would probably paint his doorposts as a sign of contempt. An unmarried woman with a child stood few chances.

In any case, she hated Milei now, and the child was his.

To her own surprise, she found that often she had no feeling for it. The little life inside her belonged to him and to this big city. She was only carrying this burden against her will. She wanted to be rid of it, turn her back on Novgorod, and flee to another world.

"I do not want it," she often murmured. "I am not ready for this. And it ties me to him."

Yet while she was full of this resentment, a part of her yearned to give life; and her instincts told her that the further she went into her pregnancy, the more terrible it would seem to lose the child.

Sometimes she did not know what she wanted. She either walked about listlessly or sat alone, staring into space.

Milei, sensing her discomfort with him, yet not troubling to find out the cause, sent for her less.

In January she finally decided. I will get rid of it.

But how? She knew that girls sometimes ended unwanted pregnancies by jumping off a gate. Somehow she had no wish to try. So what to do. For two days she wandered around thinking that perhaps she would, thanks to some divine intervention, slip and fall on an icy street and have a miscarriage. She went and prayed before Novgorod's most sacred icon—Our Lord of the Sign. But though the icon had once preserved the city against the men of Suzdal, it did nothing for her. At last, in despair, she began to search around the marketplace. Surely there must be someone there who would know how to do such things.

She found her one afternoon, in mid-January: a hard-faced old woman with a wart on one hand, who sold dried herbs at a little stall near the river.

When she explained what she needed the old woman seemed neither surprised nor shocked, but her small, brown eyes gave her a careful, cold look. "How many months?"

Yanka told her.

"Very well. But it will cost you money."

"How much?"

The old woman was silent for a minute.

"Two grivnas."

She gasped. A small fortune.

The old woman looked at her but showed no sign of giving anything away.

"Well?"

"Can you be sure . . . ?"

"You won't have the child."

"And I . . ."

"You'll come to no harm."

That afternoon, Yanka took the bale of silk that Milei had given her and sold it for two grivnas.

"Come back this evening, at dusk," the old woman told her.

As the sun fell over the frozen marshes late that afternoon, she followed as the old woman shuffled along a path that led by the southern outskirts of the city. On their left were huts; on their right, the frozen river. The sun in the west was sinking, a distant red disk going down into the snows like a sigh; downstream the palisades across the river, caught in icy shadow, looked black as a raven before the red sky.

She led Yanka to a small *izba* at the end of a little lane. Beside the *izba* was a little outhouse. She opened the door of this and motioned Yanka in. It contained various sacks, a table covered with little pots of strange-smelling herbs, and a single bench. It was cold.

"Sit there and wait," the old woman said, then vanished.

When she reappeared, she was carrying a small tub which she placed in front of Yanka. Then she went away again.

Some time passed before she came back. This time she had a large pail of hot water which she poured into the tub. A cloud of steam arose. She brought two more pails, until the tub was half full.

Then, from the table, she took several of the wooden pots and began to pour their contents into the water, stirring with a long wooden spoon. A sharp, almost acrid smell began to fill the room. Yanka had never smelled such a thing before, but it made her eyes water.

"What is it?"

"Never mind. Now take off your boots, pull up your shift, and put your feet in the tub," the old woman ordered.

Yanka did so and immediately cried out in pain. The water was scalding.

"You'll get used to it," the woman said, and pushed her feet down again. "Now stand up."

As she did so, she almost toppled over. The pain in her feet was terrible.

The old woman caught her, steadied her, then pulled her shift right up, exposing her stomach.

Suddenly she felt helpless, just like a little girl again, as if her father were making her lie down on the bench. The sharp fumes from the tub were almost choking her. She looked down and saw that not only her feet, but her legs were turning bright red.

"You're boiling me," she moaned.

"More or less," the old woman said, and poured in some more hot water.

The minutes passed. The pain in her legs had turned to an ache, then almost to numbness. She had grown used to the smell, though her eyes were still streaming. When she thought she would fall, or faint, the old woman gave her a staff to hold. And still, from time to time, she poured in more hot water and added more of the pungent herbs, whatever they were.

A whole hour passed. Then Yanka fainted.

When she came to, she found the old woman rubbing her bright red feet and legs with a paste of some kind.

"They'll hurt for a while. They'll feel scalded, but they aren't," she said calmly.

"And the baby . . ."

"Come and see me in the market, the day after tomorrow, at sundown."

Yanka slept late the next morning.

The day after, as instructed, she walked by the old woman's little stall. The old woman glanced up at her, her hard little eyes giving nothing away.

"Well?"

Yanka nodded.

"It worked. It's all right."

"As I told you," the old woman said and turned away, as if she were of no further interest.

There was nothing left for her now. There was nothing in Novgorod. She tried to avoid Milei for fear that he might make her pregnant again. But what was she to do next?

Soon, while the snows were still on the ground, she knew that the boyar meant to take the road back to the east. But where should she go? She was determined not to stay in Novgorod.

Strangely, despite all that had happened, she missed her father's familiar face. She had no wish to return to live with him, yet she would have liked to see him again. Without him, she was still utterly alone.

Yet on what possible terms should she return? Had the boyar some plans for her? Or did he intend to leave her at some town or roadside inn and pass on into the distance? She had no idea; and being completely unsure what she wanted herself, she did not care just then to ask him.

It was at this time that she found one place of sanctuary. She discovered it three days after her abortion.

It was a church: but not a stone one. It lay in the Potters' End, on the Saint Sophia side of the city, and it was constructed entirely of wood. It was dedicated to Saint Blaise.

This saint was a typical example of how, at the level of the simple people, the Christian church had wisely adapted itself to the customs and affections of the Slavs and Finns it converted. Saint Blaise protected animals. To all intents, the saint was identical with the old Slav god Veles, protector of cattle, god of well-being and wealth.

Something about the atmosphere of the dark wooden building with its tall sloping roof made her feel at home. From the outside, it was more like a high barn, yet inside, with its low ceiling and its dark little icons and gleaming candles, it had the warmth and intimacy of an *izba.* True, the logs it was made of were huge. It was as solid as a fortress. But the priests, the old men trying to look busy, the stout women patiently sweeping or polishing the candlesticks that stood everywhere, all seemed friendly. As she stood, sometimes for an hour or more, in front of the icon of Saint Blaise, she felt that, perhaps, even in her own miserable and useless existence, there might be hope.

"Lord have mercy. Lord have mercy," she would sometimes whisper to herself.

Once, as she turned from the icon, she saw a tall, dark-bearded priest who looked at her kindly and said: "Our Father loves all His children: above all He loves those who have fallen and who repent." And Yanka, knowing that he had seen into her heart, felt tears crowd into her eyes as, with head bowed, she quickly left the church.

It was a few days later that she met a young man.

There was, at first glance, nothing exceptional about him. He was about twenty-two or -three, she supposed, a little above average height, with a brown beard. His cheeks were rather high, his eyes almond shaped and brown. She noticed his hands. They were workman's hands, well callused; yet there was something fine, strong yet sensitive in the well-shaped, tapering fingers. Unusually for a workman, his nails were carefully pared. He had a serious, studious look.

When she first saw him, he was standing quietly, in reverence before an inn, but as she moved towards the door, he immediately left off his prayers, so that she smiled to herself.

He let her leave just in front of him and then caught up and fell into step beside her.

"You seem to think you are going my way." She smiled a little mischievously.

"Only to protect you. Which way do you go?"

"Towards the Leatherworkers' End."

"I, too. My master lives there."

There seemed no harm in him.

He was a slave, she discovered. He was a Mordvinian, and he had been taken captive after a raid when he was twelve. His name was Purgas. His master since he was fifteen had been a rich merchant here in Novgorod, who had had him taught carpentry.

They parted near the inn, but not before he had learned that she liked to visit the wooden church each afternoon.

She half expected, therefore, to see him there the next day. But she was surprised when he produced a little piece of carving he had done. It was a tiny riverboat, no bigger than his hand, carved out of birchwood, with oarsmen and a little sail.

It was so perfectly done that, for a moment, she caught her breath; for it reminded her of the carvings her brother used to do.

"It's for you," he said. And he insisted that she take it.

He walked her home again that day.

They often met after that. He was always friendly, rather quiet, and, she soon observed, there was a kind of shyness about him, a reserve that she liked.

When they walked through the streets, he would pause from time to time, to point out some feature of a house that she would otherwise never have noticed: a little carving, some latticework by a window; or simply the way that the heavy logs were joined at the corners.

There were dozens of ways of joining logs, she discovered. They could be cut round or square, they could be laid this way or that, notched or slotted one into another. What to her had seemed an endless collection of stout, rather brutal wooden houses to him was a mass of elaborate puzzles to be solved and enjoyed as he passed.

"There are more ways of building a simple *izba* than you would dream of," he told her. "And the master carpenters of Novgorod know them all."

Yet though he appreciated the city and knew every building in it, she soon discovered that he missed the native forests of his childhood.

"We lived in the woods, out by the Volga," he told her. And he would enumerate for her all the trees and plants of the region. When he spoke of buildings, it was with a keen professional appreciation; but when he spoke of the forests, a dreamy, faraway look came into his eyes, and she felt for him.

But the greatest surprise came the fourth day they met. She had stopped in the church in front of an icon depicting Christ holding an open book on which some words were written.

" 'Judge not according to the appearance, but judge righteous judgment,' " Purgas said, reading the text.

She stared at him in amazement.

"You can read, too?"

"Yes. I learned here in Novgorod."

A Mordvinian, a mere Finn from the forests who could read.

It was at this moment that Yanka made up her mind.

That very evening, she went to Milei the boyar and told him what she wanted.

"Well," she asked, when she had finished. "You had what you wanted from me. Will you help me now?"

To her surprise, he smiled kindly. He even gave her some useful advice.

"Now tell me again the name of this merchant and where he lives," he said. And then: "You don't actually know if this young man wants . . . ?"

She shook her head.

"But I think he will," she replied.

The very next morning, Milei arranged the matter.

"It will cost me a pretty penny, though," he remarked, with a wry smile. "However, the priests will approve." The Church encouraged the liberation of slaves.

He could be kindly, Yanka realized; for the ability to be generous is a pleasant exercise for powerful men.

And so, that afternoon, she turned to Purgas outside the church and asked: "Would you like to marry me? My master will buy your freedom if you want."

He looked thunderstruck.

"I wanted to ask," he confessed. "But as a slave, I was afraid . . ."

"There are conditions," she went on. She had thought very carefully about this; and it was Milei who had coached her, rather reluctantly, about what to do. "We shall leave the city and live near my village—but not as a boyar's peasants," she added quickly. That was one thing she knew she did not want. "We shall be free. We'll live in the Black Lands and pay rent only to the prince himself."

Despite everything, she wanted to be near her father. If anything happened, at least he would be there. But she did not want to be in the same village; nor did she wish to have Milei as a landlord anymore.

"Go to the Black Lands, then," Milei had told her. "There's Black Lands with good soil—chernozem—right next to Russka. The prince is glad to get peasants on his land. You'll get good terms and you could do very well."

And now, hearing this and to her relief, Purgas laughed. There was nothing in the world he wanted more. "That's settled then," he said.

It was: almost.

"There is one other thing," she began, hesitantly, and looked down at her feet.

He waited.

"Once, a long time ago . . ." She paused. "When I was just a girl . . . It was a Tatar, they came to the village."

He stared at her, not comprehending for a moment. Then he gently drew her to him and kissed her on the forehead.

They left two days later with Milei, who allowed them to follow him in a second sled.

When at last they reached the place on the river Kliasma where the stream led down to Russka, he parted from them.

He had been distant on the journey, as a boyar might be with a pair of almost slaves. But at the moment of parting he called Yanka over to him.

His worldly, clever face was not unkind as, discreetly, he pressed two grivnas into her hand. "I'm sorry about the child," he murmured.

Then he was gone.

The day after they arrived at Dirty Place, it began to thaw.

1262

MILEI the boyar waited.

Across the river, pale columns of dust rose from time to time, swirling across the field that had recently been harvested. The sky was a brilliant blue. There were a few thin, vaporous clouds in the high distance. Away over the forest, on the horizon, was a pinkish haze.

It was very dry; there was a scent of wormwood; no discernible wind.

He was waiting for the Tatar.

Things had been tense all that year. At any moment he had feared an explosion.

And this very morning, here in Russka, it had almost come. If he had not been there himself those two Muslim tax collectors would be dead. He was sure of it. Only when he had threatened villagers that he would turn them off his land did they quiet down.

Not that they love me for it. He smiled grimly.

They were all in the big barn now, loading sacks of grain onto the tax collectors' wagons. He still kept one ear cocked for any further sounds of trouble.

It's certainly a pity these damned tax farmers are Muslim. He sighed.

He had been right about the Tatars: right in every respect. Everything had come to pass exactly as he had told those Novgorod merchants it would, a dozen years ago.

The Tatars had taken over the northeast. True, the princes had been allowed to continue their rule; but the census and conscription had come; the northern lands were now divided up into myriads, thousands, hundreds, and tens, just as the lands of Kiev had been. And there was nothing that anyone could do about it.

Even Novgorod had had to submit to be taxed: Lord Novgorod had been humbled, too.

Prince Alexander had ridden in with the Tatar tax collectors and helped take the Tatars' tribute himself. He had crushed the local people when they resisted.

Milei smiled. What a cunning fellow this Alexander was!

He had discovered how to get the Tatars on his side; he'd used them to push aside his uncle and his brother until, now, he was the greatest prince in all the Russian lands.

He even wore an oriental helmet, given him by the Tatar khan.

The Russian people might not like him, yet his policy was not only cunning, it was also wise.

The Russians alone could not defeat the Tatars.

"Look at what happened to his brother Andrei," he would remind people who called Alexander a traitor. "He tried to fight the Tatars: so they smashed him and looted half the towns in Suzdalia."

That had been ten years ago and it was still remembered.

And what if Russians looked for help from outside?

"Consider, in that case, that fool the Prince of Galicia," he would urge. The prince in the southwest, who had been flirting with the Pope, had been even more foolish than Milei had predicted. First, he had received a crown from the Pope. Then he had looked for allies. Who should he choose but those pagan Lithuanian tribes of the north, who were expanding into the western Russian lands to avoid the Teutonic Knights? The Lithuanian chief had for a few years become a Roman Catholic, and together they had challenged the Tatars.

And the result of it all?

The Tatars thrashed Galicia and made them attack the Lithuanians. Then they made the Prince of Galicia take down all his fortifications. The Western Catholic powers, as usual, did nothing; the Lithuanian king went back to being a pagan. And that summer, he had heard, the pagan Lithuanian had attacked Galicia, which was now quite defenseless.

"Poor Galicia's finished. If Alexander had tried anything like that," he always said, "the Tatars would have taken one-half of his lands, and the Germans would have taken the other."

Alexander was wise.

But oh, he was subtle, too!

Tatar policy was never to hurt the Church. And Alexander, who served the Tatars, had made the Metropolitan Cyril a close friend.

"And bless me, now he's got every priest and monk in the land on his side. The people hate Alexander, yet every time they go to church, they hear the priests say he's a national hero. Those priests are even calling him Alexander Nevsky now, as though that skirmish with the Swedes on the river Neva back in his youth had saved all Russia."

The political astuteness of this propaganda amused the boyar hugely.

Yes, he had been right about the Tatars. They were the masters, and only a fool would refuse to work with them.

He, Milei, had been working with the Tatars and with Alexander Nevsky for more than a decade.

He also used intrigue. It was cheaper.

When Alexander's brother was briefly on the throne of Vladimir, by incredible good luck, a foolish boyar had sent him a letter that seemed to implicate the prince in intrigues against the Tatars. Milei had at once sent it to Alexander. A year later Alexander had been on the throne in his brother's place, and word came to Milei that he was in favor with the new ruler and with the Tatars.

Since then, many modest favors had come his way.

Recently, it had to be admitted, things had been more difficult.

When Batu Khan had ruled in Sarai, Milei had not found it difficult to cooperate. But at present there was a new khan in Sarai who had become a Muslim.

It was not that this new khan oppressed the Russian Church: he did not. But he had decided to allow Muslim merchants to farm the taxes from the Suzdalian lands, and these men had been exploiting their situation ruthlessly. A number of unfortunates who could not meet all the tax demands had been taken into slavery, and all over the region, from Vladimir to Murom, came news of revolts.

For once Milei sympathized with the people. The whole affair had been badly handled. But business was business. "You will see to it that the estates near Murom pay all that is demanded," he instructed his sons. "I shall go to keep an eye on Russka."

Which was what he had been doing that morning.

He had another reason, however, for being in Russka that late July day.

For with luck, today, he was to complete the biggest coup of his career. And one that would change the character of Russka forever.

When this crowning deal was done, he would hand over his affairs to his sons. He was getting old.

Anxiously Milei waited for the Tatar.

He rode in towards the evening: a quiet man in early middle age. One could tell at once from his dress and the magnificent horse he rode that he was rich and of some importance; he came alone, though, without any escort, and with just a single Mongol bow and a lasso slung on his horse behind him.

He was dressed in a kaftan of dark red silk and he wore a wide-brimmed Chinese hat.

Only one item of his dress was unexpected. Around his neck, on a silver chain, hung a little silver cross.

For Peter the Tatar was a Christian.

In fact, it was not so surprising. The Mongol state had no official religion. In their huge advance from Mongolia and across the Eurasian plain, the Mongols had encountered many powerful religions, from Buddhism in the East to Islam and Catholicism in the West.

One such faith was that of the ancient Christian church called Nestorian, which, cut off by theological disputes from the West, had expanded from its base in Persia six centuries before and set up communities as far away as China.

It was this half-forgotten Nestorian church that had given rise to a great legend in medieval Europe: that somewhere to the east, there lay a fabulous land, ruled by a mighty Christian ruler—a giant of a man.

This was the legend of Prester John.

As a boy, Milei had believed it. But in fact, this legendary empire of Prester John was simply an ancient community that was perfectly familiar to the peoples of the Orient.

The son of the great Khan Batu himself had become a Nestorian Christian.

And in Russia, too, a few Tatars had taken the Orthodox Christian faith, just as some others farther east had become Muslims. There was a Russian bishop at Sarai. And it was well known that the entire family of the senior Tatar official in the northern city of Rostov were all Christian.

Even so, it had been a surprise when, a year before, Milei had encountered the new Tatar official in Murom and found that the baskak, too, had converted to Orthodoxy a few years before.

The boyar had had some dealings with this baskak, and had found him a shrewd but quiet fellow.

"The question is," he remarked to his sons, "how can we turn this Christian Tatar to our advantage?"

For some months he had assiduously courted Peter. He had discovered quite a lot about him. Peter had taken the Orthodox faith, Milei discovered, at the suggestion of the official in Rostov. "Apparently there is a small group of these officials who have converted. They're mostly below the top grades in the khan's service but not without influence; and the Tatar authorities think it is good that some of their people follow the religion of the country where they operate. So I think this fellow could be useful," he announced to his family.

The first idea had crystallized in his mind when he discovered that the Tatar had an unmarried daughter.

His own eldest son was married, with two daughters so far. His younger son, David—a handsome boy of nineteen—was not.

"What about it?" he asked the boy. "I've seen the girl. She's not bad looking. And this baskak Peter seems to have a considerable fortune. They say he has some good connections, too."

There had been a few marriages between Russian princes and Tatar princesses already.

"Our family has married everything from Saxon to Cuman," Milei added with a grin. "So why not a Tatar this time?"

There was another consideration, too.

Milei had heard talk of a future Tatar campaign in the Caucasus Mountains in the southeast.

"They intend to attack the territory of Azerbaijan down there," he told the boy. "I know you're keen to go on a raid like that, and the pickings could be huge. It's got to help you get a good position if you're connected with a Tatar."

The boy had no objection; and to Milei's surprise, the Tatar Peter was agreeable as well.

The marriage had taken place. The Tatar had been generous. Things were looking up.

But nothing, nothing in the world had prepared Milei for what came next.

For two months before, at the start of summer, Peter had approached him and announced: "It is my intention to endow a small religious house: a church and some monks. Can you advise me where I could find a good site?"

A monastery! Even he had not realized the Tatar was so rich, nor that his religion was so serious.

"Give me two weeks," he had said. "I may have just the place for you."

Surely it was a gift from heaven. He calculated swiftly and worked feverishly.

This was just what he needed for Russka.

Over the years he had done what he could to build the place up, but it had been difficult. There was a simple wooden church there now; the population had doubled. But the troubles with the Tatars in the last ten years had made it harder than ever to find reliable settlers, and he had not been especially successful.

The presence of a monastery would bring people to the place, and sooner or later trade.

He had acquired much of the vast land—the uncultivated forest—in the area and derived some income from the furs and honey in that. His first thought had been to sell Peter some of this.

"But it won't do," he said to David. "He tells me he wants good land, and the only good land at Russka is the chernozem on the east bank."

It was then that Milei the boyar had his stroke of genius. A messenger was sent hurriedly to Alexander Nevsky himself. The monastery's needs were explained; so were Milei's; and a dutiful reminder of past services to Alexander's cause was added.

The reply came back. His request was granted, though with one proviso.

"The Grand Prince had other matters to think about. Ask no more," the message had added.

It was enough.

"You see," Milei told David, "for a very favorable price, he'll sell me a tract of his chernozem land just north of Dirty Place, and that tract is twice the size of what we have at Russka." He rubbed his hands. "If I can sell the Tatar my land at a good price for his monastery, then I'll receive enough to buy what the Grand Prince is offering me without spending my own money at all!"

The beauty of the thing made him smile with an almost artistic pleasure.

With what joy, therefore, did he now welcome the Christian Tatar and lead him to his house.

"I'll show you the whole place in the morning," he said. "I think you'll be pleased."

He told him about the trouble with the villagers that morning.

"The villagers of course know nothing about our business," he joked. "So they're probably terrified to see you."

Peter nodded slowly but did not smile.

"There have been serious riots in Suzdal and other towns," the Tatar warned. "Murom is still quiet, and I've left strict instructions with the guards; but I must go back tomorrow in case there's trouble. The khan will be furious."

"Nevsky will sort it out. The khan trusts him," Milei said confidently.

"The khan trusts no one, and no one is safe," Peter told him coldly.

His words sent a chill through the evening and made Milei more glad than ever that he had made a family alliance with these harsh rulers.

They brought fresh fish from the river, and sweetmeats, and mead. He did what he could to lighten the mood.

The next morning they went out early and inspected the land. Milei showed him the rich chernozem on the eastern bank with pride. The

Tatar walked all round the little village and saw that Milei had indeed offered him the best land.

"It's a good site for a small monastery," he agreed. "I shall endow a small church and perhaps half a dozen monks to begin. But it will grow."

Milei nodded.

"Does that mean you want to buy it?" he asked with a smile.

"Your price?"

Milei named it.

It sounded a little expensive, but not unreasonable. Milei was wise enough not to be obviously greedy.

"Very well," Peter agreed. And to Milei's delight he produced a bag of gold coins and paid him there and then.

"Now it is mine," the Tatar said.

"It is yours."

Peter began to get on his horse.

"Will you not stay?"

The Tatar shook his head.

"With these troubles . . . I want to be back in Murom tomorrow."

Milei nodded.

"All the same," he said, hardly pausing to think about it, "I should draw up a deed for the property."

It seemed such an obvious thing to say that he was completely taken aback by what came next.

"A deed? What is that?"

Milei opened his mouth to speak, then kept silent.

The Tatar looked at him curiously.

"A deed?"

Was it possible that this official did not know that in the land of Rus all property was held by deed?

Suddenly, now, it dawned on Milei that there was no particular reason why he should.

For the entire Mongol apparatus, thorough, merciless as it was, was also completely self-contained. They took their census—which no Russian ruler had ever done—they divided up the land by tens of hundreds, and they taxed. But there it ended. Their system of government was efficient, but it ran entirely parallel to the continuing pattern of Russian life. This intelligent Tatar, this Christian whose daughter had married a Russian, was still entirely a stranger in this country. He probably had no interest in being anything else. He knew nothing of Russian land transactions and law.

He had just paid for the land—but without a deed it was not his.

I have to give him the land, Milei thought quickly. And if he ever finds out that I should have given him a deed . . . Yet, he hesitated. Was there something more to be squeezed from this transaction? He would have to think about it. When in doubt, delay.

"Go back to Murom," he said with a warm smile. "We'll talk business again when I return."

Peter started off.

"Be firm with these damned people," he called after him, then turned back to the village, with his bag of gold.

In Dirty Place, too, there had nearly been a killing that morning.

Only Yanka had prevented it.

The two Muslim merchants had brought a dozen men and three large carts with them. They were not in the best of tempers when they arrived.

The Mongol administration had allowed them to collect what they could in return for a fixed amount they were to remit to the khan. They had expected to make a profit, but at present they were showing a loss.

Their visit to Russka the day before had been unsatisfactory. Milei the boyar had thought his presence had stopped the villagers attacking the tax gatherers. In fact, knowing his Tatar connections, the merchants had been careful to make quite reasonable demands at Russka. Now they needed to make up for their leniency.

The insignificant little community of free peasants at Dirty Place was somewhere to start.

"We'll fleece this village," they agreed as they approached.

And that, all morning, is what they did.

The hamlet had grown to fifteen households now and had the status of a *volost*—a commune.

In recent years the *volost* had become modestly prosperous; and this was thanks to the man whom the households had elected as their elder: Purgas, the husband of Yanka.

Ever since they married, the modest carpenter whose freedom she had arranged had never ceased to surprise her.

The first surprise had been after they had built their *izba* at Dirty Place and she had hung a little icon in the corner; for that very day he had quietly gone to the corner and hung a little chaplet of birth leaves just above it.

"Why do you do that?" she asked, puzzled. "That is what the pagans do."

He had looked a little awkward for a moment and then confessed. "I am not a Christian."

"But we were married by a priest."

It had been down in Novgorod just before they left.

He smiled gently. "It didn't seem to matter."

She had never thought to ask him if he was a Christian. Hadn't they met in a church?

"I followed you in," he confessed.

"You should have told me," she said angrily.

"I was afraid. I didn't want to lose you," he mumbled.

She thought of her own deception of him. So they had both lied for fear of losing the other's love. It was a bond.

"You must become a Christian, now," she told him. But to her surprise he refused.

"Our children can be Christian, but leave me to my own ways," he said. "In Novgorod I lived among the Christians long enough," he added with some feeling.

She understood. His escape back to the countryside with her was a return, for him, to his origins. And indeed, as she watched him find his place in the little community in the Black Lands, she saw a strange transformation occur.

At times he seemed almost like a creature of the forest. He would stand, quite motionless, with his spear on the riverbank and then, it seemed, idly dip it in the stream and come up with a fish where she, lying on the bank and staring down, had seen nothing. He would take dried fungi from a birch tree and rub it in his hands for only seconds before a little flame sprung, as it were, from the palms of his hands. He would find dried pine roots that would burn without crackling, and all manner of medicinal roots.

He got drunk rather easily, but always fell asleep. The only cause of friction between them was when he insisted she allow him to eat hare, which was forbidden by the Church.

"I worship the god Tchampas," he would say. "He is not as great as your god, but he resides in heaven and all the gods of the earth are under him."

He loved the forest, and he loved the river in a way that she realized she could not. He would touch a tree and to him it was a special being. She remembered how once she had felt about the silver birch tree, and how she had tried to assume its character.

And he feels like that about everything, she mused.

It was an ancient religion, this fetish cult of the northern forests, and she wisely did not try to disturb it anymore.

She took their children over to Russka to the wooden church there, and he did not object. This made her happy.

Her father had taken another wife. She was glad. Shortly after they had arrived at Dirty Place he had come to see them and, taking her aside, he had pressed into her hand the bag of silver coins he had brought with him from the south.

"I don't think Kiy is ever coming back," he said. "So it's all for you."

She understood it was his way of making amends, and since then they had been friends.

She had showed the coins to Purgas and he had inspected them carefully. Some, he told her, came from Constantinople and were very old. Some were Russian, from the time of Monomakh. But some puzzled him.

"The writing here seems Slav," he told her, "but what can this be?"

And he pointed to a strange, oriental-looking script.

"I think I have seen it on an icon," he said.

It was Hebrew. For the coins came from Poland and bore inscriptions both in Slavic and in Hebrew, thanks to the ancient Khazar community there.

They hid them under the floor. Who knew when they might be needed?

Purgas was not only a hunter; he worked hard on their land, and it was not long before they were living well. She had nothing to complain of.

Only one thing about her husband irritated Yanka. It was the same habit of mind that the elder had told her about when she first came to

Russka; but her Mordvinian husband seemed to have it in a greater degree. He would not plan for the future.

"None but crows fly straight," he would remind her if she pushed him for some decision. To him, each season, each day, was there to be lived through, cautiously, as if it might be one's last.

Once, after they had been arguing over some matter of this kind, he went off into the forest and returned several hours later with a deer he had killed.

"If he made plans for next week," he gently told her, "they were in vain."

"But I'm not an animal," she protested impatiently.

To which he only smiled and shrugged.

She loved him all the same. He gave her three children and great happiness. The villagers respected him.

And at least once a year the steward of Milei the boyar approached them with more and more tempting offers from the boyar to come as his tenants to Russka.

They always refused.

"We're Black people," she said simply. "We're our own master here."

As the years passed, she had grown stout. Her face had filled out. And she was content.

Yet even now she could still be amazed by her husband. What, for instance, had come over him the previous evening?

For the night before, learning what had happened with the tax gatherers at Russka, the foolish men of the hamlet had wanted to ambush and kill them. And Purgas was in favor.

News of the trouble in the northern towns had come downriver a few days before. The free peasants of the hamlet were excited.

"You're mad," she told them. "Russka didn't revolt."

"Because the boyar's in league with the Tatars," one of the men said.

"But they'll come and kill us all."

They didn't believe her.

"We're not afraid," the young men claimed.

"When I was a boy, beyond the Volga," Purgas remarked, "a young fellow wasn't ready to marry until he'd killed a man. That was the custom among the real Mordvinians."

"You foolish pagan," she shouted. "You don't understand."

And she outlined to them the might, the incredible might, of the empire on whose edge they lay.

"They would destroy us all," she told them. "They would never give up."

"So," Purgas quietly said, "you're on the boyar's side now."

She opened her mouth. Then closed it. What could she say? She remembered the evening at the inn and how Milei's words had shocked her. In a way they still did; yet now that she was older, now that she had seen the Tatars take over the north, too, she had to admit he had been right.

"Hide whatever you can," she told them. "Pay up, but make them think they've ruined you. Otherwise we'll be destroyed."

Eventually she won. Even Purgas promised to do as she asked. Then the preparation began.

That day it had gone as she had predicted. The tax farmers had arrived soon after dawn, thinking to catch the hamlet unawares. They had quickly emptied half the grain store and taken most of the livestock they could find; but before dawn Purgas and the men had hidden the rest in the marshes, which the visitors did not know how to penetrate. By early morning they were already preparing to move on.

While they took the grain, Yanka had gone for a walk. Without especially thinking where she was going, she drifted along the path towards Russka.

Perhaps I'll go and see Father, she thought.

Though it was still early, the sun was already getting warm.

The path took her by a small opening in the trees where there were some little mounds, old Viatichi tombs, and a pleasant view towards Russka. It was very quiet.

And it was just as she came to this place that she stopped, transfixed.

Surely, it must be a vision.

Peter the Tatar was pleased with his day. The setting for the monastery was just what he wanted.

It was time he made his peace with God.

"A man without religion has no peace," the official in Rostov had urged him. It was true.

The khan at Sarai, after all, was now a Muslim. Why, even the new Great Khan himself had abandoned the old sky worship and shaman cults of Genghis.

The new supreme head, Kublai Khan, had taken the Buddhist religion of the Chinese he ruled.

That all men should bow before the Great Khan Peter had no doubt. But with the passing of the years, and the shameful power struggles and intrigues among the Golden Kin for the greatest offices, Peter's bright passion for the empires of men had dimmed. Even the memory of Genghis himself, the ruler of the world, now seemed more like the vision of a bygone age than the vision of a future heaven.

There was one God in Heaven, one lord upon earth.

Perhaps, he considered, if I had been more successful, if Batu Khan had not died and I had become a general, I might yet hunger for earthly things.

His career was over, though. He would keep his position, but go no higher. He accepted it. Thanks to his sister, while Batu and her son lived, he had done well, and he had amassed a splendid fortune.

He missed the steppe. Often, just before sleeping, he would think of its huge open spaces and the swaying grasses.

Two years before, he had gone across the steppe to Sarai. It was there, from some Alans, that he had bought the magnificent gray stallion he now rode, with the black mane and stripe down its back. It was bred below the Caucasus Mountains, of the noble breed they called Hoarfrost.

"But that, I think, may be the last time I shall see Sarai," he said sadly to his wife. An instinct told him he would pass the rest of his days in Russia.

He had passed at the edge of the woods for a last look back at his new acquisition, dismounting and walking over to the highest of the little mounds for a better view.

His face softened as he gazed at it.

Idly he brushed away a fly that had decided to settle on the place where his ear had once been. Then he frowned.

Something was bothering his horse.

Afterwards, she could never explain to herself how it was that the madness had seized her: for madness it certainly was, even to think of such a thing.

And yet it was as if she could not have done anything else.

She had always sworn she would. Though she had had many other things to think about in recent years, deep down that promise to herself had remained and hardened into a certainty.

One day, she knew, I shall see him, and my chance will come.

Now, quite suddenly, there he was, standing on a mound not fifteen paces from her. Even from behind, she recognized him—the Tatar with the missing ear!

He was alone. She looked up and down the path. No one was coming.

What brought him here? He must have come to see the tax gatherers, who were about to leave.

Whatever the reason, providence had given him to her alone and unguarded. Madness it was; but she knew, with absolute clarity, that she would never have another chance like this again.

Before her, her mother's face suddenly appeared.

She crept forward. His horse was standing by a tree. On its back was a bow and a quiver of arrows.

Carefully she reached up, took the bow and a single arrow, laying the arrow across the bow and feeling the pull.

How hard it was. She could hardly bend it.

Her heart was pounding, but she began to move towards him. The horse stirred and snorted angrily.

And now the Tatar turned.

It was him. There was the scar, running to the missing ear. She remembered his face as if she had seen him only yesterday.

He looked amazed and began to raise his hand.

He had no idea who she was.

She took a deep breath and pulled on the bow. She pulled with all her strength, her face puckering up as though in acute pain. He was coming towards her. She pulled, then released.

"Ah."

It was her own outburst of breath that she heard.

Then she heard his cry.

He was still coming towards her. His hand was flailing wildly. She began to back away towards his horse.

He was on his knees now.

The arrow was sticking through him, in the middle of his stomach. What was that noise?

He was hissing something at her. She was trembling violently.

He stayed where he was, his hands on the arrow, tugging at it. Then she saw his face go very white, and he fell sideways.

And now the thought came to her. It came with huge force, like a soundless thunderclap of fear in a nightmare: what could she possibly do now?

She looked around again, and realized with a sickening terror that someone was approaching along the path.

"If they will only kill me, and not my family," she prayed, as she waited, trembling, to face them.

It was Purgas. He took in everything with one glance, then gazed at her in astonishment.

She pointed to the Tatar. He stepped over.

"He's not yet dead," he said calmly.

Then, quietly, he undid his belt and throttled the Tatar.

For a few seconds, for the last time, Mengu, now called Peter, saw before him and thought he smelled the waving grasses of the steppe.

"I thought you told us not to kill the Tatars," Purgas said with a soft chuckle.

He looked up at her.

"You knew him?"

She nodded.

"Was this the one . . . ?"

He knew a Tatar had killed her mother, but she had almost forgotten that she had told him a Tatar raped her as well. Whichever he meant, she nodded.

He looked around.

"We can't leave him here," he remarked.

"They'll kill us," she whispered.

"I don't think so. The tax gatherers have gone. That's why I was going over to Russka. There's no one to know." He looked thoughtful. "First," he said sadly, "we'll have to kill this horse. And that," he glanced down at the dead man with disgust, "is a pity."

Yanka never admired her husband's skill more than on that day.

He seemed to know exactly what to do, and he moved with such speed.

First he placed the Tatar on the splendid horse. Then, speaking softly to the animal and calming it, he led the way deep into the marshes. There, in a deserted and hidden spot, he dug a trench; and then, tethering the horse firmly so that its head was over the trench, he neatly slit open its windpipe.

Completely taken by surprise, the horse started violently, tried to break away, and then crashed to its knees. When he had gathered all the blood in the trench, he slit the Tatar's throat, too, and carefully drained the body.

An hour later he had deftly cut up both horse and man into manageable pieces and these he began to burn on a fire. He also burned all the

Tatar's equipment except his cloak and his lasso.

By noon there was nothing left but a heap of burned bones, the head of the Tatar, which for some reason he had not burned, and a heap of ashes, which he pushed back into the trench as he filled it in. When he had finished and scattered the debris on the ground, even if someone had ever found the place, he would never have known that Purgas had dug there.

"Now," he told her, "we need a tree. And I know of one quite near."

About two hundred yards away he showed her a mighty oak.

He pointed to a place, high up in its trunk, where there was a hole.

"There used to be a beehive up there once," he told her. "I found it last year. But it's empty now. But below it there's a deep hole hidden in the trunk. Now help me bring the bones here."

Carrying them in the heavy cloak, in several journeys they brought the bones to the foot of the tree.

"Now hand me the lasso," he said. And moments later he was high up in the branches by the opening in the tree. Letting down the rope, he told her to tie the cloak to it, and one bundle at a time he dropped them down into the hollow. In half an hour they had vanished.

Then he burned the cloak and the lasso and scattered the ashes.

"The Tatars will look in the river and in the ground," he said. "But they'll never look up in the trees."

"But what about his head?" she asked, pointing to the familiar face with its missing ear, which was lying on the ground and gazing blankly up at her.

He smiled.

"I have another plan for that."

It was two more weeks before Milei the boyar returned from Russka to Murom.

When he got there, he found the city much disturbed. There had been numerous refusals to pay taxes in the villages; several of the Muslim tax farmers had been attacked. The Tatar authorities were furious and retribution was expected.

The Grand Prince Alexander Nevsky was said to be preparing to travel to the khan to ask for leniency.

Times were black.

And Peter the baskak had disappeared.

Indeed, the very day Milei arrived a centurion came to ask him when he had last seen him.

"He was on his way directly to Murom," he assured the soldier.

The investigation that followed was thorough. All the villages between Russka and Murom were visited and questioned. Since Russka was the place he was last seen, a search was made and the river downstream was dragged.

There was nothing.

By late autumn, suspicion finally centered on a village near the Oka where there had been rioting; but there was no proof that Peter had even been there. It seemed that he had simply vanished from the face of the earth.

It was on the fourth day after his return that Milei told his great lie.

He had been thinking about it ever since he reached Murom. Indeed he guessed that, sooner or later, suspicion might even fall on him for the Tatar's death. But since he could prove that he had spent his time innocently at the village, he felt bold enough to take a chance.

And he could not resist it.

So when Peter's son came to him and politely requested to know whether his father had bought the land from him for the monastery, Milei shook his head.

"Alas, no. He did not like the place. A pity," he added, his eyes staring blandly at the young man. "I should have been glad if he had."

"So he gave you no money?"

Milei shook his head.

"None."

They could prove nothing. If ever they found the Tatar's body, they could scarcely expect to find any money left on him. And, by that stroke of incredible good fortune, there were no deeds to the land for anyone to find!

Peter's son had left. Short of calling him a liar, there was nothing the young Tatar could say.

The next week, using money from an ostensible sale of some land near Murom, Milei bought the extra chernozem at Russka from the Grand Prince.

Fortune had smiled on him.

1263

How STRANGE, how secret are the ways of God.

In the spring of the next year, before the snows melted, Milei the boyar went to his estate at Russka.

From the front of his house, as he looked out, the first thing he saw was the rich land across the river. And now it was all his, stretching from the river out to the north of Dirty Place for several miles.

He had come early to the village because he had great plans for its improvement.

He had brought a number of slaves from the Muslim tax farmers. Some of them, admittedly, had been made slaves illegally for failing to pay enough taxes. But no one was likely to trouble about that here. And they were good Slavs, sound peasants, as well—just what he had always needed.

The new slaves were due to arrive at Russka in early summer.

There were settlers, too. He was going to let some of the new land, and he had managed to find three families who had been ruined by the new taxes and were glad to get good new land on easy terms.

All in all, the Tatars have been good for me. He chuckled to himself.

On the first Sunday of April, the snow began to melt.

Each day the sky was bright blue, the sun warm. Soon great banks of gray slush were forming beside little brown rivulets as the land began to appear. On the river, discolored patches of brown and green could be seen where the ice was getting thin.

On the Wednesday of that week, as he gazed out from the doorway, he could see little black bumps of rich earth peeping through the snow on the river's eastern side.

And then, as he stepped over the threshold, Milei the boyar had an extraordinary sensation. It was as if someone had stabbed him in the heart.

He stopped and put his hand to his chest. Surely his heart was not giving out. He was not so old. He took a deep breath but felt no pain: no difficulty in breathing. He looked at his hands for some telltale sign of blue in the fingertips. There was none.

He walked out carefully, pulling his fur coat tightly about him, although the sun was warm. Nothing more happened. He walked around the village and went to see the steward.

The steward was about to cross the river, and so he decided to go with him. They went across in a little dugout and got out onto the small jetty opposite.

Then something stranger still occurred. As Milei stepped onto the land of the east bank, his feet suddenly felt as if they were on fire. He took two more steps and cried out with pain.

"What is it, lord?" The old steward was looking at him with astonishment.

Milei was staring down with horror.

"My feet . . . when I stepped here . . . Do your feet hurt?"

"No, lord."

He tried to take another step, but the pain was so great he could not.

"We're going back," he mumbled; and the puzzled steward had to row him across the river again.

Greatly disconcerted, the boyar went back to his house. There he inspected his feet. They were just as normal.

Later that day, as he came out again, and glanced across the river, the terrible pain struck him in the chest again like a blow, so that his knees almost buckled and he had to catch the frame of the door to stop himself falling.

The same thing happened again the next day. And the next. He could not cross his own threshold; and he could not set foot on the land opposite the river.

He thought he understood.

"It's that damned Tatar," he murmured. "He's returned to plague me."

In fact, he was more accurate than he knew.

For it never occurred to him that one starless night the previous autumn, just after he had gone back to Murom, Purgas the Mordvinian had stolen by his empty house and, with consummate skill, ripped up the threshold outside and buried, in two feet of earth, the head of Peter the Tatar right under his doorway.

Even Yanka never knew her husband had done this.

But when he had finished, had it been possible to see his expression in the darkness, a look of strange, almost diabolical satisfaction would have been discerned on the Mordvinian's face.

"If they ever find this, it is you, boyar, they will accuse of murder," he whispered, "lover of my wife."

He had always guessed. Now he and the boyar were even.

Yet though Milei knew nothing of the presence of Peter, the excruciating pains grew worse. He could hardly bear to leave his house now.

I could take over the steward's house for the time being, he thought. But how could he explain that? I'll say the ants or the mice have invaded me.

It sounded a poor excuse. Besides, what was the satisfaction of being here when he could not even set foot on his best land?

"I shall have to leave Russka," he decided.

The next day he called for his horse in the morning, and, swinging himself up into the saddle, he told the steward: "I'll be back in the summer."

Yet he had not gone half a mile from the village when his horse quite suddenly shied and threw him so that, landing on some roots, he thought for a moment he had broken his leg.

That was nothing to his astonishment, though, when the animal, looking to the left, gave a piercing whinny of fear and bolted in the other direction.

He stared at the place that had so startled his horse. And there, among the trees, was a horse of unnatural size.

It was a gray, with a black mane and a black stripe down its back. It came through the trees towards him and galloped straight across the path after his horse.

As it went by, its hooves made no sound.

Slowly Milei picked himself up.

He crossed himself.

Then he limped back into the village.

As soon as he was back, he called the surprised steward to his house, and also the old priest from the little church. "I have decided," he told them, "to make a great gift to the glory of God. I am going to found a monastery on my old land across the river."

"What has brought about this decision?" the priest asked. He had not considered Milei capable of such a selfless act.

"I had a vision," Milei replied drily, though with truth.

"The Lord be praised," the old man cried. Truly, how strange and secret were the ways of God.

Milei nodded, then, apparently lost in meditation, he walked out through the door of his house to look at the land he had just given.

He returned a moment later, smiling as if with relief, and at once he took the priest across the river and conducted him around the site.

And so it was, in the year 1263, that the little monastery at Russka was founded.

It was dedicated to Saint Peter and Saint Paul.

One other event of significance occurred in that year.

In order to beg the Tatar khan to be lenient with the rebellious taxpayers of Russia, the Grand Prince Alexander Nevsky had set out across the steppe to visit the Horde.

"He is not well," a visiting boyar from Vladimir told Milei. "If the Tatars don't kill him, the long journey may."

"I hope not," Milei answered. "His policy may have been unpopular with the people, but it has been wise."

"It will be continued," the other assured him. "But he was very distressed to go at such a time. His youngest son is only three and he wanted to see him through until he was grown."

"Ah yes, Daniel is the little boy, isn't he?" Milei knew nothing about this child beyond his name. "I wonder what his inheritance will be."

"They say," the boyar from Vladimir told him, "that Alexander has instructed his family to give him Moscow when he is older."

"Moscow! That miserable town!"

"It's not much of a place," the other agreed, "though its position isn't bad."

Moscow. Milei shook his head. Whatever talents this infant prince might have, he couldn't imagine he'd ever make much of a paltry little town like that.

FOUR

The Icon

1454

AT THE MONASTERY of Saint Peter and Saint Paul, they were summoning
the monks to Vespers; and though the spring evening was cold and damp,
there was excitement in the air. Tomorrow was the great day: the boyar
was coming; a bishop from Vladimir, too. And everyone smiled as his
assistant Sebastian led the man at the center of it all, old Father Stephen,
into the church. There was only one sadness. If only Father Joseph could
be there.

For many years there had been three very ancient monks at the monastery: now only these two remained. Father Stephen was short, Father
Joseph tall. Stephen was revered as a maker of icons; Joseph had no skills
and some thought him simpleminded. But both were very gentle, with
long white beards, and they loved each other.

For thirty-three years, however, Father Joseph had lived apart. Across
the river now, in a small clearing some way beyond the springs, there was
a group of three huts, which formed a hermitage, or skete. In recent
generations, inspired by the so-called Hesychast tradition of the famous
Mount Athos Monastery in Greece, many Russian monks had drawn
apart for a life of intense contemplation. Some, like the blessed Sergius
of the Trinity Monastery north of Moscow, had gone deep into the
forest: "Going into the desert," they called it. The skete at Russka was
quite cut off. To reach the monastery the hermits had to walk about a
mile to the river, then call for the ferryboat kept on the opposite bank.
But they came in, each day, for Vespers.

Except Father Joseph. For a year, they had had to carry the old man.
Now, however, he was too weak even to be moved. Death, everyone
knew, could not be far off. Yet still each day, a thousand times, he
whispered the Jesus prayer: "Lord Jesus Christ, Son of God, have mercy
upon me."

Vespers: the start of the day. Following the ancient Jewish custom, the
Orthodox Church began its day at sundown. The evening psalm was
sung. Throughout the Orthodox service, however long, everyone stood.
Nor were any musical instruments allowed, but only the human voice,
"Right Praising," as the Slavs call worshiping. The singing was lovely:
the whole church year arranged in sequences of eight tones, adapted from
the idea of the eight musical modes of the ancient Greeks, so that the
calendar presented an endless, subtle variation of sound, week by week.

The Great Litany began, and after each supplication the monks intoned the refrain *Gospodi Pomily:* Lord have mercy. This little phrase, repeated again and again, sounded like tiny waves breaking upon a shore.

Sebastian looked around him happily. The monastery had many treasures. Since the marriage of his forbear David to the Tatar girl, the boyar's family, besides acquiring a rather Asiatic look, had been granted more land, including the local Black Land at Dirty Place. The peasants there, once free and now under his steward, had no love for the boyar; but the monastery had gained much. The boyar had given the monks their fine church, built of gleaming white limestone, with its fashionable pyramid roof of false pointed arches and its bulbous onion dome; also a tower with a splendid bell—still a rarity in that region—and a lovely icon of Saint Paul by the great master, Rublev. But nothing, surely, could be finer than the great screen of icons—the iconostasis—that Father Stephen had been painting for thirty years and which would be revealed tomorrow.

How splendid it was. Stretching across the eastern end of the church, dividing the sanctuary from the main body, its five tiers of icons reached almost to the roof. The Holy Family and the saints, the roof. The Last Supper, the Saviour, the Mother of God and the saints, Holy Days, prophets and patriarchs: all were depicted in gleaming colors and in gold. In the center was the great double door, called the holy or royal door, on which were painted the Annunciation and the four Evangelists. And old Father Stephen had painted it all.

One part of the screen was still covered with a cloth. That night the old man was going to complete the last, small icon of the top tier. In the morning, Sebastian would fix it in place in time for the ceremony. Then the work would be complete: to the glory of God.

And the glory of Russia. For one thing was clear to Sebastian, it was that now, in these last days before the world's end, God intended Russia to be glorified.

How she had suffered. For two centuries now she had lain, dismembered, under the Tatar yoke. On every side she was threatened. To the south, Tatars swept across the steppe; to the east, the Tatar khan—the tsar, as the Russians called him—and his vassals the Volga Bulgars held their vast Asiatic dominion. And to the west now, a huge new power had arisen: for in the vacuum left by the collapse of old Russia, the Baltic tribe of Lithuanians—first pagan, now Catholic—had swept across western Russia and taken the land even as far as ancient Kiev itself. Poor Russia: no wonder that even the icons of the Mother of God, in those times, have a special quality of sadness.

Yet Russia was slowly recovering—thanks to Moscow.

The rise of Moscow was astounding. It began when a clever ruler of the little principality married the Tatar kahn's sister and became Grand Duke. As agents for the khans, the Moscow princes slowly surpassed all their rivals—Riazan, the eastern city of Nishni Novgorod, even powerful Tver—all now acknowledged her supremacy. Then, in 1380, blessed by the famous monk Sergius, Moscow had actually defeated a Tatar army at the great battle of Kulikovo by the river Don. The Metropolitan of the

Orthodox Church resided at Moscow, too. And who knew, though the Tatars still raided the land and demanded tribute, one day Moscow might help Russia to break free.

When the last hymn, the Troparion, was finished, Sebastian escorted Father Stephen to his cell. The long Easter fast had weakened the old man and he looked very frail. Sebastian gazed at him fondly. By chance they were distant cousins, sharing an ancestor in Yanka the peasant woman. Chiefly, however, Sebastian felt full of gratitude. He had always been Stephen's pupil. As a boy, the old man had explained the points of the Orthodox cross, with its two extra bars, the headrest and diagonal footrest, which distinguish it from the Catholic cross.

And now he had learned, thoroughly, the art of the icon: choosing the dry wood of alder or birch; planing the surface but leaving a rough border around the edge; attaching the linen; coating its surface with fish glue and alabaster; pricking the outline with a stylus; applying the gold leaf for the haloes; and then painting layer after layer, binding each with egg yolk and brass, to give the icon its wonderful depth. Finally, days later, one added the coating of linseed oil mixed with amber, which soaked through and gave the icon its divine warmth. For the icon was not a picture, but an object of veneration.

Once in his cell, Father Stephen dismissed Sebastian and sat at his worktable alone. One icon, of the patriarch Abraham, to complete—a last layer, which would transform the whole. It could go into the iconostasis for the service tomorrow: the coating would have to come later. He was a humble man. "Beside the simple beauty of the great Rublev," he would say, "my icons are nothing." But such as it was, the iconostasis was his. Now, gazing at the unfinished icon, he said a prayer.

It was strange, he often realized, that his screen would only stand for thirty-eight more years. For the Church had decided, after many calculations, that the Russian year 7000—1492 by the Western calendar—would be the end of the world. Sebastian, he supposed, would see it. But it was not for him to reason about such things. He must paint icons, to God's glory, to the end.

He bowed his head. Then something happened.

It was hard for Sebastian to keep still. Despite his own humility, the whole monastery was in awe of Father Stephen's accomplishment, and the coming day would be a triumph. Sebastian could think of nothing else as he paced in the damp night air. Hours passed, but he did not dare disturb the old master. Nor, when Stephen failed to appear at the midnight service of Nocturne did anyone think anything of it. For afterwards, through the little cell window, Sebastian could see Stephen before his table, his head occasionally moving to and fro, as he worked. And so the night grew deeper.

Father Stephen sat still and wrestled with his body. The stroke he had suffered after Vespers had made him only unconscious for a short while. But he could not speak and he could not move his right arm and he stared, helplessly, at the unfinished icon before him. Hours passed. He prayed. He prayed to the Virgin of the Intercession.

It was in the early hours of the morning that Sebastian awoke and went outside. The candle in Father Stephen's cell was still burning; and perhaps he might have approached if, looking over the monastery wall, he had not seen the strangest sight in the distance.

It seemed to be a little boat with a white sail, coming from the woods opposite towards the river. He rubbed his eyes. Impossible. Then he saw that it was not a boat at all, but a man, moving with great speed. And next, wonder of wonders, the shining figure moved across the water. "I'm bewitched," Sebastian was certain: for the figure suddenly floated, with apparent ease, over the monastery gate and went swiftly to Father Stephen's cell. And then Sebastian saw that it was old Father Joseph. Trembling, he ran to his cell.

And he would, in the morning, have convinced himself that this whole business had been a dream, but for one curious circumstance. For while it so happened that both Father Stephen and Father Joseph had departed this world, from their separate abodes, at about dawn that day, the icon, duly finished, was also found in the iconostasis, in its proper place.

FIVE

Ivan

1552

VERY SLOWLY.

Very slowly.

The oars' lilting refrain on the water.

Mother Volga, mighty Volga: the ships were coming from the east up the river.

High in the endless autumn sky, pale clouds passed by from time to time, as the ships, like their shadows, crossed the sullen waters and the sun dipped slowly to the distant shore. Mother Volga, mighty Volga: the ships were coming from the steppe to the homeland.

Sometimes they hoisted sails; more often they rowed. From the bank of the huge river their oars could not be heard; only the boatmen's faint rhythmic singing plaintively echoed across the stream.

Mother Volga. Mighty Volga.

Boris did not know how many boats there were. Only a part of the army had been left behind as a garrison in the east. The main force was returning to the frontier city of Nizhni Novgorod, and they were returning in triumph. For the Russians had just conquered the mighty Tatar city of Kazan.

Kazan: it was many days behind them now, on its high hill by the Volga where that huge stream at last turned southwards across the distant steppe and desert to the Caspian Sea. Kazan: by the lands of the ancient Volga Bulgars; gateway to the empire once ruled by mighty Genghis Khan.

Now it was Russian.

From dawn each day the boats traveled, until their shadows grew so long that they joined each vessel with the one behind so that, instead of resembling a procession of dark swans in the distance, they seemed to turn into snakes, inching forward on waters turned to fire by the western sunset ahead. While on the bank, the last red light from the huge sky eerily caught the stands of bare larch and birch so that it appeared as if whole armies with massed lances were waiting by the riverbank to greet them.

Boris was sitting in a boat some way down the line. He was sixteen, of medium height with a frame that was still rather spare, a broad face with a hint of Turkish in it, dark blue eyes, dark brown hair, and a wispy beard. Being a young cavalryman, he wore a quilted woolen coat—thick enough to stop most arrows. Over his shoulders he had draped a coat of fur, against the cold breeze on the river. Behind him was slung a short Turkish bow and at his feet lay an axe in a bearskin sheath.

He was of noble birth: his full name was Boris, son of David, surnamed Bobrov, and if asked where he came from he would answer that his estate lay by Russka.

No one paid any attention to him, but if anyone had bothered, he would have observed a brooding, nervous excitement in the youth's face, especially when he glanced forward at the first boat that was leading them back towards the west.

For in the first boat rode a twenty-two-year-old man: Tsar Ivan.

Ivan: Holy Tsar, Autocrat of all the Russias: no ruler before had taken such titles. And his capital was Moscow.

This was the state known to history as Muscovy, and it was already a tremendous power. One by one, in the process known as the Gathering, the mighty cities of northern Russia had fallen to Moscow and her armies. Tver, Riazan, Smolensk—even mighty Novgorod—had given up their ancient independence. And this new state was no federation: the Prince of Moscow was as great a despot as was once the Tatar khan. Absolute obedience to the center: this was the doctrine of the Moscow princes.

Only in this way, their supporters claimed, would the state of Rus return to her ancient glory.

There was still a long way to go. Even now, most of western Russia and the lands of ancient Kiev in the south were still in the grip of mighty Lithuania. Farther yet, across the Black Sea, a new Muslim power, the Ottoman Turks, had seized old Constantinople—henceforth called Istanbul—and their Ottoman Empire was expanding each generation. Catholics to the west, Muslims to the south. And to the east the Tatars had regularly swept in from the eastern steppes, over the Oka, past little Russka, and even to the white walls of mighty Moscow itself.

It was not just that the Tatars looted and burned: it was the children they stole that made Boris hate them. He remembered how he himself as a boy had stood, quivering with fear and rage, inside the monastery walls as they came riding by, with huge panniers strapped to their horses, into which they tossed the wretched little boys and girls they caught. There were several lines of defense against them: the settlements of vassals—formerly hostile Tatars themselves—across the Oka; then there were little forts, wooden barriers and stout-walled towns with garrisons. But no one had been able to control them.

Until this year, when they had found a master.

Boris smiled darkly. At his feet, with their hands manacled, lay two Tatars he had captured himself, and whom he was going to send down to his poor estate at Russka. That would teach the Tatars who was their lord.

Soon he would get more. For this campaign was only the beginning. Kazan was the nearest of the Tatar khanates. Far away to the south, by the Volga delta where once the Khazars ruled, lay another Tatar capital: Astrakhan. Astrakhan was weak. That would fall next.

And then would come the chief of all the western Tatars, down by the warm Black Sea—the khan of the Crimea, at his stronghold: Bakhchisarai.

He was a terrible figure. The palace of Bakhchisarai was like the famous Topkapi palace of the Turkish sultan in Istanbul, and even the Ottoman ruler was glad to use the Crimean khan as an ally. But in time he, too, would fall, and after that, eastward across the Volga, the Kazaks, the Uzbeks, the Nogay horde—the fierce but fragmented tribes who dwelt in the Asian deserts—they too would fall: the power of Muscovy would crush them all.

This was the great destiny that Tsar Ivan had seen: that a Christian Russian tsar would one day rule over the vast Eurasian empire of mighty Genghis Khan. Besides this even the largest ambitions of the western crusaders of old would look puny.

For the first time in all history, the men of the forest were going to conquer the steppe.

Indeed, even as they were leaving Kazan, Boris had heard some Tatars refer to Ivan as the White, that is western, khan. No wonder therefore if he should gaze ahead at the young tsar's boat with such excitement.

Besides, he had another reason to be excited that day. That very morning, the young tsar himself had spoken to him. Even now, Boris could hardly believe it. Tsar Ivan had not only spoken to him, but, it seemed, taken him into his confidence. Ever since, while those around him chatted or gazed at the passing scenery, Boris's mind had been full of the encounter with his hero.

And how heroic he was, this tall, dark young tsar with his huge destiny. It had not been easy for him: Boris knew that. Yet he had overcome all obstacles. Only three years old when he inherited the crown, he had been forced to watch, humiliated, as the great princes and boyars fought to rule Russia in his place.

There were two mighty groups: the princes, who descended either from the old Russian royal house or from the rulers of Lithuania; and the greatest boyar families—some thirty-five clans who made up the central core of the boyar duma.

These were the powerful schemers that Ivan had overcome. They hated his mother because she was Polish; and they despised his wife. For when, like the ancient khans, he had summoned fifteen hundred eligible girls to be brought before him, he had chosen this girl, from an ancient family, to be sure—but not from one of theirs. Yet Ivan had made them submit to his will. He had ruled through his own inner council of trusted, lesser men; and he had married his wife for love.

Anastasia. Boris had never seen the tsar's wife, yet he thought about her often. He thought about her because, when he got back to Moscow, he was due to marry himself; and already, in his dreams, he had created for his wife the same role that everyone knew the lovely Anastasia played.

"She comforts him in all his troubles. She is his rock." That was what they told him. "She is the one person in all the world he knows that he can trust."

Her family might not be among the greatest magnates, but they were distinguished. Their name at that time was Zakharin: a little later they were to change it and call themselves by another: Romanov.

Boris had no love for the princes and magnates. Why should he support them when they wanted to take all the great positions and leave nothing but the scraps from their table for the mere gentry like himself? Under the autocratic princes of Moscow, however, men like him could rise.

For the rule of the autocratic princes gave hope to obscure families like the Babrovs. While the Moscow rulers had set out to break the power of the mighty clans, they had advanced men of lesser family like the great Morozovs and Pleshcheevs to enormous fortune. Indeed in Russia the gentry, men like Boris Bobrov, instead of opposing autocrats, as they did in much of Western Europe, welcomed them as providing their way to fortune past the princes and magnates.

Two years before, Ivan had chosen a thousand best men—"sons of boyars" as the gentry were called, or even humbler fellows—and ordered that they be given estates near Moscow so that they should be near to hand. Boris, to his chagrin, had been just too young to be selected, for service began when you were fifteen; but he had been glad to see that not all those chosen had actually been found estates nearby. And Russka, though a minor place, was not so very far from the center.

The estate I have is nearer Moscow than some of the thousand, he reminded himself with satisfaction. I'll not be left behind for long.

These were the thoughts that filled the mind of Boris Bobrov as he moved up the river, and went over, again and again, his meeting with the tsar.

The camp had been still asleep, the boats drawn up in long lines upon the bank, shadow merging into shadow in the silence before dawn. Nothing moved upon the water; the sky was empty; not even the few birds of the night, it seemed, chose to infringe any longer upon the vast peace of the slowly fading stars.

Boris had stood by the riverbank. Before him the nearby water seemed black, although far out into the huge river a swath of silvery grayness across its surface gave a hint of the pale starlight above. He gazed towards the eastern horizon, scanning it for the first signs of the dawn: but as yet there was nothing to see.

He had awoken early and got up at once. It was cold and there was a slight dampness in the air. Pulling on a fur coat, he moved quietly out of his tent into the darkness and began to walk towards the river.

He nearly always had a particular sensation at this hour. First, beginning in the pit of his stomach, rose a sense of melancholia. In the silence, under the unending darkness of the sky, he experienced an extraordinary feeling of desolation. It was as if he had stepped from the close womb of sleep into another womb—that of the universe itself which, perhaps, had no end: so that he was at the same time forever trapped, yet utterly alone.

He came down to the water, to the boats by the bank, the long line of shadows. Before him lay the river, vast, soundlessly proceeding on its way.

His melancholy was bittersweet. It was like a conversation in which no words were spoken aloud. It was as if he had said: "Very well. I accept that I am eternally alone—I shall wander forever on the empty roads of the night."

And yet, even in making this sad submission to the universe, even as he moved into this region beyond tears, rather like the relief after weeping, he felt a warmth in his stomach that spread with a tingling sensation. It was a secretion, deep inside him, of tremendous joy and even of love, that made itself known to him only in these silent times before the dawn.

As he stood by the shadows, his mind had turned to his parents.

Boris could only just remember his mother—a gentle presence who had faded from his life. She had died when he was five. For him, therefore, family meant his father.

It was a year since he had died; but for as long as Boris could remember, he had been a tragic figure, disabled by terrible wounds he had received fighting the Tatars soon after Boris was born. For ten years he had been a widower. Once, one could see, he had possessed a big, burly frame; but the blue eyes in his broad, rather Turkish face were sunken, with dark hollows under them, his broad chest showed the bones, and it was only by a great effort of will that he managed to hold his ravaged body together, with some semblance of dignity, until his son came of age and could fend for himself in the world.

It was this feat of endurance, this drawing upon deep reserves, that had made its deep impression upon the boy. More than any vigorous warrior, his father's fallen figure represented to him something heroic. It was almost as if the emaciated figure who cared for him was both a living father and, at the same time, an ancestor from beyond the grave. And though he was only of medium height, and sometimes rather clumsy, broad-faced Boris grew up with a single, towering passion: to fill the heroic role his father had been denied.

"The family is in your hands now," his father told him. "Our honor rests upon you alone."

If he closed his eyes, he could see them, his ancestors—tall, noble figures resting in their graves, figures receding into the mists of time, warriors of forest, steppe, and mountain. And if they were watching him, he vowed that they would not be disappointed. The family of Bobrov, with its ancient trident *tamga*, would rise again to glory.

Either that or I will die, he had promised himself.

Gazing over the river under the huge, empty sky, he wondered—could his father see him in the darkness now? Did he know that they had triumphed over Kazan?

"You are with me," he whispered, with a little rush of emotion.

It must be so. God would not deny to his father the knowledge that his son was restoring the family fortunes, completing the circle that would atone for his own broken life. It must be so. If it were otherwise, then God's universe could never be perfect.

Surely the universe was perfect. Surely one day, whatever trials God made him undergo, he would be granted success, respite from his loneliness and—ah, the thought of what was soon to happen!—with his wife he would find the love and friendship he had dreamed about but never known. He would find it: perfect love.

It would be so. He had smiled and drunk in the cold air before dawn.

A footfall, quite soft, somewhere behind him. He turned. At first he could not see anyone, but then he heard a faint rustle and saw another tall shadow move out from the line of boats.

He frowned, wondering who it could be. The shadow came forward slowly, but not until it was only three paces away could he clearly see this figure's face; and when he did, he had gasped with astonishment, then bowed low, as he saw it was Tsar Ivan.

He was alone. Without speaking a word he had advanced to the riverbank and stood beside Boris for a minute or so before asking him his name.

How softly he spoke. Yet Boris thrilled to hear his voice. He asked the youth where he came from, who his family were and, though he did not say anything, seemed satisfied, perhaps even pleased, with Boris's answers. Having ascertained these facts, Ivan said no more but continued to stand silently by the young warrior staring at the broad expanse of water that stretched away, a pale glimmer, into the blackness.

What should he say? Boris wondered. Nothing, perhaps: yet it seemed madness to lose this extraordinary chance to impress the tsar. After a little time, therefore, Boris ventured to murmur: "Thanks to you, my sovereign, Russia is breaking free."

Had it pleased him? Boris hardly dared to look; but when he stole a glance at the tsar's tall figure, he could see on his long, aquiline face only a faint frown as he continued to stare at the water; and not daring to say more, Boris waited in silence. The moving river, huge though it was, went by soundlessly.

It was some time before Ivan spoke, but when he did, it was with a deep, quiet murmur that was only just distinct enough for Boris to hear.

"Russia is a prison, my friend, and I am Russia. Do you know why that is?" Boris waited respectfully. "Russia is like a bear, kept in a cage, for men to mock at. Russia is trapped by her enemies—she cannot reach her own natural borders." He paused. "Yet it was not always so. In the days of Monomakh it was not so." He turned to address him directly. "In the days of golden Kiev, tell me, how did the men of Rus trade?"

"From the Baltic to the Black Sea shore," Boris answered. "From Novgorod to Constantinople."

"Yet now the Turks occupy the Second Rome; a Tatar khan controls the Black Sea ports. And in the north"—he sighed—"my grandfather Ivan the Great broke the Hansa merchants in Novgorod, yet still those German dogs control our northern coasts."

Boris knew how Ivan the Great had ended the near cartel of the Hansa merchants in Novgorod. But alas, rich though Novgorod was, it still had to trade with the West through the Baltic ports, which were mostly in the hands of the old German knightly orders or of German merchants. The only ports belonging to Russia herself were too far north, iced up for half the year.

"Russia is landlocked," Ivan said bitterly. "That is why she is not free."

How it touched Boris to hear these words. It was not just what the young tsar said, but the pain that he heard in his voice that stirred him. This mighty sovereign, whom he already revered, suffered pain just as he did. He, too, felt a sense of indignity—in his case for Muscovy itself— just as poor young Boris suffered all the pangs of impotent fury when he considered his pitiful little inheritance at Russka. Truly the tsar, in his noble and bitter rage, was a man like himself; and forgetting for an instant his own lowly position, he turned and whispered urgently: "But it is our destiny to be free, to be great. God has chosen Moscow as His Third Rome. You will lead us!"

He meant it, passionately, every word.

Ivan turned and Boris felt his piercing eyes upon him; yet he was not afraid.

"You truly believe what you have said?"

How could he not?

"Yes, lord."

"That is good." Ivan nodded thoughtfully. "God led us to Kazan and gave it into our hands. He answered the prayers of his servant."

Indeed the campaign to the Tatar city out on the eastern reaches of the Volga had resembled, at times, a mighty pilgrimage. Not only were the icons carried before the troops, but Ivan's own crucifix, containing a piece of the true cross, was brought from Moscow; priests had sprinkled holy water all over the camp to drive away the bad weather that was hampering the siege. And Ivan's prayers had indeed been answered. He had prayed so long in his tent that some had even said he was afraid to join his troops; but Boris could not believe that. Was it not at the very moment in the liturgy when the priest had exclaimed: "Your enemies shall bow down before you," that the Russian mines had exploded and breached the stout oaken walls of Tatar Kazan? And was it not the feast of the Protection of the Mother of God when this had occurred?

He had never doubted the tsar for a moment. Nor had he any doubt that Moscow was destined to lead the Christian world—she was the Third Rome, until the end of days. God had given so many signs.

Sixty years before—in the year, by the Western count, 1492—the Russians had assumed the world would end. Indeed, it is a historical fact that for the year 1493, or 7001 by the old Russian count, the Orthodox Church had not even troubled to calculate the date of Easter. When, therefore, the millennium failed to arrive, there was genuine and official astonishment. What could it mean?

It meant, certain important churchmen decided, that a new age was beginning—an age that Moscow must surely be destined to lead. And so, in the reign of Ivan the Great and his successors, began in the state of Muscovy the idea that Moscow was the Third Rome.

After all, the imperial city of Constantinople, the Second Rome, had fallen to the Turks. Saint Sophia was now a mosque. Though the Russian Church had waited patiently for the Greek Patriarch to assume his former authority, he had continued to be no more than a puppet of the Turkish ruler; and as the years passed, it became clear that the Metropolitan in Moscow was, for all practical purposes, the true leader of Eastern Orthodoxy.

An imperial destiny. The young tsar's grandfather, Ivan the Great, had married a princess of the old imperial family of Constantinople; from this date the Russian royal family had proudly taken the double-headed eagle—the crest of the rulers of the fallen Roman city—as their own.

Boris looked across with reverence at the tall figure by his side. The tsar had fallen silent and seemed to be lost in thought again.

Then he sighed.

"Russia has a great destiny," he remarked sadly, "yet I have more to overcome within the borders of my land even than outside."

How Boris felt for him. He knew how the bold Shuisky princes—of more senior descent than Ivan from Alexander Nevsky—had humiliated him as a boy; he knew how they and others had tried to undo the work of the great House of Moscow and replace the tsar's rule with that of the magnates. He thought of how, when a terrible fire had swept through Moscow only five years before, the Moscow mob had blamed his mother's Polish family and dragged his uncle out of the Assumption Cathedral itself and butchered him. They had even, he remembered, threatened to kill Ivan, too.

Ivan's enemies tried to block all he did; there were many, Boris had heard, who were even saying that the expedition of Kazan was a waste of money.

And now the young tsar was turning to him—to him, Boris Bobrov from a miserable little estate by Russka—he was turning to him by the dark waters of the Volga and saying quietly: "I need such men as you."

A moment later he had gone; and Boris, trying to see him, could only whisper fervently after him, into the shadows: "I am yours," to which he added that most awesome of all titles—"Gosudar"—sovereign, lord of all.

He had stayed there, trembling with excitement, as the faint dawn at last began to appear in the east.

As the boats continued their journey up the great river Volga that day, Boris was still just as excited by late afternoon as he had been early that morning. What might the meeting with the young tsar lead to? Was this a prelude to a step forward for his family?

Boris, son of David, surnamed Bobrov. The custom of naming people had changed in recent generations. None, nowadays, but the princes and the greatest boyars used the full form of patronymic, with its ending *vich*. Tsar Ivan, for instance, was Ivan Vasilevich; but he, a humble noble, was only Boris Davidov, son of David—not Davidovich. To define his identity more precisely, however, a Russian might add to these two names a third—usually the name by which his grandfather was best known.

Sometimes this was a baptismal name, like Ivan, so that the third name became Ivanova, shortened to Ivanov. Or it might be a nickname.

It was in this way, during the sixteenth century, that family names began to appear, somewhat late, in Russia. For this third name was sometimes held over into the later generations—though the practice was still at the individual's choice—and a family, having chosen a surname, might easily alter it several times.

Boris's family were proud of their name. It was, they always insisted, Ivan the Great himself who had given Boris's great-grandfather the nickname Bobr, meaning "beaver": though whether it was because he liked to wear a beaver coat, or that he was hardworking, or whether that awesome monarch decided this minor nobleman looked like a beaver, no one seemed to know. But Bobrov the family had decided to be called, and that was that. The mighty Beaver, they called this ancestor respectfully. It was his father who had given the monastery at Russka its beautiful icon by Rublev, and the family saw to it, with progressively more modest donations, that both men were still remembered by the monks in their prayers.

For the family of Bobrov had fallen from what they had been in former times. The decline had been gradual and was entirely typical of Russian noble families.

In the first place, the estates had been divided many times over the generations, and the last three had failed to acquire new ones. The greatest blow had been when Boris's grandfather, having become, like so many of his class, hopelessly in debt to the local monastery, had handed over to it the entire village of Russka, keeping for himself only the lands at Dirty Place. The family still had a house within the walls of Russka that the monastery let them have at a modest rent; and since Boris felt that the name of Dirty Place sounded undignified, he preferred to say that he came from Russka.

One day he hoped to build Dirty Place up into something, and then perhaps he'd change its name to something better. But until that time it was just a shabby little hamlet and it was all he had.

In some ways he was lucky. The estate at Dirty Place, though rather reduced by a subdivision, was still on good soil and he was the sole heir. It was also a *votchina*—it belonged to him absolutely by inheritance. In the last half century, less and less land was being held as *votchina,* and more and more was being held, either by impoverished landowners or by new men, as *pomestie*—that is, on condition of service to the prince. And though in practice *pomestie* land often passed to the next generation of a family, it only did so at the prince's pleasure. Even so, Boris's income was hardly enough to pay for horses and armor and support him through the year. If the family was ever to recover its former state, he must gain the favor of the prince.

The meeting with the tsar had been the most important thing that had happened to him so far in his life. But even though the tsar now knew his name, he must do more to attract his hero's attention. The question was, what?

In late afternoon they passed an area on the left bank where the woods gave way to a long strip of steppe; and it was while they went by that Boris saw a motley collection of houses about a mile away. He gave a faint snort of disgust as, staring at them, he saw that they were moving.

"Tatars," he murmured.

The Tatars on Muscovy's borders often lived in these strange, mobile houses—not so much caravans, like the gypsies of Western Europe, as wooden huts with small wheels underneath them. To the Tatars, the fixed abodes of the Russians, attracting rats and all kinds of vermin, were like pigsties. To Boris their mobile homes proved that they were shifting and untrustworthy.

The sight of these vagrants made him think about the two he had captured. He looked down at them. They were a pair of stocky, flat-faced fellows with shaved heads; when they spoke, their voices were deep and loud.

They bray like asses, he thought.

And they were Muslims.

Though the campaign had been a crusade, it was the tsar's policy that the Tatar populations he conquered should be converted to Christianity by persuasion, not by force. Indeed, to weaken their resistance, his emissaries were careful to point out to the Tatars that the empire of Muscovy already contained Muslim communities whom the tsar allowed to worship in peace. But of course, if a Tatar wished to enter the tsar's personal service, he must be a Christian; for Ivan himself was strict and devout.

"If I am to impress the tsar," he considered, "I must show that I, too, am devout."

The two Tatars would convert that night. And soon, he felt sure, he, too, would become one of the tsar's chosen few—his best men.

The afternoon was overcast, but ahead of them a break in the gray clouds had allowed mighty shafts of sunlight to descend, which lit up an area of broken forest and caused it to shine with an almost unnatural gleam. And to Boris, gazing eagerly towards the west, it seemed as though this sunlit patch of land, aspiring to escape from the endless, dull stasis of the plain, had gathered itself together in a pool of golden fire, and was being drawn up into the sky like a huge pillar of prayer.

At dawn the next morning the two Tatars were baptized in the river Volga by one of the priests traveling with them. Following the Russian custom, they were fully immersed three times.

The young tsar could not have failed to notice it.

Two days later they arrived at the great frontier city of Nizhni Novgorod.

It lay on a hill, frowning over the junction of the Volga and the Oka, the last eastern bastion of old Russia. Eastward from Nizhni Novgorod lay the huge forests where the Mordvinians dwelt. Westward lay the heart of Muscovy. Its high walls and its white churches stared out over the Eurasian plain as though to say: "Here is the land of the holy tsar—unshakable."

At Nizhni Novgorod was the great Macarius Monastery, with its enormous fair. As he walked its streets, Boris smiled. It was good to be home.

The returning army was popular at Nizhni Novgorod. The Tatars had so often disrupted their affairs in the past—and besides, Kazan was their rival in the trade with the East. The people showed their gratitude in every way.

It was midafternoon, the end of the working day, when he met the girl. She was standing outside a long wooden building that contained a public bathhouse. She was typical of her kind. Whereas the women of the upper classes were kept in virtual seclusion and did not show their faces in public, the women of the people liked to make a display of themselves.

Her face was painted white, her lips bright red. Her eyes were set wide apart and shaped like almonds. She was at least half Mordvinian, he supposed. Her eyebrows were painted black. She wore a long embroidered gown that must have been expensive, and from under which peeped two bright red shoes that tapped out a little rhythm on the ground, from time to time, to keep themselves occupied. On her head was a red velvet cap. Her eyes looked bored, because nothing was happening, but when she saw young Boris staring at her, they became first watchful, then faintly amused. As he walked up to her she smiled, and he saw that her teeth were black.

It was done with mercury, this blackening of the teeth, and Boris had heard the custom was borrowed from the Tatars. The first time he had gone with one of these women, her black teeth had repelled him, but he had learned to get used to it.

They stopped, briefly, at a little drinking booth, where they were serving vodka. He liked this spirit that went down one so easily, even though at this time it was mainly used by the lower classes. It was not a Russian drink at all, but had entered Russia from the West through Poland in the last century. Indeed, its very name was only the mispronounciation by Russian merchants of the Latin name it bore: *aqua vitae.*

They finished their drink. He felt a warm surge run through him as she took him to her lodgings.

She proved to be warm and surprisingly supple.

Afterward, when he had paid her, she asked him if he were married, and hearing he was about to be, she laughed merrily. "Keep her locked up," she cried, "and never trust her." Then she moved lightly away, in her red shoes, humming to herself.

It was with a shock, at that very moment, that Boris turned to see that a group of people had just come out of a church opposite. They were dressed in furs and did not seem eager to attract particular attention, but Boris immediately recognized the tall young figure in their midst.

He knew very well that Tsar Ivan could not even ride near a church without paying it a visit: obviously this had been another of his sessions of prayer. But had the devout sovereign seen him with the girl? He looked at him nervously.

It was obvious that he had. His piercing eyes shot after the girl, then bored into Boris. The youth held his breath.

Then Ivan laughed—a sharp, rather nasal laugh—and his party moved rapidly away.

Boris had no doubt he had been recognized: Ivan missed nothing. But had it altered the sovereign's opinion of him—had it affected his prospects? There was no way of knowing.

It was two days before the end of October when they entered the mighty city of Moscow.

How thrilling the journey had been. They had come overland from Nizhni Novgorod, through the very heartland of Muscovy. First they had come to the ancient, high-walled city of Vladimir, where they learned that Tsar Ivan's wife had just given him a son. Then, despite his eagerness to reach the capital, Ivan had taken a large party first to nearby Suzdal, and then across to the great monastery of Trinity Saint Sergius, forty miles north of the capital, in order that he could give proper thanks to God at each place.

And as he followed the tsar to these fortress monasteries and powerful old cities, deep in the forest and meadowland of Russia, it seemed to Boris that he saw God's purpose and the destiny of the young tsar more clearly than ever before. Truly, he thought, the endless steppe will be conquered at last by Russia's mighty heart.

There was the lightest snow in the air that day, so thin and sparse that it hardly seemed to be falling at all, but danced in the air instead, brushing carelessly against the rooftops without settling and only dusting the ground.

The city occupied a noble setting at the meeting of the Moskva and Yausa rivers, with the long, low line of the Sparrow Hills behind. Boris still found its size overwhelming.

Indeed, though Boris did not know it, Moscow was then one of the greatest cities in all Europe—as big as sprawling London or powerful Milan. Its suburbs stretched so far out into the surrounding villages that it was hard even to say where the city began. First one encountered great monasteries with walls like castles, then the outer suburbs with their mills, orchards, and gardens. And then one came to the great earth rampart that enclosed the Earth Town, where the humble classes lived; then the masonry walls of the White Town, the middle-class quarters; and at last the Kitaygorod, the rich quarter beside the towering walls of the mighty Kremlin itself.

Already, as they moved through the outer suburbs, there were crowds by the road. Everywhere, it seemed, bells were pealing through the snow. Huge shapes—walls, towers, the golden domes of the monasteries— loomed in the middle distance out of the gray haze of the snow-dusted sky.

And then, as they finally approached the citadel—as though in welcome—the snow died away and there before them, glowing strangely under the lowering orange light of the snow clouds, lay the mighty city.

Boris caught his breath at the sight. The cavalrymen in their pointed helmets or their tall, cylindrical fur hats rode so proudly towards the city gates; on each side of them marched the tsar's new crack infantry corps of musketeers—the *streltsy*—and other halberdiers who, Boris could see, were already having trouble containing the thickening and enthusiastic crowd that was streaming out of the gates in Moscow's mighty walls.

How splendid, and how powerful. Great towers rose at intervals along the city walls—towers with high pyramidal roofs like pointed tents. And enclosed behind them lay the great sea of wooden houses, interrupted by stone towers and domes, that was the city.

Moscow: city of the imperial tsars. When they had crowned Ivan, they had put a cap of fur and gold upon his head and claimed it had belonged to Monomakh, greatest of princes in the days of the ancient Rus. But the autocrats of Moscow went far beyond anything that Monomakh would have dreamed of in the ancient days of Kiev. Each time a city fell, its princely family was broken and made servants of the state; and its leading boyars were resettled in other provinces. When the young tsar's grandfather had taken over Novgorod, he had even taken away the bell they used to summon the *veche,* in order to mark that the citizens' ancient freedoms were gone forever. The Moscow family had even invented a genealogy which traced their ancestry to the great Roman emperor Augustus, at the time of Christ. In the Kremlin now, splendid buildings and cathedrals by Italian architects had appeared beside the onion domes and towers of its older churches and monasteries so that, here in the heart of this northern forest empire, one might, for an instant, think oneself before a Florentine palazzo.

Moscow: city of Church and State. In the opinion of many churchmen, the state and religious authorities should rule together in perfect sympathy. This was the Byzantine ideal of the old Roman Empire of the east. And so it was in Moscow. Had not young Ivan already set out two great programs of reforms, one for his administration and one for the Church? The young tsar would not tolerate magnates who oppressed the people, nor clergy who were lax or immoral in their habits. Did not each great law code have a hundred chapters? For Ivan liked such mighty symmetry.

Moscow: heart and mind of Russia. Inside the great stout walls that ringed the city dwelt some merchants and others from abroad; but never were they allowed to defile the inner life of the mighty people of the north. Catholics and Protestants could visit but not make converts. Orthodox Russians knew better than to trust the treacherous people of the West. Though there were many Jews and other foreigners down in the southern lands of Kiev, here in the north none were allowed to come.

The state of Muscovy might yearn to possess the Baltic ports that would give them free access to the West; but here at Moscow, her heart and mind would be safe, impenetrable, protected by mighty walls that should never be broken down. Neither Tatars with sword and fire, nor treacherous Catholics, nor cunning Jews should ever enter and conquer here. This was Russia's protection against fear.

A great procession was coming from the city gates. The clergy was coming, led by the Metropolitan. Banners, icons, shining vestments, they came from the huge walled city with its gleaming domes, under the heavy gray-and-orange sky, while the air was riven with a thousand crashing bells. They were coming to greet the tsar.

"Slava—all praise. Conqueror, savior of Christians."

And it was on this day that Boris heard the soldiers give a new name to the conquering Tsar Ivan. They were calling him *Grozny*—meaning

"Awesome," "Dread," or, as it is usually if inaccurately rendered: "Terrible."

The snows had already fallen when his wedding day arrived.

A few friends, all made in the last year, came to the little house in the White Town suburb to collect him; but despite their attempts at gaiety, he felt very much alone.

Already, though it was less than a month before, the triumphant return to Moscow seemed far away. He had felt like a hero in those early days as he drank in the taverns with the other young fellows. He had felt like a conqueror when he came out into the night and walked about the citadel admiringly. He loved to wander in the huge space of Red Square. In summer it was full of market stalls, but in winter the whole market moved down onto the frozen river below. The big open space stretched away before him like the empty steppe. Beside it rose the massive, impenetrable walls of the tsar's fortress with its vast, high towers. The tallest soared up two hundred feet into the starlit night; and somewhere in that vast, closed fort dwelt the tsar.

Someday, he thought, I'll be asked to go inside those walls.

Sometimes he would go into the quarter just east of the Kremlin. This was the Kitaygorod—the so-called Basket Town—a walled area within which great nobles and the richest merchants dwelt. Here were big houses not only of wood but even of masonry too. Often, the rich nobles were celebrating and the street would be full of big sledges pulled by magnificent horses as the coachmen drank and talked together. Even by the torchlight, he could see splendid furs and oriental carpets piled in the empty sledges, for the comfort of the burly, wealthy men who would in due course stomp out into the night.

He would know that his prospective father-in-law was probably in there somewhere. True, he did not live there: he lived in a substantial wooden house in the White Town; but he was often at the feasts of these powerful men in this noblest quarter.

And it was only then that his spirits would sink a little. For this knowledge reminded Boris of the central fact of his life: that he was poor.

Indeed, as his future father-in-law Dimitri Ivanov had made clear, he was only giving Boris his third daughter as a favor to Boris's father, who had been his friend in bygone years. Not that Boris was making a brilliant marriage; but it was the best that his poor father had been able to arrange.

For Dimitri, it was certainly a sacrifice. The possession of three good-looking daughters was an asset to a noble like him. They were kept in seclusion in the women's quarters upstairs and they could be used to make marriages that would benefit the family. Though young Boris was acceptable by his birth, that was all; and so the dowry that Dimitri gave his youngest daughter Elena was very modest and caused Boris sadly to realize a simple truth: The richer you are, the more people think they ought to give you. He sighed.

As for his feelings about Elena, Boris was both excited and uncertain. His father had arranged the betrothal long before, and it was only when he had come to Moscow before leaving for the Kazan campaign that he had met her.

He would never forget it. He had entered the big wooden house late one morning. They had offered him bread and salt and, in the proper manner, he had gone to the icons in the red corner, bowed three times, and murmured—"Lord have mercy." It was as he crossed himself from right to left and turned that the girl and her father had entered the room.

Dimitri was short, fat, and bald. He wore a dazzling blue-and-gold kaftan. His face was broad and narrow-eyed, revealing the existence of a Tatar princess in his family some generations before, of which he was very proud. His beard was full and red, and it reached luxuriantly down his swelling belly, over which it was carefully brushed outward like a fan.

Elena was at his side. She was wearing a long embroidered dress of pinkish red. Her hair was golden and plaited in a single braid down her back. On her head was a modest diadem, and over her face a veil.

With a faint grunt of satisfaction, Dimitri whipped off the veil and Boris found himself staring at his future wife.

She was not like her father at all. Boris noticed at once that her eyes were blue. They were set rather far apart and were, perhaps, somewhat almond in shape; but that was the only hint that she might be related to this short, cruel-looking man. Her nose was narrow, yet slightly and nervously flared above her broad, rather full mouth. She seemed pale and tense. The muscles in her neck were standing out as she looked up at him.

She is afraid I may not like her, he saw at once, and this made him feel tender and protective. She does not realize that she is beautiful, he also shrewdly observed. That, too, was good.

And best of all, as he stared at her thoughtfully, he realized something else: he wanted her. He wanted her with the simple, definitive passion that says: She will be mine to order as I please; and I can make her beautiful.

"I had a fine offer for her the other day," Dimitri told him frankly. "But I had kissed the cross on this with your father, and there's an end to it."

Boris gazed at her. Yes, she was lovely. He started to smile.

And it was then that the little incident had taken place that on his wedding day caused him to be uncertain. It was a small thing now, really. He told himself it meant nothing at all. Elena had looked down at the floor. Yet what was the expression that had flitted across her rather anxious face? Was it disappointment? Or, could it be, conceivably, disgust?

He had looked carefully but been unable to see. Surely if she had utterly disliked him she would have said so to her father? He would not have held Dimitri to his oath in such a circumstance. Or was she remaining silent out of a sense of duty?

In the few meetings they had had since, he had tried to suggest to her that if she was unhappy in any way she should tell him; but she had modestly assured him that she was not.

All was well, he told himself, as the party came near Dimitri Ivanov's house. All would be well.

And surely, he thought, as they stood together before the priests, surely this was meant to be.

The Russian marriage service was long. The tall tapers, decorated with marten skins, filled the church with brightness; the air was heavy with the smell of wax; and the priests with their long beards and their heavy robes coated with pearls and gemstones seemed almost like heavenly presences as they solemnly moved about while the choir chanted. Candlelight, incense, hours of standing: like every Orthodox ceremony, by the time it was over, "you know you have been to church."

Boris made his vows and gave the ring, which, in the Russian Orthodox manner, was placed on the fourth finger of her right hand. But the most moving moment for him was the point, towards the end of the service, where his bride reverently went down on her knees and prostrated herself before him, lightly tapping his foot with her forehead as a token of her submission.

It was a very real submission. Like all women of the upper classes, she would be kept in near seclusion. Indeed, it was a point of honor with both of them that she should be.

She will never demean herself by appearing in public, like a common working woman in the street, he promised himself.

And similarly, it was a point of honor with her that she should obey her husband. To disobey him would be, to her, as disloyal as if a soldier disobeyed an order from his commander. To contradict him before others would be the act of a mere plebeian.

Some men made a point of beating their wives and, Boris had heard, the wives took it for a sign of love. Indeed, the famous guide to family conduct, the *Domostroi,* which had been written by one of the tsar's close advisers, gave precise instructions as to how a wife should be whipped, but not beaten with a stick, and even told the husband how to speak to her kindly afterwards, so as not to damage their marital relations.

But as he looked down at this young woman at his feet whom he scarcely knew, but now intensely desired, Boris had no wish to punish her. He wanted only to merge himself with her, to take her in his arms and, though he scarcely realized it himself, to receive from her the warm affection that he had never known.

So he now experienced a sudden, sharp emotion as, following the custom, he cast the bottom of his long gown over her as a sign of his protection.

I will love her and protect her, he swore in a silent prayer, and believed that in this moment, before the blazing candles, he had truly become a man.

At the end of the ceremony, the priest handed them a cup from which both drank and then, in the best Russian manner, he crushed it under his heel.

As they walked out, the guests, who were almost entirely hers, threw hops over them. They were married. He sighed with relief.

There was only one small event that remained in his mind to mar the happy day. It took place at the wedding feast afterwards.

There were many guests and, as is usual on such occasions, they treated the young man kindly. This being an important family occasion, the women also attended the feast, and he made a low obeisance before Dimitri Ivanov's old mother who, it was said, ruled the whole family down to all her grandchildren from the splendid seclusion of her room on the upper floor. She gave him, he noticed, a nod but not a smile.

The tables were already piled high with food. At this season he knew there would be goose and swan, well seasoned with saffron. There were blini served with cream, caviar, the meat pies made with eggs called pirozhki; there was salmon and all manner of sweetmeats—all the rich diet that caused the swollen figures of so many of the men and women crowding the room.

On a table set to one side, he noticed something else that impressed him—red and white wines from France.

For though the men of Moscow were not permitted to travel to other lands—indeed, to do so without permission might mean death—the nobles and rich merchants were as familiar with foreign luxury goods as they were ignorant of the way of life of the countries from which they came. To afford such wines at one's table: this was to be upper class, Boris considered; in his own house he usually drank mead.

Poor as he was, proud as he was, and small as the dowry had been, Boris could not help feeling a sense of gratification that he had joined himself to these people who were so obviously rich.

The company sat down to the wedding banquet with the bride and groom put in a place of honor.

At once, before the meal properly began, wine was served. Boris drank some and immediately felt a renewed surge of warmth. He had some more, looked at his bride with a little frisson of excitement, and smiled at those around him.

All was well. Almost. For though he had no great love for Dimitri Ivanov, there was only one person in the room that he hated, and for some reason he had been seated opposite him.

This was Elena's brother Feodor. He was a strange creature. While the elder of her two brothers closely resembled his stocky redheaded father, Feodor, aged nineteen, was slim and fair-haired like Elena. His beard was clipped very short and was curled. The rumor was that he had had all his body hair plucked out. Sometimes his face was lightly powdered, but in honor of the occasion he had restrained himself that day; however, it was clear that his face had been massaged and patted with some unguent: and even across the table Boris could pick up the heavy smell of his scent.

There were many such dandies in Moscow: they were quite fashionable, despite the stern Orthodoxy of the tsar. Many, though not all, were homosexual. But as Feodor had informed him at their first meeting: "I love what is beautiful, Boris: boys or girls. And I take whatever I want."

"Sheep and horses, too, no doubt," Boris had replied drily. The practices some of Feodor's friends were said to be varied.

But Feodor had not been at all abashed. He had fixed his hard, shining eyes on Boris. "Have you tried them?" he had asked in mock seriousness; and then, with a harsh laugh: "Perhaps you should."

Boris did not care for this, coming from the brother of his bride; but there was something harsh and cruel in Feodor, despite his wit and occasional humor, and he had avoided him since.

For some reason Elena was fond of him. She did not seem to think that his nature was truly vicious—unless, which God forbid, she condoned him. Boris had tried not to think about this possibility.

But this was the wedding feast. He must try to love them all. Dutifully he raised his glass and smiled when Feodor proposed a toast to him.

The blow, when it came, was completely unexpected.

It was halfway through the meal that Feodor, eying him calmly, remarked: "How nice you two look together." And then, before Boris could think of any reply: "You should enjoy sitting in your place, Boris. After this, I'm afraid, you'd be sitting much farther down the table from any of us." It was said, apparently, with ironic humor, but loud enough for many people to hear.

Boris started violently. "I do not think so. The Bobrovs are at least on a level with the Ivanovs."

But Feodor only laughed. "My dear Boris, surely you realize, no one here could ever serve under you."

It was an insult: the greatest and most calculated that could have been given. But it was not an idle taunt, as if he had said: "Let a dog puke on your mother." Boris could not get up and strike him for it. Feodor had made a highly technical statement about his family that could be verified in a book. And it was possible, he feared, that what he had said might be true.

For the entire upper class of Russia, even down to an impoverished little gentleman like himself, was recorded in an enormous and hotly disputed table of precedence. This was the all-important *Mestnichestvo*. It was not a simple system, though, like that still existing in England, where a clearly defined structure of office, rank, and title allows, to all intents and purposes, the entire upper and official classes to be assigned a place about which there can be no reasonable argument. For the Russian system did not depend upon the position of the individual but of all his ancestors, vis-à-vis the ancestors of another man. Thus a man might refuse to sit lower down the table than another at a banquet, or even to take orders from him as an army commander, if he could prove that, say, his great-uncle had occupied a higher position than the other's grandfather. The *Mestnichestvo* was huge; every noble family brought the most elaborate and impressive family tree they could to the officials who were in charge of it. This tiresome system, towards which most aristocracies are prone, had been developed over the last century or so and brought now to such a point of absurdity that Tsar Ivan had ordered it be suspended when the army went on campaign. To do so was the only way to get any order obeyed.

At public functions, for instance, great magnates had even been known to refuse to sit in the place allocated even when the tsar commanded—to risk his displeasure and possible ruin rather than yield. For once his family yielded place to another, then that fact, too, became a precedent in the *Mestnichestvo* system that might reduce his family's standing for generations to come.

Boris had always understood from his father that the Bobrovs, thanks to their former service, need yield nothing to the Ivanovs although they were somewhat poor. Was it really possible that his father had been mistaken or had misled him? He had never made inquiries: he had just assumed.

Could it be that the clan of the three-pronged *tamga,* of warriors who went back to Kievan times, were of such small account in the state of Muscovy?

As he looked at Feodor, so confident, so quietly mocking, he began to lose confidence in his own position and started to blush.

"This is no time for such a matter." It was Dimitri Ivanov's voice, cutting through the pause in the general conversation, and for once Boris was grateful to his father-in-law. But for the rest of the evening that sense of embarrassment, as if the ground under his feet had given way, remained with him.

Late that night the young men of the party escorted the couple back to Boris's house. It was a small house, which, because it had belonged to a priest, was painted white as a sign that the occupant paid no taxes. Boris had been lucky to find it.

Everything was ready. Following the custom, he had laid sheaves of wheat upon his nuptial bed. And so at last he found himself alone with Elena.

He looked at her. Did she look thoughtful? Did she look sad?

She smiled, a little nervously. He realized that he had not the remotest idea what she was thinking.

And what was she thinking, this rather quiet, shy fourteen-year-old with the golden hair?

She was thinking that she could love this young man: that he seemed to her better, if a little slower-witted, than her brother. She was afraid that, being young and inexperienced, she might not know how to please him.

She saw that he was lonely; that was obvious. But she also perceived that there was something brittle in him. While she wanted to comfort him and help him grow out of what she sensed was a morbid state, her instinct told her that, as he came up against an unyielding world, he might turn back into his loneliness and demand that she share it. And it was this sense of danger, this dark cloud on the horizon, that made her a little hesitant to subjugate herself to him too quickly.

But the simple discoveries of passion, in two very young people, were enough to form the beginning of their marriage on that and the succeeding nights.

In two weeks' time they were due to visit Russka.

*   *   *

It was a sparkling winter morning as Boris and Elena, wrapped in furs, and in the first of two sleds, each drawn by three horses, approached the little town of Russka.

Meanwhile, in the marketplace at Russka, a small but significant meeting was taking place.

To look at them, one would not have guessed that the four men—a priest, a peasant, a merchant, and a monk—were all cousins of each other; and of these four, only the priest knew that he was descended from Yanka, the peasant woman who had killed Peter the Tatar.

It was Mikhail, the peasant from Dirty Place, who was especially anxious. He was a squarely built, broad-chested fellow with soft blue eyes and an aureole of wavy, dark brown hair that rose almost upright from his head. Now his usually placid face looked worried. "You are sure her dowry is small?"

"Yes," the tall priest replied.

"That's bad. Very bad." And the poor man stared at his feet miserably.

Stephen gazed down at him with sympathy. For four generations, ever since his great-grandfather had been named after the old monk Father Stephen, the icon painter, to whom they were related, the eldest sons in his family had been called Stephen and had entered the priesthood. His own wife was also the daughter of a priest. Stephen was twenty-two, a tall, imposing figure with a carefully trimmed dark beard, serious blue eyes, and an air of quiet dignity that made him seem older. His information about Elena was sure to be good. He had contacts in Moscow and since he could read and write—an unusual accomplishment in the priesthood at this time—he could even correspond with the capital.

"A wife with no money—just think what that means for me!" Mikhail lamented. "He'll squeeze me till he breaks my bones. What else can he do?"

The question was asked without any rancor. Everyone understood the problem. Dirty Place was all Boris had. With a wife, soon a family, to keep, the only way he could possibly survive would be to get more from his estate and the peasants on it. Under his ailing father, things had been lax; but who knew what might happen now?

"You two are lucky," he remarked to Stephen and the monk. "You're churchmen. As for you," he turned to the merchant and said, with a rueful smile that contained a trace of malice, "what do you care? You live in Russka."

Lev the merchant was a stout man of thirty-five, with thin black hair swept back over his head, a stringy beard, and a hard, Tatar face. His Mongol eyes were black and cunning although, as now, they could soften with faint amusement when simpleminded men like his cousin Mikhail assumed that his elementary business practices were some kind of fiendish cunning.

He dealt chiefly in furs, but he had extended his activities into several ventures and in particular he had prospered as a lender of money.

As was often the case in Russia, the largest moneylender in the area was the monastery, which had by far the greatest capital. But the generally expanding economy of the last hundred years had created opportunities for many merchants to supply credit as well, and in Russia all classes borrowed. A prosperous small-town merchant like Lev might be owed money even by a magnate or a powerful prince. Interest rates were high. Some loan sharks even charged a hundred and fifty percent and more. Mikhail was sure that his rich cousin would go to hell when he died, but meanwhile he envied him. They were all the same, he thought, the people who lived in Russka—rich and heartless.

Since Russka had been taken over by the monastery, it had grown. There were now several rows of huts, of which some were quite large, with their main rooms upstairs to keep them dry throughout the year. Over five hundred people lived within its walls, which, like those of the monastery across the stream, had been strengthened. Over the gateway now was a high tower with a tall tent roof made of wood. This served as a watchtower for town and monastery, to give them warning of the approach of the Tatars or the bandits who had appeared in the area several times in recent years.

There was a busy, prosperous, and orderly air about the little town. In the marketplace, beside which there was now a stone church as well as an older wooden one, bright stalls were regularly set up. People came from all the nearby villages and hamlets. There was a tax collector in the place who received the customs dues from the traders; but the original impetus for the market was the fact that the goods supplied by the monastery were exempt from taxes. Here one could buy salt, brought in shallow draft boats from the north, and caviar. Local pork, honey, and fish were all excellent. Wheat came upriver from the Riazan lands to the south.

But above all, Russka was known for its icons. The monastery was a regular little workshop. There were no fewer than ten monks, working with assistants, producing a constant flow of icons that were sold in the Russka market. A number of artisans, brought in by the monastery, were housed in Russka, where they turned out handicrafts, some religious, others not, for sale in the stalls. People came from Vladimir, and from Moscow itself, to buy.

Now Lev turned to Mikhail and put his arm around him. "I shouldn't worry," he counseled. And then he spoke aloud the thought that only Mikhail, among the four of them, had failed to grasp. "Don't you realize—if this fellow has his way"—he indicated the monk beside him— "young Lord Boris won't have his estate much longer anyway."

The gentle, joyful hiss of the sleds. The two sleds ran down the gleaming road of the frozen river Rus, between the lines of soft snow-laden trees until, around a curve, the banks opened up to several broad white meadows.

In the first sled rode Boris and Elena. In the second the five Tatar slaves, Elena's maid, and a huge quantity of baggage.

And now at last there lay Russka before them, with the monastery below it. How quiet it was. Under a clear, light blue sky the wooden tent roof of the tower, glistening in the sun, reminded Boris of a tall sheaf of wheat or barley, tied just below the top, standing in a field after harvest.

He squeezed Elena's hand and sighed with pleasure at the familiar childhood sensation of being enveloped in the peace of the Russian countryside.

The tower, it seemed to him, was like a token of summer and of
fulfillment, hanging in the bright winter sky.

Elena, too, smiled. Thank God, she was thinking, that the place was
not quite as small as she had feared. Perhaps there might be a few women
there that she could talk to.

In no time they were gliding up the slope and around to the gate. As
they entered the main square, she noticed the four men standing together near the center. Seeing the sleds, they turned and bowed respectfully. It seemed to her that they were also observing her carefully.
They appeared friendly enough. She pulled the furs up to cover her
face as the sled came towards them; she noticed that one was a priest
and one a monk.

It was impossible to see the expression on the face of Daniel the monk,
because his thick black beard covered so much of it that one could really
only make out the two small, bright eyes that looked out watchfully at
the world, and the top of what were obviously broad, pockmarked
cheeks.

He was on the short side, stockily built, but with slightly rounded
shoulders. His quiet, stooping manner indicated a submissiveness proper
to his religious calling; he spoke rather quietly; yet there was something
about his hard brown eyes, an occasional suddenness in his movements,
that suggested a passionate nature either repressed or concealed.

He was watching the young couple intently.

Stephen the priest, observing both, felt sorry for Boris and Elena. He
had liked Boris's father, admired his long fight with sickness, and buried
him with a sense of personal loss. He wished young Boris well.

As for Daniel the monk, Stephen did not approve of him.

"People say that I love money," Lev had once remarked to him, "but
I don't come near that little monk."

It was true. The merchant's rapaciousness had bounds; there was the
ordinary give and take of the marketplace in his dealings. But Daniel the
monk, though he had nothing of his own, seemed to be obsessed with
acquiring wealth: he wanted it for the monastery.

"He is greedy for God," Stephen had sighed. "It's a crime."

The great battle between those who thought the Church should give
up its riches, and those who thought it should keep them, had been
fought for generations. Many churchmen believed the Church should
revert to a life of poverty and simplicity—especially those, followers of
a saintly monk named Nil Sorsky, who lived in the simple communities
in the forest hinterland beyond the northern loop of the Volga. This
faction, encouraged by these stern Trans-Volga Elders, became known to
history as the Nonpossessors; though most people in Russka, and many
in the capital, too, referred to them affectionately as the Nongreedy.

But they lost. A little after 1500 the church council, led by the formidable Abbot Joseph, declared that the Church's lands and wealth gave
her a power on earth that was wholly desirable. Those who thought

otherwise were in danger of being called heretics.

Stephen the priest privately favored poverty. His cousin Daniel, how-ever, had shown such diligence in everything relating to business that the abbot of the Monastery of Saint Peter and Saint Paul had made him the supervisor of the monastery's activities in the little trading town. To hear Daniel talk about the fall of Kazan, you might have mistaken him for a merchant or a tax collector.

"We can pick up some of the extra trade through Nizhni Novgorod and from the south," he would explain eagerly in his soft voice. "Silk, calico, frankincense, soap . . ."—he would tick them off on his fingers. "Perhaps we can even get some rhubarb, too." For some reason this luxury was still imported from the East.

But above all, Daniel's secret mission in life was to help the abbot enlarge the monastery's lands.

He would probably succeed. For generations the Church had been the one section of the community that had continuously increased its land-holdings. Two years before Tsar Ivan had tried to limit the scale of this growth by insisting that the monasteries and churches must have his permission before they accepted or bought any more land. But these rules were always hard to enforce. In the central regions of Muscovy at this time the Church owned about a third of the land.

There were two desirable estates close by. One was just to the north and east, a tract of land that had passed back into the hands of the Moscow princes. Perhaps Ivan would grant them this: for despite his recent attempts to limit them, he was still a huge giver of land to the Church himself. And then, there was Dirty Place.

Boris's father had held on to his estate; but would the young man with his wife and small dowry be able to? Daniel smiled. Probably not. They might give the land to the monastery in return for a life tenancy: this was often done. Or they could sell it outright. Or they could get them-selves ever deeper into debt until the monastery took over the estate. Boris would be well treated. His family's long connection with the mon-astery would ensure that. He would live out his life with honor. The monks would pray, after his death, for this noble benefactor who gave his lands to the service of God.

"We'll look after him," he would say.

There was only one problem the monk foresaw. Knowing the monas-tery's intentions, the young man would try very hard to keep his inde-pendence, as his father had done. He would do everything he could to avoid borrowing money from the monastery.

"Which is where you come in," Daniel had told Lev the merchant the day before. "When the young man wants to borrow, offer to lend to him, and I'll guarantee the loan," he suggested. "I'll see that you don't suffer by it."

At which Lev had laughed, and his Tatar eyes had shown a flicker of amusement.

"Ah, you monks . . ." he had replied.

And now the young man was approaching.

*   *   *

Elena was surprised, as the sled crossed the square, to hear her husband mutter a curse. What a strange, moody fellow he was, this young man. But when she glanced at him, he gave her a rueful grin.

"My enemies," he whispered. "They're all cousins." The four men looked harmless enough to her. "Especially beware of the priest," he added.

Boris's fear of the priest was founded upon a single fact: that Stephen could read. He himself could make out a few words. There were many nobles at court, he knew, who read; and the monks and priests in the great monasteries and churches read and wrote in their own rather stylized church language. But what was this parish priest, in a little village, doing with books? To Boris it seemed foreign and suspicious. Catholics, or those strange German Protestants who traded in Moscow, probably read books. Worse yet, so did Jews.

For there was always the Jewish danger: Boris knew about that. By this, however, he did not mean the Jewish faith as such, nor Jewish people. He meant the Christian heretics known as Judaizers.

They were a strange group. They had appeared rather briefly in the Orthodox Church the previous century and been rooted out in the reign of Ivan the Great. Some of them, like the Jews, considered Christ a prophet rather than the Messiah. But even at the time the exact nature of the heresy had been confused. What was clear, though, to succeeding generations of faithful Russians like Boris, was that these people relied on logic, subtle arguments and books—and were therefore not to be trusted.

Boris knew that Daniel the Monk was after his land: that he could understand. But Stephen—who knew what he might be thinking?

The little group greeted the new arrivals politely. They smiled respectfully at Elena. Then the sled moved on towards the little house, just past the church at the far end of the square, where the steward, his wife, and the servant girls would be waiting for them.

Elena smiled, trying to make her husband happy; but she felt uneasy.

Boris inspected the estate at Dirty Place the next morning.

The old steward conducted his round. He had been there since Boris was a child and was not a bad fellow. Small, quiet, close-knit, his thick hair was all gray now and the lines on his brow were so deep that it looked as if someone had scored them there with half a dozen blows from an axe. He was honest, so far as Boris knew.

"It's all in good order, just as your father left it," he remarked.

Boris looked around thoughtfully.

In certain ways he was lucky. When the tsar's land assessors, after Ivan's recent tax reforms, had visited Russka, they had carefully inspected the Bobrov estate. It contained a little over three hundred chetverts, or some four hundred and ten acres of land.

The Bobrovs had been lucky on two counts. First, the assessors had kindly decided that some of the land was low quality, which lessened the taxes. And second, the area of the estate was just a little larger than their standard measurements allowed for.

For the Russian land assessors could not compute fractions. Certain ones they knew: a half, an eighth, even a thirty-second; a third, a twelfth, a twenty-fourth. But they could not express, for instance, a tenth; nor could they add or subtract fractions with different divisors. So when they discovered that the good land at Dirty Place consisted of almost two hundred and fifty-four chetverts, which came in tax terms to a quarter of a plow plus another fifteenth, they contented themselves with a quarter plus a sixteenth—the nearest fraction they knew—thus leaving over four acres free of tax.

Thus, as they so often did, the Russians made ingenious accommodations where their expertise failed them.

Compared to many of those to whom the tsar had granted the service, *pomestie,* estates, Boris was not bad off. Most of these had only half what he had. The present income from the estate, however, was ten rubles a year. To go on campaign cost him seven rubles for himself and his horses; his armor and equipment he already owned. He owed four rubles a year in taxes, though; and he had some modest debts in Russka, including one to Lev the merchant. As things stood, therefore, he would slip slowly into debt over a few years unless the tsar did something for him.

Yet he was not discouraged. In time, he was determined to win Ivan's favor: and who knew what wealth that might bring him? As for the present . . .

"I think we can double the income from the estate," he announced to the steward. "Don't you?" And when the old man hesitated, Boris merely snapped: "You know very well we can."

Which was exactly what poor Mikhail the peasant had feared.

There were two kinds of payment that a peasant could make to his lord. He could pay rent, in money or kind; this was termed *obrok;* or he could work his lord's land: this was boyar-service, called *barshchina.* Usually peasants gave a combination of both.

The peasants at Dirty Place worked only one or two days on the land that Boris retained in his own hands—the demesne. In addition they paid him *obrok* for the land they held. During the last twenty years, the estate had lost three tenants: one had left for another lord, one had died without heirs, and one had been sent away. They had not been replaced and thus an extra hundred acres of good land had been retained by Boris's father. And while rents had been increased several times, they had not quite kept up with the steady rise in prices over recent decades.

Mikhail paid twenty-four bushels of rye, the same of oats, a cheese, fifty eggs, eight dengi of money, and a wagonload of firewood. He also had to work nearly three acres of Boris's land, which took him rather under one day a week.

His agreement with Boris did not stipulate how his obligations were to be organized. If Boris wanted to change them, he could. And the price of grain was rising.

"So," Boris remarked cheerfully, "we can reduce the peasant's *obrok* and increase their *barshchina.*"

The grain he could produce on the spare land, if the peasants worked it two or three days a week, would be worth far more than the rents they currently paid. He would hugely gain. The peasants, of course, would lose.

"We'll start with two days right away," he said.

With the extra work from the peasants, and the two Tatar slaves, things would soon begin to look up.

It was two months later that Lev the merchant, upon Boris's request, paid a respectful visit to his house. He knew the reason.

The sky was gray, the street a grayish brown. Only the snow that rimmed the wooden fences gave a pale reminder that not all the world was dreary.

It surprised Lev that the young man and his bride had not already returned to Moscow. He supposed it must be dull for them here. Not that Boris had been idle in the country: he had carried out a thorough review of everything the estate possessed. The merchant's poor cousin Mikhail had lamented to him: "His father was never like this. He seems to miss nothing. He's a Tatar like you, Lev."

Though the merchant sympathized with his cousin, he admired Boris for this. Perhaps he'll surprise them all and keep his estate yet, he thought with wry amusement.

Not that he cared. As he stomped along the street, Lev knew very well where he stood in all these intrigues. He had no strong ties to any of the parties, nor did he intend to have. He was a survivor. The times were good for merchants like himself. And with this energetic young tsar, who knew what new opportunities might open up? One had only to look at the Stroganovs up in the north for instance, a family descended from peasants just as he was, yet who had already built themselves a huge merchant empire and, it was said, had the ear of the tsar himself. They were people to watch, and emulate.

And the way to survive was to keep on good terms with everyone. First, in Russka, that meant the monastery that owned the place. But even there one had to be careful. For if there was one part of the Church's possessions that the tsars in Moscow coveted, it was these valuable little towns; and sometimes the government found excuses for taking them over. If ever that happened, the young lord of Dirty Place, who served the tsar, might be a figure of importance. You never knew.

It was in this cautious frame of mind that he arrived at the stout, two-story wooden house, with its broad outside staircase, and was shown into the large main room, where Boris was waiting for him alone.

He seemed a little pale, held himself rather tensely; but he did not waste time. "As you well know, the income from Dirty Place will go up sharply this year. But in the meantime, I need a loan."

"I am glad you came to me," Lev answered politely, as though he were not aware that Boris had already approached two other lesser merchants who had offered him terms he did not like.

"I think I need five rubles."

Lev nodded. It was quite a modest sum.

"I can lend it to you. Your estate of course is ample security. The interest rate would, on this loan, be one ruble for every five."

Twenty percent. Boris's mouth opened in astonishment. These were lenient terms indeed—less than half what the others had offered; and that very winter in Moscow he had even heard of one fellow who had been charged one percent a day!

Lev smiled.

"My calculation is that I prefer friends to enemies, lord," he said disarmingly. "I trust the lady Elena Dimitrieva is well," he added politely.

"Yes, indeed." Did he see a look of faint strain appear on the young face that, a moment before, had been flooded with relief?

He was not sure. The reports in the town were that Boris's young wife was a kindly, gentle creature. Few people in Russka saw her besides the two servants and the priest's wife, who called upon her. She did not go out in public and, quite rightly, Boris summoned the priest to say the service with her rather than subject her to the prying eyes of ordinary people in church.

After a few more polite expressions he withdrew, and soon afterward he was crossing the marketplace again.

And it was when he was halfway across that he stopped in surprise to see two large sleds, pulled by handsome horses, come jingling into the square and make towards the house he had just left. Something about the cries of the driver and the rich furs he detected within told him that they had come from Moscow.

Life at Russka had seemed strange to Elena. It was so quiet.

Yet she hardly knew herself what she had expected.

The priest's wife who called on her was a pleasant young woman of twenty called Anna with two children of her own. She was a little plump, had a pointed nose and slightly red face, and when she spoke of her husband it was with a little smile that let you know she was entirely happy with that tall man's physical attentions.

Boris did not seem to mind her visits, and she would often sit with Elena in the upstairs room as the afternoons closed in. From her Elena soon got a good picture of the local community and was even able to reassure Boris that he need not be quite so suspicious of the priest, who in fact wished him well.

But it was so quiet. Somehow she had supposed that being married, sharing a house with her husband, she would find her days occupied. And there were things for her to do, managing the house. Yet with Boris often out at the estate or in Russka, time hung heavily on her hands. She had paid three visits to the monastery her husband's family had founded. She had been warmly and respectfully received by the monks. She had also gone with Boris to look at Dirty Place. She had been welcomed with low bows and a few small gifts. But it was obvious that the inhabitants of the stout huts in the hamlet regarded her as the cause of their new obligations, and she had not been eager to go there again.

And that was all. How far away the bustle of Moscow seemed, and the busy life with her family. Why did he not take her back there? Surely he must have finished his business in Russka now: what could he do here anyway, in midwinter?

Boris still puzzled her. She was used to her father's often dark moods, when he would become withdrawn and sullen. She knew that most men were subject to sudden changes of temper that one must accept, and even admire. Her own mother had often said of her husband, with some pride: "He can throw such rages," as though this were an athletic accomplishment.

She would not have been shocked if Boris had exhibited these features, or even if he had beaten her occasionally. That was to be expected. Lev the merchant, she now knew, beat his wife, on principle, once a week.

"And look how many children they have," Anna had remarked to her, with a wry laugh.

But Boris's moods were quite different. He was always kind. If he grew gloomy, he would retire to the stove or the window by himself; if she asked what was the matter, he would only smile wanly. When she tried to characterize his behavior to herself, she could only think: It's as though he is waiting.

That was it: he was waiting, always waiting. But for what? For something wonderful, or something terrible? She knew that he was waiting for her to be his perfect bride, the Anastasia to his Ivan. Yet what did that mean? She did all she could to please him; she would put her arms around him when she saw him troubled. Secretly, though she did not tell him this, she even planned to go to her father and ask for extra money to help him, as soon as they got back to Moscow.

But something about her, it seemed, disappointed him, and he would not let her close enough to discover what he wanted. She was not sure if he knew himself.

And then he was waiting for disaster, too—for things to go badly at Dirty Place; or for some trickery from the monastery, or some other trouble. True, when things went well he would return home elated, full of great plans for the future, confident of the tsar's favor. But even hours later he would be expecting ruin or betrayal again.

It was as though the specter of his father kept rising up before him—encouraging him one moment, then exhibiting his own slow ruin the next.

Sometime after midwinter, disturbing news had come from the east. The city of Kazan had been left with too small a garrison, and now all the territory around the conquered Tatar city was in a state of revolt.

"Tsar Ivan has called the boyar duma together, but they won't act," a merchant from the capital had told Boris. "Half of them never wanted to take Kazan in the first place."

It was this event that had caused the first friction between Boris and his wife.

"Those damned boyars," he had cursed. "Those magnates. I wish the tsar would crush them all."

"But not all the boyars are bad," she had protested. Her father had friends and patrons in those circles. Indeed Dimitri Ivanov did not altogether approve of the vigorous young tsar himself, and he had taught his daughters to be cautious of him, too.

"Yes, they are," Boris had snapped defiantly. "And we'll teach them their place one day, as well."

He knew there was a covert insult to her father in these words, but he could not help himself; and when Elena looked down at the ground sadly, it only irritated him.

After this, however, several weeks had passed with no definite news, and she supposed the incident had passed from his mind. And only one question obsessed her: how much longer before they returned to Moscow?

It was strange that, despite understanding his financial position fairly well, she did not realize that the real reason he delayed was expense. He never told her, because he did not want to discuss his finances with her; and for her part, living in her father's comfortable house in Moscow, she had never realized what a burden the social life of the capital might be to a man of modest means like Boris.

As January ended and February began, she knew only one thing: that she was still at Russka and that she was lonely.

Which was why she had sent the message to her parents.

It had been quite easy. Anna had given the message to a merchant traveling to Vladimir. He in turn had given it to a friend on his way to Moscow. The two women had not even needed to tell Stephen about this arrangement, and the message itself was quite simple: Elena had not complained of being unhappy, but just let them know that she was by herself. Could they not send her someone—she had suggested a certain poor female relation—for company?

So it was with a cry first of joy, and then astonishment, that she saw, on the gray February day of Lev's visit, not one but two sleds draw up by the house and realized that they contained not her poor relation, but her mother and her sister!

They stayed a week.

It was not that they behaved unkindly. Elena's mother was a tall, imposing woman, but she treated Boris with a friendly politeness; her sister, a stout married woman with children of her own, was full of laughter, seemed delighted with everything she saw, and paid two visits to the monastery, each time making flattering remarks about its church, the icon by Rublev, and the other benefactions from Boris's family.

Of course there were the extra expenses—providing wine for them and extra fodder for six horses. A week of entertaining them and Boris knew that his loan from Lev the merchant would not be quite enough. But even that was not so bad.

It was that he felt excluded.

On the simplest level, Elena insisted on sleeping beside her sister, while her mother occupied the other upstairs room and Boris slept downstairs on the big stove. The two sisters seemed to find this a great joke, and he could hear them chattering half the night. He could, he supposed, have forbidden this, but it seemed pointless.

If she prefers her sister's company to mine, he thought gloomily, let them chatter away all night.

But the daytime was worse. The three women were always together, talking in whispers upstairs. He supposed they were talking about him.

Boris's ideas about women were similar to those of most men at that time. There were many essays by Byzantine and Russian authors in circulation, among those who could read, which testified to woman's inferior nature. All Boris knew came from people under these influences or from his father during his long widowhood.

He knew that women were unclean. Indeed, the Church only allowed older widows to bake the communion bread, not wishing younger, profane female hands to contaminate the loaves. Boris always washed himself carefully after making love to his wife and even avoided her presence as much as possible when her time came each month.

But above all, women were strangers to him. He might have his little adventures from time to time, like the girl at Nizhni Novgorod, but when he came upon women as a group, he felt a certain awkwardness.

What were these women doing here in Russka? Why had they come? When he had politely asked them, Elena's sister had answered gaily that they had come to look at the bride and at her husband's estate and that they would be gone "in the twinkling of an eye."

"Did you ask them to come?" he asked Elena, on one of the few occasions he could catch her alone.

"No," she answered, "I did not."

It was, after all, the truth. But he noticed a slight awkwardness about her when she said it.

She is not mine, he thought. She is theirs.

At last they left. As they were leaving, Elena's mother, thanking him kindly for his hospitality, said pointedly: "We look forward to seeing you soon in Moscow, Boris Davidov. My husband and also his mother await you eagerly."

It was a clear enough message—a promise of possible help from Dimitri together with a suggestion that the old lady would consider it disrespectful if he did not present himself before her soon. He smiled wanly. Their visit had cost him almost an entire ruble. If this was any hint of what married life in Moscow might cost, he would take his time before returning.

But what had these untrustworthy women been up to while they were eating him out of house and home? What had they done to his wife?

At first all seemed well. Once again he joined her at nights, and their lovemaking was passionate. His hopes rose.

It was two weeks later that he happened to suffer a change of mood. There was good reason for it. He had discovered certain deficiencies in the farm equipment and in the grain stores that had apparently escaped the steward. At the same time, one of the Tatar slaves had sickened and suddenly died. What little hired labor there was in the area was all contracted to the monastery. So he would either have to buy another

slave or farm less land that year. He could see that a second loan from
Lev the merchant was going to be needed.

Whichever way he turned, just then, it seemed that all his efforts were
thwarted.

"You'll work something out," Elena told him.

"Perhaps," he had replied gloomily. And he had gone to the window
to be alone with his thoughts.

A few hours later she had come to talk to him. "You worry too much,
Boris," she had begun. "It's not so serious."

"That's for me to judge," he told her quietly.

"But look at your gloomy face," she went on. There was something
new in the way she said this, something faintly mocking, as though she
were trying to laugh him out of his mood. Where did she get this new
boldness from? Those women, no doubt. He glowered.

He was perfectly right. Elena had several times asked her mother and
sister what they thought of Boris, and it was her sister who had assured
her: "When my husband gets moody, I let him see it doesn't bother me.
I just go on cheerfully and laugh him out of it. He always comes around."

She was a busy young woman, rather pleased with her role as older
adviser. It did not occur to her that Boris and her own husband were
entirely different.

And so now, when Elena made clear to Boris that she did not take his
mood seriously, when she continued, a little smugly, to look cheerful in
his presence, it made him think only: So: they have taught her to despise
me.

He had been brooding angrily about this for several hours when she
made her greatest mistake. It was only a casual remark, but it could
hardly have been worse timed. "Ah, Boris," she said, "it's foolish to be
so downhearted."

"Foolish!" Was his own wife now calling him a fool? In a sudden flash
of frustrated rage, he leapt to his feet, his fists clenched.

"I'll teach you to smile and laugh at me when I am worried," he roared.

And as he took a step towards her he hardly knew what he might do,
when a hammering on the door, followed by the sudden entrance of
Stephen the priest distracted him.

The priest, looking deeply concerned, hardly noticed Elena, and before
even crossing himself before the icons, delivered a message that drove
everything else from Boris's mind.

"The tsar is dying."

Whichever way Mikhail the peasant looked, he could see trouble.

Young Lord Boris was away in Moscow with his wife, though he paid
brief visits from time to time. But no doubt he would return for another
protracted stay before long, and who knew what he would think of doing
next?

The new *barshchina* was a heavy burden. In addition to this service and
some small payments to Boris, he also had to pay the state taxes, which
usually cost him about a quarter of his grain crop. It was hard to make

ends meet. His wife wove bright, cheerful cloths decorated with red bird designs, which she sold in the Russka market. That helped. There were small ways of cutting corners too: he was allowed to pick up any dead timber in the landlord's woods; and like everyone else, he ringed a tree here and there to kill it. But there was no money left over at year end and he had only enough grain of his own stored to get him through one winter after a bad harvest. Those were his total reserves.

Then there was the problem of Daniel the monk. More than once Daniel had hinted to him that if his work on the estate was poorly done—if, to put it bluntly, he discreetly sabotaged Boris's efforts—it would be no bad thing.

But in the first place, he didn't care to do it, and secondly, if the steward caught him, the consequences could be serious.

"We could leave," his wife reminded him. "We could leave this very autumn."

He was considering it, but there was nothing he could do yet.

The laws that now regulated when a peasant could leave his lord had been drawn up by Ivan the Great fifty years before, and renewed by his grandson the present tsar.

No longer could a peasant go at any time, but only at certain dates stipulated by his master—the most common of which was a two-week period centered on the autumn Saint George's Day: November 25. There was logic to this: the harvest was all in by then; but it was also the bleakest time in the year for the peasant to travel. There were conditions, of course: heavy exit fees had to be paid. But all the same once he had given notice and paid his dues, the peasant and his family were free to go, to put on their Sunday best and present themselves to a new master. Whence came the ironic Russian expression for a fruitless enterprise: All dressed up for Saint George's Day, with nowhere to go.

Yet here was Mikhail's dilemma. Even if he could ever afford to leave, where should he go?

So much of the land now was *pomestie*—service estates. They were small, and the men who held them often bled their peasants dry and neglected the land that was theirs only conditionally. At least an old *votchina* owner like Boris had more care for the place. Alternatively there were the free lands up in the north and east—but who knew what life might be in those distant hamlets beyond the Volga. Or there was the church.

"If the monastery doesn't get the estate, we could always go and take a tenancy on the lands they have," his wife suggested.

Yet he wondered. Would he be so much better off? He had heard of other monasteries raising rents and increasing the *barshchina*.

"Let's wait a bit and see," he said.

His wife would wait patiently. He knew that. She was a stout, heavy-legged creature who always made a point of glaring at any strangers; yet behind this rather harsh facade was a gentle soul who even felt sorry for Boris and his young wife, their oppressors.

"He'll be dead or ruined in five years," she prophesied. "But we'll still be here, I daresay."

Mikhail was not so sure about his two sons, though. The elder, Ivanko, was a stolid young fellow of ten, who reminded him of himself; with a fine singing voice. But Karp, his little boy, was an enigma to him. He was only seven, a dark, sinewy, athletic little creature who already had a mind that was entirely his own.

"He's only seven, and yet I can't do anything with him," he would confess with puzzled wonder. "Where does he get it from, the little Mordvinian? Even if I beat him, he does whatever he wants."

There was no place for a free spirit like that on the estate at Dirty Place. There wasn't room.

As Mikhail the peasant looked about him, and did not know what to do next, he decided to consult his cousin Stephen, the priest.

Boris gazed at the city of Moscow from the Sparrow Hills above. The message from Stephen the priest had said that he would call upon him that evening. There was plenty of time before he need ride down. Therefore he looked, with neither bitterness nor, as he supposed, any strong emotion, at the great citadel spread out below.

Moscow the center: Moscow the mighty heart. On that warm September day, even the chattering birds in the trees seemed hushed.

The summer had been slow, and silent, and large, as only Russian summers can be; it had browned the whispering barley in the fields all around; it had made the silver birches gleam until they seemed as white as molten ash. Around Moscow, in high summer, the leaves of the trees—the aspen, the birch, even the oaks—were so light, so delicate, that their tiny shivering in the breeze rendered them translucent, so startlingly green that they might have been so many emeralds and opals glittering in the sun that danced through them. Only in Russia, surely, were the leaves able to say in this manner: See, we dance in this fire, infinitely fragile, infinitely strong, with no regrets at the constant message of this huge blue sky, which tells us every day that we must die.

Now as autumn approached, the trees, and the heavyset city itself were left with a light covering of the finest dust as, like a silent, shining cloud that has hovered half a lifetime, summer now began to depart, drifting away into that huge, ever present, ever receding blue sky.

Over the thick walls of Moscow, over the huge Kremlin, whose long battlements frowned over the river, everything was quiet.

And who would have guessed that only months before, within those walls, death and treachery had ruled?

Thick-walled city of treachery: darkness within the huge heart of the great Russian plain.

They had betrayed the tsar. No one was talking; but everybody knew. There was a watchfulness, a fear, in every street, at every gathering. Boris saw it in the way Dimitri Ivanov stroked his beard or passed his hand over his bald head, or occasionally winked his rather bloodshot eyes.

He understood. They had wanted the tsar dead: and now he was alive.

It had been close. In March, struck down with what was probably pneumonia, Ivan had been dying, almost unable to speak. On his deathbed, he had begged the princes and boyars to accept his baby son. But most had been unwilling.

"Then we shall have another regency, and run by the mother's family, those damned Zakharins," they argued.

What was the alternative? Strictly speaking there was, on the outer fringes of the court, the harmless but pathetic figure of the tsar's younger brother—a weak-headed creature, seldom seen. Even when they remembered his existence, he was generally dismissed again as unfit. But what about the tsar's cousin Vladimir? Of all the many princes, none was more closely related to the reigning monarch, and he was a man of some experience. Here was a better candidate than this baby boy.

Over the dying man, they argued. Even Ivan's most trusted friends, the close counselors he had made himself, were skulking in corners, whispering. They were all betraying him as he watched and listened, scarcely able to speak. And what would happen to Muscovy, after he was gone? Anarchy, as they fought each other for power, these cursed, treacherous magnates.

But then he had recovered. The veil, having been lifted, descended once again. His courtiers bowed before him and greeted him with a smile. The subject of his cousin Vladimir's succession was not spoken of, as though it had never been. And Tsar Ivan said nothing.

Yet all around the court there was an air of gloom. In May, Ivan had taken his family to the far north, to give thanks for his life at the very monastery where his own mother had gone when she was pregnant with him. It was a long way: far, far into the forests towards the arctic emptiness. And there in a distant river, his nurse had accidentally dropped Ivan and Anastasia's baby son, who had died in a few moments.

Over the warm, dusty citadel that summer the sun had hung, like a silent companion to the dry, parching sadness within its massive walls. In the northwest, at Pskov, there was plague. In the east, at Kazan, the troubles with the conquered tribesmen were getting worse.

And for Boris, too, these long months had been touched by a kind of sadness.

Boris and Elena had hurried back to Moscow in March and taken up their modest quarters in the little house in the White Town.

Elena would make daily visits to her mother or her sister; whispered news of the dark developments in the court would reach them each day, either through Elena's father or from her mother, who had friends among the elderly ladies who had been granted quarters near the royal women in the palace.

Boris found himself often alone and with not much to do. To fill the time he took to walking about the capital and visiting its many churches, often hovering for some time before an icon, and saying a perfunctory prayer before moving on.

Yet although their life was quiet, he could not avoid expense. There were the horses to be stabled, the giving of gifts, and above all the yards of silk brocade and fur trimming for kaftans and dresses required to visit those who, he was assured, might be useful to him.

He could not help it: he resented these expenses which he could not really afford. Sometimes, when his wife arrived back happily from a visit to her mother, full of the latest news, he felt a kind of sullen anger, not because she had behaved badly towards him in any way, but because she seemed always to believe that all was well. Then, when they lay together at night, he would lie almost touching her, wanting her, yet holding back, hoping by this little show of indifference to worry her enough to break through the wall of family security that seemed to surround her. How can she really love me, if she does not share my anxiety? he wondered.

But to young Elena, these little shows of indifference only made her fear that her moody husband did not care for her. She would have liked to cry but instead her pride made her shrink from him, or lie there surrounding herself with an invisible barrier so that he, in turn, thought, See, she does not want me.

It was a particular misfortune that he should have encountered a young friend in the street one day who had retired to a booth to drink for a time, and after asking about his health and that of his wife this world-weary and unmarried young worthy had remarked: "All marriages turn to indifference, and most to hatred, they tell me."

Was it so? For weeks this foolish little sentence preyed on his mind. Sometimes he and Elena made love for several nights, and all seemed well; but then some imagined slight would interrupt the uncertain course of their relationship and as he lay beside her in secret fury, the words would come back into his mind and he would decide: yes, it is so; and he would even will it to be so, as a self-fulfilling prophesy.

So it was that the young Russian stood on the first, small chasm of self-destruction, and gazed into it.

Sometimes in front of the icons in the churches he visited, he would pray for better things; he would pray that he might love his wife always, and she him, forgiving each other's faults. But in his heart he did not really mean it.

It was on one of these occasions, as he was standing before a favorite icon in a small local church, that he happened to fall into conversation with the young priest named Philip. He was about the same age as Boris, but very lean, with red hair and a hard, intense face that seemed always to be bobbing forward as though, like a chicken looking for food, he could seize the subject under discussion with a few quick dabs beyond his beard. When Boris had expressed an interest in icons and told him that his own family had given a work by the great Rublev to the monastery at Russka, the priest had become wildly enthusiastic.

"My dear lord, I make a particular study of icons. So, there is a Rublev at Russka. I did not know it. I must go there. To be sure. Perhaps you would allow me to journey with you one day. You would? You are very kind. Yes indeed."

And before he knew it he had acquired, it seemed, a friend for life. Philip never failed to continue to meet him, at least once every two weeks. Boris thought him harmless enough.

Elena did not tell him she was pregnant until July. She expected the baby at the end of the year.

He was excited, of course. He must be. Her family all congratulated him. It seemed that this news must make all the women busier than ever.

And when he thought of his father, and realized that this might be the son who would continue their noble line, he felt another rush of emotion, a determination that, at all costs, he must succeed, hand the estate on in good condition, and more.

Yet as he sat beside her and saw her smiling at him as though surely now he must be pleased, he would think, She is smiling at me. Yet it is also her treasure that she guards in there. This child just completes her family: it will be theirs more than mine. And anyway, what if it's a girl? That will be no good to me, yet I shall have to pay for it."

In this way, often, the joy they told him he must feel turned to secret resentment.

He did not make love to Elena once he knew she was pregnant. He could not. The womb suddenly seemed to him mysterious, sacred—both vulnerable and for that reason rather frightening. Like a pea in the pod—at some times, that was how he saw it; and who but a monster would break open that pod, disturb the little life inside, or destroy it? At other times it made him think of something darker, subterranean, like a seed in the earth that must be left in the warm, sacred darkness before, at its season, emerging into the light.

In any case, Elena was often away these days. Her father had an estate just outside the city. She often went there, in the weeks of late summer, to rest with her family.

As Boris gazed over the city now, on this warm September afternoon, he told himself that he must accept what fate had in store. Elena was due back the following morning with her mother.

The afternoon was wearing on. There was a heaviness in the golden afternoon haze; yet at the same time, in the blue sky, a slight hint of the autumn chill ahead.

What the devil did Stephen the priest want with him, though? It was time to go and find out.

The tall young priest was polite, even respectful.

He had come to Moscow to visit a distant relation, a learned monk, and before leaving the city he had requested a brief audience, as he almost too elaborately put it, with the young lord.

The matter was very confidential. It concerned the peasant Mikhail.

Boris was slightly surprised, but told him to go on.

"Might I ask, Boris Davidov, that you not mention this conversation to anyone at the monastery?" the priest asked.

"I suppose so." What was the fellow up to?

Then, very simply, Stephen outlined poor Mikhail's dilemma. He did not tell Boris that the peasant had actually been encouraged to sabotage the work on the estate, but he did explain: "The monastery may well be tempted to take him from you. They would gain a good worker, and you would lose your best peasant—which in turn would make it harder for you to keep up the estate."

"He can't leave," Boris snapped. "I know very well he can't afford the fees."

Under the law, a tenant wishing to depart upon Saint George's Day not only had to clear any debts he had to his landlord, but he also had to pay an exit fee for the house he had occupied. The rates for this were stiff—more than half a ruble—that was more than the value of Mikhail's entire yearly crop—and Boris was quite right in thinking he could not pay it.

"He can't afford it, but the monastery can," Stephen quietly reminded him.

That was it. An underhanded way of stealing another man's peasants was to pay their exit fees for them. Would Daniel the monk do such a thing to him, a Bobrov? Probably.

"So what are you suggesting, that I should remit some of my peasants' service?"

"A little, Boris Davidov. Just enough to help him make ends meet. He's a good peasant, and I can tell you he has no wish to leave you."

"And why are you telling me this?" Boris demanded.

Stephen paused. What could he say? Could he tell the young man that, like many churchmen, he disapproved of the monastery's growing wealth? Could he tell Boris that he felt sorry for him and his rather helpless young wife? Could he tell him that, as things were, he was worried that Mikhail's sons, if they did not eat enough, might be tempted towards a life of crime when they were older, or towards some foolish act? He could not.

"I am only a priest, an onlooker," he said with a wry smile. "Let us say it is my good deed for the day."

"I shall bear what you have said in mind," Boris answered noncommittally, "and I thank you for your concern and the trouble you have taken."

With this they parted, the priest believing that he had done both the peasant and his lord a Christian service.

After he had gone, Boris paced about the room, going over the conversation carefully until he was sure he had it straight in his mind.

What kind of fool did they think he was? Did that tall priest think he had not noticed the little smile of cunning on his lips? On the face of it, he had come to help; but he had learned better than to believe that. He thought of Tsar Ivan, betrayed by all. He thought of the four cousins, standing together on the day he had arrived with Elena at Russka. He thought of Elena, too, who sometimes shrank from him in bed. No, they were none of them to be trusted, none. "I must stand alone," he murmured, "and I must be cleverer, more ruthlessly cunning, even than they."

What was the priest up to, then? Why, he was baiting a trap, of course: an obvious trap, too, damn him.

For if he reduced Mikhail's service, who would benefit? The peasant, of course—Stephen's cousin. And what would be the effect? To leave him, Boris, short of money: so that he would have to borrow more and bring himself a step closer to losing the estate to the monastery. "They just want to ruin me," he muttered.

That cunning priest. Only one thing he had said might be true. It was possible that the monastery, if it couldn't get the estate yet, might try to steal Mikhail.

How, he wondered, could he prevent that?

All that month he considered the matter; yet strangely, of all people, it was the curious priest Philip, with his bobbing head and his passion for icons, who gave have him his answer. It lay in a palace intrigue.

The strange business began in the Kremlin—in the dark recesses of the tsar's innermost court. It had been festering there for a long time, and it concerned the Church, and the fact that one of Ivan's advisers hated another.

With the increasing need for *pomestie* estates for Ivan's loyal followers, some of his closest counselors wanted him to support the Nonpossessors and take the Church's lands. The Metropolitan was looking for a way to head them off. And that year he found it.

The fellow who was leading this campaign, a priest named Sylvester, was foolish enough to be friends with a man who could be accused of heresy. From this small beginning, the Metropolitan saw, a huge intrigue could be put together. Other, worse heretics were found: the accusers constructed a chain showing that if one man knew a second, the second a third, the third a fourth, then, to be sure, the first man and the fourth were plotting together. Better yet, a link between some of these conspirators and the family of Prince Vladimir, Ivan's cousin and possible successor, could be discovered.

The Metropolitan was delighted. The dangerous Sylvester could now be shown to be the friend of heretics and of Ivan's enemies. A show trial could be called as a warning, a shot across Sylvester's bows.

Admittedly some of the evidence against the heretics was a little weak. While two were clearly heretics, a third could only be accused of going to a meeting to argue the case for Orthodoxy against some Roman Catholic. Even that was enough, though. "For if this man had to argue about the matter," the prosecution pointed out, "if he did not *know* the answer, then how can he be of the true faith?"

A trial was called for late October. All Moscow was buzzing with speculation. The Metropolitan, the tsar, the high dignitaries of the Church and the court would all be there. Already the party of Sylvester and his friends were badly frightened. The talk of Church land reform had subsided into a nervous silence.

And this show trial might have been enough for the Metropolitan; but it was not enough for Sylvester's rival in the council. Suddenly, now, a second case was brought—this time directly against Sylvester himself. The subject of the charge was—icons. They were in the great Cathedral of the Annunciation, in the very heart of the Kremlin; they had been recently executed under Sylvester's authority and, the charge said, they were heretical.

Even though Boris did not understand the details of the charge, like everyone else in Moscow he knew how serious it might be. To speak heresy was dangerous; but a work of art that was heretical . . . that was something permanent, a matter of record: it was like erecting a totem, a statue of a pagan god from olden times, in front of the holy of holies itself.

It was some days before the show trial was due to start that Philip the priest offered to take Boris into the Kremlin to look at the icons in question. He accepted eagerly.

The day was heavy, gray, and somber. The clouds were as thick and as solid as the ramparts of the city as the two men made their way across the emptiness of the Red Square. They passed through the tall, grim gateway, under the watchful eyes of the *streltsy* guards, and made their way between barracks, armories, and other thick-walled buildings until they came finally to the central square of the Kremlin. It was a medium-size stone square on each side of which quietly loomed the high, thick-set, gray-white presences of the cathedrals and palaces. The cathedrals of the Assumption, the Archangel Michael, the Annunciation; the Italianate Palace of Facets; the Church of the Deposition of the Robe; the Bell Tower of Ivan the Great: here they all rose, with their massive walls and high, gleaming domes in this innermost heart of the vast empire of the Eurasian plain.

"Come, I will show you the throne first," Philip said, as he turned towards the simplest and most stately of the buildings, the Cathedral of the Assumption.

It was amazing how he seemed to be able to gain admittance everywhere. He spoke a few words to the priest at the door, and a moment later they were ushered in.

It was a splendid building, made for the tsar's grandfather by an Italian architect, but modeled on the splendid old cathedral at Vladimir—a simple, pale stone Byzantine cathedral with five domes. Here, Boris knew, the Metropolitans were buried; with awe he looked around at the huge, high bare walls and round columns with their layers of enormous frescoes staring out into the airy spaces they owned.

In this cathedral was housed the most sacred of all Russian icons, the Virgin of Vladimir, Our Lady of Sorrows, which had given the men of Moscow their great victory over the Tatars at Kulikovo, back in the time of the great Saint Sergius.

But to Boris even this great icon seemed less important than the narrow, canopied golden throne that stood to one side. "So this," he murmured reverently, "is where my tsar was crowned." And he stayed there staring at it for several minutes, until at last Philip had to drag him away.

They crossed to the Cathedral of the Annunciation.

The icons in question, which had caused such fear and trembling, did not look so unusual to Boris. Indeed, until Philip started to speak, he could not see anything wrong with them at all. But the intense young priest soon disabused him: "Look at that—did you ever see such a thing?"

Boris looked. Before him was a figure of Christ, with wings and with his palms closed. "It's perhaps unusual," he ventured uncertainly.

"Unusual? It's outrageous. Idolatry. Don't you see, the artist has in-

vented that. Invented it *for himself.* There is no authority for depicting Our
Lord in such a way. Unless," he added darkly, "it comes from the Catholics in the West."

Boris looked carefully. It was true. There was something markedly
individual about the thing if one considered it. He was still considering
it when he heard a gasp of outrage from Philip.

"See here." He was in front of another icon. "Our Lord depicted as
David, dressed like a tsar. And over there." He had glanced across at
another: "The Holy Spirit depicted as a dove. Never. Never in Orthodoxy."

He turned to Boris confidentially. "There are frescoes in the palace,
they say, that are even worse. Heretics. Cunning fiends." His head
bobbed so violently it was as if he feared contamination. "I tell you," he
said, with his eyes, it seemed, focused angrily upon the tip of his beard,
"I tell you, young Lord Boris, those accursed Catholics in the West may
be rascals, but they have one good idea, and that is the Inquisition. That's
what we need in Russia. Root them out."

They left quietly; but all the way back to the Kremlin gate and beyond
he would mutter, every few paces, "Root them out. Root and branch."

And just as they came out into Red Square, Boris had his idea. "I
think," he said quietly, "that they make icons like that in Russka."

On an overcast day in early November, the two visitors appeared in
Russka. There was a cold, wet wind biting into one's face and threatening
to bring heavy rain or possibly snow; and if Boris had not been eager to
make the journey at once, Philip the priest would have preferred to wait
until a better traveling season.

They went straight to Boris's house and the young lord of Dirty Place
soon sent a friendly message to Stephen the priest asking him to call.
Meanwhile Boris had sent his servant scurrying to summon a pair of
plump chickens from his steward, a bottle of wine, and anything else he
could think of for their comfort.

Despite the fact that they were both rather chilled, Boris was elated
in a nervous way.

Within two hours they were dining, and while Philip was still eating,
which he did with the same emphatic bobbing motion that he used for
everything else, Stephen arrived.

Stephen was glad to see Boris. He wondered if this visit could signal
something good for the unfortunate Mikhail: Boris's slightly nervous
gaiety suggested to him that the young man might have been through
some kind of minor crisis in his thinking recently; since he had brought
a priest with him, Stephen hoped it had been of a religious nature.

Under the influence of the wine, apparently, both men were very
affable. Boris informed him that his friend had kindly agreed to spend
a few days with him while he attended to his business in the country and
he ventured to hope that Stephen would show him the village and the
monastery.

"For if he has to stay with me at Dirty Place all the time, I'm afraid he'll be awfully bored," Boris explained with a boyish grin. "He's a learned fellow, like you," he added amiably.

During this conversation, Philip said little, concentrating on his eating. But now he began to talk a bit. He asked Stephen a few ordinary enough questions about the small town, said a few words about his own humdrum life, and spoke with veneration, but very little understanding, about the icons in his own church.

"A pleasant, rather simpleminded fellow," Stephen thought, "of no great education."

He promised to show him around the next day.

Two days, and the trap was set. Boris sent for Daniel the monk. And when their conversation was over, the young man reflected that, including even the best moments of his brief marriage, these were the most exhilarating and most satisfying minutes that he had ever passed in his life.

"I find myself," he began, with perfect insincerity, "in a most difficult position."

He was sure, yes he was sure, that the monk did not know what was coming. Through the thick beard he saw Daniel's eyes gleaming with a burning furtiveness.

"It might not matter," Boris went on, "but for recent events in Moscow." He paused. It seemed that the monk's face was frowning in puzzlement. "I am referring of course to the heresy trials," he said sweetly.

The first trials had taken place on October 25, and they had been a triumph for the Metropolitan. The evidence, such as it was, had been enough to secure for all the accused torture and life imprisonment; and now all Moscow was terrified.

As a staunch supporter of the Metropolitan's line, Daniel was delighted. But what could these trials have to do with this young landlord and himself at Russka? He looked up at Boris inquiringly.

"It seems," Boris said, with apparent concern, "that we have heresy in our midst—right here." And he tapped the table reprovingly. Daniel stared at him.

It had been so easy. Though he had been astonished at how neatly and cleverly the priest Philip had played his part.

Bobbing his head, asking rather simpleminded questions, the devious fellow had gone around Russka all day with the obliging Stephen. Never once had he asked Stephen's opinion on any but the most trivial matters. He had been shown the icons for sale in the market, had visited the monastery, and walked around the big fields near the monastery walls. Now and then, it appeared, he had been struck with disapproval by something he had seen, and then tried to hide it. Only towards sunset, as they stood by the gate of the town and gazed down at the rich monastery below, did he seem to forget himself and burst out, bitterly: "A rich little monastery."

"You find it too rich?" Stephen curiously inquired.

At once Philip became guarded and looked at him nervously.

Stephen had smiled, then taken his arm gently. "I understand."
Philip looked relieved.

"One must be careful nowadays, my friend," he said softly.

"Of course. You are a Nonpossessor then?"

The priest from Moscow bobbed his head in acknowledgment.

"And you?" he asked Stephen.

"I, too," the simpleminded Russka priest confessed.

They had walked quietly back together to Boris's house, where they
had embraced before Stephen returned to his home.

The next day Philip had inspected the icons in the market and at the
monastery carefully. Then he had given Boris his opinions.

"The priest is a Nonpossessor. At present it's not clear whether he's
a heretic, but he reads too much and he's a fool. There's no knowing what
heresy he might easily tumble into. As for the icons, I find four designs
that are a disgrace."

"Heretical?"

"Absolutely. As bad as anything I've seen from Novgorod."

In the minds of some purists, the products of that city were always
suspect, because of its proximity to the Baltic ports and to Lithuania with
their dangerous Catholic and Protestant influences from the West.

"So I could prosecute."

"I think you should."

Boris had smiled. "I promise you, the matter will receive my full
attention," he replied.

And so now, to the astonished monk, he blandly outlined his conclu-
sions.

"It seems, Brother Daniel, that the icons that the Peter and Paul monastery is producing are heretical. They are being sold in the market under
your direction." Seeing Daniel look baffled, he continued quietly. "I'm
afraid that it is so. I have it on very good authority; and as you know,
in the current climate . . . it places the monastery—or some of those in
it—in danger."

There was no question about it, Daniel was beginning to look nervous.
For, the matter of the heretics having been disposed of, the charge concerning the icons was still under consideration in Moscow. Who knew
what would happen?

"If this is so," Daniel began, "of course we should take advice."

"Certainly," Boris agreed. "Although, of course, by raising the matter
with higher authorities, you also run a risk."

"But surely no one could think we intended . . ."

"Brother Daniel," Boris cut in, "I have come from Moscow. I must tell
you that the atmosphere there . . ."

It was true. The atmosphere was electric. Already the condemned
heretics, under the customary torture, were starting to denounce anyone
they could remember talking to. Search parties were going out to arrest
supposed heretics among the Volga elders far out in the forests of the
distant north.

"Besides," Boris explained smoothly, "I am very much afraid your own
family connections may be linked to the business."

"My family."

"Of course. Your cousin Stephen, our priest. He is, I suppose you know, a Nonpossessor."

Even under the thick beard, it was possible to see Daniel blanch. He had long ago guessed, of course, that his cousin had these feelings.

"But I am utterly opposed to such views—if he has them," he protested quickly.

"I know that as well as you. But we also both know that at times like this, when the authorities are looking . . . It is not the truth that counts but what may be perceived, what may be said. They will look at you, the icons, and your cousin—with whom you are often seen—and they will create a pattern that will speak the word *heresy.*"

The beauty of the thing, the exquisite irony. Though monk and priest were exactly opposed in their central beliefs, it was possible by a neat analysis and synthesis to bind them together like a pair of felons.

There was a long pause.

"I do not need to tell you of my regard for you both, nor of my family's regard for the monastery to which we gave its most cherished icon."

Daniel bowed his head. The icon by Rublev was certainly the best thing they had. He could not deny that the founders' family had been steadfast. He also saw clearly that Boris was offering an opening. "How might we proceed?" the monk inquired.

Boris took a long breath and looked thoughtful. "The question is," he mused, gazing at the ends of his fingers, "whether I can persuade my friend, a priest from Moscow, that this matter does not require reporting."

"I see."

"It is he who has pointed all this out to me, and he is zealous."

"Perhaps if I spoke with him . . . ?"

"Unwise. He would take it as guilt." He paused a moment. "I have also my own position to consider."

He allowed the silence to spread around the room and to settle in every crevice.

"I should certainly be sad," Boris remarked after a time, "to see misfortune fall upon a family—a large family, with many members—whom we wish well."

Many members. He watched as Daniel worked this out. Himself the monk, Stephen the priest; there was Lev the merchant; and then, ah yes, of course, Mikhail the peasant was also his cousin. Boris waited until he saw that Daniel had thoroughly understood.

"I am sure we all wish yourself and the estate at Dirty Place well," the monk murmured carefully.

They understood each other.

"Well, I shall see what I can do," Boris remarked briskly. "Let us say no more of this for the present."

But as the monk was leaving, he said casually: "By the way, Brother Daniel, if you chance to see Lev the merchant, would you send him to me."

And later that afternoon, with perfect equanimity shown by both sides, Boris borrowed another eight rubles from the merchant at the derisory interest rate of only seven percent.

Before returning to Moscow the next day with Philip the priest, he assured him that the offending icons would be altered at once and that Stephen the Nonpossessor had been sternly warned. He also made him an interest-free loan of a ruble which, as he had suspected, the stern enemy of heresy accepted with alacrity.

How sweet was the taste of victory. He departed in great good humor.

He did nothing for Mikhail the peasant. There was no need, now that he had nowhere to go.

In the winter of that year, when the snow lay on the ground, a huge expedition set out from Moscow led by Ivan's best men, including the brilliant Prince Kurbsky. They were going to Kazan.

Among the ambitious young men who went with it was Boris.

He had been gone a month when Elena went into labor. It was a long labor, but as she suffered, she prayed: "Surely now, if I endure all this pain, God will make him love me."

When the child was born, it was a girl.

In the year of Our Lord 1553, from the kingdom of England, with a message of universal brotherhood from their boy king to any they might encounter, there set out three ships under the command of a brilliant member of one of England's most illustrious aristocratic families: Sir Hugh Willoughby. His pilot general was the skillful Richard Chancellor. They were looking for a trade route around the northeast of Eurasia that might lead them to Cathay.

Sadly, in those treacherous northern waters, two of the three ships were separated; for months Willoughby and his men wandered the northern seas until, at last, trapped on an island off the Lapland coast, they froze to death in the terrible darkness when the sun completely departs for the months of arctic winter.

But while Willoughby wandered, lost, a very different fate befell the remaining ship, the *Edward Bonaventure,* in which Chancellor sailed. For in the summer months he proceeded north—so far north that he entered a strange region where, at that season, the sun never went down at all. And it was here, in the month of August, that he put ashore in a curious land where the local fishermen prostrated themselves at his feet.

So it was that the first Englishman in centuries came to the land now called Muscovy.

George Wilson liked Moscow. No one had ever taken much notice of him before, but in this place he seemed, along with his shipmates, to be something of a celebrity.

He was a ratty little man: small, thin, sinewy, with a narrow face, hard, cunning eyes set too close together, and a shock of yellow hair that these strange Russian folk would sometimes pat with curiosity. Indeed, in Muscovy, where most men, and women, were stout, he looked rather like a jackal in a company of bears. He was thirty years old.

He had only come on this voyage because, after a small business failure as a draper, he had been rather at a loose end.

His cousin, a sea captain, had warned him about these northern waters. There were ice floes big as mountains, he had said. No place for a skinny little fellow like him. Well, here he was, halfway to Cathay, in a land of men like bears. And, as far as he could see, things were looking up. For his narrow eyes glinted as he saw how much money there was to be made.

How immense the land was: hundreds of leagues from town to town. How cheap was human life. When they had arrived in summer, he had watched the great barges being dragged upriver from the northern estuary by parties of men with ropes tied around them. He had heard their mournful singing; he had seen the overseers cut with whips those who fell. He wondered how many of these unfortunate survived the long journey.

Yet how fabulously rich it was, too. Since no one knew who these visitors were or where they came from, the English party had been kept almost in confinement in the north while their hosts awaited instructions from the capital.

"These people's hospitality is so great I can hardly tell if we are guests or prisoners," Chancellor had ruefully remarked to him.

So it had been winter before they were taken to the capital, and so Wilson had seen the cargoes from these barges off-loaded onto a thousand sleds to be carried from the collecting points to the inner cities.

He had never seen such a concourse of vehicles. Every league, every day, hundreds of sleds passed them on their way to or from the cities that rose out of the snowy wastes. Goods, all manner of goods, passed by: grain, fish, but above all he saw furs, furs, and more furs. Could there be so many sables, ermines, beavers, and bears in all the world? This forest hinterland, he thought, must be greater than all the lands he had ever heard of.

But above all, one huge realization opened in his mind—an understanding that grew greater, more insistent, more awesome with every league they went: they were going farther and farther from the sea. This is the hugest country in the world, he thought, yet it has no shores.

How utterly different from his English home in London: nowhere in England were you far from its indented coastline; how utterly unlike the French, the Germans, the other folk who plied the busy North Sea and Baltic ports. These folk in their vast, landlocked world of forest and snow were different, cut off, a race apart. "Truly this is a rude and barbarous people," Chancellor had remarked to his companions.

Yet their welcome in Moscow had been astounding. It had made an unforgettable impression on George Wilson. For no sooner had they arrived than they were summoned to attend the tsar.

Even George Wilson, cunning and cynical little fellow that he was, found his knees shaking as they were ushered into the royal presence. He had already heard that, in this huge land, all men were the tsar's slaves: now he understood what that meant.

Ivan stood at the end of a great hall in the Kremlin palace. On each side of him stood the huge forms of his boyars, in their heavy, rich kaftans.

How tall he was—made taller by the high pointed hat he wore, trimmed with fur. A pale, hawklike face; a terrible, piercing eye. He commanded all, dominated this heavy, Asiatic magnificence. The party were awestruck. Ivan meant them to be: for he was anxious to impress these merchants from this strange and distant country. They might be useful to him.

He was friendly. Their letter of recommendation, written in Latin, Greek, German, and other languages, was explained to him. Then they were invited to a feast.

It passed anything they could have imagined. A hundred sat down: they ate off solid gold. Stuffed fish, great roasts, strange delicacies like elk's brains, caviar, blinis. Wine served in goblets encrusted with gems. Everything was lavish, splendid, heavy. Tsar Ivan sat apart from the mere mortals he was honoring. From time to time he sent a morsel of food to one of the guests as a mark of his favor. Each time, all stood while the name of the recipient was called out, and the tsar's own long title was proclaimed. Wilson noticed that the pious tsar crossed himself, from right to left, each time he raised food to his own mouth. He also noticed that it was the fashion, among these huge, bearded people, to drink off a goblet of wine at a single draft.

The banquet went on for five hours.

"I think we are at the court of Solomon himself," he whispered to one of his companions.

"Or the court of Babylon," the other replied.

But it was only afterwards, when they were escorted around the royal palace, that Wilson truly appreciated that this strange, mighty empire was like no other.

For how splendid, yet how barbarous it was. Room succeeded cavernous room. It was like being in some endless succession of antechambers to a Russian church. Candles lit up the gloom. By their soft, gleaming light he saw walls painted with riotous patterns of plants, winding around each other like snakes, and of dancing animals—of reds, ochers, greens. No mirrors reflected the light, but everywhere hung icons that glimmered sadly with gold. There was little of the furniture to have been found in an English palace: only plain chairs and benches, great studded trunks and huge stoves; but rich oriental carpets and hangings of silk and brocade more than compensated. It was a noble palace.

And yet. And yet, there was something else that made him fearful. It was a feeling of heaviness, of dark power. In this churchlike gloom, the painted passages seemed to Wilson like tunnels, the chambers like halls in a labyrinth. As they went in, farther and farther, it made him think of something deep, subterranean, like a womb where a man might hide; and who knew what other passages, what chambers, there might be, behind thick walls that would muffle any cry?

Life for the English merchants was sunny, though. They were in the tsar's favor. Nor did it take them long to get to know the huge market into which they had accidentally come.

For Moscow, with its great fairs upon the ice, was a huge emporium. From the east, up the Volga and the Don, came cotton, sheep, spices. Each year, the Nogay tribesmen from the Asian steppe arrived with huge herds of horses. From Novgorod came iron, silver, salt; from other cities leather, oil, grain, honey, and wax.

"The opportunities are endless," Chancellor said excitedly. Although Russia was rich in these raw materials, except for making arms she had few manufactured goods. Wilson could think of any number of luxury goods he could sell here. They could use a good English broadcloth, too, he considered. As for the return voyage home: This wax is no cheaper than I can buy in England, he calculated, but their furs . . . He could get a fortune for those furs.

Despite their powerful, burly appearance, his shrewd intelligence soon detected that the big Russian merchants were essentially passive. "They only know their own country," he remarked to Chancellor. "In a way, they are like eager children."

"I agree," the leader replied, "but remember, our customer is firstly the tsar himself."

For, they had quickly discovered, the tsar had the monopoly of many of the chief goods in the market, including liquor. Every drop of vodka sold to the eager people at the little drinking booths belonged to him. All sables, all raw silk, all grain for export, was in the hands of his agents. And foreign merchants like themselves had to offer all their goods to him first.

Such was the all-pervading power of the centralized Muscovite state.

"The tsar wants chemicals, too, for explosives," Chancellor told him, "and he wants us to bring him men of learning. I have already promised to come again with doctors and men skilled in mining."

At first some of these requests puzzled Wilson. He had already made the acquaintance of several German merchants who were allowed to reside in the city. He had seen there was a German doctor, too. Why, he wondered, should the tsar want men from distant England who could be found closer to his borders?

One of the Germans, a large, burly man who spoke some English, explained it to him. "About six years ago, my friend, a German fellow, offered to bring the tsar all kinds of experts. He collected more than a hundred and brought them to the Baltic ports. If he'd got them into Muscovy, I daresay the tsar would have made him a rich man indeed."

"And why didn't they get here?"

The German grinned. "They were stopped, that's why. Arrested by the authorities." He looked at Wilson seriously. "And the highest powers were behind it—the very highest."

"Because?"

"Do you suppose, my friend, that the Livonian Order, which controls many of the Baltic ports, is eager to strengthen Ivan's hand? He's longing to walk in there and take over those Latvian and Estonian lands. Do you think Lithuania and Poland, or the Emperor of Germany want to see Russia any stronger than she is?"

He gazed around the marketplace.

"Look at these people," he went on. "You can see for yourself: they're backward. They have few industries, no learning at all. They eat and drink, they whore and pray to their icons. And that's it. Their army is huge but badly trained. When they try to get to the Baltic ports, the well-trained Swedes and Germans can cut them down in no time. And that's how we like them. Who needs a civilized Russia? That's why Tsar Ivan is so pleased to see you. You came round by the extreme north—it's a long and inconvenient way, frozen half the year, but it still suits him very well. He can circumvent the Baltic that way and get the skilled men he knows he needs. You're gold to him."

While the English might be useful to the tsar, he in turn could be very useful to them.

"We sought a passage to Cathay by sea," Chancellor told him, "yet it seems to me we can reach the East by land. Down the Volga, beyond the lands of the Tatars, lies the Orient. Below the deserts lies Persia. With his protection, our merchants might reach such places after all."

George Wilson soon decided that this strange huge land was the best opportunity he could ever have to make his fortune. But he found it a disquieting place all the same.

It was not the violence, the crudity, or even the cruelty of the people. He cared nothing about any of these. It was their religion.

It was all pervading. There seemed to be priests and monks everywhere. People crossed themselves for, it seemed to Wilson, no reason at all; and in every house there were icons to which people bowed.

" 'Tis like popery," he remarked, "only the idolatry of the Russians is even greater."

Like most of his compatriots, George Wilson was a Protestant. He had been a boy when Henry VIII of England broke with the Pope in Rome. Now Henry's son was on the throne, and all good Englishmen were supposed to be Protestant. This was a faith which suited Wilson very well, not from any profound religious conviction, for he had none, but rather because he had a rooted if secret dislike of all authority and also because a certain harsh pride made him enjoy reading the tracts that attacked the abuses, or even the theology of the old religion with fierce logic.

These Russians are fools, he concluded. But since he thought that of most people anyway, it did not greatly signify.

And when, in January, Chancellor told him that, after their return to England that spring, he intended to lead another expedition to Muscovy, and asked him if he wished to join it, he instantly replied: "I do."

He would make his fortune here. Besides, he had another reason in mind, too. The German merchant, also a Protestant, had an unmarried daughter and no son. The girl was a little heavy, but handsome. A nice, plump girl, he thought.

He would return.

To Elena, it seemed that Boris had slowly grown another skin on top of his own. Sometimes she had the impression that he was still moving about, rather uncomfortably, inside this carapace; that if she could find a way to break through she would still find him within. At other times it would be as if this new, ever thicker layer were stuck fast, glued onto his own skin and all of one piece with it. Then, even when he came to her intimately, it felt as if she had in her hands a strange animal with a thick hide, whose mind she did not know.

Not that, in the succeeding years, she saw him very often.

For three years the armies of Russia, led by Kurbsky and others, smashed the Tatar revolts around Kazan. They went farther, across the eastern Volga into the land of the Nogays; even the distant Tatar khan of West Siberia, beyond the Urals, acknowledged Ivan as his overlord. Twice, huge fleets went south down the mighty Volga, through the steppe, to the desert lands of Astrakhan, and they took that city, too.

Tsar of Kazan, Tsar of Astrakhan: how exotic Ivan's new titles proclaimed him to be. Huge new chronicles were prepared, glorifying Ivan and his family, and where necessary rewriting history so that the sacred mission of the Russian royal house should be clearly understood. All references that ever hinted at former cooperation of the Russian princes with their Tatar overlords were removed.

It was now that, at one end of Moscow's Red Square, the Metropolitan ordered the building of that fantastic collection of exotic towers, apparently grafted together to make a new Russian life form unlike any other, that later became famous to history as Saint Basil's Cathedral.

Ivan would have liked, next, to defeat the mighty khan of the Crimea as well; but for the present that was too tough a nut to crack.

So it was that Tsar Ivan, trying to open the doors of his landlocked prison, turned northward to threaten his neighbors—those rich Livonian ports he needed so much—on the shores of the Baltic.

At first it seemed he might succeed.

No wonder, then, that Elena saw little of her husband. The life of the servitor was hard. Often there was little to eat. Blistering heat or tremendous cold: these were his lot. Before leaving for the north, Boris had returned from Astrakhan with some modest plunder—a few rubles' worth, that paid off some of his debts—and a hardened man.

His relationship with her father, never warm, now became distant. This was not a personal matter—indeed, Dimitri was pleased with his son-in-law's career—it was a question of politics.

The trouble had begun when Boris had returned from Astrakhan. Behind the new skin that had already started to form, Elena sensed a kind of elation in him. For while his armies had been subduing the steppe and desert by the Volga, Ivan and his inner counselors had been pressing through another kind of victory at home: the reform of the realm.

Once again, in common with all the centralizing rulers of the era, it was the magnates and their clients that he was determined to crush. The old rewards for service, though they were not what they had once been, were curtailed. Instead of a boyar or serving prince being given a city to feed off, local men, chosen by the gentry and merchants, were to administer each locality. But most important of all, it was now decreed that all holders of estates—whether the service *pomestie* or the privately inherited *votchina*—must give the tsar military service when summoned.

"That will teach those lazy devils who is master," Boris grimly remarked in front of his father-in-law. "Do you know that half the estate holders in Tver were giving no service to anyone?"

"Then tell me," Dimitri Ivanov asked acidly, "exactly what is the difference now between your estate, which you inherited, and a mere *pomestie?* Since the tsar usually allows the son to carry on after the father on the service estates."

Boris considered. "There's a legal difference, technically; but in practice you're right. There's no difference. If you don't serve, the tsar will take your estate away."

"And you are happy with that?"

"Yes. Why should I not want to serve the tsar? Don't you want to?" It was a wicked question, for he knew very well that his wife's family held several estates and that, at present, none of them were actually serving.

Dimitri said nothing, but he passed his hand over his bald head with obvious irritation.

"If a man doesn't want to serve the tsar," Boris went on coolly, "I personally would have to conclude that he must be the tsar's enemy."

"You should conclude no such thing, young man," Dimitri thundered.

"I am glad to hear it," Boris answered drily.

Elena's mother had managed to separate the two men after that. But the damage had been done.

Nor was it just a dispute between two men. Elena knew very well that the bad feeling between her husband and her father represented a deep divide between those who were behind the reforming tsar, and the old ruling classes, great and small, who disliked the whole tone of his rule. Indeed, there were whispers in her father's house—things said that she would never have told Boris about, but which made her wonder if the young tsar would last.

And so their life had proceeded, with brief visits from Boris, and increasing suspicion in the air around them.

If only he were not so distant when he came. If only she could break through his armor of reserve.

There was only one way to do so—only one way to make her husband happy. If only she could give him a son! Why was it denied her? There had been a boy, David, who had died when he was a week old, while Boris was away on the first campaign in the north. And after that, try as she might, nothing. Perhaps if they could win a great victory in the north. If Russia signed a peace and Boris returned home for a longer period: perhaps then there would be a son. She was still young. She prayed for sunnier days. But after some early successes, things started to go badly in the north. The Baltic cities looked for protection to Sweden, Lithuania, Denmark. It seemed the conflict might go on forever.

Then, in August 1560, Anastasia, the tsar's beloved wife, the light of his life, died.

And when she heard this, Elena's heart sank. For she had a woman's premonition that a time of greater darkness was ahead.

1566

OCTOBER. A cold, dank, windswept day at the little town of Russka: the vaporous clouds so low that sometimes their skirts almost seemed to touch the tent roof of the watchtower.

A single figure is approaching, riding slowly up to the gates. His horse is black; on the front of its saddle are two little emblems: a dog's head, because the rider is watchful, and a broom, because he will sweep away his master's enemies.

The rider, too, is dressed in black. He looks carelessly from side to side, because he is master of all in this region. A monk by the monastery gates, seeing him, ducks out of sight nervously. Even the abbot is awkward in his presence. In the town and in nearby Dirty Place, they are terrified of him.

It is over a year since he took his vows. They were biblical in tone, for he swore to love his master more than mother or father, son or daughter. He also swore to inform, instantly, upon anyone he suspects of disloyalty to his master, the tsar.

The figure in black is powerful and feared. It is true, as his wife knows, that he is not happy. But it has never occurred to him to be so.

It is his wife, now, that this grim figure has come to visit: for this is his home. His name is Boris Bobrov.

For at last Ivan had struck at all his enemies. The blow was devastating and took them completely by surprise.

In December 1564, without a word of explanation, he had left the city of Moscow with a huge baggage train and by Saint Nicholas Day had turned up at a fortified hunting lodge known as Alexandrov-skaya Sloboda some forty miles northeast of the capital. No one knew what this evacuation meant. Then in January, word came: he had abdicated.

Was it just a ruse?

"In my opinion," Elena's father told her, "the tsar hasn't been quite right in the head since Anastasia died. He's decided the boyar's poisoned her and he wants to get even with them. All the same," he added grimly, "there's a kind of cunning in this business."

There was indeed. The boyars, fearing the people, had to ask him back. And when he came, it was on his own terms.

They were astounding. No ruler, perhaps in all the world, had ever done such a thing. For after receiving a solemn oath from the boyars and the Church that he was free to rule exactly as he pleased and punish whom he would, Tsar Ivan split his realm in two. The greater part he left to be ruled in his name by boyars he trusted. But the smaller part he turned into a vast private estate, under his personal rule and peopled by his own handpicked servants.

This personal fief he called, with dark irony, the Oprichnina—which meant the widow's portion, the land a widow received for her upkeep after the husband died. His servitors were called Oprichniki. They formed a close order, like the old Livonian and Teutonic orders of German knights; and they dressed in black.

It was a state within a state. It was a police state. The Oprichniki could only be tried by their own courts—in effect they were above the law. Part of Moscow was included; so was Suzdal and pockets of land above the Oka and southwest of Moscow. Most of the Oprichnina however, lay up in the north, in the huge forestlands that spread above the loop of the Volga up to the distant northern port where the English mariners had landed. It was away from the old princely towns, a land of icebound monasteries, furs, huge salt beds, and rich northern traders. The mighty Stroganovs, a family of former peasants turned merchant princes, who never missed a trick, immediately petitioned the tsar to be included in his personal realm.

And only those loyal to Ivan might live there. At every estate the tsar's inquisitors held a court. If the landlord were loyal, he might remain; but if he had any connection with a magnate or one of the many princely families, he would almost certainly be thrown out, and given a poorer estate, if he were lucky, outside the Oprichnina instead. In this manner, the Oprichniki could be given the vacant estates for their upkeep, which they held, naturally, as service *pomestie.*

The town of Russka was included in the Oprichnina. When the inquisitors had come to interview the young landlord of Dirty Place, he had been glad. "I serve the tsar," he told them, "in all his wars. Let me, I beg you, be one of the Oprichniki. What could I desire more?" And as he saw them make a note of this he added: "The tsar himself may remember me. Let him know that he spoke with me, at dawn one morning, when we were returning from Kazan."

At this the inquisitor had smiled grimly. "If that is so, Boris Davidov, the tsar will remember you. The tsar forgets nothing."

They continued to examine him carefully. They found no fault with his family. Though old, it boasted no great connections that might make it suspect. But there was one problem. "What of your wife's family?" they had asked him. "Your father-in-law has friends in quarters whose loyalty we are not sure about. What can you tell us about him?"

And it was then that Boris had seen his chance.

"What," he had asked quietly, "would you like to know?"

A week later Boris was summoned to Moscow, and after a brief interview was told he could keep the estate on service tenure and what he was accepted into the Oprichniki.

"The tsar remembered you," they said.

Soon afterwards, though she did not know why, Elena heard that her father was deeply worried.

The wind had dropped and the afternoon was already drawing to its close when Boris was served his meal.

As soon as he sat down, the old serving man placed before him a plate of rye bread and a little jug of vodka. Staring straight in front of him, Boris steadily poured himself three small cups, throwing back his head as he downed each with a single draft. Elena said nothing. To her it seemed a rather vulgar habit which, no doubt, he had picked up from the other Oprichniki.

He ate, for the most part, in silence. Elena sat at the other side of the heavy table and picked lightly at a few vegetables. It appeared that neither quite had the courage to start the conversation: which was not surprising; for the matter they would have to discuss was, if the rumors from Moscow were true, too terrible to speak about.

The silence continued. Occasionally Boris, a little guardedly, allowed his eyes to rest on her, as though he were mulling over some abstract calculation of which she might, or might not, be a part. Once he turned to her and quietly asked after the health of Lev the merchant. On hearing that he was well, he nodded his head but said nothing. Lev was in charge of the collection of local taxes now and was therefore a fellow servant of the Oprichnina with Boris. They acted together in all official matters.

"And our daughter?" she asked him at length.

The girl had been given in marriage to a young noble at the start of the year; he did not live within the Oprichnina, but he was modestly well-off and Boris had satisfied himself about the family's loyalty. Elena suspected that he had been glad to get the girl—who was only twelve—out of his house and into that of her in-laws. Though he was always kind to his daughter, she knew that Boris had never really accepted her existence in place of the son he should have had.

"She is well," he answered briefly. "I spoke to her father-in-law." And as he obviously had other things on his mind, she did not pursue the subject.

Elena seldom went to Moscow now. Since the Oprichnina began, the atmosphere in the capital had been tense and often frightening. Right from the start there had been disappearances and word of executions. From the old princely cities came news of wholesale confiscations, great princes and magnates losing all their lands and being sent to miserable little farms on the distant frontiers of Kazan. "The whole business is disgusting," Elena's father told her on one of her few visits to the city. "Half the people being executed have done nothing at all."

She had heard that the other day one brave fellow called Gorbachev, following his father on the block, had picked up his father's head and told the people watching: "I thank God we both die innocent." Two Metropolitans had already been forced out because they could not stomach this terror state.

"You know what's most frightening," her father had continued: "people think he's kicking these people out to make room for his henchmen—these cursed Oprichniki—forgive me, I know your Boris is one. But look carefully and you'll see that's not what he's doing. Most of these confiscations haven't been in Oprichnina lands at all. They've been outside. His black shirts are all provided for. Do you understand? He's breaking up all the opposition before he turns on the rest of us. It's a plot to destroy us all."

She had found the Oprichniki terrifying. Some were nobles and gentry, but many were little more than peasants. "Some were even foreigners—just common mercenaries," her mother exclaimed in disgust. "They have no ties, nothing." Indeed, in their black uniforms and cloaks they looked to Elena like some strangely vicious order of monks.

There was something else her father told her.

"Do you know what the latest orders from the tsar have been? That if any foreigner asks about what's happening, we are to deny that the Oprichnina exists. Can you imagine it? I was in a magnate's house the other day, and an envoy from Lithuania was there. 'What about this Oprichnina?' he asks our host. 'Never heard of it,' says he. 'But the tsar's holed up in a fort outside the city,' the fellow protests. 'And what about these fellows in black shirts?' 'Oh,' says the magnate, 'that's just a summer residence and those are some of his servants, a sort of new regiment.' There were thirty of us in that room and none of us knew which way to look. But we all kept mum, of course."

And now had come this latest appalling news.

As he looked at Elena, Boris tried to analyze what he saw. She was still the same girl he had married: quiet, a little nervous, eager to please yet, at the same time, capable of taking refuge from him in the web of family and women's relationships, from which he felt himself excluded. But there was something else now: suffering had given her a certain quiet dignity, a self-sufficiency that sometimes made him admire her and sometimes made him angry. Was her dignity a reproach to him; was it, even, a sign of scorn?

Only when Boris had finished eating, only when to delay the question any longer would have been absurd, did she quietly ask: "So what really happened in Moscow?"

What indeed? It had been Ivan's own idea to call the great council of the people—the Zemsky Sobor. Not of course that it was representative in any true sense. They had just collected together nearly four hundred of the gentry, clergy, and some leading merchants into an assembly. But even so, it was an impressive body. "The war in the north's been going badly," Boris had explained. "We need those Baltic ports, and the Poles want to stop us. The tsar needs money to show the enemy that the whole country is behind him."

The great assembly had met that July. They had agreed to all the tsar proposed. Except for one problem. "Those impertinent assemblymen and the cursed Metropolitan petitioned the tsar to give up the Oprichnina. Can you believe it?" Boris had cried.

Now Elena watched her husband thoughtfully. It seemed to her that he hesitated. Did he feel guilty? Was he uncomfortable inside his protective skin?

"They were traitors. The tsar treated them like traitors," he said gruffly. "There are still many traitors, many Kurbskys to be rooted out."

Ah yes, she thought: Kurbsky. Of all the things that had turned the mind of Ivan on its present, dark path, perhaps nothing—at least since the death of Anastasia—was more important than the desertion of his childhood friend Prince Kurbsky, who had suddenly defected to Lithuania.

Historians since have long studied a lengthy correspondence between

Tsar Ivan and this exiled prince. It has been the centerpiece of several biographies. Recent scholarship reveals that this correspondence, like that other great classic of early Russian Literature, *The Lay of Igor's Host,* may be a later forgery; but forgery or not, it is significant that the terror of Ivan began only months after the departure of this minor prince.

"Is it true that the tsar locked up the whole assembly?" she asked quietly.

"Only for six days."

"How many were executed?"

"Only three."

"In public?"

"Certainly."

"Then in front of all the people he had the tongues of all the others cut out?"

"No. Fifty of them were beaten, that's all. And quite right, too."

"They had their tongues cut out?"

"No. Only some of them." He paused, his face still giving nothing away. "There was a plot, you know. They had plotted treason."

"Was it proved?"

"There was a plot. That's all." He got up from the table. "There'll be no more assemblies, I can tell you that," he added, with a short, awkward laugh.

Elena did not ask any more. She did not ask if he had taken part. She did not want to know. What could she say? What could she do? Slowly, a little tentatively, she went over to him and put her arm around him in the hope that, perhaps, her love might cure his evil. But he knew that her love included forgiveness, and, being unable to submit to that, he turned silently away. Only by the just perceptible hunching of his shoulders did she know that he was protecting himself from her.

If only she could help him, and help herself in this darkening night. Indeed, she secretly decided in her inner heart, she would even sacrifice herself to save what she saw—how could she not?—as his lost soul.

But saving a soul, perhaps, took more skill than she had.

That night when they were lying together, she tried to give herself. Yet he, like an animal that has tasted blood, wanted no other diet. How could she abandon herself to the simple, wild passion, the exercise, as she saw it, of a cat in the night, when it was just this animal in him that she feared. And how could he, seeking escape, seeking a companion who could match her strength to his, who could ride with him on his wild chase around the night, how could he find solace in her love, which came with a prayer?

He slept fitfully. She, having given herself but knowing instinctively that it was not enough, pretended to sleep.

He moved about. At dawn she saw him gazing through the parchment that covered the window at the gray light at dawn.

He turned and, seeing her awake, knowing her to have been long awake, remarked: "I go back to Moscow, tomorrow."

Should she beg him to stay? She did not know. Besides, a feeling of failure, of lassitude, began to overtake her.

"Stephen the priest's wife is sick," she remarked dully. I forgot to tell you."

Whenever Mikhail the peasant surveyed his family, he knew that his plan was right. His eldest son was married now and living at the other end of the village. He was not worried about him.

He also had another son and a daughter living, both under ten.

And then there was Karp: there was a problem.

"He's turning twenty and not yet married," he would comment ruefully. "What am I to do with him?"

"More to the point, what are half the husbands in the region going to do to him?" the old steward had remarked.

He was undeniably attractive to women: slim, dark haired, athletic; it was not only that he moved with such ease and grace, that he rode a plow horse and made it seem like a charger; it was not even his bold, rather smoky brown eyes that scanned any crowd for a pretty face; it was something inside him, something wild and free that did not belong in the confines of the village. Many women experienced a little frisson when they saw him. A few girls in Russka had allowed themselves to be seduced. Several more of the married women had secretly made themselves available. It delighted him first to conquer, then to search out, which he did neatly and deftly, what would give pleasure.

In a way, worried as he was, Mikhail was not sorry to have Karp in the house. For he was certainly a help. Despite the difficult conditions and the extra labor he had had to give Boris, the peasant and his son had managed to produce good profits from their grain.

There was one other, quite unexpected source of income that had come their way.

It had come three years before when Mikhail had found, in the forest nearby, a bear cub whose mother had been killed by some hunters. Seeing the poor little creature, only a few weeks old, he had not the heart to leave it or kill it, and to the amusement of the village he had brought it home. His wife had been furious.

"Am I supposed to feed it?" she cried.

But to his surprise, Karp had been delighted. He had an extraordinary way with animals; by the time the bear was eighteen months old, Karp had taught it to do a little dance and to perform several tricks. He would happily unchain the animal to let it perform better.

Often he could earn a few coins for the bear's performances in the little Russka market. Twice already he had gone up the river all the way to Vladimir and returned with several dengi.

"He won't make our fortune," Karp had remarked, "but he pays for his keep with a tidy profit besides."

By this and other means, very secretly so as not to arouse jealousy or suspicion, Mikhail had been putting by money. His aim was simple. "I'll make enough to buy myself out from Lord Boris. And I'll leave some over so that Ivanko can follow us in a year or two if he wants," he told his family.

For things in Russka were going to get worse. His cousin Lev, who collected the taxes locally, admitted as much to him.

"The tsar would like to tax the rest of Muscovy and let the Oprichnina lands off," the merchant said. "But the fact is, he needs money desperately. It's going to be hard."

No doubt Boris would squeeze him further too. It was time to leave.

"And where will we go?" Karp had asked.

That was easy.

"East," he had replied, "into the new lands where people are free."

It made sense. In the new settlements far out in the northern forests, authority was still far away and people lived under fewer restrictions.

"As you like," Karp had obligingly replied.

In the spring of 1567, the wife of Stephen the priest died.

Under the rules of the Orthodox Church, he was not allowed to marry for a second time but had, instead, to join the order of monks.

This he did, giving up the little house he had occupied in Russka and taking up quarters in the Peter and Paul monastery across the river. He continued, however, to officiate at the little stone church in Russka, where he was greatly respected. As for his views on Church lands, whatever Stephen might think, he certainly was not so foolish or so impolite as to say anything about them when he entered the monastery, though for some weeks Daniel kept his ears open, in case his cousin should say anything objectionable.

Elena missed her friend, who had so often kept her company, and she felt sorry for the priest, now monk.

By that September, it was clear that a new campaign in the Baltic was imminent, and Boris was looking forward to it.

During the summer he had made numerous visits to Russka and even spent some calmer, happier times with Elena. Perhaps, yet, there might be a son.

He had also paid a visit to the tsar at Alexandrovskaya Sloboda.

It was a strange place, about fifty miles north of Moscow, just east of the road up to ancient Rostov; not far away lay the great monastery of Trinity Saint Sergius. And indeed, the tsar's headquarters was run rather like a monastery itself.

His first evening inside the heavily guarded enclosures, he was shown to a small hut where two other Oprichniki were sleeping and offered a hard bench. "We shall be up early," they told him with a grin.

But even so, he had not expected to be awoken long before dawn, by the harsh clanging of a bell.

"To prayer," they muttered. And then, with more urgency, "You'd better hurry."

In the blackness of the large courtyard he could see only his two companions, one on each side of him, and a distant square of light that he took to be an open church door. But as they crossed, he heard from somewhere high above a harsh, ringing voice accompanying the clanging of the bell.

"To prayer, dogs," it cried out. "To prayer, my sinful children."

"What foolish old monk is that?" he whispered.

But he had hardly got the words out before he felt a hand clapped over his mouth, and his companion breathed in his ear: "Shut up, you fool. Didn't you realize? That's the tsar himself!"

"Pray for your souls," the voice cried, and, though he had been party to executions himself, and had cut down traitors without a second thought, there was something eerie in the cry from the tall, invisible figure in the darkness above that sent a chill of fear down his back.

It was three in the morning; the service of matins lasted until dawn. He realized that the tsar was there among them, watching him perhaps, yet he did not dare turn around to look. After a time, however, there was a rustling sound, and the tall, dark figure moved quietly past him to the front. Looking neither to right nor left, he walked to the front of the men at prayer and stood there, silently, occasionally stroking his long, reddish beard that was streaked with black.

Then, at a certain moment, he slowly prostrated himself on the floor and knocked his forehead firmly on the ground.

Never, since that dawn on the Volga, had Boris been so close to the tsar. It filled him with awe.

But that was nothing to his feelings when later that day, after mass and the midmorning meal, he was summoned into the presence of the tsar, all alone.

He was dressed in a simple kaftan, black in color but lightly embroidered in gold and trimmed with fur. His tall, lean figure, his long aquiline face, were as Boris remembered from the days of Kazan; but how much older he looked. It was not just that his hair had grown thin so that the upper part of his face had a bony, almost skull-like appearance. It also seemed to Boris that, under his long, drooping mustaches, Ivan's mouth had assumed the shape of a thin crescent moon, downturned, strangely animal. Part Russian prince, part Tatar khan and . . . something else: Boris was not sure what.

And yet, within moments, it was as though he were with the young tsar again; once more he felt that same melancholy charm, that inner passion that belonged to another, mystical world. When he smiled at him, rather sadly, there seemed to be kindness in the tsar's dark eyes.

"So, Boris Davidov, it is many years since we met, you and I, on the bank of the Volga."

"It is, Gosudar."

"And do you remember what was said to each other then?"

"Every word, lord." He could even hear it, now; that quiet, mournful, thrilling voice and the faint lapping sound of the water.

"I, too," the tsar confessed. He paused.

Boris felt himself tremble, and a wave of emotion ran from his gorge down to his chest. Tsar Ivan remembered their words. Once more, he and the sovereign were sharing the religious destiny of mighty Russia.

"And tell me, Boris Davidov," he went on quietly, "do you still believe now what you said then, about our destiny?"

"Oh yes, lord."

Yes, for all the terrible times of recent years, for all the treachery, the violence; he passionately desired to believe it. Without that holy destiny, then what was he? An empty husk, dressed in black?

Ivan gazed at him thoughtfully, sadly it seemed, as though, perhaps in Boris he was remembering something in himself.

"The path to Russia's destiny is hard," he murmured. "The straight and narrow way is hemmed in by thorns. Sharp thorns. We who travel that noble path, Boris, must suffer. There must be shedding of blood. We must not shrink from it. Is it not so?"

Boris nodded. The realization of what this meant choked him with emotion.

"The duties of the Oprichniki are often stern." He looked at Boris carefully. "Your wife does not like my Oprichniki," he remarked.

It was said as a statement, yet clearly, since Boris was now silent and watchful, he was being given an opportunity to deny it. He had an instant urge to do so; and yet, at the same moment, a little warning voice told him to say nothing.

Ivan waited in silence. Could it be that, far from being a friendly conversation, this meeting had been arranged so that the tsar could make his accusation in person: was this the end? Boris waited.

Then Ivan gave him a slight nod.

"Good. Never lie to me, Boris Davidov," he said very quietly. He turned, went to gaze at the icon in the corner and, without turning back, went on in a deep, melancholy tone. "She is right. Do you think, Boris Davidov, that the tsar is unaware of what kind of servants he has? Some of these men are dogs." Now he turned back. "But dogs can catch and kill a wolf. And there are many wolves to be destroyed."

Boris nodded. He understood.

"It is not for the servants of the tsar to think, Boris Davidov," Ivan reminded him quietly. "It is not for them to say—'I wish this,' or 'I will not.' It is for them to obey. Do not forget," he concluded, "that the tsar is set to rule over you by the grace of God, not by the changeable will of men."

Since Ivan said no more, it seemed that the interview was at an end. His eyes were wandering back towards the icon. Boris realized he should go.

But before he left, there was one thing Boris wanted to ask.

"May I stay here, Gosudar," he inquired, "until the next campaign?"

To be here, with the tsar, and at such a time, was what he wanted more than anything.

Ivan looked back at him once more. The interview being over, his eyes had begun to glaze over as he entered some other world of his own.

How quickly, Boris thought, the great man could bring down a curtain that separated him from the rest of the world. There was something that in another man he might have taken for caution or awkwardness: as though there were things he did not wish Boris to see.

"No," he said quietly, "things are quiet here today but . . . this is not the place for you."

A little sadly Boris withdrew.

That afternoon the tsar went riding. In the evening there were more prayers. Then, the next morning, the same summons to church before dawn. By midmorning some prisoners were brought into the fort and led quickly away to a stout building at the far end of the enclosure. Soon after this, Boris left.

As he had made his way back to Moscow he had experienced a wonderful lifting of the spirit, as if his whole being and his commitment to the cause had been renewed.

It was in Moscow, on a clear September day, that Boris came upon the Englishman. They met near the Kremlin wall.

He was a thin fellow, with narrow-set eyes, and when Boris saw him, he was standing by the Neglinaia River gazing curiously across it.

The sight that greeted George Wilson's eye was a recent addition to Moscow, specially constructed for the increased safety of the tsar. It was the Oprichnina palace.

It lay opposite the Kremlin, only a gunshot away—a fearsome fort with twenty-foot walls massively built of red brick and stone. The gate opposite them was sheathed in iron; above it a lion statue raised its paw angrily at the outside world. On the battlements they could see some of the several hundred archers who guarded the place.

As Wilson gazed at this sight wonderingly, Boris in turn looked at him with curiosity. He had heard a lot about these English merchants who were now to be found in several northern cities. They were a troublesome collection, but the tsar apparently thought they could be useful to him. This fellow was so thin he might be a poor monk.

In fact, at that moment, Wilson was thinking of breaking the law.

Life had treated him well. He had married the German girl. Her plump young body had delighted him; her placid round face, he had soon discovered, could turn to a lecherous hardness that made him laugh for pleasure. They had two children now and he had become rather contented.

He was still a militant Protestant. He always carried some printed tracts inside his cloak as a sort of talisman against the all-pervading presence of the Orthodox churchmen with their incense and icons. Occasionally he would be stopped, usually by a blackshirt, who would demand to know what these sheets of paper were. They especially did not like the fact that they were printed. He knew that when Ivan had introduced a modest printing press a few years before to promulgate his laws, an angry mob led by the scribes had broken it up. The simple barbarism of these people amused him. When challenged about the tracts, however, he would always solemnly reply that they were his prayers, a penance for his wickedness, and this usually satisfied them.

He had undertaken a number of profitable deals, but none so profitable as the one he was contemplating now. It was a pity that, strictly speaking, it was illegal.

The problem was not the Russians, but the English. For since Chancellor's return to Russia in 1555, the English trade had been organized as a monopoly under the charter of the Muscovy Company. Trade had been excellent. Wilson had been active in the trading depots from Moscow to the distant northern seas; and he would have had nothing to complain of but for two things: the fact that Ivan had now managed to get his hands on some of the Baltic shore, especially the port of Narva; and that a few years back a cunning Italian had managed to sow ugly rumors about the English traders in Moscow, on behalf of a group of Antwerp merchants. As a result, the English trade through the distant northern sea was not quite so easy as it had been.

"And the fact is," he told his father-in-law, "if I break the company rules and ship some goods through Narva on my own account, the profits could be excellent." He would not be the only English merchant to do so.

Wilson had no great love for his countrymen. In recent years half the fellows they had sent out had been wild young men, who seemed to the Russians, and to Wilson, to be searching for women and drink as much as for trade. The question was, where could he get goods undetected by his fellow traders?

There was an added urgency about this business, too. For Wilson was nervous about the future. The war in the north was sure to continue. When the chief representative of the Muscovy Company had last returned to England, it was with an urgent request from the tsar that he should bring back both skilled men and supplies for the war in the north with Poland. They had recently arrived. If he was to make a shipment out through the Baltic, the sooner the better, before the trouble started.

But there was another piece of news, a whispered rumor that had gone through the English community like a shock wave in the last few days; and it was this new rumor that had caused him to look at the tsar's stout fortress so carefully.

For to the departing company envoy Ivan had given a secret message, which had at once been shared with the tight English community. He had asked Queen Elizabeth of England for asylum, should he ever wish to flee Russia.

"Is he in such danger?" "Are there things we do not know?" The merchants asked one another.

Whatever Ivan's reasons for this strange request, it cast a cloud across the sky. Wilson wondered what to do.

And here was one of the blackshirts, standing right beside him. Wilson had learned to speak a passable Russian: one had to in a country where no one spoke any foreign languages. As an English merchant, he was not especially afraid of the Oprichniki. He decided to address the fearsome figure in black and see what he could find out.

Boris was surprised to be addressed by the merchant, but answered him politely enough. Indeed, pleased to find that the foreigner spoke Russian, he conversed with him for some time.

Wilson was cautious. He gave no hint to the blackshirt of what he knew; but by careful questioning he soon satisfied himself that Boris at least, who had recently been at the tsar's headquarter's outside Moscow, had no sense of impending disaster.

And for his part, Boris made a great discovery. This Englishman wanted a cargo of furs, and he wanted to obtain them discreetly. Boris did not have many, but he was sure he could find more. What a stroke of luck.

"Come to Russka," he said. "None of your English merchants have ever been there."

That autumn and the following spring were busy times for Daniel the monk. They were also disturbing.

The fact of the matter was, he was losing the abbot's favor.

It was his fault. In his zeal to make money for the monastery, he drove the traders in Russka too hard. Nothing they did escaped him; and as a consequence, they tried all the harder to cheat him. The net result of this was that both the monk and the traders were in a state of irritation with one another and the monastery's profits benefited very little.

Though discreet complaints were made to the monastery, the abbot, who was an elderly man, did little more than halfheartedly reprove Daniel from time to time. And when, in reply, Daniel assured the abbot that the townspeople were all rogues, the old man usually found it easier to believe him.

And so matters might have continued indefinitely, if Stephen the priest's wife had not died, forcing him to enter the monastery.

It did not take long for the traders to suggest that things would go better if Stephen, whom they liked, were to be put in charge of Russka.

The abbot was loath to act. He was, truth to tell, a little nervous about the determined monk. "He's very efficient, you know," he lamented to an old monk who was his confidant. "And if I took Russka away from him"—he sighed—"one never knows what he might do. He'd make a fuss, I'm afraid."

But all the same, he began to drop small and not very subtle hints: "You have done good work in Russka, Daniel. One day we must find you a new challenge." Or: "Are you tired, sometimes, Brother Daniel?"

It had only taken one or two such conversations to whip Daniel up into a fever of anxiety and activity, which had made the abbot in turn more afraid of offending him, and at the same time made him wish there was some way to get rid of him.

Stephen for his part was aware of these developments but did nothing to encourage them. He was not afraid of Daniel and privately disapproved of him; but he concluded he had enough souls to pray for, including his own.

Besides, he had other and more personal problems to deal with.

It was the greatest pity for him, however, that he did not realize the strength, and desperation, of Daniel's passion.

He was still the priest at the little church in Russka. The people of the town still looked to him for spiritual guidance, just as people in the area had looked to his father and grandfather before him. It was also only natural that he should continue to minister to Elena in her own home and, perhaps, to visit her a little more often than he had before, simply because her former companion, his wife, was no longer there to do so.

God knows, he often thought, her life must be lonely enough.

And so it was. She had even made two visits to Moscow that autumn to see her mother; she had gone back the second time because she had sensed her mother was worried about something—though what she would not say. At one point her mother had suddenly asked: "Your Boris: is he still our friend?"

And when she had hesitated, because she did not know herself, her mother had quickly said, "No matter. It's of no consequence." And then a moment later: "Do not tell him I asked you."

"Would you like me to stay here for a while?" she had asked. Little as she now liked Moscow, it seemed to her that her mother needed company at present.

But her mother had put her off. "In the spring, perhaps," she had said absently.

Elena was lonely, and concerned. How, therefore, could she help smiling with pleasure when the priest arrived to see her?

It was not long before there existed between them a friendly intimacy that could safely last as long as neither allowed it to be established, by any word or gesture, that they were half, perhaps more than half, in love.

The tall, dark-bearded priest, in his late thirties, was showing the first streak of gray hair in his beard, which if anything, in her eyes, added to his attractiveness. She admired him: indeed, he was to be admired, for he was a fine man. And they experienced the passion of those who have first come to terms with suffering, which is more measured and therefore potentially more powerful than the instantaneous passion of the young.

He would read the service to her. She would pray. At other times they would talk, though never of personal matters.

This, had it been possible, would have been the courtship of these two serious people, amid the gathering storm of events that their own decency prevented them from fully anticipating.

What extraordinary good fortune it was, Daniel thought, that God had given him the gift of observing two things at once.

Had it not been so, he might have missed one or another of the highly significant though small events that transpired in the marketplace on an early October afternoon that year.

The first concerned the English merchant, Wilson, who had arrived the evening before with Boris. After spending time with Lev the merchant, the two men had ridden off to Dirty Place, and the monk had not seen either of them again until he had chanced, when he was taking the little ferry across the river to the monastery, to see the Englishman coming along the path deep in conversation with Stephen.

He had waited and then taken the ferry back again, so that he could follow them. What might they be up to?

In fact, they had met by chance—Wilson returning ahead of Boris to Russka, and Stephen going for a walk. The priest, curious to meet an Englishman, had plied him with questions; and Wilson, who was a good judge of character, soon decided that this literate fellow was safe to talk to and told him what he wanted.

It was not long before the subject turned to religion. Here Wilson was cautious; but the priest reassured him.

"I know about you Protestants. There are people like the Trans-Volga elders, who are a little like you, in Russia. Our own church needs reform, too, though it's a little unwise to say so at present."

And it was after quite a long talk on the subject that Wilson had finally shown the priest one of his printed pamphlets.

Stephen was delighted.

"Tell me what it says," he begged. And so, to the delight of the normally solemn priest, he translated it as best he could.

The little tract was vituperative. It called the Catholic monks vipers, leeches, robbers. It called their monasteries rich and vain, their ceremonies idolatrous and much else besides.

"It's against the Catholics, of course," Wilson assured him, but the priest only laughed. "It applies to us, too," he said, and he made Wilson go over the sheet with him once again, memorizing it.

Before they reached the town, Wilson had wisely secreted it under his cloak again; but it was as they reached the far end of the market square, where the priest took his leave, that Wilson, as a little gesture of friendship, put his hand into his cloak and slipped the piece of paper into Stephen's hand.

What does it matter? he thought. They couldn't understand a word of it even if they could read.

This was the gesture that Daniel saw.

And it was at the same moment that he noticed, at the other side of the marketplace, another tiny movement. It was made by Karp, the son of that foolish fellow Mikhail the peasant.

Karp and his bear had just done a few tricks to amuse some merchants who had come down from Vladimir to buy icons. They had thrown a few small coins on the ground, and Karp had just scooped them up and handed them to his father, who was standing nearby.

That was all. Nothing more. The handing of the coins had taken place at the very same moment that the Englishman handed Stephen the piece of paper. Why should it have been significant?

Because—and here, in all its glory, was the near genius of the observant monk—because he had noticed the faces of Mikhail and his son.

He could not have put it into words. Was it a look of complicity? Perhaps, but more. It was something about the way Mikhail stood and looked about him: a sort of defiance. No, it was not just that. It was that the sturdy peasant had, just for an instant, taken on the character of his son. He had looked, he had thought, like a man who is free. Indefinable. Unmistakable.

And in a flash Daniel guessed. They were hoarding money.

He stored both these pieces of information in his mind and decided to learn more.

In November 1567, just after he had set out northward across the winter snows, Tsar Ivan abruptly canceled his new campaign against the Baltic and hurried back to Moscow. Boris returned with the rest of the army.

A new plot had been discovered. The conspirators were hoping to kill Ivan in the northern snows, with the connivance of the king of Poland. There was a list of names; and who knew how many more might be implicated in this business?

In December the Oprichniki went to work. With axes under their cloaks and a list of names in their hands, they rode about the streets of Moscow making house calls. Some were exiled. Some impaled.

At the end of the second week in December, a party of Oprichniki came to the house of the bald, stout nobleman Dimitri Ivanov. His son-in-law Boris was not one of them. They conducted him to a chamber in the armory in the Kremlin. There they had prepared a huge iron pan, underneath which was a fire. In this they fried him.

His death was recorded briefly in a secret list prepared for the tsar. In common with over three thousand others who died in the coming months, the names upon this list, since known as the Synodical, were consigned to oblivion and it was forbidden to mention them.

At the same time all the monasteries in the land were instructed to send their chronicles to the tsar for inspection. By this means, Ivan ensured that no records of events were kept for these terrible years.

Daniel the monk was confident, even cheerful.

Thank the Lord that a century and a half ago, the monks had made such a good job of writing the chronicle. There was little in it that could possibly embarrass the tsar. Throughout, the references to the Tatars were offensive and the Moscow princes were treated as heroes in the struggle against them.

Five years before, to celebrate Ivan's victories over the Muslim khanates of Kazan and Astrakhan, the monastery had added crescent moons under the crosses above the church domes in the monastery itself and in Russka, as symbols of the triumph of Christian armies over Islam.

Our loyalty cannot be questioned, he thought contentedly.

The new purge in Moscow had had a satisfactory side effect for him. The old abbot had been so distressed by the whole business that he had been scarcely capable of conducting ordinary business, and the question of the Russka administration seemed to have slipped entirely from his mind.

Besides, Daniel was more confident than before that he could defend his position there. Once again, therefore, in early spring, his mind turned to the old question: how could he enlarge the monastery's estates?

Boris's land, now that he was one of the Oprichniki, was of course out of the question. That left one other piece of land, a little to the north, that now belonged to the tsar himself. Might Ivan be persuaded?

It was not a foolish idea. Despite his restrictions on the church acquiring new land, Ivan himself had remained a handsome donor.

"He strikes down his enemies; then he gives the church some more, to save his soul," one of the monks had cynically remarked.

Might this latest purge in fact be a good time to approach him?

It was with this in mind that Daniel the monk went to the brother who had been keeping the chronicle, and set to work.

The document they produced, and which, in the month of February, they persuaded the nervous abbot to sign, was a splendid concoction. It reminded the tsar of the many privileges granted to the Church in the past even under the Tatars. That some of these were Church forgeries Daniel himself did not know. It pointed out the loyalty of the monastery and the purity of its chronicles. And it begged for much-needed land. Written in the high ecclesiastical style, it was long, bombastic, and somewhat ungrammatical.

If it succeeds, Daniel thought, my position in the monastery will be unassailable.

Before sending it, the abbot rather doubtfully showed it to Stephen, who read it, smiled, and said nothing.

On the morning of March 22, 1568, in the Cathedral of the Assumption in Moscow, a terrifying event took place.

Metropolitan Filip, while celebrating the Eucharist, suddenly turned and, in the presence of a large congregation of boyars and Oprichniki, publicly rebuked the tsar for his murder of innocents in the latest purge.

Ivan, in a fury, struck his iron-tipped staff upon the rostrum, but Metropolitan Filip stood his ground.

"They are martyrs," he announced.

It was an act of huge moral courage. The boyars trembled.

"Soon," Ivan responded, "you will come to know me better."

Within days, the Metropolitan took refuge in a monastery and Ivan began to execute members of the brave churchman's staff.

And it was unfortunate for Daniel that it should have been on the very day following this event that a clerk brought to the tsar the Russka monastery's request for land.

Tsar Ivan's response was immediate and frightening, and when Daniel saw it, neither he, nor the terrified abbot, were sure what they should do.

Saint George's Day had come.

Mikhail the peasant, his wife, his son Karp, Misha the bear, and the peasant's two other children were ready.

The work of the year was done. The harvest was long in. Indeed, there had been little enough to do since, as if in punishment for the terrible deeds of its ruler, God had sent Russia that year a dismal crop.

Over the brown-and-gray landscape a chill wind was bringing with it light flurries of snow dust that was speckling the wet, hardening ground. The stout wooden huts of Dirty Place smelled dank; bare trees and bare fields, having shed their last covering, waited gauntly for the snow to submerge them. Saint George's Day, harbinger of the bleak winter to come.

Mikhail and his family were ready to go. The exit money was all there in the peasant's hand. Unlike many other peasants in the area, he had no debts, having discreetly cleared them the month before. He had a good horse and journey money besides. He was a free man. Today he could leave.

The peasants' plan was ambitious, but quite simple. They would go across country, through the woods, to Murom. Then they would stay there until, probably in the spring, they could take a boat up the Oka to Nizhni Novgorod. From there they would find a boat that was traveling out to the east on the mighty Volga to the new lands where the settlers lived free.

It would be hard. He was not sure how they would find money to survive the whole journey; but they could find a way. Misha the bear would help them by earning a few kopeks here and there.

Yet, though the family was all packed up and ready to leave, they had not departed. For a week now, they had sat in the little hut and waited. Each day, either Mikhail or Karp would go into Russka; and each day would glumly return.

It was Karp's turn that day. He came sadly along the path.

"Well?"

Karp shook his head.

"Nothing. No sign." He suddenly kicked the door violently, but though it made him jump, Mikhail did not reprove him. "Cursed swindlers!" the young man cried.

"Perhaps another day," his mother said, but without conviction.

"Perhaps," Mikhail said.

But he knew it was hopeless. He had been cheated.

The rules of departure from Boris's estate were simple. The peasant must be free of debt and, a week on either side of Saint George's Day he might inform his lord that he wished to leave and pay his exit fees. That was all.

But there was one small catch. The lord, or his steward, must be there to receive the request to depart, and the necessary moneys.

A few days before the allotted time, Boris and his wife had abruptly departed for Moscow, and the house in Russka had been shut up. Mikhail had at once gone into Russka to seek out the steward and had returned pale with shock.

For the old fellow and his wife had mysteriously disappeared, too.

They had never left the town before; no one knew they were going, nor where they might be. Their house was empty.

Even then he had scarcely been able to believe it. He had heard stories of such trickery, to be sure; but here in Russka, beside a monastery, could such things be?

They could. As the days passed, there was no sign of them.

"But don't think they've really gone," Karp said furiously. "That steward's about somewhere, he's hiding in the area. And if we try to leave without paying our dues, he'll appear out of nowhere with half a dozen men. You see if he doesn't. He's waiting to follow us and arrest us as runaways. Then he and our cursed landlord will take more from us than ever. I'll bet you we're being watched right now."

He was exactly correct. The only thing that neither Mikhail nor Karp guessed was that it was their cousin Daniel the monk who was behind it all.

For Daniel, the whole thing had been a simple matter.

After the tsar's terrifying message, it was clear that the monastery, and he in particular, might need friends, wherever they could find them. The obvious first choice was the tsar's servitor Boris.

It had not taken the cunning monk long to discover that Mikhail was quietly paying off his debts. Early that morning he had sought out Boris himself and discreetly warned him that his best peasant was planning to leave. He had also reminded him of how he could prevent him.

Boris had been duly grateful.

"I am always your lord's friend," Daniel had said, and though Boris was not deceived by that, he nonetheless concluded that the heavily bearded monk might be useful to him.

"Very well," he had remarked. "Keep me informed of anything else I should know."

So Saint George's Day passed. And the next day. And the next.

On the seventh day after, when he woke up a little after dawn, Mikhail was shocked, but not altogether surprised, to find that Karp and the horse had gone. On the table lay a little pile of money.

Three days later a man from a village five miles down the river arrived at the door with a message.

"Karp passed through our village the other morning. He has gone. He said he left money for the horse. He's sorry it wasn't more."

Mikhail nodded.

"Did he say where he was going?"

"Yes. Into the wild field."

Mikhail sighed. It was what he had suspected. Perhaps it was where, after all, he belonged.

The wild field: the open steppe: the land where, in recent decades, other wayward young fellows like Karp had been going to join those bands of half brigands, half warriors who had nowadays taken to calling themselves Cossacks.

Yes, he belonged in the wild field. They would never see him again.

"He said please to look after the bear," the fellow concluded.

It was later that day that another, chilling piece of news reached Russka.

Tsar Ivan's men had carried off the Metropolitan.

Elena kept her faith. She could still have a son.

It was Stephen who encouraged her. Though she had never spoken a word to him about Boris, the priest thought he could guess what their life must be like. He felt sorrier than ever for her, the more he knew her; yet he always advised her correctly as a priest.

"It is not by seeking for personal happiness that we are rewarded by God," he reminded her. "It is by denying ourselves. The meek shall inherit the earth, as Our Lord told us. Therefore we must forgive; we must suffer; and above all, we must have faith."

Elena had faith. She had faith that, after all, God would give her a son; she had faith that, one day, her husband would turn from his path.

For a time, after her father's disappearance, she had had faith that he, too, might be saved. But Boris, who had investigated the matter, informed her that he had been executed. He did not say how. It seemed to Elena that this event had shocked her husband.

Perhaps this, she hoped, may turn him back towards the paths of righteousness. So at least she prayed, though as yet in vain.

How to have a son? There was a remedy the village women used, that the priest's wife had once told her about. It consisted of rubbing the body, and especially her intimate parts, with oil and honey.

"They say it never fails," her friend had assured her.

And so now, while the man she truly loved gave her spiritual comfort, she prepared herself, as best she could, as a sacrifice for the husband whose darkening soul it was her duty to save.

The spring of 1569 brought cold weather and the promise of another poor harvest. From the Baltic came news that the enemy had snatched a fortress town. Everyone seemed depressed.

It was in early June that Daniel the monk had another talk with Boris.

By now the monk was worried. Things at Russka were looking bad. Not that he was entirely to blame. The events of recent years—the ever-higher taxes for the northern war, the disruption of the Oprichnina, and the land confiscations—had hurt the Russian economy. That, with the failed harvest, was causing a grim recession. The revenues from Russka were sharply down, and the old abbot seemed to be a loss, complaining to him one day about the shortfall, yet the next suggesting: "Perhaps we are too harsh with our people in these difficult times."

He had several times seen the old man looking appealingly at Stephen after these conversations. Something had to be done.

And then there had been the business with the tsar the previous spring. That had not helped Daniel's reputation either.

For instead of agreeing to, or refusing their request for land, Ivan had sent a strange but insulting message. It was an ox hide: no more, no less. The messenger who brought it, a young blackshirt, obviously following the tsar's instructions to the letter, threw this object derisively at the old abbot's feet, in front of all the monks, and cried out: "The tsar says to you: lay this hide upon the ground and the land within it he will give you."

"Is that all?" the terrified abbot had asked.

"No. The tsar himself promises to visit you and give you the land you have chosen, and anything else you deserve."

"It is you, Daniel, who have brought this upon us," the abbot sadly remarked, after the messenger had gone. "As for this ox hide"—he sighed—"I suppose we shall have to keep it."

The hide had remained, ever since, in the abbot's room—an uncomfortable reminder that Ivan would be coming to see them one day.

The first task for Daniel, therefore, was to put Stephen in his place. It was not difficult.

"I think you should know," he told Boris, "that the priest spends more time at your house, now that his wife has died." And for good measure he added: "You once told me he was a heretic. I saw him taking something from that Englishman you brought here. The English are all Protestants, I hear; and this was a piece of paper."

It was enough. He was sure of it. Boris had said not a word; but he was sure it was enough.

Already for Boris, it was a year of evil portent. In the north, there was doubt about the loyalty of the cities of Novgorod and Pskov. Far in the south, in the Crimea, the Ottoman Turks with the Crimean Tatars were reported to be preparing an offensive against the lower reaches of the Volga. And now, this summer, word had come that the two powers of Poland and Lithuania, though they had acted together for generations, were being formally unified into one kingdom, ruled by a Catholic Polish king.

"And that means one thing," he had told Elena. "It means that we shall have Catholics from Kiev to Smolensk—right at our doors."

And now the monk was telling him that his wife might be unfaithful with the priest. He said nothing, but for long hours he brooded about it.

He hardly knew what to think. Part of him was filled with rage and with a loathing of both the heretic priest, whom he had never liked, and his wife. Yet if Daniel had thought that this was a good way to get Stephen disgraced, or at least banned from Russka, he was to be disappointed.

For Boris decided to take no action for the present, except to have the two of them discreetly watched.

There were two reasons for this. The first was that, having mastered the first wave of his jealousy, his intelligence told him that the suspicion might not be true. The fact that the priest saw his wife was hardly proof of anything. The second was a more devious thought: for if he could prove she was unfaithful, he could, with good conscience, divorce her.

Look at Tsar Ivan, he thought. He had married again and had had sons by both marriages. The tsar had an heir. Perhaps with another wife, who did not secretly shrink from him. . . .

And so began a new phase in his marriage.

Elena was entirely unaware of the pattern of his thoughts. How could she guess, when he was always something of a stranger to her. The thought that she might be unfaithful both hurt and enraged him; and yet, at the same time, it made her seem more desirable so that he found himself completely torn between the desire to keep her—a contaminated woman—at a distance, and the desire to possess her.

And poor Elena could only think: He suffers his black moods and yet, after all, he cares for me.

Sometimes, lying beside her, enclosed in the armor of his secret rejection of her, he would even, scarcely knowing that he did so, will her to be unfaithful. Though whether it was to be free of her, or to satisfy some deep, destructive tendency in his own nature, he himself would have been quite incapable of analyzing.

In this way he passed the month of June.

The weather had been changeable after late frosts in the spring. The harvest would be ruined.

On a hot and unusually sultry afternoon in late July, when even the breeze had stopped, as though realizing the futility of doing anything, Boris had ridden back from Dirty Place to Russka; and he had just come into the dusty little square when he saw, a hundred yards away, Stephen the priest slowly coming down the staircase from the upper floor of his house. He must have been seeing Elena.

His heart missed a beat.

The square was empty. The wooden houses around it and the stone church seemed to be sunk in a kind of empty stasis, as if they were awaiting a breath of wind that, with its gentle kiss, might bring them back to life.

As Boris approached his house, Stephen was walking away from him, his head sunk in meditation. He rounded a corner and disappeared.

Quietly Boris went up the stairs and opened the door.

She was there, by the open window. She was gazing out at the street, at the place where Stephen had been a few moments before. Her fingers, he noticed, were resting on the wooden frame of the window and a shaft of sunlight fell just across them as they lay there, very still. She was wearing a simple dress of light blue silk. He, having been in the fields, was for once not in black, but in a white linen smock, tied with a heavy belt, like one of his peasants.

Although his heart was pounding, he breathed very quietly; he wondered how long she would stand there, gazing after the man. He tried, without moving, to see the expression on her face. A minute passed. Then another.

At last she turned. Her face was very calm; but she started a little when she saw him and, when he did not speak, but only looked at her, she blushed. "I did not hear you come in."

"I know."

Had she made love to him? He looked for some telltale sign: a faint glow about her, perhaps; some disarrangement in her dress or in the room. He could not see anything.

"You love him."

He said it very quietly, not as a question but as a statement—as though it were something they were both quite agreed upon. Then he watched her.

She blushed deep, swallowed hard, and looked miserably confused. "No. Not as a man. As a priest."

"Is he not a man?"

"Of course. He is a fine man. A pious man," she protested.

"Who makes love to you."

"No. Never."

He stared at her. Did he believe her?

"Liar."

"Never!"

She had said *never*. She could have used other words. She might have denied that she even wished it. But she had said: *never*. That meant she had desired it. As to whether she had or not . . . who knew? His reason told him she probably had not, but he was too proud to trust her, in case he was deceived.

Yet had he not secretly wanted her to be unfaithful—to give him grounds for divorce? Suddenly, all that was forgotten as he looked at this modest, rather ordinary woman he had married, and who had committed these crimes against his pride.

She was pale now. She was trembling, afraid. "Never! You insult me."

Very well. It might be so. But then he saw it in her eye, a little look that he had never seen before: a flash of contempt, of anger.

He would show her. He stepped forward suddenly, swung his hand and struck her with the open palm across the face. Her head jerked violently; she cried out, gasped. Turned back to him in rage and terror. He struck her with the other hand.

"Bully!" she screamed suddenly. "Murderer."

It was enough.

He struck her. Again and again. Then he raped her.

He left for Moscow the next morning.

In September 1569, Tsar Ivan's second wife died. The next month his cousin Prince Vladimir, still a possible successor to the throne, was accused of conspiracy and made to drink poison. The unlucky prince's family were then killed, including his elderly mother, who lived in a convent.

But these events were followed by something far more terrible. Late in the year Ivan discovered another conspiracy: the cities of Novgorod and Pskov were planning to break away.

There may, in fact, have been some truth in it. To this day the details are not quite clear. These once independent centers, near to the Baltic ports, may well have been tempted to escape the increasing taxation and tyranny of Muscovy by joining the newly united and formidable Commonwealth of Poland-Lithuania. They had always been closer to the busy Baltic shores than to the slow, deep heartland of Moscow.

Whatever the facts of the case, at the end of 1569, and accompanied by a large force of Oprichniki, Ivan the Terrible set out in great secrecy for Novgorod. He did not want the city to know he was coming. Even the commander of the advance guard did not know where they were going. Any passing traveler they met was immediately killed, so that no news of the advance would travel.

In January Novgorod was punished.

Exactly how many died in the torture, burning, and executions that followed is not clear. They certainly numbered thousands. The city of Novgorod, so valuable to Russia over the previous centuries, was so utterly devastated that it never recovered. Having already killed most of its more important citizens on the road, Ivan only executed forty people at Pskov and burned a few priests at the stake. Then he returned to Alexandrovskaya Sloboda.

It was just after this that two small events of interest took place at Russka.

The first was the birth, to Elena, of a baby son. Boris had still not returned from the Novgorod campaign and so she and Stephen the priest had to choose a name. They chose Feodor, and so Stephen baptized him.

That same day, the priest sent a letter to Boris to let him know what he had done.

The second event centered upon Daniel the monk. For in April 1570, still anxious to enrich the monastery, he hit upon a plan.

It concerned the ox hide that the tsar had sent. It was so cunning and so daring that for centuries afterwards it would be known as Daniel's Ruse.

When the abbot first heard of it, he went white with terror.

1571

BORIS scowled, as well he might. The snow in the marketplace at Russka had long ago been trampled and packed down until it was hard as stone. The few stalls in the marketplace that had opened out of habit were now being shut. No chink of sunlight had appeared in the cloud cover and none had been expected; and now the short day, like the stalls, was closing down.

He scowled because he saw Mikhail and his family. They were standing beside the remains of the single fire that had been lit in the center of the marketplace. Mikhail did not answer his look, but stared at him without hope. What was there to hope for, after all?

There was a week to go before the beginning of Lent; yet what could the Lenten fast mean that year, when the harvest had failed for the third time running the summer before? That morning, in Dirty Place, Boris had seen a family eating ground birchbark. Bark from the trees—the peasant's last resort when the grain was all gone. Few had supplies to last them through two failed harvests. None could get past three.

The monastery had helped feed the worst cases, but even its reserves were running low. There had been plague in some of the northern areas. Two of the families in Dirty Place had run away last year. There had been greater desertions in other villages.

"The people are leaving the land," a fellow landlord had remarked to him, "and there's nothing we can do."

Where did they go? East, he supposed, east to the new lands by the Volga. But how many of them, he wondered, ever got there in the mighty, icy winter?

Mikhail and his cursed family. How they must hate him.

Since Karp had gone off with their horse, the family had not recovered. They had replaced the horse and got through the second bad harvest; but they had had to dig into their money reserve to keep going. There was no more talk of buying their freedom. As for running away, like the others, he guessed that Mikhail had concluded he was safer with his young children near a monastery than trying to survive out in the great eastern wilds.

Now Mikhail spoke to him. "Spare a kopek, Boris Davidov. At least for the bear."

He noticed the bitter irony in the request. Let my children starve but take pity on the animal—that was the message.

"Damn your bear," he said and walked on.

The bear was as gaunt as the peasants now. It had never performed its tricks for Mikhail the way it had for Karp; in its raging hunger it would probably turn nasty. It stood there, haggard in its chains. Why on earth didn't they kill it?

Boris turned to look up at the watchtower that rose, tall and gray over the gateway. He had been going up there every day of late. For, on top of all their trouble, word had come that an attack was expected from the Crimean Tatars from the south. So far nothing had come, but Boris scanned the horizon anxiously each day.

He had just come down from there. Alone, up in the high, pointed tent roof, gazing out through the eastern window at the huge flat spaces, he had been alone with his thoughts. Out there, far away, lay the Volga and distant Kazan. Out there lay the huge eastern empire of the tsar. Why, after their holy crusade, had the heartland been turned to icy stone, famine, dejection?

As he stared out of the endless grayness, it had seemed to Boris that Russka was swallowed up and lost in the long half night of winter. Nothing moved upon the landscape. The sky, though always overcast, was empty. The snow, which he usually thought of as a protection for the earth, now seemed to him like a coating of misery that had been hardened in the biting winter wind. Everything was gray. From his high place, he could make out the big field at Dirty Place, which that day looked like a large, unmarked grave.

And then he had thought about his own little family, and the boy, Feodor. And that had made him scowl, too.

Was the boy his? It was a question that had been exercising his mind for nearly a year and a half. It was possible, of course. It might be that on that afternoon when he had struck her and forced himself upon her. It could be that then she had conceived. But what if it were not that day? What if the priest had already been with her, or if he had called the next day, or the next?

As the months passed, he had brooded upon this frequently. When the child had arrived, he had received the message not from his wife, but from the priest, who had chosen the boy's name. It was the name, moreover, of Elena's brother whom he had hated. Was there irony in that? When he had finally returned, he had examined the child minutely. Who did it look like? It was hard to say. It did not seem to him to resemble anyone. But time would tell; features would appear that would tell him the truth: he was sure of it.

Meanwhile he had observed them both. The priest had congratulated him with a smile. Was there a trace of mockery in it? His wife had smiled faintly at the priest, who had stood beside her in a manner that, to Boris, appeared protective. Was there complicity between them?

The more he allowed, even encouraged these thoughts to grow in his mind, the more luxuriantly did they grow, like some morbid but fantastic plant, which, as it grew, took on in Boris's imagination a kind of dark beauty, like one of these wondrous, magical plants that are said to flower only at night, in the depths of the forest. He watched the flower, he fed it; in a strange way he even came, in the dark recesses of his mind, to love it like a man who learns to feed upon poison and then, even, to crave it.

It was in December, when the baby was nine months old, that he had begun to feel sure it was not his. Whether this was the natural growth of his imagination, whether the dark flowers of this plant he had nurtured required this belief in order that he might more completely admire their beauty; or whether something exterior had prompted him, he now became convinced. The child's face, at certain angles, started to seem long, like the priest's. The eyes looked solemn. The ears, above all, were neither his nor his wife's. They were not the same as Stephen's either, but they were more like his than Boris's. Or so it appeared to the landlord on one of his routine, secret inspections of the little boy.

He had stayed up in the high watchtower that day, alone with these thoughts, gazing out at the endless wastes, until he had definitely decided that this was so. The little fellow who crawled across the wooden floor and, sometimes, smiled up at him, was not his. He had not yet decided what he would do.

He had just come level with the church when he heard a shout from the gates and turned to see what it was.

Daniel the monk first saw them: two large sleds, whisking down the frozen river from the north. They were each drawn by three magnificent black horses.

They sped over the bank and came straight towards the monastery gate.

Only as they drew close did he see that the men in the sleds were all dressed in black. And even then, they were almost at the gate before he clearly saw the face of the tall, gaunt figure wrapped in furs who sat in the first sledge.

And then he crossed himself and, in stark terror, fell to his knees on the hard snow.

It was Ivan.

As usual, he had come from Alexandrovskaya Sloboda secretly, without warning, his swift horses eating up the miles as he sped, sometimes by day, sometimes by night, from monastery to monastery in the icy silence of the forest.

The party did not waste any time. They drove straight into the center of the monastery courtyard, and the monks were still looking out in surprise when the tall figure rose from his sled and began to stalk slowly towards the refectory. He wore a high, conical fur hat. In his right hand he carried a long staff, with a gold-and-silver top and a pointed iron tip that pierced deep holes in the snow as he advanced.

"Call your abbot," his deep voice echoed around the icy yard. "Tell him his tsar is here." And the monks trembled.

About five minutes passed before they were all assembled in the refectory. The old abbot stood at their head, some eighty monks behind him, including Daniel. The dozen Oprichniki with the tsar were stationed by the door. Ivan had seated himself in a heavy oak chair and was facing them gloomily. He had not removed his fur hat. His chin was sunk upon his chest, so that his long nose partly obscured his mouth. His eyes, glinting under his heavy brows, looked up at the monks, darting suspiciously from one to the other. His long staff rested beside him, leaning at a sharp angle over the back of the chair.

For a little time he said nothing.

"My loyal servant, Boris Davidov Bobrov: where is he?" he quietly inquired.

"Up at Russka," someone said, and then shut his mouth as though he had not spoken.

Ivan looked neither to right nor left.

"Fetch him," he intoned.

One of the Oprichniki vanished through the door. Several long moments of silence followed. Then the piercing eyes fell upon the abbot. "You were sent an ox hide. Where is it?"

If the old abbot looked terrified, it was no worse than the stark fear that now came over Daniel. Suddenly, in this new and awful light, face to face with the tsar, the plan that once had seemed so daring now appeared pitiful. It was also impertinent. His legs suddenly felt cold. He wished that he were hidden at the back of the room.

"Brother Daniel was put in charge of it," he heard the abbot say. "He can explain to you what he has done."

Now he felt the tsar's eyes upon him.

"Where is my ox hide, Brother Daniel?"

There was nothing for it.

"As you said we might, Gosudar, we used it to mark out a patch of ground, which, if your majesty is so gracious, might be granted to your loyal monastery."

Ivan stared at him.

"You ask for no more?"

"No, great lord: it is enough."

The tsar rose. He seemed to tower over them all.

"Show me."

The idea had been nothing if not ingenious. After all, the tsar's message had been quite explicit: they were to use the ox hide to enclose the land. Why not, then, cut it into strips? Better yet, why not subdivide the strips? Or even better still . . .

It had been at the end of the summer that Daniel had set the monks to work. Using sharpened combs and knives they had proceeded, day after day, to take the ox hide apart, making from it not just fine strips of leather but a thread. With care and ingenuity this thread, now wound carefully around a block of wood, could be unraveled to enclose no less than a hundred acres. The area had been staked out by Daniel on Saint Nicholas Day.

Now, with the spindle of thread in his hand, he trudged across the snow, followed by Ivan, the abbot, and the Oprichniki, to the place where the stakes began. He had just begun to unwind the thread when he heard Ivan's voice.

"Enough. Come here."

This was it then. Death, he supposed. He went and stood before the tsar.

Ivan reached forward his long hand and took him by the beard. "A cunning monk," he said softly. "Yes, a cunning monk." He looked bleakly at the abbot. "The tsar keeps his word. You shall have your land."

The two monks bowed low, both praying fervently.

"I shall remain here tonight," Ivan went on. He nodded his head thoughtfully. "And before I depart, you shall learn to know me better."

He turned, and now he smiled. For hurrying across the snow came a figure in black.

"Ah," he cried, "here he comes, a loyal servant. Boris Davidov," he called, "you shall help these cunning monks to know me better." Then, gazing down at the abbot, he announced, "Come, Abbot, it is almost time for Vespers."

It was already dark outside when, amidst the bright glow from all the candles they could muster, the trembling monks sang the service of Vespers.

Facing them, having donned the golden robes used on the highest feast days, Tsar Ivan stood and, with a strange, grim smile, conducted them with his staff. Once a terrified young monk sang a wrong note and Ivan, his eyes suddenly boring into the malefactor, brought down the iron tip of his staff with a crash upon the stone floor and made them start the hymn again.

So the service continued. Twice, as though suddenly attacked by a spasm, Ivan turned away, let his staff fall with a crash to the ground, and prostrated himself, beating his head upon the stone and crying out: *"Gospodi Pomily:* Lord have mercy."

But a moment later he would rise, pick up his staff, and, with the same grim half smile as before, conduct the singing as though nothing had happened.

At last the service ended. The shaken monks dispersed to their cells, and Ivan returned to the refectory, where he ordered food and drink to be brought for himself, Boris, and the other Oprichniki.

He also sent for the abbot and for Daniel, who, when they arrived, were told to stand just inside the door.

There was something strange about the tsar, Daniel noticed, as Ivan sat down to eat.

It was as if the service had excited him in some way. His eyes were a little bloodshot, yet seemed to be slightly absent, as though he had entered another realm while his body, almost in derision, went through the motions of existence in this world.

They had given him their best wine, and whatever food they could find. For a few minutes he ate and drank thoughtfully, the Oprichniki beside him carefully tasting everything first, to make sure it was not poisoned. The other blackshirts ate silently, including Boris, whom Ivan had seated opposite him.

After a time Ivan looked up.

"So, Abbot, you have cheated me out of a hundred acres of good land," he remarked calmly.

"Not cheated, Gosudar," the abbot began tremulously.

"You and this hairy-faced dog beside you," Ivan continued. "You shall learn now that the tsar raises up and casts down; he giveth and he taketh away." He looked at them with contempt. "On my way here, I was hungry," he intoned. "Yet in the forests here, I found no deer. Why not?"

The abbot looked baffled for a moment.

"The deer have been scarce this last winter. People are hungry . . ."

"You are fined a hundred rubles," Ivan said quietly.

He turned to Boris.

"Is there no entertainment here, Boris Davidov?"

"I had a fellow who could play and sing well, lord, but he died last spring." Boris paused. "There's a fellow with a performing bear," he said doubtfully, "but he's not very good."

"A bear?" Ivan suddenly brightened. "That's better. Take a sled and bring them, good Boris Davidov. Bring them now."

Boris rose and went to the door. He had just reached it when Ivan, having taken a draft of wine, suddenly called out: "Stop!" He looked around for a moment to observe the reaction of the others in the room. "Take two sleds, Boris Davidov. Take mine and the second. Put the bear in the first. Dress him up in my furs. Let him wear the cap of the tsar." And taking off his high hat, he threw it to Boris. "Let the tsar of all the bears come to visit the tsar of all the Russias."

At this he roared with laughter and the Oprichniki, following suit, banged their plates upon the table.

"And now," he said, turning to the abbot—and Daniel saw with amazement that every trace of mirth, in a split second, had completely vanished from his face—"tell that hairy-faced rogue beside you to bring me a jar of fleas."

"Fleas, lord?" the abbot mumbled. "We have no fleas."

"A pot of fleas, I said!" Ivan suddenly rose and strode over to them, his staff held in his hand at a rakish angle, tapping upon the floor.

He stood, towering over them both. Daniel noticed, in his terror, that the tsar was a little stouter than he had thought. It made him only more frightening.

"Fleas!" he roared. "When your tsar commands, it is treachery to disobey. Fleas!" He struck his staff a tremendous downward blow on the floor in front of the abbot. "Fleas! Seven thousand. Not one less!"

It was a favorite trick of his to demand the impossible. Though the abbot did not know it, Ivan had used this demand for fleas before. The old man quaked and Daniel thought that perhaps he was about to have a heart attack and die.

"We do not possess them, lord," Daniel said. He tried to keep his voice steady but it came out as a hoarse whisper.

Ivan turned to him. "Then you are fined a hundred rubles, Brother Daniel," he remarked calmly.

For a second, just for an instant, Daniel opened his mouth to protest.

But then he remembered that recently the tsar had tied a monk, like himself, astride a small keg of gunpowder before lighting it, and he fell silent, praying that his impulse had not been noticed.

Tsar Ivan returned to his table, indicating to the two monks that they were to remain where they were.

Now, ignoring them completely, he began to talk and laugh with the black-robed Oprichniki. He made some reference to another monastery, something—Daniel could not hear what—he had done to a monk there, which made them all roar with laughter, and sent a chill down Daniel's spine.

Half an hour passed. Tsar Ivan drank steadily, but he was obviously in control of himself. Each time his hand raised the goblet to his lips, Daniel noticed the dull flash of the big jeweled rings on his fingers. His eyes, every few minutes, darted suspiciously around the big room, piercing the shadows.

"Bring more candles," he commanded. "Let there be light." He did not seem to trust the darkness.

So they brought candle stands from the church and set them up in the corners.

It was just as they were doing so that there was a commotion at the door, and one of the Oprichniki announced that the bear was arriving. Led by the tsar, they all went to the entrance to watch.

It was a grotesque sight. Preceded by four men with burning torches, the sled came into the courtyard. The terrified monks peeped out of windows and doorways.

In it sat the bear. His gaunt frame had been hung with a magnificent sable coat. On his head was the tsar's conical hat. Around his neck Boris had hung a golden crucifix he had taken from the chapel.

With a baffled Mikhail guiding him, the bear was coaxed to walk on its hind legs from the sled into the refectory.

"Bow!" Ivan cried in a loud voice to the monks in the doorways. "Bow to the tsar of all the bears!"

He himself conducted the bear to his own chair, on which it was persuaded to sit. Then, with mock ceremony, the tsar made them all, including the abbot, bow low to the bear, before they removed the hat and coat.

"Come then, peasant," the tsar said sharply to Mikhail. "Show us your tricks."

It was not much of a performance. While the tsar and his men sat, Mikhail led the animal through its routine. It stood up, danced ponderously, clapped its paws together. The creature was a sad sight, its skin hanging loosely for want of food. After a little time Ivan grew bored and banished Mikhail and the animal to a corner.

Outside the night grew deeper. The cloud cover broke so that here and there a few stars could be glimpsed. Within, Ivan sat, apparently brooding, telling Boris to fill his goblet, and his own, with wine from time to time.

"They say," he murmured softly, "that I may retire and become a monk. Have you heard that?"

"Yes, lord. Your enemies say that."

Ivan nodded slowly. In the early days of the Oprichnina many of the boyars had suggested this solution.

"And yet," he went on quietly, "it is true. Those whom God chooses to rule over men are given not freedom, but a terrible burden; not a palace, but a prison." He paused. "No ruler is safe, Boris Davidov. Even I, chosen by God to rule over men according to my will—even I must watch the shadows on the wall: for any one of them may possess a knife." He drank thoughtfully. "Better, perhaps, the life of a monk."

Boris, too, as he sat with Tsar Ivan, felt the oppressive silence of the shadows. He had drunk deeply, but his head was still clear; instead of confusion, he felt within him a slowly rising melancholy as he entered into the twilight world of this ruler he revered. He, too, in his small way, knew what it was to be troubled by the treacheries and phantasmagoria of the night. He, too, knew that a terrible phantom may, in the cold light of dawn, turn out to be real.

They will kill him, he thought, if he does not first kill them.

And here he was, sitting opposite this great and troubled man, his tsar, who was taking him once again into his most intimate confidence. How he longed to share the life of this mighty figure, so close yet so all-powerful, so terrible yet so deeply wise, who saw into the dark hearts of men.

They drank in silence.

"Tell me, Boris Davidov, what shall we do with this rascal priest who has stolen land from the tsar?" Ivan asked at last.

Boris thought. He was honored to be asked. He had no love of Daniel, but he must make a wise answer.

"He is useful," he said at last. "He loves money."

Ivan looked at him thoughtfully. His eyes were more bloodshot, but still piercing. He reached out his long hand and touched Boris's arm. Boris felt a thrill of excitement.

"Well answered." He smiled grimly. "Let us beat some money out of him." He signaled to two of the other Oprichniki and whispered instructions. They went over to where the monks were still standing and quietly conducted Daniel out.

Boris knew what they would do. They would tie him up, probably upside down, and beat him until he told him where all the monastery's money was hidden. Priests and monks always had money and usually disgorged it fairly soon. He did not feel sorry for him. It was the smallest of all Ivan's chastisements. The fellow probably deserved worse.

But now the tsar's long evening had begun.

It was by a little sign, an involuntary winking of Ivan's left eye, that Boris understood what was to come. He had heard of it from other Oprichniki and he knew that it frequently followed a church service. The sign meant that Ivan was in a mood to punish.

"Tell me, Boris Davidov," he now said in a quiet voice. "Who is there here who is not to be trusted?"

Boris paused.

"Remember your oath," Ivan murmured gently. "You have sworn to tell your tsar all that you know."

It was true. He had no reason to hesitate.

"I am told there is one," he said, "who is guilty of heresy."

It took Stephen quite by surprise when the four strange men came to search his cell.

They were thorough. Systematically, with the skill of long practice, they ransacked his box that contained the few possessions he had brought from his former home; they investigated the bench on which he slept, his few clothes; they examined the walls and would have torn up the floor had not one of them, in the gap between the thick logs of the wall, discovered what he was looking for.

The little pamphlet.

How strange. Stephan had almost forgotten the existence of the little English tract. He had not even looked at it for months, and he only kept it in order to remind himself, from time to time, of what might be said about rich monks by those who were free to do so.

He might even have pretended he did not know what it was, but for one thing: the very day that Wilson had given it to him, while it was fresh in his mind, he had written down Wilson's translation in the margin.

When they had dragged him to the refectory, it was this that they showed to the tsar.

Ivan read it slowly; he read it aloud. From time to time he would stop, and, in a deep voice, point out to Stephen the precise nature of the disgraceful heresies written down in his own hand.

For though some Protestants, like the English merchants, were tolerated because they were foreigners—and better at least than Catholics—Ivan was deeply affronted by the tone in their writings. How could he, the Orthodox tsar, condone the insolent, antiauthoritarian arguments they used? Only months ago, the previous summer, he had allowed one of these fellows, a Hussite from Poland, to expound his views before him and all his court. His reply had been magnificent. It had been written out on parchment pages and delivered to the ignorant foreigner in a jeweled box. In rolling phrases the Orthodox tsar had crushed the impertinent heretic forever.

"We shall pray to Our Lord Jesus Christ," he had ended, "to preserve the Russian people from the darkness of your evil doctrines."

And now here was this tall, solemn monk, hiding such filth in a monastery.

When he had finished the pamphlet he glowered at Stephen.

"What have you to say to this?" he intoned. "Do you believe these things?"

Stephen looked at him sadly. What could he say?

"They are the views of foreigners," he said at last.

"Yet you keep them in your cell?"

"As a curiosity." It was true, or nearly enough.

"A curiosity." He repeated the word with slow, deliberate contempt.

"We shall see, Monk, what other curiosity we can find for you."

He glanced at the abbot.

"You keep strange monks in your monastery," he remarked.

"I knew nothing of this, lord," the old man miserably answered.

"Yet my faithful Boris Davidov did. What am I to think of such negligence?" He paused for a moment. "I need no church court to deal with this," he remarked. "Isn't that so, Abbot?"

The old man looked at him helplessly.

"You did well, Boris," Ivan sighed, "to expose this monster."

And indeed, even Boris had been astounded by the pamphlet Ivan had read out.

"How shall we punish him then?" the tsar wondered aloud, his eyes moving around the room.

Then, when he saw what he wanted, he rose from his chair.

"Come, Boris," he said, "come to help me mete out justice."

It took some time, yet even so, Boris did not feel pity. In that terrible night, heavy with wine, swept up in the tsar's hypnotic power, what they did seemed to him a final, fitting vengeance for the wrongs that he had suffered.

Let the priest die, he thought. Let the vipers—a heretic too—die a thousand deaths.

He had seen many worse deaths than this. But the particular method seemed to amuse the tsar that night.

Softly, almost gently, he had crossed the floor to where Mikhail was standing and taken out of his hand the chain by which the bear was led.

"Come, Misha," he had said softly to the bear. "Come, Misha, tsar of all the bears; the tsar of Russia has something for you to do." And he had led him over to the priest.

He had nodded to Boris, and Boris had quickly attached the other end of the chain to Stephen's belt, so that now bear and man were attached together with just two paces between them.

Putting his long arm around Boris's shoulder, he led him back to the table; then he called to the other Oprichniki.

"Now let the good tsar of the bears deal with this heretic!"

At first they had had some difficulty. Stephen, saying nothing, had gone down on his knees, touched his head to the ground and then, crossing himself as he rose, stood quite still before the bear with his head bowed in prayer. The wretched bear, starved and miserable though it was, had merely looked from side to side in confusion.

"Take my staff," Ivan had commanded, and the blackshirts had circled the pair, prodding first one and then the other, pushing the priest at the bear from behind and jabbing at the animal with the sharp iron tip of Ivan's staff.

"Hoyda! Hoyda!" Ivan cried. It was the cry of the Tatar drivers to their horses—his favorite encouragement. "Hoyda!"

They struck beast and man; they goaded the bear until, at last, confused, enraged, stung by the pain, it began to strike out at the man chained to it, since there was no other object within reach. And Stephen, bleeding from the blows from the mighty claws, could not help trying to ward them off.

"Hoyda!" cried the tsar. *"Hoyda!"*

But still the bear did not finish the business in hand and, in the end, Ivan signaled his men to drag Stephen out and complete the execution in the yard.

Yet still the night was not over. Tsar Ivan had not done.

"More wine," he commanded Boris. "Sit close by me, my friend."

It seemed as if, for a time, the tsar had forgotten the others in the room, put out of his mind, perhaps, even the priest he had just killed. He gazed at the rings on his fingers, moodily.

"See, here is a sapphire," he said. "Sapphires protect me. Here is a ruby." He pointed to a huge stone set in the ring on his middle finger. "A ruby cleanses the blood."

"You have no diamonds, Gosudar," Boris remarked.

Ivan reached out and took his hand gently, giving him a smile of surprising intimacy and frankness.

"Do you know, they say that diamonds keep a man from rage and voluptuousness, but I have never liked them. Perhaps I should."

Boris almost needed to pinch himself to make sure he was not dreaming—that it was really the tsar sitting here, side by side with him, talking to him like a brother, as intimately, as sweetly as a lover?

"Here." Ivan took a ring off another finger. "Hold it in your hand, my Boris. Let us see. Ah yes." He took the ring back after a few moments. "All is well. That is a turquoise. If it loses color in your hand, it means your death. See"—he smiled—"the color is still there."

He said nothing for a minute or so. Boris did not interrupt his thoughts.

Then suddenly Ivan turned to him.

"So," he asked, "why did you hate that priest?"

Boris caught his breath. It was not said unkindly, rather the reverse. "How did you know, lord?"

"I saw it in your face, my friend, when they brought him in." He smiled again. "He really was a heretic, you know. He deserved to die. But I would have killed him for you anyway, you know."

Boris stared down. Hearing such words from the tsar, he felt a welling of emotion. The tsar, terrible though he was, was his friend. He could scarcely believe it. Tears started to his eyes. He himself had no real understanding of how lonely he had been all these years.

Suddenly he had a great urge to share his unhappy secrets with the tsar who cared for him. Whom else should he tell, if not God's representative upon the earth, the protector of the one true church?

"You have a son, Gosudar, to continue your royal line," he began. "I have no son."

Ivan frowned.

"You have time to beget sons, my friend, if it is God's will," he murmured. "Have you then no son?" he asked, surprised.

Boris shook his head slowly.

"I hardly know. I have a son. Yet I think I have not a son."

Ivan looked at him carefully.

"You mean . . . the priest?"

He nodded.

"I think so."

Ivan said nothing for a little while, raising the goblet of wine to his lips.

"You could get other sons," he said. He looked at him meaningfully. "I have had two wives. Both gave me sons. Always remember that."

Boris pursed his lips. Emotion choked his throat. He nodded.

Ivan's eyes traveled around the room slowly. They were a little glazed. His mind seemed far away.

After a little time he rose. Boris hastened to rise also, but Ivan motioned him, with a single, royal gesture, to prostrate himself before him on the ground. Then he gently lifted the hem of his long robe and cast it over Boris's head, just as a bridegroom covered his bride at the marriage service.

"The tsar is your only father," he quietly intoned. Then, turning to the other Oprichniki, he called out, "Bring us our cloaks, and then await us here." And having put on his sable coat and his tall pointed fur hat, he said to Boris in a low voice, "Come, and follow me."

There were more stars now, in the depth of the night. Gray, ragged clouds passed slowly over the monastery, as Tsar Ivan, his tall staff tapping on the frozen snow, made his way like a ship with unfurled sails, across the empty yard and out through the gate towards the river Rus. Boris followed just behind.

Solemnly the tall tsar strode down the path, over the river's thick ice, and up the track to the little town above.

How silent it was. The high tower, with its sharp, pointed tent roof, stood out boldly against the patches of starry sky behind.

Still, speaking no word, Ivan led him up the path from the river to the gateway. The little gate at the side, manned by a single night watchman, was still open. Ivan passed through, into the starlit market square. And now he turned. "Where is your house?"

Boris pointed and was about to lead the way, but already the tsar had faced around again and was striding on, across the open space, his long staff's *tap, tap* the only sound in the town except for the faint rustle of his long robes.

Boris wondered what he intended.

The tsar did not pause as he came level with the little church whose dome shone softly in the starlight; he continued down the street until Boris ran to open the door of his house. Here, before the door, Ivan halted.

"Call down your wife. Let her come without delay," he ordered in a deep voice.

Not knowing what was to follow, Boris ran up the staircase and opened the door.

A single lamp was burning in one corner. Elena lay dozing, with the baby boy in her arms. She started to see Boris's pale face, in such a state of nervousness, suddenly at the door. But before either of them could utter a sound, they both heard Tsar Ivan's deep voice below: "Let her come down at once. The tsar is waiting."

"Come," Boris whispered.

Still not fully awake and completely mystified, Elena got up. She was dressed only in a long woolen shift and felt slippers. Holding the sleeping infant in her arms, she came out to the top of the staircase, scarcely understanding what was going on.

As she came out, she stared at Boris and, glancing down at his hands, her eyes suddenly opened wide in horror. He, too, looked down.

He had not noticed before; it must have happened when he was goading the bear.

"Your hands are covered in blood," she cried.

"I stabbed your dogs; they barked too loud at a late guest," came the deep voice from below. It was an old, bitter Russian jest. "Come down," the voice went on.

She turned to Boris.

"Who is this?"

"Do as you are told," he whispered urgently. "Hurry."

Uncertainly she descended the stairs.

"Now come to me," the tsar's voice softly commanded.

She felt the icy night air on her face and tried to cover the child. She walked over the frozen snow to where the tall figure stood, not knowing, in her confusion, how she should salute him.

"Let me see the child," Ivan said. "Put him in my arms." Letting his staff rest against his shoulder, he stretched out his long hands.

Hesitantly she passed over the child. He took it gently. It stirred but did not wake. Nervously, under the dark stare from his eyes, she stepped back a pace or two.

"So, Elena Dimitrieva," Ivan said solemnly, "did you, too, know that the priest Stephen was a heretic?"

He saw her start violently. There was, at that moment, a large gap in the clouds and the whole of the sky above Russka was clear. A quarter moon, now visible over the gateway, sent a pale light along the street. He could see her face clearly. Boris was standing to his left.

"The heretic priest is dead," he said. "Even the bears could not abide him."

There was no mistaking it. He saw her face. It was not just the horror that some weak women felt at hearing of a death, even a grisly one. It seemed as if she had received a body blow. There was no doubt: she had loved him.

"Are you not pleased to hear that an enemy of the tsar is dead?"

She could not answer.

He transferred his gaze to the child. It was a small, fair infant, not yet a year old. Miraculously it was still sleeping. He looked at it carefully in the moonlight. It was hard to tell anything by its features.

"What is the child's name?" he murmured.

"Feodor," she whispered back.

"Feodor." He nodded slowly. "And who is the father of this child?"

She frowned. What was he talking about?

"Was it my faithful servant, or was it a heretic priest?" he gently inquired.

"A priest? Who should the father be if not my husband?"

"Who indeed?"

She looked innocent, but she was probably lying. Many women were deceitful. Her father, he remembered, was a traitor.

"The tsar is not to be deceived," he intoned. "I ask you again: did you not love Stephen, the heretic priest I have rightly killed?"

She opened her mouth to protest, yet, because she had loved him, because this tall figure terrified her, found herself unable to speak.

"Let Boris Davidov decide," he said, and looking towards Boris asked: "Well, my friend, what is your judgment?"

Boris was silent.

Now, standing between them both, and with this child, half a stranger to him, in the freezing night, an extraordinary mixture of ideas and emotions crowded into his brain. Was Ivan offering him a means of escape, a divorce? No doubt the tsar could arrange such a thing: the abbot, to be sure, would do whatever the tsar said.

What did he believe? He scarcely knew himself. She loved the priest; she shrank from him. She had, by this and other means, humiliated him, tried to destroy the pride that was—should it not be?—at the center of his being. Suddenly all his resentment of her over the years came together in a single, overpowering wave. He would punish her.

Besides, if he gave way now, if he acknowledged the child that might not be his, then she had won. Yes: her final triumph over him. She would laugh to all eternity and he, the bearer of the ancient, noble *tamga* of the trident, would lay it down in the dust at her cursed feet. Not only he, but all his ancestors. At this thought, another wave of rage went through him.

And what had the tsar told him? What had he said, with such meaning?

"You can have other sons." Of course, that was it. Other sons, with another wife, to inherit. As for this boy. Whoever his father, let him suffer—for that way, infallibly, he would hurt her.

He would punish her, the child, even himself. That, he now saw, in this deep, dark night: that was what he wanted.

"The child is not mine," he said.

Ivan said not a word. Taking his staff in his right hand, holding the infant, who now began to cry, in his other, pressed against his dark, flowing beard, he turned and began to walk, with the same *tap, tap* from his staff, towards the gate.

Boris, uncertain what to do, followed at a distance behind.

What was happening? Only gradually, in her confusion and fright, had Elena understood what was being said. Now, shivering in the snow, she stared after them in horror.

"Feodor!" Her cry ran round the icy marketplace. "Fedya!"

Slipping in her felt shoes, almost falling, she threw herself wildly after them.

"What are you doing?"

Neither man looked back.

She caught up with Boris, seized him, but he pushed her aside so that she fell.

And now Tsar Ivan reached the gateway where the frightened keeper, his hand on his heart, was bowing low in mortal fear.

Ivan pointed to the door to the tower. "Open it."

Still bearing the child, he went inside. Slowly he began to mount the steps.

They were barring her way. Her husband and the foolish gatekeeper: they were barring her way at the foot of the tower.

She understood now: instinctively she understood them, and the terrors that lay in the dark labyrinths of their minds.

Forgetting everything, she clawed at the two men, fought them like an animal and, with a sudden rush, burst past them, slamming the heavy door behind her and shooting the bolt.

She ran up the wooden stairs.

She could hear him now, somewhere in the darkness above her: the creak of his footfall on the stairs, the *tap, tap* of his iron staff on every second step. He was high above.

Desperately, her heart sinking, she ran up after him. She could hear her baby crying.

"Gospodi Pomily: Lord have mercy." The words came involuntarily on her breath. Still he was high above her, so high.

It was halfway up, at the point where the tower steps came out onto the battlement that ran along the wall, that she realized she could hear nothing from above.

Ivan was already up there, in the high chamber in the tent roof where the lookout windows faced over the endless plain. She stared up at the tower that rose sheer, harsh, and silent above her, and whose wooden roof made a dark, triangular shadow across the night sky. For an instant she was uncertain what to do.

And then she heard it, her child's cry, high in that great roof above; and looking up she suddenly saw a pair of hands hold out a small white form that then, as she herself cried out with a cry, she thought, that must have reached the stars, they tossed, like a piece of jetsam, out into the night.

"Fedya!"

She threw herself against the battlements, reaching out, in a futile gesture, into the blackness, as the small white form, shocked by its fall into silence, fell past her into the deep shadows beneath where she heard the faint thud upon the ice.

At dawn the tsar left. Before doing so he insisted that he receive the traditional blessing from the frightened abbot.

He added two sleds to his little cortege: one contained a substantial quantity of the monastery's coin and plate. The other contained the bell that Boris's family had given the monks in former times, and that he intended to melt down for the extra cannon he was making.

Soon afterwards, word came that the Crimean Tatars were indeed approaching the Russian lands. The tsar, giving credence once more to the belief that he was a physical coward, absented himself in the north. The environs of Moscow were ravaged.

It was two weeks after the death of her child that Elena discovered, to her astonishment, that she was pregnant. The father of the child in her womb, as it had been before, was Boris.

There is, in the service books of the Orthodox Church, a very beautiful reading.

It is an address of the great Saint John Chrysostom, the golden-mouthed, and it is read only once a year, at the point in the late night vigil that welcomes in Easter Day.

It was with some surprise during the Easter Vigil at the Monastery of Saint Peter and Saint Paul in the year 1571—at which most of the diminished population of Russka and Dirty Place were present—that the congregation noticed a single figure enter, very quietly, at the back of the church a little after the vigil had begun.

Since the beginning of Lent, Boris had not been seen out of doors. No one was sure what was going on.

It was said that he was fasting alone. Some also said that his wife would not see him; others that they had heard him addressing her.

Again, some declared that he had tried to stop the tsar from killing his son; others that he had stood by.

So it was hardly surprising that people glanced back at him now, every few minutes, to see what he was doing.

Boris stood with his head bowed. He did not move from the back of the church, the place reserved for penitents, nor did he look up or even cross himself at the many points in the service where this is called for.

The Easter Vigil, celebrating as it does the Resurrection of Christ from the tomb, is one of mounting joy and excitement. After the long fast, almost total in the final days of Passion Week that follow Palm Sunday, the congregation is in that state of weakened, cleansed emptiness that is conducive to receiving the feast of spiritual rather than material food.

The vigil begins with Nocturne. At midnight the royal doors of the iconostasis are opened to signify the empty tomb and, with tapers in their hands, the congregation makes the Easter procession around the church. Then begins the service of Matins, and the Easter Hours, which rise towards that climactic point where the priest, standing before all the people, proclaims: *"Kristos voskresye:* Christ is risen."

And the people cry back: *"Voistino voskresye:* He is risen indeed."

Since Stephen had gone, the young priest had taken his place. This was the first time that he had stood, cross in hand, before the Holy Doors.

His own knees felt weak from fasting, but now, as he faced the congregation with their lighted tapers and smelled the thick incense that filled every corner of the church, he had a sense of exaltation.

"Kristos voskresye!"

"Voistino voskresye!"

Despite their hunger, despite everything, it seemed to the priest that a wonderful joy was filling the church. He trembled a little. This, truly, was the miracle of Easter.

"Kristos voskresye!" he cried again.

"Voistino voskresye!"

He saw that the solitary figure at the back of the church, too, was mouthing the joyous response, but was not aware that no sound proceeded from Boris's throat.

And then came the Easter kiss when, one by one, the people come forward to kiss the cross, the Gospels, and the icons, and then, greeting the priest himself, they kiss him, saying: *"Kristos voskresye"*; and he to each one of them replies, with a kiss: *"Voistino voskresye!"* Then the people kiss one another, for this is Easter, and this is the simple, affectionate way of the Orthodox Church.

But Boris, of all the people, did not come forward.

And it is then, after the Easter kiss, that the priest begins that most lovely sermon of Chrysostom.

It is a sermon of forgiveness. It reminds the congregation that God has prepared for them a feast, a reward: it speaks of the Lenten fast, by which is also meant repentance.

"If any have labored long in fasting, let him now receive his reward," the priest read out, in his gentle voice. How kindly the sermon was. If any have delayed, it said, let them not despair. For the feast of the Lord is not denied to sinners so long as they come to Him. For He shows mercy to the last, just as the first. "If any have wrought from the first hour," he read out, they should be rewarded. "If any have come at the third hour," they, too. "If any have arrived at the sixth hour," they should not now fear. "If any have delayed until the ninth hour . . ." let them approach. "If any have tarried . . ." Ah, that was it, even until the very last . . . "If any have tarried"—he glanced towards the back—"even until the eleventh hour, let him come . . ."

Whatever had been passing in his mind—whether it was that he now understood that his wife was innocent; whether it was because of his guilt for the death of Stephen and Feodor; or whether it was that, being unable any longer to sustain the burden of evil that his pride and fear of the loss thereof had placed upon him—it was certain that, as he stood in the place reserved for penitents, Boris, when he heard these lovely words, at the eleventh hour, sank to his knees and, at last, entirely broke down.

In the year 1572, the dreaded Oprichnina was officially ended. All reference to its existence was forbidden.

In the year 1581 came the first of the so-called Forbidden Years during which peasants were forbidden to leave their landlords even on Saint George's Day.

In that same year, Tsar Ivan, in a fit of anger, killed his own son.

SIX

The Cossack

1647

FREEDOM: freedom was everything.

The steppe lay all around him. How quiet it was—golden, brown, violet at the horizon, stretching forever eastward. A single hawk hovered in the sky; a tiny marmot scurried into the cover of the long, dry stalks. There was no breeze.

Here and there, unexpectedly, an ear of wheat whose seed, no doubt, had been dropped in that place by the wind in bygone years, grew among the myriad wild grasses of the endless plain.

Andrei Karpenko rode his horse slowly, making a large, lazy curve out from the big wheat field, past the little kurgan that marked its end, and away some two miles out into the wild plain before returning slowly in the direction of the little river Rus that flowed down towards the mighty Dnieper in these ancient Kievan lands.

The young man took a deep breath, so full of contentment that it was almost a sigh. How sweet was the scent of the grasses—the cornflower and broom, the wild hemp and milkwort, and, always, the unending, now withered feather grass that covered all. It was as though all these, and thousands of varieties more, had been thrown by the hand of God into a huge, flat basin, burnished by the sun all summer long, moistened with dew each day and then heated in the glowing pan once more until they gave off, in their last extremity, a final quintessence that arose from the land like a shimmering haze on this slow, late summer afternoon.

His father's farm lay just inside the line of trees, about a mile from the little settlement still known, after all these centuries, as Russka.

Andrei smiled. His father, Ostap, had been amused by the name of the place when he first came to it. "Russka—that's where my father Karp ran away from, in the north," he had often told his son. It was from this runaway that they had been given the typically Ukrainian family name of Karpenko. But the fact that he had returned to the home of far earlier ancestors was something Old Karp never knew.

Freedom: the birthright of every Cossack. It was appropriate that the family name should commemorate a rebellious love of liberty.

And now his turn had come: it was a thrilling prospect. Only the day before, the two men had appeared at the farm. They were disguised as wandering monks, and so Andrei had taken them to be; but the instant old Ostap set eyes on them he had given a broad grin and conducted them inside.

"Vodka!" he shouted to his wife. "Vodka for our guests! Andrei, listen and attend. And now, gentlemen," he had continued in a businesslike way, the moment they were seated, "what news from the south—from the camp?"

They were Cossacks. And when they had announced their exciting news, old Ostap slapped his thigh and cried out: "It's time you were off, Andrei. What an adventure! The devil—I've a good mind to go, too!"

To ride the steppe with the Cossacks: it was what young Andrei had been dreaming of since he was a boy. His horse, his equipment, everything was ready.

There was just one problem.

He was a handsome young fellow of nineteen, recently returned from the academy at Kiev where the Orthodox priests had taught him to read and write, some simple arithmetic, and even a smattering of Latin.

His hair was jet black: his skin was dark but smooth rather than swarthy; his beard was thin, like that of a Mongolian, and mostly sprouted on his chin, but he was growing a long, fine, drooping mustache. His face was round, with high cheekbones, and he had handsome, brown, almond-shaped eyes. Though some of these features came from the beautiful Tatar wife that his grandfather Karp, the runaway, had taken, Andrei's tall frame and graceful bearing were Karp's exactly. Slavic charm and ruthless Tatar eyes—it made him magnetic to many women.

Since he was still young enough to believe that human nature was consistent, it sometimes puzzled Andrei that he seemed to have two souls at war within himself: one devoted to his family and their farm; the other a wild, free spirit with neither home nor conscience, who yearned to roam the steppe to the horizon and beyond.

He was a perfect young Cossack.

And how he longed to go with those men, to the south. He could set out the very next day. Only one thing held him back—the question his worried mother had asked: "If you go, Andrei, what will become of the farm?"

Slowly and thoughtfully he rode back to the little kurgan, where he paused for a few moments to gaze around the fields and the steppe. What wonderful land it was, with its long summers and its rich black earth! For some time now, this ancient Kievan territory had acquired another name: for this was the Ukraine.

The rich Ukraine: the golden land. Why then should old Ostap complain as he surveyed his swaying wheat? "God gave us the best fields and then sent a plague of locusts to devour them." It was because the Ukraine was ruled by the Catholic king of Poland.

Four centuries had passed since Ostap's ancestress Yanka and her father had fled from the Tatars to the north. Since then, the Tatars had slowly lost their hold over the old Kievan territories, and mighty Lithuania had moved down to take their place. But the lands around the Dnieper, rich though they were, had been half deserted. Only very gradually had settlers moved back into the countryside and the shells of the once great cities.

They were dangerous frontier lands. Every few years huge raiding parties of Tatars from the Crimea would come sweeping in from the steppe to take slaves; smaller raids were constant. Like all the other settlers, when Ostap and his men went out to plow, they took their muskets with them.

Yet they were free lands. The rule of Lithuania was generally easygoing. In the countryside the land was there for the taking. As for the towns, the greater ones like Kiev and Pereiaslav were allowed pretty much to govern themselves under the long-established free burgher system from the West, known as the Magdeburg Law.

And so this part of the Ukraine might have remained: a rich frontier inhabited by Cossacks, Slav peasants, free townsmen, and Lithuanian petty gentry, who nearly all followed the old Orthodox faith of ancient Rus.

Until some eighty years before. For at the Treaty of Lublin, in 1569, the two states of Poland and Lithuania, though they had long been linked, were formally merged into one. The gentry began to convert to Catholicism, great Polish magnates started to take over huge tracts of land around the Dnieper; and though the cities kept their Madgeburg Law, the rest of the Ukraine discovered what it meant to live under contemptuous Polish lords.

How dare a Polish noble despise a Cossack! Were not the Cossacks free?

There were three main sections of their great fraternity. Four hundred miles away to the southeast, where the great river Don came down to the Black Sea shore, dwelt the Don Cossacks in their many settlements. Here, in these southern Kievan lands, lived the Dnieper Cossacks, proudly independent men like his father on his little farm by Russka. And lastly, far to the south, in the wild steppe below the Dnieper rapids, lay the Cossack horde—the Zaporozhian host—wild, unpredictable, living in a huge camp where no women were allowed, thousands strong and answerable to no man.

That was where the two fellows disguised as monks had come from.

How proud he was to be a Cossack! He had learned their exploits at his mother's knee. Who had been hired by the powerful Stroganovs, late in the reign of Ivan the Terrible, to explore and conquer the huge wilds of Siberia? Ermak the warrior and his brother Cossacks. Indeed, though Andrei did not know it, other Cossack adventurers, at this very time, were reaching those distant shores, five thousand miles away, that stared across the narrow straits to cold Alaska.

It was the Don Cossacks who had seized the great fortress of Azov, by the Black Sea, from the mighty Ottoman Turks. And it was the Zaporozhian Cossacks who had not once, but twice taken their long boats down to Constantinople and burned the Ottoman fleet under the very noses of the Turks.

Everyone feared the Cossacks. The Tatars in the Crimea feared them, so did the Turks who were the Tatars' overlords. Poland had needed their services again and again. Even the Pope had sent an envoy to the Zaporozhian camp.

"And without us Cossacks," old Ostap always said, "the tsar and his family would never have gained the throne of Muscovy."

Even this boast was half true.

Poor Muscovy. What awful torments the northern land had suffered. Soon after Ivan the Terrible's death the ancient ruling house of Muscovy had ended. For a time a great boyar related to the royal house—Boris Godunov—had tried to hold the land together, but he had sunk under the burden. Then had come those dismal years—the Time of Troubles—when plague and famine swept the land, when one after another false claimants to the throne seized power, until it was hard at times to say if any tsar ruled in Russia. Other powers had seen their chance; Sweden had invaded; and worst of all, using every kind of treachery and guile, the Polish king had tried to take the throne of Muscovy and make her Catholic.

And then, at last, great Russia had risen. She had suffered the terror of Ivan, plague and famine, and foreign invasion; but now having suffered, she arose. It was not the great princes and magnates, not the leading gentry who turned like an irresistible tide against the Poles. It was the simple peasants, the small landholders, and the grim, bearded elders of Orthodoxy from beyond the Volga River who massed with spears and axes to sweep the Catholics out.

"And we Cossacks helped them, our Orthodox brothers," Ostap would say with truth. And with rather less truth: "Without us, they would have lost."

The Poles had been driven out. A great meeting, a Zemsky Sobor, had been called, and a popular boyar family had been chosen to found a new dynasty.

In this way the family of Ivan the Terrible's first, kindly wife, who had been despised by the great magnates only fifty years before, was, in the year 1613, chosen to be their ruler, and the new Romanov dynasty was begun.

Andrei had mixed feelings about the Muscovites. Like most Ukrainians, he thought them crude. With all Cossacks, he was suspicious of any authoritarian ruler like the tsar. But the Russian people were his brothers, for a very simple reason: they were Orthodox.

"They drove the Catholic Poles out of their land: perhaps one day we can drive them out of ours, too," he sometimes said. For several generations Dnieper Cossacks had served the Polish king. Some had been given special officer status and entered on a service register that entitled them to regular pay. But the majority had been ignored. Moreover, as non-Catholics, they had fewer rights anyway.

Several times they had revolted to improve their conditions. But the revolts had been crushed, and in recent years the service Cossacks had not even been allowed their own leaders. Their chief, the *hetman,* had been a Polish appointee and many of their officers came from the Polish lesser nobility, the Szlachta. No wonder even the better-off Cossacks were discontented.

And now it seemed some kind of new campaign was afoot. That was the message the two Cossacks from the Zaporozhnian camp had brought. They were going to teach the Poles a lesson. The question was: could he go?

The sun was still high, the afternoon deliciously warm as he walked his horse towards the farm. He could not help breaking into a smile of joy as he looked at it.

A wide clearing in the trees, which approached the buildings closely on three sides. Outhouses, some of timber, some of wattle and, in their midst, the broad, stout farmhouse with its shady porch, and whose whitewashed clay walls and bright red-and-green shutters gleamed in the afternoon sun. All the buildings had thick overhanging thatched roofs that resembled so many haystacks gathered from the endless steppe before them. On the dusty turf before the farm, some chickens, half a dozen geese, a cow, and a goat picked at the ground in a desultory way: to right and left the long grass was still in the heat.

And there was his father, in front of the porch. Andrei smiled with affection.

He was a little taller than his father, but even now, strong as he was, Andrei was not sure if the old man might not have bested him in a fight.

"He's so quick," he would remark proudly to his friends.

One could see instantly that they were father and son, though old Ostap's face was a little broader than his son's. He shaved his chin, but he had a splendid drooping mustache, all gray, that hung almost to his chest. He was dressed in wide, baggy trousers and a shirt, both of linen, tied with a silk sash rather than a belt. On his feet were silk embroidered shoes with long curling toes. On his bald head was a silk cap. His face was cheerful but florid, his nose mottled. He was smoking a short Cossack pipe.

For some reason his strength, and his quick rages, seemed all the more formidable to Andrei because he knew that at any moment the old man might suddenly breathe his last. The red face, the telltale signs of breathlessness—the old warrior would not live long. He knew it, they all knew it; but with the bravado of a true Cossack he would look his son in the eye and then, quite deliberately, to challenge fate, lose his temper over some trifle. Andrei loved him for it.

But what will happen to the farm when he goes? the young man wondered. He would be the only one left. His two sisters were long since married. His brother had died a brave Cossack death, fighting, six years before. "Died like a man," old Ostap would say, raising his glass in salute, as if he did not regret it. "Mind you do the same, if things so fall out," he'd add sternly to Andrei, lest the handsome young man should think he feared to lose his last son, too.

It was not only the prospect of Ostap dying that worried his son. There were debts. He liked to live well, as befitted a Cossack gentleman: for that was how he saw himself. He liked to drink. All Cossacks drank. When he went into Pereiaslav on a market day, he'd be sure to enjoy himself. For though, as a good Cossack, he despised most townsmen, he'd usually encounter some brother-in-arms and drink the night away with him. Nor could he ever resist a fine horse. He had only to see it to buy it.

"Where does he get the money?" Andrei would sometimes ask his long-suffering mother.

"The Lord knows: but he casts his net broadly," she would reply.

There were the itinerant merchants in Pereiaslav and even Kiev who went out to join the caravans that followed the ancient salt route across the steppe to the Crimea. They lent money. So did a merchant in Russka. And so did the Jews. And they all lent to Ostap, on the security of his farm. It was a fine farm. There were excellent crops of wheat and millet. There was part of the big wood, upstream, where Ostap owned a hundred beehives. "But we need you," his graying mother had told him frankly. "Because if someone doesn't manage the farm—and your father—we'll lose everything. And I can't do it."

He wanted to go. He longed to go. Yet as he reached the farm, Andrei was still uncertain what to do. He was a little disconcerted therefore, as he dismounted by his father, when the old man abruptly said: "You're leaving in the morning. I've prepared all you'll need."

Even as Ostap spoke, Andrei saw his mother coming out of the house looking worried. He glanced at them both while his father chewed contentedly on his pipe.

"Andrei!"

It was all she said.

He paused. The prospect of going thrilled him, but he looked at his father with concern. "What about the farm, Father?" he brought himself to ask.

"What about it?"

"How will you manage?"

"Very well, damn you. Are you ready to leave?" Sensing opposition, Ostap was starting to grow red.

Andrei hesitated. He caught his mother's eye, saw her look of pleading. "I'm not sure. Perhaps I should leave later."

"What!" his father roared. "Are you disobeying me?"

"Not exactly."

"Silence, you young cur. You'll obey your father." Suddenly Ostap's heavy brows knitted and his eyes gleamed with anger. His whole body seemed to grow rigid. "Or is it," he asked menacingly, "that I've bred a coward? Is that it? Are you a coward?" The last word was said with such apparent contempt and loathing, and it was such a calculated insult, that Andrei felt his own body tense and his face go white with anger. It seemed, at any moment, that father and son might fly at each other's throats.

The cunning old fox, the youth suddenly thought. He's goading me deliberately so that I won't do as Mother wants. And even though I know what he's up to, I'm still getting angry.

"Well?" Ostap thundered. "Have I bred a coward? Are you really afraid to fight? Must I go and die in shame?"

"Die as you please," Andrei cried with frustration.

"So, is that how you talk to your father!" Ostap was now beside himself. He glanced left and right for something to strike Andrei with.

And who knew what might have happened next if, at this moment, three figures had not come riding out of the woods straight towards the little group? For the sight of them reduced both men to silence.

One was splendidly dressed and rode a magnificent bay. The other two, dressed in long black coats, rode smaller horses. The first was a Polish noble; the other two were Jews.

That a Polish noble should ride in such company was no particular surprise. For generations now, the Polish Commonwealth was the one country in eastern Europe where the Jews could live at peace. Indeed, the authorities even allowed Jews to carry swords, like noblemen.

They drew up in front of the porch without dismounting. The Pole glanced down at the family before him coolly, then surveyed the farm thoughtfully. Andrei noticed that the gold brocade on his beautiful coat glinted in the sun; his long, aristocratic hands rested easily upon the saddlebow. His face was oval, pale, and except for a thin, dark mustache, clean-shaven. His eyes were large, blue, and rather luminous. A kinsman of the great Lithuanian-Polish magnate, Vyshnevetsky, who owned vast tracts of land in the eastern Ukraine, Stanislaus was the local official of this region, overseeing numerous little forts like Russka, which Vyshnevetsky owned, on the edge of the steppe.

He remained silent for a few moments, but when he finally spoke, Andrei could only stare at him dumbfounded.

"Well, Ostap," he remarked casually, "we're taking over the farm."

For several moments there was complete silence. They were all too astonished to speak.

"What do you mean—take over?" Andrei suddenly burst out. "This farm is ours."

Stanislaus looked at him with mild interest.

"No, it isn't. It never was. You are just tenants."

Andrei was so astonished that he even forgot to wait for his father to speak.

"We pay nothing to anyone for our land," he burst out.

"Correct. It was granted you for thirty years free of obligations, and now the time is up."

Andrei looked at his father. Old Ostap for a moment appeared confused.

"That was thirty years ago," he mumbled.

"Exactly. And now the Vyshnevetskys have sold the estate to me. You owe me service."

It was not an unusual situation. In order to attract settlers to the frontier lands, the Polish magnates in the past had often granted lands with exemptions for ten, twenty, or even thirty years. Men like Ostap took such lands and then, as the years passed, came to think of them as perpetually free: so much so that Ostap had entirely omitted to mention the original condition of his tenure to Andrei, even if he had remembered it himself.

"I've been here thirty years," the old man now stated angrily, "and that means I own it." As far as he, or many like him were concerned, this statement was correct.

"Have you a charter that says so?"

"No, damn you. My charter is this." And he held up his clenched fist as though wielding a sword.

Stanislaus watched him calmly.

"You owe labor service for this land," he remarked.

"Labor?" Ostap now erupted.

"Naturally," the Pole replied.

Andrei gasped. Labor! The Pole was suggesting that his father, a man of honor, should work for him in the fields like a common peasant, a serf.

"I have worn the white coat, you Polish dog," the old Cossack fumed. "I am an officer. A registered Cossack. No man can make me work in the fields."

Stanislaus shook his head.

"You were on the register. But not now."

Nothing was more vital to the Dnieper Cossacks than the register. Normally it contained about five thousand names of the Cossacks recognized as military servitors by the king of Poland. These were the free men treated, roughly speaking, as an officer class. Sometimes after a Cossack rising, the register had been enlarged. But then it would be contracted again. Ostap had once, briefly, figured in the white coat of a registered officer, but had since lost his place.

And the problem was that, so far as the Polish king was concerned, any Cossack not on the register was a peasant—and therefore liable to labor like a serf.

This was just the life that Karp had gone south to escape. Not only was it degrading, it was outrageous.

"Back in the reign of Stefan Batory, all Cossacks were made noblemen," Ostap had always told Andrei; and although the Polish king had in fact done no such thing, most Cossacks firmly believed that they were, if not quite noble, just as good as any noble.

So it was from the bottom of his heart that Ostap now cried out: "A Cossack is a gentleman, you Polish swine." He spat with disgust. "But what would a Pole know about nobility?"

Stanislaus looked at him with secret amusement. He understood the old man but despised him.

What, he wondered, could old Ostap know of the life of a Polish noble, let alone the great magnates? What could this crude farmer know of the splendid palaces of Poland—those great European houses filled with French and Italian furniture, Renaissance paintings, Gobelin tapestries; a glittering world of ballrooms, libraries, huge receptions, where Polish lords in rich brocades or hussar uniforms cultivated their minds as well as their manners and might converse in French or Latin as easily as Polish? Even the French remarked that the Polish lords seemed to live in paradise.

The Polish lords were proud. They were not the slaves of their ruler, as the Russians were of their tsar. They chose their kings—and circumscribed their power in the great Sejm, the nobles' parliament. Not for nothing was the great Polish state, of which the Ukraine was a part, called the Commonwealth.

But the Commonwealth was for the nobility. Like most Polish lords, Stanislaus looked down upon the Cossacks. Though they were brave, he saw them as little more than brigands and runaway peasants who gave themselves airs.

Above all, he despised their Orthodox religion and their illiterate mumbling to their icons.

"It is," he would say definitively, "a religion fit only for serfs."

How far indeed it was from the romantic Catholicism of this Polish gentleman who, for all his cruelty and contempt towards the peasants, saw himself as a crusading, courtly knight in a twilight world, under dark clouds of foreboding.

This religious split between lord and peasant in the Ukraine had, if anything, been made worse half a century before, when the subtle Catholic Church had come to a great historic compromise with the old Orthodox bishops centered at Kiev. By this arrangement the Orthodox bishops had agreed to acknowledge the Pope as their spiritual head, so long as he would allow them to celebrate their services in, for all practical purposes, the Orthodox way.

This was the start of the so-called Greek Catholic, or Uniate Church.

The trouble was that many of the Orthodox had refused to accept the compromise, so that now in the Ukraine there were three Churches instead of two: Catholic, Uniate, and Orthodox. The Cossacks, moreover, had decided to champion the old Orthodox faith. In every city, especially in the eastern Ukraine around Kiev, the citizens formed brotherhoods to defend their faith so that now there was a powerful religious movement dedicated to opposing both the Catholic Poles and any kind of compromise with them.

It was, Stanislaus thought, just the kind of movement that would appeal to a Cossack like Ostap. He felt very little sympathy for him.

So now, with a casual wave of his hand, he indicated the thinner of the two Jews who had accompanied him.

"This is Mordecai," he said casually. "I have given him the lease of this place, so you'll be working for him. He'll tell you what to do, won't you, Mordecai?" he remarked easily.

It was the final insult. As Ostap looked from the Pole to the Jew, he could not himself have said which one he hated the most. Religiously, he distrusted the Catholic more than the Jew. For although his grandfather had come from Muscovy, where the fear of Judaism was often deep, Ostap had lived all his life in the Ukraine, where, ever since the time of the Khazars, the Orthodox and Jewish communities had usually tolerated each other well enough. The hatred he now felt for the Jew was not in fact based upon his religion but upon the particular role in which the Polish overlords had used them—usually as tax collectors, liquor-stall concessionaires, and rent agents. Consequently, men like Ostap found that, though in fact they were always in debt to the Poles, the face of the creditor they saw was nearly always Jewish. It was an arrangement that suited the Poles very well, for whenever their extortions went too far, they blamed their agents.

It is generally agreed that the root of the endemic anti-Semitism in South Russia lay in this cynical and unfortunate Polish system.

And no part of the system was worse than the practice of leasing, which Stanislaus was now planning to use. It was simple enough: Mordecai would hold the farm, probably on a short lease of only two or three years. For this he would collect and pay Stanislaus a stiff rent; and in turn, Stanislaus would support him in whatever exactions he made to get extra profits out of the peasants. Whereas Stanislaus might demand three or four days' work from Ostap, therefore, this adding of an intermediary who was also looking for his profit might mean that Ostap finished up working five or even six days for someone else. And since justice lay in the Polish courts, there was probably nothing he could do about it.

The old man said nothing at all. Outwardly he seemed calm, though Andrei knew that this only masked a seething rage within.

"Good," Stanislaus said cheerfully. "That's all settled then." Now he glanced at the other Jew. "There's just one other matter. It seems you owe Yankel here for your liquor. He says you haven't paid him in two years. Give me the bill, Yankel. Ah yes." He handed it down to Ostap, who took it glumly, glanced at it, and looked distressed.

"The Jew is lying," Ostap said firmly; but Andrei knew from the tone of his voice that his father was not certain of his ground.

Mordecai was a stranger; but Andrei knew Yankel well enough. He was a fat, rather cheerful fellow who operated the liquor store in Russka. Almost everyone in the area owed him money, but, though he charged interest for it, he was not unduly harsh. He had two children—a girl and a little boy; and as Andrei considered his father's formidable intake of vodka, he suspected that Yankel's claim was perfectly justified.

"Well, are you going to pay it?" the Pole demanded.

"I am not," Ostap replied.

"As you please. Yankel," he went on, "go to the stable there and pick out the best horse you see. That should do it."

Yankel hesitated a moment. He had been tempted to go to the Pole after twelve months of trying to get Ostap to pay what he owed, but now he was starting to regret it. He had no wish to make the Cossack his sworn enemy.

"Get on with it," Stanislaus ordered peremptorily, and Yankel, with a look of embarrassment, went off. A few minutes later he returned with a horse that was by no means the Cossack's best.

"Is that it?" Stanislaus asked.

"It will do, your High Nobility."

The Pole shrugged.

"Good-bye," he said, carelessly, and with that he was off, the two Jews following behind.

For some time no one spoke. Then Andrei turned to his father.

"I ride south tomorrow," he said quietly.

Ostap nodded. Even Andrei's mother did not complain. There was nothing to lose anymore.

"When I come back with our brothers," Andrei remarked with cold

fury, "we shall kill every Pole and Jew in the Ukraine. Then the farm will
be ours."

"Good idea," Ostap replied.

There was one thing left to do that night; but Andrei waited until he
could hear his father's snores in the yard before he slipped out of the
house.

Cautiously he crossed the yard. Old Ostap liked to sleep outside in the
summer; he would wrap himself in a blanket and lie in front of the porch
gazing up at the stars and humming quietly to himself until he fell asleep.
It reminded him of the years past when he slept in the open on campaign.

"I give each star a name, you know," he once told Andrei. "Each one's
an old comrade and I choose the star that seems to suit their character
best. So I look up at the Plow and I say to myself: 'Yes, there's old Taras;
and there's my friend Shilo! God knows how many Tatars his strong arm
killed.' They flayed him alive when they caught him, you know." He
sighed. "I see their faces, up there in the night sky. And then I fall
asleep."

Each year, when summer was over, the old man would stay out a few
nights longer than he should, wrapping himself in a sheepskin instead
of a blanket, and downing God knows how many tots of vodka to keep
out the cold. After a week or so of this he'd stagger in grumbling that
his bones ached, and then give it up.

The night was still warm now, however. His snores were comfortable.

Softly Andrei made his way along the path. There was a half moon,
low on the horizon, that gave the forest an agreeable sheen. He was so
full of youth and his heart was dancing so lightly that, scarcely thinking
about it, he began to run, gathering new energy and joy with every step
he took. In the darkness it almost seemed to Andrei that he was flying
along the starlit path.

He passed the still pond where, the children said, *rusalki* dwelt. A few
minutes later he was emerging onto the edge of the village's big field. He
was at Russka.

Nothing had changed. True, the little stone church from the days of
Monomakh had been burned down by the Mongols; and later the village
had lain deserted for two hundred years. And yet nothing had changed.
For in this land, every wooden house sooner or later was lost to fire, or
age. Settlements, like the fields around them, had their seed time and
harvest: it was as if Russka had been left fallow for a time and was now
under cultivation once more. And how else should the place look, but a
group of huts on one side of the stream, and a little fort with a palisade
around it on the other? There was a wooden church, with a little tower,
inside the fort. In the Ukrainian manner, it was arranged as a simple
Greek cross with a cupola over the center and smaller cupolas over its
eastern and western ends and over the two transepts. In the tower was
a single bell.

Andrei did not need to cross the river. Instead he crept stealthily up
to a large wooden hut at the edge of the hamlet. A watchdog cocked its

head at his approach and came forward wagging its tail and whimpering softly until Andrei quieted it.

The building had an upper story; in the end wall, a single window looked out under the eaves, with carved shutters and a little balcony in front of it. The shutters were open, to let in the night air.

Carefully, but easily, Andrei climbed up and sat astride the balcony, before tapping gently on the window frame.

"Anna."

Silence.

"Anna, I'm coming in."

This time there was a faint sound from within. A pale form appeared in the shadows of the room. There was a soft laugh.

"So what do you want, my young brave, calling on a girl at night?" The low voice laughed again. "Be off or I'll set the dogs on you."

Andrei chuckled.

"They won't do anything."

"I could call my father."

"You could. But you won't." He started to swing his leg over the window frame, but she moved forward quickly, caught his ankle, and pushed it out again.

"No you don't."

Now he could see her, and it made him catch his breath. Anna was the daughter of a Cossack like his father; but her mother was from the faraway Caucasus. The result of this union was a girl unlike any other in the region; the villagers called her the Circassian. She was almost as tall as he was, slim, with dark brown hair, pale creamy skin, and she held her head so high that she seemed to stare at the world as proudly as a young warrior. Indeed, her bold eyebrows, straight, strong nose, and firm chin might almost have been those of a handsome youth; but a slight upturning at the end of the nose, and the wonderful, full lips, both proud yet always, it seemed, about to open into a warm kiss, converted any masculinity in her other features and made her, for Andrei and many others, tantalizingly desirable.

She was sixteen and unmarried.

"Nor will I be, until I see a man I like," she had announced to her parents and the village in half-mocking defiance.

In the manner of the Cossack girls, she lived a free and easy life with the young men of the village. Some of them might even steal a kiss— though if they tried to go too far they would find her more than a match for them and like as not be sent sprawling.

But since Andrei had returned from the seminary a few months before, there had been a subtle change in her manner.

Little as the Poles might think of the Orthodox Church, in the last twenty years it had made great strides. Under an ambitious young churchman, a Moldavian noble by birth called Peter Mogila who had come first to the Monastery of the Caves and then become Metropolitan at Kiev, an academy and numerous schools had been set up. Though they imitated the Jesuit schools of the Poles, they were strictly Orthodox—

Ostap would never have sent Andrei otherwise. The new movement set up printing presses too, and already literacy was becoming widespread.

To Anna, therefore, young Andrei was the nearest thing to a gentleman she had come across. He could read and write. He spoke a little Latin and Polish. His father's farm was a fair size. And young Andrei was undeniably handsome.

It was not long before people were whispering: "He's the one," or "a fine couple"; and she found that she had no objection.

For above all, she sensed that within Andrei's charm and youthful exuberance lay the one quality she admired above all others—the one thing that truly attracted her.

"He has ambition," she remarked to her father.

This had not meant much to the Cossack; but she had taken care to let young Andrei know where she stood before the harvest was begun.

"Most Cossacks are fools, Andrei," she remarked bluntly. "They dream about fighting and they drink themselves stupid. But a few are wiser and they rise. Some of them even enter the gentry. Do you agree?"

He had nodded. He understood her.

And he would already have suggested that his father approach hers to arrange a marriage, but one thing held him back. First let me go on campaign, he thought. I will see a little of the world before I marry.

But now he was to leave. He looked at her.

She was wearing only a linen shift, which had come half loose as she hurriedly got up. Not only could he see her pale form; to his delight he suddenly realized that he could see her breast, almost all of it. It was not large: it was rather high and narrow; through the gauzelike linen he could see the dark tip of it. His heart pounded.

She realized what he was staring at but did not even deign to rearrange her dress. Her pride was her protection. "Look if you dare" her body seemed to say.

In a few whispered words he told her that he was leaving. He told her they were going to fight the Poles. He almost told her about the loss of the farm, but he suddenly felt embarrassed and ashamed and did not mention it.

She'll find out soon enough, he thought gloomily.

He could not tell what she thought of the news of his departure.

"When I get back, I shall marry you," he said boldly.

"Will you indeed!"

"You like me, don't you?"

She laughed lightly.

"Perhaps. Perhaps there are other handsome men too."

"Such as? Who's better than me?"

She cast about in her mind, wondering how to taunt him.

"There's Stanislaus the Pole," she said with a playful smile. "He's a handsome man. And rich."

For a second he gasped, but then he remembered she did not know about today's episode.

"He's a Pole," he said grimly.

She wondered why he suddenly looked so downcast.

"Maybe I will, maybe I won't," she said. "Maybe you won't come back. Then what would I do?"

"I'll come back. If I come back, you'll marry me?" he suddenly said, realizing belatedly she had just given him an opening.

"Maybe."

"Let me in."

"Not until we're married."

"Try me out. Make sure you like me."

"I'll take it on trust."

"And if I die, I'll never have made love to you. Let me at least—just once—take that with me to the grave."

She burst out laughing.

"You can die thinking about it."

"Perhaps I will," he said unhappily.

"Perhaps."

"A kiss at least."

"A kiss then."

Now they kissed; and it seemed to Andrei that while they kissed the moon must have moved across half the glittering stars in the night.

When he looked back, a little later, she had closed the shutters.

1648

ALL around, that April day, the huge camp was bustling with activity. In the warmth of early spring, the ground itself seemed to be steaming.

New contingents had been arriving every day; the number in the camp had swollen to some eight thousand men.

Only Cossacks came here. No one interfered with the well-defended island below the Dnieper rapids. Once, a dozen years before, the Poles had built a stout fortress a little way upriver, in the hope of intimidating the unruly Zaporozhians. They had called the fortress Kodak. The Cossacks had sacked it within months.

The island was full. The usual brushwood and log cabins, some covered with horsehide, others with turf, had been supplemented by every kind of temporary shelter. The latest arrivals had been putting up felt tents on the opposite bank. There were corrals of horses and baggage wagons everywhere.

This was the Cossack host. It contained all manner of men. There were fellows of Tatar blood, Turkish tribesmen from the east, Mordvinians from beyond the Oka River, renegade Poles, and runaway peasants from Muscovy; there were farmers, small landowners, even noblemen from the Ukraine. Rich and poor, this colorful collection made up the huge fraternity of the host. There was not a woman in the place.

The Ukrainians, who now counted themselves as part of the Zaporozhian host, mostly wore the loose, baggy trousers and broad cummerbunds that the Zaporozhians had originally copied from the Tatars of the steppe. Then there were their brothers, the Don Cossacks, who had come in large parties to join them and brought with them other Cossacks from even farther away, across the Don by the foothills of the Caucasus Mountains. These looked more like Georgians and Circassians, with open coats, slanting pockets, and heavy braiding. They wore black sheepskins and, when they rode, enveloped themselves in their huge capes, called *burkas,* which they used for sleeping blankets as well. There were even Cossacks from Siberia and the Urals, who favored red shirts and high, Muscovite hats trimmed with fur.

There was tension in the air. At any moment, everybody knew, they would be off; but since this was the Cossack camp, where things must be done democratically, no one could assume anything until the meeting had been held and the vote taken.

Meanwhile, on every side, the Cossacks were passing the time and relieving the tension in the usual ways. Many were drinking. Once they set off, however, drinking would be forbidden, even on pain of death. Here and there a Cossack was playing an eight-stringed lute and humming to himself some endless ballad about the great exploits of the past. In one place a group of energetic young fellows had got one of the older men to give them a tune on a balalaika while another joined in with an instrument rather like a small set of bagpipes: they were dancing wildly, squatting down, kicking their legs out, then leaping up high into the air.

And in the midst of all this commotion, a splendid young Zaporozhian Cossack and his companion were striding through the middle of the camp.

If old Ostap could have seen Andrei at this moment, how proud he would have been.

Over his wide, baggy trousers he wore a fine satin kaftan. His cummerbund was made of silk, his boots were of red morocco. Usually he wore a tall sheepskin hat, but at present he was uncovered, revealing a head that had been carefully shaved except for a patch in the middle that had been gathered into a topknot. At his side was a splendid curved sword.

As soon as he had arrived the previous autumn, Andrei had undertaken the first initiation of a Zaporozhian and taken a boat through the treacherous Dnieper rapids. He was itching to go on campaign so that he could be accepted as a full Cossack. But already, not just in his appearance but in his whole manner, there was a new toughness that, joined to his youthful elegance, made him stand out from the rest.

His companion was a strange fellow. He was huge, also wore a topknot, like a Zaporozhian, but his coat and black sheepskin suggested he had come from somewhere near the Caucasus region. He also wore a full brown beard, like a Muscovite.

"My father ran away to the Don and he kept his beard, so why shouldn't I keep mine?" he had explained to Andrei, who had admired its length. "It's a sign of respect," he added, quite seriously.

Stepan was thirty. He was immensely strong and there was no one in the whole camp who could outwrestle him; but like many large men, he was gentle. Only in battle did he work himself up into a kind of transcendental rage that made even brave men scatter before him. For all this strength, however, he had the mind of a child. He was also immensely superstitious. The other Cossacks called him, affectionately, the Ox.

It was strange that the graceful young man from the Dnieper and this naïve giant from the Don should have become close friends, but each admired qualities in the other and they shared their secrets unreservedly.

Though the ethos of the camp was strictly military—women were only a useless distraction when the Cossacks went on their raids—Stepan had long ago confided in Andrei that when this business was over, he intended to give up his wandering life and get married.

"I'm not like you, though," he said, gazing at Andrei's fine clothes. "I've got nothing except the clothes I stand in." Indeed, his heavy blue coat was badly frayed at the edges and in several places the gold braid was coming off.

"If the Poles take our farm I shan't have anything either," Andrei had confessed. "But don't worry, old Ox. I'll get the farm back and you can go home with a wagonload of plunder. Tell me, though," he asked curiously, "who's the girl you're going to marry?"

Stepan smiled.

"The one."

"What one?"

"The only one of course. The one fate has reserved for me."

"You haven't met her?"

"Not yet."

"Do you know anything about her?"

"Nothing."

"So she might be a Tatar, or a Georgian, a Mordvinian, or"—he laughed—"a Polish lady?"

Stepan nodded and smiled.

"Any of those."

"You don't mind which?"

"How can I mind? It's not for me to choose. I keep my mind blank. I form no picture. I just wait."

Andrei smiled. "You sound just like one of the priests at the seminary. He told me that's how he tries to pray."

"Ah, that's right," Stepan said earnestly, "that's just it. That's how we should lead all of our lives."

"I daresay you're right," Andrei replied. "But tell me—this magical girl—how will you recognize her when you see her?"

"I shall know."

"God will tell you?"

"Yes."

"Dear old Ox, how I love you," Andrei had said, suddenly embracing him.

Today, however, as they walked through the camp, there was a very different subject on their minds. At any moment they would be off, striking into the heart of the Ukraine. Moreover, as Andrei had discovered during the winter months in camp, the rebellion this time was no minor revolt. Since the Poles had put down the last Cossack uprising, some fifteen years before, the peace of the Ukraine concealed a seething resentment. Only when he got to the camp and met scores of others like himself did Andrei realize that the kind of treatment his father had received was commonplace. In the western parts, nearer Poland, conditions were even worse and most of the population had already been reduced to utter serfdom. About half the small estates in the Ukraine were now in the hands of Jewish leaseholders.

And the current preparations for an uprising were due to a man rather like his own father, though richer and better educated, whose estate had not only been illegally seized by a Polish subprefect, but whose ten-year-old son had been beaten to death for protesting. His name, ever since revered in the history of the Ukraine, was Bogdan Khmelnitsky; and though writers since often refer to him, for simplicity, as Bogdan, the Cossacks at the time called him Khmel.

It was Khmel who had come down to the Zaporozhians to ask for help. It was he who, for months, had been sending secret agents to villages all over the Ukraine. And it was Khmel—understanding very well the strength and disposition of the Polish forces, and seeing the weaknesses of the fearless but rather disorganized Cossack cavalry—who had undertaken the most brilliant stroke of all. That February Khmel had crossed the steppe to Bakhchisarai, the headquarters of the Tatar khan of the Crimea, and by a ruse had convinced him that the Poles were planning to attack him. That was why, this very day, news had come that no less than four thousand of the devastating Tatar cavalry would reach the Zaporozhian camp the next day.

The combined force would strike into the heart of the Ukraine; and, as it did so, the entire country was going to rise.

"We'll teach those Poles a lesson," Andrei predicted. "And then the farm will be ours."

Even with such a force, it was a daring plan. The armies the Poles could muster were still much larger, and well trained. But even if the Cossacks succeeded, the question remained—what next? What would they demand—what were they fighting for?

Hardly anyone seemed to know. The Polish oppression would have to end, of course. Then men like his father would be restored to wealth and honor. There would be a lot of booty for everyone, naturally: there always was after a big Cossack expedition. But beyond that, Andrei confessed to himself that he had no clear idea.

Strangely, it was simpleminded Stepan who had not only considered the matter but had a detailed answer. "You must have a free Cossack state," he told Andrei, "with equality for all and every man an equal vote. Just like the Don Cossacks. No rich men, no poor men: no landlords and serfs; no best men and lesser men. We're all equal brothers on the Don."

And although Andrei knew that this view of the Don Cossack state was a little romanticized, he also knew that this communistic democracy was widely favored by the poorer Cossacks everywhere.

How noble it sounded. A brotherhood of man.

"Of course," the Ox added, "we'll kick out all the Catholics and Jews first: you can't have a brotherhood of man with them. But then everything will be all right."

Andrei supposed so. Yet he was not sure. Didn't he want to get richer?

Didn't he want to become a gentleman and own estates, with ambitious Anna at his side?

His thoughts were interrupted by a sudden roar from the edge of the camp. That was the signal. Usually they beat the kettledrums to summon an assembly, but with so many present they were using cannon.

In the space of a few minutes, thousands of men had gathered at the meeting place where the Cossacks' little wooden church now looked like a carnival float being carried by the crowd.

To loud cries of approval, the head of the camp—the *ataman*—now led out Bogdan to address them.

He was a big, bluff fellow with a rather coarse, bearded face. He looked like the heavy Cossack squire he was. But when roused he had an unexpected gift for oratory. Now, in a few short sentences, he recounted to them once again his woes, and the disgraceful treatment he had received from the Poles. Everyone knew the tale well, but they wanted to hear it again: it was a question of form, and he did not let them down.

"Is this, brothers, how brave Cossacks should be treated?" he bellowed.

"Never," they shouted back.

"Is this our reward for services—that we should be asked for our lives in war, and in peace treated worse than any of us would treat a dog?" The peroration was coming. He looked from side to side. "Are we to suffer forever, while the brotherhood, wives, families, children are butchered, or are we going to fight?"

"We fight," they roared.

Now the *ataman* stepped forward.

"I have a proposal, brother Cossacks," he cried.

"Say it!" a hundred voices yelled back. The matter had long been agreed, but the vote must still take place.

"I propose that Bogdan Khmelnitsky be elected our grand chief, the representative of all the Cossacks in the Ukraine. I propose he be *hetman*. Who agrees?"

"We agree!" the whole camp shouted.

"Let the standard be brought forth, then."

And now even Andrei's heart missed a beat. They were bringing forward the famous horsetail standard of the Cossacks; and once that was raised, even Polish lords and Ottoman Turks might tremble, for the free Cossacks of the steppe would fight to the death.

"We march at dawn," the *hetman* announced.

There have during human history, in many countries, been worse years than was the year of 1648 in Poland.

But in all the long annals of human cruelty and stupidity—which, alas, do not seem to change—the year 1648 deserves, for several reasons, a particular mention.

It also changed Russian history.

From mid-April the Cossack army—eight thousand Cossacks, four guns, with four thousand more Tatars just behind—advanced up the western side of the great river Dnieper, across the steppe. Ahead of them they carried a huge red banner sewn with an image of the archangel.

The Poles knew that the Cossack rebels were coming and made preparations.

The Polish military commander, the magnate Potocki, made his headquarters on the west bank about eighty miles below Pereiaslav. From here he sent forward a vanguard in two parts. In the first, under command of his own son, were fifteen hundred Poles together with some twenty-five hundred regular service Cossacks; in the second, another twenty-five hundred service Cossacks and a contingent of German mercenaries. The idea was that the vanguard was to garrison and refortify Kodak.

It was either an act of foolishness or of extraordinary arrogance to assume that these troops would remain loyal: especially since Bogdan's agents had already infiltrated them.

The group with the Germans, as soon as they saw the rebels, voted to join them. They killed two of their officers and the Germans. The next day, May 6, unlucky young Potocki found his Cossacks had gone too; and after a useless stand by a stream known as Yellow Waters, he and his Poles were slaughtered.

The Cossack army came up with the main Polish force ten days later, near the modest town of Khorsun, which lay only some thirty miles southwest of Pereiaslav. Here the combined Cossacks and Tatars fell upon them.

The battle of Khorsun was a complete victory. Potocki and no less than eighty Polish lords were taken. The loot was splendid. The Cossacks also acquired forty-one pieces of artillery and thousands of horses.

News of the victory spread like wildfire. And the Ukraine rose in revolt.

Andrei and Stepan were rich.

They had fought side by side, carved a swathe through the Polish soldiers; and where Stepan would plow forward in a blind ecstasy of rage, Andrei had not only fought bravely, but had protected his friend's back and wisely steered him so that Bogdan himself had noticed them and remarked: "The big one is brave, but the young one's cunning as well."

At the end of the battle, when the whole force had erupted into a wild orgy of drinking and dancing, the *hetman* himself had strode over and, in addition to the loot that every Cossack got, presented each of the two men with six of the finest Polish horses.

"Another battle like this," Andrei remarked to his friend, "and you'll be able to buy your farm."

The largest rewards, however, went to the Tatar cavalry. They were given all the Polish nobles to ransom. Large parties set off with these captives towards the Crimea.

"The Tatars always get rich," Stepan told Andrei.

"They fight like devils, though," the young man replied enthusiastically.

"Perhaps," Stepan said sadly. "But I know them better than you: just wait and see."

For Andrei, it was a thrilling time. He had become a fully fledged Cossack, and he felt it. Not only was this an exciting adventure for him personally, but the larger, political events in which he was playing a part were taking a dramatic turn.

For Bogdan's revolt could not have happened, for the Ukrainians, at a better moment. Just after the humiliating victory of Khorsun, news reached the camp that the king of Poland had died. In the Polish capital of Warsaw, until a new king was elected, the Catholic primate and the chancellor were in charge. Bogdan had caught the Commonwealth at its weakest moment.

The whole of Eastern Europe was in a diplomatic uproar. Messengers flew from the Polish capital to Moscow and to the Ottoman Turks. The sultan was urged to recall the Tatars, who were his vassals. The tsar was asked, if he valued peace with Poland, to send troops to attack the Crimean khan. The Polish nobility was appealed to, to raise troops from their estates.

Meanwhile, in the days that followed the battle, news came from all over the Ukraine of peasants rising against their Polish landlords; and a stream of men started to arrive at the Cossack camp—some mounted and fully equipped, others with no more than the jawbone of a horse tied to a staff—but all longing to do battle.

And in the midst of all this, Bogdan calmly sent messages of his own to the Poles and to the tsar of Russia, and prepared to play one off against the other.

"Now we shall see a change," Andrei exclaimed to his friend.

"Perhaps," Stepan replied.

It was in the middle of this time of consolidation that Andrei obtained permission to make a brief visit to Russka. He took Stepan with him.

His reason for going was twofold: he wanted to see that his parents were safe, and he wanted to leave his loot and his horses at the farm. His father might sell some of the horses and keep the money hidden for him.

But in fact, the *hetman* Bogdan was glad to let the young man go, for he had an important mission for him.

"The magnate Vyshnevetsky owns your village, doesn't he?" he asked. "Well, I hear he's collecting men to attack us. Take ten men with you; find out all you can and bring me news." He gave Andrei an encouraging smile. "You went to a seminary, they tell me."

"Yes, *Hetman.*"

"Good. I'll be watching you next time we fight."

Andrei knew what that meant. In a year, perhaps, he might even be made an *esaul*—a Cossack captain. If the rebellion succeeded, the path to fortune might be opening up before him.

The party rode off in high spirits.

How beautiful the country was, as they made their way eastward over the plain under the warm June sun.

Occasionally they encountered stretches of woods and little coppices;

sometimes there were willows and pines growing along the banks of the streams. But for the most part they saw only the broad, open steppe, with its delicate, waving feather grass.

There was plenty of game, and fish to catch, but they rode steadily, resting at noon, traveling swiftly in the morning and evening.

Although he possessed the fine Polish horses, Andrei preferred to ride his smaller, Cossack steed. Bred for strength and endurance, these sturdy unshod animals could carry a man as much as fifty miles a day across the steppe. By the end of the second day, the party had reached the mighty Dnieper and crossed it by raft. In another day, they would be at Russka.

They came upon the first sign of trouble at midmorning. It was at one of the tiny wooden forts, smaller than Russka, that served as outposts for the Polish administration. As they approached, the Cossacks saw that the place was deserted, and they would have passed by without stopping if Andrei had not noticed something strange hanging from the open gateway.

It was a Polish official—one could see that at once from his fine clothes. He had been hanged. But the Ukrainian peasants had not been content until they had been cruel; and so they had first killed his wife and children in front of him and then hung their heads, on a rope, around his neck. It was a miserable ending that many Poles were to suffer that summer.

An hour later they came to a Cossack farmstead, not unlike his father's. This had been burned to the ground and thoroughly looted. But when Andrei began to curse the Poles, Stepan stopped him.

"Look." He picked up an arrow from the ground. "It wasn't the Poles. It was the Tatars on their way back."

Andrei looked and nodded.

"We gave them all the Polish nobles," he remarked sadly. "Wasn't that enough?"

"Nothing's ever enough for the Tatars," Stepan replied.

"Let's move on," Andrei said. He wondered what they would find at Russka.

They rode, for the most part, in silence. The others had sensed Andrei's anxiety and the whole group pressed ahead as fast as it could.

Only one tiny incident provoked a conversation. This was when a wildcat darted across the path in front of them and disappeared into the long grasses. Andrei would not have thought about it at all, if he had not heard Stepan mutter a curse beside him.

"What's the matter, my Ox?"

"Nothing," the huge fellow gruffly replied, but he didn't sound very convincing.

"Come on, what is it?"

"That wildcat: did it look at us?"

Andrei considered.

"I don't think so. Why?"

"Nothing. Perhaps it didn't."

Anxious as he was, Andrei could not help smiling. In a superstitious age, in a superstitious land, he had never met anyone like Stepan. Time and again on the campaign, he had seen the big fellow gaze at trees, rocks, the flight of birds, any number of everyday things that had some special, magical significance for him.

"So what does it mean, where you come from, if a wildcat looks at you," he asked with a laugh.

But Stepan would not tell him.

At last, late in the afternoon, they drew close to Russka. Anxiously Andrei looked from side to side, searching for signs of Tatars, but he saw nothing.

And then, just before they reached the marshes below Russka, they met a peasant from the forest; and when he told them what he knew, Andrei saw what he must do.

"Prepare yourselves for a battle," he told his men.

"This will need careful timing," he added.

The little fort of Russka was closed tight. Inside, a garrison of twenty Polish soldiers, sent there from Pereiaslav in the general confusion, waited for further instructions.

The fortress also contained Yankel the liquor concessionaire, three Jewish craftsmen, and two other Jewish merchants, all with their families. Since the Poles did not trust them, the local Cossacks and peasants had all been left outside to defend themselves as best they could if the Tatars came.

When they left Pereiaslav, they had been told that the magnate Vyshnevetsky was raising a large force, but since then they had heard nothing of this force's movements. They had been waiting for news for two days.

The sun was already getting low when, at the edge of the woods, on the Pereiaslav side, they saw the detachment approaching and, shielding their eyes against the sun, it was with huge relief that they saw from their shining uniforms and their splendid mounts that they were Poles.

From his position behind some bushes, just a hundred yards below the fortress gate, Stepan also watched the Poles approach.

As the Poles came close the men on the walls called down: "Where are you from? What news?"

"We're Vyshnevetsky's men," came the welcome Polish reply. "His main force is just behind us. Come down and open the gates."

From behind his bush, the intrepid Stepan grunted: "Good. Very good. We'll kill them all."

The men from the walls came down and, as their brother Poles reached the gates, opened them.

Then something very strange occurred. Unseen by the defenders, as they opened the gates to the Poles, the huge figure of Stepan, together with about twenty villagers, rushed from their hiding places to swarm into the fort behind the horsemen. Only as they reached the gate itself did the garrison see them; but as they cried out in alarm, the Polish horsemen, instead of turning on the insurgent, jammed the gates open.

And then, too late, the Polish garrison realized they had been duped.

As he cut down an astonished Pole, Andrei laughed to himself. The splendid horses he and Stepan had been given, and the various Polish uniforms, swords, and finery that his companions had looted in the big battles had come in very useful in this little deception.

I'm even glad they made me learn Polish at the seminary, he thought.

Taken completely by surprise, the Polish garrison lost a quarter of their men before they even realized what was happening. But they rallied bravely and fought well. There was no quarter given; they did not suppose that there would be any captives taken. The fighting went from house to house.

It was in this way that Andrei almost lost his life.

Pressing a Pole slowly back past the stout wooden hut where Yankel the Jew sold his liquor, he failed to see another Pole who had crept up onto the little balcony above. Only a shout from Stepan caused him to glance up and ward off a blow as the fellow leapt down on him. He fell to the ground and would have been done for if his friend's huge figure had not burst upon the scene and dispatched both Poles with a couple of mighty blows.

As he got up he saw that the battle was over. He could see the last two Poles surrounded by four of his men.

"Don't kill those two," he shouted cheerfully, "we'll see if they have any information."

Then he saw something else.

The rest of his men, and the villagers Stepan had collected, were killing the Jews.

Andrei grimaced. He didn't like the Jews any better than the Poles, and if these fellows had been armed he wouldn't have thought about it. But they were not armed. One man was trying to defend himself with a stick, but he soon went down. Then he saw them dragging out the women and children.

"Stop that," he ordered.

The men took no notice. He saw a woman fall.

"Leave them," he bellowed. "That is an order."

The Cossack hesitated this time. But he had not reckoned on the villagers.

"Jewish children down the well," one of them shouted.

"No, we use the well."

"To the river, then!" another voice cried.

They were going to drown them; and he realized, with a sense of self-disgust, that there was nothing he could do to stop them.

He turned away.

"Lord Andrei." The loud whisper came from the window of the house. "Lord Andrei."

He looked in. It was Yankel. In all the excitement he had forgotten about the fellow.

"Lord Andrei, I recognize you. Save us, noble sir. You see what is happening."

Andrei looked at him dully.

"I never did you any harm," Yankel went on, eagerly. "You're my only hope."

Because he was not sure if he had the power, Andrei replied testily: "You took my father's horse."

"But not the best. The one I took was worth half what he owed me, and you can have it back if you want." He paused for breath. "Send me out to die. Kill me yourself. But at least have pity on my children."

"Open the door."

They went in. The main room of the house was not very light and it had an unmistakable aroma of vodka, not unpleasant. Before him he saw, besides the stout old Jew, a girl of about fifteen, and a boy of eight or nine. He suddenly realized he had not seen the girl for some years, since before he went away to the seminary. She was a striking, dark-haired beauty now, with almond eyes and a curving nose that looked Turkish. The boy, too, was a handsome little fellow.

"All right," Andrei said. "I'll try. But I'll need help." He turned to his friend. "Will you help me, my Ox, to protect these Jews?" he began. But then he stopped as he realized that his huge companion had not even heard him. For Stepan was staring at the girl openmouthed, as though he had seen a ghost.

It was Yankel's own fault that, a few moments later, he lost his life.

He was so relieved and excited to have the protection of Andrei and his huge friend that, without thinking, he went out through his front door first. Two villagers standing nearby, one with an axe, the other with a scythe, took one look at him and, before the poor fellow even had time to tell them about his protector, fell upon him. He was dead when, moments later, Andrei emerged.

There were several things to be done. One was to question the two captive Poles to see what they could tell him. Another was to make two graves, one for the Poles, another for the Jews. He instructed the villagers to do this. A third was to ride over to see his father.

He took the boy with him.

The sun had just gone down when he reached the farm. He found old Ostap in robust good humor. With all the events of recent months, Mordecai had not been able to visit the farm to claim his labor service and Ostap had ignored the whole business. He had been drinking less and sleeping in the open.

"I've heard it all!" he cried, as Andrei rode up. "A boy from the village came by. Pity you couldn't have let me know in time—I would have enjoyed that fight."

He was delighted with the horses, but when Andrei made his other request, his brow clouded. "You want me to shelter a Jewish boy?"

Andrei explained everything that had happened.

"I can't take him to the camp. The villagers will kill him. Do you want me to leave him to them?"

Old Ostap frowned, unwilling to admit that he might have a soft heart. "He must convert," he announced. "Then he can help on the farm."

Andrei went over to the boy.

"This is the only place where you may be safe. People won't bother my father. But you have to become a Christian."

"Never," the boy said defiantly.

Andrei paused, then he looked carefully into the boy's eyes.

"I promised your father to save your life, and I must keep my promise. You have to help me. Do you understand? As long as you stay here, you're Orthodox."

The boy looked at him, still defiant, but understanding him.

"He's converted," Andrei announced.

The Polish prisoners couldn't tell them much. The Cossacks took all their possessions and let them walk off through the forest.

As soon as this was done, and while his men were setting up their quarters for the night in the fort, Andrei went across the river on his next errand. This was to see Anna.

He had not noticed her so far, but there had been so much to do that it was not particularly surprising. He was taken aback therefore, on reaching her house, to find it closed and boarded up.

"Where are they?" he asked.

"The old man's gone off with his sons to your Cossack camp," their neighbor told him. His wife's gone to her sister in another village near Pereiaslav."

"And Anna?"

"Anna?" The man looked surprised. "Why, didn't you know? She's gone. The Pole took her. Stanislaus came by here just after the men left. Stayed a few days. Then off he went and took her with him. Stole her at dawn."

Andrei could scarcely believe it. First the arrogant Pole had tried to take his farm and humiliate his father. Then he had abducted his girl.

"Where did they go?"

"Who knows? Probably in Poland by now," the man said.

Thoughtfully Andrei returned to the fort. It seemed he had lost his bride.

"But I'll find her," he vowed. As for Stanislaus, there could be only one solution.

If anything could take Andrei's mind off his loss, it was the extraordinary thing that had happened to his friend. For if Andrei had lost a bride, it seemed that Stepan had found one.

And whoever could have imagined that, of all the possibilities, his choice would have fallen on the Jewish girl! Despite his own troubles, Andrei almost burst out laughing.

"But she's Jewish, my old Ox," he protested as they sat together by a little fire inside the fort.

"She'll convert," Stepan said.

"Does she say so?"

"I know she will."

"But why this girl?"

"I don't know why," the strange fellow confessed. "I just know that it's so."

"You just saw her and . . . it was fate."

"Yes. That's it."

He seemed to be in a kind of daze. Even when they spoke, his eyes had a faraway look and Andrei was not sure if his friend was truly with him.

"Oh dear, poor old Ox," he said. "What are you going to do with her? You can't take her on campaign."

Stepan nodded his large head slowly.

"I know. I've been thinking about that. I'll find a priest to marry us. Then I'm going home to the Don with her."

"You're deserting me?"

"The time has come," Stepan said solemnly.

"You'd better talk to her."

"Yes." The huge fellow got up slowly. "We must talk." And with that he walked slowly over to the place where the girl was sitting in the shadows. Quietly he led her to the fire and made her sit by him. Andrei, curious though he was, left them alone. Then, very softly, Stepan began to talk to her.

For some time, from a distance, Andrei watched them. The other Cossacks glanced at them, too. What a strange fellow the bearded giant was, to be sure!

The girl seemed to be saying little, watching Stepan with her large, thoughtful eyes, interjecting a word here and there as if to prompt him. There she was, a fifteen-year-old who had seen her own father hacked to death just a few hours before and was now sitting with this strange Cossack who had taken it into his head to marry her. And, Andrei thought, it was as if she were the teacher and he the child; for something in her composed, tragic young face made her look older than Stepan— older than any of them, perhaps.

At last Andrei went to sleep. But several times that short summer night, he awoke to see them still sitting there, quietly conversing by the glowing embers of the little fire.

What was Stepan saying to her? Who knew what strange jumble of thoughts might be coming from that solemn head? Was he trying to convert her? Was he perhaps telling her about the lands past the Don that were his home? Was he telling her his life story, or God knew what tales of magic and superstition with which his simple head was full? Perhaps he was describing the endless, scented steppe, or his belief that all men should be equal brothers. Whatever it was, it was clear to Andrei that his friend, believing that this Jewish girl was his fate incarnate, had chosen that night to pour out his whole soul.

And the girl was listening, always listening.

She probably knows more about that fellow than some wives learn in a lifetime, he thought with a smile, the third time he went to sleep.

It was just as the sky was beginning to lighten that he half awoke, to find Stepan rummaging through his baggage beside him. He noticed two things—that the girl was standing up, by the fire, and that his friend had upon his simple face a look of extraordinary exaltation, as if he had just been told some wonderful, mystical secret. More than ever, he seemed to be in a sort of daze. More asleep than awake himself, Andrei remembered vaguely seeing the two of them going out of the fort together, and thinking that Stepan looked like a man who was sleepwalking. Then he fell unconscious again.

The shout that woke the whole fort came only minutes later.

Startled wide awake, Andrei rushed to the gate, to find several of the guards already there, gazing out in puzzlement. He darted through them, and down the path.

Stepan was standing by the riverbank. In his hands was a pistol. The girl was lying on the grass a few feet in front of him, dead.

He did not move. Even when Andrei reached him, he was still staring at her with a look of mystified disbelief on his face; and when Andrei tried to take him by the arm, he found that the big man was completely rigid.

For several minutes they stood there together, in the pale light of early morning; then Stepan let Andrei take the pistol out of his hand and, his body suddenly sagging, he walked slowly up the slope with him.

Only when he had sat the strange fellow down and made him drink a little vodka did Andrei get a confused account of what had happened.

During their long talk that night, it seemed the girl had understood the foolish, superstitious fellow only too well. She had told him she would marry him. He had been ecstatic. She had entirely won his confidence. And then, towards the end of the night, when Stepan had entered a state which, to him, seemed to be mystical, she had told him her wonderful secret.

"It is true we were fated to meet, Stepan. I was expecting you." She had smiled. "You see, I am magical."

She could even prove it to him, she said. If he came to a private place, she would show him.

"You can fire your pistol through my heart," she promised, "and it will not even hurt me. Come, let me prove it."

And that was what the simple fellow had done.

Even now, he could not fully understand that his faith in his destiny had been shattered. Still, he shook his head: "There must be a mistake. Perhaps she only fainted."

Nor, it seemed, did any of the Cossacks except Andrei understand that, to the girl, death was better than to be sullied by Christian hands, even when those hands were kindly.

A little later he went to see to the burial of the girl.

He wondered whether to bring her brother there, but decided it was better not to. Feeling that the little fellow should at least have something to remember her by, he searched her and was surprised to discover, on a little chain around her neck, a small, ancient metal disk with a trident on it. He had no idea what this might be, but he took it for the orphaned boy all the same.

So it was that the girl was buried in an unmarked grave by the edge of the steppe. That her journey with Stepan to the lands beyond the Don would have taken her to the homeland of her ancient Khazar ancestors, she had not remotely guessed.

As for Stepan, he gave his puzzled judgment later that morning: "It was that wildcat we saw. It must have looked at me. That's what did it."

At noon the party departed, to seek out news of the magnate Vyshnevetsky and his army.

The massacre of the Ukrainian Jews in the year 1648 followed a pattern
very similar to the events at Russka. Indeed written records survive of
incidents just as strange as Stepan's courtship.

How many Jews were actually killed is a matter of dispute that is
unlikely ever to be resolved; but it is certainly true that the death toll ran
into tens of thousands and that, for the rest of its history, this year
marked the start of the systematic pogroms that have been a recurring
feature of that region.

As for the magnate Vyshnevetsky, he gathered by early June a force
of some six thousand men from his own vast estates and then crossed the
Dnieper to its western side. Under his direction this force burned, looted,
and massacred virtually every Ukrainian settlement in its path, thus
ensuring once and for all that the Ukrainians would loathe the Poles and
demonstrating, with awesome stupidity, that singular genius for vengeance and incapacity for government that was the chief distinguishing
trait of the seventeenth-century Polish Commonwealth.

In July the fighting was resumed. And in the succeeding months,
Andrei achieved the rank of *esaul*.

He did not forget, in the campaigns that followed, to look out for
Stanislaus and Anna.

1649

It was a day, in later years, that he would always remember: for, in a
sense, it marked, for him, the end of the bright days of his youth.

At first it had seemed that things were going well. The uprising had
been universal. By the end of 1648 half the population of the Ukraine
were calling themselves Cossacks; Bogdan and his men had won more
crushing victories over the Poles, captured another hundred guns with a
baggage train containing a hundred million Polish zloty; and the victorious Cossacks had entered Kiev to be greeted by the free townsmen and
the Metropolitan himself as the saviors of the ancient lands of Rus.

A new Polish king had made a truce; treaties of friendship had been
signed with the Turkish sultan and his East European vassals; and for a
time it even looked as if the dream of a free Cossack state might come
true.

Yet despite these triumphs, Andrei could see that his friend was not
happy.

After that terrible day at Russka, Stepan had never spoken of the girl
again; but Andrei sensed that something important had changed within
his friend. Stepan's faith in himself, his simpleminded belief in his destiny, had been broken.

And though he continued to fight alongside his brother Cossacks, it was clear as the months went by that Stepan was losing faith in this cause as well. It was this disappointment on his part that caused the two friends, however sadly, to drift apart.

For the cause of a democratic Cossack state in the Ukraine was lost, even before it started.

There were two reasons. That very first season, when Poland was at its lowest ebb, Bogdan had been unable to take advantage of his victories. And as Andrei watched the peasants drift back to their farms, he could see why.

"We aren't strong enough to mount a long campaign without allies," he remarked.

True, there were the Tatars. But like most mercenaries, the Tatars were only there for profit. By the following spring they refused to fight unless they could see the battle was going to be won; and in early summer they started to make their own terms with the Poles.

The role of the Cossacks in history would always be the same: they could make or break another state; but there were never enough of them to form a viable state of their own.

They needed a protector—either Poland, the Crimean khan, the sultan of Turkey, or the tsar of Russia. They could only fight for the best terms possible. But what were those terms to be?

In the summer of 1649 the Cossacks reached an agreement with the Polish Commonwealth. The terms, by Polish standards, were remarkable. In effect, at that point, Bogdan and the Cossacks were promised a state within a state. No less than forty thousand of them were to be fully registered. Ancient Kiev and two other cities were to be the headquarters of Cossack regiments: Jesuits and Jews would be forbidden to live there.

"It was worth the fight," Andrei had said joyfully to Stepan, but the other had only shaken his head sadly.

"No. We have sacrificed everything—for nothing." And when Andrei had looked genuinely surprised he had reminded him: "No free state; no equality; privileges for rich Cossacks, nothing for the poor ones and the peasants."

It was true of course. Andrei could not deny it. For men like Bogdan—for Andrei and his father, too—the terms were excellent. But those poor peasants, inspired by Bogdan's promises of freedom, who had risen with their makeshift weapons, suffered the magnates' revenge—for them there was nothing at all.

When challenged about it, what had Bogdan and his council replied? "Let the Cossack be a Cossack, and the peasant a peasant."

This simple statement, which would long be remembered, had served as the epitaph for a free Ukraine. It left many of the participants disgusted.

"That is not what I came to fight for," Stepan said grimly.

"It's as good as we could get," Andrei remarked.

Truth to tell, it was as much as he wanted. He realized that. Why in truth should he want a free peasantry now that he was in a position to buy an estate? But in any case, the whole idea was impossible.

"You can't have complete freedom. It's an illusion," he suggested.

The big man shook his head.

"It's no illusion, but you fear it," he replied sadly.

"I just know it can't work. And anyway, who would protect us from attack? Freedom leaves us defenseless. We need authority, a big power. Don't you see that?"

"I see that treachery brings only evil," the big man replied.

And now, within days, he was being proved right.

The peasants, furious at being sold out, were beginning to rise up again; and now it was the Cossack council, not the Poles, who decreed they must be put down at once. The orders had been issued. Andrei prepared to ride.

He knew it was the end of his friendship with Stepan: he knew it the moment he heard the order.

Yet even so, he was in for a small surprise.

He found the big man already prepared to leave. Though he greeted Andrei gruffly, Andrei guessed that his friend might have been waiting for him before departing. His horse was saddled; some modest possessions were strapped to a packhorse. He saw a spare horse standing nearby.

"You've heard the order then?"

"I have."

"You're going?"

"Of course. I want no part of it."

Andrei sighed. He didn't try to dissuade him.

"So you're going back to the Don?"

"Perhaps."

Andrei looked around, a little puzzled.

"Where are your Polish horses? Where's all your loot?"

"I gave them away."

"Gave them away? To whom?"

"To some peasants. They needed money more than me."

It was a stunning rebuke, but Andrei did not try to justify himself, nor did he feel insulted. Stepan thought one way; he thought another.

"But haven't you kept anything for yourself? What about your farm back on the Don?"

"Perhaps I won't go back to the Don."

"Men are free there, my Ox, even if they aren't in the Ukraine. That's where you belong."

For a moment or two, the Ox did not reply. It seemed there was something on his mind, something he had been brooding about for some time. He shook his head slowly. "Men," he muttered at last, "are never free. Not when they are ruled by their own desires."

Andrei looked at his friend. There was a kind of finality in this statement that suggested that, whatever path it was that Stepan had been traveling in his thoughts, he had come to the very end of it and had, so to speak, returned before setting off again.

"Don't you have faith in men anymore, my Ox?" Andrei asked affectionately.

The fact that Stepan did not reply at once told Andrei that his faith in the affairs of men had been destroyed.

"We are all sinners," he grunted with a frown.

"Where will you go then?"

"I don't know."

"What will you do?"

"I don't know."

"Then you still have faith of some kind."

"Perhaps." Stepan glanced down at his feet. "One day I may become a priest," he said gloomily.

"A priest?"

"Or a monk. But not yet. I am unworthy."

Andrei scarcely knew what to make of this.

"Will I ever see you again, old Ox?" he asked.

"Perhaps." He wiped a fly off his long brown beard. "Perhaps not." He glanced at his horse. "I must be off."

Andrei embraced him.

"Good-bye, my Ox. God be with you," he said.

He did not expect to see him again.

1653

AND now, on a sharp, cold morning, in the spring of 1653, young Andrei was riding northward with the Cossack envoys.

They were going to see the tsar.

His own career, since the departure of Stepan, had gone from strength to strength. He had increasingly come to Bogdan's personal notice, and the *hetman,* with his long, crafty face, had often given him sensitive missions.

Old Ostap had died—not of his bad heart, as Andrei and his mother had always expected, but of a plague that had visited the Ukraine a little after the peasant revolt. The incident had saddened Andrei and reminded him of his own mortality.

"Time you married," Bogdan had told him. But for some reason, though he had taken to enjoying conquests wherever he went, Andrei had not yet done so. Could it really be that he still remembered Anna? And if so, what could he possibly hope for? He did not know; and he was, besides, too busy to think about it.

The present mission, he understood very well, was by far the most important of his life. The letters the little party was carrying from the *hetman* were designed to do nothing less, this time, than save the Ukraine.

For events had been moving towards a crisis.

Poland had not been content with even a partial Cossack state. Neither the Catholic Church nor the Uniates could tolerate the success of Orthodoxy in the Kievan lands; the magnates wanted their lands back; the Szlachta nobility and every taxpaying Pole were indignant at the huge increase in the Cossack register and the large number of Cossacks who therefore might suppose the Commonwealth should pay them salaries. Soon there was more fighting. The Poles added large numbers of German mercenaries to their forces, and Bogdan was not always successful. Gradually his hold was weakened. Jews began to return to the Ukrainian lands. And twice, now, large parties of Cossacks and peasants had crossed the border into Russia and been given asylum.

What should the Cossack *hetman* do?

He's still a crafty fox, Andrei had often reminded himself, with admiration.

Indeed he was. At any one time he might be negotiating with the sultan, the Tatars, the tsar, and the Poles all at once; he even tried to get the throne of the little state of Moldavia, down in the south by the river Danube, for his son. But above all, it was becoming clearer each year that the only hope for the Cossacks lay to the north and east, with Russia. Only the tsar would respect the Orthodox religion; only he could protect the Ukraine from mighty Poland.

The problem was that Russia was unwilling. The great empire of the north had troubles of her own; she had no wish to risk a costly war with a furious Poland if she accepted the Ukraine. Bogdan had sent messengers, threatened to give the Ukraine to the Turkish sultan, even harbored a strange adventurer who claimed the Russian throne—anything to get the tsar's attention.

Now, this spring, the Poles had sent another large force to reduce the Ukraine. Yet again, the *hetman* was appealing to Moscow. But this time things might be different.

"So far we've had nothing but offers of cheap bread and salt," the *hetman* told Andrei, as he handed him the letters. "But there may still be one way to sway them."

Andrei nodded.

"The Church."

"Exactly." The *hetman* leaned back in his chair and half closed his eyes. "Holy Russia. That's how they like to think of Muscovy now. Moscow, the Third Rome. Remember, the old Moscow Metropolitan became a Patriarch after Ivan the Terrible—just like Constantinople or Jerusalem. That's very important to them. There are powerful men in the Church, and among the boyars, who think they should protect their Orthodox brothers in the Ukraine. What's more, they're getting stronger." He opened his eyes again and grinned. "Shall I tell you something else? Our Ukrainian priests are better trained than the Russian ones. I'm told that the new Patriarch wants to import more of them to civilize his own priests. Let them pay the price then—don't you think?" He closed his eyes again. "I've told him I'm ready to give the Ukraine to the sultan again. Of course I know our people wouldn't like it because the Turks are Muslims, but the Orthodox Russians will like it even less."

Bogdan had given the envoys three letters: one for the tsar, one for his adviser the boyar Morozov, and one for the Moscow Patriarch.

"Send word by messenger on how you are received. Then, if things look promising, stay in Moscow and keep your ears open."

These were the instructions Andrei carried with the letters as he went on his thrilling mission.

*   *   *

Muscovy. Two Cossacks led the party—Kondrat Burlay and Silvian Muzhilovsky. Andrei was their aide.

Swiftly they made their way eastward from the river Dnieper, through the thinning woods until finally, leaving the trees behind them, they ventured out onto the open steppe. They traveled east another day before turning northward. The winter had been long and bitter. The ground was still hard, with little snowdrifts in places.

It was a strange frontier region, this. Andrei had never been here before, though he knew that many Cossacks and Ukrainians had fled to these broad borderlands where they had come, at least in name, under the protection of the Russian tsar.

"And the tsar has been making his presence felt here, too," Burlay told him. "In the old days, the Russian fortress line against the Tatars was a long way north, almost up at the river Oka. They've just finished a new line now, though. It runs right across the steppe." He laughed. "It's quite impressive."

Nothing, however, had prepared Andrei for what he saw when they came to it the next day.

He simply gasped. So this was the might of Muscovy!

The new, so-called Belgorod line of the Muscovite state was an awesome undertaking. The completed line ran across the steppe from near the fortress town of Belgorod all the way to the distant Volga as it descended towards the deserts by the Caspian Sea. Huge earth walls with trenches in front of them, wooden palisades above, stout towers with sharpened wooden stakes pointing outward from their tops: this was Muscovy's mighty barrier against the Crimean khan who, even now, a century after Ivan the Terrible had conquered Kazan, still demanded tribute, from time to time, from the Russians in their forest empire. Such was the proud memory of the one-time conquerors of the Eurasian plain.

It was as he gazed upon this tremendous wall that the young Cossack received his first impression of the true character of the Russian state of the north.

These people are not like the Poles at all, he suddenly realized. The Poles would never build like this. Poland had simply given the huge tracts of the Ukraine to a few magnates to exploit as they thought best. True, they set up forts to protect their income; they employed Cossacks to keep the raiders at bay. But they were just a collection of great lords, concerned with reaping a profit from these rich borderlands, to keep themselves in comfort in their European palaces in the West.

This colossal fortification, though, was not the work of mere aristocrats. It was the work of a mighty emperor—of a great, dark power, half Slav, half Tatar.

It's like a Tatar city on the steppe, he thought, looking at the high pointed stakes on the parapet, but huge, endless.

And indeed, the great wall itself seemed to speak, as though to say: "We know you horsemen of the steppe, for we are partly of your blood; but see, we can outbuild you—for our heart is greater than yours. Thus we shall carry our mighty Russian forest even across the endless steppe until, one day, even the proud khan shall bow before our Holy Russia."

It was Burlay, riding beside him, who now remarked, "If you want to understand the Russians, Andrei, always remember—whenever they feel threatened, they rely upon size."

So it was that the little party continued, into the great fortress of the Russian state.

At first Andrei noticed nothing very different. When they began to encounter woodland again, the broad-leaved forests seemed very like those around Kiev: the villages with their thatched roofs and timber stockades seemed familiar, too.

Yet gradually he began to see a change. The thatched roofs petered out, to be replaced by heavy logs. It grew colder: the snow lay more thickly upon the ground. Somehow the woods, and the fields, looked gray.

And there was something else.

He was used to Russians: there had been plenty of them at the Cossack camp. They spoke Great Russian of course, but that was not difficult for a Ukrainian to understand. Not that they compared with a man from the south: "Those Russians are crude fellows," the Ukrainians used to say. For just as the Poles despised the Ukrainians, so they in turn liked to despise their Orthodox cousins in the north.

Yet now that he had entered Russia Andrei was surprised to feel a faint sense of unease as he traveled north. It was something to which, at first, he could not put a name. Something oppressive.

The forest grew thicker and darker. Sometimes, in the forest, they encountered little settlements where the people produced potash. In these, Cossacks noticed, the peasants looked healthy enough. But in the ordinary village it was a different story.

"This is the third year the winter has gone on too long," the people told them. "Even in a good year, we only have just enough. With these poor crops, another year and we'll be starving."

When Andrei looked at their villages and heard their sad story, there was one thing that puzzled him.

"Your fields are huge," he exclaimed. "Surely you should have enough even in bad years."

"No," they told him, "it's not so."

And only at the third such village did Andrei discover the reason.

"You see, for every measure we sow, we only get three back at harvest," a peasant explained.

A yield of three to one. A miserable rate, unthinkable in the rich Ukraine.

"Our land is poor," the man said sadly.

And badly cultivated, he could have added. For this three-to-one crop yield in North Russia was no more than farmers in Western Europe had been getting in the Dark Ages, a thousand years before.

But if the poverty of these little villages struck Andrei, he was soon to see something very different.

The party was about fifty miles below the great eastward loop of the river Oka when they came to the old frontier line. Though not as impressive as the new Belgorod line, it was another sign of the formidable power of the Muscovite state. The stout wooden forts and palisades were still intact.

"They stretch another hundred miles, all the way to Riazan," Burlay remarked.

In many places there was long established open parkland in front of the line; but where there was not, huge swaths had been burned through the woodland so that the Tatar raiders would not have any cover.

And it was just past this great line that they came to the sprawling industrial town of Tula.

Andrei had never seen anything like it. It was a town, yet not a town. Everywhere there seemed to be long, stout houses of wood or brick filled with the sounds of men hammering. Half the buildings appeared to be smithies.

"The whole place is like a giant armory," he remarked.

And most impressive of all, there were the big, grim buildings with continually smoking chimneys that contained the blast furnaces.

These were the first blast furnaces that Russia had seen. Operated by the Dutch family of Vinius, they had been set up at Tula because of the ancient iron-ore deposits in the region. Not only were the mighty furnaces here, but innumerable workshops where armaments were made.

"They make more weapons here than anywhere except Moscow itself," Burlay remarked. "They say these Romanov tsars are bringing in new foreigners all the time, because they're the only ones who know how to operate these new machines."

Cannons, muskets, pikes, and swords: Andrei saw wagonloads of them. As a soldier he was impressed; but he found the huge, smoky place rather frightening and was glad, soon, to be on his way to Moscow again.

They reached the capital a week later.

It had been a long, hard winter. The huge city of Moscow was still under snow, although the Lenten Season had begun.

Over the vast, snowbound city, the skies were gray, heavy, and monotonous. In the streets, where the snow had not been cleared, there was also grayness, as though at some point the clouds had let fall not flakes of snow, but a dismal settling of ice-dust and cinders in their place.

Yet the scene was not without color. The roofs of the houses were white. Above, the domes of the churches were gold, silvery, or brightly painted. Occasionally in the street one might encounter a noble in a large, fur-trimmed cloak of red or blue; there might be a glimpse of rich brocade beneath; the patrols of musketeers, the *streltsy,* were to be seen in the citadel with their red coats and gleaming pikes; even the simple towns-women often went out with brightly colored scarves wrapped over their heads.

It was hardly surprising that, for some time after his arrival in Moscow, Andrei lived in a state of happy excitement. After all, it was a fine thing for a young Cossack to enter a mighty capital and find himself well received.

For they had been warmly welcomed. When they delivered their letters to the Kremlin, a senior functionary let them know that the tsar and the boyars were well disposed; and when they left the Kremlin and went to the palace of the Patriarch on Ilinka Street, they were told that the great churchman would give them a personal audience in a few days.

Andrei was full of hope. After the hard months of fighting and uncertainty, he felt like a schoolboy suddenly granted a holiday.

And if Tula had been impressive, he found Moscow awe-inspiring. He would walk across the vast expanse of Red Square towards the extraordinary building already called Saint Basil's Cathedral. The floor of Red Square was slightly curved so that, as one walked, Saint Basil's seemed to rise up over a shortened horizon. He would advance three-quarters of the way, to the tribune platform where announcements were made, and stare at those strange, barbaric, Asiatic towers and domes with wonder. Nearby, the high, massive Kremlin walls, so blank, so pitiless, seemed both threatening and protective. On one of the towers there was now a huge English-designed clock, as though to suggest that, despite the huge, tomblike silence of the Kremlin, it was still watching each minute of the present, passing world.

Sometimes he would wander through the suburbs, through street after street of dark brown, stolid wooden houses, whose roofs were still thick with snow. At every corner, it seemed, there was a church. Many were wooden, with high tent roofs; but often, over the wooden houses, he would see the big, squat, pale shape of a masonry church looming over the quarter, with softly glowing domes and, perhaps, those gay little tiers of false arches, arranged in a pyramid, that the Russians called *kokoshniki,* meaning headdresses, such as women wore.

And above all, as he wandered about in the icy city, he noticed the endless sound of bells. How many churches could there be, to produce such a continuous noise? They say there are forty times forty, and I believe it, he concluded.

Indeed, a friendly priest assured him, in the summer, when the nights were short, the monastery bells could be heard all through the night. "Just like so many nightingales," the priest said, laughing.

Truly this was the capital, the northern fortress of the Orthodox Church.

But what a study in contrasts Moscow was. He had always heard that the Muscovites were given to whoring and drinking.

"They get as drunk as us Cossacks after a victory," his father had always told him.

And to be sure, Andrei saw plenty of people getting drunk, even lying helplessly in the freezing streets by dusk. Yet at the very same time, he would see crowds of men and women moving in a solemn stream into the churches to pray.

And how they prayed! While the priests appeared before the iconostases in their gorgeous vestments, the people stood for hours—longer even than in the great cathedral in Kiev. Many of the faithful even suffered from an incurable foot ailment because of this, he learned. There was a communal zealousness about some of them, too, that he had not seen in the Ukraine. A little knot of women was often to be seen by the church doors and he had supposed they might be asking for alms until one day he saw a drunken man approach and watched, astonished, as the woman suddenly turned upon the fellow with scorn and shoved him brutally away. Truly these Russian women were devout.

Everything is done to extremes in this land, he concluded.

He noticed something else, too. There were quite a few foreigners in the streets, each wearing different national costumes. Some were merchants, but most seemed to be soldiers.

The tsar is drawing men from all countries into his service, he thought, with some satisfaction.

It was at the end of his first week that Andrei made a new friend.

He had gone into the Kremlin to visit the cathedrals. His mood was lighthearted. The sun had appeared once or twice through the clouds that morning. And just as he had left his lodgings, he had had a delightful experience. A young girl had gone tripping by, so close that he had nearly bumped into her as he came out. She could not have been more than fifteen. She wore a long, pink cloak trimmed with fur, a tall, cylindrical fur hat, and her hands were tucked neatly into a fur muff. She was very fair, her fresh young face glowing in the sharp air, and the long golden plait of hair that hung down her back was gaily tied with a bright red ribbon.

Before he had time to collect his thoughts, she was gone; but he smiled to himself as he thought, When this business is over, it will be time to think of getting married. Perhaps I'll take one of these pretty Russian girls with me.

Now, as he walked past the palace in the Kremlin, he paused for a moment below the window in the Terem Palace where one of the *streltsy* guards stood to receive the people's petitions.

How remarkable it was that anyone, even the lowest peasant, could come here, place his petition in the little box provided, and know that it would go straight to the tsar's personal secretariat in the famous Golden Room above—very likely be read out to the tsar himself. The mighty autocrat was like a personal father to his people.

And a kindly one, too. Andrei had already heard stories of the young tsar's kindness, how he would visit the prisons in person, give the poor fellows sheepskin coats, even sometimes set them free by paying off their debts.

"The tsar is like a sparkling sun," the Russians liked to say.

He had just turned towards the cathedrals when he heard a friendly voice behind him:

"Well, if it isn't my friend the Cossack."

He turned and saw a young fellow in a beaver coat grinning at him. He had to think for a moment to remember where he had seen him before, then realized that it had been in the government office where they had delivered their letters: this was the young clerk who had greeted them and conducted them to the senior secretary who had interviewed them.

He was a pleasant young man, about his own age. Andrei now noticed that he had pale, rather ivory skin and a broad, handsome forehead crowned with thick, wavy black hair parted in the middle and brushed carefully back. Yet if this upper part of his face made Andrei think of a Polish nobleman, the rest seemed to derive from a quite different source. His high cheekbones and rather slanting eyes, despite the fact that they were blue, suggested a Turkish or Tatar ancestry. It was as though a high, European face had been compressed in its middle section to produce a slightly squashed though quite agreeable effect.

He introduced himself as Nikita, son of Ivan, Bobrov. The name meant nothing to Andrei.

The two young men fell into an easy conversation. The young clerk seemed eager to talk to this visitor from the south, and it was not long before he warmly suggested: "Come to my lodgings today. We can talk better."

It seemed an excellent chance to reason more about this great state that the Ukrainians were trying to join, and Andrei accepted willingly. He agreed to come that afternoon.

The lodgings of Nikita Bobrov were in the fashionable Kitaygorod quarter; but they were modest, consisting of three rooms on the upper floor of a stout wooden house belonging to a merchant.

His host was not alone when Andrei arrived. Standing at one side of the main room was a middle-aged man in a heavy sheepskin. At the far end stood a plump woman with a younger one beside her, whose face Andrei could not quite see in the shadows.

The man in the sheepskin was of medium height; his bad-tempered face might once have been pale but now it was blotched; he had small dark eyes; his hair was parted in the middle and pulled tightly down his head so that it seemed to become one with his flowing beard. Everything about him, his body, his eyebrows, his entire character appeared to be close-knit. He might have been a small merchant. And he was obviously as angry as he dared.

Nikita briefly excused himself while he turned back to this man, whom he now addressed with an air of finality. "I can talk to you no more, Ivan," he said firmly. "My mind is made up. You see for yourself that Alyonka has hurt her leg and needs Maria to help her. She can't even get to the market. You can't object to your wife helping her mother. And even if you do, I'm ordering you, so there's an end of it. You're to leave now and return here after Easter with those missing rents."

"I should never have brought her," the fellow mumbled angrily.

"That's beside the point. And take care you bring those rents when you return," the young man added severely, "or I'll have you thrashed."

The man glowered in the direction of the two women but reluctantly placed his hand on his heart and made a low bow to Nikita before going out. His heavy steps could be heard going down the stairs outside. Andrei thought he detected a stifled laugh from the younger of the two women, but a moment later they, too, bowed and vanished into the next room.

"My steward," Nikita explained with a smile. "A difficult fellow." He indicated two benches by the window and they went over to them. "The fact is," he confessed, "I brought a widow from my village as house-keeper to save myself the expense of hiring servants in Moscow. Now," he added ruefully, "I have family quarrels on my hands. The penalty of being poor," he grinned. "Let's talk of other things."

Andrei soon discovered, rather to his surprise, that he and his host shared several things in common. As his face suggested, young Bobrov's mother, who had come from Smolensk, was Polish and thanks to her he had early on been taught to read and write and scan a little Latin—in fact, a similar education to the one Andrei had got in Kiev. He even knew some Polish courtly tales. But while this degree of education was becoming more common in the Ukraine, it was still very rare in Russia, and the young clerk had been delighted to discover someone his age who shared these attainments.

As Andrei had hoped, his friend was happy to give him all the information he wanted about the politics of Moscow.

"You came at a good time and you took your letters to the right people," Nikita assured him. "The tsar and the boyar Morozov are your friends, and that's important. The people hate Morozov because he has a silver-plated carriage and he put high taxes on bread and salt, but he's powerful. His wife and the tsar's wife are sisters and their family, the Miloslavskys, control a lot of the court." He grinned. "Morozov even owns part of the big iron works you saw at Tula."

"But we asked for the tsar's protection before, and nothing came of it," Andrei reminded him.

"True, but things have changed. The first time you asked, the tsar was younger and your letter arrived in the middle of a popular revolt here. Half the suburbs were in flames and Morozov nearly lost his life. Moscow wasn't ready to take on a commitment that risked war with Poland. But we're stronger now and the tsar's in control."

"What about the Church?" Andrei asked, remembering Bogdan's words.

"The Church wants union. You know the Patriarch of Jerusalem himself came to Moscow to plead your cause. And we already value your Ukrainian scholars."

Andrei knew that the Patriarch of Jerusalem had been in Kiev at the very time of Bogdan's triumphal entry and that after this he had gone north. He also knew that a number of Ukrainian scholars had recently been set up in a house in the Sparrow Hills at Moscow's edge. All this seemed to augur well.

"But the greatest and most powerful friend you have is not even our master the tsar," the young man solemnly told him. "It's our new Moscow Patriarch." And now Andrei noticed that his host unconsciously dropped his voice a little with respect: "Patriarch Nikon."

Andrei had noticed that although this new Patriarch had only been chosen the previous year, people already seemed to speak of him with a kind of awe.

"They say," Nikita went on, "that he may be a new Philaret."

This was a remarkable claim. For when, forty years before, the amiable Michael Romanov had been chosen by the Zemsky Sobor as the first tsar of the new dynasty, it was not long before his father, the austere Patriarch Philaret, was virtually ruling the state for him. Could this new Patriarch, whom he knew to be of humble origins, really be so powerful?

"Wait till you see him," Nikita said.

Nikon's interest was simple, it appeared. He wanted to see Moscow recognized as the equal if not the highest of the five patriarchates of the Orthodox Church. The dignity of the Moscow Patriarchate had to be raised. They needed more saints. Only a year before, the body of Metropolitan Filip, whom Ivan the Terrible had murdered, had been ceremoniously brought back to Moscow to be venerated in the Kremlin church. He also knew that the Russian Church was backward, its texts corrupt, and its scholarship inferior. He wanted to correct all this and, together with the Ukraine, to make the ancient lands of Rus a mighty bulwark against the Catholic and other religions of the West.

"He's already started to reform the prayerbook and the liturgy," Nikita explained. "It seems we've even been making the sign of the cross the wrong way."

"Is there any opposition?" Andrei wondered.

"Yes. A bit. There's a small group among the senior zealots who don't approve. They hate change." He laughed. "I got waylaid in the Kremlin not long ago by some fellow from the provinces called Avvakum—I ask you, what a name!—who went on about it for half an hour until I shut him up. But Nikon's very powerful and he'll make short work of any opposition. You can be sure of that. And then, my dear fellow, Moscow will truly be the Third Rome," he added enthusiastically.

It was an enthusiasm Andrei could share. This was what the Cossacks wanted to see.

They were briefly interrupted by a rustling at the entrance as the older of the two women appeared and began quietly to set food on the table. It was a modest meal: fish, a few vegetables, and a sort of gingerbread she had made without eggs or milk, so as not to break the Lenten fast. To wash this down, however, Nikita had allowed himself some of the vodka that was now the drink of classes in northern Russia.

Andrei had idly watched these preparations, curious to see whether the younger woman would appear; but she had not.

They moved to the table and at once Nikita poured them both a liberal quantity of vodka.

Andrei was curious to know more about his host. What sort of man was he?

"I'm a small landowner," Nikita explained. "My family have been service gentry—boyar's sons, they call us—for a long time. Our estate's a small place in the Vladimir region. But I hope to rise," he confided. He explained that the next step up would be to join the more select, so-called Moscow Gentry that Ivan the Terrible had founded with his chosen thousand retainers. "And who knows, after that? People like me have even become boyars—the highest rank of all."

His modest education, it turned out, was a great advantage to him because it allowed him to make himself useful in his government department.

"It was because my mother taught me Polish that I was chosen for this part of my department," he added. "We have special responsibility for Cossack affairs."

Andrei knew that the government department—the *prikaz*—was one of the ways to advancement in the tsar's service, and he was curious about it. Nikita was happy to tell him more, describing the work of his unit with pride. Yet the more Andrei listened, the more puzzled he became.

For as well as Cossack affairs, it seemed Nikita's *prikaz* dealt with honey production, the tsar's falcons, and numerous other matters that seemed to be completely unrelated to its main task. When he questioned Nikita about this, the young clerk only grinned.

"Every *prikaz* is the same in Moscow," he said. "You see, each department grew up because some particular matter had to be dealt with; and when something new turns up, it's just given to whoever happens to be free. There are at least three other departments dealing with you Cossacks, as well as my own."

"Isn't it confusing?"

"It is until you know your way around. But it's useful too, you know. The thing is to try to get your finger into as many pies as possible."

As Nikita began to describe the large and hopelessly confused Russian bureaucracy, Andrei's head began to swim. How, with so much red tape, so much overlapping of responsibilities, was it ever possible to get anything done? Try though he might, the more he listened, the less he could see any answer to this question—which, indeed, was not surprising, since any Muscovite at that date could have told him that there was no solution to the problem of government red tape.

They drank numerous toasts: to the Ukraine, to Holy Russia, to the Cossacks.

Nikita was eager to know the Cossacks' military strength and Andrei assured him of their fitness.

"Because if we accept the Ukraine, it will mean war with Poland," the young man remarked seriously.

For his part, Andrei wanted to know about the many people from other countries he had seen in Moscow. Who were they? At this, Nikita became vehement.

"Damned foreigners," he cursed. "We need them, that's the trouble. Do you know why, my dear Cossack?"

Andrei was not sure.

"Because you and I aren't good enough, that's why." He sighed. "It's the same problem Ivan the Terrible faced. Most of our history, you see, our enemy has been the horsemen, usually from the East. People like my ancestors—and nowadays you Cossacks—know how to fight the Tatars. But now we have even more powerful people we need to fight: the Germans, the Swedes, the powers up in the Baltic. We want to conquer the Baltic and dominate its trade, but these people have science and military expertise that we do not possess.

"Why do you think I am a clerk in a *prikaz* when my ancestors were warriors? It's because the tsar doesn't need poor amateurs like a Bobrov to lead his men. He needs Dutch and German engineers, Scottish mercenaries, even English adventurers. They're the people who we're recruiting to be our officers now. They know how to fight trained infantry. They understand siege warfare and modern artillery."

"What about the *streltsy?*" Andrei had always understood the famous musketeers were formidable.

"Good in their day—in the time of Ivan the Terrible. Hopelessly out of date now, both in tactics and weapons. They've got lazy too." He shook his head sadly. "No, we must be humble and learn from the West, my friend. They possess so much knowledge."

These thoughts seemed to depress him. They depressed Andrei, too, for this new world hardly sounded promising for the half-disciplined Cossacks either. Nikita poured them both more vodka, which they downed. Nikita poured again. Then he suddenly brightened. "Of course, once we've learned their damned Western science—Dutch cunning, we call it in Moscow—then we'll kick them all out."

"Ah," said Andrei appreciatively. "I'll drink to that."

And so, though they did not know it, the two men, with their poor smattering of education, drank cheerfully to the greatest weakness of the Muscovite state.

For, like almost everyone, even among the elite in Moscow, these young men were entirely unaware of the centuries of culture that these uncomfortable Western neighbors represented. Of the great philosophical debates of the Middle Ages they were entirely ignorant. Of the Renaissance they knew almost nothing. For the slow growth of a complex political and economic society in Western Europe, they cared not at all. That Russia was, now, many centuries behind the West in its development they had not the least idea.

The Russians had seen only the military power of the West and supposed that if they copied it, they had discovered all they needed. Thus they reached out to touch, not substance, but merely the dancing shadows cast upon Russia's walls.

"What about the foreign merchants?" Andrei asked. "I've noticed a great many."

Nikita shrugged. "They're all heretics. Patriarch Nikon has known how to deal with them, I must say. The reason you notice them is that the Patriarch made them all wear their own national dress, even if they've been here a generation or more. That way they can't conceal themselves. You know they're not allowed to live in the city anymore?"

Andrei had heard of the so-called German Quarter—the contemptuous Russian words actually meant "Dumb People's Quarter"—outside the city, but had not realized that it was a sort of ghetto.

"That was Nikon, too," Nikita said approvingly.

"I don't see any Jews."

"No. The tsar won't have them."

"That's good," the Cossack said.

"There's only one other kind of foreigner that's banned—at least from the capital."

"Who's that?"

"The English of course."

"The English?" The young Cossack from the south did not know a great deal about these people or their distant nation. "Are they terrible heretics?"

"Worse. Didn't you know?" Nikita involuntarily lowered his voice even to speak of the horror. "They cut off the head of their own king, Charles I, not four years ago."

Andrei looked at him. As a Cossack, he supposed that it was a terrible thing to kill a king, though it did not seem so very terrible to him, so long as the king wasn't Orthodox.

But the effect upon Nikita, even of mentioning this awful deed, was quite extraordinary. His face puckered up into an expression of utter contempt and loathing. "They killed their own anointed king," he repeated. And then he said something that stayed in Andrei's mind for a long time afterwards. "They are worse than the Poles. Thank God we know that we are the tsar's slaves."

Several times before Andrei had noticed this manner of speaking. The common people would call themselves the tsar's orphans, and the official service classes seemed positively proud to call themselves his slaves. So far he had assumed it was a figure of speech; but watching his new friend Nikita now, he was not so sure. It was strange.

It was just after leaving that he caught sight of the younger woman. He had glanced back at the house and seen her face, quite clearly, at an open window.

It belonged to a girl about his own age: a pretty face, lightly freckled with regular features. He could just see the top part of her body. It was obviously slim. Definitely a handsome girl.

She was watching him. He smiled at her. She smiled back, then, quickly turning her head, she ducked back inside the window.

He frowned. How strange. It looked almost as if the girl had a black eye.

Perhaps it was not altogether by chance that he happened to pass near Nikita's lodgings the next day and strolled about in the little market nearby. If he had been curious to see the girl, he was rewarded, for he had only been there a short time when she and her mother came by. He noticed that the mother, despite what Nikita had said, was hardly limping at all.

They saw him and greeted him politely. And as they came close he saw clearly that, though it was fading, the girl had certainly had a black eye.

He engaged the older woman in conversation, and she seemed quite happy to talk; but all the while he noticed the girl. There was something about her, a lightness on her feet, a faint humor in her lips, that almost reminded him of Anna. He knew she was staring at him. He tried to listen to what the older woman was saying.

And then suddenly he started. What had the woman said? She had just remarked that they came from the town of Russka.

He questioned her more closely. She described the place, where it was; there could be no doubt about it: his young friend's estate was undoubtedly the place from which his grandfather had run away.

Which means, he thought with a smile, that if he hadn't, I should very likely be a peasant of Nikita's instead of a Cossack he entertains in his own house.

He was just about to blurt all this out when some instinct for caution held him back. Nikita might yet be useful to him, and who knew how he might feel about the grandson of a runaway? Nonetheless, he supposed he must have relations in the place. "Perhaps I shall visit it someday," he said lightly.

They talked a little more. He told them about his companions and where they were lodged; then they parted. As they did so, he saw that the girl was looking at him intently.

It was not a complete surprise, therefore, when he met her in the street the next day near his lodgings. She came up to him with a smile. Despite the dark mark around her eye, she looked cheerful, even radiant. She had a light, springing step.

"Well, Mr. Cossack," she said, "may I walk with you?"

Most of the women one saw in the street moved rather cautiously; even if they wore a headdress, they placed a large scarf over it, tied under the chin; they seldom smiled.

But though she wore a scarf and a long, rather threadbare cloak, there was something in this girl's easy, almost dancing gait that reminded him of the free, self-confident Cossack girls of the south.

"You should call me Maryushka," she said, using the diminutive. "Everybody does."

"Well, Maryushka," he said, "tell me about yourself. Why do you have a black eye?"

She laughed. It was a gay little sound, though with a hint of sadness and bravery in it that was very appealing.

"You never need to ask a married woman that," she replied. Then with a sigh she added: "They say it's a fault in my character."

Her story was simple, though unusual. When she was younger, she had refused to marry.

"There was a boy in Russka." She laughed again. "He was so handsome! Slim, and dark like you. But he married someone else. He didn't want me. And the other boys—well . . ." She made a gesture of contempt. "My father was dead. My mother goes on at me every day: 'Marry this one, marry that one.' I say, 'No! He's too short. No, he's too tall.' She says I'm a wicked girl. I need training. I'll get a bad name. So . . ." She shrugged.

"So you married the steward? The man I saw at Bobrov's?"

"His wife died. He told my mother he'd tame me. 'Give her to me,' he says."

"You didn't refuse?"

"Yes. But he's the steward. He could make it very awkward for us. He has the power. So—that's life. I married. I was old, you know. Nearly twenty."

"And he beats you?"

She shrugged again. "That's part of being married. He hits with his fist.

Sometimes I can get out of his way. But he's quick. She gave a mournful laugh. "Oh yes. He's quick. So. That's all."

Andrei had always heard that these women in North Russia suffered harsh treatment from their husbands. The Cossack girls he knew, though their husbands often called them weak women and pretended to despise them, would not have put up with much of this kind of treatment.

"What does your mother say?"

"At first she says: 'Obey him and don't be headstrong, then he won't beat you.' Then she says: 'You must work to make him love you. Have children.'" She gave him a little smile. "You know what she says now? She says: 'Maryushka. All men are the same, to tell you the truth. Obey him, submit, but keep your own council. Men are despicable,' she says, 'but there's nothing you can do about it.' So I say: 'Why didn't you tell me that before?' And she says: 'Because I wanted you to get married.'" She laughed aloud. "So I'm married."

"And how did you get to Moscow?"

"Ah. I tricked him. He had to bring the rents to our landlord. So I say: 'Take me to Moscow and I'll do anything you want.' Then when I get here I say to my mother: 'You have to keep me here. I can't stand it anymore. Not this month.' So she pretends to hurt her leg and the landlord's sent him back to Russka without me!" She laughed happily.

"Look," she cried suddenly, "there's a church. Let's go in and pray."

What a strange, wayward girl she was! But what spirit she had. Before they parted that day, Andrei had already decided: It's time I had a woman: this will be the one. Because of business, however, he had to put her out of his mind for a couple of days.

It was on the third day that he saw a strange sight. He was just walking out of the White Town when, turning a corner, he saw a wagon that had been stopped in the middle of the street; and at the same moment he realized to his surprise that it was being attacked by a small mob. Thinking they must be robbers, he was about to rush to the aid of the wagoner when he noticed that the attackers were being led by a pair of priests.

"What's this?" he asked a bystander.

"Those are zealots." The fellow grinned. "And they've found what they're looking for."

To his amazement Andrei now saw the mob pull down from the wagon a lute, a balalaika, and several other musical instruments.

"A fire!" he heard one of the priests cry. "Burn these iniquities."

And sure enough, moments later, the wagon itself was set on fire. Not only that, but the gathering crowd of onlookers was roaring its approval. He had been curtly told by a priest the day before not to smoke his Cossack pipe; and he had also seen a drunkard dragged away to be flogged. But what kind of land was this, where priests burned musical instruments? Scarcely thinking what he was doing, he opened his mouth and began to utter a curse of disapproval, when he unexpectedly felt a hand held across his lips.

It was a female hand, and before he could even look down, he heard a familiar voice softly at his shoulder.

"Take care, Cossack."

Her hand was a little longer than he had realized; as she took it away, Maryushka gently squeezed his cheeks and then ran the tips of her fingers across his lips.

"Don't you realize, Mr. Cossack," she whispered, "there are probably people in the crowd who are listening—they'll tell the priests if they hear you swearing."

"What then?"

She shrugged.

"Who knows? The knout perhaps."

The Russian leather-thonged whip was a fearsome instrument.

"Are these zealots so strict then that they burn musical instruments and give the knout for swearing?"

"Oh yes. The Patriarch is for it, and some of the zealots in the church are even stricter. They are determined to cure us Russians of our whoring and drinking. All sorts of pleasure are forbidden." She laughed. "You know, the landlord's even afraid to go home because the priest at Dirty Place preaches such sermons. And Bobrov has a lute from Germany hidden in his house, I know."

Andrei frowned. Was this dour zealotry the Orthodoxy he was fighting for? Was everything in the Muscovite state so dark, so claustrophobic? The sense of unease he had felt on his journey northward from the Ukraine seemed to come back to him now with more force.

But Maryushka had reached up and gently touched his lips again. "Is there anyone in your lodgings now?" she asked.

He knew there was not.

He looked at her. "What if we're caught? The knout?"

She smiled. "No one will catch us."

A blue sky appeared the next day, and the spring sun. By noon the thaw had set in. And though, in the succeeding days, the sky was often overcast, it was clear that winter was ending at last.

The streets became sodden, gray, and brown. A rich, damp smell began to emanate from the millions of logs of the wooden houses, like a sharp, resinous incense. The wet wooden walls were almost charcoal; icicles, thinning to mere needles, hung from the glistening eaves; and here and there the white walls of a church, or the slender shape of a silver birch glimmered above the dull slush and endless puddles of the street. The smoke from the fire in every house rose to be carried, like the modest sound of the church bells, over the still somber morass of the city whose high, golden domes alone gave promise of the light and warmth to come.

In this melting season, Andrei made love to the girl Maryushka.

She had a slim, strong body; the light freckles on her legs and breasts petered out to a surprisingly pale whiteness. Her breasts were rather small.

She would visit his lodgings in the afternoon, and they would lie on his bed in the shadowy room that was almost overheated by the big stove at one end. She liked to undress herself and stretch out luxuriously to await him. Sometimes, having arched her back with a catlike movement, she would raise one of her strong, slim legs and admire it before asking him, cheerfully: "Well, Mr. Cossack, what are we going to do today?"

The first day they made love, he noticed that she winced when he first touched her, but when he looked surprised she gave a wry smile and held up her arms.

"A little reminder from my husband," she remarked drily, and Andrei saw that along the side of one arm were ugly dark marks where the steward had obviously punched her. "He's quite strong," she said mildly, and then, as though the bruises were not there, pulled him gently to her.

"You are strong yourself," he remarked a little later, "like a cat," he added.

"Yes," she replied, "a cat with sharp teeth."

And so they passed the time each afternoon while the dull light outside slowly turned to dusk, then darkness, and, apart from some occasional footfalls in the street and the faint hiss from the hot stove, the only sound was the slow dripping of melted ice from the overhanging eaves, or the little rustle and soft thud of snow slipping off the roof onto the ground below.

Sometimes, afterwards, she would sigh. "You will be gone, soon, my Cossack."

"Don't think of it, my little cat."

"Ah. Easy for you to say. You're not trapped."

It was hard for him to reply to this.

"Sometimes I wish that Ivan would die," she would muse. "But . . . what then? I've nowhere to go." And then she would manage a short, ironic laugh. "All dressed up on Saint George's Day—but Saint George's Day has been taken away. What do you think of that, Mr. Cossack?"

This was a subject to which she often returned in their conversations, and it was one that made Andrei rather uneasy.

For his affair with Maryushka was turning out to be not only a sensual pleasure, but a very important piece of education: and it was an education that was by no means pleasurable.

Only since coming to know her, Andrei now realized, had he truly begun to understand the nature of this powerful Muscovite state. And the more he understood the more he became uncomfortable.

Above all, the feature of the state that he disliked was one that— though it had for a long time been developing—had only recently passed into law. And this was what, nearly every time they talked, Maryushka complained about.

For she was no longer a free peasant. Saint George's Day had been abolished.

It was the law code of the present tsar, Alexis, which had so decreed just four years before. Until that time, though the right had been limited in practice, it was still possible in theory, once a year, for the Russian peasant—technically free since the days of ancient Kiev—to leave his master for another. The old institution of Saint George's Day was still in force.

It was the service gentry, the small men with modest estates, who disliked the rule. Invariably short of money, they could never match the terms the Church and magnates could afford to offer for the labor that, thanks to Russia's endemic famine and plague, was always in short supply.

Pitiful the service gentry might be, individually. But taken all together they were a large and formidable force. It was they who kept order in the land, they who could, when the need arose, raise troops in every village in the vast, ungainly land. In short, as the rest of Europe entered the modern age, in the backward land of Muscovy there remained an essentially feudal state of petty landed retainers and a holy tsar.

It had been the riots of 1648, when the administration had briefly lost control of Moscow, that had reminded Alexis that he should ensure the loyalty of the service class.

He had done so brilliantly.

In 1649, the famous Russian law code known as the Ulozhenie was proclaimed. Among its provisions it stated that no peasant might leave his master's land for another; and that there was no time limit for the recapture of runaway peasants by their owners. It also stated for good measure that the lower orders in the towns were likewise unfree to move.

To most of the peasants in Dirty Place, these provisions made no difference in their daily lives. They greeted the news, as it filtered down to them, with an apathetic shrug.

But Maryushka did not. Her sharper intelligence perceived the law for what it was. She saw that now there was nothing to prevent the landlord owner from treating his peasants like chattels.

And she was right. As history was to show, with this great law code, the road to the final subjugation of the Russian peasant had been quietly opened. For over two centuries, longer than the actual subjugation to the Mongols, most Russians would be born serfs.

"Do you understand?" Maryushka demanded. "Your young friend Bobrov owns me like a slave. He can probably even sell me. If I run away, he can get me back as long as I live." She laughed bitterly. "You Ukrainians revolt against the Poles. Then you want to become part of Russia, which is worse! You'd be better off under the Turkish sultan!"

It was a thought that had recently occurred to Andrei too. But he could only answer: "The sultan is not Orthodox."

Surely that was the point; at least, he hoped it was.

Then, as if to resolve his doubts, came Palm Sunday.

The morning was overcast, but with only a thin film of gray cloud, which was seamed with glimmering gold-and-silver fissures from the bright spring sky that was hidden above.

Nikita had suggested Andrei should accompany him, so that they could go into the Assumption Cathedral in the Kremlin afterwards; accordingly they had set off together, followed respectfully by Maryushka and her mother, for the citadel; but when they arrived at Red Square the crowds were so thick that they had to stop some way from the Kremlin walls.

As they waited, Andrei glanced at the older woman and then at Nikita. Did either of them guess about his relationship with Maryushka? He supposed not.

They did not have long to wait.

The ceremony of Palm Sunday in the holy state of Muscovy was, at that time, an extraordinary affair. Setting out from before the towering, exotic mass of Saint Basil's Cathedral, the long procession of boyars, officials, and priests moved towards the little tribune near the middle of Red Square, where the choir of boys was singing hymns. Somber, rich, magnificent, the greatest men wore huge chains of gold around their necks, tall hats, and coats of ermine or black fox. Splendid embroidered robes adorned the boyars, heavy enough, it seemed, to crush lesser men. And how imposing the bearded Muscovite priests looked, in their glittering vestments covered with gold and gemstones; they had become still more gorgeous in recent years by adopting oriental headgear. The bulbous jeweled miters of the bishops, like so many church domes, caught the dull glow from the broken sky and glimmered with an eerie magnificence.

On a wagon pulled by four horses was a tree, hung with fruit, to symbolize the day; on each side the *streltsy* guards, arranged in open formation across the square, now sank to their knees and bowed their foreheads to the ground. And last of all, to enact for the people the entry of Christ into Jerusalem on that great day, came the tsar himself, walking humbly on foot and leading a donkey, upon which sat the tall figure of the Patriarch.

At the little platform the procession paused. The tsar himself spoke a few words. Then it moved on, across Red Square, and into the Kremlin through the great Gate of the Savior. The tsar was going to the cathedral to pray.

Surely, Andrei thought, surely this must be the ideal state: the land where the Church and monarch were as one. How was it the Russians liked to style their ruler? "Most Pious and Orthodox, the most Gentle Tsar." Wasn't that what he had just seen?

He and Nikita went into the Kremlin. There was too much of a crush to get into the Assumption Cathedral itself, but they waited outside in the hope of seeing something more.

Their patience was rewarded. At the end of the service, with the bells pealing, he saw not only Tsar Alexis but the sweet-faced tsaritsa, too, emerge from the cathedral uncovered.

"The Patriarch insists that she show herself to the people on these great occasions," Nikita whispered, as they both bowed low.

Yes, Andrei thought, all is well. I have seen Holy Russia.

It had been a memorable day.

It was also the end, at least for a while, of his affair. He had not especially thought about it, but when, later that day, he encountered Maryushka again at Nikita's lodgings, and she suggested she should come to him the next day, he shook his head.

"Not in Holy Week," he said. It was one thing to sin, but during this, the most sacred week of the year, he simply felt he could not; and he was a little surprised that even her wayward and rebellious spirit could wish for such a thing.

She shrugged, a little sadly, but said nothing.

* * *

Holy Week passed quietly. Feeling guilty after his previous sins, Andrei fasted strictly.

On one day he, Burlay, and the other Cossacks rode out to look at the tsar's country residence at nearby Kolomenskoye. Sited by the Moskva River, it was a curious jumble of buildings—some wooden, others of brick covered with white stucco. Its tent roofs, onion domes, and towers flanked by ascending pyramids of *kokoshniki* suggested a silent, powerful peacefulness like an Indian temple.

They returned to the city feeling refreshed.

By the end of the long and lovely Easter Vigil in the Kremlin at the end of the week, Andrei felt both weak in the knees and elated. The next morning he saw the tsar ceremonially give the brightly painted Easter eggs to the great men and the soldiers at the Kremlin. Then he went to Nikita's lodgings for the feast that marks the end of Lenten fasting.

It was a happy occasion. Blinis, honey cakes, gingerbread, all manner of foods had been procured. Maryushka and her mother, both a little pale after their vigil the night before, served the collection of friends Nikita had invited. Appropriately the sky had cleared to a pale blue that morning and this Easter Day Andrei felt suddenly as if he had been made anew.

Yet as his head began to swim pleasantly with the kvass and mead and vodka he was offered, and a delightful warmth began to fill his stomach, his pious thoughts of the preceding week soon began to fade into the background, and looking across the room at Maryushka, he thought happily, Soon I'll make love to her again.

The week after Easter is known in the Russian Orthodox Church as Bright Week.

And it was on the Tuesday that the Cossacks were at last received in person by Patriarch Nikon at his palace.

Only now, seeing him at close quarters and without his miter, did Andrei realize the dominating presence of this legendary figure.

The Patriarch stood an astounding six feet six inches. Years of prayers and rigorous fasting had left an unmistakable mark on his face, which, like his tall body, was gaunt but commanding. His eyes were not unkind but were piercing.

He treated the Cossacks in a friendly but businesslike manner.

"Though the Metropolitan of Kiev properly comes under the Patriarch at Constantinople," he said, "Holy Russia can and should give him its protection. This I am determined to do. As for the Church in Moscow, it is backward. I welcome our brothers from Kiev who have so much that we need." He looked at them severely. "This is the dawning of a new age—an age of renewed and purified Orthodoxy, led by a pious Russia. You Cossacks will have a splendid role in the defense of our Orthodox state. You may rely upon me, therefore," he concluded, "to support your application for the tsar's protection. Indeed"—he smiled—"I think you may be sure that your mission here will succeed."

It was not only the ringing words: it was the tone of them, the force of the man that commanded, uplifted.

As he left, Andrei suddenly felt that he was no longer just a rebel against Poland, but the servant of a mighty cause.

Maryushka's husband arrived the next day.

Andrei saw Maryuska briefly at Nikita's lodgings, but it was only possible to talk for a few moments. She told him she was to return to Russka with her husband in three days.

"So I shan't see you again," she said quietly. Then she was gone.

He was surprised by the effect this news had on him. A strange melancholy seemed to invade his whole spirit, a sense of loss rather like a foreboding. Yet why should that be. If he were truthful with himself, the ending of an affair usually left him with a small elation—a sense, however mingled with regret, of freedom, of new pastures and, it had to be said, the pleasant, self-satisfied feeling of a conquest completed.

Yet this time it was different. He felt a cold sadness he had not known before—and he realized soon that it was not because she had meant so much more to him than any of the many others, but that, this time, he was afraid for her.

It's not just the steward and what he'll do to her, he realized. It's something in herself. Without fully understanding it, he was looking at the inner fate of a woman who wished to protest in the endless land where all must submit.

He did not want to lose sight of her. It was absurd.

A partial reprieve, at least, was suggested the next morning when Burlay, the leader of the mission, announced that their work was nearly completed and that they would soon be returning home.

"How soon?" Andrei asked.

"About a week," he was told.

"Then I have a request to make," he said.

"Very well," Burlay said when he had heard it. "As long as the landowner there has no objection. You can follow on as you please."

And so it was that Andrei made preparations to accompany Maryushka to the northern village of Russka.

Nikita Bobrov was amused when Andrei told him of his desire to visit the estate and explained his own connection with the place.

"My dear friend." He laughed. "Do you mean your own grandfather ran away from the Bobrov estate?"

"I think so," Andrei admitted.

"What a pity he didn't leave later. If he'd been in a more recent census I could probably claim you back!"

"A grandson?"

"Well, not in practice I daresay. But," he grinned, "have you ever seen the Ulozhenie?"

The law about which Maryushka had complained.

Andrei confessed that he had not.

"Well then, I'll show you."

Some twelve hundred copies of the great law code of 1649 had been printed—a huge figure for that time—and Nikita Bobrov had one of them.

It was a remarkable document, written not in stilted chancery language but in plain, vernacular Russian, so that it would be readily understandable to all.

"Here we are," Nikita showed him. "Chapter eleven."

And now, for the first time, Andrei truly understood what it meant to be a Russian peasant.

There were thirty-four clauses dealing with peasants. They covered every imaginable circumstance. Not only was there no time limit whatever on when a lord could claim a runaway back; if he married, the lord could claim his wife back; if he had children, the lord could claim them, their wives, and their children, too.

It was forbidden for a lord to kill a peasant—if he did so with premeditation. But if he did so in a fit of anger, it was not a serious offense. If, in a fit of anger, he killed the peasant of another lord, he must replace him.

Andrei asked to look at other chapters. They covered everything, from blasphemy to forgery, from monastery lands—whose growth was now limited—to illegal taverns.

One thing in particular struck him. It was the mention, time and again, of the knout.

"There's plenty of flogging in Muscovy," he remarked.

"Only peasants can be flogged," Nikita quickly assured him.

There were in fact one hundred forty-one offenses in the twenty-five chapters of the law code that carried a punishment by the knout. More severe offenses carried the death penalty. But since fifty lashes with the knout was usually fatal, the code could in practice be even more brutal than it looked.

As he read this stern, dark law code, Andrei realized with some shame that, though he had been here some time, and had received many hints, he had failed to look carefully beneath the surface of Muscovite life. More than ever, now, he understood the sense of oppression and claustrophobia that had assailed him ever since he passed the huge Belgorod fortress line across the steppe. And as he thought of the sunny, open lands of the Ukraine, of the unruly Cossack farmers, and of the free cities of Kiev and Pereiaslav who still governed themselves under Western laws, he could only shake his head.

"If the tsar wants to take the Ukraine under his wing," he remarked thoughtfully, "he will have to sign a contract to guarantee our people better rights than these."

But now it was Nikita who shook his head. "We know the Ukraine has other customs, which will be respected," he assured Andrei. "But surely you understand, if the tsar accepts you under his protection, he does not sign contracts with you. That is beneath his sovereign dignity. You must trust in his kindness and understanding."

"The king of Poland signed contracts with us," Andrei protested.

"The king of Poland is only an elected monarch," Nikita smiled, with faint contempt.

"Cossacks," Andrei said carefully, "are not slaves."

"And our most pious, Orthodox, and most gentle tsar is appointed by God to do with us all as he wishes," Nikita replied firmly. "You must remember," he went on, with a trace of condescension, "that the tsar is the heir of Saint Vladimir, of Monomakh, and of Ivan the Terrible." He smiled a little grimly. "Ivan, I can assure you, knew how to command obedience. He had one of my own ancestors roasted in a frying pan."

It was curious, Andrei thought, how these Russians seemed to take pride in the cruelty of their rulers, even when it was directed against themselves. He had several times heard Muscovites speak admiringly of the terrors of Ivan: they seemed almost to long for his return.

How different from the Cossack way. The Cossack warrior gave his *hetman* power of life and death over everyone during a campaign; but woe betide him if he tried to exercise any authority in time of peace!

This little altercation had produced a slight tension between the two men. Nikita broke it with a laugh. "Well, my Cossack, you are welcome to visit my poor estate. I've told my steward to put you in my house and look after you. I'm only sorry I can't come with you myself." He paused. "By the way"—he gave him a sidelong glance—"I know I can rely upon you not to subvert any of my peasants to your Cossack ways—of either sex."

So. He knew. Andrei looked at the floor awkwardly. But as they parted he reflected that, in Muscovy, one could never be sure what people knew, and what they did not.

Russka.

He supposed it was what he had expected.

Spring had come to the little town and its monastery. As they approached the place, the woods opened out to large fields; their long, gentle undulations of raw turfs, dark earth, and long slivers of graying snow seemed to be an echo of the endless spaces beyond. At Russka itself the ice had cleared from the center of the stream; at the edges the women still knelt on boards by holes in the ice, washing their clothes in sight of the monastery's pale walls.

On the trees, even before the last traces of ice had melted from the ground around them, little green buds were already opening staunchly under the hard, bright blue sky. Just outside the walls of Russka, a cattle pen was already a little sea of mud.

It had been a strange journey. Maryushka and the steward traveled in a light, two-wheeled cart while Andrei rode. Despite the surrounding dampness, the tracks through the woods were fairly passable and they made good speed. At nights they rested in the villages or hamlets along the way.

The steward was sullen. Now and then, as if to prove that he was really an interesting fellow, the steward would engage Andrei in conversation. But Andrei politely discouraged him and remained aloof. To Maryushka he was similarly distant, so that the steward more than once growled to his wife: "A cold fellow, that."

Sometimes Andrei would trot on ahead of them; or he might hang back and watch their two heads from behind, Maryushka's held rather still, the steward's bobbing forward constantly as though he were nodding off to sleep. But more often he would walk his horse beside them, glancing across from time to time at Maryushka, who would always be looking, dully, straight ahead. How pale she was.

Twice however, when her husband had taken the horses down to one of the nearby streams to drink, she had moved swiftly over to Andrei and whispered, "Now, quickly. Take me now."

And in the damp chill of the forest, for a few minutes, they had continued their urgent, surreptitious lovemaking before resuming their places, apparently distant from each other.

When they reached Russka, Andrei was to stay at Nikita's house near the church while the steward returned to Dirty Place. As they approached the town Maryushka remarked to her husband: "I don't want to wait on that damned Cossack."

"You'll do as you're told," he answered gruffly. "The master said I was to look after him so that's that. He'll be gone in two days," he added, by way of encouragement.

She had sullenly obeyed.

And the two days in Russka had been even more memorable than the journey.

First there had been the village of Dirty Place, where the steward had obligingly taken him.

It was a small village, no different from any number of damp little hamlets he had seen on the way. Were there still relations of his there? No one seemed to know anything about his grandfather, who had fled eighty years before, until one old woman was able to tell him that yes, she had heard that one young man had disappeared into the wild field a few years before she was born. The grandson of that family lived at one end of the hamlet. And so it was that Andrei found himself confronted with a sturdy, pleasant-faced fellow with a thick shock of wavy black hair and four children, living in one of the stout huts. They welcomed him when they heard his story, looked with admiration at his fine clothes, and through this sturdy peasant Andrei learned that he was, in some way or other, distantly related to many of the village folk, including even Maryushka's mother.

"And you are free—you have your own farm? You are not a serf?" his cousin asked in wonder.

It almost hurt Andrei to admit it and to see the look of friendly envy on the man's face.

He enjoyed his visit to the monastery rather more. The monks and the artisans of Russka still made icons, but in recent generations they had made no attempt to produce their own style, preferring to copy the work of others.

"Here," one of the monks said proudly, as he showed Andrei a beautiful miniature icon, done in bright colors and lavishly decorated with gold, "is a Mother-of-God in the style of the Stroganov masters. And here," he showed his guest a large, imposing icon of Christ, the Ruler of the World," is a fine one in the present Moscow manner. This is for one of the tsar's own churches."

He thanked the monks for their kindness and gave a suitable donation before he left.

The last forty-eight hours had been difficult. There was the danger of discovery for a start.

Not that he was afraid for himself. He was a Cossack after all. But there was a wildness, a desperation in her that made him afraid, more than ever, that she might do something foolish that could harm her.

She was cunning, though. She complained grumpily to the neighbors and townspeople at having to clean and cook for the Cossack. She would be seen going irritably about her work while he was out, and she even made it appear that she left the house as much as possible when he was there.

Yet on both days she had slipped quietly into his bed in the early morning, and already managed, on four other occasions, to make brief but passionate love to him when they could not be seen.

Several times, though, she had come close to him and whispered: "Take me away with you. Take me to the Ukraine."

It was impossible.

"You've a husband," he reminded her.

"I hate him."

"And I'm going on campaign."

Did she love him or was he a means of escape? He did not know. He did not really care either. For the fact was, even if running off with Maryushka were possible, he did not want her.

Yet she did not give up. She would ask, wait a few hours, then gently ask again.

"Take me away, my Cossack. Take me with you. You needn't keep me. I'll go away and not trouble you. Just take me away from this place. Don't leave me here."

It was a litany he had already come to dread.

And on his return in midafternoon, he expected it to begin again, when instead she turned to him, with apparent calm and asked: "Have you any money, Cossack?"

"A little. Why?"

She looked at him in a matter-of-fact way, then pursed her lips. "Because I think I'm going to have a baby."

"You're pregnant?"

"I'm not sure but . . . maybe. My time never came."

"And it's mine?"

"Of course."

He looked at the floor.

"I know you won't take me away." Her voice was flat, monotonous, and far sadder than he had heard it before. "A Cossack can do anything, but you don't want me. Anyway, it was just a dream."

He said nothing.

"But if you have some money," she said, "you can give me that."

"Perhaps you're not pregnant," he suggested hopefully.

"Perhaps."

Could it be a ploy? He did not think so.

"But do you want to have it?"

"Better yours than his."

"Won't he know?"

She shrugged.

"We'll see," she replied.

He had a considerable amount of coins with him, some Polish, some Russian. He took out all the Russian and gave it to her.

"Thank you." She paused. "You can still keep the money and take me with you," she said with a sad, wry smile.

"No."

Neither of them spoke for a little time, but he was aware of her long fingers opening and closing over the little leather pouch of coins, kneading them. He knew that she was silently crying now, but he did not move to her side, fearing it would make her worse.

When she spoke again, through her tears, it was in a soft voice that was little more than a moan. "You didn't know, do you, Cossack? You don't know what it is to be alone."

"I am often alone." He said it, he supposed, not to justify himself but to comfort her.

She shook her head.

"You're alone with hope. You may be killed, but you're on an adventure. You're free, Cossack—free as a bird over the steppe. But I'm alone with nothing—don't you see? Just the sky; just the earth. There's no way out. It's so terrible, don't you see, to know that. To know you're alone, forever . . ."

He thought of her mother, the village of Dirty Place, and of her child.

"You're not alone," he said.

She did not reply.

"I'm going," she said finally. "When do you leave?"

"At dawn."

She nodded, then smiled weakly.

"Remember me."

She had a bright red scarf which she placed, in the manner of all Russian women, over her head before departing.

The sky was clear, a wonderful pale blue, as he rode southward from the little town of Russka in the early morning.

Two miles below the town there was a huge meadow that had been made by a monastery a few decades before.

And it was as he skirted this that he saw her, standing on one side of it, wearing her red scarf. For a moment, he thought of riding over to see her, but he decided not. It was better not.

Some time later, he looked back.

She was still there, a tiny patch of redness in a huge expanse of green; a lonely figure on an endless plain. She watched him until he was out of sight.

Andrei rode south. Soon he would see the steppe again, and thatched cottages, and swaying fields of wheat.

What a strange and contradictory land this Muscovy was. Now that he was leaving it, his spirits seemed to lighten, as though a door to a dark room were being opened.

His mind drifted back to earlier days—to Anna. And then, suddenly, he thought of his old friend Stepan, the Ox. He did not suppose he would see him again.

Freedom. That was the thing. Life was good. He was a dark and handsome fellow: there was no doubt about it. He felt his mustache—a true Cossack one.

His wide Cossack trousers flapped as the sun rose in the east and a little breeze got up.

SEVEN

Peter

MANY TIMES BEFORE in Russian history it had been thought that the end of days was approaching. But it was only in the second half of the seventeenth century that the new and ominous development began that convinced many that, this time, surely, the Apocalypse and the coming of the Antichrist must truly be at hand.

In order to understand Russia, it is important to remember that, while events in the center may sometimes move quickly, and new ideas may be introduced there, in the vast land itself, things change only very slowly. There is thus almost always a huge gap between what is said and what is done. And often confusing for the historian is that even the reaction of the endless hinterland to events at the center may be so delayed that it becomes like an echo, returning long after the original sound has been forgotten and the person who made it has departed.

While historians may argue about the origins of the cataclysm that was to mark the end of old Muscovy, there is no doubt that for many Muscovites the cataclysm began in the year 1653.

It began with the church reforms of the mighty Patriarch Nikon. And most visibly, it concerned the way that the Russians made the sign of the cross.

If this seems strange, it must be explained that the Russian Orthodox was unlike other orthodox churches. Over the centuries, isolated from the rest of Christendom, it had developed its own spirit and its own practices, which, as Patriarch Nikon had correctly seen, were out of line with the Orthodox mainstream. At certain points in their service, Russians sang two Hallelujahs instead of three; they used a different number of communion loaves and made too many genuflections. They misspelled the name of Jesus in their texts, along with sundry other errors. And of all these differences, none was more obvious than their manner of making the sign of the cross.

The Orthodox do not make the sign of the cross in the manner of the Catholics. Instead of touching his forehead, his chest and then crossing his hand from left to right over his chest, as do the Romans, the Orthodox with great care and solemnity touch first their forehead, then the middle of their chest, and then swing their hands first to the right and then to the left breast—in the opposite way, that is, from the Western churches.

Further yet, however, the Russian Orthodox, in crossing himself or making the sign of benediction, held his fingers in a special way. For instead of closing the thumb against the fourth finger and raising the other three, the Russian would place his thumb against the fourth and little finger, raising only two fingers, the index and third.

This was the famous two-fingered sign—the single hand as they often called it—that the Russians believed to be the pure and ancient practice. And it was this, together with his textual and liturgical corrections, that the Patriarch Nikon had set out, back in 1653, to change.

He was a titanic figure. Like many Russian reformers, the tall, austere Patriarch was in a hurry. He began to build a great monastery outside the capital, which he called New Jerusalem. The river beside it he renamed the Jordan. Its architecture was massive, plain, and severe. He planned five thrones there on which, one day, he hoped to see all five Patriarchs of the Orthodox Church sitting, with the Russian Patriarch at the center.

His sense of ecclesiastical power, however, was his downfall. For Tsar Alexis, often away on campaign, had left Nikon in charge in his absence and even given him the highest title of Great Sovereign; and it was not long before Nikon had started to suggest, like a medieval Pope, that the Patriarch and the Church should have authority over the tsar and the state—an idea that neither Alexis nor the boyars would tolerate. Mighty Nikon was exiled: his rule was over.

But his church reforms remained.

At first, even in 1653, there had been opposition. A small group of conservative clergy—the best known of whom was the archpriest Avvakum—had opposed the changes. At once he had crushed them and exiled Avvakum to the far north; but the opposition had continued.

In 1666 the Great Church Council called to settle the dispute agreed that, while the overambitious Nikon should be deposed, his reforms should stand and, among other things, the three fingers should be raised in making the sign of the cross, instead of the traditional two. Those who refused to follow the new practices were to be excommunicated as heretics.

And thus began the great fissure in Russian society known as the Raskol—the Schism—and the appearance on the scene of a new and important group of Russians. In the nineteenth century they would come to be known as the Old Believers. But in these times they were called by the more general term for religious dissidents—the Raskolniki, the Schismatics.

It has sometimes been suggested that the reformers represented progress and the Raskolniki were obscurantist priests supported by illiterate peasants. This is not so. Indeed, Nikon's new translations were done in such a hurry that they were full of inconsistencies, and he himself insisted upon details that other Patriarchs from the Orthodox churches declared to be unnecessary. As for the Raskolniki, many were literate merchants and well-to-do peasants.

The Raskolniki also had a cogent objection, which was hard for the reformers to answer. "For if Moscow is, as the Church has long claimed, the Third Rome—after which, we know, there shall be no other—then how can all these things the Church has taught and practiced now, suddenly, be wrong? Are we to say the practices of the Russian saints, and the liturgy confirmed by the Great Church Council of Ivan the Terrible were heretical?"

In a church that had always relied on the power of tradition, rather than textual analysis or logical proof, these objections were especially telling.

This was the quarrel at the center. And who could guess what echo would return, after a time, from the hinterland?

Meanwhile, in the years that followed, there were other mighty rumblings in the land.

1670

It was summer and the normally quiet little town of Russka was in a frenzy of excitement.

For the rebels were coming.

The monks, uncertain what line to take, looked to the abbot for guidance; but he himself could not make up his mind whether to defend the monastery or open its gates to them. In the town, and the nearby village of Dirty Place, opinion was similarly split. Many of the younger folk thought it would be a liberation: "He's going to free the peasants," they said. "They'll hang the Bobrovs and the land will be ours." But many of the older folk were more pessimistic. "If those rebels come," a small merchant remarked, "they'll be like a plague of locusts."

And nobody was even sure where the rebels were. The other side of the Volga, thought some; close by Nishni Novgorod, suggested others; already across the Oka, declared some alarmists.

And what of their leader, the daring Cossack, Stenka Razin? In the space of a few short years his name had already become a legend. "He'll rule in Moscow," they said, "like a true tsar."

It was amidst all this excitement that the little children of Dirty Place found a new amusement. This was to taunt a quiet, serious, sixteen-year-old girl. She paid no great attention to them, although their persistent question, accompanied by giggles and peals of laughter, hurt her more than they knew. Her name was Arina, and the question they asked was always the same. "Arina, is Stenka Razin really your father? Is he coming to save us? Tell us, Arina, is it really your father coming?"

It hurt her because she did not know.

Who was her father? No one would tell her.

Until she was five, she supposed it was the steward: after all, they lived with him. He was a stern, sour-faced man; and although he sometimes took her on his knee, it made little Arina sad because she sensed he did not love her. No doubt it was her fault. But when she was five, he died, and she and old Elena moved into her uncle's large *izba*. And it was a little after this that a little girl told her: "Your father was a Cossack."

She did not understand; and when she asked her grandmother about it, old Elena just said: "What nonsense."

But Arina soon realized, instinctively, that there was something strange about her. Something wrong. There were whispers and giggles. And finally, when she was seven, Elena abruptly told her: "The steward wasn't your father. It was a Cossack. That's all. Don't talk about it."

She didn't. But from that day she understood, in the minds of the village people, this strange, unseen figure of the Cossack in her past was like a mark upon her.

A Cossack? What did it mean? She had never seen one, but she knew that they were wild, terrifying fellows, that each had a single lock of hair sprouting out of his shaved head, and long mustaches; and that they rode the steppe like the Tatars. Could it really be that one of these devils was her father? Once, hesitantly, she had asked her grandmother what he was like. "Just a Cossack. Dark. Forget him," Elena had replied curtly. And an entire year had passed before Arina had dared even to ask: "What was my father's name?"

"I don't know. It's not important." Old Elena sounded irritable. "What difference does it make? He's probably dead; and even if he isn't, you'll never see him anyway." Then, seeing Arina's disappointment, she had added more kindly: "Don't worry, my little dove, you've got all the family you need here, thank God."

It was true. Besides her uncle—who was her mother's brother—about half the village seemed to be related to her in some way or other. Even the priest who came to the little wooden church in Dirty Place was a distant cousin; so were two of the merchants in Russka. No, Arina supposed, she had no excuse for feeling lonely.

Life in the village was often grim: the peasants expected to suffer. Their parents could remember the last days of Ivan the Terrible and the Time of Troubles that followed. Twice in Arina's short life the harvest had failed and they had nearly starved. One year news came that a huge population of wolves—three or four thousand of them—had invaded the city of Smolensk in the west and roamed the streets in search of food.

But the greatest hardship was war. There seemed to be no end to the fighting. As feared, a new war with Poland had broken out the moment the tsar took the Ukraine under his protection. For thirteen years not a season went by without another batch of men leaving Russka for the tsar's army; many did not return.

It was a piece of bad luck for the village that Nikita Bobrov had made a good marriage. It happened just after Arina's birth, for what was good for the landlord was certainly not so for Dirty Place. "He's got other estates now," Elena complained. "What's it to him if half our men are killed? He just hands them over to Germans and heretics who drive them like cattle. He doesn't care."

Indeed, in his eagerness to please the tsar, Nikita was generous in supplying serfs from this village—which he seldom visited—to fight under the foreign officers who so often commanded in the tsar's army. All through Arina's childhood, the village seemed only half alive, waiting for the return of those who never came.

Yet despite these troubles, her own family had emerged unscathed. For some reason Arina's uncle had not been sent away to fight. By good fortune his three boys, when they came of age, were not chosen either. The family prospered. Arina's uncle was the only man in the village who was not in debt to the Bobrovs for paying his taxes, and the family even had a hired laborer of their own to help in the fields.

It was only gradually that Arina realized her uncle bribed the steward. The old steward had been a peasant, but when he died, Nikita Bobrov had sent a slave in his place, and the reason her uncle's sons were never sent away to fight was that, somehow, he could afford to bribe this man. When she came to understand this, she was rather shocked. Wasn't it wrong, she asked old Elena?

"Perhaps," Elena said. "But be glad he does it."

"Where does Uncle find the money?"

"Don't ask."

"It isn't just, though," Arina said.

Elena only smiled ruefully. "You know the saying," she answered: "'The wolf is near; but on a cold, dark, night the tsar is very far away indeed.' Don't worry about right and wrong, just survive."

The family were kind to Arina and she certainly made herself useful. She would prepare the big earthenware pot to cook on the flat-topped stove overnight and salt the food to preserve it through the long winters. When one of her cousins made a fine gingerbread board, it was she who helped him design the peacock that was to be carved on it. She embroidered well.

It was strange, given her parents, that she was so plain. From Andrei she had inherited dark hair, and from her mother a certain grace of movement. But that was all. Her face was pale; her nose, by general consent, was too long; she had a slight squint, and there was a small wart on the left side of her chin. This lack of physical beauty, however, was modified by the fact that, when she allowed herself to show it, she had a smile of extraordinary sweetness.

To compensate for her shameful birth, Elena had brought her up very strictly. Grandmother and granddaughter would always be seen, at every possible church service in Dirty Place, Russka, or in the monastery, hurrying quietly by, their kerchiefs over their bowed heads, scarcely even looking up to speak as they crossed themselves before the doorway of the church, and again inside; they would light candles before every icon and say a prayer.

Above all, she loved to sing in the little wooden church in Dirty Place, with what became by her fifteenth year a beautiful contralto voice, so that the priest there would say: "She is our nightingale." And often he would remind the village people: "See how God, though He has not chosen to give this girl good looks, has instead given her a voice and a spirit of great beauty, by which He is praised."

It was as well that Arina should have a religious nature, for as her grandmother told her bluntly, "You will never be married." She saw it very well. Thanks to the war with Poland, there were five women to every man in the district around Russka. "And of all the girls, I'm afraid you'd be the last to be chosen anyway," Elena said, "so you may as well get used to the idea."

If Arina ever felt bitter about any aspect of her fate, she never showed it. "I thank God," Elena would say to people in the girl's presence, "I thank God, at least, that she isn't headstrong like her mother." Submission, her grandmother taught her: submission and obedience were her only hope. She must never be like her mother.

When she was a little girl, Arina had often wondered about her mother. What sort of person had she been?

Fortunately, old Elena would often talk about Maryushka. She had loved her so much that she couldn't help it. Indeed, the memory of the vanished girl still, after all these years, seemed to exercise a fascination over the stout old woman. "She was a beauty, there's no denying it," she would say to Arina, with a shake of her head.

Her mother's crime, Arina discovered, was not so much her affair with the Cossack. Such things were wrong, of course, but they happened. Her crime was being headstrong.

"The steward, you see, he didn't know he wasn't your father. Not at first," Elena explained. He might never have known if he had not continually beaten Maryushka.

"Whenever something annoyed him, he'd take it out on her," Elena remembered sadly. "He used to hit her with his fist. She should have just taken it like most women do, but no, she had to lose her temper one day, just after you were weaned. She told him what she thought of him. Then she told him he wasn't your father."

She sighed. "Ah, Maryushka, my poor dove. 'I've done it now,' she says to me. 'You have,' I said. 'He'll bide his time,' she says, 'then he'll kill me. I know him.' 'Yes,' I said, 'I think you're right.' 'So will you take Arina?' she says. And then, next morning, without even saying good-bye to me, she's gone."

So had begun Elena's life with the steward. He had told her bluntly that since her daughter had left him like this, she had better look after him. And since he had power over her family, she had agreed. "But don't you try hitting me, though," she had warned. "I'm not your wife."

Even then, the village assumed that wild Maryushka had run away because of the steward's cruelty, and no one would have known about the Cossack if the steward himself, in his occasional drunken rages, had not blurted it out. "Curse him," Elena would remark. "He doesn't mind dishonoring himself, so long as he can blacken her name. My poor Maryushka."

"Where did she go?" the little girl would ask.

"How should I know? To the steppe. Or across the Volga."

"And is she there now?"

"Perhaps. If the wolves didn't get her."

"Will she come back?" Arina had sometimes asked hopefully.

In fact, Elena felt sure Maryushka was dead. What hope of survival had a lone woman walking off into the unknown? At best she had been captured and taken as a serf by a landlord somewhere. "No. She won't come back," she would say bitterly. "What for?"

Yet although she never dared to say so, the little girl had always believed that one day her mother would come. Sometimes, at harvest, when the women were out with their sickles in the field, she would watch their long, bobbing line and suppose to herself that just once, even if only for a moment, one of them would detach herself from the line and come towards her, smiling and saying: "See, my little dove, I have returned to see you after all."

And at harvest's end she liked to go over to the big meadow that seemed to stretch to the horizon and stare at the squat haystacks that dotted the empty spaces. For some reason, then, she would become convinced that her mother was out there, concealed behind one of the haystacks, and she would run from one to another, peeping around them, half expecting to find a strange yet familiar form, who would take her into her arms. But each time she played this solitary, foolish game with herself, she would find nothing in the empty silence of the endless meadow except the freshly cut stubble and the high, sweet-smelling stacks so that, by the time the shadows lengthened, it seemed to the little girl in her sharp imagination as if God Himself had hidden His face behind a cloud and left her all alone.

By the time she was ten, however, the village people seemed to have forgotten about her parents; at least, no one bothered to talk about them. And her life at Russka had been quiet.

But now Stenka Razin was coming. And who knew what that might mean?

There had been similar risings before, and there would be others in the future, but no Russian rising has ever attained such romance in Russian legend as that of Stenka Razin in 1670. Perhaps this was because it was the last real cry from the old, free Russia of the borderlands.

It had begun, far away among the freedom-loving Cossacks of the Don. For by 1670 even their democratic way of life had broken down, and a new class of rich Cossacks had appeared, who cared little for their poorer brothers. It was these poor Cossacks and peasants who, around 1665, had first rallied to the daring leader known as Stenka Razin, who was operating in the southern lands between the Volga and the Don.

It might have been only some local raiding, scarcely heard of across the endless steppe. But something about the character of Razin made it more. The raids soon turned into a rising, then a full-scale rebellion. Promising free assemblies of the people in the old-style Cossack way, he swept up the Volga taking town after town. By the summer of 1670, the rebel army was huge, had taken over half of southeast Russia, and seemed about to strike across at Moscow and the Russian heartland itself.

And now, suddenly, the village remembered Arina's father.

"Arina's father's coming," the little children cried. And the older ones, with more cunning: "How much loot has Razin got, Arina? Is he going to make you rich?"

For three weeks the taunts went on, and the girl inwardly cringed.

Then suddenly it was over. In early autumn the tsar sent an army that smashed the rebels. The democratic hero fled back to the Don, where the rich Cossacks captured him and handed him over to the tsar. The following June he was executed in Red Square. So ended, to all intents, the old free ways of the Cossacks.

"The tsar's killed Arina's father," the children now cried with glee.

She tried to take no notice. Yet, long after they had forgotten to taunt her, she remained feeling sad. Somehow the death of the dashing Razin seemed like another loss, reminding her vividly how that other Cossack, her father, had vanished from her life so many years ago. And it prompted her to ask Elena, one day in early spring: "The Cossack, my father—did he know my mother was going to have me?"

"Perhaps," Elena answered reluctantly.

"Then," she pursued, "didn't he ever come to see her again? Didn't he even want to see me?"

At first, it seemed to Arina that her grandmother had not even heard the question, because for a time she did not even deign to reply. Then at last she answered.

"No."

Arina said nothing. She would not raise the subject again. Clearly neither of her parents had loved her. She supposed that, for some reason, she did not deserve it.

It did not occur to her that the real reason Elena had paused before she replied, was that she had told a lie.

1654

THERE were, by the year 1654, three Russias. The first, Great Russia, was the Muscovy of the tsars. The second was the newly added Ukraine, which the Muscovites chose to call Little Russia. The third was the broad band of territory, about two hundred miles across, that lay on the west side of the great R of Russian rivers—more precisely the lands west of the ancient city of Smolensk and which extended to the marshes of Poland. Once ruled by the ancient princes of Rus, they had long since fallen into Polish hands. The Muscovites called this western, Russian-Polish territory White Russia.

And it was from White Russia, in 1654, that Andrei was returning that late summer's day.

It had been a strange year for the young Cossack. Bogdan and his council, after mistrustful negotiations, had finally joined the Ukraine to Muscovy with an agreement that gave them huge estates. The simple peasants of the Ukraine, needless to say, got nothing.

In March, Andrei had returned to Moscow and attended the marriage of Nikita Bobrov to an heiress. And it was then that the Russian did his Cossack friend a great favor: he arranged for Andrei to join him when the Muscovite army went on campaign against the Poles.

The war with Poland—which the tsar's annexation of the Ukraine had made inevitable—was part of a greater and longer process. The foreign officers Andrei noticed in Moscow were part of this general preparation. For this new war with Poland was really little more than an excuse for Russia to strike a still greater blow. As Nikita gleefully told his friend: "We're going to attack White Russia."

The campaign was successful. In the south, the Cossacks of the Ukraine struck across the Dnieper; farther north the Russian army advanced westward from Moscow to the ancient city of Smolensk.

Before it was over, Andrei had twice been addressed personally by the fair, blue-eyed tsar; and when they returned to Moscow he was informed that Alexis had granted him a new estate as well.

Andrei and his friend did not return to Moscow until July.

Nikita had asked Andrei to remain in the capital in the new and much larger house that he and his wife now occupied; but on their return to the capital they learned that an outbreak of plague had begun. At first they hoped that it would die down; after a few days, however, Nikita came home with grim news. "The rumor is that they're going to seal the royal family's apartments in the Kremlin. The tsaritsa and her household are leaving the city. I should get out, Andrei. Go and enjoy your new estate in Little Russia."

Andrei had taken his advice. And so it was that late in July he had left the city to return home.

He decided to go by way of Russka.

He had not been able to discover anything about the fate of Maryushka. Nikita, who had not been near the estate for a year, had an idea that the steward's young wife might have had a child; but he was not sure. So it was with some curiosity that he rode out eastward towards Vladimir and then turned south.

He was in a strange mood. Things had gone very well for him. He was becoming rich. Yet his friend's marriage, and a few close brushes with death on the campaign, had reminded him vividly that, even well into his twenties, he was still alone in the world. "This child, if it exists, will be all I have given to the world," he mused, as he made his way through the late summer countryside. "Even if I cannot claim the child, I'd like to see it."

He brought some presents with him.

Often he felt melancholy. Once, just past a village on the river Kliasma, he saw a raft moored in midstream. It had a single mast from the top of which hung a rope: and at the end of the rope, with a large iron hook under his rib cage, hung the body of a man. Obviously he must be a robber of some kind, for this kind of death was the standard Muscovite punishment for river pirates. But as he drew closer Andrei saw from the man's baggy trousers and long mustaches that he had been a Cossack. He had obviously hung there for a week already.

A Cossack: a brother. Yet not, of course, a brother.

"He was poor. I am rich."

For some reason even his own good fortune, compared to this fellow's, filled him with a sense of desolation.

Three days later he came in sight of Russka.

*　*　*

He was still half a mile from the little town when he met Elena. She was walking through the woods.

She recognized him at once, but her stolid, sturdy face gave no sign of pleasure or even of interest at the meeting.

After a brief greeting he asked.

"Did Maryushka have a child?"

"Yes."

"A boy?"

"A girl."

"Where are they now?"

"The baby is at the village. Maryushka—who knows?" And Elena explained her daughter's departure.

He was appalled.

"She just walked off?"

"Into the forest. Or the steppe perhaps. She'll be dead now."

"Perhaps not," he suggested.

"Perhaps."

He looked at her thoughtfully. "I must see the child."

"What for?"

It was hard to say. But he knew he wanted to.

"Stay away," the older woman said. "He knows about you—the steward. You can only make things worse for us, and the child, if he sees you." And reluctantly Andrei realized that she was probably right.

He drew out a purse of money. He had brought it for Maryushka. There was also a little golden bracelet—rather fine, in which was set a large amethyst. "Give the little girl these, when she gets married."

Elena took them without comment. "Good-bye," she said bleakly.

He paused, looking down at her, feeling awkward. "I'm sorry," he said finally.

She glanced at him, but there was no hint of forgiveness in her eyes. Then she spat.

"For what?"

He was silent.

"Leave now, Cossack," she said in a voice that was full not of hatred, but of a dull contempt.

Andrei returned her sullen gaze. For a second, that word—*Cossack*—and the way it was said annoyed him. Am I to be despised by a Russian peasant? he thought irritably.

It seemed that old Elena had read something of his thoughts, for now she decided to speak again. Yet when she did, it was not quite what he had expected. "Do you know, Mister Cossack, what the difference is, between you and a Russian man?" she asked quietly. "Just one thing: that you can ride away." She spat again. "The steward gets drunk and beats Maryushka. You get her pregnant and ride into the steppe. And we women, who suffer, we remain, like the earth. You trample us, yet without us you are nothing." Then she shrugged. "God made us want you. Our eyes make us despise you."

Andrei nodded. He understood. It was the eternal voice of Russian womanhood.

Slowly he mounted and, without another word, rode quietly away. He did not expect that he would ever see his daughter. Only when he was several miles away did he realize that he had forgotten to ask her name.

Elena never told Arina about her father's visit, though she carefully hid the money and the bracelet under the floor. Why cause trouble? she thought. If the steward gets to know about the money, he'll want it. As for that Cossack—better Arina shouldn't think about him. And, as the years went by, and she saw how plain Arina was, she thought: The poor girl will never get married, anyway. What use has she for a dowry?

And so she had given the money to her son; and he had used it to bribe the steward.

1677

HER life had been blameless. Of what, then, should Arina be afraid?

She was twenty-three and had not married, nor even been close to it. She knew very well that she never would be. Womanhood had only made her plainer. The wart on her chin had grown larger. It was not absolutely disfiguring; she was not unsightly; but when one came near her, it was impossible to overlook it. This, she told herself, was God's way, in his infinite wisdom, of ensuring that she would be always humble. She prayed each day. She made herself useful. She had no enemy in Russka or Dirty Place. Yet always there was a nagging fear in her mind. She was afraid that they would take her church away from her.

This fear was not unreasonable. For she was one of the Raskolniki.

The development of the religious schism at Russka had been typical of many provincial settlements: which is to say, it had been slow.

It had taken two years for the Patriarch's new prayerbooks to reach the monastery. When they had, the abbot put them quietly away in his room and refused to acknowledge that he had even received them. The monks were never told about it.

In many ways the abbot admired Nikon. Hadn't the Patriarch stood up for the dignity of the Church? Hadn't he fought the tsar when Alexis had tried to limit the gifts of property the Church might receive? Undoubtedly Nikon was a fine Russian churchman. But the abbot also had friends among the party who opposed the reforms and who objected to Nikon's high-handed ways. He mistrusted the Ukrainian and other scholars whom Nikon brought in. He was jealous of their influence and considered them too Catholic—too Polish—for his taste.

He preferred to stick to his old loyalties, both personal and liturgical. And so at the little monastery of Saint Peter and Saint Paul, the monks had continued with the old service and made the sign of the cross with two fingers; and since few people from Moscow came there, no one was much the wiser.

Except for some of the monks. For even in that backwater it was not long before they came to learn of the new form of service, and they asked the abbot what was to be done. Only after a year had passed did he even show the new books to the more senior and trustworthy brethren. And having shown them, he ordered them to obey him in all things. When Nikita Bobrov or any churchman of significance visited the monastery, he used the new form of service. As soon as they were gone, he reverted. And so they continued until the time of the Great Church Council of 1666.

Even in the little monastery at Russka, however, there could be no more dodging the issue after this. Reluctantly the abbot followed the new rules. And the monks were ordered to do the same. Authority was authority. The council was acting with the tsar. All must obey.

Except at Dirty Place.

Not that anyone knew. The abbot, if he guessed, said nothing. Nikita Bobrov, who owned the village, had no idea. The local peasants knew, but then, who ever talked to them?

For the little community at Dirty Place was led by Silas the priest.

He was a quiet fellow. His grandfather had been the son of the priest Stephen, who had been killed by Ivan the Terrible; Silas was the first of the family to take up the priesthood since that time. His own father had been a modest trader in Russka.

His thoughtful face and serious blue eyes resembled his ancestor's but he was only of medium height, and an accident as a boy had given him a slight limp. Though he lacked any great physical presence, there was a quiet, rather passionate determination about him that gave Silas authority among the peasants.

It was when he went to Nizhni Novgorod to study for the priesthood that he had come in contact with the priests who were to protest against the reforms. This was not surprising. Besides being a great trading center, the old city at the meeting of the Volga and the Oka was still something of a frontier. Once past Nizhni Novgorod, one was in the vast wild emptiness of the northeastern forests. Here were all manner of remote communities and hermits; here were the true, simple Russians, who made their houses in the forest with their axes and who struck every blow for the Lord.

Near Nizhni Novgorod, also, had come the family of the great opponent of reform, the priest Avvakum; and it happened that, while serving as a deacon there, Silas had met a kinswoman of the fiery priest and married her.

He was not a learned man. At Nizhni Novgorod they had taught him to read; but his objections to the reforms were not sophisticated, like those of the abbot. Indeed, apart from his wife's connection with Avvakum, he would scarcely have been able to say who was right about many of the issues in the dispute between the priest and the Patriarch.

Silas's feeling of disgust had deeper roots. It was instinctive. And it concerned the very core of the Russian Church, indeed of Russia itself. It was a feeling that Russia's heart had been invaded, her soul perverted: and that it was the work of outsiders. "Why does the tsar need so many foreigners?" he would ask. "Why are our troops led by Germans? Why does the tsar import craftsmen and let the boyars keep musical instruments in their houses?"

And if at first he had been confused by the technical details of the church dispute, by the time of the Great Church Council of 1666, Silas no longer had any doubt about what was wrong. "First they let Poles and Greeks tamper with the liturgy; now the foreigners have taken over," he exclaimed to his wife. And then, dropping his voice at the horror of the thing: "I've even heard that some of the new translations were done by Jews."

And to his little congregation at Dirty Place the priest would declare: "To us Russians, to simple Christians, dear brothers and sisters in Christ, only one thing is of importance. It is not worldly knowledge: for where shall worldly knowledge and foreign cunning lead us if not into greater sin? It is not subtle argument: for what can we humble people know, compared to the wisdom of God? It is love; it is devotion; it is the blessed quality, the sacred and burning ardor in each one of us to serve God faithfully, reverently in the way shown us by Our Lord and by the saints. That is all that matters." And here he used a word that was, and would long remain, close to the heart of every Russian: "We must live our lives with *blagochestie.*"

Blagochestie: it meant piety, ardent devotion, loyalty, faithfulness. It was attached, always, to the tsar in old Muscovy—the pious tsar. And above all, for men like Silas, it meant faithfulness to the old ways, to sacred tradition. It meant the humble love and religious awe of the Russian peasant, against the proud, rational, legalistic Western world towards which they sensed the authorities were trying to drag them. It meant the world of the icon, and the axe.

In Dirty Place therefore, Silas continued to use the old forms of the service; he said two Hallelujahs. And he made the sign of the cross with two fingers.

It was dangerous. The authorities in Moscow were determined to be obeyed. Far in the north, when the abbot of the great Solovetsky Monastery by the White Sea had ordered his monks not to use the new liturgy and even told them not to pray for the tsar, troops had besieged the obstinate rebels and finally massacred them.

No one knew how many other communities were secretly doing the same thing, but it seemed that the underground movement was growing. Some protesters, like Silas, were purely religious; others complained at the tsar's high taxes and at their harsh living conditions. Whatever their reasons, the sense of sullen protest was growing and Moscow knew it. There was going to be trouble.

So far, the little community at Dirty Place had received no official attention; but what if it did? What would Silas and his congregation do then? No one seemed to know, but Arina had good reason to be worried.

It was in the spring of that year, on a cool, damp day, that the stranger appeared at Russka.

Like any traveler, he went to the monastery, where the monks gave him food and shelter. Though he said that his name was Daniel, he seemed unwilling to explain anything more about himself; and when the monks asked him where he came from he answered only: "From Yaro-slavl."

Which, when they reported it to the abbot, made him smile and re-mark: "He looks it. They have real Russians up there."

Yaroslavl was ancient. Like other northeastern cities—Vladimir, Ros-tov, Suzdal—it dated back to Kievan times. It lay to the north, on the loop of the great river Volga, and beyond it was the vast taiga forest that stretched to the arctic tundra. The symbol that the city bore on its shield was, appropriately, a bear carrying an axe.

They were mighty men up in those parts: the same simple, determined men who had come down with their scythes and axes to drive the Poles out of Muscovy in the Time of Troubles.

The stranger was such a fellow. He was huge, with a shaggy head, a massive, grizzled beard, and a large nose which, with the passing of the years, had spread outward so that it took up the middle of his bearded face like a large smudge. Often he sat very still, staring before him, or holding out one of his huge hands to feed a bird. Gentle in all his gestures, it was also obvious that he was enormously strong.

But what was he doing there? No one had any idea. He possessed a little money. He did not seem to be a runaway peasant. He carried with him a tiny icon, black with age, and a little book of psalms, from which it appeared he could read. Yet he said he was not a priest.

On the third day of his stay in the monastery he became ill. A fever seized him and for a short time the monks thought he would die. But he recovered and soon he was to be seen wandering about the countryside nearby.

A week after his first walk, he had a private conversation with the abbot. After this the monks learned two things. The first was that, during his fever, a voice had commanded him to stay at Russka. The second was that he could paint icons, and he had asked the abbot if he might take lodgings in the town and join the other painters there. To this the abbot had agreed.

So it was that Daniel came to live at Russka.

He was a good craftsman, but though he would paint parts of icons under the directions of others, he would never paint the figures them-selves, claiming that his skill was not sufficient. The icons in question, being run-of-the-mill copies for sale by the monastery, were by no means great works of art; but his modesty pleased the other painters.

He kept to himself. Not only could he paint, but he was an excellent carpenter. He observed every fast strictly and spent several hours each day praying and genuflecting. Following the Old Testament to the letter, he would not eat any of the forbidden meats, including veal, rabbit, and hare.

It was noticed also that on Sundays Daniel went to the little church at Dirty Place where Silas conducted the service. But since he went to the monastery, too, no one thought much about it.

In Dirty Place, the villagers soon got used to the strange, quiet fellow who used to appear among them. The men had nothing against him; the women decided they liked him because he was reputed to be hardworking, and they sensed something gentle, almost reverential in his bearing towards them. They decided he was a holy man of some kind. And one old woman remarked: "He's a wanderer. One of these days you'll turn around and he'll be gone." For it was surely true that there was something about him that was apart.

Above all, they took their tone from Silas, who on several occasions had been seen talking quietly to the big fellow and who pronounced, firmly: "He is a godly man. He has the true *blagochestie.*"

For two years the strange fellow came each week to Dirty Place, keeping to himself and scarcely speaking to a soul. And still no one was any the wiser about him. All they knew, with satisfaction, was that when he made the sign of the cross, he did so with two fingers.

1684

FOR Nikita, the whole business had been a disaster.

It might have been all right, despite everything, if he hadn't quarreled with that damned Tolstoy. That was the trouble. "And now we're completely out of favor," he lamented to his wife.

The question was—what could they do about it? Which was when she had made her curious suggestion.

It was doubly galling because the family had been doing well ever since the Romanovs came to the throne. The first Romanov had rewarded Nikita's grandfather in two ways. He had allowed him to convert the old estate—held on *pomestie* service tenure under Ivan the Terrible—back into the hereditary *votchina* that could not be taken away. And he had given him some more *votchina*, from the good land beside the monastery, as well. Nikita's marriage had brought him fresh estates. He kept them all in good order. His peasants worked three days *barshchina* and paid him modest rents in cash and kind. They were, he supposed, no better and no worse off than most peasants. In addition, he had bought several small parcels of land south of the river Oka in Riazan province, on the edge of the steppe where the soil was rich and where his stewards used slave labor—a combination of men who could not pay their debts and captured Tatar raiders. The returns there were excellent.

Nikita had done well. Indeed the family's status had never been higher. For though the tsar had finally abolished the old *mestnichestvo* records of precedence—which, though terribly inconvenient, had guaranteed the Bobrovs a certain status—Nikita had managed to get himself raised into the coveted ranks of the Muscovite nobility. This meant that he lived in Moscow, close to the tsar, and he even dreamed of being a candidate for the provincial governorship. If only he had been able to take that one, further step into the tsar's favor, he might become a rich man.

And though his wife and he had known the sadness—all too common in Russia—of losing children, in 1668, praise the Lord, a robust little boy had been born who showed every sign of surviving. They had named him Procopy.

As he approached his fifties, therefore, Nikita had been sanguine. He enjoyed good health and high rank. Though growing stout, he was elegant. All he had to do was attract the favorable notice of the tsar.

Things had certainly been changing in the capital. The court of Alexis had been growing more cosmopolitan, more Western. Great men like the tsar's friend Matveev encouraged Western manners; a few of the inner court circle even shaved their beards. As an ambitious man with some education himself, Nikita was drawn towards these court circles. The great Matveev had liked him and become his mentor. Though he still had a healthy suspicion of all foreigners, Nikita occasionally changed his kaftan for a Polish coat. He had heard German musicians play at Matveev's house. He occasionally attended a church with a choir that performed part-singing in harmony, in the Western manner. And in 1673 he had even obliged his wife to attend one of the new entertainments arranged by the tsar—a play.

She had approved.

Her name was Eudokia, or in full: Eudokia Petrovna Bobrova. She was Bobrova because, like all Russian married women, she took the feminine form of her husband's name, Bobrov. Her patronymic came from her father Peter, whose memory she still revered. And people usually addressed her, respectfully, as Eudokia Petrovna.

She was a powerful woman: black haired, thick-set, with a round face whose placid gentleness completely belied her character. A strict conservative, she was fully conscious of her wealth and her late father's high position as a military commander. When guests came to their house, she remained out of sight until she was summoned to serve the men brandy after their meal; then, having saluted the guests, she would discreetly depart again. But in private, with other women, or alone with her husband, she had no hesitation in expressing her views. On no subject were they stronger than the changes favored by the court. A man without a beard, she told him, looked like a chicken that had just been plucked. The Western music, like the plays, was sacrilegious: "I go to church to hear the Word of God, not some Polish whining," she would say.

Above all, honoring her father's memory, she was contemptuous of the tsar's army with its foreign officers. "These Germans: what do they know? They know how to give orders. Good." She would stand up and mimic an unfortunate peasant standing in utter confusion with his musket. "I've seen them," she would cry. "The officer calls out. Nobody understands. He tries again—ah, now they understand. So this one turns left. This one goes right. This one fires his musket. One advances, one retreats. They don't know what they're doing. And why? Because the officer who drilled them the week before had a different method altogether. Imbeciles!"

And Nikita would roar with laughter because it was perfectly true, the officers from different countries often brought with them their own drill books, which did not agree with each other, and which they utterly refused to change.

On this, as on many other matters, Eudokia would conclude with the words: "Things were better in the time of Ivan the Terrible. He'd have sorted them out."

It was strange, therefore, that she did not approve of the tsar's wars. To Nikita, the absorption of the Ukraine and the drive into the Polish territories to the west meant glory for Russia. To his practical wife, however, they did not. "War just means ruin for our poor peasants," she complained.

Even Nikita admitted she had a point. There were at this time a hundred thousand men under arms. The military took up sixty-two percent of the state's budget; and as always the taxes fell on the peasants. "If we go on like this, we'll have another rebellion like Stenka Razin's," Eudokia predicted.

She began to insist, each year, that they inspect their villages, which Nikita found a great bore; and she personally would interview the peasants and frequently give them money. "It's lucky we're rich, with so many peasants to feed," he would remark wryly. But she paid no attention.

Given her conservative views, therefore, it did not surprise Nikita that in religious matters his wife should sympathize with the Raskolniki. Nor was she alone among the noblewomen of the day. The tsar's first wife had done so. And a little group of prominent ladies, including one of the great boyar family of Morozov, had not only supported the followers of Avvakum but even gone to prison for it. Such sympathies, however, were becoming unfashionable among the noble class, as well as dangerous; and Nikita had told Eudokia she must keep her thoughts to herself.

He supposed that she had.

The troubles of Nikita Bobrov began with a change in the court, when suddenly, and quite unexpectedly, Tsar Alexis died, leaving behind him a court split into two factions.

By his first wife he left several daughters and two sons: Fedor, pleasant but sickly; and Ivan, an unfortunate child, mentally retarded and with a growth of skin over his eyes. By his second wife, a woman of modest birth, Alexis had left two infant children—a baby girl and a boy of three.

The little boy's name was Peter.

The family of Alexis's first wife, the mighty Miloslavskys, had not been pleased at the appearance of the second wife's family, the humble Naryshkins. Above all, they hated the tsar's friend Matveev, who had first introduced the couple.

It was a predictable Muscovite business. Young Fedor became tsar; Peter and his mother were kindly treated; but the Miloslavskys took over all the reins of power; and it did not take the Miloslavskys long to find a pretext for arresting Matveev. That educated gentleman was foolish enough to be found with a book of algebra in his baggage, which was, naturally, taken to be a form of black magic. Even Nikita, when he heard of the arrest of his mentor, could only shake his head and remark: "He was asking for trouble. What did he want with such stuff anyway?"

Though he had lost a powerful patron, the change at court did not mean the end for Nikita Bobrov. He was not important enough to worry the Miloslavskys. He had friends. Given time, he might have continued his advance.

Except for those fatal words to young Tolstoy.

The palace of Kolomenskoye lay not far outside the city of Moscow on gently rising ground beside the river.

It was an extraordinary collection of buildings. For generations a summer residence of the tsars, Alexis had added to its stone churches and bell towers a large, sprawling set of wooden houses and halls as exotic and striking to the eye as the twisted cupolas of Saint Basil's Cathedral in Red Square. Great bulbous domes, high tent roofs with windows peeping out, huge, onion-shaped gables, and massive exterior staircases—the place was a riot of the Russian forms taken to ornamental extremes. Like much of the church architecture of Alexis's reign, it was exuberant and ornamental. It was as though, seeing their own architecture for the first time with partly Western eyes, some of the builders in Russia had decided to take their traditional forms and play with them, twisting them, piling one next to another until the final result was a tremendous, exotic stage set, a gigantic Muscovite honeycomb imbued with an impressive, rich heaviness.

And it was on a sunny summer's day, walking in the gardens before Kolomenskoye Palace, some years into Tsar Fedor's reign, that Nikita encountered Peter Tolstoy.

Why was it that he disliked the fellow so much? Tolstoy was a strong man—no doubt about it—with heavy black eyebrows and piercing blue eyes. He was intelligent. Perhaps too intelligent, perhaps cunning. He was about ten years younger than Nikita, but he knew more—and both of them were aware of it. His family's no better than mine, Nikita thought irritably; yet something about Tolstoy told Nikita that he was going to the top.

When, therefore, young Tolstoy started to walk along beside him, Nikita experienced a wave of irritation. As far as he could, without being rude, he tried to ignore him. He only vaguely listened to what was being said. And so three or four minutes passed before, to his surprise, he suddenly realized that the damned fellow was talking about Eudokia, his own wife.

He started to listen. What was Tolstoy saying? Schismatics? Danger? Now he really began to pay attention; and what he heard made him tremble.

For it seemed that Eudokia had been talking. Behind closed doors, to other women, thank God; but she had been talking all the same: arguing, in her usual way, in favor of the Raskolniki.

And very quietly, like the smooth courtier and diplomat he was, Tolstoy was warning him about it. Women's talk of course. Things were being said. If such things came to the wrong ears . . . "We men are always the last to know," Tolstoy remarked with a smile. It seemed all Moscow knew. And as Nikita looked across at the other's calm, impassive face, he was filled with a sudden fury. Why was Tolstoy saying all this: as an act of kindness? Or was it a threat—a piece of information he could use at a future date? Was the fellow trying to establish a hold over him for some reason?

Worst of all, he was being made to look a fool. He had little doubt that Tolstoy was telling the truth. Eudokia was disobeying him, and this young man was quietly telling him that he couldn't control his own wife. Yet even then, he might have kept his temper, had it not been for one tiny thing.

The two men had paused in their walk. Nikita, full of resentment, had been staring at the ground when, feeling the other man watching him, he looked up into his face—and met Tolstoy's eyes.

Nothing in the world is more unwise than to give an expressive look to a person one does not know very well. For it is sure to be misinterpreted, usually because the other sees therein the reflection of his own thoughts. So it was with Nikita and Tolstoy. By the look of worldly cynicism Tolstoy then gave Nikita, he had meant to convey: Ah, my dear fellow, there's no accounting for women's chatter. But what Nikita saw was: My God, what a fool you are, and we both know it. It was the last straw. He exploded.

"You vile young rascal," he abruptly burst out. "Do you think I haven't always known you for what you are. If you want to spread gossip about my wife, you'll find it rebounds on you. I promise you that." And then, very quietly: "Take care, or you may regret this."

It was foolish. He knew it almost before he had finished. But seeing Tolstoy wince in surprise, he mistook this, also, for a look of contempt, and he turned on his heel.

As for Tolstoy—who in reality had only meant to do a favor to a useful fellow—he at once concluded that Nikita must be an enemy: just important enough to be dangerous and who might one day need to be neutralized.

"Yet how," as Nikita afterwards moaned to himself, "could I have been so stupid?"

For the Tolstoys, though only of the minor aristocracy themselves, had married into the family of the mighty Miloslavskys.

Nikita continued to serve, and to hope. He made friends in high places. He even came to know the great prince Basil Golitsyn—a powerful westernized noble whom he hoped to secure as a patron. From Tolstoy he heard nothing, and he put the incident at Kolomenskoye out of his mind. A few years more, a little luck, and he still might secure that governorship.

He was away, visiting a distant estate, when in the early summer of 1682 news reached him of the unexpected cataclysm in Moscow; and the whole business was so quick that, though he hurried back, it was all over before he reached the capital.

Poor Tsar Fedor had died. He had produced no children and so there were two possible heirs—the unfortunate Ivan, last son of Alexis by his

Miloslavsky wife; and the handsome young Peter, still only nine years old, son of the Naryshkin girl. A half-blind, simpleton cripple and a boy; the mighty Miloslavsky clan and the upstart Naryshkins.

But there was one other factor, which Nikita had never considered: poor Ivan had a sister.

Princess Sophia was not a beauty. She was fat; she had an oversize head; her face was rather hairy and, as time went on, carbuncles appeared on her legs. As a princess, she was also expected to live in seclusion in the royal palace. But Sophia was both intelligent and ambitious. She had no intention of staying in seclusion, or of allowing the Naryshkins to push out her Miloslavsky relations.

In an astonishing series of events, and taking advantage of a sudden revolt of the powerful Moscow regiments of *streltsy,* Sophia had the Naryshkins hacked to pieces in the Kremlin palace itself. It was an appalling and terrifying affair, taking place before the very eyes of young Peter and his mother—a terrible reminder that this was old Muscovy still, as dark, as morbid as in the days of Ivan the Terrible.

Then she had both Peter and the unfortunate Ivan declared joint tsars—and herself made regent.

The strange coronation took place in late June. Nikita Bobrov, having returned, was present. The two boys, robed in vestments glinting with gold and heavy with pearls—one youth blind and half dumb, the other only a child—were each crowned, in solemn state, with the so-called Cap of Monomakh. But behind them was Sophia. For the first time in Russian history, a woman held the reins of power.

And as he watched, Nikita thought of something else, which made him much afraid. For when Sophia began her bid for power, two men had ridden into the *streltsy* quarter to whip them up. One was Alexander Miloslavsky. And the other was Peter Tolstoy.

"My dear Nikita Mikhailovich, my dear friend. We must have a talk."

There was no more urbane man in all Russia than Sophia's new chief minister, Prince Basil Golitsyn. Some whispered that he was also her lover. Could it really be so? Nikita was not in a position to know. But Golitsyn was certainly powerful and, Nikita believed, looked upon him with favor.

When he had been summoned to attend upon the prince in the Kremlin, therefore, he had dared to hope it might be good news. And now, seeing the great man advancing towards him with these friendly words, he scarcely even noticed all the other people in the room, or the expressions on their faces. He saw only Golitsyn, and the fact that he was smiling.

For even to a man of some importance, like Bobrov, the prince was dazzling. He was, in truth, the first of the great, cosmopolitan Russian aristocrats who were to impress even the grandees of Europe for the next two centuries. Had it been anyone else, Nikita might even have been shocked by Golitsyn. It was not just that he spoke Latin; nor even that he drank only moderately and that his palatial house contained Western pictures, furniture, even Gobelin tapestries; but he would welcome foreigners to his house, including even—Nikita had heard with horror—the dreaded Jesuits. Yet no one could deny that Golitsyn was a true Russian. No family was nobler or more ancient. And besides all this, as he now came towards Nikita, the modest noble was aware of the wonderful quality that God had given to nearly all members of that family: an extraordinary charm.

Instead of a kaftan, Golitsyn wore a close-fitting Polish coat with buttons down the front. His beard, instead of flowing broadly over his chest, was trimmed to a neat point. His calm, slightly Turkish face suggested a subtle, perhaps veiled intelligence.

Gently he took Nikita by the arm and walked with him to one side of the large room. "You know, my dear friend, I had hoped to see you a provincial governor," he said quietly. Nikita's heart missed a beat. What did he mean? Some other promotion? But seeing his agitation, Golitsyn only sighed. "I want you, my friend, for both our sakes, to be very calm," he murmured. "As I say, I had hoped. But alas, it will not be possible. You see, our local administration in Russia is, as you know, less than perfect."

Even in his nervousness, Nikita could not help a smile at this delicious understatement. The local administration was a bribe-ridden shambles.

"Consequently," the prince went on, "we must place huge reliance on the governors. They're all we have. And unfortunately, even the slightest shadow upon a candidate, in certain circles, makes an appointment impossible." He paused. "You'll also know that one of the most urgent tasks at present is for each governor to help the church stamp out these heretics, these Raskolniki. The Regent Sophia is adamant . . ." He waited a moment to give Nikita time to register.

"There are rumors—whether or not they are unfounded, I hardly need to tell you, my dear friend, is perfectly irrelevant—there are rumors in certain high quarters that suggest that—he let the words fall gently— "were you to prosecute the Raskolniki, you might possibly find yourself embarrassed. I'm sure you understand." He paused again, then gave Nikita a smile. "Do not despair, Nikita Mikhailovich, you may rise again tomorrow. And I myself might fall. But today, I can't help you."

Nikita swallowed. His throat felt very dry.

"What can I do?"

"Nothing."

"I shall always be ready to serve," Nikita said, with what dignity he could muster.

Golitsyn was silent.

"You may of course prefer to reside in Moscow," he said after a few seconds, "but you should feel free to visit your estates if you wish."

So it was truly over. They didn't want him in Moscow. For a second— he could not help it—he felt tears in his eyes; but he managed to blink them back.

"Come, my dear fellow, let me escort you to the door," Golitsyn said kindly.

Only as they went back across the room did Nikita look up and realize that about thirty people were watching; at the same moment, he noticed

that in one corner, with calm, expressionless faces, two of the Miloslavskys were also quietly watching. And beside them stood Peter Tolstoy.

Then he understood that it had been a public execution.

So it was that the distinguished ancestor of Russia's great novelist dealt
with Nikita Bobrov.

It was only human nature that, in the days that followed, it was not his
known enemy but kindly Golitsyn whom Nikita came to resent. So he
executed me to please Tolstoy and the Miloslavskys, he brooded. But
then, that man would do anything for power. And in his mind he conjured up, in some detail, what he supposed might be the relations between Golitsyn and the Regent Sophia, dwelling in particular upon her
known imperfections, and some others he imagined for himself.

Nikita was finished; his career was over. What should he do now? Above
all, how could he advance the family interests—what should be done
about Procopy?

He was a pleasant youth. He looked remarkably like his father, with
the same broad forehead and black hair; he was somewhat given to
enthusiasms—perhaps too much so. But his excitement was infectious
and gave him great charm. It would be tragic if the cloud over the family
should prevent him from having a fine career.

To Nikita's great surprise, it was Eudokia who supplied the answer.
"We'll get nothing from Princess Sophia," she argued. "So our only hope
is to gamble on the next reign. Let Procopy go and serve the boy. Let him
serve young Peter."

Peter? Who knew anything about the boy? Would he ever be allowed
to come to power by Sophia and the scheming Miloslavskys?

"He's our only chance," Eudokia repeated. "Just leave the whole business to me." And, rather to Nikita's surprise, it was not long before
Eudokia was summoned to see the boy tsar's mother, and returned with
an invitation for Nikita to pay young Peter a visit.

He was to go, not to the Kremlin, but to a little village just outside the
capital, called Preobrazhenskoe.

It was two months later, as the leaves were beginning to fall, that Nikita
Bobrov and Eudokia came to Russka.

Procopy had been successfully placed in Peter's household. No one
wanted Nikita in Moscow. So he had decided to visit his estates.

He found his house in the town needed repair, and he sent for men at
once. He visited the monastery and gave the monks some more money
to say masses for his father. He carefully inspected Dirty Place. And
Eudokia, as was her way in the country, took care to inspect everything,
too. It was in this way that she discovered, as she put it, "just the man"
to undertake the more elaborate carpentry needed in the house.

"He's an icon painter," she explained, "but a wonderful carpenter, too.
You must meet him, Nikita. His name is Daniel. His wife's a treasure,
too."

Nikita met them. The fellow was huge; the woman of no interest. Yet Eudokia was always talking to them. Indeed, after a couple of weeks she seemed to think the sun shone out of their eyes. Personally, he couldn't think what she saw in them.

Silence—some believe—gives a man power. So it seemed to be with Daniel. For though he said little, and asked for no consideration at all, the people at Russka looked up to him.

Not that they knew him. Even now, after seven years, he was still a mystery. Yet, like some huge old oak tree in the forest, his whole presence suggested permanence and a comforting stability that seemed to come from the earth itself.

He even looked like a tree, his wife thought fondly. In the winter months he would wrap himself in a thick, dark gown that reached to his ankles and which looked like a monk's cowl. On his head he would wear a high, conical cloth hat, trimmed with fur so that his wife, glancing up at the old watchtower with its high, tent roof, would say: "Why do we need a watchtower with my husband here?"

At other times, emerging sedately through the swirling snow, he would look like some ancient winter god, coming from the endless grayness of the forest.

In his presence she always had a sense of perfect peace. She knew him, as well as it is possible to know another being; she knew that at the core of this mighty oak resided a man of huge wisdom. When they slept together she experienced frequently, not only that oceanic feeling within herself but also the sense that, like all truly simple people, he possessed a life without end.

Yet she knew nothing of his past. She knew only that, for some reason he would never explain, he had not been married before; and that, thanks be to God, he had changed his mind.

She also knew that sometimes, in private, Daniel was deeply troubled.

He had not planned to marry when he came to Russka. I am too unworthy, he told himself. How can I ask another to share my life when I am confused and so steeped in sin? Nor would he have stayed, if it had not been for Silas.

It was not only that Silas made the sign of the cross with two fingers. The priest seemed instinctively to understand his troubled soul. "Remember," he would quietly admonish him, "we are here to suffer; but we are forbidden to despair. If you are troubled by the world, still more are you called to rejoice in the Risen Lord."

And gradually, in the little wooden church, as he looked around at the simple villagers and as he felt that intense, emotional warmth that is the hallmark of the Russian Church, Daniel found, for the first time in years, that he had no further urge to move on. For wherever I wander, it can only be the same, he considered. What else could there be, after all, but the warmth of the little village community, huddled together, naked before the Lord, in the endless Russian plain?

It was one Sunday after he had been there two years that old Silas had quietly come up to him and said: "It is time, I think, that you married."

Greatly as he revered the priest, he had wanted to contradict him. "I am too old—I'm over fifty," he protested. "And I am unworthy."

But Silas had been firm. "Not so. It is not for you to decide you are unworthy."

"But . . . I had not thought. Whom should I marry? And who would have me?"

Silas had smiled quietly. "If, as I believe, it is the Lord's will, you will know." And seeing Daniel for once look utterly confused, he had continued: "You should marry one who is beautiful—not unto men, but unto God. You should marry one by whom God is rightly praised." He smiled again. "You will be guided."

That week, and the next, Daniel had considered the matter. He felt uncertain, yet also a little excited. He thought of all the women in Russka and Dirty Place, but he came to no conclusion.

It was on the third Sunday, as he stood in the little wooden church at Dirty Place, that he found his attention caught by one person in particular. Why had his head slowly turned that way? Why, because she was singing of course: she was singing with a voice of extraordinary beauty. And then, looking at her poor, plain face with its unsightly wart—a pale face that would have been almost ugly but for the lovely expression of rapt, religious attention that it wore—he saw what the priest had meant.

He spoke to her uncle and her old grandmother immediately after the service.

And so it was that, to old Elena's astonishment, and at the unheard of age of twenty-five, Arina was married to Daniel.

On her wedding day Elena solemnly gave her granddaughter a golden bracelet set with a large amethyst. She did not say where it came from. Then Elena, with all the rest of the family, escorted Arina to Daniel's little house in Russka.

Both husband and wife had been astonished at their own happiness. They were each of them so surprised to be married at all; neither had any vanity; they could only try, rather humbly, to give happiness to the other, and as a result their love progressed with extraordinary speed.

For Daniel, the sight of this plain woman, who had never dared to hope for love, moved him profoundly. His natural tenderness, which his feelings of self-doubt and unworthiness had always held back, now suddenly found expression. Nothing prevented him: the priest had told him it was his duty to love.

He was tender, and determined to succeed. He studied her, observed her secret doubts and needs for reassurance until, with a sense of delight, he saw that like a tree after winter she was quivering into life.

Like many Russians, they called each other not by their first names, but in the ancient manner, by their patronymics. At first this had led to a small discussion. "For," as Arina confessed with a blush, "my real father was a Cossack and I do not know his name; but my supposed father was called Ivan." His father, he had told her, was called Peter; and so, since the full form of patronymic was now in general use, he was, to her, always Petrovich; while she was Ivanovna.

If only Daniel could have felt that his personal joy was a harbinger of better days to come.

He had wandered so many years, all over Russia, troubled by his sinful past, seeking peace yet never finding it. He had sought out holy men. But it was only during his time in Yaroslavl that he had truly found them. For it was there, in the wild Black Lands beyond the Volga, that he had met the stern Trans-Volga hermits and their followers. These were the true Russian believers, these austere and godly men who lived in the forests. In the manner of ancient Israelites, they felt their daily lives were close to God. Some were prophets. They shunned the evil world they saw around them. Like Avvakum and the other Raskolniki, they were shocked at the changes in the Church, and with even more certainty than Avvakum they declared that these signs of wickedness meant the coming of the Antichrist himself. "Prepare with prayer and fasting," they advised, "for the end of days is nigh."

Sometimes, having found such happiness at Russka, Daniel had wondered if perhaps the hermits over the Volga had been mistaken. By chance, after many years of the harshest winters, the climate in north Russia had become milder the year after his marriage: the cold season had been shorter, the crops better. Might it be a hopeful sign? But when, after four years of marriage, his wife had failed to become pregnant, he sadly concluded: It is probably a sign that, for the faithful, the world is becoming too wicked a place for children to live in.

In 1684, if any confirmation were needed of the wickedness of the world, the blow fell.

An edict from the Regent Sophia outlawed the Raskolniki. Suspected Schismatics could be tortured and anyone sheltering them would lose his property. For obstinate offenders the penalty was death. On the day that news of this terrible edict had reached Russka, Silas had come to Daniel's house near the market square and spent an hour talking with him urgently. He emerged looking grim.

Arina had remained outside while the two men talked and did not venture back until some time later. But when she did, she found Daniel so deep in prayer that he was unaware of her presence. She had never seen him so agitated before. With tears in his eyes, he was prostrating himself before the blackened little icon in the corner, knocking his forehead on the floor, and murmuring: "Lord have mercy. Let this cup pass from me." Feeling that she was intruding, Arina had begun to back out of the room.

It was just as she was doing so, however, that her husband said something else that seemed to her very strange. Suddenly, staring up at the icon with a look of desperation, he cried out: "Who am I, Lord, to ask for mercy—I who have murdered, not once but many times?"

Arina gazed at him. What could he mean? Surely the words were not to be taken literally: for it was hard to imagine her husband hurting a fly, let alone committing a murder. What, then, was in his mind? And it struck her, with a greater force than ever before, how little she still knew about the life of this man whom she unreservedly loved. And being ignorant, she thought, how can I help him now, in his hour of need?

When they were alone that evening, Daniel told her about Silas's visit. Faced with the terrible new threat of the edict, even the old priest had been uncertain what to do. "He honored me by asking my advice," Daniel gravely told her.

"And what did you tell him, Petrovich?"

"For my sins, I advised him to go on." He looked at her with troubled eyes. "If we continue, even in secret, it may bring great misfortune upon us—upon you, too, Ivanovna," he confessed.

She bowed her head. Whatever suffering might lie ahead, she knew that she only desired to share it with him.

"It is all I have—this faith," Daniel suddenly burst out. "I have wandered all my life in search of truth, Ivanovna. I cannot turn back now."

And it was then, because the moment seemed right, that Arina begged him: "Will you not tell your wife something of your past life, Petrovich?"

It was a strange tale he had to tell: a story of solitary wanderings that seemed to have taken him all over Russia. He told her about the elders he had met at Yaroslavl. "And before that, for a time, I was a lay brother in a monastery. That is when I learned to read."

And now Arina told him what she had overheard that day and gently asked him: "What did you mean, Petrovich, when you said that you had murdered?"

To which, to her surprise, he sadly answered: "Yes, it is true: I have killed."

For several moments after this confession he was silent; then he slowly continued. "You see, Ivanovna, even when I was a child, I had a passion for justice. Indeed, I would be so offended by anything that, to my childish eyes, seemed unjust that I would even pretend to be a fool—not to understand what was going on—so that often the other boys thought me simple in the head." He smiled regretfully. "Nowadays, of course, I know that justice belongs only to God, and that goodness can only be found in prayer. But when I was young, I believed there could be true justice in the government of men: and when I did not find it, I became angry."

"What did you do?"

"I fought. I joined Stenka Razin."

"You were in his rebellion?"

He nodded. "And we killed, Ivanovna. In the name of justice we killed not only soldiers and wicked officials, but God knows how many innocents, too. At the time I thought it right: now I can only throw myself at God's feet and beg for mercy."

"You were a Cossack then?"

"I was. A fighting Cossack. I fought with Bogdan, too. I thought nothing of killing in those days." He paused. "Later I wanted so much to break with my evil past that—as though I had taken holy orders—I changed my name to Daniel."

"What was it before?"

"Stepan." He smiled gently. "Though since my brother Cossacks thought me big and simple, they gave me another name. They used to call me Ox."

1698

PROCOPY BOBROV was an enthusiast. He was thirty-one, yet, to his mother at least, he sometimes seemed like a child. Often she would say: "It was the worst thing I ever did in my life, to send him to Preobrazhenskoe." And when the nice, sensible wife she had chosen for him complained that he shamefully neglected her, Eudokia could only sigh sympathetically and remark: "I'll do what I can, my dear. But it's that accursed Peter who makes him so."

For this was how, in private, she referred to the tsar.

Preobrazhenskoe. It was a pleasant spot—a modest wooden hunting lodge with large stables, only three miles from Moscow's walls and close by that other satellite of the city, the German Quarter. All around stretched broad meadows, dotted with silver birches; farther away lay a white-walled church whose blue dome looked rather cheerful against the paler blue of the sky. And it was there that the sixteen-year-old Procopy Bobrov had made the acquaintance of a striking twelve-year-old boy, already as tall as he was.

The women's network of Eudokia's family had worked well. The young tsar's Naryshkin mother had been only too grateful to greet a friend for her son from a sound old family like the Bobrovs. For her state was pitiable: except when he was needed for some ceremonial appearance, the boy Peter was ignored; their allowance was so small she had even had to beg the Patriarch for extra funds; and fearing for their safety, she was glad enough to keep out of sight at Preobrazhenskoe.

But if only, Eudokia thought, she had not sent Procopy there to join him. "There is nothing—nothing!—good that one can say about Peter," she would cry contemptuously. "He's nothing but," she'd search for words, "a German lout!" The boy's mother was at fault. He had not been properly supervised. Allowed to run wild, mix with all sorts of company. He ate like a peasant—even Procopy admitted that. And he was forever playing soldiers with his friends. Including Procopy, thanks to her folly.

Preobrazhenskoe. The tsar had taken the name of his little village and given it to one of his new household regiments: the Preobrazhensky Guards. Procopy was an officer in it now. How she despised them, with their foreign uniforms! And Peter's childish games, his endless playing at soldiers—they had developed into real wars now.

And to think she had supposed that nothing could be worse than the rule of Sophia and that terrible Golitsyn—the Pole, as she called him. Their foreign wars had been their downfall. In return for another peace treaty with the Poles, Golitsyn had foolishly promised to help them against the Turks and their vassal the Crimean khan.

A war against the Tatars on the steppe. It had been a disaster, and a costly one. The great men of the state had turned to Peter, and in 1689

Sophia and her favorite had fallen from power. She was sent to a convent, Golitsyn into exile.

Peter was seventeen. Though technically he was still co-ruler with poor Ivan, it was time for him to rule.

"But did he rule? Did he behave like a man?" Eudokia would furiously demand. "No. He played his games like an evil child, which is exactly what he still is."

Briefly she had been hopeful. The old Patriarch, having at last got rid of Golitsyn, was determined to rid Holy Russia of all these foreign influences. But then he had died, and Peter's strange regime began.

And strange it certainly was. While a small council, including his mother and some of the Naryshkins, acted as an informal regency, the hulking boy refused to take any interest in his empire at all. Often he stayed at Preobrazhenskoe. But even worse, he spent more and more time in the German Quarter, among the foreigners. And it was not long before his behavior became scandalous.

"The German suburb! What kind of people does one meet there?" she would say contemptuously. "And see what kind of games these heretics like to play."

It cannot be denied that the behavior of Peter and his friends, some of whom were old enough to be his grandfather, was totally outrageous; and while historians have tended to gloss over it as either the high-spirited buffooning of an adolescent, or else as a calculated political message, it is very hard to see why they should do so.

At the heart of all this was the so-called Jolly Company—a group of friends who might at any given moment number a dozen or two hundred. Some were Russian, but many were foreigners. They included a brilliant Swiss adventurer, Lefort, and an otherwise sensible old Scottish general, Gordon.

It was not the drunken parties, which might go on for days at a time. That was perfectly Russian. It was not even that they might, if you were a merchant or nobleman, visit your house and smash all the furniture. Russians were rather proud of tsars, like Ivan the Terrible, who wreaked havoc at the slightest whim.

Russians could even forgive, when he was sober, Peter's fascination with foreign crafts, and his learning the rudiments of mathematics and navigation—though these interests were certainly eccentric.

But what could anyone make of his open and insulting mockery of religion?

For in these years, the young tsar formed what he called his Drunken Synod—the All-Joking, All-Drunken Synod of Fools and Jesters. One of his drinking companions—his old tutor—became Prince-Patriarch, though this was changed to Prince-Pope. Dressed up in ecclesiastical regalia, he would appoint a drunken synod of cardinals, bishops, abbots, and other priests. And then, mocking the liturgy, making lewd benedictions over the company continually, the Prince-Pope under Peter's direction would lead the Drunken Synod in its all-night drunken revels. They were not just held indoors, out of sight in the German Quarter. The young tsar and his friends used to take to the streets of Moscow, even in Lent, taking good care to outrage every religious sensibility of the people he was to govern. So that even the foreign ambassadors from the West—who were themselves entirely used to the high jinks of young aristocrats, or the occasional calculated outrages of the students in their ancient university towns—could only conclude that the young tsar had little interest in his people and that, ingenious or not, he was vulgar without being amusing.

For several years this extraordinary regime had gone on. No one could control the wayward youth, it seemed. His mother, as Eudokia had done with Procopy, found him a wife. But Peter seldom even visited her. Then his mother died, but still his strange adolescence continued.

What was the young tsar thinking of?

As time passed, it seemed to Eudokia that when he was sober young tsar Peter thought only of two things. One was war.

"And the other is boats. Boats—everything with this man is boats!" she would complain. And when Procopy laughingly reminded her that Russia was a land of rivers she would brush him aside irritably. "You know very well what I mean. It's these accursed boats that go to sea. No Russian has ever needed to go to sea."

"Not so. The ancient Rus went to sea. They went across the Black Sea to Constantinople. And that's what we'll do now."

"First it's the Crimean khan and his Tatars, now it's the Turkish sultan himself you want to attack," she said drily.

"Precisely."

For though Peter's conduct might be odd, there was no doubt that he had, from the first, dreams of conquest. They were very natural dreams.

Who, after all, were Russia's heroes? Were they not great men like Saint Vladimir, Yaroslav the Wise, and mighty Monomakh in the days of ancient Kiev?

And in those times had not the state of Rus traded freely from the Baltic to the warm Black Sea? Did they not crush the tribesmen of the southern steppe? Had not the ancient Rus kept a settlement by the mouth of the Don in old Tmutarakan? Was there not a colony of Rus in the imperial city of Constantinople herself?

Yet now Russia possessed only a miserable little toehold, at the frozen northern end of the Baltic Sea, while the rich Baltic ports were still in the hands of the Swedes and Germans. In the south, the mouth of the Don was closed to Russians, guarded by the Turkish port of Azov, and the Turkish fleet entirely controlled the warm Black Sea.

Finally, most insulting of all, and centuries after Moscow had thrown off the Tatar yoke, the Tatar khan of the Crimea still sent huge raiding parties across the steppe, stealing Slavs by the thousands from the villages of the Ukraine and sending them to the slave markets of the Middle East. He even had the impertinence to claim tribute from the tsar; and though his claim was ignored, the Russian government—humiliatingly—still found it wise to send him handsome gifts.

So if Peter, like Ivan the Terrible before him, wanted to break out to the north and south, it was not so surprising.

Boats: they were the answer. Young Peter had discovered boats—real

boats—from the foreigners in the German suburbs. He had built a boat
of his own. He had seen, up in the north, the foreign vessels that came
to distant Archangel or plied the Baltic Sea.

That was what he needed—a fleet to go down the mighty Don and
break through, past Azov, to the warm Black Sea. It was time to turn his
war games into the real thing. They would build galleys first, for the Don;
then real ships for the sea.

Strangely, if Procopy Bobrov had been excited by this adventure, his
father was equally so. For though he was not required on the campaign,
the sixty-five-year-old former official had now acquired a new lease on
life. The young tsar needed timber for his fleet. Above all, he needed ash
trees for masts.

"They're getting some from Tula, but we have plenty on our estates,"
he had declared happily, and he had immediately made the tsar a present
of one of his woods.

When news came, in 1696, that the Turkish fort of Azov had fallen,
he was ecstatic. "Can't you feel it?" he cried to Eudokia. "I can. I feel a
warm wind blowing into our northern forests—a warm wind from the
south."

One other development had taken place during the Azov campaign:
Peter's invalid brother Ivan had died. It was not an important event; but
it meant that now, as he returned to Moscow in triumph, Tsar Peter at
the age of twenty-four sat alone upon the throne.

"He may be wild," Nikita had assured his wife, "but now we shall see
great things."

Even he, however, had been thunderstruck by what happened next:
Peter's triumphal entry into the capital.

It took place on a sunny, October day in 1696. By the Moscow river
a triumphal arch had been erected in the Roman manner, with huge
statues, one of Mars, the other of Hercules, on each side. Below it was
a model of the Turkish pasha in chains.

When the procession came, it was headed by Peter's tutor—the man
who played Prince-Pope in the infamous Drunken Synod—dressed up
in armor. Then in a gilded carriage came the Swiss Lefort. Then more
carriages. Then came a cart containing a traitor who had foolishly helped
the Turks during the campaign. The instruments of the torture and
execution he was to suffer were displayed beside him.

And at last, towards the rear of a procession that went on for miles,
came Peter.

To many who had never had a good look at him, he was an astounding
sight. He was built like an athlete. He had a mop of dark hair, a mustache
like a Cossack, and piercing, staring eyes. He stood no less than six feet
seven inches tall. Yet this young Russian giant was not wearing Russian
dress. He wore a German uniform, a black coat, and a huge black three-
cornered hat in which he had jauntily stuck a long white feather.

And there was not a priest in sight.

No icons came before the procession; no priests with banners. No
welcoming speech from the Patriarch; no church bells rang. A Roman

caesar had come, wearing a German uniform; a pagan procession was entering the capital of Holy Russia.

"Yet even the Romans had their gods," Nikita murmured. "And even Genghis Khan, pagan that he was, did not despise the church." And as he gazed at the procession and thought he saw a new, harsh sun that would burn away all the shadows.

As for Eudokia, she stared with furious disgust. "When his mother died, and he would not even stay at her bedside, I said he was unnatural," she remarked. "Now I have seen the face of evil itself."

Yet even this horror had been as nothing to what was happening now.

For in 1698, Peter had, once more, done something that no ruler of Russia had ever done.

He had traveled abroad. And he had taken Procopy with him.

While they were away, Eudokia had scarcely even visited Moscow. The place had become hateful to her. Instead she had spent most of her time alone down at Russka, where she continued to pass long hours in the company of the priest Silas, and Daniel and his family.

But now Peter and her son were back. And in Moscow, all hell had broken loose.

Daniel approached the capital with a mixture of curiosity and dread.

Could the rumors he had heard since Tsar Peter's sudden return from abroad really be true? It was many years since he had been to the capital, but when he received the summons from that godly woman Eudokia Mikhailovna, he had not hesitated but had come, bringing with him his wife and little daughter.

For—it often puzzled Daniel that God should have granted such a gift in these evil days—he and Arina, after nearly fifteen years, and long after they had given up hope, had unexpectedly been blessed with a daughter. She had been born in 1693 when Arina was thirty-nine; and he was in his late sixties. And now, here he was, age seventy, with a wife and a six-year-old girl.

At first, when he and Arina had gazed at the little baby who had so wondrously appeared, they had been astonished by one thing: She did not in the least seem to resemble either of them.

It was old Elena who, with a smile of delight, solved the mystery.

"To think that in my last days, I should have been granted such a thing," she muttered. "The child is my Maryushka, to the life."

So that was what they called her: Maryushka. And old Elena, in the last three years of her life, would sit with the child every day with as much pride as if it had been her own.

Yet if little Maryushka had come into their lives like a ray of sunshine, what dark years they were into which she had been born. All over Russia, but especially in the north, the government had continued to persecute the Raskolniki. Some sought martyrdom by challenging the authorities. Others continued in secret.

The early years, after the terrible edict, had been especially difficult. No one had been sure what to do. But Silas and Daniel had consulted the friends of Avvakum and with them had reached a wise conclusion.

"There is no merit in challenging the government and calling down its wrath," Daniel would tell his little family. "The edict is wrong, but perhaps in future it will be changed. We shall continue to pray, in secret, as we have been taught. We shall not seek trouble, but if persecution comes, we must suffer it as best we may, secure in God's protection."

It was a course that hundreds, even thousands of little congregations had followed in that vast land. No one, neither the government nor the congregations themselves, knew how many.

If Daniel was cautious as he approached, it was understandable. The capital was not only the seat of persecution, it had also become a place for danger. For that very summer, while the strange young tsar had still been abroad, the *streltsy* had revolted again, plunging Moscow into temporary chaos.

Had Sophia, still furious in her convent, put them up to it? No one knew. Fortunately for Peter, his counselors had managed to smash the rebellion very quickly. But Peter had hurried home anyway and now, a month after his arrival, all Russia was waiting to see what their young ruler would do.

As Daniel entered the suburbs, however, the huge city seemed to be quiet. His little cart made its way slowly towards the city's outer wall, passed through, and came eventually to the Kitaygorod, where the Bobrovs had their substantial house.

And there at last, with the late afternoon sun pleasantly warming his back, he led his wife and daughter into the large dusty courtyard.

It was a big wooden house on two floors, with a massive outside staircase. Around the courtyard were a number of lesser buildings, in which he would be given lodgings.

He placed his hand on his heart and bowed low as the gray-bearded figure of Nikita himself appeared and gave him a courteous greeting. A moment later, from the upper floor, Eudokia came out, smiling; before her walked a pleasant-looking serving girl carrying bread and salt in welcome.

"Welcome, faithful Patriarch," she said.

How the old man's heart warmed. His face, usually rather solemn, creased into a smile. That little word *faithful* meant so much to them both. It meant that, despite their different stations in life, they were friends. It meant that she relied upon him for emotional support. He knew it. And lastly, it meant something else, which was never spoken of before her husband.

"My lady, Eudokia Mikhailovna," he said fervently, bowing low in greeting.

He had only seen her in Russka before, never in Moscow. In Russka she dressed simply. But here in the capital she was magnificently attired, with a dress of rich red brocade and a high headdress studded with pearls. Though he despised all the trappings of worldly wealth, old Daniel could not help thinking that she looked very good in her finery.

Though they were in the heart of Moscow, the afternoon seemed to be completely silent. Hardly anyone was passing in the street outside. In the courtyard, a single mulberry tree gave a shade in one corner—which shade was scarcely needed on such a pleasant autumn day. The horse in the shafts, sensing that he was at journey's end, had dropped his head and was moving his lips thoughtfully as the flies settled on him.

And so, like old friends, the rich landlord and these poor artisans talked gently together in low tones, exchanging a little news. For even Nikita, now that he was getting old, found the presence of these simple people from the country strangely comforting.

It was while they were conversing like this, and just as Daniel was thinking it was time to unharness the horse from the little cart, that he suddenly saw Eudokia stiffen and a curious look of awkwardness pass over Nikita's face.

At that moment he also became aware that someone was coming through the gateway behind him; and at the same time he heard Nikita Bobrov say, in a voice whose heartiness was not quite natural, "Ah. Here is my son Procopy."

And then, as Daniel turned to look, his mouth fell open in horror.

Procopy was charming. Peter had always found him so: and intelligent.

The young tsar's friends at the village of Preobrazhenskoe had included all kinds of people. There were men of the old princely and boyar families; there were sons of the nobility, like Procopy; there were lesser gentry, and there were even low-born men like his favorite Menshikov, who was said to have sold pastries in the street as a boy.

One thing united them all. They were devoted to Peter.

And then, of course, there were the foreigners in the German Quarter.

Procopy was lucky that, with his ready wit, he was included by Peter not only in the military company he kept at the village, but in the frequent parties in the German Quarter. Not only did it bring him closer to the boy-tsar, but it had also opened for him another world.

For the German Quarter was utterly unlike the rest of Moscow. Its broad streets were neatly laid out. Its houses were frequently of Dutch brick or stone; with pleasant little formal gardens. Its little Protestant churches seemed light and open compared to the dark Muscovite churches that glimmered with gold. In short, it was a small oasis of Europe, of bourgeois order and culture, cleanliness and discipline, fenced off in its compound across the fields from the huge, untidy, and exotic Asiatic jumble of Moscow.

Some of the several thousand merchants and soldiers who lived there were second- or third-generation immigrants. But to the Russians— unless they had converted to Orthodoxy and made the effort to Russian- ize themselves entirely, they were contemptible: dumb foreigners. In the slang of the day, the German suburb was often called the Kokuy—which was the name of the brothel quarter in the city proper.

Yet here lived Englishmen who understood the weaponry and tactics of modern war; here could be found Germans who, far from being "dumb" as their Russian name implies, spoke many languages. Here were Dutchmen who understood how to build seagoing ships and how to navigate.

These were wonders about which the Russians were not only ignorant: they were not even curious. Procopy himself had been present when one day a faithful general, thinking to please the boy-tsar, proudly brought back an astrolabe from abroad, by which means, he explained, the cunning foreigners could navigate by the sun and stars. Peter had been delighted. No one had ever seen such a thing before.

"How does it work?" he had asked.

"How?" The general was nonplussed. "I never thought of asking," he replied.

And that the astrolabe had been in use for nearly two thousand years they had not the least idea.

But nothing had impressed Procopy more than the way that the young tsar had not only found a Dutchman who could explain it to him, but had sat down with an exercise book day after day, week after week, until he had slowly mastered the unfamiliar mathematics of the thing.

"I tell you," he explained to his father, "I admire him as a tsar, for behind his wildness is something formidable. But I love him as a man. It's not just his curiosity, which is past anything I've ever seen. But he struggles so hard. I watched him with his mathematics. It didn't come easily to him at all. But he wouldn't give up. That's what I like. He makes mistakes, but he just won't give up."

Procopy had come to know the German suburb very well; and though he did not possess the driving passion for information that Peter had, he began to have some understanding of the wealth of knowledge that it represented. Indeed, he even began to think of himself as rather advanced, as a man ahead of his time.

Until he went on the great embassy abroad.

The great embassy of Peter of Russia to Western Europe has become such a part of the folklore of world history that its true nature is often forgotten.

The folklore is that Peter, thirsty for Western civilization, visited Europe and then returned to civilize his country and make it as much like the rest of Europe as he could.

This is not true.

As to Peter's reason for going, there is not a shadow of doubt. It was to prepare for war—as a start, against Turkey. Diplomatically the embassy was to persuade Western countries to join an anti-Turkish alliance. The practical side of the tour of Europe was to learn shipbuilding, so that Russia could build a proper seagoing fleet.

Already in 1696, soon after his victory at Azov, Peter had sent fifty horrified Russians, without their families, to Western Europe to learn navigation and shipbuilding. Among them, amazingly, was the fifty-two-year-old Peter Tolstoy, who had somehow, despite his close links to Peter's Miloslavsky enemies, managed to get into the tsar's favor.

His own embassy, therefore, followed soon after.

But why did Peter himself go, and why did he go incognito—officially only as a junior member of the party led by his ambassadors?

We do not know for certain. But it was probably to give himself more freedom to roam unofficially in the dockyards of the West. Certainly he spent months working as a ship's carpenter and learning the whole business very thoroughly.

It also perhaps gave this devotee of the Mock Synod and the Jolly Company more opportunity to play the fool. This he and his friends also did. In London they were installed near the docks, in the house of the distinguished diarist John Evelyn, and so effectively wrecked both house and garden that the great Sir Christopher Wren, who inspected the place afterwards, estimated the damage at the then astounding sum of three hundred and fifty pounds. Among other items, the floors had to be renewed; the tiles from the Dutch stoves had been pulled off; the brass door locks had been broken open and the feather beds ripped apart; and all the lawns and a four-hundred-foot-long, nine-foot-high holly hedge—one of the horticultural prizes of London—had been completely destroyed.

In this manner, in 1697–98, Tsar Peter came to learn about the civilization of Europe.

The Baltic: the port of Riga; the German states of Brandenburg and Hanover; Holland; England; Hapsburg Vienna; Poland.

It was not, Procopy would say in later years, that he had entered other lands. He had entered another century.

He never really understood how great the difference was. This was not lack of intelligence on his part. The huge, two-thousand-year-old tradition of philosophical inquiry, from Socrates to Descartes; the splendors of the Renaissance; the beginnings of modern science; and, most of all, the complex and flexible Western societies with their ancient institutions, professions, legal and moral codes, and brilliant culture—all these things, despite some imported books and furniture at the tsar's court, were simply not comprehended by more than a handful of Russians. None of Peter's entourage really understood what they were seeing. Peter himself certainly did not, nor could he have.

But if Procopy did not understand what he saw, it still made a profound impression on him, and he intuited much that he did not comprehend.

With Peter he had been impressed with the ships and the huge ports. The cannon he had seen on board the ships had hugely excited him; and, with Peter, he had been delighted to discover that one could obtain greatly superior gunpowder in the West.

But when his father had questioned him upon his return and asked him which country he admired most, he replied, "I think it was Holland."

"Why," Nikita inquired: "is it their ships, their trade?"

Procopy shook his head.

"No. It is . . ." He searched for a word: "It is their order." And seeing Nikita look puzzled, he went on. "They have even tamed the sea. I saw great walls—not like our wooden walls across the steppe, to keep out the Tatars—but huge walls of stone to keep out the sea itself. They call them dikes. They have taken land back from the sea and laid out fields—thousands of them, all so neatly arranged in squares and rectangles,

within their dikes. You can scarcely credit that men could accomplish
such a thing. And they have canals, straight as arrows, that stretch to the
horizon."

Nikita looked unimpressed. "We do not need such things in Russia.
We have land without end."

"I know. But don't you see," Procopy went on excitedly, "that's not
the point." It was something he had been brooding about ever since he
had first seen these wonders. "The point, Father, is that they have conquered nature. They have imposed a pattern, order on the land, even the
sea itself." He paused and then added, with a sudden flash of insight, "It's
as if, in their own hearts and minds, they ordered themselves."

Nikita laughed.

"I can't see us Russians ordering ourselves. Can you?"

Procopy agreed. "No, I can't. But we can impose order from above.
That's the only way to do it, as the tsar himself has said to me many
times."

Nikita sighed.

"So do you mean that you and the tsar have come back meaning to
impose your will upon mother nature?" he asked with a wry smile. "My
poor Procopy, nature in Russia is mightier than any tsar. You cannot
impose anything upon her. The land," he repeated, "is endless."

Now it was Procopy's turn to smile.

"Wait until you've seen Tsar Peter try," he remarked drily.

If these comments depressed Nikita, because he thought them impractical, it was nothing to the effect they had on Eudokia. "God made
nature," she warned him, "and if you seek to impose your order upon
nature, too, then I say that this is nothing but pride. You and your tsar
are evil."

And to Procopy's great sorrow he found his mother estranged from
him.

Strangely enough, all three parties to this argument were profoundly
and equally Russian: Eudokia in her religious conservatism, Nikita in his
fatalism, and perhaps most of all young Procopy in his optimism. For,
having seen the outside world and its order, but unaware of its complex
underpinnings, Procopy had assumed that, just as the villagers in Russia
can build a house in a day, so, with a strong leader and a titanic effort,
a new order can be imposed from above. This belief is the perennial
tragedy of Russia.

What, then, had the embassy really accomplished?

In fact a great deal. Peter had wanted to study shipbuilding: he and
others had done so quite thoroughly. He wanted new armaments, gunpowder that did not continually misfire, and knowledge of modern
fighting methods, especially at sea. He obtained all of these. He also
opened up new avenues for trade.

The Russian's diplomacy failed. No one wanted to fight the sultan of
Turkey at that time. But if his drive to the warm seas of the south might
be stalled, Peter had discovered in his travels that there might be other
alliances he could make that would get him access to the other trade route
he needed: the Baltic Sea in the north.

Above all it was the long-term consequences of the embassy that were the most important. Men like cunning old Peter Tolstoy might not have learned a great deal about shipbuilding, as they had been told to do; but they came back with a wealth of observations, a knowledge of foreign languages, and some insight, at least, into European education and culture. These were the early Europeanized Russians, the group of which Sophia's counselor Golitsyn had been the forerunner. These were the men who, in the long run, would open Russia's windows on the West.

Was Procopy Bobrov such a man? Not quite. But though he lacked the desire to educate himself profoundly, he had still taken in enough to see that his homeland was centuries out of date.

This had one sad consequence. For while her sense of religious propriety had separated Eudokia from her son, Procopy also found a subtler barrier between himself and his father. Nor could he help it.

For to Nikita, his son had become a stranger. It was not his Western style of dress; nor his travels as such. But Nikita could sense, in that faint but unmistakable reserve in Procopy's manner, by the distant look in his eye, that his son no longer warmed to the same things; he knew something his own people did not. He had seen German and English officers look at their Russian troops that way.

He's not really a Russian anymore, he thought. And, hardest of all to bear for a man who had always thought of himself as more educated than his fellow nobles: He secretly despises me.

This, then, was the young man who had just walked into the courtyard, and at whom Daniel was staring in disbelief.

For Procopy was wearing a smart green uniform, close fitting, with buttons down the front in the German manner. His legs were encased in breeches and stockings. And apart from a neat mustache, he was clean-shaven.

Of course, in the old Cossack days in the Ukraine, when men still called him Ox, Daniel had been used to clean-shaven men. But here in the north—that the son of Nikita Bobrov should do such a thing!—he could only stare in wonder.

Nikita, following his gaze, smiled a little apologetically.

"The tsar's friends came back from their journey clean-shaven," he remarked.

"The tsar himself has shaved the beards of the boyars at court," Procopy reminded him. "He says he won't tolerate people at his court looking so primitive. He told me so today."

Primitive. Daniel winced at the word. He saw Eudokia start as if she had been slapped and then look away from them. It was a calculated insult.

Yet Nikita Bobrov appeared to ignore this rudeness. It seemed he had something else on his mind. For now he turned to his son with a look of inquiry. "You came from Preobrazhenskoe?"

Procopy nodded.

"Well?" Nikita asked.

"It's decided. We have some confessions. We begin the executions tomorrow." He took his father by the arm. "Come," he said. "I'll tell you about it." And he led him into the house.

Only now did Eudokia turn to face Daniel and his little family again. He saw there were tears in her eyes.

"Thank God," she cried softly. "Thank God that you have come."

Only gradually did Daniel realize the full horror of what was going on. Only during the course of that winter did he come to understand why the Lady Eudokia had felt so in need of his presence. And he himself was not sure how he could comfort her.

As Procopy had announced, the executions of the mutinous *streltsy* had begun the day after Daniel's arrival.

Indeed, they might have started sooner if the interrogations—which had been going on down at Preobrazhenskoe—had not been so difficult. For very few of the mutinous soldiers were prepared to talk, despite some extensive persuasion.

It was at that time in Russia normal procedure in all cases of this kind to give prisoners the knout to elicit a confession. The use of torture in interrogation was normal in most countries at that time, whereas it is used in far fewer countries today, but a word of explanation may be needed about the Russian method.

For it is sometimes thought that the famous Russian knout was just a kind of whip, or a flail like the English cat o' nine tails. But whereas the English navy, in the last century, would give a man a thousand lashes with the cat and reckon he might live, a twentieth of that ration with the knout would have killed him. And though, say, a Bobrov might have thrashed a peasant on his estate for some misdemeanor, he would probably have used the rods called batogs, not a knout.

The knout was three and a half feet long and made of leather. Much thicker than batogs, they were also very heavy. As a result, when a blow was struck, which the knout-master did by leaping forward and swinging with all his force, it actually sunk a wound like a bar into the victim's back for the depth of half an inch or so. The skin was completely pulverized. Blood and tissue flew with every stroke. If the knout-master worked down your back, by the second time around he would be at the bone.

In order to appreciate how thorough the Russians were in this matter, however, it should further be explained that the more severe method was first to tie the victim's hands behind his back and then haul him up by the hands with a rope over a beam. This meant not just that he hung before the knout-master but that his arms were actually dislocated from their sockets while the knouting went on. When lowered, the arms could then be forced back into their sockets again.

This was the Russian knout, with which most prisoners were interrogated.

Tsar Peter was very concerned about the mutiny of the *streltsy*. He had seen his own uncle hacked to pieces by them when he was a boy and he knew they were capable of overturning him and putting Sophia back in his place. The questioning was urgent therefore. Not only the *streltsy* but two of Sophia's maids were stripped and knouted—although Peter leniently allowed one of these a simple execution when he discovered she was pregnant.

As well as the knout, Peter, in person, supervised the putting of some prisoners to the rack and also had them roasted on a fire in front of him. Yet the *streltsy* were still so obstinate in their silence that on at least one occasion Peter tried to cure a mutineer's silence by breaking open his clenched jaws with a stick.

Procopy Bobrov was present at a number of these interrogations.

He was there for a particular reason. For as soon as they arrived back, Peter had joined the young man to his newly formed government department. It was called the Preobrazhensky Prikaz—in effect, a secret police bureau. And right from the start, it would make itself feared.

"The *streltsy* aren't talking much, even under torture," Procopy told his father. "But we do know they planned to replace Peter and they were going to kill every foreigner in Russia too."

The executions that autumn went on for three weeks, from the last day of September to October 18.

On October 12 there was a sudden, dense fall of snow, plunging Moscow directly into winter, but the daily public executions went on.

Daniel witnessed several. The victims died in several ways, though usually they were beheaded or hanged. Peter also demanded that his boyars and friends should take a hand in the executions, and Daniel heard Procopy say to his father one evening: "The tsar's curious to see some people beheaded tomorrow in the European way, with a sword instead of an axe. Have you a good heavy sword you could lend me?"

Daniel saw Procopy at work the next day. Someone else in the crowd told the old man that he had seen the tsar himself behead several men.

All these events Daniel witnessed with sorrow, but not with horror. The knouting, the executions: the *streltsy* had rebelled and it was only to be expected that they would be punished.

His horror began one morning when they brought out the regimental priests.

It was in Red Square. There, before the great, exotic towers of Saint Basil's Cathedral, Peter's men had erected a huge scaffold—but not just an ordinary scaffold: this one was in the shape of a cross. They led out the priests to the scaffold. Daniel braced himself to witness a monstrosity.

But what happened next took his breath away entirely. For now, to perform the hanging, came the court jester. He was dressed as a priest.

The same day, in the gardens of the Norodevichy Convent, a hundred and ninety-five more of the *streltsy* were hung on gibbets, near Sophia's window.

All these corpses were to be left dangling, strange, frozen specters, for five long months through the winter.

And what was Daniel to make of all this? He thought he knew. As the months passed, he became increasingly certain. Yet even then, he did not wish to form the thought himself.

* * *

Why had Eudokia summoned him? For comfort. Because, Daniel soon realized, there was no one she felt she could trust.

Her son was godless. Her husband, wanting success for his family, said nothing.

"You see for yourself, all around, what has come to pass," she told him privately. "Help me, good Daniel, to know what to do."

Ostensibly he was there as a carpenter. And indeed, he did some beautiful joinery in their house, so that Nikita himself soon forgot his irritation at his wife's unexpectedly sending for the fellow. He would proudly show Daniel's workmanship to visitors, and had Daniel not refused to work for anyone else, he could have had many commissions.

In a way, both the Bobrovs came to be glad of this addition to their household. For while his wife was devoted to the parents, Nikita found himself delighted by the presence of the little girl.

Maryushka was, indeed, an enchanting little girl. With her bright, freckled face and shining eyes she seemed to suppose that it was only natural that all the world should be her friend.

"She's a dainty little thing," old Nikita would marvel. "She could be a dancer."

Even Procopy, whose impatience with Daniel was not always concealed, used to pick her up and carry her about with him whenever he visited the house. He had a wife and two little children of his own. "So you," he would tell her, "must be my sweetheart."

"Where's your beard?" she would always, fearlessly, ask him. "Why haven't you got a beard?"

"The tsar tore it off." He would laugh.

She revered her father. She knew that he was older than the father of the other children, but knowing also with what respect he was treated in Russka, she supposed that he was therefore someone quite out of the ordinary. When she was very little, she had for some time thought that he and God the Father must be one and the same.

If Nikita was amused by Maryushka, Eudokia did indeed find the comfort she sought with Daniel and Arina. Each day she came quietly to pray with them. Often, when Daniel was working in the house, she would stand near him, watching silently. He was, Daniel saw at once, necessary to her. And as she once confessed to him herself:

"I have been a strong woman all my life, but in this new world I feel as if all that I have known is being taken away. Do not leave me just yet, faithful friend."

When she could slip out undetected, she would even put on a simple peasant's cloak and go with Daniel and his family to their secret church services. Even Daniel permitted himself a smile when he remarked: "They'll think you are my wife, and that Arina is my daughter, and Maryushka our granddaughter!"

She herself was amazed to discover what Daniel had managed to learn in his first week: that these services of Raskolniki were taking place in secret all over Moscow.

Nearly always, in the capital, they were held in private houses rather than churches. There, sometimes in the room of a modest artisan, they would take out their icons, darkened with smoke and age, place them on the walls, and pray earnestly together, making the sign of the cross with two fingers.

If Daniel brought Eudokia comfort, he found none for himself.

While the *streltsy* executions continued by day, Peter was still seen, by night, at the houses of his friends in the German Quarter. With him, it was well known, was his mistress Anna, while his wife, despite the fact that she had given him a son, scarcely saw him at all.

By late October, the executions temporarily stopped. Peter left the capital to go down to the river Don, where he was once again building a new fleet. The seven weeks of fasting that preceded Christmas began and for a time Moscow was quiet.

At Christmas, Peter was back. Peter and the Mock Synod paraded through Moscow and the German suburb on two hundred sledges in a wild effort at carol singing, which Daniel, then at prayer, fortunately missed.

With January and February came the traditional celebration of Epiphany and the pre-Lent carnival; the public executions also began again. On February 3, Peter insisted that all foreigners in the Moscow area attend to witness the execution of three hundred more of the *streltsy* who had wanted to murder them.

It was also at this time that Peter began in earnest his campaign to force his court into Western clothes by personally cutting the long kaftans of the boyars at a feast, just as he had cut off their beards a few months before.

To complete his political and personal arrangements, Peter now made Sophia formally take the veil as a nun; and he sent his own wife, who so bored him, despite her miserable protests, into a convent at Suzdal. Their son, whom Peter had not much bothered with, was now sent to his sister and given a German tutor.

It was not, however, until the carnival week just before the start of Lent that Daniel finally saw the horror of Peter's Drunken Synod.

The revelers were on their way to the sumptuous house of Lefort; at their head, as usual, was Peter's old tutor dressed as the Patriarch. Beside him went another, representing Bacchus, god of wine. He, too, wore a bishop's miter: but that was all he wore, since he was otherwise stark naked. Some of the party carried wine and mead, others huge dishes of the offensive, ungodly tobacco weed, which they had lit. Others yet were swinging censers that Daniel realized were also smoking not with incense but with tobacco.

He had heard, from young Procopy, that the tsar, when he was in England, had given Lord Carmarthen a monopoly to import the evil plant into Russia. Now here were the tsar's companions putting tobacco in church censers!

When, soon afterward, he heard that the tsar's friend Lefort had suddenly died, he could only say: "It is God's judgment."

In April, as if as a further punishment from God, food shortages began in Moscow and prices soared.

Yet all these things, Daniel soon realized, were only the advance signals of the great evil that was to come.

So far, the tsar's attention had been directed only upon his own court and the *streltsy*. Now, in the months that followed, he was to turn his fearsome gaze upon his people. And Daniel was brought from shock and misery to despair.

It began one evening when Procopy strode into the courtyard and, seeing Daniel, casually remarked, "Well, Daniel, you'll be shaving your beard off tomorrow." And seeing Daniel's look of amazement: "You haven't heard? Yes. You're going to look just like me. The tsar is issuing a *ukaz* tomorrow morning."

The *ukaz:* the edict. All tsars had used them, but from Peter they would flow in a torrent.

And the *ukaz* he issued in 1699 was devastating. All the people—not just the boyars, but simple men like Daniel, even peasants—were to shave their beards!

"It's all right," Procopy added with a grin, "you can pay a fine instead."

The *ukaz* was very simple: all except priests must shave. Anyone who refused must pay a fine and wear a bronze medallion around his neck on a chain. The scale of fines was carefully calculated. For the enserfed peasants it was a modest half kopek. But for a free man, an artisan, or even a coachman, it was a stiff thirty rubles; for a tradesman, a punishing sixty; for a noble like Bobrov, a hundred.

There was no way that Daniel could afford to pay.

Though he had been shocked by the sight of Procopy, the doings of the court nobles had always belonged in a world apart. This, however, was different. "I do not know how it is for nobles," he declared to Arina, "but for ordinary men there is no question—to shave one's beard is a mortal sin. I cannot do this thing."

"You must not," Arina agreed, while little Maryushka gazed at him in astonishment. She could not imagine the reverend figure of her father without his gray beard.

Within the Bobrov family the *ukaz* also created a storm.

"Never," cried Eudokia. "The idea is unthinkable." And when Nikita muttered irritably about the expense, she stormed: "I'd rather give all that I have than allow such a thing."

The next day, looking triumphant yet rather sheepish, Nikita suddenly appeared before her with only a mustache. She turned on her heel and would not allow him near her for a month. And when he complained she only replied coldly: "You can beat me, if you're enough of a man, but you'll get nothing else from me."

Meanwhile, she secretly bought a bronze disk for Daniel and insisted that he accept it from her.

"At least we shall have someone who looks like a God-fearing man in the house," she said firmly.

And so the terrible year went on until, at year end, came the events which were, at last, to take Daniel to the edge of the abyss.

* * *

Procopy was cheerful. He was busy, too. The *streltsy* had been utterly crushed and Peter's power was unassailable.

His own position was good: the tsar was his friend.

"And if he trusts you," he told his father, "he's the kindest fellow in the world."

For it had to be admitted that, for all his brutality, Peter could be tolerant of human weakness.

"He'll forgive you almost anything as long as you never lie to him," Procopy said. "Once, when I was late on parade, he looked so angry I thought he was going to have me knouted; but when I told him I'd been drunk the night before and only just woken up he just laughed and told me not to do it again."

Above all Procopy was cheerful because he knew that Peter was preparing for a great adventure—he was going to seize the Baltic ports.

It was a secret. The Swedes were strong and it would be necessary to take them by surprise. Brandenburg, Denmark, Saxony, all wanted to attack the Swedes and share out the rich Baltic lands of the Latvians, Estonians, and Lithuanians among themselves. But Peter could not strike north until he was sure that he, in turn, would not be attacked by the Ottoman Turks in the south. All that year, therefore, Peter assured the Swedish envoys to Moscow that he was their friend, while his own envoy in Constantinople tried to conclude a satisfactory treaty with the sultan.

Meanwhile, Russia was arming.

The new English flintlocks were a huge improvement on the old muskets of the *streltsy*, which had been completely unreliable. Equally impressive were the new bayonets from France.

"See how neatly it's done," Procopy explained to his father and Daniel one day. "Instead of firing and then fitting the bayonet into the barrel, and then removing it if you want to fire again, these cunning Frenchmen have thought of fitting the bayonet onto the outside of the barrel, so you can actually fire with the bayonet fixed!"

Neither man had ever seen such a weapon, and even Daniel, the former Cossack, agreed that the thing was well done.

Above all the state would need money.

"We're going to tax everything we can get our hands on," Procopy declared. "Even people's beards." He laughed. "And since trade will improve when we've got our Baltic ports, we'll make the merchants cough up, too."

"How will you do that?" Nikita asked.

"Simple," his son replied. "Administrative reforms."

And he explained how Peter was now going to allow all local tradesmen to be completely free of the control of the provincial governors and let them elect their own officials.

"That will please them, I should think," Nikita said. For though he himself had once hoped to be a governor, he knew very well how corrupt their administration was.

"Not really," Procopy grinned. "You see, we're doubling their taxes!"

Indeed, though many of Peter's reforms were for the ultimate good of Russia, it is certainly true that many were actually thought of originally as ways of raising revenue more efficiently.

Not only money, but men were pouring in. Procopy insisted that Nikita send a good complement from his estates, including Russka.

"And make sure they're all shaved," he remarked. When his father remarked that, for his part, he couldn't see why it mattered whether the peasant recruits were shaved or not Procopy quickly cut in: "Of course it does. That way we can spot deserters at once."

There was another way of getting men as well as applying to landlords. "We're going to make sure the peasants who've been freed by their masters don't get off," Procopy explained. "They're to report to the recruiting officers or lose their freedom."

"So their freedom will be the army?"

"That's right."

And Nikita could only shake his head at such ruthless efficiency.

But what, in the long run, did all these changes mean? This was what puzzled Nikita.

He was not shocked, as Eudokia and Daniel were. And though he found Procopy's air of superiority hurtful, he tried to be humble and to interest himself. He saw whole regiments dressed like Germans. He saw his son lead his wife out in a new German dress, in which she looked rather bashful. He saw the church mocked and the tsar's only son taken from his mother and given into the care of foreigners.

"And all I want to know," he burst out to Procopy, when they were alone one day before Christmas, "all I want you to tell me is, where are we going? Are we to stop being Russians altogether? Is that the idea? I even heard someone say the tsar would prefer us all to speak Dutch."

On this subject, to his surprise, his son reassured him. "For while I daresay the tsar would be delighted if we did speak Dutch, he won't attempt such a thing." Procopy laughed. "But you see, Father," he went on, "to understand what's going on you have to look not to Russia, but outside."

"What for?"

"Because no one in Russia realizes how backward we have become. If you went to London or Amsterdam, you'd see at once. Didn't Tsar Alexis import foreign officers and methods in your day? Yet wasn't he a good Russian?"

"He was," said Nikita piously.

"We Russians must use whatever seems good to us, then, and reject the rest," Procopy continued.

"But why does the tsar hate religion?"

"He doesn't. But the church is so backward, so superstitious, so opposed to any change, that he cannot work with it." He paused. "Tsar Peter, Father, is like a giant dragging a great army up a hill. Only the army is all facing the wrong way and pulling downward. He has to be strong. He has to be firm. He has to act, if you like, like Ivan the Terrible to achieve anything at all. Only in this way can he make Russia strong."

"Then we are not to become Westerners? We can still be Russians once we have caught up?"

Procopy put his hand on his father's arm. "Of course. I will tell you what the tsar said to me only last week. He said: 'Procopy Nikitevich—we need Europe for twenty years. Then we can turn our backs on her.' "

1700

THEN came the blow.

Old Russia ended.

To many of the population it was a cataclysm, as though the firmament of heaven had been risen. By this terrible sign, Daniel knew, as he had long suspected, that the end of days was indeed at hand. And gathering together Eudokia, Arina, and little Maryushka, he told them gravely: "The Apocalypse has begun. The Antichrist is here."

It was, indeed, the dawn of a new era.

For in December 1699, Tsar Peter had decided to change the calendar.

To understand the significance of this event, it must be remembered that in Russia, as yet, it was not the year 1699 at all. It was the year 7207 from the Creation, which system of counting, in all the centuries since the times of ancient Kiev, the Russians had never given up.

It must also be remembered that the year began not in January, but in September.

This, too, any Russian could have explained, was logical. For did not the story of Adam and Eve in the Book of Genesis speak of the apple on the tree? Clearly, then, when the world began, it must have been the autumn season!

The fact that the rest of the world used a different system was only further proof of how wicked other countries were.

This was the calendar that Peter in December 1699 decided to change. He issued a *ukaz* that the very next month, the new system, a new year, and a new century were to begin. Thus, in January, it became the year 1700.

He made only one concession to Russian sensibilities. The Catholic countries of Europe had by now adopted the modern Gregorian calendar. The English, being Protestant, were then still using the older Julian calendar. The small difference between the allocation of solar days to the year meant that as each century passed, the small gap between the two calendars grew larger. By this time, the Julian was already eleven days behind the Gregorian. But it was better to be a little late than to agree with the Pope! Peter therefore decided to use the Julian calendar and, as a result, until 1918 the Russians would continue to be nearly two weeks behind the West.

This, then, was the new age that Peter brought to Russia. He decreed that in the first week of January a branch of pine or juniper should be hung over every door, in celebration.

To Daniel, and many like him, this was the final confirmation of all that they had feared.

The idea that the world was approaching its end, though not new, had been growing enormously in Daniel's lifetime. It was not only the Raskolniki who thought so.

The collection of Ukrainian tracts predicting the end, called the *Book of Cyril*, had been widely read long before the Schism. The followers of Kapiton, whom Daniel had known on the Volga, had been urging the peasants there to prepare for the Apocalypse since Daniel was a young man.

Indeed, it had been a regular monk who had remarked to him one day: "You know, after the Church Council, Nikon himself began to think the end was coming."

The end was near. The question was: when exactly would it come? By the time of Daniel's arrival in Moscow, it was widely believed that it already had.

Endless calculations of the date were made, especially by the Raskolniki. About a thousand tracts on the subject have survived. All took as their premise that the number of the Antichrist was 666, and while some made their calculations from the split between the Orthodox and Catholic churches, and others argued that the Antichrist lay bound for a thousand years and then waited for his number, nearly all the calculations pointed to a year between 1666 and 1691.

In Russia, Daniel had been torn. While he feared that the end was near, the new joy he had found in his little family had made him hope that it might not be so.

But in Moscow that hope had evaporated.

Strangely enough it was a former monk, who had just joined the Raskolniki, who convinced Daniel. He was a small, intense fellow, and they had met at one of the secret prayer meetings at a private house. The monk had been an icon painter, which had drawn them together in the first place, and he had a formidable collection of pamphlets. He also had numerous prints that depicted Tsar Alexis and Nikon as the horns of the Antichrist, or Nikon as the Beast of the Apocalypse.

He knew the Book of Revelation thoroughly, and he quoted passage after passage explaining how each referred to a current event.

As Daniel became daily more appalled by what he saw in Moscow, his head also became more full of the monk's formulas and quotations. The fellow is certainly learned, he concluded. And it seems to me that what he says must be true.

But if indeed the end had come, then that must mean that the Antichrist himself had arrived upon earth. Many thought so. And in that case—who was he?

Some said Tsar Alexis. Others believed that it was Nikon, who, many of them added, must also have been Jewish!

But here again, the little monk had better information.

"Tell me this, who was Peter's real father?"

"Tsar Alexis."

"Perhaps. But why then is he such a dark giant? Can you think of another?"

Daniel gazed uncomprehendingly.

"Ah my friend, you are a good man: you do not see evil. I tell you, the father of this Peter was none other than the wicked Nikon himself. And this foul, illegitimate offspring is not a true tsar at all. Does he behave like a true tsar?"

Daniel could only agree that he did not.

"It is Peter himself who is the Antichrist," the little monk concluded in triumph. "It is he who is here to begin the Apocalypse. Be warned."

And it must be said that, with each passing month, Peter was giving his subjects good cause for thinking that this must be the case.

And no wonder, too, that if any final proof was needed, it came with this new and infamous act of changing the counting of the years.

"For is it not said," the monk reminded Daniel, "that the Antichrist shall change the time? Is it not said that the years of God shall be abolished when the years of Satan are proclaimed?"

"All this is true," Daniel agreed.

"Bear witness, then," his friend admonished him, "that this is indeed the Antichrist."

The festival of Epiphany, which falls on January 6, was always celebrated in Russia in a very beautiful way.

Deriving from the ancient Jewish Feast of Lights, the festival of Epiphany—or Theophany as the Orthodox usually call it—means "The Shining Forth." At this festival are especially remembered Christ's appearance to the Wise Men, and his baptism by John in the river Jordan.

It is a lovely and a delicate festival calling to mind images of light, water, and a dove descending.

At Epiphany, in Russia, it was the custom to bless the waters; and in Moscow this ceremony was of particular beauty.

Little Maryushka was excited therefore when her father announced that morning that they would all go to the river to watch.

She had been aware of a tension in the air for the last three weeks. She had seen her parents and the lady Eudokia consulting each other and heard such murmured words as *wickedness* and *the Second Coming*. She had seen the decoration over the doorways and heard people say it was the New Year; but since her father sternly told her it was not, she supposed everyone else must have made a mistake.

Today, at least, all seemed to be well. There was only the faintest wind. The cloud cover was high and thin, so that the pale presence of the sun was sensed, if not seen. The streets were full and by the time they reached the river a huge crowd was gathering. She could even see people sitting on the roofs of the houses. They crossed the frozen river and took up a position opposite the high walls of the Kremlin.

In the middle of the frozen river, inside a large area enclosed by rails, stood a little wooden building, like a shrine, densely hung with icons. Before it she could see a broad circular hole in the ice, like a well. Young priests and deacons were standing about there.

Maryushka looked up at her father. Although she already understood what it meant to be one of the Raskolniki, she hoped it was all right to enjoy these ceremonies performed by the ordinary church; she was glad, therefore, to note a look of approval on Daniel's face as he gazed at the river, and she held her mother's hand happily.

Soon, she knew, she would see both the Patriarch and the tsar himself as they sat in splendor, on twin thrones upon the ice, to watch the blessing of the waters. She was so fascinated that she forgot even to glance up at her parents again.

Across the ice now, she could see the front of the procession. A banner was waving; there was a faint glint from the jeweled miters of the priests. They were coming.

But then, suddenly, another sound was heard: The sound of pipes and drums—brisk, cheerful, but harsh. And now onto the ice swung column after column of soldiers, marching smartly in step. They wore close-fitting German coats of red, green, or blue, with gaiters and tricorn hats. They carried flintlocks. And they were clean-shaven. In front of each company marched a man with a banner; and before the first column strode a huge, tall man dressed in a green uniform. While the drums rolled and the pipes squeaked, some twelve thousand foreign-looking soldiers marched out onto the ice and formed a huge square around the area where the priests were to bless the waters.

Only when the troops were in place did the priests come onto the ice.

But now at last they came. How stately, how gorgeous the procession was. A large gold cross was followed immediately by an enormous lantern with mica windows, carried on the shoulders of a dozen priests, in which candles were burning brightly. Some five hundred priests in their golden robes and jeweled miters followed in stately procession behind. Archbishops, bishops, archimandrites, priests, and deacons; and as they gathered, hundreds of tall tapers were lit. On a raised dais a deacon stood holding aloft a huge banner on which, in gold, was depicted the double-headed eagle of the Russian tsars. On a throne sat the Patriarch. Here, indeed, was all the gorgeous panoply of old Russia.

But where, she wondered, was the tsar? Why was the Patriarch sitting alone?

"Where is Tsar Peter?" she whispered.

"He's there," Arina replied.

Maryushka frowned. Which one was he then?

The blessings had already begun. A mitered priest was passing the censer over the water: one, two, three times. Long candles were being dipped in the water. The waters were being blessed.

It was a sacred moment. At this instant, Maryushka knew, the waters of the river were mystically transformed into those of the river Jordan. This, indeed, was Holy Russia.

During all this time the massed troops had remained silent. At each important point in the service of blessing, the huge standard with the double-headed eagle had been waved, and the standards of the soldiers, as if in reply, had at once waved back in unison. As the ceremony ended, they were brought forward to be sprinkled with holy water.

Then it was done. The priests began to turn. When suddenly the whole sky appeared to crack.

To Maryushka, for a second, it seemed as if the world must have come to an end. The great thunderclap was followed by a roar that seemed to fill the whole sky, the whole day. She started so violently that she left the ground. And then, even as the mighty roar of the cannon massed along the Kremlin wall was reverberating back and forth across the river, a second awful crash followed as the twelve thousand men before her raised their muskets and fired a volley into the air; a few moments later there was another; then a third.

And the little girl, completely taken by surprise, burst into tears.

This was Tsar Peter's contribution to the celebration of Epiphany.

Only afterwards did her parents explain to her that the tall man in green, standing far away from the Patriarch, was the tsar and that the roar of the guns was meant to be a happy celebration.

As for Daniel, it seemed to him that, for the first time, he had truly seen the face of the Antichrist.

It was hard. It was cold. It was unlike anything seen in Russia before. For the Antichrist, this Peter, he now realized was the state itself, without religion. And he remembered a phrase he had heard some Moscow Raskolniki use only the week before, and which he had not quite understood.

"That's it," he murmured: "All power is Antichrist because all men are subservient to it."

Peter was the new state. And he was about power.

It was a week later that his friend the little monk disappeared.

He heard that they had taken him to the Preobrazhensky Prikaz for questioning. Ten days later he heard from the community of Raskolniki that the little fellow was dead. He had freely confessed to saying that Peter was the Antichrist. He even told his guards that they should not obey the tsar. But he had refused to name any accomplices. They had punished him by the death known in Russia as *kopchenie:* the victim is slowly smoked to death like bacon.

It was the week after this that Daniel left Moscow for Russka.

Andrei was pleased to be going to Moscow again—all the more so since he had discovered by letters that his old friend Nikita Bobrov was still alive.

"And I understood he's still rich, like me," he added with a grin.

Life had been good to him, Andrei considered. There had been tragedies: he had lost three children and his first wife. But there had been a happy second marriage and three more children, of whom his greatest joy was his son, Pavlo.

What a handsome, brave young fellow he was—a true Cossack.

As for their estates—they were considerable. "Which is why," he would remark slyly, "I am a good Russian!"

Since the days of Bogdan and the union with Muscovy, the Ukraine had suffered some terrible times while Poland and Russia fought over her and Cossack factions had fought between themselves in the period usually known as the Ruin.

But that was over now. After numerous disputes, Russia and Poland had finally signed a perpetual peace: Poland kept the land west of the river Dnieper, with the exception of ancient Kiev, and Russia held the land to the east, known as the Left Bank. At this time also, the Orthodox churchmen in Kiev finally placed themselves under the Patriarch of Moscow instead of Constantinople. There was some grumbling—because these Ukrainians still considered themselves more sophisticated than the Muscovites—but they did it.

It was also at this point that Russia found a new and satisfactory *hetman* to rule the Left Bank. He was a nobleman of polished manners and education who had at one time served the Polish king. His name—almost as famous as Bogdan's in the Ukraine—was Ivan Mazeppa.

His aim was very simple: control the land for Russia; strengthen the Cossack gentry; leave the poor Cossacks and peasants as they were; and, of course, enrich himself. This policy made the ordinary people hate him; but it certainly worked.

Ivan Mazeppa, in a feat rarely equaled in the highest days of feudalism, managed in thirty years to amass very nearly twenty thousand estates. He also gave estates to his faithful officers, including Andrei and his son.

"Thanks to Mazeppa we have ten estates," Andrei would remind his son. "And see how cleverly he has managed to make a friend of young Tsar Peter."

It was true that Mazeppa had managed to form a close and very profitable friendship with the new tsar, who trusted him more than most of his court.

And, thank God, young Pavlo was in the good graces of Mazeppa. Better still, he had fought his first campaign with Mazeppa, whom the Cossacks helped at the taking of Azov. Pavlo had been only seventeen, but he had caught the attention of Tsar Peter himself. Who knew what sort of career he might one day have! He could even be *hetman.*

He was a dark, handsome young man of twenty-five, a little shorter than Andrei had been, but very strongly made. The previous month he had broken his arm in a fall and returned home to visit his parents while it mended.

And though at first young Pavlo had been furious to be out of action, Andrei had suddenly remarked to him one day: "My boy—I think perhaps this is an opportunity after all."

The times were certainly exciting. Russia had begun her great war on the Baltic coast with Sweden. And Charles XII, that country's bold young king, was still so confident he could defeat his half-trained Russians that he had calmly attacked Poland as well. For a good Cossack, all this could only mean one thing—an opportunity to fight and enrich oneself. "The tsar needs good men for his northern campaign. And Mazeppa's going to ask his permission to take back some of the Polish lands across the

Dnieper," Pavlo had told his father. "Either way, I can't wait to get into action."

"But there are more ways of getting ahead than fighting," old Andrei had reminded his son. "Look at Mazeppa."

What better time could there be for Pavlo to go to Moscow and recommend himself to Tsar Peter?

Everything had worked out well: Mazeppa himself had given Pavlo a letter to Peter; Andrei had discovered that his old friend Nikita Bobrov had a son who was close to the tsar. It was with high hopes, therefore, that he rode northward into Russia.

Of the young tsar he did not know a great deal. The poor Cossacks hated him. They respected his conquests in the south and the fact that he had finally ended the payments to the khan down in the Crimea. But they hated the new religious ways—many had already become Raskolniki; and they detested the new war in the north. Their wild and undisciplined ways were useless against the trained infantry of the Swedish king. Losses had already been high.

"We're cannon fodder for English and German officers," they truly said.

But none of this greatly concerned Andrei now. A Cossack landowner was a very different fellow from these poor fighting peasants.

It was spring when he left Kiev. The weather was getting warm, and the rivers were settling down again into their new courses. For each year, in their full spate, the melting rivers carried downstream such a mass of branches, ice floes, and debris of all kinds, that their courses were subtly altered. Here a bank would collapse; there silt pile up a new one; fallen trees might turn a stream into new channels; a meadow might become a swamp. Each year it was the same river, yet not the same.

So, too, Andrei reflected, he was taking the same journey that he had taken half a century before: the same, but different, and this time with his son.

Though he felt healthy, a little voice within had told him that he should not expect to make any more large journeys after this one. He was strong, but he was seventy-four. And so it was with a certain nostalgia that he prepared to see Moscow for the last time.

How many memories rose up before him as he rode: memories of his youth, of Ox, of the girl Maryushka.

Faces, he thought, that I shall never see again, on this side of life's river.

In the year 1703, the Bobrovs had a new Moscow house.

It was stout, heavyset, on two floors: and it was built of stone. The rooms were low but large; the floors were made of massive wooden planks, which were polished. The furniture was simple—a stout table, some wooden chairs. And in the main room, after the icon in the corner of course, the place of honor was occupied by a tall square stove with a chimney, which was covered with Dutch tiles.

Procopy Bobrov had taken six months to persuade his father to import these tiles, but old Nikita, now that he had this stove, was proud of the thing.

"Dutch," he would say, as he conducted his guests to look at them. "Yes, they're Dutch, all right."

So it was to the new stove, in the month of May that year, that Nikita Bobrov delightedly conducted his old friend Andrei and his son Pavlo.

"What a delight this is," he cried. "After so many years. And as you see," he added, with a wave of the hand at the stove and the house in general, "things have changed since you were last here."

They had indeed.

How strange it was to find his old friend both clean-shaven, apart from a mustache, and in a tight-fitting German coat.

"Why"—he laughed—"my dear Andrei, you almost look like a Cossack!"

"Ah yes," Nikita looked a little sheepish, yet also rather proud. "The tsar's orders, you know."

For within a year of the beard tax, Peter had struck again. This time all classes above the peasant were to wear Hungarian or German short coats instead of their long kaftans, which, though undoubtedly warmer in the Russian winter, Peter had decided were too old-fashioned and impractical. He had even hung dummies, correctly dressed, by the city gates to instruct his subjects what to do.

"Yes," Nikita went on, "you'll find everything's very Western now. Young people allowed to meet each other before they're married; our women not to be kept in seclusion—he even has them attend court with their husbands. Progress of all kinds, I daresay."

Though Andrei also noticed, when Eudokia came in to greet him, that she wore a long Russian dress in the old style and greeted him in the traditional reverent manner.

"My wife preserves the old ways in the house," Nikita remarked, with a trace of embarrassment.

For their parts, the two Ukrainians thought it rather graceful.

Andrei was fascinated by all that he saw and learned in the coming days.

Nikita was obviously happy to see him, insisted he stay in his house, and took him everywhere. But it was not just the changing face of the city but the subtle change in attitudes that he noticed.

For where, in their youth, Nikita had been harsh towards foreigners, now there was in his tone something faintly but unmistakably apologetic.

"We have apothecaries in the city now, you know," he would say. "And a newspaper." Or: "There's a new school of navigation here, and another for foreign languages about to start. But of course, I daresay you're used to such things in Little Russia."

On another occasion, he even remarked humbly: "The tsar has authorized Protestants; do you think that is right?"

Above all, Nikita noticed the change in the power of the church.

Once again, another department for the church had been set up; but this time, Andrei gathered, the tsar was effectively taking some of the church revenues for the state.

"He's also taken a lot of church bells," Nikita explained, "for the cannon."

But far more striking, and shocking, was something Peter had simply failed to do. The old Patriarch had died three years earlier. And since he was nowadays their Patriarch, too, the Orthodox in the Ukraine had wondered who the new one would be. So far only a temporary stand-in had been appointed. But when Andrei asked his host who he thought would succeed, Nikita shook his head. "You don't understand. The word is that there isn't going to be one. Peter doesn't want one."

"What do you mean? The tsar can't abolish the Patriarch. He isn't God."

But Nikita only shook his head. "You don't know him," he said quietly.

Yet if these matters depressed him, the news of the war, at least, was very encouraging. After some false starts, Peter had succeeded in getting his first foothold on the Baltic. He had not yet managed to hold any of the great Baltic ports like Reval or Riga; but the previous year he had got back a fort up by Lake Ladoga, by the entrance to the river Neva where, centuries before, the legendary Alexander Nevsky had driven back old Russia's enemies. "There's only one more fort up there—it's where the Neva runs into the sea," Nikita explained. "Once he has that, he's got a hold on the sea. Not much of one," he added with a smile, "but enough for him to claim a victory!"

A week later the news came. It was brought by Procopy. "He's got the fort. There's been a battle on the river Neva with a Swedish flotilla: he won that, too. The tsar's got his foothold in the north."

He had indeed. It was a desolate, marshy place: the name Neva, in Finnish, meant "marsh." There was really nothing there but a fort. However, the river Neva led to Lake Ladoga, and from there one could penetrate one huge river system of north Russia. Compared to Reval or Riga, it was nothing much, but in 1703, it was what Peter had. And he was delighted. He awarded himself and his favorite Menshikov the Order of Saint Andrew, which he had recently instituted. He let it be known that he would enter Moscow in triumph in June. And he immediately set to work to build a new and stronger fort at the place, having a stout log house built for himself on the riverbank near its foundations.

"So what are we to call this new fort of the tsar's?" Nikita asked.

"The Peter and Paul fortress," Procopy replied. "When I left," he added, "he was talking of building a town up there, too. You know how he gets these sudden ideas."

"A town. Up there in the marshes."

"I know. It doesn't make much sense. Perhaps he'll change his mind."

"And what does he want to call that?" Nikita demanded.

Procopy grinned.

"Saint Petersburg, I believe," he said.

And it was just while they were digesting this preposterous news that a messenger arrived with news that drove all thought of Peter's little victory from Nikita's mind.

It was his steward from Russka.

And it seemed that the whole place had gone completely mad.

All along, perhaps, Daniel had known that it would come to this.

He had known it in his heart three years before, when old Silas the priest had died. That had been in the summer, just six months after his own return from Moscow.

It was remarkable, really, that the little community had been able to continue for so long, even up to then. It could not have done so without friends.

In the first place, there was the abbot. Daniel had always strongly suspected, but only in his last few months did old Silas positively tell him that the abbot was a sympathizer. "He knows what we do and says nothing. That is why nobody bothers us," Silas had explained.

The other danger might have been the Bobrov steward: but he was one of the Raskolniki himself and attended their secret services.

The third, and equally important friend, was Eudokia Bobrov.

Her interest in the community had to be secret. Only Silas and Daniel and his family knew, and they all agreed that there could be no other way. The villagers themselves did not know. Had Nikita himself ever guessed, needless to say, he would have clamped down at once. But if ever an icon, a prayerbook, some candles were needed, mysteriously Silas or Daniel had always found the money and the needed articles had appeared.

"We remember you in our prayers, good lady," Daniel had told her.

The monastery was lax but conformed. If once the Bobrovs had been suspected under the old regime, under Peter they were trusted. Russka was rather a backwater anyway. So for nearly two decades, while many Raskolniki left the center of Russia for the frontier lands, and while there might be trouble at Nizhni Novgorod or on the Don, the authorities just assumed that Russka was quiet. As for Dirty Place—who had even heard of it?

In the early spring of 1703, Silas had told Daniel he was dying.

"I shall go this summer. You must take over."

"I, too, am old," Daniel protested.

"You are the only one who can lead them," Silas replied.

"Yet how shall I be ordained a priest?" Daniel asked.

For this was now, and would always remain, the central problem of the Raskolniki.

They were the true church yet outside the church. No bishops had joined them and so there was, technically, no one to ordain priests. As the last of the original priests in the movement—men like Silas, who had been ordained before the Schism—died out, how were they to be replaced?

Some Raskolniki were prepared, if they could find one, to take on a discontented priest from the new church, as long as he underwent a ritual purification. Others used the old method, which the church now frowned on, of electing their own parish priest. In the old days, such a man was submitted to the bishop for ordination. Now, without bishops, he remained an elder, recognized by his congregation alone.

Officially, then, when Silas died, it was decided that the congregation at Dirty Place should go to the church at Russka—though a priest from the monastery would go to the little church in the hamlet from time to time to hold a service in the proper manner.

In fact, the official priest seldom went there, while the hamlet made a meager attendance at Russka.

And, having carefully washed and purified the little church whenever the priest from the monastery had come there, the Raskolniki of Dirty Place, led now by Daniel, continued their own services in secret.

At the end of the year there came another crisis. The steward died.

What if Bobrov should send a new man who was not of their persuasion?

Immediately Daniel wrote a letter, and Nikita was rather puzzled, a few days later, when Eudokia said to him: "Let me choose a new steward for Dirty Place. I know the estate far better than you."

Since he had many other things on his mind, Nikita had agreed, and rather forgotten about the matter; while at Christmas Daniel had been delighted to welcome the new young steward in the little church at Dirty Place.

But the greatest threat to their safety still remained.

It is sometimes thought that Peter was liberal over matters of religion. And up to a point this is true. A year before, in 1702, he had not only authorized Protestants to worship freely but his laws had proclaimed the principle of religious toleration—certainly something no tsar before would ever have dreamed of.

That same year, encountering a whole area of Raskolniki up in the north, he had told them they might worship as they pleased so long as they produced a certain quantity of iron for his war effort. As time went on, though Peter often fulminated against them and their old-fashioned ways, he also, rather contemptuously, issued laws that allowed Raskolniki to practice—but made them pay double taxes and wear a distinguishing yellow badge on their coats.

It was freedom—though of a rather poor kind; but some found they could live by it.

Yet to many Raskolniki, Peter had done nothing at all. For the one thing that he still absolutely demanded of all men, was the one thing they could not give: total loyalty and obedience to the tsar and his new, secularized state. How could they, when they were coming to see that he was the Antichrist himself?

Above all there was one unchanging requirement to which they could not yield.

"We cannot, in conscience, pray for the health of the tsar," Daniel declared. "That is impossible. If we do that, then we deny all that we believe in."

*   *   *

Maryushka was with some other Russka children, fishing in the river on the monastery side, the morning that the abbot died.

They knew that something must have happened when they saw the monks hurrying about at the gate, calling the lay brothers in from the fields. A few moments later the church bell started to ring.

That the abbot would die one day was to be expected. He was very old. But in fact he had dropped quite suddenly, in the monastery library, and hence the confusion.

Curious as always, the children had run to the monastery gates. At first the monks ignored them. But a lay brother soon told them; and immediately they pushed their little boat across the stream and Maryushka ran off to tell her father.

And when she saw the look that Daniel gave Arina, she understood that this death meant something very serious indeed.

Yet at first, Maryushka thought she liked the new abbot. He was a pleasant-looking man in his fifties, with a round face, very pale blue eyes, and would stop to talk to children in Russka.

But he was an outsider. The death of the old abbot had brought a visit from the authorities. They had not been impressed with what they saw; the election of a new abbot was stopped and the monks, to their great annoyance, had had this new man imposed upon them from Vladimir.

He arrived in early May. Two weeks later he had become suspicious about what was going on at Dirty Place. A week after that, two strangers arrived at the monastery and were closeted with him for some time.

How warm the church always seemed to Maryushka.

It was a simple, wooden building with a little octagonal tower over its center. One came up a flight of wooden steps to the covered porch by the west door; though beneath this was an undercroft with a stove where they often gathered in the depth of winter.

Inside the church, though the wooden ceiling hid the tower itself from view, the room was high and light streamed in through the open windows. There was a little iconostasis of four tiers: although the top row, the prophets, was so close to the ceiling that it had to be set at an angle. All the painting had been done by local artists, some of it very crude; overall, it looked reddish, rather squashed, and friendly.

It was a warm, late afternoon in early summer. The sun was gently lighting up the icons of the local saints beside the Royal Doors. In the shadows in the corners, candles had been lit before other, darker icons.

The whole village was there, standing together in the stillness, while little particles of dust danced in the long shafts of sunlight above. Sometimes, when the village was at prayer like this—the men with their long beards, the women with the scarves tied over their heads—it seemed to her as though they were timeless: as though the present itself, having been foreshadowed, was also a memory, dreamlike in its quality.

This was her family: the people with whom—such was the will of God—she was to live and die. And for that very reason, she belonged to them and they to her. This was the gentle, warm intimacy of the little church.

Her father was conducting the service. Still, though she was nine, she saw him as a Patriarch—as unshakable, as timeless as one of the prophets on the iconostasis.

He, like Silas, will die, she knew. Yet he will never die. He will be with me here, always.

She stood beside her mother. As she sang the responses, how lovely yet how sad her voice sounded.

They had just reached the Litany when Maryushka noticed the two visitors quietly enter the little church. Other heads turned also.

She saw them bow and make the sign of the cross with two fingers before standing reverently at the back.

Her father, too, had seen them. For an instant, as he began the prayers, she saw him hesitate. But then, looking up as though for guidance, he solemnly went on.

As he went through the prayers, she tried to concentrate. But she could not help looking back to see what the strangers were doing. Nothing, it seemed.

Was there something even more fervent than usual in Daniel's prayers? Was there, on that quiet, late afternoon, some particular tinge of sadness yet of warmth in her mother's singing?

It was as Daniel raised his hand for the final benediction that the two men suddenly stepped forward.

"Stop the service!" one cried.

"This is an affront to the Church and to the tsar," announced the other.

Slowly, carefully, Daniel completed the benediction.

Then, gazing down at them, he asked, "You have something to say to me?"

"You make the sign of the cross with two fingers," the first called out.

Daniel said nothing.

"Why have you not prayed for his majesty the tsar?" demanded the other.

Again, Daniel did not answer.

How fine he looks, Maryushka thought. Truly this is Elijah himself.

No one in the congregation moved.

"We shall take you with us," the first said to Daniel.

"I shall stay here."

It was a simple statement. As the two men glanced around at the congregation they saw a dozen silent, bearded faces that told them they would not.

"We'll see how you like to argue with the tsar's troops," they said. "They will persuade you to pray for the tsar."

Daniel shook his head slowly.

"The tsar is Antichrist," he said simply.

The man gasped.

"You dare to say so?"

Daniel looked at them steadily. The words had been spoken. It was inevitable, one day, that they must have been. What choice did he have?

He continued to stare at them, silently.

"Shall we deal with them, Father?" It was a young man from the back. "We could drown them."

Daniel turned his gaze towards him.

"God forgive you for your angry thought," he said quietly. "Let them depart in peace."

As Maryushka watched the two men leave, she could feel the little congregation fill with dread. They all turned back to Daniel, looking for guidance.

"My children," he said, "we must continue to pray together, hopeful always of deliverance. But we must also be prepared. For now, it may be, the time of suffering is at hand."

It was an hour later that he wrote the letter, which, it was agreed, the steward should carry to Moscow.

Nikita Bobrov was beside himself.

The news this wretched fellow brought was bad enough. But the letter! It was beyond his worst nightmares. He shook with anger.

"What in the world is to become of the Bobrovs now?" he cried. And suddenly, for the first time in years, the clever, mocking face of Peter Tolstoy rose up in his imagination. "So, you devil," Nikita shouted to the empty room, "you expect to see me humiliated a second time!"

The fact was that the young steward had panicked. Though he was a sympathizer of the Raskolniki, he was not made of such stern stuff as Daniel and his friends. Nor was he part of their community. When the two spies came he had been terrified. His first thought was to flee into the forest; but that he rejected as impractical.

It was just as he was wondering how to escape that Daniel came to see him with his letter.

"Go to the lady Eudokia with this," the old man ordered. "You are the steward. No one will hinder you if you leave quickly."

It was all the bidding he needed. Long before dark, he was riding towards the capital. But when he got there—what should he say? What should he do?

The first thing to do was to open the letter. He did so carefully, read it slowly, and sealed it again. It was as he suspected. Daniel had given Eudokia a brief account of what had taken place, asked for help if she could give any, and if not, ended with an expression of their mutual faith.

And I'm part of it, he thought grimly. Lady or not, they'll find out: she'll die for it along with them, and so will I.

There was only one chance. Give the letter to Nikita himself.

Perhaps, somehow, he can hush it up, he thought. Anyway, he's the only man who can protect me.

So it was that the distraught fellow had arrived at the house and handed the letter to Nikita.

Nor was it surprising that Nikita should be beside himself.

"What can have possessed you?" he shouted to his wife. "No one of us nobles has taken an interest in these accursed people for twenty years!"

"It may not be the fashion, but I did what was right," she answered stiffly.

"Right! You think it right to refuse to pray for the tsar and call him Antichrist? Can't you see? It's not a question just of religion. Your carpenter isn't just one of the Raskolniki—he's committed treason!"

"Because of his faith."

"The tsar isn't interested in his faith. He's interested in treason," Nikita yelled.

That was the point, Eudokia thought. That was exactly why so many Russians called him Antichrist.

"Nor will the tsar take kindly to our family being involved," Nikita pointed out. "If we didn't know, the fact that some of our peasants were traitors might be overlooked. But"—he waved the letter, "there is proof we are involved. I myself, and perhaps you, could be knouted. Our lands will very likely be taken away. Procopy's career is probably finished. Whatever your views, I do not understand how you can do this to your family—a second time."

And at this reference to her part in his own ruin, he thought he saw a trace of awkwardness in her manner.

"Whatever we do," he concluded grimly, "we shall have to act fast."

That evening a family conference was held between Nikita and his son, together with Andrei and Pavlo. As Nikita truly said, he needed any good advice he could get. And never, as he said afterward, had he been more glad that the old Cossack had become such a canny fellow.

As a result of this meeting, two pairs of men rode out of Moscow that very night.

The first pair was Procopy and the steward. They set out for a distant Bobrov estate.

The second pair consisted of Andrei and his son. They rode quickly, taking with them spare horses.

They were making their way to Russka.

The abbot was not a bad man. But he had no intention of allowing such things to go on in a village beside his own monastery lands.

It would make him look ridiculous.

He guessed, moreover, that several of his own monks were secret sympathizers with these folk. The old abbot certainly must have been. Well, this would show them.

For himself, he had no sympathy whatever for the Raskolniki. He had been only six years old when the Great Church Council condemned them. All he knew was that they took support from the official church.

"They are an unnecessary thorn in our side," he told his monks.

He had been appalled, the previous year, by certain signs that Tsar Peter might tolerate the existence of these people. He shrewdly guessed that the tsar would turn against them once he discovered how obstinate they were.

As for Daniel and his friends, when the abbot heard the report of the two inspectors he had sent for from Vladimir, he could only breathe a sigh of relief. "Thank God," he said, "they spoke treason."

Now he could send for the troops.

In the village of Dirty Place, the people were resigned.

And with good reason.

For twenty years they had continued to break the law, while stories came through every few years from distant communities of how others had suffered martyrdom for their faith.

Now the troops were coming. It was their turn.

There would be no question of mercy. Every Russian knew that. The rebellious monks at the Solovetsky Monastery had been slaughtered to a man. Since then, not dozens but scores of communities had been butchered. Worse yet, the authorities would certainly want to torture the ringleaders first.

It was therefore not surprising that in the last few decades many threatened communities had preferred, rather than falling into the hands of the authorities, to meet the inevitable end in their own fashion.

And so, in Dirty Place, they had gone to work at once. A day after the two strangers had come, the villagers had coated the roof of their church with pitch. Then they began to fill the undercroft with straw. More bails of straw were carried into the main church. At the same time, under Daniel's careful direction, some of the men made doors that fitted inside the windows of the church and chopped down the staircase that led to the main door. Then ladders were placed—five of them—below the windows and the main door. By the end of a single busy day everything was ready.

They were going to burn themselves.

Ritual self-immolation was a well-known practice among the Raskolniki.

It had been done all over Russia, though especially in the north, and since the 1660s it is estimated that tens of thousands had perished in this way by their own hands, sometimes in acts of willful martyrdom, at other times to avoid a worse fate at the hands of the authorities.

The practice was to continue in Russia, sporadically, until at least 1860.

As Maryushka watched these preparations she hardly knew what she felt. She was nine years old. She knew what death was.

Yet what was it? Would there be pain? What did it mean, to cease to be? Did it mean darkness, nothingness—forever? Her head reeled at the thought. What would it be like, this unconscious journey across a plain, without any ending?

Her parents would be with her—that was the thing. The thought was like a ray of sunlight, lightening and warming the frozen darkness. Her mother, her father: even here, at the approach of death, she wanted with all her heart not to escape the flames but to be with them, her hands in theirs.

Love was stronger, surely, than death. Even if not, it was all that she had.

They stayed in the hamlet now, most of the time; and as the sun shone upon the little church, prepared to receive them, they waited and prayed and watched.

Andrei and Pavlo rode quickly. Two days passed. Three. They were drawing near.

In a way, Andrei was excited. This was certainly an adventure. He was glad, also, to be able to do his old friend a favor.

"After all," he remarked to his son, "you and I have nothing to lose in this matter. But if we pull it off, then Bobrov will certainly be in our debt."

It was strange that now, near the end of his life, he should be revisiting the scenes of his youth again, so unexpectedly and in such circumstances. Destiny seemed to be playing a curious game with him.

It was on the second day that he remarked casually to his son: "Do you know, I once had a child in the village we're going to? A girl."

"God be praised, Father, did you really? What was her name?"

"I don't know."

"What became of her?"

"God knows. Perhaps she's dead."

"Or one of these Raskolniki."

"Perhaps. There's nothing I can do about it."

"Well, our task is clear enough anyway."

"Yes. It is."

By now, they both assumed, the luckless steward who knew too much had been disposed of by Procopy Bobrov.

"Kill him and throw him in a marsh somewhere," Andrei had advised. "No one will ever ask—but if they do, say he ran away."

As for their own mission to Russka, Andrei had been adamant. "Neither of you Bobrovs must go near the place. You know nothing. We'll take care of the whole thing for you."

As long as they were right in thinking that the villagers did not know about Eudokia's role, the plan should work.

It was very simple. The torturers must not get to Daniel and his family. There must be no confessions.

They were going to kill them.

It was already dusk, and, at that season of the year in those northern regions, the nights were very short.

The sky was overcast. The air was sultry, with a threat of thunder, as the hamlet prepared to sleep.

But little Maryushka could not sleep.

Each night she had slipped out to stand by the river in the darkness, eagerly drinking in each night, which might be her last. As usual now, she stood near the village, gazing northward.

Despite the sultry atmosphere, the clouds were thinning. Here and there, as if to light her upon a journey, strips of stars were appearing in the night sky.

It was what the Russians call a Sparrow Night. On the horizon soundless flashes of lightning appeared, like distant white flames, flickering as though to suggest that, vast as the land was, all the great plain on such a night might still be drawn together in a huge intimacy—from the arctic wastes to the warm steppe—to witness this tremulous show.

How beautiful it is, she thought. And it occurred to her that perhaps the earth was bidding her farewell.

An hour passed. Still she did not sleep. Then another. Another still.

And then a boat came slipping swiftly downstream from Russka. A boy was paddling frantically.

"They're coming," he cried. "Soldiers."

And she turned and ran.

Andrei and Pavlo were lost. The old Cossack was sure that Russka lay somewhere down this little river, but in the many years since he had been there he had forgotten just where.

It was well into the evening when they had finally given up and made their camp for the night.

The two men were astonished then to be suddenly woken, an hour before dawn, by the sound of voices and tramping feet nearby.

They were good Cossacks. In a flash both men were up and armed. Andrei was with the horses, keeping them quiet. Pavlo was watching, listening.

The sounds were from across the river. They were soldiers marching through the shadows. In the faint light from the stars, Pavlo saw the outline of bayonets. Two people, the officers presumably, were talking in low tones: in the stillness, their voices carried easily across the river.

"I did this before once, up by Yaroslavl," he heard the officer say. "Catch them at dawn, that's the thing. We'll have the whole village in our hands before they even know we're there."

From the sound of their tramping feet, Pavlo estimated there were forty or fifty men. He waited until they were past.

There was not a moment to lose. The village must be closer than they thought. Quickly the two men saddled their horses and started downstream. "We'll go down the river on this side and get ahead of them before we cross," Andrei said.

It was not easy to make much speed in the darkness. The troops had already passed the little town of Russka when the two Cossacks reached it. As they did so, they noticed the boy who had seen the troops go sliding down the stream in his little boat.

Daniel moved from house to house, waking the villagers.

In the darkness before the gray dawn they came out, a little confused, obviously frightened, some of them wrapping themselves in cloaks against what seemed to them to be a morning chill.

At each house, Daniel calmly entered and, waking the head of the household, said quietly: "It is time."

Maryushka stood inside the little hut they had been occupying, watching her mother. Though she had been up all that warm night in only a linen smock, the little girl had now started to shiver uncontrollably.

Arina seemed very calm. By the light of a taper, she quickly arranged her dress and put her feet into her shapeless bast shoes. She took a long shawl and draped it over her shoulders. Then she tied a scarf over her head. Then she ran her hands once, carefully, down her thighs. It was a little gesture she always made before she went to church.

Today, however, she did one other thing that the shivering girl noticed.

Slowly, rather meditatively, she reached over to her left wrist, on which she always wore a gold bracelet. It was a fine piece of work, set with a single large amethyst, and Maryushka knew that her mother was very attached to it. Now, however, she took it off carefully and laid it down beside her stove.

"What are you doing?" the girl whispered.

Arina smiled at her kindly. "These are earthly things, Maryushka," she said gently. "But now we are going to a heavenly kingdom."

Then her mother went quietly over to a corner of the room and came back with a small container.

She had seen her mother and some of the other women go out into the woods a few days before and return, after several hours, with some unusual berries. They had been several hours more in one of the huts, making something with these berries, and then Arina had come home with this little container; but she would not tell Maryushka what it was.

Now Arina poured some liquid out into a little wooden cup and brought it over to her.

"Drink this."

It looked dark.

"What is it?"

"Never mind. Just drink it."

The liquid tasted strange. A kind of bitter juice.

Arina looked at her carefully.

"You'll stop shivering soon."

"Did the other children get this?"

"Yes. Some of the grown-ups too, I daresay."

There were many berries in the Russian forest. Some had extraordinary properties. One, in particular, was used by the Raskolniki upon these occasions.

They went outside.

All the villagers were coming out of their huts now, and making their way silently towards the little church. Maryushka looked around for the soldiers, but there was no sign of them yet.

At the church some of the men were putting the ladders in place. She saw her father, watching over everyone, as they gathered.

For several minutes they waited. She saw Daniel and three of the older men go around from hut to hut, to make sure that no one was missing. When they gravely returned, she saw her father give a nod.

It was time.

Silently, slowly, the villagers began to go up the ladder into the church. As it happened, she and her mother were at the back. She glanced around. Still no sign of the soldiers.

Five of the men were to remain outside. Four of them, at the signal, would light the straw in the undercroft. Then they would quickly mount

the ladders, pull them up after them, and barricade the door. Properly
prepared, the building would be ablaze in moments, and there would be
nothing the tsar's troops could do except bear witness to the sacrifice.

The fifth man was up on the roof, acting as lookout. It was he who
would give the word.

The villagers were mostly in. Now it was Arina and Maryushka's turn.

Strangely, Maryushka found that she had stopped shivering. She
mounted the ladder quite calmly. She even felt a curious, rather agreeable
warmth inside her.

She entered the church.

The candles were lit—more of them than usual. All around her she saw
the familiar faces, looking taut and pale.

Soon afterwards Daniel entered.

He addressed them from before the doors of the little iconostasis.

"Brothers and sisters," he said solemnly, "it seems the time has come.
For those who are fainthearted, remember, it is an easier death by far that
we go to than that which would otherwise await us. And to you all, I say:
Our God, in His Kingdom, awaits us. He is with us now, already. His
arms are open. He is Our Father and He welcomes us, at last, from this
evil world. Prepare therefore to enter, through Christ's perfect love, into
His Kingdom of eternal light."

Then he began to read the prayers.

How familiar, and yet how strange, it all seemed. Her mother was
beside her. Her sweet voice, singing the responses, was so lovely, so
comforting. The candles seemed to be glowing with an extraordinary
brightness. How sweet, how lovely their warm flames. She felt a little
dizzy.

For it was now that the berries took their effect and Maryushka began
to hallucinate.

They were coming. In the pale first light of dawn, the man on the roof
saw the figures crossing the river.

He hesitated and then, drawing a deep breath, called down to the men
below.

He, too, must go down now. He knew it. He must go inside. But for
a few moments more he remained up there, looking at the dawn, peering
at the figures approaching.

Then he frowned. He stared again. Surely there must be more. But no,
into the village were riding not a contingent of soldiers, but only two
men. And in the half-light they did not look like the tsar's men at all.

They were Cossacks.

Below, he could see that three of the men had already gone into the
undercroft with their torches. The fourth was just following them.

He looked all around. The two Cossacks were quite alone.

"Stop!" he called down. "It's not the tsar's men at all."

Could it be that, after all, it was a false alarm, a reprieve? Cossacks—
why, they might even be Raskolniki!

"Stop the fire! There are no troops," he cried urgently again.

*　　*　　*

It was not until they were actually in the village that Andrei and Pavlo realized what was happening.

"My God," he muttered, "they're burning themselves."

Pavlo nodded.

"Our work's done for us then."

Andrei nodded.

"As long as the man Daniel dies. We still have to make sure of that."

They rode slowly forward.

And as they did so, they saw that people were starting to come out of the church, down the ladders.

It was the one thing Daniel had not foreseen. A false alarm. He had not planned for it.

Nor, therefore, had he calculated the effect that it might have on some of the congregation.

For it is one thing to stand to face death with the rest of the community; it is another to hesitate when there is an offer of reprieve.

About a third of the village, nearest the exits and hearing the shouts from outside, made for the ladders.

Arina was taken by surprise, too. As people pushed past her, she tried to continue the responses. Then after a few moments, Daniel stopped the prayers. Only then did Arina suddenly realize that Maryushka was no longer by her side.

Below, meanwhile, everything was in confusion.

The men in the undercroft were now trying to put out the fire they had started. But it was not so easily done, for the straw had been well prepared.

At the foot of one of the ladders, about a dozen people were standing and staring at the two Cossacks, who in turn were calmly watching them.

And no one, it seemed, had noticed the little girl.

In the confusion inside, with people jostling near the window, she had been accidentally shoved into the path of a large man making for the exit. Scarcely troubling to think, and finding the child in his path, he had casually picked her up, tucked her under one powerful arm, and carried her down with him, dropping her when he reached the ground.

Now she was wandering about by the huts, hardly knowing where she was.

"Where is Daniel?" Andrei called out.

"Inside," they replied. "What do you want with him? Who are you?"

And Andrei was just wondering what to reply when another cry rang out, this time from the roof.

"The troops! I see them!"

They had arrived.

It was now that Andrei looked up and saw a huge figure coming down the ladder from the other window.

This must be Daniel: from Nikita Bobrov's description, there could be no mistaking him. And from the moment he reached the ground it was obvious that, whatever his uplifted thoughts a few minutes before, he was now in a furious temper.

"Get up the ladders," he roared at the people who had dared to come down. "Get up at once, you fools. It's probably a trap." With a furious glance towards the two Cossacks he rushed to the entrance of the undercroft, moving with astonishing speed.

"Light the fire!" he bellowed. "The troops are here. Hurry!"

The people were running up the ladders again. Daniel, satisfied that the fires were now lit, was ordering the men from the undercroft up the ladder by the front of the church.

"Up," he shouted. "Up and bar the door."

Already Andrei could hear a shout from near the village gate. The troops were entering.

He looked at Pavlo.

"Better take no chances," he murmured. And urging his horse forward towards the church, he drew his sword.

The flames were already licking up the side of the building. Smoke was pouring from the undercroft. Andrei saw the ladders being drawn up into the building, heard the heavy doors slam and bars drop into place. One ladder remained, and Daniel was walking swiftly towards it as Andrei reached him.

As the huge fellow turned to look up at the Cossack with his raised saber, there was not a trace of fear in his face: only anger and contempt. And his expression scarcely altered even when the Cossack stopped, openmouthed, and cried out: "My God. It's Ox!"

And it was as the two men stared at each other that a pale woman appeared above with a cry which, as he turned to look at where she was pointing, caused old Andrei to gasp once more, and wonder if he might not, after all, be in a dream.

Everything was swaying. But at last she knew where she must go. For now she saw the flames.

The flames. Like a huge candle. So comforting. She knew she wanted them.

She was walking towards them. The friendly flames, and the church, and her parents. Why did the church keep moving? She frowned. But still she pressed on.

Ah, she could hear their crackle. Feel their warmth now. If only she could just find a ladder: that was what she needed.

"Maryushka!" Her mother's voice. She smiled, went forward. Wasn't that her father, with someone else by the ladder? It was. He would take her up the ladder. She cried out, tried to run towards him.

"Maryushka!" A man's voice. But not her father's. Why did the strange figure on the horse cry out her name? Why was the huge horse coming towards her?

Suddenly she felt herself scooped up, high. She was on the big horse with the stranger.

Yet why was he carrying her away from the flames, away into the darkness?

*   *   *

The destruction of the Bobrov estate at Dirty Place was complete.

That is to say, its principal assets—the peasants Bobrov owned—were completely destroyed.

When the troops arrived, all the ladders were drawn up. They just had time to see a large figure, with a furious backward glance, go in as the last door crashed shut.

They could do nothing about the fire. It had already seized hold.

And so there the matter rested. The abbot was satisfied. The authorities were content. Nikita Bobrov, when he was told about the matter, professed himself astonished and horrified.

Very wisely, Andrei had kept little Maryushka well out of sight. No one knew she had survived. But upon his return, he had given her to Nikita.

It was a hard decision. She was his granddaughter. There was no doubt about it. Quite apart from the astonishing likeness to her grandmother—which made Andrei feel almost as if fifty years of his life had never happened—she had begged them later that day to let her retrieve a last reminder of her mother.

When the troops had gone, therefore, they came back to the deserted village and found, where she had left it, Arina's bracelet. Andrei had recognized it at once as the one he had given old Elena. The troops had been so shocked by what they saw they had even forgotten to loot the place.

Yet though Andrei carefully explained his relationship to little Maryushka, and offered to take her with him, she was obdurate.

"Let me stay with the lady Eudokia," she begged.

Andrei understood, she was the girl's only link with her vanished family, her only friend.

He did not tell her that Nikita Bobrov and his son had wanted to kill them all.

So it was, in the year 1703, that little Maryushka returned to Moscow to the house of Nikita Bobrov.

Her Cossack grandfather left a little money for her, so that, when she grew up, she could be free.

1710

A PALE, chilly, damp spring day.

The ice broke late up in Saint Petersburg. Sometimes the sounds of its cracking were like gunshots, they were so loud. Then would come a spring so bleak, in some years, that it was scarcely worth the having. After that a warm, dusty summer whose days, in those northern latitudes, were so long that even the three hours of so-called night were but a pale twilight in which, on the horizon, the aurora danced.

It had begun with the stout, grim fort of Saint Peter and Saint Paul. Then, at Peter's direction, a town had begun to appear.

It was built on marshland. Hundreds of acres of wooden piles were sunk in the mud. Canals were dug. It was almost as if, in this desolate terrain, Peter had decided to construct a new and unnecessary Amsterdam.

But unlike the rich, reclaimed land of Holland, around this place stretched not fertile fields but poor, chilly marshland; not pasture for cattle, but wilderness from which wolves in search of food would come into the town itself.

This was the place to which, three years before, they had brought Maryushka.

She hated it.

Why did Peter decide to build his new city here? What prompted him to make it his capital?

In all probability, had the northern war been more successful, the capital of Russia might have been one of the great Baltic ports in those very regions nowadays called Latvia, Estonia, and Lithuania.

But the northern wars had been slow and difficult, and Peter, as usual, was in a hurry.

So it was that, against all advice, he insisted on building in this inhospitable place.

Right from the start he had encouraged those close to him to take a house in the new town. In 1708 he had compelled all senior officials to live there. The next year he began forcibly to transfer whole villages of people to the rising city.

It was bleak. The fortress with its thick stone walls was built. A little nearer the sea, on the other side of the river, rose the Admiralty—a huge, fortified shipyard with a tall wooden spire with a weathervane at its center. Numerous other brick and stone structures were rising on the marshy banks: here a church, there a palace or a warehouse. Already, in the fortress and elsewhere, the great Swiss-Italian architect Trezzini was hard at work. But for the most part, as yet, the city consisted of log-and-wattle huts.

There were two problems: the marshy countryside around had few of the stout trees needed for building; nor were there any stone quarries. Everything had to be brought from other ports—sometimes a hundred miles away.

Thus Peter began his new western capital.

A chilly spring day in Saint Petersburg, and Procopy Bobrov, a heavy woolen cloak over his uniform, was walking briskly along a muddy path by the river Neva.

A damp, salty wind from the sea was driving up the Neva from behind him, catching the back of his ears so that they were wet, red, and tingling.

He was quite alone. But from time to time he would glance back and stare behind him, despite the fact that the wind then smacked him harshly in the face; and even as he screwed his eyes to peer into it, like a sailor before the mast, something indefinable in his manner suggested he was embarrassed.

The fact was, he was afraid of being seen by Maryushka.

He pressed on in this manner for some distance, turning repeatedly to make sure she was not following him.

It was, undeniably, a confounded nuisance that, just when he thought he was rid of her, she should have embarrassed him like this. But she had come to him, pleading, in such a way that . . .

The fact was, his conscience troubled him.

Maryushka. They had all been kind to her. She had no complaints about that.

She had spent the first few years with the elder Bobrovs in Moscow until first Nikita and then Eudokia had died. If she could not have been happy, those years had at least been peaceful.

After the disaster at Dirty Place, Nikita had ruled his household with a rod of iron. The Raskolniki were never even to be mentioned. The family went to the authorized church. Even Eudokia, now, was so shaken that she did not speak of the forbidden subject to the little girl, even in private. Occasionally, after Nikita had gone, the old woman had spoken tenderly about Maryushka's parents; but that was all.

Then Eudokia had died and Procopy had taken her on.

Procopy had not wanted Maryushka. She knew it perfectly well. But he had promised his mother that he would look after her until she married; and so she had been taken to the new city on the Neva.

Procopy's house was large. Like everything in Saint Petersburg, its size was regulated by the tsar. Since Procopy owned five hundred peasants, his house had to be two stories high and built of timber and plaster in the English manner. Thanks to this, it leaked. Each spring, the Neva overflowed and flooded the cellar.

Two of the houses nearby had been destroyed by fire; everyone in the city—merchants, nobles, even Peter himself—were part of the fire-fighting force. The tsar himself had been present with his axe at one of these fires and had saved the nearby houses. When the other one burned, he had been away on campaign, and people had just watched as three more houses had caught fire and been destroyed as well.

How Maryushka longed for Russka and the hamlet at Dirty Place.

Alas, however, Dirty Place was empty.

When the Bobrovs had lost all their peasants there, they had intended to move families from their other estates to repopulate the place.

"After all, we own plenty of souls elsewhere," Procopy had remarked.

But even so, they never had enough. The trouble was Tsar Peter's endless war.

It has been calculated that in over two decades, Peter enjoyed only a few months of actual peace. The wars in the north dragged on interminably. Everything was subject to them. Nobles, merchants, peasants—the entire huge country was bled by the huge cost.

And so it was that, year after year, when the Bobrovs told their stewards to choose people to send to Dirty Place, the word came back that all the spare men had already been dispatched to the recruiting officers.

"For we can't ruin three other estates just to get one started again," Procopy would point out.

There was another reason—though she did not know it—why Maryushka would never see Russka again.

"People might recognize her there," Procopy confided to his wife. "And although the business with Daniel and my mother is all over now, it might be embarrassing for us."

So what was he to do with her? Old Andrei the Cossack had left a little money. The girl was to be free. He had supposed he would marry her to an artisan or someone of that class.

In the meantime she had lived in apparent contentment, in their house, acting as a maidservant to Procopy's wife. Procopy supposed he was fond of her, in a way.

In recent years Procopy had become rather somber. Partly this was the result of years of campaigning. But it was not only war that wore him down. "It is my country as well," he would say sadly.

Why was everything so impossible? Why could one never impose order on this huge, backward land?

"The tsar is a Titan!" Procopy would exclaim admiringly. "Yet this country is like a stubborn sea."

Sometimes he wondered if anyone was truly with the tsar. The people certainly weren't. Even many in the established church, let alone the Raskolniki, thought he was the Antichrist. The richer merchants were coming to hate him, because he taxed them, literally, into ruin. The nobles and others whom Peter had compelled to live in Saint Petersburg would have been glad to see the back of him and return to the comfort of Moscow. They hated the sea; their houses here cost a fortune; even the price of food, shipped in from hundreds of miles away, was exorbitant. It was difficult even to build a road across the desolate marshes to Moscow.

In the south there had been two Cossack revolts—one down by the Caspian, at Astrakhan, another on the Don led by Bulavin—that had been nearly as big as Stenka Razin's.

Who did like Peter then? Men like himself, he supposed: those who served him: the new aristocrats.

For Peter was creating a new kind of state in Russia—one based on service, where any man could rise. It was beyond anything that even Ivan the Terrible had tried. He was even giving titles on the basis of service now, and that rogue Menshikov, the former pie seller, had been made a prince!

And he, Procopy, had done well serving Peter. He had nothing to complain of. He had only two fears. One was of losing Peter's favor. The other was of losing Peter.

"He's always exposing himself to danger. It's a miracle he hasn't been killed a dozen times," he would lament. "And if Peter goes, I don't know what will happen to us. For I have nothing to hope for from his son."

Tsarevich Alexis. Not many people liked him, but he was the heir. And no one knew what he would do.

There was something about him. He didn't say much, but there was a kind of silent resentment in the tall, saturnine young man that was rather frightening. He was twenty. After sending his mother to a convent, Peter had given him to German tutors, then to Menshikov to bring up. After that, the tsar had tried to make a military man of him, without much success. His only enjoyment seemed to be getting drunk.

But if the boy was reserved and resentful, Procopy couldn't altogether blame him.

Not only was Peter rough with the boy, but he had taken a new wife now—a former Lithuanian peasant who had given him more children! A mere peasant—a Lithuanian prisoner of war. She had changed her name now to Catherine. She was the tsaritsa. Peter openly adored her. And the boy's own mother, whom he was forbidden to see, was still locked up in her convent at Suzdal! No wonder he was moody!

"And the trouble is, no one knows where he stands on the reforms," Procopy told his wife. "He daren't oppose his father, but he certainly prefers to be in Moscow with his mother's people and those damned Miloslavskys. We can't trust him."

Peter was planning to send the boy abroad. He wanted to find him a German wife.

"And the sooner he goes the better!" Procopy remarked. "Perhaps marriage will improve him."

There was so much to think about. The northern war was reaching an important juncture. Since last year Sheremetev and thirty thousand men had been besieging Riga. Procopy wanted to get there himself, quickly, before it fell.

Peter did not like his friends to miss the action.

He must leave in a day or two. But first there was this tiresome business to attend to. He strode along the river: where was the place she said she had seen the fellow?

Maryushka was in love. It had all been so simple, so natural.

She had just seen him and known that instant sense of peace and happiness, followed by an extraordinary lightening of the spirit.

It had been so simple, yet so miraculous. For the young man had felt it, too.

After that, there was nothing more to say.

He was a peasant, from one of the Bobrov estates just west of Moscow. He had been sent to Saint Petersburg the previous month in charge of half a dozen sleds full of provisions for the household.

When she had told Procopy that she wanted to marry him, he had looked thoughtful and said, "He's a peasant."

"I don't mind," she had said quickly. "I'm used to life in a village."

Procopy's face had cleared. Maryushka, being innocent, had not realized that he had only been afraid that she would want him to give this valuable young fellow his freedom.

"Very well, then. If it's what you want, you shall go down to the village this spring, as soon as my wife can replace you," he said. And he had given her a third of the money old Andrei had left for her. Not that he wanted the rest: but he judged that, as a peasant's wife, to have more might be bad for her.

Maryushka was happy. She was in love, and in a few days she was to leave Saint Petersburg forever. Though she still often thought of her parents, the pain of the past was fading as she looked forward to her new life.

She had been walking by the Neva only the day before when she had seen the men digging a trench. That was nothing unusual. There were hundreds of such gangs of unfortunates—peasants, conscripts, prisoners of war—who made up the army of workers that Tsar Peter had ordered to build his new capital.

Indeed, she would hardly have glanced at these poor fellows if she had not noticed that one of them seemed to be staring fixedly at her.

She looked down.

There in the broad, half-frozen trench stood a dark fellow of middle height who might have been handsome once. Even now, he had tried to trim the graying stubble of his beard, but without complete success. His eyes were sunken. He had lost several teeth. And as they gazed at each other, she saw him tremble.

It was Pavlo, her Cossack uncle.

There could be no doubt about it. Though she had been young at the time, she would never forget the faces of the two men who had rescued her from the fire and brought her back to the Bobrovs in Moscow.

"Pavlo."

"Maryushka."

"Why are you here?"

He tried to smile; then his mouth began to work, and she realized that it was difficult for him to speak. Something came out she did not understand. Then he was racked by a fit of coughing.

He tried again.

"Mazeppa."

Then she understood.

For in the few years since they had last seen each other, everything had changed in the Ukraine. And to the Great Russians of the north, then and ever since, the name of Mazeppa has meant only one thing: treachery.

The reasons Peter fell out with the Little Russians of the Ukraine were as inevitable as they were tragic. Basically they failed him. The huge contingents of Cossacks who came to help him fight the Swedes were no match for the highly trained northern Europeans. They suffered appalling casualties—often over fifty percent. As a result, Peter despised them; he not only gave them Russian and German officers but started quartering his own troops in the Ukraine, too. This was exactly what the Ukrainians hated most. Why should they be humiliated? And what was Peter's distant war to them anyway?

In the autumn of 1708 the crisis broke. The war had been going badly for Peter. No one thought he could win, and the powers of Europe, while they laughed at his new capital in the icy marshes of the north, were looking forward to seeing his empire broken and then dismembered.

And it was then that the victorious Charles XII of Sweden joined the Poles for a great drive against poor Russia. They were expected to attack Moscow. That would be the end of Peter. But then the Swedish king instead swung south—against the Ukraine.

And Mazeppa joined him.

Was it treachery? Undoubtedly. Was Mazeppa a schemer; had he been negotiating with Peter's enemies for years? Of course he had. He was the Cossack *hetman.* Was Peter blameless then?

Certainly not. Quite apart from his ruthless treatment of the Little Russians, he had also sent a message, at this moment of crisis, that they must defend themselves without his help. And though he was hard-pressed himself, the Ukrainians quite rightly claimed that this broke the agreement they had made with Russia back in Bogdan's time—that Russia would protect them. To save his land, Mazeppa did what he thought he had to.

It was a mistake. In a lightning strike, Peter's favorite Menshikov took Mazeppa's capital and stores and butchered almost the entire population of the place, soldiers or not.

The Ukraine hesitated. The Russians clamped down. Some Cossacks joined Mazeppa. Many did not.

The following spring came the great battle of Poltava.

This battle was, perhaps, Peter's finest hour. Peter himself, whatever his faults, was completely fearless. One musket ball knocked his hat off, another hit his saddle, and another was stopped by a silver icon he wore around his neck. But at the end of that great day the mighty Swedes were utterly routed.

Europe was astounded. The eccentric young tsar had won after all, defeated mighty Sweden. The map of Europe was changed in a day: a new and tremendous Russia was arising. And Europe, having laughed, was now afraid.

For the Ukraine, too, it changed everything. From now on, Peter pursued a new and ruthless policy. The old south was to be Russianized. Big Russian landowners, especially Menshikov, appeared. Cossack districts were headed by Russians. Even the Ukrainian presses were censored, to ensure they printed nothing that disagreed with Great Russian publications.

And soon, instead of a stream of Cossack soldiers going north, there came dismal lines of conscripts, by the thousands, to work on the tsar's building projects.

For Peter meant to be firm. As he told his advisers, he intended to model the subjugation of the Ukraine on the pattern set by the Englishman Cromwell, in Ireland.

In a way, Pavlo had been lucky. Had he not been stricken with a fever, he would have ridden with his patron Mazeppa. Had he done so, he would either have fled in exile to Sweden, or else been hanged if taken captive.

But in his case, when the inspecting officers found him at Pereiaslav, there was doubt. His case was referred to Peter himself. The answer was brief and to the point:

> *This officer once brought me*
> *a letter. He is a close*
> *associate of Mazeppa and*
> *cannot be trusted.*

> *He is to lose all his estates*
> *and be sent with the*
> *conscripts to Saint Petersburg.*

And now, with a hundred others, he was digging a trench. While Procopy Bobrov went to look for him.

And what the devil will I do if I find him? he wondered.

It was a ticklish situation. He could, of course, have ignored the girl when she begged for his help. But no—their families had been friends and . . . well, there it was, he was ashamed. But what could he do—ask the tsar for clemency? He dare not. Peter could forgive many things, but never treachery. Even the name of Mazeppa was enough to make him burst out with fury.

Perhaps he could bribe the fellow in charge of him. That was risky, though; and besides, the Cossack knew too much anyway about his family and the Raskolniki. He didn't know what he'd do: but he was sure he didn't want the girl to see him not doing it!

Ah, here was the place. He gazed down into the trench, scanned the faces he saw. But he could not say any of them resembled Pavlo.

He called the foreman over and did his best to describe the Cossack. The foreman nodded.

"Yes, sir, indeed, we had such a fellow. I had to thrash him yesterday, as a matter of fact."

"Why?"

"I saw him talking to a stranger. A girl."

"Ah yes. He's not here today?"

"No sir."

"Tomorrow, perhaps."

" 'Don't think so, sir."

Procopy looked at him carefully.

"He must've been weaker'n I thought," he mumbled.

"You mean he's dead?"

" 'Fraid so, sir. Is that all right?"

Oh yes. It was all right.

Indeed, it would hardly be noticed. For though history is uncertain how many workers died of disease, fatigue, and starvation in the building of Saint Petersburg, it was certainly tens of thousands, some say hundreds of thousands.

Another morning, rather warmer, two days later.

There was a light breeze stirring the waters of the Neva, like those of the sea beyond, into short, choppy waves.

Maryushka was leaving at last. In a way, the news about Pavlo seemed to sever her last link with the past. She knew she must only look forward now. But to what, exactly? For herself, to happiness with her husband, she hoped. Yet what did that happiness mean, in this huge land of Russia?

The clouds in the sky were high. The whole day was filled with a strange, bright grayness. Farther east, beyond the fort of Saint Peter and

Saint Paul, and high above the waters, three sea gulls were soaring and swerving in the sky. As they turned, one after another, their bodies assumed an unearthly luminous glow.

She allowed her gaze to run along the Neva. At that moment, for some reason, she suddenly felt her father's presence with her. Old Daniel. At the thought of him she smiled.

But then her smile disappeared. For as the wind caught her face, and as she stared at the huge, harsh geometry of that mighty place, it was as if another presence were emerging from that city to face her father— something frightening, grim as a Mongol khan from ancient times.

And then she saw it.

It was a vast sun, hurtful to the eye—yet cold as ice. It was rising implacably from the northern sea into the endless Russian sky. It would, she sensed, dry the very blood from her body with its terrible rays.

And by this vision she, too, understood that, as her father had told her, the awful days of the Apocalypse had come.

And the name of the Antichrist was Peter.

In 1718, after conspiring against his father, the Tsarevich Alexis was foolish enough to be lured from his exile back to Russia by promises of forgiveness from his father.

He was persuaded to do so by an elderly and cunning diplomat: Peter Tolstoy.

Soon afterwards the Tsarevich Alexis, after torture, died in the Saint Peter and Saint Paul Fortress.

It did not matter. There were other heirs.

In 1721, by the Treaty of Nystadt, the Baltic lands, including those known as Latvia and Estonia, were formally recognized as belonging to Russia. They would remain in her hands for two centuries, until 1918.

For this the newly created Russian Senate gave Tsar Peter the grandiose titles of *Pater patriae, Imperator, Maximus:* Father of his country, Emperor, the Great.

In 1722, after the unexpected death of Procopy Bobrov, his son decided to revive a village of his, called Dirty Place, near the little town of Russka. So he transferred half the population of another of his villages to the place.

Among the villagers was a woman with three fine children. Her name was Maryushka.

EIGHT

❧

Catherine

1786

ALEXANDER BOBROV sat at his desk and stared at the two pieces of paper in front of him. One was covered with figures scribbled in his own hand; the other was a letter that had been brought there by a liveried servant just half an hour before. As he looked at them now, he shook his head in puzzlement, then murmured, "What the devil can I do?"

Outside the college, as the ministries were called, it was already dark; for during December there were only five and a half hours of daylight in Saint Petersburg. Most people had gone home: the Russians normally dined at two; but it was not unusual for Bobrov to be in his office this late, since he often dined in the fashionable English Quarter, where they liked to eat at five.

The icy wind in the street outside could not be heard because, like every house in Saint Petersburg, the college's double windows had been put up in October and every interstice was caulked tight.

For months Bobrov had been playing the most difficult and dangerous game of his life; and now, when the prize was in sight, he could hardly believe what had happened. For one sheet of paper was a tally of his debts; and the other was an offer of marriage. In fact, it was a demand.

"Yet surely," he murmured again, "there must be a way out."

At this moment, he could only think of one.

With a sigh he pushed the papers away from him and then called to the anteroom beyond. Immediately a respectful young man appeared, dressed in a light blue coat with yellow buttons and white knee-breeches—the uniform of the Saint Petersburg government.

"Tell the lackey to find my coachman. I'm leaving."

"At once, Your Highly Born." The young man disappeared.

Your Highly Born. This honorific referred not to Bobrov's ancestry, noble though it was, but to the fact that he had already, though only in his early thirties, reached the dizzy height of fifth rank in the fourteen service ranks established by Peter the Great. Nobility could be achieved by service. Lower ranks were only addressed as *Well Born;* then *Highly Well Born;* then *Highly Born.* If Bobrov continued his brilliant career, he might hope to reach the final and most coveted appellation of all: *Your Highest Excellency.*

*   *   *

Alexander Prokofievich Bobrov was a good-looking man of above average height. He had a rather round, clean-shaven face with a broad forehead, slightly hooded brown eyes, and a thin mouth, which, when it moved, might have looked sensual if he did not disguise it with a faint, ironic twist. His hair, in the fashion of that decade, was powdered and arranged like a wig, with a single curl over each ear, which was produced with heated tongs every morning. His frock coat used a plain cloth: tight-fitting, knee-length, and of an English cut. His waistcoat was embroidered, his breeches white with a blue stripe. In short, he was dressed in the best European fashion of the day.

It was hard to guess his character from this carefully controlled exterior. Seen in profile, his face assumed a slightly Turkish look, and the long, hooked nose was noticeable: was there, in this refined face, a hint of cruelty? But then, in company, seeing him unconsciously making that gentle caressing motion with his arm towards some person he was talking to, it was impossible to believe he could be harsh.

In the golden era of Catherine the Great, in the gracious city of Saint Petersburg, there was no more accomplished gambler than Alexander Prokofievich Bobrov. He did not gamble for money. Though he would often be seen at the card tables in the best houses, he only played for pin money. "Only fools or rogues try to make their fortunes at cards," he would observe; and he was neither. Bobrov the gambler was interested in a greater and more secret game: he was gambling for power. Or perhaps something even more. "Alexander," a shrewd acquaintance once remarked, "is playing at cards with God." Up to now he had been winning.

Yet he had worked for his success too. By God, he had tried! He might so easily have been a nonentity, like any other provincial noble of his day. As a child on one of the family estates near Tula, his education had consisted of little more than reading from the Orthodox Psalter and learning fairy tales and Russian songs from the serfs. And so he might have continued, but for one stroke of luck. For when he was ten, a friend of his father's, apparently on a whim, had taken a fancy to him and invited him to live in Moscow and share tutors with his children. That had been his break—and it was all that he had needed.

"From then on," he recalled proudly, "I did everything myself." He had worked like a demon, amazing his teachers. Though only a boy, he had recommended himself to people at Moscow University and others with influence. Somehow he had been chosen for the elite corps of pages at the Saint Petersburg Court; and while most of those young men gambled, drank, and made love, he had studied as hard as ever until—the greatest triumph of all—he had been one of a handful of youths chosen to be sent to the great German University of Leipzig. What some thought was effortless superiority was nothing of the kind. *I paid with my youth,* he would reflect.

And what drove him forward? Ambition. He owed all his success to ambition, but it was a cruel master. It drove you forward; but if you faltered, if you met an obstacle that stopped you, it leapt like a huge fiend onto your back, first screaming abuse, and then weighing down on you like a mountain, crushing the life out of you. Yet strangely it also gave Alexander Bobrov a kind of purity. Whatever he did, however deviously he played his cards, it was all in the service of this single, secret idea that drove him on.

Yet what exactly was it that he wanted? Like most ambitious men, Bobrov did not really know. It had no name. The whole world, perhaps; or heaven; or both, more likely. He even wanted to be a benefactor of mankind one day.

But that December evening there was a more urgent question on his mind, as he looked again at the sheet of paper covered with figures and shook his head. He had known he was in trouble for a long time; but he had tried to put off the reckoning. Now it had come.

For Alexander Bobrov was completely ruined.

He had been luckier than many: he was the first to admit it. Despite subdivisions over the generations, his father had still left him three estates: the one near Tula; another on the rich land south of the Oka, in the province of Riazan; and one at Russka, south of Vladimir. There were also part shares in two others. In all, Alexander owned five hundred souls—as the adult male serfs were termed. Not a great fortune nowadays, for the population had been growing that century, but still a good inheritance. It was not enough, though.

"Half the men I know are in debt," he used to say cheerfully. It was quite true—rich and poor noble alike. The authorities were very understanding: they had even set up a special bank to lend—to the gentry only, of course—on easy terms. And since a noble's wealth was reckoned by the number of serfs he owned, the collateral for these loans was expressed not in terms of rubles, but in souls. Thank God, that very year, the credit limit had been raised from twenty to forty rubles per soul. That had kept him afloat for the last few months. But the fact was, the Tula estate, where he grew up, had had to be sold, all his remaining three hundred souls were mortgaged, and God knew what he owed to merchants.

The final blow had come that morning, when his majordomo had asked for money to buy provisions in the market, and Bobrov had discovered he had none. He had told the fellow to use his own, then paid a visit to his bank. To his astonishment, they had refused to advance him any more cash. It was iniquitous! On reaching his office he had forced himself to do his accounts and discovered to his horror that the interest he owed was far greater than his income! There was no question: he was bankrupt. The game was up. "It's no good," he sighed. "I can't play this hand anymore."

And now he turned again to the letter. The way to safety: marriage to the German girl. How the devil could he get out of it?

He had been married once before, long ago. His bride had died in childbirth after only a year, and he had been heartbroken. But that was far in the past and he had not married again. Instead, he had a charming mistress. In fact, the German girl had been only one of several desultory courtships he had begun in recent years, as a kind of insurance policy.

Her family belonged to the Baltic nobility—descendants of the ancient Teutonic Knights—some of whom had taken service in Russia after Peter the Great had annexed their hereditary Baltic lands. She was fifteen; and the trouble was, she had fallen desperately in love with him—for which he should have been grateful since she was an heiress. Her name was Tatiana.

All that year the innocent girl had been putting pressure on her father to conclude the matter. As weeks and months had passed, and Bobrov himself had become increasingly uncertain of his finances, he had been forced to get further and further committed. For if things don't go as I plan, he calculated, I can't afford to lose the girl. Indeed, he had been increasingly afraid that her father would find out the truth about his debts and call the whole thing off. "Then I'll have nothing," he sighed. Day by day he had played for time: and now on this day of all days, had come her extraordinary letter.

It was straightforward enough. He had avoided her for three weeks, Tatiana pointed out. Her father had other candidates in mind. And it ended firmly:

> I shall ask my father tomorrow night whether he has heard from you. If not, then I shall not wish to hear from you again.

By the standards of the day the letter was utterly astounding. For a young girl to write like that, in person, to a man: it was a breach of every rule of etiquette. He could scarcely believe that she had done such a thing. He hardly knew whether he was shocked or secretly impressed by this daring. But of one thing he felt certain: she meant what she said.

He leaned back in his chair and closed his eyes. What if he gave up? Would it be so terrible? With Tatiana's money he could keep his fine house in Saint Petersburg and the estates. He'd be rich, secure, respected. People would say he'd done very well. "It's time to leave the gaming table while I'm still ahead," he muttered.

Why then should he hesitate? Why not seize the lifeline fate had thrown him? He opened his eyes and stared at the window and at the winter darkness outside. There was just that one, last chance: a final, dangerous, throw of the dice. The old woman.

He sighed. It was horribly risky. Even if he got what he wanted, she could still change her mind. Then he would probably lose everything—money, reputation, even the chance of recovery. I'd be a beggar, he realized. And yet . . .

For several minutes more, Alexander Bobrov the gambler sat at the big desk pondering the chances. Then at last he sat upright, with a faint, grim smile on his face. He had decided on his play: I'll go ask the old woman tonight.

For Bobrov the gambler was playing a secret game, with higher stakes than even young Tatiana's fortune.

He was playing for Saint Petersburg itself.

* * *

Saint Petersburg. Truly it was a miracle. At a latitude parallel with Greenland or Alaska, twelve hundred miles farther north than the city of Boston, and nearer the Arctic Circle than to London or Berlin, the Russian capital was a second Venice. How lovely, how simple it was: built around the broad basin where the Neva, nearing its estuary, was divided into two forks by the big triangle of Vasilevsky Island, whose apex gently pointed inland and whose broad base out in the estuary protected the city from the sullen rages of the sea.

Bobrov knew no greater joy than to approach by ship from the west, along that long, wide inlet of the Baltic known as the Gulf of Finland, to come through the markers, up the narrow channel around the island, and out into the basin of the river that lay before him like a huge, placid lagoon.

Was there any more beautiful sight in northern Europe? Nearby, in midstream, the tip of the island, the Strelka, with its houses and ware-houses like so many little classical temples. Away to the left, in the middle of the north shore, and forming a little island itself, the old Peter and Paul fortress. It contained a fine cathedral now, built by Trezzini, embellished by Rastrelli, whose needlelike golden spire, softly gleaming, soared a thin four hundred feet and linked the low lines of the city by the water with the huge open sky above.

Off to the right, on the southern shore, lay Peter's Admiralty buildings, and the baroque and classical facades of the Winter Palace and the Hermitage. How calm and serene it was: the distant stucco facades mostly painted yellow, pink, or brown in those days, blended so softly with the wide gray waters.

"Perfect city"—Bobrov would sigh—"that can be both masculine and feminine."

City of Peter: he had laid it out. As if to remind the place perpetually of its military and naval origin, the three huge avenues—of which the famous Nevsky Prospect was the greatest—which radiated from the center of the south bank, converged not on the palace but upon the Admiralty. Yet the city's topography and its soft lines were so sugges-tively feminine. And strange to say, ever since Peter's death, his city had been ruled almost entirely by women.

First Peter's widow; then his German niece, the Empress Anna; then for twenty years Peter's daughter Elizabeth. Each of the possible male heirs had either died or been deposed in months.

It had still been the reign of Empress Elizabeth when Bobrov was born. He remembered it with a smile: those were voluptuous, extravagant years. It was said the old empress had fifteen thousand dresses and that even her French milliner had finally refused her credit! Yet she had talent: she had built the Winter Palace; her many lovers included some remark-able men, like Shuvalov, who had founded Moscow University, and Razumovsky, the lover of music—men whose names would not only usher in Russia's greatest age, but would grace European culture too. Saint Petersburg had become cosmopolitan, looking to the dazzling court of France for inspiration.

And then had come the present golden age.

Saint Petersburg: city of Catherine. Who would ever have guessed that this insignificant young princess from a minor German court would become sole ruler of Russia? She had come there as a nice, harmless little wife for the heir to the throne, Elizabeth's nephew Peter; and so she would have remained, if her husband had not become unbalanced. For though he descended from Peter the Great through his mother, the young man was German—and obsessively so. Frederick the Great of Prussia was his hero. He loved drilling soldiers. He hated Russia and said so. And in his poor, long-suffering young wife, he had no interest at all.

What a strange contrast they had made: a blustering youth and a quiet, thoughtful girl; an heir who hated his inheritance, and this foreign princess who converted to Orthodoxy and diligently learned Russian. Though they did produce an heir, Peter soon turned his back on her, took a mistress, and virtually goaded her, out of desperation, into taking lovers of her own. Did he mean, subconsciously, to destroy himself? Bobrov thought so. In any case, when this dark and hated young man succeeded to the Russian throne, and the palace guards led by Catherine's lover deposed and killed him, Alexander Bobrov was one of many who heaved a sigh of relief.

And who should replace this young monster? Why, who better than his popular young wife, mother of the next male heir, and such a lover of things Russian. Thus, by a strange fluke of fate, had begun the glorious reign of Catherine II.

Catherine the Great. Worthy successor to Ivan the Terrible and Peter the Great, whose work she would complete. Russia was throwing off the last of its chains. In the west, she had already taken back the rest of White Russia from a weakened Poland. In the south, the Turkish fleet had been smashed; and the ancient menace of the Tatar steppe had finally been crushed when Catherine deposed the Crimean khan and annexed all his lands. To the east, Russia now claimed the entire north Eurasian plain to the Pacific. Across the Caspian Sea, Russian troops had struck into the Asian deserts to the borders of ancient Persia. And only last year, Bobrov had heard, a Russian colony had been set up beyond the Bering Straits, by the coast of Alaska. Perhaps, soon, the western American lands would be hers, too!

More daring yet, Catherine even hoped to take Constantinople itself, seat of the Turkish empire—the ancient Roman capital and home of Orthodoxy! She wanted to set up a sister empire there; and already she had named her second grandson Constantine, in preparation for this Black Sea empire she planned that he should rule.

Catherine the reformer: like Peter before her, she wanted Russia to become a modern, secular empire. Slavs, Turks, Tatars, Finns, tribes without number: they were all Russians now. To help colonize the vast steppe lands she had even imported German settlers. In imperial Saint Petersburg, eight religions were freely practiced, in fourteen different languages. In the lands taken from Poland, there were even Jews. The church's lands had already been taken away and put under state control.

The laxer monasteries had been closed. New cities—at least on paper—
had been created by the score. She had even tried to reform Russia's
outdated laws and organize the gentry and the merchants into representative bodies.

Catherine the enlightened. This was the Age of Enlightenment. All
across Europe in the eighteenth century, rational philosophy and liberal
political ideas had been making progress. In America, just freed by its
War of Independence from the English king, the new age of liberty had
begun. And now, to the astonishment of the whole world, this extraordinary, enlightened woman was ruling the vast and primitive land of forest
and steppe.

Catherine the giver of laws. Catherine the educator. Catherine the
champion of free speech, the patron of the philosophers who sang her
praises. Voltaire himself, the most free-thinking man in France, used to
write her endless letters. Catherine the sage, Catherine of the many
lovers. Saint Petersburg and its voluptuous palaces were hers: and how
serene, how calm it seemed.

Nobody took any notice of the quiet figure in the heavy coat who waited
in the shadows near the entrance to the college. It was a talent he had,
not being noticed.

He could have gone in. They would have welcomed him respectfully,
without a doubt. This, however, he did not wish to happen. Alternatively, of course, he could have given his message to a servant to carry.
But he preferred not to, and for this, too, he had his reasons.

And now at last, here was his man: State Councillor Bobrov was at the
entrance, under the lamp, dressed in a thick fur coat and ready to go
home. He looked rather pale. For some reason his sled was not ready and
the lackey at the door had gone along the street to summon it.

The quiet figure left the shadows, walking quickly towards Bobrov. As
he drew close, Bobrov glanced at him and seemed to start in surprise. The
stranger made a little signal, reached him, and with an almost impercepti-
ble gesture handed him the message. Then, without a word being spoken,
he withdrew, and in a few moments had turned the corner and was out
of sight.

Bobrov stood quite still. The place was still deserted: no one had seen.
He broke the seal and, in the lamplight, quickly read it. The message was
very short:

> *You are requested to attend a*
> *special meeting of the brothers*
> *at the pink house, tomorrow*
> *at six.*
>
>   *Colovion*

That was all. There were not a hundred people in all Russia who would
have known what it signified, but to Alexander Bobrov the message
meant a great deal. As soon as he got home he would destroy it, for all
communications of any kind were to be burned: that was the rule. For

the moment, however, he pushed the letter into his coat pocket. Then he sighed. "The voice of conscience."

His sled was coming. There was much to do that night.

Before Alexander, on the big mahogany table, were several dishes: a chicken, bought frozen from the market that morning, a bowl of sour cabbage, a plate of rye bread, beluga caviar, and a glass of German wine. But he had scarcely tasted anything. He was dressed for the evening in a blue velvet coat and, nervous though he was, his face wore the gambler's mask.

He gazed around the large, high room. Its walls were papered dark green. On the side walls hung biblical scenes done in the classical manner, with somber backgrounds. In the corner stood the big stove, tiled in green and red. The solemn effect was lightened, however, if one looked closely at the tiles: for half of them depicted some heavy, usually dirty joke. These tributes to Russian humor were to be found everywhere, even in the formal rooms of the imperial palaces. At the far end of the room hung a portrait of his great-grandfather Procopy, the friend of Peter the Great, staring down morosely and looking rather oriental. Alexander had been brought up to revere the great man. "But I wonder if you ever attempted anything like this," he murmured.

It was time to go and face Countess Turova.

Though the empire's hierarchy—the fourteen ranks—was open to any gentleman, there were still families who commanded special status outside the official system. There were a modest number of old boyar and gentry families like the Bobrovs, who had managed to survive through the turbulent centuries; there were men with old princely titles—descendants of either the Tatar khans or of Saint Vladimir himself; there were men with foreign titles, usually of the Holy Roman Empire; and nowadays there were also families with new titles, created by Peter and his successors for their favorites—princes, counts, and barons. Count Turov had been one of these, a formidable man. As for his widow, Countess Turova, even Alexander had to admit he was afraid of her.

She was his father's cousin. She and the count had lost their two children, and at his death the magnate had left a portion of his huge estate to his widow, absolutely. "She can do what she likes with it," Alexander's father had always told him. "Perhaps you can get your hands on some of it—though don't ever count on her," he had added. "She's always been eccentric."

Yet this was Alexander's dangerous mission tonight.

He could not ask the old lady for money outright. He knew she would show him the door if he did that. But was there a chance of an inheritance? There were other cousins who were also candidates: but a quarter of her fortune, even an eighth would do. Bobrov sighed. Although he had paid court to her for years, he still had no idea what his prospects were. Sometimes she showed him marks of favor, at others she just seemed to enjoy taunting him.

And what if tonight she said yes? His calculation was simple. She was over seventy now: the prospect of a legacy would give him confidence to take the extra risk; he even knew one or two moneylenders who would let him have enough to tide him over another year on the strength of it. Then he would turn down the German girl, burn his boats, and wait out events.

It was a horrible risk, even so. After all, his great gamble might fail. Or what if, after promising him, Countess Turova changed her mind? Or what if she lived to be ninety? "The old bitch!" he suddenly swore.

But he had made his decision and he would stick to it. It was very simple. He felt the little silver coin in his hand. When he got to Countess Turova's he would toss the coin: just once. "If it's tails, I marry the German girl. If it's heads, and the old woman promises me a legacy, I'll take a chance." He liked that kind of gamble. There was something almost religious about tossing a coin to decide one's life. He smiled: he knew a card player who used to say that gambling was a kind of prayer.

The sled raced through the icy streets of Saint Petersburg, the faint glow from lamps and lighted windows rushing by in the gloom. A few stars could be seen.

The sled was splendid and enclosed. Two lackeys clung on behind; on the box in front sat the coachman—a huge fellow wrapped in a sheepskin, his big boots lined with flannel, a fur cap on his head. His neck, in the Russian peasant manner, was bare. Like all Russian drivers before and since, he drove at breakneck speed; and although there were few people about at such an hour, he still found the opportunity to cry out: *"Na prava*—keep to the right! Look out, soldier, damn you! Careful, Babushka!"

A boy rode on the offside horse. Both he and the coachman whipped the horses along unmercifully. What did they care? They were not Bobrov's horses. For though he had fine horses of his own, the state councillor preferred, like most people in Saint Petersburg, to use hired ones for ordinary journeys like this; and so these wretched beasts would be driven by all and sundry until they dropped and were replaced, in the usual careless Russian manner.

Bobrov sank back into the rich upholstery. The south bank of Saint Petersburg was divided into inner, middle, and outer half rings by three concentric canals. The outer canal, the border of the city's rich heartland, was the famous Fontanka. Bobrov's house lay in the fashionable First Admiralty Quarter, in the middle ring, and his route soon brought him out onto the granite embankment of the great frozen Neva. As the sled raced eastward, the ice of the river appeared on the left, the big, solid houses of the English merchants on the right. In a few moments they would be at the very heart of the capital.

He took the coin out and held it in his hand, feeling it in the darkness. What an astounding gamble it was: he was going to toss a coin for the whole Russian empire!

This was the prize in the secret game he had been playing for so long. This was the reason why he did not wish to marry, and why he needed to keep afloat financially just a little longer. For the prize was still, tantalizingly, in sight—perhaps only months away. The most brilliant position in the Russian state.

For Alexander Bobrov was planning to become the official lover of Catherine the Great.

It was no idle dream. For years he had been carefully maneuvering towards his goal. And now at last—he had it on the best authority—he was the next in line. He had been promised the position by the man who was, almost certainly, Catherine's secret husband.

At the court of Catherine the Great of Russia, there were a number of paths to power. But for a truly ambitious man, no career offered such brilliant prospects as those available to the man who shared her bed.

Though sometimes portrayed as a monstrous consumer of men, Catherine was in fact rather sentimental. Having been humiliated in her marriage, her own letters make clear that most of her adult life was spent in the search for affection and an ideal man. Nor was she hugely promiscuous. History records the names of something less than twenty lovers.

But the opportunities for those who held this position were almost boundless. Mostly they were men from families like Alexander Bobrov's, though some were more obscure. Their names were to go down in Russian history: like Orlov the brave guardsman who had won her the throne and whose brother had killed her hateful husband. Or Saltikov, the charming aristocrat: was he, as some said, the real father of Catherine's only official heir? Or Poniatowski: she had even made him king of Poland! And greatest of all, that strange and moody genius, the one-eyed warrior Potemkin who was now her mighty proconsul in the Crimea, where he was building her a new imperial province greater than most kingdoms.

When a new lover was chosen, he could usually expect a present of a hundred thousand rubles after the first night. After that . . . Potemkin, it was said, had received close to fifty million! Had the empress secretly married Potemkin, years ago? No one knew for sure. But whether he was her husband or not, one thing was certain. "It's Potemkin who chooses her new lovers," the courtiers would say.

It had not been difficult for Alexander to make friends with the great man because he really admired him. He had become one of his most loyal men. And when Catherine's poor young lover Lanskoy had suddenly died two ago before—having ruined his health with love potions, the court whispered—Alexander had seen his chance and gone straight to Potemkin himself, to put himself forward.

It had been close. A young guards officer had been sent in before him and found favor. But Potemkin had been impressed by Bobrov as a prospect, not least because he trusted his loyalty. "Even I have enemies," the older man confessed. "They'd love to see a man in that position who could be turned against me."

Several times Alexander and his patron had discussed the matter. "If things don't work out," Potemkin had promised, "I'll send you in to see her. After that . . ."

That had been a year ago. Alexander had waited anxiously. He knew the young officer slightly and now he gathered every scrap of information about him that he could. He had several friends at court. They soon told him the young man had cast amorous glances at one of the court ladies, and that he was tiring of his position. Within months he might even get himself dismissed. And then, by God, it will be my turn, Alexander had promised himself. How he would astonish her! She liked men who were daring and intelligent, and he was both. He was sure he would charm her.

Only one worrying thought had crossed his mind: could he satisfy her? The empress had never been beautiful. Though her strong, German face and broad, intellectual forehead were fine, she was squat and frankly stout these days. She was fifty-seven and, he'd heard, sometimes a little short of wind.

But she was also Catherine, Empress of all Russia. In all the world there was no other being like her. Her power, her heroic position, her extraordinary mind—all these, for a man like Bobrov, in search of the summit of the world, made her desirable beyond all others. And anyway, if there's any problem in bed, I know how to get by, he considered. He was strong, fit, and not too sensitive. I'm always all right if I eat a good meal, he reminded himself.

And then . . . What a destiny! Mother Russia and all her mighty empire at his feet: he would be one of the innermost circle who ruled with the empress. There was no greater position in all the world. If he could just hold out a little longer.

Outside, Saint Petersburg slipped silently by, huge and magical. They were coming into the huge expanse of Peter's Square, in front of the Admiralty. On his left he could see the long pontoon bridge that stretched across the frozen Neva to Vasilevsky Island. The bridge was not really needed, for the huge lagoon of ice was a busy thoroughfare in these winter months. Huge fairs were held upon it. He could see half a dozen roads across it, marked out by avenues of cut trees, or lamps that gleamed dimly until they almost faded in the darkness by the distant northern shore. A bonfire burned by the tip of the island. Farther away, opposite the Winter Palace, was the faint shape of the Saint Peter and Saint Paul Cathedral's slim spire against the night sky.

And it was now, as he came out onto the big expanse of the square, that something else, quite nearby, caught his eye; and for a few moments he seemed to forget himself, pulling the window of the sled open, letting the icy air freeze on his face as he gazed at it, with a look so strange that one would almost have thought he had been hypnotized.

It was the Bronze Horseman.

This huge statue, which had taken the French sculptor Falconet years to make, had been put up only recently; but already it was the most famous statue in all Russia. On a colossal granite rock a mighty horse, three times life size, reared up on its hind legs. Below it lay a serpent. And astride the horse, dressed in a Roman toga, was the living image of great Peter himself. In his left arm he held the reins, while his right, in a tremendous, imperial gesture, was stretched out, pointing across the broad Neva that lay before him.

Nowhere in the world, they said, was there a greater block of granite; never had such an enormous casting in bronze been made. The splendid horse, copied from the finest in Catherine's stables, seemed to be launching itself in an almost impossible leap forward into space. And now, as it did every time he saw it, the great statue took Alexander's breath away. All his dreams and ambitions seemed to be expressed in this huge bronze hymn to Russia's might. It had to be huge: had not Russia already cast, in Moscow, the biggest cannon and the greatest bell the world had ever seen? Of course Saint Petersburg should cast the largest statue in bronze. And although the narrow-minded priests had objected to Peter's Roman, pagan dress, Bobrov saw that the French sculptor had captured the very essence of the new, imperial destiny that Peter had created for his country and that the genius of Catherine would complete. Russia, by her unconquerable will, would make a final, mighty leap and rule half the world.

The statue's granite plinth bore only the simple legend:

To Peter the First,
From Catherine the Second.

Like a great phantom it dominated the dimly lit square. It was unassailable. And as Alexander stared, the statue seemed, like the inner voice of his own ambition, to speak to him and say: Little man: would you turn back now?

No, Alexander thought. No. I cannot turn back. I have come too far. Better to gamble—to win an empire or lose all—just one more time.

And he took the silver coin he was to have tossed and threw it out of the window, into the night.

"Dear Alexander!" She was smiling. "I am so glad you have come."

"Daria Mikhailovna." He bent down to kiss her. "You are looking wonderful."

In fact, the countess wasn't looking too bad. One could even see that she had once been attractive. Her little face, rather too heavily painted, always reminded him of some bright little bird, especially as now, with age, her hooked nose had become more prominent. Her small blue eyes were lively, darting glances from place to place. She was wearing a floor-length antique dress of mauve gauze, decorated with white lace and pink ribbons, which made her look like a figure of the previous generation of the French court. Her hair was fine; but somehow, despite the fact that it was powdered, it had a strange yellowish tinge at the sides, like tarnished silver; it was swept up high above her head into a daunting coiffure topped with curls and decorated with pearls and a pale blue ribbon.

To receive her guests, Countess Turova was seated on a gilt chair in the middle of her salon, which lay up one flight of the staircase in the great marble hall. Like most such rooms in Russian palaces, it was huge and magnificent. Its ceiling was over twenty feet high; its gleaming parquet floor contained at least a dozen woods. A gigantic crystal chandelier glittered above.

The guests were still arriving; many of them Alexander recognized. A German professor, an English merchant, two young writers; a distinguished old general, an even older prince: it was one of the pleasures of Saint Petersburg that one might find people of all nations and classes in such an aristocratic setting. For there was a warmer and easier spirit in Russia than in the noble houses of Western Europe.

And it was a long tradition that, once a week, such people should come to the great Turov house on Vasilevsky Island. For the count had been a remarkable man. He had helped the great Shuvalov found Moscow University thirty years before; the writers of the mid-eighteenth century—the first such intellectual group in Russia—counted him as their friend; even Lomonosov, Russia's first philosopher and scientist, used to call upon him. Turova had traveled widely—even visited the great Voltaire—and brought back many treasures of European painting, sculpture, and porcelain as well as a fine library, all of which were still housed in this splendid palace. And the countess, whose magpie mind had picked up a number of ideas in the course of her life with him, now clung to these with a tenaciousness that was in perfectly inverse proportion to her understanding of them. She kept open house for the intellectuals who, partly from habit, and partly amused by her eccentricity, continued to come. "They rely upon me," she would say. "I am their rock." She was certainly unchanging.

And upon nothing was the Countess Turova more constant than her devotion to the chief object of her worship. For if she revered her late husband, to her greatest hero she had erected nothing less than a temple. "In this house," everything seemed to say, "the enlightened worship the great leader."

Voltaire. His quizzical image was everywhere. There was a bust of him on a pedestal in the huge marble hall, and another at the turn of the great staircase. There was a portrait in the large gallery at the top, and another bust in the corner of the salon. The great philosopher was her icon. His name came into the conversation ceaselessly. If someone made a good point, the countess would say, with finality: "So Voltaire himself might have said." Or even better, and with warmth: "Ah, I see you have read your Voltaire." Something which, Bobrov was sure, she had never done herself. It was astonishing how any subject could be suddenly brought back to the great man and his authority invoked. For all I know, she thinks he regulates the weather, Alexander thought.

In deference to Voltaire, Diderot, and the other philosophers of France, only French was spoken in Turova's house.

And one had to be careful what one said. It was amazing what the old woman could hear, and what she knew. She loved to catch people out. Indeed, after invoking the blessed name of Voltaire, her favorite phrase was a sharp: "Take care, *monsieur*. For I sleep with my eyes open." And it was never clear whether this was a figure of speech or whether she meant it literally.

Now, however, still beaming, she tapped his arm lightly. "Do not go too far, *mon cher* Alexandre: I have special need of you tonight." He wondered what she was up to. "For the moment, however, you may go. Indeed, I see someone waiting for you."

Alexander turned. And smiled.

Countess Turova's house was a very large building with a heavy, classical portico in the center of two wings. The basement rooms were almost on street level, and though many nobles let such places to fashionable merchants and shopkeepers, the countess did not, preferring to live in the house entirely alone with her servants.

With one exception. She allowed a widowed Frenchwoman, Madame de Ronville, to occupy a suite of rooms in the eastern wing. This suited the countess very well, for though this Frenchwoman was not a paid companion, she was dependent in that her charming quarters were let to her at a very low rent, and it was understood that she would be available when the countess wanted her company. "It's so convenient for her to be near me," the countess was often pleased to say.

It was also quite convenient for Alexander Bobrov. For Madame de Ronville was his mistress.

Was there anyone more charming in Saint Petersburg? As he always did, he now felt that sudden tingle of almost adolescent excitement and joy in her presence, which was accompanied, usually, by a little trembling down his back. They had been lovers for ten years, and he never tired of her. She was almost fifty.

Adelaide de Ronville wore a pink silk dress, a little shorter than the countess's, tightly gathered at the waist and opening out over a hoop skirt. The bodice was decorated with the appliqué silk flowers that the fashionable French called "indiscreet complaints." Her hair, starched and powdered, was charmingly crowned with two little clusters of diamonds. As she stood quietly at his side, almost, but not quite touching him, he was aware of her slim, pale form concealed beneath. Now, her large blue eyes twinkling with amusement, she explained what was going on. "Her two stars for the evening have failed to arrive," she whispered. "Radishchev and the Princess Dashkova." She smiled. "She needs you to be the star—and her gladiator. Good luck!"

And now Alexander really had reason to smile. Nothing in the world could have been better. Now, he thought, I can please her so much she'll want to leave me the lot!

There were probably no more brilliant figures in enlightened Saint Petersburg than these two. Princess Dashkova, almost a rival personage to Catherine herself, a fearless champion of liberty whom the empress had placed in charge of the Russian Academy. As for Radishchev, Alexander knew him quite well: he was already writing brilliant essays. How mortified the countess must be that they had failed to turn up. And what a chance for him.

For despite all his efforts, Alexander was never quite sure that the old countess took him seriously. He had written articles that were widely praised. He had even, like Radishchev, contributed anonymous articles for journals on such daring subjects as democracy and the abolition of serfdom—subjects which, even in Catherine's enlightened Russia, were still too radical to be discussed officially. He had shown her these articles and let her into the secret of their authorship; but even then, he did not really know if he had impressed her. Tonight would be his chance.

The role of gladiator, as Countess Turova's regular guests called it, was always the same. For where other salons encouraged the gentle art of civilized debate, Countess Turova liked to watch a massacre. The victim was always an unsuspecting newcomer of conservative views who was confronted with a man of the Enlightenment—her gladiator—whose job it was to defeat and humiliate his opponent while she and her guests watched.

As Alexander glanced towards the countess now, he could see that a circle was already forming in front of her. On her left he noticed a newcomer, a general—a dapper, gray-haired man, short but erect with piercing black eyes. So this was the victim. The countess was beckoning. As he approached, he smiled to hear her reproving one of the young writers for something he had said. "Take care, *monsieur.*" She was wagging her finger at him. "You cannot deceive me. I sleep with my eyes open." She did not change.

It was one of the joys of these evenings that Countess Turova never troubled to be subtle. When she was ready to start the argument, she merely picked up one of the fighting cocks, so to speak, and threw it at the other. Now, therefore, she turned abruptly to the unfortunate general. "So," she said accusingly, "I hear you want to close all our theaters."

The old man stared at her in surprise. "Not at all, my dear Countess. I just said that one play went too far and should be taken off. It was seditious," he added calmly.

"So you say. And what do you think, Alexander Prokofievich?"

He was on.

Alexander enjoyed these debates. Firstly, he was good at them because he was patient; secondly, though the countess herself might be shallow, the debates in her salon often concerned important matters, touching the very heart of Russia and her future. For this reason, while he was anxious to defeat the general, he hoped also that he would be a worthy opponent.

The countess had set up the subject: freedom of speech. It was a key tenet of the Enlightenment and was supported by the empress. For not only had Catherine allowed private presses to operate legally, she had even written social satire for the stage herself. And so the debate began.

BOBROV: I am against censorship—for a simple reason. If men are free to speak, the voice of reason will eventually prevail. Unless of course you have no faith in men's reason.

COUNTESS: (nastily) Have you faith, General?

GENERAL: (cheerfully) Not much.

BOBROV: History may be on your side. But what about the future? Men can change and so can the way they are governed. Look at how the empress is bringing up her grandsons. Do you disapprove of that?

Everyone knew that Catherine had personally taken charge of her grandsons, Alexander and Constantine. She had put them under a democratically minded Swiss tutor who was teaching them how they might be enlightened rulers of the vast empires she planned to leave them.

GENERAL: I admire the empress. But when her grandson rules, enlightened or not, he will find his choices for action are limited.
COUNTESS: (impatiently) No doubt you look forward to the reign of Grand Duke Paul, instead.

Bobrov smiled. The Grand Duke Paul, Catherine's only legitimate son, was the countess's pet hate. He was a strange and moody fellow, and whether or not he was actually his son, Paul certainly modeled himself on the murdered Tsar Peter III. He hated the empress for taking over his sons and seldom came to court. An obsessive military disciplinarian, he had no interest in the Enlightenment, and there was a rumor that Catherine might one day bypass him in the succession for his son. Even so, no sensible official like the general was going to speak ill of this man who might still one day be ruler. Wisely, therefore, the older man said nothing.

BOBROV: To return to censorship. What practical harm comes from showing a play?
GENERAL: Probably none. But it is the principle of free speech I object to. For two reasons. The first is that it encourages a spirit of opposition for its own sake. But the second, and worse danger, is not the effect on the people, but on their rulers.
BOBROV: How so?
GENERAL: Because if a so-called enlightened government thinks it must defend its action by reason, then it starts to believe it is morally obliged to win every argument. Now what if a powerful and determined group—which cares nothing for argument and free speech—opposes such a government. It becomes helpless. It's no use asking a philosopher to defend us against Genghis Khan! That's the whole lesson of Russian history.

It was a powerful argument. The countess looked put out.

BOBROV: Yet the Tatars overcame Russia because she was disunited. I believe that nowadays and in the future, only those governments that have the trust of a free people will be truly strong and united.
GENERAL: I disagree. Freedom weakens.
BOBROV: You fear the people?
GENERAL: Yes. Certainly. Remember Pugachev.

Ah. Pugachev. There was an almost audible sigh among the onlookers. The little phrase would reverberate in Russia for another century. For only twelve years had passed since the last, awful peasant revolt, which

the Cossack Pugachev had led. Like all the others—like the great revolt
of Stenka Razin the previous century—it had begun across the steppe by
the Volga and swept towards Moscow. Like Razin's revolt, it lacked
strategy and organization and had been crushed. But it had reminded the
whole Russian gentry and the imperial government once more of that
dark belief that plagued all Muscovy's history: the people were dangerous and to be feared. That's all one had to say: Remember Pugachev.

GENERAL: Russia is huge and backward, Alexander Prokofievich: an empire of villages. We are in the Middle Ages still. Only a strong
autocrat and gentry can hold it together. As for the merchants
and peasants, they have no common interests with the gentry
and if you let them debate with each other, they can't agree
upon anything. Our enlightened empress knows it very well.

It was certainly true that Catherine ruled as an autocrat. The senate and
council that Peter had set up did nothing but ratify her decisions. As for
debates, when Catherine—trying to reform Russia's antiquated laws—
had convoked a huge council with representatives of all the classes, they
had refused to cooperate with each other and had been disbanded.

BOBROV: These things take time.
GENERAL: No. The nobility is the only class in Russia that is capable of
governing: they have their privileges because Russia needs
them. Do we want to lose our privileges?

The noble class set up by Peter was there to serve the state: and they
were proud to do it. Catherine, needing their support, had showered
them with favors. She had placed all local government in their hands. The
charter she had enacted the previous year had confirmed almost every
privilege they could desire. All their estates, including the old *pomestie*
service estates, were theirs absolutely now. No other class could own
land. Yet though they usually chose to serve the state, they were no
longer obliged to. They paid no taxes. They could not be knouted. They
were even allowed to travel abroad. Thus, from the state servants of the
Russian autocracy had arisen a privileged class with few responsibilities,
yet more protected than any other in Europe. The general had shrewdly
appealed to the self-interest of most of the people in the room.

But privilege was one thing: philosophy another. It was time to
counterattack.

BOBROV: But you forget Natural Law.

And now the countess gave a smile of relief. Natural Law was one of
the favorite ideas of the Enlightenment.

BOBROV: The peasant is downtrodden and illiterate. But he is not less
human than I. He, too, is capable of rational thought. That is
our hope for the future.

GENERAL: You wish to educate him?

BOBROV: Why not?

A gleam came into the general's eye. This clever civil servant had gone too far.

GENERAL: Why, Alexander Prokofievich, if the peasant is as rational as you say, and you educate him, then who will till the land? He will want to be free. He will want to turn out the government and the empress too. You will have to emancipate your serfs and your own rule of reason will sweep you away. This is not America. There would be chaos. Is that what you want—chaos and emancipation?

The old man felt sure of his ground here. Over ninety-five percent of the population were peasants—half state peasants, with a few insignificant rights; and half privately owned serfs, like Bobrov's. During that century their rights had even diminished: they could be bought and sold like cattle. Even the enlightened empress had only dared to recommend that the nobility be kind to them. And Countess Turova herself, to the general's knowledge, owned more than four thousand souls. It seemed to him he had won the argument.

The countess looked at Alexander anxiously. He smiled faintly. It was time for the kill.

BOBROV: Permit me to disagree. Voltaire showed us the absurdity of superstition—which I take, General, to be a belief in that which reason shows us cannot be so. And reason, General, does not oblige me to pretend that my serf is an animal and deny him his human rights. Perhaps my serf is not ready to be a free man yet; but his children may be. Reason does not oblige me to say that peasants who are free will not work my land. How are estates worked in other countries, where the peasants are free? You say that if a peasant has any education, he will deny all authority and try to overthrow the empress. Then why do we, educated men, gladly serve an autocracy ourselves? Because Reason tells us it is necessary. I suggest rather that Reason gives us wise laws, and as much freedom as is good for us. I am happy to know that my empress will decide these matters, and that she also allows rational men, without censorship, to discuss them. In short, I am content to serve my empress and to take my inspiration from the great Voltaire. I have nothing to fear.

With which he made a pleasant bow to the countess.

It was perfect. It was exactly what Countess Turova wanted to hear. Like the empress with her subjects, she would decide what was best for the four thousand rational beings she currently owned; and no doubt they would be grateful that their owner should be so enlightened, in this best of all possible worlds.

The little circle burst into applause. He heard the old lady murmur: "Ah, my Voltaire." The general remained silent.

And did Bobrov believe what he had just said? Yes, pretty much. He wished his serfs well. One day perhaps they would be free. And meanwhile, the enlightened era of Catherine was a fine time to be alive, if you were a noble in Saint Petersburg.

At last the moment had come. As always at such gatherings, the main part of the evening, after the gladiatorial debate, had been devoted to cards. He had played for an hour, and played badly. For how could he concentrate? Every few minutes his eyes strayed back to the table where the countess was playing, as he waited for a break in the game. As soon as he could, he excused himself and then stood discreetly at the back of the room, watching her. How small and bent her back looked, seen from that angle, how strangely frail. And yet, when at last he saw her rise and turn towards him, all his nervousness of her instantly returned. He stepped forward.

"Daria Mikhailovna, may I speak with you privately?" She started to frown. "A matter of great importance."

If he had thought his conquest of the general would earn him a good reception now, it seemed he was wrong. Obviously, having served his purpose, he was no longer of interest to her that evening. She gave him a cold little stare, muttered, "Oh very well," and started to move towards an anteroom. As he followed just behind her, he noticed that she was beginning to walk with a slight shuffle. Having reached the anteroom, she sat down on a small gilt sofa, sitting very erect, and did not offer him a seat.

"Well, what is it you wish, Alexander Prokofievich?"

This was the moment. He had prepared himself, of course. But even so, how the devil did one ask an old woman tactfully if one was in her will? He began cautiously.

"As you may have heard, Daria Mikhailovna, there have been some negotiations with various parties concerning my possibly marrying again." Her face was impassive. "As a preliminary to such discussions, some of the parties naturally asked me to make a disclosure of my fortune." It was a complete fabrication, but it was the best excuse he could think of. He paused, wondering how she was taking it.

Countess Turova, face quite still, stretched out her hand in her lap and looked at the back of it with, it seemed, some admiration. Then she turned it over and looked at the palm. That, too, appeared to be satisfactory. Then she raised her hand onto the gilt arm of the sofa and drummed out a little tattoo to herself, as though she were becoming bored. Alexander pressed on.

"The question has arisen," he continued delicately, "as to whether, besides my present estates, I have any further expectations." Again he paused, hoping she might help him.

She looked up with apparent interest. "I did not know you had any," she remarked sweetly.

Very well. If she wished to play with him he could only defend himself by seeming frank.

"I expect I haven't, Daria Mikhailovna. But I dared to hope that perhaps, as my kinswoman, you might have considered some mention of me in your will. If not, of course, I shall act accordingly."

The old countess remained expressionless. He had no idea if she believed him, or what she thought.

"You mean to marry?"

"I hope so. One day." He was careful not to commit himself. He saw the countess frown.

"Can you tell me the name of at least one of the families with whom you are negotiating?" Obviously she didn't believe him. He mentioned the German girl's family.

"I congratulate you. A good Baltic family. It could be worse." Then she smiled at him. "But from what I hear, Alexander Prokofievich, this girl is a considerable heiress. I'm sure you will have no need of more than she already has." She glanced at her hand again, as though sympathizing with that limb that it had been forced to endure this boring conversation for so long. "Unless of course," she said quietly, and without changing her expression, "this has nothing to do with your getting married. Perhaps you are embarrassed financially in some way."

"No, no." The witch.

"You have debts perhaps."

"All men have some."

"So I hear." She sniffed. "I have none." This, he knew, was an understatement. She ruled her stewards with a rod of iron. God knows what income she had.

For a few moments the countess's attention seemed to wander and her eyes fixed on something in the middle distance.

"Well, well. If you marry, I suppose we shall see less of you here."

He ignored this allusion to Madame de Ronville.

"Not at all, Daria Mikhailovna," he countered evenly. "I should bring my wife to see you frequently."

"No doubt." And now, quite suddenly, she gave him a brilliant smile. "Are you entirely ruined?"

"No," he lied, while she watched him thoughtfully. There was a brief pause.

"Well, Alexander Prokofievich. I should tell you that at present you are not in my will."

He bowed his head. Though his face did not flinch, he could feel himself going very pale; but knowing she was observing him, he looked up bravely.

"However"—she sniffed—"your father was my kinsman and you are obviously in difficulties." She said the last word with a kind of placid contempt. "I shall therefore include you. Do not expect a great fortune. But there will be, I daresay, enough."

Dear God, there was hope after all.

"It is time for my cards." Without even waiting for his arm, she abruptly rose to her feet. Then she stopped. "On second thought, Alexander Prokofievich, I will add one condition." She turned back to him. "Yes, I think it is time you married. So you will receive your legacy—but only if you marry this Baltic girl." She smiled happily. "That is all I have to say to you, *monsieur.*" And with that she moved away.

He watched her go. How did she know, by what infernal instinct had she guessed, that this was the one answer in all the world he did not want?

"I bet she really does sleep with her eyes open," he muttered bitterly.

The great house was silent; the guests had left. Alexander and his mistress had withdrawn to her apartment in the east wing and now at last they could talk alone. Naturally, they were discussing his marriage.

The wing was easily reached along a passageway from the main house; it also had a private entrance down a little back staircase that gave onto the street. It was perfectly arranged, therefore, for the conduct of a discreet affair. Adelaide de Ronville's rooms were entirely delightful. They might have been in her native France: Louis XV and XVI furniture; an Aubusson carpet with a garlanded border; thick curtains of flowered silk with heavy valences and tassels; lush draperies on the furniture; tapestries with charming pastoral scenes; soft pinks and blues; gilt, but not too much. These were the elements that she had arranged with a lightness, simplicity, and concealed sense of form that had their own special charm.

When Alexander had told her about the countess's decision, she took his arm affectionately and smiled. "You must marry the girl, my friend."

What an unusual woman she was. Half French, half Polish: she was above average height, rather square in the shoulder, with alabaster skin. She had been a brunette until she was thirty-five, but now her natural hair color was iron gray. She had an oval face, almond-brown eyes that were sometimes a little sad, and a broad ironic mouth. Her figure was slim, her breasts rather high; but it was, for some reason, a slight thickening about her thighs that, in their lovemaking, aroused Alexander to heights of passion.

It was remarkable how little she had altered in their ten years together. Only now was she entering her change of life; but that did not matter. Her slim, strong build had kept her trim; she moved with a wonderful, lithe grace; and if, with the passing of the years, Alexander had noticed in certain places a boniness and looseness of the skin that she could not help, he just directed his hands to other caresses, which better produced the illusion that nothing had changed. Indeed, the knowledge that they were cheating time gave him a sense of poignancy unlike any other he knew. It was the beauty of autumn—golden and warm.

Adelaide was grateful for the affair. As an old Frenchwoman had once told her: "An older woman improves a young man. But he is also good for her because he accepts her as she is." It was true. She savored, as a little triumph, the fact that she could still drive this rather self-centered man to erotic delight.

In his way, Bobrov loved her. His affairs with younger women had never meant so much to him. He had only to watch one of her perfect little gestures, see the elegant way she moved, to forget all the others. "Besides, I can talk to her," he would say. They had few secrets. She knew of all his plans, even his desire to desert her for the empress's bed. As she drily said: "It's a career."

And now she was firm with him.

"You must secure this German girl at once."

"I don't really want to, you know."

"Be grateful that she loves you, *cher ami.*" She smiled wryly. "Perhaps it will be good for you."

"And for you?"

She gave a little shrug. Even now, he could still be heavy-footed. What did he want—a confession of her despair to wear like a trophy? A dismissal? Forgiveness? "One must be practical," she said calmly. "You will like it. It is good to have a family."

"Perhaps."

"Enfin." There was the faintest hint of impatience in her voice. "You will not come here."

"I certainly shall." He would try to be a good husband; but he had no wish to desert Adelaide.

She, however, shook her head. "You must spend time with your wife, you know. It is very important."

He sighed. "I know. But you will not forbid me to see you?"

"Oh . . . that." She shrugged. "Who knows? We shall see."

Would she take another lover? He disliked that idea, although he felt he could not in conscience lay further claim to her.

"And this girl," she said at last, "what is she like?"

He considered.

"She has a round, simple face; blue eyes; fair. Her cheeks get a little too red. She's entirely innocent, though not stupid." He paused. "I should certainly be grateful, but I suppose my years with you have left me finding all other women inadequate."

"How charming he is, this gallant monsieur." Her lips twitched with amusement. "And do you include the empress among these other women, may I ask?"

He laughed. In fact, he had sometimes wondered whether this affair with an older woman would be helpful in coming to terms with the now-aging body of Catherine. He guessed not.

"I was speaking," he smiled, "of women; not of the Russian empire!"

A certain look told him that there was no need to say more. Her bedroom lay up a little staircase and he followed her there.

How lovely, how desirable she still was, as she slowly stretched and then, luxuriously, arched her slim, pale body. He smelled the thick, musklike scent that was one of the secrets about her he had learned to cherish. He moved his hand softly over her breast.

Did a lover, he wondered, in the great act of passion, gain a glimpse of eternity? Possibly. In his love of Adelaide, this ten-year passion that defied the passing of the years, he did not think he saw eternity, but

rather something else that he preferred. Their love, it sometimes seemed
to him, was like a drop of amber that has trapped some tiny animal,
centuries ago, in its warm embrace—and in doing so, captured the sunlight itself from that distant, long-forgotten day. He liked the analogy.
The amber falls to the earth and is buried; yet it is preserved, as long as
the earth shall last, he thought. At other times, he felt as if he and
Adelaide were together on the vast, endless plain, enjoying their brief,
passionate moment before they disappeared. And because their physical
love was complete, he felt, This is enough. This is what I am. When it
is done, I am content to be no more. And if the great darkness that
followed was eternity, then he saw that, too. One thing at least was
certain. When he encountered Adelaide's body he knew with certainty
that this, and this alone, was his true homecoming and that, for the rest
of his life, it would be his years with her against which all things would
be compared.

For Adelaide, it was a little different. She did not look for eternity
because to her that meant only age, and death. She knew that all sensations are passing. When she was younger, as her mind drifted after
lovemaking, she would sometimes feel like a little boat, floating away
upon a huge ocean; but nowadays the images and sensations that came
into her thoughts were rather different, and she felt herself more often
like a spectator watching the progress of her own life: at which times it
seemed to her that she and her lover were not in a boat, but rather upon
an island, slowly eroding in the middle of a river, and that the river was
the passing of the years.

It was past one in the morning when Alexander woke. After making love
he had fallen into a sudden, deep sleep; but his sleep had been troubled.
For an image had repeatedly come to him—he was not sure how many
times—so vivid, so insistent, that it seemed more like a vision than an
ordinary dream.

It was the countess. She was very pale as she rose up before him; she
had an accusing look on her face; and, for no reason he could understand,
she was shaking a reproving finger at him and saying, in a voice that
seemed to explain the whole universe: "Voltaire. Voltaire." The fact that
this made no particular sense did not make it any less impressive or
alarming.

He woke up with a shiver and lay for several minutes collecting his
thoughts. It was comforting that Adelaide was dozing beside him: her
pale form was not quite covered and after a little while he began to feel
better. He looked at her: could he make love again? He thought so. As
he touched her lightly, her eyes slowly opened and she smiled a little
drowsily: "You want more?"

He was looking down at her; his mouth began to part into a grin.

"Ah. I see." She reached out her arms. "Come then." Yes, he decided.
He certainly could.

Yet it was just as he had gently entered upon this second, late-night
communion, that to his surprise, before the pale form of his lover, an-

other, paler image seemed to arise before his eyes, interposing itself between them.

It was the old countess again. She did not speak this time; indeed, her white face was so motionless that it seemed she was sleeping—except for one thing: her eyes were wide open and staring. Try as he might to banish the phantasm, she remained obstinately between them, gazing at him stonily, as if to say: "You see, I sleep with my eyes open."

It was absurd. He tried to ignore her, but it was no good. It was as though the phantasm refused to let go of him. Did she sleep with her eyes open? While his body continued to perform, slowly, a little absently, the act of love, his mind could not seem to tear itself away from this proposition. Was she sleeping now, thinking of him perhaps, and all the time like some still Roman statue, staring out into space? Perhaps it was because of his earlier dream about her, or because of their conversation that evening, but the question seemed to become more important with every moment that passed.

Suddenly he stopped and slowly withdrew himself from Adelaide's embrace.

"What is it?"

"I must go."

"Where?"

"I have to see her. The old woman."

"Countess Turova? You're mad. She's asleep."

"I have to see her asleep. I have to know."

"Know what?"

"If her eyes are open."

Adelaide sat up and looked at him carefully. "You are serious?"

"Yes. It's all right. I know the way."

"You mean to go into the house, to her bedroom?" She shook her head, not sure of she was angry or amused by this eccentricity. "You did not choose a very good time to go on your expedition," she remarked.

"I know. I'm sorry. Do you want to come along?"

She threw herself back on the bed and put her hand to her forehead. *'Mon Dieu!* No."

"I shan't be long." He did not fully dress but, thinking it might be cold in the passage, he pulled on his coat. Then, still in stockinged feet, he made his way along the darkened passageway, through the connecting door, and into the main part of the house.

It was silent. By the great marble staircase, a guttering lamp gave a little light, but the corners and passages were in deep shadow. Downstairs by the main door, an old footman was sleeping on a bench; Alexander could hear him snoring. The floor above, he knew, would be deserted except for the countess's room and another little room across the passage, where an old serving woman slept in case the countess should require anything in the night.

He did not need much light. He knew the house well. Softly, making only two slight creaks, he mounted the wooden stairs that led to the countess's room. At the top of the stairs there was a little landing. On the right, through the open doorway, he could hear the rhythmic, heavy breathing of the servant. On the left, the door of the larger room was just ajar. Light came through the opening, but no sound. He moved silently to the doorway and peered through the crack.

On a painted wooden table he could see a large, three-branched silver candelabra. The candles had burned low but they shed a bright light. He could see pictures on the wall, and the edge of a gilt mirror; but the bed was hidden from view. He stood there fully a minute, hesitating. If she were not asleep and he opened the door, she would certainly see it. She would cry out; the house would be woken; and how would he explain himself then? He listened intently, hoping to hear her breathing, but could not.

Surely she was not still awake. Besides, having come this far, he did not want to give up now. Very carefully he began to push the door. It creaked. He stopped, waited, his heart pounding: still no sound; he pushed again. Now the door swung wide open, and he stepped into the room.

Her bed was to the right. It was a heavy affair with four carved posts and a canopy covered with huge festoons of heavy silk. On each side, on a night table, a single candle burned. And in the middle of this stately tableau, propped nearly upright with cushions, sat Countess Turova. Her hair had been undone. It had been parted in the middle and hung loosely down over her shoulders, the ends arranged in little strands tied with pale blue ribbons. Her chin rested on the thick lace that decorated her night-dress, so that her mouth was only just open.

And as he turned, Alexander found himself staring straight into her open eyes.

He stood stock-still, waiting for her to speak. How could he explain himself now? Would she scream; would she be furious? Her face registered no expression at all. It was just possible to see that she was breathing, lightly, through her mouth, but her eyes remained fixed, on a point somewhere just past his head. For perhaps half a minute they both remained there, silently; the little trickles of warm wax down the candles seeming to be the only things moving in the room. Then her lips made a dry, smacking sound; there was a single, faint snore. And only at that moment did Alexander finally realize: My God, it is true. She sleeps with her eyes open.

He knew that now was the moment to leave. He had discovered what he wanted. Yet somehow he could not pull himself away. He looked round the room. In one corner there was another little bust of Voltaire. On a table, some books; beside it a chair. But otherwise it was more sparsely furnished than he had expected. There was only one thin rug on the floor. As he moved quietly across the room, her eyes remained fixed. He stood at the foot of the bed and gazed at her. What should he do now? For no particular reason, he made her a low bow. The eyes did not move. He grinned, made her another.

How did he feel about her? Did he hate her for what she had done to him? Not really. She had always been willful and eccentric. Indeed, at this moment he felt only a sense of relief and light-headedness that he could stand before her like this without being afraid of her for once. Truly, he thought to himself, it is a wonderful thing to be awake when someone else is asleep. It gave one a feeling of extraordinary power.

He went over and glanced idly at the books upon the table. There were some French plays, a book of Psalms, and several journals. One journal, he noticed, contained a radical article by Radishchev; but then he looked at the others—and smiled in astonishment. They all contained articles by himself! These were the anonymous articles, the daring compositions on the very borderline of what could be said, about democracy and the serfs, and of which he was most proud. He opened the journals. Besides his articles there were numerous underlinings and little notes, in the countess's own hand. So, she really had taken an interest. Could it be that, after all, she did approve of him?

He sat down and turned the pages, glancing up at her from time to time. Did her eyes flutter once? How strange: he was not even afraid anymore. I could just sit here and discuss my articles with her, he thought pleasantly.

Finally Alexander got up and, in a sort of celebration of this curious little interview that Providence had granted him, he did a little dance on the floor in front of her. Then he made her a solemn bow and withdrew. As he made his way back, no one stirred in the big house.

Except for the Countess Turova, who, when she was sure he had gone, called her maid.

Tatiana was in love so much that it hurt. If Alexander came close, she trembled; if he smiled at her, she flushed; if she heard no word from him for a day, she became pale and silent. By now, therefore, her face was thin: she had scarcely eaten for two weeks.

Since early morning she had been at the window, watching. Countless times she had seen a sled approaching that she thought was Bobrov's and pressed her face to the window uselessly until it had gone past. Once, catching sight of a muffled figure walking through the snow, she became convinced it was he, and she hurried frantically from room to room, keeping pace with him until he turned the corner and vanished.

It was dusk when, having been persuaded by her mother at last to sit down, she suddenly heard a small commotion downstairs, followed by a lengthy pause. Then her father was in the doorway.

"Alexander Prokofievich is here to see you. He has something to say." She rose, very pale, trembling slightly. With terror she noticed that her father was looking concerned. "Before you go down, Tatiana, I must ask: are you sure, truly certain that you want this man?"

She stared at him. Then Alexander had come to claim her. She flushed. How could her father ask? "Just a minute, Papa." She rushed to her room, followed by her mother, while her father was left, still frowning. He had some reservations about Bobrov.

Below, Alexander waited. The minutes passed and no one came. My God, he thought, what if, after all this, she's changed her mind? It was nearly a quarter of an hour before the door opened.

Tatiana's entrance took him by surprise. She was wearing a dress of dazzling blue that perfectly complemented her fair complexion and made her pale blue eyes look brilliant. He had always thought of her face as rather round and placid; but now it had grown thinner, shedding its puppy fat and allowing the form of her cheekbones to show through. She had a fresh glow on her skin that was wonderful and she advanced towards him with a calm smile.

"Alexander. My father tells me you wish to speak to me."

And Alexander, gazing at this commanding heiress, could only think: Well I'm damned: she has taken charge. Yes, he could see now that this strong young woman was capable of writing that amazing letter that had brought him so abjectly to heel. He was impressed.

There was only one thing that Alexander did not know. Tatiana had not written the letter at all. To be exact, she had written out the words, but not composed them. And even as she wrote them she had trembled, hesitated, and looked up with large, tearful eyes at the older woman who was calmly dictating them to her.

For her mother, when she could bear the girl's agony no longer, had called upon the one person who, though they hardly knew each other, she felt sure could resolve the business. She had secretly taken Tatiana to see Countess Turova.

It was the countess who had taken the firm tone in the outrageous letter; the countess who had given Bobrov the deadline. She had been rather proud of her handiwork and quietly confident of the result. "He'll be yours, if you want him," she had predicted coolly.

And why had she gone to such trouble? Not, certainly because she cared particularly for Alexander or this poor little German girl. For she did not. But Alexander was a kinsman; the girl was an heiress. Properly established with a rich wife he might yet be a credit to her. Besides, it was a wonderful opportunity to exercise power—and such chances, it had to be admitted, did not come to her very often these days.

She had kept the business to herself. But when the unsuspecting Alexander had come to her asking about an inheritance—the very same evening—she had almost laughed out loud. Only by inspecting her hands had she been able to keep a straight face. And hadn't she played her cards to perfection? How she enjoyed that—defeating the gambler at his own game!

As for the girl . . .

"You know of course that he has a mistress?" she had remarked with cold casualness to Tatiana, as soon as they had finished the letter, watching curiously to see how she took it.

Tatiana blushed. She did. Her mother had found that out. But one expected such a thing in an older man; it even made him more mysterious and exciting.

"I daresay with a young girl like Tatiana he'll have no need to think of a mistress," her mother had remarked hopefully.

"Not at all," the old woman had contradicted her. "The more a man gets, up to a certain age, the more he wants." She turned to Tatiana. "You mustn't give him time or opportunity if you want a faithful husband. That's all there is to it."

Armed with this information, and the stern letter, the lovelorn girl had returned home and waited.

Grief and pain had strengthened Tatiana. If she was distraught while she waited for Bobrov's response, now in her moment of triumph she had steeled herself to be cool; however much she wanted him, she must not give him another chance to humiliate her. From now on she would make him see that it was he who was lucky, not she. And I'll take him from that Frenchwoman, she thought. Indeed, it was this last determination that helped her, at this moment of crisis, to astonish him by her calm detachment.

So it was that Alexander Bobrov came to claim his bride.

A light snow was falling that evening as Alexander Bobrov made his way across the city. The little fires by the watchmen's huts at the street corners looked orange; the houses loomed as though in a mist. All of which pleased Alexander. For he did not wish to be seen. At the Fontanka Canal he got out of his sled and, telling the coachman to wait for him, walked across the little bridge alone. In moments he had disappeared.

He walked briskly but carefully, occasionally turning, almost furtively, to make sure that he was not being followed. The quarter was respectable enough: about half the houses were wooden, half brick and stone. He passed a church and turned into a quiet street.

Only one thing puzzled him. What the devil had become of that letter? When the stranger had brought it to him the night before, he had intended to burn it as soon as he returned home. But then he had forgotten. Only after leaving Tatiana in the early afternoon had he remembered it, felt in his coat pocket, and discovered that it was gone. He shrugged. It didn't really matter. The letter would be completely meaningless to anyone who found it.

Now Alexander turned through a covered archway, into the shadowy courtyard of a large building. Its walls were covered with peeling pink stucco, and like many such buildings, it contained a series of sprawling apartments, two per floor, most of which were occupied by merchants of the middling sort. With a last, backward glance, he ascended the ill-lit stone staircase to the second floor. The stairs were deserted, with the sole exception of a very large black cat, which sat by a window and which Bobrov ignored.

When he reached the apartment he knocked carefully, three times, before the door opened a fraction and a voice from the gloom of the hall said quietly: "What do you seek?"

"The Rosy Cross."

The door opened wide. For Alexander Bobrov the gambler, unknown to even his mistress, was a member of the innermost circle of that great, secret brotherhood—the Freemasons. And they had important business that night.

Perhaps she should have expected it. But she was very young. That was the conclusion Tatiana herself came to, in the years that followed.

She loved him. When she saw his carriage approaching or watched the lackey at the door help him off with his coat, a thrill of excitement would go through her. He had known how to make her love him. Even in the early days of their marriage he had seemed to control everything. In their lovemaking, when he was finished himself, he would still arouse her in other ways, again and again, leaving her glowing, yet always wanting more of him. She loved the way he looked, the way he dressed, his knowledge of things beyond her. Even the slight thickening around his waist, which had begun in their first year together, seemed to her to suit him very well: he looked neat, yet powerful.

And surely he, too, was excited by their love. She knew he was: she could tell. She was learning, too. She was eager to learn, both to experience new delights and to please him. She was happy; she was enthusiastic; she would—and did—astonish him!

Tatiana had great gifts. She was warmhearted and practical. She liked to supervise the women in the kitchen; she would proudly make dainty pastries with her own hands, sitting opposite him, her face flushed with excitement, to watch his reaction. How delighted he seemed, how charmed.

It was therefore a shock to her when, six months after they had been married, he failed to come home one night and she began to suspect that he was still in love with Adelaide de Ronville.

She was right. And as Alexander often reminded himself, it was his fault. Indeed, he reflected, I cannot blame her at all.

It was not her fault that she was so young. It was not her fault if, like most girls of her kind, she had little education. She could not share a joke in French like Madame de Ronville, or even the old countess. It was not her fault if, on the occasions when he took her to salons like that of Countess Turova, she sat rather meekly to one side; not that the countess, having quickly asked after her health, would promptly ignore her for the rest of the evening.

It was not her fault if, after a few months, the subject of her pastries bored him; or that, without either of them saying anything, he usually went alone to the countess.

Nor was it her fault, Alexander knew, if their lovemaking left him only half-contented. That had seemed delightful at first, too; he had been aroused by her slightly plump young body. Yes, he had thought, this is how nature meant things to be. A young girl, full of energy, swept away by the first excitement of love. It was not her fault if she craved passion with either a submissiveness or a violence that were far from the varied subtlety of Madame de Ronville.

In short, he found that his young wife was cloying; and that married life destroyed the delicate balance, the sense of silence within which is the mark of the confirmed bachelor.

He felt guilty. He had known how to make his young wife love him and want him; yet he found he could not give up Adelaide. He did not wish to hurt her. But what could he do? Only with the older French-woman did he find peace. "Only with you," he would tell her, "can I sit, *tres chère amie,* and listen to the ticking of the clock." Indeed, his passion did not diminish but increased. The little wrinkles on her face, so finely drawn, so expressive of her character, represented for him as he gazed fondly down at her, no diminution of her sexuality but rather a distilla-tion. Her body, still young in many ways, filled him now with an extra tenderness. It was strange, but his wife's very youth made him love the older woman more. So it was that, discreetly but often, he had gone to call upon Adelaide.

It was a week after this first failure to return at night that Alexander was to go to Countess Turova's salon. Tatiana said nothing but made discreet arrangements; and shortly after he left, she followed him in a hired carriage. She saw him go in and waited quietly outside. Sure enough, at about eleven o'clock, the guests departed and the lights in the big rooms went out. She waited another twenty minutes. The lights in the main body of the house were all out now. In the east wing, however, where Madame de Ronville's apartment was, she could see a faint flick-ering of candles. Then they went out. A little later she went home. Tatiana supposed she must expect such treatment. But the pain was very great. Wisely, however, she said nothing. What was to be gained? He would deny it and then, more hurtful still, there would be a lie between them that would be more humiliating still.

So the weeks passed. She tried to shut the Frenchwoman out of her mind, yet thought of little else. And Alexander, for his part, supposed he was kind to her. For it was not her fault if she did not make him happy: she was a good wife and, despite the pain he guessed he caused her, never complained. No, he had nothing to reproach her with. And because he knew all this in his head, it did not even occur to him that secretly, in his heart, he blamed her for everything.

It was in the autumn of 1787 that two new circumstances arose in Tatiana's life. The first was her discovery that she was pregnant. This brought her only joy. Surely it will bring Alexander closer to me, she thought.

The second, however, was a puzzle. For she began to sense there was something else going on in Alexander's life—something secretive—about which she knew nothing. The most obvious sign was his unexplained absences.

Several times during the previous months he had gone off in the evenings on unexplained business. Once he had done so late at night—but at a time when she knew for certain that Adelaide de Ronville was out of the city. Could it possibly be that Alexander had another—a second—mistress?

Then in September, just after she told him she was pregnant, he abruptly went to Moscow for two weeks, giving her an explanation that was strangely vague. And Adelaide was in Saint Petersburg. So it must be another woman—but who?

It would have surprised Tatiana very much if she had known the truth: and still more had she understood that the person Alexander was going to see was both her greatest friend—and also her enemy.

The history of the Freemasons in Russia is, by its nature, shrouded in darkness. Its records were nearly all hidden or destroyed. Yet, about its general shape, a good deal is known.

There were many Masons in Saint Petersburg. The English lodges were especially popular. After all, the English were fashionable: every rich man wanted an English thoroughbred, every lady an English dog; and the smart place for a fellow like Bobrov to be seen was the English Club. Besides, English Freemasonry reflected the character of that easygoing country. It gave no trouble. Nonpolitical, not too mystical, concerned with philanthropy, the English lodges were patronized by foreigners and Russians alike.

When, therefore, back in 1782 some of Bobrov's English friends had invited him to join, he had accepted gladly.

And he would probably never have given it another thought, but for a chance encounter in Moscow a year later. An old acquaintance from his student days, discovering that he was a member, had assured him: "But, my dear fellow, you must meet some of the Masonic circle here—they're the best people in society." And so it was, upon his next visit to the old capital, that Alexander Bobrov encountered two highly significant people: the prince and the professor.

The first was a rich aristocrat and patron of the arts; the other a middle-aged, balding, rather abstracted figure who was head of the Moscow University press. Indeed, one would almost have called Novikov nondescript, had it not been for a certain strange though kindly light in his pale blue eyes. This was the man Alexander liked to call the professor.

It was the professor with whom he had had his secret rendezvous that snowy December night, in the pink house beyond the Fontanka Canal; it was the professor who had become his mentor and led him into the very different and secret world of higher Masonry; and it was the professor whom, ever since they met, Alexander had always thought of in the same way; as the voice of conscience.

There were several reasons why Alexander should have become fascinated by his new friends in Moscow. They were enlightened and educated—the center of the university circle. The prince and his friends were the cream of the capital's aristocratic society: that appealed to Alexander's vanity. And also, though he scarcely realized it himself, the secret hierarchy of higher Masonry reminded him of the bureaucratic ladder— and Bobrov was one of those men who have only to see a ladder to want to climb it.

For three years, making numerous visits to the professor in Moscow and corresponding by letter, Alexander had studied as the professor led him through the first of the higher degrees of Masonry—first to the rank of Scottish Knight, then the Theoretical Brother. "Our mystical secrets go back to the very dawn of Christianity," his mentor explained. "To ordinary Masons, the secret signs we use—the hieroglyphs—are mere playthings. These men do good works, which are admirable, but they understand little. The true meaning is revealed only to those who are worthy."

There was something very pure about the quiet scholar that Alexander found impressive. Indeed, at first he had hesitated to engage in higher Masonry because he had heard rumors that these inner orders practiced alchemy and magical arts. But there was nothing like that with the professor. "The way I shall lead you," he promised, "lies along a pure and Christian path. Our only motive is a burning desire to serve God and our blessed Russia."

The professor worked tirelessly. Besides his official duties at the university press, it was he who ran the private Freemason's press that turned out books and pamphlets for the membership. Dozens of bookshops distributed these in the main cities. "We spread our gospel," the professor would say happily.

And in many ways, Alexander realized, the Masonic brotherhood was like a secret church. For ever since Peter the Great had made Russia a secular state, the ancient prestige of the Orthodox Church had declined. Peter had abolished the Patriarch; Catherine had taken all the church lands and put them under state control. Though the peasants still followed the church, were often Raskolniki—for the enlightened Catherine tolerated these old Schismatics with polite amusement—for men of Bobrov's class it was different. Few of his friends took the church seriously, yet they often felt something was missing from their lives. It was not surprising that they were sometimes attracted to the religious and mystical atmosphere of the Masonic brotherhood. It salved their consciences that they were, truly, doing good.

And he himself, he had to admit, was drawn to the professor's Christian piety. Though they only met from time to time, he often felt the older man's influence upon him. It was not strong enough to divert him from his worldly plans; yet, there was no denying it, he felt it like a reproach. Perhaps, he acknowledged, in this matter, too, I am gambling: that if I fail to win the world, I shall still through the professor save my soul.

Yet during his studies, Alexander was also conscious of something else—an inner, organizing force at work in the brotherhood that for some reason was hidden from him. Two years passed, however, before one day in the autumn of 1786 the professor said to him, "I think it is time for you to take another step." And he gave him a certain little book and said: "Take it and read it through. Then, if you wish to become one of our number, make your application to me." And thus Alexander finally discovered the inner circle. "We call ourselves the Followers of the Rosy Cross," the professor said.

The Rosicrucians: the secret elect. There were only about sixty of them in all Russia, and it was a tribute to his talents that they had chosen Alexander to be of their number. Though this secret circle controlled most of their activities, ordinary Masons did not know they even existed. "They know us, but not our true identity," the professor explained, "in order that we may protect our mission from ignorant eyes." Indeed, their secrecy was such that, while every Freemason had a secret name, the Rosicrucians among themselves had yet another set of coded identities. And so when the professor, that cold December night in 1786, had summoned Alexander to his first Rosicrucian meeting at the pink house beyond the Fontanka Canal, he had signed his message not with his Knights Templar name—*eq. ab. ancora*—that was used in the ordinary Masonic lodges, but by his secret Rosicrucian name: Clovion.

For Alexander, that first meeting of the inner circle had been a powerful revelation. It was a small group—the prince and the professor from Moscow, himself and one other from Saint Petersburg. And for the first time the professor began to show him the real purpose of the brotherhood. "We seek no less than to create a new and moral order in society," he declared. "We shall lead it forward."

"You mean all Russia?" He knew that there were Masons in high places in the government.

"Not only Russia, my young friend. In time, the whole world," the older man said seriously. And though he did not elaborate, Alexander had a sense that the Rosicrucian network extended far indeed. Even so, he was awestruck by what the prince then added. "I can also tell you that an approach is being made to the Grand Duke Paul, to ask him to be our secret patron." He smiled. "And I am hopeful that he will accept."

The heir to the throne! He might not particularly like that strange man, but Alexander could see at once the huge possibilities if Paul were their patron.

We Rosicrucians could finish up ruling Russia, Alexander had thought excitedly. How strange that, on the very day when he had reluctantly committed himself to Tatiana and given up hope of entering Catherine's inner circle, this new possibility should have opened up before him. He smiled to himself. Perhaps Bobrov the gambler was being saved by fate for even greater purposes.

There was just one problem. The professor was not satisfied with him.

"I find in you a coldness, a lack of fervor," he had sometimes complained when Bobrov studied with him. He had been delighted when Alexander told him he was to marry. "Ah, that is good, my friend. It will open your heart." But less than a year later he wrote:

> I cannot forbear to mention, dear brother, certain news that has reached me. It is widely known in Saint Petersburg, I am told, that despite your recent marriage, you neglect your wife and continue your affair with a certain lady.
>
> I must inform you that your membership in our order places burdens upon you; and this conduct is not acceptable. Look into your heart, I beg you, and decide what you must do.

Though Alexander dutifully burned this letter, as was the rule with all Rosicrucian correspondence, he still seemed to see it before him every day. He knew the professor was right. His conscience troubled him. Yet he could not give her up.

A message came from a visiting Mason from Moscow. "The professor told me to tell you he is praying for you." It did no good. His next letter was noticeably cool. And when Alexander met him in Moscow later that year, his mentor was very angry.

"The members of our inner order must be men of good conscience, Brother Alexander. We expect you to follow the example of Grand Duke Paul, who is devoted to his wife, not that"—and now his pale eyes suddenly blazed—"of the profligate and wicked court of his mother the empress!" Then more gently he added, "Marriage is not always easy, Alexander, but all of us count on you to mend your ways."

And Alexander, rather shaken by the professor's vehemence, told him he would try to reform. At the time he even meant it. Little as Tatiana knows it, the professor is her greatest friend, he thought.

There was, however, another cause of friction between Alexander and Tatiana, which the professor could certainly not do anything about. This was the issue of money.

It had come up so gradually that he could hardly say when it began. At first it had been an occasional inquiry about the estates, or the household expenses, which he took to be childish curiosity. Yet after a little while, he began to notice that there was a certain quiet persistency in her questions.

"Do you know how many servants we have, Alexander?" she had asked after they had been married three months. He had no idea, and no interest in finding out. Sixty? Eighty? "And how much do they cost?" she had gone on.

"Nothing," he replied shortly.

In a way, this was true. For though merchants and foreigners hired their servants at great expense, Russian noblemen just brought in serfs from their estates. A hundred was nothing. The women worked in the kitchens or elsewhere out of sight; the men dressed in livery like lackeys. One might see a footman who had just pulled his livery coat on over his peasant's smock and failed to do up the buttons; none of them was really presentable; but things were the same in most of the houses he knew. Alexander did not even know where they all lived. In the basements, he supposed.

"But they eat food," Tatiana reminded him. "What does that cost?"

How the devil did he know? Food came. It was eaten. The Russka estate brought some cash payments and the rest in kind. Cartloads of provisions would arrive at the Saint Petersburg house—and immediately disappear. The peasants on the Riazan estate paid him in *barshchina* labor: his steward sold the grain and sent him the proceeds. He knew he spent it all, but he had no idea how.

Sometimes these questions amused him. But after a time they began to annoy him. How much did the mountains of wood for the stoves cost? Why did they have so many carriages they never used? Shouldn't they go and inspect their estates?

"Your father gave us plenty of money. We've no need to worry," he would assure her.

Indeed, Tatiana's father had discovered the truth about Alexander's financial position soon after the marriage; and although Tatiana's dowry had been ample to pay all his debts and leave them an estate to spare, the Baltic nobleman had not been pleased, and relations between him and Alexander were cool.

So Alexander could not help suspecting that her father's influence was at work when, one day just before she discovered she was pregnant, she had astounded him by remarking: "Don't you think, Alexander, that you should give me some accounting of how you have spent my dowry?"

It was a calculated insult! She was his wife, and barely seventeen years old to boot. What impertinence! Furiously he had burst out: "You damned foreigners! You Germans—the Dutch and English are just the same—you count every kopek. Why"—he searched for an insult—"you're like so many Jews!" But he could see that, despite the fact that she submissively bowed her head, she was not satisfied.

Besides, there was something he could not tell her.

The costs of the Masonic press were considerable. The program of books was ambitious. And, it had to be admitted, the professor was sometimes a little vague about keeping accurate accounts. Already, at the time of his marriage and in addition to the contributions to the brotherhood, Alexander had been asked to help support the press. How could he refuse, when men like the prince were contributing handsomely? Indeed, he had been amazed to discover that some students of higher Masonry were prepared to consecrate almost their entire fortunes to the cause. He certainly did not want to lose face before his new friends. So it had been with some satisfaction that, soon after his marriage, he had been able to announce: "I shall be able to make a contribution."

Tatiana would have been surprised indeed to know, when Alexander left for Moscow just after she became pregnant, that he was also going to see the professor at his estate; that he was hoping for a reconciliation with his mentor; and that with him he was taking a further contribution, which amounted to nearly a fifth of her dowry. Had she known it, she might indeed have concluded that, if the professor was her friend, he was also her enemy.

1789

It was on a raw, dull day in March in that year so fateful in the history of the world, when the ice on the Neva was still solid, that Alexander Bobrov the gambler struck a last bargain with God. It was not the deal he had wanted; but it seemed to be the best he could get at the time.

The morning was gray: a faint wind, on its way westward from the icy waters of Siberia, hissed through the huge open squares of Saint Petersburg. In the big salon of their house, Alexander Bobrov was facing his wife. He had not returned home until dawn that morning, but they were not speaking of that. He was sitting, and Tatiana was standing, to ease her back: for she was eight months pregnant with their second child. And he was glowering at her.

Damn her. Didn't she trust him? How dare she defy him?

She trembled for a moment but did not reply. Damn her. Damn her a thousand times. Or was she taunting him deliberately, because of Adelaide?

Tatiana stood quite still, holding on to the back of a chair for support. If she did not speak for a moment, it was because she was having to prepare herself, and she was nervous. Why did all these things have to come to a head when she was so pregnant?

Did he love her? It was not only the Frenchwoman: there were those unexplained disappearances to Moscow and these mysterious evenings out in Saint Petersburg. What was she to make of it?

Strangely, she did not hate Adelaide de Ronville. Sometimes she would meet her rival at Countess Turova's. The Frenchwoman was always polite and never made the faintest reference to her relationship with Alexander. Tatiana supposed she should be grateful for that and even admired the other woman's poise. Madame de Ronville did not even try to patronize her. She will be old soon, Tatiana had told herself at first. It will pass. Indeed, she even thought she could guess how the other woman felt. We're both his mistresses, after all, she realized, but I am young and have his children. It must be hard for her.

She could not help loving Alexander: perhaps it was his combination of strength and weakness that made her do so. Even his vanity, strangely, pleased her. For she understood him better than he realized. Large though his talents were, she saw that his ambition was always a step ahead of them, leaving him never satisfied, never secure. He loves her, but he will need me, even if he only exploits me now, she told herself.

But on one subject she could not give way.

Alexander was short of money again. It was not a crisis. He was not ruined; but he had started to incur debts and he was short of cash. Naturally, therefore, he had asked Tatiana to apply to her father. She was the heiress, after all. Where had the money gone? In their usual, lavish life-style, he supposed. And also, of course, to the Rosicrucians.

His admiration for the professor had, if anything, increased—despite his mentor's vigorous opposition to his way of life. The older man over-came every adversity. The Masons had encountered some opposition recently. Their enemies had even complained that their works were sacri-legious. But the professor had got his friends in the Church to issue an almost complete vindication. The debts had mounted; but he had quietly continued printing away, on presses down on his estate. Alexander could not help feeling affection and admiration for him.

It was getting damnably expensive, though. Hardly a month went by without some fresh appeal for help from the Brothers; and had it been any lesser cause Alexander might have been tempted to hold back. But still the prospect ahead thrilled him. Any guilt he might have felt about spending his wife's money was tempered by this one thought: The Rosi-crucians may yet rule everything.

So when, that morning, he had asked his wife to apply to her father for extra funds, it had come as a shock to him when she refused. How could she? It was her duty to do so. But she had maintained an obstinate silence. And now, despite her condition—and perhaps because, in his heart, he felt somewhat guilty—he shouted at her: "Tatiana, I command you to do this."

It was with astonishment, therefore, that he watched her turn and look down at him with an expression he had never seen before. It was angry and, yes, contemptuous. As for her words, it was a moment before he could even take them in.

"I'm sorry, Alexander, but I see no reason why my father or I should trust you with any more of my fortune when you have still failed to account for the dowry money which, I must remind you, is mine. And if you do not know where it is, then perhaps I, and not you, should control our affairs."

He stared at her. He felt his face go white with anger. Trembling with rage he roared at her, in a voice he scarcely recognized himself: "Jewess!"

Then he leapt up and struck her in the face so hard that she crashed to the floor.

An hour later Alexander was still in his study. He had not yet been able to bring himself to go out. How could he have done such a thing? He knew very well why: because he was guilty.

Am I going to ruin my wife and family? Even for the Rosicrucians and my own endless ambition? he asked himself.

Before him lay several letters. One canceled the purchase of a splendid English horse, another the purchase of a magnificent new carriage, of which he had no real need. But more significant by far was the much longer letter he had just completed. It was to the professor and it ended:

> Perhaps at a future date it may be vouchsafed me to enjoy those blessings which alone, I know, can come from our Holy Order's uncontaminated source, but I confess, highly worthy Superior, that at present I find myself unable to make those sacrifices which you rightly demand of me, and therefore respectfully withdraw until I can prove myself worthy of our brotherhood.

He had left the Rosicrucians. He smiled ironically. That would save more than his household expenses every year.

It was just as he sealed this letter that they brought him the news: Tatiana had gone into labor.

The day had passed, then the night. An anxious, interminable morning. And still Tatiana was in labor. The gray light outside gave the room a dull tone.

The afternoon before, a Polish midwife had been summoned; a German doctor in the evening. By midday they had both been shaking their heads. Since midday, there had also been one other figure in the room. The serfs from Russka who worked in the house had been urging Alexander to let her in all morning. They had no faith in the midwife from the city; as for the German doctor, they viewed him with silent contempt. But this was one of their own, a midwife from the country, a true Russian from the hamlet of Dirty Place. She was sitting in a corner now, doing what the foolish city folk should have been doing from the start: reciting the strange mixture of Christian prayer and pagan spell without which no child in the Russian countryside should be born. Alexander had glanced at the old woman and shrugged: God knew if she was doing any good, but he supposed she could do no harm.

And now the doctor was leading him out of the room. His face was grim. "It's blocked," the doctor told him. "The baby can't get out. There's a chance, maybe, that I can save the child. But the mother . . ."

"I don't understand."

"They may bleed."

"To death, you mean?"

"Perhaps. Some do, some don't."

"What should I do?"

"Nothing. Pray."

The doctor went back in, leaving him outside. He went to his little study, mechanically sorted through his papers, then tried to recite prayers, but got only a sense of his own emptiness. After a time he went back again and let himself into the bedroom.

How shocking it was. Tatiana's round face was drawn and ghostly white; sweat had matted her fair hair and her eyes were large with fear. The contractions were making her shiver. "At any time," the doctor whispered, "the vessel of blood may break."

Alexander gazed at Tatiana helplessly. It was terrible to be so useless. He went over to her and took her hand. She looked up at him and tried bravely to smile. He squeezed her hand. She winced as a contraction reached its peak, took a deep breath, and kept her large blue eyes fixed upon him; for at that moment, he realized guiltily, he was her only lifeline. He smiled, tried to make her feel, at her hour of death, that he loved her. What else could he do?

"I am having your child," she whispered.

He squeezed her hand but could not speak. She was about to die. He thought she knew it. And she was afraid, so much more afraid than she had ever been in her life, as she looked up at him with frightened eyes that said: Even if you cannot help me, tell me, this once, that you love me.

And it was then, a little after three o'clock on that March afternoon, that Alexander Bobrov, seeing little more to gamble for in the earthly or the heavenly kingdoms, made his final bargain with God.

Let her and the child live, merciful God, he silently vowed, and I will be faithful to my wife and give up Adelaide de Ronville.

It was, it seemed to him, the last card he had to play.

1792

THERE is no stranger or more magical time in the city of Saint Petersburg than midsummer. It is the season known as the White Nights.

For around the summer solstice, in those northern climes, the endless days do not give way to darkness. Instead the daylight lingers, far into the evening and beyond until, at last, for the space of half an hour or so in the early hours, it is transformed into a pale, glimmering twilight. The atmosphere is charged, the world unreal. Buildings seem like gray shadows; the water wears a milky sheen; and on the distant northern horizon, the twilight grayness is punctuated by the flashes of the aurora borealis.

Season of White Nights: electric season. Surely it must have been some dangerous magnetism in the atmosphere that led Alexander Bobrov to commit such acts of complete insanity. No other explanation is possible.

For by that summer, the world had entirely changed. It was as if some huge electric storm were about to break. Who knew what monarchies might fall, what societies dissolve into chaos? Each day Saint Petersburg waited for news from the West, where just three summers before with the storming of the Bastille in Paris, the epoch-making cataclysm had begun.

The French Revolution. Already the king of France, his queen Marie Antoinette, and their children were virtual prisoners. Who knew what these revolutionaries—these Jacobins—would do next? The monarchs of Europe were outraged. Even now, Austria and Prussia were at war with this disruptive new revolutionary power. Britain was ready to join. And no one was more shocked than the enlightened Empress Catherine of Russia. The principles of freedom and enlightenment were one thing— splendid theory. Revolution and mob rule were quite another! Remember Pugachev! She had crushed that desperate Cossack and his peasants' revolt years ago; she was not going to invite another peasant rising.

Small wonder therefore if enlightened thinkers, from the empress down, looked at these results of the Enlightenment with horror and concluded: "It went too far, too fast." Instead of reform, they saw only chaos. "These Jacobins have betrayed us all."

And if, in France, the revolutionaries believed they were witnessing a new springtime of the world, at the distant court of Saint Petersburg, it seemed rather that a golden era was passing—as though Catherine's long summer, having extended too far into autumn, had suddenly been exposed by this harsh, cruel wind blowing in the world; and that now her leaves were suddenly falling, revealing a bare forest before the unrelenting winter.

The empress was lonely. The faces about her were changing. Above all she had lost her one true friend, her gallant old warhorse, the great Potemkin.

What a loyal friend he had been. He had given her the Crimea. Just two years before the Revolution, together with the awestruck ambassadors of the great European powers, he had taken Catherine on a magnificent tour of that huge southern province by the Black Sea. The path had been almost literally strewn with flowers. He had even erected delightful stage-set hamlets—the famous Potemkin villages—along the way to charm them. The villages might be artifice, but the new empire was not: it was rich indeed. And so it was that at last a Russian ruler had come to sit in the fabled palace of the Crimean khans, at Bakchisarai, and receive the final homage of the Tatars.

And that, both for Catherine and Potemkin, had been the end of their long, late summer. The winds had started to blow; the French Revolution had come; they had failed to take the last, glittering prize of Constantinople; and sadly for both of them—just as Alexander Bobrov had foreseen—Catherine's young lover had been unfaithful, and this time Potemkin's enemies had succeeded in putting their own protégé, a vain young man, into her bed. It was the end of the game for Potemkin and he probably knew it. He came to Saint Petersburg, gave the most gigantic party for the empress that the capital had ever seen, and then departed south once more, in deep depression. In a year he was dead.

She was lonely. What had she left? A vain young lover—at least she was not alone in bed. A son who had come to hate her, and who grew daily more like her late, impossible husband. Her two grandsons, educated by her own instructions, and adored. And the empire. She would preserve it and strengthen it for her grandsons. As with everything she did, she was thorough.

How changed was Saint Petersburg now. France was quite out of fashion: even French dress was frowned upon. The newspaper reports of the terrible French contagion were kept to a minimum. "Thank God," wise men declared, "that our peasants can't read." Public discussion of the Revolution was forbidden, republican books burned, plays banned. It was the philosophers who had brought all this to pass: even enlightened men had to admit that now. If she was firm with others, Catherine was firm with herself; sadly the empress ordered that the bust of her old friend Voltaire be removed from her rooms, as she mustered her strength to face this new, gray world.

And who could blame her if she turned with bitterness upon those she feared might weaken the state in these dangerous times? When Radishchev the radical was foolish enough to publish a book—at such a moment!—calling openly for the ending of serfdom, she was so angry that he was lucky only to be sent to Siberia. What, she demanded, were the Freemasons up to, with their secret activities? Were they convening with her son? Were they Jacobins of some kind? It seemed not, but she had ordered that the professor be questioned carefully, just to find out. "Russia is looking," she made clear, "for loyalty."

In all Saint Petersburg, in the autumn years of Catherine the Great, there was no more loyal man than Alexander Prokofievich Bobrov.

"The Jacobins are traitors," he often said. On the Enlightenment, he was in total agreement with the empress. "Freedom of speech, like reform, is only possible when things are stable," he would declare firmly. "We must be very careful"

For in all Saint Petersburg, there was no more careful man than he. He lived in a modest house, no longer in the first Admiralty quarter, but in the less fashionable second. He kept only thirty servants and seldom gave dinner to more than a dozen guests. His carriage and equipage were modest; even his debts were modest. Indeed, he almost lived within his income.

He was still a state councillor. For some reason his career had come to a halt. And with his old patron Potemkin gone, it seemed unlikely that he would rise higher. "He's a very nice man," people now said: and a wise fellow knows he is going no further when they say that. Yet he appeared to be content. He still had hopes of minor appointments in the future that might supplement his income; and if he had such hopes, it was because people these days said something else about him, too. "Bobrov," they would agree, "is sound."

He had worked hard at that. From the very moment of the Revolution, he had severed his ties with all radicals. When Radishchev had been arrested, he had even submitted a brief article to a journal exposing the monstrous errors of his former acquaintance. By good luck, also, he had never had any contact with the Rosicrucians since the day he had sent his resignation to the professor. Indeed he had even avoided the ordinary Masonic lodges. If his life was duller, it was also very safe. And indeed, how else should it be, for a cautious family man?

For if Alexander had struck a bargain with God, that terrible day in 1789 when Tatiana lay near death, the Almighty had kept His side of it. Tatiana had lived. Not only that, she had produced a fine baby boy and then, two years later, another. For his part, Alexander still saw Adelaide de Ronville as a friend, but no longer as a lover. He was a model husband: a little paunchy now, but dependable, so that his old friends said with a smile: "Ah, Bobrov—a very married man."

There had been one unexpected setback: Tatiana's father had died and, to everyone's surprise, left only a pittance. It seemed that, unknown even to Tatiana, the Baltic nobleman had been speculating in the grain from his southern estates and had lost heavily. Alexander and the family were not ruined: the estates were only about half mortgaged now. "But thank God for the countess," he remarked to Tatiana. "Without her, there'd be almost nothing to leave the children." They both visited the old woman regularly, and she had long ago promised them that their legacy was secure. "God knows," Alexander would say, "she can't last much longer now."

This then, in the autumn years of Catherine the Great, was the modest family life of Alexander Bobrov, whose gambling days were over.

Season of White Nights: it was on one of the first of these magical evenings that Alexander made his way over the Neva for one of his routine visits to the countess.

She had been growing rather frail of late, but she still insisted on entertaining. Her evenings were quieter now. Only a few old faithfuls came; but the eccentric old lady carried on exactly as before. Indeed, it sometimes seemed to Alexander that she must be confused about the date, for she always ignored the French Revolution. Perhaps she had even forgotten it! But then nothing, he mused, should disturb the tranquil certainty of the old lady's temple.

When he entered the salon, the huge, white silk window blinds had been three-quarters lowered, but the windows were open so that the faint breeze gently ruffled the bottom folds of the blinds. Outside, the evening was light; within, the room seemed filled with paleness and half shadow.

As he expected, there were only a few people there, mostly old men, though one or two of the younger generation had appeared. He saw Adelaide de Ronville, talking quietly with one of the old gentlemen, and they exchanged a smile. She looked a little thinner, more brittle nowadays. It was a pity that she had no lover at present. And there was the countess, in the middle of the room, sitting on her gilt chair. What a curious old creature she was, with her long dress and ribbons, still just like something out of the old French court as she sat in state to receive her guests. He bent down to kiss her, noticing that she seemed rather listless that evening. Did she like him? Even now, after all these years, it was impossible to say. One moment she would seem to smile at him; but then, a few minutes later, he would see her watching him with a look of such cynicism, even malice in her sharp old eyes that it almost made him cringe. Who knew what she was thinking? She seemed pleased to see him now, however, spoke a few words, and then let him go.

He wandered about the room. One or two people were still drifting in and since he did not particularly feel like talking, he just stood and watched them or listened to them idly. He heard nothing of interest until he chanced to overhear one rather excitable young man, who had apparently just arrived from Moscow.

"Who knows what you can publish nowadays," he was saying. "It's not only the censorship. Why they even arrested old Novikov, who ran the university press. Is no one safe?"

"They say he was a Freemason," someone objected.

"Perhaps. But even so . . ."

Alexander almost sighed. What memories that name brought back. Poor old Novikov. Though it was more than three years since he had had any contact with the professor, he suddenly felt a desire to write to his old mentor, or at least to his family. He questioned the young fellow from Moscow. Had any charges been preferred? Not yet, it seemed.

"What is the professor to you?" the man asked.

And then, after pausing only a second, Alexander heard himself say: "Nothing at all. I just met him once or twice, years ago."

No, he would not write. The old man was a fool to get himself into trouble like that. He preferred to be careful. He moved away.

Some time passed. There was an air of quiet lethargy in the room, which was not unusual at Countess Turova's these days. He managed to catch a few words with Adelaide, who complained of the heat. Then he stared out of the window at the bright evening street for some time. How boring everything was.

So he scarcely noticed that there had been a subtle change in the atmosphere of the room. People were changing position. The countess was suddenly coming to life. A little group was gathering about the old lady, drawn there, it seemed, by some new arrival. Only now did he realize that she was beckoning to him. Wearing a faint smile to hide his boredom, Alexander strolled over. No doubt they wanted him to supply some repartee. And it was only when he reached the countess, and saw the figure who was standing on her right, that his smile froze.

It was the old general: the man he had humiliated in this very place five years ago. Alexander could hardly believe it: he hadn't even set eyes on the old man since then, and might have forgotten his existence if he had not heard that the general had acquired a surprising influence at court in recent years. Now, as he bowed politely, he saw two things, to his dismay. The first was that the old man's eyes were glittering with dislike; obviously the general had not forgotten him. The second was the look in the countess's face, and with it came the awful realization: My God, he thought, she thinks I'm going to humiliate him all over again.

Didn't she realize that five years had passed? Didn't she know that the Enlightenment was out of fashion and that the general was now dangerous? But of course she didn't. Or if she did know, he supposed that she didn't care or that she simply wanted to be amused.

Already she was smiling with happy malice. "Well, General," she began, "I understand you mean to burn all our books now, as well as close our theaters."

If only there were some way out: but there was none; and the general knew it. Alexander was trapped.

What followed was worse than anything Alexander could have imagined. The general played his hand to perfection. He understood precisely how the universe had changed since the French Revolution: he had no need to defend himself from the Enlightenment. Instead, repeating their previous argument, point by point, he calmly and bluntly stated his case, pausing after each statement to announce: "But Alexander Prokofievich, I know, will disagree."

It was brilliant. The old fellow had him exactly where he wanted him. Every time he invited Alexander to take up Countess Turova's cause, he also gave him the chance to proclaim himself against the government: and, Alexander guessed that the general would be delighted to take any statement he made and repeat it, verbatim, to the highest circles at court. Once, as a further taunt, he even remarked: "But you, as a friend of Radishchev, will no doubt disagree."

What could Alexander do? He squirmed. It was humiliating. Once or twice he managed, lamely, to take the countess's part; but most of the time he was reduced to defending himself, even weakly agreeing with the general, so that the old fellow, with quiet sarcasm, was able to say several times: "You seem to have changed your tune, young man," or: "I'm so glad that, after all, you agree with me."

And all the time, Alexander could see the old countess becoming more and more irritated. She gave him a stern look at first, then tried to interrupt, then began to drum with her fingers on the arm of her chair. After a time she lifted up her hand and gazed at the back of it, as though to say, "I am so sorry that you, too, should have to be present at this debacle." Couldn't she really see the danger he was in? Obviously not. With each exchange he could feel her growing colder until, at last, she retreated into an ominous silence.

The general saved the coup de grâce for the end, and he executed it with all the confidence of a card player who is taking the last, inevitable tricks. He set Alexander up nicely.

"The Enlightenment," he said calmly, "has led to these Jacobins. But perhaps Alexander Prokofievich may have something good to say about these fellows."

"I have nothing good to say about Jacobins," Alexander replied quickly.

"Very well. Yet these same Jacobins have claimed as their hero that Monsieur Voltaire, who they say inspired them. The empress, as you know, has repudiated Voltaire. Do you?"

The trap was sprung. Please go on—the general's eyes seemed to glint triumphantly—and give me something I can use at court to break you.

And as Alexander wondered what to say, the silence was interrupted only by Countess Turova's voice, cold as ice: "Yes, Alexander Prokofievich: what would you like to say about the great Voltaire?"

"I admire the great Voltaire," he said carefully, after a pause, "just as the empress does. As for the Jacobins, they are utterly unworthy of such a great man."

It was a clever answer. There was nothing there for the general to use, but it seemed to mollify the countess. The grim expression on her face seemed to relax a little.

But the general had scented the kill.

"Very good," he said with lethal blandness. "Yet since his writings have caused such trouble, would it not be better if they were removed from the eyes of those dangerous gentlemen?" And he looked around the little group with a smile.

"You mean censorship?" the countess cut in sharply.

"I do."

"Censor the great Voltaire?"

"Perhaps the empress will decide to make a bonfire of all his books, my dear countess. But no doubt Alexander Prokofievich would not agree to it?"

The countess stared first at the general, then at Alexander, in horror. It was one thing to ban a few seditious tracts, even if she disapproved of it; but to burn the entire works of the great Voltaire, to cut off civilization itself . . . "Unthinkable," she murmured.

But it was not. How cunning the old general was. A trap within a trap. For only a few days before, a friend who frequented the court had whispered to Alexander that the enemies of the Enlightenment were secretly pushing for just such a terrible act. "And with the empress in her present mood, they may get their way," he had said. "Before a year is out, Voltaire may be banned." Clearly the general hoped Alexander did not know this: a denunciation of the idea was all he needed: then Alexander would be an enemy of the government. There was no way out. The general had trapped him and he knew it.

"Well, Alexander Prokofievich?" the old man gently inquired.

"I am the loyal servant of the empress," Alexander lamely replied.

The general shrugged; but from the countess there was a little gasp, then a terrible silence. The little group around her watched in fascination;

the old general gazed at them all with a contemptuous satisfaction.

Then at last Countess Turova spoke. "I am interested to learn, Alexander Prokofievich, that you would burn the works of Voltaire. I had not known this before." She stared down at her hands thoughtfully. "I am sure that your wife must be waiting for you. So we will bid you goodnight."

It was a dismissal. He bowed his head and left.

A few days later, when Alexander called at her house, he was told that she was not receiving. Two days after that, when Tatiana went at her usual time, she was told the countess was not at home. A third time the servant at the door informed Alexander, insolently, that he was not to call again; and that very day, he received the following ominous message from Adelaide de Ronville:

> I must tell you, dear friend, that the countess absolutely refuses to see you. She also says she intends to cut you out of her will. I can do nothing with her. But you should know that her lawyer, who is in Moscow, will return in three days, and if she does not change her mind, he will be sent for as soon as he is back. I fear the worst.

Alexander looked at the letter with dull horror. The children's inheritance—gone. The entire business was insane, but he knew the old lady too well to think she would change her mind. He had insulted her idol; that was all she knew, or cared about. He showed the letter to Tatiana, remarking with shame: "See what your foolish husband has done."

She would not let him take the blame, however. "The old woman is mad, that's all," she said firmly; and even in his distress, Alexander smiled to himself as he embraced her. How much closer they were nowadays.

But what could be done? The first day he wrote the countess a letter. It was returned. On the second, Adelaide wrote to her. That, too, was returned. Early on the morning of the third came a message from Adelaide.

> I have spoken again on your behalf—to no avail. She is obdurate. The lawyer has been sent for and he comes tomorrow. If you wish to talk, if there is anything I can do, I shall be at the Ivanovs all evening. So you can find me there.

Alexander sighed. What was the point? There was nothing to be done now. Sadly he told Tatiana, "It's no good. I'm afraid we've lost it." The stupidity of the whole business disgusted him. Miserably he retired to his study to think.

Yet even at this moment of crisis, he did not despair. Perhaps the shock even gave him strength. If the inheritance was gone, he must think of some other way to get money. All morning, grimly determined, he pondered this question. His aims were modest: the days of Bobrov the gambler were long over. He would pay off his debts and put a little money by. It might take years and sometimes be humiliating: he did not care. He would make a start, right away.

And so it was, at midday, that he came out, kissed his wife, and ordered his best carriage and horses.

He was going to Empress Catherine's summer palace.

It was in the early afternoon that, unbeknownst to Alexander, Tatiana and her children set out in a modest hired carriage and crossed the Neva to Vasilevsky Island. When they arrived at Countess Turova's house, however, it was not to her door that they went.

It had not been easy for Tatiana. But the Frenchwoman is the only person, she reasoned, who might get me in to see the countess. If it meant she must suffer the small humiliation of asking her husband's former mistress to save her, so be it. And when the children asked who they were going to see, she told them, "an old friend of mine."

Her plan was quite simple. Once the countess knew she was in the house, surely she would see her. And when the old woman saw the children, could it fail to soften her? Then Tatiana would explain everything. It was a mother's plan.

And so it was that an astonished Adelaide de Ronville found herself confronted with three little children and their mother who, staring with clear, blue eyes straight into hers, declared simply: "We are in your hands."

"Mon Dieu." Adelaide gazed at the children. Alexander's children. She realized, to her surprise, that she had never seen them before. Then she looked quickly at this simple, strong woman. Their mother. And because it had happened so unexpectedly, leaving her no time to prepare herself, she experienced a sudden, terrible sense of loss and loneliness so that, for a moment, she found she could not speak.

"Wait here," she said, after a few moments. "I promise nothing, but I will do what I can."

She was gone some time. While she waited, Tatiana looked around her curiously. Though she had little understanding of what she saw, she perceived that there was something about the subtle arrangement of the Frenchwoman's salon that was charming in a way that no room of her own could ever be. Yet what was it? Some of the hangings were old and worn. The colors were muted compared with the bright blues and heavy greens of the Bobrov house. Yet this, she realized, was what he liked. That the art of Adelaide's seduction lay in the mind, that the joy of the room's restful silence was that it evoked a whole civilization—said, in effect: "In this house there are countless rooms in which your imagination may wander"—never occurred to her.

She sat there, holding her children, for nearly an hour. Then Adelaide returned, looking grim. "She won't see you. I'm sorry."

And this, too, Tatiana was not able to understand.

The Catherine Palace. The huge park containing the imperial summer quarters lay only a short distance to the southwest of Saint Petersburg. Alexander had reached it in under two hours. He loved the place.

For if anything symbolized the cosmopolitan era of eighteenth-century Russia, it was this building. Like the huge Winter Palace, it had been principally designed by the great architect Rastrelli in Empress Elizabeth's reign. It was the Russian Versailles. The ornate, rococo facade of the central section was three stories high, and it stretched for well over three hundred yards. Pilasters, caryatids, windows, and pediments were picked out in white; the walls were painted blue. At each end, a little cluster of onion domes served to emphasize even further the incredible horizontal line of the place. Catherine had abolished some of the formal gardens for an English park, laid out by John Bush. She had also decided to replace the gilt on the domes with a duller but more sensible paint. "But God knows" people would remark, "there's enough of Rastrelli's gold left inside."

There was indeed. For here was European elegance blended with true Russian sumptuousness. There were huge halls of multicolored marbles, rooms decorated with jasper and agate; there was even, unique in all the world, a room whose walls were entirely made of amber. The magnificent parquet floors used dozens of woods. And everywhere was the gold that Rastrelli loved, set off with alabaster, lapis, deep reds, and dazzling blues in such brilliant profusion that even visitors from the greatest courts in Europe gasped. How should it be otherwise when this was the capital of the vast Eurasian empire, which could take such treasures from lands that stretched from the Baltic shores all the way to the desert and mountains of the fabulous Orient?

The Russian Versailles. Yet it was profoundly different from the great French palace. For where the French king had laid out his vast, proud palace and park with a cold classical geometry, this gorgeous Russian palace was essentially simple. It was a long, brightly painted house in the forest. That was all. Despite its magnificence, there was a charming humility about the place, as though to say: man is still dwarfed, under this sparkling northern sky and this ever-receding horizon, here at the corner of the endless plain. In this, the rococo Catherine Palace was still entirely Russian.

"State Councillor Bobrov." They gave him directions immediately, and Alexander entered boldly. Yet all the same, he could not help feeling mortified as he made his way through the huge gilded halls. With every step a little voice, long smothered, seemed to say: This should have been yours, not his.

For the man he had come to see was young Platon Zubov—the Empress Catherine's new lover.

How inscrutable, indeed, was fate. The very position he had once aspired to occupy now belonged to a handsome young man in his early twenties, who was vain, shallow, and ambitious. He was so obvious about it all. Nobody liked him. Yet the whole court sensed—perhaps the empress also knew—that in the autumn of her life, this young lover would be her last.

And this was the young man whose favor Alexander had, for some time, been trying to cultivate. It had not been pleasant. But what else do you do, when you've got a family? he told himself. A little while ago he had actually been very useful to the young favorite, hoping to build up a debt of gratitude with him in the future. But now, in this present crisis, it seemed time to cash in the debt at once. That was what he was counting on today.

The pavilion rooms in which the young man was holding court had been built into one end of the palace, together with a long gallery, by Catherine's Scottish architect Cameron. It was beautifully designed—smaller in scale but in the style of a sumptuous Roman palace, with a Roman bathhouse underneath. Before the doorway of one of the rooms stood a crowd of people: venerable courtiers, rich landowners, important military men. Three years ago they would not have looked at Zubov: now they waited meekly for admittance to the favorite. It should have been his—Alexander shut out the thought and sent in his name. As the door opened, he heard laughter inside.

He was only kept waiting an hour before they let him in.

The room was splendid, done in Pompeian style, with severe Roman furniture. Young Zubov himself stood in the middle of the crowded room, smiling. For his amusement, he had dressed himself in a Roman toga that day: and indeed, with his classically perfect face, the vain young man looked very good in this dress. Holding his hand was a monkey.

"My dear Alexander Prokofievich"—his large eyes seemed surprised but delighted to see the modest state councillor—"what brings you here?"

This was the moment. Great men easily forget they owe favors; but Bobrov did not give him the slightest chance. "Why naturally," he replied, "I came here to congratulate you upon our triumph in Poland." And Zubov positively beamed at him.

Poland. If the great Potemkin had given Catherine the Crimea, it was young Zubov's intention to have his name linked to another important addition to the Russian empire. For fate had given him Poland.

If the great feudal magnates of Poland and her partner Lithuania had advanced like a steady tide into ancient Russia in those centuries when she was struggling with the Tatars, that tide had long since ebbed away. Moreover, Russia's former rival was still ruled by its famous diet—the *sejm*—that hopeless body of magnates, which, having elected a king, could frustrate any course of action by the veto of a single member. Poland's weakness had suited Russia very well. Twenty years ago, had not Catherine been able calmly to take another bite out of its borderlands and then have her former lover elected as a puppet king? By what folly then had the Poles, just a year ago, declared a new constitution that allowed for a normal voting system in the diet and a hereditary, constitutional monarchy? The poor king had even been stupid enough to endorse it. Did her former lover really suppose that Catherine would tolerate his ruling over a strong and stable Poland on her borders?

Her reaction was instant. "They are revolutionaries—Jacobins!" she declared. It was nonsense, of course: the reformers were conservative monarchists. But rulers are entitled to lie. Something would have to be done.

Here, then, was the opportunity—for Zubov to make his name, and for

Russia to enlarge her mighty empire. While many, including the great fading star, Potemkin, had recommended caution, the new favorite urged: "Europe's powers are distracted by the war with revolutionary France. They've no time to worry about Poland. Now is the time to invade her." That spring, with Potemkin now dead, Zubov had got his way. Even now, following plans he had meticulously drawn up, a Russian force was sweeping easily across the Polish plains.

"My dear Alexander Prokofievich," Zubov now declared. "You have timed your visit perfectly. I have just heard this morning that Vilnius is ours." The ancient Lithuanian capital. Another Baltic province to add to the lands of Latvia and Estonia that Peter the Great had secured for Russia. "By the end of the year," the young man went on, "Poland will be half its present size. We'll give a piece to Prussia and keep the rest for ourselves." It would certainly be a triumph.

"I share your joy," Alexander said carefully, in a voice that, once again, gently reminded him that a favor was due.

"Ah yes." Zubov looked at Alexander thoughtfully. "You were rather useful to us, weren't you?" Alexander bowed. "Of course. I remember it all." And the young man gave him a smile of total understanding.

It had not been anything to be proud of. At a time when Zubov was still unsure of prevailing on the subject of Poland, Bobrov in his modest way had done useful work for him in the bureaucracy. In doing so he had deliberately betrayed his old patron, the sick Potemkin. He was still secretly ashamed of it. And all this Zubov perfectly understood.

"So," the favorite said quietly, "tell me what you want."

It was not much: just one of those many positions that existed throughout the cumbersome Russian administration and carried a handsome salary for minimal duties. It would not make him rich, but it would supplement his income nicely and let him save some money until some better chance arose. He had rather despised these sinecures before, but this was not the time to be too particular. Zubov let him finish, then turned to his monkey.

Alexander had heard of the monkey. It was Zubov's favorite pet and was often present at audiences. It was said that important courtiers had been sent out of the room because the monkey did not like them. He was not sure what kind of monkey this little object with a long, curling tail might be, but he eyed it rather nervously.

"Alexander Prokofievich wants a present," Zubov said to the little brown creature. "What do you think?"

Alexander held his breath.

What happened next took place so fast that Alexander never actually saw it. All he knew was that the little creature must have sprung—for suddenly the monkey was on his chest, its little arms clasped round his neck, and its face, like that of a tiny old man, pressed close to his—and that the force of its landing was so unexpected that it had made him topple and fall with a crash onto the marble floor.

The whole room burst out laughing. The monkey was still pressing its face to his, squealing excitedly, opening and closing its little mouth so that Alexander wondered if it was going to bite him. He struggled to get up, slipped and fell. The little creature was all over him again, tugging at his ears, pushing its nose against his. And above it all he could hear, almost a squeal of mirth, Zubov's voice. "He likes you, Bobrov! He loves you!"

And then, suddenly, silence. Alexander turned his head: legs in silk stockings, uniforms, all around, and all motionless. He looked up; and now he saw, standing in the center of the room, a short, stout figure in a simple, pale silk robe, rather like a dressing gown.

It was Catherine.

Awkwardly, scarlet with humiliation, and trying to straighten his clothes, he rose and bowed. The monkey had disappeared somewhere. He was conscious only of the circle of twenty or so courtiers watching him, and of the empress, whose face was like a mask.

So at last, after all, he had met her face to face. Humiliating though it all was, he looked at her with curiosity. This was the woman whose bed he had hoped to share.

Her face was still fine. The brow was noble. But her short, stout body looked coarser and flabbier than he had realized; and some of her teeth were clearly missing. Her golden autumn had shed nearly all its leaves, and she knew that nothing could disguise it. Alexander gazed at her, and he did not envy Platon Zubov anymore.

"Who is he?" The empress's voice cut coldly, authoritatively through the silence.

"Alexander Prokofievich Bobrov," Zubov answered, and he gave Alexander an encouraging smile. "He came to ask for an appointment," he added kindly.

Catherine looked at Alexander, apparently searching the large store-house of her mind for scraps of information, saying nothing while she did so. She might be getting old, perhaps unwell, but her prominent, calm blue eyes were still rather alarming. For years Alexander had vowed that when they met he would astonish her. Now in her presence, after this ridiculous beginning, he was idiotically speechless. He felt himself growing hot. And then he saw a faint recognition in her eyes.

"You are State Councillor Bobrov?"

He bowed. Perhaps Potemkin had spoken of him formerly and she remembered. She must, at least, be aware of his family's ancient services. Was it possible that, after all, his hour had come? God knows I have deserved it, he thought. Then she spoke.

"Aren't you a relation of that tiresome and ridiculous Countess Turova?"

It was not a question. It was a cold, contemptuous accusation. At this signal of royal displeasure, it seemed to him that he could feel the whole room grow instantly cold towards him.

"I am distantly related. I'm afraid she is rather absurd," he said lamely.

"Quite. Now I know who you are."

And with that she turned her back and began to walk out of the room. Just before the doorway, and without turning her head, she called: "Come, Platon." Then she swept out.

Zubov started after her quickly; from somewhere the monkey reappeared and loped along behind him. At the door, Zubov turned, gave a regretful little shrug to Alexander, and then suddenly grinned. "Oh well, Alexander Prokofievich," he called out, "at least my monkey liked you! Good-bye." Then he was gone, and all the room was laughing.

It was over. He would never, as long as he lived, get any court favor. And why? Because the empress associated him with Countess Turova and her stupid views.

My God, he thought, I might as well have kept on the right side of the old witch and her damned Voltaire.

Sadly, his head down, he left. He was broken. As he made his way back to where his carriage was waiting, he scarcely noticed the old general going into the palace, with a faint smile on his face.

All the way back to Saint Petersburg he brooded. He was finished. He could see it all. They would move to a smaller house. There would be almost nothing for the children. Even his most modest hopes had been dashed.

Perhaps I should just go and live at Russka, he thought. There would be nothing to do, but it would be cheap. "A fellow from Riazan," he muttered. That was the popular phrase for a country bumpkin. Twice during the journey back he put his head between his knees, in a gesture of despair.

It was eight o'clock in the evening when he reached Saint Petersburg: the bright haze in the streets would continue, growing gradually paler until midnight, when the strange, electric luminosity of the White Night would begin. Shortly he would have to face Tatiana with the news of his failure. As his carriage approached the second Admiralty Quarter, however, an idea occurred to him and he ordered the coachman not to stop but to continue across the Neva to Vasilevsky Island. Once there, he told him to wait by the Strelka, the tip of the island; then he proceeded on foot. He would have one last try. After all, he had nothing to lose.

The great house of Countess Turova was quiet. It might have been deserted. It was as though, having no wish to take part in that interminable, pale summer night, it had retreated into itself, behind its large, heavy, and slightly dusty facade. Its big, silent pillars and their deep recesses made Alexander think of a mausoleum, or a government office on a Sunday. Yet he knew the old woman was in there somewhere.

He approached discreetly, keeping out of sight of the main door, where some lackey might observe him, and made instead for the little side entrance that led to Madame de Ronville's quarters. Her note had said she would be out at the Ivanovs that evening: so much the better. He had no need to involve her, only to get access to the building. When he reached the door he pulled out the ring of keys that he always kept with him. Although they were no longer lovers, he had never been able to bring himself to part with the key to that little side door. He let himself in and went up the stairs.

How still it was. Inside the house there was not a sound—not even a scratch or a whisper. He passed through Adelaide's rooms. The evening sunlight outside softly lit up the tapestries and damasks. There was a faint smell of roses in the salon. A moment later he passed into the main body of the house. Since this, too, was silent, he guessed that the old lady had probably retired early. He made his way carefully up the little staircase to the landing and paused. The door of the maid's room was closed: obviously she had not come up yet. But the door of the countess's bedroom was open. He listened. Was she there?

Then he heard her. At first he thought she must be talking to someone; she was muttering with such conviction; but after a few moments, hearing no answering voice, he moved into the doorway. Then he was sure: the countess was muttering to herself. What was she saying? He could not make it out; but suddenly the thought crossed his mind—perhaps the old woman was going a little mad. Mad or not, it was time to act. Calmly he stepped into the room.

She was reading, sitting in bed, just as she had been that night five years ago. She looked older and frailer now; her hair, tied with ribbons, was getting thin. Her shoulders, slightly exposed, showed the bones sharply through the sagging skin. She was propped up on pillows, leaning slightly forward, following the text of a newspaper by holding a magnifying glass close to the page, and muttering irritably to herself while she did so.

She started with a little cry when she saw him. He saw her swallow with alarm. But then, quickly collecting herself, she noisily slammed down the newspaper on the bedclothes and hissed furiously: "What do you want? How dare you come here!"

He tried to look soothing.

"I wanted to speak to you, Daria Mikhailovna, but"—he gave a wry smile—"you would not let me in."

"Get out."

He wondered if anyone could hear them, but he stood his ground. It was all or nothing now.

"Daria Mikhailovna, permit me at least, and with great respect, to say that you have done me an injustice. And even if you are unfairly angry with me, do not, I beg you, destroy my poor wife and children, who are innocent."

"You sent them to pester me already once today, and I sent them away," she retorted sharply. "Now leave my house."

His wife and children here? What was she talking about? "I did no such thing," he replied truthfully.

But the old woman's attention seemed to wander now. She began to mumble. "First one comes, then the other, pretending they don't know. Liars. They'll get nothing from me." Could it be, Alexander wondered, that the countess was really becoming senile? The thought had just formed when she abruptly hissed, "Or their children: filthy creatures. Snakes!"

This last was said with such vehemence, in a manner so insulting, that he could not help tensing with anger.

"You do not understand, Daria Mikhailovna," he went on patiently. "You are angry with me, but I assure you, no one admires the great Voltaire more than I do. But at the moment, my dear Daria Mikhailovna, even those of us who think as you do, cannot speak. The empress won't hear of it. I'm a state councillor. Surely you know that I have to be careful."

He paused, wondering if she had understood. For a moment she did not reply. She stared down at the newspaper that lay before her. Then she looked up at him, with contempt, and spat out a single word: "Deceitful!"

What a foolish, vicious old woman she was. And now she continued muttering, though whether to herself or addressing her remarks to him, it was impossible to tell. "He says one thing to this one, another to that. Two-faced. You can't trust him an inch." And just because, in his heart, Alexander was ashamed of the way he had deserted his old patron Potemkin, and because it was true that he had altered his views to the prevailing wind, the crazy old woman's accusations made him all the more angry. First the hot drive out to the summer palace, then his utter humiliation, now this.

"You don't understand. I assure you," he began.

But she cut in. "You think I don't know you for what you are. This is the second time you've come sneaking in here, you snake."

"I most certainly have not," he retorted hotly.

"Liar!" She fell silent, then continued her colloquy with herself. "Oh yes, I saw him creeping in here in the middle of the night like a wolf. Thief! Thinks he can just come in here and mock me. Blackguard! Picking up my books, dancing about in front of me like a lunatic. Snake! Viper!" She spat out the words.

My God! Then she had not been asleep that far-off night. Her eyes had been open because she was awake. It had never occurred to Alexander that the old lady had been brooding secretly about his foolish nocturnal visit for the last five years. And how on earth could he explain it now?

"Who do you think you are?" she suddenly demanded furiously. "You think you can deceive me, too? Liar!" she rasped.

He was shattered yet furious. He was not a liar!

"All this because I said a word about Voltaire! What about my children—your own kinsmen? You mean to disinherit them?"

" 'You mean to disinherit them?' " She mimicked his words with surprising accuracy and a vicious contempt. "I care nothing for your children. Serpent's brood. Let them starve! Now get out of here. Traitor!"

It was too much. It was cruel beyond reason. The rage and frustration of the day, perhaps, of his whole life, suddenly welled up and flooded over.

"You old witch!" he cried out. "You stupid, senile old hag! What do you know about anything? Damn your Voltaire! Damn you, too!" He raised his fists above his head, tightly clenched. "My God! I'll kill you!" And he took a step towards her.

It was a gesture of frustration. He had meant, perhaps, to shock her. He hardly knew himself. But now to his horror he saw her shudder, watched her eyes open very wide, then roll up. Then she fell back on her pillow.

He stood still. It was very quiet. He glanced at the door, expecting to see servants, but there was nobody. It suddenly occurred to him that in that huge house, the servants on other floors had probably never heard them. He looked back at her. Her mouth had fallen open, making a small, rather pathetic little O. Her few yellow teeth seemed very long, like a rat's. She did not seem to be breathing.

Trembling, he went over to her. What should he do? Gingerly he felt her pulse. He could feel nothing. He continued to gaze at her nervously for some time before he fully realized that she was dead.

Because he was so afraid of her, a simple and obvious fact had never entered his mind—that the frail old woman had been terrified of him. He must have given her a heart attack. He crossed himself.

And only after several moments more, as he stood there wondering what to do next, did the true significance of what had happened occur to him.

"Praise be to God," he whispered. She was dead—and she hadn't yet altered her will. "I'm saved after all."

Cautiously he went to the door and looked out onto the landing. Everything was quiet, just as it had been before. He glanced back once more at the figure of the countess. She had not moved. He went out, descended the staircase to the main body of the house, then slipped quietly along the passage to Madame de Ronville's quarters.

A few minutes later he was letting himself out of the little street door. No one saw him. He locked the door behind him. Then, walking swiftly, he made his way through the tenuous late evening light to the Strelka, where his carriage was waiting.

It was just as his carriage was rolling over the bridge towards Peter's Square that, in the great house on Vasilevsky Island, Countess Turova's eyes fluttered and slowly opened.

The dead faint into which she had fallen had lasted some time. She had, indeed, been lost to the world and had herself no idea how long she had been unconscious. Nor was it surprising that Alexander should have believed her dead: for having little experience of old people he did not know that their pulses often become almost impossible to feel. For some while she lay very still, collecting her strength. She called for her maid, but obviously the woman was still downstairs somewhere. Her face puckered up into an expression of disgust and she muttered something to herself. Carefully she levered herself round, so that her legs hung over the side of the bed, and she slowly lowered them to the floor. Holding the bedside table, she made sure that she could walk. Then she went over to the little writing table. Feeling in one of the drawers, she pulled out a piece of paper and looked at it thoughtfully; she had no idea what it meant, but she was sure it meant something.

It was the letter Alexander had unknowingly dropped from his pocket when he had done his foolish little dance in her room that December night, five long years before. And it was signed—Colovion.

Then, unaided, Countess Turova started to make her way towards the stairs.

* * *

Alexander could not sleep that night; perhaps it was the excitement of what had passed, or perhaps it was merely the season: but a little after midnight he set out from his house and began to walk.

There were others about in that pale gloaming: young couples, even children, walking along the broad embankments of the Neva or beside the silent canals traversed by their little bridges, enjoying the warm magic of those early hours. Sometimes a little party would go by, singing and laughing in the glimmering grayness.

Alexander made his way to the embankment. Slowly he walked along, across the great square where Peter's mighty statue reared up, past the long, bare walls of the Admiralty, and out onto the broad expanse before the Winter Palace and its extension, the Hermitage. On his left lay the wide pale expanse of the Neva. On the Strelka in midriver, a little light was glowing. Now and then people passed by like shadows. And as he stood gazing northward, the little flashes of the aurora, like silent lightning, ignited past the horizon over the arctic wastes.

Unreal season. Unreal city. As he looked back over the last ten years of his life and thought of the strange events of that day, it seemed to Alexander that his whole existence had been like a tiny walk-on part on this huge Saint Petersburg stage set. For wasn't it all just a play? Wasn't poor Empress Catherine, with her young lovers, a pathetic personal sham? Wasn't this enormous city, built on a northern marsh, with its Italian facades gazing over an icebound wasteland, another kind of improbable deception? The city is built on wooden piles, he thought. One day they will rot and it will all fall back into the marshes. Wasn't the enlightened noble class, to which he belonged, the greatest sham of all—speaking of Voltaire, yet ruling as it did over a vast empire of villages and serfs, stuck in the Middle Ages, or even the Dark Ages, if truth be told? Was Peter the Great's vision of Russia as a great continental empire—was the boundless energy and ambition of the Bronze Horseman—just a wild dream, impossible ever of being? As he stared over the river and then looked back at the great open space beside the palace, he suddenly had an overwhelming sense that the vast Russian land of marsh and forest might advance, at any moment, into the emptiness of this unnatural city.

"Why, the whole city," he murmured aloud, "is just a huge Potemkin village—a facade." And if so, what had his life been—his gamble for power, his love of display, his desire for earthly and even heavenly rewards? Was it all a great illusion?

It seemed to him, all that moment, that it was so. As he slowly made his way home, revolving this thought in his mind, he would glance up from time to time to notice a piece of broken-off stucco here, or the rotting bricks on the corners of the houses there, and murmur to himself: "Yes. It is vanity. All is vanity."

And so deep in contemplation of this grand futility was Alexander, that returning at last in the early morning he did not even notice the little carriage standing in front of his house, or the little group of men who stood waiting to receive him: so that he looked up in astonishment as one of them stepped forward and said to him quietly: "State Councillor Bobrov, you are to accompany us. You are under arrest."

The cell was pitch black. There was no light from any source.

He did not know how long he had been there, but since the door had half opened twice and a hand had pushed in a crust of bread and a little pitcher of water, he supposed it must be between one and two days.

The cell was very small. If he stood with his back to the heavy door and reached out his right hand and his left, he could place the palms of each hand flat against the two walls. From this position he discovered he could take two full paces before his head hit the wall opposite. The first few hours he thought there was a rat in one corner; but now he was not sure. Perhaps it had found a hole somewhere and gone away. For this was the dreaded Peter and Paul fortress. He wondered whether the cell was above or below the water level. Below, he thought.

Only one thing puzzled him. Why had they arrested him? For what crime? The arresting officer had not told him—probably had not known. And since they had thrown him in here, no one had spoken to him. There was only one thing to do: keep calm.

Another day passed. No one came. He wondered if they would leave him there to die. Then, at the end of the third day, the door opened and they pulled him out, and a few minutes later he found himself standing, rather unsteadily, in a large room, blinking at the pain of the light and becoming vaguely aware of the fact that, after his confinement, he was stinking. There was a single guard in the room and when Alexander asked him what was going on he replied gruffly: "You'll be questioned."

"Oh. By whom?"

"Don't you know?" The guard grinned. "By Sheshkovsky himself, of course." Then he laughed. "You'll talk."

And now, despite his determination to be calm, Alexander trembled. Everyone knew about Sheshkovsky—the most feared inquisitor in all Russia. The great interrogator had easily broken poor Radishchev, the radical writer. They said that his victims were lucky if they lived. Yet, Alexander reminded himself, I am a noble. By law he can't torture me. He can't give me the knout. The court had to strip him of his noble status before he could suffer those indignities.

He was still thinking nervously about these matters when he felt hands forcing him to sit on a bench. A table with a lamp on it was put in front of him. Then, a moment later, he became aware of another figure in the room—somewhere out in the shadows, past the bright lamp—a figure he could not see but whose voice he could hear.

"So," the voice said quietly, "tell me about Colovion."

In the three weeks that followed, Alexander Bobrov was often confused. Some days they would leave him alone in his cell, but usually they would wait until he was falling asleep and then drag him back to the lighted room and shine the lamp in his eyes, or force him to move about so that he could not sleep.

His inquisitor came at irregular intervals. At first Alexander thought this was a ploy, but after a time it seemed to him that the inquisitor had other business elsewhere, and that he, Alexander, might be of only marginal interest. Yet each time he asked why they were keeping him there, the reply was indirect, and therefore all the more frightening: "I think you know, State Councillor," or, "Perhaps you would like to tell me, Alexander Prokofievich."

They did not use torture: they did not threaten him with the knout. Yet no torture, he realized, can be worse than never being allowed to sleep. As for the interrogator, Alexander understood, now, why he was so feared. It's not what he does to your body, he thought. It's what he does to your soul.

For gradually, session after session, day after day, the inquisitor was taking over his mind.

It was a subtle process. When, for instance, he had denied all knowledge of Colovion, the interrogator had not contradicted him. But toward the end of the session, quietly, imperturbably, he had let him know by a few words that he knew about the professor and the Rosicrucian circle. So he has probably been interrogating the professor too, Alexander realized. Yet how did he know about their connection? There were no written records. Had the professor talked? Perhaps. It began to occur to him that the interrogator might not be seeking information from him at all, but only trying to discover how much he would lie.

It was the same when they discussed other matters. His interrogator wanted to know about the articles he had written, years ago, on subjects like the emancipation of serfs. Yet those articles had been anonymous. No one knew who had written them. How was it then that, each time he denied having done so, the invisible voice would quietly accept his assertion and then, with incredible accuracy, recite a line or two that he had written an entire decade before.

Slowly, as the process continued and the gentle, reasonable voice, never accusing, allowed him to see, again and again, that he knew the truth, Alexander, to his own surprise, began to feel guilty.

By the seventh day it seemed to Alexander that the interrogator knew everything there was to know about him. By the fourteenth day it seemed to his confused brain that the interrogator knew more about him than he did himself. By the twentieth day Alexander knew that the interrogator was all-knowing, godlike. What reason was there to try to hide anything from this voice—this kindly voice, who was only helping him to open his heart and then at last to sleep?

On the twenty-first day he talked.

It was a cool, damp October morning when Alexander Bobrov left the Peter and Paul fortress, with his hands and feet manacled, and sitting in the back of a little open cart. In the front of the cart sat the driver and a soldier with a musket. There were two outsiders.

The sky was gray. The waters of the Neva were high, and above the Admiralty he could see the little flags flying that warned that there was a risk of flooding. For it was not unusual, at such a season, for the waters of the Gulf of Finland to sweep in past Vasilevsky Island and take over the cellars and even the streets of the city of Peter.

Strangely Alexander felt at peace with the world. Though manacled, he sat quite calmly, almost cheerfully, and watched the huge world go by. His clothes were in tatters, his head bare, yet it did not seem to concern him unduly. In the distance, across the river, he caught a glimpse of the Bronze Horseman. There was the Winter Palace and the Hermitage. The empress and her lover Zubov were in there somewhere, no doubt. Good luck to them.

It was odd: he had lost everything, yet he actually felt more comfortable now than he had in years. Here in a cart, his head open to the elements, he felt absolved of all earthly cares. Perhaps it was personal to Alexander, or perhaps it was a trait often found in Russia, but he realized that he only felt truly himself at life's extremes. It was as though he had never really felt comfortable when he was striving for mediocrity, as he had been these last few years. Give me a palace, he considered, or a monk's cell.

Anyway, he had been lucky. He had only been sentenced to ten years.

He had learned of it the day before. For several weeks now, he had been in a small cell with a window. He had not been allowed any visitors, nor any news of the outside world. He still did not even know what crimes he had been charged with. Then, that morning, the interrogator had come and told him his sentence.

"Your trial went well," he blandly announced. Like other such trials, it had been a brief, informal affair at which the accused himself had not been present. "The empress had wanted to give you fifteen years. That's what we gave your friend the professor. But your wife wrote to the empress—a very fine letter, I must say—and so we've been lenient. In fact, you've been even luckier than that. But I'll let your wife tell you about it."

Tatiana had come a few hours later. It was only now that he learned that the countess was still alive. "But she has told everyone in Saint Petersburg that you tried to murder her," Tatiana explained. "She went to the police that very night and told them to arrest you. And then"—she paused—"it seems there were other charges." She looked at him anxiously. "They say you were a Freemason. I do not understand."

He sighed. He thought he was beginning to.

The crackdown of Catherine the Great on the Freemasons in the summer of 1792 was sudden. It was probably caused by Novikov when, under questioning, he had inadvertently revealed the existence of the secret inner order of Rosicrucians. Historical evidence shows that, even afterward, the authorities had only a very imperfect idea of how the order worked. Since the Rosicrucians always burned all their correspondence, the full membership was never established. The links to Grand Duke Paul were never proved; the international network only vaguely understood. But the empress was adamant. The order was secret, its members probably radical; they might be plotting with her son. She trusted no one nowadays. They were to be eliminated.

The business, it must be said, was planned intelligently. The men with important connections, like the prince, were to be quietly exiled to their estates. The bookseller who had sold Masonic tracts would be arrested and let out with a terrible warning. The professor was to be made an example of. "But I wish," the empress had declared, "we had someone to make an example of from Saint Petersburg as well as Moscow."

It was most fortunate therefore, on the very eve of the crackdown, that the inquisitor Sheshkovsky should have come to her with the surprising news: "I think we may have discovered just the man we need. Moreover," he added, "it seems the fellow's a dangerous radical." And the empress, when she heard who it was, had been delighted.

But how, Alexander wondered, had they known so much about him? Tatiana soon supplied the answers.

"Madame de Ronville told me what was happening," she explained. "She came to see me after you were arrested. It seems there was a letter of some kind that the countess had—from Professor Novikov the Freemason. She didn't know what it was, but she showed it to the authorities. She was using anything she could find to have you prosecuted."

Alexander could imagine it.

"Then a man called Sheshkovsky went to see her. Do you know him?"

"Yes. I know him."

"He spent a whole afternoon talking to her. She showed him a lot of articles you had written, years ago. He was very interested."

"I expect he was." He could imagine the scene: the old countess and the skillful interrogator. How easy it would have been for the inquisitor to get the information he wanted out of her. How the subtle fellow must have smiled to himself: and no wonder he had seemed to know everything!

And yet . . . even as Alexander considered the matter, a new and even grimmer thought suddenly came into his mind. Had the interrogator cunningly coaxed the information out of the foolish old lady, or, in a terrible act of irony, was it possible that she had done it deliberately: revealed those articles to him—the very articles she had praised and which represented her own, most passionate views—*knowing* that they would seal Alexander's fate?

He would never know.

"Yes," he said sadly, "she had her revenge."

"There is one piece of good news, though," Tatiana told him. "You are not to be imprisoned in a fortress, like the professor. Guess where your prison is?"

Alexander had looked blank.

"You're to be imprisoned in the monastery"—she smiled—"at Russka."

And so it was, he reflected, as the little cart bumped out of the city on that chilly October morning, that Empress Catherine had, in the end, found a use for Bobrov the gambler after all.

1796

How slow, how quiet was the passing of his years.

He would listen to the bell that tolled the monks to prayer, and by this means he would always know the hour. Yet sometimes it seemed to Alexander that the little monastery was half empty: one day, he fancied, he might wake up to silence—which would tell him that the remaining monks were gone, leaving him alone in his cell with only his strange companion.

The cell was quite spacious; its walls were painted white, and there was a high, barred window. With a small jump he could catch hold of the bars, pull himself up, and look out at the top of the monastery wall and one of the corner towers, also painted white. So he could see the outside world—the sky at least.

They let him have books, but no writing materials. One of the monks gave him a book of psalms. Every month Tatiana, who spent most of the time at Russka, was allowed to visit him, and usually she brought the children. Indeed, if I were ready to be a hermit, I should almost be contented, he thought.

And so the years passed quietly, almost, one could say, untroubled—but for certain thoughts that occurred to him by day; and at night, by a certain dream.

How strange it was to be so near one of his own estates, yet so far. The place was much the same as in former times—and yet it was not. The monastery certainly was only a shadow of its former self. When he had visited it as a young boy, it had still owned the lands around as far as his own estate of Dirty Place. But since Catherine had taken over all the Church lands, the peasants who worked them all belonged to the state now: the monastery was no longer the local landed power, but only a rather forlorn collection of religious buildings, set in the midst of state-owned fields. As a young man he had welcomed the change. "Let the church stick to religion," he had said. But now, even cut off in his cell, he could sense the different atmosphere in the place, and he was not so sure. Part of Old Russia had gone from the land; the monastery had been hollowed out into an empty shell.

It was never a prison before, either, Alexander reflected. But twenty years ago Catherine had decided that the little Russka monastery would be a convenient place to keep prisoners awaiting trial, and it had been used that way ever since. Nowadays, however, there were just two prisoners, both kept in the same cell; Alexander and his curious companion.

Was it chance, or some malicious afterthought of the empress, that had caused Alexander to be put in a cell with this fellow? Probably the latter.

He was very tall and gaunt and a little older than Alexander, with a long, straggling black beard and deep-set black eyes that gazed out from their hollows with a kind of fervent intensity. It had seemed strange therefore, given the complete absence of physical likeness, that he should have announced to Alexander, on their first day together, that he was none other than Catherine's husband, the late Tsar Peter.

He was entirely harmless. At some time the empress must have decided he was a nuisance and locked him up. Perhaps he had been forgotten. Who was he? Alexander guessed he was a state peasant from somewhere in the north. The fellow could not read and write and mostly sat there, staring fervently at the wall: occasionally he would speak, earnestly, about Holy Russia, and denounce the empress as an atheist and a harlot. When he did so, Alexander would quietly nod and say: "Yes, Your Majesty." In his own mind he called the man, like the pretenders of olden times, the False Peter. They shared the cell quite peaceably.

The thoughts that disturbed his peace of mind by day took many months to form. Indeed, at first he was not even aware that they were taking shape.

When Tatiana came, Alexander was taken to another cell, where they were allowed to talk undisturbed. He enjoyed these meetings. Tatiana was always very calm and quietly affectionate. She would sit there with the children and give him news of the outside world. Thus he learned about the terrible events in France: how the Jacobins had executed the king and his poor queen Marie Antoinette. He heard how Catherine and her son Paul were on worse terms than ever, and that it seemed increasingly likely she would try to pass him over for her grandsons. He learned that Poland finally had been completely taken over by her neighboring powers and that most of it was now virtually a Russian province. "One cannot deny," Tatiana remarked, "that Empress Catherine has been hugely successful."

And whenever she came, he never failed, with a playful smile, to ask: "What news, then, from the big city?"

It was their special joke, and it referred not to Saint Petersburg, or even Moscow—nor even to the provincial capital of Vladimir, but to Russka.

For the little town was now, officially, a city. True, it mustered little more than a thousand inhabitants; true, the road that led to it was only a dirt track, so deeply rutted that it was almost unusable—indeed, the river was still the best approach until the snows of winter came; but when Catherine had reformed the local administration fifteen years before, it had been decided that the little backwater should be raised, at least on paper, to the dignity of a city. There were dozens, perhaps hundreds of such cities in the Russian empire now—depressed little villages carrying this grandiose designation, in preparation for the splendid new world that was to come. It was a contrast between official and actual reality that Alexander nowadays found rather amusing. "Have they mended the gate," he would ask, "in the big city?"

How he admired Tatiana. He came to do so more with every month that passed. His father had built a modest wooden house on the slope above Dirty Place—then never used it. But she had completely cleaned it up; she watched over the estates herself; the children seemed healthy. "But aren't you terribly bored down here?" he would ask. "Shouldn't you go to Moscow or Saint Petersburg?"

"Not at all," she always replied. "I find the country suits me very well." And gradually, as the months went by, a new realization began to dawn upon him. "I've sold the Saint Petersburg house," she informed him early in the first year. Then, two months later: "I hope you won't mind, Alyosha, but I've dismissed the steward." A year later, after a good harvest, she told him: "I'm adding two little wings to the old house. I think you'll like them." And to his astonishment, when he once remarked that one day, when he was finally released, he'd try to pay off some of their debts, she smiled, kissed him, and whispered, "We haven't got any, my dearest."

"But how? Who gave us money?"

"No one, Alyosha. The estates are quite profitable, you know. And"— she smiled wryly—"our expenses in the country are modest, you see."

He had said nothing, but after she had gone he sighed to himself and murmured: "The truth is, the best thing I ever did for the Bobrov family was to go to jail." It was an uncomfortable thought, and it was soon followed by another: What use, then, will I be to my family even when I am released? The German girl had taken over.

Though he loved and admired his wife, he came often to ponder this, grimly, by day.

The dream that came to him by night was so absurd that it was laughable. It did not come very often; sometimes weeks, even a couple of months might pass in between occurrences. But whenever the dream reappeared, it was always exactly the same.

It was the countess. She came to him just as she had that night years ago—a pale, insistent vision, staring at him, wagging her finger and hissing with an urgency that was as terrible as it was meaningless: "Voltaire. Voltaire."

Why should this foolish dream upset him so? It was hard to say. Yet each time he had it, he awoke with a sense of emptiness and desolation that was hard to bear; he would awake with a cry that echoed around the monastery, and in the dim light from the dawn, he would find, even in the staring, angry eyes of the False Peter, a certain sense of comfort.

Once, after he had been in the cell for three years, the vision appeared as usual, but instead of speaking, the old countess just stared at him, with a quiet satisfaction; and then, obscenely, as if they were sharing some obscure joke about the world from beyond the grave, it seemed to Alexander that she winked. After that, the dream did not occur again.

It was a little before Christmas, in the year 1795, that Alexander heard a sledge arrive in the courtyard of the monastery; its arrival was followed by a long pause; then, to his surprise, he was taken out of his cell and brought to the one used for visits, and a few minutes later a figure in a fur coat and hat was ushered in.

It was Adelaide de Ronville.

She had been visiting Vladimir. "And you know," she explained with a little shrug, "it's not so far to Russka, in a sled."

Alexander smiled. How moved he was that she should have made the journey. "How did you get in here? Did you bribe the monks?" She nodded. "And where will you stay? You must go to our estate. You can't get back to Vladimir tonight."

"Yes. They are expecting me there."

He did not argue. "Let me look at you," he begged, and he helped her off with her coat.

She stood before him. She was sixty. The lines on her face were more deeply scored, making an intricate network; yet when she turned her face up to his, it seemed to Alexander that, more than ever, the lines only accentuated and further defined what had been there. She made a slightly ironic little gesture with her mouth. "I grow old. These days, you know, there is nothing so wonderful to see."

"I do not agree."

They talked for a little time. He asked after the countess, and learned that she was very frail, but otherwise unchanged. Had she forgiven him? "Of course not." He asked Adelaide about her own life. Had she a new lover?

"Perhaps. Perhaps not. It's not important." They talked quietly, just as usual, until a monk came to indicate that Adelaide must leave. As Alexander held her coat for her again, he lightly touched her arm.

For many hours after Adelaide had gone, he found to his own surprise that he was trembling; and by this he understood, more certainly even than in years gone by, that he would always be the prisoner of this, the nearest that he had come to passion in his life.

On the last day of the year 1796, some seven weeks after the Empress Catherine the Great of Russia died, Alexander Bobrov was released from prison, having completed only four years of his sentence. For one of the first acts of the new tsar, Paul, was to give an amnesty to almost all the enemies of the mother he detested. Alexander went to his estate nearby.

It was just three months later that Countess Turova also died. "Truly," everyone said, "an era has really passed." She left the bulk of her huge estate to Alexander's distant cousin. And a quarter of it to Adelaide de Ronville, who married soon after.

NINE

∾

The Duel

1802

HIGH IN THE BLUE September sky, a pale sun hovered, while from time to time small white clouds drifted over the endless plain.

As they passed, the clouds assumed many forms. One resembled a fish, openmouthed as it crossed the azure sky; another a horse and rider; a third, perhaps, the witch Baba Yaga sweeping by.

They came from the east, in a leisurely procession, past the old frontier city of Nizhni Novgorod, where the mighty Volga meets the sluggish Oka, and into the huge loop in the R of Russian rivers that is the Russian heartland. Westward towards Moscow they came, over ancient Russian cities—Riazan, Murom, Suzdal, and stately Vladimir. And some of them, too, passed over the small, shining ribbon of river that cut through the forest down to the little town of Russka and the village beyond.

Seen from above, how insignificant these places looked: with modest wooden houses and the town, perched on its high riverbank, staring at the little white-walled monastery opposite. How still everything was. Did the sound of the monastery bells, tolling over the trees, reach up to the passing clouds? Surely not. The sky was silent but for the faint hiss of the breeze. For what were the lives, the loves, and the fates of men to those clouds, which came from the vast eastern spaces where the natural order of things is, like the endless sky, unknowable, beyond mere human comprehension?

And could anything be less important than the subject the two peasants were discussing that afternoon? They were speaking of silk ribbons.

They were standing by the riverbank. Behind them was the little village that belonged to Alexander Bobrov. The place had improved recently. There was a wooden footbridge over the river and walkways made of boards traversed the muddiest places. The huts, mostly raised off the ground, were in good repair. One or two, though retaining the arrangement of the traditional peasant *izba,* had an upper floor as well, and elaborately carved shutters as proof of the wealth of their occupants.

The two men were cousins, though separated by two generations. In common with fifteen other families in the village, they shared a descent from the girl Maryushka, the sole survivor of the terrible church fire in the reign of Peter, who had returned to the village long afterward. As it happened, both men had been christened Ivan.

But there the resemblance between the two men ended. Ivan Suvorin was a giant. In him, it might be suggested, the genes of Maryushka's father, once called Ox, had miraculously reproduced themselves without dilution. He was a head taller than any other man in the village. His arms were so powerful it was said he could lift a horse. He could chop down a tree in half the time it took anyone else. As for his face, even his massive black beard could not conceal its heavy features or the huge, shapeless promontory that was his nose.

His cousin, by contrast, was of only medium height and in shape almost perfectly square. He had a mass of wavy brown hair, soft blue eyes, and, when he chose, sang beautifully. He was a kindly man, though given to moods of depression that would lead him to sudden rages or morbid tears. But these would pass as quickly as they had come, and he seldom hurt anyone.

His name was Ivan Romanov.

It pleased him that his name was the same as that of the royal house: but in fact it was not an unusual distinction. The name that the imperial dynasty had chosen in the sixteenth century was among the fifty most common in Russia, meaning simply: "the son of Roman," and pronounced, with the stress on the second syllable, Romahnoff. Nevertheless, Ivan Romanov was proud of it.

The two men were both serfs belonging to Alexander Bobrov. But there again, the similarity ended. For while Romanov worked the land and did wood carvings to help earn money to pay the landlord his *obrok,* Suvorin had been more enterprising. Starting with a single loom in the family *izba,* he had begun to weave cloth and sell it in the little market at Russka. Recently, however, he had discovered he could get a better price in the ancient city of Vladimir, a day's journey away.

And now he wanted to make silk ribbons: and the question was, would his cousin Romanov like to come in with him?

The two men were accompanied by a ten-year-old boy, Suvorin's son. He was called Savva and he was, as far as it was possible to be, a smaller replica of his father. As Romanov looked at the two Suvorins now, there was something about them that, he had to admit, made him feel nervous. What was it in those four piercing black eyes? He wanted to say it was cunning, yet there was no doubt that Suvorin was scrupulously honest. Perhaps they were just calculating. Yet it was more than that. There was something proud yet relentless about them, that was it, something unbending as if to say: "We are tall in stature and in spirit." Whenever he saw them, he remembered his mother's favorite proverb: It's the tallest blade of grass that's the first to be cut down.

"These silk ribbons are very profitable. We could all do well if you care to join us," Suvorin said.

Romanov still hesitated. He could use the money. He looked at them thoughtfully. And it was then that something struck him.

It was the boy: Savva. He was ten years old. And yet Ivan Romanov had never seen him smile.

"No," he said with a smile. "I think I'll just stick to my wood carving."

"Suit yourself," Suvorin replied.

And they parted, not in any anger, but both parties understanding that, the offer having been refused, it would never be made again.

It did not seem significant to Romanov at the time.

It was on that same day that, once again, Alexander Bobrov became a father. More or less.

As he held the child in his hands and inspected it, he felt conflicting emotions. There was, there must be, something wonderful, something holy about a newborn child. As he looked down at Tatiana, who had gone through so much for him during many years, he gave her a kindly smile. "It's a boy," he remarked.

Unfortunately, it was not his.

It had come as a shock to Alexander when, at the end of the previous year 1801, Tatiana had been unfaithful to him. Strangely enough, it had come just as a new hope had entered his life.

The previous five years had been discouraging. Though Tsar Paul had released Alexander from prison, he had shown no desire for the former state councillor's services, and Alexander had remained, feeling rather useless, on the estate that his wife had run so competently without him. In a way, however, he was well out of Saint Petersburg, for the tsar's strange nature had soon turned to morbidness, then madness; and when a group of patriotic officers, in 1801, had murdered him and placed his son on the throne, all Russia had heaved a sigh of relief.

And Bobrov, too, had been filled with excitement. Young Tsar Alexander: the grandson whom Catherine herself had trained: autocrat of all the Russians, yet child of the Enlightenment. Youthful, beautiful to look upon, charming: the complete antithesis of his gloomy, narrow-minded father. The Angel, some called him. The Bobrov family had been planning to spend the winter in Moscow that year. In the month of November, suddenly fired with a new energy, Bobrov had left Tatiana and the children in Moscow and set out for Saint Petersburg alone. Perhaps, now, there would be some appointment for a man of his attainments. For two months he drifted about the capital and received various promises that gave him hope, but nothing definite. In January he had returned.

It was a dashing young captain of Hussars who had found Tatiana alone, and who had quite captivated her before moving on with his regiment to the Ukraine. The officer was witty, amusing, and already had a score of such affairs to his credit. He was twenty-five; Tatiana thirty-one.

The young captain was discreet. One had to say that for him. Indeed, Alexander was not even sure that the affair had actually taken place until the incontrovertible signs began to appear in Tatiana that spring. What should he do? He thought of a duel, but then he learned that the fellow had been killed in a border skirmish; for a week he even dreamed of giving the bastard child away to one of his serf families—that would teach Tatiana a lesson! But he knew he would not. After all, he told himself bitterly, any husband who leaves his wife alone in Moscow for two months is a fool. And besides, he would tolerate no scandal. Nothing more was said about the affair: the baby would be treated as his.

He had already recovered his self-esteem by taking up with a pretty serf girl who worked in the house. Though he was cool towards Tatiana, he remained polite. He told himself that the child was an accident and that it was beneath his dignity to think about it any further.

It only remained to name the boy. The custom was simple: the firstborn son was usually named after his grandfather; others, often, by the saint's day nearest their birth.

"You are fortunate," the priest remarked to them when he came. "His name day is the feast of St. Sergius."

Sergei it was therefore. That gave a name and patronymic of Sergei Alexandrovich, since he was the official father. Not bad.

"Sergei." Tatiana smiled. And then, looking at the child, she called to him, using the diminutive of Sergei: "Seriozha. Come to your mother."

"Of course," Alexander said to her calmly, "this one will not inherit anything of mine. When I die, you will receive a widow's portion. You can provide for him out of that. Meanwhile, I'll provide for his education."

Tatiana inclined her head. The subject was not mentioned again.

And so Sergei Alexandrovich Bobrov came into the world.

Six months later, Alexander resumed relations with his wife. In 1803, a daughter was born. They called her Olga.

1812

MARCH. What tumultuous days they were, these days of war and peace. Who would have guessed that out of the fire of the French Revolution—the fire of liberty, equality, fraternity—would emerge this astounding conqueror who had made the whole world tremble? Napoleon: hero to some, ogre to others. Did he mean, like Julius Caesar or even Genghis Khan, to rule the world? Probably. And though the enlightened Tsar Alexander—the Angel, they still called him—had tried to preserve Russia from the horrors of these European wars, it seemed now, in the early spring of 1812, that Napoleon and his formidable Grand Army were preparing to sweep into Russia from the west.

All Russia trembled. The Orthodox Church of Holy Russia declared that Napoleon was the Antichrist. The tsar called the country to arms. And if there had been some among the gentry who felt that the golden age of Alexander had not lived up to its promise, that the expected reforms had been few and unimportant, all this was suddenly forgotten as, in drawing rooms all over the empire, the tsar once again became the Angel.

It was a chilly, overcast day before the start of spring. The snow still lay, hard, upon the ground, and the Bobrov family were sitting in the salon of their country house, waiting for news.

The house was typical of its kind: a narrow, two-story wooden structure, about eighty feet long. The walls had been painted green; the windows picked out in white. The center boasted a simple classical portico with four pillars, all in wood and painted white, which provided a spacious veranda. Two little single-story wings that Tatiana had added, of two rooms each, extended from the ends. From its position near the top of the wooded slope, the village was hidden by some trees, but there was a pleasant view down to the river. Behind it were various outbuildings. A little to the left was a wooden hut, half submerged into the ground; this was the icehouse, where ice from the frozen river in winter was stored through the warm summer months. On the right of the house was the bathhouse: another squat building made of huge, unpainted logs. So peaceful did this ensemble appear that one might have supposed it had always been there. In fact, however, there had been nothing before Alexander had come, and it represented a profound change in the life of the family and of the village.

For the notion of a country house was still new to Russia. The knight's manor and the magnate's castle, so much the rule in England or France, could be found as far east as Poland—but in old Muscovy they had been completely unknown. As for the country villa of the Renaissance, with its cultivated leisure—the idea would have been unimaginable. Until the eighteenth century, when the Bobrovs visited their estates, they had always stayed in houses within the walled town of Russka. Though a noble who was very poor might find himself living in a village, almost indistinguishable from the peasants, only after the reign of Peter the Great did landowners even begin to live like European squires.

Their country houses were nearly always modest. While Russian rulers and their favorites had palaces that might rival those of Germany or France, the houses of men like Bobrov would have seemed makeshift to an English gentleman. Indeed, their construction and scale were far closer to those of the landowners in the newly freed colonies of America.

Only one thing had spoiled the tranquillity of the Bobrovs—the name of their village: Dirty Place. When they had lived in Russka it had not mattered: but when he came to live on the estate, Alexander had found the name offensive and absurd. He had toyed with various new names before deciding upon one derived from that of his own family: Bobrovo. Bobrovo, therefore, was now the official designation of the village and estate, though some of the older peasants still referred to it as Dirty Place.

Today there was a sense of expectancy in the house. In the area around Moscow, new regiments were hastily being raised. The previous afternoon Bobrov had received a personal letter from the military governor of Vladimir asking him to supply more serfs as recruits. The peasants in the village had been drawing lots that very morning, and shortly he would hear who had been chosen.

His own second son, Alexis, though only nineteen, was proudly serving as an infantry officer. Every time anyone approached the house, Tatiana would rush to the door, hoping the visitor might be bringing a letter from him. Patriotism, excitement, seemed to be in the air.

And yet, in all these preparations, there was one great problem that filled Alexander Bobrov with a special foreboding. "For it's not Napoleon's troops I fear so much," he told Tatiana. "It's our own people." The serfs.

When the story of Napoleon's great invasion of Russia is told, it is often forgotten that, in the months leading up to it, many Russian landowners feared an internal revolution more than they feared the invader. And for this view there was good reason. All over Europe the conquering emperor of the French had claimed to be liberating people from their rulers in the name of the Revolution: to many of them he was a hero. Indeed, of the huge force who were to march with him into Russia in 1812—the legendary Grand Army—fewer than half were French at all. And of all these European contingents, none fought more eagerly than those from the next-door Polish territories—formerly grabbed by Austria and Prussia when unhappy Poland was partitioned—whom Napoleon had indeed liberated. No wonder then if Russian leaders feared that their own subjugated Poles, and their oppressed Russian serfs, might rise in sympathy with this liberating army. "He'll do what Pugachev failed to do, and give us a real revolution," Bobrov had predicted gloomily.

If the outside world was full of danger, however, the salon where the Bobrovs were sitting was a scene of quiet, domestic calm. There were several pieces of rather stiff English furniture, two ancestral pictures, and some somber classical landscapes, all brought from Saint Petersburg. But the general impression of the room was still one of friendly disorder.

Alexander and Tatiana were sitting in armchairs. He wore an old blue English coat, a cravat, and silk stockings; she wore a long, high-waisted pink dress, with a bright shawl draped over her shoulders. In her hands was a piece of embroidery. Near the fire sat their eldest son, twenty-two-year-old Ilya. He had his mother's round face and fair hair. He was reading a book. In Alexander's opinion the young man should have been away fighting, like his brother. But perhaps because, back in '89, she had so nearly lost him at birth, Tatiana had always kept him at home, insisting he was delicate. "He doesn't look delicate to me," Alexander would grumble. "He just looks fat and lazy. It was a pity he had let Tatiana spoil the boy, because Ilya was intelligent. But Alexander could not be bothered to do anything about it now.

And then there was little Sergei. It would have surprised Alexander to know that his face lightened into a smile whenever he looked at this ten-year-old boy. Yet what a bright little fellow he was, with his black hair, his laughing brown eyes—the other Bobrov children's eyes were blue—and his merry ways. He was sitting by the window now, with his sister Olga, inseparable as usual, drawing funny pictures to make her laugh.

Lastly, close by the children, sat a plump peasant woman in her early forties. This was the children's nanny, Arina. A few minutes earlier, she had been telling the children one of her inexhaustible fund of fairy stories, and Alexander, too, had half listened, marveling as he always did at the richness of the Slav folk tradition.

On the nanny's lap sat a baby girl of one, an orphaned niece that the Bobrovs had allowed her to bring to live in the house, and to whom she had given her own name: Arina.

It was a pleasant scene. On a table in the center of the room, in woven baskets, were rice and egg pirozhki and other pastries; on a plate, some cinnamon crescents; on another, an apple pie. In a little bowl was some raspberry syrup, with which Tatiana liked to flavor her tea, and slices of lemon for everyone else. For Alexander there was also a little flask of rum. And on a little side table stood the most important item of all: the samovar.

It was a splendid one. Alexander had bought the samovar in Moscow and was very proud of it. It stood some two feet high, was silver, and shaped rather like a Grecian urn. Heated by charcoal, the water in the samovar was always boiling hot, and from time to time Tatiana herself would go to fill the teapot with a fresh supply from the samovar's tap.

So, on that cold, snowy day, the family quietly awaited news from the outside world.

It was little Sergei who, glancing out of the window, suddenly stood up and said: "Look, Papa. Visitors."

Several things were striking about Ivan and Savva Suvorin. The first was that, at twenty, Savva was now as tall as his father, so there were two giants in the village. The second was that, unlike most Russian peasants who wore felt or bast shoes, the Suvorins both wore stout leather boots, which proclaimed their wealth. The third was that each wore a huge hat: the father's shaped like a bulbous dome, the son's high and rounded, with a large brim—almost like an old English Puritan's hat—so that as they walked along they resembled nothing so much as a tall wooden church and belltower, moving along.

Both wore heavy black coats. From the older man's belt hung a bag of coins. He made no secret of the fact that he had money. What was concealed, however, was the equal quantity of coins that were sewn into the inside of the other's clothing. "God knows if we shall need it," Ivan remarked. "You can never tell with that greedy wolf."

For the rich serf was going to see his master Bobrov; and the money was to save his son's life.

"Cheer up, Savva," he added. "You drew the lot; it was fate, but I can save you. It may be expensive, but better a serf than dead—eh?" To which his son did not reply.

Savva very seldom smiled: he could not see the point. Though he was only twenty, something in his square young face suggested that on this matter, as upon most, his opinion had long ago been formed. With his black hair, his huge nose, and his black, watchful eyes, he was already as formidable as his father. His mouth was usually pursed into a thin line of silent defiance, and his firm, determined walk somehow suggested that, wherever he was going, it was because he didn't much care for the place he was coming from.

It was in silence, therefore, that they completed their walk up the slope to the house of Alexander Bobrov.

Alexander Bobrov could scarcely believe it had happened. Fate, for once, must have decided to smile upon him. As he gazed at the two Suvorins who now stood before him in his study, he had to fight to suppress a grin.

For this could only mean one thing. Money. The question was: how much?

Bobrov was not a greedy man. Though he had once dreamed of riches, he had always rather despised money grubbing, as such. But time, failure, and children to provide for had left their mark, so that it might be said, nowadays, that he was sporadically greedy.

"So, Suvorin, your son doesn't want to be a soldier?" he remarked pleasantly. He turned to Savva. "You would get your freedom, you know," he added.

Since the time of Peter the Great, when a fixed proportion of all the souls in Russia became liable for military service, it was the rule that the serfs chosen—usually, as at Bobrovo, by lot—were granted their freedom upon discharge. But what was that worth when the twenty-five-year service was usually a sentence of death? Men had been known to mutilate themselves to avoid this fate. And now young Savva had drawn the unlucky lot: and Alexander Bobrov could hardly believe his luck.

For though the Suvorins were owned by Bobrov, they had money. Their achievement in the last ten years had been considerable. Not only did they turn out large quantities of silk ribbons, but they now ran a whole network of other serfs, taking their cloth to Vladimir market in return for a cut of the profits. Suvorin had a dozen looms working for him these days, and he was adding more all the time.

All of which suited the landowner very well. For whatever he does, he knew, he still belongs to me.

The rich serf was profitable to Alexander for a very simple reason. For while the serfs down on the Riazan estate still paid their dues with three days' *barshchina* labor, he nowadays made all the Bobrovo serfs give him a cash *obrok:* and the amount of the *obrok* to be paid was set, exactly as he pleased, by the landowner! Twice in the last three years he had raised Suvorin's *obrok;* both times the fellow had grumbled but paid. "God knows what he's still hiding from me," Alexander had complained. Now was the chance to find out.

For there could be only one reason for this visit. Bobrov knew it very well: and he intended to enjoy every moment of it. He leaned back in his chair, half closed his eyes, mildly inquired—"So, what can I do for you?"—and waited. And just as Bobrov had known he would, Suvorin bowed low, and announced: "I have come, Alexander Prokofievich, to buy a serf."

Then Alexander Bobrov smiled. For he had serfs to sell.

It had taken many centuries, but by the turn of the nineteenth century the legal position of the Russian peasant had finally reached its low point. Peasants now—whether serfs owned by a landlord or state peasants bound to crown land, whether well-off like the Suvorins or semi-starving—were all virtually slaves. A serf had almost no rights at all. Bobrov knew one landowner who insisted on a first night with every serf girl when she was married. He had heard of an old lady who had sent two serfs to Siberia because they forgot to bow to her carriage as it passed. The landlord was employer, judge, and executioner. Indeed, even the one right he did not have—that of sentencing a serf to death—was easily circumvented by whipping the offender until, by accident, he died.

Above all, serfs could nowadays be bought and sold like chattels. A pretty girl or a man with special skills could fetch a high price. In a celebrated case, a magnate had sold an entire serf orchestra for a fortune.

Of course, it was wrong. It was monstrous. In his radical days, in the salons of Catherine's Saint Petersburg, Alexander would have conceded as much. Nowadays, it was well known, the tsar himself considered the practice of serfdom utterly repugnant.

"But he can't change it, not yet. The gentry won't let him," Alexander would correctly argue. And in the meantime, I must provide for the family, he told himself. At least on the Bobrovo estate, serfs were seldom flogged and never killed.

In all this terrible selling of souls, probably no practice was more common than the selling of men as military recruits. And it was not the landlords who usually bought these.

It was other serfs.

For the recruiting officer cared not a rap whence the soldier came. As long as he had a body for cannon fodder, it was enough. A rich serf like Suvorin, therefore, did not let his sons go to war. He simply went to the landowner and bought another fellow to go in his place.

So here he was, and the only question was, how much? Slowly Bobrov considered, while the Suvorins waited.

It was quite by chance that, at this moment, Tatiana and young Sergei should have entered the room. The landlord's wife had run the estate long enough to guess what business the Suvorins must have called upon. She had always rather liked the stern couple. Perhaps it was her Baltic ancestry, but their businesslike ways appealed to her. She looked at her husband inquiringly. As for young Sergei, he just smiled at them cheerfully, as he did at everyone.

And why was it that their entry should have caused Bobrov to change his price? Was it a sudden memory of his humiliation at Sergei's birth? Was it a sense of his failure at his career and his wife's success at running the estate when he was in prison? Whatever the cause, instead of the five hundred rubles he had thought of asking for, he calmly announced: "The price is a thousand rubles."

The two serfs gasped. He had struck home this time; he could see it in their faces. The amount, of course, was outrageous. The top rate being asked for substitutes, even by the greediest landlords, was about six hundred rubles at that time. But it was not unknown for landlords to charge even greater sums if they thought the purchaser might have the means.

"Of course," he added coolly, "I could just decide to send Savva anyway." It was within his power. Then he watched as the two serfs looked at each other.

They had brought eight hundred rubles. To get another two hundred they would have to dig under the floorboards. It was all they had in the world.

"I could bring such a sum tomorrow, Alexander Prokofievich," Suvorin said glumly.

"Very well, I will send for one of the Riazan serfs to take Savva's place." Alexander concealed his smile, but he felt a glow of triumph. It was not easy to run the estate better than his unfaithful wife, but he had discovered that milking the richer serfs was one way. And he had certainly got the better of Suvorin today. In his triumph over the serf, he scarcely gave young Savva more than a glance.

Savva looked at the Bobrovs. Tatiana he did not mind. She was fair and she was practical. He correctly saw, from the distant look on her face, that she had no part in this. But the rest of them, father and sons, he hated and despised. He might have admired them, although they oppressed him, if they were strong. But he knew that they were not. He glanced at Sergei. Somehow he looked different. His bright brown eyes were watching him with apparent amusement: was the boy laughing at him?

Savva knew little of the past. Back in Peter the Great's time, his grandmother had told him, her grandmother had escaped from fire when the villagers burned themselves in the church. Then she had returned here later. "We've been here as long as the Bobrovs," she used to say. But that was all he knew. Of his earlier ancestors, cheated by a Bobrov one Saint George's Day in the faraway reign of Ivan the Terrible, he knew nothing. He had never heard of Peter the Tatar and his severed head. All that was lost, long forgotten, buried in the ground.

What Savva knew was that these Bobrovs were his enemies: he knew it in his soul. And as he looked at them now, he made a simple, irrevocable decision. He would be rid of them. It might take him many years; he would need to be cunning and to be strong; but he had strength and endurance.

Master versus serf: it would be a duel, perhaps to the death.

1812

OCTOBER. Somber blue-gray skies; dark trees. First refugees had come by, then troops, each followed by complete silence—as when, after a shot has been fired and its echo died away, one continues to listen intently and the silence seems so much greater because one hears nothing.

The Russians had fought; they had defended the fatherland; the serfs had been loyal. And was it not natural to fight when they saw before them not only the French, but their traditional enemies from the ancient days of Alexander Nevsky and Ivan the Terrible—the German Prussians and the Poles?

First there had been the day when news came of the huge but inconclusive battle of Borodino; soon afterward that Napoleon had entered Moscow. And then, the fire.

It could be seen from over thirty miles away—that tower of fire and smoke that rose, for three days, like a vast pillar into the September sky to announce that Moscow itself was burned down and that the mighty conqueror had been robbed of his prize. Still the emperor of the French lurked in the charred city. What would he do next?

Russka had been busy. Troops had come streaming through as the Russian army prepared to shadow the foe along the great curve of the river Oka. A few days earlier a whole regiment of infantry in their green coats and white leggings had come swinging by. Then squadrons of cavalry.

It was one October morning, during these days, that Sergei and his sister Olga were sitting with Nanny Arina and her baby girl by the fire in the nursery.

There had been fresh news, and fresh rumors, every day. Napoleon was still cooped up in the burned and empty city of Moscow. Would he try to strike up at Saint Petersburg, where the tsar was fortifying the approaches? Would he try to pull back to Smolensk? If so, the crusty old veteran General Kutuzov and the main Russian army were waiting for him on the way. Or would he attempt to sit out the winter in Moscow?

How thrilling it all was. Sergei was so excited, so eager to see Kutuzov, or even the French, that Alexander had laughingly told him: "You won't be satisfied until Napoleon himself has paid a visit to Russka!"

"If he comes, we'll all fight, won't we?" he had anxiously asked. He would stand, side by side with his father, and protect his mother and sister to the end. Which had just caused Alexander Bobrov to laugh and ruffle the boy's hair. "I daresay we should, Seriozha," he had replied affectionately.

The last few days had been quiet, though. No troops came by. Russka was as silent as usual.

Sergei was a passionate little fellow. He not only loved his family: he was in love with them. His mother at forty-two had matured into a classic, rather Germanic beauty. She was unlike any other woman the boy had seen and, for some reason too wonderful to understand, she seemed to treat him with a special softness that gave him a secret pride. Then there was stern Alexis, away at the wars. Alexis was tall and dark like their father. Sometimes Sergei was a little afraid of Alexis, who could be rather cold and aloof. But hadn't he the right to be? He was an officer. A hero.

Here at home was Ilya. Some people laughed at his fair-haired brother because he did nothing and was so fat. But Sergei didn't. "He's read so much," he would say in wonderment. "He knows absolutely everything."

And then there was his father. It always seemed to Sergei that Alexander Bobrov was everything a nobleman should be. He would look splendid, like Alexis, in uniform. Yet he was cultivated like Ilya. He would be stern; yet, with that ineffable little Bobrov gesture of the hand, he could seem wonderfully gentle. He had suffered in prison for his beliefs. And above all, he had that most desirable of all qualities in the eyes of the schoolboy: he was a man of the world. How lucky he was to have such a father.

These were his heroes. There remained his childhood playmate, the little girl with the long, dark brown hair and the sparkling eyes: little Olga. He called her little because she was a year younger and he felt

protective towards her. Yet at times she was like an extension of himself.
Each always knew what the other was thinking.

How lucky, how supremely blessed by God he was to be one of such
a family.

Sergei and Olga sat on each side of Arina. As usual, she had been
telling them a story. How comforting her dear, shiny, round face was!
She was going gray, she had lost a front tooth that summer, yet she was
always the same. "Pretty I never was," she would admit cheerfully. How
old was she? The two children often tried to guess or to trick her into
telling them. But all she would ever say was, "I'm as old as my tongue,
my dear, and a little older than my teeth." Perhaps she didn't even know
herself.

And she was just about to start a new tale when, suddenly, they heard
a commotion downstairs and then, suddenly, his mother's voice, crying
out: "Alexis."

How handsome he looked. How utterly splendid in his fur-lined coat. In
the gray light of the hall, with his dark, brooding features and deep-set
blue eyes—like some warrior from another age, a *bogatyr,* from the days
of ancient Rus. Sergei was beside himself with excitement to see his hero.

Alexis even smiled at him. "Here," he called out, and to Sergei's surprise he produced a musket ball. "This is a French bullet. Just missed me
and hit my supply wagon." Sergei took it with delight.

"Did you see Napoleon?" he cried.

"Yes." Alexis grinned. "He's nearly as fat as Ilya."

Soon, round the dining-room table, he gave them all the news. After
the battle of Borodino, he proudly told them, old General Kutuzov had
actually complimented him in person. Since Moscow fell, he had been
specially picked to carry out sorties against the French. And now he came
to the most exciting news of all.

"Napoleon's leaving Moscow. The French are going home." Alexis
nodded thoughtfully. "It's too late, though. Napoleon's supplies are already low and he must think he can make a dash for the border before
the snow comes." He smiled at Sergei. "If so, Seriozha, he's forgotten one
thing." He paused. "Our Russian mud. He'll get bogged down. Our
Cossacks will destroy every sortie he sends to find food. Then winter will
get him long before he even reaches Smolensk."

"And will we engage again?" Tatiana asked anxiously.

"Yes. Probably. But if there's another big battle like Borodino, we'll
crush him this time."

Soon Alexis had to hurry on. He could not even stay the night. The
family watched as he and his father embraced and Alexander Bobrov
gave his brave son his blessing. Then he was gone, and as always happens
when a soldier departs, each of them wondered if they would see him
again.

It was at dusk that young Sergei came upon his father, standing alone
on the veranda, gazing out at the last glow of the sunset. Alexander did
not see him. There were tears in his eyes, and he was muttering to
himself: "A true Bobrov. A true Bobrov."

And for the first time it occurred to Sergei that perhaps his father might love Alexis more than him; and he wondered what he could do to be worthy of this greater love.

Three weeks had passed; the first snows had fallen, and the shattered Grand Army of Napoleon was already reduced to a dark, straggling mass, leaving corpses along its route as a snail leaves a trail, when the Bobrovs were surprised to receive a very different sort of visit.

It was young Savva Suvorin.

Alexander Bobrov had decided that he really did not like the Suvorins. Perhaps he felt a little guilty for the way he had treated them over the recruit substitute. But there was something dark and calculating behind their reserve that made him feel uneasy. An instinct told him that they neither feared nor respected him. He was not inclined to help them, even though his wife would laugh and remind him: "They're the best source of income you've got."

Now he stood before Bobrov, this solemn, twenty-year-old serf, with a strange gravity already in his walk, calmly making a most extraordinary request.

"I wish, lord, to ask for a passport. To visit Moscow."

As a serf, Savva could not travel anywhere without a passport from his owner. He even needed one to go to the regional city of Vladimir. It did not seem a matter of great significance, but Bobrov looked at him with suspicion. "What the devil for?" The whole city had just burned down!

Savva permitted himself a half smile. "Exactly, lord. So if there's one thing the people there will need, it is warm clothes. We should get a good price for our cloth just now."

Bobrov snorted with disgust.

How typical. Here they were, in the middle of the great patriotic war, and all this fellow could think about was profit.

"That's profiteering."

"Just business, lord," the serf replied calmly.

"Well I won't have it," Alexander snapped, and then, casting about for another reason: "It's unpatriotic." With which he waved the serf away.

And why, he always wondered afterward on this trivial matter, had Tatiana decided that evening to interfere? Perhaps it was some instinct, or just that she felt sorry for Savva. But as soon as he told her about it she had begun to plead: "I beg you to reconsider." Until at last he had given way and signed a passport. It did not seem very important.

1817

THE plan that young Sergei Bobrov had hit upon was daring—but with careful timing it should work. Two friends would answer for his whereabouts, a third would answer his name at a roll call. By bribing one of the school servants he had secured horses for each stage of the journey out and back.

The school at the tsar's summer residence of Tsarskoe Selo, near Saint Petersburg, was both strict and elite. It adjoined the great blue-and-white Catherine Palace, and not only had the tsar given its pupils the use of his own library but the imperial family would come to watch the chapel services from a private gallery above. Alexander Bobrov had had to pull some strings to get young Sergei in there.

The illicit journey would not be easy. It was April. The snow was melting and everywhere the ground was sodden. The roads were like a quagmire. And if he got caught . . .

From under his bed he pulled out the box in which he kept his personal papers. There was the letter to his parents he had begun the previous evening. And there was the letter from his little sister, smuggled in three days before. Written in her large, childish handwriting, it was quite brief and to the point.

Dear Seriozha,
I am very unhappy. I wish I could see you.
                                        Olga

He read it again and smiled. Life at the prestigious Smolny convent school for girls in the city of Saint Petersburg could be grim. He was not surprised that his lively, bright-eyed little sister was hating her first year. And though the risks might be great, he had only asked himself one question when he received the letter: what would Pushkin do? For Pushkin would have gone to her. Pushkin was his hero.

Sergei Bobrov was happy at Tsarskoe Selo. He was quick, intelligent, and even had talent. He could draw well and make up a verse in French or Russian better than any other boy in his class. "But if only I could do these things like Pushkin," he would sigh. Pushkin: the boy writer of daring verses; the cartoonist. Pushkin with his mop of curly hair, his soft but brilliant eyes, his wayward humor. He was always getting himself into scrapes—and always after women, too. That year was his last at the school, and though some of the masters thought he was a mischief-maker, to the boys he was already a celebrity.

It was thanks to a common interest that Pushkin had taken notice of Sergei—a love of Russian folktales. His nanny Arina, the serf woman, had taught Sergei most of what he knew: the tale of the fabulous firebird, the hero Ilya of Murom—"You should see my fat brother Ilya for a real comparison with the legendary hero!" he would laugh—and countless others. Even Pushkin was impressed with his knowledge. "Always keep those folktales in your mind, my young versifier," he would say. "They contain the true spirit, the special genius of Russia." It was Pushkin, however, who had led Sergei into serious trouble. It had begun with a cartoon—scandalous but lighthearted—that Pushkin had drawn after the final defeat of Napoleon. It showed the angelic Tsar Alexander returning in triumph—but having grown so fat in the west that the triumphant arches were hastily being widened for him! It was some months later that Sergei followed his hero. His target, however, was the new and intensely pious minister of education—one of the noble Golitsyn family. And his cartoon showed the minister making a detailed personal inspection of the girls at the Smolny school, to ascertain their morals! It was outrageous, and though few of the teaching staff at the school had any love for the authoritarian minister, he was solemnly warned: "Any more trouble from you, Bobrov, and you'll be expelled."

Whatever the risk of trouble, however, Sergei knew what he must do. It'll be all right, he told himself. And anyway, I won't let Olga down.

The early morning was still dark when Sergei slipped out. A groom was waiting for him with a horse half a mile from the school and soon he was clattering down the road to Saint Petersburg. The road was empty. Sometimes he passed between long, dark lines of trees that seemed about to come together and smother him. Then the land would open out into a waterland of dark brown spaces traversed by gray gashes of unmelted snow. More than once he half expected to hear the cry of a wolf. The icy wet air stung his face.

And yet he was happy. A day before, he had sent a message to Olga, telling her where to meet him, and in his mind's eye he could see her pale face and hear her voice saying: "I knew you would come." It made him feel warm inside. How lucky he was to have such a beautiful sister. How happy he was to be a Bobrov.

And how fortunate to be alive—and a Russian—at such a time! Never had the world looked so exciting. The great threat of Napoleon had finally been laid to rest in 1815 at the battle of Waterloo. Now the British had put the disturber of Europe on the distant Atlantic island of Saint Helena, from which there would be no escape. Russia, meanwhile, was now stronger than ever before in her history. Down in the southeast, in the Caucasus Mountains, the ancient kingdom of Georgia had at last been joined to Russia's empire. In the north, Finland, long under Swedish control, had also been taken over by the tsar. In the distant east, across the sea, Russia not only possessed Alaska but had now established a fort in California, too. And, most splendid prize of all, at the great Congress of Vienna where, after Napoleon, the assembled powers had redrawn the map of Europe, Russia had been given almost the whole of her ancient rival Poland, with her lovely capital of Warsaw.

But what really excited young Sergei was Russia's new place in the world. No longer the barbarous Asiatic kingdom cut off from the Western world; no longer the backward pupil of Dutch and German adventurers, English and French. At the congress the Russian tsar had taken the lead. More even than this, Russia had proclaimed her own special mission.

"Let us put a final end to these terrible wars and bloody revolutions," the tsar had proclaimed to the governments of Europe. "Let the European powers come together in a new and universal brotherhood, founded solely on Christian charity."

This was the famous Holy Alliance. It was, by any standards, an astonishing document. Russia even proposed a shared European army—the first international peacekeeping force—to police this universal order.

Admittedly such grand ideas had existed before, in the days of the

Roman Empire or the medieval church; but the Holy Alliance with its mystical language was profoundly Russian. And if the devious diplomats of the West signed it with a cynical smile, and the pragmatic British refused even to do that, every Russian knew that the West was corrupt. Simple, straightforward, warmhearted, fervent: the Holy Alliance was the Russians at their best. No wonder that young Sergei Bobrov the schoolboy felt exalted.

The city of Saint Petersburg was already in sight, under a platinum sky, when Sergei reached the post house where he changed horses; and the harsh, bright morning was well advanced by the time he entered the capital.

The Smolny convent school lay some three miles east of the Winter Palace, at the far end of the Neva basin, where the river curved around to the south. Since he had time, Sergei took a leisurely route along the embankment beside the pink granite of the quays, past the great statue of the Bronze Horseman, the old Admiralty, and the palace. The Admiralty—though it still contained shipyards—was being refashioned to a severe neoclassical design, surmounted by a high, golden fleche to echo the slim golden spire of the Saint Peter and Saint Paul Cathedral across the water. Sergei breathed a sigh of contentment. How wonderful it was to be in Saint Petersburg.

There was another reason, too, for his excitement.

For in the northern capital of Saint Petersburg, in the month of April, it was the season of the breakup of the ice. Though much of the snow and slush had been cleared from the gray streets, there remained, through the center of the city, the great white lagoon of the frozen Neva, and at this time it began to melt. The roads across it had been dismantled. Soon, before the ice floes began to move, they would take up the pontoon bridges too. And today, as he rode along the embankment, he could see great fissures across the Neva's surface and, from time to time, hear a great crack, loud as a pistol shot, as another section broke up. How thrilling it was, on this chilly, damp morning, to feel the wet air on one's face and know that here, too, the huge northern world, in its own indomitable fashion, was making life anew. As Sergei rode along, his young heart was dancing.

And it was dancing with excitement still as he came to the long, closed wall of the Smolny convent.

He had told Olga in his message exactly where to go and when. Pushkin himself had told him about the little window in the wall where one could enter unobserved. Sure enough, it was there, about twelve feet up. Having left his horse at an inn, therefore, Sergei discreetly made his way to this spot and waited. He waited an hour. Then at last the window opened.

There were two hours before she would be missed. They sat side by side in the little whitewashed room, his arm around her shoulder, and her head from time to time resting upon his chest as they talked softly together.

He loved her. Of the other Bobrovs, she resembled Alexis the most.

Her build was slender though there was nothing weak about her long limbs and elegant, tapering hands. She had her brother's slightly Turkish features with a long chiseled nose, and a mouth that turned down with faint irony at the corners; but whereas there was a trace of cruelty in Alexis's face, in hers there was only refinement. Her eyes were deep blue and sometimes seemed a little startled at the world, although they could suddenly become transformed into a glowing gaiety. And how gratefully, now, they looked up at him.

She was not happy. No wonder. The education at the Smolny school was outstanding. As well as the embroidery, dancing, and cooking one might expect young ladies to learn, the girls were taught languages, geography, mathematics, and physics—a progressive education that astonished visitors even from America. But the discipline was harsh. "We sing psalms before every meal," Olga said sadly. And then, shaking her head: "It's a prison." For from autumn until the end of spring, when the school year ended, the Smolny girls were virtually locked in the convent precincts. "I hate them all, even the other girls," she whispered.

He understood that she was only lonely. He held her gently, her long brown hair falling across his arm, and let her talk for nearly an hour until, gradually, she became more cheerful and even began to laugh. Then, nestling close to him, she murmured: "Enough of my boring life, Seriozha. Talk to me. Tell me about the world."

It made him so proud, to know that she looked up to him. And since his own mind was so full of such ideas, it was no time before Sergei was excitedly outlining to her his hopes for the future.

"The tsar will create a new Russia," he told her. "Serfdom is going. There'll be a new constitution. Look at what he's already done in the Baltic states and in Poland. That's the future."

For as well as now abolishing serfdom in the Lithuanian and Baltic territories, Tsar Alexander had just amazed everyone by granting the newly acquired kingdom of Poland a very liberal constitution, with almost no censorship, an elected assembly, and votes for a wide section of the population.

"And that's only the start," Sergei assured her. "When Russia itself gets a new constitution, we shall be like Britain, or even America!"

The enthusiastic claim was not as wild as it sounded. The enlightened Tsar Alexander had in fact sought the advice of English diplomats, and of President Jefferson of the United States, about how to devise a new government. Years ago his talented minister Speransky had drawn up a proposal that included separated powers, an elected parliament—a duma—and even elected judges. Even now, an official group had started to prepare a plan for dividing Russia into twelve provinces that would each have considerable autonomy. True, the tsar was enigmatic—one could not be sure quite where he stood. But this was Russia, where all change was slow and difficult.

"And what will your part be, Seriozha, in this wonderful new Russia?" Olga asked.

Oh, he knew that. He was certain about his own life. "I'm going to be a great writer," he said boldly.

"Like your friend Pushkin?"

"I hope so. Do you realize," he went on, enthusiastically, "that until the time of Catherine, Russian literature hardly existed! There was nothing but a lot of moldy old psalms and sermons in Church Slavonic—the devil to understand. People like us wrote verse or plays in French. No one wrote a thing worth reading in actual Russian until Lomonosov, when father was young, and dear old Derzhavin the poet, God bless him, who's still with us. So you see," he exclaimed happily, "it's for us to begin. No one can tell us what to do. You should hear Pushkin's verse. It's extraordinary."

Olga smiled. She loved to watch her brother and his enthusiasms. "You'll have to work hard at it, Seriozha," she said thoughtfully.

"Of course." He grinned. "And what are you going to do, when you get out of this convent-prison?" he asked playfully.

"Get married of course."

"But who?"

"A handsome officer, in the guards." She smiled. "Who writes poetry in Russian."

He nodded thoughtfully and then, to his surprise, felt sad. I wish I could be that man, he thought.

Soon afterward it was time to go.

The afternoon was drawing in when, tired but happy, Sergei returned the horse and walked the last half mile through the cold slush towards the school. No one was about; he slipped inside and made his way towards his quarters, where his friends would be waiting. With luck he had not even been missed. There was the door. He opened it. And started with surprise.

The high room was empty, except for a single, tall, slim figure in riding boots and uniform who stood by the gray lightness of the window and who now slowly turned toward him.

"Alexis!" His heart gave a jump; a little wave of joy swept over him. "How long have you been here?"

And then, suddenly, his smile faded.

"Where have you been?" Alexis's voice was cold, cutting as a razor.

"Nowhere."

"Liar. They've been searching the school for you for two hours."

"I'm sorry." Sergei hung his head. There was nothing he could say.

"Being sorry is useless," Alexis said with a cold rage. "I came to see you as I happened to be here on business. While I've been waiting, I have heard a good deal about you. You drew cartoons of the minister and you're under threat of expulsion. I suppose you know that?"

"Yes."

"I persuaded them not to expel you. You ought to be whipped. I offered to do it myself—for the family honor." He paused, waiting, it seemed, for this last statement to have its full effect.

What was it, at that moment, that prompted Sergei to say something that he didn't even mean? Was it irritation with Alexis's lecturing tone, the shock of being caught, the fear of his punishment, or, perhaps, a sudden impulse to strike out because the brother he loved and worshiped was seemingly turning against him? Whatever the cause, he suddenly blurted out: "To hell with the family honor!"

Alexis gasped. He had not gone to a school like this; he had gone, as soon as he could, into his regiment. Service to the tsar, family honor—these were his gods. He had no idea how it was possible for this boy to be so disloyal. Yet what was it that now made Alexis do the unforgivable? Was it a row he had had with a superior officer the day before and his fear for his own career? Was it a mistress who had dismissed him contemptuously the week before? Was it a streak of cruelty in his nature that secretly had been awaiting an excuse to inflict pain ever since, six months before, he had heard for the first time a certain piece of information in Moscow? Whichever of these, in a voice that was both icy and venomous he hissed: "That may be. But to me, to the rest of us, it matters a great deal. And kindly remember that, though you are not one of us, you still carry our name and we expect you to behave accordingly. Do you understand?"

"What do you mean, 'not one of us'?"

"I mean, you brown-eyed little interloper, that you are not—to our parent's shame, a Bobrov. But—because we do care about honor—we treat you as if you were." And then, coldly, as if it were a head cold that he had caught one day and lost: "At a time when she was lonely our mother committed an indiscretion in Moscow. Long ago. It was over at once. Nobody knows. You don't belong, but we pretend you do. And since we have lent you our name, you will honor it." He paused. "If you ever breathe a word of this to anyone, I will kill you."

Then, having wantonly destroyed, he left.

Later that night, finishing his letters home, which, through cold tears, he found difficulty in seeing, Sergei wrote:

> I am very happy here at school, my dear parents. Today I saw Alexis, who is also well, and this, too, made me happy. Give my love to Arina and her little niece.

He had always supposed his mother was perfect and that his parents loved him. Perhaps, if he was not a Bobrov, if he was unwanted, it scarcely mattered what he did with his life.

1822

JANUARY. Tatiana gazed around the little marketplace. For the first time after a month of dull days the morning sky was clear and all around Russka the snow was shining. Savva the serf was about to get into his sled. He was returning to Moscow. How smart he looked in his new coat. He turned and made her a low bow, and she smiled.

For they shared a secret.

Though Russka was quiet that morning, there were many indications that nowadays it was a busier place than before. True, the walls frowning from the high riverbank were still as stout as in the time of Ivan the Terrible; the tall, forbidding watchtower with its steep tent roof still rose into the sky; but within the walls there were two wide streets of wooden houses on each side of the market, intersected by three more. Behind the church there was now a broad avenue with rows of trees down the center and on one side three neat stone merchants' houses with classical features. At the end of this avenue was a small park, and past that the old fortification wall had been lowered and a small esplanade laid out with a pleasant view over the river and the surrounding countryside. Outside the walls, on the side away from the river, the scattered huts and small holdings had grouped themselves into several lanes that petered out into fields about a quarter of a mile away. The total population was about two thousand. In short, though certainly not the city designated by Catherine, Russka had still managed to assume the character of a small town.

Dear Savva: how close they had grown in the last four years. She was rather lonely sometimes. Alexander had become sick and this had made him rather uncommunicative. Sergei was employed in the foreign ministry nowadays, which kept him busy in Saint Petersburg and Moscow. Olga had recently married a handsome young guards officer with an estate near Smolensk, so she was absent. And Alexis, now married, had been posted down to the Black Sea, at the great port of Odessa. The previous month he had had a son, whom he had named Mikhail. But it might be years before Tatiana saw her first grandchild. "So there's only Ilya and me, really," she thought sadly. And though Ilya was at home, his large, placid head was usually in a book; one couldn't talk to him about anything practical.

But Savva and his father were practical: that was what she liked about them. They ran two little factories in Russka now, each employing a dozen people. One wove woolen cloth, the other linen. And the two men were so well organized that they still had time to spare. Indeed, the previous year she had persuaded her husband to let Savva's father go down to supervise the Riazan estate—with the result that its revenues immediately rose sharply. She often went into Russka to watch the Suvorins' activities and talk to Savva about his business.

And it was these talks that had first led to a great realization, and her present secret plan.

For—though one would never have guessed it in the country houses of the gentry—Russia was slowly changing; and the change was taking place in the very region in which she lived.

There had always been several sources of wealth in Russia. The salt beds and the furs in the huge northern wilderness, which had once made the merchants of ancient Novgorod rich; the wonderful black earth; the chernozem, of the warm Ukraine; and since the time of Ivan the Terrible there had gradually been added the minerals of the Ural Mountains, far to the east, and some very modest trade from the huge, barely colonized wastes of Siberia that lay beyond.

Yet it was here in the old Russian heartland around Moscow, where the weather was terrible and the land was poor, that the greatest strides were now being made. For here was the home of Russian manufacturing.

Leather goods, metalwork, icon painting, cloth, linen, the printing of silks imported from the East, and, most recently, cotton manufacture: these were light industries that could be set up in town or village. Then there were the old ironworks at Tula and the huge armaments factories of Moscow. The greatest market for iron, as well as many other commodities, lay only a few days to the east, where the Volga and the Oka met at the ancient frontier city of Nishni Novgorod. In Catherine's reign, an enterprising merchant family had even set up a glass factory in a village not twenty miles away from Russka. And above all, the provincial capital city of Vladimir, with a new industrial town called Ivanovo to the north of it, was becoming a huge new center of the textile business.

By the standards of Western Europe this new industrial and commercial activity was unimpressive. Under five percent of Russians lived in towns, against twenty percent in France and over thirty in England. But it was a beginning.

And to Tatiana, the more she understood it, the more it was exciting. Often Savva would remark to her: "Ah, Tatiana Ivanovna, what I could do if only I had more money to invest!" She saw what huge opportunities there were, and, having nothing else to occupy her active nature, she brooded about them constantly.

"If our serfs can set up little factories," she would challenge her husband, "we could set up big ones."

It was a perfectly reasonable statement. Though most of the gentry despised such merchant activities, there were others who did not. Indeed, some of the greatest magnates were also owners of large industrial enterprises that were worked by their serfs. Bobrov could have set up a plant like the nearby glass-making factory without loss of face.

But he was not interested. "Who would run it after I am gone?" he demanded. "Alexis? He's a soldier. Ilya? He'd be incapable." He shook his head. "Far better to build up the estates for them than get into risky projects none of us understand. Besides," he would remind her, "it's far simpler to let the serfs do it all: we get our reward by taking their profits in *obrok* payments." And when she was still unsatisfied he remarked wearily: "You're just a German."

Tatiana had long supposed that she knew Savva; yet it was only a year before that she had fully realized the secret passion that drove him. It came to light one day when she was quizzing him gently about his personal life. The two Suvorins, as well as being entrepreneurs, were highly unusual in another way, too: they were both single. Savva's father was a widower. But Savva himself, though thirty-three now, was still unmarried. It was unheard of. The priest at Russka had spoken to him about it many times; Bobrov had threatened to force him to marry. But he had been strangely evasive. And only then had he at last confessed to Tatiana: "I'll never marry until I'm free. I'd sooner go into the monastery."

"Who will you marry?" she had asked.

"A merchant's daughter," he replied. "But no merchant will let his daughter marry a serf, since then she becomes a serf, too."

So that was it. He wanted to buy his freedom. Several times already he had approached Bobrov on the subject, but the landlord had waved him away. "Every landlord has a price, though," he told Tatiana. "And then . . ." Then she suspected he would do great things.

And so Tatiana had formed her plan. It was very simple, if somewhat unusual. And it rested on a perfect understanding that she now reached with Savva.

At first Alexander Bobrov was puzzled by his wife's desire that he should sell Savva and his father their freedom. "What's it to you?" he would inquire. But weeks and months went by, and she continued to badger him: "Let them go, Alexander Prokofievich. You say you want to put money by: take your profit now then, and sell them their freedom."

"I sometimes think you prefer those serfs to your own family," he would remark drily.

But still she had persisted until, just a week ago, and in order to get some peace, he had at last promised wearily: "Very well. But if they want their freedom, they can pay me fifteen thousand rubles for it and nothing less." After bleeding them white for so many years, he calculated, there was no possibility that they could raise such a sum.

Tatiana only smiled.

Her understanding with Savva was very straightforward. "I shall persuade Alexander Prokofievich to sell you your freedom, Savva. I will also lend you the money you need, free of any interest. A year after you get your freedom, however, whenever that may be, you will repay me exactly twice what I lent you. Is that agreed?" He had bowed low. "Very well then," she had told him. "Leave it to me. But tell no one."

It might be highly unorthodox for a lady to concern herself with a serf like this—especially behind her husband's back; but the plan was entirely sensible. Suvorin would get his freedom, Bobrov a substantial sum of money to pass on, and she would discreetly increase the little nest egg she was building up for Sergei.

And though the sum Bobrov had demanded for the Suvorins' freedom was huge, she had faith in Savva. It might take time, but he would find it.

Already she had lent him a thousand rubles. Now, this bright January morning, she had come into Russka with more—another thousand. "Take it to Moscow and use it well," she told him.

And now, as he mounted the sled and bowed again, she did not know that Savva had another secret, one that he was concealing from her. He would have enough money now to buy his freedom by the end of that very year.

The duel between master and serf was nearly over.

JULY. Olga gazed at her husband fondly. They had spent the last month together on the estate near Smolensk, and it seemed to her she had never known such happiness. There was a glow upon her skin, a softness when she came near him that made even the serfs on the estate smile and declare: "Truly they are man and wife."

Then, with a laugh, she passed him Sergei's letter.

He had always written to her regularly, ever since their schooldays, often enclosing a poem, too, or some funny drawings. She kept the letters and loved to go over them again, when she had nothing to do. This one was characteristic.

My dear little Olga,
No doubt your husband is beating you regularly, in the old-fashioned way—so I send you news to cheer you up.

I have found a charming group of friends. We meet in the Archives of the Foreign Ministry in Moscow and call ourselves the Lovers of Wisdom. (For that goddess, you know, like all women, needs many lovers.) We read the great German philosophers, especially Hegel and Schelling. And we discuss the meaning of life and the genius of Russia; and we are ardent and altogether pleased with ourselves.

Do you know that the universe is in a state of becoming? It is so. Each idea has an opposite. When they combine, they produce a new and better idea, which in turn finds its opposite, and so on, until in this wonderful way the whole universe approaches perfection. Our human society here on earth is just the same. We are all of us just evolving ideas in the great cosmic order. Is that not wonderful?

Do you feel the grand cosmic forces, my little Olga—or does your husband beat you too much? Sometimes I feel them. I see a tree and I say: "That's the cosmos, evolving." But then sometimes I don't. I hit my head against a tree the other day and didn't feel cosmic at all. Perhaps if I'd hit it harder.

I must stop now. My friends and I have to follow our cosmic destiny and go out drinking. Then I shall seek the cosmos with a certain lady of my acquaintance.

I will now tell you an interesting fact. Our esteemed Minister of Education is so suspicious of philosophy that no chair in that subject is allowed in Saint Petersburg. I know of one man who discreetly lectures on philosophy in the botany department, another who teaches from his chair in agriculture. Only in our beloved Russia can the nature of the universe be considered a branch of agriculture!

I'm awfully sorry your husband is such a brute. Write to me at once if you want me to rescue you.

Your ever loving
Seriozha

SEPTEMBER. It was the end of summer, which had been long that year. The buggy bumped along the dirt road. It went at an unhurried pace because old Suvorin was careful to avoid the numerous ruts and potholes; besides, what was the use of hurrying anywhere when one was driving Ilya Bobrov?

It was three days since they had left the city of Riazan. Tomorrow they would get to Russka. "And it would have been tonight, sir, if you could get up in the mornings," the gray-bearded serf had remarked. To which Ilya had replied with a smile and a sigh: "I daresay you're right, Suvorin.

I don't know why I find it so hard, I'm sure."

The sunlight was already tinged with red. The track passed between endless silver stands of birch and larch trees, their leaves now turning to a rustling gold against the pale blue sky. Soon, as the sun sank lower, the pigeons would come dipping over the treetops.

And now the trees opened out and large fields appeared. Like many in the area, this village grew flax, barley, and rye. The harvest was done. Little yellow-brown haystacks dotted the field. Along its boundary, a bank of wormwood and nettles lent a faint, bitter smell to the air. As they approached the first *izba,* they were greeted by a barking dog and a large woman with a basket of mushrooms in her arms. Soon afterwards they came to an inn.

"We'll have to stop here for the night," Suvorin remarked gloomily.

The inn was typical of its kind: a large room with tables and benches, a big stove in one corner, and a grumpy tavernkeeper, who immediately became obsequious when he caught sight of Ilya. While Suvorin saw to the horses, Ilya sat down near the stove and called for tea.

It had been a satisfactory journey. He was glad now that Tatiana had at last persuaded him to go with old Suvorin. They had thoroughly inspected the Riazan estate—at least Suvorin had—taken their rents, sold the crops and some timber, and were returning to Russka with a considerable sum of money. Since the Riazan estate was one day to be his— Alexis would get Russka—he supposed it was as well he should get to know the place. Suvorin had even induced him to walk about outside so that his color had improved from its usual pastiness.

Ilya Bobrov was not an invalid; yet thanks to Tatiana's folly he had grown up genuinely uncertain whether he was well or not. He was no fool. Kept often in bed as a child, he learned to read voraciously, and he had learned from his father both a love of French literature and an enlightened philosophy. Unfortunately, however, and because his father had, ultimately, been defeated by life, he had taken in, without even knowing it, a subconscious belief that everything was useless. Failure and impotence seemed, to Ilya, inevitable. A kind of torpor descended upon him. And though he often had an acute sense that he was wasting his life, that he must shake off this torpor—somehow, because he never had to, he did not. Now, at the age of twenty-eight, he was amiable, lazy, unmarried, and decidedly fat. "I am too stout," he would say apologetically, "but I don't know what's to be done about it."

This journey, however, had rather stirred him up. Indeed, it had even given him a new idea, which he had been thinking about all day. So that when Suvorin appeared with his portmanteau, and the landlord with a glass of steaming tea, he just nodded to them both, put his feet up on the traveling chest, and, half closing his eyes while he sipped his tea, considered: Yes, it's certainly time I stopped vegetating. I think I shall take a trip abroad. I shall go to France.

It was time for his life to change. And old Suvorin, watching him and thinking of his own son, Savva, in Moscow, concluded, If that fellow had half my son's energy, he could still make something of himself.

So the time went slowly by as the sun sank and the landowner and the elderly serf contemplated their destinies. And the journey might have ended the next day, quite without incident, had it not been for the landlord.

For the little tavern saw only modest business. The landlord did not intend to let an obviously rich gentleman like Ilya slip through his hands too cheaply. As soon as Ilya had his tea therefore, the fellow had slipped out and hurried off down the street. He did not return for half an hour.

Ilya was delighted with the landlord's proposal. He had enjoyed a short catnap and now, stimulated by the journey and the new plans hatching in his brain, he felt particularly lively.

"Stop grumbling, Suvorin," he said. "It's a capital idea." And then to the landlord, still bowing low: "Go and fetch them. And bring wine and vodka too."

The landlord smiled. It was certainly good luck that those gypsies should have been passing through: if they would entertain the fat gentleman, he had already agreed to split whatever they were paid. As darkness fell, the little inn suddenly became a hive of activity. There was a smell of cooking. Wine and vodka appeared. So, miraculously, did a number of people. And then, with the food, came the gypsies.

There were eight of them, brightly dressed, swarthy skinned and not bad-looking. They sang: two of the women danced. Ilya grinned and tapped his foot. Yes, he felt livelier than he had in years. He did not usually drink much, but tonight . . . "More wine," he called to the landlord.

One of the girls was singing now, while the men strummed. What a strange sound the song had. Where did it come from? Was it Asiatic? He had no idea. The girl was about fifteen, he supposed: rather a scrawny little thing, really. And yet . . . he felt a definite stirring. She was coming towards him, almost touching . . . My God, he thought, I must live: that's it. I must travel.

By the time the evening finally ended, he had treated everyone in the inn to half a dozen drinks, had danced, ponderously, with the fifteen-year-old girl, and was quite in love—not exactly with her, but with life itself.

And it was well past midnight when, having cleared away some of the debris, the landlord made up a bed for him on one of the benches and Ilya lay down to sleep. "For the fact is, dear old Suvorin," he muttered, "I think I may be rather drunk."

"Yes, sir." The serf quietly arranged himself on another bench and closed his eyes.

Five minutes later, still lying there with his eyes open, Ilya was suddenly struck by a thought. The portmanteau on the floor beside him was not locked. It was his own fault. Somehow he had mislaid the key while they were in Riazan; it would scarcely have mattered except for one thing. All the money was in there.

And now, through the haze of his drunkenness, this idea seemed to grow in importance. It was urgent. The dim awareness that he had probably made a fool of himself with the gypsies became translated into the idea that they had wanted to make a fool out of him. One of those devils, probably the girl, would sneak in there and rob them—with the landlord's help no doubt. He sat bolt upright.

"Suvorin. Wake up," he hissed. The old man stirred. "Come over here and open the portmanteau." Suvorin came. "Take the money out. The bag and the packet. That's it."

The bag contained silver rubles; the packet the banknotes, in use since Catherine's time, which the Russians called assignats.

"You keep them, Suvorin. They'll never be able to rob you, I'm sure." The old man shrugged but complied. Then they both lay down again. "You're a capital fellow," Ilya said. Then he fell asleep.

An hour later something woke him. Was it a sound? Or the moonlight outside the window? Scarcely awake, he was vaguely aware that there was something important he had not done. What the devil was it? Ah yes: the money. Somehow, in the deep recesses of his sleep the thought had formulated—what if all the gypsies crept up on poor old Suvorin and took the money. They'd get it all. But he'd outwit them.

Slowly, with difficulty, he managed to rise and lurch across the room and shake Suvorin awake. "The packet. Give me the packet." Unquestioningly the serf fumbled in his clothing and produced it. Then Ilya lurched back and sat down heavily. Where could he conceal it? He opened the portmanteau and peered inside at the jumble of his possessions. His head fell forward: God, he was sleepy. Ah yes: that would do.

In the bottom of the portmanteau lay a book of Derzhavin's verses. Unfortunately the spine had broken and he had tied the book together with a cord. Fighting off sleep, Ilya undid the cord, slipped the packet in the book, and tied it up again. I don't suppose a gypsy would think of looking in a book, he thought as he closed the portmanteau. Suvorin was snoring. "I must keep watch," he muttered, and he instantly fell back into a deep sleep from which he did not awake until well into the morning.

One of Ilya's first acts when he was back in his room at home, was to put the volume of Derzhavin's verses back in his bookshelf. He had no memory whatever of waking up and putting the money there; and so he never gave the book a thought.

He was therefore completely mystified when, after he and old Suvorin had showed the accounts to his father, half the money was missing.

"But you've got it, Suvorin," he said plaintively to the old serf.

"You took back the notes, sir," the other replied with the faintest hint of impatience.

"Do you swear to that?" Alexander Bobrov demanded sharply.

"I do, sir."

And poor Ilya could only look baffled.

"I just remember giving it all to you," he said.

It was not, however, until Tatiana herself had gone through his clothes and the portmanteau, and returned puzzled and shaking her head that Alexander Bobrov made his terrible decision.

"Suvorin, you have stolen it. I shall decide what to do with you tomorrow."

*   *   *

In a way Alexander Bobrov was glad. He had regretted giving way to his wife over the Suvorins, though he would not go back on his word: and now that he had an excuse to think old Suvorin was a thief, he was determined to believe it. "Either he's a liar or your son is," he snapped when Tatiana pleaded with him. And when she reminded him that, according to Suvorin, Ilya had been drunk, Bobrov merely remarked: "All the easier to steal from him, then. You see," he added in justification, "if you offer a man like that the chance to buy his freedom, it just tempts him to steal the money to pay you."

It was nonsense. Tatiana told him so. In his heart of hearts he perhaps knew it. But the facts seemed unassailable; even Tatiana admitted that. And it had to be admitted this turn of events worked out very nicely for the Bobrovs.

For the next day Alexander Bobrov held court. This meant that he summoned Suvorin before him and acted, as was his right, as the serf's accuser, judge, jury, and executioner. Since he judged Suvorin guilty of a serious theft against him, the sentence was harsh.

"I am sending you to Siberia," he announced.

He did not even need to add what the sentence also assumed—that everything the Suvorin family possessed would pass directly into his hands. So whatever money he would have paid for his freedom became Bobrov's anyway. His son, now penniless, would remain a serf. It was certainly all very convenient.

"But you can't," Tatiana protested. "It's against the law." For the law said that a master could not send a serf of over forty-five to Siberia. And Suvorin was forty-eight.

But the law was not strong, when confronted by a landowner.

"I'm sending him to the military governor of Vladimir." Alexander said bluntly. "He's a friend of mine." And though she tried all day, there was nothing Tatiana could say this time to change his mind.

Alexander Bobrov was quietly triumphant. He was within his rights, more or less. He had outmaneuvered those cunning serfs and decidedly added to the value of the estate. Several small signs had told him recently that he might not have many years left to do that.

In a way, of course, he felt sorry for Suvorin—even though he was determined to believe him guilty. But then, he thought, these sudden and arbitrary reversals of fortune must be expected by any man. After all, it had happened to him, too, when Catherine had thrown him in jail. That was how things were and how they had always been, in Russia.

The very next day, wearing chains, Suvorin was taken to Vladimir from where, quite regularly, little parties set out on the long, long road to Siberia.

And the same day Tatiana sat down to write a letter.

Savva took the little blackened object in his hands. And for once, he smiled. He had promised himself this treasure for a long time, and now at last he felt he could afford it.

For they were home and dry. Two more weeks in Moscow and he would have the money for his and his father's freedom. All I have to do now, he thought with a grin, is get out of this store.

"It's good," the gray-bearded seller said simply. "Very old. Before Ivan the Terrible, I think." Savva nodded. He knew.

It was a little icon—nothing to look at. There were dozens of bigger and brighter ones in the store. As with many ancient icons the paint had grown dark with age, been overpainted, grown dark again. In its long life this icon had probably gone through this process two or three times; and even now the solemn figures of the Mother of God and Child could only dimly be made out against their darkening amber background. Why then should Savva value it so much?

It was because he knew the art of the icon was only visible to the trained eye, and even then, could only be apprehended by the spiritual sense. The icon was not just a painting, it was prayer. The intimate little forms in their receding world were revered for their simplicity and grace—and this came from the religious intention of the hand that painted them. Most icons, therefore, were false, impure: only in a few, a very few, did the invisible fire of the spirit—as pure as in the dawn of Christianity in the ancient Greek and Roman world—show through. Painted and overpainted by religious hands, these icons were to be venerated by those who understood. Like Savva.

With a deep sense of satisfaction, Savva paid the old man. And now it was time to leave.

But, as usual, that was not so easy. The old fellow had somehow managed to get between him and the door. Two other younger men with friendly but solemn faces had joined him. "You would receive a warm welcome, you know," the old man reminded him for the twentieth time, "if you were to join us." And then, very seriously: "I would not sell this icon to most men."

"I thank you, but no," he replied, as he had done so many times before.

"We can help you buy your freedom," one of the younger men remarked. But still Savva did not react. He had no wish to join them.

They were Old Believers. This was, nowadays, the name usually given to the sectarians—the old Raskolniki—who had split off from the church a century and a half before. There had been none in Russka since the burning of the church, and most had fled to the outer provinces during that period of persecution. But during the reign of Catherine they had been officially tolerated and there was now a sizable community in Moscow. There were several rival groups: some who had their own priests, some who did without. And of all these there were none more remarkable than the group to which the fellows who ran this store belonged.

The Theodosian sect was rich and powerful. Its headquarters were by their cemetery, in which had once been the village and was nowadays the outlying suburb of Preobrazhenskoe. They had numerous communes inside and outside the city. They owned public baths. They engaged in manufacturing and trading enterprises, and thanks to monopolies granted them by Catherine it was the Theodosians who sold all the best icons. But the most striking thing about the sect was its curious economic organization.

For the Theodosians ran what were, in effect, cooperatives. Members of the sect could obtain loans from their coffers at low interest rates to start businesses. In all their enterprises—some of which were quite large textile factories—the poor were cared for by the community. And though some of its successful members grew extremely rich in their lifetimes, their assets at death were taken over by the community. Puritan, upright, its stricter members even celibate, this strange, almost monastic mixture of capitalist factory and village commune was a uniquely Russian solution to the challenges of the early industrial revolution.

Since he had encountered them in Moscow, the Theodosians had urged him many times to join the sect. They could certainly have financed him. But each time he passed the high walls of the community's compound he had thought: No, I do not want to give all I have to them. I want to be free.

He left the Theodosians in their store at last and made his way across Moscow to his own modest lodgings. This was a pleasant wooden house in a dusty street. On the door was a little sign with a name upon it—not his own, for being still a serf he could not legally own anything, but that of his landlord: BOBROV. Soon, he thought, that sign will say SUVORIN. And he went inside contentedly.

It was five minutes later that a messenger arrived with the letter from Tatiana.

She told him everything. That his father was already on his way to Siberia in chains; that he had lost all he had; that Bobrov was sending a man to take him back to Russka, where, once again, he would be a poor serf. It ended with an act of generosity and a none too subtle hint.

> Whatever you think fit to do, the money I lent you is yours—I do not wish to be repaid and will be glad only to know that you are well.

His landlord's wife was telling him to run away and keep the money. It was, he knew, an astonishing act for a member of the gentry class towards a serf.

But he only sighed. It was no use. If I take the money and I'm caught, they'll only say I stole it. Her letter won't do me any good. Carefully he wrapped up notes to the value of her loan. He would leave them with a merchant he could trust who would get them to her. Then he considered what to do.

He would not go back. Not to the Bobrovs after what they had done. He would sooner die—As I daresay I shall, he thought. No, he would run away. There were ways of doing it. Some men pulled the barges down the Volga. Backbreaking work. Several thousand men died at it every year. But you could get away like that—far away to the south and east with few questions asked. Or perhaps head east, for the distant colonies of Siberia where they wanted men, no matter who. Perhaps he would even try to find his father. It's lucky, he considered, that I'm strong.

It seemed that, after all, he had lost his duel with the Bobrovs. But even so, he would not give up—not in a thousand years.

One thing at least was certain: he would never see that cursed place Russka again.

It was on the very day his father sent poor Suvorin away from Russka that, far away in the northeastern province of Novgorod, Alexis Bobrov made a remarkable discovery.

The day was bright, with a sharp, damp wind blowing, when he arrived at the place. The three young officers who rode with him were in cheerful spirits. "Though I'm sure I shall hate anything devised by that oaf," one remarked scornfully. But Alexis, as he passed through the gates and along the well-kept road, was filled with curiosity.

The oaf was the famous General Arkcheyev.

It was one of the strange features of the reign of the enlightened, even poetic Tsar Alexander that he should have come to choose General Arkcheyev as his closest adviser. Perhaps it was an attraction of opposites. The general was half educated and bad tempered; his face was coarse, his hair close-cropped, his body perpetually stooped forward as though under the weight of the stern tasks he set himself. Alexis had come to admire him for the brilliant way he had directed artillery in the great campaign of 1812. "He may be crude," he told his companions, "but he is loyal to the tsar and he gets things done." Like many straightforward soldiers—that was how Alexis liked to see himself—he had been delighted when the tsar made Arkcheyev his closest counselor.

And it was here in Novgorod province that the general, upon the tsar's command, had now undertaken one of the greatest social experiments in Russian history.

The moment they entered the huge estate, Alexis sensed something strange about the place. The peasants looked odd; the road had no ruts in it; but only when they came to the village itself did the party gasp with astonishment.

It was not a Russian village at all. The haphazard collection of peasant *izbas* that had once stood there had been completely razed; in their place, row upon row of neat cottages. They were identical—each painted blue with a red porch and white fence. "Good God," Alexis muttered: "it's like a barracks." Then he noticed the children.

They were little boys, some no more than six years old. They came swinging by, in perfect step and singing, under orders from a sergeant. They were in uniform. And then Alexis realized what had seemed so strange since he arrived: everyone was identically dressed, and none of the peasants had a beard.

"Yes, you'll find perfect order," explained the young officer who showed them around. "We have three sizes of uniform for the children—quite enough. They wear uniforms at all times. The men are clean-shaven: it's neater. Iron discipline: we beat a drum when it's time to work in the fields." He grinned. "We can almost make them mow a meadow in step!"

And a few minutes later, when they were shown inside the cottages,

Alexis was even more astonished. They were all spotless. "How do you do it?" he asked.

"Inspections. See"—the young man pointed to a list hanging on a wall—"that's an inventory of everything in the house: everything has to be checked and clean as a whistle."

"How do you keep discipline?" one of the officers asked.

"The cane is enough. Any slip and they get it. We salt the cane, actually," he added.

Alexis soon noticed something else. Unlike a normal village, there seemed to be as many men of all ages as women.

"Everyone has to marry," their guide explained, then laughed: "whether they want to or not. The women should be grateful, actually. No widows or old maids here—we give them a man."

"You must have plenty of children then," Alexis remarked.

"We certainly do. If the women don't produce regularly, we fine them. The empire needs people to serve it."

"Are they happy?" one of the others inquired.

"Of course. Some of the old women wept," the young man conceded, "but the system is perfect, don't you see: everyone works, everyone obeys, and everyone's looked after."

For this was General Arkcheyev's Military Colony. It covered a huge area in the province, where the army settled and the local peasants were forcibly converted into reservists and militarized state workers. Further colonies were already being set up down south in the Ukraine. "Within three years," their guide said, "a third of the entire Russian army will be settled like this." There was no doubt: it was impressive.

But why should the enlightened Tsar Alexander have encouraged his henchman to set up these totalitarian districts? Was it just for convenience? For they were certainly a cheap way of keeping a standing army occupied and fed in time of peace. Was it, as some suspected, that the tsar—hoping one day to weaken the grip of a conservative gentry upon the army and the land—was experimenting with these colonies as a way of doing so? Or was it perhaps that Tsar Alexander, imbued with a military streak like his father, and frustrated almost beyond endurance by the chaotic, refractory nature of the endless Russian land, had resolved—like Russian reformers before and after—to impose order somewhere at least, whatever the cost? Whichever explanation comes nearest, it was certainly true that the military colonies, with their iron discipline, terrible symmetry, and their complete dedication to the state, would have delighted old Peter the Great himself if only he had thought of them.

To Alexis Bobrov, the colony was a revelation. Hadn't he dedicated his life to military service? Arkcheyev's creation was the most perfect thing he had ever seen. How far it was from the shabby chaos of Russka and a thousand estates like it. Just as the army was, for him, a relief from the ineptitude of his own family, this place seemed an escape from everything that irritated him in Russia. He saw only that the people here were industrious and well fed: he saw what he wanted to see. For just as one man will be attracted to power, another will be fascinated by order. He was quite seduced.

And from that day there was rooted in his mind a single, unalterable precept which, whatever difficulties he encountered, seemed to make sense of everything. It was simply this: the tsar would be served by imposing order. And from this principle derived a second: that which is most conducive to order must be right. Good enough, he told himself, for a straightforward soldier like me.

It was in the summer of the following year, when Ilya had already departed with a family friend on his tour abroad, that Alexis, visiting Russka, chanced one day to take down the battered volume of Derzhavin's verse. When he discovered the banknotes, he guessed at once what had happened. But there was nothing to be done. Suvorin was in Siberia. His son had run away, God knew where. Alexander Bobrov was unwell.

Besides, to suggest Suvorin's sentence was a mistake would look bad for everyone: bad for the family, bad for their class, not congenial to order.

He put the money in a safe place and said nothing.

1825

IF a Russian is asked for the date of the most memorable event before the present century, he or she will almost invariably reply: 1825, December.

For this was the date of the first attempted revolution.

The Decembrist conspiracy—so named after the month in which it took place—is almost unique in human history on account of its curious character. For it was an attempt—a very amateurish one—on the part of a handful of nobles, acting from the highest motives, to secure freedom for the people.

To understand how this came about it is necessary only to go back to the reign of Catherine, when the ideas of the Enlightenment and of liberty had first taken root in Russian noble circles. Despite the shock of the French Revolution and the fear of Napoleon, the idea of reform in Russia had continued to grow under the enlightened Tsar Alexander. And God knew there was much to reform: a legal system that might have come from the Dark Ages; the institution of serfdom; a government that, despite the nominal existence of a judicial senate, was in reality a primitive autocracy. Yet what was to be done! No one could ever agree. The representatives of the gentry, merchants, and serfs called together by Catherine had simply quarreled with each other. There were no ancient institutions, as in the West, to build upon. Tsar Alexander had found the same thing: great schemes were drawn up, but any attempt to introduce them promptly foundered upon the great Russian sea of obstruction and inefficiency. The gentry were loyal but would not hear of freeing their peasants: by 1822 the tsar had even restored their official right to send serfs to Siberia. Everyone feared another Pugachev uprising. The government found in practice that it could only tinker with the system, try to maintain order, and conduct experiments like the military colonies, to seek new forms that might lift the country out of its ancient social stagnation.

It was not surprising then, as the years went by, that some liberal young nobles began to feel that their angelic tsar had cheated them. Their minds were opened by the Enlightenment. The great patriotic victory over Napoleon and, in some cases, contact with mystical Freemasonry had filled them with a romantic fervor towards the fatherland. Yet while Tsar Alexander's Holy Alliance might inspire them as they looked outward, the scene within Russia seemed increasingly dominated by the stern authoritarianism of General Arkcheyev. So it was, in the years after the Congress of Vienna, that a loosely knit group began to form, dedicated to change and even revolution.

They were quite alone. Within their own class, an idealistic few. The middle, merchant class, still small, was conservative and uninterested; the peasants completely ignorant.

Nor had they an agreed plan. Some wanted a constitutional monarchy on the English pattern; some, led by a fiery army officer, Pestel, down in the south, wanted to kill the tsar and set up a republic. In secret they planned, plotted, hoped, and did nothing.

And then quite unexpectedly, in November 1825, Tsar Alexander was no more. A sudden fever had apparently carried him off; and he had left behind no son. The succession fell to the tsar's two brothers: Constantine, the grandson Catherine had hoped would rule in Constantinople, and a younger brother, a well-intentioned but unimaginative fellow named Nicholas.

While the conspirators wondered what they should do, a series of bizarre events took place. Grand Duke Constantine, commanding the army in Poland, had already married a Polish lady and renounced his rights to the throne. Tsar Alexander had accepted this and issued a manifesto designating Nicholas the heir—but which was so secret that no even poor Nicholas had been told. Now, therefore, Constantine immediately swore allegiance to young Nicholas; while Nicholas and the Russian army naturally swore allegiance to him! When at last the confusion was sorted out, it was agreed that everyone should, in December 1825, swear allegiance all over again, this time to the bemused Nicholas.

It was now that the conspirators, rather confused themselves, decided to stage a coup. There were only a handful of them: most of their colleagues had panicked at the thought of real action. They decided to incite a mutiny by persuading the troops to support Constantine against the new tsar. After that—no one was quite sure. There were two groups of conspirators—one in Saint Petersburg and one, under Pestel, down in the Ukraine. They were badly coordinated and had different aims.

On the morning of December 14, when the army and the Senate were to take the new oath, a group of officers led some three thousand confused troops into the Senate Square. They arrived late, after the senators had already taken their oath. On the conspirators' instruction the troops began to shout: *Constantine and Constitution.* It was believed that the soldiers supposed that this strange word, *constitution,* must be the name of the grand duke's wife.

Nicholas, wanting to avoid bloodshed, had them surrounded; but at dusk, when they did not budge, some rounds of canister were fired and several dozen men killed. Then it was over. Soon afterwards, in the south, Pestel's rebellion was strangled at birth. Five ringleaders, only, were executed.

This was the Decembrist revolt. Aristocratic, amateurish, slightly absurd. Yet despite—perhaps even because of—the heroic folly of these nobles, they came to be seen as an inspiration, like the Christian martyrs of ancient times, for those revolutionaries who came after them.

To the new tsar, Nicholas, the revolt was a shock. He was a simple man who believed in service. He assumed his nobles did. What possible reason could there be for these fellows to betray their sacred trust? He had all their confessions copied and bound in a book that never left his desk and which he studied carefully. From it he learned of Russia's need for laws, liberty, and a constitution. He was not a clever man, but he thought about it.

First, however, there must be order.

1827

SUMMER was beginning and Tatiana was contented: for now, suddenly, in place of silence and sadness, the house was full of happy voices. And as she looked forward to the coming summer months, it seemed to her that nothing more was likely to shatter their tranquillity. My children, she thought with a smile, have come home.

In the year and a half since Alexander Bobrov had died, she had often been lonely, with only Ilya—who seldom went down to his Riazan estate—for company. In that time, too, tragedy had struck the family twice more. A year ago Olga had lost her handsome husband—killed while on service—leaving her with one baby and pregnant with another. Thank God, at least, she was well provided for, the Smolensk estate being large. Then, late last autumn, poor Alexis had lost his wife in a cholera epidemic, just before he was due to go off with his regiment; and one winter's morning a sled had arrived at Bobrovo containing—small, cold, and miserable—his five-year-old son Mikhail, to be taken care of by his grandmother. "Just until Alexis marries again," she told Ilya.

Tatiana had been philosophical. Old Arina had been brought back into service as nanny, with her niece to help her. And under their care little Mikhail—Misha they called him—turned out to be a gentle, sweet-tempered version of his stern father. Arina found him a child of his own age from among the serfs in the village—Ivan Romanov's youngest son, Timofei: and soon the two little boys were playing happily together each day and old Arina pronounced confidently: "He'll mend."

And then, in spring, had come good news. Olga and her two babies would come there for the summer. And a week later a letter arrived from Alexis. A new campaign against the Turks was expected that autumn. But for the summer, he had obtained a three-month leave: "which I intend to spend with you and my son," his letter declared. "So we shall have our hands full," Tatiana told the old nanny cheerfully.

Indeed, of all her children, only Sergei would be missing. "And that," Tatiana had to confess, "is probably just as well."

At first Olga never saw the danger. She certainly meant no harm.

How happy she was to be back in the simple green-and-white house, and to gaze down the slope to the riverbank where the sweet-scented pine trees grew. It was a return to her childhood and her family. And how good it was to see her two baby girls safely in the hands of the two Arinas. Her old nanny had only three teeth left now, and a hint of beard on her dear, round face; but her niece—young Arina they called her—was a pretty, cheerful girl of sixteen who was quickly learning all the older woman knew. Olga would spend happy hours sitting out on the veranda with them, accompanied by young Misha, listening to old Arina's wonderful stories.

The pain of her husband's death, terrible though it had been, was passing; and in the huge, silent Russian summer, she felt a sense of healing.

Indeed, there was an atmosphere of particular gentleness in the house that summer. Alexis, too, had suffered a loss and it had softened him. "I'd always supposed," he confessed to her, "that if I were killed—as I may be this autumn if we go to war with Turkey—Misha would at least have his mother. Now, I'd leave him an orphan." And though he did not care to show it, Olga knew that he treasured each day that he spent there with the little boy.

There might, perhaps, have been more laughter. Often as she sat with old Arina, she thought of Sergei, and his infectious gaiety. She had not received his usual letter for several weeks now, and she wondered idly what he was up to. But she was grateful, all the same, that he was not there.

It was eighteen months ago, at her father's funeral, that the relationship between Sergei and Alexis, always strained, had reached breaking point. The attempted coup of the Decembrists was, at that time, only two months past. And when the family, all in black, had gathered in the salon, Alexis had gravely remarked that he thanked God, at least, that the conspirators had been so easily rounded up. Why Sergei could not keep his mouth shut, Olga did not know, but he had replied quite cheerfully: "I knew several of those fellows. If only they'd told me what they were up to I'd have joined them at once." And then, almost plaintively: "I can't think why nobody told me."

Despite the occasion, Olga had found it hard not to laugh. She could see exactly why the conspirators hadn't told her indiscreet brother their secret.

But the effect upon Alexis had been terrible. His already pale face had gone completely white with anger, and after a second's pause, he had said in a voice that, had it been more than a whisper, would have been shaking: "I scarcely know, Sergei, why you are here. And I am sorry that you are." The two had not spoken after that.

No, much as she loved him, she was glad Sergei was not there to disturb the tranquility of this precious summer.

And perhaps because it was so peaceful she did not see the danger.

His name was Fyodor Petrovich Pinegin. He was a friend of Alexis's—an acquaintance, perhaps, rather than a friend—whom Alexis had brought down with him to stay. Pinegin was a quiet man, still in his twenties she supposed, with a thin, hard face, sandy hair, and pale blue eyes that seemed to have no particular expression. "He's a good fellow, a bit lonely," Alexis told her. "He's seen a lot of service but never talks about it." Indeed, he would sit quietly while others talked, just sucking on a short pipe, expressing few opinions. He had one peculiarity: he always wore a white military tunic and trousers—though whether this was from preference or because he had no other clothes, Olga did not know. When asked what he liked to do best he mildly replied: "To hunt."

Since Alexis was busy with the estate and Ilya seldom moved from his chair, she found herself often in his company when she went for walks; and he made a surprisingly pleasant companion. He would only talk a little, he listened well, and there was a kind of quiet strength about him that she found rather attractive.

Olga knew that she was beautiful. She was twenty-four now, with a long, elegant build, large and luminous blue eyes, flowing brown hair, and a high-spirited grace that reminded any horse-fancier of some pure-bred Arabian. Marriage had added to this a comfortable good humor, which she had kept in her widowhood and which made both men and women feel relaxed in her presence. She had the impression that Pinegin liked her, but she had not thought about it very much.

There were many delightful places to wander. Close by the house there was a long, shady alley in a grove of silver birches. Or one could stroll by the river, where the pine trees gave their scented shade. But Olga's favorite walk lay through the woods to the monastery.

She loved the monastery. Since the reign of Catherine ended, a number of Russian monasteries—taking their inspiration, as in former centuries, from the great center at Mount Athos in Greece—had found a fresh vigor and dedication to the things of the spirit; and some ten years before this movement had reached Russka. A few monks had even revived the ancient hermitage, the *skit,* that lay across the river past the springs.

Twice Olga walked over to the monastery with Pinegin and proudly showed him the little icon by Rublev that the Bobrovs had given so long ago. Though he said little, it seemed to her that he was impressed.

The second time they went, Olga took little Misha with her. For some childish reason, he seemed to be shy of Pinegin and would not walk beside him; but on the way back, when he got too tired to walk, the soldier quickly picked him up and carried him home, for which Olga gave him a grateful smile. "One day, if you like, we can walk over to the old springs and the monks' hermitage across the river," she suggested. To which Pinegin gladly agreed.

So the days had passed: Pinegin sometimes out with a gun in the early morning; Ilya reading; walks in the late afternoon. In the evenings they played cards. Tatiana usually won, with Pinegin never far behind. Olga had a feeling that, had he chosen to do so, the quiet officer could have won more often.

Indeed, the only thing that gave her any cause for worry during those days had nothing to do with Pinegin at all. It concerned the estate.

There was nothing much wrong. It was more a succession of little things that, Olga was sure, could easily be put right. If, that was, Alexis would allow it. For if a new cart or a pump were needed, he would brusquely order the serf to try harder with the old one; he was also cutting down timber a little faster than he replanted. "Discipline's needed, not money," he would say. "I watch over things in his absence," Tatiana told her, "but he won't let me make any improvements. And of course," she confided, "now that the Suvorins are gone, the income from the estates is less." Two years before, news had come from Siberia that Ivan Suvorin had died. As for Savva, no word of him had ever been heard. Olga was sad to see these small signs of decline in her old home, but not unduly worried. There were still miles of trees to be cut down before Alexis would be in any real trouble.

The only hint she might have had, in retrospect, came when one morning she was starting out for a stroll through the woods and casually asked Pinegin if he would like to join her. "I'd be glad to," he said, "but I'm afraid a plain soldier must be rather dull company for you sometimes."

And just to be pleasant she had replied, with a warm smile: "Oh, not at all, Fyodor Petrovich. In fact, I find you very interesting indeed." To her great surprise she thought she had seen him blush. But apart from an almost unconscious feeling of satisfaction, she had scarcely given it another thought.

It was one of the worthy but slightly tedious aspects of Alexis's character that, like his mother and the majority of the village people, every Sunday he liked to go to church—and though nothing was said, it was quite clear that he expected everyone in the house to accompany him. He went not to the little wooden church in the village, however, where once a week a priest came to hold a service, but to the old stone church by the marketplace in Russka.

"I wouldn't mind going," Ilya told her grumpily, "except for that damned priest."

The priest at Russka, it had to be said, was not a pleasant man. While the monasteries of Russia, at this time, were experiencing a revival, the ordinary priesthood was not. The priestly class was looked down on socially and, quite often, for its morals; and the priest at Russka did little to improve this general image. He was a large, bloated man with red hair and a brood of children who, it was said, stole food in the marketplace. The priest himself never let slip any chance of coming by either food or money. But every Sunday Alexis insisted on standing through the long service to receive a blessing from this man's large, fat hand; and Olga naturally accompanied him.

It was on the way back, one Sunday, when he and Olga were walking across the market to their carriage, that he turned to her and remarked: "Of course, he's got no money, but if you want to marry Pinegin, you know I've no objection."

Marry? She stared at him.

"Whatever put that idea into your head?"

"You seem to spend a lot of time with him. I'm quite sure he thinks you're interested."

"Has he said so?"

"No. But I'm sure."

Had she led him on? She really didn't think so. "I just never thought about it," she truthfully replied.

He nodded. "Well, you're a widow and you're rich. You can do as you please. But be careful." And then he added something that surprised her further. "Don't trifle with Pinegin, though. He's a very dangerous man."

She wondered what he meant, but he wouldn't say more.

She was very careful, therefore, in the coming week. She did not try to be distant, for that might have seemed rude. She was as friendly as before. But now several times she went out alone, or took her mother or Alexis if she strolled out with him. And all the time she watched the quiet soldier and pondered: was he so dangerous?

It was one afternoon in the first week of June, when the family was sitting at tea on the veranda, that they saw what appeared to be a small whirlwind approaching. The whirlwind came along the lane, vanished behind the trees, and then appeared at the gates of the little park. "Good God," Ilya exclaimed, "it's a troika."

There was in Russia no more noble conveyance. No one knew exactly when the fashion had begun—some said it came from Hungary—but if a young nobleman nowadays wanted to impress the world, he found the smartest coachman he could and harnessed up a troika.

The troika—also know as a unicorn—consisted of three horses running abreast. In the center, between the shafts and under a brightly painted headboard, was the leader, who trotted. On each side were two wheelers, fanning outwards, who galloped—one furiously, the other coquettishly. It was difficult to handle, stylish, and the ultimate in elegance. And it was this aristocratic carriage that now, in a cloud of dust, came whirling up the slope towards them.

As it reached the house, they could see two passengers within; but it was the splendidly dressed coachman, who now leapt down with a cry, who looked strangely familiar and caused Alexis to mutter: "What the devil's this?"

It was Sergei. And as he strode forward and in the Russian manner kissed each of them three times, he cheerfully announced: "Hello, Olga. Hello, Mama. Hello, Alexis. I've been exiled."

He was bound to have got into trouble sooner or later. And as Olga reminded Alexis, one didn't have to do much to be in hot water these days.

For one of the first acts of Tsar Nicholas, to ensure political order in his empire, had been to set up a new, special police bureau—the so-called Third Department—and place at its head one of his most trusted friends, the redoubtable Count Alexander Benckendorff. Benckendorff's task was simple. The tsar, who meant well, would consider reforms at the proper times; but meanwhile—however long this process might take—there were to be no more Decembrists. Benckendorff was thorough. Already his gendarmes, in their light blue uniforms, seemed to be everywhere. And in particular the department paid close attention to enthusiastic young gentlemen with too little respect for authority—men like Sergei.

In fact, it was Sergei's boyhood hero Pushkin who had really started it. Pushkin was making a name for himself. Already some of his first, brilliant writing had been published. And already the young poet's "Ode to Liberty" had landed him in trouble with the authorities. The tsar had told Benckendorff personally to censor young Pushkin's work. It was not surprising therefore that Sergei, longing to step into the limelight with his hero, should have hastened to produce something shocking of his own.

Sergei Bobrov's poem, "The Firebird," was printed at his own expense—a huge sacrifice for a young fellow on a modest salary of seven hundred rubles a year. Pushkin, to whom he immediately dispatched a copy, had sent a letter of generous encouragement: and in truth, for a first effort, it wasn't bad. The firebird of his story was—needless to say—a harbinger of liberty. And in two days, before the ink was dry, Benckendorff had impounded it.

The author was so little known, the action of the Third Department so quick, that a week later Sergei found himself not a celebrity, but under orders to return straight to the family estate at Russka and stay there until further notice. And here he was.

"There's a letter for you, Alexis," Sergei went on. "Very important," he added, as he drew it from the recesses of his coachman's coat.

It was from Benckendorff himself. Alexis took it without a word.

At first it seemed all might be well. Besides his manservant, Sergei had brought with him a pleasant young man from the Ukraine, called Karpenko, whom he had met in Saint Petersburg. Between herself, Pinegin, and this Karpenko, Olga hoped she could keep Sergei and his soldier brother apart.

Alexis, she could see, was doing his best to be pleasant. He was somewhat mollified by Benckendorff's letter.

"We think," the great man had written, "that the young man is a harmless scamp; but it will do him no harm to cool his heels in the country for a while. And I know, my dear Alexis Alexandrevich, that I can rely upon you to keep a wise and fatherly eye on him."

"I'll do that, all right," Alexis told Olga.

But about Sergei's high spirits he could do nothing.

Dear Seriozha. He made light of everything. No one could resist his good humor for long. Since Benckendorff, like Tatiana, came from the Baltic nobility, he insisted on bringing her his verses for censorship. Once he even wrote out the Lord's Prayer for her. "For under the Third Department's rules," he explained, "most of the Lord's Prayer will have to go."

And when he was able to prove that this was indeed the case, even Alexis could not help smiling.

He set about teasing old Arina at once. "Dear old nanny, my dove," he would say, "we can't have an old thing with her head full of fairy tales looking after young Master Misha here. He needs an English governess. That's the thing nowadays. We'll send for one at once." As for the little boy, he was immediately fascinated by this wonderful uncle who made rhymes and drew funny pictures. "Misha, you are my little bear," Sergei would say. And the little fellow followed him around everywhere.

Sergei and his friend made an amusing pair. Karpenko was a small, dark twenty-year-old with rather delicate features, and very shy. It was obvious that he was devoted to Sergei, who treated him kindly. With Sergei's encouragement, the Ukrainian's soft brown eyes would light up and he would give brilliant imitations of everyone from a Ukrainian peasant to the tsar himself. Karpenko taught Misha to do a little dance like a bear. And after the priest of Russka had come to call one day, the Ukrainian did such an explosively funny imitation of the fat man greedily ordering a meal and trying to rearrange his red beard over his huge stomach, that Alexis actually burst out laughing.

To little Misha it seemed that, after the cold winter and his mother's death, he had found himself in a strange new world of wonderful sunlight and magical shadow that delighted him, but whose signals he could not always decipher.

For everywhere now, at the Bobrovo estate, a rich sensuousness hung in the air.

Young Arina: with her rather plump young body and her reddish-gold hair: Misha thought she was beautiful. Her blue eyes seemed to light up with excitement whenever she saw his uncle Sergei or Karpenko. She was a little shy of Sergei, though, whereas she would let the dark Ukrainian put his arm around her.

Uncle Sergei was a marvel: there was no doubt. Everyone loved him. He would talk with clever Uncle Ilya by the hours, often in French. And he was always happy to come and sit at old Arina's feet, where he would declare: "I've read all Krylov's folktales, but even he never told them like you, my dear." He was puzzled therefore when once he saw his father glaring at Sergei when the latter's back was turned, and he asked his aunt Olga: "Doesn't Papa love Uncle Sergei?"

"Of course he does," she told him. And when, rather shyly, he asked his father, Alexis said the same thing.

Often, when they all went for a stroll in the alley of birch trees behind the house, he would notice that Karpenko tried to walk beside Aunt Olga. Once he heard her say to Uncle Sergei: "Your friend's in love with me," and then she had given a ringing laugh. Could Karpenko be in love with two women? the little boy wondered. And then there was Pinegin, with his pipe, his pale blue eyes, and his white tunic. He was always there, quietly watching, giving a faint smile from time to time. Yet there was something about him, something hard and reserved that made the boy afraid. Once, when they were all sitting on the veranda, Misha asked him: "Are you a soldier?" And being told yes: "And soldiers kill people?" Pinegin puffed on his pipe, then nodded. "He kills people," the little fellow announced solemnly to all the grown-ups, and everyone burst out laughing. Since he couldn't see the joke, Misha gave up trying to understand things that afternoon, and he ran off to play with Timofei Romanov.

To Olga's relief, over a week passed without incident. Everyone knew that Sergei and Alexis must be kept apart. Everyone was careful.

She had forgotten how amusing he was. He seemed to know everyone and to have seen everything. He would tell her scandalous stories of the scrapes, duels, and illicit affairs of everyone in Moscow and Saint Petersburg, but always with such unbelievable detail that she laughed so hard she had to hang on to his arm.

One evening, after listening to his stories, she asked him curiously about his own love life. Had there been many women? she wondered. Whatever answer she expected, it was not what came next. Leading her to a quiet corner, he took a little book from his pocket and handed it to her. There were columns of names on each page, each with a little comment. "My conquests," he explained. "The ones on the left are platonic friendships. The ones on the right, I've had."

It was outrageous. Nor could she credit the names. "The virtuous Maria Ivanovna slept with you, you rascal?"

"I swear." He gave her a graphic account. And she burst into peals of laughter.

"I don't know what we shall do with you, Seriozha," she said.

As the days passed, only two things troubled Sergei Bobrov. Neither could be mentioned to anybody.

The first was a tiny incident that had taken place the day before he left Moscow. He had been walking along the street with his manservant—a young serf from the Russka estate—when it had happened: and he had been so surprised that, before he could think, he had let out several incautious words—words that could be very serious for others. He had been unsure how much the young serf had taken in, but immediately afterwards he had sternly said: "Whatever you think I just said, you heard nothing—unless you want a thrashing. You understand?" Then he had given him a few rubles.

He had kept an eye on the fellow since they had arrived at Russka and, as far as he could tell, all was well. After a week he put it out of his mind.

But the other matter could not be so easily dismissed. It was in his thoughts every day; and for once he did not know what to do.

It seemed a harmless idea. Even Alexis agreed when, in his second week there, Sergei suggested they should get up some theatricals. He had found some French versions of Shakespeare's plays in the library. "Ilya and I will translate some scenes into Russian," he announced. "Then we can all play them." After all, it was something to do.

So why did Olga feel a sense of misgiving? She was not sure herself. At the beginning, as it happened, this new activity brought her two pleasant surprises. The first concerned Ilya.

She had never, in truth, had much respect for her oldest brother. She remembered how, five years ago, everyone had hoped that his tour of Europe would improve his health and inspire him to do something. Indeed, after staying in France, Germany, and Italy he had finally returned looking slimmer and even purposeful. He had obtained a good post in Saint Petersburg and it seemed he might make a career. And then, after only a year, it was over: he resigned, left the capital, and returned to Russka. True, he had tried to take part in provincial affairs, but he soon became discouraged by the lack of progress and by his boorish fellow gentry. A sort of lethargy seemed to overtake him. And now here he still was, living with his mother, reading books all day and hardly getting out of bed before noon—behaving just as he had when Olga was a girl.

But she had never before seen Ilya roused to such enthusiasm. He and Sergei would work together for hours. His placid face would take on a look of furious concentration. He would even waddle about, warming his hands excitedly as Sergei wrote down what he dictated. "He translates, I polish," Sergei explained. "He's awfully good at it, you know," he added. And for the first time Olga had an inkling of what poor Ilya might have been.

The theatricals began lightheartedly. In the long, warm evenings, with the shadows slowly lengthening and a faint, delicious smell of flowers wafting from some bushes nearby, they would gather by a linden tree before the house and practice their parts. Their first attempt was some scenes from *Hamlet,* with Sergei as Hamlet and Olga as Ophelia. Tatiana joined in; Alexis, too, as Hamlet's wicked uncle; Karpenko and Pinegin split the other parts between them, the soldier turning in a quiet, accurate performance, the Ukrainian hilarious as the ghost. "And what shall I be?" little Misha had demanded.

"You are the bear!" Sergei told him. And to Olga's murmur that there wasn't a bear in *Hamlet,* he whispered: "But Misha doesn't know that." He paused. "Nor does Alexis, come to think of it," he added mischievously, which sent her into a fit of giggles.

Olga's second discovery surprised her even more. It was about Sergei. They were playing a scene as the two awkward lovers when it first struck her. Then, as she listened carefully to other scenes, she suddenly realized. For while Ilya had made the translations, it was Sergei who had turned them into Russian verse.

And it was brilliant—so lovely, so full of feeling, that she was taken aback. Sergei's voice, too, she noticed, when he spoke this wonderful verse, became musical, beautiful to hear.

She remembered the wayward boy who had befriended her; she knew the scamp and womanizer who made her laugh. Yet here, suddenly, was another Sergei, hiding beneath the frivolous surface—a poetic nature, perhaps even profound. She found that she was moved, and with a new respect she told him: "You must go on writing, Seriozha. You have real talent."

The trouble was Alexis.

It was not his fault. His acting, though stiff, was not so bad. It was his language. For while Ilya and Sergei, as educated men, spoke both French and Russian elegantly, poor Alexis—never a scholar, and joining his regiment when almost a boy—had learned French from fifth-rate tutors and Russian from the serfs at Russka. The result was rather unkindly but accurately summarized by Sergei: "He speaks French like a provincial and Russian like a servant." It was a curious condition, not unusual among men of his class at that date. Nor did one notice it so much in everyday conversation; but now, reciting Sergei's beautiful verse, he frequently stumbled awkwardly and Sergei, with a laugh, would have to correct his grammar to prevent him from making nonsense of a line. "I speak well enough for a plain soldier," Alexis growled; but Olga could see he felt awkward.

All the same they managed to do quite well with *Hamlet,* and it was agreed that they would next attempt some scenes from *Romeo and Juliet.* "In which," Sergei added, "there is of course a bear."

It was while Sergei and Ilya were busy with their translation that Olga decided one afternoon to go with young Karpenko and Pinegin on one of her favorite walks, along the low ridge behind the house.

The weather was perfect. The silver birches were gleaming in the sun and shedding a dappled shade. Karpenko, though he gazed at her with adoring eyes, was still too shy to say much. As usual, Pinegin was wearing his white tunic and puffing on his pipe. After two weeks of Sergei's lively conversation, Olga found the soldier's silence rather agreeable.

Olga had long ago decided that, if Karpenko was in love with her, he was certainly harmless. Indeed, he was so shy that she liked to bring him out of himself. She had learned, for instance, that he came from Poltava, a province southeast of Kiev, from an old Cossack family. "My brothers are strapping fellows—it's only me that's so small," he apologized. After some coaxing, he had one day admitted that he, too, hoped to make a literary reputation in the future.

As usual, therefore, after they had walked awhile, they began to talk, and, encouraged by Olga, the young Cossack started to speak of his beloved Ukraine. It was a delight to hear him, a pleasure to see his soft eyes glow as he described to them the whitewashed houses and their thatched roofs, the huge fields of wheat on the rich black earth, the vineyards and lemon groves down by the Black Sea, the huge melons that were grown in his own village. "It's another world in the south," he confessed. "Life is easier. Why even now, if we need more land, we just take our plows out into the empty steppe, which has no end."

So wonderful was his description that Pinegin nodded his head thoughtfully and remarked, "It is so. I have been there, and it is just so."

And it was this statement that suddenly prompted Olga to turn to the quiet soldier and try to draw him out for once.

How little, still, she knew of him. What sort of life had he had? Where had he come from? Where had he served? Was he always so much alone, or had there been others close to him in his past—lovers perhaps? And above all what did he really think about his life, this man who seemed to know so much, yet say so little?

"It is your turn, Fyodor Petrovich," she said softly. "You say you have been in the south. What can you tell us about it?"

"I passed through the Ukraine," he replied. "But I have served farther south, in the Caucasus Mountains. Do you wish to know about that?"

"Most certainly." She smiled. "I do."

He took a little time to reply, but when at last he did, his thin, hard face took on a faraway look. His voice was very quiet. And the words he used were simple soldier's words, yet very carefully chosen. Olga was riveted.

He told her about the high Georgian passes that now belonged to Russia, and the passes beyond, where wild tribesmen still dwelt. He described the mountain goats; the huge ravines one could look down and see the shepherds in the gullies a thousand feet below; the swirling mists over which, as far as the eye could see, the snowy peaks hung pink and white in the crystal sky. He told her about the tribesmen in their bright tunics and shaggy sheepskins—Georgians, Circassians, and those distant descendants of the radiant Alans, the proud Ossetians—who might suddenly appear from nowhere: "Friendly one day, with a bullet for you the next." She could see it all, as though she had been there.

"I was down in the eastern steppe once," he continued, "on the edge of the desert. That's a strange region." And he told her about the little fortresses between the Black and the Caspian seas, and about the Tatar and other Turkish tribesmen who made the frontiers such a dangerous place. And now Olga had a vision of something huge, harsh, unknowable, yet pitilessly clear.

And as she listened, she wondered. There was something about him: something distant, something one could not touch. Had he, perhaps, drunk in something of the character of these harsh, lonely regions where he had lived? Was he, as Alexis said, dangerous? If so, she was not sure it wasn't strangely attractive.

It was just as she was considering this, and hoping to draw him out further that, out of nowhere, Sergei suddenly appeared along the path. "Our work is done!" he cried. "I am Romeo, and you are Juliet." And then in a whisper, which she hoped Pinegin could not hear: "Has he been boring you?"

But if Pinegin heard, he said nothing. And they all three walked back together.

Misha Bobrov watched the grown-ups. Young Arina was beside him. It had been very hot that day and everyone was lethargic. They were rehearsing a scene from *Romeo and Juliet.*

He had seen his father make two mistakes with his lines and Uncle Sergei had had to correct him. But it didn't seem to matter because Uncle Sergei was laughing. His father looked rather red.

"It's beautiful, Seriozha," his aunt Olga said. "But enough for today. I must sit down."

"Tea," called Sergei to young Arina. "We need tea."

As the girl went off to the house, little Misha went over to his Uncle Sergei. He felt very hot, too. Perhaps, he thought, if they all sat down, Uncle Sergei would tell him a story. "Well, my little bear?" his uncle said. "What can we do for you?" And Misha let him ruffle his hair.

But now his father was turning towards him.

It was such a small incident; yet, like one of those little flashes of lightning on the horizon that warns of the approach of a summer storm, Olga should have seen its true significance.

She was hardly surprised, when Alexis abruptly announced he was going for a walk, that no one was anxious to join him. But this caused him to turn to his little son, who at that moment happened to be standing beside Sergei, and ask: "Well, Misha, are you coming?"

It was such a small gesture: it was nothing really. The child just glanced up at Sergei and hesitated. That was all. But it was enough. Olga saw Alexis flinch for a second, then instantly stiffen.

"You prefer to be with your uncle Sergei rather than me," he said, with quiet bitterness.

The little boy, sensing his mistake, looked confused. Then he blushed. "Oh no," he said seriously. And then: "You are my papa." And he went to Alexis's side.

Alexis turned and the two of them walked away, but Olga saw that he did not give the little boy his hand and, remembering that he would soon be leaving them to fight the Turks, she felt sorry for them both.

It was probably just as well, Olga thought, that on the following evening Sergei had arranged for some musicians to come over from Russka so that they could have a little dance—a *bal*, as he called it. Perhaps, Olga hoped, this would break the tension.

How delightful it was. Just as if she were in the city, Olga would pile up her rich hair, put on a gossamer ball gown with billowing sleeves and her dainty, flat-heeled dancing slippers with their pink ribbons; the men would put on uniforms and take turns dancing with her and Tatiana by the bright light of a hundred candles, while the servants and the two Arinas watched with broad smiles.

But the star of the evening was little Karpenko. He borrowed a balalaika and led the musicians in haunting Ukrainian melodies. Then he danced for them—wild Cossack dances, crouching almost on the ground while he kicked out his legs, and next leaping high into the air while the musicians kept up a frenzied beat. Once, drawing himself up and arching his back, and jamming a tall, sheepskin hat upon his head, he gave a brilliant version of a stately Georgian dance—moving across the floor with precise little steps, turning his body from side to side as he went, so that he seemed almost to be floating. "He's good," Pinegin remarked. "I've served down there so I should know." He smiled quietly. "He even manages to look two feet taller." And it amused Olga very much that a few minutes later the Cossack disappeared onto the veranda outside with young Arina, and they were gone for some time.

It was towards the end of the evening, when the others were outside, that Olga found herself dancing with Pinegin. As usual he was wearing his white uniform, but now it seemed to her rather becoming. She also noticed that he really danced very well—nothing flashy, his movements firm but controlled and easy to follow. It was a pleasant sensation.

Then, suddenly, everyone was back. Sergei cried to the musicians: "A mazurka!" And scarcely waiting to ask Pinegin, he swept her away in a wild dance, whirling her around the room, stamping his feet, while Pinegin stood silently to the side. "I was lucky," Sergei explained to her. "I got lessons from the great dancing master Didelot himself."

But Olga found, rather to her surprise, that she would have preferred that he had not interrupted her dance with Pinegin.

The opening thunderclap of the great storm that was about to engulf them took everyone, including Olga, completely by surprise. It came the very next morning, when Sergei was in the bathhouse.

No one in Russia, from the imperial family to the most miserable serf, could imagine life without the traditional Russian bath. Similar in kind to a Scandinavian sauna, the bathhouse contained a stove that heated a deep shelf of large stones, upon which the bather tipped water to fill the room with steam. To stimulate the blood he might also swat himself with birch twigs. In a city, the communal bathhouse would take scores of people at a time; the little bathhouse on the Bobrov estate took only three or four.

Sergei loved to take a bath: in summer he would run down afterward and throw himself into the river; in winter he would roll in the snow. And it was just as, tousle-haired and gasping, he emerged from the water that morning that little Misha came running down the slope towards him crying out: "Uncle Sergei! You'll never guess what's happened. They've come to arrest the priest at Russka."

It was true. Two hours earlier the big redheaded priest had been astonished by the arrival of three blue-coated gendarmes of the Third Department who methodically proceeded to ransack his house. Within an hour the town, the monastery, and even the village of Bobrovo were buzzing with the news. What could it mean?

Olga guessed at once. She guessed—and her heart sank.

"Oh, Seriozha," she whispered. "What have you done?"

"Nothing much," he confessed with a sly grin. He had sent an anonymous letter to the department saying the priest was operating an illegal Masonic press and distributing pamphlets. And to her protest that this accusation was unlikely he replied, "It's unbelievable. But the gendarmes don't seem to think so, do they?"

"Oh, Seriozha," She didn't know whether to laugh or cry. It was well known that Benckendorff's department was being snowed under with false accusations from all quarters, and that some of their investigations had been strange, to say the least. "God help you when Alexis finds out," she said.

It was noon, just as the gendarmes, having found nothing, were leaving, when Alexis, returning from a morning ride, passed through Russka and the shaken priest told him his story. Like Olga, Alexis guessed the cause at once.

And so it was that, seeing Sergei that afternoon sitting with the family, he gave him a look of chilling scorn, and without the need of any further explanation said quietly: "You will regret this very much, I promise you."

Alexis was surprised, early that evening, when Sergei's manservant requested a discreet interview with him.

To the Bobrov serfs, Sergei's position had always been a little puzzling. When his father died, they saw that the estates went to his brothers; but though Sergei's different looks had caused some ribald speculation, it was more generally assumed that his youth and wild ways were the reason for this exclusion. One thing was certain, however. If there was any choice to be made between their master Alexis and young Sergei, there was no doubt about whose side to be on.

Nothing is ever hidden from household servants. The growing rift between Alexis and Sergei had been noticed at once. Within minutes of their angry encounter that day, everyone knew. And it had caused the young serf to consider his position very carefully before, that evening, giving the older brother a careful account of certain matters. When he had told his story, the landlord seemed pleased.

"You were quite right to tell me this," Alexis said. "You will speak of this to no one," he added, "but if it ends well, then I'll let your family off a year's *obrok.*" The manservant was delighted.

And that very day Alexis put certain inquiries in motion.

Afterwards Olga blamed herself. Yet she had meant so well.

All the next day the tension in the house was terrible. Alexis looked like thunder. They dined in near silence. In the evening she tried to persuade Sergei to come out for a stroll with her, but he obstinately refused and sat at one end of the salon while Alexis, at the other end, ignored him entirely. Everyone spoke in low tones, but Olga, looking at the two brothers, was terrified that at any moment, some careless word might start a quarrel. Sergei, in particular, looked as if he were ready to provoke his older brother. What could she do to keep the peace?

It was then that, looking at Karpenko, she suddenly thought she had had an inspiration.

"Why don't you tell us," she suggested, "a Cossack story?"

He blushed with pleasure. He understood very well what she wanted. How glad he was to be useful to Olga and Sergei, these two people he loved. And so, in a quiet voice, he began.

He was intensely proud of his Cossack ancestry. In no time they were all spellbound as he told them tales of the ancient days, of the wild Cossacks riding over the open steppe, and of the great river raids from the Zaporozhian camp down the mighty Dnieper. Tatiana sat with mouth open in wonder; Ilya put down his book; Pinegin nodded with approval and murmured: "Ah, yes. That is good." And even Alexis did not notice when Sergei moved his chair closer, in order to hear better.

What a gay, thrilling world the little Cossack opened before them. What mad feats of bravery, what good fellowship, what wild freedom! Olga congratulated herself on her choice: and if the young fellow was a little carried away, surely there could be no harm in that.

For there was something else about the tales, too: a haunting beauty, an air of nostalgia and even melancholy that she discerned in his tone—as there always is when one speaks of a world that has entered its twilight. "The old Zaporozhian *sich* is gone," he said quietly at one point. "Catherine the Great destroyed that." And later, rather sadly: "The Cossacks are all good Russians now." If he felt a tinge of regret for the past, Olga didn't blame him. The disciplined tsarist regiments of today's Cossacks were fine in their way: but a far cry from the freedom of older times.

Ilya in particular was captivated. "My God," he exclaimed, "you tell your stories so well that if you want to make a literary reputation, you should write them down. Have you considered it?"

And it was then that the trouble began. For having blushed with pleasure and admitted that he had, Karpenko then added a curious and unexpected statement. "Actually," he confessed, "what I really want is to write them in the Ukrainian language. They sound even better that way."

It was a perfectly innocent remark: though undoubtedly surprising. "Ukrainian?" Ilya queried. "Are you sure?" Olga, too, found herself puzzled. For the Ukrainian dialect, though close to Russian, had no literature of its own except one comic verse. Even Sergei, always willing to support his friend, couldn't think of anything to say in favor of this odd idea.

And it was now that Alexis spoke.

Though he had obviously enjoyed the Cossack's stories, Olga had noticed her elder brother's expression gradually becoming rather thoughtful. She had not attached too much importance to this; though when the Ukrainian spoke of Russia, she had noticed that once or twice he frowned. Now at this last suggestion he shook his head.

"Forgive me," he said calmly, "but the Ukraine is part of Russia. You should write in Russian, therefore." His tone was not unkind, but it was firm. "Besides," he added with a dismissive shrug, "Ukrainian is only spoken by peasants."

There was silence. Olga glanced anxiously at Karpenko. Then Sergei spoke: "How boorish."

And Olga trembled. Was this the start of the quarrel she dreaded?

The little Cossack saw her face and understood at once. "It's quite true that Ukrainian is the peasant's language," he readily agreed. "But that's why I'd like to use it for writing about village life, you see." If he thought, however, that he had saved the situation, he was premature.

"Quite right." Sergei was determined to defend his friend. "After all, our own Russian literature has only existed for a generation. Why shouldn't the Ukrainians start their own?" He smiled contemptuously. "Or is having their literature strangled at birth by an illiterate Russian to be another benefit of the tsar's rule?"

Olga caught her breath: a gratuitous insult. Alexis went pale; but with an effort he ignored Sergei. Turning to Karpenko, however, he asked dangerously, "Do the people of the Ukraine dislike the tsar's rule?"

The Cossack smiled gently. He could have said that the Ukrainian peasants had no special love for Russia; he might have mentioned that, under the program of Russification, the towns were losing all their ancient liberties. He could have remarked that even his own family remembered bitterly that their ancestor, a proud Cossack landowner, was sent in chains by Peter the Great to his new capital in the north and never heard from again. But instead he was tactful.

"When Napoleon invaded," he quietly reminded Alexis, "the tsar had no more loyal troops than the Cossacks. And on the eastern side of the Dnieper, where I come from, the landowners have been glad of Russian protection since the time of Bogdan. On the west side of the Dnieper, however, where there's more Polish influence, Russian rule is accepted but not particularly popular." It was a fair assessment, and even if it was not quite what Alexis wanted, he could hardly argue. For the moment he lapsed into silence.

And it was now that, casting about in his mind for a more cheerful topic, and without thinking too much, young Karpenko rattled on. "Do you know," he remarked, "funny enough, about ten miles from where we live there's a place where my family used to have a farm once. It has a new name now, but in Peter the Great's time it was called Russka."

This, as he hoped, diverted their thoughts. Nobody had heard of it, though Ilya at once remarked: "Many northern place names derive from the south. The Bobrovs anciently came from near Kiev, you know, so the village you speak of may once have been ours." He smiled. "There's something we have in common, my friend." The fact that the Cossack's ancestor had run away from the northern Bobrov estate and discovered this Russka in the south was unknown to them both.

"I wonder what sort of place it is now," Olga said.

And then Karpenko made his great mistake. "Actually," he confessed awkwardly, "it's a military colony."

He realized his error the moment he had spoken. Alexis sat bolt upright. Sergei grimaced. And Alexis suddenly smiled. Now was his chance to put them all in their places.

"A military colony," he said with a triumphant look. "There's a splendid improvement." And despite himself—he could not help it—the Cossack winced.

For of all the changes that the tsar's government had made in the Ukraine, the military colonies were the most universally loathed. There were about twenty of them, each large enough to support an entire regiment, and they covered a huge area. Since Karpenko could think of nothing to say in favor of these terrible places, he bit his lip and said nothing.

But Sergei, quietly simmering, had no such inhibitions. "If Alexis had his way, you see," he said quietly, "the whole of Russia would be a single military colony. Like Ivan the Terrible and his Oprichnina, eh, Alexis?"

Alexis's face became stony. "Young people should speak of things they understand," he stated with dry scorn. "Like making rhymes," he added bitterly. And he shifted his chair so that Sergei was presented with his back. Then, looking about for someone trustworthy, he remarked to Pinegin: "If all the empire were governed like a military colony, things would be a lot more efficient." To which Pinegin quietly bowed his head.

It was time to end the discussion—and end it quickly. Olga glanced around, wondering what to do. She signaled to her mother, who nodded, remarked placidly—"Well, well, this has all been very pleasant"—and made as if to rise. But before she could do so, Sergei's voice cut through the air.

"You're surely not suggesting, Alexis, that the military are efficient?"

Why, oh why, could he not for once keep silent? Olga saw a muscle flicker in Alexis's cheek. But he did not turn. He merely ignored the interruption. Olga began to rise.

"I said," Sergei repeated with an evenness that showed he was now angry, "do you believe the military are so efficient?"

In the silence that followed, one might have thought Alexis had not heard. But then he turned to Pinegin again and coolly remarked: "I think, my friend, I heard a dog yapping somewhere."

And Sergei went scarlet. And Olga knew that there was nothing she could do. "Do you know how our wretched soldiers are taught to shoot a volley?" Sergei exploded to the whole room. "I'll tell you. All together. Perfect timing. There's only one problem. They aren't trained to point at anything. It's a fact. I've seen it. No one minds where they shoot, as long as it's together. The chances of a Russian volley hitting the enemy are almost nil! But this"—he sneered contemptuously—"is my brother's military efficiency."

Alexis had lost his calmness now. He seemed about to turn and strike. But it was Pinegin who spoke. Olga had never seen him like this before. He was very quiet, but his eyes glittered, and there was something strangely menacing as he asked: "Are you insulting the Russian army?"

"Oh, much more than that," Sergei shot back. "I'm criticizing the whole Russian empire, which thinks that by imposing order on the human spirit—no matter how absurd or cruel the order—it has achieved something. I'm criticizing the tsar and that dog Benckendorff with his idiotic gendarmes and his censorship: I despise your military colonies, where you try to turn children into machines, and the institution of serfdom, which makes one man the chattel of another. And yes, by all means I'm insulting the army, which is run by the same incompetents who are in charge of this whole, vast sea of stupidity and rottenness that is called the Russian government." He turned back to Alexis. "Tell me, my efficient brother, how many rounds are Russian soldiers given each year for target practice? How many?" And when Alexis, too angry for speech, made no reply: "I'll tell you then. Three rounds. Three a year. That's how your men are trained before you go off to fight the Turk." He laughed savagely. "And no doubt military organization is just what you are using so effectively to run down this estate—now that it no longer has those Suvorins to prop it up!"

Olga gasped. It seemed that Alexis was about to throw himself upon Sergei. She looked at Pinegin desperately, beseechingly.

And the soldier in his white tunic smiled. "Well, Bobrov," he remarked with a dry laugh, "if your brother had said that to me in our regiment, I suppose I should have had to play target practice with his head. But we won't mind. Let's have a game of cards." And before Alexis could speak, Pinegin led him firmly away.

Thank God, Olga thought: thank God for Pinegin.

The following morning Alexis announced that he had to go to Vladimir to see the governor. He expected to be back in a week.

"Would you stay here, my dear fellow, and keep an eye on my brother?" he asked Pinegin, to which the other quietly agreed.

By noon Alexis was gone. With him he carried a letter that he had written late the night before. It was addressed to Count Benckendorff.

Did she still love Sergei? She was fond of him, of course; but could one love a man so self-centered? The quarrel with Alexis had been so unnecessary and his insults unforgivable. The next morning, when he took Misha out fishing, she ignored him.

All morning she was occupied with her two baby children. Old Arina was unwell that day, but young Arina helped her.

It was in the early afternoon, while young Arina was putting the two infants down for a nap, that Olga, strolling towards the birch wood above the house, noticed the white uniform of Pinegin alone in the alley. Feeling she should speak to him, she followed, and soon came to his side.

"I owe you many thanks, Fyodor Petrovich," she said quietly, as they walked along.

He gave her a quick look. In the flickering light and shadow of the alley his eyes looked a deeper blue than usual. "I am always at your service," he said, and quietly puffed on his pipe.

They went slowly up the alley. Despite the fact it was high summer, the short grass in the shade was still green and springy. There was the faintest breeze. "I am very angry with Sergei." She sighed.

He did not reply for a few moments. Then, taking his pipe out of his mouth, he said calmly, "If you will forgive me, he is still a child."

"Yes, I suppose you're right."

He glanced at her again. "Even children, Olga Alexandrovna, can be dangerous, though."

Sergei? Dangerous? Yet that was what Alexis had said of this man. They walked on in silence. What did she make of him? she wondered. If a man is to be judged by his actions, she must think well of him. It was certainly restful to be in his quiet presence. She looked at his hard, impassive face and remembered how he had danced with her, then smiled to herself. Perfect control: she could imagine him as a patient hunter, biding his time.

Yet still there was something distant about him, something she could not fathom. And, emboldened by the sense of intimacy they shared at that moment, she suddenly turned to him and said: "You told me something of your life once, Fyodor Petrovich. But may I ask you—what do you believe in? Do you believe in God, for instance? And what guides you when you are in danger?" She stopped, hoping she had not offended him.

He puffed on his pipe for a moment, then shrugged. "Fate," he said at last. "When you never know if a tribesman's going to put a bullet in your head, you start to believe in fate." He smiled. "It's restful."

"You're not like my brothers, are you?"

"No. That's true." He nodded thoughtfully. "Your brothers are always hoping for something. If they can't hope, they get angry—or give up, like Ilya."

"You don't hope?"

He turned towards her. "As I said, I believe in fate. Things happen as they are meant to. We just have to recognize our destiny."

She was conscious of his pale blue eyes, watching her. Yes, she thought, she had a strange sensation of being safe with him, yet also in danger; and she found it rather fascinating. "I think," she said, "that I understand a little."

He nodded. "Yes, Olga Alexandrovna," he said quietly, "I think we understand one another."

And sensing that this was a compliment, and not knowing quite how to respond, she reached out and lightly touched his arm.

Then they walked back.

And why not, after all? Pinegin was alone. After leaving Olga, he had decided to walk along the lane to Russka; and now he was sitting on one of the little burial mounds beside the path, enjoying the view of the monastery, as the afternoon sun glanced off its golden domes.

Why shouldn't he? He was a gentleman, wasn't he? And this woman was special: she was not like the others.

He had had his share of women. There had been that Jewish girl, when he was stationed in the Ukraine. And the Circassian, down in the mountains. Pure beauty. There he had lived far from the clinging dross of civilization. And some others. But because he was so ridiculously poor, he had always felt awkward with the daughters of the gentry. He told himself they were shallow, vapid, and of no interest. I, who have stood so often on the edge of the abyss, between life and death, he used to think, what can they say to me? But Olga was a being apart. She has suffered, he told himself. She might understand me. He suspected he might never find another like her.

He was poor of course. Yet he had noticed that when other poor men married rich women, people thought well of them, even admired them. Besides, he had other things to offer. He was not some young fool with only a few thousand serfs to recommend him. He was a man who could take care of himself, who had stood alone. And there was something else—a secret that he was strangely proud of. He had never known fear.

Quietly he puffed on his pipe. After all, why not?

Alexis would be back in a few days. If he hadn't changed his mind, he would make his proposal then.

Young Karpenko looked at Sergei with a puzzled frown: something strange was happening to his friend.

There was something about him, some profound inner tension and excitement whose causes Karpenko could not fathom. He knew that behind the facade—behind the Sergei who played idiotic practical jokes, behind even the moralist who so furiously protested about the State of Russia—there was a still, poetic soul. This was the Sergei he loved. And, he could sense, it was this inner man who, for whatever mysterious reason, had been raised to a pitch of secret, nervous exaltation. Why, he had no idea.

And now, this strange request. What could his friend be up to? Why was he so insistent?

"I'll do what I can," the Cossack said, "though I'm not sure it will work." He gave Sergei a puzzled look. "It's just that I don't under-stand . . ."

Sergei sighed. How could anyone understand? "Don't worry," he reas-sured his friend. "It's very easy. Just do as I say, that's all." He hardly understood it himself. But he knew one thing, more certainly than any-thing in his life. "It must happen," he muttered. "It must." He planned it all so carefully.

It was June 24, the feast of Saint John. The last week, since his quarrel and the departure of Alexis, had not been easy. Everyone had been keeping to themselves and he had felt rather an outcast. Ilya stayed with his books; Pinegin frequently went out hunting alone; his mother would scarcely speak to him; even little Misha seemed to be shy of him. And after three days Olga had told him sadly: "I tried so hard to keep the peace, Seriozha. And you spoiled it. You have hurt me."

But the coming feast had lightened the atmosphere. People had begun to look more cheerful. And when, two days before, Sergei had made his suggestion, it had been quite warmly greeted. "I always promised to take you there," Olga had said to Pinegin.

And Tatiana announced: "Ilya and I will come, too. I haven't been to that place in years."

And so it was agreed that, after the celebrations that day, they would all make an expedition to visit the old sacred springs. "We'll take the two Arinas as well," Sergei suggested. "Then old Arina can tell us fairy tales." It was a charming thought, for it was a delightful setting and appropriate to the day.

For it was the custom, upon Saint John's night, for people to go into the forest.

The feast of Saint John the Bather, as the Russians liked to call the Baptist, was a strange and magical day. Everyone dressed up, and in late morning the two Arinas appeared before the company in all their finery.

How lovely, Sergei thought, and how stately was the traditional dress of the Russian peasant woman. Today both the old nanny and her niece wore embroidered blouses with billowing sleeves, instead of the usual simple skirt and shirt. Over these blouses, and reaching to the ground, was a long sleeveless gown—the famous *sarafan*—colored red and em-broidered, as was the style in that village, with geometric birds of oriental design. And crowning this splendid ensemble was the high, tiaralike headdress—the *kokoshnik*—a diadem embroidered with gold and silver threads and river pearls. The only difference in their dress was that young

Arina, as a still unmarried girl, wore her hair in a single, long plait tied with ribbons down her back. In such a dress, it was impossible not to walk in a stately fashion. As well they should, since, like every Russian peasant woman, they were arrayed—though they did not know it—like the ladies of the great half-oriental, Roman court of Constantinople, a thousand years before.

At midday they all went down the hill to watch the celebrations.

It was a curious feast, this day of John the Bather—half Christian, half ancient, pagan Slav—and it was hard to say where one began and the other ended. Upon this day, at the village of Bobrovo, the villagers made little dolls of Yarillo the old fertility god and his female counterpart, whom they called Kupala; and having paraded them around the village, they drowned them in the river, in a ceremony that was half baptism and half ritual killing, and which in either case signaled an ancient rebirth.

Then, under the warm sun, they walked back to the house, where a charming meal was laid out: meat pirozhki, cold *shchi*—the summer version of cabbage soup; trout, turkey, and blini. There were cherry, apple, and raspberry pies, accompanied by mountains of sour cream. To drink there was kvass, wine, and half a dozen different flavored vodkas.

The mellow atmosphere was made softer yet when a little later the village women, all in their wonderful dresses, arrived in front of the house and, standing in a circle, sang those most lovely of all the Russian folk melodies, the ancient Kupala songs.

It was perfect, Sergei thought. Everything was just right. And as the afternoon's lengthening shadows stole across the threshold of evening, he waited.

Misha and the two babies had been put to bed, and the reddening sun was glowing softly over the forest when they all set out to visit the springs.

Tatiana and Ilya went in a little cart, with one of the serfs driving. Everyone else walked. They took the lane that led through the woods past the old burial mounds and came out by the monastery. Then they crossed the river under the town. And soon afterwards Tatiana and Ilya had to abandon the cart, to walk along the little path that wound along near the water's edge towards the site of the springs.

How quiet it was. Only the faint sound of lapping water disturbed the darkness. High in the starlit summer sky, the three-quarter moon rode to the south.

They were walking now by twos: Olga and Pinegin in front; then Karpenko and young Arina; then Sergei and old Arina; and slowly bringing up the rear, Ilya and Tatiana.

The air was warm; there was almost no breeze. Once or twice Sergei smelled the delicate scent of wild strawberries, hidden in the darkness. Once, in a glade, they saw by the moonlight a bank of the blue and yellow flowers the Russians call John and Mary flowers.

The moon gave light enough to show the wanderers their path; and Sergei watched them all. He saw the way Pinegin, still in white, walked beside Olga: never too far, never too near. He watched Olga's easy, swinging gait. He saw Karpenko surreptitiously slip his arm round young Arina. He saw Ilya stumble on a root that his mother had entirely avoided. Each of them had their thoughts that night, he supposed: each their secret hopes. But none, surely, like his.

Sergei had never felt this way before: unless, perhaps, it had always been so, and he had never known it.

In childhood, she had always been his friend, his confidante—his soul mate. How he had loved her pale and lively face, her long brown hair, her light and gentle laugh. She seemed a part of him, and he of her: they knew each other's thoughts, always, without speaking. But then, as was to be expected, they had been parted.

Life had been hard on Sergei. His literary career was slow; money was short. He was often rather lonely. Yet she is there, he always told himself; and his jaunty letters only bore half the tale.

Night after night he would sit down to write. His verse came slowly; often he gave up. His hopes for fame seemed dismally far away.

He invented a method, though, when he composed. Olga became his audience: in his mind's eye her image was always hauntingly before him. If what he wrote was moving, he had moved her; if gay, it meant that he had made her laugh. And once or twice he saw he made her cry. And so, unknown to Olga, through these years, she was Sergei's companion in his thoughts: and often alone in his lodgings he would cry: "My Olga, you—at least you—will understand."

Would it, he had wondered, be a disappointment, living in the family house with her again? Married, then widowed, with children—he imagined she would have changed. Nothing had prepared him, therefore, for what took place in June.

His discovery was made the first day. It was so overwhelming, so absolute, that at times it made him tremble; and at times he wanted to laugh. It cleaved the whole sky, like a silent flash of lightning. It was so natural, so inevitable: surely it was fated, predestined, fashioned by the gods from the beginning of time, enduring, who knew, even to the end. She filled his thoughts. His entire existence seemed to take place under her blue eyes' gentle gaze. Everything was for her. The translations of Shakespeare she loved had been written, every word, for her alone. And everything else that he did—the practical jokes, the foolish quarrel with Alexis—was only an insane game, played to distract them both, by a man who must wear a mask because his true love was forbidden.

Never before, he now understood, had he known passion. And now he could go on no more. Tonight, he had vowed. It must be resolved tonight.

The springs had not changed in centuries. They still burst out of the high bank in these silvery cascades that drained away to the river. It was fully dark. The stars were out. The small, moonlit glade in front of them made a perfect resting place and, charmed by the spot, the company sat on the grass, while the little waterfalls made a low, splashing sound a few yards away. Then Sergei turned to the old woman: "Come now, Arina my duck," he gently said, "tell all your children a story."

And so, in a quiet but musical tone, old Arina began to speak. She told them about the sacred springs and the spirits that inhabited them. She told them about the magic ferns and flowers in the forest. She told them about the souls of lovelorn girls—the *rusalki*—who lived in the river; she recounted the story of the firebird, Ilya of Murom, and several others. And all of them were entranced, grateful to be sharing this most magical night of the Russian year.

Only when she had finished, and everyone was sitting, contented, yet half hoping for something more, did the little Cossack say: "Recite us some of your poems, Sergei. He's written some wonderful ones recently," he added. And when Sergei made a show of reluctance Olga softly chimed in, in a tone that showed she had forgiven him: "Yes, Seriozha. Let us hear."

He had prepared himself so carefully. The mood of the company was just as he had hoped, as quietly he began. The first poem was an old folktale about Baba Yaga the witch, which made them laugh. The second was a poem to autumn. But the third was a love poem.

It was not very long—just five short stanzas. But he knew it was the best thing he had ever written. It spoke of the poet meeting a loved friend after a long absence and finding his love had turned to passion.

> *I shall remember till my ending*
> *How I first saw my love, my light;*
> *Just as the darkness was descending;*
> *A fleeting angel in the night.*

He told how, in the years of his own unhappy life, when they were parted, it was her memory that sustained him:

> *Your spirit calmed me, waking: sleeping*
> *I saw your face across the night.*

And that now, meeting his angel once more, she had awakened a passion; he was born again; and in his heart:

> *Divinity and inspiration,*
> *And life, and tears, and love.*

No one was looking at Olga. They did not realize. When Tatiana, after a pause, asked him who this lady was, he answered: "A woman I knew in Saint Petersburg." Everyone was quiet. Then he heard Ilya murmur: "Beautiful, my dear Seriozha. Exquisite. What a heart you have."

And still, dear God, no one thought to look at Olga.

She was sitting a little back from Tatiana. She had only to move her face two inches to place it in shadow, and now she had done so, and bowed her head. But he had seen—even in the moonlight—he had seen her blush, then seen the tears upon her cheeks. Dear God, she knew. At last she understood.

They sat for several moments, and then Sergei suggested, "The night is young. Why don't we walk to the *skit* where the monks live!" The little hermitage lay at the end of the path. Karpenko at once endorsed the idea; Pinegin seemed agreeable. But Ilya and the two older women were disinclined. "We'll go back to the cart and go home," Tatiana declared. "Let the young people go on." And so the party divided.

Those who continued were led by Sergei along the path. He had young Arina and Pinegin close beside him. Olga, seemingly lost in thought, walked just behind with Karpenko. Sergei moved along briskly, telling Pinegin something of the history of the little hermitage as they went. And so intent on this was he that, it seemed, he was taken by surprise to find after a few turns of the path that the Cossack and Olga had fallen behind so far that they were out of sight.

"Walk on," he said to Pinegin. "I'll go and hurry them up." And a few minutes later the little Cossack came up to Pinegin, looking back over his shoulder as if the others were just around the corner, and remarked: "Olga's talking to her brother. They'll catch us up. This way." And he led them forward.

It was a couple of hundred yards farther that the track forked. "Sergei said it's this one," the Cossack said firmly. And they had walked on more than half a mile before the track petered out and Karpenko said: "Devil take it. I must have made a mistake."

They stood together, Sergei and his sister. They had moved just off the path to the riverbank, where they could watch the reflection of the moon and stars on the water. How pale she looked, in her long white summer dress. For a time they were silent.

"The poem was for me?"

"Of course."

She gazed at the water. "I . . . had no idea." She stopped, then seemed to smile. "Dear Seriozha. It was very beautiful." She paused. "But the words . . . were not for a sister."

"No."

She sighed. She shook her head gently. "Seriozha . . . your poem spoke of love of the kind . . ."

"Of passion."

She took his hand and looked up at him for a moment, then down again at the water.

"I am your sister."

For a moment he did not speak. Then he said simply, "I daresay we shall never in our lives speak of this again. But, so that I may know, when I die—could you love me as I love you?"

She paused so long he thought the moon had moved upon the water. Then she shrugged. "What if I could?" And then: "I love you as a brother." She squeezed his hand gently and turned her face up to his. "What is it you want, Seriozha, my poet of a brother? What is it you want?"

He smiled a little sadly. "I scarcely know. Everything. The universe. You."

"You want me?"

"The universe, you: for me it's one and the same."

"You brought me here, my dearest Seriozha, to seduce me?" She smiled almost playfully.

"You know that."

She blushed. "I do now. Impossible—even if I would do such a thing. Not with my brother."

"Did you know," he asked softly, "that I'm only your half brother?"

"Yes, I did."

She gave a little laugh that floated across the river.

"Does that make it only half a crime?"

"I don't know. Perhaps. It's stronger almost than I am. An impulse."

"We can resist our impulses."

"Can we?" he asked, in genuine surprise.

She did not move, however, and soon, he put his arm around her while they stood and gazed silently at the sparkling night. He did not know how long they stood, but eventually he felt her give a little shiver, and taking his cue said softly: "Let me this only time in my life, kiss you, just once."

She looked down at the ground and slowly shook her head, and then she sighed and looked up, with a strange, sad smile, as she turned and put her arms around his neck.

By the time they got back to the fork in the path, Pinegin was getting irritable.

"We'd better go on towards the *skit,*" Karpenko said. "They must have passed us."

But something—he did not know what—made Pinegin think otherwise.

"I'm going back," he said.

"They said to go on this way," the Cossack said anxiously.

But Pinegin took no notice. To Karpenko's dismay, he went smartly off down the path; and after a minute or two of hesitation, the Cossack said, "I suppose we'd better follow."

He might not have noticed them through the screen of trees if they had not moved. But suddenly Pinegin caught sight of a swaying shape as the two stood locked in each other's arms. For a moment, just then, they seemed to draw apart, so that by the moonlight he saw their faces clearly. After a second's pause, they moved again so that he could not see them.

For almost a minute he could not move. Olga, for whose hand he was about to ask, was with another man—her cursed brother. Stricken, he waited and wondered what to do. Then cold anger seized him. Wasn't she, after all, almost his own? Why should he let this happen? He started to turn off the path and move towards them.

But then he corrected himself. What was the point? This woman, whom he had loved, was dead to him now. And as he was thinking this, along came Karpenko.

"Pinegin!" the Cossack called out, so that his voice echoed through the trees. "What are you doing here?"

"Nothing."

"Let's go to the springs and wait for them there," Karpenko suggested loudly, so that the lovers could hear. And they walked back to the springs. Pinegin was very calm now. Coldly he counted the minutes. So many and Sergei had had her; fewer, and perhaps he had not.

It was just as he was on the point of deciding that, yes, this horror must have happened, that the two of them came down the path. Olga looked very pale, Sergei a little cautious. "We looked for you everywhere," he briefly said. And Pinegin nodded slowly.

"It's late," Olga then murmured.

"Let us go home." She came to Pinegin's side. "Arina," she ordered the girl, "you walk with us. The young men can follow behind."

On the long walk home, they did not say much. After a time, Pinegin lit his pipe. Sergei and his friend had fallen far behind. As they came, at last, in sight of the house at Bobrovo, dawn was almost breaking, and Pinegin felt a trace of dew on his face.

Several thoughts had gone through his mind on the way back. For a short time he had even considered forgetting the incident. It had been, perhaps, a moment's madness. But then he had considered: If I were to take Olga now, all my life that young man would be looking at me and thinking . . . Thinking what? That there was Pinegin, a poor nonentity, acting the husband for his sister and lover. The thought filled his proud nature with icy rage. Whatever Olga's guilt—and all women, he supposed, were weak—it was Sergei who had made a fool of him. He guessed, Pinegin thought. He saw my interest, and then he did this.

The simplest course would be to challenge Sergei. But a duel, whatever the outcome, is always talked of: and that would lead to Olga's complete dishonor. And that, he realized, would be beneath him. But something would have to be done. I shall have revenge, he thought coolly.

For Pinegin was very dangerous.

As dawn was breaking, young Arina waited.

After leaving Olga at the house, she had wandered about by herself, unable to sleep. It had been a magical night. She could hardly believe her luck when she and her aunt had been summoned to join the party. Then, when she was left with Olga and the others, she had been ecstatic.

It seemed to the girl that Olga was the most beautiful creature she had ever seen. As for the two young men, she had been studying them, fascinated, ever since they arrived. They were made in heaven, she thought, not upon earth.

And now, after this magical night, all her senses were awakened. She could still feel the Cossack's arm around her. She remembered his kiss, on the veranda at the dance. She had not understood what was passing in the woods that night—it had never occurred to her. All she knew was that she was warm, and sixteen, and that the night had been enchanted.

She was standing by the bathhouse. She saw the two men come from the lane and pause at the bottom of the slope. She watched intently. Then they parted, Sergei remaining by the water's edge while the Cossack started up the slope to the house.

The girl smiled. It couldn't have been better. The one she loved—alone.

It was a few minutes later that Sergei looked up to see the girl walking quietly along the bank towards him. The first rays of the sun were catching her hair. It did not take long for him to understand what she wanted. And a little while afterwards, in a pleasant clearing in the woods above the house, though the girl was not Olga, he managed, almost, to pretend to himself that she was.

Old Arina was furious. She had seen them, in the early morning, sneaking down from the woods towards the house. She had not even needed to question her niece to guess at once.

Now it was noon and the old woman was alone with Sergei on the veranda. She might be a serf, but she had also been his nanny. She was not afraid of him. And she was giving him a piece of her mind.

"You are shameless. You write pretty poems, but you're a selfish monster. And God will punish you, Sergei Alexandrevich, I swear He will." She positively glowered at him. "And so He should!"

"I'm sorry, my duck," he said with a lame smile. "I daresay nothing will come of it."

"I shall marry her to someone in the village, straightaway, just in case," Old Arina said. "I'll get your mother's permission and you'll be lucky if I don't tell your brother Alexis. I just hope we can find a young man. They're not so keen to be father to your brats, you know . . ." And she went on for some time before she noticed that Sergei's attention was riveted elsewhere.

"Look," he said softly. And she turned.

The large carriage swept up the track to the house. It pulled up now by the main door, but in front of the stables to one side; and moving along the veranda, Sergei and the old woman could see its occupants getting out. First came his brother Alexis, a look of grim triumph on his face. Then a stern-looking soldier.

And now Sergei went completely white.

For from the back of the carriage, his hands in chains, they were pulling down a grim, bearded figure who, when he finally straightened up, towered over them all.

They had captured Savva Suvorin.

And Sergei knew it was his fault.

That single moment of carelessness in a Moscow street.

He had been so surprised to see the tall figure of Savva Suvorin that without even thinking he had called out his name. And when it seemed that Savva had not heard him Sergei had foolishly run across to him and taken him by the arm. Only as he did so and felt Suvorin stiffen did he remember—of course the tall serf was still a runaway.

Sergei had always been appalled by the way the Suvorins had been treated. "Don't worry, I won't give you away," he quickly said. But Savva was taking no chances. "A mistake," he muttered. "My name is not Savva." And he turned and disappeared through a doorway.

Sergei did not go after him. He stood there for a moment or two, looking up and down the street. It was as he did so that he suddenly realized they were only a few yards from the walled compound of the Theodosian sect. "The Theodosians," he muttered. "Of course that must be it."

He had heard how these Old Believers took people in and sometimes gave them false names and papers. No doubt this was the case with Savva Suvorin. Well, good luck to him. He turned away.

And it was only now that he realized that his manservant was standing beside him, and he remembered, too, that he was one of the serfs from the Russka estate. How much had the fellow heard? It was then that he had threatened him with a thrashing if he repeated anything.

Evidently it had not worked.

There was a round-faced woman, too. That must be his wife. And a little boy of two. They were each taken down. They stood there silently. Then Savva Suvorin saw Sergei. His face did not register anything. He just stared at him. Sergei had an urgent desire to rush over and explain that he had not given him away. But what was the point? It was his carelessness and stupidity that had done it. He could only stare back apologetically.

He heard Alexis say: "Well, Suvorin, you'll be thrashed tomorrow." And then Alexis turned and caught sight of Sergei.

"Ah, Sergei"—Alexis smiled, which should have been warning enough—"I have some news for you. Come inside."

And morosely Sergei went in.

Alexis was businesslike. Almost cheerful. He came to the point at once.

"As you see, Sergei, we have recaptured a runaway serf. It seems that you saw him in Moscow but did not see fit to inform me. That, I suppose, makes you an accessory to theft. But we'll say no more about that.

"The real point, Sergei, is that, as you know, I was asked by Count Benckendorff to keep an eye on you. And I'm afraid I haven't been able to make a very favorable report.

"Count Benckendorff therefore—I'll show you his letter—has decided that it would be better for you to go away for a while. Tomorrow I shall send you to the military governor at Vladimir. He will make arrangements for you to travel east—not to Siberia, by the way, just to the Ural Mountains. You'll be staying there for three years, I believe."

Exile. Three years' exile in the Urals, hundreds of miles out beyond the river Volga.

"Perhaps," Alexis suggested brightly, "you can make a study of mining conditions while you are there."

Little Misha did not understand. His uncle Sergei looked white and scarcely noticed him when he came by; Karpenko was walking about shaking his head and muttering. His aunt Olga was weeping. Even Pinegin, sitting in his white tunic and puffing on his pipe, looked grim. It seemed Uncle Sergei had to go away, but Misha could not work out why.

Nobody saw the little boy slip into the salon and stand behind a chair. His father was there, standing. His grandmother was sitting on a sofa.

Misha was about to step out into the room when his grandmother spoke.

"Wolf! That is what you are."

Misha stared. She was speaking to his father.

"You are responsible for this. I know it very well. My own son—a viper!" She spat out the word. "I have nothing more to say to you. Please go."

He saw his father wince, then coldly turn. He hid behind the chair as Alexis walked slowly out. Then, trembling, he sneaked out himself.

What did it mean? Was his father wicked?

1844

The duel between Savva Suvorin and the Bobrov family entered its final stage in the year 1844. It was between a master who respected but hated his serf, and a serf who hated and despised his master.

Savva Suvorin had never given up. The day when he had fled Moscow after receiving Tatiana's letter about his poor father, Savva had taken with him only some money sewn into his clothes and the little blackened icon. For two terrible years, to keep out of sight, he had pulled barges on the river Volga. It was backbreaking work. He saw many die at it. But God had made him strong. And each night he took out the little icon and prayed: "Lord have mercy on me and keep me safe from the evil doings of unworthy men."

After two years he had gone to the great fair of Nishni Novgorod: but it was hard to get anything except menial work without proper papers: and so he was led, finally, back to Moscow and the Theodosian community, who welcomed him gladly and gave him forged papers.

He had been happy in Moscow. Though the community existed to look after its poorest members, it contained many vigorous men of business; and it was not long before Savva was noticed by them. He married the daughter of one: a quiet girl with a round face, pointed nose and, he soon discovered, an astonishing practical sense. They had a child they called Ivan.

And then Sergei had seen him.

On the day after he arrived back at Russka, Alexis Bobrov had him flogged. As the lashes fell on his back, however, he concentrated his mind on one thought: I shall live; and I shall one day be free. And, God be praised, at only the twentieth lash a figure had appeared and a voice cried out in fury: "Enough! Stop this at once!" And so great was Tatiana's anger that even Alexis had dared proceed no further.

The relationship between Savva and Alexis was uniformly sour. Only Tatiana had been able to save the serf from being systematically destroyed. When Alexis wanted to use Savva as a menial house serf "to teach him a lesson and some manners"—as Alexis put it—it was Tatiana who stopped him, pointing out: "Common sense at least should tell you he's worth far more to you doing what he does best." And it was Tatiana who lent Savva money to get started again.

In the years that followed, Savva Suvorin wasted no time. Having been cheated of his object twice before, he pressed ahead with relentless urgency. When, right at the start, his old cousin Ivan Romanov offered to help—"I've three grown sons and a young boy growing, too"—he politely refused. He would have no partners, no interference, no one to slow him down.

In 1830, while Alexis was away at the crushing of another Polish uprising, Savva set up a small business for printing cottons. The profits were extraordinary. But when Alexis returned and saw what he had done, he tried to charge an *obrok* so high that it would almost have closed the business, and Savva told his wife grimly: "That fool doesn't want to profit by me; he wants to ruin me."

Only Tatiana, who ran the estate in Alexis's absence, was able to restrain her son—and make it possible for Savva to operate. Thanks to her, and paying a reasonable *obrok,* he was able in ten years to build up a cloth mill with hired workers at Russka and to become richer than he had ever been before.

Yet despite this working arrangement, Alexis continued, each year, to become a little poorer. The reason was very simple. For though Tatiana could talk some sense into him about the running of the estate, she could do nothing about his personal expenses. And severe though he was, Alexis liked to live well. As his son Misha, destined for the guards, grew up, Alexis insisted on providing lavishly for him, too. "For the honor," he said, "of the family." The result was that the extra *obrok* from Savva's activities, instead of being plowed back into the estate, just encouraged him to spend more, and still his expenses often exceeded his income.

By contrast, Savva's treatment of his own son was harsh. While he and Maria were sad that God had only granted them a single son: "One is enough," Savva would say. Young Ivan, though not of his father's towering build, was a shrewd boy with a fine singing voice. Though Savva had no objection to this, he knew where his son's interest in music must end. When Ivan, aged thirteen, foolishly appeared in the house with a violin he had just acquired, Savva took it from him, examined it, and then with a blow that almost stunned the boy, broke it over his son's head. "You've no time for that," he said simply, by way of explanation.

There was another source of friction between Savva and his master. This was that the serf was an Old Believer. He had kept his contact with the Theodosians, and though he did not seek to convert others, it would be noticed that, when he ate in company, he did so in the Old Believers' manner—apart, using his own wooden bowl, and a little wooden spoon with a cross upon it.

Strictly speaking, the Old Believers sects were loyal at this time. But to Alexis this quiet profession of Savva's faith was deeply objectionable—partly because it seemed to him a sort of personal defiance, and partly for another, even more important reason. "It's against the good of Russia," he firmly declared.

For in 1832, the government of Tsar Nicholas had formulated a doctrine that, in a way, summarized the outlook of all Russian administrations that century and even beyond. This was the famous doctrine of

Official Nationality. It was declared in government, in the army, and above all in school: and it resoundingly declared that the good of Russia lay in three things: Orthodoxy, the tsar's autocracy, and nationality, which last meant a sense of communal belonging to the Russian nation.

The idea was simple. It suggested a paternal relationship between the tsar and his people; it was entirely appropriate to a state that liked to refer to itself as Holy Russia. And to Alexis, the moment this doctrine of Official Nationality was announced, it was sacred.

The dour Old Believer therefore, seemed to the authoritarian landowner to be vaguely treacherous, disloyal, and disobedient. I should have thrashed him more, he thought, and if ever I get an excuse, I'll thrash him again.

And still Savva's real goal, his freedom, seemed elusive.

In 1837, Savva asked Alexis Bobrov what it would take to purchase his family's freedom.

"Nothing, because I will not free you," was the reply.

The next year he asked again and received the same reply. "May I know why, sir?" he asked.

"Certainly," Alexis said pleasantly. "It's because, Suvorin, I prefer to keep you where you are."

And bitterly, looking at his own son, Savva remarked to his wife: "He's still just as I was at his age: a serf and the son of a serf." And when Maria tried to comfort him and told him something would turn up, he only shook his head and muttered, "I wonder what."

And then, starting in 1839, came the famine.

There had not been a crop failure for a number of years: now the crops failed two years running. Alexis was away, down in the Ukraine. Though she was nearly seventy, the burden fell upon Tatiana.

For Russka, the two failures and the resulting famine were grim indeed. "The Riazan estate's a complete wash-out," Ilya moaned. "The steward writes me they've been slaughtering the livestock because there's no winter feed." Numerous attempts were made to buy grain from other areas. "But even if we do find some," Tatiana remarked, "it gets lost on the way." By the winter of 1840 the situation was desperate.

Each day Tatiana would go down into the village and move from house to house. There were still some reserve supplies at the manor, though only enough to help the worst cases, and she used her judgment as best she could. She had two particular calls she always made. One was to the Romanovs, because their son Timofei had always been the playmate of little Misha; the second was to the *izba* where young Arina now lived with her husband and children. She owed it to old Arina, who had died five years before, to help her niece. It was a wretched business. Except for the eldest, a homely girl called Varya, the children were sickly. In the space of four weeks she saw three of them die. And almost worse, she could not persuade Arina to eat. Anything she gave her ended up with Varya. Desperate to preserve at least one child, the mother was sacrificing herself. For a long time, Tatiana was certain, Arina had subsisted off a single turnip. And if these deprivations hurt the peasants, her sharing in their pain, she was sure, had damaged the health of Tatiana herself. In the summer of 1841, when, thank God, the crop did not fail, she said sadly to Ilya: "Something has happened inside me. I don't think I shall make old bones."

It was in the early spring of 1840, when things were at their worst, that the curious rumor started. It was Ivan Romanov who told her about it when she came to the *izba* one morning. Both he and all his sons were looking excited. "It's the tsar," he said. "The tsar is coming here." He smiled. "Then everything will be all right."

"You mean Tsar Nicholas is coming?"

"Oh no," he said with a smile: "The last tsar. Tsar Alexander. The Angel."

It was one of the many strange rumors in Russian history that Tsar Alexander I did not die in 1825, but instead went wandering as a monk— usually by the name of Fedor Kuzmich. No one knows quite when it began. It is even claimed to this day that a certain English private family has papers to prove that this was true.

Each morning now, when she went down to the village, Tatiana saw people hopefully looking out for the former tsar, in the belief that somehow he would bring food. And on one occasion a monk from the monastery was stopped and carefully examined to make sure he was not the tsar in disguise.

While she smiled sadly at all this, it also offended Tatiana's practical nature. And it was this hopeful waiting for Tsar Alexander, as much as anything, that gave her a new idea. She summoned Savva Suvorin. "What we need here in future," she told that practical man, "is not a tsar, but an alternative crop. I want you to make inquiries and see what you can find."

It was not until three months later that Suvorin reported to her, but when he did, it was, for once, with a faint grin. In his hand he held a small sack, from which he now drew out a dirty, gray-brown object. "This is your answer," he said. "The German colonists have been growing these down in the south for a long time, but we haven't any up here."

"What is it?" she asked.

"A potato, my lady," he replied.

And so it was, some time before it became usual on the private estates in the province, that one of modern Russia's most important crops was first planted at Russka.

But for Savva Suvorin, though he regretted the suffering, it was hard not to take a grim pleasure in the failures of 1839 and 1840. For they gave him his chance.

"That's two years of income Bobrov has lost," he said to his wife and son. "That damned Alexis Bobrov can't hold out much longer." He nodded thoughtfully. "It's time to make them an offer they cannot refuse." And in the spring of the following year, he requested a passport from Tatiana, to visit Moscow.

And now, in May 1844, Savva Suvorin stood before Alexis Bobrov and made his astonishing offer.

"Fifty thousand rubles."

And even Alexis was struck dumb. It was a fortune. How the devil had Savva found it?

"I will return tomorrow, lord, in order that you may consider the matter." And he discreetly withdrew, while Alexis could only stare after him. This time, the serf thought, I have him.

The plan of Savva Suvorin was hugely ambitious. It centered on the gigantic loan he had negotiated, free of interest for five years, from the Theodosians. This loan would allow him to buy his freedom and also to make a single, enormous investment that would transform the Suvorin enterprises forever.

There was at this time no more booming business in Russia than the manufacture of cotton from the imported raw material—so much so that the area above Vladimir was becoming known as Calico Country. Savva's plan was not only to convert his woolen plant over to cotton, but also to speed production hugely by the purchase of a large, steam-driven jenny from England. One or two of the more powerful Russian entrepreneurs had already done this a few years before, and he knew the results had been spectacular. "But I won't do it unless I'm free," he told his family. "I'm not setting up a big enterprise like that just to have those accursed Bobrovs steal it all on some pretext like they did before."

Fifty thousand rubles. It was an extraordinary offer that the landlord had to consider.

Alexis Bobrov, at the age of fifty-one, was an impressive figure who looked rather older. His body was heavyset. His gray hair was cut short; his cheeks had filled out with age so that his long, hawkish face had become squarer, more massive. His nose had thickened at the bottom and curved down over his mouth so that, with his long, drooping gray moustache, he put one in mind of some Turkish pasha of unshakable authority. Upon the uniform were numerous medals and orders including that of Alexander Nevsky.

Having been widowed a second time, and suffering from an old wound acquired in the Polish rising, which gave him a slight limp, he had taken an honorable retirement that year and had come to live permanently on the Bobrovo estate.

When he told his mother and brother Ilya about the offer, they were both adamant: he should take it. In Tatiana's case, the argument was simple. As well as her private sympathy for Savva, it was clear to her that the money was needed. "With that," she reasoned, "you could clear all the debts we've incurred from the crop failures, make the necessary improvements in the estate, and have plenty to spare." For a generation at least, the Bobrovs would be out of trouble.

Ilya's argument was slightly different. Though he had never realized his mistake over the stolen money, he had always had a vaguely guilty feeling over the way his family had treated the Suvorins. But even aside from that, there was another consideration. "For the fact is—forgive me putting it like this, my dear brother—but every civilized man in Russia finds serfdom repulsive. Even our tsar, who most people think of as reactionary, is known to think that serfdom should be abolished. A major committee has already sat on the subject for years, and each season there's a new rumor from the capital that something is going to be done. One day I think that rumor will be true. A proposal at least will be made. And what will Suvorin offer you then, if he believes that in a year or two he may get his freedom anyway? Quite apart from my own feelings about serfdom, I say your own self-interest should make you take his offer."

Yet as Alexis listened, he was not convinced. Ilya's argument he rejected out of hand. "People have been talking about freeing the serfs all my life," he said, "but it never happens. The gentry won't allow it, not in my lifetime. Perhaps not in Misha's either."

There was also something else that he found offensive about the business. He was shrewd enough to guess at once the likely source of Savva's finances. Even he couldn't come up with that much. It must be those damned Theodosians, he thought. And he remembered something the redheaded priest at Russka had told him the previous year. "You know, Alexis Alexandrovich, wherever these Old Believers set up factories, they start converting all the local peasants, and the Orthodox church loses its flock." Alexis could imagine just what might happen if Suvorin were free of his authority. The whole place would be riddled with Schismatics. As an upholder of the doctrine of Official Nationality he was appalled by the idea.

And thirdly, most important of all, he was secretly convinced of something else. My mother, he told himself, is admirable in her way, but now that I'm here to manage the estate full-time, things are going to change. All that was needed to increase the income dramatically, he believed, was the bringing of what he called "a bit more discipline" to things. Moreover, while his respect and affection for Tatiana would not allow him to offend her by doing so yet, she would not always be there; and when she was gone, he faithfully promised himself: I'll squeeze that Schismatic Suvorin until the pips squeak. He might not get fifty thousand rubles out of him, but over the years he'd surely get enough. Let him make money, he vowed, but I'll see he dies poor.

And so, when Savva appeared the next day, Alexis Bobrov looked at him coldly and declared: "I thank you for your offer, Suvorin, but the answer is no." And when the dumbfounded serf—who knew that this decision could not possibly be in Bobrov's own interest—asked him when he might discuss the matter again, Alexis gave a smile and replied: "Never."

That night, therefore, when Savva discussed it with his wife, he told her, "That obstinate fool is immune to reason." And when she suggested that perhaps one day something would change his mind, Savva grimly replied, "He'll never give in, until he's ruined."

And he wondered when that might be.

It was at this time that Ilya began to behave strangely. No one quite knew what had got into him. Usually, as the warm weather approached, he would be found sitting by the window in the salon, or about on the veranda, reading. Seldom before high summer would he spend much time out in the open.

Now, however, his pattern of life had completely changed. He spent hours up in his room, from which he would emerge with a furrowed brow, frequently muttering, and generally locking the door, so that the servants could not clean it. He would pace up and down in the alley above the house for an hour at a time. And if Alexis or Tatiana asked him what he was up to, he would give them some meaningless reply such as—"Aha!" or "Why, nothing at all!"—so that they could only wonder what his secret was.

It was on one of these days, when Ilya had been passing excitedly in the alley, that Tatiana experienced the first sign. It was nothing much: a sudden dizziness. But a few hours later, as she was sitting in the salon, she blacked out for about half a minute.

She said nothing to anyone. What was there to say? She went about her daily business. But from that moment the thought entered her mind and remained there quietly but insistently: the days to come were numbered, and the number might not be large. A week later she had another blackout.

If these signs were not unexpected, Tatiana still felt rather lonely and afraid. She found she liked to go to church each day; but the redheaded priest at Russka was not much comfort. She visited the monastery and conversed with the monks, which was a little better. But it was after a Sunday service, when the bread that had been blessed was distributed, that a peasant woman she scarcely knew came up to her with a kindly smile and said, "You should go and see the old hermit beyond the *skit.*"

She had heard of this man. He was one of the monks at the little *skit* beyond the springs who, two years before, had been allowed to move farther into the woods to a hermitage of his own. Stories had come back that he was a man of great holiness, but nothing more definite than that. There was no talk of miracles; he kept to himself and few knew much about him. His name was Father Basil.

For a week Tatiana put the idea at the back of her mind. It was far away, and she felt rather shy. But then she had another blackout and a pain in the chest that frightened her. And so it was two days later that she had the coachman harness up a little single-seat cart and, without saying where she was going, she set off.

It took them all morning. She had to leave the coachman and walk the last part on foot. But the place, when she got there, was not what she expected.

The clearing was quite large. In the middle stood a simple but well-built hut. Before the hut was a little vegetable garden. To one side, near the trees, were two beehives made of hollowed logs. Just in front of the door was a table with some books and papers upon it, and sitting at the table was a monk. She could see from a hoe beside the vegetable garden that he had been working there recently, but now he was engaged in writing. Seeing her, he looked up pleasantly. She had heard that he was an ascetic and that he was seventy-five. So she was surprised to see before her a refined but vigorous-looking man whose beard was still mostly black and a face that might have belonged to a man of fifty. His brown eyes were clear and looked at her with great straightforwardness.

"Ah yes," he said, "I thought I felt somebody coming."

He nodded politely when she introduced herself, and he produced a stool for her to sit on. Then, as if he were waiting for something, he said, "Perhaps you would sit here for a little while, until I return." With that he disappeared into the hut, she supposed, to pray.

It was warm and pleasant. The light breeze that rustled the leaves could hardly be felt in the glade below. While she waited she tried to work out what it was, exactly, she wanted to ask this holy man, how she should say it. And in this way some twenty minutes passed.

When she saw the bear she very nearly screamed. It seemed to come from nowhere and lumbered across the clearing straight towards her. She had just risen to rush into the hut when the hermit appeared.

"Ah, Misha," he said gently. "Back so soon?" He smiled at Tatiana. "He comes to beg for honey because he knows he's not allowed to touch the beehives." And he stroked the bear's head affectionately. "Off you go, you naughty fellow," he said kindly, and the bear lumbered away.

When the bear was gone Father Basil resumed his seat and indicated that she should do the same. Then, without asking her any questions, he began to speak quietly, in a deep, firm voice.

"On the subject of our life after death, the Orthodox faith is very clear and quite explicit. You must not think that, at the moment of death, you suffer any loss of consciousness, for this is not the case. Indeed, quite the opposite. Not for an instant do we cease our existence. You will see the familiar world around you but be unable to communicate with it. At the same time, you will encounter the spirits of those who have departed, probably those you have known and loved. Your soul, released from the clinging dross of the body, will be more lively than before; but you will by no means be free of temptations: you will encounter spirits both good and evil and be drawn to them according to your disposition. For two days—I speak in terms familiar to us here on earth—you will be free to roam the world. But on the third day you will face a great and terrible trial. For, as we know from the story of the dormition of the Virgin, the Mother of God herself trembled at the thought of that day when, as we put it, the soul passes through the tollhouses. This day you must fear. You will encounter first one and then another evil spirit; and the extent of your struggle with those evils in life will give you strength, or not, to pass through. Those who do not, go straight to Gehenna. On this day the prayers of those on earth are of great assistance."

Tatiana looked at the hermit thoughtfully. If she had hoped for comfort, she had not found it. Who would pray for her upon that day? Her family perhaps? Stern Alexis?

The hermit gave her a quiet smile. "I will pray for you then, if you like," he said.

Tatiana bowed her head. "But perhaps you will not know of my death," she suggested. The hermitage was so cut off.

"I shall know," he replied. Then he continued. "For thirty-seven more days, after the third, you will visit the regions of heaven and hell, but without knowing your own destiny. Then you will be allotted your place to await the Last Day of Judgment and the Second Coming."

He turned to her kindly. "I remind you of this so that you may know that your soul suffers no loss in death, but rather passes, instantly, into another state. Your life is only a preparing of the spirit for its ultimate journey. Prepare yourself, therefore, without fear. Repent your sins, which stand against you. Beg for forgiveness. Make sure that your spirit, on the threshold of its journey, is humble." He got up.

Tatiana also rose. "Will it be soon?" she asked.

"The hour is always late," he replied quietly. "You must prepare. That is all."

He gave her his blessing and a little wooden cross. And then, just as she was leaving, he motioned her to stop.

"I see," he said thoughtfully, "that before you pass over, you are to undergo a trial." He paused, gazing past her; then, turning his eyes back to her, he remarked: "Pray earnestly, therefore, as you prepare to receive a visitor."

As she walked slowly back to the cart, she wondered what he meant.

It was a week later that a modest carriage, driven by an ill-dressed and rather grumpy-looking coachman drew up to the house. In it sat Sergei. And with him was his wife.

At the age of forty-two, Sergei Bobrov looked like what he was—a man whose talents had brought him minor standing, and who hoped for more. The two literary geniuses of his generation—his old friend Pushkin and, more recently, young Lermontov—had both appeared like meteors in the sky only to lose their lives in their prime. People looked to Sergei as a man who might, in his middle age, continue what they had begun when young. And perhaps part of the reason for the deepening lines down his face was that, so far, he had not quite managed to produce works to justify this hope. His dark hair, worn long, had thinned at the front. He had thick side whiskers now, which were graying. His eyes looked a bit strained. He had a slight paunch, which somehow suggested a kind of irritability. He came only seldom to Russka, and Tatiana knew he had constant problems with money; but he never complained.

And now, as soon as the couple were inside the house and the first civilities were done with, Sergei drew his mother to one side, and explained: "The fact is, I've come to ask you all a favor."

His old friend Karpenko, now living in Kiev, had invited him to tour the Ukraine. An arduous journey was planned, some of it on horseback and quite unsuitable for a woman. "If I'm going to do any good work," he confided, "I need a change of scene, the chance to get away." He expected to return in two months. In the meantime, he had come to ask: "Could I leave my wife with you?"

It would have seemed strange to Tatiana to refuse.

It was a pleasant gathering at dinner. In particular it made Tatiana happy to see Alexis and Sergei together.

Over the years they had achieved a measure of reconciliation. And they had evolved a cast-iron rule for avoiding quarrels—which was simply never to discuss certain matters like the military or Savva Suvorin.

And if she knew they had done all this chiefly for her sake, at least it was something.

If Alexis went out of his way to be agreeable, Ilya was beaming with pleasure. It was hard for this highly educated man to share many of his thoughts with her—still less with Alexis. But ever since Sergei's appearance, Ilya had been galvanized, and before dinner she had heard him waddling about in his room, pulling out books and papers and muttering: "Ah. Seriozha. There are so many things we must discuss." If anyone would discover Ilya's secret, it would certainly be Sergei.

The one figure of mystery at the table was Sergei's young wife. What could one make of her?

Sergei had married Nadia three years before. She was well born, a general's daughter, whose fair hair and pretty appearance upon the dance floor had made her referred to in society, one year, as an "ethereal beauty." It happened, that year, that Sergei, too, had been briefly in fashion. And it seemed that the girl and the rake had each fallen in love with each other's reputation in the short-lived season. "She's certainly blond," Ilya had complained after their first meeting. "But I can't see anything ethereal about her." Since the marriage, Sergei's family had seen little of the girl. There had been a baby, lost when it was a week old, and no news of further pregnancies since. And now she sat quietly, looking a little bored, but talking mostly to Alexis, with whom it seemed she felt more at ease than with Ilya. If she were staying there all summer, Tatiana thought, no doubt she would know all about her before long.

At the end of the meal, Tatiana and Nadia both felt tired and decided to retire, while the men moved out onto the veranda to smoke their pipes and talk. The atmosphere between them now was mellow. Even Alexis, after talking to Sergei's wife, was in a cheerful good humor; and when Sergei had given them the latest gossip from the capital, he turned to Ilya and remarked: "Well, brother: now that Seriozha is here, are you going to tell us, at last, what the devil you've been up to these last few weeks?"

And it was then that Ilya revealed his secret.

"The fact is," he replied with a placid smile, "I'm leaving Russka." And as they gazed at him in astonishment he explained: "I'm going abroad to write a book. I'm calling it *Russia and the West*. It will be my life's work."

Perhaps it had been a sudden inspiration; perhaps the culmination of years of study. Or perhaps it had been the sight of Alexis's medals, especially the Nevsky order, resting so ceremoniously upon his brother's chest, which had suddenly brought it home to Ilya that while his brother had already retired with proof of a lifetime's accomplishment, he himself had absolutely nothing to show for his fifty-five years on earth. Whatever the cause, he had now decided to make a supreme effort: Ilya Bobrov, too, would leave some memorial.

He had spent a lifetime in study; he was a European, a progressive: what, then, could be better than to write the book that would lead his beloved Russia forward upon her destiny, so that future generations might look back and say: "Ilya Bobrov showed us the way."

And now, with obvious pride, he outlined his plan. "My thesis," he explained, "is very simple. Russia has never, in all her history, been

capable of governing herself. It has always been outsiders who brought
order and culture to our land. In the days of golden Kiev it was Norsemen
who ruled us and the Greeks who gave us our religion. For centuries we
lived in darkness under the Tatar yoke; but when we emerged, who led
us forward into the modern world? Why, the English, Dutch, and German scientists and technicians imported by Peter the Great. Who gave
us our present culture? Catherine the Great, who brought us the Enlightenment from France. What philosophers inspire you and me, Sergei?
Why, today's great thinkers from Germany.

"It must be so, for Russia has so little to offer of its own, and what we
have belongs to the Dark Ages. Look at our laws!" He turned from one
to the other. "Just a few years ago our noble Speransky at last completed
the great codification of Russian laws, and what do they reveal? A con-
cept of justice that would have looked barbaric in the West a thousand
years ago. The individual has no rights, there are no independent judges,
no trial by jury. Everything may be done—even to landowners like
us—at the whim of the tsar. And to this we Russians cheerfully submit
like oriental slaves. No wonder progress is impossible.

"My plan is simple. I shall go to England, France, Germany to gather
material for an outline for a new Russia. A Russia modeled on the West.
A complete restructuring of our society." And he gazed at them in triumph.

"But, my dear brother"—Sergei laughed—"if you say things like that,
people will say you are mad." It was true that only a few years before,
a distinguished Russian thinker who had written a similar view had been
declared officially mad by the infuriated authorities.

Ilya, however, was not at all abashed. "The fault of that author," he
declared, "was that even he did not go far enough. For here"—he tapped
the arm of his chair excitedly with his finger—"here is the true originality
of my approach. For I shall show that the key to our spiritual salvation
lies not in religion, not in politics, not even in justice, but in economics.
And here"—he smiled complacently—"I have my bible and my prophet:
I refer of course to the great Scotsman, Adam Smith, and his book *The
Wealth of Nations.*"

Indeed, the writings of Adam Smith, the father of capitalist economics
and free markets, were well known to Russian intellectuals at this time.
The first Russian translation of Smith had appeared back in 1803. Ilya
now expounded, with relish, the great economist's ideas on enlightened
self-interest and economic efficiency. "Everything flows from this," he
declared, "even the freeing of the serfs."

If Alexis had looked bemused during most of this, he now suddenly
became attentive. "Freeing the serfs?" he demanded. "Why?"

"Because, my dear brother," Ilya explained, "numerous Russian
economists over the last two decades have conclusively shown that, all
other considerations aside, if you free your serfs, you yourself will actually be better off." He smiled. "Think of it. A free peasant, paid for what
he produces, has incentive. Your serf, forced to work for no reward, does
as little as he can get away with. It's as simple as that." He paused. "I

promise you, this view is well understood even in official circles. Only our Russian inertia holds us back."

For several moments Alexis was quiet while he considered this. But when at last he spoke, he did so not in anger but in genuine puzzlement.

"Do you really mean then," he asked, "that each individual in society should act for himself, considering his own interest paramount? Do you mean that the peasant should strive to get as rich as he can and rely only upon his own hard work?"

"Yes. Pretty much."

"And if his fellow peasant, who is weaker, falls behind, is he to be allowed to suffer?"

"He may be helped, but yes."

"And what about families like us? Our whole role in history has been to serve the tsar and our country. Should I be at home looking for profit like a merchant instead?" He shook his head sorrowfully.

"We all want to serve a cause, Alexis," Ilya explained, "but I am speaking of money and of markets."

"No," the other rejoined. "You are speaking of men and their actions. And if all men act only for themselves, as you suggest, then where is religion, where is discipline, where is obedience and humility? I see only chaos and greed." It was not often that Alexis was brought to such eloquence. It was obviously heartfelt. "I'm sorry, Ilya, but if that is your idea of progress, it is not mine. This is the evil, self-centered way of the West—and you are certainly right that it comes from the West. It is what Russia has fought against for centuries. And both I, and our church, and even I suspect our serfs, will oppose it as long as we have breath."

And sadly he got up, bade them both good night, and left them.

For a long time after he had left, Sergei and Ilya continued to talk. They discussed Ilya's journey, which he planned to begin that very autumn; they discussed literature, philosophy, and many other matters. And it was far, far into the night when Sergei finally turned and said, "You know, my dear brother, Alexis was not altogether wrong about your ideas. You insult our poor old Russia, yet you are also wrong about her."

"How so?"

Sergei sighed. "In the first place, you want to bring efficiency to Russia. I tell you frankly, it cannot be done. Why? Because Russia is too big, and the weather is too bad. This is the wasteland the Romans never conquered. The West joins its towns by roads. Yet what have we got? One! One metaled road in the whole empire, from Moscow to Saint Petersburg—planned by Peter the Great but not executed until 1830, when he'd been dead a hundred years. Europe has railways. What have we? They started building one from the Russian to the Austrian capital last year and the tsar himself has declared he thinks it is dangerous for people to move about so much. Russia is not the bustling West, my brother, and it never can be. Russia will be slow and inefficient until the Second Coming. And shall I tell you something? It doesn't matter.

"Which brings me to my second objection. Your prescription for Russia comes from the head. It is logical, reasonable, clear-cut. Which is exactly why it has nothing to do with the case.

"The Russians will never be moved by such things. That is what the West will never comprehend. It is the deep weakness of the West, as we see it, that it does not know that to move Russia, you must move her heart. The heart, Ilya, not the mind. Inspiration, understanding, desire, energy—all three come from the heart. Our sense of holiness, of true justice, of community—these are of the spirit: they cannot be codified into laws and rules. We are not Germans, Dutch, or English. We are part of Holy Russia, which is superior to all of these. I, an intellectual, a European like yourself, say this to you."

"You are one of this new group then, who claim a special destiny for Russia, apart from the rest of Europe, who people call Slavophiles, I take it," Ilya remarked. He had read a little of this group lately.

"I am," Sergei said, "and I promise you, Ilya, it's the only way."

And so at last, their minds full of these grand and universal thoughts, the two brothers affectionately embraced each other and retired to their beds.

At eleven o'clock the next morning, Sergei departed for the Ukraine.

As he strolled through Vladimir that August morning, Alexis Bobrov was in a rather good temper.

Just before leaving he had received a letter from his son Misha to announce that he would be joining his family at Russka for ten days on his way from his regiment to Saint Petersburg. He should be arriving at the very time I get back, Alexis thought contentedly. How pleasant that would be.

The summer had gone rather well. That accursed Savva Suvorin had kept quiet. On the estate, despite widespread failures in some areas, the prospects for an excellent harvest looked promising. In the village there had been a marriage: Arina's daughter Varya had married young Timofei Romanov, Misha's childhood playmate. He liked them both. The Romanovs were always respectful. He had taken a particular interest, let the young couple off a year's *obrok,* and thoroughly enjoyed giving them his blessing at the wedding. Whatever Ilya might say, that was how things were meant to be in Russia.

He had been busy in the district, too. He had become an assistant to the marshal of the nobility—whose duties largely consisted in keeping up the registers of the gentry in the area. But it gave him a sense that he was participating in the province, and now, with time on his hands, he was making numerous visits to his fellow landowners—"to make sure I'm in touch," as he put it.

Above all he had been pleasantly surprised by Sergei's wife. It was amazing really, he thought, that such a sensible young woman would have married Sergei. He found they agreed about most things, and though he was too well bred to pursue the matter, certain hints she had dropped suggested that she had a sensible view of Sergei's writing, too. "I must confess," she had confided to him the previous week, "I didn't realize when I married him that he just scribbled all the time. I supposed he did something else as well." It must be very trying for her, he thought.

It was a pity that Tatiana and Ilya didn't seem to get on with her very well. But she certainly put herself out to be pleasant to him. "I really do think it's too bad of Sergei to leave me in the country like this," she said to Alexis, "where there's nothing to think about all day." And then she gave him a pretty smile. "I'm so grateful to have you for company."

Alexis was in Vladimir that morning because he was on his way to spend a few days with a landowner nearby. He had just seen the governor and was planning to visit the great cathedral. And no person, certainly, could have been further from his mind when he suddenly paused, opened his arms, and cried out: "My dear fellow! What brings you here? Aren't you coming to see us?"

It was Pinegin.

The house party was delightful. Misha was so happy to be home. He had arrived at Bobrovo a couple of days earlier than expected and been pleased to find Sergei's wife Nadia there. She was only a few years older than he was and he thought her rather beautiful.

It was easy to see why young Misha Bobrov was popular in his regiment. Though he looked like his father Alexis, there were some important differences. Physically he was an inch or two shorter, and more thick-set. Intellectually he was far more educated. He loved to sit with his uncle Ilya and discuss life. "And though I shall never read a hundredth part of what he has, I like to think a bit of his learning has rubbed off on me," he would say pleasantly. And lastly, by temperament he was optimistic and easygoing, so that even Alexis once remarked to Tatiana: "Frankly, he's the best fellow this family has produced for a long time: I'm the first to admit it." He had the same little gesture as his grandfather, that gentle, caressing motion of the hand when he touched someone's arm or ushered a guest into a room. And even Alexis's occasional dark moods would usually dissolve at the sight of his son.

As was his habit, Misha spent the first day visiting all those he loved. He sat with his grandmother for an hour. The rest of the morning he spent with Ilya. He found his uncle in a strange and excitable state, but he put it down to the great book he was writing. He also visited the village, kissed Arina, and called upon his childhood playmate Timofei Romanov and his wife Varya. In short Misha was home, and all was well in the world.

He was curious about the stranger, Pinegin. He had a vague memory of this man from his early childhood—a figure then, as now, in a white tunic and usually smoking a pipe. Pinegin was somewhere in his forties now, but scarcely changed except for a few more lines around the eyes, and the fact that his sandy hair had turned iron gray. He greeted Misha with a friendly if slightly guarded smile, and Misha's only thought about him was: Ah, there's another of those quiet, rather lonely fellows from the frontier forts. He was glad to see that Pinegin was making himself pleasant to Sergei's wife Nadia, sitting with her and Tatiana on the veranda telling them anecdotes, or accompanying her if she wanted to walk in the alley. After all, that was what a houseguest was meant to do.

And therefore, on the second afternoon, as he strolled up to join them in the alley above the house, Misha was completely dumbfounded when he caught sight of them, standing in the glade just off the park, and saw that Nadia was folded in Pinegin's arms.

Misha stood quite silently, hardly able to believe it. And still Nadia and Pinegin kissed.

How easy it had been. Perhaps in a way, Pinegin thought, it would have been better still if the girl had, at least a little, loved her husband. But it was not so, and so it was futile to concern oneself with that.

It was strange to be back at Russka. "You must come, my dear fellow. I'll return in a few days to join you: amuse the ladies at least, I beg you, until then." Those had been Alexis's words. And as he bumped along the road, Pinegin shrugged. How strange that they should have met like that in the street, when he was on his way to take some leave in Moscow. But then, if one believed in fate, nothing was surprising.

Seventeen long years had passed: seventeen long years of distant campaigns, border fortresses, and frontier posts. Often he had been in danger; always he had been cool, protected by fate. A man could be a hero, though, but still be forgotten at the center, where promotions were made. A rich man, a husband of Olga, would find himself promoted: but Pinegin was still a captain. Possibly one day he would be a major. But something about him, something distant and rather lonely, made that uncertain. He preferred, it seemed, to remain a law unto himself.

Seventeen long years. After the Turkish campaign of '27, he had lost touch with Alexis. But even in distant places he had received news. He knew when Olga had remarried. He heard of Sergei's return from exile; he read Sergei's works when they appeared. Word of Sergei's marriage to a general's daughter reached him, and a fellow he knew even managed to send him a little miniature picture of the girl. He heard that they had lost a child. And always these little items about the family who had insulted him were filed quietly away in his memory, like a weapon in an armory, locked up but always kept clean in case of some future need.

For to Pinegin, believing as he did in fate, there was nothing to do but wait for the gods, in their proper time, to give him their signal. When it came, they would find him ready. And clearly now the sign had come, and with icy calm Pinegin had gone about the business. It was very simple, quite inevitable: tit for tat, humiliation for humiliation. He would seduce Sergei's wife.

For as Alexis had long ago observed, Pinegin was dangerous.

All the rest of that afternoon, Misha wondered: what the devil should he do? He loved his uncle Sergei. He couldn't just let this terrible business go on. Besides, since Pinegin had only been here a few days, surely the affair could not have gone too far as yet.

That evening, therefore, while the others were sitting out on the veranda playing cards, he found an excuse to walk alone with Pinegin and take a turn up the alley. He was very careful to be pleasant and polite. But when they reached the place opposite where Pinegin had kissed

Nadia, Misha quietly observed, "I was here this afternoon, you know."

Pinegin said nothing, but gave him a thoughtful sidelong glance and puffed on his pipe.

"I hardly know my sister-in-law," Misha went on quietly. "She has been left alone here all summer of course. And I probably misunderstood what I saw. But you will understand I'm sure that in the absence of my father and my uncle, Captain Pinegin, I must ask you to make sure that nothing takes place that would bring dishonor to my family."

And still Pinegin puffed on his pipe and said nothing.

He had not counted on this young man. The deed was the key. He had even left to fate the question of whether or not Sergei discovered. If he did, so much the better: Pinegin had no fear of the consequences. But young Misha was a bystander whom, for some reason, the gods had added to the scene, and there it was. The young man's speech, of course, was absolutely correct. He found no fault with it at all. And he wondered what to do.

Slowly he turned and began to stroll down the alley again, Misha at his side.

"I certainly have no quarrel with you, Mikhail Alexeevich," he remarked at last. "And you have spoken wisely. I will not say whether or not there has been a misunderstanding: but I believe that you should no longer feel any concern about the matter. Please put your mind at rest."

And taking this for an assurance, Misha was satisfied.

It was therefore with stupefaction, on rising early the following morning, that he saw Pinegin quietly come out of Nadia's room.

An hour later, he challenged him.

"I'm afraid I cannot accept your challenge."

Misha stared at him.

"I'm sorry?"

"I refuse to fight you," Pinegin told him calmly.

"Do you deny sleeping with my uncle's wife, in this very house?"

"No."

"May I ask why you refuse my challenge?"

"I do not wish to fight you."

Misha was completely at a loss.

"Then I must call you a coward."

Pinegin bowed.

"For that, Mikhail Alexeevich, I will fight you." He paused. "Are you content to fight at a time of my choosing?"

"As you wish. The sooner the better."

"I will let you know when I am ready. Next year perhaps. But I promise you, we shall fight." And with that he walked away, leaving Misha completely mystified.

Now, he thought, what the devil do I do?

At ten o'clock that morning, a small event took place at Bobrovo that was almost unnoticed.

Ilya Bobrov came slowly downstairs, crammed a large, wide-brimmed hat on his head, took a stout walking stick, and left the house without a word to anyone. A short time later the villagers were surprised to see his cumbersome figure wheezing along, his face red with the unwonted exertion but set with a look of the grimmest determination. Nobody had ever seen him go walking like this before. Once through the village, he took the lane that led through the woods towards the monastery. Several times, as he went along, he muttered nervously.

No one had taken much notice of Ilya recently. If he had seemed to be more abstracted than usual, if there had sometimes been a hint of desperation in his manner, Tatiana had put it down to hard work and thought nothing of it. She was quite unaware, therefore, that after all his months of labor at this great project, Ilya had reached a point of absolute crisis and near breakdown. He had been up all the previous night; and had anyone met him as he walked through the woods, he would have noticed that his eyes, which usually gazed out so placidly upon the world, were fixed ahead, staring wildly as though the sight of only one object in the universe could satisfy them. He looked like a haggard pilgrim in search of the grail.

Which in a way he was.

It was at noon that day, when Tatiana had gone over to Russka, taking Pinegin with her, that Misha, alone with his thoughts in the quiet house, was suddenly disturbed by a clatter at the door and the sound of laughing voices.

It was Sergei. He was back from the Ukraine. And he had brought his friend Karpenko with him.

He bounded into the hall. He looked sunburned, rested, full of life and good humor. Encountering Misha, he gave a cry of joy and embraced him. "Look at this," he called to Karpenko. "See what has become of little Misha the bear!"

In front of Misha now stood a very different man from the nervous youth who had once gazed adoringly at Olga. Karpenko was a charming man at the end of his thirties with a gleaming black beard, wonderful, sensitive eyes, and a reputation of huge success with women—"who always seem to stay his friends, whenever he discards them," Sergei would say with puzzled admiration. Karpenko had reason to be contented. Most of his hopes had been realized. For himself he had three plays to his credit and he edited a successful journal in Kiev. Even better, in a way, he had seen his beloved Ukraine achieve literary honor. His fellow Ukrainian, the satirist Gogol, had already made an important name for himself in Russia. And best of all—confounding all those who would dismiss it as a peasant's language—his country had at last found a writer of true greatness, the national poet Shevchenko, who wrote his exquisite lines in the Ukrainian tongue. So now Karpenko could truly say, "See, the ambitious hopes of my youth have not been dimmed: they have been vindicated."

And Misha stared at this happy pair and wondered what to say.

"We shall go to Moscow tomorrow," Sergei gaily announced. "Then to Saint Petersburg. Karpenko and I are full of ideas. We shall take the capital by storm!" He looked about him. "Where the devil's Ilya? We're both longing to see him." And servants were sent to look for him.

It was only after running upstairs to see his wife that Sergei returned looking puzzled. "That's the strangest thing," he remarked to Misha. "I thought she hated the country. Now she says she wants to stay down here another week or two while we go on to Moscow. What do you make of that?" And then, staring in perplexity at Misha's troubled face: "Now what's the matter with you, my Misha?"

And now, it seemed to Misha, he had to tell him.

The arrangements were discreetly made that afternoon.

The place chosen was the little clearing by the burial mounds off the lane that led to the monastery. No one was likely to come by there at dawn. Pinegin having no person to be his second, Karpenko had unwillingly done as Sergei asked and assumed that responsibility.

The dinner that afternoon passed quietly. Sergei, Pinegin, and Karpenko made polite conversation, in which Misha attempted to follow them. By agreement, neither Tatiana nor Nadia were given any inkling of what was passing.

Indeed, the only mystery that day lay in the whereabouts of Ilya, who still had not returned by afternoon. Since he had been seen going along the lane towards Russka, however, it was hard to believe that much harm could have come to him. After dinner, Karpenko undertook to amuse the ladies while Sergei retired to his room to make his preparations.

There were a number of letters to write. One was to Olga, another to his mother, another to his wife. He wrote them very calmly and carefully. The one to his wife contained no reproaches. The letter on which he spent the most trouble, strangely, was the one to Alexis.

It was in the late afternoon, as the sun was starting to sink towards the tall watchtower at Russka, that another, even more curious sight was seen by the villagers at Bobrovo.

It was the return of Ilya.

He came, as before, on foot. He was very tired now and his feet were dragging, but he did not seem to mind. And upon his face was a look which, insofar as was possible in a man so overweight, could only be described as religious ecstasy.

For Ilya had found that which he sought.

And it was this wonderful discovery that he shared with Sergei, in the latter's room that night, long after the sun had gone down.

It was a strange little scene: the one brother tired, shaken, longing only to be left alone with his thoughts until the dawn; the other, entirely unaware of what was going on, his face flushed with excitement, intent upon telling his companion the things that were passing in his mind and seemed to him so important. "Indeed, Seriozha," he said, "you couldn't have come at a better time."

The great crisis Ilya had suffered was easy enough to understand. All summer he had labored at the plan of his great book. Every waking moment all his mind had gone into it. And by August he had produced a blueprint for a new Russia, a modern Russia, with Western laws and institutions, and a vigorous economy—"maybe like that of the merchants and free farmers of America." There was really nothing wrong with Ilya's plan. It was intelligent, practical, logical; he could see just how Russia could become a free and prosperous nation like any other.

And then the crisis, for Ilya, had begun.

In a way, as Sergei listened to his brother's urgent explanation, the business was almost comic. He could just see poor Ilya waddling about in his room with furrowed brow, shaking his head at the problems of Russia and the universe. And yet at the same time he understood and respected Ilya's problem, which was not really comic at all, but represented the tragedy of his country. And this tragedy was expressed in a single statement.

"For this was the trouble, Seriozha. The more my plan made sense, the more every instinct inside me said, 'This is nonsense. This will never work.' " He shook his large head sadly. "To lose faith in your own country, the country you love, Seriozha—to feel that *because* your plan makes sense, that is exactly why it is doomed: that is a terrible thing, my friend."

It was not uncommon. Sergei had known many thoughtful men, some in the administration, who suffered from exactly this agony of mind. Like many before, no doubt like many after, Ilya the civilized Westernizer was being undermined and mocked by his own instinctive understanding of his native Russia.

Yet still, all summer, he had pressed on. "This was to be my life's work, Seriozha. I couldn't just toss it aside. I couldn't just accept it as an exercise in futility, don't you see. It was all I had." Week after week he had plowed on, refining, improving, and yet no less troubled. Until finally, after a sleepless night, the crisis had come that morning. He could go on no longer.

It was then, in a state of extreme nervous excitement, that Ilya had walked out of the house and gone—as he had not done in years—to the monastery. He hardly knew what had led him there himself. Perhaps a childhood memory. Perhaps an instinctive turning to religion when all else had failed.

He had wandered about at the monastery for several hours without receiving any enlightenment. Then it had occurred to him to go and look at the little icon, the Rublev, which his family had given to the place all those centuries ago. "At first," he said, "I felt nothing. It was just a darkened object." But then, slowly, it seemed to Ilya that the little icon had begun to work upon him. He had stayed before it for an hour. Then another.

"And then, at last, Seriozha, I knew." He took Sergei's arm excitedly. "I knew what was wrong with all my plans. It was exactly what you—you, my dear Seriozha—had told me. I was trying to solve Russia's problems by using my head, by logic. I should have used my heart." He smiled. "You have converted me. I am a Slavophile!"

"And your book?" Sergei asked.

Ilya smiled. "I have no need to travel abroad now," he said. "The answer to Russia's problems lies here, in Russia." And in a few brief words, he sketched out his new vision. "The church is the key," he explained. "If Russia's guiding force is not religion, then her people will be listless. We can have Western laws, independent judges, perhaps even parliaments—but only if they grow gradually out of a spiritual renewal. That has to come first."

"And Adam Smith?"

"The laws of economics still operate, but we must organize our farms and our workshops on a communal basis—for the good of the community, not the individual."

"It won't be like the West then, after all."

"No. Russia will never be like the West."

Sergei smiled. He did not know whether his brother was right or wrong, but he was glad to see that, for him at least, the agony seemed to be over. The debate between those who looked to the West and those who saw Russia as different would no doubt go on. Perhaps it would never be resolved.

"It's very late," he pleaded. "Please may I get some rest?" And he finally persuaded a reluctant Ilya to depart.

There were still a few hours to go before the dawn. For some reason he found himself thinking almost continuously of Olga.

The little glade was very quiet. There was a faint sheen of dew upon the small mounds nearby that caught the early rays of the sun. In the middle distance they could see the monastery, whose bell had just stopped ringing.

The two men had stripped to their shirts. There was a faint chill in the air that caused Sergei to shiver involuntarily.

Karpenko and Misha, both very pale, had loaded the pistols. Now they handed them to the two men.

And all the time Misha kept thinking, I know this must be done. It is the only honorable way. And yet it's insane. It is not real.

There was no sound, for some reason, not even a bird, as the two men paced slowly away from each other. All that could be heard was the faint sound of their feet brushing the short, damp grass.

They turned. Two shots rang out.

And both seconds ran, with a cry, to Sergei.

It was not surprising that the bullet had struck him precisely in the heart. Ever since he was a young man, Pinegin had never been known to miss. Down in the frontier forts he had an enviable reputation for it: which was why, years ago, Alexis had remarked that Pinegin was a dangerous man.

When Alexis returned to Russka that afternoon and heard the news, he broke down and wept. At his request, Pinegin left at once.

But the most unexpected event took place that evening.

Sergei's letter to Alexis was a very simple but moving document. It asked his forgiveness, first, for any hurt he had brought the family. He told Alexis, frankly, how hard it had been for him to forgive the exile in the Urals that Alexis had engineered; but he thanked him for his restraint in the years since. And it ended with a single request.

> For there is one great wrong I have done in my life—you may not agree because you follow the legal rules applying to serfdom—but to me, when I foolishly gave the game away and caused Savva Suvorin to be caught again, I did him a terrible wrong. You have a clear conscience about it, I know. But I have not, and there's nothing I can do about it.
>
> I know from our mother that he had offered you a huge sum for his freedom. If you have any love for me, Alexis, I beg you to take it and let the poor fellow go free.

Twice Alexis read this. Twice he noticed that little phrase—"you have a clear conscience about it"—and twice he shook his head sadly as he remembered the banknotes he had hidden all those years ago.

And so it was that evening that, after struggling uselessly for decades, Savva Suvorin was astonished to be summoned to the manor house and told by Alexis, with a weary smile: "I have decided, Suvorin, to accept your offer. You are a free man."

1855

SEVASTOPOL. At times it seemed to Misha Bobrov that no one would ever get out of it.

We're marooned, he used to think each day, like men on a desert island.

Yet of all those defending the place, of any man fighting in this whole, insane Crimean War, was there anyone, he wondered, in a stranger position than he? For while I struggle to survive in Sevastopol, he considered, I'm under almost certain sentence of death if I ever get out of it. The absurd irony of the situation almost amused him. At least, he thought, I can thank God I shall leave a son. His boy, Nicolai, had been born the previous year. That was one happy consolation at any rate.

His sense that he was on a desert island in Sevastopol was not so fanciful. The great fortified port lay in a circle of yellowish hills near the southern tip of the Crimean peninsula—not far from the ancient Tatar capital of Bakchisarai—and was therefore some hundred and fifty miles out from the Russian mainland into the waters of the warm Black Sea. To the south, before the port's massive, jutting fortifications, the forces of three major European powers—French, British, and Turkish—were encamped. The bombardment from their artillery—superior in every way to anything the Russians possessed—had been pounding at poor Sevastopol for eleven months. Its once graceful squares and broad boulevards were mostly rubble. Only the endless obstinacy and heroism of the simple Russian soldiers had prevented the place from being taken a dozen times.

Those approaching the city from the north crossed the harbor on a pontoon bridge. To the west, across the harbor mouth, the outdated Russian fleet had been sunk to prevent the allied ships from getting in. The best use for our ships really, Misha considered, since they're quite incapable of actually fighting the modern fleet of the French or the English. Beyond the line of sunken hulks, out in the open waters of the Black Sea, the allied ships lay comfortably across the horizon, blockading Sevastopol very effectively.

What a mad business it was, this Crimean War. On the one hand, Misha supposed, it was inevitable. For generations the empire of the Ottoman Turks had been getting weaker, and, whenever she could, Russia had taken advantage and expanded her influence in the Black Sea area. Catherine the Great had dreamed of taking ancient Constantinople itself. And if ever Russia could control the Balkan provinces, then she could sail a Russian fleet freely through the narrow strait from the Black Sea into the Mediterranean. No wonder then if the other powers of Europe watched with growing suspicion every time Russia looked at the Turks.

Yet the actual cause of the war was not a power play at all. In his chosen role as defender of Orthodoxy, the tsar had found himself in dispute with the sultan when the latter had removed some of the privileges of the Orthodox Church within his empire. Troops were sent by Tsar Nicholas into the Turkish province of Moldavia, by the Danube, as a warning. Turkey declared war, and at once the powers of Europe, refusing to believe that the tsar was not playing a bigger game, entered the war against Russia.

There were in fact three theaters in the war. One by the Danube, where the Austrians contained the Russians; one in the Caucasus Mountains, where the Russians took a major stronghold from the Turks; and lastly, the Crimean peninsula in the Black Sea, which the allies attacked because it was the home base of the Russian fleet.

It was a messy business. True, there were moments of heroism, such as the insane British charge of the Light Brigade at Balaclava. But mainly it had been stalemate, with both sides entrenched upon the peninsula, and typhus carrying off far more, despite the ministrations of Florence Nightingale and others like her on all sides, than did the actual fighting.

Above all, win or lose, the war was a humiliation for Russia. The weapons and techniques of the Russian army were shown to be hopelessly out of date. Her wooden fleet could beat the Turks, but confronted with the French or British, it was a joke. The prestige of the Russian tsar abroad plummeted. The belief in the autocracy at home, too, was severely shaken.

"Our country simply doesn't work," people complained. "Do you know," a senior officer remarked irritably to Misha, "the allies out there can get relief supplies from their own countries far faster than we can get them from Moscow. These are modern countries fighting an empire that is still in the Middle Ages!"

The war had started in 1854. By the end of that year, everyone knew, even down to the most ordinary enlisted peasant, this simple but devastating fact: The tsar's empire, Holy Russia, did not work.

If I get out of this, Misha had decided, I'm going to resign my commission and go to live in Russka. His father and Ilya were both dead. The estate needed looking after. And anyway, he concluded, I've had enough.

It was only after he had been in Sevastopol a week that he encountered Pinegin.

He had almost forgotten about the man, yet suddenly there he was, hardly changed: still a captain, his iron-gray hair hardly any thinner, his weather-beaten face as calm as ever, and a pipe usually stuck in his mouth.

"Ah, Mikhail Alexeevich," he said, as if their meeting were the most expected thing in the world, "we have a matter to settle, I believe."

Was it really possible, Misha sometimes wondered, that after all these years Pinegin could really be serious? Indeed, at first he had been inclined to treat the matter as a sort of macabre joke.

But as the months passed he came to realize that for Pinegin, with his rigid code, there was nothing to argue about. Misha had called him a coward; therefore they had to fight; the fact that ten years had passed before they happened to meet again was a mere detail, of no importance.

It was out of the question, against all rules of military conduct, to settle such matters during an active engagement. "But when this is over, if we both live, then we can settle our differences," Pinegin remarked pleasantly. And there was nothing to be done about it. Which means that, excluding a miracle, he's certainly going to kill me, Misha thought.

They met, quite often, as it happened, during that terrible siege. There, with men dying by the thousands in the beleaguered and disease-ridden port, these two—separated by their strange understanding, Misha thought, like two visiting spirits from another world—continued to meet quietly, politely. The encounters were almost friendly. Once, after a heavy bombardment, with hundreds of casualties, they found themselves helping each other to remove bodies from a burning building. On other occasions, Misha saw Pinegin calmly moving among the sick, apparently oblivious to the risk of infection himself. He would quietly write letters for the men, or sit there, smoking his pipe and keeping them company by the hour. He was a perfect officer, Misha considered, a man without fear.

And yet this was the man who had killed Sergei and would surely kill him, too.

So the months had passed. In March that year, Tsar Nicholas had died, and his son Alexander II had come to the throne. There were rumors that the war would end: but although there were negotiations, they failed, and the dismal siege went on. In August a Russian relieving force had been checked by the allies. Three weeks later the French had taken one of the main redoubts and refused to yield it.

It was on the morning of September 11 that the word finally came. It spread through the port like a whimper; it turned into a mutter, then a huge, excited, restless moan. "Retreat." They were going to retreat. Suddenly packhorses were being prepared, wounded men loaded into wagons. Confusion was everywhere in the street, along the boulevard, as the vast, untidy business got under way by which a weary army makes a last, huge effort to pull itself together sufficiently to remove itself, with some semblance of order, from the scene of conflict.

It was midmorning when the special units were sent into action. There were several dozen of these and their task was simple but important. They were to blow up all the remaining defenses of Sevastopol. "If the enemy wants this place, we shall leave him only ruins," Misha's commanding officer remarked. "I've been asked to supply some officers and men right away. You're to report to the Ninth Company at once," he told Misha.

And so it was that Misha found himself under the command of Captain Pinegin.

It was unpleasant, dangerous work as they moved forward towards their first objective. As they crossed a small square, a shell whistled overhead and exploded on a house a hundred yards behind them, sending a shudder through the ground. In the narrow street they had to negotiate next, there were two unexploded shells lying in the rubble. At last, however, they came to the place. It was a section of wall that had been built up to provide a gun emplacement. To reach it, however, one had to walk along a section of wall which, whether through laziness or stupidity, had not been properly protected. And since a party of French snipers had established themselves in the section of ruined city beyond, it made for a hazardous journey. Twice, as they had made their way along, Pinegin had pulled him down as a sniper's bullet whistled overhead.

The task was easy enough. The men brought up kegs of powder. Misha and Pinegin arranged everything carefully, setting a fuse and laying it along the wall. Meanwhile, they sent the men away with the rest of the explosives.

For some reason, while the two men worked it became very quiet. The snipers were certainly still out there, but waiting for them to show themselves. The bombardment had briefly paused. There was a faint breeze and the sun felt pleasantly warm. The sky was a pale blue.

And it was then that Misha Bobrov suddenly realized that he could commit murder.

They were quite alone. Their men were several hundred yards away and out of sight. The place was otherwise deserted. Pinegin, as it happened, was not armed. He was kneeling with his back to Misha, fiddling with the fuse, while Misha crouched by the wall, keeping out of the snipers' sight.

So who in the world would ever be the wiser? It would be so easy to do. He had only to show himself for a moment upon the parapet—just enough to draw the sniper's fire. Even a single shot would do—something their men would hear. And then . . . His hand rested on his pistol. A single shot, it hardly mattered how it was done. The back of the head would do. He would leave Pinegin there, blow up the emplacement, tell the men a sniper had caught the captain. No one would even suspect.

Was it really possible that he, Misha Bobrov, could commit a murder? He was surprised even to find that he might. Perhaps it was the months in that hellhole that had made him more careless of human life. But he did not think that was it. No, he admitted frankly, it was the simple human instinct for self-preservation. Pinegin was going to kill him in cold blood. He was just doing the same, getting his shot first.

And what was there to prevent him? Morality? What morality, ultimately, was there in a duel where both men agree to commit murder? Was Pinegin's life really worth so much compared to his? Hadn't he himself a wife and child, a home, while this fellow had nothing but his cold heart and his strange pride? No, Misha decided, there was nothing to stop him from killing Pinegin, except for one thing.

Convention. Just that. Was mere convention so strong as to allow him to die for it? Convention—a code of honor that was, when you really looked at it, insane?

His hand rested on his pistol. Still he did not move.

And then Pinegin turned and looked at him. Misha saw his pale blue eyes take in everything about him. And he knew Pinegin guessed.

Then Pinegin smiled, turned his back again, and continued fiddling with the fuse.

It was several minutes later that they lit the fuse and watched the little spark run away from them, along the wall, to its destination. Just before it reached the barrels, they both ducked down and held their breath. But then, for some reason, nothing happened. "Damned suppliers," Pinegin muttered. There had been problems recently with all kinds of supplies, even military, reaching the army. "God knows what's wrong now. Wait here," he ordered. And he ran up and, keeping his head low, made his way swiftly along the wall. Just before he reached the barrels, a single sniper's bullet whistled harmlessly overhead.

Then the barrels blew up.

1857

ONLY one thing puzzled Misha Bobrov when, late in 1857, he returned at last to Russka.

It concerned Savva Suvorin and the priest.

Of course, there were better things to think about. The new reign of Alexander II seemed likely to bring many changes. The Crimean War had been concluded on terms that were humiliating to Russia. She had lost her right to a navy in the Black Sea. But no one had any stomach for further hostilities. "First," Misha would declare, "the tsar must sort things out at home. For this war has almost ruined us." Everyone knew that things had to change.

And of all the reforms that were being spoken of, none was more important, and none would affect Misha more, than the possible emancipation of the serfs.

Upon this great subject, in the years 1856 and 1857, the whole of Russia was a seething mass of rumor. From abroad the radical writer Herzen was dispatching his noble journal, *The Bell,* into Russia, calling upon the tsar to set his subjects free. Closer to home, returning soldiers had even started a rumor—that spread like wildfire—that the new tsar actually *had* granted the serfs their freedom, but that the landlords were concealing the proclamations!

But amid all this excitement, Misha Bobrov—though he personally believed the emancipation was desirable—was very calm. "People mistake the new tsar," he told his wife. "They say he'll be a reformer and perhaps he will. But actually he is a very conservative man, just like his father. His saving grace is that he is pragmatic. He will do whatever he has to do to preserve order. If that means freeing the serfs, he'll do it. If not, he won't."

Many landowners, however, were nervous. "I'll tell you a useful trick," one fellow landlord told him. "Some of us reckon that if the emancipation comes, then we'll have to give the serfs the land they till. So what you can do is to take your serfs off the land—make them into household domestics for the time being. Then if this awful thing happens you'll be able to say: 'But my serfs don't till any land.' And you may not have to give them a thing!"

And indeed, Misha actually discovered one landlord in the province whose lands were completely untilled, but who had suddenly acquired forty footmen! "A trick," he remarked to his wife, "which is as stupid as it is shabby." The Bobrov serfs stayed where they were.

Whatever changes were coming, Misha was looking forward to being at home. He had inherited not only Bobrovo, but also the Riazan estate from Ilya. "I shall devote myself to agriculture and to study," he declared. After Ilya's death five years before, he had discovered the huge unfinished manuscript of his uncle's great work. Perhaps he would be able to complete it for him.

No, there were plenty of things to think about. But the matter of Suvorin and the priest still intrigued him.

"The one thing I regret about giving Suvorin his freedom," Alexis had always told him, "is that once he's not under my thumb, he'll start bringing his damned Old Believers here and converting people. And I always promised the priest I wouldn't let that happen."

In his years away on military service, Misha had rather forgotten about this; but now he had returned and he began making some inquiries, it was soon clear to him that, indeed, this transformation had taken place.

The Suvorin enterprise was growing rapidly. The jenny imported from England for the cotton plant had been a huge success. Savva Suvorin now employed half the people living in the little town of Russka. His son Ivan ran the business in Moscow. And while it was not clear to Misha whether all those Suvorin employed were Old Believers, there was certainly a core of them at the factory; and although recent legislation had broken up a number of the Old Believer groups, including the radical Theodosians, some sort of observances continued almost openly. Indeed, Timofei Romanov once obligingly showed Misha the house in the town where the local group met to pray.

Yet—here was the puzzle—there was no word of protest from the priest at Russka.

The first time Misha had asked him about this, the priest had denied it. "The congregation at Russka is loyal, Mikhail Alexeevich. I don't think you need worry about that." His red beard was turning gray now. He was fatter than ever. Congregation or not, Misha thought, he certainly looks well fed.

Misha even once, out of curiosity, confronted Savva Suvorin himself. But that worthy, gazing down at him contemptuously from his great height, merely remarked with a shrug, "Old Believers? I know nothing of that."

It was on a Sunday morning, one day in December, that Misha received his little moment of enlightenment. He was standing in the snow-filled market square in Russka, shortly after the church service, which had been rather poorly attended. He would have gone home; but it was at just this time, as it happened, that the sled bringing newspapers from Vladimir often arrived, and he had hung around for a little while in hopes of getting the latest news.

He was still waiting there when he saw the redheaded priest emerge from the church and begin to walk ponderously toward his house. With him, Misha noticed, was a rather surly-looking fellow, also with reddish hair, whom Misha vaguely recognized as the priest's son, Paul Popov. Misha had heard he was a clerk of some kind in Moscow: one of that tribe of underpaid petty officials who in those days made ends meet by whatever small-time bribery and corruption they could come by. Misha gazed at the priest and his son with vague contempt.

And then he saw the strangest thing. Savva Suvorin entered the square and walked close by them. As he drew near, he gave the priest a curt nod, almost as he might to an employee. But instead of ignoring him, both the priest and Paul Popov suddenly turned and bowed low. Nor was there any mistaking the meaning of their gesture. It was not the polite bow that Misha made to the priest, and the priest to him. It was the bow of servant to master, of employee to paymaster. And they had both given it, father and son, to the former serf.

And then Misha understood.

It was at just this moment that the long-awaited sled came in through the gates of Russka and jingled across the square.

Misha ignored it. He could not resist the sudden impulse that had suddenly taken hold of him. He had never cared for the redheaded priest, and now the opportunity was too perfect. He strode across the marketplace and, just as the priest reached the center, he accosted him, in a loud voice. "Tell me," he cried, "how much is it? How much do Suvorin and his Old Believers pay you for giving up your congregation to them?"

The priest went scarlet. He had hit!

But Misha never received his answer. For at that moment there was an excited shout from the far side of the square, where the newspapers were being unloaded. And as they all turned, a voice excitedly cried out: "It's official. From the tsar. The serfs are going to be freed."

And Misha forgot even the priest, and he hastened across the square.

TEN

Fathers and Sons

1874

With a slow hiss and clank the train approached the ancient city of Vladimir, and the two unexpected visitors gazed out with curiosity.

It was spring. The snow had mostly departed, but here and there they saw drifts or long grayish slivers across the terrain. All the world, from the peeling white walls of the churches to the brown fields by each hamlet, had an untidy, blotchy look. There were huge puddles everywhere; rivers had overflowed their banks; and the roads, turned into quagmires, were almost impassable.

Yet if, upon earth, all movement had temporarily ceased, the skies were full of traffic. Throughout the woods, where light green buds had appeared seemingly overnight on the bare silver birches, the air was full of the raucous cries of birds who came flocking and wheeling over the forest. For this was the Russian spring, and the rooks and starlings were returning.

The journey had been long, but the two travelers were in good spirits. The train conductor—a tall, thin man with round shoulders, large ears, flat feet, and a habit of cracking his knuckles—had engaged their attention; and long before they reached Vladimir, young Nicolai Bobrov had refined his imitation of this man until it was a fine art.

Nicolai was twenty; a handsome, slim young man with the Bobrovs' regular faintly Turkish features, a small, neatly trimmed mustache, a soft, pointed beard, and a mass of dark brown, wavy hair. His blue eyes and pleasant mouth looked manly.

His companion, though only twenty-one, looked a little older. He was a thin, rather sulky-looking fellow about two inches taller than Nicolai, with a shock of bright ginger hair. His face was clean-shaven. His mouth was thin, his teeth small, rather yellowish, and uneven. His eyes were green. But the thing one noticed most, after the first glance, was the area around the eyes, which was slightly puffy, as if he had been punched at birth and never quite recovered.

When the train arrived at Vladimir, the two men got out and Nicolai went in search of transport. Horses were not enough, for they had a considerable quantity of heavy luggage, and he was gone over an hour before he eventually returned with a grumpy-looking peasant driving a carriage so battered it was little more than a cart. "Sorry," he said cheerfully. "It was the best I could do." And a few minutes later he and his companion set off.

Mud. Everywhere he looked, it seemed to Nicolai Bobrov, there was mud. Brown mud that stretched to the plowland's horizon; mud that stretched down the road like an endless penance; mud that took hold of the carriage wheels and dragged them down like some evil spirit trying to drown a stranger in a pool. Mud splattered their clothes, mud caked the carriage, mud said to them, plainly and without fear of contradiction: "This is my season. None shall move, because I do not allow it. Neither horse nor man, rich nor poor, strong nor weak, neither armies nor the tsar himself have any power over me. For in my season I am king." It was not the snow that first broke Napoleon on his retreat from Moscow, Nicolai remembered: it was the mud.

Yet despite their slow progress, young Nicolai Bobrov felt elated. For it seemed to him that perhaps all his life—and certainly the last year or two—had been a preparation for this journey and this spring.

How he had prepared. Like all the other students in the house they shared, he had read, listened, debated week after week, month after month. He had even practiced mortifications like a monk. One month he had slept on a bare board, which he covered with studs. He generally wore a hair shirt. "For I am not yet as strong and as disciplined as I should be," he would confess to his friends. And now, at last, the hour was approaching at which, he hoped, both he and all the world would be born again.

And what luck, Nicolai considered as he glanced at his companion— what incredible luck that he should be undertaking his mission with this man above all others. He knows so much more than I do, he thought humbly. He had never met anyone like him.

As they made their way, at a snail's pace, through the endless mud, only one thought secretly troubled Nicolai. His unsuspecting parents. What would become of them?

Of course, he realized they would have to suffer: it was inevitable. But at least I'll be there, he thought. I daresay I can keep them from the worst.

Slowly the little carriage made its way toward Russka.

Timofei Romanov stood by the window of the *izba* on that damp spring morning and stared at his son Boris in disbelief.

"I forbid you," he cried at last.

"I'm twenty and I'm married. You can't stop me." Young Boris Romanov looked around his family. His parents' faces were ashen; his grandmother Arina was stony faced; and his fifteen-year-old sister Natalia was looking rebellious, as usual, while the two little girls looked frightened.

"Wolf!" Timofei roared. And then, almost pleadingly: "At least think of your poor mother."

But Boris said nothing and Timofei could only look outside at the clamorous birds wheeling over the trees and wonder why God had sent the family all these troubles at once.

The Romanov family consisted of eight people. Over the years Timofei and Varya had lost two children to disease and malnutrition; but such tragedies were only to be expected. Thank God at least the remaining four were healthy. Arina, too, though she had never quite recovered her health from the terrible famine of '39, was a source of strength: small, somewhat shriveled, sometimes bitter, but indomitable. Together with Boris's new wife, they all lived together in a stout, two-story *izba* in the center of the village.

To have four healthy children living should be counted as a blessing— except for one thing: three of them were girls. After Boris was born, Timofei had been overjoyed. When Natalia had come, he had been glad. But when, years later, not one but two more girls had followed, he could not believe his bad luck. Every peasant needed sons to help him; daughters were just an expense; you had to give them dowries. And what have I to give them? he would sadly wonder, as he gazed at Natalia and the two little girls. He was fifty-two now: he would have liked to take things more easily. Instead the future looked bleak.

And then, a month ago, Varya had told him that she was pregnant again. "I couldn't believe it at first," she said, "but now I'm sure." And so, although in reply to her uncertain look he had smiled bravely and remarked, "It's a gift from God"—in his heart he had said, "It's a curse."

And now, on top of all this, Boris had just announced that he was going to ruin them.

The Emancipation of the Serfs had changed the lives of Timofei and his family, but not much for the better. There were several reasons for this.

While the peasants on land owned by the state had got a moderately good deal, the serfs of private landlords had not. For a start, only about a third of the land had actually been transferred to the private serfs, the rest remaining with the landlords. Secondly, the serfs had had to pay for this land: a fifth in money or labor service, the other four-fifths by means of a loan from the state, in the form of a bond, repayable over forty-nine years: so that, in effect, the serfs of Russia were forced to take out a mortgage on their holdings. Worse even yet, the landlords managed to have the prices of land set artificially high. "And it's not only those damned repayments," Timofei would complain. "It's us peasants who still pay all the taxes, too. We're supporting the landowners as much as ever!"

It was perfectly true. The peasants paid the poll tax, from which the nobles were exempt. They also paid a host of indirect taxes on food and spirits, which were a greater burden on the poor. The net result of this was that, after becoming free, Timofei the peasant was actually paying ten times as much to the state for each desiatin of land he held as Bobrov the gentlemen did for his. No wonder then if, like most peasants, Timofei often muttered: "One day we'll kick those nobles out and get the rest of the land for ourselves."

He did not hate the landowner—not personally. Hadn't he and Misha Bobrov played together when they were children? But he knew that the nobleman was a parasite. "They say the tsars gave the Bobrovs their land," he had explained to his children, "in return for their services. But the tsar doesn't need them anymore. So he'll take their land away soon and give it to us." That simple belief was shared by peasants all over Russia: "Be patient. The tsar will give." And so he had waited for better times.

Young Boris Romanov was a pleasant-looking boy—square and stocky like his father, but with hair that was lighter brown and already rather thin at the front. His blue eyes, through defiant, were gentle.

He did not want to hurt his family; but in the last few months since his marriage, life had become impossible. The arrival of his wife—a kindly, golden-haired young girl—in the household had produced a new pecking order. While Arina and Varya had previously expected obedience from his sister Natalia, they rather ignored her now and concentrated their attention on Boris's wife. "They think they own me," she would sadly remark.

But it was his mother's unexpected pregnancy that really brought about the crisis. "We shall be starting a family, too," the girl reminded Boris. "And where will that leave us, when it's her new child who'll be the important one?" His father Timofei, too, always moody and feeling the strain of the new situation, had taken to shouting at him on the slightest pretext. "Call that a way to stack wood, you Mordvinian?" he would bellow; and to Boris's wife he had promised: "I may have failed with my son, but I'll thrash some sense into my grandchild when you give me one—you can be sure of that!" By the time the spring thaw came, Boris had decided it could go on no longer.

And this was why, that very morning, he had made the fateful announcement that he was moving out.

He had several friends who had done the same thing in recent years. "It's hard when you start with your own *izba*," they had warned him. "But then it gets easier. And it's better really once you've done it, because you don't quarrel with your family so much." He was sure it was a good idea.

Indeed, he would have made the break sooner but for one consideration: his sister Natalia.

For what would become of her? What would the family do to the fifteen-year-old girl with the pouting mouth and the air of secret defiance? "They'll break her," he told his wife ruefully. "They'll work her into the ground to make up for us." When he talked it over with Natalia, however, she had been adamant. "Go, Boris," she told him. "Don't worry about me." And when he asked her how she would manage: "I'll be all right, you'll see." She grinned: "I have a plan."

He wondered what it was.

An hour later Timofei Romanov, rather pale, stood staring across an open field. Beside him was the man who would now decide his fate.

The village elder was a small, gray-bearded peasant with a loud voice and a decisive manner, whom Timofei respectfully addressed in the old-fashioned way, by his patronymic only, as "Ilych."

Nervously Timofei explained the situation, scarcely daring to look at the elder; but when he was finished, unable to bear the suspense, he turned to him abruptly and asked, "Well, Ilych, am I ruined?" Whatever the other said, he knew it would be final—and there would be nothing in the world he could do about it.

Timofei Romanov was free: and yet he was not. In this he resembled most of the former serfs in Russia. For when the tsar's advisers had given the serfs their land, they had encountered one other, most difficult problem: what if these peasants, no longer owned by their masters, started wandering about, doing what they liked? "How will we control them? How can we ensure that the land is tilled and taxes collected?" Freedom was all very well, but one couldn't have chaos. And so, in their wisdom, the authorities had derived a simple solution. The peasant, though legally free, would still be tied to his place. The land taken from the landlord was not given to the peasant individually, but to the village commune, which was made responsible for taxes and everything else. If, for instance, Timofei wanted to travel to Moscow, he would have to apply to the village elder for a passport, just as he had formerly applied to Bobrov. Even minor matters of justice rested with the commune. And above all it was the village elder who periodically redistributed the scattered strips of land—so many good, medium, and poor for each family. In short Timofei Romanov was now, in effect, a member of a medieval village without a feudal lord, or, to use a modern term, a compulsory peasant cooperative. The terms do not matter for, in reality, they are one and the same.

And this was the problem: if Boris left home and set up on his own, the land would be repartitioned. Timofei's share would probably be reduced. The land he had now was not enough to support the family and its obligations. How would he manage?

"I'll have to cut your holding," Ilych said brusquely.

"How much?"

The elder considered. "By half." It was even worse than Timofei had feared. "I'm sorry," the elder went on, "but there are more young people in the village now. There isn't enough land for them all as things are." Then he shrugged irritably and left.

Yet whatever his troubles that morning, Timofei Romanov would have been dismayed had he known what was passing in his mother-in-law's mind.

Arina was sixty-three. She was the senior woman in the family, and she let no one forget it. And above all, she loved her daughter Varya. "I didn't nearly kill myself for her in 'thirty-nine," she would say, "to see harm come to her now." As the years went by, it became clear that the mark left by that terrible time was never going to leave her. And she herself would often remark: "I lived on one turnip for a month that year and my stomach's never been the same. That's why I'm older than I should be." And it was true that though she was still at first glance a comfortable, round little babushka like any other, there was concealed within her a ruthless instinct for survival that made her formidable.

And now her daughter was going to have another child. She had watched quietly as the little family drama began to unfold. Several times poor Varya had turned to her miserably and said: "God knows it'd be a blessing if I lost the baby before it was born." And now, as she saw how events were shaping, Arina came to her own private conclusion. If it's another girl, she decided, it will have to die. Such things were not uncommon. She had known a woman who had drowned her child; exposing them was easier and less obvious. If it has to be, then I shall do it, she thought. That's what grandmothers are for.

But she kept this decision to herself. And when he returned gloomily from his talk with the village elder and told them the news, Timofei had no idea of the meaning of his mother's grim look. Instead he remarked to his wife: "We may have to send Natalia to the factory. Send her to me."

As Peter Suvorin followed in the wake of his grandfather Savva, a new idea took shape in his mind: Perhaps I should kill myself.

For some reason the thought had an extraordinary beauty. How would he do it, though? That was something else to ponder. Whatever he did, one thing was certain: he must escape from this terrible trap.

If only his father had not died. Remembering his own harsh upbringing by Savva—and also because Peter's mother had died when the boy was only ten—Ivan Suvorin had been a kindly father with the wisdom to let his two sons be themselves. Vladimir, five years the older, was a born businessman and Ivan had let him manage one of the Moscow plants when he was only seventeen. But Ivan had intellectual leanings and—to old Savva's disgust—had even allowed Peter to go to university.

Then, six months ago, Ivan had suffered a massive stroke: and Peter's sunlit world had abruptly come to an end.

I'm completely in his power, he realized. For old Savva had asserted himself with extraordinary force. Within a week he had taken personal control of everything. Peter's studies were canceled at once; and while young Vladimir was left to manage the factories in Moscow, Savva had curtly ordered Peter to accompany him back to Russka. "It's time," the old man told his wife, "that we took this one in hand."

To Peter, it had been a revelation. As a child in the comfortable Moscow house, his grandparents had been distant figures whose occasional visits were treated with a kind of religious respect. His grandfather was the tallest man he had even seen: with his thick shock of hair, his huge gray beard, and piercing black eyes, he was as terrifying as he was silent. Even since he had gained his freedom, Savva had dressed in a long black coat and an immensely tall top hat: so that once, as a little boy, Peter had dreamed that the great tower in the Moscow Kremlin had turned into his grandfather and gone stalking across the city like an avenging fury. Many times, with a wry smile, Ivan had told his sons how Savva had broken a violin over his head. Peter avoided the old man as much as possible.

But now that he had been forced to live in his grandparents' house, Peter's feelings had changed. The childhood fear still remained; but it was accompanied now by something else: and this was awe.

Savva Suvorin was something more than a mere mortal. He was a law unto himself and unto God: fixed, immutable, and merciless. He was eighty-two and stood as straight as he had at thirty. He strode everywhere on foot. The Theodosian community to which he had belonged had been broken up by the authorities in the 1850s and, like many other merchants, he had found it necessary to subscribe, nominally, to the Orthodox Church. But he remained an Old Believer in private and still ate alone out of a wooden bowl, with a little cedarwood spoon with a cross on it. The breakup of the Theodosians also removed any last chains that community might have had upon the Suvorin enterprises. They belonged entirely to Savva and his family. And they were huge.

Peter knew the holdings at Moscow: the dye factory by the river, the plant for printing calico, the glue factory, the starch factory, and the little printing press his brother Vladimir had set up. But never, until now, had he really understood what had taken place at Russka.

Russka had never been beautiful, but now it was hideous. On the steep slope down to the river, the huddled huts, lean-tos, and straggling fences seemed to topple into the water as though they had been tipped out of the town like so much refuse. Inside the walls, the huge brick cotton mill with its rows of blank windows dwarfed the church, and its belching octagonal chimney outmatched even the ancient watchtower by the town gate. The cloth mill was nearly as big; these were long, barnlike buildings containing the linen factory. People were drawn there from miles around, and old Savva Suvorin ruled it all.

The force of will that had built this place up was frightening to contemplate. And it's all there, in his face, Peter thought. The great square head, the smoldering eyes, the heavy brows, and that mighty, shapeless promontory of a nose. Did they still make noses like that? His father's had been large, his own inclined to heaviness; but history itself might have paused, he thought, before Savva's features, like a sculptor before a stubborn granite rockface. My God, he realized, he's like one of those elders of ancient times, from beyond the Volga—only turned into a merchant. Such was Savva Suvorin.

At first life had not been too unpleasant. His grandparents lived in a simple stone house, not a tenth of the size of the big Moscow house. It was furnished simply, with heavy, rather ugly furniture, which was impressive for being solid and highly polished. But what did the old people want with him? When he took Peter with him on his rounds, Savva gave no indication of what he expected; and after a few weeks Peter supposed the old man was bored with his company and would soon send him back to Moscow.

It was his grandmother, soon after Christmas, who had actually dealt the blow. "We've decided you should start work in the linen factory," she calmly announced. "You'll get to know the village, too, that way."

Maria Suvorin's face was still, in older age, perfectly round; her nose, if anything even more pointed; her compressed mouth, despite her huge riches, never smiled. And behind two narrow slits resided the same pair of hard gray eyes. Like most simple Russian women, her white hair was parted in the middle, drawn tightly around her head, and fixed at the back. The only luxuries she allowed herself were the rich silk brocade dresses that ballooned out to the ground like a bell. Over her head she liked to wear a big shawl that spread over her shoulders and upper arms and was pinned under her chin so that she exactly resembled one of those brightly painted little Russian dolls—a comfortable image that was quite contradicted by her ruthless character.

"But I'm unsuited to this kind of work," he protested.

"We think it's best," she calmly replied.

"But what about my studies?"

"That's all over now," she said placidly. And then, not unkindly: "You surely can't expect your eighty-two-year-old grandfather to do all your work for you, can you?"

And now, on this cold, damp spring morning, as the starlings wheeled over the rooftops, it seemed to Peter that he could bear it no more.

He had tried to take an interest and find something to excite his imagination. When Savva told him—"The American Civil War hit our cotton supplies for a while"; or: "We can get cotton from Asia now"—Peter conjured up images of distant ships from the New World, or caravans across the desert, and told himself that the Suvorin enterprises were part of some larger, exciting adventure. But each day as he was faced with the same grim chimneys, the endless lines of spinning machines, and the monotonous, grinding work of the factories, he knew in his heart: Russka was a prison.

That morning they were doing what he hated most of all: inspecting the workers' living quarters.

Life was not so bad out in the villages, where the flax for the linen was grown and every peasant *izba* produced its own handicrafts. But the living quarters in Russka were completely different. There were three long rows of wooden houses for worker families, which might not have been so bad except that three to five families were crammed into each house. "We are all one family," Savva would remind these people as he moved among them like a grim Old Testament patriarch: "We live together."

And then there were the dormitories. Why was it that, as the two men now entered one of these, Peter's heart sank?

It was not that the place was squalid. It was spotlessly clean, light, airy, and well heated. The long room was painted white, with a line of wooden pillars running down its center and beds on each side. The beds consisted of a wide, shallow wooden tray divided in two so that in each half there was room for a narrow mattress and a few other possessions. Two people therefore, separated by a low partition, slept on each bed, and there were thirty people on each side of the dormitory. Under the bed was a wooden box that could be locked; and above, hanging from the wooden ceiling, was a rack over which the rest of the worker's clothes could be hung. Men slept in one dormitory, women in another. It was all very orderly.

And yet depressing: and Peter knew exactly why. It was the people.

There was, as yet, no urban working class outside Moscow and Saint Petersburg—and scarcely there. The people who lived in the dormitories mainly belonged to two types. There were the children of peasant families from distant villages, who returned periodically to their families to give them their modest wages; and there were the former household serfs who had been given their freedom at the Emancipation but who, having no land to claim in any village, were cast loose and who were entirely homeless. These were the wretched creatures who now cringed as he and his grandfather passed. They are just peasants, he thought, who are lost. And the very tidiness of the place made it seem even more inhumane.

And I am supposed to live here, he considered, and continue this terrible system. These people and these hideous factories will feed my family. It was all so terrible. He did not know quite what he wanted out of life, but with a kind of desperate urgency he muttered under his breath: "Anything, anything—I'd even haul barges up the Volga—but not this."

It was just as they were leaving the dormitory that Peter Suvorin chanced to glance back and caught sight of something he was not meant to see.

At the far end of the dormitory, with his back to Peter, a youth of about his own age was doing an imitation of Savva Suvorin for his friends. He knew the young man slightly. His name was Grigory. Considering that he was small and pinched in appearance, his imitation wasn't bad. Seeing Peter watching, however, the others made warning signs, and the young fellow stopped and turned.

It was a shock to Peter. He had seen most kinds of expression on men's faces, but he had never seen naked hate before. Grigory either did not know it showed or didn't bother to conceal it. Either way, it was unnerving.

My God, he thought, this fellow thinks I'm like my grandfather. If only he knew the truth! And then, even worse, he realized: But why would he even care that I sympathize with him, when I'm a Suvorin? And he fled.

Natalia walked briskly along the path towards Russka. As soon as she had seen her father returning glumly from his interview with the village elder, she had slipped away. No doubt he would be looking for her by now.

She knew exactly what was in store for her. She would be sent to the Suvorin factory and expected to stay there as long as the family needed her wages to make ends meet. She dreaded it. I'll be a spinster and a slave all my life, she calculated.

She was determined to do better than that. When she was a little girl, because Misha Bobrov had always been friendly towards her father, both she and Boris had been sent to the little school in Russka for three years, where they had learned to read. Poor though she was, this unusual accomplishment had given her a secret pride, a belief that somehow—she had no idea how—she would amount to something.

But although she had guessed what it would mean for her, she had encouraged Boris to go. She loved him. She knew it had to be. At least he may be happy, she thought. And her plan—the plan of which she had spoken to Boris?

There was no plan. She had no idea what to do.

She pulled her scarf more tightly around her head as the damp air made her face smart. She could only think of one possible way out.

She was going to see Grigory.

Misha Bobrov and his wife Anna were beaming with pleasure.

It was just as dusk was falling that day that the little carriage arrived at the Bobrovo estate. To their amazement Nicolai jumped out, ran to embrace them, and announced, "I got leave from the university to come home early—so here I am." And when he added that he had brought a friend, Misha happily replied, "The more the merrier, my dear boy." And, taking his son by the arm with that gentle Bobrov gesture, he led the way inside.

Misha Bobrov always counted himself a lucky man that he got on so well with his son. He still remembered the brooding atmosphere that surrounded his stern old father Alexis and had always resolved never to allow such bad feeling at Bobrovo again—which came naturally to him anyway, for he was a kindly, easygoing man.

Above all, he was always delighted to let the boy argue with him. "Just like dear Sergei and old Uncle Ilya," he'd say. Indeed, he was rather proud of his own skills in debate; and even if—as one expected with young people—Nicolai sometimes became heated, Misha never minded. "The boy's basically sound," he'd tell his wife afterwards. And when she thought he'd let Nicolai go too far he would reply: "No, we must listen to the young people, Anna, and try to understand them. For they are the future." He congratulated himself that this strategy had clearly proved correct.

The two travelers were tired after their journey, and after eating they both expressed a desire to retire early. "But I can see we shall have some splendid discussions with these young men," Misha remarked to Anna, as they sat in the salon afterwards. "One may not always like what goes on at universities, but our young people always come back full of ideas." He smiled contentedly. "I shall have to be on my mettle."

Only one thing puzzled him. It was absurd, really, but he had a curious sense, the moment he had set eyes on him, that there was something vaguely familiar about Nicolai's friend. Yet what the devil was it?

Yevgeny Pavlovich Popov. That was how the ginger-haired fellow had been introduced: it was a common enough name. "Have I seen you before?" Misha had asked.

"No."

He had not pursued the subject. Yet—he was sure of it—there was something about the fellow. And that night, as he lay for many hours too excited to sleep, this little conundrum was one of many matters the landowner turned over in his mind.

The arrival of his son always made Misha Bobrov think about the future. What sort of estate would he be able to hand on to the boy? What sort of life would Nicolai have? Above all, what did the boy think about things. I must ask him about such-and-such, he'd think. Or, remembering some pet project of his own: I wonder if he'd approve of that. So it was that, in the darkness, a host of subjects crowded into his thoughts.

And it was typical of Misha Bobrov that, although for him personally things had gone rather badly, he remained convinced that in general they were going well. "I am optimistic about the future," he would declare. This was one of the few matters upon which his wife could not agree with him.

In fact, on the Bobrov estate, things were going extremely badly. For if the Emancipation had disappointed the peasants, it had hardly been any better for the landowners.

The first problem was old and familiar. By 1861 Misha Bobrov, like nearly every landowner he knew, had already pledged seventy percent of his serfs against mortgages at the state bank. In the decade after Emancipation, half the money he received as compensation went straight to the bank to pay down these debts. Furthermore the state bonds that he was given in part payment—the bonds that the peasants were struggling so hard to pay off—were slowly losing their value as Russia suffered a mild inflation. "Those damned bonds are already worth only two-thirds of what they were," he had remarked to Anna just the week before.

Because he was in debt and short of cash, Bobrov found it hard to pay for labor from his former serfs to cultivate the land he had left. Some had been rented out to peasants; some leased to merchants; and some, he feared, would soon have to be sold. Most of his friends were selling land. Each year, therefore, he grew a little poorer.

Why, then, should he be optimistic?

There were several reasons. The Russian empire was certainly more settled and stronger than when he was a young man. After centuries of conflict, the vast empire seemed to be reaching out, at last, to its natural frontiers. True, the huge territory of Alaska had been sold to the United States in 1867. "But it was too far away," Bobrov would say. And meanwhile Russia was consolidating her hold on the distant Pacific rim of the Eurasian plain, where the new port of Vladivostok, opposite Japan, gave promise of a vigorous Far Eastern trade. Down in the south, after the debacle of the Crimea, Russia had once again secured the right to sail her fleet in the warm Black Sea; and to the southeast she was gradually absorbing the desert peoples beyond the Caspian Sea, with their fierce ruling princes and rich caravans. In the west the last uprising of the Poles had been crushed, and Russia—closely allied now with Prussia—was at peace with her western neighbors. And if, some said, the Prussian kingdom and its brilliant chancellor Bismarck seemed a little too hungry for power, what was that to the empire of the tsar, which covered a sixth of the land surface of the globe?

But the real source of Bobrov's optimism resided in what he saw inside Russia itself.

"We've seen more reform in the last fifteen years," he would point out, "than at any time since Peter the Great."

It might be that, in private, Tsar Alexander II only wanted to maintain order in Russia; but having decided that reforms were needed to do so, he had made amazing progress. The creaking, ancient legal system had been totally revised. Now, for the first time in eight hundred years of Russian history, there were independent courts, with independent judges and professional lawyers. These courts were open to all men and conducted not in secret but in the open. There was even trial by jury. The military had been reformed: all men, noble and peasant, were liable to be chosen by lots for service—but for six years only, not twenty-five. And in all but the elite regiments, a man of humble birth could even become an officer. "God knows, we can only do better than we did in the Crimea," Misha liked to say to fellow gentlemen who complained of this mixing of classes.

But the reforms that pleased Misha Bobrov the most were the new local assemblies.

For these were the bodies known to history as the *zemstvos*—*zemstvo* meaning: "of the land, the community"—in the country, and the dumas—the duma being the ancient tsar's council—in the towns. And Russia had seen nothing like them before. In every district, town, and province, these assemblies for local government were elected by all taxpayers, whether gentry, merchant, or peasant. "So now," Misha cheerfully claimed, "Russia has entered the modern world of democracy, too."

True, the *zemstvos* and dumas had only modest powers; and key posts like that of governor and police chief were all appointed by the tsar's government.

True, there were also some special features in the election. In the towns, for instance, the votes were weighted by how much the voter paid in taxes: the great majority of the people, therefore, who only contributed a third of the taxes, could only elect a third of the council members. In the country, similar weighting, and a series of indirect elections, ensured that in the provincial *zemstvos,* over seventy percent of the members belonged to the gentry. "But it's the principle of the thing that matters," Misha declared. "And all the classes have a say."

Besides—and this was, perhaps, the thing Bobrov liked best of all—these *zemstvos* gave men like him a role in society. As a service class the nobles might have been passed by; their serfs might have been taken from them; but in these local *zemstvos,* however modest their power, a noble like himself might still preserve the illusion that he was important and useful to his country. "We have always served Russia," he could still say, with a trace of satisfaction.

Just before he fell asleep a possible solution to the puzzle concerning his familiar guest occurred to Misha Bobrov.

Devil take it, he thought. Didn't the young fellow say his patronymic was Pavlovich? And didn't that horrid old priest at Russka, with the red hair, have a son called Paul Popov—a petty official of some kind in Moscow. Could this ginger-haired fellow be the priest's grandson, then?

It was an amusing thought. He decided to ask him in the morning.

Yet when morning came, and Misha descended to the dining room where he expected to find the two young men at breakfast, he was greeted by his manservant with a most curious bit of news.

"Mister Nicolai went out with his friend just before dawn, sir," the fellow said.

"Before dawn? Where to?"

"Down to the village, Mikhail Alexeevich." And then, with obvious disapproval: "They were dressed as peasants, sir."

Misha looked at the man. He was not usually given to inventing stories.

"Why the devil should they be doing that?" he demanded.

"I can't understand it, sir," he replied. "They said"—he hesitated for an instant—"they said, sir, that they were going to look for work."

And Misha Bobrov could only wonder what on earth this could mean.

Grigory was nineteen, with a pinched face and long, oily black hair that was parted, rather sadly, down the middle. He was not strong physically, and God had cursed him with teeth that gave him pain almost every day. But he was determined, in his quiet way. Determined to survive.

He was also frightened of Natalia Romanov, who loved him.

He had been one of a family of eight. His father had been a household serf who had drifted into casual labor in Vladimir and who, as soon as they were ten, had sent his children out to work. About once a month he had flogged Grigory with birch twigs that he had thoughtfully wetted first. Yet despite this, Grigory had been fond of him.

His father had not minded when, at the age of thirteen, Grigory had said he wanted to leave home. Indeed, Grigory had the impression that his parents were rather glad to get rid of him. But before he left, his father had given him one piece of advice to take with him on his road through life. "Take what you can from women, Grigory. But watch out. Sometimes they seem kind, but deep down they want to hurt you. Remember that." He always had.

And now this girl. What did she see in him? She was pretty, lively; her father had his own holding. By Grigory's standards, the Romanovs were rich. He could make her laugh: but then, with his sharp, rather cruel humor, he could make almost anyone laugh. He could make people laugh who hated him, and whom he hated.

So what could she want with him? The way she hung around, the way she looked at him, you'd have thought she wanted to marry him. That was what one of the men in the factory had said she wanted—which had only caused Grigory to look at the fellow with suspicion before gruffly replying, "I'll have to think about that."

When the two young men dressed as peasants appeared in the village that morning nobody at first knew who they were, until Arina, coming out of the house, took one look and called out: "Holy Master Nicolai, how you've grown!" And a moment later, at the old woman's insistence, they were inside the Romanov *izba* sitting by the big warm stove and eating sweetmeats.

When the family heard that Nicolai and his friend wanted to work in the village, they were mystified. Who could fathom the mind of a noble?

But when Timofei cautiously inquired if they wanted to be paid and was told they did not, his eyes opened wide at this stroke of good luck. "Go no further, Nicolai Mikhailovich," he said. "I can give you just what you want."

And so it was, two hours later, that a puzzled Misha Bobrov encountered his son and young Popov quietly helping the peasant at the edge of a large field and, wise enough not to interfere, shook his head in amusement at the strange eccentricities of young people and returned to his house. "They'll be hungry tonight," he remarked to his wife, and he went to read a book.

Natalia watched the two visitors with curiosity, too. She had been a little girl when Nicolai Bobrov went away to school, and the landlord's son was hardly more than a name to her. He was handsome, she thought, with his neatly trimmed mustache and beard and his bright blue eyes. Very handsome. But his friend with the ginger hair was different; she did not know what to make of him. He didn't say much to Natalia and her family, leaving Nicolai to do the talking; and Natalia decided he must belong to some class of person that she had never seen before. Still, she considered, he's nothing to do with me. She had other things to think about.

Especially Grigory.

Natalia loved her family. She did not want to hurt them. But when Boris said he was moving out, something had snapped inside her. She felt suddenly very lonely. She knew her father and mother needed her; yet when the previous evening Timofei had told her, as she feared, that she might have to go to the factory, she couldn't help feeling resentful. If I do that for them, she decided, then I want something to make me happy, too. Strangely, that meant Grigory.

Why him? The fact was, her prospects in the village were not good. The Romanovs were poor: with this new baby, her father certainly had nothing to give her as a dowry. And as she wasn't a particular beauty, she would be lucky to get one of the better village boys. But in any case it was the little fellow in the factory, with his sly wit, who had captivated her. There was something about him, an inner drive, that fascinated her. None of the village boys had that. When they had first struck up an acquaintance she had started to teach him to read, and she had been astonished by his quickness. He did not seem to study things like other people: he attacked each subject, devouring it ferociously until he had mastered it. He's like a tiger, she thought, wonderingly. And yet he was also vulnerable: he needed looking after. She found this combination attractive, compelling; and by the spring she had concluded that he might not be perfect but that there was no other man on earth like him.

Was he interested in her? At first she was not sure. But gradually, as they continued to meet, it seemed to her that behind his gruff manner there was an awakening of something else, and she waited eagerly for some further sign.

What if they married? Her idea was simple enough. Either he could come and live with them in the village, and then there would be two wages to bring home, or, if they wouldn't take him in, then she would go and live with him in Russka and they would get nothing. It was a way of asserting her independence, at least.

And so, all day, while Nicolai and Popov worked with her father, she thought about him.

She was quite surprised when, at dusk, Nicolai announced that he and his friend would be back again the following morning.

Nicolai was pleased. The first day had gone well. Yevgeny seemed to be satisfied too. "We'll get their confidence," he said. "But remember," he added sternly, "we mustn't say anything for the time being. That's the plan."

"Of course." The plan was everything.

How lucky he was, Nicolai thought, to be with Popov. Admittedly he could sometimes be rather mysterious, so that you felt he was withholding information; but he seemed so certain about things, so definite. And now they were partners in this all-important business. He supposed that one day their names might even be listed with the others in the history books.

Meanwhile he was looking forward to this evening. He had seen Yevgeny in action many times, and he wondered with amusement what his friend would do to his parents.

As Misha Bobrov waited in the salon for the two young men to come down for supper, he tried to conceal his excitement.

Not only did he long to find out what they were up to, but, as he told his wife, "You can be sure we have a great many things to discuss." He believed that he would give a good account of himself. Indeed, he thought that the students might be rather impressed.

The salon was a long, pleasant room, simply furnished with chairs and sofas of French design, and was graced with heavy blue curtains, parted at the center and tied at the sides with large tassels. A fine mahogany glass-fronted bookcase, its decorative panels carved in the shape of classical lyres, stood handsomely at the far end of the room; on the mantel over the fire, a black marble clock, shaped like a rather stolid little Greek temple front, stared out into the room with confident self-satisfaction. In one corner, a round table was covered with a bright Turkish rug. And everywhere a mass of family pictures, from large oils to tiny cameos, were strewn around the walls in no particular order.

As well as these conventional furnishings, however, there were several indications that Misha Bobrov was a gentleman somewhat out of the ordinary.

On each side of the bookcase was a picture—not the classical scenes his grandfather would have favored, but bright, informal studies, one of a country landscape at sunset, the other of a wrinkled peasant's face. These paintings by the new school, known as the Wanderers, gave him huge pleasure. "They are the first truly Russian painters since the makers of icons," he would say. "These young fellows paint Russian life as it really is." Indeed, in his study, he even had a little sketch by the best of the younger artists, the brilliant Ilya Repin, which showed a humble barge-hauler on the Volga, straining on his harness as if he were trying to be free. And when young Nicolai had shown some talent for drawing at school, Misha had urged him: "You try to draw like these young men, Nicolai—just as you really see things."

Further evidence of the landlord's character lay on the round table, in the form of several thick periodicals. These were the so-called fat journals, which had become such a feature of Russian intellectual life at that period. In these might be found, in serial form, the latest works of the great novelists of the day: Tolstoy, Dostoyevsky, and Turgenev. But they also carried political commentaries and essays of the most radical kind, so that their presence in the salon was a declaration by Misha Bobrov that said: "You see, I keep abreast of all that is going on."

It was by this table that the landowner, with a great show of cheerfulness, greeted the two young men when they came down. It was clear to them both that he was holding himself in. As if nothing unusual had happened he conversed idly about the capital, the weather, the fact that his wife would be down shortly. And only after several minutes, with a show of nonchalance that almost made Nicolai burst out laughing, did he remark: "I hope you enjoyed your time in the fields today; but might one inquire what exactly you were doing?"

To which the young men answered just as they had agreed they would.

It seemed to Misha that the meal was going well. The red wine was excellent. In the warm light of the candles, under the gaze of his ancestors on the walls, he sat at the head of the table, happy and flushed and doing most of the talking. His wife Anna—tall and dark, not clever but with decided opinions—graced the other end.

So the young men wanted to study village conditions. It was a novel idea, to work side by side with the peasants like this, but to Misha it seemed rather commendable. And when young Popov added that he was collecting folktales, Misha was delighted. "I know most of Krylov's fairy tales by heart," he told his visitor. "But my old nanny Arina is the one you should really talk to. She knows hundreds."

Misha Bobrov believed he got on well with students. For a start, he was interested in education. He had been busy all that year with the district *zemstvo* trying to improve the local schooling. "We now give a basic education to one boy in six and one girl in twenty at Russka," he told them proudly. "And it would be twice that if Savva Suvorin didn't place every obstacle in our way."

He also let them know that he hated the minister of education. For some reason the tsar was devoted to this man, a certain Count Dmitri Tolstoy—a distant kinsman of the great novelist—whose regime at the Education Ministry was so reactionary that he was known as the Strangler. And when Misha learned that Popov had studied at the medical school, where there had been a huge student strike some years before, he was quick to declare, "With that cursed Tolstoy at the ministry I can understand any student who wants to revolt."

He spoke easily of literature, the latest radical essays in the journals, and politics: where he even took the line—highly unusual for a provincial landowner—that as well as the local *zemstvos* there should also be a constituent assembly, freely elected by the people, to advise the tsar on national affairs. In short, Misha Bobrov gave such proof of his progressive views that he felt sure that, although the two young men did not say much, he must have impressed them.

It was towards the end of the meal that he received a surprise.

He had been watching Yevgeny Popov with some interest during these conversations. In his day nearly all the university students had come from his own gentry class; but since midcentury, a new generation of educated people had begun to appear; sons of priests, minor officials, and merchants—men like young Popov. Misha was all in favor. The doctors, teachers, and agricultural experts whom the local *zemstvos* were employing mostly came from this class. But he sensed that Popov was more intellectual than most. What kind of fellow was he? Misha also noticed that Popov was rather abrupt when he spoke, as though scorning useless civilities. So much the better, Misha thought. He's direct. And he took care to be direct himself whenever he addressed him.

But he could not quite restrain his original curiosity about the ginger-haired student's family; and so it was, when they were well into their second bottle of wine, that he politely inquired: "I noticed, my dear sir, that your patronymic was Pavlovich. Would you by any chance be the son of that Paul Popov, whose father was once the priest at Russka?"

It was a perfectly polite question, but Popov scarcely bothered to look up from his food when he answered: "Yes."

Fearing that he might have offended him in some way, Misha graciously added, though with flagrant untruth: "A most distinguished man."

"Was he? I've no idea." Popov continued to eat.

Slightly puzzled, still curious, and feeling vaguely that, having begun to ask after his family it would be impolite not to follow through, Misha plowed on. "I hope your father is well."

Still Popov did not trouble to look up. "He's dead."

"I'm sorry." It was Anna Bobrov who, scarcely thinking, had spoken. After all, it was only common courtesy. But to her amazement, Popov now looked up at her calmly.

"No, you're not."

"Excuse me?"

"You're not sorry. How could you possibly be sorry if you never even met him?"

Anna looked confused, Misha frowned, and Nicolai smiled with amusement.

"Yevgeny hates shams. He believes one should only tell the truth."

"Quite right," said Misha, hoping to smooth over the little awkwardness. But to his surprise, young Popov only turned to look at him with a mild contempt.

"Then why did you say that corrupt old idiot my grandfather was distinguished?"

This was gross impertinence; yet, to his astonishment, Misha Bobrov felt himself blushing guiltily. "You're my guest," he muttered. Then, irritably: "One should show some family respect."

"I can't see why, when there's nothing to respect."

There was an awkward pause. Then Anna spoke. She was not sure if she understood any of this, but one thing at least she knew. "Family feeling is the most important thing in the world," she said firmly.

"Nonsense. Not if the feeling is insincere."

Her mouth opened in astonishment; but Nicolai, with a laugh, smiled at her, then at his father, and explained: "Popov is the most sincere fellow in the world. He believes we must strip away falsehood from everything. Destroy it no matter what it is."

"You mean," Anna tried to fathom this, "that anything, even kindness to others, good manners, should be destroyed? What on earth would you have if everyone did that?"

And now, for the first time since he had arrived, Popov smiled. "Truth," he said simply.

Misha Bobrov also smiled. Now he understood the fellow. "You're what they called a Nihilist," he said. Every educated Russian knew something of these radical fellows after they had been described in Turgenev's famous novel *Fathers and Sons* a few years before. They followed the Russian philosopher Bakunin, who urged that all society's falsehoods must be destroyed and that this destruction of outworn ideas, no matter how painful, was creative. "I am with you absolutely, my dear sir," he declared. "I understand." He felt rather pleased with himself.

"No, you don't." Popov was looking at him with a calm disdain. "You're just typical of your generation. You talk endlessly, make a few halfhearted reforms, and, actually, do nothing." He shrugged contemptuously.

Misha Bobrov gasped. His fist clenched. For a moment he said nothing, but forced himself, very carefully, to drink the rest of his glass of wine. As he did so, he noticed that his hand was shaking. It really was outrageous: this rudeness in his own house. And yet—this was the awful thing—could it be that there was some truth in what the young man said? Misha suddenly had a vision of dear old Uncle Ilya, sitting in his chair, as the weeks, months, and years passed, reading, talking—and doing nothing—just as Popov had described. Surely he was not like that himself: was he? "The reforms of the present reign have been real," he said defensively. "Why, we abolished serfdom before the Americans abolished slavery."

"In name but not in fact."

"These things take time." He paused and looked seriously at the young man. "Do you really believe that everything in Russia is rotten?"

"Of course. Don't you?"

And there, of course, was the problem. Misha Bobrov gazed at Popov; he could not honestly deny the charge. Russia was still pitifully backward. The bureaucracy was famous for its corruption. Even the elected *zemstvo* assemblies, of which he was so proud, had no influence at all on the central government of the empire, which was the same autocracy as in the days of Peter the Great or even Ivan the Terrible. Yes, of course his beloved Russia was rotten. But wouldn't it improve? Weren't enlightened, liberal-minded men like him making a difference? Or was this rude and frankly unpleasant young man right?

Only now, as he silently pondered this question, did Anna Bobrov suddenly speak up. She had listened to their exchange. Of the philosophical content she had understood not a word. But one statement she had clearly grasped. "You say that the state of Russia is rotten, Mr. Popov," she declared, "and you are absolutely right. It's a disgrace."

Nicolai turned to his mother in surprise. "And what should be done about it, Mother?" he inquired.

"Done?" She looked astonished. "How should I know?" And then, speaking unconsciously for the vast majority of the Russian people, and in a tone of voice that proclaimed that the statement was obvious: "That's for the government to decide!"

"Madame"—Popov smiled ironically—"you have just solved the entire problem."

And it was clear to them all that—God bless her—she certainly thought she had.

The discussion ended after that. But, as well as feeling hurt by Popov's words, Misha Bobrov was left with the sad and uncomfortable feeling that a gulf had opened between him and his son: that there was something about Nicolai and his friend that he did not understand.

In the days that followed the weather swiftly grew warmer. In the Bobrov house everything seemed very quiet. The two young men went out each day to work with the villagers and returned home tired. Everyone avoided further discussions, and when Misha occasionally asked if their researches were progressing well, they assured him they were. "Young men do get strange enthusiasms sometimes," he remarked doubtfully to his wife. "I suppose there's no harm in it."

"Being out of doors is very good for Nicolai," she replied. And Bobrov had to agree that the boy looked uncommonly fit. Young Popov, he thought, sometimes looked rather bored.

For his part, Nicolai was delighted with everything. He enjoyed the physical work and the company of the peasants who, though he could never really be one of them, seemed to get used to him; indeed he was delighted when, after a week, Timofei Romanov actually forgot for a moment who he was and cursed him as thoroughly as his own son for digging a trench in the wrong place.

Above all, though he had moved among the peasants since his childhood, it was only now, he realized, that he really understood what their lives were like—the crippling payments, the shortage of land, young Boris's need to get out from the nagging claustrophobia of his parents' house, and the resulting miserable prospect of the Suvorin factory for Natalia. And it's our fault, the gentry's, that they have to live like this, he thought. It's true that we are parasites upon these people, who have nothing to gain from the way that Russia is run.

Yet as he observed the village, he noticed other things, too. He had learned a little from books about agricultural methods in other countries;

and so he now understood that the practices followed at Russka, as in most of Russia, were medieval. The plows were wooden, since iron ones were too expensive. The plowland, moreover, was still arranged in strips, with wasteful ridges of unplowed earth between them. And since these strips were regularly redistributed, no peasant ever had a personal holding he could call his own, which he might have cultivated more intensively. When Nicolai once suggested this solution to Timofei, however, the peasant only looked doubtful and remarked, "But then some people might get better land than others." Such was the immutable way of the commune. "Anyway," Timofei confessed to him, "our greatest problem now is that every year the crops we sow yield less and less. Our Russian soil is exhausted and there's nothing you can do."

It was this statement that, for the first time, led Nicolai to question his father in detail about the village. Was Timofei correct? To his son's surprise, the landowner's answer was remarkably informed.

"If you want to understand the Russian village," he explained, "you have to understand that many of its problems are of its own making. This soil exhaustion is a perfect example. Six months ago," he went on, "the provincial *zemstvo* hired a German expert to study the question. The basic problem is this: our peasants use a three-field system of crop rotation— spring oats or barley, together with potatoes; winter rye; and the third field fallow. And quite simply, it isn't efficient. In other countries they're using four-, five-, six-year rotations and growing clover and lea grass to replenish the land. But in our backward Russia we don't.

"However, the greatest problem here," he continued, "is Savva Suvorin and his linen factory."

"Why so?"

Misha sighed. "Because he encourages the peasants to grow flax for making linen. It's a valuable cash crop. The trouble is, they substitute it for oats or barley in the spring sowing and the flax takes more goodness from the land than anything else. So—yes—the land here is getting exhausted, and flax is the main culprit. It's the same all over the region.

"But do you know the two greatest ironies of all? First, our people do grow lea grass, which would replenish the land: but they grow it in a separate field instead of putting it into the rotation. So it does no good. Second, in order to compensate for the lower yields, they take more pastureland and put it under plow. By doing that they reduce the livestock they can graze—the livestock whose manure is the only other thing they have to put goodness back into the exhausted land!"

"But that's a cycle of insanity," Nicolai said.

"It is."

"And what's to be done about it?"

"Nothing. The peasant communes won't change their customs, you know."

"And the *zemstvo* authorities?"

"Ah," his father sighed, "I'm afraid they've no plans. It's all too difficult, you see."

And Nicolai could only shake his head.

Yet there were cheerful times too. Nicolai and Popov would often sit in the *izba* with the Romanov family, and Arina would relate the very folktales she had told Nicolai's father as a child. Popov usually sat quietly to one side; he had not become close with the family. But Nicolai would happily sit at her side and encourage her to tell him not only tales, but stories of her own life too. She several times told him of the awful famine of '39. And she would happily relate her life as a serf girl in the Bobrov household.

"I see you have that same gesture," she once remarked to Nicolai, imitating the Bobrov's gentle, caressing motion of the arm, "that your father has. Ilya Alexandrovich had it, too. And your great-grandfather, Alexander Prokofievich."

"Really?" Nicolai was not even aware of this family characteristic. "And Uncle Sergei—did he have it?"

But for some reason this set the old woman off into a high cackle of laughter. "Oh no. He had something else, Master Sergei did!" And she went on laughing for several minutes, though nobody there knew why.

It was after one of these pleasant conversations, however, when Popov had gone out, that Arina one evening drew him aside. She seemed unusually agitated. "Master Nicolai, forgive a poor old woman, but I beg you, don't you get too mixed up with that one." She gestured to the door.

"You mean Popov? He's a capital fellow."

But she shook her head. "Stay away from him, Master Nicolai."

"What's he done?"

"That's what I don't know, see? But please, Nicolai Mikhailovich. He's . . ." She looked confused. "There's something wrong with him."

Nicolai kissed her and laughed. "Dear Arina." He supposed Popov must seem strange to her.

Many subjects went through Popov's mind as he had made his way, one afternoon, along the lane that led through the woods to the little town of Russka. One of them concerned a hiding place. What he needed, he thought, was a small but private spot. A shed would do. But it would have to be somewhere that could be locked up and where nobody ever came. There was nowhere like that at Bobrovo.

The article in question, carefully dismantled, was packed in pieces in a locked box in his room, which he had told his host contained only books. Soon, he judged, it would be time to use it.

Well, no doubt something would turn up.

Generally speaking he was pleased with his progress. Though he had some doubts about young Bobrov's character, it seemed to him that Nicolai would serve his purpose here quite well. He had also kept his eyes open for others who might be useful. Young Boris Romanov, for instance, had engaged his attention: a fierce spirit, he thought. Popov had spoken to him several times in a general way but had given the young man no inkling, as yet, of what was afoot. One had to be careful.

There was only one thing, really, that had taken him by surprise when he arrived at Russka. This was the influence of the nearby factories and the Suvorins who owned them. Clearly they were important, and he needed to learn more about them. So, leaving Nicolai at work in the fields that day, he had come past the monastery, over the bridge, and into the busy little town.

For some time he wandered about looking at the grim brick cotton mill, the warehouses, and the sullen rows of workers' cottages. He was becoming rather bored when his attention was suddenly engaged by a lone figure walking dejectedly by some stalls in the marketplace.

Popov moved towards him.

It seemed to Natalia that she was making progress.

Grigory had kissed her.

The kiss had not been very satisfactory. It had been salty, and she had felt him tense, uncertain what to do with his lips. She realized he had never kissed before. But it was a start.

Though Natalia had not been sent to the factory yet, she was sure it was imminent. Boris had not changed his mind, and, since there was nothing to be done about it, the family would all help him to build a new *izba* at the far end of the village. Once he left, her own fate seemed inevitable. And though she had not yet told her father anything about her young man or her hopes, she continued discreetly to meet Grigory every few days.

She often talked to him about life in the village. She also told him about the two strange young men. Grigory enjoyed hearing about Nicolai and Popov. He was not able to understand why anyone would go and work in the fields if he did not have to, and he tried to imagine what they were like. So it was with great curiosity, early one evening, that he turned when Natalia suddenly pointed across the marketplace in Russka and declared, "Well, I never. There he is—the ginger-headed one. I wonder what he's doing."

And so indeed did Grigory. For the curious stranger was deep in conversation with young Peter Suvorin.

A month had passed. The ground was dry; spring was giving way to early summer. At Bobrovo all was quiet.

Why, then, should Misha Bobrov be so worried?

It was Nicolai. At first he had looked so well: he had come home each day from the fields, flushed from his work, but relaxed; he had even caught a little sunburn from the spring sun. Misha, though he was still consumed with curiosity about the two young men, had left them alone and carefully avoided any further discussions. So the days had passed: everything had been peaceful, even pleasant. And then something had begun to go wrong.

It was around the end of the second week that Misha had noticed the difference in his son. At first it was a slight paleness; then his face had started to looked pinched and worried; and when they spoke together, there seemed to be a barrier between them. Nicolai had sometimes been defiant in the past, but he had never been cold and distant before. Yet now he seemed determined to become a stranger to both his parents. In the last few days he had become increasingly irritable, too. What had got into the boy? Was it something about the village, perhaps? Misha asked

Timofei Romanov if he had noticed anything; but the peasant told him that Nicolai seemed cheerful enough at his work.

It must be that friend of his, Misha concluded. I wish I knew more about him. Indeed, he confessed to himself, I wish I knew anything about what these two young men are thinking.

His chance came, rather unexpectedly, on a Sunday. Anna Bobrov was the cause.

Misha only went to church on the great feast days, but his wife went every Sunday, sometimes twice; and it had always been the custom for Nicolai, when he was at home, to accompany her. She had been disappointed, therefore, when he had made excuses all this month. But the worst had come that morning when she had asked—"Are you leaving me to go to Russka alone again?"—and Nicolai had turned on her irritably and, in front of Popov, told her in a cruel tone: "I've better things to do than waste my time on you and your God." She had been so shocked and hurt that Misha had put on his coat and gone with her himself; and that afternoon he had resolved that something must be said.

It was late afternoon when he came upon the two young men. They were sitting in the salon. Outside, the light was starting to fade and Nicolai, who had been making a drawing of his friend by the window, was just closing his sketching book when Misha quietly entered the room, lit the lamp on the round table, picked up a journal, and sat down comfortably in an armchair. He nodded to Popov, who was staring thoughtfully out at the park, and then remarked pleasantly to Nicolai, "Forgive my saying so, but your mother was rather hurt by you this morning."

The rebuke was merited, yet instead of acknowledging his fault, Nicolai only turned and stared at him. Then quite suddenly he gave a high-pitched laugh. "You mean because I didn't go to church?" He shook his head. "The church is just a tavern where people get drunk on religion. I can get drunk on vodka if I need to."

Misha sighed. He was not shocked. There was hardly an educated man since the Enlightenment who had never had doubts about God and organized religion. But why did Nicolai need to be so abusive? "You can doubt God without insulting your mother," he remarked irritably, "and as long as you stay in this house you will show courtesy to your mother. I hope that is understood." Then, having made his point, he turned grumpily back to his journal and assumed the conversation was over.

He was rather surprised, therefore, when Nicolai wished to continue it. Whatever thoughts had been bottled up inside the young man in recent weeks, it seemed that this little incident had made him wish to let some of them out. For now, turning contemptuously to his father, he remarked, "You have never heard of the philosophy of Feuerbach, I suppose."

As it happened, Misha had heard of this philosopher, who was in vogue among the radicals, but he had to confess that he had never read him.

"Had you done so," Nicolai said coldly, "you would know that your God is nothing more than a projection of human desires. No more, no less." He looked at Misha with pity. "You need God and the church because they belong to the society of the past. In the society of the future, we won't need God anymore. God is dead."

Misha put down his journal and looked at his son with interest. "If God is dead," he asked, "what will you replace Him with?"

"Science, of course." Nicolai looked at him impatiently. "Science has proved that the universe is material. Everything can be explained, don't you realize, by physical laws. There is no God pulling the strings—that's mere superstition. It's like thinking the earth was flat. But science, and only science, makes men free."

"Free?"

"Yes. Masters of themselves. In Russia a superstitious church supports an autocratic tsar, and the people live in darkness, like slaves. But science will sweep it all away, and then," he concluded impressively, "there will be a new world."

"What sort of world?" Misha inquired.

"Quite unlike yours," Nicolai told him bluntly. "A world of truth and justice. A world where men share the fruits of the earth together and where one man is not set over another. A world without exploitation of man by man."

Misha nodded thoughtfully. He recognized that these were noble sentiments, yet he could not help observing, "Your new world sounds to me a little like a Christian heaven."

"Not at all," Nicolai replied quickly. "Your Christian heaven is an invention. It exists in a nonexistent afterlife. It's an illusion, a cheat. But the new world, the scientific one, will be here on earth and men will live in it."

"So you despise my hope of heaven and you think my religion is a fraud?"

"Precisely."

Misha considered. He did not object to his son's desire to build a heaven on earth, even if he could not himself believe in it. Yet it seemed to him that there was a flaw in the whole argument.

"You speak of a new world where no one will be exploited," he ventured. "You also say that there is no God. But tell me this: if the universe is material, if I face no threat of hell nor hope of heaven in the life to come—then why should I trouble to be kind to my neighbor and share the fruits of the earth with him? Won't I exploit him, materially, for all I can get, since I've nothing else to look forward to?"

Nicolai looked at Popov and laughed. "You don't understand anything, do you?" he remarked contemptuously. And then, coldly: "I'm afraid I've nothing more to say to you."

Misha gazed at his son sadly. It was not the argument he minded, nor even the rudeness. He and Nicolai had often had hot disputes before. But something in the tone of this last dismissal worried him profoundly. He could sense that it implied some deeper parting of the ways. He turned to Popov. "Perhaps you can enlighten me," he said quietly.

"Perhaps." Popov shrugged. "It's quite simple. You can't understand because you are a product of the old world. Your thinking is so condi-

tioned by your society that you can't imagine a moral world without a
God. In the new world, where society will be organized differently,
people will be different." He stared at Misha with cold green eyes. "It's
like Darwin's theory of evolution—some species don't adapt, and they
die out."

"So a person who thinks like me won't exist anymore?" Misha suggested.

And then Yevgeny Popov gave one of his rare smiles. "You're already
dead," he said simply.

And why now, Misha wondered, should Nicolai suddenly jump up, his
face very pale, and run out of the room?

Misha Bobrov was so disturbed by this conversation that he watched
repeatedly for a chance to spend time with his son alone. He had never
felt that they could not speak to each other before. And I cannot leave
matters like this, he thought. Not until two days later, however, did an
opportunity present itself.

It was early evening. Popov had gone over to Russka, and Nicolai,
having come back from the village, was wandering about alone. Misha
had hesitated to approach him in the house, for fear that Nicolai might
rebuff him and retire to his room. But in a while he saw Nicolai set off
for a walk in the woods above the house, and after giving him a little
time, he hurried after him.

He caught up with his son just as Nicolai had reached the top of the
little ridge and was turning eastward to walk along it. This was a pleasant
path that led for nearly a mile, first eastward, then curving to the south,
until suddenly it ended and one encountered the river again below. By
happy chance it was a walk they had often taken together when Nicolai
was a child, though it was several years since Misha had gone that way
himself. Nervously he approached the young man; but when Nicolai,
having given him a look of slight surprise, said nothing, Misha thank-
fully fell into step beside him.

They continued together for some minutes before Misha gently inquired: "Do you remember when you were a little boy that I used to carry
you on my shoulders along this path?"

Nicolai nodded. "I remember."

They had walked on another hundred yards when Misha added, "Just
here, if you look north, you can see Russka and the monastery." And
pausing to gaze over the woods below, they saw the golden domes of the
little religious house glinting over the forest floor, and the pointed watchtower of the little town opposite. It was warm and very peaceful. After
a little while, they went on.

Not until the ridge turned south did Misha remark, "I am sorry you
cannot speak to me anymore. It is sad for a father when that happens."
And although Nicolai did not reply, it seemed to Misha that he could
sense a softening in his son. I'll say no more, he thought. We'll come to
the end of the ridge, turn back, and then perhaps I'll try again. And so,
hoping that he might still regain his son's affection, he strolled along
while Nicolai, lost in his own thoughts, walked beside him.

In truth, Nicolai was torn by many emotions, and his father had not been wrong to perceive a softening in his manner. The walk along the ridge had brought back a flood of childhood memories—of his mother's simpleminded devotion, of his father's kindness. Misha had been a good father; he could not deny that. And although, for the last month, he had been steeling himself to hate him, Nicolai found now that he could feel only pity for the landowner. Yet what was he to do? Was a reconciliation possible? Could he even now, at the eleventh hour, save his father from the coming storm? These were the thoughts that chased each other around Nicolai's mind as the two went along in silence.

Until they came to the end of the path and saw what had happened to the woods.

It had always been a charming spot, a pleasant place to rest. The ground fell away sharply to the river below and there was a delightful view southward over the silvery water and the forest. This was what both men had expected to find.

Yet the scene that now met their gaze was completely transformed and they could only stare in astonishment. A hundred yards before the end of the ridge, the woods suddenly ceased. Before them, stretching to left and to right, was a huge, unsightly scar of bare ground dotted with rotting stumps. As they made their way to the end of the ridge, they could see that the ground had been picked completely bare, and at the end, where the wooded slope down to the water had been, there was now a large gully and below it a constriction in the river where a landslide had silted up the stream.

Both men stared at this scene of devastation in horror. Then Nicolai very quietly asked: "Did you do this, Father?"

To which Misha, after a pause, could only mutter, "It seems I must have." And then, shaking his head: "That damned merchant."

In fact, as he looked at this terrible sight, Bobrov should not have been surprised. For what he saw was only the result of a practice that had become very common and was already leaving its mark over considerable areas of Russia. This was the practice of leasing.

It was very simple. Like most landowners after the Emancipation, Misha Bobrov had retained a very little plowed land, rather more pasture, and most of the forest. Short of cash, unwilling to part with his remaining land forever, he had therefore compromised and leased part of the woodland to a merchant. The provisions of the lease were fairly typical. For a fixed sum, half paid in advance, the merchant received a ten-year lease on the woodland, during which time he could do as he pleased. Naturally, therefore, to recover his money, the merchant cut down all the trees as fast as he could and sold the timber. Having only a short lease, however, the merchant had no interest in replanting, but instead grazed livestock on the cleared ground, destroying any chance of natural regrowth by the time the lease ran out.

The resulting soil erosion and gullying, in numerous provinces, was one of the most disastrous evils ever to befall the Russian landscape until the twentieth century.

Long ago Misha had leased the wooded parts of the Riazan estate, and these had now been completely destroyed. A few years back he had done the same with these outlying woodlands at Russka, but then he had forgotten all about it. Now, as he gazed at the ruins, he felt a deep sense of shame.

It was fortunate for him, however, that he could not at this moment see into his son's mind. For as Nicolai looked at the unsightly gully and pondered what had happened, the issues that had so troubled him of late were finally resolved. Popov is right, he thought. There is nothing that can be done with these landowners—even my own father. They are useless parasites. And once again he dedicated himself to the great task which, he knew, was now almost upon him.

So the two men slowly returned, Misha noting, rather sadly, that they spoke no further words to each other.

As he strolled back from Russka that same evening, Yevgeny Popov considered that, all in all, things were in a satisfactory state.

Young Bobrov was a bit emotional, but it didn't matter. He would serve his purpose.

Peter Suvorin, too, had been helpful. An artist at heart, Popov judged, an idealist. He's very confused, but malleable, he considered. Above all the young industrialist felt guilty, just like Nicolai Bobrov, and it was amazing how you could manipulate people who felt guilty. Men like this, moreover, men whose families had money or influence, were especially worth cultivating because one never knew when their resources might come in useful.

He had as yet told Peter Suvorin almost nothing. It was better that way. I'll keep him up my sleeve, he thought. But the young man had been able to provide him with one most useful thing: a private place.

It was a storeroom at one end of a little-used warehouse. The store contained various shovels and other items of equipment used for clearing snow in winter; during the summer months, therefore, no one even went there. It had a lock, to which Peter Suvorin had given him the key. He had told Peter some foolish story about storing books in this place, which seemed to satisfy him; and then, by mid-May, he had set to work.

The little hand-printing press he kept there was quite sufficient for his needs. In a few days he had produced all the leaflets he needed for the time being, disassembled the press, and hidden its parts under some floorboards.

For now, he decided, it was time to begin.

It was a book—a novel in fact—badly written, by a busy revolutionary; in parts it was absurdly sentimental: and yet to Nicolai Bobrov, as to thousands of his generation, it was an inspiration. Its title: *What Is to Be Done*.

It told of the new men and women who would lead society into the new age when all men would be free. It told of their sufferings and their dedication: it created for the reader the image of a new breed of human being—half saint, half superman—who would, by sheer moral force, lead his weaker brethren toward the common good. It was in imitation of this mythic ideal that Nicolai had undergone his ascetic regime as a student and lain on a bed of studs. It was with this valiant new man in mind that he had come with Nicolai upon this mission to Russka. And so it was upon the eve of the great day that he turned to this little novel, reading late into the night, to prepare himself for the ordeal ahead.

Natalia watched young Bobrov with fascination. He was standing on a wooden stool in front of her parents' *izba,* and a little group was gathered before him.

The evening sun was catching the side of his face, creating a sheen like a little golden river down the thin curve of his youthful beard. Dear God, how handsome he looked.

Natalia had been working in Russka for two weeks now: long, boring shifts at the cotton factory—ten or twelve hours each shift—which they relieved by singing songs together, above the din, just as though they were women going to mow a field. Quite often, before walking home to her parents, she saw Grigory, who still had not made up his mind about her; but she was usually so tired that she scarcely cared, some days, whether he married her or not.

But now her eyes were fixed upon Nicolai Bobrov. And it was not just because of his good looks. It was because of what he was saying. She could hardly believe it.

Nicolai had started several minutes before. He would not have stood on the stool, where he felt rather foolish and uncomfortable: but Popov had told him he really should. Indeed, despite his preparation, he had suddenly found himself so shy that he would gladly have let his friend do the talking. Popov had pointed out, however, with perfect truth: "You're closer to them than I am, Nicolai. Have courage and do it."

So here he was. Quite a little crowd—five or six households—had gathered around as soon as he got up to address them; others were coming; and since, despite going over the thing a thousand times in his head, he could never decide how to begin, he found himself unconsciously falling back on the biblical formula he knew they would understand.

"My friends," he began, "I bring you good news."

They listened carefully as he outlined to them the many problems of their lives. When he spoke of their heavy repayments, there were murmurs of assent. When he spoke of the need to improve the yields on their plowland and stop the rape of the woodlands, there were nods of approval. When he apologized for the part his own family had played in their miserable lives, there were looks of surprise, several grins, and general laughter when a friendly voice cried, "We forgive you all, Nicolai Mikhailovich, if you'd just let us string up the body of your old grandfather!" Which was followed by an even louder laugh when someone else called out, "If you want your serfs back, young sir, we'll surely let you have Savva Suvorin!" And when Nicolai calmly announced that they ought to have all the land, including everything his father still owned, there was a cheerful roar of approval. "So when's he going to give it to us?" A woman called out.

And then Nicolai came to his extraordinary message.

"My father will not help you, my friends," he declared. "None of the landowners will. They are parasites—a useless burden from a former age." Now that he was getting into his stride, Nicolai became quite carried away.

"My dear friends," he cried out, "we are entering a new age. An age of freedom. And it is in your hands—this very day—to bring the new age to pass. The land belongs to the people. Take then, what is rightfully yours! We are not alone. I can tell you that all over Russia, at this very moment, the people in the villages are rising up against the oppressors. Now is the time, therefore. Follow me—and we shall take the Bobrov estate. Take it all—it is yours!"

He had done it.

Few events in Russian history have been more curious than the occurrences in the summer of 1874.

Nicolai and his friend were not alone: their strange mission to the peasants was being repeated in other villages all over Russia, in the movement known to Russian history as the Going to the People.

The young people—both men and women—were nearly all students. Some had studied abroad. About half were the children of landowners or high officials; the rest came from families of merchants, priests, or minor bureaucrats. Their politics followed the ideas of those who believed, like the French philosopher Fourier, that the peasant commune in the countryside was the best kind of natural socialism. Indeed, many claimed that Russia's very backwardness would be her salvation. For she was scarcely corrupted by the evil of bourgeois capitalism at all. She could move straight from feudalism to socialism, thanks to the natural communism of the village. And though few of them knew much of peasant life at close quarters, they believed that after working in the villages and gaining the peasants' confidence, they had only to give the word for a natural revolution to take place. They told themselves that the peasants would rise and establish a new and simple order in which the whole empire of Russia would be freely shared among the peasant brotherhood.

It was not surprising that Nicolai was drawn to this movement. Many of his most idealistic friends were volunteering. What was amazing was that, at first, the authorities did not realize what was happening. Some two and a half thousand students quietly slipped out into hundreds of villages that summer: some to their own or nearby estates; many others across the Volga or to the old Cossack lands by the river Don. Even now some of these last were telling the Cossack peasants that the time of Pugachev and of Stenka Razin had come again. And out of this, they all hoped, a new world would be born.

Nicolai looked at the faces before him. He had done it. At last, after all these months of preparation, the die was cast.

The way had been hard. How could it be otherwise? He had never minded the sacrifice of his own inheritance—he cared nothing for that; but his parents were going to be dispossessed—he thought, and that would destroy them. Whatever their faults, he still loved them. How nearly, when they took the walk along the ridge, he had come to explaining everything to his father. Until he had seen the ruined woodlands and decided that Misha was past saving. And he supposed it was better he had kept silent. His father would never have understood. Anyway, he told himself, soon nobody will have estates. His parents' way of life was finished. At least, after the revolution, he thought, I'll be there to show them the way.

For this was it. The word had been spoken and there was no going back. It was the revolution. And now that it had finally begun, he felt a sense of exaltation. Flushed and excited, he waited for the villagers to respond. "Well," he called, "are you with me?"

And nobody moved. There was absolute silence. They just gazed at him. Had he convinced them? It was impossible to say. What was in their minds? He suddenly realized he had no idea. Wasn't anyone going to say anything?

It was only after a long pause that, at last, a small, black-bearded man stepped forward. He looked up at Nicolai with cautious suspicion. Then he asked his question.

"Are you saying, young sir, that the tsar has given us the rest of the land?"

Nicolai stared at him. The tsar?

"No," he replied truthfully. "It's yours to take."

"Ah." The man nodded, as though his suspicions had been confirmed. "Well, then." He stepped back. "The tsar has not given." And there was a sympathetic murmur that said, more plainly than any words: This young fellow doesn't know what he's talking about.

Nicolai felt himself go pale. Was this the revolution—the spontaneous uprising of the commune? What had gone wrong? Had his arguments been defective in some way? He scanned their faces for a sign. But they continued to watch him placidly, as though curious to see what this young eccentric might do next. He glanced questioningly at Popov, who only shrugged. Almost a minute passed, awkwardly, until some of the villagers started to turn away. "I shall speak again tomorrow," he announced, with what he hoped was a calm smile, and got down off his stool.

In front of him now was a group of about ten people, including the Romanovs. Nicolai wondered what to do next. It seemed, however, that his words had had some effect upon Timofei Romanov; for the peasant was looking agitated and was clearly eager to speak.

"Have I got it right, Nicolai Mikhailovich," he asked with a worried frown, "that you want your father to lose his land?"

"Yes."

"That's what I thought." He shook his head. "I don't know what's got into all the young people nowadays. My own son is doing the very same thing to me. Why is it?"

"But you don't understand," Nicolai protested. "The land would go to the commune so that there would be plenty for everyone. It's what you've always wanted."

"And this is to happen all over Russia?"

"Yes. Right now."

Timofei shook his head again. "That is terrible," he said. "There will be bloodshed." And seeing Nicolai look confused, he took him by the arm. "I expect you mean well, Nicolai Mikhailovich," he explained kindly. "And one day, when God decides, we shall be given all the land, just as you say." He smiled. "Yes, it will all be so natural. The tsar will see that we have need, and he will give. Perhaps even in my poor lifetime. And then he will say to me: 'Timofei, the land is yours.' And I shall say 'I thank Your Highness.' And that will be all." He looked at Nicolai earnestly now. "But we must be patient, Nicolai Mikhailovich. That is God's will, and it is our Russian way. We must suffer and be patient, until the tsar decides the day has come." And satisfied that he had said all that could possibly be said, he let go of Nicolai's arm with a friendly pat.

Nicolai sighed. If his speech had failed to enlighten the older man, perhaps he had done better with his own generation. He turned to young Boris. "Well, Boris, what do you think?"

Boris looked thoughtful. The motives of this young nobleman were a mystery to him. But then, what sort of madman deliberately went to work in the fields when he could be sitting comfortably in the manor house? Boris knew the size of the Bobrov estate, though, and he knew how to calculate.

"If we shared out all your father's land," he estimated carefully, "then I'd have enough to take on two, maybe three hired laborers of my own." He grinned. "Why, a few years like that, a few good harvests, and I could even get rich." He nodded. "If that's the revolution, Nicolai Mikhailovich, then I'm all for it—if you and your friends can really pull it off."

Nicolai gazed at him in astonishment. Was this all the young fellow had in mind—personal gain and the exploitation of others? What had become of the spontaneous revolution? "I'm afraid," he said sadly, "that wasn't quite what I meant."

As Nicolai and Popov walked up the slope to the manor, both were lost in their own thoughts. Perhaps, Nicolai considered, he had just expected things to happen too soon. A few more speeches, a few more days, weeks, even months, and the message would begin to get through. He would try again tomorrow, and the next day. He'd be patient.

It was Popov who finally broke the silence. "We should have told them the tsar was giving them the land," he said gloomily. "I could even have forged a proclamation."

"But that would be against everything we stand for," Nicolai objected.

Popov shrugged. "It might have worked, though," he said.

Yet if Nicolai thought he had failed to win any converts, he was wrong; and he would have been surprised indeed to see into the mind of one member of the Romanov family the following morning. Natalia's mind was in a whirl. It had not occurred to anyone to ask her opinion about the speech the evening before, but it had deeply moved her. Now, as she made her way out of the village in the early morning, the phrases were still echoing in her head: a new age, the end of oppression. Until that day she had believed her father and put her faith in the faraway tsar. Didn't everyone? But as she had listened to Nicolai, it seemed to her that a whole world had opened.

He was so beautiful. He's like an angel, she had thought, as the sun caught his face. Despite his peasant's dress, he was so obviously a noble from another world. He was educated. Surely he must know many things that her poor father could not possibly understand.

She knew that what he said about the land was true. But recently she had experienced another kind of oppression, as bad as any in the days of serfdom: that of Suvorin and his factories. That was where the peasant was truly enslaved. Already she had come to hate it: and as for Grigory, she knew that his loathing of Suvorin was almost an obsession. Is there really a new age dawning, she wondered, where we shall all be free? And if so, won't the peasants in the factory benefit from this revolution, too? If she could just ask young Nicolai.

It was just as she started along the path into the woods that she saw Popov.

He had gone for an early stroll. He was ambling along, wearing a wide-brimmed hat like an artist, and as she approached he gave her quite a pleasant smile. Normally she would not have spoken to him; for though she had nothing against Nicolai's friend, she had always felt rather shy in his presence. However, encouraged by the smile, and eager to find out, she asked him: "This revolution and the new age that Nicolai Mik- hailovich spoke of—will it change things in the factory, too?"

He smiled again. "Why certainly."

"What will happen?"

"The factories will all be given to the peasants, too," Popov promptly replied.

"We wouldn't have to work such long hours? And Suvorin would be kicked out?"

"That's right."

"I have a friend," she said hesitantly, "who would be interested to hear Nicolai Mikhailovich. But he is at the factory."

And now Popov looked at her with interest. "I shall be in Russka this afternoon," he said, "if your friend would like me to speak to him." And seeing a trace of doubt on her face, he added, "I know somewhere very private."

Nicolai did not go to work in the fields that day. But in the late afternoon, when he went down to the village and mounted the stool in front of the Romanov *izba,* he noticed that the crowd assembling was much bigger than it was the day before. This pleased him. He had not really wanted to speak again that day. Popov had deserted him to go into Russka for some reason, and he might have waited for another occasion to speak if his friend had not urged him on. "Courage, my friend. They've had time to think about what you said yesterday. You may have made more converts than you think. Go to it, Nicolai."

Not only was the crowd bigger, it was excited. Several of the senior men were in the throng and the village elder himself was standing at the back. They had been waiting for him.

It had not occurred to Nicolai that the villagers were planning to arrest him. Indeed, some of the men had wanted to go and fetch the local police officer from Russka beforehand, but the elder, bearing in mind that this was the landowner's son, had refused. I'll hear what he says myself before I take action, he had decided. And now, as Nicolai prepared to address them once again, the elder listened carefully.

"Once again, my friends, I stand before you with good news. I stand before you at the dawn of a new age. For today, all over our beloved Russia, great events are occurring. I speak not of a few protests; not of a hundred riots; not even of a huge uprising such as we have seen in the past. I am speaking of something more joyful, and more profound. I am speaking of the revolution."

As the crowd gave a little gasp of anticipation, Nicolai saw the village elder start. But he did not notice Arina, hurrying out of the village.

Yevgeny Popov gazed calmly into the agitated face of Peter Suvorin. What a kindly, sensitive face it was, despite the overlarge nose. How strange that grim old Savva Suvorin's grandson should be such a poetic fellow.

For the document he had given Popov to read was almost a poem. Not that poor Peter Suvorin realized it, of course. He thought he had written a call to revolution.

They had a strange relationship. It had not taken Popov long to become Peter's mentor. He had soon discovered Peter's hatred of the Suvorin factory, his guilt about the workers there, his vague, poetic longings for a better world. Popov had given him a copy of *What Is to Be Done* and talked to him about his responsibilities for the future. More recently Popov had indicated that he was part of a larger organization with a Central Committee. He could see this had intrigued Peter. He had dropped other hints about future action and made references to the existence of the little printing press. And, above all, he had achieved mastery over Peter by the simple art of giving or withholding approval. It was amazing how people needed approval. But though the heir to the huge Suvorin enterprise was obviously an important catch—potentially far more important than Nicolai Bobrov—he was so confused and idealistic that Popov was not sure how to use him.

The composition he had now brought Popov, sheet after sheet in his nervous handwriting, was the passionate distillation of all his thoughts. It was a cry for social justice, an almost religious invocation of human freedom; it spoke desperately of the oppression he saw in Russia—not so much of the body as of the spirit. And it concluded with a call to revolution. A gentle revolution.

It had taken him many hours to produce and now, with an anxious frown, he awaited his mentor's verdict.

"You mean," Popov asked, "that the people can take power peacefully, without bloodshed? That their oppressors will just give up without a fight when the people refuse to cooperate?"

"Exactly."

"It would be like a sort of pilgrimage," Popov remarked.

"Why, yes." Peter's face cleared. "I hadn't thought of that."

Popov looked at him thoughtfully. He couldn't imagine how he was going to use him, but he'd think of something. "I'll keep this: it could be important," he said. "I shall report it to the Central Committee. In the meantime, hold yourself in readiness."

Peter Suvorin flushed with pleasure. Popov put the paper in his pocket and turned to go. He was due to meet the girl Natalia and her friend in a short while. He wondered if that would be any more interesting.

By the time he arrived at the village, Misha Bobrov was red in the face. Arina had been so insistent that he had come on foot straightaway, almost at a trot. If he hadn't known Arina all his life he would not have believed what she had told him. Yet now, arriving just in time to hear Nicolai's final words, he went completely pale. Those terrible words. Spoken by his own son.

"Rise up! Take the Bobrov land and all the other estates. For this, my friends, is the revolution!"

It was true, then, what she had said. Yet even now he could scarcely take it in. His only son a betrayer. He means to ruin me and his own mother. Is that how much he cares for us? For a second this was all that Misha Bobrov could think. Then he felt Arina tugging urgently at his sleeve.

"Look."

He suddenly realized that the villagers were quite silent and that they were turning to look, not at Nicolai but at the village elder, who was making his way grimly towards Nicolai, accompanied by two of the senior men. "They're going to take him to the police," Arina whispered. "He'll be arrested. You must do something, Master Misha." And he realized she was right.

It was not often that Misha Bobrov had to think quickly, but now he did. And in a flash he saw what he must do.

"Nicolai!" His voice rang out. The crowd turned in surprise. "Nicolai. My poor boy!" He strode forward, Arina just behind him.

He was an impressive figure when he wanted to be. The crowd parted before him. Even the village elder and his two men hesitated as the landowner marched up to his astonished son. When he reached Nicolai, Misha turned to the villagers angrily. "Why didn't anyone tell me sooner?" he thundered. Then, with a peremptory nod to the elder: "Quickly now. Help me lift him down. The poor boy."

Nicolai was so taken aback by the entire proceedings that he let them lift him to the ground almost before he knew what was happening; and he was even more surprised when his father, giving him a pitying smile, swiftly mounted the stool and addressed the little crowd.

"My friends: the fault is mine. I should have warned you." He looked a little embarrassed. "My poor son has been suffering from a nervous disorder. The doctors in Moscow recommended country air and heavy exercise. That is why he has been working in the fields." He shook his head sadly. "It seems the treatment has not worked and the fits of delusion have returned." He raised his hand and let it fall, helplessly. "A family tragedy. We can only pray for his recovery with time." He turned politely to the elder. "Perhaps your men would help me get him back to the house."

There was a moment's pause. Had it worked?

"We were going to arrest him, sir," the elder began, uncertainly.

"My good man," Misha retorted sharply, "it's not a policeman he needs but a doctor."

The elder seemed to hesitate. The crowd looked confused. And then, dear Arina's voice, a clearly audible cackle from just behind him. "He used to have those fits when he was a boy. I thought he'd grown out of them." Thank God she had taken her cue.

There was a murmur in the crowd. This explained it all: no wonder the young man's behavior had seemed eccentric. There were even one or two chuckles.

Only the village elder looked thoughtful. Quietly now, he came to Misha Bobrov's side. "I shall still have to report this to the police, sir," he said softly.

Misha looked at him. "That will not be necessary," he said calmly. "The boy needs rest. He's quite harmless, and I don't want him agitated." Then, with a sidelong glance: "Come and see me tomorrow and we can discuss it."

The elder nodded. They both understood that a little money would change hands. Moments later two of his men were helping Bobrov and Timofei lead poor Nicolai away.

Nicolai went quietly. Indeed, he scarcely knew what to do. The indifference of the peasants the first day had come as a shock; but the discovery that they were about to arrest him . . . He could scarcely believe it. And now, he thought miserably, they actually believe I'm mad. He hung his head. Perhaps I am. He had not himself realized the strain that the last few days had been. Now, suddenly, he felt strangely depleted, unable to do anything. Silently they all went up the slope.

It was when they were halfway to the house that Timofei Romanov was struck by a thought. He turned to Misha Bobrov. "The other young man, sir, with your son—the quiet one. Would he be a doctor then?"

To which Bobrov smiled grimly. "A sort of doctor. Yes," he muttered, "I suppose you could say that."

An hour later, in the privacy of the house, Misha Bobrov was beside himself.

The two young men were standing before him. And they did not even seem to think they owed him an apology.

"You, sir," he addressed Popov. "I hold you equally responsible. Whatever your beliefs, you have abused my hospitality. As for you"—he turned to Nicolai—"you have just incited the peasants to attack your own parents. Have you nothing to say?"

Nicolai looked pale and exhausted. As for Popov, it was impossible to know what he was thinking. The insolent young man seemed slightly bored.

"You have both lied to me, too," Misha went on furiously, "with these stories about collecting folklore. Yet you dare to preach to me about morality!" He glowered at them. "Well?"

Yet whatever response the landowner expected, it was not what he got.

For now Popov laughed. It was a dry, contemptuous sound.

"Poor Mikhail Alexeevich." His voice was quiet, deadly. "What a fool you are." He sighed. "But you *liberch* are all the same. You talk about liberty, and reforms. You praise your ridiculous *zemstvos.* And it's all a lie—a dirty little compromise to hold on to your own power and wealth. And you don't even realize we all see through you. We know what you really are: you're even worse than the autocrat, because you want to corrupt the people into thinking they are getting somewhere. But you will be completely destroyed, and there's nothing you can do about it. The march of history is inevitable. So there's nothing for you to get excited about."

For a moment Misha thought he was going to strike this loathsome Popov; but he contained himself. If nothing else, he was determined to get to the bottom of this young man's ideas, which had such an influence on his son. "Your real reason for being here is to foment a revolution that will usher in a new age—this heaven on earth of yours, without a God. Is that correct?"

"Yes."

"The revolution will destroy everything—the tsar and the landowners—for the good of the peasants?"

"For the common good."

"Would you have the peasants kill the landowners?"

"If necessary, certainly."

"But the peasants don't follow you. They almost arrested Nicolai. Where does that leave you?"

"The peasants aren't politically aware yet. They don't understand the common good."

"That's the new world of perfect equality."

"Yes. The peasants still need to be educated."

"By you?"

"By the new men."

"Who understand what is really good for them. And to achieve this end—for the common good, will new men like yourself use any means?"

"Possibly. Why not?"

"This means that the new men are superior to all of us. They are above the ordinary rules because of their higher mission and understanding. You're a sort of superman."

Popov smiled faintly. "Perhaps."

Misha nodded. Now he thoroughly understood. "You'll leave my house tomorrow morning," he said drily. "At dawn. As for you"—he turned to Nicolai—"you will stay in the house for the time being. Your nervous illness is the only thing protecting you from the police. You understand?"

But if Misha thought he had settled matters, he had not reckoned with Yevgeny Popov; and it was with astonishment that he now turned as the redheaded student calmly addressed him.

"Actually, I shall be staying here for some time."

What new impertinence was this? "You'll do as you are told and be gone at dawn," Misha snapped.

Yet still Popov only gazed at him imperturbably. "I think not," he replied. And as Misha started to grow red, he went on quietly: "Consider, Mikhail Alexeevich, your true position. Your son has incited the peasants to revolution. I didn't. In the eyes of the authorities, it is Nicolai who is a criminal now. So your position is very weak. For myself, I care nothing about the authorities or anything they can do to me. But if you force me to, I could certainly make things very unpleasant for you and your son. If I say, therefore, that I wish to stay here for a while, it would probably be wiser of you to let me." And then he smiled.

Misha was dumbfounded. He looked first at one, then the other of the young men. "And you call this man your friend?" he said to Nicolai with disgust. And then, furiously, to Popov, "Do you really suppose you can get away with this?"

"Yes."

Misha was silent. He supposed it was true that the young troublemaker could be a danger to Nicolai. I wish to God I had more information—something I could pin on this Popov, he thought. Perhaps something would turn up. In the meantime, though he hated to show any weakness before this loathsome interloper, he decided to be cautious. "You can, perhaps, be useful," he said at last. "You can remain here awhile on the following conditions: you are to refrain from any political activities; and you will tell people that Nicolai is sick. But if you start any trouble, or implicate Nicolai in any way with your activities, then you may find I have more influence with the authorities here than you think. Do you understand?"

"That suits me very well," Popov said blandly, and he strolled out of the room.

It was half an hour later that Nicolai came to Popov's room. He found his friend in a calm but thoughtful mood. "That was a brilliant trick of yours, telling father that you'd expose me," Nicolai said. "He didn't know which way to look." He had never admired his clever friend more.

"Yes. It was, wasn't it?"

"But what shall I do now?" Nicolai asked urgently. "I can't just give up. Should I go to another village, do you think, and try to raise the peasants there?"

To his disappointment, however, Popov shook his head. "For the moment, Nicolai," he said, "I want you to stay in the house and do just as your father asks." And when Nicolai began to protest, he stopped him. "The fact is, my friend, I have some business to attend to at Russka and your being here gives me just the cover I need. So do cooperate, there's a good fellow."

"If you think that's best," Nicolai said reluctantly. He looked at Popov curiously. "What are you up to?"

For several moments Popov did not answer. Then, rather thoughtfully, he remarked, "He's right of course, your father."

"Is he? What about?"

"The peasants. They won't follow us."

"Perhaps in time," Nicolai suggested.

There was a silence.

"God, how I despise them," Popov murmured.

Which left Nicolai rather confused.

Two weeks had passed since Nicolai's attempt to start the revolution, and in the village of Bobrovo everything was quiet.

No one had set eyes on Nicolai Bobrov. It was known that he was up at the manor house. The serfs there said he sometimes went for walks in the woods above the house; the rest of the time he seemed to rest or read books.

As for his friend Popov, he was often to be seen nowadays, wandering about with a notebook and sketching pad. Somewhere in the Bobrov house he had found an ancient, wide-brimmed hat that had once belonged to Ilya and which gave him the look of an artist; and the people at Bobrovo would often see him wandering over the little bridge to sketch the village from the footpath on the other side of the river. Frequently, too, he would take the lane through the woods to Russka and draw the monastery or the town. And if anyone asked him about Nicolai Bobrov he would shake his head sadly and say, "Poor fellow. Let us hope he will recover soon."

If the village was deceived, however, Arina was not. She said nothing, but she knew very well that Nicolai wasn't ill; as for Popov: What is he up to, that evil one? she would ask herself. As the days went by, Arina several times confided to her daughter, "Something bad's going to happen, Varya." But when asked what, she could only shake her head and say, "I don't know."

Perhaps, she realized, it was her own family troubles that gave her a sense of foreboding. Things were looking bad for the Romanovs. Young Boris and his wife were gone, and already she could see the strain was telling on Timofei. All alone now, the peasant's simple face looked pale and abstracted, as if he were suffering pain. The money Natalia brought from the factory was a help, but there was something about the girl recently that made Arina wonder if she was reliable. I don't like the look of her, she thought. She'll run away or do something stupid. Varya's pregnancy was not agreeing with her either. She was looking pale and unwell; and once, when the two of them had gone into the woods to pick mushrooms, the younger woman had tripped on a root and fallen facedown. Instead of getting up, she had just lain on the ground and moaned, "This baby's going to kill me, Mother. I know it."

As she considered these matters, it seemed clearer than ever to Arina that when it was born, the baby must be disposed of. It's easier to be hard when you get old, she considered. You see things as they are. And if anything confirmed this opinion, it was the interview that took place between Natalia and the family one evening.

Natalia was rather proud of herself when she made the announcement.

Right up to the end she had been uncertain. His reluctance and shyness had remained a constant challenge. Overcoming them had become a game she played with herself each day, and even Natalia was not fully aware how much this game had turned into an obsession. How slowly they had progressed from that first kiss, as she patiently cultivated the small flower of his trust and affection: how hesitantly it had grown from the cold, bare ground of his barren life. And what a sense of excitement it gave her to hold his small, bony form in her arms and feel him gradually spring into life. What was it, this result of her careful labors? Was it love? Was it affection? She supposed that, since there was life where before there was nothing, it must be. Above all, it gave her a strange and wonderful sense of possession. This, she thought, is mine. And since the completion of this process, the flowering, must be marriage, it seemed to her that when that took place, it would be the solution to everything.

As for Grigory, he allowed himself to be persuaded. Gradually their innocent embraces became, for him, full of a new excitement. As his confidence grew he began to want, urgently, to explore her body and to possess her. And since she would only let him go so far, he understood well enough that they must be married if this new world of wonder was to be opened and revealed to him. All right then, I'll do it and have her, he thought. We'll get married.

And what then? He would lie with her. Her whole body would be his. The thought had become so thrilling that it made him laugh. What else would happen? He could hardly see beyond this except for one thing. As soon as we're married, I'll hit her in the face and give her a beating, he thought. That way I'll be master in my own house. It wasn't much, but it was the only thing he knew about marriage.

So it was that, one sunny evening, Natalia told her parents the good news. Now that Grigory had proposed, she felt such a sense of achievement that she almost forgot that they might not be pleased. It was a shock, therefore, when, instead of smiling, her father went pale and then roared: "Never!"

"But why?" she stammered, taken aback.

"Why? Because he's a penniless factory laborer: that's why! He hasn't a yard of land. He hasn't a horse. He's got nothing but the clothes on his back! What the devil do you mean by asking me to accept such a son-in-law?" He pounded his fist on the table. Then, turning to his wife: "Varya, Varya. First the child; then my son leaves; now this. What the devil am I supposed to do?" And he buried his face in his hands.

Natalia looked at her mother. She, too, was pale, and she was shaking her head. "But he could help us," she said, and she explained her plan for having Grigory live with them. "It would mean we'd get his wages, too."

But after only a short pause her father went on, with a groan, "Yes, and then you'll produce a brat of your own, and then where will we be?"

"There are young men in the village who'd have you, you know," Varya said gently. "It's better if you have your own place, Natalia. You'd find that out quite soon."

"You're not to see this boy anymore," Timofei interrupted. "I ought to take you back from that cursed factory, except . . ." He threw up his hands helplessly. Except that he couldn't afford to.

There, they all knew, lay the real point. But it was only because she was hurt that Natalia suddenly decided it was time to speak the truth.

"The fact is," she said quietly, "that you don't want me to marry at all because you need me here to support you. As for your talk of finding me a peasant with land, you can't give me any dowry, so who'd have me? The boys in this village have enough girls to choose from. But I shall get married, whether you like it or not—and Grigory is the best chance you've got." It was humiliating, but true. She turned to walk out.

"You're only fifteen. I can refuse my consent," Timofei shouted after her. "I forbid you to see him."

She went outside and started to walk out of the village. Only when she got to the riverbank did she start to cry.

Inside the *izba,* Timofei put his head in his hands, Varya shook her head sadly, and Arina, who had said nothing, looked thoughtful and grim. She was sure of it now. Whatever happened, there was no room for this baby.

How easy it was, Popov discovered, to go about his business unmolested. With his hat and his sketchbook—and his careful references to Nicolai's malady—no one seemed to suspect him of anything. It excited no suspicion if he loitered in the Russka market sketching. Even old Savva Suvorin had seen him near the cotton mill and done no more than give him a bleak stare. And this last was important to Popov. For he was starting to make remarkable progress.

There was no question: young Grigory was a wonderful find. Who'd have suspected, Popov thought, that a chance encounter would lead to such a treasure? The fellow was intelligent, quick: and above all, he was bitter. He has judgment, Popov considered. He wouldn't do anything rash like Nicolai Bobrov or Peter Suvorin. But no one who had heard Grigory speak his true mind about old Savva Suvorin and his factories could be in any doubt: If he needs to, he would kill. It seemed to Popov that there might be an important future awaiting Grigory—perhaps even a great one.

The girl was not bad, either. Natalia didn't have her young man's cold fire. But she was a rebel, too, with a mind of her own. She hated the old order. Popov judged that they would make a good team. He could see himself working with them for a long time, as things developed.

For the moment, however, until he was sure he could trust them, he was cautious. Though it was clear that Grigory would gladly burn down the factories and slit Suvorin's throat, if he thought he could get away with it, Popov kept their conversations general. He would speak vaguely about the better order that was to come; he dropped faint hints about his friend Nicolai Bobrov's connection with the mysterious Central Committee; he told them that he himself was only a new disciple of the cause. "Bobrov hasn't told me much, and unfortunately he's sick," he explained. And so, over two weeks, he found out far more about them than they did about him.

It was on the day after Natalia's quarrel with her parents, when they were meeting in the storeroom where he had hidden away the printing press, that Popov told them in a confidential tone, "I have a message for you from Bobrov. He is impressed with what he hears of you and he wants to entrust you with a mission." He paused and, seeing they were interested, lowered his voice. "There is someone else in Russka who has contacts with the Central Committee. Tomorrow he will give you some leaflets, which you are to distribute selectively—to people you can trust—in the factories and in the village." He looked at them carefully. "But one thing is of the greatest importance. You must not speak to this person, and you must never reveal his identity to anyone." He looked grave. "The committee knows how to deal with those who betray them."

He could see they were impressed.

"Don't worry, we'll do it," Grigory said with a grin.

It was the next day that young Peter Suvorin went to a quiet place near the dormitory where Grigory lived and, finding the young man and Natalia waiting there, gave them a package wrapped in plain white paper.

Peter followed his instructions precisely. He had no idea what the package contained. He spoke no word to Grigory or the girl; nor did they address him. But as he left the astonished couple, his heart was singing.

As well it might. For hadn't Popov told him that this Grigory was in touch with the Central Committee? And were not these—the very young people who had good reason to hate and despise him—now his comrades? He was accepted. He was breaking free of his terrible inheritance at last. For the first time in weeks, he smiled.

Boris gazed at his sister with affection and also with guilt. They had found a quiet spot by the river where they would not be disturbed; and only as they sat down did he suddenly realize that weeks had passed since they had last been alone like this.

Was it all his fault? When he and his wife had not asked her to live with them, they had not meant to desert her. But somehow they had always been so busy in the last few weeks. As he thought about it now it occurred to him that she must have felt terribly alone. Was that why she was running after this Grigory?

He listened carefully, though, as she poured her heart out to him. "I won't let them stop me," she told him. "I'm going to marry." And finally his heart sank when she said, "They may not like Grigory, but when I get pregnant by him they won't have much choice, will they?"

"Do you love him?" Boris asked.

"Of course I do."

He said nothing, but he was not convinced.

If only, it seemed to Boris, they had more money. Then his sister would not have been working in the factory, and she could have had a husband from the village. And who had made everything so difficult? He had, by moving out. If I'd realized, he thought, maybe I'd have acted differently. Yes, he was to blame, and money was the problem. But what could he do now? I'll think of something, he promised himself.

He put his arm around her. "Don't do anything unless you're sure," he said. And the two of them remained that way for some time, enjoying their renewed intimacy and the peace of the little river.

Boris was surprised therefore when, after about twenty minutes, Natalia suddenly reached into her shirt and pulled out a leaflet. "Read this," she said, with a faint smile.

It was a remarkable document: brief and to the point. Using some of the same phrases that Nicolai Bobrov had employed, it urged the peasants to prepare for the coming day when a revolution would usher in the new world. It was aimed at the landlords, of course, but it was particularly scathing about the new class of exploiters, the factory owners like Suvorin, "who use you worse than animals." These were the people who must be utterly destroyed, the leaflet said. "Organize," it urged. "Be ready." It was a telling composition, and as he read it, Boris's heart sank.

"Where did you get this?"

"Never mind."

"But this is dangerous, Natalia."

"I thought you were in favor of the revolution. That's what you said to Nicolai Bobrov."

"I want more land. But this"—he shook his head—"this is different. You stay out of it. You could get in a lot of trouble." Then, as she only shrugged: "Did Nicolai Bobrov give you this?"

"No."

"Who then?"

"You'd never guess in a million years."

"Promise me you'll drop all this."

"I promise nothing. But keep quiet yourself. Don't tell I showed it to you."

"You can be sure of that." He had a sudden thought. "Is this Grigory in this business with you? Did he get you into this?"

"Maybe yes, maybe no. Maybe I got him into it."

He handed the leaflet back to her.

"I never saw this, Natalia. You burn them if you've any more." And he got up.

It was his fault. He knew it: his fault that his sister had gone to that accursed factory; that she had decided to marry Grigory; and that now she was getting mixed up in God knew what danger. He must do something—if only he knew what.

Savva Suvorin was a thorough man. When he walked around the workshops each day, his sharp old eyes missed nothing; and he was proud of the fact that he never used spies. True, his foreman told him everything that was going on. "But only because they're afraid I'll find it out anyway," he would say. And no doubt by some similar logic, he was informed about everything that passed in the village of Bobrovo, too.

Savva was also in a good temper. Two weeks before, he had been seriously worried about his grandson. The boy had become so morose and moody that both Savva and his wife had feared for his health. But just in the last few days, for some reason, a change had come over Peter: his face had cleared; he seemed to be taking an interest in life again; he was almost cheerful. "I daresay," old Maria said, "it took him a while to get used to things here, after the big city." And Savva looked forward to better days.

It was one morning, just three days after the change in Peter, that he saw young Grigory pass a piece of paper to a fellow worker. At first he thought nothing of it. When he happened to see the man slip the paper under his machine a little while later, he still did not imagine it could be anything important. And it was only idle curiosity that made him push his stick under the machine that evening, pull out the paper, and so discover one of Popov's leaflets.

The spasm of fury that passed through Savva Suvorin caused him to break his heavy stick over his knee. For a moment, he wanted to confront young Grigory. He would break him as completely as he had broken his stick. But it was one of the great strengths of the old man that a lifetime of hardship had taught him never to act rashly. Where, he wondered, had Grigory come by the leaflet? Was it likely that the impoverished young peasant could have instigated such a thing by himself? For a time he became deeply thoughtful.

Then he put the leaflet in his pocket.

Just a few hours later, by the side of a field of barley, Timofei Romanov was looking at his son in puzzlement. For the proposal that Boris had put to his father had taken the older man by surprise. "You're saying we should go to Bobrov for money. Enough to give Natalia a dowry?"

"And to pay off your debts, too."

"On what grounds?"

"Let's say his friendship for you. Didn't you play together as children? Hasn't he helped you before?"

"He's also short of money himself," Timofei objected. "I don't want to ask, and he'll certainly refuse."

"Maybe he can't refuse."

"What do you mean?"

"Because I think he's vulnerable. Remember how Nicolai was nearly arrested?"

"But he's sick."

"So they say. But he isn't, you see. They really are preparing a revolution. I'm sure of it."

"How can you know?"

"I just think so, that's all. But if I'm right and Bobrov's just pretending Nicolai's sick and he thinks we know something, he may decide to help you—see?"

"You mean blackmail him?"

Boris grinned. "More or less."

Timofei looked horrified. "I couldn't do it."

"Not even for Natalia—to get her away from this Grigory?"

Timofei shook his head in perplexity. "I couldn't," he repeated. It was against his entire nature.

"I'd come with you," Boris suggested. "You don't have to be blatant. Just feel him out. You'll see if he's nervous soon enough." And as Timofei still looked unhappy: "Just think it over, Father. That's all," he suggested.

The noon sun was high the next day when the villagers of Bobrovo trembled to see the tall figure of Savva Suvorin, in his high top hat and black coat, and carrying a new walking stick, come striding down the lane towards them. He passed straight through the village, however, looking neither to right nor to left, and made his way up towards the manor house.

He was going to see the landowner.

The journey brought back many memories. It was sixty-two years, the old man remembered grimly, since he had walked up that very path with his father to ask permission to visit Moscow. Forty-seven years since Alexis Bobrov had brought him back after his recapture and ordered him to be flogged as a runaway serf. And every detail of those events was as fresh in his mind now as on the day they had happened. Savva never forgot.

Nowadays, of course, his wealth could have brought the Bobrov estate twenty, a hundred times over. The landlords who had treated him like a dog were frightened of him now. And today they had given him the means to destroy them.

Having reflected on the matter, there was little doubt in his mind about the basic facts. He had heard, of course, about the incidents concerning young Nicolai Bobrov in the village—how he had worked with Romanov, then preached revolution. The story that Nicolai was sick had struck him as unlikely. He had also observed the ginger-haired student hanging around near his factory and once seen him with Grigory, the boy who was sweet on the Romanov girl. Now, suddenly, Grigory was distributing revolutionary leaflets. The coincidences were too many. He had no doubt that the police would easily discover a link between the two. "So young Bobrov and his friend are revolutionaries," he muttered. He could have them both put in jail. And then the Bobrovs would be destroyed—it would be a final and terrible revenge. He had thought about it with pleasure for some time.

Misha Bobrov was surprised indeed when the tall figure of the factory owner appeared at the house. As it happened, Nicolai had retired to his bed with a headache that day, and Anna was visiting a friend near Vladimir, and so the landowner was alone. He ushered Suvorin into the salon at once, where the old man glanced around him with grim curiosity. He refused the seat Misha offered him, so that the landlord was left standing rather awkwardly himself, until he finally decided to sit down anyway, staring up at the industrialist with a vague sense of misgiving.

Savva never wasted words. He came straight to the point. "Your son," he said simply. "He's a revolutionary." And when Misha began to protest that Nicolai was unwell: "I found this in my factory. It comes from your son and his friend." Taking out the leaflet, he gave it to the landowner. "Read it," he ordered.

As Misha Bobrov did so, his face went pale. There before him were the very phrases he had heard his son speak. Word for word. Only with one difference: they called for violence. Kill Savva? Burn down his house? "Oh my God! Are you sure? . . . I mean, I had no idea . . ." His voice trailed off miserably. His face alone was all the confirmation that Savva needed. "What will you do?" Misha asked, helplessly.

And it was now that Savva Suvorin showed his greatness and the source of his power. He was eighty-two. For fifty-two years of his life he had struggled to get free of the tyranny of the Bobrovs, and for thirty more he had kept a grudge. Now, at last, he could destroy them.

But he was not going to. Not yet. For Savva Suvorin, better than anything else, understood power, and the Bobrovs, though he hated and despised them, were no use to him destroyed. Misha might be a fool, but he still had influence in the *zemstvo* and he had irritated Savva with his activities there more than once. With this information, however, Savva could control him forever. Suvorin does not revenge himself on small men, he thought proudly. He uses them.

Calmly, therefore, very quietly, he told the unhappy landowner what he should do. "Firstly, you will tell this Popov that he is to leave Russka forever. He is to remain in your house, communicate with no one, and be gone by dawn tomorrow. Can you organize that?"

Misha nodded miserably.

"You will also speak to Timofei Romanov. His daughter is always with this Grigory, whom I caught distributing the leaflets. You can be sure, therefore, that she is in this, too." He glowered at Bobrov. "Didn't you have that girl sent to your damned school once? Now perhaps you see what that leads to." He shook his head at the folly of educating working peasants. "You will also instruct your friend Romanov to keep his daughter at home until further notice. She is not to be told why; and she is to have no contact with Grigory of any kind. I shall have him watched for a few days to find out what else he is up to. Then I'll deal with him."

He gazed down coldly at Misha. It occurred to him with some satisfaction that their roles had been reversed now—he was the master, a Bobrov the servant.

"If any of you disobey these instructions in even the smallest way," he concluded, "then I shall turn the entire matter over to the police, who will quite certainly be able to prove a conspiracy involving your son, Popov, and the Romanovs. They will all go to Siberia, or worse."

And with that he turned his back on the shaking landlord and stomped out of the house.

Several times in the last twenty-four hours, Timofei and Boris Romanov had returned to the subject of approaching Misha Bobrov for money; but so far Timofei had not been willing to do so. He was surprised, therefore, in midafternoon, to be summoned urgently to the manor house. And as soon as the summons came, young Boris announced, "I'm going with you."

When they arrived, it was to find Misha in a frightened but thoughtful state. He had spent half an hour in the sickroom with his son. Though he was not quite sure whether to believe him, it seemed that Nicolai was not aware of Popov's recent activities in Russka. But he admitted to knowing Popov had a handpress for printing. And that's quite enough to send him to Siberia, Misha thought.

With the two Romanovs before him, Misha proceeded cautiously. "Tell me, Timofei," he asked, "is your daughter friendly with a boy called Grigory?"

"Ah, Mikhail Alexeevich," he cried, "if only she were not." And he would have started upon his litany of woes if Misha had not cut him short.

"This is what young Grigory had been distributing," he said, and he showed Timofei the leaflet, reading out a few sentences from it for the illiterate peasant. During this he noticed that poor Timofei looked first confused, then horrified and lost, but that young Boris, the moment he set eyes upon the leaflet, went pale as a ghost.

It was true then. Suvorin was right.

Calmly he outlined Suvorin's instructions. Though he made no direct reference to his own son's part in the conspiracy, he let them know: "The person behind this is Popov. It seems he has abused my hospitality and duped us all. He leaves at dawn, never to return." Then, looking at Boris carefully, he remarked: "You'll agree that, regarding Natalia, we should do exactly as Suvorin asks?"

To which the young man, looking glum, replied, "I agree."

And it was at this moment that Yevgeny Popov walked cheerfully into the room.

Popov had had a disquieting day. He had received a letter that morning that let him know, in carefully disguised language, that the peasant revolution was failing. Everywhere the villagers had behaved like those at Bobrovo. Several hamlets had called the police, and news of the movement was spreading to the provincial authorities. Several young idealists were already in custody: a general clampdown was expected.

The letter had worried Popov, but it was his habit to disguise his thoughts and so now he smiled, almost pleasantly, at the three men in the room.

Misha Bobrov did not waste time. With undisguised loathing he snapped at Popov, "Your game's up. Suvorin's found your leaflets." And in a few words he summarized what the old man had said. "I won't bother to ask for your comments," Misha remarked contemptuously, "since I know you will lie. But you're to leave here by dawn, so I suggest you prepare for your journey."

How cool the young monster was. He did not flinch: indeed he was still, faintly, smiling. Yet even Misha was astounded when Popov quietly replied: "Not at all. I already told you I shall leave when I choose."

"You go tomorrow."

"I think not."

"You've no choice. Suvorin will arrest you."

"Perhaps." He shrugged. "I can see that all of you are frightened. But you really needn't worry. Nothing will happen." He yawned. "I'm too tired to eat supper tonight. Besides I have letters to write. But I shall be famished tomorrow evening, I'm sure." He turned to Bobrov. "I really shall be here for some time," he said blandly, and he went upstairs.

For several seconds all three men were speechless. It didn't make sense. Then Timofei Romanov looked at Misha and asked helplessly, "What do we do now?"

Yevgeny Popov sat in his room and considered. His calm refusal to leave had been partly a bluff. There was no doubt, after the disquieting letter this morning and Suvorin's threat, that it was time to move on. But he was not going to let that stupid landowner and those damned peasants— or even Savva Suvorin—think that they could push him around. He was a revolutionary, infinitely their superior.

So, what should he do? Whatever he did, Popov always left himself escape routes: it was his nature to deal in ambiguities; and whatever these people planned, he felt sure he could outwit them. For several minutes he pondered; then a smile appeared on his face. Going over to the locked box by the foot of his bed, he took out a handwritten document. Then, sitting at a little table by the window, and making constant reference to the document, he began to form letters and words on a fresh sheet of paper until, after a time, he became confident. And then, taking a new sheet, he began, very carefully, to write.

He had been writing for several minutes when he heard someone creep along the passage and pause outside his door. Then he heard a key being inserted in the lock and softly turned. He shrugged. So they thought they could make him a prisoner. He continued to write.

Twenty minutes passed. He wrote two letters, then a short note. Having read them all carefully and satisfied himself that they were perfect, he got up.

Next he went to the cupboard and took out the peasant's clothes he had worn when working in the fields, together with a peasant's hat that covered his red hair. Only when he was fully dressed in this did he bother to try the door. As he expected, it was locked. He went to the window and looked out. It opened wide enough to get his head and one arm out; if he wanted to leave that way, he would have to force the window out of its frame and then take a fifteen-foot drop onto hard ground. As he looked around, however, it occurred to him that the window of Nicolai's room was only the third along from his. He took a small coin out of his pocket and tossed it; then another. After the fourth coin had rattled against the glass, the tousled head of his friend appeared.

"Hello, Nicolai," he called. "They've locked me in. You'd better let me out."

*   *   *

At first, it seemed to Misha, it was clear what they should do. And so it would have remained, but for Boris.

It had only taken a few words, whispered by his son, to make the confused Timofei fully understand the danger Natalia was in from the leaflets; and once he understood, he was ready to do anything.

Certainly it was in all their interests that they should take care of the whole business themselves. "I don't want him talking to outsiders, or even my own coachman," Misha frankly confessed, "because there's no knowing what this accursed Popov might say about any of us." It was agreed, therefore, that before dawn the two Romanovs would come in their cart, collect the redheaded student, and take him all the way to Vladimir. "I've a stout club," Timofei remarked, "and we'll strap him to the cart if necessary."

"When you get to Vladimir, you're to put him on the Moscow train. And don't go until you've watched it out of sight." This would complete Suvorin's instructions, and after that, Misha fervently hoped, he would never see the loathsome young man again.

At this point it had occurred to Misha that perhaps he ought to lock Popov in his room. Fetching the key and going upstairs had taken several minutes. He was surprised, however, when he came down, to find both the Romanovs looking as if they had decided something separately between themselves.

Boris took the lead. He had a sharper mind than either of the older men. He had not given up his hope of making some money from the landowner, and he also saw some real danger to all of them in the plan. His reasoning was simple. "After all, Mikhail Alexeevich, we've all seen what this fellow's like. Even threatened with the law and Savva Suvorin, he refused to go. He obviously wants to stay here and create some kind of trouble. And if that's so, then what's the use of us putting him on a train to Moscow when he can just get off at the next station and be back here in a day or two?"

Misha couldn't deny this. "But what can we do?" he asked.

Boris paused, thoughtfully. "The fact is," he said coolly, "I'm worried about my sister, sir. She's mixed up with this Grigory because she has no dowry. And that's because of my father's debts." He looked at Bobrov politely but with meaning. "You've always been very good to our family, sir. You put Natalia and me in school. Do you think you could see your way to helping us again?"

Misha frowned. "What did you have in mind?"

"Maybe I could arrange for this Popov to make a long journey, so he'd be sure not to bother us again, sir."

"A long journey?"

"Yes, sir. Very long."

Misha felt himself tremble. The proposition was unthinkable. Yet—it was useless to deny it—he was tempted. At this moment there was nothing in the world he wanted more than to be rid, forever, of Popov's evil presence.

"I could never countenance . . ." he began.

"Of course, sir, we'd just be doing what you said," Boris said calmly, "taking him to Vladimir." He looked at Misha carefully. "No one's waiting there for him?"

"No." There was a long pause. Then Misha shook his head. "Just put him on the train," he said. "Come back before dawn." And though Boris looked doubtful, he waved them away.

After they had gone, he sat in the salon for several minutes. Boris's argument had worried him. It was perfectly true: there was nothing to stop Popov from returning and no knowing what new troubles he might start for them if he did. And what of the young revolutionary? As far as Misha knew, no one was expecting him to turn up anywhere. The fellow was a wanderer. He might just go off into the country, of his own accord, for the rest of the summer. If he disappeared, it could be months before any inquiries were made about him. And by then . . .

He shook his head. It's people like me, he reflected, decent people, who are always helpless when faced with vicious beasts like this Popov. In my place, I don't suppose he'd hesitate for a second.

And it was just at this moment that Boris Romanov suddenly reappeared. "Popov's gone, sir," he said. "He was seen going through the village towards Russka. What shall we do?"

Misha leapt up. "Impossible." He rushed upstairs and opened the door to find the room empty. The devil: Suvorin had told him to keep Popov in the house. Now he'd probably gone to warn his associates or start some new trouble: and then what would Savva Suvorin do? Was there no limit to the danger this redheaded fiend could cause them? "You've got to stop him," he cried. "Quickly!"

But Boris did not move.

"If we catch him today, he'll be back tomorrow," he pointed out quietly. "What's the point, Mikhail Alexeevich?"

"Just stop him, for God's sake," the landowner almost pleaded.

Still Boris did not move. "About my sister, sir," he said gently. "And my father."

For a long moment both men were silent. Then at last, staring down at the floor, Bobrov murmured, "I'll give your sister a dowry. As for your father—I'll help. Will that do?"

"Yes, sir. Thank you."

"And . . ." Misha did not know how to go on.

"Don't worry, sir. We'll take the young gentleman to Vladimir. You won't be troubled with him anymore." He turned to go, only pausing for a moment to remark, "He'll be needing his luggage if he's traveling. If you could pack his bags, sir, we'll collect them before dawn."

Then he was gone.

It was unfortunate that, though they hurried, the two Romanovs were just too late. By the time they came to the end of the wood opposite the monastery, Popov had vanished. The path leading across the fields and over the bridge into the town was empty.

"God knows where he is," Timofei muttered. There was nothing to be done. But one thing was certain. "We'll catch him on the way back," the peasant said.

Timofei had a club, Boris a knife. Their plan was easy enough. "When we've killed him," Boris had explained, "you hide with him in the woods while I go and bring his luggage in the cart. Then we just put him in the back, like he's sleeping, and drive off towards Vladimir. Later we'll bury him and his luggage somewhere." It should be straightforward. There was nothing but forest and a few hamlets on the way. "Plenty of room in which to bury him," Timofei remarked cheerfully.

The spot where they chose to wait was the little clearing by the old burial mounds, with its clear view to the monastery. Even if Popov chose to return after dark, they would be able to see him by starlight as he came along the path.

They settled down to wait.

Yevgeny Popov waited patiently by the old springs along the path to the *skit*. He had not wished to go into Russka by daylight, but fortunately he had met a boy by the monastery and given him a few kopeks to deliver the note. He had only waited an hour before the young man he had summoned came in sight.

Peter Suvorin was in a state of some excitement. What could the urgent summons mean? But when Popov gravely told him, he positively trembled. "The message from the Central Committee was very clear," he explained. "We have only hours. Are you ready to suffer for the cause?"

"Oh yes."

"Very well." They ran over all the details together. Young Suvorin had money. He quickly made a plan. Indeed, faced with a crisis, Popov noticed with interest that the young idealist was surprisingly practical. "How will you leave?" he asked.

Peter considered. "My grandfather has a boat he uses for fishing. I'll take that."

"Excellent. Go at dusk." Popov embraced the young man. "We shall meet again," he promised.

The light was just fading as Yevgeny Popov made his way back along the path from the springs towards Russka. When he found a good vantage point, he sat down in the warm shadows and watched the river. The pale stars had begun to shine in the turquoise sky. He waited as the turquoise deepened to indigo. There was no one about.

Then he saw the little boat. It was scudding along, hugging the bank. He watched as it slipped away, southward, with the gentle flow of the stream. It would be at the river Oka in the morning. And as he watched, he smiled to himself. He had judged young Peter Suvorin well. He had fallen completely for the story that the police were coming to arrest them all the next day. He had genuinely supposed that the invented Central Committee wanted at all costs to preserve him. And he had at once volunteered to go into hiding for a few months. But underneath all this was another motive, of which perhaps young Peter himself was not fully aware. "I just gave him his excuse to escape from his grandfather," Popov thought. He was seldom wrong about people.

And now that Peter was safely gone, it was time to begin.

Popov moved carefully. Pulling his hat well down on his head, he did not enter the town by the main gate, but skirted it and came in by the open lane on the side away from the river. There were a few people about, but no one paid any attention as he walked quietly by in the darkness.

As he expected, the narrow street by the warehouse was deserted. When he reached it, he first unlocked the little storeroom where he had hidden the printing press and then entered the main warehouse. After moving about for a while, lighting a match now and then, he found exactly what he wanted: against one wall, bales of straw were piled high; in a corner were some empty sacks; and on some shelves were a dozen lamps in which, heaven be praised, there was still some oil. Carefully, without hurry, he took bales of straw from the pile and arranged them around the walls. Then he twisted the sacks into several large torches and collected the oil into two containers. Finally, just for good measure, he carried half a dozen bales of straw around and placed them against the walls in the storeroom. Even taking his time, he was through in under half an hour.

Now, however, came the daring part of his plan. Inside the little storeroom he carefully unearthed the parts of the printing press and the packet of leaflets. Then, checking to make sure the street was empty, he went outside.

The streets were silent. Keeping to the shadows, he made his way past the church by the marketplace and into the broad avenue that led to the little park and the esplanade. Three houses lay on the right-hand side, behind fences. The first of these was Savva Suvorin's.

There were no lights at the window. The Suvorins did not retire late. Gingerly, looking about, Popov opened the gate in the fence and went into the yard. Though the house was made of stone and masonry, the entrance, on one of the end walls, consisted of a stout wooden staircase, covered over, which rose some six feet up to the main floor. It was to the space underneath these stairs that Popov went, and there he deposited his things.

It was necessary to make this journey twice. The second time, as well as the leaflets and part of the hand press, Popov brought with him a trowel from the storeroom.

Then, on his hands and knees beneath Suvorin's staircase, he set to work.

So far, all was going to plan. Indeed, he had only made one mistake that evening, of which he was not aware. For when he left the storeroom for the second time, he did not pause to lock the door, but only pulled it to. He did not look back a few moments later, and therefore he did not see that the door, improperly fastened, was swinging silently open again.

Popov worked noiselessly. The earth under the staircase was not too hard. In a few minutes he had made a hole nearly a foot deep. Steadily, careful to make no sound, he went on. As he did so, he smiled to himself.

It was the perfect symmetry of this business that he liked. By the end of the evening, Savva Suvorin and Misha Bobrov would neutralize each other. He would be in the clear. Young Peter Suvorin would be the criminal. And the printing press and revolutionary leaflets would have been buried, apparently by Peter, under the house of Suvorin himself. This last, he had to admit, was an artistic flourish; but he could not resist it. I have completely outmaneuvered them all, he thought.

True, there were a couple of loose ends. Young Grigory and Natalia, for instance. He had no special plan for them. But they were harmless. All they knew was that Peter Suvorin gave them the leaflets.

No, his scheme was perfect: he was, infinitely, superior to them all.

When the hole was nearly two feet deep and he was about to stop, the trowel struck something hard and Popov, reaching down, felt a smooth, rounded surface. Curiously he scraped the earth away from it and after a minute or two he was about to pull it up. The object looked pale.

It was a skull. God knew what it was doing here. He examined it. He had enough knowledge of medicine to notice that the shape suggested the skull might be Mongolian rather than Slav. A Tatar, perhaps. He shrugged. He couldn't imagine what it was doing buried by Suvorin's house.

Soon afterward the printing press and the packet containing the leaflets were in the ground. He spread earth on top and patted it down. Then, taking the skull with him, he slipped out and made his way back towards the warehouse.

A little before he got there, he passed a street corner where a small well had been sunk. He paused only a second to drop the skull into this, hearing it splash into the water far below. And so it was that the head of Peter the Tatar, the unknown founder of the monastery, found a new resting place in the waters under the town.

Natalia and Grigory had lingered by the dormitory until after dark, talking. She had warned him about her father's attitude but told him that he'd soon get over it. And anyway, as far as she could see, Grigory did not care about her father's opinion. Her campaign had been so successful that, indeed, the young man had only one thought now—how to enjoy her body. When, therefore, sometime after dusk, she suggested that they go somewhere to be alone, he raised no objection.

It was the custom of young couples seeking privacy, in the warm summer months, to walk in the woods outside the town. They were just making their way towards the lane that led out of Russka, when, passing the warehouse, they noticed that the door of the little storeroom was open. Looking inside, they saw to their surprise that it contained a number of bales of straw; and it occurred to Natalia that this was a fine and private place. It was the work of only a few seconds to make a little bed of straw in one corner. Then, motioning to her lover, she closed the door. Soon, she promised herself, very soon, she would be pregnant, and married.

* * *

When Popov reached the warehouse he went straight to the main building. Quickly he poured the oil over the torches he had made out of the
sacking. Lighting one of them, he put it against the main pile of straw.
One after another he lit the rest of the torches and put them against the
bales he had prepared around the walls. Then, when he had just two
torches left, he ran around to the storeroom.

He had not realized how quickly the fire would take. He had only put
the straw in the storeroom because, since it was locked, it would be hard
for anyone to put out a fire in there. Yet even as he reached it, the flames
were licking the rafters in the main building. He must hurry. Quickly he
opened the door, lit the two tapers and tossed them onto the nearest bales
of straw. Then he pulled the door shut again and locked it. Since it had
never occurred to him to look, he did not see the two young people in
the corner who, a few minutes before, had sunk into sleep.

Rapidly he sped away through the shadows and out of the town. It was
time to return to Bobrovo.

Misha Bobrov sat in the salon alone. Upstairs Nicolai was fast asleep, and
the landlord thanked God that he was. For if his son had come into the
room just then, he was not sure he could have clung to this absurd
pretense until finally, disgusted with himself, he gave it up. He had paid
them to murder the young man: that was the truth. No doubt by now
he was dead.

Murder. He recalled that time, almost twenty years ago, when he had
been tempted to kill Pinegin at Sevastopol. He had been a murderer in
his heart then, but he had not done it. Was he a less moral man now?
Or was it just that, this time, he had others to do the deed for him? Filled
with fear, and with self-loathing, he at last put his head in his hands and
murmured, "Lord my God, what have I done?"

It was with a mixture of astonishment, relief, and terror therefore that,
some time after midnight, he heard a sound, glanced up, and saw Popov
standing before him, staring at him curiously.

Misha opened his mouth, but he could not speak.

Popov had had an uneventful journey back. Not wishing to be seen, he
had once again slipped out through the rear exit from the town. By the
time he reached the river, he could see a red glow over the roofs and hear
shouts within. Instead of crossing the main bridge and the open area by
the monastery, he had decided to take the path by the springs, follow the
winding river downstream, and finally cross the little footbridge at Bobrovo. It was a long way around, but completely deserted.

As he approached the manor house, it had been impossible not to feel
a sense of satisfaction, even glee. Everything was in place. And in his
pocket he had the two letters.

It had not been difficult to copy Peter Suvorin's handwriting. He had
a talent for that sort of thing anyway. But it was the tone of the two little
compositions that he was so proud of. From the long revolutionary essay
that Peter had given him, he had caught not only the young man's turns
of phrase, but the way his mind worked. I've got his very soul, he had

thought with a smile as he wrote the two letters. Their authenticity was wonderful.

The letters themselves were very straightforward. One was to Nicolai Bobrov, his supposed fellow conspirator. It told him that he was leaving, that he was going to try to burn down his grandfather's factory and that the printing press and the leaflets were safely hidden in Savva Suvorin's house, where no one would find them.

All that was needed was to give this letter to Misha Bobrov. As soon as the landowner threatened Suvorin with it, the angry old industrialist would be completely neutralized. "If he threatens to arrest Nicolai, his own grandson goes, too." This was the perfect symmetry he was so pleased with.

The other letter was just a piece of extra insurance for himself, for possible future use. It was from Peter to Popov, telling him that he was about to leave and thanking him for his kindness. Above all, it delivered Popov a wonderful exculpation.

> You have been a good friend to Nicolai and to me and I know that you have begged him, as you have me, to stick to the path of reform and give up our ideas of revolution. But you do not understand these things, my friend, nor how far this matter goes—and I can't tell you. I can only hope that one day, when the bright new dawn appears, we shall meet again as friends and that you will see that all has, truly, been for the best. Adieu.

Having outwitted them all and proved his superiority, it seemed to Popov that he would probably stay a few more days at Russka, shake down the Bobrovs for some money, and then depart.

Only two things had surprised him. Upon entering the yard at the manor house, he had found all his luggage outside the door. Why should Bobrov be so confident he would leave that night? And now, having gone inside, here was the landowner staring at him speechless, as if he had seen a ghost. Yet he must have known he'd gone out, since he had packed up his luggage.

Popov stared at Misha thoughtfully. His mind was working quickly. "Surprised to see me?" he inquired.

"Surprised?" Misha looked flustered. "Not a bit, my dear fellow. Why should I be?"

"Why, indeed?" Why, for that matter, should the landowner be blushing scarlet and calling him "my dear fellow"?

And now, as his own mind raced, it occurred to Misha that if the Romanovs had missed Popov, they might turn up at any time now. And then what? Drag him off in their cart and butcher him? No. He couldn't face that anymore. Yet what the devil should he do? Anxiously, without realizing he even did so, he glanced at the door.

It was all Popov needed to comprehend. He did not know the details but the sense was clear. Someone was coming to get him, and the landowner was terrified. Very well, he would stay ahead.

"If I could completely neutralize Suvorin for you, what would you give?" he mildly inquired. And in answer to Misha's look of desperate hope, he told Misha about the existence of the letter from Peter Suvorin to Nicolai and explained its contents.

"You have this letter?" Misha asked eagerly.

"It's hidden, but I can get it—for a price."

"How much?"

"Two thousand rubles."

"Two thousand?" The poor man looked flabbergasted. "I haven't got it."

He was so nervous that Popov thought he was probably telling the truth. "How much have you?" he asked.

"About fifteen hundred, I think."

"Very well. That will do."

Misha looked relieved; then anxious again. "There's one other thing," he said nervously. "If I give you money, you must leave right away."

"What, you mean now, in the middle of the night?"

"Yes. At once. It's essential."

Popov smiled faintly. It must be as he had guessed then. Fancy this fool having the courage to have me killed, he thought. And how typical to panic afterwards. Aloud he said, "You'll have to give me a horse. A good one."

"Yes, of course."

That would be worth some money, too. It was amazing what power someone's guilt gave you over them.

"Go and get the money," he commanded.

A quarter of an hour later he was ready to go. He was riding Misha Bobrov's best horse. He had fifteen hundred rubles in his pocket, and Misha had the precious letter. Before leaving the house, Popov had paused for a moment, wondering whether to go and wake Nicolai, to say good-bye. But he had decided against it. His friend had served his purpose. He had nothing to say to him. He looked down at the anxious landowner.

"Well, good-bye, until the revolution," he said pleasantly. Then he was gone.

It was an hour later that the two Romanovs appeared at Bobrovo to ask if Popov had been there. To make sure they didn't try to follow Popov, the landowner told them he had not returned.

The fire at Russka took both the warehouse, another next door, and four of the little row houses in whose roofs flying embers had lodged. Not until the following morning did anyone realize that Natalia and Grigory were missing, and their charred remains were found only hours later.

Because of an interview that took place in the early morning between Savva Suvorin and Mikhail Bobrov, no police investigation of the fire ever took place. It was declared an accident. How Natalia and Grigory came to be trapped inside was never explained. It was remarked, however, that the local police chief and his family all had new clothes a few weeks later.

*   *   *

Varya Romanov had her baby at the end of the year. It was a little girl, whom they decided to call Arina. Varya was so attached to the baby, who replaced her only daughter, that the little girl came safely through the winter, entirely unaware that her grandmother and namesake had more than once stood over her cradle and murmured, "I know I ought to leave you out there, but I haven't the heart."

Nor was the child ever aware of another small event that had taken place just a week after winter ended.

It was the habit of Misha Bobrov, each spring, to sort out his papers. Since this was a yearly event, there were always plenty to sort. Letters, notes he had made to himself, memoranda from *zemstvo* officials, unpaid bills, the papers accumulated on the big table in his study on top of the books that lined the walls, and in the drawers of his desk. He enjoyed this business; it allowed him to survey the previous year of his life and, proceeding in a leisurely fashion, it often took him three or four days. The letters, in particular, he liked to read over; and many of these he would then tie up with ribbon and store in boxes in the attic. And when his wife suggested this was a waste of time he would calmly reply, "You never know," and continue happily with his work.

There had been much to read and ponder this last year. He had even considered writing up an account of the extraordinary events of the last summer. How strange and interesting for Nicolai's grandchildren to read about one day, he had thought. However, he had put this task off for the time being—"until I'm not so busy"—and so the only memorial of those days among the papers was the letter that Popov had given him from Peter Survorin. I must certainly keep that, Misha considered. After all, one could never know when it might come in handy against the Suvorins in the future. And since the strange document did not belong with anything else, he tied a piece of red ribbon round it, labeled it "Suvorin Fire," and put it up in the attic with the other letters.

It was the day after finishing this task that Misha received an unexpected visitor—young Boris Romanov. The landlord had not seen the young peasant for some time, and he was surprised that he was not accompanied by his father. He had him shown into his study, smiled at him pleasantly enough, and inquired, "Well, Boris, what is it?"

The speech that Boris had prepared was so slow and convoluted that at first Misha could not make out what he wanted; but there was a look of sullen awkwardness on the peasant's face that made the landowner uneasy. Carefully Boris reminded him of the family's poverty, their need for more land, and their loyalty to the Bobrovs. Then, finally, he came to the point. "I was thinking about last summer, sir," he said.

So that was it. Misha was cautious. "Well?"

"We had an agreement then, sir. About helping my father and giving my sister a dowry." Still Misha said nothing. "My sister's dead now, sir."

"God rest her soul."

"But as you know, we have a new baby in the family." He looked at the floor. "So I wondered if you could see your way to helping us like you said, sir. Natalia's dowry could go to the baby Arina, you see."

Misha gazed at him thoughtfully. In truth, the young man's speech had touched a raw nerve. Since that terrible night the previous summer, no word had ever been spoken about the evil bargain he had made with the Romanovs. After all, the murder had not taken place; poor Natalia had died and Misha had tried to blot the whole episode from his mind. Apart from some help with his repayments, Misha had not thought it necessary to give any money to Timofei Romanov, nor had the peasant dared to ask. Yet more than once Misha had secretly thought to himself, It's we, really, who brought misfortune on the Romanovs. I ought to do something for them one day. Young Boris's suggestion of a present of money for the child appealed to him. Perhaps, quite soon, he would. And because he was turning the matter over in his mind, he did not trouble, at first, to reply to the peasant.

It was then that Boris Romanov made his great mistake. Misunderstanding Misha's hesitation, he suddenly looked up and announced, "After all, sir, what with my sister being killed in the fire, we wouldn't want you getting into trouble now, would we?" With which he gave the landowner a nasty grin.

And Misha stared at him in amazement; then he blushed. What the devil did the fellow know?

In fact, young Boris knew nothing at all. But had Misha possessed any idea about what the young peasant suspected, he would have been shaken indeed.

For if the authorities had dismissed the fire at Russka as an accident, Boris had certainly not. The memory of his poor sister Natalia seemed to haunt him; the more he brooded about it, the more sure he was that the whole business was suspicious. Time and again that winter he had challenged his father. "If it was an accident, then how come Natalia and Grigory were locked inside?" he would demand. Why would anyone want to kill them? "Maybe they knew too much." And the identity of the killer? "That redheaded devil, Popov. It must have been." Even old Timofei conceded that this last was possible. But it was the next step in Boris's logic that his father was unwilling to take.

"For," Boris reasoned, "there's still more to this than meets the eye. Think about it." He jabbed his finger down on the table. "Bobrov let us go after Popov, but we never caught him. Who tipped that devil off? Must have been Bobrov himself. Sent a servant, or even Nicolai, around to warn him. And how come Popov escapes—vanishes? And nothing's ever said about either the fire or Nicolai Bobrov? There has to be something going on that we don't know about. And that landowner's hiding it. He knows who lit the fire, he knows who killed my sister—and maybe a lot more."

To which Timofei would only listen sadly, shake his head, and reply, "I still don't believe it. But even if it is so, what can you do about it?"

And here Boris was stuck. He had no proof. The authorities would never listen to him. He'd only get into trouble. Yet as the winter months went by, his sullen conviction became an obsession. He could not let it go. And finally, just as the snows were melting, he decided, "I'll shake down that damned landlord anyway. I bet I can frighten something out of him."

Though he had blushed, Misha collected himself quickly. In a moment, he was outwardly calm. His mind, however, was working rapidly.

The fire. The peasant was insinuating something about the fire. Yet his only crime was in concealing the letter that Popov had given him that revealed the culprit. Was it possible the peasant knew about the letter? It seemed unlikely. With a face that, he hoped, was completely serene, he gazed at Boris and remarked, "I don't think I understand you."

"I just mean, sir, you and I know who did it," Boris said boldly.

"Do I? And who might that be?" It was said with a faint smile, but to his annoyance, Misha could feel his heart pounding. Could the fellow really know?

"That red-haired devil Popov," Boris replied with confidence.

Thank God. He knew nothing. The insolent young peasant was bluffing.

"Then you know more than I do," Misha replied blandly. "And now, since you are being impertinent, you'd better get out." He glowered at Boris. "If I hear another word of this, I'll lodge a complaint with the police," he added, then turned his back while, crimson and furious, Boris departed.

This interview marked the beginning of an unspoken but permanent coolness between the Bobrovs and the Romanovs. No further help came from Misha Bobrov even to Timofei; the landlord preferred to ignore them. Timofei regretted this, but as he said to his son, "After what you did, I can hardly look him in the eye."

As for Boris, though he had been humiliated, the interview had done nothing to shake his suspicions. Indeed, as time went on and he brooded about the subject further, he found more and more reasons to confirm his belief. "I saw him blush," he remembered. "He knew something, all right." And it seemed ever clearer to Boris that, even if he could not fathom the business, there had been a conspiracy. "That redhead, those damned Bobrovs, maybe even the Suvorins, too, for all I know—they're all in it somehow," he concluded. "They killed Natalia."

And in his rage he came to two decisions that he would never alter as long as he lived. The first, which he shared with his father, was very simple: "One day I'll meet that accursed redhead Popov again, and when I do I'll kill him."

The second decision he kept to himself, though he was no less determined to carry it out. "I'll ruin that landowner who sits on the land that should be ours," he promised himself. "Before I die I'll see those damned Bobrovs thrown out. I'll do it for Natalia." And so, in the village below their house, the Bobrov family acquired a mortal enemy.

But these secret thoughts caused no ripple on the placid surface of the village's life. By the following year, it seemed that the events of 1874 had receded into silence. The redhead student Popov was apparently forgotten. And in the town of Russka, only occasionally did anyone trouble to ask: Whatever became of young Peter Suvorin?

ELEVEN

Revolution

1881 September

THE tsar was dead: assassinated. Even now, months later, the ten-year-old girl found it hard to believe.

Why were there such wicked people in the world? For the last three years there had been killings—policemen, officials, even a governor. And now, with a terrible bomb, they had killed the good man, the reforming tsar Alexander II himself. Rosa could not understand it.

Who would do such a thing? A terrible group, it seemed: the People's Will, they called themselves. No one had known who they were or how many: perhaps twenty, perhaps ten thousand. What did they want? Revolution: the destruction of the whole apparatus of the Russian state that ruled its people from on high. Month after month, the People's Will had hunted the tsar; now they had destroyed him, as if to say: "See, your mighty state is only a sham. Against us, even the tsar himself is impotent, to be destroyed when we wish." And now, with the poor tsar dead, they had supposed the people would rise up.

"Which shows how little these revolutionaries know," her father had said.

For nothing had happened. Not a village had risen, nor a single factory. The shocking event had been greeted only by a huge Russian silence. The tsar's son—the third Alexander—had succeeded to the throne and at once imposed order. There had been a huge crackdown; many of the revolutionaries had been arrested and most of the Russian empire was at present under martial law. The People's Will had failed—God be praised. Russia was calm and at peace.

Or so it had seemed. Until this new and horrible business—so inexplicable to her, so terrifying—had begun. And once again, as she had done so many times in recent months, Rosa wondered: why were there such wicked people in the world?

They will not come here. Her father had promised. But what if he were wrong.

It was early afternoon—a quiet time in this peaceful southern village at the border of forest and steppe. Few people were moving about; Rosa's parents were resting on the upper floor of the stout thatched house. Although it was autumn, down here in the Ukraine the weather was still warm. Through the open window, Rosa could see the apple tree in the courtyard and smell the sweet scent of a honeysuckle bush nearby.

Rosa was a beautiful girl. Her long, pale, oval face, long neck, and a certain slow grace in her movements had made some of the villagers call her "the swan maiden." Her raven hair was worn in a thick braid down her back. She had a long nose and full lips. But her most striking features were her eyes. Dark lidded, framed under the strong, black arch of her eyebrows, they were huge, blue-gray, and luminous; and they gazed solemnly out at the world like those of a figure in an ancient mosaic.

She sat by a piano. She was not playing now, but the music she had been practicing that morning—a piece by Tchaikovsky—was echoing in her mind. As she stared out at the blue sky, she went over each phrase, each haunting melody, trying them this way and that until she was satisfied.

It was the only piano in the village. She would never forget the magical day when it arrived on a little barge coming upriver. Her father had saved for a year to buy it and brought it all the way from Kiev. All the neighbors had come out to watch as he and her two brothers proudly escorted this wonder to their house. By what instinct had he known that she was musical? She had been only seven when a visiting cousin, a musician, had told them she was a prodigy. The very next year she had gone to live with that family, during term time, down in the big city of Odessa on the Black Sea coast, where there were fine music teachers. Already she had given a public performance, and people were saying she would be a professional musician.

"As long as her health holds up," her mother would gloomily say. It was true: that nagging problem with her chest was often with her. Sometimes she would have to rest for days at a time, when she was longing to go back to school. "You'll grow out of it," her father promised her: and how she prayed that he was right. How she wanted to live her life for music.

For once Rosa stepped into that kingdom, everything else became unimportant. Sometimes it seemed to her that music was in everything: as absolute as mathematics, as infinite as the universe itself: music was in the trees, in the flowers, in the endless steppe; music filled the whole sky. She wanted only to play, and to learn.

And here was the strange conundrum that had puzzled her for several months, and that today made her thoughtful and melancholy.

For if God had made this beautiful world, and given it music, and if she, it seemed, might have been chosen to serve His musical purpose and to play for Him, then why were there evil men planning to kill her?

Laid out on the east side of the little river, the village's comfortable thatched houses with their whitewashed walls stretched on each side of the broad dirt road for nearly a mile. Several, like the house where her parents lived, had little orchards behind them. Near the river there was a market square; and just downstream stood a distillery. Indeed, in the poorer Russian north, where settlements were smaller than in the Ukraine, such a place would have been called a town.

It was also quite prosperous. To the huge fields of wheat on the rich black earth of the steppe, two new and valuable crops had been added in recent times: sugar beets and tobacco. Both crops were sold to merchants who exported them through the ports on the warm Black Sea, and thanks to this trade and the region's natural abundance, the peasants lived well.

Rosa's grandfather had first come to the region to farm. He had died five years ago and her father had taken over. An enterprising man, he also traded wheat and acted as local agent for a firm that manufactured agricultural equipment down in Odessa, so they were now among the better-off families in the village.

She was not aware that once, in former times, this southern settlement had borne the name of Russka.

It was not surprising. The settlement had had two names since then; of its past little sign remained. The little fort on the western bank was only a few marks upon the turf; of the church the Mongols had burned down, there was not a trace. Even the landscape had somewhat altered. Centuries of farming had cut down many trees, and there were no woods on the eastern side of the river now. The pool and its haunting spirits had gone, dried up. Even the bee forest had disappeared. From the last house in the village, the open steppe of south Russia extended to the horizon, and the only way that the place might have been identified from ancient times was by the tiny mound of an ancient kurgan that appeared upon the steppe in the middle distance.

Rosa walked until she reached the end of the village, where she stopped to gaze over the steppe. There was a pale sun. High overhead, trailing white clouds, coming from the west, receded over the endless, browning grassland towards a violet horizon.

She had been standing there for some time when the cart came in sight. It was a stout affair, containing two people: a huge, thick-set man with big black mustaches, who was driving; and a slim, handsome boy, also dark haired, and just a year older than Rosa. These were Taras Karpenko, a Cossack farmer, and his youngest son, Ivan.

Seeing them, Rosa smiled. For as long as she could remember, she had played Cossacks and Robbers with the Karpenko boys and the other village children; young Ivan was her special playmate. And ever since, some years before, her father had sold Taras some farm equipment that had proved successful, the burly Cossack had looked upon the family with a kindly eye.

There was also another reason Rosa's father had found favor with Taras.

It was strange to think that the heavyset farmer was the nephew of the illustrious poet Karpenko, whose delicate features still looked out from drawings and prints on the walls of several local houses. Taras was enormously proud of this fact, however, and would mention his uncle's name in the same breath, and with the same reverence, as that of the most famous of all Ukrainian poets, the great Shevchenko. When he discovered, therefore, that Rosa's father not only possessed a copy of Karpenko's verses, but genuinely loved them and knew many by heart, he had clapped him on the back and always thereafter, if anyone mentioned Rosa's family, he would announce: "Not a bad fellow, that." Which stood them in good stead in the village and often caused Rosa's mother to remark: "Your father is very wise."

He was indeed wise—and very unusual—since this knowledge that formed a bond between him and the Cossack was becoming increasingly rare.

For the rule of the tsar in the Ukraine, with each decade that passed, had become even more heavy-handed. The tsars liked uniformity. True, in their huge empire it could not always be achieved. In Poland and the westernmost parts of the Ukraine, they had to put up with the Catholics: as the empire continued to expand eastward into Asia, they had to tolerate increasing numbers of Muslims. But insofar as possible, everything should be Russified: autocracy, Orthodoxy, nationality—that was the thing. In 1863, therefore, with that genius for official blindness in which it specialized, the Russian government announced that the Ukrainian language that was spoken by much of the southern population did not exist! In the years following, Ukrainian-language books, newspapers, theaters, schools, and even Ukrainian music were banned. The works of Shevchenko, Karpenko, and other Ukrainian national heroes passed out of sight. Intellectuals spoke and wrote in Russian. As for the people, while in the north education was spreading, in the south it declined; and by the late nineteenth century, eighty percent of Ukrainians were illiterate. The tsars were pleased: the Ukraine was not disturbed by discordant voices. And no wonder, then, if the proud Cossack Karpenko would occasionally remark to Rosa's father: "Well, my friend, at least you and I seem to know what's what."

As the two Cossacks drove by, therefore, they acknowledged her in a friendly manner: young Ivan with a happy grin and his father with a smile and a nod; and seeing this, Rosa felt a sense of reassurance.

They will not come here. There was nothing to be afraid of, she reminded herself.

For Rosa Abramovich was Jewish.

Until a century before, when Catherine the Great took most of Poland, there had been hardly any Jews in the empire of Russia. Upon adding these western lands, however, Russia gained a large Jewish community.

Where did they come from? The history of the Diaspora is confused and often obscure, but the Jews of Russia indirectly derived from Germany, from the Mediterranean and Black Sea ports, and also, it can hardly be doubted, from the remnants of the Turkish Khazar community that had spread into many parts of southeastern Europe. Of their racial origins, therefore, it is hard to say anything except that they were mixed.

But they believed in the one God of Israel.

What should be done with them? Some thought the Jews devious, like the Catholics; others called them obstinate, like the Old Believers. But two things were certain: they were not Slav and they were not Christian—therefore suspect. Like every other nonconformist element in the tsar's empire, therefore, they must be first contained, then Russified. And so it was, in 1833, that the tsar decreed that henceforth the Jews must be confined within a particular area: the Jewish Pale of Settlement.

In fact, the famous Jewish Pale was not the ghetto it sounded. It was a vast territory comprising Poland, Lithuania, the western provinces known as White Russia, and much of the Ukraine including all the Black Sea ports—in other words, the land where the Jews already resided, and some more besides. The purpose of the Pale was, mainly, to limit the immigration of Jews into traditional, Orthodox north Russia, although even in this respect it was often only loosely enforced, and there were sizable Jewish groups in both Moscow and Saint Petersburg.

The Jews lived mostly in towns or in their own villages—the traditional, tightly knit shtetl communities. They usually spoke Yiddish among themselves. Some were craftsmen or traders; many were poor and partly supported by their fellows. But there were also those who, like Rosa's grandfather, went to live in ordinary country villages to farm the land.

But still they were not conformist: something had to be done about that. And the solution of successive tsarist governments was always the same: "Let them convert."

It was a steady pressure that the regime applied, over decades. Jews paid extra taxes; their own system of community government—the *kahal*—was made illegal; their representation in local elections limited by unfair quotas. More subtly, they were allowed into the school system, then encouraged to convert; less subtly, they were recruited into the army, then beaten if they didn't. Conversion was enough. Though some people might be suspicious of those whose ancestry was Jewish, as far as the state was concerned, once the Jews had converted to Orthodoxy, they were good Russians.

This policy met with some success: numbers of Jews did convert. More important, a gradual process of assimilation had begun: for among the younger generation there had arisen a liberal movement, the Haskalah, which argued that Jews should participate more actively in Gentile society. Rosa's eldest brother, who was married and lived in Kiev, had told her all about it. "If Jews are going to get anywhere in the Russian empire, then we should go to Russian schools and universities. We have to take part. That doesn't stop us from being Jews." But her father was very suspicious. Though he did not take the view of many strict Jews, who isolated themselves as far as possible from the gentile world, he frowned on the Haskalah. "It's the first step down the slippery slope," he would say firmly. "First you put secular learning on an equal footing with religious education. In no time, the world comes first, religion second. Then you forget even your religion. And at last you have nothing." Rosa knew there was truth in this: she had heard of a number of these liberals turning into little better than atheists. So while Rosa's family kept on good terms with their Ukrainian neighbors, they always observed their religion strictly with the other Jewish families in the area. Both of Rosa's brothers received a religious education, the elder reaching the highest rung, the yeshivah; and her father had even hoped the young man might become a religious teacher.

There was one exception to her father's strict rule, however, for which Rosa thanked God. "Studying music in Russian schools is different," he always said. That did not compromise one's faith. It was the best way for a Jew to advance in Russia.

They will not come here. Why should they? The village was such an out-of-the-way little place. Besides, they had done nothing wrong.

Of course she knew there had always been bad feeling between her people and the Ukrainians. The Ukrainians remembered the Jews as the agents of the Polish landlords. They also usually lived in towns instead of in the country—they were foreign heretics. To the Jews, on the other hand, the Ukrainians were not only Gentiles—the despised *goyim*—but they were also, mostly, illiterate peasants. Yet even so, they might have lived at peace but for one thing: their relative numbers.

Perhaps it was a Jewish tradition of having large families; perhaps their communal self-help saved children's lives; perhaps their respect for learning led them to pay more scientific attention to hygiene or make more use of doctors: whatever the reason, it was a fact that in the Ukraine in the last sixty years, while the general population had risen by a factor of about two and a half times, the number of Jews had risen by a factor of over eight times. And the cry was beginning to be heard: "These Jews will take our work and ruin us all."

It was that year that the trouble had begun. No one could say exactly what started it. "When people get angry," her father had told her, "almost anything can set them off." But whatever the true causes might be, it was in the year that the tsar was assassinated that, all over the south, a series of disturbances began that made the world familiar with a grim and ugly word: pogrom.

Surely not here, though. Not in the quiet village at the border of forest and steppe. With this thought in mind, Rosa turned to go home.

People were moving about in the village as Rosa retraced her steps; but the place was still quiet. A cloudbank had arisen in the west and its shadow was advancing towards her. There was a faint chill now in the breeze.

She was halfway down the street when she noticed the little group. It was nothing much: just two women, both neighbors, and three men who looked like strangers, standing in the street in front of her house. From a distance, they seemed to be arguing. She saw two more villagers, both men, going to join them. A few moments later, she saw her father come out.

He was dressed in a long black coat and he had put on his round, wide-brimmed black hat. The ringlets that hung down the side of his face were black but his handsome beard was gray. She saw him wag his finger at them severely. He's telling them off, she thought with a smile.

And then she heard it: a single shout that echoed down the street and suddenly made her cold.

"Kike!"

She started to run.

They were already jostling her father by the time she reached him. One of the men knocked his hat off; another spat on the ground. The two village men made a halfhearted attempt to restrain them, but then they drew back: though why they should be afraid of three strangers Rosa could not think—until, a moment later, she glanced again down the street, and saw the reason.

There were six carts. They had just crossed the little bridge over the river. Riding in them, or walking beside, came about fifty men: some of these were carrying clubs; a few looked drunk.

Rosa looked at her father. He was picking up his hat, with what dignity he could muster, while the three men watched him. He was fifty years old, rather delicately built with a fine, thin face and large eyes like hers. Instinctively she wanted to take his hand for comfort, and she realized now with a shock that the poor man was as frightened as she was. What should they do? Retreat to the house? Two of the men were moving round to block their way. The party down the street was getting close. Behind her, Rosa now saw her mother coming out to join them; and though her father waved her back she took no notice. If only her brothers were with them, Rosa thought; but they were both away in Kiev that month. Helplessly she and her parents stood there, waiting.

When the men arrived, they formed a circle around the little family. Rosa looked at their faces. Some looked hard, others wore a look of foolish triumph. For a moment nobody spoke. Then her father broke the silence.

"What do you want?"

It was not immediately clear whether the party had a leader, but one of them, a huge peasant with a brown beard, now answered, "Nothing much, Jew. We're just going to burn your house down."

"And give him a thrashing," another cried.

"That, too," remarked the first, to laughter.

Rosa could see that her father was shaking but trying to appear calm. "And what have I done to you?" he asked.

This was greeted with a chorus of derision. "Plenty!" several cried out.

"What have you done to Russia, yid?" called another.

"Damned Jewish profiteers," screamed a third. "Usurers!"

But it was another cry, coming from somewhere at the back of the crowd, that really startled Rosa and made her turn pale.

"Who drinks the blood of children?" the voice shouted. "Tell us that!"

She had heard about this terrible accusation before. "Once," her father had told her, "long ago, foolish people used to accuse the Jews of the strangest things. They even said we killed Christian children and drank their blood." This was the infamous Blood Accusation of the Middle Ages. "Simple people actually thought it was true," he had said with a sigh. How strange, and how terrifying, to hear it echoed now.

Yet it was another voice that, in a way, surprised her even more. For now, suddenly from the back of the crowd a little old man with a completely bald head and a white beard pushed his way through to the front of the crowd and, pointing to Rosa's father, bellowed: "You can't fool us, Jew. We know what you are. You're a foreign traitor—a tsar killer. You're a revolutionary!" To which, to Rosa's amazement, there was a roar of approval.

How strange it was, indeed. For whatever her poor father might have been accused of, this surely was the most unlikely.

She knew about the Jewish revolutionaries. Some years before, it was true, a few radical students from Jewish families had joined the movement that, in the famous Going to the People of 1874, had tried to take revolution to the peasants in the countryside. These were the most radical of the Jews who had chosen to assimilate into Russian secular life. Indeed, in a double irony, many—not out of religious conviction but in order to feel closer to the peasants they wanted to influence—had actually converted to the Orthodox Church. These young people were exactly the ones Rosa's father, and most conservative Jews, hated most. Their example, her father had warned his children, was exactly what became of those who strayed into the world and lost their religion. As for the tsar: "We should always obey the law and support the tsar," her father would declare. "He is still our best hope." And indeed, until the terrible assassination, the reforming tsar had relaxed some of the restrictions on the Jews in his empire. The vast majority of Jews at this date were therefore conservative and tsarist; but one cannot argue with a mob.

The men surrounding them had already burned down some Jewish houses in Pereiaslav the week before and now they were traveling around the local villages looking for more fun.

"Time to get started," someone cried. There was laughter. The huge man with the brown beard, accompanied by the little old man, stepped towards Rosa's father, as she looked around desperately. She wanted to scream.

And it was just then that, twenty yards away, the stout cart bearing the massive form of Taras Karpenko and his son creaked into the street, and the two Cossacks caught sight of them.

"Thank God," Rosa heard her mother whisper. "He can save us."

The big Cossack did not hurry. He drove his cart calmly towards them, and the men parted to let it through. With his flowing mustaches and his powerful frame, he was a commanding figure. When he reached the edge of the circle around the little family, he pulled up and glanced down inquiringly at the fellow with the brown beard. "Good day," he remarked pleasantly. "What's up?"

The peasant looked up at the Cossack and shrugged. "Nothing much. Just teaching this Jew a lesson."

Karpenko nodded thoughtfully. "He's not a bad fellow," he remarked placidly.

Thank God. Thank God indeed for the big, powerful farmer. Rosa looked up at him gratefully. He would send these men about their business. She was so relieved that, for a moment, she did not fully take in the conversation that followed.

"He's still a Jew," the peasant objected.

"True." The thick-set Cossack glanced round at the men. "What do you plan to do?"

"Burn his house and thrash him."

Karpenko nodded again and glanced a little sadly at Rosa's father. Then he spoke to him. "I'm afraid, my friend, you're going to have rather a rough time."

What was he saying? Rosa stared at him in disbelief. What could he

mean? Her father's friend, the man whose children she had played Cossacks and Robbers with—wasn't he going to help them? In astonishment
she saw him take up the reins. He was turning the horse's head—leaving
them.

A mist seemed to form in front of her eyes; she felt suddenly nau-
seated; and before her a great, cold gulf—something she had never imagined was there—seemed to be opening wide: wide as an ocean.

He was on the side of these men.

"Father!" It was young Ivan. Rosa blinked though the haze of her tears
and stared up at him. The boy was white, trembling; he was standing up
in the cart. How slim, almost frail he looked, yet so tense, so passionate
that he seemed to radiate an extraordinary strength. He was looking
down at the heavyset Cossack. "Father! We can't."

And Taras stopped the cart.

Slowly, rather unwillingly, Karpenko turned to the big peasant with
the brown beard. "They come with us," he said gruffly.

"There are fifty of us, Cossack," cried the little old man. "You can do
nothing."

But Taras Karpenko, though he glanced around at the crowd, only
shook his head. Then, turning to the big peasant again, he explained, a
little sheepishly: "I owe this Jew a personal favor." Then he motioned
Rosa and her parents to climb into the cart.

"Call yourself a Cossack? Jew lover! We'll come and burn your farm
down, too," shouted the old man. But nobody stopped the Abramoviches
from getting into the cart.

"I'm afraid your house will be burned down," Karpenko said in a
matter-of-fact way to Rosa's father. "But I've saved you a thrashing."
Then he flicked the reins and the cart started slowly down the street.

As they went out of the village, Rosa stared back. The men were busy
smashing the windows of her house. She saw the old man going inside
with a lighted torch. They are going to burn my piano, she thought: the
piano her father had saved a whole year to buy for her. She looked at
him. He was sitting in the cart shaking. There were tears in his eyes, and
her mother's arms were around him. Rosa had never seen her father cry
before and she supposed it was not possible to love anyone more than,
at that moment, she loved him.

Then her thoughts turned back to the Karpenkos. Ivan had saved
them. As long as she lived, she told herself, she would never forget that.

But she would also remember his father; their friend. He would have
left them. And she thought of something else her father had once told
her: "Remember, Rosa, if you are a Jew, you can never trust. Not completely." She would remember.

1891 December

NICOLAI Bobrov told himself he should not worry too much.

The message from his father had been disquieting, of course—there was no denying it. He also felt a pang of guilt. But I daresay when I get there, it won't be so bad, he reasoned. Then he sighed.

It was a long way to be traveling alone. As the covered sled whisked him though the broad streets of Saint Petersburg towards the station, Nicolai gazed out comfortably. He loved the mighty city. Even on a gray day like this, it seemed to have a dull, almost luminous glow. And, it had to be said, Nicolai was a comfortable fellow.

Like any other gentleman in the Western world, he wore a frock coat. Somewhat shorter than in earlier decades, with a single vent behind and two small cloth buttons in the small of the back. His trousers were rather narrow, of a very thick cloth: and to a later generation might have seemed rather untidy, for the fashion of giving trousers a crease had scarcely come into use as yet. His shoes were polished and boned so that they twinkled and gleamed. Across his waistcoat hung a gold chain from his fob watch. His shirt was white with a stiff detachable collar; around this was a narrow silk cravat with polka dots, tied in a loose bow that gave him a faintly artistic appearance. The only parts of his clothing that were particularly Russian were the big greatcoat with a fur collar, which he had undone inside the enclosed sled, and the fur hat that lay on the seat beside him.

Nicolai Bobrov was thirty-seven. The hair on his head and the neat, pointed beard he favored were prematurely graying. His nose seemed to have grown more hooked, giving his face something of the Turkish cast of his ancestors'; but the face had few lines and still often wore the same, open look it had possessed in the days when he was a student trying to persuade his father's peasants to usher in a new world.

How far away those days seemed. Nicolai was a family man now. He had a daughter, and an elder son, named Mikhail after his grandfather; and this last year there had been a new baby, a boy they had called Alexander. In his pocket now he was proudly carrying a little photograph, pasted on board, of the baby. If asked his politics nowadays, he would certainly reply, in a general way: "I am a liberal."

If the revolutionary fervor of his student days had not lasted, it was not surprising. Nicolai had never forgotten the humiliation of 1874. "The peasants weren't even interested," he had soon confessed. He had felt cheated by Popov, too. "He was just an opportunist who made a fool of me," he told his parents. A few years later, when the terrorists killed the tsar, he had only shaken his head sadly. "Even a tsar is better than chaos," he nowadays declared. To which he would add: "Russia will be a free democracy one day; but the truth is, we aren't ready yet. It'll take a generation, maybe two." Until then, thank God, Russia was quiet.

And quiet, nowadays, Russia certainly was. Immediately after the assassination of his reforming father, the new tsar Alexander III had moved decisively. The murderous People's Will inner circle had been discovered and smashed; that good old reactionary, Count Dmitri Tolstoy, had been brought back as minister of the interior and soon had a special police service of no less than a hundred thousand gendarmes. Most of the empire had been placed under martial law by the tsar's so-called Temporary Regulations. These had been in force for ten years now—but then, as Nicolai liked to say: "When our rulers do something good in Russia, they say it's permanent and then revoke it; but when they do something bad, they say it's temporary, and it stays forever!"

There was censorship, internal passports; in the universities, all student organizations were forbidden; in the countryside, new officials called land captains had been appointed to deal out government justice to the peasants without benefit of independent law courts. And the most perfect expression of the official attitude came from the Procurator of the Holy Synod, who, when asked the government's role in education, replied: "To keep people from inventing things."

It was a police state. And yet, Nicolai thought, perhaps it was for the best. At least there was order. True, there had been a few strikes; true, down in the south there had been some pogroms against the Jews. One could not approve of that. But there had been no more bombs. And as he looked out at the winter city a thought suddenly occurred to him, which made him smile.

For the truth is, he concluded, it's as if the Russian empire has been under snow for the last ten years. Yes: that was it exactly. Winter was harsh and cold. Nothing could grow; the snow stifled everything; people might complain at this huge Russian stasis. But the snow also protected the land; under it, delicate seeds could survive the howling winds above. Under the great snow covering of tsarist rule, perhaps Russia could slowly prepare herself for her new and different future in the modern world. And when the time is right, he thought, our Russian spring will be beautiful. The idea pleased him.

Now the sled was crossing the frozen river Neva. On the embankment opposite lay the Winter Palace; to the left, the thin spire of the Peter and Paul cathedral gleamed in the pale light. In the middle of the ice stood a remarkable construction: a towering wooden scaffolding, over fifty feet high, from which a steep runway covered with ice descended. This was one of the city's favorite winter pastimes—an ice mountain, as the huge slide was called. As he watched, Nicolai saw two couples in tiny sleds go whirling down it with shouts of glee. And he smiled: police state or not, life in the Russian capital was not so bad.

A few minutes later they were on the south bank, past the palace, and turning into the broad, handsome vista of Nevsky Prospect. And here again, Nicolai smiled.

"The Street of Toleration" they affectionately called the Nevsky in those days. On it, almost side by side, could be found the churches of Dutch Calvinists, German Lutherans, Roman Catholics, and Armenians, as well of course as the many Orthodox ones. Off the Prospect lay the famous concert halls, theaters, and the fashionable English Club. The royal confectioner had a store here where one could buy chocolates that very likely had lain uneaten in the Winter Palace the night before.

Nicolai had been living in Saint Petersburg for nearly ten years now. He was not rich, but thanks to a sinecure at one of the ministries, where he appeared only once a week, his income was enough to get by on. He was a member of the Yacht Club, where there was an excellent French chef. Frequently he took his wife to one of the capital's four opera houses, where one could nowadays hear not only the masterpieces of Europe but also the new home-grown operas by those Russian geniuses who had suddenly burst upon the world in the last few decades: Tchaikovsky, Mussorgsky, Borodin, Rimsky-Korsakov. Or they would go to the Maryinsky theater to see the finest ballet performances in the world. In the summer, the family would go to a pleasant summer house they rented, just a few miles away on the Gulf of Finland. And once a year, he bought his wife a present from Fabergé the jeweler—for while that master produced his fabulous Easter eggs for the tsar, the Fabergé store also had hundreds of charming little items for more modest purses like that of Nicolai Bobrov.

Truly, in Saint Petersburg in 1891, a liberal-minded man like Bobrov had little to make him want to worry about the future.

But the summons from his father had been worrying.

This last year, all over Russia, the harvest had failed. Saint Petersburg was still supplied but reports were coming in from the central provinces of shortages in the countryside. "You needn't worry, though," a friend at the relevant ministry assured him. "We're organizing relief. We've got everything in hand."

Nicolai had been surprised, therefore, when the previous week he had received the letter from his father Misha: ". . . Frankly, my dear boy, the situation in the villages here is desperate and getting worse. We are doing what we can, but my health is not what it was and I can scarcely cope. If you possibly can, for the love of God, come."

He had also realized, with a pang of guilt, that nearly two years had passed since he had last been to see his parents. He felt sure that his father must be exaggerating; but even so, it was with some misgivings that, on this gray December day, Nicolai Bobrov set off for Russka.

A hiss of steam, a whistle, a succession of puffs like a drum roll, and the train was gliding out through the suburbs towards the snowy wastes beyond.

The Saint Petersburg to Moscow express. In its beautifully paneled and richly upholstered coaches, one could dine and sleep in luxury unmatched on any other railway in the world. How delightful just to sit, hearing the soft hiss of the samovar that was ready in every carriage, and gaze out as the train rushed along the rails that crossed the endless plain.

For, to Nicolai, the railway meant the future. The government of the tsar might be reactionary, but this very year it had begun a vast and daring enterprize: a railway line that would eventually stretch all the way from Moscow across the huge Eurasian landmass to the Pacific port of Vladivostok thousands of miles away. The Trans-Siberian Railway: there would be nothing quite like it in the world.

And this was the new Russia that was to come. The Russian peasant—the muzhik in his *izba*—might be a poor, ignorant fellow, still in the Dark Ages; the newly conquered tribesmen in the Asian deserts might still be living in the world of Genghis Khan and Tamerlane; but over the surface of this huge, primitive empire, the modern world was running bands of steel. Huge coal reserves were being mined in the distant deserts and mountains above Mongolia; there was gold in the bleak wastes of eastern Siberia. German and French capital was flowing in to finance huge government projects: the vast resources of the empire were only beginning to be tapped.

And this was the point. No one doubted Russia's military might. She had put the humiliation of the Crimean War behind her. Though she had sold the huge, empty territory of Alaska to the United States two decades ago, her empire still covered most of the vast north Eurasian plain, from Poland to the Pacific. The Turkish empire trembled before her; the British Empire watched her advance across Asia with cautious respect; in the Far East, the crumbling empire of China would give her whatever she wanted; Japan was eager to cooperate and trade. And now, gradually, Nicolai believed, we shall bring our people into the modern world by exploiting this vast wealth we now own. That was Nicolai Bobrov's hope, and his joy in the railway.

He was sitting alone in the restaurant car. They had just brought him caviar and blini and a glass of vodka. The table was laid for four people, but the other chairs were unoccupied. It was a bore, having no one to talk to.

So when the waiter asked if he might seat two other gentlemen at the table, Nicolai nodded that he had no objection and he looked up curiously to see what sort of companions he was getting.

The two men sat down quietly opposite him, scarcely looking at him. One was a curious-looking fellow he had never seen before.

And the other was Yevgeny Popov.

There was no mistaking him—the shock of carrot-red hair, the same greenish eyes. He had not changed much except that in his face there was now a certain maturity, a settled strength that suggested he might have suffered. Noticing that Nicolai was staring at him, he looked carefully into his face. And then, without smiling, he quietly remarked: "Well, Nicolai Mikhailovich, it's been a long time."

How strange: though they had not met for seventeen years, Nicolai expected his former friend to look awkward. After all, Popov had used him cynically and then extorted money from his father. But Popov looked neither guilty nor defiant: he just gazed at Nicolai calmly, taking him in, asked him where he was going, and on hearing, said thoughtfully—"Ah, yes, Russka"—before turning to his companion and remarking: "The big Suvorin factory is there, you know."

And now Nicolai looked at the other man. He was indeed a curious-looking fellow. He might, Nicolai guessed, be in his early twenties, though his ginger hair was already receding fast. He had a small, reddish, pointed beard. His clothes and bearing suggested that he might belong to the minor provincial gentry and probably be destined for a career as a minor official of some kind.

But what a strange face.

"This is Vladimir Ilych Ulyanov," Popov introduced him. "He's just taken his legal exams in Saint Petersburg and now he's going to be an attorney." The lawyer politely acknowledged Nicolai and gave him a slight, rather grim smile.

Ulyanov? Where had Nicolai heard that name before? Though his hair was ginger, his appearance was definitely Asian. He had a stocky body, a dome-shaped head, high cheekbones, a rather broad nose and mouth, and unmistakably Mongolian eyes. He didn't look Russian at all. But that name: what was familiar about it?

Of course. Ulyanov: Alexander Ulyanov. Four years ago a young student of that name had gotten mixed up with some idiotic plot to kill the tsar. The business had been quite isolated—a madcap plan of some stupid young people. But the unfortunate young man had refused even to apologize and had paid with his life. Nicolai remembered his own revolutionary career as a student and inwardly shuddered. Might he, in different circumstances, have done such a thing? Ulyanov. It had been a respectable family, he remembered: the father had been a schools inspector of humble origin, but had done well enough to reach the rank that gave the family hereditary nobility. He wondered if this young lawyer had anything to do with them.

For the first few minutes, the conversation was hesitant. Nicolai was curious about what his former friend had been doing; but Popov gave him evasive answers, while Ulyanov seemed content to sit quietly watching them. Nicolai gathered that Popov had spent some time abroad, but that was all.

Yet it was a pity to let the opportunity go. He's sure to be up to something, Nicolai thought. And then he'll mysteriously disappear for another twenty years. So after a few more indirect passes he suddenly asked him bluntly: "So tell me, Yevgeny Pavlovich, are you still working for the revolution—and when is it coming?"

He noticed Ulyanov look questioningly at Popov, who answered with a little shrug. But nobody said anything. A few moments later, Ulyanov got up and left them for a while.

"There's an interesting man," Popov remarked pleasantly after he had gone.

"Where does he come from?"

"Nowhere important: a small provincial town in the east, on the Volga. He actually owns an estate there—just a small one with a few poor peasants." Popov smiled wryly. "So he's both a landowner and noble, technically. Don't you recognize his name?"

Nicolai mentioned the student who was executed.

"Exactly. This man's his brother. The whole family was devastated at the time, of course. Vladimir was very shaken."

"He wouldn't get mixed up in a plot like that himself?"

Popov grinned. "Vladimir Ilych is a lot more cautious."

Nicolai commented on the lawyer's Asiatic looks and Popov nodded. "You're right. Actually, on the mother's side I believe he's part German and part Swedish; but the father's family are Asiatic, certainly. They were Chuvash tribesmen."

Of course. He should have guessed from the hair. The Chuvash were an old tribe of Asiatic origin, settled on the Volga, and who frequently had reddish hair. "I was sure he wasn't Russian," Nicolai said.

"No. Actually, I doubt if he's got a single drop of Russian blood in his veins."

"And what's your interest in him?" Nicolai asked.

For a moment, Popov only gazed at him blandly, saying nothing. Then, very quietly, he murmured: "I will tell you this, Nicolai: whatever this fellow may be, I have never met any man like him before."

Just then, Ulyanov returned and this interesting discussion had to end. Nicolai was rather sorry. He had just been becoming curious about the quiet Chuvash lawyer-landowner. But any sense of disappointment he had was soon forgotten as Popov turned back to him and remarked with a faintly ironic smile: "So, Nicolai Mikhailovich—you were asking about the revolution."

In after years, it always seemed to Nicolai, the hour that followed was the most interesting he had ever spent in his life.

Popov spoke quietly, and well. Though from time to time Nicolai recognized flashes of the cold, conspiratorial fellow he had known in his student days, it soon became clear that Popov had developed into something broader since then—a man of larger ideas. A few details of his personal life also emerged. He had been married, but his wife had died. He had been sent to Siberia for three years and spent another year in prison. He had visited a number of European countries, including Britain.

Nicolai knew that, over the years, quite a number of Russian radicals had had to leave and live abroad. He had some ideas of their life: constantly on the move, often traveling with forged papers and different identities; agitating, attending revolutionary conferences, writing articles for illegal journals smuggled into Russia; picking up a meager living by tutoring and translating, or borrowing from sympathizers, or possibly stealing. It was hard not to pity this state of rootless wandering: such people, it seemed to Nicolai, became trapped in a tiny, conspiratorial world, dedicated by sheer force of habit to the service of an idealized revolution which, quite probably, would never come.

Yet now, as he listened to Popov, it soon became clear to Nicolai that his former friend knew far more about the world than he did. Popov gave him an account of the radical movements in Western Europe, from the worker trades unions to the revolutionary political parties: how sophisticated they sounded, compared to anything in Russia. He gave an amusing account of some of the exiled revolutionaries abroad. But above all, as the cosmopolitan Popov explained the European situation, there was something else that struck Nicolai even more. It was his certainty.

For whereas, when he was young, Nicolai remembered men speaking of revolution and a new world order as articles of faith, he noticed that Popov now spoke in a very different manner, as if everything that was passing were part of some concrete, historical process that he well understood. When he expressed this thought, Popov smiled.

"Of course. Have you not read Karl Marx?"

Nicolai had heard of Marx, and he tried to remember what he knew.

The fellow was a German Jew who had lived a long time in England and died a few years ago. An economist and a revolutionary. And there had been a disciple who was still active: Engels. But the works of these formidable men were only just beginning to appear in Russia, and Nicolai had to confess he had read nothing.

The theories of Marx, Popov explained, derived from the great German philosopher, Hegel, at the start of the century. "And no doubt you remember the great world system of Hegel from your student days, don't you?" Popov chided.

"I think so." Nicolai searched his mind. Yes: he did remember. "It was called the dialectic," he said.

"Exactly. The dialectic. That is the key to everything."

Nicolai remembered it all now—Hegel's beautiful, cosmic system, which showed that the world was progressing towards an ultimate state of perfection: the Absolute. And the process for getting there? It was all done in stages—a seemingly endless clash of ideas, but each clash marking a step forward. Thus a thesis—one seeming truth, met its opposite: antithesis. And from the two emerged a new idea: synthesis—better than the idea before, but still imperfect. And so the synthesis would now become thesis—and the whole business would start again. Normally, Nicolai recalled, each thesis collapsed because it had some flaw, some inner contradiction. Thus for instance, men had thought the earth was flat—until the evidence contradicted what at first had seemed obvious. Then they supposed the earth was the center of the universe with the sun circling around it—until this, too, was shown to be false. He liked the dialectic: it suggested progress. It was compelling.

"And the greatest master of the dialectic was Karl Marx," Popov stated. "For by it he has explained the whole history of mankind—and its future, too," he added.

Marxism: Nicolai listened, fascinated, as Popov outlined the system. "Only matter exists," he began. "That is the great truth that underlies everything; and hence the name we give Marx's system: dialectical materialism.

"For it's the material means of the production that determines everything," he expounded. "How we feed ourselves, clothe ourselves, how we extract minerals from the earth and manufacture. Man's whole consciousness, his society, his laws all derive from this economic structure. And in every society to date there are two classes fundamentally: the exploiters and the exploited. Those who own the means of production and those who sell their labor."

"And the dialectic?"

"Why, the class struggle: that's the dialectic. Think of it. In feudal Europe who held the land? The nobles. And the exploited peasants worked it. But gradually that structure fell apart. A new world arose: the bourgeois world, which has led to full-scale capitalism. Now the exploiters are the factory owners and the exploited are the workers—the proletariat. Thesis and antithesis."

"And the synthesis?"

"The synthesis is the revolution. The workers take over the means of production. Capitalism destroys itself and we enter the new age. It's quite inevitable."

"What happens in the new age?"

"First socialism, where the workers' state owns the means of production. Later we progress to perfect communism, where the state, as we know it, will not even be needed."

"So we are still progressing towards the new world we dreamed of as students?"

Popov nodded. "Yes. But our mistake back in 'seventy-four was to try to make a revolution with the peasants. The revolution can only come from the proletariat. And the big difference is that now, thanks to Marx, we know what we're doing. We have a framework." He tapped his finger on the table. "The revolution has become scientific."

Though Nicolai was not sure he understood perfectly, he was impressed. "Are there many Marxists in Russia?" he asked.

Popov shook his head. "Only a few so far. The leader of Russian Marxism is Plekhanov, and he mostly lives in Switzerland." He reeled off a few more names, none of which meant anything to Nicolai.

"And what does all this tell us about the revolution in Russia?" Nicolai asked. "How and when will it come?"

Popov gave a wry grin. "Sometimes, Nicolai Mikhailovich, it seems there are as many opinions as revolutionaries." Then he grew serious. "Briefly, however, there are two views.

"Consider," he went on. "Formal Marxism says that everything happens in its proper time. First an agricultural, feudal economy, then a bourgeois state. From this, capitalism develops, becomes more and more centralized and oppressive until finally it collapses. The workers break their chains: the socialist revolution takes place. A clear and logical sequence.

"Now Russia," he explained, "is still primitive. She has only just entered the bourgeois stage of development. Her proletariat is small. If we had a revolution of our own, it would probably be like the French Revolution—throw out the monarchy and leave the bourgeoisie in charge. Only Europe can have a socialist revolution: and then—maybe—Russia could become absorbed into the new world order that Europe will create."

"So, the revolution can't start in Russia?"

"According to classical Marx—no. But I said there were two views. The other—which even Marx himself admitted was possible—is this: What if Russia is special, a unique case? Consider, Nicolai: a rotten autocracy; a weak noble class completely dependent on the tsar and with no economic power of its own; a small middle class, hardly developed; and a peasantry traditionally organized in communes. Nothing like England or Germany at all, therefore; a brittle, outdated regime. Maybe Russia could have a sudden revolution therefore that would move directly to some kind of primitive socialism after all. No one knows."

Nicolai listened, fascinated. "And what do you think?" he asked.

Popov shrugged. "I've no faith in the peasants, as you know. I believe the main doctrine of Marx—Russia must first pass through a bourgeois and capitalist state. The proletarian revolution can only follow after that."

"So you don't think the revolution will begin here?"

"I'm sure it won't."

During all this time, Nicolai had noticed that Ulyanov had been content to say nothing, though once or twice, when Popov had been talking of Marx, the lawyer had nodded in agreement. Now, however, he spoke, very quietly.

"Marxism is clearly correct. But we should remember, Marx was also a revolutionary, and revolution is a practical as well as theoretical business." He nodded to Popov. "Russia is immensely backward, of course. But industry is developing rapidly now. The proletarian class is growing. The basic Marxist conditions for revolution may exist in Russia in our lifetimes. And then—this is the key—the proletariat will need to be educated and led. You'll need a trained cadre at the center—otherwise it won't work." It was said quietly, yet with certitude. Clearly when this lawyer gave his considered opinion, he did not expect it to be questioned.

Nicolai studied Ulyanov. A revolutionary cadre: the leaders: the new men, as he and Popov used to call themselves years ago. And suddenly remembering the arguments with his own father in those days, he asked the strange-looking fellow: "Tell me—your cadre: should it use any means to promote the revolution?"

The lawyer stroked his beard thoughtfully. "I should say yes."

"Including terrorism."

"If it's useful," Ulyanov responded calmly, "why not?"

"I just wondered," Nicolai said.

The conversation moved on after this, to other things. Nicolai tried to find out a little more about what Popov was doing, but he soon gave up, and shortly afterwards Ulyanov announced that he felt tired and would retire to his carriage.

It was just before they parted, however, that one scrap of conversation occurred that, for some reason, always stuck in Nicolai's mind afterwards. They had been discussing the famine, and he had told them about his father's letter.

"It's quite true," Popov said. "Things are terrible in the central provinces."

And then Ulyanov spoke. "It's a great mistake," he remarked.

"What is?" Nicolai asked.

"This attempt at famine relief. We should do nothing to help. Let the peasants starve. The worse things are, the more the tsarist government is weakened." It was said quite calmly, without any anger or malice, in a detached, matter-of-fact voice.

"He's been saying that all week." Popov laughed.

"I am correct," the lawyer replied in the same tone. It occurred to Nicolai that it was this very lack of emotion that might make this curious Chuvash rather formidable.

They parted in a friendly manner. Nicolai supposed he might never see either of them again. And he certainly had no premonition that, formidable or not, the balding lawyer with the little reddish beard would ever place himself at the head of a revolution.

It is a favorite hobby of those who study Russian history to choose—each having his own theory—a particular year from which, he will argue, the Russian revolutionary process began, and was perhaps inevitable. "This was really the beginning," he or she will say.

For Nicolai Bobrov, however, there was not just a year, but a single day: it was a day on which a tiny domestic scene took place, that was witnessed only by himself. And though he participated afterwards in many of the great events that were seen on the stage of world history, it was to this small and unknown incident that he would always return in his mind and say: "That—that was the day when the revolution began."

It took place some five months after the conversation in the train.

If Nicolai had wondered if his father might be exaggerating the difficulties at Russka, that suspicion died the day he arrived home.

The situation was desperate. The harvest of '90 had been poor, not only at Russka, but down on the Bobrovs' other estate in Riazan province, too. In '91 therefore, Misha Bobrov and his fellow members of the *zemstvo* board had tried to save the situation by urging the peasants to sow a mixed crop. "Extra potatoes," Misha had said. "Even if the cereals fail, there will be something to eat." But nothing had gone right. The entire potato crop had been blighted; every other crop had failed, too. There had been nothing like it since the terrible year of 1839, and by autumn it was clear there would be famine.

Something else Nicolai quickly realized was that, for his father, the famine was also a personal crisis. Though seventy, and not in the best of health, Misha Bobrov had plunged into activity with a fervor that was almost reckless. "For the fact is," he confessed, "as a member of the *zemstvo* gentry, I feel a double burden these days."

Nicolai knew very well what he meant. Ever since the elected *zemstvo* assemblies had been set up by the reforming tsar Alexander, the government had tinkered with its membership. Sometimes the present tsar had simply refused to confirm people, even when elected, if their loyalty was suspect. But the crunch had come in 1890, when the present tsar had simply decided to alter the voting rules—so drastically, that the electorate was often reduced by more than half, and the gentry composed the vast majority of the board members. It was a shameful business, a calculated slap in the face of the simple Russian peasants, and Nicolai knew that his liberal-minded father had felt deeply embarrassed. "We gentry really have to prove ourselves," he repeatedly said. "Otherwise what are we good for?" The result of this was that Misha Bobrov had worked himself into the ground; the tragedy was that he had achieved so little.

It was not his fault. The *zemstvo* had organized grain stores; it had carefully monitored food allocations; Misha and others had toured the area continuously. But nothing could alter the fact that supplies were running low. "In another eight weeks, all the grain will have gone," Misha had told him. "After that—God knows. We've been trying to buy grain from other provinces not so badly hit. But . . ." He spread his hands. "Nothing."

While they themselves were not short of food, it was clear to Nicolai that the strain of the famine around them had been too much for his parents. His father looked gray and sunken, his usual optimism entirely gone. Anna, usually so decisive, seemed wan and hesitant. But she did take him aside and tell him firmly: "Nicolai, you must take over. Your father can't go on."

Nicolai toured the village. It was always the same. To his delight he found that Arina was still alive—a small, shriveled little babushka, but her eyes as keen as ever. Timofei Romanov and his wife gave him a warm welcome. Their daughter, baby Arina as Nicolai thought of her, was now a pleasant, rather square-faced girl of seventeen. Only Boris seemed cold towards him; but Nicolai did not place great importance in that. Throughout the village, he found a calm resignation. The elder saw to it that each family had a little bread. There was still salted meat in some *izbas.* And most families went out each day to try to catch fish through holes in the ice. "But," as Timofei remarked, "I daresay you'll bury us, Nicolai Mikhailovich."

At the monastery, which had grain stores, the monks had taken over the feeding of the nearby peasants, taking them flour each day. "We have nine weeks' supply," they told him.

"But the man upon whom everything now depends is at Russka," his father told him. "And that's Vladimir Suvorin."

Vladimir: the elder grandson of that old terror Savva, and the brother of the unfortunate Peter Suvorin. Back at the time, deeming it unwise, Misha had never told his son about the incriminating letter of Peter's and how he had used it to blackmail old Savva. Since then he had preferred to keep the incident closed. Of Peter, therefore, Nicolai knew only that he had run away, and appeared again sometime later. "I believe he's a professor in Moscow," Misha told him. "He never comes here." Of Vladimir Suvorin, on the other hand, Nicolai had heard more. The powerful industrialist ran his factories firmly in Moscow and Russka but fairly. His workers never labored more than ten hours a day; no children were used; there were numerous safety precautions and both work and living quarters were clean; there were no cruel fines for minor infractions. And unlike some of Russia's leading industrialists, he had never suffered from a strike. In Moscow, Nicolai had heard, Vladimir had a huge house; but he came to Russka often. Having been away so much himself, however, Nicolai had never met him. "What's he like?" he asked.

"Huge. And impressive," his father had replied, so that Nicolai had a vision of some tall and forbidding figure like old Savva.

It was on the second morning that Vladimir Suvorin arrived at the Bobrov house. He was huge, all right. But not as Nicolai had supposed. In fact, he was unlike anyone Nicolai had seen before.

Vladimir Suvorin was six feet tall and built like a bear; but there any resemblance to the animal kingdom ended. Even as he stepped off the sled and walked towards the waiting family, his presence seemed to fill the place with a sense of authority as, pulling off a gray glove, he extended a huge, rather fleshy hand to old Misha and smiled kindly.

"My dear friend." He seemed to envelop them all.

This impression, once they were inside, was even more striking. His big frame was encased in a beautifully cut coat that made his slight paunch seem only a fitting adjunct to his imposing chest. His large, square-cut face had just enough fleshiness to suggest controlled good living. His hair was thinning but cut short; his nose large but regular; his dark brown mustache and short beard perfectly manicured. Around his neck was a soft, gray silk cravat fixed with a large diamond pin. And about his person there was a faint and pleasant scent of eau de cologne.

Nicolai watched him, fascinated. Like all those who lived in Saint Petersburg, he had a slightly superior attitude to Moscow. Moscow was provincial, a place for merchants. In Saint Petersburg, Nicolai had moved in the best circles. He knew the men of the imperial court, cosmopolitan aristocrats. He knew nobles with great houses. Yet here was a man— grandson of one of the Bobrov serfs—who did not belong to these upper-class circles and yet who was, Nicolai sensed at once, even more cosmopolitan than they. He spoke Russian elegantly; by a few words he let fall, it was clear he spoke French. And in fact, though Nicolai did not then know it, Suvorin was comfortable in German and English, too.

But what was this extraordinary aura that Suvorin had? He's like a monarch, or an Eastern potentate, Nicolai thought. His black eyes, set wide apart, seemed to possess a comprehensive intelligence; above all, there was about him an astonishing sense of comfort and of power. He has perfect manners, yet he says and does exactly as he likes, and everyone obeys him, Nicolai guessed. It was the first time he had met a member of that very special group, the cosmopolitan very rich. For though only age forty-one, Vladimir Suvorin had long ago grown accustomed to the pleasant idea that, if he chose, there was almost nothing he could not buy. This knowledge, when combined with intelligence and culture, could make even the grandson of a serf into a prince.

And so, at once, the great man took them all over. Nicolai he immediately treated as a trusted colleague. "Thank God you are here, Nicolai Mikhailovich." Towards old Misha, he was both courteous and protective. "You have done so much, dear friend. It's time to let the younger generation take some of the burden now. But I know you will keep an eye on us all." In two minutes, Nicolai felt proud to be swept into his orbit.

"There is news from the provincial governor," he said. "The government will supply grain. It's being shipped from the Ukraine and we shall have it in a month. As you know, we still have about eight weeks of grain left. I am going myself to speak to the governor, to make sure there are no slipups. So all we have to do is keep everyone in good heart. Yes, thank you, *chère madame*, I should love a glass of cordial." And he sat down among them comfortably.

During his visit, Nicolai learned a little about Suvorin. He had lost a wife, married again, and had a son. Normally he liked to travel two months a year. He knew Paris as well as he did Moscow. He knew personally such artists as Renoir and Monet; he knew the great writer Tolstoy and had been down to his estate at Yasnaya Polyana. Tchaikovsky he also knew. "And his unfortunate wife," he added with a sigh. This was a glittering world of literary men, crowded salons, conoisseurship and judicious patronage—a world where high rank or extreme wealth were passports to entry, as they are everywhere, but where only talent and excellence were tolerated. It was clear that, on top of this, Suvorin was a formidable man of business. Nicolai also learned much about the work that the *zemstvos* had done in the last few months. "Without men like your father," Suvorin told him frankly, "the local administration of food would have broken down entirely. It's the *zemstvo* people in town and country who have held things together, not the central government at all."

And after he had gone, Misha remarked admiringly, "Thank God we have him with us. He makes things happen. The authorities daren't ignore him."

Though he had noticed Boris Romanov's coolness towards him, Nicolai would still have been surprised to hear the dispute raging in the *izba* of Timofei Romanov that same time.

The disputants were old Arina and Boris. Timofei and his wife said little; as for the subject of the quarrel, the seventeen-year-old girl, her grandmother's namesake, no one thought of asking her at all.

"You can't do it," Boris was fairly shouting. "Those people are our enemies, only you're all too stupid to see it." At this Timofei looked uncomfortable and old Arina shrugged contemptuously. "Besides," Boris cried, "she should be here to help her parents." But old Arina was obdurate. "It would be one less mouth to feed," Timofei's wife remarked at last.

"Better to starve," Boris growled.

The years since the tragic fire that killed Natalia had done nothing to assuage the feelings of Boris Romanov. Indeed, as time passed his sense that the Bobrovs and the entire gentry class were conspiring against him had grown even stronger. To Boris, the evidence was clear. Ten years ago, for instance, when it was rumored that the government would finally abolish the burdensome payments the peasants had been making to their former owners ever since the Emancipation, the administration finally announced only a niggardly reduction of twenty-five percent. "And what the devil is the use of that?" Boris protested. Now the peasants' voting rights to the *zemstvo* assemblies had been almost wiped out. "Another swindle by the gentry," Boris stormed. "Now they even take our votes away." And when, during the famine, old Timofei had pointed out the good work that Misha Bobrov was doing, Boris had only replied contemptuously: "If that old criminal can do it, an honest peasant could do it better."

His grandmother's decision that her granddaughter Arina should join the Bobrov household had therefore filled him with fury. Yet, since his father was head of the family, and Timofei was not prepared to contradict the determined old woman, there was nothing he could do.

"I think it would be best," old Timofei finally agreed, "if they will take her."

And the old woman was certainly adamant. It was astonishing what force of will could be contained in that small frame; it was strange, too, how her determination to ensure the family's survival had now caused her to shift all her thoughts from her own beloved daughter to the next generation. Her memories of the last great famine; perhaps some guilt from the time she had nearly exposed her as a baby now caused old Arina to fight for the girl with an implacable determination. If things got worse, there was only one house where there would certainly be food. "I'll speak to them," she said quietly. "They'll take her."

So it was that, shortly after Vladimir Suvorin had left, the Bobrov family was faced by old Arina and the girl. The old woman did not even have to say much. Anna Bobrov understood perfectly. "Of course we'll take her," she told the old woman. And then, with a thoughtful smile: "My husband is tired. I'm sure he'll be glad of her help."

By that afternoon the girl was installed. "Now you'll be safe," her grandmother whispered to her as she left. But it was one other message that remained, for some time, in the girl's mind. For just as she had departed the village, Boris had pulled her to one side and muttered: "Go to those damned Bobrovs if you choose; but just remember, if you ever become their friend, you won't be mine anymore."

The next six weeks were busy for Nicolai Bobrov. His mother's prediction that the young Romanov girl would be useful soon proved to be wise: for a few days later, relieved of the strain of coping with the famine alone, Misha Bobrov suddenly fell sick. Day after day he lay on his bed, seemingly too weak to move, and if it had not been for the calm, steady presence of this peasant girl who nursed him, Nicolai believed they might have lost the old man.

What a treasure she was, this baby Arina. She was fair, with very light brown hair, and though one could not exactly call her pretty there was a simplicity in her rather square peasant's face that was very attractive. She had a quietness about her, like a nun, that made her a pleasant, peaceful presence in any room she entered. She was very devout. Anna and she would often walk over to the monastery, shawls tied over their heads, so that from a distance one could not have said which was lady and which was peasant. Yet she had also learned from her grandmother a huge fund of folktales, and when she recited these, her gentle face and blue eyes would seem to glow with pleasure and with quiet amusement. Besides her daily nursing, it was this knowledge in which old Misha rejoiced. "Tell me, little Arina, about the Fox and the Cat," Nicolai would hear his father's voice weakly rasp as he passed the room. Or: "Pass me that book, little Arina—those fairy tales by Pushkin. He has a story like the one you tell."

"Your tales remind me of when I was a boy," he would tell the girl. "Isn't it funny, we used to call your old grandmother Young Arina then. And the tales you know come from another Arina—her aunt, I suppose— who was still alive when I was young." And to Nicolai he would say:

"This young Arina, you know, she is the real Russia, the enduring heartland. Always remember that." And sometimes, looking at her affectionately, he would doze off and dream of those sunlit days when Pushkin was still alive, and his uncle Sergei was putting on theatricals at Bobrovo.

"If your father gets his health back, it'll be thanks to that girl," Anna told her son. And indeed, Misha did seem to be gradually recovering his strength.

After three weeks Nicolai made a brief visit to Saint Petersburg to see his wife and children. Then he returned.

But there remained one huge problem: the promised grain supplies never arrived. "And I shan't get well," old Misha declared, "until they do." Messengers were sent to the governor by the *zemstvo* and by Suvorin. Nicolai offered to return to Saint Petersburg to try to see certain high officials there. Every few days, news came that the arrival of the grain was imminent, and everybody prepared. They still had a month's supply in hand: then three weeks', then two.

It was in mid-February that the message came through to the local *zemstvo*. The message was quite simple.

It is regretted that, owing to problems of transport and storage, the grain shipments previously notified will not be made.

And that was all.

"Do they realize what this means?" old Misha gasped from his bed. "It means the people here are going to die. No one's even caught a fish in the river for two weeks. Two-thirds of the livestock has gone. Our people will be finished. I can't believe that even those fools in the bureaucracy would do such a thing."

The news was round the whole area in hours. And when Nicolai went into the village that day, he was hardly shocked when Boris Romanov shouted at him: "So, the people in Saint Petersburg have decided to kill us—is that it? Do they want our carcasses for meat?" Nor was he surprised that this was greeted by nods of approval from the other villagers.

A week passed. The peasants were sullen. Another week. Many of the grain stores were now empty. A silence descended upon the village.

And then, one morning, grain began to arrive.

It was an extraordinary sight: lines of sleds, arriving from God knew where: a dozen; two dozen; three dozen. It was like a supply train for a small army. The sleds made their way ponderously into Russka, where, it seemed, Suvorin's managers were ready to receive them, at one of the warehouses. But a dozen of the sleds peeled off and made their way through the woods towards the village of Bobrovo. When they reached it, they continued up the slope to the house of Misha Bobrov; and as they approached, and people came to the windows of the house to watch them in astonishment, it could be seen that, riding in the front sled was a large and powerful figure—a figure who, wrapped in furs, his face glowing in the icy air, for once truly did resemble a mighty Russian bear.

And it was this bearlike Vladimir Suvorin who now, with a happy grin, got down from the sled, strode over to where Misha—so excited that he had insisted on leaving his bed—was standing wrapped in a blanket, and gave him a mighty bear hug.

"There, Mikhail Alexeevich, I've brought you and your village some grain. We can't have my old friend going hungry."

"I told you he'd do it!" Misha cried to his son and his wife. "I told you only Suvorin could pull it off. But how the devil," he remarked of the industrialist, "did you manage to prize it out of the governor, after they told us they had nothing."

"My dear friend, you don't understand. The authorities have nothing. No one is being supplied."

Misha frowned. "Then this?"

The other grinned again. "I bought it myself. My agents found it and shipped it all the way from the south. It's nothing to do with the authorities."

For several seconds Misha was silent, unable to speak. Nicolai saw tears well up into the old man's eyes. He held on to Suvorin's sleeve, then muttered: "How can I thank you, Vladimir Ivanovich?" And shaking his head: "What can I say?"

But it was after a moment's thoughtful silence that Misha Bobrov suddenly made his extraordinary outburst. Throwing back his head, and gathering all his strength, he shouted out in a paroxysm of frustration, shame, and contempt: "Damn those people! Damn that governor! Damn the government in Saint Petersburg. I tell you these people are useless to us. Let them give power to the local *zemstvos* since they are incompetent to govern themselves."

He shouted it in front of the servants, the drivers, and several villagers. He did not seem to care. It came straight from his heart. Misha Bobrov, landowner, noble, liberal but loyal monarchist, was done with his government. So, Nicolai knew, were other landowners and *zemstvo* men all over the central provinces that winter of famine.

And so it was this day, in after years, that Nicolai Bobrov would look back and murmur: "That: yes, that was the start of the revolution."

It was in early spring that the first outbreak began.

It started in the group of huts that straggled along the riverbank below the little town of Russka. Why it should have started there no one knew. Perhaps because there was an old rubbish heap there—perhaps not.

At first, when several people suffered from diarrhea, no one took much notice. But then, after two days, one man suddenly experienced a violent discharge from his stomach of whitish and yellowish matter, like whey. Shortly after, he vomited more of the same, then cried out that the pit of his stomach was on fire and screamed for water. The next day he suffered acute cramps in the legs and his body started to turn blue. His eyes became so sunken he resembled a skeleton and, when he spoke, his voice was only a hoarse whisper. When his wife tried his pulse, she could feel nothing. Just before the following dawn he died.

After his death, his body remained strangely warm for some time. His wife said it had grown hotter. She also noticed that, well after death, the corpse suffered muscular twitches and spasms, which frightened her.

And within a few more hours, all Russka knew that cholera had arrived.

"If we can just keep it out of the village." This was Misha Bobrov's litany each day. "Of course," he would say, "if Russia was properly run, the whole area would be sealed off. There'd be a *cordon sanitaire.*" But neither local nor provincial administrations could attempt such a thing: people came and went. Thanks, however, to the efforts of the two Bobrovs and of Suvorin, a sort of informal quarantine was in force that seemed to be limiting the terrible cholera's spread.

Indeed, their modest success was soon confirmed by a young doctor that the *zemstvo* managed to employ to help deal with the outbreak. "In other parts, it's raging almost out of control," he said. "The famine has weakened everyone and made them terribly prone to diseases."

It was not long before Nicolai had made himself extremely familiar with the disease. "It especially attacks the young and old," the doctor informed him. "The most serious cases usually seem to go straight to the white-vomit-and-diarrhea stage. They usually die in a day or two. There is one small comfort, though," he added. "Generally, the bulk of the fatalities occur at the very start of the outbreak. So the first week or so is the worst. After that, many of them pull through."

There were several dozen cases in the town; a few in the monastery; and several in the villages in the area. Nicolai greatly admired the way the young doctor went about his work. "Though the truth is, I can't do much," he confessed. "The early stages I dose with opium or nitrate of silver; mustard flannels and chloroform for when they get the cramps. If they're sinking and there's a chance they might pull through, brandy or ammonia to give them a jolt back to life. And that," he said wryly, "is about it."

The unfortunate doctor was soon short of everything. Once more, the central government promised medical supplies, but this time the Bobrovs did not even expect them to arrive—which they did not. "All my best brandy went in the first week," Misha said with a sad smile. Nicolai went to the provincial capital to get supplies but found none. In Moscow, however, Suvorin was able to obtain some nitrate. And the young doctor worked without ceasing.

"How do you avoid getting it yourself?" Nicolai had asked him when they first met.

"Some people believe it's carried in the air," the doctor told him. "But I believe the chief cause of infection is through the mouth. Never drink water or eat food touched by someone with cholera. If you get vomit or any bodily fluid from sick people on your clothes, change and wash yourself very thoroughly before you eat or drink anything. I don't say it's foolproof, but I haven't got cholera yet."

And though Nicolai several times accompanied the young doctor to places where the disease was raging, he carefully followed this advice and came to no harm.

A week passed. A second. A third. And still the cholera did not spread to the village of Bobrovo. Strangely enough also, while the rest of the world was trembling before the sickness, Misha Bobrov was getting his strength again. He would often walk out now with his wife or young Arina and stroll in the woods above the house. It was pleasant, too, for the old man and his son to come to know each other better again. Indeed, it nowadays caused Nicolai some amusement to remark to his friend the doctor: "Do you know, since he turned against the government my old father's far more radical than I am. I thought it was supposed to be the other way round!"

Gradually the deaths from the disease grew less, the new cases fewer. After a month it seemed to have subsided. "You've been lucky," the doctor told him. "And I've just been asked to go to another bad spot over by Murom. Good-bye."

Soon afterwards, in mid-May, Nicolai decided it was time for him to return to Saint Petersburg. "I'll be back in July," he promised his parents. "And if there's no more sign of cholera in the region, I'll bring all the family to see you." It was with a considerable sense of relief, therefore, that he set out once more for the capital.

He did not go alone. To their surprise, the Bobrovs had discovered that young Arina had always wanted to see the capital. And since Misha was now recovered, and Nicolai's wife had written to say she had need of a temporary nanny for their children, it was agreed that young Arina should accompany Nicolai and remain with his family for the summer. The girl seemed delighted.

And if, just before leaving, she had had an unpleasant interview with her brother Boris, she kept it to herself.

It was three days after they had left that old Timofei Romanov showed signs one afternoon of being ill. Within an hour he was vomiting a whitish substance with little ricelike grains in it.

He had cholera. It had gone straight to the second, deadly stage.

By the time darkness fell, he was in agony. By morning he was transformed. The terrible discharges had left his body wracked and almost purple. His eyes were hollow caverns; the pallor of death was upon him. His wife and old Arina, who had changed his sodden clothes a dozen times already, stood in the pale light of dawn and gazed at him mournfully. The old fellow's eyes were staring, sometimes at them, sometimes at the little icon in the corner; but he could no longer utter. Once, with a huge effort, he managed to smile, as if to tell them that he was resigned.

Misha Bobrov was surprised early that morning to find Boris Romanov at his door. He could not remember when the surly and suspicious fellow had last been up to the house. But today he seemed polite: almost friendly.

"I'm afraid, sir," he explained, "it's bad news. My father." And he told Misha the details.

"My God." So, just when he thought they had been spared, the plague had come to Bobrovo after all. Thank God I'm fit enough to deal with the crisis, Misha thought, and he immediately gave orders to send for a doctor and warn the people in Russka about the outbreak.

He was rather surprised, a few minutes later, to find young Boris still hanging around.

"The fact is, sir," the younger man explained, "he's asking for you. He wants to say good-bye." And just for a moment, Misha saw tears form in Boris's pleading eyes. "He won't last the day," he said simply.

Misha hesitated. He could not help himself. The fact was, he had no desire to go into a house where there was cholera. I can't afford to get it myself, he thought. There's too much to do. But immediately he felt ashamed. God knows, I asked the doctor to do it. Besides, I've known old Timofei all my life.

"Of course," he said. And put on his coat.

How confoundedly hot it was in the Romanov *izba.* There was a suffocating smell, despite the fact that a window had been opened.

There before him lay his childhood playmate Timofei—or what was left of him. Poor devil. It seemed his mind might have wandered a bit, for he now gazed at Misha with a kind of astonishment; but it was hard to know what was in his mind since the old man could not speak. My God, but he's the same age as me, Misha remembered. He looked a hundred. Well, now I'm here, I must go through with it.

Misha glanced round the room. Despite everything, old Arina and her daughter had kept it spotlessly clean. The floor had been scrubbed recently, and the table. Timofei lay in clean bedclothes by the stove. The morning light was streaming in through the window. He glanced at the little icon in the corner, taking what comfort he could from it. Boris offered to take his coat: the heat felt a little less oppressive once it was off. But though they offered him a chair, he preferred to stand, some distance away from the patient; and he was careful to touch nothing. And now dear old Timofei was trying to smile.

He spoke what words of comfort he could. To his surprise, he did not find it so difficult. He recalled times past, people they had known, and the gentle old peasant seemed to receive pleasure from it. Boris, with a grateful smile, slipped out of the room for a minute. It was strange how, in the presence of death, foolish antagonisms could disappear.

Boris moved swiftly and quietly. He could hardly believe how easy the whole thing had been. His father had looked so surprised to see the landowner that for a second Boris had feared Misha might guess that the old man had not sent for him at all: but he hadn't guessed; all was well. Now he slipped across the passageway into the open storeroom opposite.

The bedclothes and three of his father's shirts were lying in a corner where they had been thrown a short time ago. Old Arina said they should burn them, but no one had had time yet. Carefully he opened out Misha Bobrov's coat and laid it on the pile. Then he turned it over and did it again, gently pressing the coat down. He repeated this, making sure that the coat was thoroughly impregnated. Then, with a look of polite respect on his face, he went back into the room, carrying the coat carefully.

"This," he whispered to himself, "is for Natalia."

* * *

What a business that had been, Misha considered a short time later as he walked hurriedly back to the house. How horribly hot the room was. Thank God he had taken care not to touch anything. You couldn't be too careful.

But he was proud of himself. He had done the right thing, and the old peasant was happy: he could see that.

He must have been sweating himself in there, more than he had realized. As he strode back up the slope even his coat felt damp. He wiped his brow and his mustache with his coat sleeve. Yes: it had certainly been an unpleasant business and he was glad it was over.

A week later the news reached Nicolai in Saint Petersburg: his father had cholera.

1892

SUMMER. There was a subdued buzz of conversation in the room. Soon the distinguished speaker would arrive and Rosa Abramovich felt a tingle of anticipation. She had never been to a meeting like this before. There were about thirty people there, almost all in their early twenties.

Outside the evening sun was bathing the Lithuanian capital of Vilnius and its old castle hill in a soft orange light.

Rosa Abramovich was twenty now and she had lived in Vilnius for a decade. She might, she knew, have been in America. Many Jews had started to go there after the pogroms in 1881; but at the family conference her father had called in the autumn of that terrible year, they had decided instead to cross the Jewish Pale, some five hundred miles to the northwest, into Lithuania. "There's not much trouble in Vilnius," her father had remarked. "If pogroms come there, then we'll leave Russia." He still had faith.

Rosa loved her new home. From the Lithuanian capital it was only a day's train journey to the Baltic Sea, or southwest to the ancient Polish capital of Warsaw. To the north lay the Baltic provinces where the Latvians and Estonians lived and where once, centuries ago, the crusading Teutonic Knights had raided Russia. "It's very much a border province, a crossroads," her father had remarked.

And indeed, though all these lands nowadays formed part of the tsar's sprawling empire, it could not be said that their character was in the least Russian. In the rolling, prosperous farmlands and woodlands of Lithuania, the people had not forgotten that once they and the Poles, in their joint kingdom, had been masters of all these western lands and more besides. The Lithuanian farmers, with their large, handsome wooden houses, reminded Rosa of the independent Cossack farmers she had known in the Ukraine. As for the capital of Vilnius, it was a pleasant old European city, containing buildings in many styles—Gothic, renaissance, baroque, and neoclassical. It contained a fine Catholic cathedral and numerous churches. Of Russian architecture there were hardly any examples at all. And this cosmopolitan city had also a thriving Jewish community.

In fact, Rosa's father had found only one thing wrong with the place: it was home to far too many of those secular-minded young Jews who were turning their back on their religion: try as he might, it had been almost impossible to stop his two sons from consorting with them; but he had kept a strict watch over little Rosa. Until his sudden and unexpected death the previous year. And now, it was into precisely such dangerous company that Rosa had fallen that evening. It was all, she thought, rather exciting.

Friends of her brothers had brought her there. Half the people in the room were young men and women from the assimilated Jewish middle class—students, a young doctor, a lawyer. The rest were Jewish workers, including three girls who were seamstresses. It was a pleasant, lively group, but to Rosa they were all strangers. And why had she come? She hardly knew: but mainly, she supposed, because she had nothing better to do.

For though she was only twenty, life had already dealt Rosa some bitter blows. At first, after arriving in Vilnius, it had seemed that everything was going so well. Her musical career had made huge strides: by the age of sixteen she had given several piano recitals and made a small tour; a year later she was promised a major tour with an important conductor. Her parents were delighted; her brothers proud, even a little envious. She had everything she could desire. And now she had nothing.

Why, she used to wonder—why would God give her this gift, only to blight it? This must be another of life's inexplicable mysteries. The last three years had been a nightmare. Sometimes the sickness had been like a terrible weight on her chest and she would cough until it hurt; for days she would be prostrate, unable to summon up the energy to do anything. The tour had had to be canceled; even her musical studies were almost abandoned. "If I can't play properly, I don't want to play at all," she told her unhappy father; and she had slowly sunk into a depression, while her family watched hopelessly.

"If only she had friends to help her," her mother would lament. The trouble was that almost all her friends in Vilnius were musicians; and now she no longer wished to see them. Only one close friend remained: young Ivan Karpenko down in the Ukraine. Ever since that terrible day when he had saved the family from the pogrom, there had been a special bond between Rosa and the Cossack youth. It was to Ivan, therefore, that she wrote long letters during this period of pain, and from whom she received back warm letters of encouragement.

The sudden death of her father the previous year had forced Rosa to come out of her lethargy. The family's main income had gone; her two brothers were having to support her mother; Rosa was forced to consider what to do with her life. A musical career was out of the question now: so what were the alternatives. Teach the piano—for a pittance? Her mother suggested it, but Rosa dreaded the thought. There was the Teacher's Institute in the city, where Jewish students could train to teach in the state schools. Her brothers thought this was better. What does it matter, if I can't do what I want? she thought. But I must do something. I can't just be a useless person. She had enrolled at the institute. And now here she was, on a summer evening, at a Jewish workers' meeting, simply because she had nothing better to do.

There were so many meetings. Some were just study groups, teaching eager workers to read and write; others were more communal and met to discuss how they could improve working and living conditions. And a few were, more or less, political.

Today's meeting, however, was rather special. A professor all the way from Moscow had come to address them on worker movements in and outside Russia. "But I daresay it'll go further than that," one of her companions whispered. "The professor's a Marxist." And when Rosa looked blank, "A revolutionary."

A revolutionary. What did such a person look like? Would they all be arrested? It was with some interest that Rosa now looked up as the speaker entered the room.

Peter Suvorin spoke well. At first, his thin, abstracted face, small gold-rimmed spectacles, and quiet, kindly eyes might have given him the appearance of a mild-mannered schoolmaster. But soon it was this very gentleness and simple sincerity—combined with a wonderful clarity in all his explanations—that made him impressive.

At thirty-seven, Peter Suvorin had not changed. He was one of those pure and fortunate souls who, having encountered a single and powerful idea, find their destiny. Peter's idea, the theme of his life, was very simple: that mankind could—and must—reach a state where all men are free and none oppressed. He had believed it in 1874 and he believed it now.

He had had a strange life. Back in 1874, after his sudden departure from Russka, he had wandered in the Ukraine for months, and the Suvorins had wondered if he had died. Then, however, needing money, he had contacted his brother Vladimir in Moscow; and Vladimir, feeling he must, had let old Savva know that his grandson was alive.

Was it, perhaps, Savva Suvorin who had sealed Peter's fate? According to his lights, the old man had been forgiving. For the letter he had seen, supposedly written by Peter and confessing to the fire, had been a terrible blow to the old man. For months afterwards, in secret, he would mutter to himself: "To attack his own family!" It would have been hard to say whether this treachery, or the accidental killing of the two young people, shocked him more; and he was so shaken that he never told anyone, including Vladimir, about it. Now, therefore, when news of Peter came, Savva sent him a strongly worded message: return at once to make amends for his terrible crimes, it said, or be cut off from the family forever. It seemed to Savva that he was acting with forbearance. And he was shocked still further when, having received the message with a groan, Peter refused to return. "His heart is hardened into sin," the old man declared, and never spoke of the young man again. Six months later he died.

The will of Savva Suvorin was clear. The dangerous revolutionary Peter was cut out of all control of the Suvorin enterprises and left with only a modest allowance. "You could contest it," Vladimir told him frankly. "Or I'll give you part of my fortune myself." But Peter was young and proud. "Besides, I want no part of it anyway," he said. He returned to Moscow and his studies. He fell in love but was rejected. He discovered a talent for physics, studied the subject deeply, and even wrote a small textbook on the subject that was published successfully. He told himself that he was happy enough. And he continued, steadfastly, to look for a better world.

He came to Marxism in the 1880s. Ever since his first meeting with Popov, he had become a student of revolutionary thought. He had several times encountered Popov again, and that secretive fellow had put him in touch with certain radical groups; but to all these people he was seen as a kindly dreamer. In Marxism, however, he had found a system that gave him more stature. Here was his longed-for utopia, but scientifically arrived at—not by some violent, conspiratorial overthrow, but by a gradual and natural historical process. "You call my views utopian," he would say to Vladimir, "but I just call it human progress." And in his heart he secretly believed that one day the Suvorin factories would pass into the hands of the workers with scarcely a shot fired.

Strangely it was his early interest in Marxism that had convinced the tsarist authorities that the mild-mannered professor was harmless to the state. That very year a senior official had privately conveyed the government's attitude to Vladimir Suvorin himself.

"My dear fellow, as long as your brother sticks to studying Marx we're not very worried. We've looked at all these things, you know," he added wisely. "This Marx was an economist. We've even allowed some of his works to be translated and published—because right or wrong, no one can understand a word of him anyway. It's revolutionaries we're worried about, not economists—and I can't see your brother throwing any bombs, can you?"

It was a strange relationship between the brothers—the rich industrialist and the poor professor, the family man and the lonely bachelor. They were fond of each other, but some strain was inevitable. Nor was it helped by the fact that Vladimir's handsome young second wife, who loved to entertain in the great Moscow house, could not help feeling rather sorry for this kindly man whom she regarded as a poor unfortunate. "Peter should marry," she would tell Vladimir. "But I'm afraid he's too timid." Peter sensed her feelings and it hurt his pride. He did not go to the Suvorin house often.

This evening's meeting was small, but Peter Suvorin believed it was important, and he was especially anxious it should go well. As he spoke, therefore, he tried to gauge the reaction of the audience carefully. With admirable precision, he outlined for these young people the developments in Europe. Only three years before, an important socialist conference, the Second International, had been held for delegates from many countries. The last year had seen, for the first time, groups of workers in Russia celebrating May Day as a token of solidarity with the international workers' movement. "And these things, in their infancy now, will shape the future of civilization in generations to come," he assured them.

Only when he was sure he had them with him did Peter Suvorin broach the real subject that was on his mind, and the reason why he had been so anxious to address them that night. Which was that they were Jewish.

He began carefully, and subtly, by alluding to some of their grievances: for in recent years the tsarist government, for reasons never explained, had undoubtedly turned vigorously against the Jewish community and treated them shabbily. Jews had been forbidden to buy land and told they must only live in towns; education quotas were being applied against them so that only a miserably small percentage of students in higher education could be Jews, even in the big cities in the Pale. And the laws of the Pale were suddenly being enforced with such viciousness that the previous year some seventeen thousand Jews had been thrown out of Moscow. Worse yet were the repeated outbreaks of violence since the pogroms of 1881, which the government had done little to prevent.

It was hardly surprising therefore if in recent years the Jewish workers had begun to think of setting up their own workers' committees, quite independent of the others. Peter could hardly blame them. But this was exactly what he was anxious to combat.

"The workers of the world must unite," he told them. "All groups, all nations shall be one." He saw this vision so clearly. "And besides," he warned them, "as part of a larger movement, your voice will be much stronger than it ever would be as a separate group."

They listened to him politely; but he could see they were uncertain. And then a tousle-haired young man near the front quietly addressed him. "You say we should remain part of a larger brotherhood. Well and good. But what are we to do if our non-Jewish brothers refuse to defend us? What then?"

It was the question Peter had been awaiting. For it was true, he knew, that Russian workers had mixed feelings about their Jewish brothers. In Russia proper, they were foreigners; in the Pale, they were competition; and there were even activists and socialists who had failed to stand up against the pogroms for fear of alienating the workers they were trying to win over to their cause.

Peter was too honest to deny the problem; but it was a phase that would pass, he assured the young man. "Remember, we are at the very first beginnings," he said. "Even many of the activist workers have to be educated; but as the great brotherhood develops in size and consciousness, this problem will fall away. And," he added, "you will speed that process by staying on the inside, not by splitting off."

There was a long pause. He was not sure if he had convinced the young man or not. Some other questions followed.

It was just as the meeting was about to end that the girl stood up. She had been sitting towards the back, just behind a large youth, and he had only been aware of a mass of black hair. Now, suddenly, she was staring at him, with huge, luminous eyes, and a look of genuine puzzlement on her face.

And indeed, Rosa Abramovich was puzzled. She had listened intently to all that Peter Suvorin had said. She had caught his vision of the great sweep of human history and the better world to come, and it had touched her profoundly: she had never heard anyone speak like that before. Yet when she considered her own life, and her memories of what had passed in the Ukraine, there was something she found she could not understand. And so now, she faced him a little awkwardly and asked in a soft voice: "But when the new world comes, when the socialist state has been achieved, will that mean that the Jews are not persecuted anymore—that men will have changed?"

Peter stared at her. It was a question of such dazzling stupidity that, for a moment, he had not known what to say. Was she trying to be funny? No. As he gazed at her large, serious eyes and pale face, it was obvious that she was entirely sincere. What a striking-looking girl she was. He smiled. "I'm afraid you haven't understood," he said kindly. "In a socialist worker state, all men will be equal. The persecution of minorities is inconceivable." And seeing her looking doubtful: "Come to me after the meeting. I'll recommend you some books to read."

Rosa sat down. Someone was saying something, but she did not hear. Did she believe the professor? She had no idea. But one thing she did know. He was the most beautiful-looking man she had ever seen in her life.

The courtship of Peter Suvorin and Rosa Abramovich was not long. For from their first meeting it seemed as if they had known each other all their lives.

"He's almost twice your age," her brothers warned her.

"He's a revolutionary; and he's not Jewish," her mother protested. And then, more hurtfully: "Remember your father, Rosa, before you do this thing."

Rosa had loved three men in her life. One, she now understood, was the Cossack boy Ivan Karpenko. Of course, it was only a childhood affection, followed by a friendship conducted by letter. Yet as she grew older and wiser, this innocent childhood love came to seem more and not less important to her. The other man had been a conductor she had watched from afar when she was fifteen, and never spoken to. And now Peter Suvorin. None of them, as it happened, had been Jewish.

What was it that so moved her about Peter Suvorin? Was it his mind? His brilliant mastery of economic theory fascinated her, even if she could not always follow it. He seemed to possess a system that explained all the complex problems of the world. But there was also a purity about him, a passionate idealism that she loved. He was a pilgrim soul, an outsider, a sufferer. He was a bachelor who, in all these years, had never found a woman worthy to be his wife.

As for Peter, he was astounded to find himself with this magical, poetic creature who had somehow dropped from the sky into his life. True, she was Jewish; but she was one of a kind. And besides, he told himself, I really have no one in the world I have to please but myself.

If Peter felt he had begun his life again, to Rosa it seemed that her own existence had suddenly been resolved. She had a purpose now. Even her health started to improve dramatically. And though she loved her mother and revered the memory of her father, she found she could no longer think as they had. She had seen too much of the younger generation, her brothers' friends. Many of them scarcely went to the synagogue at all. "Why should I ruin my life, which has been unhappy, for the sake of religion, which has brought me no comfort," she once burst out to her mother, who was berating her. "I won't do it. I don't care anymore." She was in love. Nothing else seemed to matter.

"You are leaving me," her mother told her bitterly. "I will have nothing to do with it."

"She'll get over it," her brothers counseled.

It was in September that Rosa left with Peter for Moscow. But it was a short while later, just before they married, that Rosa took one further step. She accepted baptism into the Russian Orthodox Church. "You know it means nothing," she wrote to her brothers. "But it makes things easier in Moscow, especially if there are children. I suppose we shall have to tell Mother," she added, doubtfully.

A month later, when she finally heard of it, Rosa's mother quietly summoned her friends to sit *shivah* with her. She herself had sat, only two weeks before, with an old couple whose son had become an atheist and a socialist. "She is dead to me now," she announced sadly.

Her sons refused to take part, though they tried to comfort her. But her friends understood.

1905   July

YOUNG Ivan worshiped his uncle Boris. Uncle Boris knew everything.

He was head of the family now. Timofei and his wife had died in the plague of '91; old Arina a year later. He had a large family, some of them already full grown; and to these he added his little sister Arina, whose husband had died young, and her six-year-old son, Ivan.

The news that his uncle Boris had given the boy was certainly exciting. "This year, little Ivan, is the most important year in the history of Russia. And do you know why? Because the revolution has begun."

The revolution. It was certainly an exciting word, but the boy was not certain what it meant. "It means," his uncle explained, "that we are going to kick the Bobrovs out and take all the land for ourselves. What do you think of that?" And little Ivan had to agree that this sounded wonderful indeed.

He knew that his mother Arina liked the Bobrovs, and not everyone in the village spoke badly of them. But Uncle Boris was always right. "Long live the revolution!" he cried, to please his uncle.

The extraordinary events of 1905 had been brewing for a long time. If the reign of Alexander III had been one of reaction, the last eleven years under his unimaginative son Nicholas II and his German wife had been a sorry continuation of almost everything that was dull and oppressive in the former reign. Indeed, sometimes it almost seemed as if the unfortunate Tsar Nicholas was deliberately looking for people to oppress. For nearly a century, the people of Finland had been an autonomous duchy within the empire; now, suddenly, the government had decided to Russify them, as it had the Ukraine, with the result that now the Finns were rioting. In the Ukraine, meanwhile, there had been a peasant uprising, and in 1903 a terrible pogrom. Meanwhile the government, frightened and determined to control everything, had become almost irrational. For no reason, there was a sudden clampdown on the universities; and when students protested they were treated like political agitators and sent into the army. It had even alienated the last supporters who might have helped them, by curtailing the work of the liberal gentry in the *zemstvos*.

Police spies were everywhere. So tangled had the government's system of supervision become, that in order to prove himself to the terrorists he had infiltrated, a government agent had been forced to shoot the minister of the interior! Illegal political parties were forming.

True, there were bright spots. Under the brilliant finance minister, Sergei Witte, Russia's railways and heavy industry had made great strides. The Trans-Siberian line reached as far as the Pacific now. Foreign capital was pouring in, especially from France. But these developments, important though they were, hardly as yet meant a great deal to the ordinary people, and indeed, in recent years, there had even been a mild economic depression.

But the cause of the cataclysm, when it came, was the war.

It was the same story as before, when Russia had so disastrously become involved in the Crimea. This time it was in the Far East, where the Trans-Siberian Railway had caused Russia to extend her influence, bullying the Chinese and coming into conflict with Japanese interest in the region. Overconfident in her army and navy, the mighty land empire had allowed herself to get into a war with the little island nation. And now she had been catastrophically beaten.

It was humiliating. Month after month, news came of Russian failure. Russian troops, fighting a distant war that neither they nor their families understood, were suffering appalling casualties. The cost of the war had caused economic chaos. There was a famine. And the government had not a friend. Even the Temporary Regulations—the martial law still in force since 1881!—were useless to contain the situation. The liberal gentry of *zemstvos* begged the tsar to grant the people an assembly.

And then, in January of that year, had come Bloody Sunday.

This incident—the spark which, most believe, ignited the great Russian conflagration—was a strange and confused affair. The demonstration, led by a Ukrainian priest and demanding only the redress of grievances, wound its way in some confusion through the frozen streets of Saint Petersburg. The massacre did not, as always portrayed, take place in front of the Winter Palace. (The tsar, in any case, was not in the city that day.) But in one of several incidents, frightened soldiers fired upon the crowd, causing the deaths of a number of people at the city's Narva Gate.

And then all hell broke loose. The liberal *zemstvos* protested at the outrage. Strikes broke out. With consummate foolishness, the government closed the universities, leaving the student population on the streets with nothing to do. Every dissatisfied group in the empire, sensing a looming crisis, saw its chance to protest. There were riots in Finland, the Baltic states, and Poland, as well as in Russia proper. By summer, police records detailed 492 significant disturbances. The huge textile mills at Ivanovo, north of Vladimir, were in an uproar. In journals and leaflets circulating in the cities, revolutionary articles began to appear under a pseudonym that until then had been known only in revolutionary circles: V. I. Lenin. During May and June came yet more crushing news from the East: the whole Russian fleet had been sunk. Soon after this, down at the Black Sea port of Odessa, the Russian battleship *Potemkin* had mutinied.

What was the government to do? The police could not cope; the army was mostly in the East, defeated and beyond recall. All Russia waited.

And now little Ivan was in a fever of excitement. What was happening at Russka?

Until that morning, the town and the Suvorin factory had remained quiet. But just before noon, a man returning from the town reported: "Something is going on there in the weaving shops." By midafternoon word came: "It's a strike." And soon afterwards three girls from the village who worked at the cotton mill appeared and reported: "they told us to go home." And by these signs little Ivan understood that the revolution had come to Russka.

It was late that afternoon, however, that his uncle Boris began to behave strangely.

Alexander Bobrov was still brooding irritably as he entered the market-place at Russka that day.

He was a handsome, fair-haired boy, just fourteen, with the first faint down of a mustache on his upper lip. He had hurried towards the town as soon as he heard about the trouble. But not before certain words had passed between him and his father—words that could not be unsaid. Which was why he was still frowning when he reached the town. Why couldn't he control himself?

They were a strange couple, father and son: so alike in looks, yet mentally so different. I suppose, Nicolai had thought, as he gazed at the boy that morning, some people are just born conservative.

The sad death of Nicolai's older son some years before had left Alexander as his only heir now, and the boy took his position very seriously. A religious fellow, he liked to go to church with his grandmother Anna and was extremely proud of his family's ancient connection with the monarchy. Above all, he was eager to take over the estate: and this, for a long time, had been the source of the tension between them.

How well Nicolai remembered his own disgust with his father Misha's handling of the estate; now it was his turn. Had he done any better? No. The Riazan estate, bit by bit, had gone; he had had numerous offers for pieces of the remaining woodlands and pastures at Russka—one from the village commune, and two, for small parcels, from Boris Romanov. But each time he had refused because of the protest of his mother Anna and young Alexander. Now, he knew, he could not hold out much longer.

"The fact is," he would say, "since the Emancipation there hasn't been enough land for the peasants or for me." His fate was not uncommon: half the landowners he knew had sold their estates in recent years, as the Russian nobility slipped into its final decline. But it was no use telling that to young Alexander.

And even this shortcoming was nothing compared to Nicolai's latest crime. "For why," his son had accused, "are the workers making these wicked demands of the tsar? It's because of the *zemstvos,* Father—because of you."

Nicolai knew that he should have chastised the boy for such impertinence. Yet as he looked at his son standing there with indignant tears in his eyes, he couldn't bring himself to. For the fact was, the charge was perfectly true. It had been last year, even before the troubles broke out, that he and the other liberal men of the *zemstvo* councils had met in Saint Petersburg and drafted their proposal to the tsar, asking for an elected assembly, a parliament, to help govern the nation. How heady and exciting those meetings had been. Some present had declared that it was like the meeting of the Estates General before the French Revolution; and Nicolai himself had suddenly felt the same wonderful exaltation he had briefly known as a student, during the Going to the People, thirty years ago. If my son's a born conservative, I suppose I'm a born radical, he thought with a smile. And it was certainly true that when the troubles broke out after Bloody Sunday, the workers and revolutionaries, having no prepared political plan, had simply taken over the demands of the *zemstvo* men and demanded an elected assembly. And how much it says about our backward Russia, Nicolai reflected, that even now, in the year 1905, for the people to demand a vote in their country's affairs is seen by the government as little short of treason.

It was certainly treason to young Alexander. For that was what the boy, in a flood of tears, had called back at his father as he rushed out of the room: "Traitor!"

Alexander was halfway across the market square when he saw a familiar figure: and at once he smiled. It was Vladimir Suvorin.

The relationship between the young noble and the industrialist was very simple. The industrialist was Alexander's hero. Suvorin had hardly changed with the years: he was slightly heavier; there was a just perceptible graying at the temples; but as long as Alexander could remember, his robust and perfectly tended figure had always been the same. It was not only Suvorin's extraordinary charm that captivated the boy; nor was it his great culture, of which Alexander was only dimly aware. The figure that the boy saw at Russka was the practical man of affairs: and above all, he was a conservative.

Though he took little interest in politics, it was almost inevitable that Vladimir Suvorin should be a conservative. Knowing young Alexander's tsarist loyalties, he used to laugh and say: "You must not give me too much credit, my friend. It's only self-interest that makes me love the tsar."

Sometimes Suvorin would try to enlighten the boy. "The tsars have always seen the larger merchants as arms of the state, to make Russia strong," he would explain. "Peter the Great just taxed the great merchants into bankruptcy; but later administrations have been more intelligent, and nowadays they give us government contracts and protect us from outside competition with tariffs." Once or twice, trying to give the boy a better appreciation of the world as it really was, he would caution him: "Russian industry mostly prospers, Alexander, by exporting raw materials and by selling manufactured goods, usually of rather inferior quality, to our own huge empire and to the poorer countries of the East. So the tsar and his empire are good for me. That's all." But even these blunt explanations did little to modify Alexander's view of Russia or his hero. Suvorin supported the tsar. That was all that mattered. And it amused the older man, in a bluff way, to rest a large hand on the boy's shoulder and remark: "My grandfather was your grandfather's serf, my friend. But I don't mind if you don't."

When Alexander caught up with him, Suvorin was walking towards the cotton mill. He nodded briefly as the youth fell into step beside him. "It is really a strike?" young Bobrov asked.

"Yes." The industrialist seemed quite calm.

"What will you do?" Alexander whispered. "Call in the Cossacks?" He knew several strikes had already been broken up by the dashing Cossack cavalry squadrons. But to his surprise, Suvorin shook his head. "I'm not such a fool," he replied.

For half an hour they walked around various parts of the Suvorin enterprise—the mill, the weaving looms, the dormitories. All the machines lay idle, but there was no sign of other trouble. The workers were mostly standing around in groups, talking quietly, and as Suvorin went by, he exchanged polite greetings with them. "The strike's not against me or the working conditions, you see," he explained to Alexander in a low voice. "This is different. People from outside have come and persuaded them to strike in sympathy. They're demanding political reforms." He smiled ruefully. "Calling in the Cossacks would only make things worse."

Alexander groaned. "It's those *zemstvo* men, like my father, isn't it?" he muttered. "They've stirred up all this trouble."

But to Alexander's surprise, Suvorin shook his head firmly. "Don't blame your father," he replied. "Wait." And for several more minutes he said nothing.

Only when they were outside in the warm and dusty street did Suvorin explain. Taking the boy by the arm, he walked up and down with him, speaking quietly but with conviction. "You don't understand what is happening, my friend. Do you know the story of the emperor who had no clothes? Well, that's what is happening to the tsar now. Think of it. Russia is huge, inchoate, disorganized. A vast land of peasants where a semblance of order is maintained by an autocratic tsar, his army and police, and a few privileged persons like you who have few links with the people. But the whole state is a huge sham—don't you see? Because— this is the key—*no one has any real power.* The tsar has no power because his army is in the east and he has no true link with his people. The government is not for the people, it's against them. You and your father have no power: you depend upon the tsar for all your privileges. I have no power: I depend upon the tsar to maintain order and protect my business. The people have no power, because they have no organization, and no idea what they want anyway." He shrugged. "The present crisis shows that the tsar is actually unable to lead our society or to control it. The emperor has no clothes. And in this huge mess we call the empire, it will only take one spark to set off a huge fire. We could have a revolt any day, that would make the Pugachev look like a tea party. Total, mindless chaos." Suvorin sighed. "That's why I'm being careful."

"So what can the tsar do?"

"Head them off. The only organized forces out there are two. There are the unions, still forming, and except for the railway men all professionals—the doctors, teachers, and lawyers. And there are the *zemstvo* men like your father—the only people with a program. The tsar has to come to terms with them and hope that the people will quiet down. The longer he takes, the worse it will be."

"But what about the tsar and Holy Russia?" he cried. "The peasants believe in that."

Suvorin smiled. "They do on Feast Days, I daresay," he replied. "But only two people believe in Holy Russia every day of the year."

"Who are they?"

"The tsar himself, my young friend. Just the tsar." He grinned. "And you!" He liked to tease the boy.

It was as they continued their walk around the town that Alexander noticed that Suvorin seemed to be looking for something. His eyes were constantly scanning the street before him: several times he turned abruptly to glance to one side. When Alexander asked him, however, what he was searching for, the industrialist quietly smiled. "Not something, my friend. Someone." He glanced down at young Bobrov.

"Hasn't it occurred to you," Suvorin asked, "that all the time we went round inside, we saw only familiar faces. No sight of the outsiders who stirred up the trouble. But I've discovered who it is: a single man." He nodded thoughtfully. "They call him Ivanov."

"Will you arrest him?"

"No. I'd like to, but it would only create more trouble."

"Are you going to speak to him?"

"I offered to, but he avoids me. He's a cunning devil." He paused. "I'd like to get a good look at him. Just so I'd know him another time."

They continued to walk. They strolled to the little park by Suvorin's house and gazed down from the parapet over the woodlands and river below. Then they went back, past the church, into the market square. And then they saw him.

He was standing about a hundred yards away talking to a group of men and, for a moment, he was not aware that Suvorin and the boy were watching him. He was an unusual figure. One might have guessed he was in his late forties. His face was clean-shaven and marked by two deep lines that curved down his cheeks from the outer corner of each eye. There was a slight puffiness around the eyes themselves. And his head was covered with close-cropped orange-red hair. "So that's him," Suvorin murmured. "What a curious-looking fellow." He would certainly know him again.

A moment later, the stranger caught sight of them and slipped away.

Alexander, too, took careful note of the face. So this, he thought, is the face of the enemy. For some reason he had a feeling that he might see him again.

Little Ivan watched his uncle Boris, fascinated. His uncle had not seen him enter the passage and was unaware of his presence.

Only a few minutes had passed since Boris had been talking to the man from the Suvorin factory outside. He had seemed quite casual then. "A ginger-haired fellow, eh? Well, I never. About my age. Who did you say he was? Ivanov, eh? Never heard of him. And where did you say this fellow was staying? Out of Suvorin's way, I suppose. Ah yes. Just outside the town. Well, well. Good luck to him and to you all."

Yet there was nothing calm about his uncle now. Little Ivan had never seen him so excited as he paced up and down the big storeroom muttering to himself. "Ivanov indeed. It's that devil. That ginger-headed devil. Murderer. This time I'll get you, though. I'll not miss you this time. Ah, my poor Natalia."

He was muttering so vehemently that little Ivan was rather frightened. After a minute or two he slipped out again. But whatever could it mean?

It was unusual for Uncle Boris to go out hunting on a summer night, and especially to walk for miles. But tonight, for some reason, was an exception.

"I'm going down south to the marshes," he remarked blandly. "Find myself a good spot and see what the dawn brings." The nights were short and warm. All kinds of game came over the marshes in the early morning. Dusk saw Boris preparing his gun cheerfully. Before he went, Ivan saw him slip a large hunting knife into his belt. "Can't I come too?" he had begged; but Boris had just ruffled his hair and remarked, "Next time." Then as night fell, he had taken his boat and paddled away towards the south.

It was only some time later, when she was putting him to bed, that the little boy had told his mother Arina about Uncle Boris's strange behavior and asked, "Who was Natalia?"

How oddly people were behaving that evening. Why had his mother turned so pale, then tried to hide it? And why, having told him to go to sleep and that she was going to join the rest of the family at a neighbor's, had she instead slipped silently out of the village?

He had watched her out of the window. She had gone up the slope, towards the Bobrov house.

But if all these things were puzzling to little Ivan, the scene the next morning was terrible.

The dawn had just been breaking when he had awoken and gone outside; and he had just been enjoying the first, tentative sounds of the birds when his uncle had appeared, walking through the gloom. He could see that his uncle was furious about something, but it seemed that the fury was not directed at him: for Uncle Boris had even smiled as he paused to exchange a few words.

"Anyone go up to the Bobrovs' last night?" The question was asked so casually, so easily, that the little fellow had not even thought as he answered.

"Only Mama."

And now, as the family stood before him in the *izba,* Boris Romanov was trembling with rage.

"You warned him, didn't you?"

Arina quailed; yet even now, there was a hint of righteous defiance in her manner. "What if I did?"

"What if you did? I'll tell you what." And with a sudden spring he was upon her, knocking her down and hitting her twice, hard, in the face. "You stupid cow! You Mordvinian!"

"Don't! Don't!" the little boy screamed, rushing to protect his mother.

But Boris picked him up and tossed him across the room so that he crashed into a bench and lay there, half-stunned.

Damn Arina; damn the witch. Having taken his boat a little way downriver, Boris had hidden it on the far bank, then doubled back and walked through the darkness into Russka. At dead of night, armed with his long hunting knife, he had crept around the edge of the town to the house where that accursed ginger-headed villain had been staying. It was a warm night. Two men were sitting outside the door of the house opposite; he had waited, patiently, in the shadows for them to go inside. At last they had slowly risen to go. One door had shut. Then another. He had let a minute pass in silence. He had smiled to himself. He would place his hand over Popov's mouth, then slit his throat, whispering his name as he did so. "Remember Natalia." That would be it. Just so the devil knew—just so he understood, as he went down, into the depths. With a bit of luck, they'll suppose one of Suvorin's men did it and arrest him, too, he thought cheerfully. Revenge—even if one had to wait thirty years—was so infinitely sweet.

And then, suddenly, two horses, pounding along the little road. One with a rider, the other spare. What the devil? The two horses pulling up sharply by the very house where Popov lay. The rider springing down and hammering on the door.

"Yevgeny Pavlovich! Popov, damn you! I know it's you. You've got to get out. Listen, it's Nicolai Mikhailovich, come quick."

Bobrov. How the devil did he know? Who tipped him off? And why should he save the fellow's skin anyway? Damn them all. They were all in league. And now when would he get his chance at revenge again?

He turned back to his sister.

"You traitor!" he bellowed. "Do you know what you've done?"

"Yes," she cried back with equal rage. "I asked Bobrov to stop you. What of it? You can't go round killing people."

"Not if he killed my own sister?"

"No."

He glowered at her. "I see you're a friend of Bobrov and the redhead," he said, suddenly quiet. "But I promise you one thing: I shan't forget this."

And both Arina, and the terrified little Ivan, knew that he would not.

It was two days later that an unexplained fire burned down a section of Nicolai Bobrov's woods. People took it to be one more sign that the revolution was getting very near.

1906   May

It was early evening, and over the great Moscow house, preparations were under way. Indeed, there was more than the usual air of expectation among the servants, for this evening, they knew, some very strange guests were due to arrive. But then, they reflected, after the extraordinary events of the last year, anything might be expected.

In the comfortable upstairs room, however, everything was quiet. Mrs. Suvorin, in a long, mauve silk gown, her heavy, rich brown hair only loosely pinned so that perhaps, at any moment, it might tumble down her elegant back, was sitting writing letters at a little desk.

Her daughter Nadezhda was sitting on a French empire chair, with a tapestry cover. In front of her was a small round table covered with a heavy, tasseled cloth upon which she was resting her elbows, while gazing at her mother.

She is certainly a handsome woman, Nadezhda thought, but I should make Papa a much better wife. Which was, perhaps, a rather strange thought for a little girl of eight.

The first thing people noticed about Nadezhda Suvorin was her auburn hair. She was allowed to wear it long and loose so that it fell in lustrous masses over her shoulders to her elbows. In a taffeta dress, silk stockings, shoes with satin ribbons, and a big, wide-brimmed hat from under which her hair poured down, she looked enchanting. And then people would notice her eyes. They were deep brown, and they knew everything.

It was amazing what Nadezhda knew. Yet how should it be otherwise? Fate had decreed that her brother should be older: by the time she was six, he was already studying abroad. It was natural, therefore, that her father should turn to this bright little girl to be his companion.

She knew every painting in the great house. There were the contemporary Russians—wonderful natural evocations of the country by Repin, Surikov, Seron, Levitan. Levitan had done a huge landscape of Russka—a haunting vision of the little town on its high bank, seen from across the river under a deep blue sky full of retreating clouds. In the dining room hung portraits of her mother by Repin and her father by Vrubel. But her greatest delight was to take visitors through the rooms reserved for Vladimir's collection of European painters, which was dazzling; and middle-aged Russians who were scarcely familiar with such wonders themselves would be astonished as she prattled: "This is a Monet; here's

Cezanne. Renoir's nudes always seem to have the same two faces, don't you think?" Or: "This is by Gauguin. He ran away from his wife and children and went to live in Tahiti." On his last trip to Paris, her father had even brought back small pictures by two new artists: Picasso and Matisse. "These are just getting started, so I bought them for you," he had told her.

Vladimir delighted in taking this bright little person with him and showing her his world. As a patron of the arts he went everywhere and knew everyone. Already she had been to Saint Petersburg and seen the great Pavlova dance; she had visited the great Tolstoy at his Moscow house; at the Moscow Arts Theater, which Vladimir helped support, she knew all the actors and she had even met the playwright Chekhov. When she had been unimpressed by this modest man with his pince-nez, compared to the leonine figure of the great novelist, her father had told her: "Never judge by appearances, Nadezhda. For Chekhov is great also. It's what people do that matters." Which had caused her several times to demand, quite innocently, of distinguished old gentlemen visiting the house—"Now tell me, Ivan Ivanovich, what exactly you have done"—to their great confusion and Vladimir's huge amusement.

Only one thing puzzled little Nadezhda. Why was her mother often cool towards her father? To the outside world they seemed devoted, but the sharp-eyed child knew better. It was her, not her mother, that Vladimir took out: she had watched him approach her in private and seen her gracefully drawing away. It was very strange. And no wonder therefore if the girl considered: I should look after him better.

It was now, having finished her letter, that Mrs. Suvorin turned and stood up.

She was indeed a striking woman. With her tall, powerful body, her head thrown proudly back, and her brown eyes gazing, apparently, down upon the world, she seemed more like a member of one of the princely families than a merchant's wife. When men looked at Mrs. Suvorin, however—as they always did—it was the fine points of color on her cheeks, the creamy flesh of her wonderful, sloping shoulders, her splendid, rather low breasts that they noticed, while becoming instantly conscious of the powerful, controlled sensuousness that her elegance did not trouble to conceal. If she'd let me, strong men thought, I could make that body glow; while others, less certain of themselves, could only muse: Now, that, my God, would take a proper man. A few, more poetic, thought they saw in those proud eyes a hint of sadness; but then, watching her in her drawing room, it was hard to know whether this might not be just an element of her art. One thing in any case was certain: Mrs. Suvorin was in full bloom of her maturity.

As she rose, Mrs. Suvorin noticed Nadezhda's eyes fixed upon her, and she gazed at her daughter thoughtfully, before nodding to herself.

It would have surprised Nadezhda to know that her mother understood very well what was passing in her mind. Indeed, she had guessed it all long ago, and it made her feel guilty. But as she looked at the girl's accusing eyes, she could only sigh inwardly and reflect that there were things about her life that she could not explain to Nadezhda. Perhaps when the child was older. Perhaps never. At least, she thought sadly, whatever my faults, I am discreet.

"I must dress now," she remarked briskly.

It promised to be an interesting evening. For these were certainly astonishing times.

Young Alexander Bobrov could only gasp. Of course, he had always known that his hero Suvorin was rich. "He's a director of the Merchant's Society and the Commercial Bank, you know," his father had explained. "He's one of the elite." And his name matched his position, being one of the half dozen former princely palaces which had, in recent decades, passed into the hands of the new merchant magnates like Suvorin who had supplanted them in power.

Since they had special business to conduct, they had come a little before the other guests, and now as they awaited him, young Alexander stared around the huge room to which they had been shown.

It was very long, high and vaulted like a church. Down the center, on an immense oriental carpet, ran a massive table covered with a green cloth upon which, he supposed, a hundred people could easily have stood. Above, three huge brass chandeliers lit what would otherwise have been a cavernous gloom, and caused the golden patterns inlaid in the vaulting to glow. Around the sides of the room, stout upright chairs and tables of dark wood were lined. Heavy, opulent, almost oppressive, it was like the palace of some tsar from ancient Muscovy. But most astonishing of all were the walls: the paintings were hung so densely that their frames touched. Russian scenes, Impressionists, historical paintings—their brilliant colors blazed out like new-made icons.

One of these, just above Alexander, especially caught his attention. It was a large historical picture of Ivan the Terrible. The mighty tsar was standing in a long robe of gold brocade edged with fur; in his hand was a heavy staff; and his fearsome eyes were glaring down accusingly, straight at Nicolai Bobrov. As well they might, thought Alexander, considering his father's disgraceful errand.

For Nicolai had come to sell the merchant his estate.

It wasn't really his fault. He couldn't hold out any longer. He was in good company, too. Since the troubles had begun in the countryside last year, landowners all over Russia had been selling off. Suvorin, moreover, had offered him an excellent price for the place. "More than it's worth," he reminded his furious son. But now, seeing the boy's miserable face, he looked down awkwardly at the long table and muttered, "I'm sorry."

Vladimir Suvorin did not keep them waiting long. He swept into the room with his lawyer, embraced Nicolai warmly, gave Alexander's arm a friendly squeeze, and in a moment the papers were all on the table before them.

Suvorin was in a good mood. He had long considered having a country retreat near his factories at Russka. In recent years, also, he had become interested in Russian crafts. "I'm going to set up some workshops for woodcarving and pottery on the estate," he had told Nicolai. "And a little museum for folk art, too." Now, seeing the father and son standing gloomily before him, he understood perfectly what was passing in their minds.

"Your father's made a wise decision," he said firmly to Alexander. "Though I want the estate for my museum, I shan't be able to make it pay any more than he could." He smiled. "All the wise men are selling, my friends, and only fools like me are buying." Turning back to Nicolai, he remarked, "Naturally, my friend, I rather envy you. You're free as a bird now. You should make a tour of Europe. All the Russians are doing it, and nobles like you are treated with great respect in Paris and Monte Carlo. You should show your son the world."

But even these kindly words failed to draw a smile from Alexander. Not that he felt any resentment towards the industrialist—quite the reverse. All he knew was this: the Bobrovs had held estates as long as Russia had existed; his father, with his liberal ideas, had lost them. His father had failed in his duty. And looking with renewed admiration at Suvorin, he thought once more: How I wish you were my father.

But now Vladimir was beckoning. "Enough of business, my friends. It is time to meet our other guests."

Mrs. Suvorin's entertaining was justly famous. Everyone came to her house. Artists, musicians, and writers were especially welcome. But the aristocracy did not disdain the merchant's hospitality and even a proud Saint Petersburg sophisticate like Prince Shcherbatov was a regular visitor. The Suvorin influence spread everywhere—theaters, journals, art schools. Even a strange young man named Diaghilev, who seemed to want to make himself a one-man ambassador for Russian art and culture, found patronage and encouragement in the Suvorin house. Indeed, of Russia's celebrities, perhaps only Tolstoy, for some reason, had never come there.

Mrs. Suvorin liked her guest list to have a theme, and this evening was no exception.

"Tonight," Vladimir had murmured to Nicolai Bobrov as they went into the huge salon, "will be all about politics."

It was certainly appropriate. The political events of the last nine months had been astonishing. All the previous summer the situation had grown worse while the tsar delayed. There had been constant terrorist acts, and industrial trouble. "Why the devil won't he listen to the *zemstvos?*" Nicolai would fume. But still the tsar delayed. And then, in October, the unthinkable had happened. There had been a general strike. For ten terrible days, as winter approached, nothing had moved in the entire Russian empire. The government had been completely powerless. "Either we shall have reform," Nicolai had declared, "or we're all going to die." And then at last the tsar had given way. He would grant the people a parliament—the duma. "At last," Nicolai had explained, "that poor man has seen some sense. We'll have a constitutional monarchy, like England. We'll be civilized, like the West."

Except that this was Russia.

The first duma of the Russian state was organized as follows: Elections were held in which most Russian men could vote, but they did so grouped by class, each class able to send only so many deputies. The arithmetic of this system meant that each vote of a gentleman like Bobrov was worth that of three merchants, fifteen peasants, or forty-five urban workers. At the very time when the voting was taking place, however, the government also issued a package known by the old-fashioned title of Fundamental Laws. These added a second chamber on top of the first, half appointed by the tsar and the rest selected by the most conservative elements. This effectively hamstrung the duma. "Just in case they wanted to do anything," Nicolai Bobrov commented wryly. Even if the two houses were in agreement, they still had no real control over the bureaucracy that actually ran the empire. Further, the tsar confirmed the autocracy, reserved the right to dissolve the duma at his pleasure, and affirmed that, whenever the duma was not in session, he could govern by emergency decree as he saw fit.

"In short," Nicolai had summarized, as these measures became known, "it's very Russian. It's a parliament—and it isn't. It can talk—but it can't act. The tsar gives—and the tsar takes away."

Why then, as he walked into Mrs. Suvorin's drawing room that evening, should he have been so pleased? The answer was: two simple reasons. First, the socialists had to boycott the entire proceedings, and so put up few candidates; second, the tsar's assumption that the majority of the gentry and of the peasants would be loyal and vote for conservative candidates was completely wrong. The overwhelming majority voted against the regime—and returned a large number of progressive liberals. "And do you know," Nicolai declared gleefully to his wife, "I'm not sure next time I won't stand myself." And as he entered the room, he looked about him with interest.

Mrs. Suvorin greeted him pleasantly. "I have done my work well." She smiled. "We have someone from almost every political party here."

Nicolai smiled in return. It was typical of the situation in tsarist Russia that at present almost all the political parties remained, technically, illegal. The duma was beginning its deliberations arranged in parties that, officially, did not exist!

Her claim was true. Nicolai soon identified men of impeccable right-wing credentials who wanted the duma abolished. "Friends for you," he said with a grin to his son. There were conservative liberals who wanted the duma to cooperate with the tsar; and there were men like himself, Constitutional Democrats, known as Cadets for short, who were determined to push the tsar towards a proper democracy. "And what about the parties of the left?" he asked her.

There were two of these nowadays. There were the Socialist Revolutionaries, who represented the peasants, but some of whom were unfortunately dedicated to terrorism. "I'm short there," his hostess remarked lightly. "Though if a bomb goes off I suppose I'll know I had one after all." And there was the party of the workers, the Social Democrats. "And there I have done better. Come and meet my brother-in-law, Professor Peter Suvorin."

Peter and Rosa Suvorin did not often come to his brother's huge house. Not that they were unwelcome: the two brothers were fond of each other; but their ways had long parted. Rosa and Mrs. Suvorin had little to say to each other, and Peter found that there was a subtle patronage towards him in her manner that plainly said: "I shall be charming, of course, but you are a poor, unfortunate creature." Indeed, but for one circumstance the two families might scarcely have met at all: and this was the friendship of their children.

Three children had been born to Rosa, but only one had lived: Dimitri, a dark-haired little boy three years Nadezhda's senior. They had first met one Christmas when Nadezhda was three, and had at once taken a liking to each other. Since the girl constantly asked for him, Dimitri was frequently invited, although for some reason Mrs. Suvorin never cared to let her daughter go to her cousin's modest house. But it seemed to please her to see the children together and she would say to Rosa, with obvious sincerity: "It's so nice for Nadezhda to have another child to play with."

But tonight Mrs. Suvorin had been positively eager to see the Marxist professor. "He is my link to all these people on the far left," she had said to her husband. "And I think it's time I came to understand them better."

She knew a little about the Social Democrats. She was aware that they had split, in recent years, into two camps, the smaller of which was the more extreme. "With typical Russian confusion," Vladimir had remarked, "the majority call themselves the little party, and the minority call themselves the big party—the Bolsheviks." Mrs. Suvorin was sure that kindly Peter must belong to the less extreme majority, but she was curious about the Bolsheviks, and a few days before she had asked him: "Do you know any of these fellows? What are they like? Could you bring one to our house?" To which Peter had replied: "I do know such a man who's in Moscow at present. But I don't suppose he'd come." "Ask him anyway," she had requested, which Peter had done.

Nicolai Bobrov was curious to meet Peter Suvorin, whom he only vaguely remembered from his youth; and the two men found they liked each other. "We Cadets," Bobrov assured him, "are going to oppose the tsar all the way until he gives us a real democracy."

"We both want that," Peter agreed pleasantly. "But we want democracy to usher in the revolution, and you want it to avoid the revolution!" In answer to Nicolai's further question, he gave his opinions of the future freely. "The workers' organization will be the key to everything now," he explained. "And the Marxist's job is to keep them political, committed to a socialist revolution when the time is ripe."

"Who will do that?" Bobrov asked.

"In the western provinces, the Jewish workers' organization, the Bund," Peter answered. He was sorry that his earlier efforts to persuade the eager young Jewish reformers not to follow their own path had failed. But he could not deny that the Jewish Bund had been solid and strong in the months of crisis; and they were good Marxists.

"And in the rest of Russia?"

Peter smiled. "The new workers' committees. They got started last year and they're very effective. Political cells in every city. They're the answer."

"What do you call them?" Nicolai asked.

"We call them soviets," the professor replied.

Nicolai shrugged. It seemed to him that if the duma did its work well, these soviets would soon be forgotten.

While they talked, he found himself, from time to time, watching his host and hostess as they moved in their separate paths about the room. There was no doubt about it, they were very good at managing these things. Mrs. Suvorin was stately. She had a knack of moving from group to group with a quiet grace that earned the respect of every woman, and left every man surreptitiously gazing after her. She flirts by not flirting, he realized. As for Vladimir, the men liked and respected him, but for the women, one could see, he had a special talent. Why was it that they seemed to flush with pleasure when he talked to them? After observing him a little while, Nicolai thought he saw. He understands the way they think, he decided. He gets inside their minds. It was another facet of his extraordinary intelligence, and Nicolai suddenly wondered: is he unfaithful to her, perhaps? He had no doubt that many women in the room would gladly have encouraged any interest Suvorin showed.

Nicolai was still musing in this manner when he noticed that Vladimir was talking to Rosa Suvorin. Nicolai also noticed that Vladimir's usual, comfortable smile had disappeared. His face wore a look of tender concern and he was speaking to her earnestly. Whatever was he saying with such urgency? Peter, too, was now looking at his wife with puzzlement. Rosa, looking suddenly very pale and tired, was shaking her head, apparently resisting him. Then, giving her arm a gentle squeeze, Vladimir moved off, while Rosa suddenly turned away towards a window. To Nicolai Bobrov, and no doubt to Peter, it seemed rather strange. And Nicolai would have thought more about it if, at this moment, something had not happened to deflect everyone's attention.

For now the door opened, and a new figure appeared. It was Yevgeny Popov.

Young Alexander Bobrov had found himself standing beside Vladimir at the moment when Popov entered and, for once, he heard even the perfectly controlled industrialist gasp with surprise.

"Well, I'm damned!" He glanced down at Alexander. "It's the fellow we saw during the strike."

It was indeed. The redheaded man they had called Ivanov. "Will you throw him out?" Alexander whispered.

"No." The industrialist smiled. "Don't you remember, my friend, I wanted to talk to him then; and now here he is. Life is wonderful indeed." And with outstretched hand he strode across the room to where the revolutionary was standing and smiled. "Welcome."

But if this action took the youth by surprise, it was nothing to his horror when, a moment later, the redhead walked over to his father, embraced him warmly, and then, when Mrs. Suvorin asked in confusion—"You two know each other?"—replied calmly: "Oh yes: we go back together a long way."

His father was a friend of this creature. It seemed to Alexander that there was no limit to his father's foolishness and disloyalty.

The little group that gathered around Popov eyed him with curiosity. Nicolai in particular, seeing his old acquaintance in this strange new setting, looked on with some amusement, while Mrs. Suvorin, gazing at his calm, rather detached expression and comparing him with her Marxist brother-in-law, quickly came to the conclusion that this was a very different sort of man: one who recognized no barriers.

"You wanted a Bolshevik," Peter said to her wryly. "Here he is."

And Mrs. Suvorin smiled.

"You are welcome indeed," she said. Which was certainly true. For, excellent though the company always was at her house, Mr. Suvorin knew that recently she had been missing out on something: the true revolutionaries.

In a later age it would be called radical chic, this fashion among some of the privileged classes of inviting revolutionaries to their home and even making contributions to their cause. A few industrialists, convinced that the tsar was on a road to catastrophe, may have courted the revolutionaries as a kind of insurance policy against the future. But others of the rich and idle certainly did so only because they thought it amusing, or smart, or perhaps to receive a little frisson from the knowledge that they were playing with fire. Mrs. Suvorin had always eschewed these activities before, but recently she had feared that, without an occasional revolutionary, her salons might begin to look a trifle dowdy. She needed Popov, therefore: he completed her arrangements.

And, it had to be said, he made himself rather agreeable. It was evident at once that he was well informed. He had recently returned from the socialists' latest congress, held in Stockholm; and while he was obviously careful about what he said, he seemed quite willing to answer questions. To Mrs. Suvorin's inquiry about the Bolsheviks he was very straightforward.

"The difference between the Bolsheviks and the rest of the Social Democrats—the Mensheviks, as we call them—is not that large. We all want a socialist society; we all follow Marx; but there are disputes about tactics." He smiled at Peter Suvorin. "And sometimes personalities." He reeled off the names of some of the Menshevik leaders: young Trotsky, Rosa Luxemburg in Poland, various others. "But it's the Bolshevik leader who really makes the split, though." He grinned. "That's my friend Lenin. He never compromises about anything."

"And who is he, this Lenin?" Nicolai Bobrov asked. "I don't know a thing about him."

"Oh, but you do." Popov smiled. "For you've already met him—fifteen years ago, on a train. Remember?"

"The lawyer? The Chuvash lawyer with an estate by the Volga?"

"One and the same. He's been living in exile most of the time. He's in hiding now, because the authorities don't seem to like him. But he's the man behind the Bolsheviks."

"And what does he want? What makes him different?"

"He writes carelessly," Popov replied, "but the key to Lenin lies in his book. That's his manifesto." And he told them a little about it.

This all-important work had been written only four years before, and smuggled into Russia from Germany; but for most revolutionaries, it had already become a bible. Choosing the same title as the little novel that had so inspired the previous generation of radicals, he had called it *What Is to Be Done*. And it was not so much a political tract as an instruction manual—on how to make a revolution. "Marxism tells us the old order will collapse." Popov smiled. "Lenin tells us how to give it a push." And then carefully: "Roughly speaking, our Menshevik friends want to wait until the masses are ready to create the socialist order of a new and just society. We Bolsheviks are skeptical. We think that a small and highly organized cadre is needed to push for the great change in society. It's only tactics: but we believe the masses will need leading, that's all."

"Some of us think," Peter Suvorin observed, "that Lenin regards the workers as nothing more than cannon fodder."

To his surprise, however, Popov only nodded. "It's probably true," he replied. Then, smiling again: "That's part of his greatness."

For a moment or two the little group was silent, digesting what Popov had said. Then Nicolai Bobrov slowly spoke. "I can see your point about the masses needing leaders, and you may be right. But isn't there a danger of such a group becoming too powerful—a sort of dictatorship?"

And to his surprise also, his Bolshevik friend was extremely frank. "Yes. It is a danger, in theory. But remember, Nicolai Mikhailovich, that the political objective we seek is not that far from yours. The only way forward for Russia, the only way to socialism, is through the people— through democracy." He paused. "Whatever else, always remember this: all socialists, including the Bolshevik faction, are trying to reach the same thing: a democratically elected body—one man, one vote—with sovereign power. We don't want to overthrow the tsar to put another tyrant in his place. We want a constituent assembly, just as you do. Democracy will lead to socialism; but democracy is the all-important means."

It was said with great seriousness and great force. And all who heard him believed.

Or so it seemed, until young Alexander Bobrov broke his silence.

He had been standing beside Vladimir Suvorin all this time, watching Popov carefully. True, he had been listening as well, but for Alexander it was not a question of argument. The redheaded Bolshevik was his enemy. He knew that in his bones. His enemy unto death. For the youth, therefore, it was only a question of observing the object of his hatred so that he might know him better.

And now the revolutionary's words had infuriated him: not because of what had been said but because, Alexander could see, the hearers had been impressed. Are they all going to be as stupid as my father, he wondered; and he had a burning urge to expose Popov, to throw down the gauntlet, and to humiliate him.

"I've heard that all the leading revolutionaries are yids," he said softly but distinctly. "Is it true?"

It was a calculated impertinence, a sort of generalized insult that those on the right liked to use—to anger Jews by calling them all revolutionaries and revolutionaries by calling them all Jews. There was a horrible, embarrassed silence.

But Popov, gazing at the boy, who was now flushing, only chuckled. "Well, of course, Trotsky and Rosa Luxemburg are both Jewish," he said. "So are several others I can think of. But so far, my friend, I have to tell you that the Jews are in a minority in our party. Mind you," he added, with a wink at Peter Suvorin, "Lenin, who's not a Slav himself, always says the only intelligent Russians are the Jewish ones. So you'll have to make what you can of that."

It was well handled, and the company laughed gratefully. Alexander felt Vladimir Suvorin's large hand resting on his shoulder give him a gentle, warning squeeze, but he ignored even his hero.

"What about terrorism? I hear that the Bolsheviks are behind some of the bombing, and that they've been committing robberies, too."

These charges were entirely true. Lenin advocated both methods at this time, to maximize disruption and to get funds for the Bolsheviks—a fact that embarrassed party men like Peter Suvorin who tried to cover it up.

"I, too, have heard of these incidents and expropriations," Popov replied blandly. "But I know absolutely nothing about them."

Now Vladimir's hand moved down to Alexander's arm, squeezed firmly, and the boy heard the great man whisper: "Enough, my friend." But he had not finished.

"Do you know, I have seen you before," he said, more loudly. "When you were inciting the workers of the man in whose house you now dare to come. But you avoided meeting him then. You used another name— Ivanov—and ran away like a dog. How many names have you, Mr. Popov?"

For a moment, as Popov turned his green eyes upon him, it seemed to young Alexander that he was looking at a snake. But then, very calmly, the Bolshevik replied: "It is a sad fact that for a long time—since any opposition in Russia is under police surveillance—many people have had to use more than one name. Lenin, to my knowledge, has used more than a hundred." Though cool, Popov had turned pale.

"You deny that you're a thief and a coward, then?" Alexander pursued, into the terrible silence.

This time Popov did not reply at all, but only looked at him, for a moment more, with a faint half smile. Then Mrs. Suvorin, with an easy laugh, led Popov away.

"You've made a dangerous enemy," Alexander's father warned him a few minutes later.

To which the youth only replied sulkily: "It's better than having him as a friend."

Despite Alexander's embarrassing attack, it was generally agreed, afterwards, that the evening had been a success. Indeed it was one of those special occasions, which for long afterwards and for different reasons remains as a landmark in the minds of all those concerned.

For Nicolai Bobrov, it was the evening when his son made an enemy of Popov. For Mrs. Suvorin, it was the occasion upon which, after spending half an hour with her, this strange, redheaded Bolshevik had promised to visit her salon again, when he was next in Moscow.

For two people, however, the evening was to be remembered by small events that took place just as it was ending.

It was only after leaving his brother's house that Peter Suvorin turned to his wife and asked curiously: "Whatever was Vladimir talking to you about?"

"Oh. Nothing."

He waited, but she said no more.

"It must have been something," he suggested. "You looked upset."

"Did I? I don't think so."

Why, even now, should his dear wife, at this harmless mention of a conversation with his brother, suddenly look as though she might burst into tears? Surely Vladimir could not have said anything to hurt her.

"I think my brother's kind," he said, to see if there were any reaction. "People say he's wise," he added, for no particular reason.

And then came the reply that he remembered always, afterwards, and never understood.

"He knows everything. That's just the trouble. Please don't speak of him again."

It was certainly very strange. It made no sense at all.

For young Alexander Bobrov, the event that changed his life came just as he was walking out through the great hall behind his father. And it was only chance that made him glance up at the marble gallery above. But when he did, he found he could not move. Little Nadezhda loved to watch the guests departing. She would lie awake while her parents' parties were in progress, then sneak out in her nightdress and peer through the marble pillars, taking note of all that passed below. As it happened, most of the guests having departed, she was standing up now, clearly visible, her long brown hair cascading down.

Which was how Alexander saw her. A youth, almost a young man, staring up at a little girl of eight.

"She must be Suvorin's little girl," he murmured. He had never seen her before. Yet an angelic face. What lustrous hair. And she was the daughter of Vladimir—his hero—and straightaway, at that very moment, it came to him. "One day," he whispered to her, though she could not hear, "one day you will be mine."

1906   July

NICOLAI Bobrov stared sadly at the long wooden house that had always been his home. He could scarcely believe he might never see Russka again.

The rest of the family had all departed a month ago: his old mother Anna, his wife, and young Alexander. They were all in Moscow now, while he had returned to remove the last vestiges of his family's long occupation.

It was midmorning and he was finished. The three carts by the stables had been piled high by the peasants who now stood expectantly beside them. A last search around the empty house had revealed only a few old boxes of papers left in the attic. He thought they would just fit onto the third cart. Then it would be time to go.

Nicolai was leaving things in good order: he was proud of that. He had stopped a leak in the roof and had the little bathhouse repaired. He had also arranged for Arina to move up from the village and live in as housekeeper with her son. She would take good care of the place. Suvorin would have nothing to complain of. Indeed, as he had taken his last walk up the alley of silver birches above the house, and gazed down the slope of the little river Rus below, he had thought what a pleasant spot it was, and brushed away a tear.

Now, however, as he glanced towards the door of the house and saw Arina and her son watching him, he took a sharp breath and threw his chest out. He was a Bobrov. They would see him leave with dignity. "It's time," he muttered, "to begin a new life." True, he was fifty-two; but though his hair was gray, his blue eyes were clear and his figure, unlike that of his father and grandfather at that age, had put on little weight. He might have lost the estate, but there was still the future.

Yet who knew what that future would be? The last three months had hardly been promising. The duma, having met, had been a shambles. He had made a visit to Saint Petersburg and found everyone quarreling. The peasant members had little idea what to do. Some of them had gotten drunk and started brawls in taverns. One was arrested for stealing a pig. Yet comic as these antics were, the behavior of his own party, the liberal Cadets, had shocked him even more. Having demanded a wholesale distribution of land to the peasants, which the tsar refused to consider, they would not cooperate with the government about anything. Worse yet, while the terrorists continued their campaign all over Russia, the Cadets refused even to condemn the violence until the government gave in to their own demands.

"I'm a Cadet," he complained to Suvorin on his return to Moscow. "But thousands of people are being killed. We liberals are supposed to be responsible: I can't understand it."

Suvorin, however, had been philosophical. "You forget, my friend, that this is Russia," he said. "Throughout our history we have only known two political forms: autocracy and rebellion. This business of democracy and parliament, which only work through compromise, is all new to us. We think we want democracy, but we don't really understand it. It will take time."

Days before, having sat only two months, this duma had been dissolved and new elections were expected later that year. Nicolai had heard, however, that the socialist parties would probably take part next time. "And God knows whether that will make things better or worse." The future looked uncertain indeed.

Time to be going. There were only those few boxes in the attic to bring down; if they left soon, they could be in Vladimir by nightfall. Nicolai turned to go inside.

It was just then, however, that he noticed a figure coming up the slope towards him, and realized to his surprise that it was Boris Romanov.

He had not expected to see him. When he had gone down the day before to bid farewell to the peasants in the village, he had been aware that Boris had quietly avoided him. He had long known that Boris harbored a grudge of some kind against his family. "Watch out for that fellow," his father Misha had cautioned him once. "I had some trouble with him." Misha would never say exactly what, though. For his part, however, Nicolai had nothing against Boris. He remembered with a wry smile how he had once incited him to revolution when they were young. And as I'm a Cadet, these days, trying to get more land for the peasants, he really ought to be my friend, he considered. Perhaps, after all, the head of the Romanov family had relented and come up the hill to say good-bye. Nicolai went forward to greet him.

They met by the end of the house. Nicolai gave the peasant a friendly nod while Boris paused a few paces away from him. It was some time since Nicolai had examined Romanov so closely. He, too, was going gray, but he looked strong and healthy. They were a typical contrast: the noble in his straw hat, open linen jacket, waistcoat, fob watch, and tie, looking so Western he might just have come from watching an English cricket match; the Russian peasant, the perfect muzhik, in loose trousers, bast shoes, red shirt, and broad belt, unchanged since the ancient times of golden Kiev. Two cultures, both calling themselves Russian, yet with nothing in common except their land, their language, and a church in which neither of them usually bothered to worship. And now, having lived side by side for centuries, they were bidding each other farewell.

"So you're going." The burly peasant was standing with his arms hanging loosely by his sides. His broad face, Nicolai noticed, seemed to have closed up somewhat so that his eyes were now like slits.

"As you see, Boris Timofeevich," the noble answered politely.

For a moment Boris surveyed the carts silently, and then the front of the house where Arina and little Ivan were watching. He nodded thoughtfully.

"We should have smoked you out long ago." It was said in a matter-of-fact way, yet it was a far from friendly statement. The process of vandalism and arson by which, in recent years, many landlords had been encouraged to sell their lands to peasants was generally known as "smoking out." Nicolai remembered the fire in his woods the previous years and looked at Boris thoughtfully. "But Suvorin's got the land now, not us," Boris added bitterly.

"The Cadets want land distribution. There are state lands hereabouts you may get which would be far better than my poor woods," he reminded the peasant.

But Boris ignored him. He seemed to be following his own train of thought. "The revolution's started, but it hasn't finished yet," he said quietly. "We'll have all the land soon."

"Perhaps." Nicolai was beginning to get bored with the peasant's sullen rudeness. "I must be going," he said irritably.

"Yet"—Boris allowed himself a grim smile—"the Bobrovs are going at last. So, good-bye, Nicolai Mikhailovich." And he took a step forward.

It seemed he was going to say a half-friendly good-bye after all. Nicolai began to extend his hand. And then Boris grimaced. And spat.

Nicolai had never known what it was to have someone spit in his face before. It was worse, more utterly insulting, more violent than any mere blow. He reeled back. And as he did so, the peasant hissed: "Good riddance, you damned Bobrov. And don't come back or we'll kill you." Then he turned and stomped away.

So horrified, so revolted was Nicolai that, for a second or two, he could do nothing. After that he thought briefly of striking the departing peasant, or of having him arrested. Then he was overcome by a feeling of disgust and futility. He looked back at the house and saw Arina and the boy staring at him. The peasants by the carts were watching him impassively, too. Did they all, perhaps, hate him so much?

"We're going," he called out, with what dignity he could muster. And a few moments afterwards he was seated beside the driver of the first cart, as it creaked down the slope. Still red, and shaking with impotent fury, he scarcely glanced back as they went along. And only when they were halfway to the monastery did he remember, with a shrug, that he had left some boxes still in the attic. It didn't matter. They could stay there. It was over.

And so the Bobrovs quitted their ancestral estate.

1907

To Dimitri Suvorin at the age of twelve the world seemed a wonderful place. Yet there were still things he did not understand.

In particular: what was happening to his mother?

He was a strange boy, his body small and slight. His narrow face sometimes reminded Rosa of her father. Like Peter, however, Dimitri was shortsighted and wore spectacles. If he looked physically fragile, however, this was offset by an extraordinary intensity in the pale face under its unruly mop of black wiry hair, and by the sudden laughter to which he was frequently prone.

He was a happy child. Though the little family was very close—his parents obviously adored each other—the atmosphere was never oppressive. The three of them lived in a pleasant, untidy apartment with high ceilings near the center of the city. The building was three stories high and its street side was faced with cream-colored stucco. In the courtyard where the children played stood a mulberry tree. From the courtyard, one could see, looming quietly over the roof, the dome of the little church where Dimitri had been christened. The district was full of charm. Nearby was the School of Painting and close to that a strange house with a glass roof where Prince Trubetskoy the sculptor had his studio. Two streets away was a little flower market and beside it a coachmaker's workshop with a huge stuffed bear in the window.

And how delightful it was, on a warm summer evening, to walk about the city. Snobbish Saint Petersburg with its classical facades might be the empire's head, but Moscow was still the heart. Though a city of nearly four hundred thousand now, it was a curious blend of the industrial and Muscovite ages. On the outskirts, tall factory chimneys and ancient fortified monasteries dwelt side by side. In the last two decades, the so-called "Russian" style of architecture—Russia's version of the West's nineteenth-century "gothick" style—had come into vogue, so that railway stations and other public buildings now arose with strange designs of brick and plaster so ornate that they might have come from the wild Muscovite extragavanza of Saint Basil's Cathedral on Red Square. And these buildings, too, had their own heavy charm. Young Dimitri would spend hours wandering about the streets, or on the broad and leafy boulevards that ringed the inner city, or by the Kremlin walls, from inside which the silvery tinklings of the church bells could be heard. And sometimes it seemed to him as if the whole city was like some gigantic piece of music by Tchaikovsky, Mussorgsky, or one of the other great Russian composers, that had miraculously been transposed into stone.

He was four when the first clear signs of his musical talent appeared. His mother spotted them at once. By the age of six, at his own request, he was learning both the piano and the violin. When he was seven his father declared: "Perhaps he'll be a concert pianist." But at eight Rosa had said: "I don't think so." And it was true, as time passed, that though he had a remarkable gift for playing, young Dimitri would often prefer to compose little tunes of his own than spend the extra hours needed each day if he were to climb the rocky path to the performer's art. Now, at twelve, he went to the excellent Fifth Moscow Grammar School near Arbat Square and studied music voraciously in his spare time.

And prepared for the revolution. There was never any question about that in Professor Peter Suvorin's home. They all worked for it. Two years before, they had been up many times all night while Rosa typed out revolutionary articles on her typewriter, and young Dimitri had often been used to take them to various distribution points. It was thrilling to know that he was aiding the great cause.

And now something even more exciting had happened. His father was in the duma. He had gone to Saint Petersburg.

It had been a great step. After boycotting the first duma, the socialists had decided to participate in the second. "If we can get a large number of socialists in," Peter had explained, "we can smash the tsar and end this farce once and for all. Use the tsar's own duma to abolish him!"

"And then?"

"A constituent assembly elected by all the people. A democratic government. All the socialists agree about that."

Freedom. Democracy. The new world was about to begin. And his father, the distinguished Professor Suvorin, was a part of it. Life was wonderful.

Yet there were still things that were puzzling. Why was it, for instance, that his uncle Vladimir was so rich while they lived so simply themselves? "Your father has no interest in all that," his mother told him with a dismissive gesture. But as he got older this explanation did not seem quite enough. Though he and Nadezhda were like brother and sister, he knew their parents were not close. "If your father had his way," the little girl had once remarked, "Mama says you'd put us all in the street." And then, with perfect innocence: "If that happens, Dimitri, can I come and live with you?" He had promised she could, but it had always seemed odd to him that his kind uncle Vladimir did not understand the need for revolution.

And then there was his mother. Why was she always so anxious? Was it possible, Dimitri had wondered, to love people too much? When his father left for Saint Petersburg, Uncle Vladimir had offered to let Dimitri stay with them so that Rosa could accompany Peter. She had refused; yet ever since, each day, she had constantly moaned: "Do you think your father is safe there? I'm sure something will happen to him." She would even fret at night so that, by morning, there were dark rings around her large eyes.

It was late March when the incident occurred. Peter Suvorin was away in the capital and Dimitri was returning from school one afternoon, when, having followed an unusual route, he found himself in a long narrow street.

The street was empty. A few bare trees could be seen down the sides; here and there were patches of dark ice in the gutters. A dull gray light pervaded the place.

He was halfway down before he heard a scuffle and saw the little gang, and even then, it did not occur to him to be alarmed.

There were only half a dozen of them: four young men and two boys about his age. They came out of a courtyard and then walked along on each side of him for several yards before one of the young men spoke.

"I think he's one." They all continued to walk.

"You do? Hey, boy, what's your name?"

"Dimitri Petrovich. Suvorin," he added as firmly as he could. He was not sure what this all meant.

"Good Russian names, young Mr. Suvorin. Shall we leave him, boys?"

"Maybe. Look at his nose, though."

"True. We don't like your nose, Dimitri Petrovich. Why don't we like his nose, boys?"

"Looks like a kike."

"Right, Dimitri Petrovich. That's the problem. You sure you aren't Jewish? Not at all?"

"Quite sure," Dimitri answered with confidence, as they continued to walk.

"What's your mother's name, boy?"

"Rosa Abramovich," he replied.

"Aha. Where's she from?"

"Vilnius," he replied in all innocence.

"A Rosa Abramovich from Vilnius. Then your mother's a Jew, boy."

"She is not," he answered hotly. But they had stopped and surrounded him. "She's a Christian," he shouted furiously, not because he had anything especially against the Jews, but because the accusation was a lie. Seeing the boy's genuine rage, the little gang hesitated.

And it was then that Dimitri did a very foolish thing. "Don't you touch me," he shouted furiously. "My father's a deputy in the duma, and you'll be in trouble."

"Which party?"

"The Social Democrats," he said proudly. And instantly realized his mistake. He had heard of the Black Hundreds of course—the gangs of right-wing thugs who beat up socialists and Jews in the name of the tsar. But somehow he had always thought of them as the large groups their name suggested; nor, since he was a good Russian, had he ever considered they could have anything to do with him.

"Kike! Socialist! Traitor!" The little fellow went down at once.

He had only received a black eye and several kicks in the ribs when a carriage entering the street caused his assailants to break off. Half an hour later he was safely back at home, and though shaken, he was able to eat some supper.

But there was one aspect to the whole business that mystified him. "They said you were a Jew," he told his mother. And he was therefore even more astonished when she confessed that it was true. "I converted when I married," she explained. They had never told him before.

And from that day, her nervousness seemed to get worse.

Strangely, whatever these events meant to his mother, they did not mark Dimitri; and this was due to an extraordinary aspect of his makeup.

It had to do with music.

Ever since he was a little child, Dimitri had thought in terms of music. From as long as he could remember, notes had suggested colors to him. As soon as Rosa showed him the different keys on the piano, each had possessed, for him, its own distinct character and mood. At first these discoveries belonged to a musical world that he associated with the instruments he played. But then, when he was nine, something else took place.

He had been in the little church beside his home one evening listening to vespers. The church had a fine choir, and the haunting melodies of the chanting were still with him as he left. It was sunset when he stepped into the street and the sky above Moscow was gold and red. For several minutes he had stood gazing towards the glorious colors in the west.

And then, trying to express what he saw, he had chosen a chord. It was in the key of C minor. After a moment, he had added another.

It was odd, he thought: he had chosen the chords. He had imposed them on that sunset. Yet as he looked, it was as though the sky were answering him, saying: Yes, that is my sound. And in his mind the chords and the sunset became one.

He had walked back into the courtyard next. There was the mulberry tree, the reddish light catching its upper branches, warm shadow below. And now he heard another chord and a little melody; and this time the music came so instantly that it was as if he had not chosen it, but heard it.

How wonderful it was. He felt suffused with a strange sensation of warmth inside his stomach. When a moment later some children ran out into the yard, and he was afraid he might lose his thought, he found that with an effort of will he could hold the chords in his mind so that they did not slip away. And he experienced a small pang of fear, which he did not understand, as though the sunset and the tree had said to him: "If you step forward now, little boy, you will lose yourself and belong only to music." And being uncertain what this meant, he had decided to preserve this blessed state of being in his mind, as, sometimes, he would preserve a dream, that he might return to it later.

That had been the start. His life had never been the same after that. By a small act of concentration he found that he could step back into this dream whenever he wished: soon the periods of contemplation grew longer, and might last for hours, during which his concentration grew so deep that he could have entire conversations with people, or eat a meal, and emerge with no recollection of these events at all.

Very soon he had noticed other things. Once he stepped into his other world, it seemed to him that he was not inventing music, but listening to it—that the wonderful harmonies he heard came from outside himself; they were given to him, though he could not say with certainty by whom or by what. And before long, the musical otherworld began to invade the everyday world, like a light encroaching upon shadow, so that even such mundane things as a carriage passing in the street, or a dog barking, now seemed to Dimitri to contain their own music, which he would joyfully discover. His whole mind became crowded with musical phantoms: the people he saw every day, his schoolmasters, his mother, his uncle Vladimir, came to be presences, each with a voice—his father a tenor, Uncle Vladimir a rich baritone—like characters in some wonderful opera that was as yet only partially revealed to him.

And—this perhaps was the most wonderful thing of all—it was often as if, stretching before him on an endless, symphonic plain, he could perceive the lives of all people and all things, including his own small life: so that his own small joys and sorrows became part of that huge, echoing process, and were returned to him as music. When the young men from the Black Hundreds attacked Dimitri, therefore, the pain they caused him only turned to music in his mind.

Two events took place that summer, however, which did make a deep impression upon Dimitri.

In June, the tsar dissolved the duma; and on the very next day a new electoral system was announced. "The tsar couldn't stomach the socialists," Peter announced on his return. "This new system is quite amazing," he remarked. Under the tsar's new rules, the vote of a landowner counted for that of roughly five hundred and forty workers. "The conservative gentry will have a majority. And I'm out for certain."

"But is it legal? Can the tsar just break the rules like that?" Dimitri demanded.

Peter shrugged. "It's illegal according to the constitution issued last year. But since he made the rules then, the tsar reckons he can change them now." He smiled. "The tsar honestly believes it's his duty to be an •

autocrat, you know. He thinks Russia is like a huge family estate he's got to pass on to his son exactly as it was when his father gave it to him. He calls it his sacred trust." He shook his head wearily. "It's so stupid it's almost funny, really."

But though his father was philosophical, young Dimitri could tell that he was inwardly outraged. There was another worrying side to these events, also. The tsar's new minister, Stolypin, was a highly able man, bent on reforming the backward empire. "But reforms can only take place after pacification," he had declared, and his pacification had been thorough. No less than a thousand people suspected of terrorist involvement had been executed the previous year—Russians now called the hangman's noose "Stolypin's necktie." Police spies were everywhere. Popov, and others like him, had wisely disappeared, perhaps abroad, and Rosa was constantly anxious about her husband. "I've done nothing to offend Stolypin," he would assure her. "But you know people who have," she would reply. And now for the first time, young Dimitri began to think of the revolution not as a joyous state that must inevitably come in the future, but as a bitter and dangerous struggle between his father and the tsar. And it was this, rather than his encounter with the Black Hundreds, that made life seem darker to the boy.

The second event took place late that summer, when a letter arrived from the Ukraine. It was from Rosa's childhood friend, Ivan Karpenko, and it contained an unexpected request. He had a son, just two years older than Dimitri—a gifted boy, he said—who wanted to study in Moscow. "I wondered if he could stay with you," he wrote. "He would pay for his keep, of course."

"We've nowhere to put him," Peter complained. But Rosa would not hear of any difficulties. "We'll manage," she declared, and wrote at once to Karpenko that he should send his son. "He'll be company for Dimitri," she said firmly. But both Dimitri and his father knew what she really meant. She was thinking: he'll be a protector.

He arrived at the start of September. His name was Mikhail. And from almost the moment he came, Dimitri announced: "He is a genius."

Mikhail Karpenko was a slim, dark, handsome youth with sparkling black eyes, who had just entered puberty; and it was certainly amazing what he knew. Within minutes of his arrival, they discovered that he was intensely proud of his Ukrainian heritage and his distinguished ancestor, the poet. "There's been a big revival of our Ukrainian culture, you know, just in the last few years," he told Rosa. "And I'm part of it," he added rather grandly. But his interests were far wider than that. He seemed fascinated by everything having to do with culture and the arts; and he absorbed new ideas with an astonishing speed. When Dimitri took him to visit his cousin Nadezhda, Karpenko seemed in his element, and he quickly found favor there. Even the great man himself was impressed. "Why, it's quite amazing, the things you know, my little Cossack," he would say with a chuckle; and often he would come and sit with his daughter and Dimitri on one side and Karpenko on the other, his great arms around them, and relate all the latest news from the world of art.

It was an exciting time in the Suvorin family. For that year, in addition to his huge mansion, Vladimir had decided to build himself a new house, about a mile away. "A little retreat," he told them with a grin, "but an unusual one."

This was an understatement. Only a handful of men in the world would have dared to do what the Russian industrialist now proposed. Which was nothing less than a whole house, constructed entirely in the style of Art Nouveau.

The designs he showed Dimitri and Karpenko were astounding. Though the basic structure of the house was a simple, square box with a side entrance, there all conformity ended. Every window, every pillar, every ceiling was shaped in the swirling curves of the Art Nouveau style. The effect was magical, contemporary yet plantlike. "It's like some fabulous orchid," Karpenko remarked, which pleased the industrialist greatly. "It will have the latest of everything," he explained. "Electric lights. Even a telephone." Designers from France were even coming to supervise the work.

And afterwards Karpenko remarked with awe to Dimitri: "Your uncle's like a Renaissance prince."

What a joy Karpenko was. The three of them—Dimitri, his cousin Nadezhda, and Karpenko—soon became firm friends. The ten-year-old girl, sophisticated though she was, would listen, fascinated by the handsome boy with his flashing eyes and his infectious enthusiasms. This year, he was devoted to the present Russian poets who belonged to the symbolist school. "Music," he would cry, "music is the supreme art because it reaches into the perfect, mystical world. But with words we can come close." And he would quote whole verses of Russia's brilliant young poet, Alexander Blok, transporting them to a realm of mysterious goddesses, or to the end of the world, or the coming of some nameless messiah, while Nadezhda gazed at him with shining eyes. The two boys came to see her several times a week.

The gay intimacy of their afternoons together was only occasionally dampened by the presence of a rather serious sixteen-year-old.

It was November when they first began to notice that Alexander Bobrov had entered their lives. His father at that time had just become one of the Moscow deputies, for the liberal Cadet party, to the tsar's new and conservative duma—which, after losing their estates, had been some comfort to the family. Since his own father had just been cut out of the duma, however, this did not make Dimitri especially friendly towards the solemn youth. Nadezhda was polite, because he was a friend of her father's. But Karpenko, only two years Alexander's junior, made no secret of his contempt.

Alexander seldom said much. Having called upon Suvorin on some pretext, he would come in with him, or sometimes venture in alone, speak a few polite words to Nadezhda, and stand around for a short while, listening to their conversation rather awkwardly. And it was not long before Karpenko had found a nickname for him. "Look out," he would whisper, "here comes the Russian calendar."

It was a clever joke. Though Peter the Great had reformed the calendar, he had used the old Julian system for counting the days; and whereas the rest of Europe had since transferred to the more modern Gregorian system, Russia and her Orthodox Church had stuck with the Julian. As a result, by the start of the twentieth century, the huge empire now lagged thirteen days behind the rest of the world. The cruel nickname exactly captured Alexander's conservative mentality.

Whenever he saw young Bobrov, Karpenko would speak enthusiastically of the coming new age, of the folly of the tsar, and declaim the lines of Alexander Blok on Russia's years of stagnation:

> Let the ravens croak and fly
> Over us who daily die.
> God, O God, let better men
> See Thy Kingdom come.

And poor young Bobrov would watch, morosely.

The following Easter, in 1908, a small incident made plain what was in young Bobrov's mind.

As everywhere in Russia, Easter day was a busy time in the great Suvorin house. Though neither Vladimir nor his brother Peter were religious, it never occurred to either to miss the long Easter Vigil the night before; and on Easter day the house was open to a constant stream of visitors. In the huge dining room, the long table was piled high with the rich foods that were allowed now that the Easter fast was over. In the center of the table were the two traditional Easter dishes: *kulich,* the creamy, thick bread decorated with the paschal sign; and the white sweet shaped like a little pyramid—the *paskha.* And everywhere, of course, decorated Easter eggs, some painted red, some in the Ukrainian manner covered with elaborate designs: people brought them, received them— several thousand eggs would be consumed in the huge Suvorin mansion. And all washed down with iced vodka.

The Bobrovs came by in the middle of the day, just after Peter Suvorin and his family, and so Dimitri and his friend were witnesses to the little scene. Young Nadezhda and her mother were both wearing the traditional festival dresses of Russian women. Mrs. Suvorin also wore a high diadem—the *kokoshnik*—of gold and mother-of-pearl, which made her look more regal than ever. As was the custom, each arrival went from one person to another, kissing each one three times and exchanging the Easter greeting—"Christ is risen": "He is risen indeed."

When young Alexander Bobrov reached Nadezhda, however, he did not pass on but paused and reached into his pocket and drew out a little box. "This is a present for you," he said gravely. Astonished, the girl opened it, to find a tiny but beautiful little Easter egg, made of silver with decorations in colored stones. And it came from Fabergé.

"It's lovely." For once, she was so astonished that she did not know what to say. "It's for me?"

He smiled. "Of course."

Dimitri and Karpenko watched, equally amazed. It was one of Fabergé's smallest pieces, of course, but still an astonishing present for a boy still at school to give, and hardly appropriate. Nor were they alone. For the little scene had caught the eagle eye of Mrs. Suvorin. She swooped.

"What a charming present." She gathered both the boy and his ego and his egg and somehow whisked both across the room before Alexander knew what had happened. "But, my dear Alexander," she said gently but firmly, "I can't allow you to give such a thing to Nadezhda at her age. She's really too young, you know."

Alexander blushed scarlet.

"If you do not wish . . ."

"I am very touched that you should have thought of it. But she is not used to such presents, Alexander. If you wish, you can give it to me and I will give it to her when she is older," she said kindly. And feeling now that there was nothing else in politeness he could do, Alexander sadly gave it to her.

But the message was clear. He had tried to make a declaration, and Mrs. Suvorin, for whatever reason, had not let him do so. He felt embarrassed and humiliated. And even when Vladimir affectionately put his arm around him and led him off for a stroll in the gallery, he was hardly comforted.

As for Dimitri and Karpenko, they were beside themselves. "Poor young Bobrov," Karpenko mocked, "Fabergé sold him a rotten egg."

And Nadezhda, deprived of her egg, could hardly decide what she felt about it all.

1908 June

In the summer of 1908 it seemed that Russia, after all, might be at peace. The wave of terrorism was passing. Stolypin's harsh measures against the revolutionaries had greatly damaged them; and the recent discovery that the leading Socialist Revolutionary terrorist had all along been a police agent had weakened that party in the eyes of the people. There were signs of progress, too. The new duma was not, as some had feared, the tsar's lapdog. Liberals like Nicolai Bobrov spoke up boldly for democracy; and even the conservative majority backed the minister Stolypin in his plans for careful reform. Finally, that year, the excellent weather gave every promise of a bumper harvest. The countryside was quiet.

And it was in the country that the blow that was to decide Dimitri's destiny fell, quite unexpectedly, out of the blue sky.

It was Vladimir's idea that they should go to Russka. All spring Rosa had looked unwell, and both Vladimir and Peter had urged her: "Escape the city in the summer heat." In the end it was agreed that Dimitri and his friends should come; Karpenko would stay for the month of June before returning to the Ukraine for the rest of the holidays; and Rosa would try to come with Peter in July.

Dimitri found the place delightful. His uncle's remarkable vision was already at work. Thirty yards from the old Bobrov house there now stood a long, low wooden building that housed the museum and, at the far end, some workshops. In the workshops Vladimir had already installed an expert woodcarver and a pottery maker, whom Dimitri and Nadezhda loved to watch. The museum, though only just begun, was already a little treasure house. There were the traditional distaffs, elaborately carved, painted wooden spoons, presses for making patterns on bread and cakes, and wonderful embroidered cloths, featuring the curious oriental bird design that was customary at Russka. Vladimir had also begun a collection of icons of the local school from the time when the monastery had been a center of production.

In the house itself, Vladimir had provided a varied library and a grand piano. Mrs. Suvorin, evidently rather bored by the country, usually sat reading on the verandah; but the house was efficiently run by Arina, whose young son Ivan was constantly hovering, hoping for a chance to play. He and Nadezhda were almost the same age, and it was amusing to see the sophisticated ten-year-old girl go whooping down the slope after the peasant boy, play hide and seek with him in the woods above the house.

In the afternoons, Vladimir would often take Nadezhda and the boys to bathe in the river. The big industrialist was surprisingly agile and a strong swimmer. Karpenko, it turned out, could hardly swim, but Vladimir personally held him in the water and coached him so that soon he could outstrip any of them. Afterwards, their bodies tingling from the cold water, they would sit on the bank and talk.

The industrialist was a wonderful talker. He would put his great arm round Nadezhda or one of the boys and discuss all manner of things with them, exactly as if they were adults. And it was on one of these afternoons that he gave them his view of Russia's future. As usual, it was to the point.

"It's really quite simple," he told them. "Russia is now in a race against time. Stolypin, whom I personally support, knows he has to modernize Russia while he keeps the lid on the forces of revolution. If he succeeds, the tsar will keep his throne; if not . . ." He grimaced. "Chaos. Peasant and urban insurrection. Remember Pugachev, as they used to say."

"What must Stolypin do?" Karpenko asked.

"Three things, chiefly. Develop industry. Thanks to foreign capital, that's going well. Next, educate the masses. Sooner or later some kind of democracy will come, and the people aren't ready for it. Stolypin is making progress there. Thirdly, Stolypin's trying to reform the country-side." He sighed. "And that, I'm afraid, will be hard."

The attempt to change the Russian peasant, Dimitri knew, lay at the heart of the great minister's reforms. In the last two years, important changes had been made. The payments due to the former landowners, together with all arrears, had been entirely canceled. The peasant had been given full civil liberties, the use of the same law courts as any other citizen, and an internal passport for travel without the permission of the commune, which he was now free to leave at any time. At last, half a century after the Emancipation, he was a free man in fact as well as theory. But there still remained one huge problem.

"For what can be done about the commune?" Vladimir wondered aloud.

Even now, the commune's wasteful strip-farming of medieval times with its periodic redistributions had changed but little. Russian grain yields remained only a third of those in much of Western Europe. In his attempt to change this, Stolypin was trying to encourage peasants to withdraw from the commune, cultivate their own personal land, and be independent farmers. Laws were being passed; easy credit made available through the Peasant Bank. But progress so far was slow.

"Isn't Stolypin trying to make the peasant into a bourgeois, though—a capitalist?" Dimitri objected. "Of course he is," Vladimir replied. "Unlike you, Dimitri, I'm a capitalist. But I do confess that it's going to be very difficult to make it work."

"I'd have thought it would be easy," Karpenko remarked.

"Yes, my friend," Vladimir tousled the boy's head affectionately. "But that's because you come from the Ukraine. Down there and in the western provinces of White Russia there's a tradition of independent farming. But in these central provinces, in Russia proper, the commune system is solid. And if you want to know why, just look at the village here. Look at Boris Romanov, the village elder."

Dimitri and Karpenko had soon come to know Romanov. As village elder now, he was a figure of some power, which he clearly enjoyed. The family, with three strong sons, had the largest share of land in the village now and Boris's house had painted shutters and handsome carving round the eaves. Yet that spring, when Stolypin's reforms had made some state land by the monastery available for purchase, and Vladimir had remarked to him—"Well, Boris Timofeevich, I daresay you'll be buying some yourself"—he had glowered and replied: "The commune's buying it." And then, quietly but audibly: "And we'll smoke you out, too, one day."

"Nothing will persuade Romanov that the answer to everything isn't to take this estate," Vladimir continued. "And do you know the irony? In many provinces there isn't enough land—even if you dispossess every landowner—to do the peasants the slightest bit of good! Their best answer is to resettle to less populated provinces—which Stolypin's also trying to encourage." He sighed. "So the peasants support the social revolutionaries—even the terrorists—because they promise to distribute all the land."

The industrialist smiled grimly as he summed up. "So the communal peasant does little for himself but waits for a miracle that will solve everything in the twinkling of an eye. Passive, but angry. He'd prefer decades of unnecessary suffering, followed by a moment of useless violence."

Though Dimitri, coming from the socialist household of Peter and

Rosa, naturally knew that in his conservative politics his uncle Vladimir was mistaken, he had a great respect for his intelligence and recognized the truth of much of what he said. And thinking of the revolution he knew one day must come, he asked: "So do you think Stolypin will fail, and the tsar lose his throne?"

"It isn't clear to me," his uncle replied frankly. "But remember this: in 1905 we had a war and a food shortage. That's what actually caused the revolution. My guess, therefore, is that in order to win the race, Stolypin needs two things: peace, and good harvests. That is what will really decide the fate of Russia. Nothing much else."

Yet it would have been hard, that peaceful summer, to think for long about such serious matters.

It was a happy time. In the mornings, Karpenko would often go out to explore the countryside, or sketch, or devise fantastic games to amuse young Ivan and Nadezhda, who both seemed to look upon him as a god. Meanwhile, for three hours, Dimitri would practice the piano. He had concentrated on the piano now, to the near exclusion of the violin, and though he might lack the driven technical virtuosity of the professional performer, his playing was of a remarkable musical sophistication.

In the afternoons, if they were not swimming with Vladimir, they sat on the verandah and read books or played cards with Mrs. Suvorin.

One day Vladimir had taken them round the factories at Russka. It had been an impressive tour. Dimitri had studied the factory workers with interest as they quietly went about their tasks; but Karpenko had been fascinated by the mechanism of the plant itself. "Such raw power," he whispered to Dimitri afterwards. "Did you notice the incredible, harsh beauty of the place? And your uncle—he's in charge of this machine. I admire him more every day."

Several times they had visited the monastery. And in the second week of June, Arina took them across the river and along the little path to the old springs, which utterly delighted Karpenko. "How Slavic!" he cried. And then: "How pagan."

The evenings Dimitri especially enjoyed. For sometimes, while the others laughed and talked in the library, he would quietly sit at the piano and try out his own tentative compositions. It was on these occasions that he discovered a new and extraordinary feature of his uncle's character. For sometimes, as he was playing, he would be aware of Vladimir softly entering the room and sitting in the shadow. But often as not, when he came to a pause, his uncle would come over, gaze thoughtfully at the keys, and then in his rich baritone suggest: "Why don't you try it this way." Or: "If you changed the rhythm here . . ." And—this was the remarkable thing—Dimitri nearly always found that, unknown to himself, it had been what he wanted to express all along. "How do you know my mind like that?" he would ask. "Am I composing, or are you?" To which his uncle would reply, with a touch of sadness: "To some, Dimitri, it is given to create. To others, only to understand the creative act." And Dimitri could only marvel at this man, with whom he felt he was developing a bond.

*   *   *

It was the day before he was due to leave that Karpenko drew Dimitri to one side and said: "Let's go for a walk. Just the two of us."

"Where to?"

"An enchanted place." He grinned. "The springs."

Their walk was delightful. Karpenko was at his charming best, full of infectious laughter, and as they went along, Dimitri reflected how lucky he was to have such a friend. How handsome he was, he thought admiringly. Though fifteen, Karpenko had suffered few of the disadvantages of adolescence. He was nearly always in a sunny mood. The beginnings of his beard so soft he scarcely needed to shave; his smooth skin quite without blemish; his little figure might have been conceived by some Renaissance sculptor like Donatello. Their slight difference in age precluded any rivalry: Karpenko knew more than Dimitri, but shared his knowledge freely and always with kindness, like a protective elder brother. Best of all, behind his facade of jokes, and his brilliant manner, there lay a deeply thoughtful nature that Dimitri loved and respected.

And it was in this last vein that, after they had rested on the mossy ground by the springs for a while, Karpenko suddenly turned to him rather seriously and remarked: "Tell me, Dimitri, have you ever heard the proposition they call the Extraterrestrials Argument?"

Dimitri shook his head.

"It goes like this," Karpenko explained. "Imagine that beings arrived from another planet and saw how we live—all the injustice in our world. And they asked you: 'What are you doing about it?' And you replied: 'Not much.' What would they say, Dimitri? How could they understand such madness? 'Surely,' they'd say, 'any rational being would put such a state of affairs right, as his first and most pressing duty.' " He looked at his friend earnestly. "Don't you agree?"

"I do."

"So, what I wanted to say, before I leave, is—shouldn't we commit ourselves to do something, to make a new and better world, you and I?"

"Oh yes."

"Good, I knew you'd agree." Slowly and solemnly now he reached into his pocket and drew out a pin. Then he pricked his finger and drew blood and handed the pin to Dimitri. "We'll make a pact, then," he said. "Blood brothers."

And young Dimitri flushed with pride. It was the fashion just then, especially among young men in revolutionary circles, to use the ancient custom of blood brotherhood. But to think that Karpenko was doing him such an honor! Dimitri took the pin and did the same. Then they pooled their blood.

Karpenko had only been gone four days when Mrs. Suvorin, receiving a message that her sister in Saint Petersburg was ill, felt obliged to depart. Nadezhda and Dimitri remained, however; with Vladimir and Arina there, it hardly seemed that they could come to any harm. And so a pleasant week passed.

It was the custom for the stableboys to take the horses down to the river each day. If they were being watched, this was done in an orderly manner; but if not, they would mount them bareback and, with loud whoops, go careening down the slope; and little Ivan, whenever he could escape Arina's watchful gaze, would slip off to join in.

If Nadezhda had not been watching, that warm July day, perhaps Dimitri would not have done it; but seeing the nine-year-old Ivan looking cheerfully down at him from the horse in the stableyard, he suddenly decided: if the little boy can do it, so can I. And a moment later he had clambered onto a horse himself, and was moving out towards the slope.

First a walk, then a run: the horses were excited. Hooves pounding on the hard ground; wild cries. The ground both coming to meet him, yet falling away at the same time: Dimitri clung to the horse's mane. There was dust everywhere, a smell of sweat. Suddenly he felt a branch from a sapling slap him in the face and cut him. He laughed. He was losing his balance. How foolish. Next he was falling, headlong, as the flanks of the other horses rushed by. Then the ground, or was it the sky, hurled itself at him.

Dimitri heard his leg snap. In that strange, silent moment before the searing pain, he heard it quite distinctly. And he was still just conscious when Nadezhda came running down the slope to where he lay.

Dimitri did not realize, for some time, that things would never be the same.

They had put his bed downstairs, in the big, airy room where the piano was. He was not too bored. There were plenty of books. Arina frequently came in, and Nadezhda would happily sit and chatter in her inimitable way. But he looked forward most to the times when his uncle Vladimir would come and talk or read to him by the hours. The only thing he missed was that, for the present, he could not play the piano.

And then his mother came.

If there was any consequence of his accident that Dimitri would never have foreseen, it was that it would change his view of Rosa. What had she been to him until then? The loving mother who had helped him take his first steps in music; the woman who adored his father; the selfless, strangely sad figure who worried incessantly about her husband and her son. She did not look well when she arrived. Her large eyes were haggard. Her black hair was streaked with gray, and because it was both thick and long the effect was to make her seem unkempt. He loved her, but felt sorry for her, because she could not be happy.

It was Vladimir who revealed another side of her. "You must rest, now that you are here, Rosa," he urged. "And," he added firmly, "you must play. We cannot allow this young man to be without music." And to Dimitri's great surprise, the very next day, she began to do so.

How strange it was. He had never heard her play before. He had known that once she played. Often, when he was younger, she would help him over a few bars here and there, when he ran into difficulties: and from this he knew that she had considerable technique. But for some reason she would never sit down and play. Now, however, hesitantly at first, she began to do so: simple pieces the first day or two. Then a

Beethoven sonata or two. Then pieces by Tchaikovsky, Rimsky Korsakov, and other Russians. She would play for an hour, then two, her face sometimes frowning with amusement as she asked her fingers to perform tasks they had not done in years, sometimes smiling gently. And as he listened Dimitri was more and more astonished. She is formidable, he thought. A major talent. He could hear it coming through in every phrase. But the fifth day, the transformation in Rosa as astonishing. It was as if she had shed her sad persona like an unwanted skin. She had drawn her hair back more tightly, so that it no longer seemed untidy. Fresh air and several nights of sleep had relaxed her face and smoothed out the lines. Now she threw her head back, in calm triumph as the Beethoven *Apassionata* flowed like a wave from her fingers. And often Vladimir stood beside her.

"I never knew you played like that," Dimitri remarked one day; and almost added: or that you were so beautiful.

"There are many things you do not know," she replied gaily, and strolled out, with a laugh, onto the verandah with Vladimir and Nadezhda.

And then, just as suddenly, it ended. It was a sunny afternoon. Rosa had been there ten days. The day before, Vladimir had brought her the scores of some studies by his favorite of all the Russians composing just then, the brilliant Scriabin. They were wonderful pieces, as delicate and measured as a Chopin prelude, as haunting as one of the Russian symbolist poems of Alexander Blok. Rosa was playing them while Vladimir basked in an easy chair, a seraphic smile on his face. And unusually, Dimitri had fallen asleep.

Rosa had stopped playing when he began to awake, and Vladimir was standing beside her at the piano. They obviously imagined he was still asleep, and though they were speaking in low tones, he heard most of their words distinctly.

"You cannot go on. I've been telling you for three years." His uncle's baritone voice, gently persuasive. "I can't bear to see it."

"There's nothing to be done. But, Volodya . . ." Dimitri had never heard anyone use this diminutive form of his uncle's name before. "Volodya, I'm so afraid."

"You need sleep, my little dove. Stop tormenting yourself. At least stay with me here awhile." Vladimir paused, apparently to think. "I have to go to Berlin and Paris next spring. Come with me. We can go to one of the spas for a health cure. I think you know you will be safe with me."

Dimitri stared, his eyes wide open. He saw his mother touch Vladimir's large hand affectionately. "I know."

Dimitri sat bolt upright, then winced with pain. He saw their two faces turn towards him, his uncle's irritated, his mother's distraught. Then Vladimir, as calmly as though nothing had happened: "Ah, my friend. You have woken up. Let's all have some tea." And Dimitri himself could not make out what it was he had just heard.

The next morning, Rosa announced that she must return to Moscow. "I've been away from your father for too long," she told him. "I worry about him so." And once again her face looked haggard, suggesting she had not slept the night before.

The days that followed might have been sad for Dimitri. Not only did his mother depart, but Nadezhda was summoned back to Moscow by Mrs. Suvorin; and since the doctor said he must not be moved, he was left at Russka almost alone. It was Vladimir who now, quietly but firmly, took over his life.

Just two days after Rosa left, his uncle appeared with several books and scores and dumped them on the table beside his bed. "You play well, my friend, and you've made some pretty compositions in the evenings," he announced firmly. "Now that you're confined to bed, though, you should make the most of your seclusion. It's time you began to understand what you're doing. These are books of musical theory and composition. Study them."

It was hard work at first, even boring. But each evening his uncle made him go through the exercises: harmonies, counterpoint, the complex business of musical discipline. Though only an amateur, Vladimir's understanding was considerable and he was a stern taskmaster. "Now I know why your factories make a good profit," Dimitri once said with a laugh. But the results, he had to confess, were excellent. In just six weeks, with nothing else in the world to do, the thirteen-year-old made astonishing progress. And he found something else, too: that as his technical understanding increased, he began to have a burning desire, an absolute compulsion, to use this new knowledge he was mastering, and to compose. So that in September, when the doctor finally agree that he might travel back to Moscow, he remarked to Vladimir: "Do you know, I think perhaps I'm really going to be a composer."

To which his uncle, to the boy's surprise, simply smiled and replied: "Of course you are."

And it was because of this period of study that Dimitri Suvorin, long after he had become famous, always remarked: "It was a fall from a horse that made me."

The fall from the horse had one other effect. Whether it was the carelessness of the stableboys who carried him back to the house, or the fact that the fracture was multiple, or the poor technique of the factory doctor who set his leg, Dimitri Suvorin's right leg was twisted out of shape permanently and for the rest of his life he walked with a stick.

1908   September

As well as visiting whenever he could think of an excuse, Alexander Bobrov often walked past the outside of Vladimir Suvorin's great house in the hope of catching sight of Nadezhda. Despite the embarrassing incident at Easter he had never, for a moment, given up his idea. "I shall marry her," he told his father bluntly.

Once already, that month, he had found an excuse for going in and had found Mrs. Suvorin and her daughter there, and learned that Vladimir would not be back in Moscow until late that month.

This evening, however, it was already late; the curtains and blinds were all closed; and only habit had made him walk by the Suvorin house at all. A light mist had fallen; the street lamps were so many yellowish blurs; few people were about. He would probably not ever have glanced at the house if he had not heard a light footfall in that direction, a footfall that seemed to end by the front door.

He peered across the street. For a moment he could not see anyone; then, standing by the portico, he made out a muffled figure in a broad-rimmed felt hat. He paused to watch and to his surprise, a moment later saw the front door open a little and the figure swiftly step inside. But it was just as the door was closing that he caught his breath. For as the figure took off his hat, Alexander saw, without a shadow of a doubt, the reddish hair of Yevgeny Popov.

What the devil does she want with me? It was a question Popov had asked himself many times. She had everything: a brilliant husband, a huge fortune—all that the bourgeois world had to offer. Of course, the upper bourgeoisie, having no useful purpose, sometimes got bored. In a celebrated case, one of the heirs of a great Russian merchant fortune had recently blown his brains out in his brother's house—not for any reason, but purely on a whim because he happened to see a revolver on a table. *Ennui* they called it. Bourgeois decadence, of course, was what it really was.

Was she just bored? He did not think so. Unhappy, perhaps, but not bored.

He remembered a conversation he had once had with Lenin. "Don't expect too much from women," his friend had told him. "I've never yet met any woman except my wife who could play chess or read a railway timetable." Popov grinned to himself. He knew that in recent years Lenin had been having a sporadic affair with a certain countess who lived in Saint Petersburg. He wondered if the countess could do either.

As for Mrs. Suvorin, whether she played chess or not, there was no doubt about her intelligence. Although recently he had heard that the authorities wanted to arrest him, Popov had managed to come discreetly to the house several times in the last two years. Each time, she had questioned him carefully about his beliefs; and though she had declined to read any Marx, it seemed to him that she was genuinely interested in what he told her.

It was also becoming clear that she was interested in him.

But why? From the first it had occurred to Popov that Suvorin might be unfaithful. If his wife wanted to revenge herself with an affair, though, hadn't she plenty of her own kind to choose from? Unless of course she wanted him because he represented the revolution that would destroy her husband's world. That, of course, would be a special kind of insult. But whether that idea amused him, or whether it would make him feel he was being used, he was not sure.

The house was quiet. She had sent the servants to bed long ago. She was sitting on a low chair in front of the fire, which was burning low, and she wore a pale blue peignoir. She seemed to be lost in thought as he sat, his legs apart, leaning forward with his elbows resting on his knees.

"Tell me," she said slowly, "why you come here."

Popov was silent for a while before answering. There were good reasons of course. The first had been that the Bolshevik party was short of funds. Whether he could get money out of the industrialist's wife he had no idea; but it was worth looking into. He remembered how, not long ago, when a rich sympathizer had left a legacy to the party and his two daughters had disputed the will, a pair of enterprising Bolsheviks, concealing their affiliation, had somehow persuaded the two women to marry them and got the money for the party that way. Even Popov had been impressed by that piece of audacity. It showed what could be done.

Yet there was more to it than that. He was frankly flattered that this proud, clever woman should feel attracted to him. Indeed, he had to confess, he felt something for her, and if his first thought had been to humiliate her, now he found himself even wondering: could she, perhaps, be saved?

"I find you interesting," he said at last.

She smiled. "You're just curious?"

"Why not?"

Certainly he was curious. Suvorin impressed him. This was not a weakling, like a Bobrov, to be brushed aside. Suvorin was powerful and intelligent, one of the great capitalists whose final overthrow would begin the revolution. How could he not be curious about his world? When he entered the Suvorin house, Popov also realized that it represented something else that had been missing in his life.

For though he had traveled, and studied history and economics, Popov had never taken much interest in the arts. When he was with Mrs. Suvorin, he was sometimes reminded, with a wry smile, of a conversation he had had in Switzerland the previous year with his friend Lenin. They had been speaking of the countess in Saint Petersburg when Lenin burst out: "Do you know, she showed me a strange thing once. A postcard of a painting called the Mona Lisa." He had shaken his bald head. "Have you ever heard of it, Popov? I hadn't. What on earth is it about? I couldn't make head nor tail of it." And though Popov was not quite so prosaic as the great revolutionary, he had often to confess a sense of ignorance in Mrs. Suvorin's presence; and he would let her lead him to one of the rooms where her husband's modern paintings hung and would stare at them, fascinated, while she explained them.

But now she was looking at him thoughtfully. "Tell me," she suddenly said, "if you knew, for a certainty, that all this was going to continue, that there would be no revolution for at least a hundred years, what would you do?"

It was a fair question. "Actually," he confessed, "I think Stolypin may succeed. So does Lenin. The revolution may not even come in my lifetime." He shrugged, then smiled. "I suppose the truth is," he admitted frankly, "I've spent all my life being a revolutionary and I wouldn't know how to be anything else. It's a vocation, you know, like any other."

"But in the long run, you think all this"—she gestured around the beautifully furnished room—"has to go."

"Certainly. There isn't room for such privilege. All men will be equal."

"And when the revolution comes, you will destroy the capitalists and their supporters ruthlessly."

"Yes."

"Then tell me this," she continued pleasantly. "If the revolution actually comes soon, and I choose to resist it"—she smiled quizzically—"would you kill me, too?"

To which, instead of answering, he frowned and paused to think.

That, she decided, was what she liked. However devious he might be in his dealings, there was still a strange if cruel honesty about him. Something almost pure. He was undoubtedly dangerous: perhaps her fascination with him was, in part, the excitement of a forbidden love. And now, rather than lie, he was calmly considering whether he would kill her or not.

"Well?"

"I don't think it would be necessary. Actually," he added, "I think you could be saved."

He did, too. She was like a bird in a cage, he often thought: trapped in this huge mansion and her bourgeois world, certainly; yet still a free spirit, capable of leaving all this behind if called to a higher purpose.

"I suppose that's a compliment." She smiled.

"Yes. It is."

For several more minutes they sat in silence, conscious of the other, yet following their own thoughts.

And then the fire in the grate hissed, and spat.

The fire was low, just some brightly glowing embers amidst the ash, and the little piece of sparkling cinder it threw out might easily have lain on the floor and slowly extinguished itself. But by chance it came to rest upon the edge of Mrs. Suvorin's peignoir and immediately flared up with a sharp flame. She gave a little cry and, intending to whisk her peignoir away, stupidly flicked the lighted cinder onto her lap instead.

It was nothing really. An instant more and she could have risen and stamped out the tiny fire. But seeing the fear on her face, Popov suddenly thought that she was catching flame and, without thinking more, threw himself forward, plucking the burning cinder from her in his bare hands and tossing it back into the grate. Then, grabbing a cushion, he smothered the little fire.

And now, finding him almost in her arms, Mrs. Suvorin looked into his face and saw, to her surprise, a look of tenderness.

"Don't move," she said.

It was another two hours before, in the damp cold outside, young Alexander Bobrov gave up his lonely vigil. He could not understand it. The devil Popov was with her; there could be only one reason why.

And what on earth, he wondered, should be done?

1910

At first sight, in the years 1909 and 1910, it might have seemed that the household of Professor Peter Suvorin was a place of perfect harmony.

Everyone was busy. Dimitri had two music professors now and was making rapid strides. Karpenko had entered the School of Art and was already gaining a reputation as a fellow of ideas. As was his custom, kindly Vladimir had given the young man a helping hand, inviting him frequently to his house when distinguished members of the art world were gathered there, and introducing him to several artists. And Peter Suvorin himself was particularly busy: for it was during these years that he wrote his classic textbook, *Physics for Students,* which was to make his name affectionately familiar to a whole generation of Russian schoolboys.

These were quiet times for Russia, too. To Dimitri, as he walked into the shady courtyard of the apartment building, it often seemed that, if great events were stirring in the world, their sounds had been muffled by the time they reached the narrow, tree-lined streets of Moscow. Of the doings of the tsar, his German wife, and their children in their private palaces in Saint Petersburg, he heard hardly anything.

Dimitri knew, too, that Stolypin and the duma continued on their road of slow reform; though when he read the newspapers it seemed to him that the great minister, though he brought peace and prosperity, had few friends. "The liberals hate him for clamping down," Vladimir explained, "but the reactionaries hate him because his system of governing seems to weaken the absolute autocracy of the tsar. He's winning through, though," he added.

To Dimitri, the evenings were the best time of the day, when the family sat together around the table and discussed the day's events. How delightful it was, especially in the spring and summer months, when his mother would prepare tea, served with raspberries, and through the open window one could see the mellow turquoise sky and hear, faintly, the singing of vespers from the church next door.

Karpenko was a constant source of conversation. While Dimitri's studies, at this time, were of a gradual and private nature—he would be immersed for weeks at a time in the Beethoven piano sonatas, or in a Tchaikovsky symphony, which profound joys could not easily be shared in words—Karpenko was in a continual ferment of intellectual excitement; and hardly a week seemed to pass when he did not bring home some new discovery that changed the world. Sometimes it was a new school of painting, inaugurated in an exhibition with some name like the Blue Rose, or the Golden Fleece. One month he read the *Confessions* of the writer Gorky and some writings of a new group in Saint Petersburg who called themselves the God Builders, and each evening he would lecture the family: "Don't you see, all through the centuries man has been like Prometheus, chained to a rock of superstition. But now, Dimitri, man is risen. The people is God. The people will be immortal. Think of it, Professor: first the people will create the revolution and be free; then, maybe one day we'll even take over other planets, the universe." And afterwards he and Dimitri would continue these weighty discussions in the room they shared, late into the night.

But the discovery of Karpenko's that meant the most to Dimitri was something more modest. There were many poets in Moscow and Saint Petersburg just then; indeed, poetry was so popular that poets could even make a living at their craft. And one night Karpenko arrived with a collection of verses by some people Dimitri had not heard of before. "They're a new school," he explained. "Instead of using symbols and abstract ideas they write more directly, about experience." Two of these in particular Dimitri loved at once. "I feel as if they're writing about this very street, this very apartment and family," he said, delightedly. And so, at the start of their careers, he discovered two of Russia's greatest twentieth-century poets: Osip Mandelstam, and Anna Akhmatova.

Yet despite Karpenko's brilliance, it was during these evenings that Dimitri gradually came, as never before, to appreciate one other member of his close-knit family: this was his father.

Peter Suvorin seldom spoke much, but he would sit, with his gold-rimmed spectacles propped below the bridge of his nose, quietly reading a paper or looking over the pages of his manuscript. His face was clean-shaven except for a small wedge of beard on his chin; and though his hair was gray and his face, somewhat drawn, had collected little lines upon it, he still looked less than his fifty-five years. With his look of kindly serenity, one might have taken him for a Swedish pastor.

And in his gentle way, he presided over everything. "Do you know what your father reminds me of?" Karpenko once laughingly remarked to Dimitri. "He's like one of those elders at a monastery. We all worship and make a noise and believe. But the elder in his hermitage, he's quiet and serene: because unlike the rest of us, he *knows.* That's how it is with your father and the revolution."

Indeed, Peter Suvorin had reason to be content with his modest, steady course. The Bolsheviks in the last two years had little to show for their extremism. Police spies had infiltrated their ranks and made it hard for them to operate. Their lonely leader Lenin seemed to have been forced into permanent exile in Switzerland, and their membership had plummeted. But the moderate, Menshevik socialists had continued about their business, gradually building up support in the factories, organizing trade unions, educating, and publishing—mostly legal activities. Some were ready to work with the duma. There was even talk of changing the party's name to the Workers' Party. And Peter Suvorin was happy because, as he would tell his family: "It's progress."

"The new age is coming," he liked to say, "not because of your will, Karpenko, nor even the cunning of a fellow like Popov. You shouldn't worry about the now or the when: we do not know the hour or the manner of its coming. The point is that we know the process is inevitable."

Once, with a smile, the professor had remarked: "It occurred to me as I was working on my book the other day, that the Marxist dialectic is like the laws of physics. Consider an electric current. It has a positive and negative charge: thesis and antithesis—they create a tension, the potential difference. They flow together, making a synthesis. When Trotsky used to speak of a permanent revolution in the world—a continuous process—I suppose it's like an electric current: endless, dynamic, capable of powering anything." Listening to his father, Dimitri would get a wonderful sense that all things in the universe were scientifically related, and that his little family, with their different forms of expression, were all moving along the great highway to an ultimate and marvelous destiny.

Nothing ever seemed to change the professor. He taught, he wrote, his pupils came to the house. His life was as quiet and ordered as his mind. Whatever else was going on, Peter's activities gave the household a certain rhythm and purpose. It was comforting.

And by the summer of 1910, Dimitri was certainly in need of comfort. For by then it was clear that Rosa Suvorin was going mad.

For some months after Dimitri's accident, Rosa's habitual anxiousness seemed to have lessened. It was as if, fearing something worse, she was actually relieved that tragedy had struck and that now it was over. But then, just around the time Peter started writing his book, something began to change.

Why did she insist upon typing his book herself? Several times he had begged her to let him give the work to someone else, but on each occasion she had gone white with determination, as though he were somehow trying to violate her act of passionate devotion, and he had given up.

Each night, after supper was finished, she would set up her typewriter in the little dining room and start to work. She refused to do this during the day, saying she had no time then. Over and over again, she would type whatever Peter had written, until she was satisfied that it was perfect. Sometimes she would be done in an hour or so; but often she would continue, late into the night, lovingly placing her offering on the table in the hall in the early hours, and appear in the morning with eyes dark from lack of sleep. And how many nights, Dimitri wondered, had he fallen asleep to the faint sound of the typewriter going *tap, tap, tap* in the darkness?

Worse however than this obsessive behavior, which wore Rosa down, was the reawakening of her old anxiousness, which now returned with a vengeance.

It took strange forms. If there were the faintest chill in the air, Peter must have an overcoat and a fur hat; if the sun was warm, she feared for sunstroke; whenever there was ice upon the ground, she knew he must have slipped and injured himself. This anxiety soon extended to cover Dimitri as well. Sometimes, to his great embarrassment, she would even insist that Karpenko go with him to school, in case anything should happen to him on the way. She could only relax, it seemed, in the evenings, when her husband and son were safely at home again.

Then she began to follow them. At first they did not even realize that she was doing so: she would have some perfectly plausible excuse—a friend to visit, some shopping to do—for accompanying Peter to the university or Dimitri to school. But before long the excuses wore out and it became clear that she simply wanted to keep them in sight. Peter, who went in to the university only twice a week, decided to humor her; but Dimitri had to beg her to let him alone; and often thereafter he would turn irritably, to find her pale, wan face a hundred yards behind him.

More embarrassing were her suspicions.

They came, it seemed, from nowhere. Yet they tortured her. She would decide, quite suddenly, that a fellow professor was out to get Peter, or a neighbor with whom she was on friendly terms was a police spy, watching her whole family. She would earnestly warn Dimitri that there was a hidden conspiracy, coming from the Black Hundreds, to destroy all Jews and socialists. "Anyone may be in it," she would warn him, "you never know." And no one, it seemed, was above suspicion.

In the first months of 1910, Karpenko grew agitated because the government, having allowed the Ukraine some cultural freedom, became nervous over the sense of nationalism emerging there. "The word is that they are about to close all the Ukrainian cultural societies," he told them dejectedly. "We Cossacks should rise up again as we did before," he added wryly, "and take over the Ukraine again."

It was an innocent statement, said jokingly. But suddenly Rosa's face clouded. "What do you mean by that?" she demanded. "What sort of uprising?" And for some ten minutes she cross-questioned the youth suspiciously. And afterwards, when Dimitri asked her what the matter was, she turned to him with a troubled face and explained: "Don't you realize: the Cossack uprising was the greatest massacre of Jews that Russia has ever seen."

"But you surely don't think . . . ?"

"You never know, Dimitri. You can never be sure of anybody."

And Dimitri could only shake his head.

It was a week after this incident, when the two of them happened to be alone, that Rosa sat Dimitri down at the kitchen table and said to him earnestly: "I want you to make me one promise, Dimitri. Will you do it for me?"

"If I can," he replied.

"Promise me, then, that you will be a musician. That you will never become a revolutionary, like your father, but that you will stick to music."

Dimitri shrugged. Since he had every hope of devoting his life to music this did not seem too hard a thing to promise. "All right," he said.

"Your word?"

"Yes." He smiled, half irritated, half with love and pity, at Rosa. How haggard her face looked. "Why?"

She gazed at him sadly. It occurred to Dimitri that the seers of ancient times, like Cassandra in Greek tragedy, might have looked a little like his mother, with huge, sorrowful eyes that seemed to see beyond the present, into a terrible future. "You don't understand," she told him. "Only Jewish musicians will be safe. Only musicians."

And there was nothing he could say at this obvious sign of madness.

* * *

Several times, in the spring of 1910, Peter tried to persuade Rosa to see a doctor, but she would not hear of it. He discussed the matter with his brother Vladimir, who twice came to the apartment and who suggested she should go down to Russka for peace and quiet. This, however, she also rejected. "I'm going to Germany in May," he informed Peter. "I believe there's a doctor there who could help her. But though Peter was agreeable, Rosa utterly refused even to consider it. And no one knew quite what to do.

It was at the start of May that Dimitri overheard a strange conversation that, even in retrospect, continued to puzzle him.

He and Karpenko were spending the evening with Nadezhda. As usual the time had passed delightfully and after a long discussion about music he had suggested he play them the Tchaikovsky *Seasons,* only to find that the music was not in the house. He had returned to the apartment therefore, with the aim of collecting the score and hurrying back to the big Suvorin house to play it.

He knew that his mother was alone that evening, since Peter was out at a meeting nearby. He was surprised therefore, upon opening the door, to hear voices coming from the little drawing room off the hall. They belonged to his mother and to Vladimir. His mother's, for some reason, was only a faint murmur, but Vladimir's rich voice he could hear clearly.

"I'm more concerned with you. This can't go on. For God's sake, my dear, come away with me to Germany."

Then his mother's voice, too soft to make out.

"Nothing will happen to anyone."

Another murmur.

"I tell you truthfully, the boy's better off here at present. There are no better music teachers in the world than in Russia."

Now there was a longer pause. Dimly he heard his mother say something about a letter. Then his uncle's voice again. "Yes, yes. I give you my word. Of course I can arrange it. If anything happens I'll get him out. Yes, Dimitri shall go to America if that is what you wish."

After this there was a long silence, and then he thought he heard his mother sobbing. Instead of collecting his music, he quietly withdrew and returned to his friends saying that he had been unable to find it. But later that night, as he lay awake in his room and listened to the faint *tap, tap, tap* of his mother's typewriter, he wondered: what on earth would he want with America?

There was no question about it. Mrs. Suvorin had scored one of the greatest coups of her social career so far. A personal triumph.

For in mid-June 1910, the week after All Saints' Day, she entertained the monk, Rasputin.

He had said he would come in the afternoon and take tea. It was therefore an intimate gathering that Mrs. Suvorin had prepared, consisting of family members, some of her more important friends, and those few women who, over the years, had deliberately or inadvertently hurt her vanity, and who now could not fail to be impressed by this visitor who was known to be on intimate terms with the imperial family.

Vladimir was still abroad, but she kindly invited Peter Suvorin and Rosa, and naturally Dimitri and Karpenko accompanied them. And so it was that the two youths found themselves in a company of forty or so persons eagerly awaiting the arrival of the strange man.

It was five years since Rasputin had first appeared before the tsar, but much about him was still a mystery. People called him a holy man— though he was never a monk, as some supposed. Indeed, though he seldom bothered to see them, he had a wife and family in the distant Urals. And though voices had been raised in the capital about his lewd behavior, many credited him with supernatural powers. "He's a real hermit from the Russian forests," Karpenko told Dimitri. "They say he walked to the capital all the way from Siberia." He gave a little laugh: "He's supposed to have the power of second sight, you know. Just watch his eyes." What everyone knew, however, and what made him nowadays a figure to be courted by fashionable ladies, was the fact that he had a devoted admirer in the empress.

What did she see in him? Few people knew. The imperial household was a little world apart, utterly cut off from the rest of society by a phalanx of noble courtiers from old service families who thought it their duty to separate the monarchy from the barbarous Russian people as far as possible. The tsar, his German wife, his daughters, and the heir to the throne, the little tsarevich, were as hidden from even prominent subjects as the family of an oriental despot.

And that the heir to the throne had a terrible disease that made him bleed, and threatened his life, and that this extraordinary, hypnotic peasant from Siberia seemed able to cure it, not even rich Mrs. Suvorin had the least idea.

If Mrs. Suvorin had intended to stage a memorable little occasion, she was afraid for a short time that her efforts might collapse in ruins, since Rasputin was extremely late. But at last the doors opened, conversation dropped, and a black-clothed figure was ushered in. After which all the company stared in surprise. For he was not what they had expected.

"I thought he'd be taller," Karpenko whispered, in obvious disappointment.

The man who was the imperial family's confidant, and who knew the most terrible medical secret in the Russian empire, was hardly an impressive figure. He was only of medium height; the top of his head reached no higher than the base of Mrs. Suvorin's coiffure. He was rather slightly built with a narrow chest and sloping shoulders. His long, dark hair was parted in the middle; his beard, which hardly reached the top of his chest, was rather wiry. His blunt nose veered away noticeably to the left. He wore a simple long coat of black silk that reached below his knees. He might have been a small-time priest from one of a thousand villages. Though his clothes were clean and his beard combed, there was a faint, acrid smell from his body that suggested he washed himself less often than other men.

He bowed politely to everyone in the room and seemed grateful when

Mrs. Suvorin led him to a sofa and offered him tea.

The little party, however, soon seemed to be going rather well. Mrs. Suvorin, rather meeker than usual, sat and made polite conversation with her honored guest. The imperial family was mentioned and pious sentiments about them expressed. Various people were brought over to speak to Rasputin and for each, it seemed, he had kind and modest words. When Nadezhda was introduced, he politely told her mother that the girl had a beautiful nature. To Peter Suvorin he respectfully said: "You study the wonders of God's universe."

"There doesn't seem anything so remarkable about him," Dimitri remarked to Karpenko.

He was to revise this opinion somewhat, however, a few minutes later, when Mrs. Suvorin motioned him to approach. For it was only now, as he came face to face with Rasputin, that he encountered that strange man's most extraordinary feature.

While he observed him before, it had seemed to Dimitri that the fellow's eyes were rather foxy: curious, watchful, probably cunning as, from under his heavy peasant brow, their gaze darted here and there about the room. But now, finding them turned and fixed upon himself, Dimitri experienced their full effect.

They burned: there was no other word for it. They were like two searchlights boring through the darkness, and everything else about the man was forgotten as one felt their astonishing, primal force. Only when he drew very close did the hypnotic gaze seem to soften and the eyes appear kindly, if a little bloodshot.

"A musician. Ah yes." That was all Rasputin said to him. It seemed he was not especially interested in Dimitri, though for some reason, after he had returned to his place, the boy felt a strange tingling sensation in his back.

Despite this little glimpse of Rasputin's power, the rest of the visit passed quietly enough; and it might have remained in Dimitri's mind as nothing more than a social event but for two small incidents that took place shortly before Rasputin left. The first concerned his mother.

Rosa had already been introduced, just after Peter, and apart from a polite bow, Rasputin had appeared to take no notice of her at all. Indeed, he was not even looking in her direction when suddenly, as if impelled, he rose from the sofa, turned, and walking swiftly over to where she was standing, took hold of her forearm with one hand and stood there, like a doctor feeling a pulse, quite silent for almost a minute. Then, without a word, he calmly let the arm drop and returned to his place, continuing his conversation with Mrs. Suvorin as though nothing had happened. As for Rosa, though everyone else looked awkward, she did not blush, or even look startled, but stood very still, and neither then nor later did she ever refer to the incident.

The more frightening occurrence took place as Rasputin was leaving.

For some reason, after watching him for a while, Karpenko had suddenly decided he did not want to meet Rasputin. When it looked as if Mrs. Suvorin was about to summon him, he had slipped away to a far corner of the room. And as the visitor finally rose to take his leave,

Karpenko watched discreetly from behind the cover of two elderly ladies.

And Rasputin was halfway to the door when he abruptly stopped, wheeled, and came straight towards him.

The two ladies blushed and parted. Rasputin came nearer, then paused about ten feet in front of the young man. The hypnotic eyes stared at him, as Karpenko, stripped of his protection, seemed to quail before them. For a full quarter minute Rasputin looked at Karpenko. And then he smiled. "Well, well," he said softly. "I have known others like you, in Siberia and Saint Petersburg." And to Mrs. Suvorin: "What a clever young Cossack to have in your house."

What on earth did he mean? Mrs. Suvorin seemed to understand him, but she only looked a little awkward and escorted Rasputin to the door.

But the effect upon Karpenko was devastating. By the time Rasputin had gone and Dimitri had gone over to him, he was white as a ghost and shaking. When Dimitri put his arm around him and asked him what was the matter he could only whisper: "He saw through me. He saw everything. He is the devil himself." And when Dimitri gave him a look of blank incomprehension, he just grimaced, shot an awkward glance at Mrs. Suvorin, and muttered: "You don't understand. You know nothing."

And for several weeks afterwards, the young Cossack was moody and withdrawn; and Dimitri could not discover why.

1911 September

FOR some reason, Rosa noticed, her breasts felt cold. Why should that be? The chill damp air smelled faintly of smoke as she walked down the street. Darkness had fallen an hour ago. Here and there, lamps glowed.

At the corner she stopped and looked back. The bedroom she and Peter shared was the only room in the apartment that looked onto the street and for some reason—she herself did not know why—she had lit a candle and placed it in the window there. She could just see it now, a small, guttering flame set in the dark frame of the building, a strange, intimate little sentinel. A message perhaps, of love and of hope. Except for a note to say she had gone for a walk, she was leaving no other.

She walked around the corner. Her footsteps, oddly, felt light.

No one would know: that was the point. That was, in truth, her gift of love to them, that they should never know. Only Vladimir would know, and he was with his son in Paris now, not due back for a month. She had not written to him: there was no message; but he would know, and he would keep her secret.

A party of Cossacks clattered by on their horses on their way back to barracks, capes pulled tightly around them against the autumn chill.

When had it all begun? At the very start, perhaps: she had married Peter Suvorin when she was still depressed. That was her fault. Yet she had loved him passionately. No, she thought she could pinpoint the real

beginning. It was in 1900, when little Dimitri was five and the letter had
come from America.

Since her marriage, Rosa had had little contact with her family in
Vilnius. Four years afterwards, her mother had unexpectedly died, and
then her elder brother and his family had emigrated to America. Then,
in 1899 her other brother had followed. Their departures had not surprised her. Tens, hundreds of thousands of Jews were leaving; indeed, by
1914 some two million Jews would leave Russia for the United States;
and the tsarist government was glad to see them go. Rosa had been happy
that her brothers had crossed the Atlantic to find happiness; but their
lives, by now, seemed far removed from hers.

And then came the letter. It was from her second brother, who normally disliked writing and from whom she had not heard since several
months before he left. Yet now he wrote at length, giving a detailed
account of the crossing and news of the family; and his letter also contained a long final section.

> We came to Ellis Island. It was frightening for a moment. When
> I saw that great slab of a building and saw the rows of other immi-
> grants waiting for inspection in the huge hall I thought—My God,
> it's going to be like Russia, only worse. It's a prison— But it was soon
> over and then we were out.
>
> And then . . . This is why I had to write to you, dear Rosa. Then
> we were free. Can you imagine the feel of it? It's hard to describe.
> To *know* that you are free. There are no gendarmes watching you for
> the Ministry of the Interior, no police spies looking for enemies of
> the regime. You can go where you please. Everyone can vote. And
> a Jew has as many rights as anyone else.
>
> The Americans are like the Russians. They are simple and
> straightforward, and speak from the heart—the Russians at their
> best, that is! But also they are unlike Russians, because they are free,
> and they know it.
>
> And this is why I am writing to you now, dear Rosa. For being
> here, I can't help thinking of you. Of course, you have converted and
> you live in Moscow. But are you sure, are you really sure that this
> truly makes you safe? And little Dimitri: apart from your conver-
> sion, which I know was done for expediency, in Jewish eyes the son
> of a Jewish mother is a Jew. It's not that I'm personally religious: you
> know I'm not. But all I mean to say is, if things get bad in Russia,
> for God's sake come to America. Legally or illegally, you can always
> arrange something. Come and join us, I beg you, here where all your
> family will be safe.

The letter had made a lasting impression upon Rosa. If in recent years,
with her new life and her child, she had seldom thought about the past,
the letter brought it all back to her with a strange force. With poignancy
she found herself thinking of her poor father and all he had tried to do
for her. She thought of her own music, which she had never gone back
to since marriage. She remembered rather sadly, now, the pain she had

caused her mother. And picturing her brothers she thought: I wish I could see them again.

The letter worried her, too. Though her brother spoke of the Jews, she did not fail to notice his veiled reference to police spies and enemies of the regime. Peter, with his socialist activities, could also find himself in danger. She had mulled over the letter for a month before showing it to Peter one morning and asking: "What do you think?"

But even she had not been prepared for his response.

"How terrible," he said, "to want to leave Russia." And when she suggested that perhaps it might be better for them to move to America, he just looked at her with blank incomprehension and suggested she might want to lie down. She knew better than to raise the subject again. She had discovered that, though gentle and kind, Peter also possessed a strange obstinacy that made him blind to anything that did not fit his idea of the universe. They would never go to America: there was nothing more to say.

Had she resented this? She did not believe so at the time. She loved Peter. He was so good and simple; and though he had been almost a father-figure at the start, as the years passed she realized increasingly how much he relied upon her. He did so with such touching faith. "I can't imagine how I would have lived without you," he would sometimes say. "It was surely the angels who sent you." And once he had even confessed: "That day you spoke of America. That was the worst day in my life. For a moment, you know, it was as if you were suggesting you wanted to turn your back on everything I love. Thank God that madness passed."

He needed her. He plainly adored her. And how could she tell him, therefore, what was happening to her now?

It was in 1905 that the terrible dreams had begun. They came quite suddenly and without warning. And the subject was always the same: the pogrom.

Often it was her father's face that she saw, surrounded by the mob. Then she would see the burly Cossack, sitting in his cart—sympathetic but ready to leave them to their fate, and it would seem to her that this time the men got her father, and dragged him away. After a while, however, the dream would get more complex. Time would be telescoped. She would be in the village in the Ukraine, but a grown woman instead of a child. Her father would suddenly become transformed into Peter. Worse yet, under an echoing gray sky, he would turn into little Dimitri.

Night after night the dreams came, and she would awake in a cold sweat, terrified. They were so frightening that at times she dreaded even going to sleep. And in her waking hours, now, a terrible new premonition began to form in her mind—a gnawing conviction that, try as she might, nothing would shake: something awful was going to happen to Peter and Dimitri.

Only some months after the onset of the dream had the other problem begun. Whether it was related or not, Rosa could not be sure. Was it some hidden resentment, or a fear about which she knew nothing? Whatever the reason, the new misery not only came to her, it refused to go away.

She could not bear her husband to touch her anymore.

Even now, five years later, she could be proud of one thing: Peter never knew. She loved him. She knew that he could never understand. Sometimes of course she had slept with him, and, by a supreme act of will, had completely disguised her secret revulsion at the act. But week after week, month after month, she had devised excuses that allowed her to avoid lovemaking at night while she heaped her affection upon him by day; and whether it was guilt at this subterfuge and betrayal, or the recurring dreams, or whether they were all tangled up together, she found that she was becoming more and more filled with a terrible premonition that her husband and her son were in danger. This had been her frame of mind, when Dimitri had been attacked and discovered he was Jewish.

Only Vladimir had guessed her secret. Dear Vladimir. Somehow, he had guessed everything.

She found she had reached the broad boulevard that circled the inner city. The wind was driving along it, picking leaves off the little trees at the edge of the street and carrying them eastward. A carriage rattled by.

Had she briefly, when she was young, thought of Vladimir as a lover? She gave a little laugh. An impossible love: a love that could never be. Yet even a platonic love like theirs contained pleasures and pains. For what did it mean to a woman to know that it was not her husband but his brother who truly understood her? She loved his company; he made her happy. Yet she feared him. For he returned her to herself; he induced her to play again; he showed her too clearly what she tried to hide from herself—the agonizing gulf that separated her from her husband; and so she would flee from Vladimir back to her prison. "You must get away, just to sleep," he would urge, and she knew it was true. But she could not. "You'll destroy yourself, my little bird." Then so be it.

Vladimir had promised to get Dimitri to America. That was all that mattered to her now.

She passed a store where they sold newspapers and glanced in. There was a little board by the door, proclaiming a headline. Poor Stolypin, the loyal minister, had been shot in Kiev earlier that month. Now it turned out that his assassin was a double agent: a police spy who had only committed the atrocity because the revolutionary group he had infiltrated had begun to suspect him. She shook her head wearily. "Only in our poor Russia do we live with such insanity," she murmured. Was the whole Russian empire just a bad dream? she wondered. Perhaps.

A dream from which it was time to escape.

The street she now took contained tramlines. Since before the turn of the century, there had been trams in Moscow—stout vehicles with a lower and an open upper deck, and drawn by a pair of horses. They moved along at a pleasant, easy pace. In the last year or so, however, these had begun to be replaced by electrified trams—single-deckers that moved along at a far greater speed. The new age was coming, there was no doubt. A little way up the street, Rosa noticed, there was an intersection of lines at a crossroad, and she made towards that.

Dimitri would go to America. And he would be a musician. That was what her father had always said: "They often forgive Jews if they are musicians."

There was a little knot of people standing in a lighted doorway by the crossroads and they watched the woman idly as she walked up the street. One of them noticed that she looked rather cheerful. "Quite normal," as he later said. "Nothing unusual."

Peter Suvorin's book, of course, had been her standby for the last eighteen months. How many nights had she devotedly typed for her husband until the early hours, when he was safely asleep? The act of devotion that kept her from his bed and about which she had not had to explain anything. But the book had been finished last week. It was going to press. It would probably make him famous, and leave her with nothing to protect her.

It was not difficult to accomplish. Like a friend who had only been waiting for her to arrive, the electric tram hastened towards her through the night, just as she reached the crossing. Rosa paused. She had taken off her gloves, as if to fumble for something in her pockets; now, casually she put them on again, not even noticing that she had pulled her glove from her left hand onto her right. The tram, as it came closer, seemed to be whispering. "At last. Come with me." Two paces, three.

They all saw. There was no doubt about what happened. The woman standing on the curb and looking in her pockets had glanced up at the tram, turned, and slipped. She uttered a little cry as her foot, trying to find its balance on the damp stone, had shot up in an ungainly manner. She had seemed to grasp for support as, twisting, she fell into the street. The tram had been almost on top of her as she went down. It was all so absurd.

Just as the tram passed over her, Rosa saw her father.

There was no doubt in anyone's mind that, even if she was subject to moods, this wretched business had been an accident.

It was two months afterwards that Dimitri Suvorin completed the three *Etudes* in her memory, rather in the manner of Scriabin, which have always been agreed to be his first serious and mature compositions.

1913

As the year 1913 drew towards its close, Alexander Bobrov looked forward with some confidence to a pleasant future. True, there were some obstacles to overcome, but he had prepared his personal campaign carefully and he was quietly confident. The girl was fifteen now and already a dazzling young woman. Soon it would be time to begin.

Alexander was twenty-two. He was above average height, powerfully built, and had the saturnine, rather stern good looks of his great-grandfather Alexis, though, unlike him, he was clean-shaven.

He was acutely conscious of his good looks. This, however, was not exactly vanity. As the last representative of his noble family, and, despite his father's liberal tendencies, as a representative of the order that was dedicated to protecting and preserving the tsar, he felt it was his duty to be handsome. He took care, besides dressing carefully, to hold himself with a military uprightness—with what, in those days, was referred to by the French term as a proper *tenue*—and to be seen, as far as he could afford it, in the best places. His position in life, his whole desire, prompted him to seek two things and two things only. One was a court appointment; the other his marriage to the heiress Nadezhda Suvorin. For both these objects he was steadfastly preparing himself.

This preparation included his sexual experience. "I shall be faithful to my wife," he told a friend, a young officer in the imperial guard. "But I shall get some experience first. My plan is to have ten mistresses. What do you think?" "My dear fellow, why not twenty?" "No," Alexander had replied seriously, "I think ten will do."

He had gone about the business methodically. His first had been the wife of an army doctor—a pleasant woman in her mid-twenties who had been amused, as much as anything, by the solemn eighteen-year-old's evident determination to get into bed with her. That had lasted three months. There had been a charming dancer from the corps de ballet in Saint Petersburg: after all, every man of the world was supposed to have had an affair with a dancer. To make sure he had, so to speak, covered all the ground, he had a brief fling with a gypsy singer from a theater— though whether she was a gypsy he was not sure; and for a month he had gone regularly to a certain young lady in one of the capital's most select brothels, patronized only by those from a certain milieu. Notwithstanding its select clientele, he lived in constant fear of unhappy consequences and, besides, found it awfully expensive. After a month he went there no more. He was currently on his sixth experiment, an amusing blond widow in her twenties, half German, half Latvian, who, it seemed, saw no reason why a young fellow like him should sleep. And with this arrangement, for the time being, he was quite content.

When he looked to the future of Russia itself, Alexander also had reason to be hopeful. The third duma had lasted its full five-year term until the previous year and now a new, fourth duma was sitting. The tsar had succeeded in somewhat increasing the conservative element, though the radicals had also strengthened, leaving the center weaker; but taken as a whole, the new body was no worse than the last. His father, indefatigably, had got himself elected again. And, it had to be said, the condition in the country as a whole was now excellent.

"Stolypin's gone, and his place has been taken by nonentities," Nicolai Bobrov had remarked to his conservative son, "but his work lives on. Look at the results." And he would tick them off on his fingers enthusiastically. "Trade: hugely up. Agricultural yields: up, and we exported thirteen and a half million tons of cereals in 1911. The state debt's well down: we've run budget surpluses in three of the last four years. The countryside's quiet." He would smile contentedly.

"Do you know," he told Alexander once, "I met a Frenchman the other day who calculates that at our present rate of economic growth, we'll overshadow the economy of the whole of Western Europe by 1950. Just think: you'll probably live to see it." Of the revolution, little was heard in those years. "With a little luck," the elder Bobrov liked to say, "we may have headed it off."

Indeed, only if one looked abroad were there any clouds on the horizon; but neither of the Bobrov men, nor anyone they knew, was overly concerned.

"Diplomacy will sort out any problems," Nicolai would tell his son. "The great powers have to live together. That's why we have all these alliances."

The huge system of alliances, indeed, seemed rather in Russia's favor. The need for French finance and a better understanding with Great Britain had drawn these three countries into the pact known as the Triple Entente; Germany, Austria, and Italy had formed the Triple Alliance. "But they balance each other," Nicolai often pointed out. "Each keeps the other in order."

Only down in the mountainous Balkan region above Greece was there any sign of real danger. Here, as the power of the almost defunct Ottoman Empire finally crumbled, Austria was advancing. In 1908 she had taken the two provinces of Bosnia and Herzegovina, inhabited mostly by Slavic Serbs. Other Serbs felt threatened; Russia, sympathetic to her fellow Slavs, and watchful of this region so close to Constantinople and the Black Sea, monitored each development carefully. "But all these things will get worked out," Nicolai predicted. "It's not in anyone's interest to start a war." There were few statesmen in Europe who would have disagreed with him.

Indeed, in the last five years only one matter had marred the serenity of Alexander's world and caused him mental discomfort.

Yevgeny Popov: what should be done about him?

In a sense, even Alexander realized, Mrs. Suvorin's affairs were none of his business. Yet so great was his loathing of Popov, so huge his respect for Vladimir, that the thought of Popov's liaison preyed upon his mind. On that first misty night when he had seen the Bolshevik sneak into the Suvorin mansion, he had felt a kind of personal violation.

Even then, after his chilly vigil in the street, he had not wanted to believe it. Trying to fathom the mystery, he had taken to wandering about the area late at night; and twice more that very month he had witnessed Popov arriving for a tryst. There could be no doubt: the household of his future wife, and the person of his future mother-in-law, were being contaminated by the redheaded socialist.

It was terrible.

But what should he do? Vladimir was his friend. If the great man was being deceived, then surely it was his duty, Alexander considered, to warn him. It wasn't only the dishonor, either. One never knew what trouble a man like Popov could bring to a respectable family. He would be protecting Nadezhda too. To tell the older man directly was embarrassing, though. Besides, if Mrs. Suvorin discovered what he had done, he'd earn her undying hatred: hardly a satisfactory situation when he was hoping to become her son-in-law.

If he could just remove Popov from the scene somehow. He was fairly certain that the police would arrest Popov if they could find him; but he couldn't very well direct the police to him when he was anywhere near the Suvorins. Twice he waited until the early hours and tried to follow the Bolshevik; each time, though, Popov somehow managed to disappear within a few blocks.

The solution he finally hit upon was straightforward enough. He sent an anonymous letter to Vladimir. It was rather a successful production, made with cuttings from newspapers, and rather illiterate: he was proud of it. He did not refer to Popov by name, but rather as "a certain redhead revolutionary." He continued after this to walk past the Suvorin mansion whenever he could late at night, and for a month or two, catching no sight of Popov, he assumed his letter had worked. But then, some months later, he saw him lurking there again.

From time to time, then and in succeeding years, he would casually ask Vladimir questions such as: "What happened to that damned Popov, the Bolshevik, who came here once?" or "Did they ever arrest that cursed redhead we once saw at your factory? I wonder what became of him." But Vladimir never gave any sign that he knew or cared about the fellow and, it seemed to Alexander, he had done all his duty bid him do. I'll get even with that criminal one day, though, he secretly vowed. I'll put him away.

Apart from these secret nocturnal watches, he was quite often at the Suvorin house; and it was partly as an excuse for visiting Vladimir, and partly to give himself something in common with Nadezhda, that he began during these years to take an interest in painting that was almost professional.

His university studies were not too taxing. In his spare time he worked hard. He made a thorough study of the main movements of Western painting; he also—which he came to enjoy rather more—started to study the ancient art of icon painting in depth. As was his way, he was methodical and serious; but with time he also began to develop a real feel for the subject. More ambitiously, perhaps, he started to venture into contemporary art. Vladimir's son, who still spent more time in Europe than in Russia, had recently sent back astonishing works by Chagall, Matisse, and a curious new figure on the scene who seemed to be starting a whole new school of painting, full of geometric shapes and unlike anything seen before: Pablo Picasso. And whether he liked them or not, whether they were interesting or quite meaningless to him, Alexander Bobrov studied each new item as thoroughly as if it were a riddle to be solved, asking questions, relating them to other work, until he knew more than anyone else. He also began to have a shrewd idea about values so that Vladimir one day remarked to him with amusement: "Funnily enough, my friend, though you're a Russian noble you actually have the makings of a dealer."

Thanks to this knowledge and Vladimir's good opinion of him, Alexander found that Nadezhda treated him with a respect that was pleasing to him. She would be content to leave the high-spirited Dimitri and Karpenko extemporizing at the piano, and walk through her father's galleries with him for a few quiet minutes while he outlined some new and interesting discovery he had made. "You do know a lot," she would say, and look at him with large, serious eyes.

She was fifteen now and, he often noted with approval, filling out nicely. Soon she would be a young woman. Alexander was very careful, therefore, in his relationship with her, keeping a friendly distance, quietly impressing her with his store of knowledge, and waiting for her to come to him.

There was only one problem to overcome at present. He hoped it would pass before too long.

Nadezhda was in love with Karpenko.

To Dimitri Suvorin, the year 1913 was not just a time of promise, but of wild excitement.

For never before had Russian culture risen to such dizzy heights. It was as if all the extraordinary developments of the last century had suddenly come together and burst forth upon the world.

"This isn't a flowering," Karpenko liked to say, "it's an explosion."

Europe had already thrilled to Russian music, to her opera and the bass voice of the legendary Chaliapin. Now Diaghilev's Ballet Russes had taken London, Paris, and Monte Carlo by storm. Two years ago the astounding Nijinsky had danced Stravinsky's *Petrouchka;* last year, he had danced the extraordinary, pagan and erotic *L'Apres-midi d'un Faune;* and in May 1913, in Paris, he had choreographed the event that was to change the history of music: Stravinsky's *Rite of Spring.* Vladimir Suvorin, by good luck, had happened to be visiting Paris at the time.

"It was amazing," he told Dimitri. "And frightening. The audience was scandalized and went berserk. I saw poor Diaghilev afterwards. He doesn't know what to do with Nijinsky: he's terrified he's gone too far. Yet it was brilliant, I tell you. The most exciting thing I ever saw in my life."

He had also brought Dimitri a copy of Stravinsky's score and the young man went over it for days, fascinated by its titanic, primitive energy, its dissonances, never heard before, and its jarring rhythms, finally declaring: "It's like seeing a new galaxy being created by God's hand. It's a new music with new rules."

"Russia is no longer behind Europe," Karpenko had declared on this occasion. "We're ahead." And few could have denied that in this thrilling ferment of all the arts, Russia had become the avant-garde.

If Dimitri was excited by his musical discoveries, the life of his friend Karpenko was now a perpetual whirl. Since Rosa's death, they had rearranged the apartment so that Peter, Dimitri, and Karpenko each had a separate room, and these shared bachelor quarters suited them all very well. Thanks to Vladimir's kindness, Karpenko had enough money to continue his studies and rent a small studio besides; and since he was now in the thick of the avant-garde, one never knew when he would show up at home.

The avant-garde—remarkable in Russia for being led by both men and women—was seething with ideas, and whenever he appeared Karpenko would inform Dimitri and his father about some latest wonder: a riotous abstract canvas by Kandinsky; a brilliant stage set by Benois or Chagall; and invariably some new -ism, so that Peter would quietly inquire: "Well, Karpenko, what's the -ism today?"

In 1913, it was Futurism.

It was certainly a remarkable movement. Led by such brilliant young figures as Malevich, Tatlin, and Mayakovsky, the Russian Futurists liked to combine painting and poetry, producing illustrated books and pamphlets whose daring effect has never been equaled. "Picasso's Cubism was a revolution," Karpenko explained, "but Futurism goes much further." In their paintings the Futurists took the broken, geometric forms of Cubism and set them into explosive forward motion. In their poetry, language was broken down, even to mere sounds, grammar changed, creating something new and striking. To Dimitri, the Futurist productions reminded him of some huge, elective dynamo. "This is the art of the new age—the age of the machine," Karpenko declared gleefully. "Art will transform the world, Professor," he told Peter, "along with electricity." He had even put aside his own experiments in painting to write some poems for the new Futurist publications.

At the age of twenty, Karpenko had grown into a strikingly handsome young fellow. He was clean-shaven, and his slim, dark good looks were so noticeable that Dimitri would often, with amusement, watch respectable ladies in the street forget themselves and stare after him as he passed. Dimitri used to see him in the company of artistic young women who were obviously very taken with him: but Karpenko preferred to keep his love life to himself and which, if any, of these young women had success with him Dimitri could only guess.

Occasionally Dimitri remembered his friend's strange behavior the day he met Rasputin; but he never saw anything like it again, and gradually put it out of his mind. Indeed, he could find few character flaws in Karpenko. Despite being handsome, he was not vain. Sometimes in the last two years, it was true, he had retreated into short bouts of moody silence; but these, Dimitri thought, might be nothing more than periods of creative concentration. The only fault he could find with his friend, really, was that his witty remarks were sometimes a little cruel; but that was understandable in someone with such a quick and brilliant mind as Karpenko.

Though their lives were more separate now, the two young men often went out together. Sometimes they would go to visit Vladimir Suvorin. The industrialist's Art Nouveau house was complete now, and it was an astonishing work of art. The main hall especially was breathtaking, with a floor of colored marble and granite in a spiral design, lilac-colored walls, stained-glass windows that might have come from Tiffany, and a staircase of creamy white marble whose banisters, carved in elaborate, swirling shapes, looked as though they might melt at the touch of a hand. Vladimir was collecting a library of contemporary books that he had decided to place in the new house, and was then spending much of his spare time there. Karpenko, who was helping him obtain a fine collection of Futurist publications, seldom went there without bringing some new item that assured him a warm welcome.

And of course they went to see Nadezhda.

They were lively visits. Sometimes they would take some friends and then, more often than not, heated discussions would ensue in which Nadezhda, though she was only fifteen, was able to take some part. The subjects, in those heady days, were usually artistic rather than political; but they were invariably argued with extreme passion as only, perhaps, the Russians and the French can.

"Have you read Ivan Sergeevich's latest poem? What do you think?"

"It's terrible, appalling. His attitude is sentimental but without real feeling. He is false."

"It's outdated."

"He's let everyone down. He's completely discredited."

"He is dead. There's nothing more to say about him."

"No. You are all wrong."

The opinions would fly and Nadezhda would listen, gazing at Karpenko with sparkling eyes.

Sometimes Alexander Bobrov would appear on these occasions and then Karpenko, if, say, the company had just condemned the poet Ivanov, would casually ask: "What do you think of Ivanov, Alexander Nicolaevich?" So that when, as he always did, Alexander made some noncommittal reply like—"not bad"—the company would all look at each other or burst into howls of derision while Bobrov gazed at them glumly.

"Poor old Alexander Nicolaevich," Karpenko would say behind his back. "He knows everything and understands nothing." And to his face he once remarked: "You keep studying, Alexander, but you're always an artistic movement behind."

Why did Karpenko hate Bobrov so much? "He represents every pig-headed Russian who ever lived," the Ukrainian claimed. But one day he confessed: "I can't stand the interest he takes in Nadezhda. I try to expose him to her whenever I can."

Yet what did he want with the girl himself? It was increasingly clear that she was in love with him: how much it was hard to know. And he did nothing to discourage her affection. "So you truly care for her?" Dimitri once asked as they were returning home.

"I feel protective, I think," Karpenko answered frankly. "I can't bear to think of her being wasted on a booby like Bobrov."

"But what about you yourself?"

Karpenko gave a short laugh. "Don't be silly. I'm a poor Ukrainian."

"Uncle Vladimir likes you."

"His wife doesn't."

Dimitri had occasionally noticed that, while she never said anything, Karpenko's charming manner, which usually delighted older women, seemed to meet with a certain hauteur from Mrs. Suvorin. "I don't think she means anything," he said. And after a short pause: "You're not just letting her love you to spoil things for Bobrov, are you?"

To which, to his great surprise, Karpenko suddenly let out a little moan. "You don't understand anything, do you? She's like no other girl in the world."

"So you do love her?"

"Yes, damn you, I love her."

"Then there's hope," Dimitri said cheerfully.

But Karpenko only shook his head with a despondency Dimitri had never seen before. "No," he declared quietly, "there isn't any hope for me."

It was on a December evening in 1913 that the bad feeling that had long been simmering between Nadezhda Suvorin and her mother suddenly erupted.

The spark that lit the flame was the simple fact that Mrs. Suvorin had warned her to be careful of Karpenko.

What was wrong with him? the girl demanded to know. Was he too poor? Did her mother have social ambitions? But Mrs. Suvorin denied these charges. "Frankly, it's his character. And to tell you the truth, I think he's playing with you. He's not serious. So don't lose your heart." That was all she would say.

And Nadezhda decided she hated her.

She was in love with Karpenko. How could she not be? Was there anyone more brilliant, more handsome? She had admired him as a child, but now, in the flush of her adolescence, she was suffering all the yearnings of first love. She might have forgiven her mother's attack, however, had it not been for one fact.

A year ago she had discovered about Popov.

It had been late one night that she had happened to wake and, wandering out along the passage, heard a faint sound in the hall. To her surprise she had seen her mother glide across the hall to the door to let a stranger in; and crouching by the balcony, just as she used to do as a child, she had seen them mounting the stairs together. The redhead. Popov.

For a while she found it hard to believe. Her mother and the socialist? And apart from her disgust she had thought: how could she do such a thing to poor Papa? Yet he tolerates her. He is a saint. And ever since, though she said nothing, she thought of her mother as a secret enemy.

And it was unfortunate, therefore, that on the very evening of Mrs. Suvorin's remark about Karpenko, Popov should have chosen to come again.

Had Nadezhda known Popov's mission that night, however, she would have been still more astonished. Even more, perhaps, than was Mrs. Suvorin when she heard it.

"Would you like," he asked simply, "to run away?"

How strange: When he was younger, the idea would have been unthinkable, but he was wondering whether to give up.

A few years ago, he had hoped to extract money from the Suvorins for the Bolshevik cause. Knowing all he did, he supposed he might have. Yet he had not.

God knew, the party needed funds. Not long ago a new Bolshevik newspaper had been started with articles by a strange young fellow from Georgia whose writing reminded one of a priest intoning the liturgy. Stalin he had called himself, in the revolutionary manner—"man of steel." All that year Popov had tried to find funds for *Pravda,* but he had never asked Mrs. Suvorin.

She had become a being apart. He supposed he loved her. And now he was thinking, instead, of asking her to finance their personal flight.

For in 1913, Popov was weary. There was no hope of revolution. Lenin's attempt to reunite the socialist left had met with little success. There had been more arrests. Even young Stalin had been exiled to Siberia. Truly, it seemed to him, he had done all that reasonably could be done.

"We could go abroad," he suggested.

And to her own astonishment, Mrs. Suvorin, for a long moment, considered it.

He was an extraordinary man. She had learned much from him. He had caused her to think long and hard about her life; and he had even altered her political outlook. "I do think we must have democracy," she had finally confessed. "I just can't see anything else that's fair. I still want, personally, to keep the tsar; but we need a constituent assembly." It had become a point of secret passion with her.

Yet he also troubled her. Talking to him about the revolution it was as if, sometimes, he had grown a protective covering—a carapace—that shut out all human feelings that might interfere with the business at hand. At such times she would think: he would kill and never care.

And now the revolutionary had surrendered. He was smiling almost sheepishly. And she wanted to take him in her arms.

The door burst open quite suddenly, as Nadezhda stepped into the room. She was wearing a long dressing gown and her hair was loose down her back. She was shaking, yet also smiling.

"Ah yes," she said calmly. "My mother worries about my friends. Perhaps she would prefer it if they were Bolsheviks."

Popov gazed at her, but said nothing.

"Would you, Mama?" she insolently asked. Then with sudden fury: "Just so you know I know how you treat poor Papa." And turning to Popov: "You ought to be locked up. Perhaps you will be."

"Nadezhda, go to your room," Mrs. Suvorin said promptly. But to Popov she had to murmur: "You had better leave." And to his look of inquiry she could only shake her head sadly. "Impossible."

Both mother and daughter knew, from then on, that they would never mention the incident again.

1914 August

SLOWLY and solemnly, through the dusty summer heat, the procession wound through the streets. Priests in their jeweled robes and heavy miters led the way. Some carried icons, others huge banners. A choir was chanting. And as they passed, like waves unfurling themselves along a shore, a sea of hands rose and made the sign of the cross, while heads and backs bowed low. For this was Holy Russia still; and Russia was at war.

Alexander Bobrov watched with tears of emotion in his eyes. What a summer it had been. There had been a drought; and a total eclipse of the sun. Every peasant in every village had therefore known that some disaster was probably at hand. But now that it had come, here in the streets of Moscow, it was as if some wonderful, religious transformation had taken place. Suddenly all differences were forgotten, all Russians became brothers, united in defense of the fatherland.

Behind the icons, someone was carrying a huge portrait of the tsar. It might have seemed strange, had anyone paused to consider it, that this man with scarcely a drop of Russian blood in his veins, and who resembled his cousin King George V of England as much as anyone, should be the central figure in this almost Asiatic pageantry. His serious, rather unimaginative face with its short brown beard gazed out, not like some icon, nor like the grim rulers of Muscovite times, but like what he was—a puzzled, well-meaning, and rather reluctant German prince, trapped by destiny in an alien Eastern empire. But he was the tsar, the little father of all the Russians; and now, as his portrait passed, the people bowed.

Alexander bowed, too. He was in uniform now. And tomorrow he would leave to fight.

How had it begun, this gigantic mobilization that was about to shake the world?

The events down in the Balkans that had sparked the conflict were simple enough. In 1908, when Austria, backed by Germany, had annexed Bosnia and Herzegovina, she had signaled her intentions to expand, but it had seemed the threat could be contained. The summer of 1914 ended that hope. When Bosnian terrorists assassinated the Austrian Archduke Franz Ferdinand at Sarajevo, Austria had insisted it was the doing of next-door Serbia and demanded an apology with humiliating terms. Serbia had at once complied. And Austria had then refused to accept it and prepared to move on her. "There's no question now: Austria and Germany mean to dominate all the Balkan states. That means they'll control Constantinople and the Black Sea," he had declared to his father. But apart from such an obvious strategic consideration, there was another that weighed with Alexander just as much.

"The Serbs are fellow Slavs, and fellow Orthodox," he declared. "Holy Russia must be their protector. We must go to their aid." It was exactly what Russia had done.

Might it not have remained a regional conflict, though? God knows, there had been intermittent wars down in the Balkans for centuries. For a short time, with England's Lord Grey engaging in frantic diplomacy, it seemed that it might. But it was not to be: once put in motion, the juggernaut of war rolled on. Russian troops were sent to aid Serbia; Germany declared war on Russia; then France and Britain followed in. By August, the civilized world was beginning a general conflict.

At least, thank God, it would be a short war. Everyone was agreed about that. That very morning, Alexander had received a thoughtful letter from his father, still a member of the duma, in Saint Petersburg.

> The whole point, my dear boy, is this: Germany has taken a huge gamble, that she can avoid a war on two fronts, against France in the west and Russia in the east at the same time.
>
> Her vaunted Schlieffen Plan is that she can race through Belgium into northern France, encircle Paris, and win outright on the western front—in under three months—before Russia has time to mobilize. Then she will turn upon us.
>
> I can tell you, by the way, that certain people with good intelligence on this matter inform me that the Germans have quite detailed plans for us then. The empire is to be broken up into regions—the Baltic provinces, the Ukraine, and so on, leaving us only ancient Muscovy. Think of it—our mighty empire broken up!
>
> But it won't happen because the Germans have made a blunder. Russia can mobilize much faster than they plan for. And if we attack fast, with our vast resources of manpower, Germany will be faced with the very war on two fronts that she cannot sustain. She'll have to capitulate.
>
> The general opinion here—both in our government circles and in the embassies—is that the war will be over by Christmas.

Alexander had gone to volunteer at once. As the only son of his family, he was technically exempt, but he was longing to take part. Given his social status, of course, he would be an officer, and he was off the next day to begin training. "But by the time we've gotten through the existing reserve," he was told, "it will all be over. So you needn't expect to fight."

He was wearing a uniform already. he was proud of that. It added to his mood of exaltation.

And only one thought troubled him. Soon he must go to bid farewell to Nadezhda. And after what had happened, would she even speak to him?

How could he have been so foolish? It had been two days before at the Suvorin house. He had gone there to tell Nadezhda he was going into the army. He had been feeling rather proud of himself: there was, even nowadays, something glamorous about a fellow in an officer's uniform.

And then he had found Karpenko there.

He sighed. It was no good denying the fact: Nadezhda's fascination for Karpenko had not worn thin; in the last six months, she seemed to have fallen truly in love with him. How ironic it was. He, Alexander, was twenty-three and just finishing his studies; Nadezhda was sixteen and a young woman. This had been the year when he had always planned to make his move. But now, instead, he found himself thinking: she's still a child, she'll grow out of him; not yet.

They were standing together by the window when he came into the room. Karpenko had obviously just said something amusing and she was laughing. How at ease they looked together. And then Karpenko had turned, and spoken.

What had the fellow said? The odd thing was, Alexander could hardly remember. Something like: "Here comes our warrior: Bobrov the bogatyr." Something harmless enough, though faintly mocking.

And he had lost his self-control.

"As a Ukrainian, I wouldn't know how you view this war," he had said coldly.

It was true, they both knew, that there were Ukrainians living in the Austrian empire, and also a small body of Ukrainian nationalists, who saw the coming war as a chance to liberate the Ukraine from Russian rule. There was talk of interning some of these. But it was also true that hundreds of thousands of Ukrainians were, even now, being mobilized in the Russian army. Karpenko went white.

"Ukrainians are not traitors. We shall fight for the tsar," he said quietly.

But, still bitter, and pleased for once to have put his adversary on the defensive, Alexander continued: "Really. And shall we see you in uniform? Or are you, perhaps, unwilling to face such danger?"

There was a terrible silence. The question was unfair because most students were exempt and most young men with powerful friends were speedily using them to get exemptions anyway. But this time he saw Karpenko blush.

But, oh, what stupidity.

"I think that's the most horrible thing to say." Nadezhda's eyes were blazing. "And I think, Alexander Nicolaevich, that you should leave us now."

What had he done? What idiocy had made him do it? Dare he go back? He must. "I can't go away," he muttered, "leaving things like that."

It was therefore with some nervousness that he slowly made his way towards the great Suvorin house.

Alexander Bobrov would have been surprised indeed, had he known about a brief interview that had taken place just an hour before.

It was Mrs. Suvorin who had made Karpenko do it. She had summoned him that morning. Their meeting had been brief but, though she had hardly been friendly, he had to admire the calm, matter-of-fact way she went about the business.

"The girl's in love with you," she said simply, "and it's gone too far. You and I both understand what you must do."

He stood a little awkwardly by a large, upright armchair. How did one manage these things? She was standing a few feet away from him, completely unsuspecting.

"I think you know, Nadezhda, that I'm very fond of you," he began.

It was not so bad. He loved her and felt protective. He explained gently how much their friendship meant to him and led slowly towards his message. "In case, you see, I might inadvertently have misled you, there is something you should know." He paused. "Our friendship can never be more than that: a friendship."

She had helped, too. Though she went pale, she continued to look at him calmly. Now however she frowned. "You mean there's someone else?"

"Yes."

"I did not know. For a long time?"

"Yes."

She frowned again. "You're not actually married, are you?"

"No."

"Perhaps you will change."

He looked sadly at the Turkish carpet on the floor. Then he shook his head.

"My heart is engaged elsewhere," he said, and then felt embarrassed at such a ridiculous expression.

But she did not seem to notice. "Thank you for telling me," she said simply. "I think I'd like you to go now."

To Dimitri Suvorin, both then and thereafter, that warm August afternoon had the quality of a dream.

Perhaps it was the dusty heat or the sullen gray-blue sky; perhaps it was the echoing bells or the chanting of the priests; or perhaps those medieval Russian masses moving timelessly through twentieth-century streets. Or perhaps it was the people in the houses—thousands of pale faces at every window and balcony, looking strangely small and detached in this mighty city turned stage set.

It was midafternoon when he chanced to find himself near the Suvorin mansion just as the procession was about to pass by. He had known that Karpenko was going there that day, and thinking that his friend might still be there, he went in. And so it was that he came upon Nadezhda, alone, in the small salon upstairs.

She was standing by the window, staring out at the street. Her face was rather pale; she seemed unusually quiet; together they crossed themselves, along with the crowds in the street below, as the priests with their icons led the long procession past.

"It's strange," she said at last. "The last war, when we fought the Japanese, never seemed very real to me. I suppose I was just very young."

"It was far away, too."

"Did people feel like this—so patriotic—before that one?"

"I don't believe so."

"Holy Russia." It seemed she did not need to elaborate. She just left the two words hanging. "It's hard to realize," she went on, "that people one knows are going to die."

Dimitri nodded. His own limp meant that he could never pass the medical for any kind of military service. It did not make him feel guilty. It was just a fact. "Who do we know who's fighting?" he asked.

"There's Alexander Nicolaevich," she replied.

"That's true." He paused. "By the way, have you seen Karpenko?"

"Yes. He left."

"Any idea where to?"

"No." She was silent for a short time. Then she remarked: "It's a commitment, isn't it. I mean, you say: 'I'm ready to lay down my life,' and perhaps you do lose it."

"I suppose so. Yes."

She continued staring at the long procession, most of them simple peasants in their shirts, for a while before remarking: "I'm rather tired, Dimitri. Come and see me again soon."

A few moments later, outside, it was only a whim that decided Dimitri to see if Karpenko might have looked in at his uncle Vladimir's new house. As he made his way towards it, the side streets were almost deserted. Apart from the occasional pealing of patriotic church bells, the afternoon seemed to have withdrawn itself into silence. There was no breeze. He noticed that a fine dust had settled on everything, even the leaves of the trees he passed.

When he reached the Art Nouveau house, standing on its larger corner plot, it, too, seemed dusty and deserted, as though the plasterers had just finished working on the house and left it empty. He went up the steps to the entrance and pulled the bell.

He heard it ring but there was no reply. He waited. Vladimir only kept a skeleton staff there, but it was odd for there to be nobody in the place. "Asleep, I suppose," he muttered, and pulled the bell again, though without conviction. Still nothing. Probably gone to watch the procession, he decided with a shrug. I may as well go.

It was an idle impulse to turn the handle of the heavy door. He certainly didn't expect anything to happen. Yet to his great surprise, it opened. They had forgotten to lock it. And since he was hot, and had nothing better to do, he stepped inside.

How delightfully cool it was. The high hall with its creamy white staircase was still. Blue-and-green light filtered softly through the high windows. It made him think of being a fish in some beautiful grotto. The main drawing room, the dining room, and the library all gave off the hall. Quietly he went from one to another to see if he could find anyone; but there was nobody.

Should he go? He might as well. But before doing so, he thought he might as well look upstairs. Even if there was no one about, it was rather pleasant exploring the house like this, by himself.

Although he was familiar with all the rooms on the main floor, Dimitri had only once been to the upper floor of the house; he knew there was a sitting room and a study up there, but he could not remember where they were. Having reached the top of the curving stairs, he went slowly round the landing, opening one door after another. He found the sitting room and a bedroom, but not the study, and was about to go down again when, down a short passage on his left, he noticed a single door. That must be it. He went towards it, and he turned the handle.

It was a handsome room. The walls were blue; the window depicted a strange, dreamy landscape with mountains in the distance and trees in the foreground, whose fruits were red and gold. On the far wall was a painting by Gauguin, depicting two naked women, with a Tahitian sunset behind them.

It was not the study, however. Though there was a desk on the left and a chaise longue in the center, at the far side of the room stood a large bed.

And upon it lay his uncle Vladimir and Karpenko.

They were both naked. Vladimir's large, hairy form was turned away from him, but there could be no mistaking it. His powerful arm was resting across Karpenko's back. Karpenko, however, had his head turned towards the door and now his handsome face looked straight into Dimitri's.

Dimitri stared. Then Karpenko gave him a strange, rather guilty smile, as though to say: Well, now you know, don't you?

And not knowing what to do, Dimitri very quietly retreated, closed the door, made his way down the stairs to the silent hall, and walked out of the house.

For some time, as he walked towards his home, he could not make out his own feelings, the shock and horror were so great. And it was with surprise, perhaps, as he finally turned into the courtyard with its dusty mulberry tree that he realized that, for his friend, he felt a new kind of protectiveness. As for Uncle Vladimir, he felt a kind of betrayal together with one determined thought: Nadezhda must never know.

And on that dreamlike day it also came to him how much there was about people he did not understand.

It was late that afternoon, having at last summoned up the courage, that Alexander Bobrov entered the Suvorin mansion and, rather to his surprise, was told that Nadezhda was free to see him.

Still more surprising was the fact that, before he could stammer out the apology he had carefully prepared, she reached up, touched him on the lips, and said: "Never mind." Then she linked her arm in his and suggested they walk through the gallery.

Looking at her face, it seemed to Alexander that earlier she might have been crying; but whether for that reason or some other, there was a quietness, a tenderness in her manner he had never seen before.

But this was nothing to his surprise and joy when, as he was about to leave, she turned to him and said: "Well, Alexander, you're going off to war. Don't forget to come back to me, will you." And then, turning up her face and looking at him with a little smile: "Perhaps you would like to kiss me."

And she reached up her arms.

1915

THERE had been a shower. The ground was wet and steaming in the sun as Alexander waited with his men. In front of them lay a huge Polish field; behind, a line of trees.

Soon the action would begin.

Alexander Bobrov surveyed his men. There were thirty-three of them, all, except one, raw recruits, conscripted that winter and given four weeks' basic training. The single veteran, a reservist of twenty-seven, Alexander had deputed to act as sergeant.

The trench in which they were standing was not very deep. Once they had gotten to six feet down, the captain inspecting the line had told them impatiently, "That'll do. We've come here to fight, not dig."

He was a short, fat man, the captain: an officer of the old school with fierce gray whiskers and a red face who, it sometimes seemed to Bobrov, secretly regarded the war as an exasperating diversion from his proper military business of sitting in his club. This morning, though, he had been bustling and brisk.

"Won't be long now," he had told them an hour ago. "Be brave, lads." Then he had disappeared.

Alexander gazed at the huge, muddy field before him. About half a mile away it dipped down, and past that one could see only a lightly wooded ridge some way beyond. Would German helmets suddenly appear? Or puffs of smoke? Alexander hardly knew. For this was his first action, his first real taste of war.

War. In their primary objective the Russian command had been successful. Her immediate, lightning strikes in the summer of 1914 had taken the enemy by surprise. In the north, Russian forces had raced across Poland and smashed into the Germans in East Prussia, causing a momentary panic-stricken retreat. In the south, a Russian army had swept westward from the Ukraine into Austrian territories, and only just been prevented from cutting north, through Silesia, into Germany and towards Berlin itself.

True, the initial success was achieved at appalling cost. The offensive in the north was not properly supported. When the Germans counterattacked, the losses were horrific. About 250,000 men were killed in the August offensive in the north; by the end of 1914, Russian losses, including prisoners-of-war, reached an amazing 1,200,000 men.

But Germany was fighting on two fronts. Her master plan had failed. And the empire of Russia, having been humiliated in her last two wars— the Crimean and the war with Japan—had shown herself a military power to be reckoned with. By the start of 1915, Germany was concentrating its main effort against her. And by March 1915, so necessary was she to France and Britain, that those allies had reluctantly to agree that when the war was over she should receive nothing less than the ancient city of Constantinople—her dream since the time of Catherine the Great—as her prize.

In 1915, however, the Germans were beginning to strike back. And now they were advancing with thunder.

Alexander Bobrov looked at his men thoughtfully. He liked them. He thought they liked him, too. But he wished they were better prepared.

For if the great offensives of 1914 had been dramatic, the second round, of 1915, had taken on a very different character.

He had never forgotten his surprise the day they were issued arms. For when twenty of his men had received rifles, the officer in charge stopped, with an abrupt "That's it."

"But what about the rest?" he had asked, surprised.

"They'll have to get them at the front."

"You mean, there are stores up there?"

The officer had looked at him pityingly. "They'll get them from their fellow soldiers," he said. "The ones that have fallen." And it was not long before Alexander discovered that, in some regiments in this section of the front, twenty-five percent of the men had been sent forward with no arms, expected to scavenge them, so to speak, from the hands of the dead. Somehow he had managed to beg and steal rifles for all his men; but he knew of one unit where half the men were armed with pitchforks, and there was a rumor that to the south, one company was preparing to fight the enemy with their bare hands.

The artillery supporting them, he knew, had only two rounds per field gun; but he had not told his men this.

Then there had been the incident of the wireless.

He had been at the company command post two days before, where they had a wireless set up. The captain was busily engaged with this, giving the colonel a detailed briefing on their position and dispositions and looking rather pleased with himself. But only one thing puzzled Bobrov. "Are we transmitting everything like that, sir?" he asked the captain when he was finished.

"How do you mean?"

"Well, there's no code. You were transmitting everything in clear."

The captain stared at him with a frown. "Whyever not, for God's sake?"

"I just thought—what if the enemy were picking up our signals? He'd know all our dispositions."

And now the captain's face cleared. "Don't be silly, Bobrov." He smiled. "We're transmitting in Russian, man. The Germans can't understand a word we say."

His attitude was not unusual. The transmissions for the entire Russian army were transmitted in clear, which, as the German High Command was later to remark, "made things simpler on the eastern front."

Why were things so badly organized? Partly, he knew, it was because the high command was dominated by men like the captain: old-fashioned parade-ground soldiers who despised modern weaponry and modern methods. The commander-in-chief, Sukhomlinov, was just such a man. There was, he also knew, a cadre of forward-looking younger officers who chafed under this regime; but these men were not in control.

But it was not just the generals. As the captain himself, in a moment of honesty, suddenly admitted to him: "The trouble is, we had enough ammunition for a short war but not a longer one. Our factories just don't produce enough."

And what, Alexander wondered, did his men make of it all? They were all in their early twenties. None of them wanted to be in the army, but they seemed to understand well enough that Russia must be defended.

Except, perhaps, for one. He was a pleasant young fellow, with a broad face, not quick of mind, from a small village in the province of Riazan. Alexander liked him and often chatted to him in the evenings. But there was one thing he could never seem to make the fellow understand.

"I mean, sir, they haven't attacked Riazan, have they?" he had said one day, with genuine puzzlement in his voice. "So what does the army want with me?"

"But if we don't fight them here in Poland, they might get to Riazan later," Alexander had suggested.

It had not worked, however. For the fellow had only looked at him earnestly, and then, with a childlike smile, replied, "Yes, sir. But, then again, they might not." And Alexander had wondered how many others, like this simple fellow from Riazan, there might be in the Russian army.

It began quite suddenly. And it was unlike anything he had expected.

There were no German helmets; no squadrons of artillery and flashing swords; no lines of men with rifles. Nothing but a distant, sullen roar.

And then the crashes. At first the German shells fell into the woods behind. Then some more smacked into the field in front of them, sending up little typhoons of mud. The enemy knew their positions, all right. And then, while his men, frightened and mystified, cowered in their inadequate trench, the roaring went on, and on.

For in the spring and summer of 1915, the Russian army experienced the full weight of an orchestrated German bombardment.

It was two hours later that the captain came by. His whiskered face was covered in mud as he peered down into the trench. They had taken only one direct hit. It was strangely clean. The young fellow from Riazan had simply disappeared.

"Come on, Bobrov. Get out," the captain cried. "We're moving back."

They clambered out of the trench and followed him, keeping just inside the wood, where the shells were not falling. After a time they came to the command post. It had been obliterated.

"Damn Germans. They know how to shoot, I must admit," the captain said to him with a wry grin.

He's not such a bad fellow, Alexander thought. Just a bit old-fashioned. And he glanced back to make sure all his men were together.

A shell screamed over. Then another.

And then there was a very loud bang. It was, really, quite extraordinarily loud. And everything went white.

1915 July

HE awoke very slowly through a haze, and to the sound of a piano.

How strange, he thought. I must have died. For how else should he be here, in his own bedroom, in his childhood home at Russka? Curiously he gazed around him. It seemed that the angels had decided to change the furniture somewhat, but there could be no doubt about where he was: he could see a familiar tree out of the window. That sound from the piano was certainly heavenly. He closed his eyes.

When he opened them again, stranger yet, it was to see Nadezhda staring down at him and smiling. He gazed at her in wonder, then frowned. Had she died also? He was sorry for that.

And then her voice, excitedly.

"Dimitri. Dimitri. He's come round." And the heavenly music stopped.

It had been Vladimir's idea. When he had been brought back to Moscow, still barely conscious, and his father had wondered what to do for him, it was the rich industrialist who had organized everything. Alexander had been lying there, delirious and tended by a doctor and a nurse, for three weeks.

Gradually he learned what had happened. The shell whose blast had so nearly killed him was a tiny part of a huge bombardment that had pushed the Russian army in the north back from Poland nearly three hundred miles.

"It's a catastrophe," Nadezhda told him, the third day he was well enough to talk. "Most of Lithuania's gone. They're advancing across Latvia. And our people are still pulling back. Old General Sukhomlinov's been dismissed. About time, too. Everyone says the government's incompetent. They say we can only hope for help from Saint Nicolas the Miracle-Worker!"

But the really fascinating news came from his father.

Though the tsar had dismissed the duma early in the year and ruled by decree, the setbacks in the war had been so great that he had been forced to call it into session again, and so Nicolai Bobrov was in the capital. So great had the anti-German feeling been since war began that the government had changed the capital's name from Saint Petersburg, with its German-sounding ending, to the more Russian Petrograd. It was from Petrograd, therefore, that Nicolai's letters were now addressed.

They were full of information. He gave his son character sketches of the important men in the parliament: Rodzianko, the chairman of the duma, portly but wise; Kerensky, the leader of the socialists—"a good speaker, but with no real political plan except to destroy the tsar"—and several others. He related all the gossip from the court. "The empress's friend, the fellow Rasputin, caused so much trouble with his lechery that he's been sent back to his family in Siberia. Let's hope he stays there." And above all, to Alexander's amazement, his father was optimistic.

The Germans can't defeat Russia for a simple reason: we continue to retreat and we always have reserves. Napoleon found the same thing. Even if we abandon the capital, we shall still exhaust them.

But this present crisis is our last and best opportunity to reform the government. The tsar didn't want to call the duma back but now he's had to. We shall force some measure of democracy on him and save Russia by doing so.

Out of defeat comes victory, my dear boy.

Alexander could only hope his father was right.

For a long time he was still very weak. It seemed the blast had damaged his insides in some way. His wounds, which were extensive, still caused him pain. "But you're young. You'll mend," the doctor told him cheerfully. They put him in a wheelchair and arranged a room for him downstairs so that he could wheel himself out onto the verandah and enjoy the company.

The house was busy. Dear Arina, as housekeeper, ran everything with wonderful efficiency. And she personally would supervise the samovar of tea and the wonderful pastries that appeared on the verandah every afternoon. Despite the war, the little museum and the workshops were functioning, and Arina's son Ivan, now sixteen, was an apprentice to the woodcarver there and showing great promise.

Though Peter Suvorin and Karpenko remained in Moscow, the rest of the family had all moved to the country and Alexander was interested to see how each person seemed to have his own appointed task. Mrs. Suvorin was busy helping a new *zemstvo* organization to house the flood of refugees from the front. "We've even got two Jewish families in the village," she informed them. Vladimir had converted the Russka cloth works into a small armaments factory, making cartridges and grenades. As for Dimitri, he was playing and composing each day. A dozen suites for piano and two movements of his first symphony were already written, the scores being kept in a locked cupboard which was treated by all the family with the reverence that used to be reserved for an icon.

And then there was Nadezhda.

Her father had set up a little nursing home where wounded soldiers could convalesce in Russka, and every day she would go there to nurse them. Sometimes those that were fit enough were brought over for tea at the house. And though Alexander sometimes observed a slight coldness of the girl towards her mother, it seemed to him that there was a new gentleness in her manner: a gentleness that, in particular, was meant for him.

And so the month of July passed peacefully; and August. During August the doctor allowed him, twice, to be taken by cart to the monastery. How delightful it was, he thought, to be back among such familiar sights.

Except for one thing: the village.

"It's extraordinary," he remarked to Vladimir. "What happened? I never saw the place so prosperous."

It was true. For while, by the summer of 1915, the great cities were suffering from the war, in the huge Russian countryside, the First World War ushered in a time of plenty. How could this be?

"Actually," Vladimir explained, "it's quite simple. Like most administrations in wartime, the government's paying for things by printing money. Consequently there's inflation. And the one thing everyone needs, which the peasants have, is grain. Grain prices are high, we've just had a bumper harvest, and the villagers all have excess income." He grinned. "Do you know, that rogue Boris Romanov's even bought himself a phonograph. He even plays Tchaikovsky on it, I believe."

A week later, visiting Boris Romanov's comfortable house, Alexander saw this marvel for himself. And he wondered: could it be, after all, that this war would be the saving of Russia, and that his optimistic father was right.

The blow fell in late August. The tsar dismissed the duma. At the same time, he decided to take over, personally, as commander-in-chief of the Russian armies. He would go to the front himself.

In the first week of September, Alexander received a long letter from his father. It was no longer optimistic. And its ending was filled with foreboding.

> Everyone pleaded with him, from Rodzianko down; but the tsar is an obstinate fellow who believes it is his duty to be an autocrat. So democracy under tsardom is dead. I'm sure of it. As for his attempts to revive the army, they are sure to be unlucky. I can foresee only chaos.
>
> Rasputin has reappeared here. I hear he saw the tsar himself. God save us.

1917 March 2

YET even now, it was hard to believe.

The rule of the tsar was over. Russia was free.

Nicolai Bobrov stood at the window and looked out eagerly. A head cold had kept him indoors that day. It was three hours now since his son Alexander had gone over to the Taurida Palace, where the duma met to see if the news had come. Any moment he would be back.

Surely the news must have come. Surely by now the tsar must have signed the abdication. "For God knows," he murmured, "the tsar can't possibly go on." Not now that Bobrov and his friends had taken power.

For in the end, it was the duma who had deposed the tsar.

What a strange business it had been; yet not really so surprising. The fears he had expressed back in that fateful summer of 1915 had been justified.

The tsar had been frequently away at the front. True, the army had not done so badly. The great Brusilov offensive of 1916, mounted while the British were making their mass attack on the Somme, though it had failed to break the enemy, had made some gains on the western front. Down in the Caucasus, Russian troops had advanced into Turkey. But in the south, Germany and Austria had pushed to the western shore of the Black Sea through Romania and the British had been forced to pull out of Gallipoli, leaving Russia still blockaded at the entrance of the Black Sea and unable to export her grain.

The war on the Russian front, as on the western front, was a grim stalemate.

But at the center—Bobrov could only shake his head. It had been a nightmare. The empress, that foolish and ignorant German woman, had been left holding the reins of government. It seemed she had got it into her head that she was another Catherine the Great—so she once told a startled official. And beside the empress—seen or unseen, had been the terrible Rasputin.

It had been bewildering to watch. It sometimes seemed to Bobrov that anyone who had an ounce of talent was dismissed. Only blind loyalty to the tsar was rewarded. And the endless list of appointments and dismissals—over forty new provincial governors in a single year!—had made one duma wit remark that the administration was having an epileptic fit. All faith in the government had evaporated. Ugly rumors about the empress and Rasputin had even reached the troops at the front. They were said to be in secret league with the Germans.

Thank God, in December 1916, two aristocratic patriots had murdered the evil Rasputin; but by then the damage had been done.

Before his eyes, Bobrov had witnessed the signs of the breakup. Every party in the duma, even the conservatives, had turned against the tsar. Though the army held firm along the front, there had been a million desertions. And then a terrible winter had left the capital short of food and fuel.

It couldn't go on. For weeks the entire duma had been in an uproar. Those close to the tsar said he showed signs of depression. Even some of his relations, the archdukes, said he should step down to save the monarchy and spoke of a regency.

"But personally," Nicolai Bobrov would always say afterwards, "I think it was the weather that really did in the tsar."

For suddenly in February 1917, after a bitter winter, the weather turned warm, and in Petrograd everyone came out onto the streets.

The demonstrations were spontaneous. The people had had enough. Not only strikes but massive street disruptions began. The police and Cossacks were hopelessly outnumbered. And then the authorities made a huge mistake: they called out the garrisons.

They were not regular troops. Most of them were recent conscripts, taken from their villages and cooped up for months in overcrowded barracks. Why should they fire on the people? They mutinied, and joined the protesters.

And then, on February 28, it was over. The tsar, trapped outside the capital after visiting the front, sent word that the duma should disband until April. "And we refused," Bobrov would say, with a calm smile. "We refused to go, and suddenly realized we were the government."

The deputies declared it. The mobs in the street seemed to agree. After all, what else was there, if not the duma? The next day, the duma asked the tsar to abdicate, and the Russian monarch found that he had not a friend in the world.

Where was the young fellow? Nicolai was very proud of his son. Alexander was able to walk about now; he was still an officer; but he had been pronounced unfit for further active service and he had been spending the last weeks in the capital with his father. Though still a monarchist, he nowadays tolerated his father's liberal views with good humor; and even he had been shocked by the conduct of the government in recent months. "He's been gone such a time," Nicolai now concluded, "there must be some news just coming through."

And then Nicolai smiled. How strange, he thought. Here he was, a widower, aged sixty-two. He had lost his estate. His country was locked in a terrible war, with no end in sight; his monarch had just fallen. Yet today he felt as if his whole life were beginning again.

He was sorry for the tsar, personally. He didn't think he was a monster—just an inadequate man in an impossible position. But although he had worked hard for years to reach some sort of liberal compromise with the stubborn ruler, now that he was gone, he realized he was relieved. Democracy, at last, could now begin.

What was it his son had said the other day? He had argued so passionately.

"You don't see what you're doing, Father," he had warned. "The whole empire has been set up to revolve around the tsar. Everything, everyone is attached to him. It's like some huge machine that turns around a single lynchpin. Take that pin out and the whole apparatus will just fly apart."

Would Russia fly apart? Nicolai didn't see why. "The duma is there," he had said. "There are sensible men in it."

"Ah, you liberals," Alexander had replied with sad affection. "You always think people are going to be reasonable."

The duma would do very well, in Nicolai's view. At least for the time being. It was, after all, the nearest thing to a democratic body that Russia possessed. Already it had chosen a group to act as a provisional government, and almost all the parties had agreed to support it. Yesterday, he had heard, some of the workers' leaders and Mensheviks in Petrograd had formed some sort of workers' council—a soviet, they called it. He knew one or two of the leaders, not bad fellows. They could certainly help to restore some order in the factories.

And then there would be progress. The program of the provisional government was already clear. Prosecute the war—everyone except the Bolsheviks agreed to that, and the Bolsheviks didn't count for much these days—and move quickly to hold elections to a new constituent assembly, which would replace the duma. A full democratic body. One man, one vote. Everyone, left and right, was agreed about that, too.

"I can feel it," he murmured, as he gazed into the street. "A warm ray of hope."

And then he saw Alexander.

The fellow was hurrying along, certainly. He had a piece of paper in his hand and he looked excited. This must be it, then: the formal abdication. With a happy smile Nicolai prepared to greet him.

So why was the boy frowning? Had the tsar said something foolish, even now?

"The abdication came through?" he inquired.

"No. The tsar still can't bring himself to sign it. But he will. He hasn't any choice. The army chiefs are telling him to go as well."

"Then what's this?" Nicolai pointed to the paper.

Alexander handed it to him without a word. And Nicolai read.

It was not long. It was addressed to the Petrograd military garrison, and it contained seven terse clauses.

It told every company to elect committees who would remove control of all arms and equipment from the officers. Officers were no longer to be addressed by honorary titles or saluted off duty. The committees were also to elect representatives to the Petrograd Soviet, which announced that it, and not the provisional government, was now the final authority on all military matters.

It was signed by the Committee of the Petrograd Soviet, dated the previous day. And it was headed, simply and without further explanation: Order No. 1.

Nicolai stared at it in disbelief. Then he exploded with laughter.

"This is absurd. The Petrograd Soviet is just an informal workers' body. It's not elected by anyone and has no authority. Nobody's going to take any notice of it."

"But they already are. I've been to some of the barracks. They're all going to comply. Some of them just laughed at me because I was wearing an officer's uniform."

"But the regular troops, our soldiers at the front . . ."

"The order's already on its way to them. I tell you, most of the troops will follow it."

Nicolai was silent. Thunderstruck.

"Then who's in charge?" he cried.

Alexander shrugged.

"God knows."

1917 July

BORIS Romanov grunted with satisfaction as he stepped from the shady verandah into the salon. Only the ticking of the clock in its marble case could be heard.

He enjoyed the house with its green walls, its little white portico, and its cool interior. He went up every afternoon and sat on the verandah. Once it had belonged to the Bobrovs; then Vladimir Suvorin. And now, to all intents and purposes, it was his. He smiled grimly at the thought. The revolution—his revolution—had finally come.

The last few months at Russka had been strange. News of the tsar's abduction and of the new provisional government had only filtered slowly through to the provinces. Boris had not known for sure until ten days afterwards. He had met a peasant traveling from Riazan province who, a month later, still refused to believe it.

And what did these events in Petrograd mean? The provisional government had promised a constituent assembly. Good. There was complete freedom of speech and assembly now. No harm in that. But above all, the fall of the tsar must mean one thing.

"Now," he told his family, "we shall get the land."

Everyone knew it. The provisional government was discussing how it was to be done. All that spring, soldiers had been deserting from the front and making their way home, so as not to miss out on the distribution. Two had appeared back in the village.

But nothing had happened. The provisional government, as it did in all things, moved slowly, legalistically, and hesitantly.

It was in late April that he had led the villagers onto the estate. It had been very simple. There was nobody to stop them. When he entered the house, only Arina had been there to protest.

"What right have you got to do this?"

He had grinned. "The people's right." And when she had foolishly tried to bar his way he had just shoved her aside with a laugh. "This is the revolution," he had told her.

It was a curious situation—as if the place had entered a sort of limbo. Technically the estate still belonged to Vladimir Suvorin, just as did the factories at Russka. But Vladimir was in Moscow now. Arina continued to live in the house; so did her son Ivan, who for the time being continued his woodwork. Meanwhile, the villagers cut down some of Suvorin's trees and grazed their cattle on the slope before the house. And who was going to say anything? It was only a question of time before it was all made legal, whatever that might mean.

And as far as Boris Romanov was concerned, this was the revolution.

To others, perhaps, it might involve something more. That very month there had been an attempt to take over the provisional government in Petrograd. A madcap plan—an armed uprising—by those Bolsheviks. Boris knew about Bolsheviks. They were fellows like that accursed redhead Popov. They had been growing in numbers lately with their slogan "All power to the Soviets" and their screaming editorials in their paper, *Pravda*. But their revolt had been smashed. One of their leaders, Trotsky, was in jail. Another, Lenin, had fled abroad. "And let's hope that's the last of them," Boris had said.

There was a new man at the head of the government now, a socialist called Kerensky. He'd called in General Kornilov to restore order. Perhaps he'd speed up the constituent assembly and the legalizing of the land distribution, too.

Slowly now Boris mounted the stairs. During the last three months he had examined the house and its contents with interest. There were certainly some strange-looking books and paintings there. The grand piano, however, he had much admired. One of his sons had played a tune on it.

Only today had it occurred to him that there was one part of the house he had never investigated. He would go to the attic.

Rather to his disappointment, however, he found that Suvorin had made no use of it. The long low room under the roof was almost empty, the board floors bare. Only at one end did he notice, under a small round window, a few dusty old boxes.

With slow deliberateness, but not much interest, he opened them, then made a grimace. Papers. Old letters, bills, and other nonsense of the Bobrovs. He shrugged. He couldn't be bothered to look at them, and he was just about to turn away when he noticed one piece of paper that seemed to be sticking out slightly from the rest. Along the top, he noticed, was a heading: *Fire at Russka.*

He frowned and pulled it out, to find another slip of paper folded inside the first. It seemed to be a letter of some sort.

It was signed: Peter Suvorin.

1917   November 2

It was one in the morning and they were alone.

The night before, when the Moscow Kremlin had still been holding out, there had been fighting in the streets; but now the city was quiet. In Petrograd and in Moscow, Lenin and his Bolsheviks were now in power.

Or were they?

Popov smiled at Mrs. Suvorin; and despite all that was passing, she smiled back. She thought he looked younger.

"So tell me," she said, "what really happened."

And then he laughed.

The world-shattering event known as the October Revolution was, strictly speaking, nothing of the kind. It was a coup by a minority party, about which the majority of the population did not even know.

All through that year of 1917, since the abdication of the tsar, Russia had staggered along under a strange duality: a provisional government, which had little real power, and a congress of soviets, which had a growing network of local bases in factory, town, and village, but no real legitimacy. Elections were needed to a democratic constituent assembly; but the government, even after its leadership fell upon the popular socialist, Kerensky, was painfully slow. Meanwhile the economy was collapsing, there were food shortages, and the members of the government themselves were becoming weary.

It was while this government was wavering that the Bolshevik Party began to make steady progress in the soviets. In July, foolishly, they had attempted an insurrection that was crushed; but this did not stop their political advance. By the start of September, Trotsky and his Bolsheviks had a majority in the Petrograd Soviet. A few days later the Bolsheviks also had a majority in Moscow. In the country as a whole, however, they remained in a minority. With time it seemed possible that the Bolsheviks would become the dominant leftist party: but then again they might not. And it was in this rather uncertain situation that, in the month of October 1917, Lenin with some difficulty persuaded his fellow Bolsheviks to gamble once more on a bid for instant power.

It began on the night of October 24 and it was orchestrated, chiefly by

Trotsky, from the former convent and girls' school, the Smolny Institute, which had become the home of the Petrograd Soviet.

"And the amazing thing," Popov declared, "was how easy it all was." He grinned. "We did the main part by stealth."

All through that evening the conspirators had done something so simple it was brilliant. They had just gone from one vital installation to another, picketing or taking over, and few of the workers they had relieved had bothered to oppose them. They had already done their best to win over the military garrisons, but they need not have worried, for the military was not much inclined to act, and poor Kerensky failed to make any proper defensive plans. By morning, almost all the city's key points had been quietly taken over.

"Kerensky went off to get military support from outside the city," Popov told her, "but had little luck. That just left the ministers of the provisional government sitting in the Winter Palace with a guard of some Cossacks and, if you please, the Women's Death Battalion. There were forty war invalids too, God bless them!"

"Then you stormed the Winter Palace?"

"More or less. Actually, some of the women, I suppose, knew how to shoot, so our people wouldn't go near the place. Then we got five thousand sailors. But when they saw there was shooting, they went away, too!"

"I heard the Winter Palace was bombarded."

"Correct. The heroic cruiser *Aurora* fired upon the palace. They hadn't any live shells unfortunately, so they fired a single blank. Then the Peter and Paul Fortress had a go. But they missed."

"That's impossible. The fortress is directly opposite the palace."

"I was there. They missed."

"And then?"

"Oh, in the end they gave up and our people went in and looted the place." He chuckled. "Though in the future, I'm sure we shall tell the story rather differently."

Mrs. Suvorin looked at Popov thoughtfully. She had seen little of him in the last year, but they still felt an attraction for each other. She could understand why, in his moment of triumph, he should have sent a message that he would call upon her that night.

Several thoughts went through her mind. What would this change mean politically? Some people, she knew, were outraged. The civil service, the banks, and a number of unions had resisted the usurpation of the duma by going on strike. It was still possible that armed forces would be used against the Bolsheviks. Yet other people were taking things very calmly. The Petrograd stock exchange had not reacted at all: prices were firm. As a businessman had remarked to her: "These Bolsheviks are just a party within the workers' soviets: and it's the soviets, not Kerensky, who've had the real power for months. I doubt it will make much difference."

True, the first act of the new group had been to declare that all estates were now to be distributed to the peasants. But that had been coming anyway, and she knew very well that the peasants had already occupied the estate at Russka. She had reconciled herself to that.

What about the men involved? What were they like? She had seen the list of ministers. Lenin she felt she knew about; also Trotsky. She feared them. Yet Lunachazsky, the culture minister, she had met and found to be a cultivated and sympathetic man. Other names meant less. And one, the chairman for Nationalities, named Stalin, meant nothing at all.

Which brought her back to Popov. Even now, after a decade, she did not really know him. Sometimes, like that time in 1913, she had broken through and found a man of warmth; yet at other times the thick shell of the revolutionary had descended. She still felt he would kill without caring. And, perhaps worse, he would lie without hesitation.

Somehow, she felt instinctively now, he represented them. If she could gauge him, she might have an insight into these men who were his colleagues.

And it was with this in her mind that she now asked him the question that had been troubling her more than any other. "What, then, are you going to do about the constituent assembly?"

All the parties, including the Bolsheviks, had been calling for it. Before being overthrown, the Kerensky provisional government had set the dates for the elections in November. Now, with this coup, what would become of those?

He looked at her in surprise. "The elections are scheduled."

"Will they take place?"

"Certainly."

"Nothing is certain. How do I know that your Lenin isn't a dictator?"

"You have my word he isn't." Popov gazed at her earnestly. "I assure you the constituent assembly will be called. It's part of our program. Not only that, all the decisions of this government—the distribution of the land, everything—are only provisional, and subject to ratification by the assembly."

His eyes looked straight into hers. She supposed she must believe him.

"Do you promise me that?"

"I do."

1918 January

On January 5, 1918, the constituent assembly met in Petrograd. Since the elections had taken place well after the Bolshevik coup, it would be hard to deny that the results reflected the people's will under present conditions. Of the 707 members, the largest group—370—belonged to the peasants' party, the Socialist Revolutionaries. Of the lesser parties, the Bolsheviks had 170 members. Other parties included the Mensheviks, and there were over a hundred members with marginal or no party affiliations. The ruling Bolsheviks, therefore, were in a definite minority, with only twenty-four percent of the vote.

The constituent assembly met for one day. Lenin watched the proceedings from a balcony. The constituent assembly refused to agree that the

Bolshevik government was the supreme power or to bow to the decisions of the soviets. That same night, Lenin, with a show of military force, disbanded the assembly.

Thus, after centuries of tsarist rule, and after its February and October revolutions, Russia enjoyed its one and only day of democracy. "It's a pity," one of the sailors who disbanded it remarked, "but"—using the tsarist term of affection that many soldiers then applied to Lenin—"the Little Father doesn't like it."

The following day, Mrs. Suvorin sent a note to Yevgeny Popov.

> You lied. You must have known.
> It was all planned.
> Do not come to see me again.

1918 February

THE fate of Alexander Bobrov was decided in an icy Moscow street. It was foolish of him to have lost concentration—and all the more so since it was the very eve of his departure.

For it was clear that, for the two Bobrovs, it was time to leave. "It seems," Alexander said wryly, "that we shall not be required in the modern age."

And the new age had, indeed, begun. Officially it started on January 31. For on that day, by government decree, Russia moved to the Western, Gregorian calendar, and ceased to be thirteen days behind the rest of the world. Whatever the date, however, the Russia that Alexander knew was dissolving in the strangest way, before his eyes.

She was neither at war nor at peace. An armistice had been signed with Germany, but the peace terms, negotiated by Trotsky, had yet to be agreed. The assumption by some idealistic revolutionaries, that if they offered to go home, the Germans would do so, too, had been swiftly disproved. The general revolution in Europe that some, including Lenin, had hoped for, showed no sign yet of taking place. Meanwhile, in this uncomfortable half world, the old Russian empire was showing every sign of breaking up. In the north, Finland, Lithuania, and Latvia had already declared independence. In the west, Poland was sure to be lost. In the south, formal authority in the Ukraine had broken down, but while the Bolsheviks were trying to get control, the Ukrainian nationalists had already proclaimed a new Ukrainian state.

At home, everything that seemed familiar was being broken up. The land belonged to the people; the program for nationalizing industry had begun; and the Orthodox Church had been told that all its property was confiscated and all its legal rights taken away. In effect, it was outlawed. "In six months," Lenin had declared, "we will build a socialist state." It seemed he might succeed.

For if the Bolsheviks were still a minority, they were a determined one.

The opposition forces were in disarray; cleverly, Lenin had drawn some of the extremists of the peasants' party—the terrorists—into his government so that they would not oppose him; Red Guards and other units were everywhere; Bolshevik cells were growing in the factories; and, most significant for the Bobrovs, a new organization, headed by a ruthless fellow named Dzerzhinski, had begun to operate in the last two months: the Cheka.

The Extraordinary Commission to Combat Counterrevolution, Sabotage, and Speculation was a very effective body. It was remarkable what it could come up with. It seemed that a number of political opponents of the Bolsheviks had been guilty of sedition, including many of the liberal Cadets. They were declared to be enemies of the people. Nicolai Bobrov had just learned that he was one of them.

Alexander Bobrov was walking quite slowly, because he was lost in thought. He was wearing an old coat, a worker's cap, and a pair of heavy boots. The coat collar was turned up against the cold, and his face was hardly visible. He had taken to dressing like a worker a month ago. His father was in hiding.

Their escape had been arranged by Vladimir Suvorin. Mrs. Suvorin was to cross into Finland and go thence in stages to Paris, where Vladimir's son was awaiting her. The two Bobrovs, dressed as workers, were to accompany her. In the confusion that still existed everywhere, the journey itself should not be unduly difficult. "You just need to keep out of trouble until you leave," Vladimir had said.

The industrialist's own position was curious. Though the Bolsheviks wanted to nationalize all industry, they were still uncertain what to do with men like Suvorin. If he cooperated, with his wide knowledge and his many contacts, he might be useful. "They know that industry and finance still have to run," Vladimir had explained to Alexander. "I've a friend in the culture minister, Lunarcharsky, too. All the same," he added, "I fear it may not be many months before I follow you." Nadezhda, despite much scolding, had insisted she stay with her father, and Alexander had just come, an hour before, from bidding her farewell.

Since their time together in Russka while he recovered from his war wounds, they had grown very close. Twice he had proposed. But in the upheaval taking place all around them she had simply begged: "Not now." Alexander had no doubt that she and Vladimir would be in Europe, too, within the year. And then, he thought, will be the time. It was funny: they would both be nothing then—just a pair of émigrés. But he didn't mind. "Take care of yourself, my Alyosha," she had said, and had given him a long kiss.

And it was just these thoughts, as he went along the street, that made him foolishly forget.

"Got a cig?" The soldier was standing in front of him, looking up. "Cigarette?"

Alexander gazed down at him, hardly focusing. There were six or seven other soldiers, Red Guards, watching him. The one who had approached him was a disreputable little fellow. When he was serving,

Alexander would have made him clean himself up.

"You want a cigarette, do you?" he said irritably. "Well, I don't smoke." And he started to walk on.

What the devil was the matter with the fellow? The soldier had suddenly caught his coat. His hopeful look had turned into a snarl. He was calling to the other guards, who were coming towards him, one of them unhoisting his rifle.

And then he realized what he had done.

He had spoken naturally, just as he would have done a year ago. He had forgotten to disguise his voice, which had the faint but unmistakable burr of the aristocratic intonation. He had addressed him with a certain haughty disdain; and worst of all, he had used the familiar "thou" which officers always used when addressing their men.

He was discovered.

"Here's an officer. What's your name?"

"Ivanov. I'm not an officer."

"You were, though, weren't you? I think we've got ourselves an enemy here, boys. Fine suit of clothes you've got there, my lord. Nice coat. Think you're a muzhik, do we?"

And suddenly Alexander doubled up with pain as a rifle butt was swung and hit him in the stomach. He went down.

"What shall we do with him, lads?"

"Take him to a tribunal."

"Search him first, maybe."

"I think you'd like to have a nice talk with the Cheka. That's what I reckon," the first said with a laugh. "Up you get, Baron. Come along, Excellency. What a fine officer you are, sir, to be sure."

He staggered up. Thank God he had no papers on him.

"My name's Ivanov," he said weakly.

Then one of the soldiers cried out: "Here's the man we need. He's on the Committee. Let's ask him."

And Alexander looked up to see Yevgeny Popov, who gazed at him with mild surprise, while the soldiers told him what they'd found. "Says his name's Ivanov," the first one added. Then Popov smiled.

For a few, long seconds he said nothing. His green eyes rested upon Alexander, yet it seemed he was thinking of something else. At last he spoke.

"This man, comrades, is a good Bolshevik. He's one of us."

The soldier who had discovered Alexander gazed in amazement.

"But he talks like a noble," he protested. "I swear he was an officer."

Popov smiled. "Have you heard Vladimir Ilych speak?" he asked. It was often a subject of some amusement that Lenin pronounced his diatribes against the capitalist classes in an accent that was markedly upper middle class. "Besides, comrade, there are officers who served in the imperial army who are loyal Bolsheviks now." It was true that, even in the higher command, there were men who had thought it their patriotic duty to obey the new government as thoroughly as they had the old. "We just shoot them if they don't," Popov added pleasantly.

The men looked at him doubtfully. "Are you sure, comrade?"

Popov shrugged. "Ask him," he said. And he smiled, again, at Alexander.

Afterwards, Alexander often wondered how he got through the next few minutes. His life was at stake, very probably. He had not prepared himself; and there was no time to think.

"My name is Alexander Pavlovich Ivanov," he began slowly. It was not a long story. He was terrified that if he made it long, he might forget what he had said. He told them that he had been wounded in action, that on his return he had become disgusted with the old regime and that, immediately after the October coup, he had offered his services to the Bolsheviks. "I've got no money," he said. "And unfortunately I'm still sick." Then he offered to show them his wounds.

"Long live the revolution," Popov said quietly.

"Long live the revolution," Alexander repeated.

The soldiers turned to Popov.

"You heard him," he said. "I vouch for him."

"Oh, well, if you're one of us," the first soldier said. And he clapped Alexander on the back. "Pity you've got no cigarettes," he added. Then the soldiers left.

As he stood there, watched by Popov, Alexander felt physically sick. It was not only the blow from the rifle, nor the fear: it was the complete humiliation of having to swear to these pathetic lies in front of the man he hated and despised the most in the world. Head bowed, he looked up at Popov.

"Why?" he asked.

For a moment Popov did not reply. It seemed that he, too, was contemplating. "Do you remember that you once called me a liar?" he said. "I used a false name, too. That disgusted you, didn't it?" He paused, still looking at Alexander coolly. "You called me a coward, too, I recall." He nodded slowly. "And why did you lie just now, so eagerly, Alexander Nicolaevich? I will tell you. You didn't do it for a cause. You haven't got a cause. You did it to save your skin."

Alexander couldn't deny it.

"I just wanted to see," Popov said calmly. "It was interesting to watch. Tomorrow, or the next day, or the next, you'll be caught. And then I shan't save you. You'll be on your own. If they ask me, I shall tell them exactly what you are." He paused. "But in the meantime, you see"—and now it seemed that Popov was speaking for a lifetime—"you will know that you are not better than me. In fact, you are worse. You're nothing. Good-bye."

He walked away.

And Alexander Bobrov, looking after him, wondered if he was right.

The next day the Bobrovs left for Finland.

1918   July

In the months that led up to June 1918, a rather unexpected change began
to take place in Vladimir Suvorin. Whether it was the effect of the events
surrounding him, or whether it was one of those physical changes that,
sometimes, occur rather suddenly with age, it was hard to say.

The events of that spring might have shattered a lesser man.

A week after Mrs. Suvorin had left, the Cheka called him in to ask him
where she was. He told them with perfect truth that she had gone to
Finland. "We estimate your fortune at twenty-five million rubles," one
of the men remarked. "What have you to say?"

"I didn't know I had so much," he answered blandly.

"You won't for long," they promised.

In March Vladimir was informed that the Art Nouveau house belonged to the state; two days later, the great Suvorin mansion became a
museum. In April, the factories at Russka were taken over. Late in May,
after asking him to spend several days explaining various aspects of their
workings, all the Moscow plants followed. By the month of June, Vladimir controlled nothing.

It was strange. He had never taken great interest in affairs outside
Russia except insofar as art was concerned. He had no overseas investments. The only deposits in foreign countries that the great industrialist
possessed were the accounts in London and Paris that his son and he used
for purchasing works of art and enough for Mrs. Suvorin to live on for
a while, but not more. By June therefore, Vladimir was poor.

He was not personally harassed. When the house became a museum,
he received a personal visit from the minister Lunarcharsky. That kindly
man, who with his bald pate and pince-nez perched on his nose looked
more like a professor than a revolutionary, was straightforward: "My
dear fellow, the museum needs a curator. Who better than you? Nadezhda can be your deputy." And they were permitted to inhabit a small
apartment at the back of the house, which had once been used by the
housekeeper.

Each day, therefore, Vladimir would solemnly lead around the parties
of workers whom Lunarcharsky would enthusiastically send along in
lorries, while Nadezhda would try to explain a Picasso to puzzled peasant
women, or quietly sweep the floor.

The physical change in Vladimir was twofold. In the first place, he lost
weight, so that now his clothes hung somewhat loosely on his large
frame. But secondly, whether it was his thinning that showed the bone
structure of his face, or whether some other process was also at work, his
physiognomy began to change. His jaw seemed longer, his eyes more
deep-set, and his nose appeared to be longer and coarser. By the end of
June, though not quite so tall, the resemblance had become extremely
striking—he looked just like his grandfather, old Savva Suvorin.

And perhaps hardship had given him something of Savva's temperament, too. For now the man for whom all things were always possible
had become rather silent, and cautious. And determined.

He watched events carefully. Since the spring, two important events had taken place. First, the capital was transferred from Petrograd to Moscow. Second, under Lenin's direct instructions a peace had been signed with Germany at Brest Litovsk. It gave way to all Germany's demands. Finland, Poland, Lithuania, Estonia, and Latvia all became independent. So, under German control, did the Ukraine. The loss was devastating in terms of agriculture and mineral resources. But as Russia was then in no position to fight, it may have saved the Bolshevik regime. Since Russia was no longer their active ally, however, the peace also caused the Western powers to look carefully at the new socialist government whose leaders had long and actively espoused the cause of world revolution. By summer, a British force had already established a beachhead in the far north, officially to guard allied ammunition supplies; and soon a Japanese force, encouraged by the United States, had landed upon the Pacific shore in distant Vladivostok. Other forces were also at work. In the far south, the Don Cossacks were preparing to resist the Bolsheviks; other opposition was gathering in the east beyond the Volga. Lenin, clearly anxious, was busily recruiting a new Red Army. Trotsky was in personal charge. In Moscow, they had been offering steadily higher salaries all spring to get recruits. "There's going to be a civil war," Vladimir told Nadezhda. "Though God knows who'll win it."

Quietly, carefully, Vladimir watched. June passed, then July. And then, in the last part of July, the news came that decided him.

They had shot the tsar.

Dimitri looked thoughtfully at his uncle Vladimir and then his father. It was the first time he had seen a tension between them. Still stranger was it to hear his father, standing in the dining room, say in almost cutting tones to the great man: "I am surprised you should even ask me to desert my country."

They had been talking for half an hour and reached only an impasse. Patiently Vladimir had explained his reasoning. The increasing terror from the Cheka, the danger from outside. "Only one thing can result when a regime is in this kind of position," he argued. "Either it falls, or it imposes a tyranny. I'm sure now that the Bolsheviks will hold on to power. And the killing of the tsar signals their intentions. They'll stand and fight. And I for one, certainly, will be destroyed."

"The tsar was killed by the local Siberian Soviet anyway," Peter objected.

"I don't believe it. And history will prove me right."

But Professor Peter Suvorin wasn't very interested in the tsar.

There was no doubt, Vladimir considered, as he looked at his brother, that Peter could be irritating. He thought sadly of Rosa; then, with a grim smile, of his old grandfather. What, he wondered, had poor old Savva made of Peter? Not much, it seemed. To Vladimir's deep and general mind, accustomed to weighing causes and intentions as well as appreciating the beautiful, his brother's intelligence, however fine in its way, was superficial. Carefully he had questioned him about the events of recent

months, the Bolshevik seizure of power, the ousting of moderate socialists like the professor himself. All these things, Peter agreed, had disturbed him greatly. "But in the long run, don't you see, Vladimir, it may
have to be this way. We have the revolution." And he had smiled with
that sweet, clear look in his eyes that made Vladimir shake his head
and remark grumpily: "I may be wrong, but I think you see what you
want to."

Yet why, Dimitri wondered, despite my father's refusal, should Uncle
Vladimir still be putting such pressure upon me to go? For I haven't the
least desire to.

Indeed, the last few months had been thrilling. In the ferment of the
revolution, the artists of the avant-garde had been taking to the streets.
Posters and proclamations were signed by artists like Mayakovsky.
"Every artist is a revolutionary and every revolutionary is an artist," a
young friend of his had declared. Huge murals were appearing. On top
of a building near their apartment, a bristling sculpture made of metal
girders towered up as if to proclaim the new, scientific age to the blue
sky. There was a huge banner by Tatlin draped halfway down a theater
nearby. Each day, he and Karpenko had roamed the streets in wonder.
Karpenko was painting busily and he, Dimitri, planned to astonish them
all with his new symphony—a hymn to the revolution. How, therefore,
could he possibly want to leave?

It was only when Peter was out of the room for a moment that Vladimir confessed to him: "I must beg you to come, Dimitri, because I promised your mother that I would." He paused. "It was really her last request,
you know."

"But why," Dimitri asked, "why should she be so anxious for me to
leave?"

Vladimir sighed. "She had dreams."

"Of what?"

"That something would happen to you if you stayed." He paused.
"The dreams became very terrible to her, very vivid, just before the end."

"Before the accident?"

Vladimir looked at him sadly. "Quite."

But the youth was shaking his head. "I couldn't leave my father, I don't
want to go anyway." He looked down. "My mother always told me I'd
be safe as long as I was a musician, you know." Then he looked up again
and grinned. "As you see, I am."

And so, reluctantly, Vladimir gave up. Only one person in the professor's apartment agreed to go. And this was Karpenko, who, after hearing
the debate said quietly: "I will come with you to Kiev. I want to get
home."

It was the following day that Dimitri asked his father a favor. The
Symphony to the Revolution was going well. But in the slow movement
he wanted to incorporate some material he had written out, fully orchestrated, when he had been down in the country two years before.

"And the devil of it is," he explained, "I must have left it down at

Russka, in Uncle Vladimir's house. As I hear the place was hardly touched, it's probably still sitting there; but I haven't really time to go down there."

And Peter had smiled. "I'll gladly go for you," he promised.

Nadezhda had gotten used to her new life. She liked the simple workers she took around the house; she was even used to having them watch her sweep the floor. For sheer convenience now, she often dressed like a simple peasant woman herself, with a scarf over her head. And above all, she was glad to feel that in this, the great crisis of his life, she was there beside her father. I at least, she thought bitterly of her mother, remain always at his side.

Only one thing made her angry and caused her to go into a tense silence that could last an hour or more. And this was the presence of Yevgeny Popov.

"Why does he come here?" she would moan aloud. "Does he come to taunt me? To gloat?" Two, sometimes three times a week Popov would come by, curiously inspect the house, look in at their apartment, and then with a brief nod depart. "I'd like to slam the door in his face," she once said bitterly to her father, but he only warned her quietly: "Never annoy a man like that. He's dangerous these days."

Did her father know about Popov and her mother? She had always supposed he did, but never asked. How dare the man come around like this to look at her poor father now?

It was understandable therefore if, as their departure approached, she should dream happily of being rid of the intruder.

Vladimir's plan of escape was very simple.

He had noticed that the Bemsky railway station was, at certain times, a scene of general chaos. And it was from there that trains left for the Ukrainian frontier. It was still not too difficult to get forged papers. The main thing, in his position, was not to be recognized. The plan therefore was kept secret. Once the date was decided, not even Dimitri or Peter were to be told.

Everything seemed quite normal therefore, on the afternoon before their departure, when Popov came by the house.

He made his usual round of inspection, then carefully looked in upon the apartment, where he found Nadezhda alone; and no doubt would have gone if she had not glanced up at him and remarked: "Well, have you come to gloat as usual?" Adding drily: "No one's stolen anything—unless you have, of course."

He looked at her curiously. "Perhaps you should be more polite to a people's commissar. But then, you do not like me."

She shrugged. She had said too much already, and it would be madness to say more. But because she knew she was leaving, she foolishly gave way to her feelings. "I'm sure you are a thief. I imagine you are a murderer. And you tried to steal my mother from my father, who is an angel. Why should I do anything but despise you?"

For nearly half a minute, Popov said nothing. Why was it, he won-

dered, that the bourgeoisie so often lived a lie? Why should this impertinent girl, who was old enough to be someone's wife, continue in complete ignorance of the simple truth? So he told her about Vladimir.

After all, it wasn't so important. Then he left.

For a long time, Nadezhda did not move. Her mouth had fallen wide open
in shock, and as she sat, very pale in her chair, an onlooker might have
supposed that she had died.

Surely it could not be true. She had heard of such things of course.
There was a rumor that had been whispered to her, a year ago, about
Tchaikovsky. But her father, the angel she had adored and looked up to
all her life! She was too shocked even to weep.

And still she had told herself it was not true until early that evening,
Dimitri had looked in, and she had said, with calculated lightness—"So
Dimitri, do you know about my father and Karpenko?"—and poor Dimitri, caught off guard, had gone bright crimson and asked hoarsely: "How
the devil did you know?"

It was evening. To lessen the risk of detection, they did not enter the
ornate Bemsky station all together.

Vladimir as he strode along the platform, dressed in his peasant's shirt
and belt, his heavy hand holding a bag on his shoulder, looked exactly
the Russian Muzhik his grandfather Savva had been. Some minutes later,
a bashful young peasant couple, the boy dark and handsome, boarded
another part of the train. Nobody particularly remembered them.

Karpenko was elated. Firstly, the business was an adventure; secondly,
he was going to see his family for the first time in a year; and thirdly,
he was returning to his beloved Ukraine.

It was time to go home. The revolution was all very well of course.
He had supported it like everyone else. "And who knows," he had
remarked that spring to Dimitri, "if I were a Russian, I might still be a
Bolshevik." But how could he tolerate the way they were treating his
homeland. The Bolsheviks had no love of the Ukrainian nation or its
language. Earlier in the year, the Cheka chief in Kiev had shot people
in the street if he heard them speaking Ukrainian. How could a Karpenko stand for that? Since the Germans had come in, the Ukrainians
had been allowed to elect a Cossack *hetman*, just as in the old days. And
already, he had heard, Ukrainian texts were coming back into the
schools, and the poet Karpenko was occupying a place of honor again.
Yes, this Russian revolution had been exciting; but it was time to go
home.

He noticed that Nadezhda seemed tense and preoccupied, but thought
little of it. Nor did it disturb him when, as he went forward from their
carriage to let Vladimir know they were safely aboard, she asked him to
remain up front with her father. "I just want to be alone tonight," she
said. As she liked.

He was entirely unaware, therefore, that a few minutes before it was
due to leave, Nadezhda stepped off the train.

* * *

Popov was in a hurry. He had commandeered a military car to take him
to the Suvorin house; now he drove swiftly away again.

How could he have been so stupid? He should have guessed. Why
would Nadezhda take the risk of insulting him, unless she knew very
well that she would not be seeing him again? As he drove, his face set.
There were only two obvious ways for the Suvorins to try to leave the
city. He tossed a coin and headed for one of them.

As she went down the platform, Nadezhda could no longer see through
her tears.

Since last evening she had kept herself under rigid control. She had
kissed her father when he came back, exactly as usual. She had made him
supper. The following morning she had shown some factory workers
around the museum, then in the evening, just as planned, she had locked
the great house, dressed as a peasant, and slipped out to join Karpenko.

But she was not going with them, her father and his lover. She was not
going to share that secret shame and betrayal, that opened like a deep,
dark, and terrible abyss before her.

It was a horror—worse by far than the financial ruin that had befallen
them. Everything that she had believed in was shattered.

If Karpenko stayed with Vladimir in his carriage, they would not
realize she had gone until they were at the Ukrainian border in the
morning. Then it would be too late.

What would become of her? Perhaps she would be kept at the museum. Or Uncle Peter and Dimitri would help her. Or Popov might have
her shot for all she knew. She hardly cared.

She had reached the end of the platform. Dully, she heard whistles
blowing. Then someone bumped into her, holding her. She looked up.

It was Popov.

Never, in after years, did she fully comprehend what happened next.
Popov, the hateful Popov, with his arms firmly around her. Popov, surprisingly gentle, yet firm, turning her around, forcing her to walk, numb
and uncomprehending, back up the platform. His voice in her ear.

"Were you running away from them, pretty one? Because of what I
told you, eh? Was that it? I think so. Don't say a word. What else would
you be doing?" A squeeze on her arm.

"Believe me. Please believe me—there are many worse things. He's not
so bad, your father, not so bad at all. Here we are."

He was walking her up the train. He was walking up to the front,
gazing in at the windows. He was going to discover them. Dear God!
What had she done? She struggled to get away. He held her with ease.

"Don't fly, little bird. Don't fly. Ah, there they are."

He was pulling open the carriage door. She could see, as through a
haze, her father and Karpenko. Popov was murmuring something now.
What was he saying? Whispering something about her mother. Tell
her . . . tell her what? That he loved her?

Then suddenly she was pushed inside the carriage, pushed into her
father's arms, and the door slammed. For a second everything seemed

oddly still. Then there was a jolt as the train began to move.

As it did so, Popov watched with a wry smile.

For months now, he had been visiting the house to make sure the girl was safe and well. It was foolish of him to have been angry with her. When he realized that the Suvorins were making a run for it, he had certainly meant to stop them. When he entered Bemsky station, he had intended to arrest Vladimir.

But then he had changed his mind. Why not admit it? It was the sight of that foolish weeping girl. Moscow was no place for her. Let her go. Let her father take her away to where she belonged. To Mrs. Suvorin.

Mrs. Suvorin—the solitary island of love, the only one he had encountered in many years upon the great stream that carried him inexorably, now, high in its mighty flow.

Popov seldom allowed himself to be weak. Perhaps never again, he thought, would he step out from the tough, protective shell that grew, like a carapace, upon him. He turned. Mrs. Suvorin and his last connection with her were gone. There was only the revolution now. It was, after all, what he had lived for so long.

It was a strange business, one that no one could ever explain.

On a day at the end of July, Peter Suvorin had been seen at the town of Russka. From there he had gone to the village and asked the village elder if he might be let into the big house.

A few villagers, standing nearby, noticed that when he told Boris Romanov his name, the elder stared at him in complete astonishment. But then it was odd, perhaps, to realize this trim professor was the brother of the heavyset Vladimir.

The elder couldn't have been more helpful. He took Peter up to the house and found the package he was looking for. Some music, it seemed, locked in a cupboard. Then he had personally escorted him back through the woods towards Russka.

No one knew what had happened to him. No trace was ever found. It was just one of those mysteries.

And young Dimitri Suvorin completed the splendid slow movement of his Revolution Symphony from memory. It was dedicated, naturally, to his father.

1918 August

YOUNG Ivan watched tensely as the troops approached. The Red Army. They has been busy in the town of Russka that morning; they had a commissar with them, a man of some importance; and to his amazement he had just heard the commissar was coming to the village in person.

The commissar and his uncle Boris. He wondered who would win.

The village had prepared carefully. A week before, on a moonless night, the entire village, men and women, had turned out and moved all the grain to new hiding places. Because he and his mother lived up at the big house, and because his uncle hated Arina, they had not been asked to take part. But Ivan had sneaked down and watched them. Two stores were underground, at the edge of the wood. More ingenious, some fifty sealed containers had been lowered into the river a short way upstream. Some grain, however, had been left in plain view, in a large storehouse at the end of the village. "Let the thieves take that," Uncle Boris had said. And then, with disgust: "Even when my father was a serf, they never came and took away his grain."

All over Russia, the countryside was in a state of seething revolt. To the south, a week before, the people in one hamlet had chased two Bolshevik officials away with pitchforks and killed one of them.

The problem had begun last year, when the provisional government had directed that all surplus grain must be sold to the government at set prices. Naturally since the prices were low, most of the peasants had ignored this; besides, peasants had been accustomed to selling their produce at the market since time began. But now the Bolsheviks—or Communists as they nowadays called themselves—said this was speculation and the Cheka officers had been shooting people they caught. "But have you seen what these fools want to pay?" Boris had thundered. "They'll pay sixteen rubles for a pud of rye. And you know what that's worth if I can sell it in Moscow? Almost three hundred rubles! So let them come," he had said grimly, "and see what they can find."

They were coming now: thirty armed men in rather dirty uniforms. At their head walked two figures, both wearing leather coats: one young, the other perhaps sixty, with graying hair that had a reddish, sandy look. And it was only as they drew close that Ivan heard his uncle mutter, "I'll be damned, It's that accursed redhead."

Popov approached the village without particular emotion. Indeed he had only come to this region because Lenin had personally asked him to do so.

He had never known Vladimir Ilych so angry. Of course, they both knew, the fact that most of the old officials from the agriculture university had gone didn't help. Someone on the central committee had even suggested allowing grain to be freely sold for a while. "But if we're going to allow a free market, then what are we Communists doing here at all?" Lenin had countered. Meanwhile, the cities were so short of food that they were emptying. It was absurd.

The object of the exercise today was twofold. Firstly, to obtain grain. Second, to discipline the villagers. Lenin had been very explicit.

"The trouble, Yevgeny Pavlovich, is the capitalist class among the peasants—the kulaks. They're profiteers, bloodsuckers! If necessary the entire class should be liquidated. We've got to take the revolution to the countryside," he had added grimly. "We have to find the rural proletariat."

Popov smiled grimly as he remembered his experiences down here in the past. Who was a kulak? A selfish peasant? A successful one? In his own view, all peasants were petit bourgeois, but then he had never liked them. It was time to sort them out.

"If only," he remarked to the young commissar who was accompanying him, "it was as easy to organize these cursed villagers as it is to sort out a factory."

The morning in the factory had gone very well. There was a soviet there, led by a young Bolshevik he could trust. One of the factory managers had been kept on for the last few months to ensure that the plants functioned smoothly. This morning, however, in conversation with the committee, he has satisfied himself that they could operate without the manager now.

"So you're to be taken to a concentration camp now," he had told the astonished manager at noon. Lenin and Trotsky were both very keen to see these camps used more. "A new camp is just being set up at Murom," he informed the manager. "I hope you enjoy it."

"But for what crime?" the fellow had asked.

"That will be decided in due course," the young commissar at Popov's side had snapped and, grimly amused, Popov had left it at that.

And now the commissar and the village elder faced each other. If either recognized the other, neither gave any sign.

"Where's the grain?" Popov asked quietly.

"Grain? Over there, Comrade Commissar." And he indicated the storehouse.

Popov did not even bother to glance at it. "Search the village," he ordered the troops peremptorily.

It was a strange little comedy, Ivan thought, as he watched the two men. The two commissars strolled around the village, inspecting the huts, accompanied by Boris, who, it seemed, was eager to show them everything. Indeed, Ivan had never seen his burly, overbearing uncle put on an act like this. He bowed and scraped like an innkeeper from the old days, calling Popov "Comrade Commissar," "sir", and even once, in an apparent fit of absentmindedness, addressing him like a tsarist official: "Your Highly Wellborn."

But Popov's face remained only a mask.

"Nothing, Commissar," the sergeant reported.

To which Popov only replied: "No, I didn't think there would be."

Turning suddenly to Boris, he demanded: "What's up at the big house?"

"Nothing much, esteemed Comrade Commissar. Just his mother now." Boris indicated Ivan.

"Good, We'll see it."

As they went up the slope, the young commissar asked Popov quietly: "You think they have grain?" Popov nodded. "What will you do?"

"Find it and take it all."

"All? Won't the village itself go hungry then?"

"Yes." Popov glanced at him. "You should know, comrade, that hunger is sometimes very useful. It makes the people turn on one another at first—they'll attack the kulaks who have food. And then they become submissive. These things are well studied, and useful."

They reached the house. Popov made a brief tour of inspection, insisting on seeing the attic as well as all the outbuildings and the workshops.

Having satisfied himself that the place contained no stores, he came back outside. Then he called the people there to come to him in front of the verandah.

There were a half dozen villagers who had followed out of curiosity; Boris, Ivan, Arina, and three Red soldiers. Popov gave them all a faint smile. Then he turned to Boris.

"You are the elder. Do you swear you have no grain."

"I do, Comrade Commissar." Boris nodded vigorously.

"Very well, then." He beckoned one of the soldiers. "Take aim at her." He pointed to Arina. Then he turned to young Ivan. "Now tell me where it's hidden," he said gently.

The Red soldier shot Boris by the river, as soon as the last of the containers of grain had been pulled out.

"And now," Popov announced, "it's time to set up a proper village committee."

Bringing the revolution to the countryside wasn't easy. But the new plan that the leadership had hit upon had a certain brutal logic. The kulaks, the swindlers, the rich peasants, they all must be hounded out: and who better to do this than the poor peasants—the majority. Committees of the Poor must be set up at once, therefore, to seize control of the villages.

Privately this was one of the few ideas of Lenin that Popov did not agree with. "For the simple fact is," he would argue, "that the majority of peasants aren't poor: they're middling. They can't employ labor usually; but they have a modest surplus of their own. The poor peasant half the time is just an ordinary peasant who's become a drunkard."

However, if Vladimir Ilych wanted his Committee of the Poor, he should have them. Popov looked about him. "You." He suddenly pointed to young Ivan. "Your mother's a widow. What land do you hold in the village?"

It was true that, as an orphan and with no help from his uncle, Ivan actually had the smallest holding of any male in the village just then.

"I am putting you in charge of the committee," Popov said with a smile. "How's that?"

There would be a committee on paper, anyway. He wondered how long the boy would last.

It was late afternoon when Popov, satisfied with his day's work, returned to Russka. On his way, he passed the monastery. It was empty now. The monks had been forced to abandon their home after the confiscations of January; but strangely enough, hoping that the government might relent or be overthrown, they had left everything in place. An old priest who still resided in the town kept an eye on things.

Since he was here, it occurred to Popov that he might as well inspect the monastery, too. "We'll go in," he said.

It was entirely empty and very quiet. The kitchens and storehouse had been ransacked at some point, and a few of the windows had been broken; but otherwise the monastery had not been harmed. Popov walked all over it, carefully, by himself. When he had finished, he was glad he had taken the trouble; he made a brief note.

> Monastery at Russka: will make an excellent small prison or detention house. Inform Cheka.

He had certainly done a good day's work.

When he returned to the entrance, he found that the soldiers had built a small bonfire. The young commissar was busy carrying things out of the church to burn. Popov looked at him in mild surprise: the objects he was carrying were icons. "I didn't know you were so strongly anti-religion." he remarked mildly.

"Oh, yes. Aren't we all?"

Popov shrugged. "I suppose so."

He glanced at the icon the fellow was tossing on the fire. It looked vaguely familiar. "I think that one may be rather good," he remarked.

"No such thing as a good icon," the other replied.

"Perhaps." He watched the little object begin to burn. Its lines had a remarkable grace.

And so disappeared the greatest gift of the Bobrovs to the little religious house: the icon by the great Rublev.

As darkness fell that summer night, long after the little bonfire in the monastry had died down, a single figure emerged from the woods below the village to the riverbank where Arina was waiting with a small boat.

Ivan had been hiding since the soldiers left. After the events of that afternoon, he had no choice. Would the sons of Boris Romanov forgive him for getting their father killed? Would the villagers forget he had given away their grain? As for this position the Bolshevik has just given him on this committee, that in itself might have been his death warrant. "If I'm here in the morning, I'll be dead," he had told his mother, and she knew it was true.

Now she helped him into the boat.

"Which way are you going?" she asked.

"South. I daren't go past the village. I'll get down to the Oka, then follow it to Murom, I daresay."

"And what will you do?"

He shrugged. "I don't know. Join the army maybe." He smiled despite himself. "Seems the safest place to be!"

"Here's money." Arina kissed him. "You're my only son," she said simply. "If you die, I want to know. Otherwise I shall believe you are alive."

"I'll live."

Once again he embraced her, then got into the boat.

There was a quarter moon, away to the south. He pushed the boat out and began to row slowly up the silvery stream towards it.

1920   October

It was getting cold. But the work was nearly done: a simple mopping-up operation. The truck and the artillery piece before them were little more than charred metal. Half a dozen bodies lay there, and one man apparently alive. An officer.

Ivan moved forward, cautiously. All around, the empty steppe of south Russia extended to the horizon.

The war was almost over. The Whites and their foreign allies had nearly been successful once or twice. For a brief period it had seemed Petrograd itself would fall. Denikin, Wrangel, and others had fought well. But they had always lacked the coordination that the Reds enjoyed. And, perhaps the determination. Now the final White front was being rolled back, and the capitalist allies—Britain, America, Japan, Italy—had all given up.

And now here was a Cossack officer still alive. A handsome devil certainly, but doomed.

Karpenko watched Ivan draw close. It was a pity, certainly, to be dying. Two years ago he could never have imagined himself fighting like this. But to his great surprise it had brought him a kind of satisfaction. The pain in his stomach was like a fire.

It seemed to him that the young Red looked vaguely familiar; but it scarcely mattered.

"Well, comrade, you'd better put me out of my misery," he said cheerfully.

Which Ivan did, as kindly as he could. As it happened, it was the last shot he had to fire.

The revolution had been won.

TWELVE

Coda

1937

SOFTLY, softly, the music began, and although it was late at night, the eleventh hour, he felt fresh and confident.

If there were still just time.

Dimitri Suvorin's pen moved quickly over the paper.

It was a short piece, the *Suite.* A little programmatic piece inspired by Russian folklore. Children and adults, he thought, could enjoy it. Everything was written now, except the coda.

In the room next door, his wife and children were sleeping. There was one boy, named after his grandfather, Peter, and a girl, Maryushka. The little boy, people said, was very like him. As he wrote, Dimitri smiled to himself. The *Suite* was for all his family, but especially for little Peter. He had dedicated it to him that very evening and he knew that it was important he should do so. For then, when the boy heard it, perhaps he would understand.

It was the answer to the terrible secret they shared.

The *Suite* was a charming idea. It was the story of some hunters who go into the forest and meet a bear. Naturally, they are afraid of the bear, but they capture it and bring the huge beast back with them in chains. On their way back through the forest, they catch a glimpse of the magical firebird. One of the hunters, knowing its wonderful properties, races after the bird, trying to get one of its feathers. But he fails. The gleaming bird, as it always does, flies away, taunting, elusive.

Dimitri was pleased with the musical characterizations: the bear had a slow, heavily accented tune, representing his simple nature and his heavy footfall; the firebird a haunting little melody that would suddenly break out into brilliant staccato bursts of sound as its feathers glittered and burst into flame.

When the men get the bear back to the town, they train it for the circus, and the music represented the coaxing and the blows, the bear's misery and his clumsy steps as he begins to rumble around the circus, obedient to their will. It was full of pathos and humor. The children would clap and laugh.

But would it be approved?

Dimitri paused in his work for a moment. Outside, he could see over the roofs of the nearby buildings. A moon, nearly full, rode high in the autumn sky. And three miles away, he knew, in his study deep in the

Kremlin, another figure would certainly be working at this hour.

It was remarkable what Stalin had achieved: there was no question. In the early twenties, after the ruin of the civil war, how uncertain the course of the revolution had seemed. The leadership had even had to tolerate, with the new economic policy, a measure of capitalism for a time. But then Stalin had imposed his will: what Lenin had begun, he would complete. And the transformation had been astounding: the entire countryside turned into state farms and collectives; the independent peasants of the Ukraine deported en masse. The first, stupendous Five Year Plan for industry completed in just over four. Russia was now, truly, a world industrial power. Yet at what cost? How many had perished? He did not like to think how many.

Russia had risen like a great bear: that was it. There was nothing, it seemed, the mighty bear could not accomplish with its huge strength, if properly directed.

Yet he missed those earlier days. Things had been livelier then. Writers like Bulgakov and Pasternak had been free to say what they like. Eisenstein had burst upon the world with his astonishing film work. Painting had still been the province of the avant-garde, before the present doctrine of socialist realism had condemned all painting to a dreary depiction of idealized proletarian life.

Nowadays one had to be more careful. A friend of his who had foolishly recited a poem mocking Stalin back in '32—and done so only in the privacy of a friend's apartment—had disappeared within the week. Eisenstein's films were made under Stalin's personal supervision now; all the history books were being rewritten.

"I can only thank God," he would say to his wife, "that no one's found a way to control music yet." His work, like that of Prokofiev and Shostakovich, was not much interfered with.

For several more minutes Dimitri wrote intensely: the coda was taking shape. The apartment was silent as his little family slept. Dimitri completed the first section of the final entrance of the bear.

It was the latest piece of foolish legislation that had really depressed him. To educate children for a socialist world was one thing. Dimitri would sometimes smile at Stalin's passion for Peter the Great. Peter, too, had seen all men as nothing more than creatures whose purpose was to serve the state. But even Peter the Great never dreamed of legislation like Stalin's. To turn ordinary children into enemies of their own parents— everything in him revolted against that. The new Children's Law was very clear, though. Any child who discovered counterrevolutionary tendencies in either parent should report him or her. He had grinned at the time. "Your mother's a scientist and I'm a musician," he had said to young Peter, "so I don't think you need to worry about that." And the little boy had laughed. He was only nine, but already Dimitri recognized a studious, thoughtful look in his dark eyes. "Perhaps you'll be a scholar or an artist," Dimitri liked to say to him.

In the second section of the *Suite,* one of the hunters manages to catch the firebird just long enough to pull out one of its feathers, and he brings it to the circus. How the feather sparkles and crackles with light. It is as though the fellow has just discovered the power and wonder of electricity, and the music became charged with chromatic energy as the wondrous feather appeared.

It had been foolish of him, of course, to have made the remarks he had, even in private. Yet how could one not be irritated? The previous year the regime had actually declared that a number of scientific disciplines were to be abolished: pedology, genetics, sociology, psychoanalysis. The reason: Stalin's great constitution had just been published, which declared Russia to be a perfect, democratic state. How then could there be sciences which spoke of poor children, inherited differences, social problems, or troubled people?

And one evening, at home with some friends, Dimitri had turned to little Peter and said: "You realize, don't you, that this constitution is a flagrant lie?" That was all he had said; but it was enough.

It was a week later that he had known. It was a look in the boy's eyes that had told him. He had been working at the kitchen table one afternoon and suddenly had seen little Peter gazing at him with a steady, accusing stare. Then, when he had instinctively drawn the boy to him and put his arm around him, he had felt Peter suddenly draw back, then look at him guiltily and in evident confusion. He had known at once, and understood. And the boy guessed he knew. And neither had said a word.

It was a pity, though.

Would they let the *Suite* be performed? It seemed innocuous enough— just some circus scenes, based on fairy tales. He supposed they would, but perhaps he should hide the music somewhere, give it to someone. Just in case.

He worked on swiftly.

The coda depicted a remarkable scene. The firebird comes out of the forest—something it has never done before—and bursts into the circus. Swooping and wheeling around, the firebird terrifies everyone—the audience, the hunters, the bear trainer. Sparks fill the air. The electric lights flash on and off wildly. And in this pandemonium, the bear, for so long cowed, breaks free and begins his own, lumbering, tragicomic dance.

Would it be played? Would he be allowed to finish it? Three miles away, deep in the Kremlin's great stone heart, Stalin was working now. At just this time of night, it was said, the lists of those to be purged were placed before him. So many had gone already. Names, names without number, names without faces. Did they vanish from the universe, or only from the earth.

Slowly the coda formed, its syncopated rhythms coming together, parting, as the crowds shouted and the firebird and the bear contrived their wild dance of ever-mounting joy, and freedom, until they burst out of the circus into the night, and rushed towards the forest.

Midnight passed. One o'clock.

A knock on the door.

Still the firebird was flying high, brushing the top of the tent as the lights flashed madly. And the bear was hugging his trainer, not in rage but in love, while the foolish fellow howled with fright.

The knocks at the door grew louder.

His wife in the kitchen now, staring with frightened, uncomprehending eyes. "NKVD. What have we done?" His little daughter, awakened
and crying. His son, looking pale as a ghost, behind them.

The firebird was swooping now, calling to the bear. She had her stolen
feather in her claws. The bear was lumbering towards the entrance. A
minute more and they would be free.

The men were hammering on the door now. Their voices echoed,
angrily. Little Peter was turning into the hall. In a moment he would let
them in.

And now the flaps of the circus tent flew apart and with a last, huge
crash from the percussion, they rushed, the firebird and the bear, out into
the huge embracing freedom of the forest where, for a second or two
more, their timeless, joyous melodies were heard to echo.

Dimitri turned. There were three of them. They let him kiss his wife
and little girl. The music rested on the table. They turned to go.

The little boy was there in the hall. Whatever they had told him at
school had not been enough. Now, seeing his father being taken away,
he had suddenly broken down.

Dimitri picked him up in his arms and held him. He hugged him close.

"It's all right," he whispered. "You understand. I knew, but it's all
right. The music's for you."

Then he, too, went out into a colder, darker night.

1938 January

IVANOV was the local party chief at Russka that year. Not a bad sort of
fellow. He had a deputy named Smirnov.

Between them they were looking at the list. Twenty-five names were
required. They had got to twenty-three; at last found a twenty-fourth;
but they were still a man short.

He had to be found, of course. Twenty-five names of enemies of the
people. That was the funny thing about a purge. The top people, of
course, were carefully chosen: but down here, you just got a quota you
had to fill in. "There must be someone," he said.

And then he remembered Yevgeny Popov.

He was a strange figure, very quiet, who was living out his retirement
in a small house at the edge of the town. He grew cabbages and radishes
in his garden, and kept himself fit by walking each day to the nearby
village and back. Come to think of it, he hadn't seen him recently.

"Is Popov alive?" he inquired. His deputy said he was. "He'll do, then,"
Ivanov suggested.

"But he's in this eighties," Smirnov protested. "He's one of the real old
Bolsheviks. A loyal man."

The chief considered. "If he goes back so far," he said thoughtfully,
"he must have known a lot of people."

"He knew Lenin."

"Maybe. Perhaps he also knew Trotsky."

"I hadn't thought of that."

It suddenly occurred to Ivanov that the little house where Popov lived would do very well for a cousin of his wife's.

Number 25: Yevgeny Pavlovich Popov, he wrote. Suspected collaborator with Trotsky.

And so, at the age of eighty-four, Yevgeny Popov was surprised to be sent to a gulag.

1945 August

IT was a warm afternoon as Ivan walked past Russka and made his way towards the village. The sky was clear. A few clouds drifted up from the south. There was a pleasant smell in the fields and a dustiness everywhere, as there is at harvest time.

He was home from the war. In all but name, it was over—the Great Patriotic War.

He had fought well, nearly lost his life several times; but, along with every other soldier on the front, he had been sustained by two pieces of knowledge: he was fighting for the fatherland; and Comrade Stalin was commanding everything. It was well known, by now, that there was almost nothing the great leader could not do. The war, thank God, was almost done with. It was time to stay at home and build a new, bright future.

And it was smiling at this thought that he came out of the wood and saw the big village field before him where the women were slowly stooping with their sickles as they had since time began.

And then his mother Arina looked up and saw him and, forgetting her age, came running across the field, her arms outstretched, towards him.

Epilogue

1990 June

So THIS WAS the day. Paul Bobrov was up early, and before six o'clock he was ready to leave.

The Hotel Aurora wasn't a bad place. Comparatively new and situated near Red Square, it was a nine-story concrete structure whose rooms had been designed and furnished by a Finnish enterprise. The beds and chest of drawers were all of a piece, made of pale wood, and ran along one wall like a bench. The beds were not uncomfortable, but hard and narrow, and it occurred to Paul that Russian hotels were certainly not places designed for any sexual encounters, despite the opportunities that existed in the form of the score or so of pretty girls who infiltrated past his doorman into the lobby and the bars, looking for customers each evening.

A pale sunlight was coming through the windows as he made his way towards the elevator bank. Bobrov glanced at his watch. In fifteen minutes he would be on his way to the old Bobrov estate.

Paul Bobrov was thirty-three, the second of Alexander and Nadezhda's ten grandchildren. He was of medium height and though he retained the slightly Turkish look of his ancestors, these features were softened. Sometimes, in the way of numerous past Bobrovs, he would unconsciously make a gentle, almost caressing movement with his arm.

How pleased old Alexander would have been, he thought, to know of his visit. His grandmother, still beautiful at ninety-two, though rather frail, had given him a vivid description of the place and assured him: "I certainly shan't die until you get back and tell me all about it."

The old estate: a vivid reminder of how things were. Not that anybody had ever forgotten.

The little Russian community to which Paul Bobrov belonged resided in a suburb to the north of New York City. It was one of several in the region: there were other, similar communities to be found in London, Paris, and elsewhere. These were not, he could have told you, to be confused with the huge mass of Russian Jews who had come at the turn of the century; nor the later wave of those fleeing Russia at the time of the Second World War; nor, God forbid, the recent wave of Soviets who nowadays crowded into such areas as New York's Brighton Beach. No, Paul Bobrov's community was that of the Russian émigrés, the noble classes to whom, strictly speaking, even Nadezhda belonged only by right of marriage.

They were a close-knit group. A few had money, but many had not. They lived modest middle-class lives in shady tree-lined streets; and though to outward appearances they were ordinary Americans, they usually married among themselves, spoke Russian as well as English in the home, and—rare among other émigré communities—preserved a genuine inner life from their home country.

The center of this was the Church. For old Alexander, always inclined towards at least the forms of religion, this was natural. For others, careless of religion back in Russia, the Orthodox Church was now the remaining bastion that preserved their identity and added moral integrity to that preservation. There were two branches of the Orthodox Church to which people like the Bobrovs belonged, and neither recognized the legitimacy—for the time being—of the Patriarch in Moscow, who was felt to be under the thumb of the KGB.

Each Saturday, from far and wide, members of the community like Paul, already two generations removed from Russia, would bring their children to the church hall for a half day of lessons in Russian language and history. On any Sunday one might see the bearer of some proud old Russian name handing out candles in the church or singing with a fine bass voice in the choir. The old woman with a scarf over her head, praying to an icon like any babushka, might be a Russian princess. Infants were thoroughly baptized—completely immersed in the font three times.

And once a year, Paul took his wife to either the Russian Nobility Ball—a sedate affair at which elderly gentlemen might be seen wearing tsarist decorations—or the more lively Petrushka Ball. Both were elegant, held in large New York ballrooms, and well attended.

In such ways, with remarkable tenacity, the Russian community had held on and waited.

But for what? Paul was the first of the family to venture back. Did some of his uncles or cousins hope for a restitution of the tsar? Though Nicolas and his family had been destroyed, the dynasty had survived through the grand dukes, so such a restoration was technically possible. But Paul found it hard to imagine. Nor could he conceive of abandoning his home in New York. "But if things change, if things open up, then it would be good to get involved," he would say. It was a rather vague aspiration, but full of, perhaps, only half-acknowledged emotions.

What a stroke of luck it had been, meeting Sergei Romanov. They had found each other at a trade fair in New York the previous year. The Russian had been looking for opportunities to develop software programs in Moscow under license to Western companies. He had a good team of people but little idea of the business, and Paul, who marketed desktop computers, had been glad to give him some help both in making contacts and with his faulty English. Only on the second day had Bobrov

mentioned that sometime he hoped to go to the Soviet Union and visit
the family's old estate. The only trouble, he explained, was how to get
there, as it wasn't on any tourist route. "A little place called Russka," he
had said.

"But, Paul Mikhailevich," Romanov had exclaimed, "that's the very
place my own grandfather came from! I've never been there myself.
Come to Moscow, my friend," he had said warmly, "and we'll go there
together."

And now here he was, with Romanov coming to collect him.

They had agreed to meet in front of the hotel at six-fifteen. Too early
to get breakfast in the cavernous dining room: but Paul had noticed the
previous evening that on the fifth floor there was a little bar that opened
at six, and he made his way there now.

It was a small place, typical of such refreshment rooms. Under the glass
counter would be laid out plates of sliced cheese, sliced salami, pirozhki,
hard-boiled eggs, and, of course, white and black bread. There were large
jugs of apple juice and grape juice, a coffee machine, and a samovar. By
the window was a counter where one could stand to eat; down one wall
there were four small tables. The big glass doors meant that one would
see the people inside, and the opening times were pasted on the glass.

It was five minutes after six when he got there. Inside he could see the
food being laid out by a pretty but bored-looking blond girl of about
twenty. Behind her, a large, grumpy woman in her fifties was grimly
inspecting the bread. He tried to open the glass door. It was locked.

The girl glanced at him and said something to the older woman, who
did not even deign to look at him. Paul glanced at his watch, tapped on
the glass, and pointed to the opening times. The girl just stared at him.
Then the big woman turned and shouted at him: *"Zakryt."* The word
most familiar to any tourist in Russia. *"Zakryt."* We're shut.

And then the girl smiled.

"Mnye skuchno." I'm bored.

"Mnye skuchno, skuchno, skuchno."

She used to mutter the words to herself by the hour, every day, almost
as monks used to mutter the Jesus prayer. *"Mnye skuchno."* It was a litany.

Ludmilla Suvorin was intelligent: her father, Peter, had been too, until
he took to drink; and Peter's father had been Suvorin the composer.
Only, until a few years ago, one wasn't supposed to mention him, because he'd been sent to the gulags. And though his work, including the
final *Suite,* were reinstated nowadays, that fact did little good for her.
Peter had died when Ludmilla was five; her mother had married a rail-
wayman, and they lived in a drab four-room apartment that they shared
with another family, in a big, peeling concrete block in the wastelands
of the city outskirts. There were four of these blocks on that street,
standing in an isolated row, and across the top of them in large metal
letters painted red were the words: COMMUNISM'S BUILDING A BETTER WORLD.
Her building bore the letters: WORLD.

Ludmilla was also lazy. She should have been doing something better
than this, but she couldn't be bothered. She liked to dance. She had a
good figure, slim and strong. Sometimes she had thought of selling her

body like the leggy girls in the lobby. Several of those were students. One was married and saving to get a dacha in the country. Years ago, such girls often used to dream of snaring a Westerner who'd fall in love with them, marry them, and get them out of Russia. But they were wiser now: it never happened. They took the money—hard currency—and were grateful.

She hadn't done so, though. So here she was, with Varya.

And now Ludmilla watched the American with mild amusement on her sulky face. The American did not understand what he was up against as he gesticulated impatiently out there. But then, how would he?

For Varya had her own very clear ideas about the running of the bar. On two things in particular she was inflexible, the first of which was opening hours.

If the bar was due to open at six, she understood, then that was when she arrived. "They don't pay you for coming early, do they?" she would say. "And after we open at six," she explained, "then we have to get ready." During this time, while she put the food out on the trays and brewed the coffee, she naturally did not allow any customers in, since they would only be in the way. For some fifteen to twenty minutes every morning, therefore, there was an interval during which she explained, with no sense of contradiction: "The bar is open, but it is shut."

And similarly, of course, in the evenings, when the bar closed at nine, customers ceased to be served some twenty minutes before that time. "Otherwise," she would say severely to Ludmilla, "we should be closing late."

"*Zakryt,*" therefore, she shouted, as Paul waited irritably outside.

And only at thirteen minutes past six did Varya relent and tell Ludmilla to open the door.

The American spoke extraordinary Russian. Beautiful to hear. Even Varya looked awkward now and seemed eager to make up for keeping him outside. They gave him a cup of coffee, salami, an egg. And bread, of course.

"You're Russian?"

"Yes." He smiled. "American."

"So you've come back to see." She had met one or two of these émigrés in the hotel before. They all spoke this beautiful language: just listening to them could almost make you weep. "There's not much of your Russia left, they tell me," she added. She couldn't think of anything else to keep him there. He went over to the table and sat down. He drank some coffee; then ate a piece of bread. Then frowned.

Ludmilla smiled. "Something wrong?"

He made a small grimace. "Nothing much. It's just that the bread's a little stale." He glanced at her. "Haven't you really anything better?"

And Ludmilla looked at Varya. For this was Varya's second strange idea.

When had it first begun? Ludmilla had been working there only six months, so she did not know. But somehow the bar had finished one day with too much bread. Anyone else would have taken the bread or thrown it away the next day. But for some reason known only to herself, Varya had insisted on serving the old bread the following day, until it was all used up—which, as it happened, was not until closing time. The fresh bread delivered that morning had still remained untouched in the kitchen behind the bar. The following day, therefore, she repeated the process. The previous day's bread was served; the fresh, delivered sliced, was left in the kitchen. And within a short time this curious procedure had set into a pattern that had developed rules of its own.

No one was allowed to touch the bread. If you did, Varya would know. Nor could anyone tell the people downstairs not to deliver one day, to clear the backlog. "Then they'd start asking questions." Nor, even, could you use any of the fresh bread if you ran out of the stale bread during the day. "We use so much a day, no more, no less," Varya said firmly. So it was, in the fifth-floor bar, that the bread served was always exactly one day old.

Paul only stayed another two minutes. Then, with a nod to Ludmilla, he hurried off. It never occurred to either of them that they were related.

It was an easy journey down. The huge, broad street leading out of Moscow soon gave way to modest two-carriage highways; within an hour the two had merged into a single road, broad enough for two cars to drive abreast on each side, but with no markings upon it of any kind. "We don't have your freeways," Sergei remarked apologetically.

"You don't need them," Paul replied. And indeed, for a main road, the traffic was remarkably light.

Like most Russians, Sergei drove his little car at breakneck speed, feeling free to use almost any part of the road as the mood took him. Once or twice, rather unexpectedly, the road surface of even this high-way would abruptly disintegrate, and one would be traveling, still at the same speed, over a surface of caked mud or chips for half a mile or so until the metaled surface resumed again.

The weather was excellent. The sky was a clear pale blue, cloudless, and with only a faint, dusty haze along the eastern horizon. The birch trees lay on each side of the road, their silver trunks and brilliant emerald leaves producing a sparkling effect.

Sergei Romanov had a round face, balding head, and fair hair. He had been twice to the West and hoped to go again. Like many Russians of his age—and Paul put him in his late thirties—Sergei was cautious about talking about himself but extremely curious to know more about Bobrov. At first, however, as Paul had sometimes found with other Soviets of the intellectual kind, there was a slight shyness in this. When he referred to old Nicolai Bobrov, for instance, he said: "Your great-grandfather, the late esteemed member of the last duma"; his playful tone masked, Paul realized, a certain sense of respect towards his family's past.

Bobrov chatted easily with him now, therefore, speaking of his family, his Russian upbringing, the nursery rhymes and folktales he had learned as a child; and by the time they had been driving an hour, Sergei was entirely relaxed.

"Of course, we can't help being curious about you," he said frankly to Paul, "because when Russia lost all the people like you, we lost the better part of our old culture, and now we hardly know how to get it back."

"It depends what you want, I should think," Paul replied. "What do you want?"

Sergei was thoughtful for some time.

"You operated under capitalism before the revolution, didn't you? Free markets?"

"Yes. Pretty much."

"And free expression? Literature? Philosophy?"

"Certainly."

"Do you know, philosophy in Russian schools consists of Hegel, Feuerbach, and Marx? Plato, Socrates, Descartes, Kant—these are scarcely mentioned." He shook his head. "We want our history above all," he continued. "Stalin rewrote so much we don't have any idea what the truth is. Can you imagine what that feels like? To realize you have no idea what really happened, what made you the person you are? We feel like a lost generation. And we want it all back." Suddenly, and with an unexpected passion that sent the car careening to the center of the road and back, he banged on the steering wheel. "All of it!"

"How about the Church?"

"I'm an atheist," Sergei said firmly. "I can't believe. But if others wish to, they should be free to do so." Then he smiled. "My mother believed. She used to go to secret services. In people's houses. Did you know about that?"

Paul had heard of this secret religious activity. No one knew exactly how it was organized. It was known as the Catacomb Church, after the secret, underground worshiping of early Christian times; but he was aware that ever since the early days of the soviet state, there had been a large network of priests, often moving from one region to another, who held secret services for the faithful in cabins, barns, or hideouts in the woods all over Russia.

"Perhaps if Russian culture returns, you may become a religious believer, too," he said with a smile.

"I doubt it."

They drove some way towards the city of Vladimir before turning south. Several times Sergei seemed to get lost, but he managed eventually to find the narrow road that apparently led towards Russka.

Having relieved his feelings about his culture, Sergei seemed anxious to talk of other matters. He spoke of things he had seen in the West, and asked Bobrov about his business. "You market computers, don't you? Tell me exactly how it works."

This was not easy, but Paul did his best. He outlined the whole marketing plan for a new product from market research all the way through to the advertising and the sales kits. "Then," he said with a grin, "I have to sell it to the salesmen." It was the same pattern, pretty much, he explained, for any product.

And all the time, Sergei Romanov nodded and said: "Ah yes, this is what we should have."

* * *

It was late morning when they reached the little town of Russka.

It was a terrible disappointment.

Thanks to his grandmother's information, it was now Paul Bobrov who conducted Romanov around. The town was rather run down. The great watchtower, with its high tent roof still stood. So did most of the houses in the town, though he noticed that the larger, merchant houses by the little park had been split into apartments and their gardens left to grow high with bushes and brambles. The stone church by the market-place, however, was in a sorry state and had clearly not been used in decades.

He found that one of the factories there was making bicycles; but the textile business still existed, in that the other was making woolen blankets. Having made a tour of the sad little town, he led Sergei down to the river and walked him along the path to the springs. The springs, at least, had not been altered, and the two men sat for some time on the green mossy bank and listened to the sounds of the water splashing down.

By now, however, Paul was impatient to see the old Bobrov house; and as soon as they had walked back from the springs, they got into the car and drove across the bridge and along the bumpy path through the wood.

The village was much as Nadezhda had described it. There were no Romanovs there now, and Sergei had no idea which house had been his family's; but once again, remembering all Nadezhda had said, Paul was able to take him to the handsome two-story house with the carved gables and tell him: "This is where Boris Romanov used to live."

There was only one thing that puzzled him: as they went around he kept looking up the slope towards where, he was sure, the old Bobrov house should be. But he could not see it. Finally he asked a villager: "Where's the big house?" And the fellow explained: "They say there was one up the hill there. But I never saw it."

And so it proved to be. When they walked up the slope, they found nothing. Not a frame; not an outbuilding; nothing but a faint outline on the turf and, a little above it, an overgrown alley through the trees.

The ancestral house had gone. His link with the past lost, buried in the ground. His journey had been in vain. Sadly he turned to go back.

It was when they approached the monastery that they discovered something was going on.

From outside, it looked almost deserted. The walls were crumbling; the bell tower was down. The buildings within seemed to be windowless.

Yet now two monks suddenly appeared.

They were young, both in their twenties, simply dressed in black cassocks. One was tall and thin, with a small fair beard; the other had a broad, intelligent face and bright blue eyes set wide apart that looked out with an extraordinary freshness upon the world. They smiled as the car approached. Sergei halted and rolled down the window.

"There are monks here?" The great Danitov Monastery had been sending out monks to several places, but he had no idea they had come down to Russka.

"For three months." The tall monk smiled. "You are baptized?"

"Most certainly." It was Paul Bobrov who answered from the passenger seat.

"God has sent you at a propitious time," the monk with the blue eyes said. "Come and see." And the two monks turned and led the car in.

It was an unexpected sight. A dozen monks were standing near the chapel. Though, like the other buildings there, it had lost its windows long ago, huge sheets of transparent plastic had been placed to cover them. Several of the smaller buildings, Paul could see, had been partly remodeled and made habitable. Someone had started work on the inside of the gateway.

He also noticed that, for some reason, about forty peasants, mostly women but a number of men, were standing respectfully to one side; and that just by the church entrance, a casket covered with a purple cloth was lying.

They got out and stood awkwardly.

"I'm afraid we are intruding," Paul said. But the two young monks would have none of it and rushed away, returning a minute later with a man of about fifty with an intelligent, inquiring face. He made them a gracious bow of welcome and explained: "I am the Archimandrite Leonid. May I ask how you happened to be here just now?"

When Paul told him why he had come, the archimandrite seemed almost shaken. "You are a Bobrov? The family that founded this monastery? And your name is Paul: we are, as you know, the Monastery of Saint Peter and Saint Paul." He closed his eyes for a moment. "These things," he said quietly, "are sent to us as signs. They do not come by chance." And then, smiling to them both, he said, "Please stay for a little while. It appears that your coming was meant to be."

It was indeed an extraordinary coincidence, Paul considered, however you looked at it. He, a Bobrov, had arrived at the little monastery, just being reopened—and not just upon any day. For the very day before, the monks, diligently searching, had found the grave of one of their most revered elders, and that day, at the very hour when Paul arrived, they were taking his remains into the church for a service of rededication. It was the Elder Basil, who had lived as a hermit many years in the previous century, out past the springs, in the company of a bear.

The service was not unduly long and was very simple.

The casket containing the remains of the Elder Basil had been placed at the northeast corner of the church. The interior of the building was a strange sight. Apart from the sheets of plastic over the windows, only half the space was, as yet, safe for use, and a big triangle of cloth had been draped across a string to mark off this area. Behind it stood a stepladder and several buckets, apparently to catch rainwater from the roof.

Though the archimandrite had put on vestments, all the other monks were simply dressed in black, some of them showing signs of plaster dust. The people who crowded in seemed mostly poor. There was nothing of

ornament, no grandeur, nothing to delight the eye in that simple Orthodox service.

They sang a psalm and a hymn.

The sermon of the Archimandrite Leonid was, similarly, very simple
and delivered with expressions of extraordinary gentleness.

They must all be grateful, he reminded them, for signs of God's Providence, which by their very nature are wholly unforeseen. They remind
us, he pointed out, that the Wisdom of God is great indeed and that,
though we may glimpse it, we may not know more than an infinitesimal
part of His great purpose. How else was it, he suggested, that at such an
hour, on such a day, one Paul, descendant of the founder of this monastery, should appear by chance at the monastery gates, having traveled for
thousands of miles. And was it not significant, he remarked, that having
come in search of his earthly house, and found it gone, he should now
have come unaware to this, his spiritual house?

He turned then to the former life of the monastery—the centuries of
its existence—and to the fact that now life, after a short death, was
resuming again.

But it was his words on the Elder Basil himself that Paul would always
remember.

For many years, the Elder Basil dwelt in his hermitage praying and
giving spiritual guidance; to him also are ascribed a number of miracles. But today, as we have his blessed remains before us, it is to the
very start of his life as a hermit that I wish to turn.

It was always said that the Elder Basil had a gift with animals. It
was remarked that a large bear would often appear, and that he
would find this bear and talk to it like a kindly father to a child; and
people therefore decided he had a gift.

In fact, the opposite was the case. The elder, at the start of his
seclusion, was very much afraid when the bear appeared. So much
so that, the first time, he cowered in his little hut all night and almost
returned to the monastery the next day. The second night, the same
thing happened.

Only on the third night did the Elder Basil understand what he
must do.

For on the third night, Basil remained outside his hut, seated
quietly on the ground. And he said the Jesus prayer: "Lord Jesus
Christ, Son of God, have mercy upon me, a sinner." Not because he
asked any longer that his body be saved; but rather that, he considered—"What can this bear do to me, who by God's Grace has eternal
life."

And thus his fear of the bear disappeared. And so, my children,
we here are not without fear. We know what has passed in former
decades in the Russian land. But in rebuilding this monastery, and
in remembering the example of the Elder Basil, we know that we
must not fear the bear. We must love him. For perfect love casteth
out fear.

It was just then that, to his surprise, Paul realized that his friend Sergei was trembling, and that he was crying.

The monks had fed them. The two men departed in the late afternoon with an extraordinary feeling of lightness. And for a long time they drove slowly back towards Moscow in silence.

Only after an hour did Sergei speak.

"We shall do it. We shall rebuild Russia, you know."

"Yes."

"I don't think we want pure capitalism, though. A sort of mixed economy."

"I daresay it could be done."

For another hour after that Sergei did not speak. It was not until they were entering the suburbs of Moscow that he suddenly said: "How long do you think it will take? Five years?"

"Perhaps longer."

"Well, you may be right. Not more than ten, though. We'll catch up in ten years."

"I hope so."

"There's nothing Russia can't do, you know. Nothing."

"I'm sure that's right."

Sergei Romanov smiled. "It just needs the right leadership," he said. "Then we'll do it." An idea seemed to strike him then. "By the way," he continued. "There was something I meant to ask you this morning, when you were telling me about your business. Something I didn't quite understand."

"Yes?"

Sergei glanced at him with a slight frown. "What is a salesman?"

Paul Bobrov did not feel like sitting in the gloomy darkness of the dining room that night. He glanced at his watch. Eight forty-five. The bar on the fifth floor was open for another fifteen minutes. He went straight to the elevators. A minute later he arrived at the glass doors.

Varya was alone in the room. Eight forty-five had passed. She had nothing against the fellow from this morning who spoke so beautifully. But habit was not to be changed.

"Zakryt!" she called, and disappeared into the kitchen.

The sun was setting as Paul Bobrov sat at his window and gazed out over the rooftops of Moscow. To his left, he could see one of those tall thick-set towers with which Stalin had decorated the city in the last years of his rule. Symbols of a new age, like the Empire State Building; symbols of uncompromising power, like the bleak walls of the Kremlin.

Were they Russian, though?

He did not think so. Even now, he could not say, he did not know, what Russia was. That did not surprise him. She had always, down the centuries, defied definition. Was she part of Europe or part of Asia—what did those terms mean anyway? There wasn't a commentator he had read who could tell him what this vast land was or what it might become. To be sure, no one in the Kremlin knew.

But whatever it was, he thought he had caught a glimpse of it that day, at Russka.

The city was quiet that night; Bobrov, at his window, continued to watch and ponder till long after dark.

High in the starlit summer sky, pale clouds passed from time to time, drifting in a leisurely procession, glowing softly in the reflection of the crescent moon that was now arising in the south.

And softly the wind moved over the land.